THE International Directory of Little Magazines and Small Presses

LEN FULTON & ELLEN FERBER, EDITORS

16th Edition 1980-81

DUSTBOOKS

Dustbooks would like to thank the many people who by advice, counsel and criticism have helped make this directory a more useful and readable publication.

COVER DESIGN AND ART DIRECTION:
GEORGE MATTINGLY, G M DESIGN
PHOTO SPECIAL EFFECTS: RICHARD BLAIR

Systems design, typesetting format and computer programming by Neil McIntyre, Data Service, Co., P.O. Box 2066, Marysville, CA 95901.

Published annually by Dustbooks
P.O. Box 100, Paradise, CA 95969

PAPER	CLOTH
$13.95/copy	$17.95/copy
$42.00/4 year subsc	$54.00/4 year subsc
ISBN 0-913218-93-6	ISBN 0-913218-94-4

Three-across pressure sensitive mailing labels are available from the *International Directory*. These labels can be sorted alphabetically or by Zip Code. Price is $35.00 per thousand.

///DBKS//Paradise/CA

ON THE OTHER HAND...

If you are interested in only one or two of our information titles, but would like to beat inflation and get onto an automatic subscription basis (folks who did this four years ago received this 16th edition for about $4.00!) here are our '80 four-year subscription prices — again, as with the Info Library verso, good if you use the order blank below:

International Directory -$42.00/4 years (paper)
-$54.00/4 years (cloth)
Directory of Editors ---- -$30.00/4 years
Small Press Record ----- -$54.00/4 years (cl. only)
Small Press Review
(monthly) -$25.00/4 years

Dustbooks, P.O. Box 100, Paradise, CA 95969

Enclosed find $_____ for four-year subscriptions to: _____

_____

_____

_____

NAME _____

ADDRESS _____

_____

PAST and FUTURE

This directory enters its third decade of documenting a publishing phenomenon which seems to show no diminution in its growth. We have greater sobriety these days to be sure, the effect perhaps of six or so years of efforts to solve problems of distribution and promotion. But the impact of small, independent publishers on the book publishing industry as a whole is greater than ever. And it is clearly destined to continue.

The sixties were explosive, a coming on. The polemics were endless, the editing quick, the production hasty and constrained by the limited technology of the time. I remember when the "Justowriter" was the thing every publisher craved. In Berkeley the Free Speech Movement -- how many remember Mario Savio today? -- helped to begin a social process called do-it-yourselfism, which led to street poetry, the underground press, what we liked to call then the "mimeo movement", meat poetry, concrete poetry -- and a sort of internationalization of literary and political publishing. In the later sixties the move was somewhat away from polemics and towards special group- and subject-oriented magazines and presses. The literature of Blacks, Women, Chicanos and Native Americans were such early specializations. Several publishing organizations like COSMEP and CCLM were formed at the end of the decade, and with them came **grants** -- and a whole new argument. Access grew important: the availability of the tools of doing, with an emphasis on soft technology, which seeks harmony rather than war with natural forces. Stewart Brand published the first **Whole Earth Catalogue** in 1968 out of his garage.

The seventies saw the expansion of the **possibilities** of publishing from the few and select to the many. Spiritual energy gave way to craft, discipline and purpose. The emphasis was on technology and knowledge. Breakthroughs in typesetting from strike-on to film-strip gave independent publishing an absolutely critical boost, and the appearance of short-run printing manufacturers gave them another. All in all the Seventies were a period in which the work that had started in the decade before was carried forward, expanded and polished. The Subject Index of this directory indicates the wide range covered by these publishers.

The 1980's, if we get through them at all, are going to see both marketplace turmoil and continued growth for the independent publisher. Listings from new publishers for this directory arrive at the Dustbooks office at the rate of about fifty per month throughout the year, and while it is true that many operations die or suspend publication, the ratio of births to deaths is easily ten to one, creating an expanding industry that offers the new writer extraordinary possibilities for publication.

What has clearly sustained small press growth in the last two decades, and what will continue to sustain it increasingly in the future is the viability under small press conditions of the **limited press run,** and the small press will continue to serve a multitude of limited, often specialized markets. The economy in general through the Eighties will remain in turmoil, and this will spell ruination for many corporate publishing operations whose conglomerate owners will grow weary of low-profit enterprises. Literary publishers will still struggle as always, but will **survive,** while nonliterary publishers will grow at an awesome pace. But fad publishers should look out for the **Zeitgeist,** for it is in this area that the small presses could experience fortunes and misfortunes not unlike their corporate bretheren.

Micro-computer technology is going to be an increasingly important device for small publishers. Those who think not should look to the typesetting revolution that has taken place since the late sixties, a revolution based on the same sort of technology as the microprocessor. The magic is frozen in a chip known as an EPROM (erasable programmable read-only memory) and is going to be at least as important to the small publisher as offset printing technology. Along with typesetting, micro-processors will provide storage for editing, accounts receivable and inventory management, and critical support for what is essentially a mail-order industry.

And mail-order will become even more important to the small publisher. While established distributors like Ingram and Baker & Taylor will increasingly try to accommodate those smaller publishers who prove profitable to them, the 70's experiments in distribution will largely have failed. Publishing organizations and arts groups will become more important as information centers, catalysts and **facilitators.** There will be more cooperation between them and less jealous infighting, and grants themselves will have a narrowing importance to independent publishing as a whole. "In some ways," said Richard Grossinger of North Atlantic Books, "the marketplace is fairer."

Whatever else you may predict about the 80's, the true growth in publishing in anything like its traditional and creative sense, will all take place in the independent publishing business.

*   *   *   *   *   *   *   *   *   *   *   *   *

Almost every year there is some change in this directory, and this year is no different. We have, of course, expanded the Subject index a few more categories as happens every year. Eventually every U.S. state and every country

Almost every year there is some change in this directory, and this year is no different. We have, of course, expanded the Subject Index a few more categories as happens every year. Eventually every U.S. state and every country will be a separate subject! We have also enlarged the Regional Index by including all non-U.S. presses and magazines. These follow the U.S. regional index, and are organized by publisher alphabetically within country. The U.S. Regional Index is also reformatted by popular demand, so that now publishers are listed within state, alphabetically within the **first three digits** of their Zip Codes. This produces a true geographic index so publishers can be found by area.

And finally the **big** change for us is within each **book** publisher listing. Following that item in the listing which shows titles published and expected last year, this year and next year we have indicated the number of actual book titles listed in the current edition of our **Small Press Record of Books in Print.** We thought this would be another good item in the profile of a given book publisher. As always, we welcome feedback.

--Len Fulton, August, 1980

KEY TO DIRECTORY LISTINGS:

Listings are of three basic kinds: those for **magazines** (periodicals), those for **presses** (book publishers), and **cross-references.**

The **cross-references** are simply publisher imprints (usually presses but sometimes magazines) which have no listing data of their own but which are designed to lead you to a listing for that publisher which does have such data.

A complete **magazine** listing would include, in the following order: Name of magazine, name of press, name(s) of editor(s), address, phone number, type of material used, additional comments by editors including recent contributors, frequency of publication, one-year subscription price, single copy price, sample copy price, founding year, average number of pages, page size, production method (mi-mimeo; lo or of-offset; lp-letterpress), circulation, length of reporting time on manuscripts, payment rates, rights purchased and/or copyright arrangements, ad rates (page/half page), discount schedules, back issue prices, number of issues published in 1978, expected in 1979 and 1980, areas of interest for review materials, and membership in small mag/press organizations.

A complete **press** listing would include, in the following order: Name of press, name of magazine (if any), name(s) of editor(s), address, type of material used, additional comments by editors including recent contributors, average copy price, in cloth, paperback and "other", founding year, average number of pages, page size, production method, average press run, length of reporting time on manuscripts, payment or royalty arrangements, rights purchased and/or copyright arrangements, number of titles published in 1979, expected in 1980 and 1981, number of titles listed in the current edition of the **Small Press Record of Books in Print,** and membership in publishing organizations (see list in Appendix).

Certain special abbreviations apply to listings from the United Kingdom: px-postage is extra; pf-postage is free; pp-pages; p-pence.

In some cases in this edition we received no report by press time but had a reasonable sense that the magazine or press was still going. In such cases a ‡ is used before the name. Query before sending money or material however.

The following additional indicators are used in this edition to simplify yes or no in the listings: † means that the magazine or press does its own printing; § before a listing of areas of interest for review materials indicates that the magazine wishes to receive materials for review.

For those who wish to list a magazine or press in future editions of this *Directory*, Dustbooks provides a special form. Please write to us for it. Write to us also for a form to list books, pamphlets, broadsides, posters and poem-cards (i.e. *non-periodicals*) in our annual *Small Press Record of Books in Print*. However, once a report form has been filled out for the Directory, further forms and requests for information will be sent automatically. A "proof-sheet" is sent in February of each year for updating Directory listings. Deadline for this *Directory* is April 1st of each year; for the *Record* it is November 15th.

A

 # MAGAZINE, Brian Breger, Harry Lewis, Chuck Wachtel, 86 E 3rd Street, Apt 3A, New York, NY 10003, (212) 228-2178; (212) 243-1393; (212) 673-1511. 1978. Poetry, fiction, art, criticism, parts-of-novels. "We publish poetry and prose, up to six pages per author, approximately three writers in each issue. We are open to quality work from anyone. Every submission is judged collectively. Contributors include: Steve Katz, Paul Metcalf, Maureen Owen, Richard Elman, Quincy Troupe, Susan Sherman, Steve Cannon, Armand Schwerner, Joel Oppenheimer, George Economou, Joe Johnson." circ. 300. irregular. Pub'd 11 issues 1979; expects 13-17 issues 1980. sub. price: free, except libraries $25.00; per copy: free; sample: free. Back issues: Subject to discussion and availability. Please Write. Discounts: The magazine is distributed free by mail to anyone who wishes to be on mailing list. Our occasional special issues, devoted to the work of single individuals, will be available at the standard 40% to bookstores. 16pp; 5½X8½; of. Reporting time: varies; at least two months. Payment: We cannot, unfortunately, pay for work used. Contributors of course receive copies (6 or more depending on the availability). Copyrighted, reverts to author. CCLM.

& (Ampersand) Press (see also STARDANCER), Chael Graham, 415 3rd Street, Brooklyn, NY 11215. 1980. Poetry, fiction, art, photos, criticism, long-poems. "& Press will offer a new series of chapbooks beginning in the autumn of 1981. Each book will be 24-50 pages in length, and the editors will retain the right to select works to be included and their order. We will accept queries only beginning in January 1981. Please enclose a brief (2-3 pages at most) discussion of your work, your artistic philosophy and 5 sample poems with your query. We are seeking 'New Art' written outside the quagmire of New York, West Coast, London of Little Magazine sensibilities. We are seeking the very best sustained effort to transform words and worlds. We will use the Outpost method: once a writer's work is accepted we will solicit subscriptions for the volume. When enough are arranged to underwrite publication, the book will be published and distributed to subscribers and selected booksellers only. After all costs have been paid for by sales, Author will receive 50% of the actual money received on all subsequent sales. We encourage group and cooperative efforts and collections and the use of illustrations throughout the text. Please, only query if you are a serious writer. All queries should include an SASE or they cannot be returned. Additional address: 10 South Street, Colchhester, Essex, UK" avg. press run 250-500. Expects 2 titles 1981. avg. price, paper: $3.00. Discounts: 40% trade on 5 or more copies. 24-50pp; 6X9; of/lp. Reporting time: 1-4 months. Payment: 50% split after costs + copies. Copyrights for author. CCLM.

A, Alphabox Press, Jeremy Adler, 47 Wetherby Mansions, Earls Court Square, London SW5 9BH, United Kingdom. 1969. "A (1970); AB (1973); ABC (1975); ABCD (1977). Envelope magazine of visual poetry. Pages usually supplied by respective contributors. Contributors include: Bob Cobbing, Peter Finch, Bill Griffiths, D.S.H., Jackson MacLow, Peter Mayer, B. P. Nichol, Nannuci, P. C. Fencott, Paul Outton, Paula Claire etc." circ. 300. irreg. Pub'd 1 issue 1979. sub. price: 75p plus p&p; per copy: 75p plus p&p; sample: 75p plus p&p. 40pp; size A4; mi/of/silkscreen. Reporting time: 2 mos. Payment: 3 copies. copyright with author throughout. no ads accepted. ALP, CULP.

‡A Harmless Flirtation With Wealth (see also BARE WIRES), Helen McKenna, Editor & Publisher, P.O. Box 9779, San Diego, CA 92109, 714-234-9632. 1975. avg. press run 3,000. Pub'd 1 title 1979; expects 2 titles 1980. 2 titles listed in the *Small Press Record of Books in Print* (9th Edition, 1980). avg. price, paper: $3.00. Discounts: Distributors: to be arranged; 10 percent libraries; 40 percent bookstores. 80pp; 5½X8½; of. Not accepting ms. right now. Payment: Standard: 10-15 percent. Copyrights for author.

A SHOUT IN THE STREET: a journal of literary and visual art, Queens College Press, Joseph Cuomo, Ed.; Frederick Buell, Marie Ponsot, Poetry; Beverly Gross, Fiction, English Dept. Queens College, Flushing, NY 11367, 212-520-7238. 1976. Poetry, fiction, art, photos, interviews, long-poems, plays. "We are most interested in writing and art that is rooted in particular places and times. We print: long poems, long short stories, portfolios of visual art, & photoessays. Recent contributors: A.R. Ammons, James Dickey, John Gardner, Allen Ginsberg, Aileen M. Smith, W. Eugene Smith, Gary Snyder, Roman Vishniac, Diane Wakoski, Tillie Olsen, E.L. Doctorow, James Purdy, Meridel Le Sueur, Lynne Sharon Schwartz, Rene Gelpi, Ngugi wa Thiong'o." circ. 1,000. 3/yr. Pub'd 3 issues 1979; expects 3 issues 1980. sub. price: $6.00; per copy: $2.50; sample: $2.50; or free on request to libraries. Back issues: $2.50. Discounts: To Libraries: sample copy on request. To bookstores: 40 percent discount on consignment; discounts off single copy price on orders of 5 or more. 96pp; 6X9¼; †of. Reporting time: 8 weeks. Payment: in copies plus one year's subscription. With grant from

CCLM, we also offer prize money to best fiction, poetry, photography. Copyrighted, reverts to author. COSMEP.

ABBA, Abba Books & Broadsides, Eutychus Peterson, PO Box 8516, Austin, TX 78712. 1976. "Research articles, short fiction, poetry, line drawings and photographs, dealing with manifestations of God. Respond in 6 weeks, conditional on SASE. All rights, 1¢/word or $3.33 per poem. Writer's copies provided. Advertising accepted subject to editorial approval of content. No discounts. Back issues while they last, $5.00 each. 4-issue subscription, $15.00; two in print. Appears irregularly, trying for one a year" circ. 300. Pub'd 1 issue 1979. price per copy: $5.00; sample: $5.00. Back issues: $5.00. 80pp; 6X9; †lp. Pub's reviews: 50 in 1979. Ads: $75.00/$45.00.

Abba Books & Broadsides (see also ABBA), Eutychus Peterson, PO Box 8516, Austin, TX 78712. 1979. "Publishing out-of-print, out-of-copyright classics. Letterpress: handmade papers and fine printing for the collector. Rights and royalties individually negotiated. One book in 1979, one or two more anticipated" avg. press run 300. Pub'd 1 title 1979.

ABBEY, White Urp Press, David Greisman, 5011-2 Green Mountain Circle, Columbia, MD 21044. 1971. Poetry, fiction, articles, art, photos, interviews, criticism, reviews, letters, parts-of-novels, plays. "ABBEY is the Molson's Ale of Small Press rags. Recent contributors-Ann Menebroker, Merritt Clifton, Eric Greinke, Steve Sneyd. Susan Fromberg Schaeffer, Charlie McDade, John Elsberg, Ron Androla, Richard Peabody, Real Faucher, Peter Blush, Laurel Speer, Andrew Darlington, and Claudia Lapp." circ. 200. 3-4/yr. Pub'd 4 issues 1979; expects 4 issues 1980, 4 issues 1981. sub. price: $2.00; per copy: $.50; sample: $.50. Back issues: 50¢. 18pp; 8½X11; of. Reporting time: 2 minutes-2 years. Payment: nothing. Pub's reviews: 12-20 in 1979. §poetry/fiction/fanzines (sci-fi)/rock/beer-drinking. Ads: $10/$5.

ABBEY NEWSLETTER, Ellen McCrady, 5410 85th Avenue, Apt 2, New Carrollton, MD 20784, (301) 459-1181. 1975. Articles, reviews, letters, news items. "The *AN* is a professionally-oriented medium of communication for book conservators, a profession as yet unorganized and without a formal training program. It is designed to be useful also to amateur bookbinders and conservation-minded librarians. I acknowledge receipt immediately; it may be a month or more before I decide to publish it. Almost every submission is accepted, edited with loving care, and published." circ. 375. 6/yr. Pub'd 5 issues 1979; expects 6 issues 1980, 6-7 issues 1981. sub. price: $10.00; per copy: $1.50; sample: free. Back issues: $1.50. 12pp; 8½X11; of. Copyrighted. Pub's reviews: 1 in 1979. §Bookbinding and book conservation. Ads: No ads.

ABC Letter Service of Rochester (see also WOMEN STUDIES ABSTRACTS), Sara Stauffer Whaley, P.O. Box 1, Rush, NY 14543, (716) 533-1376 & (716) 533-1251. 1972. Music. avg. press run 1,800. avg. price, paper: $45.00/yr. Discounts: 40% insti. bookstores. 80pp; 5⅞X9; of. Reporting time: 2 months. Payment: None. Does not copyright for author. COSMEP.

Aberdeen Peoples Press, Editorial Group, 163 King St, Aberdeen, Scotland, 0224 29669. 1973. Fiction, articles, art, photos, cartoons, interviews, criticism, reviews, letters, news items, non-fiction. "Additional interest in material suitable for pamphlets 12pp-100pp. Libertarian socialist politics and scottish political comment." avg. press run 1,000. Pub'd 4 titles 1979. 6 titles listed in the *Small Press Record of Books in Print* (9th Edition, 1980). avg. price, other: 20p community papers. Discounts given. 16pp; 8½X12; †of. Reporting time: 14 days. Payment: negotiable. Copyrights for author. APS.

‡ABERDEEN UNIVERSITY REVIEW, E. E. Morrison, Dept Of Mathematics, Edward Wright Building, Dunbar Street, Aberdeen AB9 2TY, United Kingdom. 1913. Articles, poetry, reviews. "In general c. 3000-4000 words for articles." circ. 1400. 2/yr. Pub'd 2 issues 1979; expects 2 issues 1980. sub. price: $7.00; per copy: $3.50. Back issues: At publ. price. 96pp; 15X24½ cm. Reporting time: 1 month. Payment: none.

ABORTION EVE, Joyce Farmer, Lyvely, Box 845, Luguna Beach, CA 92652, (714) 494-7930. "*Abortion Eve* is a sex education book.".

ABRAXAS, Warren Woessner, 2322 Rugby Row, Madison, WI 53705. 1968. Criticism, reviews. "*ABRAXAS* has converted to an all-review format. We are interested in reading reviews and criticism of books of small press poetry and fiction. *Abraxas Press* has published an anthology of Jazz Poetry, *Bright Moments* ($4.00), and is presently not considering unsolicited manuscripts. Reviewers in future issues will include Ron Slate, David Hilton, Douglas Blazek, Victor Contoski, and Geoffrey Cook." circ. 400. 4/yr. Pub'd 2 issues 1979; expects 4 issues 1980. 8 titles listed in the *Small Press Record of Books in Print* (9th Edition, 1980). sub. price: 4/$6.00; per copy: $1.50; sample: $1.50. Back issues: Nos. 4-19 available as a set for $50.00. Discounts: 40 percent trade discount on orders of more than 5 copies. 50pp; 5½X7; of. Reporting time: 3 wks. Payment: copies. Copyrighted, reverts to author.

Pub's reviews: 50 in 1979. §reviews and criticism of small press poetry and fiction. Ads: exchange ads only. CCLM, COSMEP, COSMEP MIDWEST.

ABSINTHE, Indian Tree Press, Lela Crystal Neuburger, Editor, Barryville, NY 12719, 914-557-8141. 1977. Poetry, articles, art, interviews, reviews, news items. *"ABSINTHE* concerned w/poetry and related work." Pub'd 3 issues 1979; expects 3 issues 1980. sub. price: $4.00; per copy: $1.50. 20-32pp; 5½X8½; of. Reporting time: ASAP. Payment: copies. Copyrighted. Pub's reviews: 10 in 1979. §Poetry books.

Absolute O Kelvin (AOK) Press (see also INTRINSIC: An International Magazine of Poetry & Poetics; Tired Teddybear Productions), Michael Zizis, Mary Ellen Kappler, Box 485, Station P, Toronto, Ontario M5S 2T1, Canada, (416) 534-0139. 1978. Poetry, fiction, interviews, reviews. "AOK is a literary press, devoted to serving excellent literary forms in poetry and prose." avg. press run 800. Pub'd 1 title 1979; expects 2 titles 1980. avg. price, paper: $4.95. Discounts: 40%. 50pp; 6X9; of. Reporting time: at least 4 months. Payment: 10%, 30 copies gratis. Copyrights for author.

"Absolutely Furious" Productions (see MAGIC SAM)

ABYSS, Abyss/Augtwofive, Gerard Dombrowski, Craig Ellis, P.O. Box C, Somerville, MA 02143. 1969. Poetry, concrete art. "No unsolicited mss." circ. 1,000. irreg. Pub'd 1 issue 1979; expects 6 issues 1980. sub. price: individual: $5.00/yr; institution: $10.00; per copy: varies; sample: $2.00. Back issues: query. Discounts: none. pp varies; 8½X11; of. Reporting time: 1 month. Payment: Copies. Copyrighted. Pub's reviews: none in 1979. §sports. Ads: none. none.

Abyss/Augtwofive (see also ABYSS), Gerard Dombrowski, Abyss; Craig Ellis, Augtwofive, PO Box C, Somerville, MA 02143, 617-666-1804. 1966/1969. Poetry, concrete art. "Have been doing broadsides, posters, etc/current postcard series includes work by E.R. Baxter III, Bill Costley, Larry Eigner, etc/planning a chapbook series, cassettes, and more/No unsolicited mss." avg. press run 1-1,000. Pub'd 1 title 1979; expects 6 titles 1980. Discounts: Standard trade. 1-500pp; size Varies; of. Reporting time: 6-8 weeks. Payment: Copies. Does not copyright for author. none.

AC Publications, Andor Czompo, Ann I. Czompo, PO Box 238, Homer, NY 13077, (607) 749-4040. 1978. Music. "Our publications are geared toward educational and recreational dance materials in both performing arts and folk arts." avg. press run 500-1,000. Pub'd 3 titles 1979; expects 2 titles 1980. 2 titles listed in the *Small Press Record of Books in Print* (9th Edition, 1980). avg. price, paper: $5.95-$9.95; other: Booklets $3.00. Discounts: 2-9, 20%; 10-100, 40%; 100 or more, 50%. For bookstores, wholesalers, and libraries. 8½X11; of. Payment: 10% to contributors & authors. Copyrights for author. COSMEP.

Academic Publications (see also JAMES JOYCE QUARTERLY), Univ of Tulsa, 600 S. College, Tulsa, OK 74104. 1 title listed in the *Small Press Record of Books in Print* (9th Edition, 1980).

ACADEMY AWARDS OSCAR ANNUAL, ESE California, Art Sarno, 509 N. Harbor Blvd., La Habra, CA 90631, (213) 691-0737. 1968. Articles, art, photos, interviews, reviews. 1/yr. sub. price: $9.95; per copy: $9.95. Back issues: $9.95. Discounts: 2-5: 20%; 6-10: 25%; 11-29: 30%; 30 & up: 40%. 112pp; 8⅜X11; of. Payment: no.

Academy Chicago Limited, Anita Miller, Jordan Miller, Jill Sellers, 360 N. Michigan, Chicago, IL 60601, 312-782-9826. 1975. "Strong anti-sexist bias." avg. press run 5,000. Pub'd 15 titles 1979; expects 6 titles 1980, 6 titles 1981. 14 titles listed in the *Small Press Record of Books in Print* (9th Edition, 1980). avg. price, cloth: $11.95; paper: $5.95. Discounts: 1-2 copies, 25%; 3-49 copies, 40% copies, 40%; 50-99 copies, 42%; 100-249 copies, 43%; 250+ copies, 45%. Libraries: 1-10 copies, 10%; 10+ copies, 15%. 150-300pp; 5½X8½; of. Reporting time: 4-8 weeks. Payment: Standard paperback/hardcover royalties: c. 7-10 percent. Copyrights for author. COSMEP.

Acadian Publishing, Inc., Andrew Vidrine, Church Point, LA 70525, (318) 684-5417. 1978. "We plan to publish mostly fiction, but don't exclude good non-fiction. We will offer standard royalties to authors, but are filled up with mss for the next year or two, at least. Average copy price depends on number of pages per book, and, naturally, on binding. We usually publish simultaneously in both soft and hard covers. Like 500 hard, 1,500 soft. Average number of pages: our first book this year was 96 pages. Second book 204 pages. We plan a 500 page novel in 1979." avg. press run 2,000. Pub'd 2 titles 1979; expects 1 title 1980. 2 titles listed in the *Small Press Record of Books in Print* (9th Edition, 1980). Discounts: Publishers Universal discount schedule. pp varies; 5½X8½. Reporting time: We'll be as fast as we can. Payment: Standard. Copyrights for author.

ACCCA Press, Milli Janz, 19 Foothills Drive, Pompton Plains, NJ 07444, (201) 835-2661. 1978. Articles. "This is a first edition soft cover book, which was printed and published by grant awarded by the National Endowment of the Arts. Since many, many copies were published, I am still distributing the first edition. However, I soon plan to publish a second edition of *Culture Without Pain* and will include the many community cultural centers which have started, developed and are continuing as self-sustaining true cultural centers in their community in many parts of the U.S. and around the world. I know that this book has been translated into several languages." 1 title listed in the *Small Press Record of Books in Print* (9th Edition, 1980). avg. price, paper: $3.00 plus postage ($4.00). Discounts: 10%. 8½X11. Payment: When other writers will join me, I will offer a per page fee.

Acme Print & Litho (see also RUDE), Joe Thomas, Publisher, 390 Douro Street, Stratford on Avon Ontario N5A 3S7, Canada. 1978. "Write us a letter. *Quill & Blotter Annual Review, OK Sure Postcard, Find Art Poster Series*" Pub'd 7 titles 1979; expects 20 titles 1980. 2 titles listed in the *Small Press Record of Books in Print* (9th Edition, 1980). avg. price, paper: $5.00; other: varies. Discounts: negotiable. 50-100pp; 8X11; †of/lp. Reporting time: ASAP. Payment: negotiable. Copyrights for author.

‡**Acorn (see also TREES),** Joan Dibble Shambaugh, 185 Merriam Street, Weston, MA 02193. 1975. Poetry, fiction, art. "'Submissions are by invitation only.'" avg. press run 250. Pub'd 1 title 1979. avg. price, paper: $1.50. 20pp; 5½X8½; of. Copyrights for author. COSMEP.

Acrobat Books Publishers, Tony Cohan, Gordon Beam, 420 1/2 N Larchmont Blvd, Los Angeles, CA 90004, 213-467-4506. 1975. Fiction, art, photos. "Short fiction (up to novella size) only—basically open to: 1. strong documentary ideas having to do with Southern California 2. extraordinary original artistic work—fiction, art, photography, & occassionally poetry. *NINE SHIPS, A BOOK OF TALES* by Tony Cohan; *STREET WRITERS: A GUIDED TOUR OF CHICANO GRAFFITI* by Gusmano Cesaretti; *OUTLAW VISIONS* ed. by Tony Cohan/Gordon Beam; *WHO KILLED CHEROKEE MCCADDEN?* by T.M. Landmark; *THE RECORD PRODUCER'S HANDBOOK* by Done Gere; *WHAT IT IS, WHAT IT AIN'T* by Cam Smith; *HOME THOUGHTS FROM ABROAD* by Robin Williamson." avg. press run 3,000. Pub'd 2 titles 1979. 1 title listed in the *Small Press Record of Books in Print* (9th Edition, 1980). avg. price, cloth: $11.00; paper: $4.95. Discounts: 1-5 copies, 20 percent; 6-49, 40 percent. 96pp; 7¾X7¾; of. Reporting time: 60 days. Payment: one third of profits. Does not copyright for author. COSMEP, SCBP.

Acrobus, Inc., Alexander Bisbal, 1324 Lexington Avenue, New York, NY 10028, 212-534-3265. 1978. avg. press run 5,000. Pub'd 2 titles 1979; expects 2 titles 1980, 4 titles 1981. avg. price, cloth: $5.95; paper: $3.95; other: $5.50. Discounts: 30-55%. 150pp; 8X11; †of. Reporting time: 6 to 8 weeks. Payment: yes. Copyrights for author. ALTA.

THE ACTS THE SHELFLIFE, sun rise fall down artpress, Miekal And, 838a Wisconsin St, Oshkosh, WI 54901. 1980. Poetry, fiction, articles, art, photos, interviews, criticism, reviews, letters, longpoems, collages, concrete art, news items. "*The Acts The Shelflife* will be an almanac of sorts designed to compile and catalogue information about the post-maximus long poem. This journal is devoted only to the longpoem. Its emphasis will be to set down this smallpress phenomenon in the language that the longpoem has already created. I'm especially wary of critical language that is once removed from the poem itself. For more info write." circ. 500. Expects 1 issue 1980, 1 issue 1981. price per copy: $5.00. Discounts: none. 60pp; 8½X11; of. Reporting time: a couple of weeks. Payment: 2-5 copies. Not copyrighted. COSMEP Midwest.

Adam Seed Publications, Simon Jeremiah, 1561 S. Fitch Mt. Rd., Healdsburg, CA 95448. 1977. Poetry, articles, art, photos, parts-of-novels. "Publishers of *Caretaking the Wild Sinsemilla,* we seek articles on growing *cannabis americanensis,* harvesting, curing, and related topics. Also: private correspondences suitable for publication in future anthology." avg. press run 8,000. Pub'd 1 title 1979; expects 1 title 1980, 1 title 1981. 1 title listed in the *Small Press Record of Books in Print* (9th Edition, 1980). avg. price, cloth: $7.50; paper: $4.00. Discounts: 40%. 100pp; 5X7; of/lp. Reporting time: 2 mos. Payment: 10%. Copyrights for author.

ADOLESCENCE, Libra Publishers, Inc., PO Box 165, 391 Willets Road, Roslyn Heights, L.I., NY 11577, (516) 484-4950. 1960. Articles. circ. 3,000. 4/yr. Pub'd 4 issues 1979; expects 4 issues 1980, 4 issues 1981. sub. price: $20.00 instit., $16.00 indiv.; per copy: $6.00; sample: $6.00. Back issues: $7.50. Discounts: 10% to subscriber agents. 192pp; 6X9; of. Reporting time: 3 weeks. Copyrighted. Pub's reviews: 60 in 1979. §Behavioral sciences.

Adventure Trails Research and Development Laboratories, T. D. Lingo, DIRECTOR, Laughing Coyote Mt., Black Hawk, CO 80422. 1957. "Published *Consciousness Science Syllabus* by T.D. Lingo. Fundamental neurology to method of brain self-control, backward self-therapy and forward self-circuiting into the 3/8 bulk of dormant frontal lobes. Since 1957, a new order of advanced problem-solving intelligence, multiple orgasm and species conferencing telepathy to consensus democratic

4

action has been observed to emerge automatically." 1 title listed in the *Small Press Record of Books in Print* (9th Edition, 1980). avg. price, paper: $5.00. 50pp; 8½X11; †mi. Yes.

ADVENTURES IN POETRY MAGAZINE, Dr. Stella Woodall Publisher, Stella Woodall, Editor-Publisher, PO Box 253, Junction, TX 76849, (915) 446-2004. 1968. Poetry, photos, cartoons, long-poems. "The best poems published in *Adventures in Poetry Magazine* are published in the annual *Adventures in Poetry Anthology,* a beautiful hardback book containing 100 or more poems, with a short biography of poet. Only excellent poems of high caliber with inspirational value that will help people are published. Each edition has a theme; for instance the next year's themes are: Patriotic (already published), Thanksgiving, Love, Easter, Vacation, and Christmas. Each edition features the most outstanding all-around poet using the poet's photograph and biography. One edition carries the best poems submitted for the annual Patriotic Poetry Seminar, Winner of Freedom's Foundation Award, and sponsored by Stella Woodall Poetry Society International, and held the first weekend of each October. Society membership dues: $15.00. The Dr. Stella Poetry Pattern is 1st choice for publication (This is a 2-stanza 4-line each stanza, Iambic, 4-feet in 1st & 3rd lines & 3-feet in 2nd & 4th lines. The 2nd line in each stanza has a feminine ending). Each edition of this international quarterly magazine features the most outstanding poet, and the latest Poet Laureate of Stella Woodall Poetry Society International, using these poets' photographs, biographies, and poems. A copy of Dr. Stella Woodall's hard-back gold-award-winning book, *Anthology of Texas Poems,* is awarded to the author of the best poem min each edition of this international magazine. Each edition also honors poets of one of our United States, using the photograph, biography and a statement on poetry by the governor of that state and the photographs, biographies, and poems of the president of that state's poetry society, and of that state's poet laureate. Poems by members of *Stella Woodall Poetry Society International* are given preference over the hundreds of poems submitted each quarter for publication in *Adventures in Poetry Magazine,* which has been published since March, 1968. Dues for membership are $15.00 annually. To become a member, a poet must be recommended by a member and must submit his photograph, biography, and his best poem. For further information on membership poets should write to Dr. Stella Woodall, PO Box 253, Junction, Texas 76849, or call (915) 446-2004." circ. 600. quarterly. Pub'd 4 issues 1979; expects 4 issues 1980, 4 issues 1981. sub. price: free to members of Stella Woodall Poetry Society International; per copy: $4.00; sample: $4.00. Back issues: $3.00 (if available). Discounts: none. 76-80pp; 5½X8½; of. Reporting time: 1 week to 1 month. Payment: none. Not copyrighted. Ads: No ads.

ADVISORY BOARD RECORD, Kxe6s Verein R Press, Steven Buntin, PO Box 2066 or 2204, Chapel Hill, NC 27514. 1976. Poetry, fiction, articles, art, photos, cartoons, interviews, satire, criticism, reviews, letters, parts-of-novels, collages, plays. "Prefer materials on chess of tournament results, games, annotations, theory, etc." circ. 500+. 6/yr. sub. price: $5.00; per copy: $1.00; sample: $0.50. Back issues: $0.75 each. Discounts: we are our own agents. 20-24pp; 5½X8½; †mi/of. Reporting time: ASAP, tournament results have priority. Payment: case by case, most work by staff. Copyrighted. Pub's reviews. §Publishing, copyrighting, chess, board games, freedom of the press. Ads: $12.00/$6.50/$0.10 ($1.50 min.). CCLM, COSMEP, COSMEP/SOUTH, COSMEP/EAST.

THE ADVOCATE, Robert I. McQueen, Editor; Peter Frisch, Publisher, 1730 S. Amphlett, Suite 225, San Mateo, CA 94402, 415-573-7100. 1967. Articles, art, photos, interviews, letters, news items, non-fiction. "Query first, most materials assigned." circ. 65,835. 25/yr. Pub'd 25 issues 1979; expects 25 issues 1980, 25 issues 1981. sub. price: $18.00; per copy: $1.25; sample: $1.25. Back issues: none. Discounts: none. 88pp; size tab; of. Reporting time: 6 weeks. Payment: $25.00 per published column, on publication. Copyrighted. Pub's reviews. §all. Ads: $728.00/$406.00/42 spaces - $2.00. ABC.

AEOLIAN-HARP, Geneva Verkennes, 1395 James St., Burton, MI 48529. 1968. Poetry. "Want rhymed poems, no single sentences, prefer 12 lines. Those interested in Poem Patterns, write, enclosing $20.00 check to Geneva Verkennes. Send $2.00 plus SASE for sample of printing. *ALOHA TO HAWAII* $2.25 postpaid (40 pages), *FLOWERS OF HAWAII* $2.25 postpaid (27 pages)." circ. 100 up to 500. 1/yr. Expects 2 issues 1980. 11 titles listed in the *Small Press Record of Books in Print* (9th Edition, 1980). sub. price: $2.00; per copy: $2.00; sample: $2.00. Back issues: Some left from (1968) — 55 poets and writers: $5.00. 20-40pp; size varies; of/mi. Reporting time: right away. No payment; only subscribers who send in 5 short poems and $5.00 will be considered for future issues. §Will write up a review and send it to you for $10.00. Only poetry books on nature; no cheap novels or pornography. CCLM.

AERO SUN-TIMES, Wilbur Wood, 424 Stapleton Bldg., Billings, MT 59101, (406) 259-1958. 1974. Poetry, articles, art, photos, cartoons, interviews, criticism, reviews, letters, plays, news items. "Length: 15 to 20 typed pages (single spaced, 20 pages); Biases: we promote sensible, appropriate, low-cost and decentralized applications of renewable energies; Recent contributors: Wilbur Wood,

Brainerd Horner, Kye Cochran, Isao Fujimoto" circ. 1,000. monthly/bimonthly. Pub'd 12 issues 1979. sub. price: $15.00/yr; magazine is part of $15 yearly membership in our non-profit tax-exempt educational organization; per copy: $1.25; sample: one free if available. Back issues: $1.25-$1.50. Discounts: none. 24pp; 8X10½; of. Reporting time: variable. Payment: solicited material done on either consulting or contracted basis; unsolicited material can seldom be paid for. Not copyrighted. Pub's reviews: 71 in 1979. §Renewable energy (solar, wind, small hydro-electric, biomass, human, & geothermal), appropriate technology, general energy, architecture & design, construction, & owner-built housing. no ads.

Aesopus Press (see also THE WOODSTOCK REVIEW), Pat Jackson, Marilyn Mohr, Annie Jung-Blythe, 27 Oriole Drive, Woodstock, NY 12498, 914-679-7795. 1975. Poetry, fiction, art, reviews. avg. press run 500. Pub'd 1 title 1979; expects 6 titles 1980, 8 titles 1981. avg. price, paper: $1.50. Discounts: 25% in quantity, 40% bookstores. 16pp; 5½X8½; †of. Reporting time: 6-8 weeks. Payment: copies. Copyrights for author.

AEVUM, Catherine McAllister, 4 Forest Place, Fredonia, NY 14063. 1979. Poetry, fiction, criticism, reviews. "Recent Contributors: William Heyen, Dick Lourie, Dave Kelly, Helen Ruggieri, David Lunde, Doug Carlson, Alvin Aubert, Shreela Ray, Dennis Maloney. Fiction must be relatively short." circ. 500. 6/yr. Pub'd 6 issues 1979. sub. price: $10.00; per copy: $2.00; sample: $2.00. 45pp; 5½X8½; †of. Reporting time: 2 weeks. Payment: 2 copies. Copyrighted, reverts to author. Pub's reviews. §Poetry, short fiction, scholarly.

AFFORDABLE CHIC NEWS, Woman Matters Press, Barbara Schnipper, Editor-Publisher, PO Box 153, Cabin John, MD 20731, (301) 229-6765. 1978. Articles. "This consumer-fashion publication includes short articles on wardrobe planning and personal appearance, particularly as they relate to saving money and to women's personal advancement. Helping women improve their personal appear-ance without spending an outrageous amount of money is one key aim. Short articles (max. length of 2 typewritten, dbl-spaced pages) will be considered, provided a SASE is enclosed. Payment at the moment is a free subscription. Longer mss will also be considered, but SASE should be included." circ. 200. 6/yr. Expects 2 issues 1980, 6 issues 1981. sub. price: $5.50; per copy: $1.00; sample: $1.00. Back issues: $0.50 plus SASE. Discounts: 33⅓%. 4pp; 8½X11; of. Reporting time: 2 months. Payment: Free publications, newsletter or other appropriate vehicle from WMP. Copyrighted, reverts to author. Ads: $100.00/$50.00/$1.00 a line (approx. 6-7 words). WBPA, COSMEP-South, WCGE.

AFRICA CURRENTS, Africa Publications Trust, Montagu Pubications, Montagu House, High Street, Huntingdon, Cambs., England PE18 6EP, United Kingdom. 1975. 4/yr. sub. price: £3/yr; per copy: 50p. lp.

AFRICA NEWS, Charles W. Ebel, P.O. Box 3851, Durham, NC 27702, (919) 286-0747. 1973. Articles, photos, interviews, news items. "all of the above items relate to current African develop-ments" circ. 2,500. 48/yr. Pub'd 48 issues 1979; expects 48 issues 1980, 48 issues 1981. sub. price: $25.00 individuals; $48.00 non-profit; $78.00 profit; per copy: $0.50; sample: $5.00 per month trial. Back issues: rates upon request. Discounts: 3 rates, basically: individuals get special rate for (new) subscribers — $20.00/year. 12pp; 7X8½; †of. Reporting time: 2 weeks. Payment: none at present. Copyrighted, rights ververt to publ. Pub's reviews: 30 in 1979. §Africa, Third World generally. no ads.

Africa Publications Trust (see AFRICA CURRENTS)

Africa Research & Publications Project, Kassahun Checole, P.O.Box 1892, Trenton, NJ 08608. 1979. "Most of our publications are in the booklet form 4 to 110 pages. We are mainly interested in social change and human rights issues, critical perspectives on development & underdevelopment, and political and economic relations between the developed-industrialized countries and African nations and movements (North-South dialogue, NIEO, appropriate technology, etc.). Recent publica-tions: reproduction of materials from RENCONTRE ET DEVELOPPEMENT, in Algeria and the Action for Development Unit of UN's FAO, etc." avg. press run 1000. Expects 20 titles 1980. avg. price, paper: $2.00; other: $5.00 average for institutions. Discounts: 40% for orders of 10 or more. 8½X11; mi/of. Payment: 30 to 50 free to author or organization.

AFRICA TODAY, Edward A. Hawley, Exec. Editor; George W. Shepherd Jr., Tilden J. LeMelle, c/o G.S.I.S, Univ of Denver, Denver, CO 80208. 1954. Articles, reviews, letters. "Scholarly articles on AFRICA ONLY-2000-6000 words, book reviews (AFRICA titles only)-450-1800 words, occasionally use poetry, but only by African authors or based on first hand experience of Africa." circ. 2,000. 4/yr. sub. price: $10.00 Indiv., $15.00 Instit.; per copy: $2.50 plus $.50 postage and handling charge; sample: no charge. Discounts: 15% to established sub. agencies only; bulk rates available. 100-112pp; 5½X8⅜; of. Reporting time: 3-4 months. Payment: copies in which article appears. Copyrighted, does not revert to author. Pub's reviews: 40 in 1979. §contemporary Africa-various aspects:political, economic, geographic, literary. Ads: $140/$75/1/4-$40. COSMEP.

THE AFRICAN BOOK PUBLISHING RECORD, Hans Zell Publishers Ltd., Hans M. Zell, P.O. Box 56, Oxford 0X13El, United Kingdom, 0865-512934. 1975. Articles, reviews, news items, interviews, criticism. "Largely a bibliographical tool, providing information on new and forthcoming African published materials; plus 'Notes & News', 'Magazines', 'Company Profiles' sections and interviews; normally one major article on aspects of publishing and book development in Africa per issue. Since 1977 also features short concise book reviews." circ. 1,500. 4/yr. Pub'd 4 issues 1979; expects 4 issues 1980. sub. price: £24.00 ($55.00); per copy: £4.50-$11.25 back issues; sample: Sample copies only at Editor's discretion. Back issues: £18/$40 per volume; £4.50/$10 single copies. Discounts: 15% to adv. agents/10% to subs. agents. 84pp; size A4; of. Reporting time: 6-8 wks. Payment: £35/$75.00 for major feature article. Copyrighted. Pub's reviews: 102 in 1979. §books published in Africa only. Ads: £65/$142/£40/$88.

‡**AFRICAN LITERATURE TODAY, Heinemann, Africana Publishing Corp.,** Eldred Durusimi Jones, Fourah Bay College, Univ. of Sierra Leone, Freetown, Sierra Leone. 1968. Articles, reviews. circ. 3,500. 1/yr. Pub'd 1 issue 1979; expects 1 issue 1980. price per copy: £3.50/cl., £1.80/pa. Discounts: 1/3 trade. 160pp; 5½X8½; lp. Pub's reviews. §Africa.

Africana Publishing Corp. (see AFRICAN LITERATURE TODAY)

AFTA—The Magazine of Temporary Culture, Bill Marcinko, Dale Marcinko, 47 Crater Avenue, Wharton, NJ 07885, (201) 366-1967. 1977. Fiction, articles, art, photos, cartoons, interviews, satire, criticism, reviews, news items. "*AFTA* is basically a review magazine of popular culture: books, films, records, television and comic books with short news items, reviews and interviews of a recent nature. We also cover the anti-nuke, pro-gay, and feminist movements. We will trade subscriptions with other small press editors." circ. 10,000. Quarterly. Expects 2 issues 1980, 4 issues 1981. sub. price: $10.00/yr; per copy: $2.50; sample: $2.50. Back issues: none available. Discounts: 10 copies: $14.00 postpaid. 120pp; 8½X11; of. Reporting time: 2 weeks. Payment: free copy of issue. Copyrighted, reverts to author. Pub's reviews: 20 in 1979. §fiction, poetry, satire, humor, critical essays, review magazines. Ads: $100.00/$50.00/$0.20. WSA, UFO, TFN.

AFTERBIRTH, Duende Press, Box 571, Placitas, NM 87043. 1980. Poetry. "The editor will consider only his own material." CCLM.

AFTERIMAGE, Visual Studies Workshop Press, Charles Hagen, Editor, 31 Prince Street, Rochester, NY 14607, 716-442-8676. 1972. Articles, photos, interviews, criticism, reviews, letters, news items. "Features, reviews, news, notices of exhibitions. Recent contributors: Paul Byers, Howard Becker, Michael Lesy, A.D. Coleman, Les Krims, Nam June Paik, Richard Rudisill" circ. 3,800. 9 with one double issue/yr. sub. price: $15.00; per copy: $1.75 single, $3.00 double; sample: gratis. Back issues: $1.75. Discounts: Classrooms (10 or more subscriptions) 20% — Trade 40%. 24pp; 11X22; of. Reporting time: 2 to 3 weeks. Payment: minimal to nothing. Copyrighted, does not revert to author. Pub's reviews: 54 long, 248 short in 1979. §Photography, film, video, and related areas. no advertising. CCLM,.

Afterimage Book Publishers, George A. Lareau, 305 S Cottage Grove, Urbana, IL 61801, (217) 384-7319. 1978. Poetry, photos. "We are not soliciting anything at present. Our first several books are works of our own creation, in the field of photography" avg. press run 2,000. Expects 3 titles 1980. avg. price, cloth: $14.95. Discounts: Bookstores, 40%; Distributor, 55%. 100pp; 5½X8½; of. COSMEP.

AGAINST THE WALL, C. William George, Ed.-Publ., PO Box 444, Westfield, NJ 07091. 1972. Fiction, articles, art, cartoons, interviews, satire, criticism, reviews, music, letters, news items. "Usually publish in 200-500 word range. Philosophically libertarian, anything from laissez faire capitalism to voluntary communalism ok, with preference for anarchism over limited statism subclassification. Recent contributors include Robert Anton Wilson, Merritt Clifton, Barbra Brodie, Oscar B. Johannsen, A.D. Winans" circ. 5,200. 10/yr. Pub'd 10 issues 1979; expects 10 issues 1980, 10 issues 1981. price per copy: $1.00; sample: $1.00. Back issues: $1, 3/$2.50. Discounts: $50/100 copies. 30pp; 8½X11; of. Reporting time: varies considerably. Payment: Negotiable, usually copies. We do not believe in "copyright" laws!. Pub's reviews: 7 in 1979. §Libertarianism as applied to education, politics, psychology, etc. Ads: $30.00/$18.00/$0.40, $0.75 for 3x.

AGENDA, Agenda Editions, William Cookson, Peter Dale, 5 Cranbourne Court, Albert Bridge Road, London, England SW11 4PE, United Kingdom, 01-228-0700. 1959. Articles, poetry, art, photos, satire, reviews, interviews, long-poems. "Poetry must be in recongnizable contemporary

English. No 'concrete' or sound poetry considered. 'More than usual emotion, more than usual order'. At least half magazine devoted to reviews." circ. 2,000. 4/yr. Pub'd 4 issues 1979; expects 4 issues 1980. sub. price: £5 ($12) to private individuals; £6 ($24) to libraries & institutions; per copy: £1-25 ($3.00); sample: 90p ($2). Back issues: most back issues £1.50 ($4). Discounts: 33⅓%. 96pp; 7X5; lp. Reporting time: 1 month. Payment: £3 per page of poetry. Pub's reviews. §Contemporary poetry, neglected poetry from past. Ads: £40/£20.

Agenda Editions (see also AGENDA), William Cookson, 5 Cranbourne Court, Albert Bridge Rd, London, England SW114PE, United Kingdom, 01-228-0700. 1971. "New poetry. Translations." avg. press run 1,500. Expects 4 titles 1980. 15 titles listed in the *Small Press Record of Books in Print* (9th Edition, 1980). avg. price, cloth: £6; paper: £2. Discounts: 33⅓%. 80pp; 7X5; lp. Reporting time: 1 month. Payment: 10%.

THE AGENT, Georgette Munday, Jim Hol, 46 Denbigh Street, London SW1, England, United Kingdom. 1879. Poetry, fiction, articles, art, photos, cartoons, interviews, satire, criticism, reviews, music, letters, parts-of-novels, long-poems, collages, plays, news items. "*The Agent* incorporates *Invisible Art, Relevant Material,* and the New Agency Sheets. It has produced Jim Hol and each issue works out at about 40p (including postage); if you send what you think it's worth you'll help pay for the next one; or send something else in exchange. Annual subscriptions by arrangement. Most material is not copyrighted at all." circ. 700. 4/yr. sub. price: By arrangement (suggest your own price); per copy: 40p; sample: 40p. Back issues: 40p. 36pp; 5¾X8¼; of. Reporting time: two weeks. Payment: free copies. Pub's reviews: 3 in 1979. §Arts. Ads: £40/£20/Free for non-profit.

THE AGNI REVIEW, Sharon Dunn, Editor; Norman Dukes, Associate Editor; Askold Melnyczuk, Advisory Editor, P.O. Box 349, Cambridge, MA 02138, (617) 491-1079. 1972. Poetry, fiction, parts-of-novels, long-poems. "Russell Edson, Clarence Major, Kenneth Rexroth, Mary Morris, Peter Klappert, William Harmon, Linda Pastan, Mekeel McBride, Olga Broumas, David Bosworth, Joyce Carol Oates, Dave Smith, Maxine Kumin, Michael Benedikt, Paul Mariani, Bin Ramke are among past contributors." circ. 1,000. 2/yr. Pub'd 2 issues 1979; expects 2 issues 1980. sub. price: $5.00; per copy: $3.00; sample: $3.00. 128pp; 5½X8½; of. Reporting time: 2-8 weeks. Payment: $5.00 per page. Copyrighted, reverts to author. Ads: Upon request. CCLM.

AHNOI, Joel Lewis, 707 90th Street, North Bergen, NJ 07047. 1979. Poetry. "We are a small shoe-string magazine committed to publishing quality poetry. No biases, tho' we look favorably upon poets from our Garden State. Recent contributors include Ginsberg, Padgett, Waldman, Ted Enslin, T. Berrigan and Amiri Baraka" circ. 400. 4/yr. Pub'd 2 issues 1979. price per copy: $1.00; sample: $1.00. Discounts: inquire. 40pp; 8½X11; of. Reporting time: 1 month to 6 weeks. Payment: none. Copyrighted. no ads.

Ahsahta, D. Boyer, O. Burmaster, T. Trusky, Boise State University, Department of English, Boise, ID 83725, 208-385-1246. 1975. Poetry. "We publish only work by Western poets—this does not mean paeans to the pommel or songs of the sage, but quality verse which clearly indicates its origin in the West. Our first three volumes included older poets, the next three were contemporary, and we plan to alternate this way in the future." avg. press run 500. Pub'd 3 titles 1979; expects 3 titles 1980. 14 titles listed in the *Small Press Record of Books in Print* (9th Edition, 1980). avg. price, paper: $2.50. Discounts: 30 percent to trade, bulk, jobber, classroom. 60pp; 6X8½; †of. Reporting time: 1 month. Payment: copies of book. Copyrights for author. COSMEP.

Air-Plus Enterprises, Ann Saltenberger, PO Box 367, Glassboro, NJ 08028, (609) 881-0724. 1973. Articles, news items. "Length: brief - open. Primarily staff written at present but would like any first-person account of a legal abortion, particularly if complications developed." avg. press run 5,000. Pub'd 4 titles 1979; expects 4 titles 1980, 4 titles 1981. Discounts: 25%. Reporting time: 1 month. COSMEP.

AIS EIRI, Robert G. Lowery, Editor, 553 W. 51st St., New York, NY 10019, 212-757-3318. 1974. Cartoons. "Anything relating to Irish & Irish related things." circ. 2,500-3,000. 2/yr. Pub'd 2 issues 1979; expects 2 issues 1980. sub. price: $7.50/4 issues; per copy: $2.00; sample: $0.50. Back issues: $2.00/issue. Discounts: 50 percent. 56pp; 8½X11; of, lp. Reporting time: 3 months. Payment: 6 copies. Copyrighted, reverts to author. Pub's reviews: 7 in 1979. §International politics & Irish subjects. Ads: $250.00/$150.00. CCLM, COSMEP.

Akens-Morgan Press, Inc., Huntsville, AL 35801. 1 title listed in the *Small Press Record of Books in Print* (9th Edition, 1980).

Akiba Press, Sheila Baker, PO Box 13086, Oakland, CA 94611, (415) 339-1283. 1978. Fiction, photos. "Will publish historical fiction and non-fiction, as well as juveniles on same themes. Up to

8

400 pp." avg. press run 2,500. Pub'd 1 title 1979; expects 2 titles 1980. avg. price, cloth: $10.00; paper: $5.95. Discounts: 20% libraries, 40% bookstores. 250pp; 6X8; lp. Reporting time: 3 months. Payment: 10% royalty, no advance. Copyrights for author.

AKROS, Duncan Glen, Albert House, 21 Cropwell Road, Radcliffe on Trent, Nottingham NG12 2FT, United Kingdom. 1965. Articles, poetry, satire, reviews, interviews, criticism, letters, long-poems. "Mainly Scottish poetry and criticism. Contributors include Alexander Scott, Edwin Morgan, George Bruce, Alastair Mackie, Donald Campbell, Maurice Lindsay, Duncan Glen, John Herdman, D.M. Black." circ. 1,300. 3/yr. Pub'd 3 issues 1979; expects 3 issues 1980. sub. price: £2.00 for 3; per copy: 75p; sample: 75p. Back issues: nos. 1-9 kraus $22, nos. 10-15 nos. 16-22 kraus. Discounts: 25% below & 33⅓% over 4. 88pp; 9X7; of. Reporting time: a few days. Payment: £3 per page. Copyrighted, reverts to author. Pub's reviews. §Mainly Scottish poetry and criticism of Scottish poetry. Ads: £40.00/£25.00. ALP, ALMS.

AKWESASNE NOTES, Sotsisowah, Editor; Segwalise, Assoc Editor, Mohawk Nation, Rooseveltown, NY 13683, 518-483-2540. 1969. Poetry, fiction, articles, art, photos, cartoons, interviews, satire, reviews, letters, long-poems, collages. "Vine Deloria, Jr./Stan Steiner/Jack Forbes" circ. 75,000. 5/yr plus books and pamphlets. Pub'd 5 issues 1979; expects 5 issues 1980, 5 issues 1981. 12 titles listed in the *Small Press Record of Books in Print* (9th Edition, 1980). sub. price: donation basis; per copy: $.50; sample: on request. Back issues: 50 cents. Discounts: 30% on consignment, 50% prepaid. 36pp; 17X11; of. Reporting time: usually promptly. No payment-a participant newspaper. Pub's reviews: 10 in 1979. §ecology, native american, colonialism, etc. no ad rates. APS.

ALA Social Responsibilities Round Table (see also ALA/SRRT NEWSLETTER), c/o Eubanks, Brooklyn College Library, Brooklyn, NY 11201. 1 title listed in the *Small Press Record of Books in Print* (9th Edition, 1980).

ALA/SRRT NEWSLETTER, ALA Social Responsibilities Round Table, Julia McCartney, c/o Eubanks, Brooklyn College Library, Brooklyn, NY 11210. 1969. "News-little outside material solicited. Bias-small press & movement press for libraries." circ. 1,200. 5-6/yr. sub. price: individual $3.00/yr; institution $20.00; sample: 1 free. Back issues: $1.00 ea. 7pp; 11X17, fold; of. Payment: none. Pub's reviews. §Movement-general, literary-only gay, women. no ads. COSMEP.

Albacore Press, Ann Orleman, PO Box 355, Eastsound, WA 98245. 1978. Articles, photos. "Would like to publish children's books as well as books about fishing and the ocean. Also considering a book about chimney's." avg. press run 2,000. Expects 1 title 1980, 1 title 1981. avg. price, paper: $5.95. Discounts: 40% to bookstores, 25% to libraries. 80pp; 8X11; of. Reporting time: 1 month. Payment: Each agreement would be different. Copyrights for author.

ALBATROSS, Stacey M. Franchild, P.O. Box 2046, Central Station, East Orange, NJ 07019. 1974. Poetry, fiction, articles, art, photos, cartoons, interviews, satire, criticism, reviews, music, letters, plays. "We try to print all sides of feminist or lesbian issues that our readers express any interest in and keep an open forum going for women to learn to express themselves in print—we prefer short things because we don't have much of an attention span but will also do long ones." circ. about 5,000. 2/yr. Pub'd 2 issues 1979. sub. price: $7.00 (3 issues); per copy: $3.50; sample: 3.50. Back issues: Price varies depending on how scarce the issue is. Discounts: We try to offer a 25% discount and will go lower if getting money up front—mostly we work on consignment. 56pp; 8½X11; of. Reporting time: 1 month. Payment: We pay in contributors copies, ads & subs. Copyrighted, reverts to author. Pub's reviews: several in 1979. §Lesbianism-Women-Women's Movement—& like that. Ads: $77.00/$47.00/$0.77. CCLM.

ALBERTA HISTORY, Historical Society of Alberta, Hugh A. Dempsey, 95 Holmwood Ave NW, Calgary Alberta T2K 2G7, Canada, 403-289-8149. 1953. Articles, reviews, non-fiction. "3500 to 7000 word articles on Western Canadian History" circ. 3,000. 4/yr. Pub'd 4 issues 1979; expects 4 issues 1980. sub. price: $6.00; per copy: $2.00; sample: free. Back issues: $1.00. Discounts: 1/3 off. 40pp; 7X10; of. Reporting time: 1 month. Payment: nil. Not copyrighted. Pub's reviews: 20 in 1979. §In our field-Western Canadian History. Ads: none. AASLH, CHA.

ALBUM, Tom Luba, 218 N Douglas Street, Appleton, WI 54911, (414) 733-0160. 1974. Reviews, music. "Length varies, contact for specifics. Want record reviews on music that 'deserves to be heard'. Priority given to artists deserving of greater merit. Want good writing & good knowledge of subject. Recent contributors: Tom Bingham, Cary Baker, David W. Chandler, Lawrence Keenan, Doug Collette, Tom Montag." circ. 2,000. 4/yr. Pub'd 4 issues 1979; expects 3 issues 1980, 3 issues 1981. sub. price: $3.00; per copy: $1.00; sample: $.84. Back issues: $1.00. Discounts: Inquire to editor. 16pp; 11X17; of. Reporting time: 1 week - 1 month usually; sometimes forever. Ads: $45.00/$27.00/$0.10.

ALCATRAZ, Alcatraz Editions, Stephen Kessler, 354 Hoover Road, Santa Cruz, CA 95065. 1978. Poetry, articles, art, photos, interviews, criticism, reviews, letters, long-poems. *"Alcatraz* is an occasional sampler/assemblage to indicate editorial directions of Alcatraz Editions and to present vital examples of new imagination at work. Especially interested in essays connecting diverse creative & cultural/political realms, poetry that takes chances, strong black & white visuals. Issues will be assembled at long intervals, mostly be invitation, so please inquire before sending material. Our first number, *Alcatraz an assemblage,* had 43 contributors: Anderson, Alegria, Hirschman, Braverman, etc." circ. 1,000. irregular. Pub'd 1 issue 1979. price per copy: $6.00. Discounts: 40% to booksellers on orders of 3 or more. 200pp; 6X9; of. Reporting time: fast. Payment: copies. Copyrighted, reverts to author. Pub's reviews: 1 in 1979. §Poetry, translations, cultural commentary, criticism, biography. Ads: No ads.

Alcatraz Editions (see also ALCATRAZ), Stephen Kessler, 354 Hoover Road, Santa Cruz, CA 95065. 1978. Poetry, long-poems. "Biased toward excellence, honesty, courage, imagination. See *Alcatraz an assemblage* for drift of current persuasions, or any of our first four books: *Bug Death* by F. A. Nettelbeck, *Sola* by Flora Durham, *Evans Road* by Mark Bristow, *Living Expenses* by Stephen Kessler. Please inquire before sending mss. as we are scheduled well into the '80s." avg. press run 500. Pub'd 2 titles 1979; expects 3 titles 1980. avg. price, paper: $4.00. Discounts: 40% to trade on orders of 3 or more. 80-120pp; of. Reporting time: 1-3 months. Payment: copies.

Alcazar Press, Peter Miller, 570 Windsor Street, Westbury, NY 11590, (516) ED4-3538. 1978. Fiction, satire. "Full-length novels. Count Lovebite trilogy by Peter Merlin. *Count Lovebite* (already published); *Sun Up For Count Lovebite; The Count at Twilight.*" avg. press run 1,000. Pub'd 1 title 1979. avg. price, paper: $3.95. 277pp; 5½X8½; of. Reporting time: instantaneous. Copyrights for author.

THE ALCHEMIST, Marco Fraticelli, Box 123, LaSalle, Quebec H8R 3T7, Canada. 1974. Poetry, fiction, art, photos, collages, concrete art, non-fiction. "No biases in terms of length of material or number of works submitted. Although we publish good 'traditional' works we are more interested in those which explore the possibilities. We especially need graphics (pen & ink)." circ. 500. 2/yr. Pub'd 2 issues 1979; expects 2 issues 1980. 1 title listed in the *Small Press Record of Books in Print* (9th Edition, 1980). sub. price: $5.00; per copy: $1.50; sample: free. 80pp; 5½X8½; of. Reporting time: 1 mo. Payment: copies only. Copyrighted, reverts to author. COSMEP.

Alchemist/Light Publishing, Bil Paul, P O Box 5530, San Francisco, CA 94101, (415) 655-0728. 1972. Fiction, photos. "Books." avg. press run 2,000. Pub'd 1 title 1979; expects 1 title 1980, 1 title 1981. 3 titles listed in the *Small Press Record of Books in Print* (9th Edition, 1980). avg. price, paper: $4.00. Discounts: 40% bookstores. 100pp; size varies; of/lp. Reporting time: 1 week. Copyrights for author.

Alchemy Books, Brian King, Mark Pittard, 681 Market, Suite 755, San Francisco, CA 94105, (415) 362-2708. 1977. Poetry, fiction, satire, long-poems. "We publish mainly non-fiction books with strong political or philosophical overtones, but remain open to anything. Recent works include: *Tarot Revelations* by Joseph Campbell and Richard Roberts and *Iran's Revolutionary Upheaval* by Sepehr Zabih." avg. press run 5,000. Pub'd 18 titles 1979; expects 27 titles 1980, 30 titles 1981. avg. price, cloth: $12.95; paper: $5.95. Discounts: 40% on 1 copy prepaid; 20% on 2-4; 42% on 5-30; 46% on 31-50; 48% on 51 or more. 200pp; of. Reporting time: 1-2 months. Copyrights for author.

ALDEBARAN, Staff, Roger Williams College, Bristol, RI 02809. 1971. Poetry, fiction, art, photos, interviews. "Dedicated to printing fine poetry and prose. Submissions of prose, poetry, art, accepted September through May. Interested in quality material, no biases." circ. 400. 2/yr. Pub'd 2 issues 1979; expects 2 issues 1980, 2 issues 1981. sub. price: $2.00; per copy: $1.00; sample: $1.00. Back issues: $1.25 for all numbers. Discounts: 40% bookstores. 48pp; 8½X5½; of. Reporting time: 4 months. Payment: 2 complimentry copies. Copyrighted, reverts to author. no ads.

Aldebaran Review, John Oliver Simon, 2209 California, Berkeley, CA 94703. 1968. Poetry, art, photos, long-poems. "Aldebaran Review has become a series of chapbooks & small anthologies of poetry. The editor feels especially close to—work by inmates at Folsom Prison, by a group of teenagers in Berkeley, the collected poems of a 6-year-old girl, long-poems & sequences by Alta, Pancho Aguila, Steve Sanfield, etc." avg. press run 1,000. Pub'd 1 title 1979; expects 3 titles 1980, 2 titles 1981. 14 titles listed in the *Small Press Record of Books in Print* (9th Edition, 1980). avg. price, cloth: $6.00-4 issues, $8.00 for institutions; paper: $2.00. Discounts: 20-40% to trade, up to 50% to distributors. 56pp; 5½X8½; †of. Reporting time: quickly. Payment: copies only. Copyrights for author. CCLM, COSMEP, COSMEP-WEST.

ALEMBIC, David Dayton, 1744 Slaterville Road, Ithaca, NY 14850, (607) 277-0827. 1977. Poetry, art, photos, long-poems. *"Alembic* hopes to become a 4-page center section of *The Cornell Daily Sun,* published 4 times a year primarily for The Sun's 15,000 readers, but available by subscription to others. Contributors to past issues include: Joan Colby, M.R. Doty, Mark Jarman, Thomas Johnson, Mekeel McBride, Tom McKeown, Gunilla Norris, William Pillin, Felix Pollak, Bert Meyers, John Tagliabue, Doren Robbins, James Anderson, Fred Muratori, Donald Walsh, Herbert Morris." circ. 5,000. 4/yr. Pub'd 3 issues 1979; expects 3 issues 1980, 4 issues 1981. sub. price: $3.00/4 issues; per copy: $1.00; sample: $2.00 for #2, 3, or 4; $1.00 for #6 and up. Back issues: #'s 1-4, $10.00; limited quantities. Discounts: inquire. 4pp; 11X17; of. Reporting time: up to 6 weeks. Payment: copies. Copyrighted, reverts to author. Ads: $3.00 col in.

Alex Aiken, 48 Merrycrest Avenue, Glasgow G46 6BJ, Scotland. 1971. "Publish own writing solely." Pub'd 1 title 1979. 5 titles listed in the *Small Press Record of Books in Print* (9th Edition, 1980). Discounts: trade 34 percent, libraries 10 percent. 8X5½.

Algol Press (see also STARSHIP: The Magazine About Science Fiction; SCIENCE FICTION CHRONICLE), Andrew Porter, Editor & Publisher; Susan Wood, Canadian Literature Editor, P.O. Box 4175, New York, NY 10017, 212-643-9011. 1963. Articles, art, photos, interviews, criticism, reviews, letters, news items. "Not soliciting material" avg. press run 2,000. Pub'd 2 titles 1979; expects 2 titles 1980. 4 titles listed in the *Small Press Record of Books in Print* (9th Edition, 1980). avg. price, cloth: $15.00; paper: $5.95. Discounts: 40 percent trade discount. Write: F&SF Book Co., P.O. Box 415, Staten Island NY 10302. 196pp; 5.5X8.5; of. Reporting time: 1-3 weeks. Payment: Royalties percentage of gross cover price. Copyrights for author.

Alice James Books, Cooperative, 138 Mount Auburn St., Cambridge, MA 02138. 1973. Poetry. "We are a small press, publishing books of poetry. We emphasize the publication of women, but have had 3 men as members. As a cooperative we make decisions collectively. When we accept a new manuscript the poet becomes a member of the cooperative and participates in work and policy-making. Members are limited to a geographic area close enough to participate in weekly meetings." avg. press run 2,100. Pub'd 4 titles 1979; expects 5 titles 1980. 29 titles listed in the *Small Press Record of Books in Print* (9th Edition, 1980). avg. price, paper: $3.95. Discounts: 20% jobbers, 50% distributors, no discounts for libraries, 40% bookstores. 72pp; 5½X8½ (can vary); of. Reporting time: 2 months. Payment: No royalties. Author receives 100 books as part of cooperative's contract with author. Copyrights for author. COSMEP.

ALIVE, Pete Jones, Editor, P.O. Box 1331, Guelph, Ont., Canada. 1969. Poetry, fiction, articles, art, photos, cartoons, interviews, satire, criticism, reviews, music, letters, parts-of-novels, long-poems, collages, plays, news items. "National and international contributors. Various news colums. Subscription is for 52 issues rather than one year. The cost is $11.00 for 52 issues. Institutions: $30.00, prisoners: free. All material copyrighted to individual athors. 1/8 of a page; camera ready preferred; only on exchange basis." circ. 5,000. 52/yr. Pub'd 21 issues 1979; expects 52 issues 1980, 52 issues 1981. price per copy: 10¢ per 24-page demi-tab mag; sample: 10¢ or free upon request. Back issues: If available @ 10¢ plus shipping. Discounts: 50% to stores. 24pp; 8⅛X10½; of. Reporting time: 1-3 weeks. Payment: 5 copies of issue that the contributor's work appears in. Pub's reviews: 13 in 1979. §Political, economic, and cultural areas.

All About Us, Betty Nickerson, Box 1985, Ottawa, Ontario K1P 5R5, Canada, (613) 238-2919. 1972. Poetry, fiction, art, photos, plays, letters, long-poems. "Most books are anthologies by young, unpublished writers, and painters." avg. press run 3,000-5,000. Pub'd 2 titles 1979; expects 4 titles 1980, 4 titles 1981. 6 titles listed in the *Small Press Record of Books in Print* (9th Edition, 1980). avg. price, paper: $5.00. Discounts: trade—classroom. 120pp; 6X9; of, lp. Reporting time: depends on submission. Payment: no royalties. author retains all rights. ACP.

All of Us, P O Box 4552, Boulder, CO 80306. Fiction. avg. press run 1,000. Pub'd 3 titles 1979; expects 3 titles 1980, 3 titles 1981. avg. price, paper: $4.00. 28pp.

Allegany Mountain Press (see also UROBOROS), Ford F. Ruggieri, Helen Ruggieri, 111 N. 10th St., Olean, NY 14760, 716-372-0935. 1974. Poetry, fiction, long-poems, criticism. "We will be reading manuscripts for publication in our UROBOROS books & the Rebis chapbook series; see UROBOROS magazine for biases." avg. press run 500. Pub'd 6 titles 1979. 3 titles listed in the *Small Press Record of Books in Print* (9th Edition, 1980). avg. price, cloth: $8.00; paper: $3.50; other: Chapbooks $1.50. Discounts: 2-5, 25%; 6-10, 30%; 11-24, 40%; 25+, 50%; wholesale by arrangement. 32-70pp; 5½X8½; †of. Reporting time: 2-3 months. Payment: Chapbooks pay copies; books by arrangement. CCLM, COSMEP, NYSSPA.

Alleluia Press, Dr. Jose M. de Vinck, Owner, Box 103, Allendale, NJ 07401, 201-327-3513. 1969. Poetry, criticism. "Very few outside MSS. are accepted since we have our own authors. We produce books and offer our imprint and distribution *only* in the case of scholars whose works are up to our high standards and who can finance first costs of production. No limit to length: we have 1,250 pp.

and 850 pp. books. Some recent contributors: Rev. Casimir Kucharek, Rama, Sask., Can.; Liturgical Commission, Ruthenian Dioceses of Pittsburgh, Parma & Passaic; Archbishop Joseph Raya, Combermere, Ont., Can., etc. We specialize in very high quality religious books, generally printed in Belgium, but accept other works, for instance a photographic album. Our distribution, however, is geared mainly to religious customers of the Byzantine Rite, Orthodox and Catholic, and to the general Christian readership." avg. press run from 1,000 to 10,000. Pub'd 4 titles 1979; expects 3 titles 1980, 3 titles 1981. 7 titles listed in the *Small Press Record of Books in Print* (9th Edition, 1980). avg. price, cloth: $6.00-$15.00; paper: $2.00-$12.75; other: $35.00-Deluxe Morocco. Discounts: Below $20.00, 25 percent; $20.00 or over, 40 percent; no discount on all codes BW. Special discounts on very large orders. from 32 to 1,250 pp depending on type of book; size varies; of/lp. Reporting time: 1 week · Payment: Individual contracts. Does not copyright for author.

ALLIN, Nina Carroll, 27 Harpes Road, Oxford, United Kingdom. 1968. Poetry, art, concrete art · "Ted Hughes, Brian Patten, George McBeth, James Kirkup, each ALLIN is illustrated. Copyrights: copies are sent to British Library copyright department. Each author makes own arrangement." circ. limited. irreg. Pub'd 1 issue 1979; expects 1 issue 1980. 7 titles listed in the *Small Press Record of Books in Print* (9th Edition, 1980). sub. price: £1/4 issues; per copy: 30p; sample: 20p. 1pp; 15X20; of. Payment: copy. ALP.

The Ally Press, Paul Feroe, PO Box 30340, St. Paul, MN 55175, (612) 227-1567. 1973. Poetry. "Poetry chapbooks and translations, with illustrations, theme, or distinguishing feature. Strong preference for unalienated writers. Will be expanding soon to New Age 'how-to' books of commercial interest. Recent work is, *Silent Voices, Recent American Poems on Nature,* including Robert Bly, Ted Kooser, Norbert Krapf, etc., $2.95 & $6.50 (cloth). 'An Ally is a power capable of carrying a man beyond the boundaries of himself.'—from the teachings of Don Juan" avg. press run 1500. Expects 2 titles 1981. 6 titles listed in the *Small Press Record of Books in Print* (9th Edition, 1980). avg. price, cloth: $6.50; paper: $2.50. Discounts: 1-4, 20%; 4-49, 40%; handcased, 20%. 5¼X8; †of/lp. Reporting time: 4 weeks. Payment: in copies. Copyrights for author. COSMEP.

Almar Press, Alfred N. Weiner, Editor-in-Chief; Marilyn Weiner, Managing Editor, 4105 Marietta Drive, Binghamton, NY 13903, (607) 722-6251. 1977. "Publish business, technical, and consumer books and reports. These main subjects include financial, travel, career, technology, personal help, hobbies, general medical, general legal, how-to. *Almar Reports* are business and technology subjects published for management use and prepared in booklet and/or 8½ x 11 format. Other publications are printed and bound in soft or hard covers as required. Reprint publications are a new aspect of our business." avg. press run 1500-5M. Pub'd 2 titles 1979; expects 6 titles 1980, 8 titles 1981. 3 titles listed in the *Small Press Record of Books in Print* (9th Edition, 1980). avg. price, paper: $3.50-$5.00; other: $3.00-$5.00 (Reports). Discounts: standard or per special arrangement. 64pp; 8½X11, 5½X8½; of/lp. Reporting time: 4 weeks. Payment: royalty: 10%, 12½%, 15% or special arrangements. Copyrights for author.

ALPHA, Either/Or Publications, Lynda C.H. Russell, Box 1269, Wolfville, Nova Scotia B0P1X0, Canada, 542-2201 Ext 421. 1976. Poetry, fiction, articles, art, photos, cartoons, interviews, satire, criticism, reviews, music, letters, plays. "Short stories - 1,000 words up. Would very much like to see more humor, satire, etc." circ. 300-500. 7/yr. sub. price: $3.00; per copy: $0.50; sample: $0.50. Back issues: to Jan. '77 - $0.15; $0.25 Feb. '77 on. Discounts: Negotiable. 32pp; 8½X11; of. Reporting time: 1 month. Payment: None at present. Copyrighted, reverts to author. Pub's reviews. §Fiction, anthologies, nonfiction on the arts. Ads: Rates presently under revision.

Alphabox Press (see also A), Jeremy Adler, 47 Wetherby Mansion, Earls Court Square, London SW5 9BH, United Kingdom. 1974. Poetry, long-poems, collages, concrete art. "*Fenster Sieben Gedichte* by H. G. Adler, *Acht Gedichte In Faksimile,* by Franz Wurm, *The Amsterdam Quartet* by Jeremy Adler. H.G. Adler, *Spuren und Pfeiler. Gedichte,* with illustrations by Friedrich Danielis, *Vowel Jubilee* by Jeremy Adler. In preparation: Ernst Jandl, *Portraits* (Winter 1979-80). Other publications in association with Pirate Press and Writers Forum. To publish otherwise unpublishable visual poetry; poetry combining traditional techniques with experimentation; translations; at cost (non profit-making) prices. Contributions not solicited, but considered if accompanied by SAE." avg. press run 100-300. Pub'd 2 titles 1979; expects 3 titles 1980. 4 titles listed in the *Small Press Record of Books in Print* (9th Edition, 1980). avg. price, paper: $2.00-$3.00. Discounts: 33%, 40% booksellers. 20pp; size A4, A3; †of. Reporting time: 2 months. Payment: copies. ALP, CULP.

Alphaville Books (see also OXYMORON: Journal Of Convulsive Beauty), Jack Grady, Orlan Cannon, 728 Hinman Avenue, Evanston, IL 60602. 1975. "Alphaville Books publishes avant-garde/experimental literatue & related graphics. Various formats planned for 1979-80. Exchanges & inquiries (w/SASE) welcomed; moving to Chicago (6/79), so request address correction/send 1st class when possible." Pub'd 1 title 1979; expects 2 titles 1980. 4 titles listed in the *Small Press Record of Books in Print* (9th Edition, 1980). avg. price, cloth: varies; paper: varies; other: Varies. Discounts: enquire. pp varies; size varies; †of/xerox. No mss sought presently. Payment: by arrangement w/authors.

Alpine Publications, Betty McKinney, Barbara Hagen Rieseberg, 1901 South Garfield, Loveland, CO 80537, (303) 667-2017. 1976. "We publish nonfiction books for the dog, horse, and pet markets. About half of our sales are by mail order. Our books are high quality, in-depth, thorough coverage of a specific subject (breed). Authors must know their field and be able to provide useful, how-to information with illustrations." avg. press run 2,000. Pub'd 4 titles 1979; expects 10 titles 1980, 10 titles 1981. 6 titles listed in the *Small Press Record of Books in Print* (9th Edition, 1980). avg. price, cloth: $14.00; paper: $5.00. Discounts: 2-5, 20%; 6-9, 30%; 10-49, 40%. 200pp; 8½X11, 6X9, 5½X8½; of. Reporting time: 30 to 60 days. Payment: 10% on hardback, 7% paperback. Copyrights for author. COSMEP.

Alta Gaia Society, Lia Colla, Bonnie Nielsen, Dutchess Avenue, Millerton, NY 12546, (518) 789-3865. 1978. Poetry, fiction, art, criticism, reviews, concrete art. "Interested in cultural-philosophical works by women." avg. press run 2,000-3,000. Expects 2 titles 1980, 5 titles 1981. 2 titles listed in the *Small Press Record of Books in Print* (9th Edition, 1980). avg. price, cloth: $12.95; paper: $6.95. Regular trade discounts. 350pp; 5½X8½; of. Reporting time: 6-8 weeks. Payment: Upon mutual agreement. Copyrights for author.

Alta Napa Press, Carl T. Endemann, Box 407, Calistoga, CA 94515. 1977. Poetry, fiction, articles, photos, parts-of-novels, long-poems. "Reply only if S.A.S.E. Gondwana Books is now a division of Alta Napa Press." avg. press run 500 — 1,000. Pub'd 2 titles 1979; expects 3 titles 1980. 5 titles listed in the *Small Press Record of Books in Print* (9th Edition, 1980). avg. price, cloth: $7.50; paper: $3.50. Discounts: Trade 40%; Bulk 50%. 50-150pp; 5X8½, 6X9; of/lp. Reporting time: 2 mos. Payment: yes. Copyrights for author. COSMEP.

THE ALTADENA REVIEW, The Altadena Review, Inc., Robin Shectman, Editor; Carl Selkin, Associate Editor, P.O. Box 212, Altadena, CA 91001. 1977. Poetry, articles, art, interviews, criticism, reviews. "Articles, reviews, criticism, interviews, should be on subjects of interest to poets and readers of poetry. Very high standards for original poetry." circ. 300. 3/yr. Expects 3 issues 1980. sub. price: $4.50; per copy: $1.50; sample: $1.50. Discounts: 40% discount to bookstores; 10% discount on other orders of more than 5 copies. 48pp; 5½X8½; of. Reporting time: 4 weeks or less. Payment: 2 copies of issue in which work appears. Copyrighted, reverts to author. Pub's reviews: 2 in 1979. §Poetry. Ads: none. COSMEP.

The Altadena Review, Inc. (see also THE ALTADENA REVIEW), Robin Shectman, Editor; Carl Selkin, Associate Editor, PO Box 212, Altadena, CA 91001. 1977. Poetry, articles, art, interviews, criticism, reviews. avg. press run 300. Pub'd 1 title 1979; expects 3 titles 1980, 3 titles 1981. avg. price, paper: $1.50. Discounts: 40% to bookstores; 10% on other orders of more than 5 copies. 48pp; 5½X8½; of. Reporting time: 4 weeks or less. Payment: 2 copies of magazine in which work appears. COSMEP.

THE ALTERNATE, Alternate Publishing Company, John W. Rowberry, 15 Harriet Street, San Francisco, CA 94103, (415) 346-4747. 1977. Fiction, articles, art, photos, cartoons, interviews, satire, criticism, news items. "Gay audience, interested in more thoughtful material than usually appears in gay non-porn magazines. Looking for material exploring future of gays, alternative socio-political organization, lifestyles, over-all concept of gays in mainstream society, historical information, trend towards putting modern methods to work for gays deciding their own destiny. John Rechy, Daniel Curzon, Harvey Milk, Art Agnos." circ. 30,000. 6/yr. Pub'd 2 issues 1979; expects 6 issues 1980, 6 issues 1981. sub. price: $15.00; per copy: $2.50; sample: $2.00. Back issues: Sample is always current issue, back issues $2.00 each. Discounts: varies. 68pp; 8X11; of. Reporting time: immediately. Payment: varies from $1.00 printed inch up. Copyrighted. Pub's reviews: 30 in 1979. §Art, poetry, photography, new fiction, resource information. APS.

Alternate Publishing Company (see THE ALTERNATE)

ALTERNATIVE FUTURES: THE JOURNAL OF UTOPIAN STUDIES, Sans Serif Press, Merritt Abrash, Alexandra Aldridge, Human Dimensions Center, Rensselaer Polytechnic Institute, Troy, NY 12181, (518)270-6574. 1978. Articles, interviews, reviews, letters. "Essays of analytical and speculative nature; mss in duplicate w/SASE. Utopian/futures thought and literature, communitarianism & social experiment, utopian/dystopian science fiction, non-technical futures inquiry." circ. 700. 4/yr. Pub'd 3 issues 1979; expects 4 issues 1980, 4 issues 1981. sub. price: $10.00/yr individuals; $17/yr institutions; per copy: $3.00; sample: limited no. samples available. Discounts: 15%/agency. 128pp;

6X9; of. Reporting time: 3 months. Payment: 3 copies of issue in which work appears. Copyrighted. Pub's reviews: 14 in 1979. §Communitarianism and social experiment, futures inquiry, utopian literature & thought, utopian/dystopian science fiction. Ads: $100/$60/.

ALTERNATIVE MEDIA, Alternative Press Syndicate, Craig Silver, Editor, Box 775 Madison Square Station, New York, NY 10010, (212) 481-0120. 1969. Articles, cartoons, interviews, criticism, reviews, news items. "*AM* publishes articles for and about the alternative forms of journalism and media. We publish about 4 or 5 features in each of our quarterly issues as well as news items, reviews, and some ad exchange." circ. 7,000. 4/yr. Pub'd 1 issue 1979; expects 4 issues 1980, 4 issues 1981. sub. price: $5.00; per copy: $1.50; sample: on request. Back issues: Not available before 76 issues, $1.50 per issue. Discounts: 60¢. 44pp; 8½X11; of. Reporting time: 3 weeks. Payment: $20.00-$100.00. Copyrighted. Pub's reviews: 20 in 1979. §Future studies, media, journalism, film, community action, countercultural material, other. Ads: $500.00/$330.00/$0.25. ASP, COSMEP.

THE ALTERNATIVE PRESS, Ann Mikolowski, Ken Mikolowski, 3090 Copeland Rd, Grindstone City, MI 48467. 1969. Poetry, art. "Number ten includes new postcards, broadsides, bumperstickers, etc by Joanne Kyger, Arthur Okamura, Robert Creeley, Donna Brook, Andrei Codrescu, Edward Dorn, Faye Kicknosway, Jim Gustafson, Rosmarie Waldrop & Anselm Hollo." circ. 500. 3/yr. Pub'd 3 issues 1979; expects 3 issues 1980. 2 titles listed in the *Small Press Record of Books in Print* (9th Edition, 1980). sub. price: $10.00; per copy: 3.50; sample: 3.50. †lp. Reporting time: 1-3 months. Payment: copies. Not copyrighted. CCLM, COSMEP.

Alternative Press Syndicate (see ALTERNATIVE MEDIA)

ALTERNATIVE RESEARCH NEWSLETTER, Wintergreen Collective, PO Box 1294, Kitchener, ON N2G 4G8, Canada. 1979. Poetry, fiction, articles, art, cartoons, interviews, satire, criticism, reviews, letters, news items. "Serves as a bill-board of resources, reviews, trends, information, news & notes, activities, up-dates, happenings & the like, & lists resources of all sorts, of the alternative culture. All areas from anarchism to zen, world-wide. Send some different copies of your mag; anyother info (catalogs, books, etc) for review. Short articles, etc wanted. Contacts wanted too, from around the world, to help with info." circ. 1,500-2,000. 4-6/yr. Pub'd 2 issues 1979; expects 4 issues 1980, 4-6 issues 1981. sub. price: $5.00/£2/Dm 8; per copy: $1.25/50p/Dm 2; sample: $1.00/50p/Dm 2. Back issues: same prices. Discounts: write. 32pp; 8½X11; of. Reporting time: immediately. Pub's reviews. §Alternative culture, spiritual & metaphysical, counter-culture, radical, etc. Ads: $60.00/$30.00/$0.10. APS, CAPF.

ALTERNATIVE SOURCES of ENERGY MAGAZINE, Bolger Publishing, Staff, Network Contributors; Don Marier, Editor-in-Chief, 107 S. Central Avenue, Milaca, MN 56353, 612-983-6892. 1971. Articles, art, photos, cartoons, interviews, satire, criticism, reviews, letters, news items. "Need alternative energy related material with photos, art, graphics, solar, wind, water, thermo electric topics. Wood/organic fuels, greenhouses architecture, integrated systems, much more." circ. 10,000. Bimonthly. Pub'd 6 issues 1979; expects 6 issues 1980, 6 issues 1981. sub. price: 6 issue price $15.00/Foreign $32.00, air mail only Canada & Mexico, surface mail only $18.00; per copy: $2.75; sample: $2.75. Back issues: $2.00; thru #38; inquire-many now out-of-print. Discounts: Please request discount information on your letterhead. 56pp; 7X10; of. Reporting time: 3 weeks. Payment: $50.00-$150.00. Copyrighted, does not revert to author. Pub's reviews: 150 in 1979. §Alternative energy topics & appropriate technology. Ads: $436.00/$245.00/$0.35: $8.75 min. Request current rate card. COSMEP.

†ALTERNATIVES- Perspectives on Society and Environment, Ted Schrecker, Trent University, c/o Traill College, Peterborough, On K9J7B8, Canada. 1971. Articles. "Environmental-ecological emphasis, topics cover philosophical, social, political, economic and other considerations. Articles submitted should be typewritten, modest footnoting at end of article. Two copies should be submitted." circ. 12-1,500. 4/yr. sub. price: $4.00 indiv; $7.00 instit; $5.00 US & Overseas to indiv; $8.00 US & Overseas to instit; $9.95 3 yr discount to indiv; $12.95 3 yr discount to US & Overseas; per copy: $1.00; sample: $1.00. Back issues: $1.00/ea except $3.00/vol. 1,1: 2,1: 2,2; $2.00/vol. 1,2 (Available to Libraries only). Discounts: 40% bookstores and orders of 20 plus. 44pp; 8½X11; of. Payment: none. Pub's reviews. Ads: $250/$125.

Alyson Publications, Inc., Sasha Alyson, 75 Kneeland Street, Rm 309, Boston, MA 02111, (617) 542-5679. 1977. "We publish short and medium-length books on radical and feminist issues. We do subsidy publishing and co-publishing with other groups also." avg. press run 4,000. Pub'd 1 title 1979; expects 6 titles 1980, 10 titles 1981. 2 titles listed in the *Small Press Record of Books in Print* (9th Edition, 1980). avg. price, paper: $3.00-$4.00. Discounts: Standard 40% trade, 50% wholesalers. 80-200pp; 5¼X8¼; of. Reporting time: 2 weeks max. Payment: 4-8%. Copyrights for author.

AMBIT, Martin Bax, 17 Priory Gardens, London, England N6 5QY, United Kingdom. 1959. Poetry, fiction, art, photos, long-poems. "Always looking for material which excites and interests. Suggest contributors read the magazine before they submit." circ. 1,500. 4/yr. sub. price: £2.50; per copy: 60p; sample: 60p. Back issues: Recent back nos. 60p. 96pp; 9½X7½; of. Reporting time: 3 months. Payment: by arrangement. Ads: £25 page. ALP.

American Academy of Arts and Sciences (see DAEDALUS, Journal of the American Academy of Arts and Sciences)

‡**American Artists In Exhibition, Inc.,** Neal Spitzer, Director, 799 Greenwich St., New York, NY 10014, 212-989-1595. 1975. Poetry, fiction. "This is a public art project devoted to building new and wider audiences for the arts. We place literature posters in banks, supermarkets, store windows and other places with heavy pedestrian traffic. Poster 18 x 28, $2.00; Broadside 17 x 22, $2.00; Signed limited edition broadside, 100% cotton fiber 17 x 22, $10.00. Published with authors copyright notice, but author must take care of registration." avg. press run 4,000. Pub'd 6 titles 1979; expects 6 titles 1980, 6-10 titles 1981. 19 titles listed in the *Small Press Record of Books in Print* (9th Edition, 1980). Discounts: 1/3 off for quantity orders — special arrangements made for participation in public art project by arts councils and other non-profit organizations. 1pp; 18X28, 17X22; of. We do not accept submissions. Payment: $100.00 plus additional fellowship when possible, plus 100 broadsides for author.

AMERICAN ARTS PAMPHLET SERIES, Mick Gidley, Queens Bldg., Univ. of Exeter, Exeter EX4 4QH, United Kingdom. 1970. Articles, interviews, criticism. "The American Arts Pamphlet Series is an irregular series publishing specially commissioned items on the arts in America. Titles include *A Chronological Checklist of the Periodical Publication of Sylvia Plath*; *A Selected Bibliography of Black Literature* ; *The Harlem Renaissance*; *A Catalog of American Paintings in British Public Collections*; *Charles Ives and the American Band Tradition*; Robert Flaherty's *The Land.*" circ. 1,300. 1-2/yr. Expects 1 issue 1980, 1 issue 1981. 5 titles listed in the *Small Press Record of Books in Print* (9th Edition, 1980). price per copy: varies; sample: $3.00. Discounts: 33% booksellers. 33pp; size A5; lp. Copyrighted.

THE AMERICAN BOOK REVIEW, Charles Russell, Suzanne Zavrian, John Tytell, Rochelle Ratner, PO Box 188, Cooper Station, New York, NY 10003, (212) 749-5906. 1977. Reviews. "Length: ideally, 750-1,500 words. Reviewers should be primarily writers. *Unsolicited reviews encouraged.* We would like to see more reviews, or review articles, departing from the traditional review form—more innovative material. Contributors: William Denby, Fanny Howe, Joyce Carol Oates, Andrei Codrescu, etc." circ. 10,000. 6/yr. Pub'd 4 issues 1979; expects 6 issues 1980, 6 issues 1981. sub. price: $4.00; per copy: $1.00; sample: $0.75. 16-24pp; 11½X16; of. Reporting time: 2 months. Payment: $25.00 per review. Copyrighted. Pub's reviews. §Literary or closely allied fields. Ads: $125.00/$75.00. CCLM.

American Business Consultants, Inc., Wilfred F. Tetreault, J. Johnson Russell, Robert W. Clements, 1540 Nuthatch Lane, Sunnyvale, CA 94087, (408) 732-8931. 1979. Non-fiction. "These books written by the above authors covers thoroughly business opportunities, business training, and general education in the art of buying and selling your own business. The material in these books has been thoroughly researched and approved by California and Nevada Department of Real Estate. Pending in other states and the board of accountancy." avg. press run 1,000. Pub'd 1 title 1979; expects 14 titles 1980, 16 titles 1981. 15 titles listed in the *Small Press Record of Books in Print* (9th Edition, 1980). avg. price, paper: $2.00-$49.95. Discounts: standard. 6-300pp; 8½X11; †of. Reporting time: 2-6 weeks. Payment: standard. Copyrights for author.

American-Canadian Publishers, Inc., Arthur Goodson, Ed. Director; Arlene Zekowski, Stanley Berne, Herman Zaage, Art Director, Drawer 2078, Portales, NM 88130, 505-356-4082. 1972. Poetry, fiction, articles, art, photos, interviews, satire, criticism, reviews, music, letters, parts-of-novels, long-poems, collages, plays, concrete art, news items, non-fiction. "We believe through the practice of 25 years and 42 completed works (15 published books with many soon forthcoming) that the language/-literature/criticism of the year 2,000 will be a celebration of the multilinear dimensions of verbal consciousness - non-exclusive, genrebreaking and open structured new frontiers of literary possibility. Beyond grammar and the sentence and the visual. A truly perceptual extension in many media. Newest titles: Arlene Zekowski, *Image Breaking Images;* Stanley Berne, *Future Language,* 2nd printing, fall 1977. Also available: 'Literary Best Sellers' *Seasons Of The Mind* (Zekowski); *The Unconscious Victorious* (Berne). Now available on cassettes: interviews readings radio shows on: neo-narrative, poetry-prose open structure & the grammarless language. Send for free kit/catalog on 'The Grammarless Language.' Discounts available for bookstores, distributors & class adoptions." avg. press run 1,500 per title to 3,000 per title. Pub'd 2 titles 1979; expects 2 titles 1980. 9 titles listed in the *Small Press Record of Books in Print* (9th Edition, 1980). avg. price, cloth: $15.00; paper: $6.00; other: $10.00-$100.00. Discounts: 40 percent to dealers; 50 percent bulk-class adoptions: rates negotiable. 200pp; 6X9; of. Payment:

negotiable. Copyrights for author. Rio Grande Writers Assoc, COSMEP, LPSC, WIP, NESPA.

The American Conference of Therapeutic Selfhelp/Selfhealth/Social Clubs (see CONSTRUCTIVE ACTION FOR GOOD HEALTH)

American Dance Guild Inc (see also AMERICAN DANCE GUILD NEWSLETTER; DANCE SCOPE), 1133 Broadway #1427, New York, NY 10010. 6 titles listed in the *Small Press Record of Books in Print* (9th Edition, 1980).

AMERICAN DANCE GUILD NEWSLETTER, American Dance Guild Inc, Sarah Montague, Editor; Elizabeth Richter Zimmer, Contributing Editor, 1133 Broadway #1427, New York, NY 10010, (212) 691-7773. 1956. Articles, criticism, reviews, letters, news items. circ. 1,000. 9-10/yr. Pub'd 8 issues 1979; expects 9 issues 1980, 9-10 issues 1981. sub. price: regular membership: $35.00; per copy: $1.00; sample: $1.00. Back issues: $1.00. 14pp; 8½X11; of. Reporting time: 2 months. Payment: none. Not copyrighted. Pub's reviews: 15-18 in 1979. §performing arts, arts management, arts education. Ads: $50.00/$30.00. CCLM.

AMERICAN FIDDLERS NEWS, American Old Time Fiddlers Assoc., De Lores "Fiddling De" De Ryke, 6141 Morrill Avenue, Lincoln, NB 68507, 402-466-5519. 1965. Poetry, articles, cartoons, interviews, reviews, music, letters, criticism, news items. "We can use anything about Music played on the violin-fiddle. Writings must be by someone who knows the subject-(or interviewee must be expert). Must be sympathetic to fiddler-violinist. Must be authentic information-well researched, also review Records and Music books of Music, report contests and conventions." circ. International Mailing List 5,000. 4/yr. Pub'd 4 issues 1979; expects 10 issues 1980, 4 issues 1981. sub. price: $7.50; per copy: $2.00; sample: $2.00. Back issues: $5.00 per year's volume. Discounts: $6.50 per year. 20pp; 8½X11; †mi. Reporting time: 1 month or less. Payment: copies. We do not copyright for author. Pub's reviews: 10 in 1979. §Music-folk lore, dancing (folk), violin making-music books, classical violin. All violin-fiddle records/All violin-fiddle music. Ads: $25/$13 (1/4 page $6.50)/$1 per inch.

AMERICAN LITERATURE, Duke University Press, Edwin H. Cady, 6667 College Station, Durham, NC 27708, (919) 684-3948. 1929. Articles, criticism, reviews. "American Literature *only*" circ. 6,000. quarterly. Pub'd 4 issues 1979; expects 4 issues 1980, 4 issues 1981. sub. price: $10 individuals/$12 institutions/foreign: add $3.00 postage; per copy: $3.00. Back issues: Single, $4.50; Volume $18.00. 175pp; 6X9; lp. Reporting time: 2-3 months. Payment: 50 reprints. Copyrighted, rights optional with author. Pub's reviews: about 90 in 1979. §American literary criticism, scholarship, bibliography. Ads: $200.00/$125.00/15% discount for four consecutive issues.

AMERICAN MAN, Richard Haddad, Box 693, Columbia, MD 21045, (301) 997-1373. 1980. Poetry, fiction, articles, art, cartoons, interviews, reviews, letters. "Publishes articles, etc, dealing exclusively with the male role, the male experience, and related subjects. Mag is supportive of the liberation of men from destructive gender rules. Premiere issue contributors include Herb Goldberg, Phd & Warren Farrell, Phd." circ. 500. 4/yr. sub. price: $14.00; per copy: $3.50; sample: $3.50. 56pp; 5½X8½; of. Reporting time: four to six weeks. Payment: two copies issue in which contribution is published. Copyrighted, reverts to author. Pub's reviews. §Gender roles, social change. Ads: $32.-00/$18.00.

American Old Time Fiddlers Assoc. (see also AMERICAN FIDDLERS NEWS), DeLores 'Fiddling De' DeRyke, 6141 Morrill Avenue, Lincoln, NB 68507, (402) 466-5519. 1965. Poetry, articles, interviews, reviews, music, letters, news items. avg. press run 5,000. Pub'd 1 title 1979. avg. price, paper: $7.50. 8½X11; †mi. Reporting time: A month or less. Some rejections the same day received if SASE enclosed. Payment: copies.

‡**AMERICAN POET, Prairie Poet Press,** 902 10th St., Box 35, Charleston, IL 61920.

AMERICAN POETRY REVIEW, Stephen Berg, David Bonanno, Rhoda Schwartz, Arthur Vogelsang, 1616 Walnut St., Room 405, Philadelphia, PA 19103, 215-732-6770. 1972. Poetry, fiction, articles, art, photos, cartoons, interviews, satire, criticism, reviews, music, letters, parts-of-novels, long-poems, collages, plays, concrete art, news items, non-fiction. circ. 26,000. 6/yr. Pub'd 6 issues 1979; expects 6 issues 1980. sub. price: $7.50; per copy: $1.50; sample: free. Back issues: $5.00 and $2.00. Discounts: Through Eastern News for stores and newsstands. 48pp; 9¾X13¾; of. Reporting time: 6 weeks. Payment: $0.50 line for poetry; $25.00 tabloid page for prose. Copyrighted, reverts to author. Pub's reviews. §Literary. Ads: $500.00/$295.00. CCLM.

American Revolutionary Political Pamphlets, Melvyn Freilicher, 704 Nob Avenue, Del Mar, CA 92014, 755-1258. 1974. Fiction, art. "Mostly I print my own work. When I do print someone else, the ms. is solicited." avg. press run 400. Pub'd 1 title 1979; expects 2 titles 1980. avg. price, cloth: free. Discounts: These pamphlets are distributed free, so far. 45pp; 8½X11; of. COSMEP.

16

‡THE AMERICAN SCHOLAR, Joseph Epstein, 1811 Q St.NW, Washington, DC 20009, 202-C05-3808. 1932. Poetry, articles, criticism, reviews, letters. "3,000 to 4,000 words best" circ. 40,000. Quarterly. Pub'd 4 issues 1979; expects 4 issues 1980. sub. price: $8.00; per copy: $2.00; sample: $2.00. Back issues: $2.50 and up. Discounts: Vary. 144pp; 5½X8; of. Reporting time: 4 weeks. Payment: $250.00 per article. Copyrighted. Pub's reviews. Ads: $425.00/$235.00.

American Studies Press, Inc., Donald R. Harkness, President & Editor-in-Chief, 13511 Palmwood Lane, Tampa, FL 33624, (813) 961-7200; (813) 974-2857. 1977. Poetry, fiction, articles, art, photos, cartoons, interviews, satire, criticism, music, letters, long-poems, plays. "Oct 77, 'Carol for This Year,' words and melody by Don Harkness, arranged by Lin Phelps; Mar 79, *Tales from a Reservation Storekeeper* by Raleigh E. Barker. May 79 *On Being Human* by Laszlo J. Hetenyi; July 79 *A Journey to California: The Letters of Thaddeus Dean 1852* ed by Katharine Dean Wheeler; Aug 79 *American Studies Singing* by Jay Gurian; Sept 79 *Seasa 79 Proceedings* ed by Don Harkness; May 80 *California Frescoes* by Jans Juergensen." avg. press run 500. Pub'd 5 titles 1979; expects 6 titles 1980, 7 titles 1981. 7 titles listed in the *Small Press Record of Books in Print* (9th Edition, 1980). avg. price, paper: $3.75. Discounts: 40% on 5 or more copies. 50pp; 6X9; of. Reporting time: should be brief. Payment: 10% after printing expenses paid; 25% on second and subsequent printings. Copyrights for author. COSMEP.

Americana Books (see also THE BOOK-MART), David G. MacLean, PO Box 481, Pinellas Park, FL 33565. 1968. Articles, photos, cartoons, interviews, reviews, letters, news items. "ISBN 0-917902; ISSN 0161-5556" avg. press run 1,000-1,500. Expects 1 title 1980. 2 titles listed in the *Small Press Record of Books in Print* (9th Edition, 1980). avg. price, cloth: $12.50; paper: $5.95. Discounts: 1, 25%; 3 or more, 40%. 150pp; 5X8½; of. Not seeking submissions.

Amigo Press, Virginia P. Ryder, 620 Lombardy Lane, Laguna Beach, CA 92651, (714) 494-2302. 1979. "We are a new press specializing in food, nature, travel with emphasis on Mexico (often but not always)." Pub'd 1 title 1979. 1 title listed in the *Small Press Record of Books in Print* (9th Edition, 1980). avg. price, cloth: $7.95; paper: $5.95. Discounts: negotiable.

Amistad Press, Yolanda C. Carter, PO Box 5026, Austin, TX 78763, (512) 472-8992. 1975. Poetry, fiction, art, photos. "We publish: I. Miniature books, 7/8 inches high up to 2⅞ inches high, a specialized item for doll houses and miniature book collectors. Most books are original, but other people have also contributed text and drawings." avg. press run 300-500. Pub'd 10 titles 1979; expects 4 titles 1980, 4 titles 1981. avg. price, cloth: $10.50. Discounts: 30-40% to dealers. 30pp; of. Payment: 10% of wholesale price on books sold, paid once a year.

Amity Books, Bob Amos, 1702 Magnolia, Liberty, MO 64068, (816) 781-6431. 1979. Articles. "Amity has published one book. *Runner* is 70,000 words, non-fiction. All our books are designed to demonstrate alternative lifestyles and to bridge the racial, religious, age and income barriers." avg. press run 2,000. Pub'd 1 title 1979. avg. price, cloth: $9.95. Discounts: 20%-40%. 200pp; 5½X8½; lp. Reporting time: 6-8 weeks. Payment: 10%, no advance. Copyrights for author.

AMOSKEAG: A Magazine of Haiku, The First Haiku Press, Matsuo Allard, 113 Comeau Street, Manchester, NH 03102. 1980. Poetry, articles, interviews, criticism, reviews, letters, news items. "*Amoskeag* is the only haiku magazine in English to maintain fidelity with the Japanese manner of printing haiku: in one-line forms. We will not cater to those who deliberately propagate the misconstrued western form of haiku in three or so lines. It is the *only* haiku magazine *anywhere* to print only one poem per page, with the author's name on yet another individual page, preceeding his selection(s). *Amoskeag* is eclectic, printing haiku in all known forms: Teikei (traditional), Yuki Teikei (pure traditional), Jiyuritsu (free meter), Hi-Teikei (non-traditional, or 'unfixed form'), Ichygoshi (one-line-poem style); and proletarian haiku, humanist haiku, etc. Contributors include, John Wills, Marlene Wills, Eric Amann, Lorraine Harr, Hiroaki Sato, Onsey Nakagawa, etc." circ. 3-500. 4/yr. Pub'd 4 issues 1979. sub. price: $6.00; per copy: $2.00; sample: $2.00. Back issues: $2.00. Discounts: 2-10, 25%; 10 plus, 40%. Applies to lit mag dealers and classroom only. 100-180pp; 8½X2⅓; †mi, of. Reporting time: within a few weeks for manuscripts of unique quality, occasionally longer for others. Payment: At least one contributor's copy, but usually 2. Cash also for prose. Copyrighted. Pub's reviews. §Anything to do with the Japanese one-line verse forms: haiku, senryu, tanka, etc. Such works in English. One-line poems. Anything in any way connected with the above. Ads: $30.00/$15.00/$0.35.

AMOXCALLI, Luis Chaparro, Carlos Humphreys, PO Box 2064, El Paso, TX 79951, (915) 594-2222. 1978. Articles, photos, interviews, reviews, news items. "*Amoxcalli* is the official publication of the El Paso Chapter of Reforma, the National Organization of Spanish Speaking Librarians. As such, its theme is library service to the Spanish-speaking. Each issue contains contributions by librarians dedicated to serving this often overlooked but increasingly significant minority." circ. 800. 3/yr. Pub'd 3 issues 1979; expects 4 issues 1980. sub. price: $7.00; per copy: $1.50; sample: free. Back issues: $1.00. 12pp; 8X11; †of. Reporting time: 3 months before printing. Payment: $50.00 per contribution. Copyrighted, reverts to author. Pub's reviews: 6 in 1979. §Anything to do with the Spanish bilingual/-bicultural, in particular, library service to them. Ads: $58.00/$30.00/$10.00 col in.

Ampersand Press (see also CALLIOPE), Martha Christna, Director; Geoffrey Clark, David Howard, Robert McRoberts, Creative Writing Program, Roger Williams College, Bristol, RI 02809. 1980. Poetry, fiction, long-poems. "Our current project is a collection of poetry and prose by Jim Hall, to be published summer 1980. Future plans include poetry postcards, chapbooks and single volume collections of poetry and fiction. We are not accepting unsolicited manuscripts at this time." avg. press run 500. avg. price, paper: $3.00. Discounts: 40% bookstores. 40pp; 5½X8½; of. Payment: individually arranged. Copyrights for author. CCLM, COSMEP.

Ana-Doug Publishing, S. J. Scholl, 1236 Cranbrook Place, Fullerton, CA 92633, (714) 871-4060. 1975. Articles, art, photos, cartoons. avg. press run 2,500. 1 title listed in the *Small Press Record of Books in Print* (9th Edition, 1980). avg. price, cloth: $12.00; paper: $7.00. Discounts: 20 to 50 percent. 200pp; 8½X11; lp. Reporting time: 30 days. Payment: 15 percent. Copyrights for author. COSMEP.

Ananda Marga Publications, Dadajii Amita'bha, 854 Pearl Street, Denver, CO 80203, (303) 832-6465.

Ananda Publications (see also SPIRIT & NATURE), Rambhakta, 14618 Tyler Foote Road, Nevada City, CA 95959, 916-265-5877. 1968. "Material pertaining to the yogic way of life. Books by Swami Kriyananda: i.e. *Your Sun Sign as a Spiritual Guide, 1971*; *Yoga Postures For Self Awareness, 1968*; *The Path: Autobiography of a Western Yogi, 1977*; *Cooperative Communities: How to Start Them & Why, 1968*; *The Road Ahead, 1973.*" avg. press run 5M. Pub'd 3 titles 1979; expects 4 titles 1980. 11 titles listed in the *Small Press Record of Books in Print* (9th Edition, 1980). avg. price, cloth: $12.50; paper: $4.00. Discounts: 1-4 books 20% off; 5-24 books 40% off. 120/pp (paper), 600/pp (cloth); 5½X8½; †mi/of. COSMEP.

ANAPRESS, H. T. Shannon, 114 Albert Road, South Melbourne, Melbourne, Victoria 3205, Australia, 697-0100. 1948. Poetry, fiction, articles, photos, news items. "Articles approximately 1,500 words. Non-Sectarian, Non-Party political on current national problems e.g., afforestation, defence, foreign relatives, nuclear waste disposal of an informative and scientific nature. News local, pertaining to association members." circ. 5,000-7,000. 4/yr. Pub'd 4 issues 1979; expects 4 issues 1980, 4 issues 1981. price per copy: free; sample: free. Back issues: Free where available. 32pp; 8½X11½; lp. Reporting time: One month prior to printing. Pub's reviews. §Travel, biographies. Ads: $100.-00/$50.00.

ANARCHISM: The Feminist Connection, Come! Unity Press, 13 East 17 St., New York, NY 10003. circ. 2,000. price per copy: $2.00; sample: $2.00. 3½X4½; †of.

ANARCHIST REVIEW, Cienfuegos Press, Stuart Christie, Over the Water, Sanday, Orkney KW17 2BL, United Kingdom. 1976. Poetry, fiction, articles, art, cartoons, interviews, satire, criticism, reviews, music, letters, collages. "Recent contributors: Michael Moorcock, Norm Chomsky, Philip Lovine, Mike Horovitz, John Sladek. Price varies with each issue. Yearly sub includes all CP titles published in calendar year, including books, pamphlets, posters, etc." circ. 3,000. 4/yr. Pub'd 1 issue 1979; expects 2 issues 1980, 1 issue 1981. sub. price: £30.00. Discounts: 0-25, 33% plus postage; 26-49, 40% plus postage; 50 upwards, 50% plus postage. 186pp; 8¼X11½; of. Reporting time: 2 weeks. Copyrighted. Pub's reviews: 83 in 1979. §All areas, science, literature, politics, history, criminology, etc. Ads: £300.00/£150.00/15p per word.

AND, Writers Forum, John Rowan, Bob Cobbing, 262 Randolph Ave, London W9, United Kingdom. 1954. Poetry, art, concrete art. circ. 500. irreg. Pub'd 1 issue 1979. price per copy: varies; sample: 50p + postage. Discounts: 33% trade. 40pp. Reporting time: 3 weeks. Payment: copies. Not copyrighted. ALP.

‡and books (see also Around Publishing; The Distributors), Janos Szebedinszky, Stephen Raymond, 702 S Michigan, Suite 836, South Bend, IN 46618. "Encourage non-fiction mss on alternative materials. Please query first with outline." 2 titles listed in the *Small Press Record of Books in Print* (9th Edition, 1980).

AND/OR NOTES, and/or Services, Anne Focke, Director, 1525 10th Ave., Seattle, WA 98122, 324-5880. 1978. Poetry, fiction, articles, art, photos, interviews, music, letters, collages, concrete art. "Monthly publication with calendar of upcoming events, plus documentation, news pertaining to our various programs, library, video, new music, visual arts, and a forum section of discussion (and artwork) of or relating to the arts. Note: *Hindsight* no longer published." circ. 2,000. 12/yr. Pub'd 12 issues 1979; expects 12 issues 1980, 12 issues 1981. sub. price: $10.00. 24pp; 11X8½; of. Reporting time: deadline is 10th of the month. Ads: $25.00.

And/Or Press, Peter Beren, Executive Editor, P O Box 2246, Berkeley, CA 94702, (415) 849-2665. 1974. Non-fiction. avg. press run 10,000. Pub'd 30 titles 1979; expects 8 titles 1980. 28 titles listed in the *Small Press Record of Books in Print* (9th Edition, 1980). avg. price, cloth: $11.95; paper: $6.95. Reporting time: 3 months. Payment: standard arrangement. Copyrights for author.

and/or Services (see also AND/OR NOTES), 1525 10th Ave, Seattle, WA 98122. 2 titles listed in the *Small Press Record of Books in Print* (9th Edition, 1980).

Andrew Mountain Press, Candace Catlin Hall, PO Box 14353, Hartford, CT 06114. 1980. Fiction, art, photos, interviews. "Andrew Mountain Press started with publication of *Shelley's Day,* a photographic essay on the day of a legally blind child. Future projects being considered are an animal picture book, a story about a refugee, and a calligraphy project. Currently looking for manuscripts for shorter books with appeal to children. Production is not fancy - typewritten copy, and illustrations limited to black and white (and one other color), and b & w photographs." avg. press run 1,000. avg. price, paper: $2.95. 24pp; 7X8½; of. Reporting time: usually 1 month. Payment: standard. Copyrights for author.

ANDROGYNE, Androgyne Books, Ken Weichel, 930 Shields, San Francisco, CA 94132, 586-2697. 1971. Poetry, fiction, art, collages. circ. 500. 2/yr. 2 titles listed in the *Small Press Record of Books in Print* (9th Edition, 1980). sub. price: $4.00; per copy: $2.00; sample: $2.00. Back issues: No. 1, $5.00; No. 2, $2.00; No. 3, $2.00. Discounts: 40/60. 40pp; 5X8; †of. Reporting time: 3 weeks. Payment: 2 copies. Copyrighted, reverts to author. §Poetry-Collages-Criticism. COSMEP.

Androgyne Books (see also ANDROGYNE), Ken Weichel, 930 Shields, San Francisco, CA 94132, 586-2697. 1971. Poetry, fiction, articles, art, photos, criticism, collages, plays. avg. press run 500 copies. Pub'd 2 titles 1979; expects 4 titles 1980. 7 titles listed in the *Small Press Record of Books in Print* (9th Edition, 1980). avg. price, cloth: $9.00; paper: $3.00. 1pp; †of. Reporting time: 3 weeks. Copyrights for author. COSMEP.

Anemone Press, Barbara Berman, E. Ethelbert Miller, Thulani Davis, PO Box 441, Howard University, Washington, DC 20059, (202) 232-3066. 1977. Poetry. "We prefer to publish poetry by women. We have printed the work of Rikki Lights, Lee Howard, Patricia Jones and others." avg. press run 1,000. Pub'd 1 title 1979; expects 1 title 1980, 2 titles 1981. 2 titles listed in the *Small Press Record of Books in Print* (9th Edition, 1980). avg. price, paper: $3.50. 62pp; 5½X8½; of/lp. Reporting time: 1-2 months. Payment: Negotiable. Copyrights for author.

ANGEL EXHAUST, Steven Pereira, Jenny Pereira, Adrian Clarke, 59 Ilford House, Dove Road, London N1 3NA, United Kingdom, 01-354-1669. 1979. Poetry, fiction, articles, interviews, criticism, reviews, letters, news items, concrete art, photos. "ISSN: 0143 8050; Contributors: Bob Cobbing, Harriet Rose, Ted Burford, Geoff Adkins, Peter Finch, Hugh Underhill. Lengths, Max, (not rigid). Stories: 50,000; articles/interviews: 4,000; reviews/poems: 2,000. Biases: local and community activities based around literature; any good written work accepted." circ. 200. 3/yr. Pub'd 2 issues 1979; expects 3 issues 1980, 3 issues 1981. sub. price: £6.00; per copy: £2.00; sample: £2.00. Back issues: no back issues. Discounts: 1/3 for trade, etc. 40pp; 148mm x 210mm; †of. Reporting time: we hold material max one week before notification. Payment: one free copy of mag to non*subscribers, cover price to others. Copyrighted, reverts to author. Pub's reviews. §Poetry, literary, esp workshop or local group activity. Ads: £20.00/£12.00. ALP.

Angels Gate Press, H. D. Sacks, PO Box 1881, San Pedro, CA 90733. 1979. Poetry, fiction, art, photos, long-poems. "Recently published *Memories of the Future,* by Gordon Wagner. *The Proletarian Arcane* by Jack Hirschman." avg. press run 500. Pub'd 2 titles 1979. 2 titles listed in the *Small Press Record of Books in Print* (9th Edition, 1980). avg. price, cloth: $20.00; paper: $5.00; other: $1.25. Discounts: Usual trade. 80pp; 6X9; of. Reporting time: 60 days. Payment: 10% of retail sales. Copyrights for author.

ANGELSTONE, Angelstone, Beth Cloyd, Sandra S. Thompson, Carol Dennison Smith, 316 Woodland Drive, Birmingham, AL 35209, (205) 870-7281. 1977. Poetry, art, photos. "Black & white art/photos-suitable for offset-also prose poetry. We are looking for non-traditional imagistic poems with interesting use of the language that do more than convey a mood. First issue features Alabama residents and natives, future issues not limited to Alabama. Contributors must include SASE or poems will not be returned. Recent contributors: Sonia Sanchez, Pier Giorgio DeCicco, Terry Stokes, Susan Fromberg Schaeffer, Lyn Lifshin, David Spicer, Joe Rosenblatt, Carolyn Smart, Phillip Foss, etc." circ. 200. 2/yr. Expects 2 issues 1980, 2 issues 1981. sub. price: $5.00; per copy: $2.50; sample: $2.00. Back issues: $2.00. Discounts: Negotiable. 30-40pp; 7X10; of. Reporting time: 1 week - 3 months. Payment: 2 copies. Copyrighted, reverts to author. COSMEP.

Angelstone (see also ANGELSTONE), Beth Cloyd, Sandra S. Thompson, Carol Dennison Smith, 316 Woodland Drive, Birmingham, AL 35209, (205) 870-7281. 1977. Poetry. "Chapbooks by Carol Dennison Smith, Sandra S. Thompson, and Robert Lynn Penny. Forthcoming in 1980, *A Straw Hat for Everybody* by Pier Giorgio DiCicco" avg. press run 200. Expects 2 titles 1980, 1 title 1981. avg. price, paper: $3.50. Discounts: Negotiable. 30-40pp; 7X10; of. Reporting time: 1-3 months. Payment: Negotiable, according to the individual. Copyrights for author. COSMEP.

Angle Lightning Press, Wendy Wachtel, 17 E. 84th Street, New York, NY 10028, 861-5926, 877-6239. 1978. Poetry, photos, long-poems. "Angle Lightning's focus is poetic works that are both ambitious and of high quality. We are equally concerned with the quality of the production and design of our publications. Our most recent publication is *There is a Voice*: a collection of English poetry and photography by Montreal women. It allowed a real, complex, and teaching women's voice to emerge. Previous pub: *Island Fire*, a collection of poetry written by Fire Island residents. As well as focusing upon specific geographic regions, both books contain poetry that unravels the mind with the poets thought and well-crafted expression." avg. press run 1,000. Pub'd 1 title 1979; expects 1 title 1980, 2 titles 1981. avg. price, paper: $2.50. 2-4, 10%; 5-9, 30%; 10 or more, 40%; 10% discount for classroom. 100pp; 6X9½; of. Reporting time: 2-3 months. Payment: Minimal. Possible increase in future.

THE ANGLO-WELSH REVIEW, Five Arches Press, Gillian Clarke, John Davies, 1 Cyncoed Ave., Cyncoed Cardiff, Wales, United Kingdom. 1949. Articles, poetry, art, criticism, music, letters, long-poems. "Only quality material-any length. Preferably with some Welsh connexion (writer born/lived in Wales, writes about Wales or Welsh affairs, all in English)." circ. 1,500. 3/yr. sub. price: £1.85/sub; per copy: 75p. Back issues: £.50. 250pp; 8X5; lp. Reporting time: 3 mos. Payment: by arrangement. Ads: £25/page. ALP.

Angst World Library, Tom Carlisle, Kathie McKie, 2307 22nd Ave. E, Seattle, WA 98112. 1974. Fiction, parts-of-novels. "We are a literary press with macabre overtones and interested in science fiction. Recently published: *Bonstonofavitch!* by Thomas Carlisle; *Mystery Of The Pig Killer's Daughter* by Lawrence Russell; *Death Of A Whale* by A.E. Sutton. Please query prior to submitting ms. and *always* enclose SASE. *Tragedy of the Moisty Morning* by Jessica Salmonson" avg. press run 110-200. Pub'd 2 titles 1979; expects 2 titles 1980, 2 titles 1981. 8 titles listed in the *Small Press Record of Books in Print* (9th Edition, 1980). avg. price, paper: $2.00 to $4.00. Discounts: 40% on purchases over 5 copies. pp varies; 5X8; of. Reporting time: 1-2 mos. Payment: 25% of net profit + 5 copies, and/or outright purchase. Copyrights for author.

Anian Press, Colin Browne, PO Box 69804, Station K, Vancouver, B.C. V5K 4Y7, Canada. 1979. Long-poems, poetry. avg. press run 300. Pub'd 1-2 titles 1979. 1 title listed in the *Small Press Record of Books in Print* (9th Edition, 1980). Discounts: Over 5 copies, 40%. of.

ANIMA, Conococheague Associates, Inc., Harry Buck, John Blair, Karin Blair, Rebecca Nisley, 1053 Wilson Avenue, Chambersburg, PA 17201, (717) 263-8303. 1974. Poetry, articles, art, photos, interviews, criticism, reviews, music, long-poems. "ANIMA, An Experimental Journal celebrates the sources of our separate identity in the common soul of us all. Authors from the Teilhard Research Institute and the Foundation for Mind Research; anthropologists, musicologists, and philosophers explore frontiers of awareness between fields of conventional scholarship. A feminist forum, ANIMA features 'Daughters of the *New* American Revolution,' a clearing house for feminist action, women active in business, teaching, and the arts. Articles on Eastern religion and dance, French folk music, and initiation rites present a cross-cultural perspective centered on the question of creativity in a cultural source. The magazine is itself a physical example of its themes, with experimental design and art work by many new photographers, poets, and artists. Authors creating new traditions from immediate experience are welcome." circ. 700-growing. 2/yr. Pub'd 2 issues 1979. sub. price: $8.50; per copy: $5.00; sample: free. Back issues: $5.00. Discounts: 5 copies-20%. 80pp; 8½X8½; of. Reporting time: 12 weeks. Payment: copies and offprints only. Copyrighted. §psychology, religion, women. Ads: $50/$30. COSMEP.

Anjou (see also WRIT), Richard M. Lush, Roger Greenwald, 235 Queen St West, Toronto, Ontario M5V 1Z4, Canada, 416-979-2555. 1980. "no unsolicited mss" lp.

ANN ARBOR REVIEW, Fred Wolven, Editor; Gerald Clark, Assoc Editor, Washtenaw Community College, Fred Wolven, editor, Ann Arbor, MI 48106, (313) 973-3408. 1967. Poetry, fiction, articles, art, photos, interviews, criticism, reviews, parts-of-novels, plays, concrete art, non-fiction. "New and younger writers, and women writers. Also 1-act plays. New and different directions in poetry and fiction. Especially interested in writer interviews and critical essays, and Canadian, European and South American writing. Duane Locke, Richard Kostelanetz, Peter Wild, Alvaro Cardona-Hine, Deborah Tall, Linda Wagner, Elisavietta Ritchie, Robert Stilwell. See recent issue. Copyrights revert on request for reassignment or via permission to reprint." circ. 450-1,000. 3/yr (July-June). Pub'd 3 issues 1979; expects 3 issues 1980. sub. price: $6.00 ($7.00 foreign); per copy: $2.00; sample: $2.00. Back issues: $3.00 per copy. Discounts: 20 - 40 percent (inquire). 96pp; 5X7; of. Reporting time: 3 weeks-2 months. Payment: contributor's copies. Copyrighted. Pub's reviews: 3 in 1979. §New women writers, anthologies, Canadian writers, articles on writing and teaching of writing, non-fiction (current events, history), teaching children writing. Ads: $75.00/$40.00. CCLM, COSMEP.

ANNEX 21, Fredrick Zydek, Annex 21, U.N.O. 60th & Dodge Streets, Omaha, NB 68182. 1978. "Not accepting unsolicited manuscripts at this time. Recent contributors: Patrick Gray, David Wyatt, Roy Scheele, Nina Anderson." circ. 1,000. 1/yr. Pub'd 1 issue 1979; expects 1 issue 1980, 1 issue 1981. sub. price: $4.00; per copy: $4.00; sample: $4.00. 100pp; 5½X8½; lp. Payment: varies, but payment is made. Copyrighted, reverts to author.

Anonymous Owl Press (see also THE MARGARINE MAYPOLE ORANGOUTANG EXPRESS), 3209 Wellesley NE #1, Albuquerque, NM 87107. 1973. 1 title listed in the *Small Press Record of Books in Print* (9th Edition, 1980).

ANOTHER CHICAGO MAGAZINE, Thunder's Mouth Press, Lee Webster, Editor, 1152 S. East, Oak Park, IL 60304. 1976. Poetry, fiction, articles, art, photos, cartoons, interviews, satire, criticism, reviews, long-poems. "Recent contributors have included Paul Carroll, Elizabeth Libbey, Tom McGrath, Christine Zawadiwsky, Peter Michelson, John Knoepfle, David Ignatow, Phyllis Janik, Sterling Plumpp, Ralph J. Mills Jr. and Joan Colby." circ. 1,200. 2/yr. Pub'd 1 issue 1979; expects 2 issues 1980, 2 issues 1981. sub. price: $5.00; per copy: $2.50; sample: $2.50. Back issues: $2.50. Discounts: 40% on 10 or more. 80pp; 8½X5½; †of. Reporting time: 6 weeks. Payment: copies, but we are trying to raise funds to make minimal cash payments. Copyrighted, reverts to author. Pub's reviews: 1 in 1979. §Poetry, fiction, literary reviews or criticism, works on politics and art. Ads: $100.00/$50.00. COSMEP, CCLM.

ANOTHER SMALL MAGAZINE, Beth Blevins, Susie Cullen, Terrie Cullen, 1014 N Branciforte, Santa Cruz, CA 95062, 426-8698. 1979. Poetry, articles, art, photos, cartoons, reviews, fiction, letters. circ. 500. 2/yr. sub. price: Individual issues only, no subscriptions; per copy: $0.50 + postage; sample: $0.50 + postage. Back issues: $0.25 for postage. 32pp; 7X8; of. Reporting time: variable. Payment: copies. Pub's reviews: 3 in 1979. §Poetry, travel, art. Ads: bargainable.

Ansuda Publications (see also THE PUB), Daniel R. Betz, Alexander Gold, Box 123, Harris, IA 51345. 1978. Poetry, fiction, art, satire, long-poems, plays. "No limits on length, style, or material. We just stress originality and quality. We usually do chapbooks by one author/poet, but we are engaged at the moment with work on our 'psycho-horror' and 'pure fantasy' anthology entitled *Hor-Tasy),* in which we request work from a number of writers. If the writer has something really different that other publishers are uninterested in or afraid of trying, we welcome a query from him/her with an open mind, but query first."* avg. press run varies. Pub'd 1 title 1979; expects 2 titles 1980, 1 title 1981. 2 titles listed in the *Small Press Record of Books in Print* (9th Edition, 1980). avg. price, paper: $1.25 on chapbooks. Discounts: query. 28pp; 5½X8½; †mi/of. Reporting time: immediately, 2 weeks, sometimes 1-2 months. Payment: we must see material first. Copyrights for author.

ANTAEUS, The Ecco Press, Daniel Halpern, Susan Dwyer, 1 West 30th St., New York, NY 10001, 212-736-2599. 1970. Poetry, fiction, interviews, letters, parts-of-novels, long-poems. "Contributors: Michael Rothschild, Louise Gluck, James Merrill, Flann O'Brien, Brian Swann, Sanford Chernoff, Carolyn Forche, William Kotzwinkle, Norman Dubie, Octavio Paz, Robert Hass, Italo Calvino, William Harrison." circ. 5,000. 4/yr. Pub'd 4 issues 1979; expects 4 issues 1980, 3 issues 1981. sub. price: $14.00; per copy: $4.00; sample: $4.00 free to reviewers and college professors. Back issues: Issues still in print 2-36 $67.00. Discounts: 33⅓% trade. 160pp; 6½X9; of. Reporting time: 1 month. Payment: $5.00 per page. Copyrighted, will assign copyright upon author's request. Ads: $250.-00/$150.00. CCLM, NYSSPA, NESPA.

The Antares Foundation (see PARAGRAPH: A QUARTERLY OF GAY FICTION)

ANTENNA, Karen Glenn, Diane Gage, Mary Gillespie, Jill Singleton, Connie Rawlins, 5014 Narragansett #6, c/o Gage, San Diego, CA 92107. 1976. Poetry, art, photos, long-poems, concrete art. "Recent contributors: Al Zolynas, Karl Kempton, Geoffrey Cook, Wanda Coleman, Patricia Traxler, Steve Kowit. Interested in both unknown and established poets. Deadlines: 4/30; 9/30. Winter 1980 special issue on Childhood. Contributors east of Mississippi please send ms. to Karen Glenn, 631 Maryland Ave N.E., Wash. D.C. 20002" circ. 700. 2/yr. Pub'd 2 issues 1979; expects 2 issues 1980,

2 issues 1981. sub. price: $5.00; per copy: $2.50; sample: $2.50. Discounts: 40%. 80pp; 4¼X5½; of. Reporting time: 1-3 months. Payment: 1 copy. Copyrighted, reverts to author. Ads: $40.00/$20.00. COSMEP.

Anthony Publishing Company, Carol K. Anthony, 218 Gleasondale Road, Stow, MA 01775, (617) 897-7191.

ANTI-APARTHEID NEWS, 89 Charlotte St., London W1P 2DQ, United Kingdom. 1965. Articles, reviews, news items, letters. "Support for liberation movements of Southern Africa." circ. 7,500. 10/yr. sub. price: £4.50 UK/Europe, £4.50 surface/ £6.50 airmail outside Europe; per copy: 15p; sample: free. 12pp; 17X12; of. Pub's reviews: 25 in 1979. §Southern Africa. Ads: £2/col inch.

Anti-Ocean Press, Sol P. Lachman, 540 W Maplehurst, Ferndale, MI 48220, (313) 547-0790. 1975. Poetry. "1978 title is *Camptown Spaces* by David Shevin (satirical poetry on America). Future publications will be primarily Judaica." avg. press run 1,000. Expects 1 title 1980. 1 title listed in the *Small Press Record of Books in Print* (9th Edition, 1980). avg. price, paper: $3.00. Discounts: 40 percent to stores. †lp. Reporting time: 30 days. Payment: by arrangement. Copyrights for author.

Antietam Press, Ellen M. Dorosh, P.O. Box 62, Boonsboro, MD 21713, (301) 432-8079. 1978. "Especially interested in working with self-publishing authors in all phases from writing through promotion and distribution" avg. press run 500-1000. Expects 5 titles 1980, 5 titles 1981. 4 titles listed in the *Small Press Record of Books in Print* (9th Edition, 1980). avg. price, paper: $4.00. Discounts: In keeping with present industry practices. 50-100pp; 5½X8½; of. Reporting time: 2-3 weeks. Payment: Negotiated with individual author. Copyrights for author.

THE ANTIGONISH REVIEW, R. J. MacSween, St Francis Zavier University, Antigonish, Nova Scotia B2G1CO, Canada. 1969. Poetry, fiction, articles, art, interviews, criticism, reviews. circ. 600. 4/yr. Pub'd 4 issues 1979. sub. price: $5; per copy: $1.50; sample: free. 110pp; of. Reporting time: 2 months. Payment: copies only. Not copyrighted. Pub's reviews: 20 in 1979.

THE ANTIOCH REVIEW, Robert Fogarty, Editor; Sandra McPherson, Poetry Ed.; James Jordan, Bk. Rev. Ed.; Nolan Miller, Fiction Ed., PO Box 148, Yellow Springs, OH 45387, 513-767-7386. 1941. Poetry, fiction, articles, satire, criticism, long-poems, non-fiction, reviews. "Recent contributors: James Purdy, Stephen Dixon, Annie Dillard, Tess Gallagher, Heather McHugh, Charles Simic, Landrum Bolling, John J. Gilligan, Alvin Greenberg, John P. Roche, Warren Bennis, Cynthia Fuchs Epstein" circ. 3,500. 4/yr. Pub'd 4 issues 1979; expects 4 issues 1980. sub. price: $12.00 ($14.00 for Foreign)/$14.00 Institutional; per copy: $3.00; sample: $3.00. Back issues: $2.50. Discounts: 20 percent to agent. 128pp; 9X6; of. Reporting time: 1-6 weeks. Payment: $10.00 per page (approx. 425 words). Copyrighted, reverts when requested. Pub's reviews: 77 in 1979. §General interest social science, fiction, contemporary affairs. Ads: $160.00/$120.00. CCLM, COSMEP, OAC.

ANTIQUE PHONOGRAPH MONTHLY, APM Press, Allen Koenigsberg, 650 Ocean Ave., Brooklyn, NY 11226, 212-941-6835. 1973. Articles, art, photos, cartoons, interviews, criticism, reviews, music, letters, news items, non-fiction. "Ray Wile, George Blacker, Ken Barnes, Jay Gandy, Robert Feinstein, Tim Brooks 500-3,000 words—Articles on the history of recorded sound and development of recording technology, both from a scientific and cultural point of view. Also articles on popular music, vaudeville, opera, politics, etc. Anything recorded 1877-1929. Articles on the development and restoration of antique phonographs. We welcome books and records for review. ISSN: 0361-2147" circ. 1,500. 10/yr. Pub'd 10 issues 1979; expects 10 issues 1980. sub. price: $8.00; per copy: $0.80; sample: free. Back issues: $8.00 for complete year. Discounts: free samples for clubs, classroom, etc. 16-20pp; 5½X8½; of. Reporting time: 2 wks. Payment: $10 to $50. Buys American or reverts to author. Pub's reviews: 20 in 1979. §Music history, music biography, history of sound recording, patent history. Ads: $65/$35/$.10-$.15 per wd/classified. ARSC.

Anvil Press Poetry, Peter Jay, 69 King George St., London SE10 8PX, United Kingdom. 1968. Poetry. lp/of. Payment: royalty. ALP.

APALACHEE QUARTERLY, D.D.B. Press, P.V. LeForge, David Morrill, Richard Johnson, Len Schweitzer, Monica Faeth, Po Box 20106, Tallahassee, FL 32304, (904) 224-0478. 1972. Poetry, fiction, articles, art, photos, parts-of-novels, long-poems, plays. "We always need manuscripts of poetry and fiction, but we're often flooded by manuscripts from one author. Try not to do this. Send 3-8 poems and prose up to 30 pages. We often write short criticisms on our rejection notices, but unless we specifically ask you to try us again it would be better if you tried your luck elsewhere after the first attempt. We, as well as anyone else, have our prejudices. Submissions without SASE are kept for 2 years, then used for scratchpaper. We have a game where we sit around in a circle and ridicule long vitas and absurd lists of previous publications, so include these accordingly. Don't send manuscripts that are so dog-eared and gravy stained that it's obvious 19 other magazines have amused themselves by making paper airplanes and little hats out of them. We're extremely selective about what goes in to the A.Q. Be selective in submitting. We would prefer to publish quality from an unknown rather than garbage from someone with a name." circ. 400. 4/yr. Pub'd 4 issues 1979; expects 4 issues 1980. sub. price: $4.00 individual; $6.00 institution; per copy: $1.50 includes postage and handling; sample: $1.50 includes postage and handling. Back issues: $2.50 each. 44pp; 6X9; of. Reporting time: 3-8 weeks. Payment: 2 copies. Copyrighted, reverts to author. Pub's reviews: 10 in 1979. §fiction, poetry. Ads: $50.00/$30.00. CCLM,.

Apeiron Press, Jeffrey Holland, P.O. Box 5930, Chicago, IL 60680. 1978. Poetry, long-poems. "We at Apeiron are looking for book-length manuscripts (especially poetry) with a clear emphasis on the metaphysical/ontological. We inaugurated our venture with E. R. Cole's *Act & Potency,* a unique collection of poems that celebrates the hidden nature of reality. We hope to publish three or four books a year. Writers should query before sending completed manuscripts." avg. press run 500-750. Expects 1 title 1980, 3-4 titles 1981. avg. price, paper: $4.95. 48-60pp; 5½X8½; lp. Reporting time: 4-6 weeks. Payment: Negotiable. Copyrights for author.

APM Press (see also ANTIQUE PHONOGRAPH MONTHLY), Allen Koenigsberg, 650 Ocean Avenue, Brooklyn, NY 11226, 212-941-6835. 1968. Articles, art, photos, cartoons, interviews, criticism, reviews, music, letters, news items, non-fiction. "Books on the history of recorded sound: 1877-1929. Discographies, manuals, posters, etc., development of the phonograph, lives of the inventors and artists. Also APM Monograph series. Restoration of antique phonographs." avg. press run 1,000. Pub'd 2 titles 1979; expects 2 titles 1980. 7 titles listed in the *Small Press Record of Books in Print* (9th Edition, 1980). avg. price, cloth: $10.00; paper: $5.00. Discounts: 40 percent. 100pp; 6X9; of. Reporting time: 2 weeks. Payment: Negotiable. Copyrights for author. ARSC.

APPEAL TO REASON, Workers' Press, Jonathan Aurthur, Editor; Richard Santillan, Contributing Editor; Jeff Frieden, Contributing Editor; Rudy Torres, Contributing Editor; John Moore, Contributing Editor, PO Box 3774, Merchandise Mart, Chicago, IL 60654. 1971. Articles, art, photos, cartoons, interviews, reviews. "*Appeal to Reason* is a journal principally devoted to analysis of current political affairs in essay form. However, it is open to a diversity of forms of presentation. Recent issues have included articles on discrimination in sports, the dialects of G. F. Hegel, the philosophy of Mao Tse Tung, the Lysenko controversy, international oil cartels, poems by Jack Hirschman and Percy B. Shelly, book and film reviews, militarism, China, the Bahamas, etc. Forthcoming issues will feature articles on the labor movement, and the trend towards a third party. Contributions are welcome." circ. 3,000. 4/yr. Pub'd 4 issues 1979; expects 4 issues 1980, 4 issues 1981. sub. price: $8.00 indiv.; $15.00 libraries & insti.; $15.00 foreign airmail; per copy: $2.50; sample: $2.00. Back issues: shipping cost alone. Discounts: 40% bookstores, 50% distributors. 96pp; 5½X8½; of. Reporting time: 6 weeks. No payment. Copyrighted, reverts to author. Pub's reviews: 3 in 1979. §political science, world communist movement, labor movement, history, public affairs, minorities. Ads: $50.00/$25.00 or will trade ads.

Apple-Gems, Dorothy Applegate, William G. Applegate, PO Box 16292, San Francisco, CA 94116, (415) 587-9752. "*Mission A-Go!Go! 'What's an Ugly American'* An army wife's personal story of how she and her family, on overseas tours found out what it means, and more important, how they did something about it. Biographical information: Author: Thirty-two years as dependent military wife. Author of family prayer column in US and abroad. Biographical information: Illustrator: Eighty-two year 'young' father of author, widely known for his special oil portraitures." avg. price, paper: $9.95. Discounts: 1-3 books, 20%; 4-10 books, 40%; 11 and up, 42%. 248pp; 5½X8½. Copyrights for author.

Apple-wood Press, Philip W. Zuckerman, Box 2870, Cambridge, MA 02139, (617) 964-5150. 1976. Poetry, fiction, art, photos, long-poems, non-fiction. "Cloth and paper editions of poetry, and short fiction." avg. press run Limited: 100-250. Paper: 1,000-2,500. Pub'd 15 titles 1979; expects 15 titles 1980. 4 titles listed in the *Small Press Record of Books in Print* (9th Edition, 1980). avg. price, cloth: $10.00; paper: $4.00; other: $7.50 (broadside). Discounts: Inquire. 100pp; 5½X8½. Reporting time: 3 months. Payment: 10 percent. Copyrights for author.

Apple Tree Lane, Nancy Welch, 2 Fair Oaks Lane, Atherton, CA 94025, (415) 323-4534. 1978. "Titles - *Tassels* and *Doing It Yourway: A Guide to Self Publishing.*" avg. press run 2,500. Pub'd 1 title 1979; expects 1 title 1980. 2 titles listed in the *Small Press Record of Books in Print* (9th Edition, 1980). avg. price, paper: $5.00. Discounts: 30% to 12; 12-50, 40%; over 50, 50%. of.

APPLEWOOD JOURNAL, Kim Huegel, PO Box 1781, San Francisco, CA 94101, (415) 668-6691. 1978. Articles, photos, cartoons, interviews, satire, criticism, reviews, letters, parts-of-novels, news items. "We're interested in people with a modicum of brains who have been exceptionally creative in removing themselves from the 9 to 5 ratrace, via home businesses, novel ways of supporting themselves, people who grow organic gardens, who experiment and use alternative energy, who use and make natural, non-synthetic products, who are sufficiently concerned with the quality of life and the worthlessness of the 'rat-race' to have taken substantial steps in improving their lives, and whats more, can help other people improve their lives. Brains and writing ability are respected." circ. 75,000. 6/yr. Expects 6 issues 1981. sub. price: $10.00; per copy: $1.50; sample: $1.50. Back issues: Same as cover price, which, due to inflation, will rise. Discounts: 40% off cover, please contact us for our terms and credit policies. 64pp; 7½X10; of. Reporting time: 4-8 weeks, generally shorter. Payment: $20-$300. Copyrighted. Pub's reviews. §Health, environment, natural products, lifestyles, business, gardening, self-sufficiency. Ads: $350.00/$200.00/$1.00.

Applezaba Press, D H Lloyd, Richard E McManus, Dolly Ickler, 333 Orizaba, Long Beach, CA 90814, (213) 434-7761. 1977. Poetry, fiction. avg. press run 300 copies. Pub'd 1 title 1979; expects 4 titles 1980, 4 titles 1981. 7 titles listed in the *Small Press Record of Books in Print* (9th Edition, 1980). avg. price, paper: $3.00. Discounts: 40% to bookstores. 78pp; 5½X8½; †of. Reporting time: 2 months. Payment: by arrangement. Copyrights for author.

Applied Probability Trust (see also MATHEMATICAL SPECTRUM), D. W. Sharpe, Department of Pure Mathematics, The University, Sheffield S3 7RH, England, United Kingdom. 1968. Articles, reviews, letters.

April Dawn Publishing Company, Po Box 4433, Falls Church, VA 22044. 1 title listed in the *Small Press Record of Books in Print* (9th Edition, 1980). COSMEP.

AQUARIUS, Eddie S. Linden, Flat 3, 116 Sutherland Avenue, London W9, United Kingdom. 1968. Articles, poetry, fiction, reviews. "Special all Irish issue forthcoming with Seamus Heaney" circ. 1,500. 2/yr. sub. price: £3.00; per copy: £1.50. Back issues: £1.50. Discounts: 33% trade. 120pp; lp. Payment: special issues only. Pub's reviews: 40 in 1979. §Poetry, biography. Ads: £28 full page/£14 half page.

AQUILA MAGAZINE, ROQ Press, Bob Quarteroni, Executive editor; Jane C. Musala, Editor; William A. Blair, Associate editor, 116 Old Mill Road #G, State College, PA 16801, (814) 237-7509. 1975. Poetry, fiction, articles, art, photos, interviews, satire, reviews, music, letters, parts-of-novels. "Still looking for the truly different. AGUILA was started with the hope that it could be a repository of the unique. Poems that talk about eating pus-filled crotches are not *different,* they're just silly. I want to see anything that has a fresh perspective, or handling, no matter how twisted. Poems, short fiction, photos, art," circ. 200. Irreg. shoot for 3/yr. Pub'd 2 or 3 issues 1979; expects 2 or 3 issues 1980. sub. price: $6.00; per copy: $2.00; sample: $2.00. Back issues: $2.00. No discounts. 32pp; 5¼X8½; various methods of production. Reporting time: 1-4 months. Payment: copies-prizes-some small ($1-3) payments. Rights revert to author but no copyright. Ads: $35.00/$17.50. COSMEP.

ARAB AMERICAN ALMANAC, THE NEWS CIRCLE, Joseph R. Haiek, PO Box 74637, Los Angeles, CA 90004, (213) 483-5111. 1974. Art, photos. "On Arab Americans community affairs & history, & addresses etc. Comprehensive and the only almanac of its kind in the USA. 312 pages." circ. 5,000. Pub'd 1 issue 1979; expects 1 issue 1981. price per copy: $12.00. Discounts: About 40% depends on quantity. of. Payment: yes. Copyrighted.

ARARAT, Leo Hamalian, 628 Second Ave, New York City, NY 10016. 1960. Poetry, fiction, articles, criticism, reviews, parts-of-novels, art. "We prefer material in some way pertinent to Armenian life and culture." circ. 2,200. 4/yr. 8 titles listed in the *Small Press Record of Books in Print* (9th Edition, 1980). sub. price: $9.00; per copy: $2.50; sample: $2.50. Back issues: $2.50. Discounts: 15%. 64pp; 9X12; of. Reporting time: month. Payment: $10.00 a printed page (roughly). Copyrighted, reverts to author. Pub's reviews: 10 in 1979. §Ethnic Armenian. Ads: $25.00/$125.00. CCLM.

Arbitrary Closet Press (see also SCREEN DOOR REVIEW), 517 Bently, Eaton Rapids, MI 48827. 1972. Poetry. 1 title listed in the *Small Press Record of Books in Print* (9th Edition, 1980). avg. price, cloth: $1.00. †mi. Reporting time: immediate. Payment: copy only. Does not copyright for author.

Arbor Publications, Haskell Rothstein, Margaret Rothstein, PO Box 8185, Ann Arbor, MI 48107, 313-662-5786. 1979. "Material used: Almost anything of merit, but only on a subsidy basis. Author must have a well written, 'clean' (neat and error free) manuscript; author must be willing to do promotion and must know a market for his/her material." avg. press run 1,500. Pub'd 1 title 1979. 1 title listed in the *Small Press Record of Books in Print* (9th Edition, 1980). avg. price, cloth: $7.95; paper: $4.95. Discounts: 30% to bookstores on consignment. 212pp; 5½X8½; of. Reporting time: three months or shorter. Payment: subsidy only; author pays all costs; we charge a reasonable fee for

24

arrangements. Copyrights for author.

Arc Publications, Tony Ward, 6, Plane Street, Lydgate, Todmorden, Lancs, United Kingdom. 1969. Poetry, long-poems, concrete art. "Any style considered as long as in high standard. Unfortunately unable to accomodate any mss. for publication during 1980/81" avg. press run 450. Pub'd 7 titles 1979; expects 8 titles 1980. 15 titles listed in the *Small Press Record of Books in Print* (9th Edition, 1980). avg. price, paper: 75p. Discounts: 33⅓ 5 or more copies. pp varies; size variable; †of. Reporting time: 3 months. Payment: Negotiable. right remains with authors unless otherwise requested. ALP, BAAA (Beau & Aloes, Arc Association).

ARCADE-THE COMICS REVUE, The Print Mint, Inc., Belier Press, Bill Griffith, Art Spiegelman, Po Box 40474, San Francisco, CA 94140. 1975. Fiction, articles, cartoons, satire, parts-of-novels. "R. Crumb, S. Clay Wilson, Spain Rodriguez, Willy Murphy, Gilbert Shelton, Charles Bukowski, William Burroughs, George di Caprio, Justin Green, Jim Hoberman, M. K. Brown, Michelle Brand." circ. 15,000. quarterly. sub. price: $6.00; per copy: $1.50; sample: $1.50. Discounts: trade-retail less 40%, bulk (over 1500 assorted) retail less 60%. 48pp; 8¼X10½; of. Reporting time: three weeks.

Arcane Order (see also JACKSONVILLE POETRY QUARTERLY), Leonard J. Mather, General Editor; William H. Cohen, Poetry Editor, 2904 Rosemary Lane, Falls Church, VA 22042. 1950. Poetry, articles, art, satire. "We publish only material by members of the Arcane Order: Steve Lotz, Thomas Charles Chimes, Elihu Edelson, Elizabeth Hunter, etc." avg. press run 125. Pub'd 3 titles 1979; expects 2-4 titles 1980, 2-4 titles 1981. avg. price, paper: available to members only, gratis. 2-10pp; 8½X11; †mi/of. Reporting time: varies from immediately to one or two years. Payment: none.

THE ARCHER, Camas Press, Wilfred Brown, P.O.Box 41, Camas Valley, OR 97416, (503) 445-2327. 1951. Poetry, art, satire. "I do not know the considered dimensions of a 'longpoem.' We have no set limit, but rarely have used one which took more than two pages, about 64 lines. Most are less than one page. Satiric prose is sometimes used if clever and very brief, as in satiric or humorous verse. (Most received are not very funny, in our view.) Only use of art is occasionally for covers, and don't know that that is worth mentioning." circ. 500. Quarterly. Pub'd 4 issues 1979; expects 4 issues 1980. sub. price: $4.00/yr; per copy: $1.00; sample: $1.00. Back issues: 50¢ a copy while supply lasts. Discounts: $3.00/yr, $4.00/2 yrs. 28pp; 5½X8½; †lp. Reporting time: Usually within 2 days to 2 weeks. (In the past there were some considerable delays.). Payment: copies. Copyrighted, reverts to author.

Archinform, PO Box 27732, Los Angeles, CA 90027, (213) 662-0216. 1975. Articles. avg. press run 500. Pub'd 4 titles 1979; expects 7 titles 1980, 5 titles 1981. 11 titles listed in the *Small Press Record of Books in Print* (9th Edition, 1980). avg. price, paper: $35.00. Discounts: Pre publishing 10%; bookstore negotiated consignment; same special offers; five books or more; library; school. 150pp; 8½X11; of. Reporting time: 6 months - 1 year. Payment: by publication/by author. Copyrights for author.

Ardis (see also RUSSIAN LITERATURE TRIQUARTERLY), 2901 Heatherway, Ann Arbor, MI 48104. 1971. Poetry, fiction, criticism, plays. "Russian and Soviet subjects, misc. bibliographies" avg. press run 1500. Pub'd 30 titles 1979; expects 30 titles 1980, 30 titles 1981. 57 titles listed in the *Small Press Record of Books in Print* (9th Edition, 1980). avg. price, cloth: $15.00; paper: $4.95. Discounts: On request. 300pp; 5½X8½; of. Reporting time: 2 months.

AREITO, PO Box 1913, New York, NY 10001. 1974. Poetry, fiction, articles, art, photos, cartoons, interviews, reviews, music, news items. "Articles mostly on Cuban topics-either on the revolutionary govt. or about the exile community. Articles will be published in Spanish with an English summary in the English supplement. Length limited to less than 29 double spaced 8½ x 11 pages. Interview with Cuban political prisoner. 1st trip of young Cubans back to Cuba." circ. 5,000. 4/yr. Pub'd 4 issues 1979. sub. price: $4 for indiv, $8.00 for instit.; per copy: $1.00; sample: $1.50. Back issues: $8.00 (Vol. 1 number 1 Special anniversary re-issue). 60-90pp; 8½X11; of. Pub's reviews: 5 in 1979. §Cuba, the Cuban exile community in the U.S., Latin America. Ads: Quarter: $30.00.

ARENA SCIENCE FICTION, Geoffrey David Rippington, 6 Rutland Gardens, Birchington, Kent, England CT7 9SN, United Kingdom. 1977. Articles, art, interviews, satire, criticism, reviews, letters. "Recent contributors: Angus Taylor, George Turner, Paul Kincaid, Richard Lupoff, Ian Watson. 800 to 40,000 words." circ. 800. 3/yr. Pub'd 2 issues 1979; expects 3 issues 1980, 3 issues 1981. sub. price: $5.00 airmail; $3.00 surface mail; per copy: $1.50 airmail; $1.00 surface mail; sample: $1.00. Back issues: $1.50. Discounts: Trade, 33% sale. 44pp; 6X8 inches/15X21 cm; of. Reporting time: 1 week to 1 month. Copyrighted, reverts to author. Pub's reviews: 40 in 1979. §Science fiction. Ads: £18/£9.

THE ARGONAUT, Michael E. Ambrose, PO Box 7985, Austin, TX 78712, (512) 478-2396. 1972. Poetry, fiction, articles, art, interviews, letters, news items. "Fiction up to 6,000 words, poetry preferably short, articles query, artists submit xeroxes for assignments. Want speculative, scientific SF with characterization, fantasy with light or Dunsanian emphasis, articles on genre & authors. Recent contributors: Dirk W. Mosig, Albert J. Manachino, Dale Hammell, Leo Wagner, Gene Phillips, Gordon Linzner, B. F. Watkinson, Dewi McS, David Vosburgh, Michael Danagher, Larry Dickison." circ. 200. 2/yr. Pub'd 1 issue 1979; expects 2 issues 1980, 2 issues 1981. sub. price: 4/$5.50; per copy: $1.50; sample: $1.50. Back issues: No. 4, $0.75; No. 6, $1.50. Discounts: 5 copies or more, 40%. 56pp; 5½X8½; of. Reporting time: 1-2 weeks. Payment: Fiction/articles $0.005 word; poetry 1 copy of issue line; art $5.00, $2.50, copies. On acceptance. Copyrighted, reverts to author. Pub's reviews: 12 in 1979. §SF & fantasy, H. P. Lovecraft & C. A. Smith. Ads: $5.00/$3.00/$.02 per line/$.10 min.

Ariadne Press, Carol F. Hoover, Editor, 4400 P St., N.W., Washington, DC 20007, (202) 337-2514. 1974. Fiction. "Ellen Moore 'Lead Me to the Exit' publication date 12-01-77." avg. press run 2,000. Pub'd 1 title 1979. 1 title listed in the *Small Press Record of Books in Print* (9th Edition, 1980). avg. price, cloth: $6.95. Discounts: 25%-40% to booksellers. 208pp; 5½X8½; of. Payment: 10% of list price. Copyrights for author. Writer's Center, Glen Echo, Md.

Aris Books (see also GARLIC TIMES), L. John Harris, 526 Santa Barbara Road, Berkeley, CA 94707, 527-1958. 1976. Art, photos, cartoons, collages. "Aris Books co-publishes general non-fiction with *Panjandrum Press*. From 100 pages to 300 plus pages. How-to, cooking, health, biography, musical instrument construction, psychology, etc. Our next book is by Stephanie Waxman, the children's book author." avg. press run 4,000. Pub'd 2 titles 1979; expects 2 titles 1980, 2 titles 1981. avg. price, cloth: $10.00; paper: $4.95. Discounts: our discounts are typical—available on request. 250pp; 6X9; of. Reporting time: 1 month. Payment: 7½ percent, 10 percent, 12½ percent, twice annually. Copyrights for author.

ARIZONA QUARTERLY, Albert F. Gegenheimer, Univ. Of Arizona, Tucson, AZ 85721, Main Library 541-B (602) 626-1029. 1945. Poetry, fiction, articles, reviews. 4/yr. Pub'd 4 issues 1979; expects 4 issues 1980. sub. price: $2.00; per copy: $0.50. Back issues: Regular price available. 96pp; 6X9; of. Reporting time: 3-4 weeks. Payment: Copies. Copyrighted, does not revert to author. Pub's reviews: 22 in 1979. §Modern literature. no ads.

THE ARK, Geoffrey Gardner, Box 322 Times Square Station, New York, NY 10108, 612-339-5162. 1970. Poetry, fiction, criticism, letters, long-poems. "Recent contributors have included Lyn Lifshin, Lucien Stryk, Robert Dana, Faye Kicknosway, Stephen Kessler, David Ray, Paul Mann, Hayden Carruth, Edouard Roditi, Cid Corman, Ivan Arguelles, David Budbill, Erskine Lane, Marjorie Hawksworth, Colette Inez, Alfred Starr Hamilton. We want excellent work of any form and style. Please, no more MFA poetry of *any* sort! We are especially interested in translation. Our last three issues have included translations of: the 13th century Turkish Sufi Yunus Emre, Leon Felipe, Pablo Neruda, Nizar Qabbani, Alma Johanna Koenig, Shinkichi Takahashi, Francisco de Quevedo, Mahmoud Darweesh, Fujiwara No Sadaie, Rene Guy Caddou, Fernando Pessoa. Prospective contributors are advised to look at an issue or two before sending their work to us. Number 14 is a special 400 page issue in honor of Kenneth Rexroth, illustrated by Morris Graves and including work by 100 contributors. Number 15 will be a book of poems by David Budbill, *From Down to the Village*. From number 14 on, all issues will befull length books. And only full-length mss. are now solicited. A future issue will be *The Selected Plays of Paul Goodman*." circ. 1,000 plus. 2/yr. Pub'd 1 issue 1979; expects 2 issues 1980, 2 issues 1981. sub. price: $6.00; per copy: No. 14: $10.00; No. 15 and beyond: $3.50; sample: $1.50 while limited supply of back numbers lasts. Back issues: No's. 1-12 $20.00 the set; number's 7-10 $2.00 each; numbers 11 $ 12 $1.50 each, Number 14 $12.00. Discounts: 40 percent to bookstores, otherwise none. 80-100pp; 6X9; †of. Reporting time: At once to 3 months. Payment: Copies only, but generously. Copyrighted, reverts to author. no ads at all. CCLM.

THE ARK RIVER REVIEW, A.G. Sobin, Jonathan Katz, c/o A.G. Sobin Box 14 WSU, Wichita, KS 67208, 316-832-1075. 1971. Poetry, fiction. "We are now printing only issues which comprise chapbook-length selections of work from three poets/writers each. One 3-poet issue and one 3-writer issue per year. We will be particularly receptive to mss. from those who have yet to publish a full length book. Send full manuscripts (15-25 pages of poetry, 80-150 pages of fiction) of which up to one-third may have been previously published in magazines if permission to reprint can be obtained. We will be reading throughout the year. In addition to $250 cash payment we will send gratis copies in your name to several dozen agents and book publishers with an eye toward exposing your work to those who are in a position to help you toward book publication. If at all possible, at the time you submit, a copy of the issue ($2.50) for which your work is being considered, be it the fiction issue or the poetry issue. (But if you can't, that's okay—not to worry). We strongly advise you to look over back issues before submitting. We work with a number of readers, but with a system that does not require a concensus—thus we hope to be open to a very wide range of material. We always prefer to take a chance with something really new than to print what is highly competent but usual—this is especially true of fiction. Conventional fiction stands little chance. Recent contributors are: Arthur Vogelsang, Maura Stanton, John Skoyles, Albert Goldbarth, John L'Heureux, George Chambers, Stephen Dunn, Kenneth Rexroth, James Tate, Leslie Ullman, Harley Elliot; and you will be surprised by our good taste!" circ. 1,500 +. 2/yr. Pub'd 3 issues 1979; expects 2 issues 1980, 2 issues 1981. sub. price: $5.00/4 numbers (two double issues); per copy: $2.50; sample: $2.00. Back issues: Vol. 1&2 complete $20.00 each,Vol 3&4 complete $18.00 each. Discounts: 40% to the trade. 80-160pp; 5½X8½; of. Reporting time: 2 weeks to 2 months. Payment: $250.00/ms. Copyrighted, we will grant any request to reprint made by the author. CCLM, COSMEP.

Arlotta Press, 634J Millbank Dr., Dayton, OH 45459. 1977. Articles. avg. press run 1,000. 1 title listed in the *Small Press Record of Books in Print* (9th Edition, 1980). avg. price, paper: $3.00. Discounts: 40% bookstores, standard libraries. 80pp; 5½X8½; of.

Armchair Press (see also WRITERS IN RESIDENCE), Mark Berman, 123 Dorchester Road, Scarsdale, NY 10583. 1973. Poetry, fiction, long-poems. "Publish 1-4 books each year." avg. press run 1,000. Pub'd 4 titles 1979; expects 4 titles 1980. 16 titles listed in the *Small Press Record of Books in Print* (9th Edition, 1980). avg. price, cloth: varies; paper: varies; other: Varies. Discounts: write for specific information. pp varies; size Varies; of/lp. Reporting time: 4 months. Payment: 10% of print run. Share copyright with author. CCLM.

Charles N. Aronson, Writer Publisher (see also PEEPHOLE ON PEOPLE), Charles N. Aronson, RR1, 11520 Bixby Hill Road, Arcade, NY 14009. 1969. Poetry, fiction, articles, art, photos, cartoons, interviews, satire, criticism, reviews, letters, parts-of-novels, news items. "Aronson recently began publishing *Peephole on People.* Aronson has published 10 books since the press was founded in 1969. *Peephole on People* is an 8-page newsletter magazine. The longest book published by Aronson is *Free Enterprise* and it has 1,689 pages. The bias? Truth & Beauty." avg. press run 2,000. Pub'd 2 titles 1979; expects 1 title 1981. 10 titles listed in the *Small Press Record of Books in Print* (9th Edition, 1980). avg. price, cloth: $16.00; paper: $10.50; other: $1.00 for the 8-page newsletter. All get the same quantity discount. 1 copy 20%; 2-4, 30%; 5-9, 40%; 10+, 45%. Wholesalers, 50%. 112-1,700pp; 8½X11; of. I print only my own stuff. Copyrights for author. COSMEP.

Around Publishing (see also THE LITTLE AROUND JOURNAL; and books), Janos Szebedinszky, Patricia Walsh, 541 Mentone, Mentone, IN 46539. 1975. Poetry, fiction, articles, art, photos, cartoons, interviews, satire, criticism, reviews, music, letters, parts-of-novels, long-poems, plays. "*The 1984 Calendar* and assorted fantasy directed projects." avg. press run 2-5,000. 3 titles listed in the *Small Press Record of Books in Print* (9th Edition, 1980). Discounts: 25-35 percent. of. Reporting time: 3-6 weeks. Payment: 50-50 on profits. Copyrights for author.

ART AND ARCHAEOLOGY NEWSLETTER, Otto F. Reiss, Publ., Otto F. Reiss, Editor; Victor W. von Hagen, European Editor; Joseph Baicich, Associate Editor, 243 East 39th Street, New York, NY 10016. 1965. Articles, photos, reviews. "Recent Contributors:Victor W. Von Hagen; David Reese, Harvard Univ; Dale R. Grieb. Length of Material:300 to 3000 words; we often *condense* contributions. Style: not unlike 'Science' department in 'Time' magazine. We return 90%-95% of all submissions as unsuitable, often too naive, and because would-be contributors confuse us with a travel magazine and send reports from an American Express tour of Mexico and similar on-the-beaten-track spots." circ. 1,800. 4 x yr. sub. price: $7.00/4 issues; per copy: $2.50; sample: 10 15-cent stamps. Back issues: vary from $.75 to $3.00. Discounts: subscription agents 20%. 16-20pp; 8½X5½; of. Reporting time: negative, return mail. Payment: $20-25. Copyrighted. Pub's reviews: 20 in 1979. §ancient history esp. lands around the Mediterranean; archaeology (same area). Ads: $55.00/$30.00.

ART & LITERARY DIGEST, Canada Publishing Co., Roy Cadwell, Tweed, Ont K0K3J0, Canada. 1969. "Payment 1 cent a word for material used. We need digests of art, crafts, and general interest articles. Payment for poetry in copies of the magazine." circ. 1,000. quarterly. sub. price: $3.00; per copy: $1.00; sample: $1.00. Discounts: 40 percent. 4 - 24pp; 8½X11 or 5½X8; of. Reporting time: 30 days. Payment: $.01 a word. Poetry-copies. Not copyrighted. Pub's reviews: Ads: $25/$15/$.05.

Art Official Inc. (see also FILE MAG), General Idea, 217 Richmond Street West, Toronto, Ontario M5V 1W2, Canada, (416) 362-1685. 1972. Interviews. "We do not usually publish unsolicited material." avg. press run 3,000. Pub'd 1-2 titles 1979; expects 1-2 titles 1980, 1-2 titles 1981. 9 titles listed in the *Small Press Record of Books in Print* (9th Edition, 1980). avg. price, paper: $3.00. Discounts: 35 percent bulk orders, 5 or more. pp varies; 10¾X14"; of. Reporting time: varies. Payment varies. copyright reverts to authors. CPPA.

Artemisia Press, Clifton Chas S., Mary T. Currier-Clifton, PO Box 6423, Colorado Springs, CO 80934, (303) 685-5766. 1977. Poetry, articles, art, photos. "Artemisia Press currently is seeking chapbook-length mss. of poetry with a Western or Southwestern orientation. We like work with a shamanistic or magickal feel to it, and/or 'poems of place'. We will also consider photos and graphic work in the same general vein." avg. press run 300-1000. Pub'd 2 titles 1979; expects 2 titles 1980. 1 title listed in the *Small Press Record of Books in Print* (9th Edition, 1980). avg. price, paper: $3.95; other: n/a. Discounts: Trade 40%. pp varies; 3X5 to 11X8½; mi/of/lp. Reporting time: 2 months. Payment: by contract. Copyrights for author.

THE ARTFUL DODGE, Daniel Bourne, General Editor & Fiction Editor; Stephen Cape, Poetry Editor; Editor, Mike Cagle, Art & Graphics Editor, 110 South Roosevelt, Bloomington, IN 47401, 332-6296. 1979. Poetry, fiction, articles, art, cartoons, interviews, satire, criticism, reviews, parts-of-novels, long-poems, plays. "*AD* presents both established and lesser known writers. Non-English material is usually printed with accompanying English translation. Submissions are welcome, but cannot be returned unless accompanied by a stamped, self addressed envelope." circ. 300. 4/yr. Pub'd 4 issues 1979. sub. price: Indiv. $4.00; Instit. $6.00; per copy: $1.00; sample: $1.00. Back issues: $1.00. Discounts: 30%. 70-80pp; 5½X8½. Reporting time: 2 months maximum. Payment: copies. Copyrighted, reverts to author. Pub's reviews. §Poetry, fiction, speculative fiction, plays, criticism, arts, social commentary. Ads: $25.00/$15.00/$8.00.

THE ARTFUL REPORTER, North West Arts, Jonathan Hyams, 12 Harter Street, 4th Floor, Manchester, England M1 6HY, United Kingdom. 1977. Fiction, articles, art, photos, cartoons, interviews, criticism, reviews, music, letters, news items. "Includes what's on supplement." circ. 30,000. 10/yr. Pub'd 10 issues 1979; expects 10 issues 1980, 10 issues 1981. sub. price: £4; sample: free. Back issues: free, but subject to availability. 12-16pp; size A3; of. Reporting time: 3 weeks. Payment: £25 per 1,000 words, £7 per illustration. Copyrighted, retains rights only on fiction & illustration. Pub's reviews: 20 in 1979. §All arts related areas and the north west. Ads: £110/£65/5p.

Artichoke Press, Kate Page, S.E. Barrett, 3274 Parkhurst Drive, Rancho Palos Verdes, CA 90274, (213) 831-1818. 1979. Poetry, fiction, articles, art, criticism. "The purpose of Artichoke Press is a literary press which will publish quality work. It may well turn into a cooperative press because of the tremendous cost of printing etc. & also because of the difficulties of distribution. Our first & only book is poetry, and its quality is high. Art - Design - content. We use letterpress and MacIntosch & Young from Santa Barbara as our printer. We expect to continue with this formula, printer, designer is Kath Barrett who also does the illustrations. We are not necessarily solliciting any ms because of cost etc. Obviously we are an extremely small press. Our objective is one at a time with art form in mind for each publication." avg. press run 1,000. Pub'd 1 title 1979. 1 title listed in the *Small Press Record of Books in Print* (9th Edition, 1980). Discounts: 40% to bookstores. lp. COSMEP.

Artists & Alchemists Publications, Adele Aldridge, 215 Bridgeway, Sausalito, CA 94965, 914-332-0326. 1975. Art, concrete art, poetry. avg. press run 2,000. Pub'd 1 title 1979; expects 1 title 1980. avg. price, paper: $5.00. Discounts: 45 percent on orders of 5 or more when payment is enclosed and 10 percent on 1-4 books, 40 percent 5 or more without prepayment. No returns - we pay shipping. 8½X11; of. not looking for ms. now. Copyrights for author. COSMEP, NESPA.

Arts End Books (see NOSTOC)

ARTZIEN, Kontexts Publications, Michael Gibbs, Eerste Van Der Helststraat 55, Amsterdam, Holland, 768556. 1978. Art, criticism, reviews. "*Artzien* is a monthly review of art in Amsterdam, containing reviews of current Amsterdam exhibitions and events and items of general art-critical interest." circ. 500. Monthly. Expects 2 issues 1980, 10 issues 1981. sub. price: $12.50; per copy: 75¢; sample: 75¢. Back issues: all issues available at 75¢. Discounts: trade: 33⅓%. 16pp; 6⅞X8½; †mi. Copyrighted, reverts to author. Pub's reviews. §contemporary arts. Ads: Dfl 80/Dfl 40/Dfl 0.50 per word.

ARULO!, JoAnn Amadeo, 252 No. 16th Street, Bloomfield, NJ 07003. 1979. Poetry, art, letters. "Reviews arty sketches for each cover." circ. 350. 6/yr. Pub'd 2 issues 1979. sub. price: $12.00; per copy: $2.00; sample: $2.00. Back issues: $2.00. 52pp; 5X8; †of. Reporting time: 1 month or sooner. Payment: three free copies best poem in issue/three free copies cover designer. Copyrighted, reverts to author.

AS IS, L. Pablo Gamson, Paul Parsons, 118 Fleetwood Terr., Silver Spring, MD 20910, (301) 587-0377. 1971. Poetry, fiction. "Not interested in diatribes, deliberate obscurity, obscenity or superficial pious work. 'The fault of most poetry is not that it is bad but that it is boring.' We accept work from the Baltimore-Washington area only." circ. varies. irreg. price per copy: $1.00. Back issues: $.50. 24pp; various methods. Reporting time: any time. Payment: copy only. Not copyrighted. §poetry. Glen Echo Writers Center, Glen Echo, MD.

As Is/So & So Press (see also SO & SO), John(Joma) Marron, 2864 Folsom, San Francisco, CA 94110, 415-282-9570. 1973. Poetry, fiction, long-poems, collages. "Interested in process of thought as revealed in speech, gesture, dance, meditation, and also the visual rendered in one's own eye, hand, media at hand. 50-100 pages for now. Charlie Walsh: janitor, futures expert, state dept-vacation hymns." avg. press run 500-1,000. Expects 1 title 1980. 2 titles listed in the *Small Press Record of Books in Print* (9th Edition, 1980). avg. price, cloth: $5.00; paper: $3.00; other: $2.00. Discounts: But 2 of first 4 titles (20% off); 3 of 4 (30%); 4 of 4 (40%)/40% to bookstores minimum of 5. 80pp; 5X8; mi/of/lp. Reporting time: 6 weeks. Payment: 10-25% (depends on sales). Copyrights for author. CCLM, COSMEP.

ASCENT, Phyllis Dale, Yasodhara Ashram Society, Box 9, Kootenay Bay, B.C. V0B 1X0, Canada, (604) 227-9220. 1969. Articles, photos, interviews, reviews. circ. 1200. 3/yr. Pub'd 3 issues 1979; expects 3 issues 1980, 3 issues 1981. sub. price: $5.00; per copy: $1.75; sample: no charge. Back issues: $1.00. Discounts: 20%. 50pp; 6X9; †of. Payment: no. Copyrighted, does not revert to author. Pub's reviews: 5 in 1979.

ASFA POETRY QUARTERLY, Charles Ghigna, 820 North 18th Street, Birmingham, AL 35203, (205) 252-9241. 1974. Poetry, art. "Recent contributors: Betty Adcock, Ann Deagon, Elissa Bishop, D. S. Dunn, Eugene Silverman." circ. 1,000. 4/yr. Pub'd 4 issues 1979; expects 4 issues 1980, 4 issues 1981. sub. price: $4.00; per copy: $1.00; sample: $1.00. Back issues: $1.00. 25pp; 8½X11; of. Reporting time: 2 weeks to a month. Payment: Complimentary copies.

Ash Lad Press, Bill Romey, P.O. Box 396, Canton, NY 13617, 315-386-8820. 1975. Non-fiction. avg. press run 1,500. Pub'd 1 title 1979; expects 2 titles 1980. 4 titles listed in the *Small Press Record of Books in Print* (9th Edition, 1980). avg. price, paper: $4.95. Discounts: trade 40% for orders of over 5, 20% for 1-4, texts 20%, libraries 25%. 150pp; 6X9; of. Cooperative sharing of costs and income. Copyrights for author. COSMEP.

Ash-Kar Press, Strange de Jim, PO Box 14547, San Francisco, CA 94114. 1978. Art, photos. "Spiritual and occult how-to books." avg. press run 5,000. Pub'd 2 titles 1979; expects 1 title 1980. 3 titles listed in the *Small Press Record of Books in Print* (9th Edition, 1980). avg. price, paper: $5.95. Discounts: 50 or 55% to wholesaler, 40% to retailor. 112pp; 5½X8½; of. Reporting time: we do not solicit outside material. Payment: individual basis. Copyrights for author.

Ashford Press (see also SARCOPHAGUS), M. J. Westerfield, RR 1, Box 128, Ashford, CT 06278. 1973. Poetry, fiction, art. "All manuscripts welcomed, both fiction and non-fiction. Recent titles include *Bells & Clappers* (poetry) by Susan Alon and *The Los Angeles Book of the Dead* by Lewis H. Lappert II (fiction)." avg. press run 1,000. Pub'd 1 title 1979; expects 2 titles 1980, 4 titles 1981. 2 titles listed in the *Small Press Record of Books in Print* (9th Edition, 1980). avg. price, cloth: $6.50; paper: $3.00. 6X9; †of/lp. Reporting time: 2 weeks. Payment: by individual arrangement. Copyrights for author.

ASI Publishers, Inc. (see also ASTROLOGY '80—The New Aquarian Agent), Henry Weingarten, Barbara Somerfield, 127 Madison Ave, New York, NY 10016, 212-679-5676. 1972. "ASI publishes in a variety of subject areas. Our general requirements for new books are (1) the material is accurate (2) the material is unique and adds to the existing literature something not already available, and for which there is a real need (3) the material (explanations and diagrams) are clear and understandable. If you are interested in submitting a manuscript to us, your initial letter should be accompanied by an abstract, table of contents, detailed description, or outline, including if possible, information relative to approximate page length and number of tables and illustrations. Please do not send a complete manuscript to us until we have made a specific request for it." avg. press run 1,000-5,000. Expects 6 titles 1980, 8 titles 1981. 30 titles listed in the *Small Press Record of Books in Print* (9th Edition, 1980). avg. price, cloth: $15.00; paper: $6.95. Discounts: 40 percent retail; higher—dependent on quantity ordered (see ABA redbook). 128-320pp; 6X9; of. Reporting time: 3 months. Semi-annual payment; standard author contract. Most all copyrights held by publisher.

THE ASIA MAIL, Potomac Asia Communications, Edward Neilan, Editor & Publisher, P O Box 1044, Alexandria, VA 22313. 1976. Poetry, articles, art, cartoons, interviews, satire, criticism, reviews, music, letters, parts-of-novels, long-poems. "1,000 word top. We'll send a sample. Write for writer's guidelines, Managing Editor Donna Gays, c/o Asia Mail." circ. 30,000. 12/yr. Pub'd 12 issues 1979; expects 12 issues 1980, 12 issues 1981. sub. price: $11.00; per copy: $1.50. Back issues: $2.00. Discounts: on request. 24pp; 11½X14½; of. Reporting time: 8 weeks. Payment: up to $150.00 Major articles; $50.00 Reviews. Copyrighted. Pub's reviews: 24 in 1979. §Asia interest. Ads: $1760/979.20/65¢.

Asian American Perspectives Inc. (see BRIDGE MAGAZINE)

Asian Studies Center (see JOURNAL OF SOUTH ASIAN LITERATURE)

Askin Publishers, Ltd., 16 Ennismore Ave., London W4 1SF, United Kingdom, 01-994-1314. 1973. "Book length - genuine contributions to scholarship of Western magic *or* classical works on magic from earliest period to 1700." avg. press run 500. Pub'd 3 titles 1979; expects 3 titles 1980, 5 titles 1981. 7 titles listed in the *Small Press Record of Books in Print* (9th Edition, 1980). avg. price, cloth: £5; paper: £2; other: £28 (leather). Discounts: 35-40% depending on quantity. 280pp; 5¾X8¾ and 10X12¾; of/lp. Reporting time: 3 weeks. Payment: 10% royalty. Copyrights for author.

Aslan Enterprises, Steve Saran, P.O. Box 1858, Boulder, CO 80306, 303-449-1515. 1973. "Health, natural lifestyle." avg. press run 5,000. Pub'd 5 titles 1979; expects 2 titles 1980, 5 titles 1981. 10 titles listed in the *Small Press Record of Books in Print* (9th Edition, 1980). avg. price, other: $3.00 poster. Discounts: 40 percent. 17X22; †of. Reporting time: 1 month. Payment: negotiable, quarterly. Copyrights for author. COSMEP.

ASPECT, Art and Literature, Southwood Press, Rudi Krausmann, Scotland Island 2105 NSW, Sydney, NSW, Australia, 9972481. 1975. Poetry, fiction, art, photos, interviews, satire, criticism, reviews, parts-of-novels, long-poems, collages, plays, concrete art. "Recent contributors: Reiner Kunze, Bill Berkson, Frank O'Hara, Peter bichsel, Ted Hughes, Roger Garfitt, Christopher MacKel. Prose: 1,000-3,000 words, Poetry: 1-3 poems per contributor, Articles: 1,000-5,000 words: Interviews etc." circ. 1,000. 4/yr. Pub'd 4 issues 1979; expects 4 issues 1980, 4 issues 1981. sub. price: $12.00; per copy: $3.00. Back issues: $3.00. Discounts: 33⅓% Stores; 55% Agents. 72pp; 7X9½; of. Reporting time: 1-6 months. Payment: $10.00 Poetry (per page) $10.00 per 1,000 words (prose) minimum. Copyrighted, reverts to author. Pub's reviews: 10 in 1979. §Art, literature. Ads: $200.00/$100.00.

ASPEN ANTHOLOGY, J.D. Muller, Box 3185, Aspen, CO 81611, 303-925-8750. 1972. Poetry, fiction, articles, art, photos, interviews, criticism, reviews, parts-of-novels, plays. "Poems usually no more than 40 lines, stories 1-10,000 words. All forms, themes, subjects considered. Joyce Carol Oates, Kurt Vonnegut, Marge Piercy, Kathleen Fraser, Michael Dennis Browne, James Salter, Karen Swenson.H. E. Francis, Leonard Gilley, Reg Saner, Kent Nelson." circ. 1,000. 2/yr. Pub'd 2 issues 1979; expects 2 issues 1980. sub. price: $4.50; per copy: $2.50 + 75¢ p & h; sample: $2.50 plus $0.75 postage. Back issues: $2.50/all back issues + 75¢ p & h. 120pp; 6X9; of. Reporting time: 2 mo. max. Payment: 2 copies. Copyrighted, reverts with acknowl. of first pub. by AA. Pub's reviews: 20 in 1979. §all literature, arts, criticism. Ads: $50.00/$25.00. CCLM,COSMEP.

ASPHODEL, A.C. Libro, Editor; C.W. Bechtel, Production Manager, 613 Howard Avenue, Pitman, NJ 08071. 1978. Poetry, fiction, articles, art, interviews, criticism, reviews, parts-of-novels, long-poems, concrete art. "Poetry any length, Fiction, short fiction preferred, to 3,000 words. Articles, reviews,crit. poetics;words. SASE a must!" circ. 400. 2/yr. Expects 2 issues 1981. sub. price: $4.00; per copy: $2.00; sample: $2.00. Discounts: none. 50pp; 5½X8½; †of/lp. Reporting time: Four to six weeks; if more, then considering. Payment: 1 copy. Copyrighted. §art/travel/books. Ads: $75.-00/$40.00.

Bay Area ASPO News, Debbie McDaniel, PO Box 603, Belmont, CA 94002, (408) 243-1136. 1966. Poetry, articles, art, cartoons, criticism, reviews, letters, news items, non-fiction. "This newsletter is published for pregnant and new parents. ASPO is a national organization which promotes Lamaze prepared childbirth. Articles should be no longer than two pages, double spaced. Include return postage." circ. 3,000. 4/yr. Pub'd 4 issues 1979; expects 4 issues 1980. sub. price: $2.00; per copy: free, include 28 cent stamp; sample: Free, include 28 cent stamp. Back issues: Free if available, include 28 cent stamp. Discounts: none. 12pp; 8½X11; of. Reporting time: 2 months, include SASE. Payment: none. Not copyrighted. Pub's reviews: 20-30 in 1979. §childbirth, parenting. Ads: $140.00/$80.00. COSMEP.

ASSEMBLING, Assembling Press, Scott Helms, Co-compiler; David Cole, Co-compiler; Richard Kostelanetz, Co-compiler, Box 1967, Brooklyn, NY 11202. 1970. Poetry. "Also known as *Second Assembling - Eighth Assembling;* uses otherwise unpublishable creative work. *Assembling* is collaborative. Contributors print 1M copies of up to three 8½ x 11 pages of anything they wish at their own initiative and expense. Contribution is by invitation. An invitation will be sent to anyone whose work demonstrates a commitment to 'alternate' style or substance. Those wishing invitations are invited to send manuscripts. Editors of *Assembling* are really compilers-they are not interested in authoritarian procedures. Eight *Assembling* annuals have collected an unprecedented variety of avant-garde printed art. Individual books extend the bias and principles of the press. Send SASE for check-list." circ. 1,000. Pub'd 4 issues 1979; expects 6 issues 1980, 6 issues 1981. price per copy: $6.95 for Seventh; $4.95 for all previous editions; sample: (Assembling pubs.) $4.95. Discounts: 40% discount to retailers paying in advance, and incl. postage. We do not send consignments as past issues are scarce. 300pp;

8½X11; mi/of/lp. Reporting time: 1 mo. Payment: copies only. Copyrighted. CCLM, COSMEP.

Assembling Press (see also ASSEMBLING), David Cole, Scott Helms, Richard Kostelanetz, PO Box 1967, Brooklyn, NY 11202. 1970. "Work that extend the principles and achievements of *ASSEMBLING*; see our retrospective catalogue" avg. press run 700. Pub'd 5 titles 1979; expects 5 titles 1980, 5 titles 1981. 29 titles listed in the *Small Press Record of Books in Print* (9th Edition, 1980). avg. price, paper: $8.00. Discounts: 40% to dealers paying in advance. of. Reporting time: one month. Payment: 10% of edition. Copyrights for author. CCLM, COSMEP.

ASSERT NEWSLETTER, Impact Publishers, Inc., Robert E. Alberti, PO Box 1094, San Luis Obispo, CA 93406, 805-543-5911. 1970. Articles, interviews, reviews, photos, cartoons, letters, news items, non-fiction. "Special interest: assertive behavior" circ. 1,800. 6/yr. Pub'd 6 issues 1979; expects 6 issues 1980. sub. price: $4.00(US, Can, Mex), $5.00 surface, $7.00 air (foreign); per copy: 75¢; sample: free. Back issues: no discount-$.75 per issue (75¢ effective 10-1-79). Discounts: none. 6pp; 8½X11; of. Reporting time: 4 weeks. Payment: none. Copyrighted. Pub's reviews: 4 in 1979. §Assertive Behavior Therapy & Psychology in general. Ads: $125.00.

Associated Creative Writers (see also WRITING), Charles Brashers, 9231 Molly Woods Ave, La Mesa, CA 92041, 460-4107. 1979. "We'll print whatever strikes our fancy: We plan to emphasize quality: If we take 'old-fashioned, well-made literature' as the original thesis and Post-modernist experimentation as its antithesis, we'd like to see the synthesis that comes of the two. Type of material used varies: we have a report on research, *Developing Creativity* $2.50; some poetry; an experimental historical-anthropological novel, *A Snug Little Purchase* $4.95, in print." avg. press run 300-2,000. Pub'd 1 title 1979; expects 2 titles 1980, 3-4 titles 1981. 1 title listed in the *Small Press Record of Books in Print* (9th Edition, 1980). avg. price, cloth: $6.00-$10.00; paper: $3.00-$5.00. pp varies; 5½X8½; of. Reporting time: We'll try to take less than a month. Payment: Haven't worked out details yet, but are planning a flat 20% royalty to authors. May do some co-operative publishing on a 50-50 basis. Copyrights for author.

Astro Artz (see also HIGH PERFORMANCE), Linda Frye Burnham, 240 So Broadway, 5th Floor, Los Angeles, CA 90012, 213-687-7362. 1978. Art. "Interested in reproduction of drawings and in documentation of performance art activity. No submissions, please." avg. press run 2,000. Pub'd 1 title 1979; expects 2 titles 1981. avg. price, paper: $10.00; other: $300.00 short, signed edition. Discounts: 40%. 100pp; of. Reporting time: no submissions, please. Payment: variable. Copyrights for author. COSMEP, AAP.

ASTROLOGY '80—The New Aquarian Agent, ASI Publishers, Inc., ASI Publishers, Inc., Henry Weingarten, 127 Madison Ave, New York, NY 10016, 212-679-5676. 1969. Articles, art, cartoons, satire, criticism, reviews, letters, news items. "Dedicated to the promotion of scientific astrological research and practice. Contributors *must* be knowledgeable in astrology. *NO* Sun Sign Garbage." circ. International; 2,000. 4/yr. Expects 4 issues 1980, 4 issues 1981. sub. price: $12.00; per copy: $3.95; sample: $3.95. Back issues: $10.00 Volume; $32.00 for all 4 printed volumes. Discounts: 40 percent to retail outlets; with full returns privileges; 50 percent to jobbers. 64pp; 6X9; of. Reporting time: 1 month. Payment: $2.00 per page. Copyrighted, does not revert to author. Pub's reviews: 15 in 1979. §Astrology. Ads: $75.00/$45.00/$25.00.

ASTROLOGY NOW, Llewellyn Publications, Noel Tyl, Lore Wallace, Stephen Albaugh, Llewellyn Publications, P.O.Box 43383, St. Paul, MN 55164, (612) 291-1970. 1975. Articles, art, photos, cartoons, interviews, reviews, letters, parts-of-novels. circ. 10,000. Bi-monthly. Pub'd 6 issues 1979; expects 6 issues 1980, 6 issues 1981. sub. price: $10.00; per copy: $2.00. Back issues: $2.00. Discounts: 40% to discount retailers; 50% to discount wholesalers. 95pp; 8½X11; of. Reporting time: 6 weeks. Copyrighted, does not revert to author. Pub's reviews: 50+ in 1979. §Astrology, metaphysical, occult. Ads: write for rates. ABA.

THE ASTRONOMY QUARTERLY, Pachart Publishing House, Dr. Eric R. Craine, Box 35549, Tucson, AZ 85740, (602) 297-4797. 1977. "Deals with topics in astronomy, closely related sciences and their philosophical ramifications in a readable but intelligent manner." 4/yr. Pub'd 4 issues 1979; expects 4 issues 1980. sub. price: $8.00; per copy: $2.50. Discounts: 20% prepaid, us invoicing. 64pp; 6X9; of. Payment: yes. Copyrighted. Pub's reviews: 20 in 1979. Ads: $144.00/$72.00.

Ata Books, Dorothy Bryant, 1928 Stuart Street, Berkeley, CA 94703, (415) 841-9613. 1978. "I publish my own work, chiefly fiction. So far have published three novels and one book on fiction process. Plan to average one book per year." avg. press run 5,000. Pub'd 2 titles 1979; expects 1 title 1980, 1 title 1981. 4 titles listed in the *Small Press Record of Books in Print* (9th Edition, 1980). avg. price, cloth: $9.00; paper: $5.00. Discounts: 40% bookstores, 50% jobbers. 150pp; 5½X8½; of.

31

ATHAENA, Paula D. Rubenstein, 2 Sadore Lane, Yonkers, NY 10710. 1976. Poetry, art, long-poems. "Innovative or traditional, top-quality material." circ. 300. 3/yr. sub. price: $5.00; per copy: $2.00; sample: $2.00. Back issues: $3.50. 28pp; 5½X8½; †of. Reporting time: 4-6 weeks. No payment. Copyrighted, reverts to author. §poetry, articles, reviews, criticism, interviews. COSMEP.

ATHENE, Society For Education Through Art, Don Pavey, Geoff Lloyd, Joan Griffiths, S.E.A. Bath Academy of Art, Corsham, Wilts, United Kingdom. 1939. "An international platform for new ideas in arts and education. Published by the Society for Education through Art (SEA), its official aim is to further the recognition of art as an essential part of education through which the potential of every child and adult can be realised. Was first promoted by a pioneering group of artists, Eric Gill, Henry Moore, Herbert Read, Clive Bell and others. Includes contributions from abroad-Moscow, Belgrade, Rome, Japan, etc. in recent issues." circ. 4,000. 2/yr. sub. price: £1. Back issues: on application. 32pp; size A4; of. Ads: £75.

THE ATLANTIC REVIEW, Robert Vas Dias, Editor, 115-117 Shepherdess Walk, London, England N1 7QA, United Kingdom, 01-250-4011. 1975. Poetry, fiction, articles, interviews, criticism, reviews, parts-of-novels, long-poems. "Biases toward informative essays on contemporary, post modern poetry. Also reviews, poetry & exper lit. Interested in innovative work by British and North American writers." circ. 700. 2/yr. Expects 2 issues 1980, 3 issues 1981. sub. price: $5.96; per copy: $2.50; sample: $2.50. Back issues: $2.50. Discounts: 40% to the trade (three copies or more). 72pp; 7½X10; †of. Reporting time: 5 weeks. Payment: copies plus offprints. Copyrighted, reverts to author. Pub's reviews: 9 in 1979. §Poetry, poetics.

ATLANTIS, Box 294, Acadia University, Wolfville, Nova Scotia B0P 1X0, Canada. 1975. Articles, reviews, criticism. 2/yr. sub. price: $7.00 ind., $12.00 instit., $15.00 overseas; per copy: $3.50; sample: (Special issues $5.00 per copy). Back issues: $4.00. 170pp; 8X10. Copyrighted, reverts to author. Pub's reviews: 40 in 1979. §Womens studies.

Atlantis Editions, Richard O'Connell, P.O. Box 18326, Philadelphia, PA 19120. 1962. Poetry. "Poetry of the highest quality. No biases. Contributors include: Elliott Coleman, Calliepe Doxiadis, Alexandra Grilikhes, Jack Lindeman, Howard Meroney, Richard O'Connell, Eric Sellin." Pub'd 3 titles 1979; expects 4 titles 1980. avg. price, paper: $2.50. lp. Reporting time: 3 months. COSMEP.

ATTENTION PLEASE, Hearthstone Press, Harold Leland Johnson, 708 Inglewood Drive, Broderick, CA 95605. 1975. Poetry, reviews. "Average 32 lines-longer must justify space required. Recent Contributors: Stella Worley, Ann Menebroker, Michael Scott Cain, James Magorian, Paul Fericano, Joyce Odam, Robert Phillips, Mervin Lane, Harold Witt, Ben Hiatt, Gary Fincke, A.D. Winans, Bill Hotchkiss, Charles Taylor, Matt Field, Joan Colby." circ. 500. Tri-annual. Pub'd 3 issues 1979; expects 3 issues 1980. sub. price: $4.00; per copy: $1.50; sample: $1.00. Back issues: $1.00. Discounts: 40 percent trade only. 36pp plus; 5½X8½; †mi/lp. Reporting time: 4 weeks. Payment: $10.00 to 2 best of issue, 1 copy to each contrib, $5.00 to 5 or more next best. Copyrighted. Pub's reviews: 10 in 1979. §poetry. Ads: none. COSMEP.

August Derleth Society Newsletter, Richard H. Fawcett, 61 Teecomwas Drive, Uncasville, CT 06382, (203) 848-0636. 1977. Poetry, fiction, articles, art, reviews, letters, news items. "Tributes to August Derleth are always welcome. Short stories and poems — particularly if these are written on macabre themes or with a Wisconsin setting are also welcome. Also: art work on the same themes, and letters from persons who may have known or met August Derleth." circ. 200. 4/yr. Pub'd 1 issue 1979; expects 4 issues 1980, 4 issues 1981. sub. price: $2.00/yr; per copy: $.50; sample: $.50. Back issues: $.50. Discounts: none. 10pp; 8½X11; †of. Reporting time: two weeks. Payment: none. Copyrighted, reverts to author. Pub's reviews: 8 in 1979. §Macabre tales & regional literature — Wisconsin. Ads: .10 word classified.

Aura Publishing Co., Ruth Zakutinsky, 975 Elm Street, New Haven, CT 06511, (203) 397-3865. "We are interested in juvenile material of Jewish religious, cultural and historic interest." avg. press run 2,000. Pub'd 1 title 1979; expects 2 titles 1980, 3 titles 1981. 2 titles listed in the *Small Press Record of Books in Print* (9th Edition, 1980). avg. price, paper: $2.98. Discounts: 40-50%. 32pp; 8½X11; †of. Reporting time: 2-4 weeks. Payment: 10% of profit after cost of printing etc. or $100.00 for manuscript upon acceptance. Copyrights for author.

Auriga, P. H. Niles, Box F, 8 Candlelight Court, Clifton Park, NY 12065, (518) 371-2015. 1979. Fiction, criticism. "Emphasis upon science fiction, at present." avg. press run 100. Pub'd 1 title 1979. 2 titles listed in the *Small Press Record of Books in Print* (9th Edition, 1980). avg. price, cloth: $3.00. 125pp; 5¼X8¼; of. Reporting time: Self-publishing author (not accepting submissions at present). Copyrights for author.

Auromere, Inc., Santosh Krinsky, 1291 Weber Street, Pomona, CA 91768, (714) 629-8255. 1974. "Sri Aurobindo Books and Indian Spiritual Texts and Children's Books. Other addresses: Auromere, Inc., c/o Atmaniketan Ashram, Merschstrasse 49, 4715. Ascheberg-Herbern, W. Germany, Phone (02599) 1364. We are the exclusive U.S. representative of a number of publishers from India and their titles are significantly more in number. Including: Ganesh & Co.; National Book Trust of India; Samata Books: Hemkunt Books; Children's Book Trust of India. In addition we also represent Sri Aurobindo Books Distribution Agency and Dipti Publications here in the U.S., plus Vedanta Press of Hollywood list has over 1,000 titles." avg. press run 5,000-10,000. Pub'd 1 title 1979; expects 3 titles 1980. avg. price, cloth: $8.95; paper: $3.95. Discounts: Trade 40%, any quantity; Jobbers, Distributors by arrangement. 100-200pp; 5⅜X8⅜; of. Reporting time: several weeks. Payment: variable. Copyrights for author. AAIP.

AUSTRALIAN SCAN: Journal of Human Communication, Rodney G. Miller, c/o Dept of Communication, Queensland Institute of Technology, GPO Box 2434, Brisbane, Queensland 4001, Australia, (07) 221-2411 Ext. 463. 1976. Articles, interviews, criticism, reviews, news items. "*Australian Scan* seeks to promote study, criticism, research, teaching and application of communication principles, by publishing articles of general interest which discuss issues and studies in human communication. Bias is for international material of lasting importance and interest and for Australian & Pacific communication studies. Length of material: Brief note up to 200 words; short article 1,000 to 2,000 words; article 3,000 to 5,000 words." circ. 300. 2/yr. Pub'd 2 issues 1979; expects 2 issues 1980, 2 issues 1981. sub. price: $7.00 (Aust.); $10.00 (overseas); per copy: $3.50 (Aust.); $5.00 (overseas); sample: $3.50 (Aust.); $5.00 (overseas). Back issues: As for normal subscription where back issues available. Discounts: On application. (Normal trading is by advance payment subscription only). 72pp; 6¾X10; of. Reporting time: Two months from receipt of material. Payment: 3 copies of issue containing contribution. Copyrighted, require acknowledgement for reprint. Pub's reviews: 2 in 1979. §Academic & serious polular works on human communication; e.g. public communication, creative or educational literature, drama, film, and television, organizational communication, interpersonal or small group communication, mass communication and media studies. Ads: $40.00/$20.00.

THE AUTHOR, Society Of Authors, Richard Findlater, 84 Drayton Gardens, London, England SW10 9SD, United Kingdom. 1890. "The main journal of professional writers in Britain. N.B./NO unsolicited material, contributions only by invitation." circ. 4,500. 4/yr. sub. price: £1.60; per copy: 40p. 45pp; lp. Ads: £25/£14/£8.

Author! Author! Publishing Co., Dorothy Wainer, 210 E 58th Street, New York, NY 10022. 1973. Poetry, photos, long-poems, collages, plays. "Also essays, short prose, plays. Currently publishing the work of one author, Patricia Ryan, but is planning to expand. No unsolicited manuscripts acepted." avg. press run 500. Expects 1 title 1980, 1 title 1981. avg. price, other: $1.50. 24pp; 6X9; of. Reporting time: No unsolicited manuscripts accepted.

Authors' Co-op Publishing Co., varied, Rt. 4, Box 137, Franklin, TN 37064, (615) 646-3757. 1977. Poetry, fiction, interviews, satire, criticism, reviews, letters, long-poems, collages. "Biased against pornography and special diets for weight losing, and health. First book was 2,000; Science Fiction, A. E. van Vogt's 'The Battle of Forever', next publication, 'The John W. Campbell Letters', book. Query first" avg. press run varies. Expects 1 title 1980, 1 title 1981. 3 titles listed in the *Small Press Record of Books in Print* (9th Edition, 1980). avg. price, other: $9.95 signed, numbered $14.95. Discounts: 1, 25%; 2-4, 33⅓%; 5-49, 40%; 50-99, 45%; 100-500, 50%; over 500, write for terms. 160pp; 5X8½; †of. Reporting time: Several days. Payment: Percent of net profit, as with University Presses, only greater. Copyrights for author. COSMEP, SWFA.

Autolycus Press, Willard Scott, Box 23928, Webster Groves, MO 63119, (314) 645-2114. 1970. Fiction, articles, satire, criticism. "We publish about five books per year, some in paper. We do not take submissions, since we are committed already for the next two years. We specialize in the work of Vincent Starrett and Michael Murphy." avg. press run 500/4,000. Pub'd 4 titles 1979; expects 6 titles 1980. avg. price, cloth: $10.00; paper: $5.00. Discounts: 1/3 discount, most sales are direct. (We will have classroom books in comparative lit.). 225pp; 6X9; lp. Reporting time: no submission accepted. Payment: 15%. Copyrights for author. Baker Street Irregulars.

Autumn Press, Inc., Nahum Stiskin, President & Editor-in-Chief, 1318 Beacon Street, Brookline, MA 02146, 617-738-5680. 1972. Fiction. "A.P. Books cover all 'new age' concerns, with a bias toward East-West cultural confluence. Book of Tofu and Book of Miso, by Bill Shurtleff & Akiko Aoyagi exemplary. Cover natural foods, Zen and meditative practices, alternative lifestyles, self-sufficiency, low-energy technologies, temple architecture and symbolism. Forthcoming titles to deal with Kundalini-and-science, nuclear power, natural and herbal healing, vegetarianism, natural foods cooking. Developing a random list (20 titles now in print) with above focus." avg. press run 7,500. Pub'd 8 titles 1979; expects 8 titles 1980, 10 titles 1981. 26 titles listed in the *Small Press Record of Books in Print* (9th Edition, 1980). avg. price, cloth: $10.00; paper: $5.95. Discounts: Distributed to the retail and library trade by Random House, Inc. 216pp; size variable; of. Reporting time: 1-3 months. Payment: standard. Copyrights for author. AAP, NESPA.

Avalon Editions (see also DOUBLE HARNESS), Andrew Cozens, 9 Bradmore Road, Oxford OX2 6QN, United Kingdom. 1971. Poetry, photos, long-poems. "All mss. are considered though usually solicited mss. receive preference. Recent and planned booklets include: Welch, Tipton, Tweedale, Ward (UK), Eigner (US), Kondos (Greece), and traditional Bengali poetry. Inexpensively but neatly produced. The only bias, we hope, is for talent as opposed to mediocrity." avg. press run 300-500. Pub'd 5 titles 1979; expects 5 titles 1980. 12 titles listed in the *Small Press Record of Books in Print* (9th Edition, 1980). avg. price, paper: 50p. Discounts: By arrangement. 20pp; 7X5; †lp. Reporting time: 1 month. Payment: By arrangement. ALP.

Avant-Garde Creations, Mary Carol Smith, Editor and Publisher, P.O. Box 30161, Eugene, OR 97403. 1977. Fiction. "The titles of our books are *Deep Foot, Deeper Foot, The Game of Orgy,* and *The Magic Carpet and the Cement Wall* (children). Also the deluxe (boxed) *Game of Orgy.* Information about our books is available direct from the publisher." avg. press run 10,000. Pub'd 2 titles 1979; expects 4 titles 1980. 4 titles listed in the *Small Press Record of Books in Print* (9th Edition, 1980). avg. price, cloth: $7.95; paper: $2.25-$3.95; other: $7.95 for the deluxe (boxed) Orgy game. Discounts: negotiable. 125-325pp; 8½X11, 4⅛X7; of. We accept no submissions. Payment: confidential. Copyrights for author. COSMEP.

Ave Victor Hugo Publishing (see also GALILEO), Charles Ryan, Floyd Kempske, William Desmond, 339 Newbury St., Boston, MA 02115. 1971. Poetry, fiction, articles, interviews, criticism, reviews, parts-of-novels, long-poems, plays. "Published one novel in 1976, *Milk Of Wolves* by Frederick Manfred." avg. press run 40m. 1 title listed in the *Small Press Record of Books in Print* (9th Edition, 1980). Reporting time: 2 months.

The Avondale Press, Ronald Napier, P.O. Box 451, Willowdale, Ontario M2N5T1, Canada, (416) 773-5115. 1973. Music. "Specializing in books on music, preferably by Canadian or with some Canadian aspect." avg. press run 1,000. Pub'd 2 titles 1979; expects 2 titles 1980. 5 titles listed in the *Small Press Record of Books in Print* (9th Edition, 1980). avg. price, cloth: $10.95; paper: $3.95. Discounts: 20% to trade. 100+pp; 6X9; of. Reporting time: 1 month. Payment: standard. Copyrights for author.

THE AWAKENER MAGAZINE, Filis Frederick, 938 18th Street, Hermosa Beach, CA 90254, (213) 379-2656. 1953. Poetry, articles, art, photos, cartoons, interviews, reviews, music, plays, news items. "A journal devoted to the life and teachings of Avatar Meher Baba, and the spiritual Path." circ. 1,000. 1/yr. Pub'd 1 issue 1979; expects 1 issue 1980, 1 issue 1981. sub. price: $5.00; per copy: $2.25; sample: 4 for $5.75 while they last. Discounts: 40% to legit bookstores & jobbers. 72pp; 6X9; of. Reporting time: immediate. Payment: copies. Copyrighted. Pub's reviews: 5 in 1979. §Philosophy of religion, mysticism, new age consciousness. Ads: No ads.

Aya Press, Glynn Davies, PO Box 303, Station A, Toronto, Ontario M5W 1C2, Canada, (416) 782-9984. 1977. Poetry, fiction, long-poems, collages, concrete art. "Aya Press' modest output runs the gamut from Joycean poetry (*Ancient Music* by Itzy Borenstein) to sci-fi (*The Viridical Book of the Silent Planet,* by Brian Henderson); from fictions (*Craft Dinner* by Governor-General's Award Winner B. P. Nichol) to erotofantastic (*The Illustrated Universe,* by Rikki). Polished professional writing is our only criteria." avg. press run 600-700. Pub'd 1-2 titles 1979; expects 3 titles 1980, 4 titles 1981. 8 titles listed in the *Small Press Record of Books in Print* (9th Edition, 1980). avg. price, cloth: $20.00; paper: $5.95; other: $100.00-$200.00. Discounts: Trade: 1-4 copies, 30%; 5 or more, 40%. No discount to libraries. 80pp; 5½X8¾; of. Reporting time: 1-2 months. Payment: By mutual agreement. Preferably nominal amount cash and balance in copies. COSMEP, ACP, LPG, NYSSPA.

AZIMUTH, Poetry & Press, Joann E. Castagna, Box 842, Iowa City, IA 52240. Articles, interviews, criticism, reviews, letters, news items. "John Jacob & Jim McManus will be among early reviewers. Small press history by Brigham Q. Becker. Whenever possible letter press material will be reviewed by letter press printers. Focus on the midwest, but no area will be ignored. Editor returning to grad school. Mag will not continue past first year" circ. 1,000. 4/yr. Expects 4 issues 1981. sub. price: $5.00; per copy: $1.25; sample: $1.25. Discounts: 60/40 bookstores. pp varies; 8½X11; of. Reporting time: 1 month. Payment: copies. Copyrighted, does not revert to author. Pub's reviews. §All small press. Ads: $50.00/$25.00/$.10. CCLM, COSMEP-Midwest.

AZTLAN: International Journal of Chicano Studies, Chicano Studies Research Center Publications, Dr. Juan Gomez-Quinones, Teresa McKenna, Reynaldo Macias, Rosa Martinez, Managing Editor, University of California-Los Angeles, 405 Hilgard Avenue, Los Angeles, CA 90025, 213-825-2642. 1970. Articles, criticism, reviews. "*Aztlan* is a biannual publication dedicated to the social sciences and the arts as they relate to Mexican Americans here." circ. 1M-2M. 2/yr. Pub'd 3 issues 1979; expects 3 issues 1980, 2 issues 1981. sub. price: $15/individuals, $20/libraries & institutions; per copy: $4.50 to $7.50; sample: $4.50. Back issues: $4.50 to $7.50. Discounts: 20% over $100 purchase. 150pp; 6X9; of. Reporting time: 4 months. Payment: books in quantity, 2 and 10 offprints. Copyrighted, reverts to author. Pub's reviews: 6 in 1979. §books on the Mexican Americans. So Calif Bookbuilders.

B

The B & R Samizdat Express, Barbara Hartley Seltzer, Richard Seltzer, Robert Richard Seltzer, Heather Katherine Seltzer, PO Box 161, West Roxbury, MA 02132, 617-469-2269. 1974. Fiction. "We publish two titles. 1) The Lizard of Oz, a fable for all ages 2) Now & Then & Other Tales from Ome, a short collection of children's stories." avg. press run 2,000-6,000. 3 titles listed in the *Small Press Record of Books in Print* (9th Edition, 1980). avg. price, cloth: $4.50; paper: $1.95-$2.95. Discounts: trade 40% (orders of 5 or more copies) 20% (orders of less than 5). Lizard-128pp/Now & Then-64pp; 5½X8½; of. Reporting time: we do not solicit manuscripts. Payment: author is publisher. Copyrights for author.

‡BA SHIRU, Margaret Higbie, David Westley, University of Wisconsin, 866 Van Hise, Madison, WI 53706. 1970. Poetry, fiction, articles, reviews, art, criticism. "Journal devoted to African Languages, literatures and linguistics. Unique in its emphasis on African Oral traditions. We publish oral narratives in original African language and critical articles as well. Pub. retains copyright, author retains other proprietary rights." circ. 200. bi-annual. Pub'd 2 issues 1979; expects 2 issues 1980, 2 issues 1981. sub. price: indiv. $5.00/yr; instit. $15.00; per copy: $2.50 indiv/$7.50 instit. Back issues: original cost $1.00-$2.50, several issues out of print. 90pp; 6X9; of. Reporting time: ASAP. Copyrighted. Pub's reviews: 8 in 1979. §African Studies. Ads: $50/$25/$15. CCLM.

The Babbington Press, Eric Kraft, Mark Dorset, Martha Dorset, Margot Dorset, P.O. Box 98, Stow, MA 01775, (617) 897-8535. 1975. Poetry, fiction, articles, art, photos, interviews, criticism, music, letters, parts-of-novels, collages, plays, news items. "The Babbington Press and all its publications are pieces of one fiction: The Life Of Peter Leroy, author of *The Unlikely Adventures Of Larry Peters.*" avg. press run 100. Pub'd 1 title 1979; expects 1 title 1980, 1 title 1981. 4 titles listed in the *Small Press Record of Books in Print* (9th Edition, 1980). avg. price, paper: $6.00. Discounts: none. 96pp; 8½X11; †xerography. no unsolicited manuscripts. Authors are fictional characters. Copyright is held by The Babbington Press.

BACHY, Papa Bach Paperbacks, John Harris, Reviews; Lee Hickman, Poetry & Prose; Rod Bradley, Art & Photography, 11317 Santa Monica Blvd., Los Angeles, CA 90025, (213) GRU-BERG. 1972. Poetry, fiction, articles, art, photos, cartoons, interviews, satire, criticism, reviews, letters, parts-of-novels, long-poems, collages, plays, concrete art. "Serious poetry and fiction of highest quality, experimental or traditional, any length. Also related essays and reviews, black & white photography and graphic art. *Bachy* is dedicated to the discovery and continued publication of serious new writers, poets and artists. Recent contributors include Kate Braverman, Sam Eisenstein, Joseph Hansen, Jack Hirschman, Greg Kuzma, Clarence Major, Deena Metzger, Harry Northup, William Pillin, Holly Prado, Henry H. Roth, Lawrence Spingarn, John Thomas." circ. 1,000. 3/yr. Pub'd 3 issues 1979; expects 3 issues 1980, 4 issues 1981. sub. price: $10.00; per copy: $3.50; sample: $3.50. Back issues: #'s 1,3&4/$2.00; #'s 5-9/$2.50; #2/$4.00; #'s 10-14/$3.00; #'s 15-16/$3.50*. Discounts: 40% off. 170pp; 8½X11; of. Reporting time: about 8 weeks. Payment: author's copies only. Copyrighted, reverts to author. Pub's reviews: 18 in 1979. §Small press poetry and fiction. CCLM, COSMEP, WIP.

BACK BAY VIEW, Charlotte Boehm, Penelope Henes, Alicia Holmes, G.B. Macaulay, 33 Karen Drive, Randolph, MA 02368, (617) 986-5704. 1977. Poetry, fiction, art, photos, interviews, reviews, plays. "233 Beacon Street #8, Boston, MA 02115 (Business Address). *No biases* but one half of the work in each issue is from Mass. *An ocasional long poem,* Special sections in each issue (interviews, plays, reviews, etc). Contrib. Robin Becker, Don Cohen, Nick Fryar, Stanley Nelson, Irene Roman, Carol Trowbridge." circ. 2,000. 2-3/yr. Pub'd 3 issues 1979; expects 2 issues 1980, 3 issues 1981. sub. price: 4/$5.00; per copy: $1.50; sample: $1.50. Back issues: #5 (interview with Marilyn French) $2.50. 48pp; 8½X11; of. Reporting time: 3-4 months. Payment: 2 copies. Copyrighted, reverts to author. Pub's reviews: 1 in 1979. §Poetry, film, fiction, drama, nonfiction, theatre. Ads: $50.00/$35.00/. COSMEP, CCLM.

Back Row Press, M. R. Ritter, 1803 Venus Ave., St. Paul, MN 55112, 612-633-1685. 1976. Fiction, plays. "Interested in religion, bisexuality—sociology, philosophy." avg. press run 350. Pub'd 1 title 1979; expects 1 title 1980. 2 titles listed in the *Small Press Record of Books in Print* (9th Edition, 1980). avg. price, cloth: $8.95; paper: $5.50. Discounts: 40 percent to stores, 25 percent to libraries. 280pp; 5½X8½; †mi. Not currently accepting submissions. Payment: Authors have collective stock in press. Author owns copyright. COSMEP, WIFP, COSMEP-MW.

BACKCOUNTRY, Cheat Mountain Press, Michael Mazzolini, Box 390, Elkins, WV 26241, (304) 636-6236. 1977. Poetry, fiction, articles, art, photos, cartoons, interviews, satire, parts-of-novels, long-poems. "*Backcountry* publishes twice yearly in April and October. We seek poetry, fiction, graphics, and photographs of any length and subject matter. Contributors retain all rights. Sometimes we have cash prizes but usually contributors are given three copies. When submitting please include a short biography and SASE." circ. 1,000. 2/yr. Pub'd 2 issues 1979; expects 2 issues 1980, 2 issues 1981. sub. price: $2.50; per copy: $0.75; sample: $0.75. Back issues: $0.75. 28pp. Reporting time: 4 months. Copyrighted, reverts to author. COSMEP.

Backpack Media (see also FROZEN WAFFLES), David Wade, Bro. Dimitrios, 3215 Sec Ave West, Bradenton, FL 33505. 1974. Poetry, fiction, art, photos, interviews, reviews, long-poems, collages, plays, concrete art. "Poetry, prose poems; almost any kind of short work (plays, aphorisms, parables [modern], fantasy, Si Fi, futureworlds, etc.). Oral & visual qualities to be expressed in cassettes, post cards, poster poems, etc." Pub'd 1 title 1979; expects 1 title 1980, 2 titles 1981. 4 titles listed in the *Small Press Record of Books in Print* (9th Edition, 1980). avg. price, cloth: $6.00; paper: $4.50; other: Pamphlets: $2.00. Discounts: Hope to give breaks to people over 40; mental institutions, prisons, etc. 22-45pp; size varies; of. Reporting time: 5 seconds (arf!) to 5 days. If you don't hear from us, we probably never got your material. Payment: At least one free copy of your work(s). Money later; much money much later. Inflation has bloated our poverty. Copyrights for author.

Backroads/Caroline House, Box 370, Wilson, WY 83014, (307) 733-7730. 1977. Photos. Pub'd 1 title 1979; expects 3 titles 1980. 2 titles listed in the *Small Press Record of Books in Print* (9th Edition, 1980). avg. price, paper: $4.95. 72pp; 5X7; of. COSMEP.

BACULITE, Bill Lazo, Editor; Warren Nolan, Editor; Joel Scherzer, Poetry Editor, P.O.Box 11151, Pueblo, CO 81001. 1980. Poetry, fiction, art, photos, reviews. "Emphasis is on material with a Southwestern flavor, although we will consider other themes as well. Short poems are preferred. Query first before sending articles. Please include brief biographical sketch with all unsolicited manuscripts. Contributors include Helen Wade Roberts, Tony Moffeit and Lyn Lifshin" circ. 300. 2/yr. Expects 2 issues 1980. sub. price: $2.50/yr; per copy: $1.25. Discounts: 40% to bookstores. 32pp; 5½X8½; of. Reporting time: 2 months. Payment: copies. Copyrighted, reverts to author. Pub's reviews: 0 in 1979. §poetry and fiction.

Baja Trail Publications, Inc. (see also MEXICO WEST), Shirley Miller, Editor; Victor Cook, Mgn Editor; Tom Miller, Consulting Editor, P O Box 6088, Huntington Beach, CA 92646, (714) 536-8081. 1975. Articles, news items. "500-750 words. Current travel & recreational information on Baja and west coast of Mexico." avg. press run 2,000. Pub'd 6 titles 1979; expects 6 titles 1980. 2 titles listed in the *Small Press Record of Books in Print* (9th Edition, 1980). avg. price, cloth: $8.00, $15.00 2/yrs. 12pp; 8X10½; of. Reporting time: 2 weeks before 1st of Feb., Apr., June, Aug., Oct., Dec. Payment: $20.00. Copyrights for author. COSMEP.

Bakke Press, Martin Wilcox, Rt. 3, Box 119-A, Hillsborough, NC 27278. "Bakke press is currently inactive and plans for the future are uncertain." 1 title listed in the *Small Press Record of Books in Print* (9th Edition, 1980).

BALLET NEWS, Robert Jacobson, Editor-in-Chief; Karl F. Reuling, Managing Editor, 1865 Broadway, New York, NY 10023, 582-7500. 1979. Articles, art, photos, interviews, criticism, reviews, letters, news items. circ. 40,000. 12/yr. Pub'd 7 issues 1979. sub. price: $18.00; per copy: $1.75; sample: $1.75. Back issues: $1.75. 48pp; 8⅛X10⅞; of. Payment: 10¢ a word for features, 8¢ for reports. Copyrighted, does not revert to author. Pub's reviews. §Dance. Ads: $600.00/$385.00.

Balsam Flex (see also BALSAM FLEX SHEET), Dyane Citroen, c/o I8 Clairview Road, London, SW I6, England. 1978. Poetry, interviews, criticism, music, concrete art. "In 1978 - I6 cassettes, 4 books, I dried soup recipe + 2 rubber stamps were produced - a particular feature of the cassette series is that each cassette features — one contributor or event — past contributors have included — Bang Crash Wallopp, Bob Cobbing, Cris Cheek, Allen Fisher, JGJG, Iida Kajino, Jackson MacLow, Tumla

36

Nitnelav, Lawrence Upton, Rudi Schlemmer Topf, E. E. Vonna-Michell, Henri Chopin, Vlli McCarthy. In 1979, 32 cassettes, books and supper 8 films were produced. Particular attention + discounts are made to archives." avg. press run 50-500. Expects 23 titles 1980. avg. price, paper: $2.00; other: $2.50. Discounts: Negotiable. 20pp; 8X10; †of. Reporting time: 3-6 weeks. Payment: usually none. Copyrights for author. ALP.

BALSAM FLEX SHEET, Balsam Flex, Dyane Citroen, c/o 18 Clairview Road, London, SW 16, England. 1978. Articles, interviews, criticism, reviews, letters, news items. "*Balsam Flex Sheet* provides a listing of all books and materials received, plus *Balsam Flex Sheet* is primarily concerned with 'information' and as such caters to the small archivist-past + coming issues are concerned with mircofiche, tape, chemical processed books, video, reviews + criticism, length of material is not of importance." circ. 750. Expects 2 issues 1980, 3 issues 1981. price per copy: $2.00; sample: free. Discounts: Negotiable. †of. Reporting time: 4-8 weeks. Payment: Usually none. Copyrighted, reverts to author. Pub's reviews. §Media, poetry, art, electronics, critical. ALP.

BALTIC AVENUE POETRY JOURNAL, Baltic Avenue Press, Philip Shirley, Becky Shirley, 1045 Fulton Avenue SW, Birmingham, AL 35211, 788-3307. 1979. Poetry, reviews, long-poems, interviews. "Recent contributors: Anne Cherner, Lyn Lifshin, M.R. Doty, Giorgio d. Cicco, Jeanie Thompson. Don't like poems about poems. Length & style: open. No pornography. Short reviews." circ. 500. 4/yr. Pub'd 1 issue 1979; expects 3 issues 1980, 4 issues 1981. sub. price: $6.00; per copy: $1.50; sample: $1.50. Discounts: 1-10 copies, 30%; 10 or more, 40%. 32pp; 5½X8½; †of. Reporting time: 30 days. Payment: 2 copies. Copyrighted, will reassign rights on request. Pub's reviews. §poetry books.

Baltic Avenue Press (see also BALTIC AVENUE POETRY JOURNAL), Philip Shirley, Becky Shirley, 1045 Fulton Ave. SW, Birmingham, AL 35211, 788-3307. 1977. Poetry, long-poems. avg. press run 300. Pub'd 2 titles 1979; expects 2 titles 1980. avg. price, paper: $2.00. Discounts: 40% to booksellers. 16-32pp; 5½X8½; †of. Reporting time: 30 days. Payment: 10-15% of press run in copies. Copyrights for author.

Banana Productions (see also VILE), Anna Banana, Bill Gaglione, 1183 Church St., San Francisco, CA 94114, 415-648-5174. 1974. Poetry, fiction, articles, art, photos, cartoons, satire, reviews, letters, collages, concrete art, news items. "*Vile* #8 expected out fall '80 will be the last issue of *Vile*. *Vile* #7 limited edition (300) hand-stamped $20.00 standard, $25.00 for 1/25 numbered & signed editions." avg. press run 1,000. Pub'd 1 title 1979; expects 1 title 1980, 1 title 1981. avg. price, paper: $5.00. Discounts: 40% on consignment. 100pp; 8½X11; 7X10; 6X9; of. Reporting time: 1-3 months depending on busy-level here. Payment: copies only. Does not copyright for author.

BANGE DAGEN, Futile, Ric Blok, PO Box 812, Rotterdam 3000AV, Holland. 1977. Poetry, fiction, articles, art, photos, cartoons, interviews, satire, criticism, reviews, letters, parts-of-novels, long-poems, collages, news items. circ. 1,000. 12/yr. Pub'd 12 issues 1979; expects 12 issues 1980, 12 issues 1981. sub. price: dfl 18.50; per copy: dfl 1.50. 16-20pp; 100mm x 270mm; †of. Reporting time: 1 month. Pub's reviews: 5 in 1979. §Social struggle.

Banyan Tree Books, 1963 El Dorado Avenue, Berkeley, CA 94707, 415-527-2499. 1975. "We are not accepting any mss. at present." 1 title listed in the *Small Press Record of Books in Print* (9th Edition, 1980).

THE BARAT REVIEW: A Journal of Literature and the Arts, Lauri S. Lee, Barat College, Lake Forest, IL 60045, (312) 234-3000. 1966. Poetry, fiction, articles, art, photos, interviews, criticism, reviews, parts-of-novels, long-poems, plays. "Printing the finest quality contemporary literature and thought. Recent contributors: Jean Valentine, Nancy Willard, Judith Minty, Hanna Holborn Gray, Paolo Soleri, Karl Krolow, Zbigniew Herbert, Helen Chasin." circ. 2,000. 2/yr. Expects 2 issues 1980, 2 issues 1981. sub. price: $8.00; per copy: $4.50; sample: $1.00. Back issues: $15.00 per issue; available are all issues except Vol. I, No. 1, Vol. II, No. 2, and Vol. VI, No. 2. Discounts: Agencies, 30%; Bookstores, 40%; Classroom, usual. 60-75pp; 7¾X10¼; lp. Reporting time: 6 weeks. Payment: copies. Copyrighted, reverts to author. Pub's reviews: 2 in 1979. §Fiction, poetry, essays, biography, literary criticism.

THE BARD, Metloc, The Reverend Francis Edwards S.J., Chairman, Editorial Board, 10 Uphill Grove, Mill Hill, London NW7 4NJ, United Kingdom. 1975. Articles, reviews, criticism. "Recent contributors: Thomas Merriam, Francis Edwards SJ, Bronson Feldman. Scholarly articles on all aspects of Shakespearean studies, with special reference to the authorship problem. 3,000-7,000 words." circ. 400. 2/yr. Pub'd 2 issues 1979; expects 2 issues 1980. sub. price: £3.00; per copy: £1.50; sample: £1.50. Back issues: Vol. 1, Nos. 1,2,3, supplement to 3, 4; Vol. 2, Nos. 1, 2, 3, 4; £1.50 each. Discounts: 10 percent to trade. 40pp; 9X6½; of. Reporting time: 1-2 mos. No payments. Pub's reviews: 1 in 1979. §Shakespearean studies. no ads.

Bard Press, Rich Spiegel, 799 Greenwich Street, New York, NY 10014, (212) 929-3169. 1974. Poetry. "Each chapbook is a single long poem. Poets published by Bard have included Clint McCown, Barbara Holland, Pat Kelly, Matt Laufer, Janet Bloom, Lydia Raurell and Richard Spiegel." avg. press run 100. Pub'd 2 titles 1979; expects 2 titles 1980, 2 titles 1981. 3 titles listed in the *Small Press Record of Books in Print* (9th Edition, 1980). avg. price, paper: $1.00. Discounts: 30%. 32pp; 4X5½; of. Reporting time: 6-9 months. Payment: copies of the book. NYSWP, NYBF.

BARDIC ECHOES, Clarence L. Weaver, Editor, 125 Somerset Drive, N.E., Grand Rapids, MI 49503, (616) 454-2807. 1960. Poetry, art, reviews, news items. "40 lines or less; any style; good taste; preference to poems by members of Bards of Grand Rapids, and to weave pattern poems. Recent contributors: Jack Ashby, Francine Burks, Robert Casper, Angelo Deluca, Jaye Giammarino, Eleanore-Melissa Emily Romano, Paris Flammonde, Andy Gunderson, Guanetta Gordon, P. C. Niblette, Leonard Opalov, Jess Perlman, Marie J. Post, Alice Mackenzie Swaim, Arnold McLeod, Robert Ambacher, Nel Modglin, Monica Boyce, Catharine Albright Waldraff, Joseph Cherwinski, Vera Joyce Nelson, Mary Annis Peacock, Conrad Pendleton, Marion J. Richardson, Eugene Botelho, Ruth Wildes Schuler, R.C. Walker, Charles A. Waugaman, Robert F. Whisler." circ. 600. 4/yr, occasional extra issue. Pub'd 4 issues 1979; expects 4 issues 1980. 12 titles listed in the *Small Press Record of Books in Print* (9th Edition, 1980). sub. price: $2.50; per copy: $.75; sample: $0.75. Back issues: $.50/ea. Discounts: 25% to periodical sub agencies. 32pp; 5½X8½; of. Reporting time: 1-3 mos. Payment: copies only; book awards in special categories. Copyrighted, author holds all rights except first n.a. serial. Pub's reviews: 115 in 1979. §poetry. no ads. CCLM, COSMEP.

‡**BARE WIRES, A Harmless Flirtation With Wealth,** Helen McKenna, P.O. Box 9779, San Diego, CA 92109, (714) 234-9632. 1976. "Humor, quotations, illustrations, anecdotes — brief and unusual" circ. 100. irreg. Pub'd 4-5 issues 1979. sub. price: $1.00; per copy: 10¢; sample: 10¢. Back issues: 10¢ each. Discounts: 10% libraries, 40% bookstores. 6pp; 8½X11; of. Reporting time: 1 month. Payment: copies only. Not copyrighted. no ads.

Barn Hill, Helen Estes Seltzer, 825 Hallowell Drive, Huntingdon Valley, PA 19006, (215) 947-1646. 2 titles listed in the *Small Press Record of Books in Print* (9th Edition, 1980).

Barnhart Books, Robert K. Barnhart, President & Managing Editor, Box 250, Bronxville, NY 10708, 914-337-7100. 1978. "Barnhart Books publishes dictionaries and language-related works. Specialty of Clarence L. Barnhart, Inc. has been English-language dictionaries (Thorndike-Barnhart Dictionaries, World Book Dictionary, Barnhart Dictionary of New English Since 1963) authored and edited in-house in addition to Bloomfield-Barnhart *Let's Read* basic reading program published in 1963 et seq., written and published in-house. Publication of others' works within specialty of Clarence Barnhart, Inc. seemed logical. As language-related works have both popular and scholarly public." avg. press run 5,000-10,000. Pub'd 3 titles 1979. avg. price, cloth: $10.00. Discounts: 20-43% to booksellers direct, depending on size of order. 6X9. Reporting time: 1-3 months. Payment: by individual contract.

The Barnwood Press, Tom Koontz, Thom Tammaro, RR 2, Box 11C, Daleville, IN 47334, (317) 378-0921. 1977. Poetry, fiction, articles, art, interviews, criticism, reviews, letters, long-poems, concrete art, news items. "Our organization is a nonprofit cooperative. We are mainly interested in poetry, but we are also publishing a series of children's novels and are considering some other kinds of materials. Books: Tate, *Bareback Morning* (poems) 1977, *Butcher Paper* (poems) 1977, Tammaro, *Evocations* (poems) 1978, Trivers, *2 + 7* (children's poems) 1978, Hamilton, *Christmas At Metamora* (children's novel) 1978, Carter, *Early Warning* (poems) 1979, Carothers, *John Calvin's Favorite Son* (poems) 1980, Hamilton, *Daniel Forbes, A Pioneer Boy* (children's novel) 1980, Maurer, *Old State Rd 37: The Mason Cows* (poems) 1980. Broadside poem: Coghill, *What The Apache Word For Love Means,* 1978; Poetry Cards: Tammaro, *Where West Is* and *Fishing The Lake,* 1978, Whitlock, *Thrift,* 1979. Alternate address: 3768 N. Tillotson Ave., Muncie, IN 47306" avg. press run 1,000. Pub'd 3 titles 1979; expects 10 titles 1980, 8 titles 1981. 13 titles listed in the *Small Press Record of Books in Print* (9th Edition, 1980). avg. price, paper: $2.25; other: $0.50. Discounts: 50% on books of poetry, 40% other. 40pp; 5X8; of. Reporting time: Varies from 2 weeks to 6 months. Payment: negotiated. Copyrights for author. COSMEP.

Bartholomew's Cobble, Rod Steier, 19 Howland Road, West Hartford, CT 06107, 203-521-6053. 1974. Poetry. "Each poet has full artistic control over his book, this includes length, cover design, material, etc. *We normally do not seek unsolicited manuscripts,* and have published books by Russell Edson, Rod Steier, Terry Stokes, Charles Simic, Dave Kelly, Pat Bizzaro and Cynthia MacDonald. *We cannot assure return of unsolicited ms. Please do not send them.*" avg. press run varies. avg. price, paper: varies; other: $2.50. Discounts: 60-40 usually on 3 copies or more. 24pp; 8½X7; of. We only solicit. Payment: copies. Copyrights for author.

BARTLEBY'S REVIEW, Albert Stainton, Rita Tomasallo Stainton, 3152 Lyon St., San Francisco, CA 94123. 1972. Poetry, reviews. circ. 500. 2/yr. Pub'd 2 issues 1979; expects 1 issue 1980. sub. price: $3.00 individuals/$3.00 libraries; per copy: $1.50 individuals/$1.75 libraries; sample: $1.50. Back issues: $5.00 ea. for issues 1 and 2. Discounts: 40%. 48pp; 5½X8; of. Reporting time: 1-3 months. Payment: copies. Pub's reviews. §poetry. CCLM.

Basement Editions, Laureen Mar, 22 Catherine Street Floor #3, New York, NY 10038, (212) 925-3258. 1978. "2-4 color prints, suitable for framing" avg. press run 200. Pub'd 6 titles 1979; expects 6 titles 1980, 6 titles 1981. 5 titles listed in the *Small Press Record of Books in Print* (9th Edition, 1980). avg. price, other: $5.00 unsigned, $15.00 signed and numbered. Discounts: 40% to dealers. 19X25; †Hand-pulled serigraphs. Reporting time: 1 month. Payment: copies or percentage. do not apply for copyright but copyright appears in author's name.

The Basilisk Press, David Lunde, Editor, P.O. Box 71, Fredonia, NY 14063. 1970. Poetry. "We publish only full length books of poetry. So far have published Bruce Woods, T.C. Burtt, Jr., Phyllis Janik, David Lunde, Dave Kelly, Dave Smith, Greg Kuzma, Tom McKeown, Bruce Guernsey, Tom Disch, Peter Warren, Toni Zimmerman. Books forthcoming by David Rafael Wang, Harley Elliott, Lyn Lifshin. (Have published one set of poem postcards but don't know if this will continue. No unsolicited poems for cards.) Zimmerman published 1976." avg. press run 600. Expects 2 titles 1980, 1-2 titles 1981. 14 titles listed in the *Small Press Record of Books in Print* (9th Edition, 1980). avg. price, paper: $3.00. Discounts: 20% to libraries, 40% to retailers on orders of 5 or more copies. 50-75pp; 5½X8½; of. Reporting time: 1day-1month. Payment: contributor copies only. Copyrights for author. COSMEP.

The Battery Press, Inc., P.O. Box 3107, Uptown Station, Nashville, TN 37219. 1976. "We reprint scarce military unit histories." avg. press run 1,000. Pub'd 10 titles 1979; expects 10 titles 1980, 10 titles 1981. 26 titles listed in the *Small Press Record of Books in Print* (9th Edition, 1980). avg. price, cloth: $25.00; paper: $15.00; other: $10 — $15. Discounts: 5 or more, 40%; 1-4 copies, 20%;. 200pp; size varies; varies methods of production. Payment: varies. Copyrights for author. COSMEP.

Bayshore Books, Elizabeth S. Wall, Box 848, Nokomis, FL 33555, (813) 485-2564. 1978. "Juvenile nonfiction (Gr. 1-6) is our only area of publication at this time. Books are illustrated, 2 color, and deal with computer literacy, e.g, *Computer Alphabet Book Computer Sign Book*." avg. press run 3,000. Expects 3 titles 1981. 1 title listed in the *Small Press Record of Books in Print* (9th Edition, 1980). avg. price, cloth: $8.95. Discounts: Bulk. 64pp; 8½X11; of. Copyrights for author. COSMEP, COSMEP SOUTH.

BB Books (see also GLOBAL TAPESTRY JOURNAL), Dave Cunliffe, 1 Spring Bank, Salesbury, Blackburn, Lancs BB1 9EU, England, UK, 0254 49128. 1963. Poetry, fiction, articles, art, long-poems. "Mainly publish poetry collections, short novels, anarchic counter-culture theoretics & mystic tracts (zen,tantra, etc.)" avg. press run 1,000. Pub'd 4 titles 1979; expects 4 titles 1980, 4 titles 1981. 8 titles listed in the *Small Press Record of Books in Print* (9th Edition, 1980). avg. price, paper: $2.00. Discounts: 1/3 to trade. 44pp; 8X6; †of. Reporting time: soon. Payment: 20 copies.

BBB Associates, Robert Toms, PO Box 551, San Mateo, CA 94010, (415) 344-8458. 1977. Music. avg. press run 2,000. Expects 2 titles 1980. avg. price, paper: $7.00. Discounts: Assorted titles: 0-4, 0%; 5-99, 40%; 100-149, 42%; 150 and up, 44%. 170pp; of. Reporting time: 1 month.

Le Beacon Presse (see also IOWA CITY BEACON LITERARY REVIEW; LE BEACON REVIEW; M'GODOLIM; FOREIGN POETS AND AUTHORS REVIEW), Keith Gormezano, 621 Holt Avenue, Iowa City, IA 52244, (319) 354-5447. 1977. Poetry, fiction, articles, art, photos, cartoons, interviews, satire, criticism, reviews, music, letters, parts-of-novels, long-poems, collages, plays, concrete art, news items. "We are interested in all types and varities of manuscripts particularly those from writers, poets, artists who have not had their first book published... yet and those authors who are relatively unknown. Donald Justice (1980 Pulitzer Prize for Poetry) would not be published by us for obvious reasons. Publications in the work/past have included poetry, geanological research, fiction, Who's Who Among Hispanic-Americans, plays, drawings, etc. We are committed to publishing the creative works of new or unknown authors. Please mail your clean, clear photocopied manuscript along with a resume about yourself and a SASE. Everything except plays and graphic artwork should be typed, (single spaced is prefered to cut publication costs as we reduce your manuscripts 74% as they are) with a PICA typewriter or typeset by yourself. Right now, we don't have the financial resources or staff to do typesetting. Priority for publication in 1979 is being given to those writers who have previously had their work published in ICB, BR, M'g and FP&AR. If you are a writer, poet, artist who hasn't been published..yet and your friends whose opinions you trust tell you time and time again that you have talent, then *put* this book down, go *get* your manuscript, and *mail* it to us *today, now,* pronto, amigos! For 1980, we are particularly interested in anthologies and work by artists but still will have the room to print poetry, fiction, etc." avg. press run 200. Pub'd 30 titles 1979; expects 50 titles 1980. 3 titles listed in the *Small Press Record of Books in Print* (9th Edition, 1980). avg. price, paper: $1.95. Discounts: 50% postpaid, 40% billed if 10 or more, 30% 5-9, 20% 3-5, 50% for libraries postpaid. 20-80pp; 5X8; †of. Reporting time: 3-12 months. Payment: 20% and copies at cost. COSMEP, CCLM.

LE BEACON REVIEW, Le Beacon Presse, Keith Gormezano, 621 Holt Avenue, Iowa City, IA 52240, 319-354-5447. 1979. "*Beacon Review* is a monthly literary magazine from the Paris of the Praries that focuses on publishing the creative works of new or unknown authors, poets, artists, because we believe in giving new writers a chance to be read. Clean, clear, fairly dark photocopies are okay to submit along with your resume and we would prefer that you use a PICA typewriter because we reduce your submissions to get them on the multilith press. We prefer good, down to earth, emotional, thought-provoking material from our contributors so if you want to get published and you have been told by good friends and your writing instructors you trust that you have the talent, then put this book down, get your manuscript or start plugging away at it, and mail it to us today. In addition, we will review *all* magazine and books that we receive. A line if it's so-so, a paragraph if it's good and a quarter page if we think it's excellent." circ. 200. 12/yr. Pub'd 10 issues 1979. sub. price: 10/$12.00, 6/$5.00; per copy: $1.00; sample: $0.75 w/SASE. 32-40pp; 5½X8. Reporting time: 1-3 months. Pub's reviews: 40 in 1979. §should be first or second book by new or unknown authors but we do review *all* received. Ads: $5.00/$3.00/$0.05 20 word minimum, will exchange. COSMEP.

Bear Claw Press, David Robbins, Karl Pohrt, 1039 Baldwin Street, Ann Arbor, MI 48104, (313) 668-6634. 1975. Poetry. "Our books and calendars pay homage to native american cultures, although we also publish poetry concerned with wilderness and ecology. Representative works: Howard Norman's Swampy Cree translations, poetry by Jim Heynen and Greg Kuzma, an ethnographic calendar of circumpolar bear traditions, a calendar of native american songs, most of them illustrated by Tom Pohrt. Last publication: the narrated life of a great Plains Indian healer *The Seven Visions of Bull Lodge* for the Gros Ventre tribe of Montana." avg. press run 1,000. Pub'd 2 titles 1979; expects 2 titles 1980, 1 title 1981. 4 titles listed in the *Small Press Record of Books in Print* (9th Edition, 1980). avg. price, paper: $4.95. Discounts: 40% wholesale. 60pp; 6X9; of. Reporting time: 2 weeks to 1 month. Payment: negotiated. Copyrights for author.

Bear Cult Press (see GREAT CIRCUMPOLAR BEAR CULT)

Bear Tribe (see also MANY SMOKES), Wabun (editors) Sun Bear, Nimimosha (art director), P O Box 9167, Spokane, WA 99209, (509) 258-7755. 1970. Poetry, articles, reviews. "Books on native philosophy, religion, self reliance, environment. So far we have written most of the books we have published." avg. press run 5,000. Expects 4 titles 1980, 6 titles 1981. 4 titles listed in the *Small Press Record of Books in Print* (9th Edition, 1980). avg. price, paper: $3.50. Discounts: 10 copies 40%, 25 copies 45%. 100+pp; 5½X8½; of. Reporting time: 1 to 2 months. Payment: standard. Copyrights for author. ABA.

BEAU FLEUVE SERIES, Intrepid Press, Allen De Loach, P.O. Box 1423, Buffalo, NY 14214. Poetry, criticism. "Blackburn, De Loach, Mottram, Orlovsky, Bremser, Cirocco, Coleman, Kerman." circ. 500-1M. irreg. 16pp; 5X8; of. Reporting time: 3 mos. by request. Payment: 10%. Copyrighted. §experimental fiction, poetry. COSMEP, Niagara-Erie Writers.

Beaver Lodge Press (see THE NORTH WIND)

BEDFORDSHIRE MAGAZINE, White Crescent Press, B. Chambers, Crescent Rd., Luton Beds., United Kingdom. 1947. Articles, poetry, art, reviews, news items, letters. "Restricted to material of Bedfordshire interest-history, biography, topography, literature, etc. Articles 800-2000 words, with illustrations." circ. 3M. 4/yr. Pub'd 4 issues 1979; expects 4 issues 1980. sub. price: £4.32 3 years; per copy: 25p. Back issues: 25p plus 11p postage. 64pp; 8½X5½; of. Pub's reviews: 20 in 1979. §Bedfordshire matters. Ads: contact publisher.

Beekman Publishers, Inc., Joanne Michaels, John Hamilton, 38 Hicks Street, Brooklyn Heights, NY 11201, (212) 624-4514. 1971. Fiction. "Beekman is largely a distributor of titles published in England and other European countries. We do not accept unsolicited manuscripts. Beekman published an original novel last month (A Spartan Education by Albert Werder), but this was its first. We are known for our business & finance, medical and other technical lines." avg. press run 2,000. Pub'd 5 titles 1979; expects 5 titles 1980, 5 titles 1981. 34 titles listed in the *Small Press Record of Books in Print* (9th Edition, 1980). avg. price, cloth: $15.00; paper: $5.00. Discounts: 20%. 300pp; of. No unsolicated mss. 6 months. Payment: 8-10%. Copyrights for author.

BEFORE THE RAPTURE, Cynthia Gallaher, PO Box A3604, Chicago, IL 60690. 1980. Poetry, articles, art, reviews, long-poems. "*Before the Rapture* is first and primarily a magazine of Christian poetry. We seek poems that are contemporary, dynamic, original, in touch with what we confront today. The title of the magazine is derived from 'the rapture' as explained in the Book of Revelations, a time when God hand picks his followers from earth before the reign of the anti-Christ. Poems about this approaching era are particularly welcomed...as well as poems on altruistic love, the Holy Spirit, Israel and the Mid-East." circ. 300. 1/yr. Pub'd 1 issue 1979. sub. price: $7.00 3/yrs; per copy: $2.50; sample: $2.50. Discounts: 40%..net 30 days. 25pp; 8½X11; of. Reporting time: 1 to 4 weeks. Payment: contributor's copy. Copyrighted. Pub's reviews. §Religious poetry, comment (Christian or Jewish). Ads: $25.00/$10.00. COSMEP.

Belier Press, J. B. Rund, PO Box 'C', Gracie Station, New York, NY 10028. 1973. Photos, cartoons. "Publishers of U.G. Comix anthologies, adult comics, antiquarian erotica, graphics, no novels, no pocket books published" avg. press run 7,500-20,000. Pub'd 8 titles 1979; expects 8 titles 1980, 10-15 titles 1981. 4 titles listed in the *Small Press Record of Books in Print* (9th Edition, 1980). avg. price, paper: $6.50. Discounts: 40-55%. of. Reporting time: Fast response. Payment: 5%, 7½%, 10%. Copyrights for author.

Bell Springs Publishing Company, Bernard Kamoroff, PO Box 640, Laytonville, CA 95454, 707-984-6746. 1976. avg. press run 10,000. Pub'd 1-3 titles 1979; expects 1-3 titles 1980, 3 titles 1981. 2 titles listed in the *Small Press Record of Books in Print* (9th Edition, 1980). avg. price, cloth: $12.00; paper: $8.00. Discounts: Bookstores 40%; wholesalers 50%. 200pp; 8½X11; of. Reporting time: 2 weeks. Payment: negotiable. copyright in author's name if author so wishes. COSMEP, AM Booksellers ASSN.

Bellerophon Books, 36 Anacapa Street, Santa Barbara, CA 93101, (805) 965-7034. Art. avg. press run 10,000. Pub'd 10 titles 1979; expects 10 titles 1980, 10 titles 1981. avg. price, paper: $2.50. Discounts: Trade 40% for 24-99 or for prepaid single copies; 50% for 100 or more. 48pp; 8½X11; †of. Payment: outright purchase.

Bellevue Press, Gil Williams, Deborah H. Williams, 60 Schubert St., Binghamton, NY 13905, 607-729-0819. 1973. Poetry, art, photos. "All publication by our invitation only.Authors should write ahead. Poetry post-cardspoems always needed. Recently published artists and authors include: Bradford Stark, Matt Phillips, Marcia Falk, Ursula K. LeGuin, Stephen Sandy, Philip Dow, Kirby Congdon, Mac Hammond, Patricia Wilcox, Barbara Unger, James, Purdy, Tom Disch, David Posner, et. al." avg. press run 65 to 125 on broadsides, 500 to 2,500 on post-cards, 220 to 750 on books. 163 titles listed in the *Small Press Record of Books in Print* (9th Edition, 1980). avg. price, paper: $2.50 to $10.00 for books (many autographed editions); other: $4.00 to $5.00 for broadsides. $0.20 for art cards, $0.20 for poetry cards. Discounts: 40 percent on orders over $50.00, to private collectors. 40 percent off to all bookdealers. No discount to libraries, handling and postage added. 25 to 80 pp for books.; of/lp. Reporting time: Usually within 8 weeks concerning manuscripts, longer for letters and misc. correspondence. Payment: 10 percent of published edition to authors, plus $5.00 for each accepted poetry post-card poem, $10.00 for broadside poems. Payments to illustrators or for introductions varies. Copyright remains with authors. We only print one edition of our books or cards, no reprints. NESPA.

THE BELLINGHAM REVIEW, Signpost Press, Peter Nicoletta, Editor; Knute Skinner, Editor; Richard Dills, Editor; Joseph Green, Assistant Editor, 412 N. State Street, Bellingham, WA 98225, 206-734-9781. 1975. Poetry, fiction, art, photos, parts-of-novels, plays, long-poems, reviews. "No fiction over 5,000 wds. Open to all types of poetry.Summer address: 2914 Nequalicum, Bellingham, WA 98225, (206) 671-0846" circ. 500. 2/yr. Pub'd 2 issues 1979; expects 2 issues 1980, 2 issues 1981. sub. price: $4.00 for 2 issues, $7.50 for 4 issues, $10.50 for 6 issues; per copy: $2.00; sample: $2.00. Back issues: #1, $5.00; #2, $2.25; #3, $2.25; #4, $2.00; #5, $2.00; #6, $2.00. Discounts: 25 percent. 50pp; 5½X8½; of. Reporting time: 2 months. Payment: one copy plus one-year subscription. Copyrighted, reverts to author. Pub's reviews: 6 in 1979. §Poetry volumes & anth. books of fiction. Ads: $50.00/$30.00/$15.00.

Bellrock Press (see also JOURNAL OF CANADIAN FICTION), 2050 MacKay Street, Montreal, QE H3G 2J1, Canada. 1 title listed in the *Small Press Record of Books in Print* (9th Edition, 1980).

BELOIT POETRY JOURNAL, David M. Stocking, Marion K. Stocking, P.O. Box 2, Beloit, WI 53511. 1950. Poetry. "We publish the best of the poems submitted. No biases as to length, form, subject, or school. Occasional chapbooks, such as the recent chapbook of Afro-American poetry. Some recent contributors: Jerald Bullis, Albert Goldbarth, Karen Snow, L. C. Phillips, Timothy Cohrs, A.G. Sobin, Richard Jackson, T. Alan Broughton." circ. 1,200. quarterly. Pub'd 4 issues 1979; expects 4 issues 1980. sub. price: $4.00; per copy: $1.00; sample: $1.00. Back issues: $2.00 for chapbooks, most others $1.00. List available. Discounts: by arrangement. 40pp; 5½X8½; of. Reporting time:

immediately to 4 mos. Payment: 3 copies. Copyrighted, reverts to author. Pub's reviews: 20 in 1979. §books by and about poets. mags with poetry. Ads: $100. CCLM.

Beninda Books, George P. Argiry, Editor, P.O. Box 9251, Canton, OH 44711. 1977. "*Catch the Sticky Fingers* George P. Argiry, 143 pages, bar management guide. *Bartender Mixed Drinks For Everybody* George P. Argiry, 31 pages, mixed drinks. *An Author's Insight* George P. Argiry, 68 pages, self-publishing. *Sales Guidelines* George P. Argiry, 40 pages, sales impressions." avg. press run 5,000. Pub'd 2 titles 1979; expects 4 titles 1980, 4 titles 1981. 4 titles listed in the *Small Press Record of Books in Print* (9th Edition, 1980). avg. price, paper: $2.00-$5.00. Discounts: 40% — 50%. 36 — 150pp; 4½X7; 5½X8½; of. Reporting time: 3-6 months. Payment: 10% semi annual. Copyrights for author.

THE BENNINGTON REVIEW, Robert Boyers, Peggy Boyers, Alex Brown, Bennington College, Bennington, VT 05201, (802) 442-5401. 1978. Poetry, fiction, articles, art, photos, interviews, criticism, reviews, music, letters, parts-of-novels, long-poems, plays. "Recent contributors: May Sarton, Lesle; Epstein, Richard Sche- chner; George Skiner; Pat Adams; Mary Kinzic; Nichulas Del Banco; John Updike; Joyce Carol Oates; Hellen Frenkanthaler; Ronald Paulson; Stanley Kauffman; Josephine Jacobsen; Karen Swenson." circ. 2,000. 3/yr. Expects 3 issues 1980, 3 issues 1981. sub. price: $12.00; per copy: $4.00; sample: $2.00. Back issues: $4.00 @. Discounts: Agents receive 10%. 100pp; 8X11; of. Reporting time: 1-3 months. Copyrighted. Pub's reviews: 18 in 1979. §Art, film, dance, crafts,novels, cultural criticism, etc. Ads: $450.00/$250.00.

BERGEN POETS, Editorial Board, c/o Mrs. Ruth Falk, 197 Delmar Avenue, Glen Rock, NJ 07452, (201) 444-3829. 1973. Poetry, art. "We are a poetry co-op. Annual publication-(open to members of Co-op only)-30 to 40 poets. *Diversity* our vitality." circ. 250. 1/yr. Pub'd 1 issue 1979; expects 1 issue 1980. price per copy: $4.00; sample: $4.00. Back issues: $2.50 each. Discounts: none. 52 pp perfect bound; 5½X8½; of. Payment: copies. Copyrighted, reverts to author. Ads: none. CCLM.

BERKELEY BARB, Mark K. Powelson, P.O. Box 1247, Berkeley, CA 94701. 1965. Poetry, articles, art, photos, cartoons, interviews, satire, criticism, reviews, parts-of-novels. "Most BARB articles and reviews fall into the 500 to 1,000 word category. Full-page pieces average 1,500 words. Most writing styles are acceptable, providing they are not overly academic or highly experimental as to be inaccessible. to a general newspaper readership." circ. 45,000. biweekly. sub. price: $10.00; per copy: Bay Area-$.25/outside S.F. Bay Area- $.50; sample: Free. Back issues: 25¢, plus postage, if necessary. Discounts: 15%. 20pp; 11½X17½; of. Reporting time: 6 weeks. Payment: about 4 cents a word. Copyrighted, reverts to author. Pub's reviews: 40 in 1979. §A broad range of counter-cultural and non-sectarian leftist political issues. Ads: $640.00/$340.00/$1.50. APS.

BERKELEY JOURNAL OF SOCIOLOGY, Editorial Board, 410 Barrows Hall, University of California, Berkeley, CA 94720. 1955. Articles, criticism. "Cynthia Cunningham, Business Manager. Subject index: critical review of key social issues, such as Third World movements, prison reform, popular culture, and the Women's movement." circ. 1,500. annual. Pub'd 1 issue 1979; expects 1 issue 1980. sub. price: $7.00 institutions/$3.00 individual; per copy: $7.00 institutions/$3.00 individual; sample: please inquire. Back issues: please inquire. Discounts: please inquire. 250-300pp; 5½X8½; of. Reporting time: 3 months. We hold copyright, with permission. Pub's reviews: 1 in 1979. §Social trends. Ads: Available on request.

THE BERKELEY MONTHLY, Tom Klaber, Publisher; Alan Rinzler, Editor, 910 Parker Street, Berkeley, CA 94710, (415) 848-7900. 1970. Poetry, fiction, articles, interviews, satire, criticism, music, letters, parts-of-novels, long-poems. "Since 1970, *The Monthly* has established a reputation for outstanding graphics and design, and for the diversity of its editorial content. We welcome first rate poetry, short fiction, and nonfiction articles. Recent contributors include: Fred Cody, Theodore Roszak, May Sarton, Ann Menebroker, Joyce Odam, and William Stafford." circ. 70,000. monthly. Pub'd 12 issues 1979; expects 12 issues 1980, 12 issues 1981. sub. price: $6.95; per copy: $.75; sample: $.75 if available, with SASE (Needs 50/ postage for 2nd class). Back issues: query. Discounts: query. 60-88pp; 11½X15; of. Reporting time: as soon as possible. Payment: poetry - $15; short fiction - $50 & up; nonfiction - nego. photos and art work - nego. on sliding scale. Copyrighted, *The Monthly* buys all rights, but usually reassigns to author upon request. Pub's reviews: many in 1979. §poetry, fiction, science, holistic, arts, small press publications, etc. Ads: query.

BERKELEY POETRY REVIEW, Casey Finch, c/o Office of Student Activities, 103 Sproul Hall, Univ of Calif, Berkeley, CA 94720. 1973. Poetry. "Manuscripts should be no longer than 5-6 pages, and should include no more than 4 poems; most poems in the magazine are 10-25 lines, although longer and shorter poems can be considered. Prose poems and translations are encouraged; the originals should accompany translations. Lyrical, moral, erotic, political, comical, magic etc." circ. 500-750. 2/yr. Pub'd 2 issues 1979; expects 2 issues 1980, 2 issues 1981. sub. price: $6.00; per copy: $3.00;

sample: $3.00. Back issues: $3.00. Discounts: none. 75pp; 6X8½; lp. Reporting time: 6 weeks. Payment: free copy. Copyrighted, reverts to author. Ads: No ads.

BERKELEY POETS COOPERATIVE, Berkeley Poets Workshop and Press, Charles Entrekin, Managing Editor, P.O. Box 459, Berkeley, CA 94701, (415) 848-9098. 1969. Poetry, fiction, art, photos, parts-of-novels, long-poems, plays. circ. 2,500. 2/yr. Pub'd 2 issues 1979. sub. price: $5.00; per copy: $2.50; sample: $2.00. Back issues: Prices vary, write for information. Discounts: 40% trade. 80pp; 5½X8½; of. Reporting time: 3 months. Payment: 2 copies. Copyrighted. no ads. CCLM, AAP.

Berkeley Poets Workshop and Press (see also BERKELEY POETS COOPERATIVE), P.O. Box 459, Berkeley, CA 94701. 1969. Poetry, fiction, art, photos, parts-of-novels, long-poems, plays. "Book manuscripts are considered only if writer has published in our magazine." avg. press run 500. Pub'd 1 title 1979; expects 2 titles 1980, 2 titles 1981. 7 titles listed in the *Small Press Record of Books in Print* (9th Edition, 1980). avg. price, paper: $2.50. Discounts: 40% trade. 54pp; 5½X8½; of. Reporting time: 3 months. Payment: l0 copies plus 50% of profit. Copyrights for author. CCLM, AAP.

Bern Porter Books, Bern Porter, 22 Salmond Road, Belfast, ME 04915, 207-338-3763. 1911. "Owing to death of partner, Margaret Eudine Porter for past twenty years, manuscripts are no longer solicited. Type of material used vanguard, experimental and classic contempory. Arts, bibliography, short story, drama, poetry, contemporary classic literature." avg. press run 1,750 copies. Pub'd 467 titles 1979; expects 482 titles 1980, 493 titles 1981. 40 titles listed in the *Small Press Record of Books in Print* (9th Edition, 1980). avg. price, cloth: $8.50; paper: $2.10; other: $12.50. Discounts: Normal or all current standard. 167pp; 5½X7, 8½X11; lp. Reporting time: 3 weeks. Payment: 10 percent royalty on all sales. copyright in authors name. COSMEP, NESPA, MPW, STWP.

BERTRAND RUSSELL TODAY, Daniel Manesse, Editor, P.O. Box 431, Jerome Ave., Bronx, NY 10468. 1975. Articles, reviews. "We are interested in articles of a page or two in length on anything pertaining to the life and work of Bertrand Russell. We are also interested in articles on philosophy and religion." 1/yr. Pub'd 1 issue 1979; expects 2 issues 1980. 1 title listed in the *Small Press Record of Books in Print* (9th Edition, 1980). sub. price: $2.00; per copy: $2.00; sample: $2.00. Back issues: $2.00 per copy. 25pp; 8½X11; of. Reporting time: 1 week. Payment is with copies of the magazine. Copyrighted, reverts to author. Pub's reviews: 2 in 1979. §Books about Bertrand Russell, philosophy, religion. Ads: $20/$10.

‡**Best Cellar Press (see also PEBBLE),** 118 So Boswell Ave, Crete, NB 68333. 10 titles listed in the *Small Press Record of Books in Print* (9th Edition, 1980).

Between The Lines, Robert Clarke, Jamie Swift, 97 Victoria Street North, Kitchener, Ontario N2H 5C1, Canada. 1977. Articles, photos, cartoons, interviews. "popular non-fiction, national and international history, economics, politics, theory and practice" avg. press run 4,500. Pub'd 2 titles 1979; expects 3 titles 1980, 4 titles 1981. 5 titles listed in the *Small Press Record of Books in Print* (9th Edition, 1980). avg. price, cloth: $14.00; paper: $5.50. Discounts: for Canadian trade and university bookstore under 5 copies 20%, 5 copies and over 40%, no library discount, except to library services. 240pp; 6X9; of. Reporting time: 1 month. Payment: variable. Copyrights for author. ACP (Assoc. of Canadian Publishers).

BEYOND BAROQUE, BEYOND BAROQUE LIBRARY of SMALL PRESS PUBLICATIONS, Manuel 'Manazar' Gamboa, Editor; Alexandra Garrett, Associate Editor; Jocelyn Fisher, Associate Editor, 68l Venice Blvd. P.O. Box 806, Venice, CA 90291, (213) 822-3006. 1968. Poetry, fiction, articles, art, photos, cartoons, interviews, satire, criticism, reviews, parts-of-novels, long-poems, collages, plays, news items, non-fiction. "*Beyond Baroque* (absorbs *New* Magazine and New Books) will include multi-cultural, bilingual writings, translations, contemporary fiction and poetry." circ. 9M. 4/yr. Pub'd 4 issues 1979; expects 4 issues 1980, 4 issues 1981. 6 titles listed in the *Small Press Record of Books in Print* (9th Edition, 1980). sub. price: institutional subscriptions & memberships $15.00. Also available for smaller donations or free on request.; per copy: free; sample: free. Back issues: query. Discounts: none. 64pp; 8½X11; of. Reporting time: 4-8 weeks. Payment: copies only. buys first serial rights only. Pub's reviews: 6 in 1979. §literary. CCLM, COSMEP.

BEYOND BAROQUE LIBRARY of SMALL PRESS PUBLICATIONS, BEYOND BAROQUE, Jocelyn Fisher, Library Director, Beyond Baroque Foundation, 68l Venice blvd. P.O. Box 806, Venice, CA 90291, (213) 822-3006. 1973. "*BEYOND BAROQUE LIBRARY* presently consists of over 18,000 small press literary publications. The Library serves as an important link between the independent publisher and the public. It strongly urges publishers to contribute books and magazines to this lending library. In exchange *BEYOND BAROQUE* will send its literary magazine. The Los Angeles Public Library System has put *BEYOND BAROQUE LIBRARY* on the SCAN system, one of California's regional resource centers.".

BEYOND RICE, A Broadside Series, Noro Press, Geraldine Kudaka, P.O.Box 1447, San Francisco, CA 94101, 982-4316. 1979. Poetry, art, photos, concrete art. "Utilizes broadside format of poetry/-visual. Issue #1 includes Kay Boyle, Marina Rivera, Jessica Hagedorn, Wendy Rose and Naomi Clark; visual artists: Marina Winkler, Erin Goodwin, Deanna Forbes and Glenn Rogers Perrotto. Submissions of visual art and poetry welcome. Please limit poetry submissions to 6 poems, each less than 1/2 page single space typed. Visual art must be submitted as blk/wh. photo, no more than 8 per submission. All work must include SASE" circ. 300. 2/yr. Pub'd 1 issue 1979. sub. price: $10.00; per copy: $6.00; sample: $5.00. Back issues: $25.00 collector's edition — signed & numbered (1-50) in special leatherette folder. Discounts: 40% off for orders of 8 or more plus postage. 18pp; †of/lp. Reporting time: 3 weeks. Payment: 1 signed copy plus 2 copies. Copyrighted, reverts to author. Ads: $50/$25.

BIALA, PRAHRAN COLLEGE OF ADVANCED EDUCATION, Julian Gitzen, Editor, 142 High St, Prahran 3181, Victoria, Australia. 1976. Poetry, fiction, plays. "We treat manuscripts in this order of preference: 1. short or one-act plays, 2. short fiction, 3. poems (preferably short). This rating reflects our only conscious bias. *Biala* is increasing in size, and each issue from now on is expected to contain a supplement featuring the best short fiction and poems published in Australian journals during the previous year." circ. 500. 1/yr. price per copy: $4.50. Back issues: $1.50. Discounts: 33%, plus free postage. 120pp; 6X9; of. Reporting time: 2 to 3 months. Payment: plays, $100; short fiction, $25; poems, $5-$15, plus complimentary copies. Copyrighted, reverts to author. no ads.

Biblio Press, Doris B. Gold, PO Box 22, Fresh Meadows, NY 11365, (212) 454-1922. 1979. Poetry. "Interested in non-fiction ms. of Jewish content linked to feminism; also Jewish reference materials, i.e., folklore; sayings, women's history, women's organization analyses—for students of Jewish studies. Seeking 'science fiction' on Biblical miracles; essays on problems of Jewish women in the community. Have published the first: *Bibliography on the Jewish Woman* by Aviva Cantor, compiler. (52 p. paper, $3.00 ret.) *Honey in the Lion* Collected poems of Doris B. Gold (printed at the Print Center, Brooklyn, a NY State Council on Arts and National Endowment nonprofit Press, distributed by Biblio) (80 pg. paper, $3.00 ret.)Forthcoming Fall, 1980: *Jewish Women & Jewish Law*, bibliography." avg. press run 1,000. Pub'd 2 titles 1979. 3 titles listed in the *Small Press Record of Books in Print* (9th Edition, 1980). avg. price, paper: $3.00-$5.00. Discounts: Women's bookstores get 35% off; jobbers 40%, Jewish bookstores 35%; also on consignment (for poetry). 15% off to academics writing on their letterheads. 50-100pp; 5½X8; 8½X11; of. Reporting time: 1 month. Payment: Flat fee at this time. Later 1980 we will possibly arrange royalty.

THE BIBLIOTHECK, G. D. Hargreaves, National Library of Scotland, George IV Bridge; Edinburgh EH1 lEW, Scotland, UK FK9 4LA, United Kingdom, (031) 226-4531. 1956. Articles, reviews. "The supplement is entitled the ANNUAL BIBLIOGRAPHY OF SCOTTISH LITERATURE and consists of a checklist of the year's books, reviews, essays and articles in the field of Scottish literature." circ. 300. 3/yr + supplemental. Pub'd 3 issues 1979; expects 3 issues 1980, 3 issues 1981. sub. price: £5-80 (individual subscribers); £7-50 (institutional subscribers); per copy: £2-00; sample: free. Back issues: reductions for bulk orders. Discounts: no. 30pp; 6X8; of. Reporting time: c. 1 month. Payment: 6 offprints. Copyrighted, copyright to publishers and contributors. Pub's reviews: 8 in 1979. §Scottish bibliography. Ads: 12/8.

BIBLIOTHEQUE D'HUMANISME ET RENAISSANCE, Librairie Droz S.A., A. Dufour, Librairie Droz S.A., 11r.Massot, 1211 Geneve 12, Switzerland. 1934. Articles, criticism, reviews. "history of 16th century" circ. 1,000. 3/yr. Pub'd 3 issues 1979; expects 3 issues 1980. sub. price: 75 SW.FR ($46.00)-yr; per copy: 25 sw.fr. ($16.00). 600pp; 16X24 cm; typography. Pub's reviews: 100 in 1979.

Bicentennial Era Enterprises, PO Box 1148, Scappoose, OR 97056. 1978. Criticism, news items. "The press is part of a larger operation designed to educate people to their rights and to document the errors and false policies of government which have led to a loss of those rights." avg. press run 5,000. Expects 1 title 1980. 1 title listed in the *Small Press Record of Books in Print* (9th Edition, 1980). avg. price, paper: $5.00. Discounts: Trade 40%; Bulk and Class 10%; Agent, Jobber by agreement. 166pp; 6X9; of.

The Bieler Press, Gerald Lange, 4603 Shore Acres Road, Madison, WI 53716, (608) 222-3711. 1975. "Contemporary literature in its varied forms. Looking for the unique and the unusual. Authors who send gifts, and money, and who write nice long letters, and who have the virtues of patience and understanding, are more welcome than those who do not. Cause and Effect. Recent titles are *Follain/Initiation* by Frank Graziano and Jean Follain w/trans. by Mary Feeney; *First Z Poems* by Dennis Saleh; *The Compleat Melancholic* by Lewis Turco. Publications first appear in laboriously hand-printed limited editions. Larger editions are sometimes reissued in offset reproduction. Write for information regarding authors' rights, trade discounts, publication descriptions, etc. Mss require SASE or we

44

never received them." 11 titles listed in the *Small Press Record of Books in Print* (9th Edition, 1980).

BIG MAMA RAG, Tearraleen Woodsharp, 1724 Gaylord, Denver, CO 80206. 1972. Poetry, articles, art, photos, cartoons, interviews, satire, letters. "Radical Feminist Theory and Women's issues." circ. 9,000. monthly. sub. price: $6.00/individual; per copy: $.45 in state/$.55 outside Co. 16pp; 61 picas x 16 in.; of. Reporting time: 3 mos. Payment: free sub. Pub's reviews. §written by or for women. Ads: $200/$105/$3-col. in./$.10/wd. COSMEP.

BIG MOON, Christine Kyckelhahn-Wilkins, Claudia Cary-Bilan, 207 Texas, Bellingham, WA 98225, 206-671-4029. 1974. Poetry, fiction, articles, art, photos, criticism, reviews, letters, parts-of-novels, long-poems, collages, concrete art. "We publish the best poetry and short fiction we can find, though the emphasis is on poetry. We read all MSS carefully, and are interested in new poets as well as known ones. Recent contributors include: Stuart Friebert, Lyn Lifshin, John Tagliabue, Elton Glaser, Christine Zawadiwsky, William Dickey." circ. 500. 2/yr. Pub'd 2 issues 1979; expects 2 issues 1980. sub. price: $4; per copy: $2; sample: free. Discounts: 60/40. 65-70pp; 5½X8½; lo. Reporting time: 2-3 wks. Payment: 3 copies. Ads: $28/$15/class-wd: negotiable. CCLM, COSMEP.

BIG PRINT, Editorial Collective, 163 King Street, Aberdeen, Scotland. 1978. Articles, photos, cartoons, interviews, letters, news items. "Longish feature type articles about 700-800 words. Biases - community inspired action, anarchism and other libertarian perspectives. Primarily a local magazine." circ. 800. 12/yr. Pub'd 10 issues 1979; expects 10 issues 1980. sub. price: £2.50; per copy: £0.15; sample: £0.15 + postage. Back issues: £0.15 + postage. 16pp; 8X11½; of. Pub's reviews. §Community action, radical history, novels, feminism, anarchism, etc. Ads: £20.00/£10.00/free.

Big River Association (see also RIVER STYX), Michael Castro, Jan Castro, 7420 Cornell Ave, St. Louis, MO 63130. 1975. Poetry, fiction, art, photos, cartoons, interviews, long-poems. "Our overall orientation is multi-cultural, multi-ethnic. We've published works by Helen Adam, Michael Corr, Ishmael Reed, AllenGinsberg, Jerome Rothenberg, Ntozake Shange, Clayton Eshleman, Gary Snyder, Quincy Troupe, Paula Gunn Allen, David Meltzer, andmany young lesser known writers. Themes for 1980: The six elements: Earth, Water, Fire, Air, Light, Quintessence. Works connected in any way will be considered." avg. press run 1,000. Expects 2 titles 1980. avg. price, paper: $3.00. Discounts: subscriptions, individuals, $5.00 (2 issues); institutions, $10.00; bookstores, 40%; orders 10 or more, 50%; back issues and samples, $3.00. 130pp; 5½X8½; †of. Reporting time: 2 months. Payment: 2 issues. Copyrights for author. COSMEP, CCLM.

BIG SCREAM, Nada, David Cope, Susan Cope, 2782 Dixie, SW, Grandville, MI 49418, 616-531-1442. 1974. Poetry, fiction, art. "We include at least 5 pages of each writer publ.- some longpoems tend to have imagist bias tho some surrealism; prefer *personal* poems. Contributors: Michael McMahon, Eric Greinke, Dave Montgomery, Jim McCurry, David Cope." circ. 100-150. 2-3/yr. Pub'd 2 issues 1979. sub. price: $5.00; per copy: $1.00; sample: $1.00. Back issues: $1.00 per copy. Discounts: 5-10 copies 25 percent, more than 10 40 percent. 30pp; 8X8½; †mi. Reporting time: 1 week - 1 month. Payment: 3 copies.

BIKINI GIRL, Lisa Baumgardner, PO Box 319, Stuyvesant Station, New York, NY 10009, (212) 533-3561. 1978. Poetry, fiction, articles, art, photos, cartoons, interviews, satire, criticism, reviews, letters, parts-of-novels, collages, concrete art, news items. "*Bikini Girl* changes in format and content with each issue. Each issue is *pink*. Sometimes the magazines come with soundsheets or glasses (psychedelic color-burst glasses), or paper dolls, flip-books, etc." circ. 4,500. 2-3/yr. Pub'd 3 issues 1979; expects 2 issues 1980. price per copy: $2.00; sample: $2.00. Back issues: $2.50 each back issue. Discounts: 30% when purchase 10-25 copies, 40% when purchase 25+ copies. 32pp; of. Reporting time: immediately. Copyrighted.

BILE, No Tickee/No Washee Enterprises Ltd, Bradley Lastname, 5228 South Woodlawn, Loft 3E, Chicago, IL 60615, 324-7859. 1978. Art, photos, cartoons, letters, collages, news items. "Recent contributors include Bradley Lastname, Dick Higgins, Gregg 'Buddhadada' Puchalski, Philip Lamantia, Michael Gibbs, Cabaret Voltaire." circ. 200. 12/yr. Pub'd 5 issues 1979; expects 12 issues 1980, 12 issues 1981. sub. price: $8.00; per copy: $2.00; sample: $2.00. Back issues: Back issues #1-3, $2.00 each. Back issues #3-12, $2.00 ea. Discounts: 40% on consignment to be paid quarterly. 12pp; 8X11; of. Reporting time: 3 days. Payment: copies, magazine exchanges. Not copyrighted. §7/21/29/38/43/47/72/88. Ads: $30.00/$20.00. AAP, CCLM.

BILINGUAL REVIEW/La revista bilingue, Bilingual Review/Press, Dr. Gary D. Keller, Editor; Karen S. Van Hooft, Managing Editor, 106 Ford Hall Dept Bilingual Studies, Eastern Michigan University, Ypsilanti, MI 48197, 212-969-4035. 1974. Poetry, fiction, articles, interviews, criticism, reviews. "Research and scholarly articles dealing with bilingualism, primarily but not exclusively Spanish-English; U.S.-Hispanic literature; English-Spanish contrastive linguistics; fiction, poetry, etc., concerning Hispanic life in the U.S." circ. 4,000. 3/yr. Pub'd 3 issues 1979; expects 3 issues 1980, 3 issues 1981. sub. price: $12.00; per copy: $4.50; sample: $4.50. Back issues: $4.50. Discounts: none. 96pp; 7X10; of. Reporting time: 6-8 weeks. Payment: no. Copyrighted, does not revert to author. Pub's reviews: 9 in 1979. §Books dealing with our primary areas of interest: bilingualism, U.S. Hispanic literature. Ads: $100.00/$60.00/$40.00/ 2-pg spread $150.00, back cover $175.00, inside cover $150.00. CCLM, COSMEP.

Bilingual Review/Press (see also BILINGUAL REVIEW/La revista bilingue), Gary D Keller, General Editor; Karen S. Van Hooft, Managing Editor, 106 Ford Hall, Dept Foreign Languages, Eastern Michigan University, Ypsilanti, MI 48197, 313-487-0042. 1976. Criticism, poetry, fiction, articles. "Re: Types of material: We publish book-length monographs and collections of articles in the following areas: scholarly studies in the language and literature of US Hispanos; studies in contemporary methods of literary analysis; Puerto Rican and Chicano literature (anthologies of fiction, poetry)." avg. press run 1000 cloth + 1000 paper. avg. price, cloth: $14.95; paper: $8.95. Discounts: 20% for bookstores and booksellers. 288pp; 5½X8½; of. Reporting time: 8 - 10 weeks. Payment: Varies from author subsidy with repayment to author from royalties on copies sold, to standard 10% royalty with no subsidy, depending on commercial prospects of book. Yes. COSMEP.

Bilingue Publications, Robert C. Medina, PO Drawer H, Las Cruces, NM 88001, (505) 526-1557. 1975. Fiction. avg. press run 1,000. Pub'd 1 title 1979; expects 1 title 1980, 1 title 1981. avg. price, paper: $3.50. Discounts: 40%. 140pp; 6X8. Reporting time: 3 months.

Biography Press, Fremont Johnson, 1240 W. Highland Ave., Rt. 1 Box 745, Aransas Pass., TX 78336, 512-758-3870. 1970. avg. press run 500. Pub'd 20 titles 1979; expects 25 titles 1980. 2 titles listed in the *Small Press Record of Books in Print* (9th Edition, 1980). avg. price, cloth: varies; paper: varies. pp varies; 5½X8½; †of. Reporting time: 2 weeks - month. Copyrights for author on request, $15.00 including Library of Congress fee.

Biohydrant Publications, R.F.D. 3, St. Albans, VT 05478. 1976. Poetry, art. "Publish primarily the art and writings of sculptor/poet David R. Wheeler." avg. press run 500. Pub'd 1 title 1979. 1 title listed in the *Small Press Record of Books in Print* (9th Edition, 1980). avg. price, paper: $9.00. Discounts: straight 30 percent. 250pp; 8½X11. Copyrights for author.

BIRD EFFORT, Bird Effort Press, Robert Long, Josh Dayton, 25 Mudford Avenue, Easthampton, NY 11937. 1975. Poetry, fiction, articles, art, interviews, criticism, reviews, letters, parts-of-novels, long-poems, collages, plays, concrete art. "Ignatow,Peters,Berger,Wheelock,Acker,Hitchcock, Dobyns, Matthews, Matthews, Unterecker, Hays, Bruchac, Padgett, Coolidge, Giorno, Kostelanetz, Bennett,Bukowski, etc." circ. 500. 1/yr. Pub'd 1 issue 1979; expects 1 issue 1980, 1 issue 1981. sub. price: $5.00 to indiv; $6.00 to instit; for two consecutive issues; per copy: $2.50; sample: $2.50. Back issues: Issue 1/2 rare; write for details. Others $2.50. Discounts: 40% trade. 135pp; 8½X7; of. Reporting time: right away to two weeks; longer if we're in Lithuania. Payment: 2 copies; money when and if available. Copyrighted. Pub's reviews: 3 in 1979. §Poetry/fiction/criticism/translation. Ads: $50.00/$25.00 We will exchange ads with other magazines.

Bird Effort Press (see also BIRD EFFORT), Robert Long, Josh Dayton, 25 Mudford Ave, Easthampton, NY 11937. 1975. Poetry, fiction, art, parts-of-novels, long-poems, collages, plays, concrete art. "To date we've published only broadsides, but hope to get into chapbooks when we can. *Query before submitting.*" 3 titles listed in the *Small Press Record of Books in Print* (9th Edition, 1980). Reporting time: 2 weeks.

Birth Day Publishing Company, PO Box 7722, San Diego, CA 92107, (714) 296-3194. 1975. Poetry, articles, art, photos, interviews, reviews, letters, news items. "An inquiry, investigation into and experiences with spirituality in general and in particular, the life and teachings of an Indian holy man named Sri Sathya Sai Baba. Published material has been book length, non-fiction. Recent contributors include Samuel H. Sandweiss, M.D., Dr. John S. Hislop, Ph.D, and Howard Murphet." avg. press run 5,000. Pub'd 2 titles 1979; expects 3 titles 1980, 3 titles 1981. 4 titles listed in the *Small Press Record of Books in Print* (9th Edition, 1980). avg. price, cloth: $8.25; paper: $3.60. Discounts: Book trade, 40%; Bulk, 50%; Classroom/Library, 40%; Jobber, 50%. 225pp; 5½X8½; of. Reporting time: m/s by invitation only. Payment: Usually none. Copyrights for author. COSMEP, SSA.

BIRTHSTONE, Dan Brady, Peter Marti, Pam Duval, Eve Yorker, 1319 6th Avenue, San Francisco, CA 94122. 1975. Poetry, art, photos, long-poems, collages. "Poetry: any subject, graphics: pen and ink any subject. Photos: B/W-no stated biases any subject fine." circ. 500 plus. 2-4/yr. Pub'd 2 issues 1979. sub. price: $6.00 (4 issues); per copy: $1.25; sample: $1.25. Back issues: upon request. 16pp; 8½X11; of. Reporting time: 3 - 5 weeks. Payment: in copies. Copyrighted. §poetry, graphics, photography. Ads: $70.00/$35.00. COSMEP-WEST.

Biscuit City Press, Robert M. Gutchen, Sylvia Gutchen, P.O. Box 334, Kingston, RI 02881, 401-783-8851. 1970. Fiction. "The principal activity of the Biscuit City Press is fine printing on a hand-press (an 1870 Albion hand-press) in limited editions of short pieces, with or without illustrations. Editions have run from a low of 15 copies to a maximum of 250 copies, most running about 60 copies —all numbered. Much emphasis is placed on choice of paper, on typography, inking, and on the quality of the printed impression. Because the Biscuit City Press is an extra-curricular activity, only three or four items—of the proprietor's choice—are issued each year. All books are bound by hand." avg. press run 60. Pub'd 3 titles 1979; expects 3 titles 1980. avg. price, cloth: $42.00; paper: $7.00. No discounts on single items. 20 percent discount on 5 or more items. 14pp; 5X8; †lp.

Bits Press (see also PIECES), Dept of English, Case Western Reserve Univ, Cleveland, OH 44106, 216-368-2359. 1974. Poetry. "Most recent chapbooks are *Peripheral Vision* by Elton Glaser, *Detail From an American Landscape* by Merry Speece, *Man in the Attic* by Conrad Hilberry, and *Coyote* by Bruce Bennett." avg. press run 1,200. Pub'd 3 titles 1979; expects 5 titles 1980, 3 titles 1981. 7 titles listed in the *Small Press Record of Books in Print* (9th Edition, 1980). avg. price, paper: $2.00. 28pp; 8½X5¼; †lp. Reporting time: 1 month. Payment: by arrangement (usually copies). Copyrights for author. CCLM.

BITTERROOT, Menke Katz, Ed. in chief, Blythbourne Station, P.O. Box 51, Brooklyn, NY 11219, (914) 647-8861. 1962. Poetry, reviews. "We shall always discourage stereotyped forms in poetry which imitate fixed patterns and leave no individual mark. We shall inspire all poets who seek their own identity through original poetry, realistic or fantastic. Many of our poets see *Bitterroot* as a palm in a desert.u" circ. 1000+. 4/yr. Expects 4 issues 1980. sub. price: $5.00; per copy: $1.50; sample: $2.00. Back issues: complete set of 55 issues/$125.00. Discounts: 10%. 50pp; 5½X8½; of. Reporting time: immediately. Payment: one copy. Copyrighted, credit for bitterroot requested. Pub's reviews: six in 1979. §poetry. Ads: $100/$50. CCLM.

BITTERSWEET, Ellen Massey, Lebanon High School, 777 Brice St., Lebanon, MO 65536, 417-532-9829. 1973. Poetry, fiction, articles. "Most material is done by staff, but do accept authentic ozark material." circ. 3,600. 4/yr. Pub'd 4 issues 1979; expects 4 issues 1980. sub. price: $8.00; per copy: $2.00; sample: freeto libraries. Back issues: $2.00. Discounts: none. 68pp; 8½X11; of. Reporting time: 1 month. Payment: sample of magazine. Copyrighted, does not revert to author. no advertizing.

BLACK AMERICAN LITERATURE FORUM, Joseph Weixlmann, Indiana State University, Parsons Hall 237, Terre Haute, IN 47809, 812-232-6311, Ext. 2760. 1967. Poetry, articles, art, photos, interviews, criticism, reviews. circ. 950. 4/yr. Pub'd 4 issues 1979; expects 4 issues 1980, 4 issues 1981. sub. price: $4.00($6.00 foreign); per copy: $1.00($1.50 foreign); sample: $1.00 ($1.50 foreign). Back issues: $1.00($1.50 foreign). Discounts: 40 percent. 40-44pp; 8½X11; †of. Reporting time: 3 months. Payment: 3 copies. Indiana State Univ. holds copyright. Pub's reviews: 13 in 1979. §Black American literature. Ads: $40.00/$25.00/none. CCLM, COSMEP.

BLACK ART: AN INTERNATIONAL QUARTERLY, Val Spaulding, Editor; Samella Lewis, Editor; Paul G. Lewis, Editor, 137-55 Southgate Street, Jamaica, NY 11413. 1975. Art, photos, interviews, reviews. "Here you will find an extensive presentation of the art of Black cultures. BLACK ART *an international quarterly* includes illustrated feature articles and interviews from established artists — works of new artists — an art collector's column and a fhow-to section for the beginning collector — historical art sections dealing with both the recent and the distant past — a photo essay — a folk tale, a young people's section. Also, there are two additional sections — placement, grants and exhibits — reviews of books and shows. ISSN 0145-8116." circ. 7,000. 4/yr. sub. price: $12.00; per copy: $3.50; sample: $1.50. Back issues: $5.00. Discounts: 30%. 72pp; 8½X11; of. Reporting time: 10 weeks. Payment: none. Copyrighted, reverts to author. Pub's reviews: 3 in 1979. §Non Western art (African, African-American, Oceanic), music, drama. Ads: $815/$425. ASME (American Society of Magazine Editors).

BLACK BOOK, J. Garmhausen, ,Dept. of English, Bowling Green State Univ., Bowling Green, OH 43403. "Each issue contains the work of one writer: poetry, essays, notebooks-whatever fits. The first issue was a collection of poems by Anselm Hollo. Please no unsolicited mss. at present." circ. 1M. 3/yr. sub. price: $4.00; per copy: $1.50. 48pp; of.

BLACK BOX MAGAZINE, Watershed Intermedia, Alan Austin, Ahmos Zu-Bolton, Elizabeth Wray, Anne Becker, PO Box 50145, Washington, DC 20004, 202-347-4823. 1972. Poetry, reviews, music, long-poems, plays. "We are an audio magazine publishing the whole range of contemporary poetry-including tape-poetry, sound poetry, songs & other collaborations between poets and musicians, binaural translations. Issues are two to three hours long, on a pair of cassettes, in a special box. We're convinced that the age of the page is ending (at least where poetry's concerned), and that a new kind of poetry rooted in the voice and in performance is more and more the norm. Poetry submissions should be made to us on tape only-no manuscripts, please! But for interviews and dramatic material, we'd rather read first, it saves time." circ. 9M. 4/yr. Pub'd 5 issues 1979; expects 4 issues 1980. sub. price: individuals, $17.95 institutions, $37.50; per copy: $9.95-ea while current; $12.00 thereafter.; sample: $5. Back issues: No. 1 & No. 2 $25.00; others $12.00. Discounts: Trade, 40 percent on min. order of 10; on instit. subs., there is a 25 percent disc. on the second yr of a 2 yr order, and on the additional copies in a multiple-copy order. Reporting time: too long. Payment: $5.00 minute. Copyrighted, reverts to author. §records & tapes. CCLM, COSMEP.

Black Buzzard Press (see also VISIONS), Bradley R. Strahan, 2217 Shorefield Road, Apt 532, Wheaton, MD 20902. 1979. Poetry. "Not currently publishing book length mss. Currently fully occupied with *Visions.*" avg. press run 500-700. avg. price, paper: $4.00. Discounts: Schools & libraries 20%, 50 or more 30%. 20-70pp; 5½X8½; of. Reporting time: 2 weeks to 2 months. Payment: by arrangement. Copyrights for author.

THE BLACK CAT, Writers For Animal Rights, Richard Morgan, Phyllis Fischer, P.O. Box 1912OA, East Tennessee State University, Johnson City, TN 37601. 1975. Poetry, fiction, articles, art, interviews, criticism, reviews. "We are an international journal published by Writers for Animal Rights, and welcome overseas submissions. Particularly interested in poetry about animals (from humane, liberated point of view)." circ. 500. 2/yr. sub. price: $4.00 for two issues; per copy: $2.00; sample: $2.00. varies; 32-64pp; 5½X8½; of. Reporting time: ASAP. One to six months depending on time of year. Payment: generally copies. Copyrighted. §poetry, fiction, art, photography, criticism, counter-culture, general non-fiction. Ads: please inquire.

The Black Cat Press, Norman W. Forgue, 8248 Kenton, Skokie, IL 60076, 677-9686. 1961. Poetry, fiction, articles. avg. press run 249. Pub'd 8 titles 1979; expects 7 titles 1980, 9 titles 1981. avg. price, cloth: $15.00-$45.00. 32-96pp; 1¾X2½; †of/lp. Copyrights for author.

The Black Hole School of Poethnics, Grinley Nash, Box 555, Port Jefferson, NY 11777. 1978. avg. press run 500. Pub'd 4 titles 1979; expects 8 titles 1980. 4 titles listed in the *Small Press Record of Books in Print* (9th Edition, 1980). †of. Reporting time: Time is irrelevant.

BLACK JACK & VALLEY GRAPEVINE, Seven Buffaloes Press, Art Cuelho, Box 249, Big Timber, MT 59011. 1973. Poetry, fiction, art, photos, interviews, reviews, parts-of-novels, long-poems, collages. "*Black Jack*: rural poems & stories from anywhere in America, especially the West. Work that tells a story, a craft that shows experience, not only of the head, but of the heart too. I'm more than prejudice against poems that are made up or forced, even when they are concocted out of the supposed wisdom of some established school. Art is for individuals with strong images and charactizations. *Valley Grapevine* is taking material native to Central California. Contributors: Gerry Haslam, Roxy Gordon, Badger Stone, Wilma McDaniel, Bill Rintoul, Richard Dokey, Donk Thompson, De-Wayne Rail, Dean Phelps, Pat Elliott, John Moore, etc." circ. 300-500. 1/yr. Pub'd 1 issue 1979; expects 1 issue 1980, 1 issue 1981. price per copy: $2.50-$3.50. Discounts: 1-5, 10%; 6-10, 15%; 11-15, 20%; 16-20, 25%; over 20 copies, 30%. 80pp; 5½X8½; †of. Reporting time: within a week, often a day or two. Payment: copies, often other free copies. Copyrighted, reverts to author. Pub's reviews: 10 in 1979. §Western and rural, native american, hobo, the road, prisons. Ads: No ads. CCLM.

BLACK MARIA, Collective, PO Box 25187, Chicago, IL 60625. 1971. Poetry, fiction, articles, art, photos, interviews, reviews, plays. "We accept work done by women only. Interested in redefining women's position in society, family & herself. Enclose SASE for return of submissions; prefer original copies. Black & white photos specifications: 2x3 to 8x10 glossy & magazine format 6x9. Poets should submit at least 3 examples of work; 4 to 75 lines." circ. 1,000. infrequent. Pub'd 2 issues 1979. sub. price: $8.00; Institution $12.00; per copy: $2.00; sample: $2.00. Back issues: $1.50. 64pp; 6X9; †of. Reporting time: 2-5 months. Payment: Contributors copies and 1 yr. subscription to BLACK MARIA. Copyrighted. Pub's reviews. §any material done by or about women. Ads: $60/$30/$.25 per word. CCLM, COSMEP.

THE BLACK POSITION, Broadside Press, Gwendolyn Brooks, 7428 S. Evans Ave., Chicago, IL 60619. 1971. 1/yr. Discounts: 10 copies 40%. 5X8. CCLM.

THE BLACK REVIEW, Makini Tulinagwe, Black Berry Press, P.O.Box 9405, Baltimore, MD 21228. 1978. Poetry, fiction, articles, art, cartoons, interviews, satire, criticism, reviews, parts-of-novels, long-poems, collages, plays. "Restricted to writing by Black (Afro-American, African, Afro-Caribbean) writers/artists" Bi-annual. Pub'd 1 issue 1979; expects 2 issues 1980, 2 issues 1981. sub. price: $5.00/yr; per copy: $3.00; sample: $3.00. Discounts: 50 copies, $100.00; 100 copies, $180.00; 150 copies, $250.00. 60pp; 5X8; of. Reporting time: 1-2 months. Payment: copies. Copyrighted, reverts to author. Pub's reviews: 3 in 1979. §Books on any subject by Black authors. Ads: $35.00/$22.-00/$5.00, 1-50 words. COSMEP, COSMEP South, CCLM.

Black Rose Books, 3981 Blvd., St. Laurent 4th Floor, Montreal, Que H2W 1V2, Canada. 38 titles listed in the *Small Press Record of Books in Print* (9th Edition, 1980).

THE BLACK SCHOLAR: Journal of Black Studies and Research, Robert L. Allen, Editor, P.O. Box 908, Sausalito, CA 94965, 415-332-3130. 1969. Poetry, articles, art, photos, interviews, criticism, reviews, music. "Manuscripts for full-length articles may range in length from 2,000 to 5,000 words, include brief biographical statement, typewritten, double spaced. Articles may be historical and documented, they may be analytic and theoretical; they may be speculative. However, an article should not simply be a 'rap'; it should present a solid point of view convincingly and thoroughly argued. Recent Contributors: Ishmael Reed, June Jordan, NTOZAKE Shange, Alice Walker, Andrew Salkey, Andrew Young, Ronald Dellums." circ. 15,000. 10/yr. Pub'd 10 issues 1979; expects 10 issues 1980. sub. price: $16.00; per copy: $2.00; sample: free. Back issues: $2.00. Discounts: Publishers discount of 25% off above rates. 64pp; 5¾X8½; of. Payment: in contributors copies of magazine and 1 year subscription. rights become property of the Black Scholar. Pub's reviews: 20 in 1979. §the black experience or black related books. Ads: $400.00/$225.00/$50.00 (1st 50 words) $10.00 (per line, extra). CCLM.

Black Sparrow Press, PO Box 3993, Santa Barbara, CA 93105. 1966. Poetry, fiction, criticism, letters. "See our publications." avg. press run 2,500. Pub'd 18 titles 1979; expects 15 titles 1980. 114 titles listed in the *Small Press Record of Books in Print* (9th Edition, 1980). avg. price, cloth: $14.00; paper: $5.00. Discounts: Trade: 40 percent - 46 percent. 150-250pp; 6X9; lp/of. Reporting time: 60 days. Payment: Royalty on sales. Copyrights for author. COSMEP.

Black Stone Press, Peter Koch, 393 Hayes Street, San Francisco, CA 94102, 863-1933. 1974. "Visual language, design poetry, typographic printmaking." avg. press run 500. Pub'd 1 title 1979. 7 titles listed in the *Small Press Record of Books in Print* (9th Edition, 1980). avg. price, paper: $6.00. Discounts: 25% to stores. 6X9; †lp. Copyrights for author. CCLM, PCBA.

Black Swan Books Ltd., John J. Walsh, PO Box 327, Redding Ridge, CT 06876, (203) 938-2716. 1978. Poetry, fiction, music. Pub'd 2 titles 1979. Discounts: Trade 20%. Copyrights for author.

THE BLACK WARRIOR REVIEW, Marnie Prange, Editor; Brad Watson, Fiction Editor; Leslie Nail, Poetry Editor, P.O. Box 2936, University, AL 35486, (205) 348-5526. 1974. Poetry, fiction, interviews, reviews, parts-of-novels, long-poems, art, photos, criticism, plays. "Publish high quality contemporary fiction and poetry. Recent contributors include Philip F. O'Connor, Fred Chappell, Eve Shelnutt, Patricia Goedicke, Thomas Rabbitt, John Engels, R.H.W. Dillard, Dara Wier." circ. 1,000. 2/yr. Pub'd 2 issues 1979. sub. price: $5.00; per copy: $2.50; sample: $2.50. Back issues: $2.50. Discounts: none at present. 128pp; 6X9; of. Reporting time: 2 weeks to 2 months. Payment: 2 copies of magazine. Copyrighted, transferred on request. Pub's reviews: 4 in 1979. §Serious poetry and fiction. Ads: $80.00/$50.00. CCLM, COSMEP, AWP.

BLACKBERRY, Gary Lawless, Box 186, Brunswick, ME 04011. 1974. Poetry. "Chapbooks by Enslin, Sanfield, Beltrametti, Gifford, Deemer, Koller, Lawless, Ferraris, Byrd, BlueCloud. One Anthology-Sitting Frog—poetry from Naropa Institute Summer '75, edited by Rachel Peters, Eero Ruittila. Novel by James Koller, *Gulf of Maine Reader #1*, chapbooks by Brandi, Fox, Cass, Hadley, Steuding, Bruchac, Baldwin, Roottila, *Salted in the Shell #23*." circ. 200. 10/yr. Pub'd 7 issues 1979. 7 titles listed in the *Small Press Record of Books in Print* (9th Edition, 1980). price per copy: $1.75; sample: $1.75. Back issues: Sitting Frog-$3.25. Discounts: 5, 40%; library 10%. 16-20pp; 8½X7; of. Reporting time: 2-4 weeks. Payment: copies + %. §ethnopoetics/back country/Amer. Indian. NESPA.

The Blackhole School of Poethnics, Grinley Nash, Box 555, Port Jefferson, NY 11777. 1978. Poetry, fiction, art, photos, cartoons, interviews, satire, criticism, collages, plays, news items. "Writings from perspective beyond mere assimilation of scientific reality of phenomenon of Blackhole; this is it! Everything at once and the one clear line that is art. Titles: *Nothing Left to Fake*, a great American *four page* novel, Graham Everett; *Rent,* Ed Harsen (8 p.); *Plutonium,* (a broadsheet), various authors; *Pond In Chile No,* Jonathan Cohen (broadside)." avg. press run 250-500. Expects 3 titles 1980, 5 titles 1981. avg. price, paper: $1.00. Discounts: 60/40 to trade. 4-8pp; 5½X8½ // 17X22; †of. Reporting time: Usually within 2 weeks. Payment: 10% of the run.

Blackrock Printers (see also CARN (a link between the Celtic nations)), Cathal O. Luain, Celtic League, 9 Br Cnoc Sion, Ath Cliath 9, Ireland. 1973. Articles, reviews, criticism, news items, poetry, interviews, letters. avg. press run 2M. avg. price, paper: 40 p. Discounts: 20 - 25% to shops. 24pp; 8½X10½; of. Reporting time: up to 3 months. Payment: none.

BLADES, JoAnn Balingit, Francis Poole, 4, rue Mohamed Bergach, Tangier-Medina, Morocco. 1978. Poetry, art, cartoons, satire, collages. "Submissions must include SASE and International Reply Coupons." circ. 100-200. 4-5/yr. Pub'd 4 issues 1979; expects 4 issues 1980, 4 issues 1981. sub. price: $3.00; per copy: $0.75; sample: $0.75. Back issues: $1.00 + postage. 10pp; 4¼X3½; †of/xerox. Reporting time: 1 month. Payment: copies (2). Copyrighted, reverts to author.

BLAKE, AN ILLUSTRATED QUARTERLY, Morris Eaves, Morton D. Paley, Dept. of English, Univ. of New Mexico, Albuquerque, NM 87131, 505-277-3103. 1967. Articles, art, photos, criticism, reviews, letters. "Our orientation is scholarly, though we have published some non-scholarly material. Blake was both poet and artist, and we welcome material on either or both aspects of his work: news items on exhibitions, publications, etc.; essays, and notes that run from one to many pages, discussion articles for the exchange of opinion; minute particulars, which are mini-notes; reviews of books about Blake; biographical material. Many of the articles are illustrated." circ. 600. 4/yr. Pub'd 4 issues 1979; expects 4 issues 1980. 1 title listed in the *Small Press Record of Books in Print* (9th Edition, 1980). sub. price: $12.00; per copy: $3.00. Back issues: whole nos. 17-18/$5; whole no. 20/$3. Discounts: Agency disc. 15 percent; Individual subs. $10.00/yrly. 60pp; 8½X11; of. Reporting time: 4-6 wks. Payment: copies only. Copyrighted, does not revert to author. Pub's reviews: 25 in 1979. §Scholarship. Ads: $80/$55. COSMEP.

BLANK TAPE, Permanent Press, Keith Rahmmings, Box 371, Brooklyn, NY 11230. 1976. Poetry, fiction, articles, art, photos, cartoons, music, letters, parts-of-novels, long-poems, collages, plays, concrete art. "In keeping with BLANK TAPE'S policy of unceasing innovation, we are about to inaugurate what we are certain will prove a revolutionary trend in magazine publishing. Beginning with the forthcoming issue, BLANK TAPE will cease to be published in its standard offset format but will instead be tattooed on living human skin! Yes, no longer will work be circumscribed by the artificial borders of the 8½ x ll page, but will conform to the physicalcontours of its human medium, insuring that each copy is as unique and irreplaceable as the body it is printed upon. Each jam-packed quarterly issue will be imprinted by our staff of experienced professional tattooers on the bodies of five hundred volunteers who will expose themselves regularly at libraries and bookstores, to say nothing of restaurants, busy intersections, subway platforms, airport terminals, and other public places throughout the United States and the free world! Contributors may also opt to be tattooed and thus be able to wear BLANK TAPE indelibly for the remainder of their lives. Just think of that! We are secure in the knowledge that this new publishing concept will be regarded as the landmark it is, and needless to say, will consider work only of the highest caliber, the most exalted dimensions, the brightest magnitude, to say nothing of the quintessence of excellence, the pinnacle of perfection and the summit of achievement for inclusion in the new, sense-shattering, tattooed BLANK TAPE!" circ. 1,000. Irregular. Pub'd 2 issues 1979; expects 3 issues 1980. sub. price: $9.00/3 issues plus 50¢ post.; per copy: $3.00; sample: $3.00. Back issues: Inquire. Discounts: 40 percent on 5 copies or more. pp varies; 8½X11; †of. Reporting time: 2 wks-mo. Payment: Copies and autographed photo of Mister Ed. buys 1st serial rts. Pub's reviews: 1-2 in 1979. §Poetry, fiction, and you name it. COSMEP.

Blarney Books, Michael F. O'Connor, 6129 Shenandoah Drive, Sacramento, CA 95841. 1979. Poetry, fiction, satire. "Humor is the key word here. Blarney Books is interested in poetry and fiction that has a humorous-yet realistic slant, we're not looking for gutter material so consider that when submitting, however, we are not prudes either. Comic novels must not be charactatures. We are looking for plausable-yet outrageous-(is that a contradiction ?) characters. Poetry should also have at least a serious underlying theme similar to Armour and Parker. 1 title: *For White Boys Who Have Contemplated Monasteries After Being Dumped On Once Too Often.*" avg. press run 2,000. Pub'd 1 title 1979. 1 title listed in the *Small Press Record of Books in Print* (9th Edition, 1980). avg. price, cloth: $8.95; paper: $3.95. Discounts: Being new we do not yet have experience with these. 150-200pp; 5½X8½; of. Reporting time: 8 weeks max., probably less. Payment: again, we are new and will have to discuss this with authors. Copyrights for author. COSMEP.

BLIND ALLEY, Blind Alley Press, Brian Robertson, Editor, P.O. Box 1296, Edinburg, TX 78539. 1977. Poetry, fiction, satire, criticism, reviews, long-poems. "We're not looking for off the wall mondo-humor, but well craftedmaterial that shows an understanding of what humor is about. Don't rip off a TV or movie (visual) type of humor. Study it. Read Benchley, Perelman, Allen, then give us a try. Too many editors treat humor as a second rate form of writing, but, then again so do writers. Don't insult yourself by sending rhymed verse—that died when the old Saturday Evening Post went down in flames. If ever it paid to order a sample of a magazine, it's with BlIND ALLEY. If you make it in between our covers, you'll be in the best of company. We've published Fericano, Koertge, Ted Daniel, Locklin, Richard Grayson, Magorian, and others, but if themanuscript is funny and well done, names don't mean a thing to me." circ. 500. 4/yr. Pub'd 4 issues 1979; expects 4 issues 1980. sub. price: $10.00; per copy: $2.50; sample: $2.50. Back issues: all back issues sell out. Discounts: 50%

to bookstores and classrooms. 60pp; 8½X11; †mi/of. Reporting time: immediate to two weeks. Payment: pays one or more contributor's copies. Copyrighted, reverts to author. Pub's reviews: 30 in 1979. §Poetry, essays, humor, erotica. Ads: none.

Blind Alley Press (see also BLIND ALLEY), P.O. Box 1296, Edinburg, TX 78539. 1977. Poetry, fiction, satire, criticism, reviews, long-poems. "Please see our listing for BLIND ALLEY MAGAZINE. We also publish chapbooks, pamphlets, broadsheets, poetry postcards, and so on. These type projects are usually co-coperative, although we do underwrite costs on some of them. Send work to BLIND ALLEY MAGAZINE first so we can get to know each other." avg. press run 500 to 1,000, but varies. 2 titles listed in the *Small Press Record of Books in Print* (9th Edition, 1980). avg. price, paper: $1.50. Discounts: 50% to bookstores and classrooms. pp varies; 5½X8½; †of. Reporting time: immediate to two weeks. Payment: arranged.

BLITZ, Mike McDowell, Editor-in-Chief, PO Box 279, Dearborn Heights, MI 48127. 1975. Articles, photos, interviews, criticism, reviews, music, letters, news items. "Magazine is billed as 'The Rock and Roll Magazine For Thinking People'. Emphasis is on artists who are not being afforded enough exposure via other forms of the media. Magazine covers all forms of aesthetically meritous rock and roll music, with slant towards the academic." circ. 2,500. 6/yr. Pub'd 6 issues 1979; expects 6 issues 1980, 6 issues 1981. sub. price: $6.00 for 6 issues; per copy: $1.25; sample: $1.50. Back issues: Varies with each title, information supplied upon request. Discounts: $0.75 per copy on orders of ten or more; overseas $1.00 per copy, US Currency in advance only (cover lists price of 75p for U.K. 28pp; 8½X11; of. Reporting time: deadline is 15th day of month before publication (6 weeks). Payment: all submissions are non-solicited. No financial renumeration. Copyrighted, reverts to author. Pub's reviews: 25 in 1979. §Music, music related films and publications. Ads: $200.00/$120.00/$10.00 for insert any size. COSMEP.

BLOODROOT, Bloodroot, Inc., Joan Eades, Editor; Linda Ohlsen, Editor; Dan Eades, Editor, P.O. Box 891, Grand Forks, ND 58201, 701-775-6079. 1976. Poetry, fiction, articles, art, parts-of-novels, long-poems. "We prefer work by women about women's concerns, though we have published men. Beginning and established writers are read with equal care - particularily when the writing is well-crafted. In poetry our bias is toward length - both of line and poem. In fiction we look for honest stories - traditional or experimental - which read like stories rather than undistilled autobiography. In both, we tend to prefer the honest and energetic to the careful and lifeless. We are open to the poetry and fiction of all schools, but reviewers have noticed an affinity to work with a strong voice. We occasionally use interviews that we have assigned, and writers should query before submitting them. Though BLOODROOT is growing, we still try to respond individually. We needtwo line drawings (preferably pen and ink) for each issue: one for the cover and one for the frontpiece. We'll look at photocopies, but the original must be available if accepted. Drawings should be of women or of interest to women and of a shape to suit or 6 x 9 size." circ. 800. 3/yr. Pub'd 1 issue 1979; expects 3 issues 1980. sub. price: $6.00; per copy: $2.00 plus 50¢ for postage and handling; sample: $2.00 plus 50¢ for postage and handling. Back issues: $5.00. Discounts: standard. 72pp; 6X9; of. Reporting time: one week to six months. Payment: one copy or, grants permitting, $5.00 per page. Copyrighted, reverts with credit given. CCLM.

Bloodroot, Inc. (see also BLOODROOT), Dan Eades, Editor; Joan Eades, Editor; Linda Ohlsen, Editor, P.O. Box 891, Grand Forks, ND 58201, (70l) 775-6079. 1977. Poetry, fiction. "Our chapbook series is open to writers published in BLOODROOT" avg. press run 500. Pub'd 2 titles 1979; expects 4 titles 1980, 4 titles 1981. 3 titles listed in the *Small Press Record of Books in Print* (9th Edition, 1980). avg. price, paper: $1.50, poetry; $2.50, fiction. Discounts: standard. 24 pp poetry; 60 pp fictionpp; 5½X8½; of. Reporting time: one week to six months. Payment: according to NEA guidelines whenever possible. Copyrights for author. CCLM.

BLT Press (Bates, Lear, and Tulp) (see also LYNN VOICES), Peter Bates, Bill Costley, Arnold Trachtman, 72 Lowell Street, Peabody, MA 01960, (617) 531-7348. 1977. Poetry, fiction, art, interviews, letters. "*Lynn Voices* #1 is a series of monologue poems about people typifying Lynn, MA, a General Electric factory town of 85,000 on the North Shore of Massachusettes Bay. It updates Vincent Ferrini's *No Smoke* (1941). As far as submissions go, we welcome any that depict the plight of the industrial city dweller. Please, no self-indulgent lyrics, no Meir Baba poems, no Plath/Sexton death trips. We are looking for the dramatic, the stark, the oral-historical, the anti-fascist. We do not accept the view that politics taints poetry, nor do we think realism implies gloom and doom. Satire is our strongest dart, and we believe not only in aiming it well, but also aiming it at the right target: the pompous apologist, the wide-eyed wonderseeker, the blissed-out meditator, the apolitical crab scurrying under sand, and any other foolish targets the U.S. media heaves at us." avg. press run 5,000. Expects 1 title 1981. 1 title listed in the *Small Press Record of Books in Print* (9th Edition, 1980). avg.

price, other: Newsprint: $.25. Discounts: Free bundle of ten copies to any library, community group, or publication upon request. 8+pp; 11X16; of. Reporting time: 1 month. Payment: free copies.

BLUE BUILDINGS, M. R. Doty, Tom Urban, 2800 Rutland, Des Moines, IA 50311, (515) 277-2709. 1978. Poetry, long-poems. "Prose poems, translations. Recent contributors include Michael Benedikt, Gene Frumkin, Louis Hammer, George Hitchcock, Mekeel McBride, Dan Masterson, Marge Piercy, Raymond Roseliep, Stephen Sandy, Richard Shelton, Jane Shore, William Stafford, David Wagoner, Peter Wild, and many others." circ. 500. 3/yr. Pub'd 3 issues 1979; expects 3 issues 1980, 3 issues 1981. sub. price: $5.00; per copy: $2.00; sample: $2.00. Discounts: 40% trade. 40-60pp; 8½X11; of. Reporting time: 2 weeks to 3 months. Payment: copies. Copyrighted, reverts to author. Ads: $25.-00/$15.00.

Blue Flower, L. Salzmann, A. Salzmann, 1825 Pine Street, Philadelphia, PA 19104, (215) 382-1410. 1 title listed in the *Small Press Record of Books in Print* (9th Edition, 1980).

Blue Heron Press, Dawn Anne Jordan-Westcott, Heather McFarland, W.F. Westcott, PO Box 1326, Alliston, Ontario L0M 1A0, Canada, (705) 435-9914. 1979. Poetry, fiction, articles, long-poems. "We are a specialty book press, producing books of quotable quotes, collections of articles that are topical, yet timeless, poems & some short stories; all work is type set and printed via offset and has high grade paper and glossy plated covers; quotable quotes and appropriate poems are put on specialty cards & note paper. No unsolicited ms accepted; will be returned unopened. We have 5 titles selected for 1980-82 release. Will likely add 3-5 more." avg. press run 1,000. Pub'd 1 title 1979. 1 title listed in the *Small Press Record of Books in Print* (9th Edition, 1980). avg. price, paper: $5.95. Discounts: 20% trade orders less than 5; same for classroom; agent, 40% on orders 20 books or more. 5X8; of. Reporting time: do not accept. Payment: advance varies 10% 1st 5,000 copies, 15% thereafter. Copyrights for author.

BLUE HORSE, Jacqueline T. Bradley, Patrick Kelly, Dr. G. Warren Weissmann, S.J. Brunswick, Eugenia P. Mallory, P.O. Box 6061, Augusta, GA 30906. 1966. Poetry, fiction, photos, satire, collages. "*Blue Horse* is a magazine of satire, misanthropy and scurrilous language without regard to sex, religion, age, race, creed, or I.Q. *Blue Horse* is the periodical of Blue Horse Movement which recognizes the folly of human life and the inutility of politics. *Blue Horse* sees writers as the victims of their own art. Interested in scathing fiction; some poetry, and arrogant photocollage." circ. 500. 1 to 2. Pub'd 1 issue 1979; expects 2 issues 1980, 3 issues 1981. 8 titles listed in the *Small Press Record of Books in Print* (9th Edition, 1980). sub. price: $5.00; per copy: $2.50; sample: $2.00. Back issues: $3.00 except Vol. 1, $5.00. Discounts: Prisoners pay postage only. 32pp; 5½X8½; of. Reporting time: 1 month. Payment: copies. Copyrighted. Ads: exchange.

THE BLUE HOTEL, Windflower Press, Ted Kooser, PO Box 82213, Lincoln, NB 68501. 1979. Poetry, fiction, interviews, criticism, reviews, long-poems. circ. 500. Expects 1 issue 1981. price per copy: $3.00; sample: $3.00. Discounts: 40% to distributors. 80pp; 5½X8½; of. Reporting time: 3 weeks. Payment: copies only. Copyrighted, does not revert to author. Pub's reviews. §Poetry, short fiction, literary criticism. Ads: $60.00. COSMEP.

‡BLUE MOON NEWS, Blue Moon Press, Inc., James Hepworth, c/o English Dept., University of Arizona, Tucson, AZ 85721, 602-884-1387. 1976. "No manuscripts will be returned without SASE." Pub's reviews.

Blue Moon Press, Inc. (see also BLUE MOON NEWS), James Hepworth, c/o English Dept., University of Arizona, Tucson, AZ 85721, 602-884-1387. 1972. Poetry, fiction, articles, art, photos, interviews, criticism, reviews, long-poems, cartoons, satire, letters. "We are mainly interested in poetry and fiction, but are open to all good writing in whatever form it may appear. Recent books by L.D. Clark, Patricia Clark Smith, Simon J. Ortiz, Leon Felise." avg. press run 250-500. avg. price, cloth: $7.00 - $15.00; paper: $4.95. Discounts: 30 percent to bookstores, subscription rates are discounted over direct sales. Bookstores: 20% (1-2); 33% (3-4); 40% (5+); Book Jobbers: 46% (negotiable). 52-150pp; 5½X8½; of. Reporting time: 6 weeks to 3 months. Payment: Authors receive 10 percent of press run. Occasionally, we buy all rights. $50.00 honorarium. Copyrights for author.

Blue Mornings Press, Maurice Schneps, PO Box 411, New York, NY 11357. 1980. Poetry. "We expect to publish several books of poetry every year, in fine, hardcover edition. We are not currently reading unsolicited material. Our first book is *The Blind Receptionist,* by Robert J. Richkin with preface by Robert Creeley." avg. press run 2,000. Pub'd 1 title 1979. avg. price, cloth: $5.95. Discounts: 1-10, 35%; over 20, 50%. 64pp; 5⅜X8¼; of. Payment: 10% gross receipt. Copyrights for author. NYSSPA.

Blue Mountain Press (see also SKYWRITING), Martin Grossman, 511 Campbell St., Kalamazoo, MI 49007, 349-3924. 1975. Poetry. avg. press run 500. Expects 1 title 1980. 4 titles listed in the *Small*

Press Record of Books in Print (9th Edition, 1980). avg. price, paper: $2.00. Discounts: 40 percent/5 copies minimum. 28pp; 9X6; of. Reporting time: 2-4 mo. Payment: 10 percent of run. Copyrights for author.

The Blue Oak Press, Marlea Berutti, Managing Editor, P.O. Box 27, Sattley, CA 96124, 916-994-3397. 1967. Poetry, fiction, criticism, long-poems. "Recent contributors: Cornel Lengyel, Edith Snow, William Everson, Robinson Jeffers, Randy White, John Berutti, Bill Hotchkiss, K'os Naahaabii, Stan Hager. Our bias would be toward the poetry of contemporary Western America; and we have drawn significant focus on the work of Robinson Jeffers as the seminal figure of this developing tradition. Price is extremely variable, from one special edition at $30.00 to paperbacks at $3.95." avg. press run 500. Pub'd 4 titles 1979; expects 3-4 titles 1980. avg. price, cloth: $10.00; paper: $5.00; other: special editions, cloth, $15.00, $20.00, $30.00. Discounts: 40 percent to bookstores and dealers; 20 percent to libraries; 30 percent on consignment; short discounts on special editions. 80-100 pp: but this is also extremely variable, upward.; 6X9; †of/lp. We do not invite submissions. No specific payment policy. Copyrights for author.

BLUE PIG, Sand Project Press/US, David Ball, 23 Cedar Street, Northampton, MA 01060. 1968. Poetry, art, collages, concrete art. "Tom Raworth, Phillip Lopate, Merrill Gilfyllan, Jack Collom. 20-25 pages/issue. Issues rare & irregular. Choice eccentric & unyielding." circ. 250. 1-2/yr. Expects 1 issue 1980, 2 issues 1981. 1 title listed in the *Small Press Record of Books in Print* (9th Edition, 1980). sub. price: free to people; institutions pay through the nose. Back issues: Prices variable. First issues out of sight. 20-25pp; 8½X11; of. Reporting time: 1 month to never for unsolicited submissions. Payment: $25.00 - $50.00 when we have a grant. Copyrighted, reverts to author. CCLM.

BLUE UNICORN, Ruth G. Iodice, B. Jo Kinnick, Harold Witt, 22 Avon Road, Kensington, CA 94707, 415-526-8439. 1977. Poetry, art. "*Blue Unicorn* is a journal looking for excellence of the individual voice whether that voice comes through in a fixed form or an original variation or in freer lines. We publish poets who are established and those who are less known but deserve to be known better, and we are also proud to welcome new talent to our pages. We like poems which communicate in a memorable way whatever is deeply felt by the poet, and we believe in an audience which is delighted, like us, by a lasting image, a unique twist of thought, and a haunting music. We also use a limited number of expert translations. Among recent contributors to our tri-quarterly are: John Ciardi, Rosalie Moore, Charles Edward Eaton, James Schevill, John Ditsky, Janemarie Luecke, Don Welch, Barbara A. Holland, Lawrence Spingarn, A.D. Winans, Eve Triem, William Dickey, Adrianne Marcus, Stuart Silverman, Josephine Miles. Please send only unpublished poems." circ. 500 most issues. 3/yr. Pub'd 3 issues 1979. sub. price: $8.00; per copy: $2.75. 48-60pp; 4¼X5½; of. Reporting time: 1-3 months. Payment: 1 copy. Copyrighted, reverts to author. §Poetry.

Blue Wind Press, George Mattingly, Lucy Farber, P.O. Box 7175, Berkeley, CA 94707, 415-526-1905. 1970. Poetry, fiction, art, photos, satire, collages. "Recent titles: *Port of Saints* by William S. Burroughs; *So Going Around Cities: New and Selected Poems 1958-1979* by Ted Berrigan; *Finite Continued: New Poems 1977-1980* by Anselm Hollo; *Who is Sylvia?* a novel by Tom Clark; *Chances are Few* by Lorenzo Thomas; *Rhino Ritz: An American Mystery* by Keith Abbot; *Blade Runner (A Movie)* by William S. Burroughs; *This Once: New and Selected Poems 1965-1978* by David Gitin. Other titles include *Sojourner Microcosms: New and Selected Poems 1959-1977* by Anselm Hollo; *Light Years: Selected Early Work* by Merrill Gilfillan." avg. press run 1,500. Pub'd 5 titles 1979; expects 4 titles 1980. 22 titles listed in the *Small Press Record of Books in Print* (9th Edition, 1980). avg. price, cloth: $10.95; paper: $4.00; other: $25.00 signed cloth / $10.00 signed paper. Discounts: Retail: 1-4 copies, 20%; 5-49 copies, 40%; 50+ copies, 41%. Limited editions: For the retail trade - 1-4 copies, 20%; 5+ copies, 30%. Orders of 10+ copies shipped postage-paid, bookrate. Individual: Prepayment including 75¢ postage and handling required; No Institutional discounts except 15% library standing-order. 150pp; size varies.; of. Payment: royalty : 8% paper / 10% cloth / 12½% signed cloth. Copyrights for author. CCLM, AIGA, AIP.

Blue Wolf, Daniel Conroy, Stan Hartman, 1240 Pine Street, Boulder, CO 80302, (303) 442-4214.

THE BLUEGRASS LITERARY REVIEW, Marjorie Mendenhall Hoffman, Midway College, Midway, KY 40347. 1979. Poetry, fiction, articles, reviews. "Fiction, articles, reviews: 2,500-3,000 words. Poetry, flexible." circ. 500. 2/yr. Pub'd 1 issue 1979; expects 2 issues 1980, 2 issues 1981. sub. price: $6.00; per copy: $3.00; sample: $3.00. Back issues: $5.00. 52pp; 6X9; lp. Reporting time: 1 to 3 months. Payment: two copies to published author. Copyrighted, does not revert to author. Pub's reviews. §Poetry, essay, regional material, biography. Ads: No ads.

BLUELINE, Alice Gilborn, Blue Mountain Lake, NY 12812, (518) 352-7365. 1979. Poetry, fiction, articles, reviews, plays. "We are interested in material that has some relationship, either literal or in spirit, to the Adirondack mountain region in upstate New York. We are willing to interpret that relationship broadly. Short fiction and essays should be no more than 500 words, poems 40 lines or less. Recent contributors include Joseph Bruchac, Paul Corrigan, Joanne Seltzer, Charlotte Haigh, Laurence Josephs." circ. 500. 2/yr. Pub'd 2 issues 1979. sub. price: $3.50; per copy: $1.75; sample: $1.75. Back issues: $1.75. Discounts: $1.50 per copy to distributors. 40pp; 5½X8½; photo/of. Reporting time: 6 weeks. Payment: in copies. Copyrighted. Pub's reviews: 1 in 1979. §Short fiction, novels, poetry, essays with some relationship to the Adirondacks. Ads: no ads. COSMEP.

Blues Press, Paul W. McAllister, PO Box 91, Kalamazoo, MI 49005. 1979. Poetry. "Interested in new poets." avg. press run 1,000. Pub'd 2 titles 1979. avg. price, paper: $3.00. Discounts: 40%. 32pp; 5½X8½; of. Reporting time: not accepting unsolicited manuscripts at the moment. Payment: varies.

Boa Editions, A Poulin Jr., 92 Park Avenue, Brockport, NY 14420, 716-637-3844. 1976. Poetry. "Generally not accepting unsolicited manuscripts. Major poets invited to select and introduce new poets. Contributors include: W. D. Snodgrass, Barton Sutter, M. L. Rosenthal, Barry Wallenstein, Anthony Piccione, Archibald MacLeish, Henry Miller, Bertrand Mathieu, Edward Byrne, John Ashbery." avg. press run 600-1,000 half in paper and half in cloth. Pub'd 6 titles 1979. avg. price, cloth: $7.95; paper: $4.00; other: $25.00-$35.00 signed. Discounts: 20 percent to subscribers; Bookstores: 40 percent; 20 percent for signed editions. 40-60pp; 6X9; of. Reporting time: 2-4 weeks. Payment: copies and negotiated royalty. Copyrights for author. COSMEP, NESPA, NYSSPA.

Boardwell - Kloner, J. B. Boardwell, 323 S Franklin, Room 804, Chicago, IL 60606, (312) 973-2816. 1978. Poetry, art. "Very few publications anticipated in near future, about 1 per year." avg. press run 1,000. Pub'd 1 title 1979. 1 title listed in the *Small Press Record of Books in Print* (9th Edition, 1980). avg. price, cloth: $7.00; paper: $3.50. Discounts: 40%. 60pp; 5½X8½; of. Reporting time: 1 month. Payment: negotiable. Copyrights for author.

Bobbi Enterprises, Mary Sharp, Matt Niemi, Rt 1, Box 44, Mt Iron, MN 55768, 735-8364. 1979.

THE BODY POLITIC- Gay Liberation Journal, Pink Triangle Press, The Body Politic Editorial Collective, Box 7289, Station A, Toronto, Ontario M5W1X9, Canada, 416-977-6320. 1971. Poetry, fiction, articles, art, photos, cartoons, interviews, criticism, reviews, letters, news items. "Required: material from people conversant with gay liberation politics and principles-able to translate those ideas into imaginative formats. Copyright owned by Pink Triangle Press; reprinting arranged by permission of author and PTP." circ. 10,000. 10/yr. Pub'd 10 issues 1979; expects 10 issues 1980. sub. price: $7.50 Canada $10.00 U.S.; per copy: $1.00 Canada & U.S.; sample: $1.00 Canada & U.S. Back issues: $1.00 Canada & U.S. Discounts: 30% trade. 44pp; 10¼X14; of. Reporting time: 1 month. Payment: no. Pub's reviews: 200 in 1979. §gay liberation, sexuality, sexual politics, homosexual themes. Ads: $275.00/$165.00/$0.20 personal, $0.60 business. CPPA.

BOGG, Bogg Publications, John Elsberg, USA Editor; George Cairncross, British Editor, 2010 N. 21st Street, Arlington, VA 22201. 1968. Poetry, fiction, articles, art, cartoons, interviews, satire, reviews, letters, news items. "U.K. Address: 31 Belle Vue ST., Filey , N. Yorks, UK YO14 9HU. Short fiction; mainly short reviews. The magazine puts out a series of free (for postage) pamphlets of poetry, prose, comics. The magazine is divided into roughly equal British and American sections." circ. 300. 3/yr. Pub'd 3 issues 1979; expects 3 issues 1980, 3 issues 1981. sub. price: £1; $4; per copy: 40p ($1.50). 45pp; size Quarto; of. Reporting time: immediate. Payment: copy of issue first time an author appears. Copyrighted, reverts to author. Pub's reviews: many in 1979. §small press publications, U.K. and U.S. Ads: negotiable.

Bogg Publications (see BOGG)

The Bold Strummer Ltd, Nicholas Clarke, Mary Clarke, 1 Webb Rd,, Westport, CT 06880, 203-226-8230. 1974. Cartoons, interviews, music. "The Bold Strummer is relatively new to publishing and our two latest books, *The Musical Instrument Collector* by R. Willcut and K. Ball; *An Introduction to Scientific Guitar Design* by D. Brosnac represent the biggest books we have yet done. Our three previous publications are less than 50 pages. The Bold Strummer also has a catalogue of 88 pages that goes to ten thousand guitarists." avg. press run 5000. Pub'd 2 titles 1979; expects 1 title 1980, 3 titles 1981. 2 titles listed in the *Small Press Record of Books in Print* (9th Edition, 1980). avg. price, paper: $8.95. Discounts: 40%, 20% to libraries. 130pp; of. Payment: royalty 10% of retail. Copyrights for author. NAMM.

Bolger Publishing (see ALTERNATIVE SOURCES of ENERGY MAGAZINE)

BOMBAY GIN, Anne Waldman, Larry Fagin, Reed Bye, Charlie Ross, c/o Naropa, 1111 Pearl Street, Boulder, CO 80302, 444-0202. 1975. Poetry, fiction. "Recent contributors: Phil Whalen, John Ashbery, Allen Ginsberg, Mike McClure, Robert Duncan, Mike Brownstein, Dick Gallup, Ted Berrigan,

Anne Waldman, etc." circ. 500+. 2/yr. Pub'd 2 issues 1979; expects 2 issues 1980, 2 issues 1981. sub. price: $5.00; per copy: $3.00; sample: $3.00. Back issues: $5.00. Discounts: 40% (standard). 75pp; 8X11½; †mi/of. Reporting time: 4-6 weeks. Copyrighted, reverts to author. CCLM.

Bon Mot Publications, David M. Kelley, Box 606, Manchester, NH 03105.

Bonanza, Inc., Roger Snowden, PO Box 971, Reno, NV 89504, (206) 322-4900. 1977. "How to, games, gambling, self improvement, 3M - 4M" avg. press run 5,000. Pub'd 1 title 1979; expects 2 titles 1980. avg. price, cloth: $10.00; paper: $6.00. Discounts: 1-4, 20%; 5-24, 40%; 25-49, 43%; 50-99, 46%; 100-199, 50%; 200 plus, 60%. 150pp; 5¼X8¼. Reporting time: 14 days. Payment: each piece negotiated. Copyrights for author.

‡**BONSAI, Bonsai Press,** Jan Streif, Frank Robinson, Associate Editor, 1350 E Bethany House, #1, Phoenix, AZ 85014. 1976. Poetry. "*Bonsai* invites all schools of poetry, including haiku, but the standard is high. Interested in essays on same subjects. Recent contributors: Jean Battlo, Ross Figgins, Sanford Goldstein, LeRoy Gorman, Gary Hotham, Elizabeth Searle Lamb, Geraldine Clinton Little, Frank K. Robinson, Raymond Roseliep, Felix Stefanile, Selma Stefanile, L.E. Ward." circ. 350. 2/yr. Expects 2 issues 1980, 4 issues 1981. sub. price: $4.00 USA & Canada (Other $5.00); per copy: $2.00. Back issues: $1.25 (when available). Discounts: Bookstore 35 percent. 48pp; 8½X5½; of. Reporting time: 2-6 weeks. Payment: none. Copyrighted, reverts to author. Pub's reviews. §Haiku, Poetry. Ads: $15.00/$9.00. CCLM.

Bonsai Press (see also BONSAI), Jan Streif, Editor; Frank Robinson, Associate Editor, 1350 E Bethany House, #1, Phoenix, AZ 85014. 1976. "Manuscripts not needed at this time." avg. press run 150. Pub'd 1 title 1979; expects 1 title 1980, 1 title 1981. 1 title listed in the *Small Press Record of Books in Print* (9th Edition, 1980). avg. price, paper: $2.75. 40pp; 8X5; of. Reporting time: 1 month. Payment: Unsettled. Copyrights for author.

BOOK ARTS, The Center For Book Arts, Mindell Dubansky, 15 Bleecker St, New York, NY 10012. 1975. Articles, art, photos, interviews, news items. "Articles/Interviews on: books, book sculptures-/art, bookbinding, the history of some aspect of books, book restoration, papermaking, printing, calligraphy, wood engraving etc." circ. 1,000. 4/yr. Expects 4 issues 1980. sub. price: $15.00. Back issues: Vol I out of print, Vol II $5.00. Discounts: sub agency: 15%; adv. discounts: 20% to rare bookdealers, galleries, art suppliers. 4-6pp; 8¼X10½; †lp, of. Reporting time: 3 mo. Payment: in copies. Copyrighted, reverts to author. Pub's reviews: 3 in 1979. §books/mags on books & their arts: bookbinding, calligraphy, fine printing, wood-engraving etc.

BOOK BUYER'S GUIDE/MARKETPLACE, Franklin Publishing Company, Kevin K. Kopec, PO Box 208, East Millstone, NJ 08873, 201-873-2156. 1975. Articles. "Advertisements, buying tips" circ. 10,000. 3/yr. Pub'd 4 issues 1979; expects 4 issues 1980. sub. price: $5.00; per copy: $1.25; sample: $1.00. Back issues: $1.00. Discounts: None, $5.00 annual subscription, $7.00 outside U.S.A. 20-32pp; 8½X11; of. Reporting time: 3 months. Copyrighted. Pub's reviews. §all areas. Ads: $90.00/$50.-00/$10.00 (50 word) $0.20 per word. COSMEP.

The Book Department, 236 Tower Avenue, Hartford, CT 06120, (203) 728-3470. 1979. "Prophetic or prophecy." avg. press run 500. Expects 1 title 1980, 2 titles 1981. avg. price, paper: $4.95. Discounts: 39% minimum 5 books. 96pp; 5¼X8¼; of.

BOOK EXCHANGE, Pamela A. Hartley, 9 Elizabeth Gardens, Sunbury-on-Thames, Middx TW16 S 9, United Kingdom, Sunbury 84855. 1948. Articles, photos, reviews, news items. circ. 3,000. 12/yr. Pub'd 3 issues 1979; expects 12 issues 1980. sub. price: £7.50, $17.50 (airmail $30.00) (European airmail £10.50); per copy: £0.75; sample: free. Back issues: not available at present time. Discounts: 10% for institutions and trade subs. agencies. 32pp; 8½X5½; of. Payment: negotiable. Copyrighted. Pub's reviews: 1,000 in 1979. §History, art, politics, fiction, science, religion, literature, childern's books, craft books, technical, art, philosophy. Ads: £60/£30/pro rata classified 7p per word; dealers 6p per line or 50¢.

THE BOOK-MART, Americana Books, David G. MacLean, PO Box 568, 3, St. Petersburg, FL 33731. 1977. Articles, photos, cartoons, interviews, reviews, letters, news items. "We would welcome exchange advertising and/or subscriptions." circ. 2,000. 12/yr. Pub'd 12 issues 1979; expects 12 issues 1980, 12 issues 1981. sub. price: 3rd class $7.50; 1st class $10.00; foreign on request; per copy: 75¢; sample: 75¢. Back issues: 75¢. Discounts: 10 or more per issue, 50%. 24pp; 8½X11; of. Reporting time: 1 month. Payment: $.50 column inch. Copyrighted, reverts to author. Pub's reviews: 26 in 1979. §Book collecting, bookselling, bibliography, notable authors, paper collectibles, price guides on the above. Ads: $35/$18/15¢/line.

Book Publishing Co., Matthew McClure, 156 Drakes Lane, Summertown, TN 38483, 615-964-3571.

1970. avg. press run 10,000. Pub'd 1 title 1979; expects 3 titles 1980, 3 titles 1981. 7 titles listed in the *Small Press Record of Books in Print* (9th Edition, 1980). avg. price, cloth: $12.50; paper: $3.50. Discounts: 40% off for over 5 copies. 160pp; 5X8; †of. Copyrights for author.

BOOK TALK, Carol A. Myers, 8632 Horacio Pl NE, Albuquerque, NM 87111, 505-299-8940. 1972. Articles, reviews. "300-1,000 words. All contributors actively engaged in a book-related field (editors, librarians, booksellers, publishers, authors (of books), etc.)" circ. 400. 5/yr. Pub'd 5 issues 1979; expects 5 issues 1980, 5 issues 1981. sub. price: $5.00; per copy: $1.00; sample: free. Back issues: $1.00 for existing issues, $2.00 for issues needing reproduction. 12pp; 8½X11; of. Reporting time: 1 month. Payment: none — all donated by subscribers or interested bookpeople. Not copyrighted. Pub's reviews: 120 in 1979. §Southwestern non-fiction (area defined as TX, NM, AZ, CA, UT, CO and OK). Ads: $50.00/$30.00.

The Bookery, Betty Doty, 8193 Riata Drive, Redding, CA 96002, (916) 365-8068. 1977. "Subject: marriage communication, inquiry first, SASE." avg. press run 5,000. Pub'd 1 title 1979. 1 title listed in the *Small Press Record of Books in Print* (9th Edition, 1980). avg. price, paper: $8.95. Discounts: Retailers: 40%; Wholesalers: 50%. 123pp; 7¼X9½; of. Reporting time: 2 weeks. Payment: 6%, report & pay on monthly sales. Copyrights for author. COSMEP, WIP.

BOOKLEGGER MAGAZINE AND BOOKS, Booklegger Press, Celeste West, Joanne Genet, 555 29th St., San Francisco, CA 94131. 1973. Articles, reviews. "Two areas of emphasis: guides to feminist media (*Women Make Movies, Words in Our Pocket*) and on women's health and sexuality (*Guide to Feminist Erotica*)." circ. 2M-4M. 1-2/yr. Pub'd 1 issue 1979; expects 1 issue 1980. sub. price: $5.00; per copy: $5.00; sample: $5.00. Back issues: $2.00. 64pp; 7X10; of. Reporting time: 1 mo. Payment: $25-$100. Copyrighted, reverts to author. Pub's reviews: 100+ in 1979. §hot and cold running wimmen. Ads: No ads. CCLM, COSMEP.

Booklegger Press (see also BOOKLEGGER MAGAZINE AND BOOKS), Celeste West, Editor, 555 29th St, San Francisco, CA 94131. 1972. Articles, art. avg. press run 4,000. Pub'd 1 title 1979; expects 1 title 1980. 3 titles listed in the *Small Press Record of Books in Print* (9th Edition, 1980). avg. price, cloth: $10.00; paper: $5.00. 160pp; 6X9; of. Reporting time: 1 month. Payment: 10% net receipts. Copyrights for author. COSMEP.

BOOKS & BOOKMEN, Sally Emerson, P.O. Box 294, 2 & 4 Old Pye Street, Victoria St., London SW1P2LR, United Kingdom, 01-222-3533. 1955. Articles, interviews, criticism, letters. "All work is commissioned. No unsolicited MSS please." circ. not disclosed. 12/yr. Pub'd 12 issues 1979; expects 12 issues 1980. sub. price: $27.60; per copy: $2.30; sample: free. Back issues: Twice current cover price if over 6 months old. Discounts: 10% publisher/agent. 68pp; 11X8½; lp. Payment: House scale or by arrangement. Copyrighted. Pub's reviews: 1,000 in 1979. §New books. Ads: $200.00/$120.-00/$0.10.

BOOKS IN CANADA: A National Review Of Books, Canadian Review of Books Ltd., D Marshall, Michael Smith, 366 Adelaide St East, Toronto, Ontario, Canada, 416-363-5426. 1971. Fiction, articles, art, photos, cartoons, interviews, satire, criticism, reviews, letters, parts-of-novels. circ. 40,000. 10/yr. Pub'd 10 issues 1979. sub. price: $9.95; sample: free. Back issues: $1.00. Discounts: 15% advertising agency commissions. 40pp; 7X11; of. Reporting time: 2 weeks. Payment varies. Copyrighted. Pub's reviews: 600 in 1979. §literature. Ads: $725/$480/$6/line class. CPPA, CBPC, ACP.

BOOKS OF THE SOUTHWEST, W. David Laird, Editor, Univ. of Az Library, A349 Main Library, U. of AZ, Tucson, AZ 85721. 1957. Reviews. circ. 500. 12/yr. Pub'd 12 issues 1979. sub. price: $4.00; per copy: $.50; sample: free. Back issues: $.50 per issue. 12pp; 5X8; of. Pub's reviews: 600 in 1979. §Anything Southwest.

The Bookstore Press, Gene Boyington, Gerry Hausman, Lorry Hausman, Lynne Wetherell, Box 191, RFD 1, Freeport, ME 04032, 207-865-6495. 1970. "We do not accept unsolicited mss. We have enough contracted books to publish for the next two years. We are distributed to the trade by The Benjamin & Matthew Book Company, Box 191 RFD 1, Freeport, Maine 04032; 2nd Cumberland Press, Main Street, Freeport, Maine 04032. Children's books and non-fiction." avg. press run 3,000. Pub'd 4 titles 1979; expects 4 titles 1980. 23 titles listed in the *Small Press Record of Books in Print* (9th Edition, 1980). avg. price, cloth: $6.00; paper: $2.95. Discounts: on request. of. Reporting time: 3 months. Copyrights for author. COSMEP.

Bookworm Publishing Company, Ronda Gaddie, Editor-In-Chief, P.O. Box 3037, Ontario, CA 91761, 714-983-8548. 1975. Non-fiction. "We publish books of interest in the fields of natural and social ecology, broadly defined. Current titles include '*Earthworms For Ecology And Profit*', '*Don't Call It Dirt!*', by Gordon Baker Lloyd, and '*Begonias For Beginners*' by Elda Haring. *House Plants and Crafts*

For Fun & Profit by Derek Fell, *Living Off the Country For Fun & Profit* by John L. Parker. Other titles cover the fields of vermology, gardening, and botany. We are looking for well-written how-to-do-it type books on any topic related to gardening & agriculture, including business, and family self-sufficiency." Pub'd 4 titles 1979; expects 10 titles 1980. 9 titles listed in the *Small Press Record of Books in Print* (9th Edition, 1980). avg. price, cloth: $9.95; paper: $4.95. Discounts: 1-4, 20 percent; 5-49, 40 percent; 50-149, 44 percent; additional discounts available. 200pp; 5½X8½. Reporting time: 6 weeks. Payment: royalty, 5% of revenue. Copyrights for author. BPASC, BPSC.

Borderland Sciences Research Foundation (see also JOURNAL OF BORDERLAND RESEARCH), Riley Hansard Crabb, P.O. Box 549, Vista, CA 92083, 724-2043. 1945. Articles, photos, reviews, news items. "We publish the transcribed lectures of the editor and research articles by him and the Associates on borderland subjects." avg. press run 200. Pub'd 4 titles 1979; expects 5 titles 1980, 5 titles 1981. avg. price, paper: $2.50. Discounts: 40% off list in catalogue on orders of $10 or more [net] to us, cash-with-order. No discount on subscriptions, borderland gadgets or lecture tapes. 40pp; 8½X11; †of. Reporting time: a few days. Payment: none. Does not copyright for author.

Borderline Press, 96 Halbeath Road, Dunfermline, Scotland. 1977. Poetry. "Publications: Tom Scott: *The Tree,* John Cornford: *A Memoir,* Alan Bold: *This Fine Day.*" avg. press run 1,500. Pub'd 1 title 1979; expects 2 titles 1980, 2 titles 1981. 2 titles listed in the *Small Press Record of Books in Print* (9th Edition, 1980). avg. price, paper: £2-50. Discounts: Trade/bulk 35%. Reporting time: various. Payment: various. Copyrights for author.

Borealis Press Limited, Frank Tierney, Glenn Clever, 9 Ashburn Drive, Ottawa K2E 6N4, Canada, (613) 224-6837. 1970. Poetry, fiction, criticism. "With few exceptions publish only material Canadian in authorship or orientation." avg. press run 1,000. Pub'd 20 titles 1979; expects 20 titles 1980, 20 titles 1981. avg. price, cloth: $15.00; paper: $5.00. Discounts: 40% to retail; 20% to jobbers. 100pp; 5¼X7¼; of. Reporting time: 4 months. Payment: 10% once yearly. Copyrights for author.

The Borgo Press (see also SCIENCE FICTION & FANTASY BOOK REVIEW), R. Reginald, Mary Burgess, Box 2845, San Bernardino, CA 92406, (714) 884-5813. 1975. Criticism. "Four-fifths of our line (80% of published titles) consists of *The Milford Series: Popular Writers of Today,* a series of 64-page literary critiques and interviews on the modern popular authors of our time; emphasis is on science fiction authors. Twenty percent of our line consists of serious literary or historical works aimed at the library and academic market." avg. press run 1,000. Pub'd 10 titles 1979; expects 15 titles 1980, 20 titles 1981. 54 titles listed in the *Small Press Record of Books in Print* (9th Edition, 1980). avg. price, cloth: $14.95; paper: $4.95; other: Milford Series: Cloth $8.95, Paper $2.95. Discounts: 20% for trade sales. 64-192pp; 5¼X8¼; of. Reporting time: 2 months minimum. Royalty ranges from 10-15%. No advances; we pay once annually. Copyrights for author.

BOSS, Boss Books, Reginald Gay, Box 370, Madison Square Station, New York, NY 10010. 1966. Poetry, fiction, articles, art, photos, interviews, criticism, reviews, parts-of-novels, plays. "*BOSS* 5, published in 1979, includes a revealing conversation between Taylor Mead and David Bourdon on the subject of Andy Warhol, with many Warhol illustrations; also a short story by James McCourt, essay on Pasolini's *Salo,* poetry by Sanguineti, Anne Waldman, John Wieners, Frank Lima. *BOSS* 6, due fall 1980 will feature a profusely illustrated interview with Charles Henri Ford on painter Tchelitchew, augmented by provocative excerpts from Ford's Diaries on the same painter." circ. 1,000. 2/yr. Pub'd 1 issue 1979; expects 1 issue 1980, 2 issues 1981. price per copy: $4.00 Indiv.; $7.00 Instit. Back issues: Prices variable. Discounts: trade/bulk/less 40%. 96pp; 6X9; of. Reporting time: 4-8 weeks. Payment: copies. Copyrighted, reverts to author. Pub's reviews. §Poetry, novels, art. CCLM, COSMEP.

Boss Books (see also BOSS), Reginald Gay, Box 370, Madison Square Station, New York, NY 10010. 1966. Poetry, fiction, art, cartoons, interviews, plays. "Particularly interested in looking at full-length book mss of poetry, but interested in a few sample pages first, possibly as first submission for *Boss* magazine." avg. press run 1000. Expects 1 title 1980, 2 titles 1981. 4 titles listed in the *Small Press Record of Books in Print* (9th Edition, 1980). avg. price, cloth: $7.95; paper: $5.95. Discounts: 40%/5+ copies. pp varies; 6X9; of. Reporting time: 2 months. Payment: usually flat fee, negotiable. Copyrights for author. COSMEP, CCLM.

Boston Critic, Inc. (see NEW BOSTON REVIEW)

BOTH SIDES NOW, Free People Press, Staff, 1232 Laura St., Jacksonville, FL 32206. 1969. Poetry, fiction, articles, art, photos, cartoons, interviews, satire, criticism, reviews, music, letters, news items, non-fiction. "An alternative journal of Aquarian/New Age transformations. Articles on current events and thinkpieces with emphasis on alternatives having implicit spiritual content. Unique spiritual/-

political synthesis with advocacy of 'New Age Politics,' nonviolence, pacifism, human rights & social justice. Sharing information on emerging New Age as examplified in alternative lifestyles, institutions, healing, economics, technology, and philosophy. Reprints of important material which deserves wider circulation. In 1980 switched from tabloid to magazine format. 1979 contributors included John Judge, Susan Gowan, Bonnie Barnes, Elihu Edelson, Peter Maurin, Martha Gold, Irv Thomas, Kriya, Peter Blum, and Staughton Lynd (authors); Leigh Anne Eagerton, Michael Dorian, and Fred Wright (art)." circ. 2,000. irregular. Pub'd 1 issue 1979; expects 6 issues 1980, 12 issues 1981. sub. price: 8 issues $2,4 issues each addl $1; per copy: $.30; sample: $.30. Back issues: Most available at reg. prices. Discounts: $10/100 plus postage. 16-24pp; 8⅛X10⅞; of. Reporting time: erratic. Payment: copies. Authors retain rights. Pub's reviews. §'New Age'u. Ads: $50.00/$25.00/$0.10/word, $3.00 (3½ col in); $2.00 (2⅛ col in). APS.

BOTTOMFISH MAGAZINE, Frank Berry, Pamela C. Nelson, Asst Editor; James Green Jr., Publ Coordinator, 21250 Stevens Crk., Cupertino, CA 95014, 408-996-4550. 1976. Poetry, fiction, parts-of-novels, long-poems, plays. "Adrianne Marcus, Daniel Langton, Adam David Miller, Thom Gunn, Jessica Hagedorn, Stephen Vincent, Paul Shuttleworth, Frank Cady, Wm. Dickey, Joseph Stroud." circ. 100. 1/yr. Expects 1 issue 1980. sub. price: free on request, donation of $1.50 requested; per copy: $1.50; sample: $1.50. Back issues: None available. Discounts: None, free to prisoners. Free on request to libraries, mags & individual writers. 50-70pp; 7X8½; †of. Reporting time: 2 months, (not operating during the summer). Payment: two copies of magazine. Copyrighted, reverts to author. Ads: none. CCLM, COSMEP.

BOUNDARY 2, William V. Spanos, State University of New York, Binghamton, NY 13901, (607) 798-2743. 1971. Poetry, fiction, articles, art, photos, interviews, criticism, reviews. "Frequent special issues, such as Vol. 4, no. 2: 'Martin Heidegger and Literature;' Vol 3, no. 3: 'The Oral Impulse in Contemporary American Poetry'; Robert Creeley: *A Gathering*. No length limit, although 35 pages is a good rule of thumb for upper limit. Criticism submitted should deal primarily with postmodern concerns. Recent contributors: Robert Bly, David Ignatow, Jerome Rothenberg, Diane Wakoski, David Antin, Nathaniel Tarn, Jerome Mazzaro, Joseph Riddel, Roy Harvey Pearce, Richard Palmer, Albert Hofstadter, George Economou, Robert Creeley, Denise Levertov." circ. 1,250. 3/yr. Pub'd 3 issues 1979; expects 3 issues 1980, 3 issues 1981. sub. price: Students, $10.00; Individuals, $13.00; Institutions, $20.00; per copy: $4.00; sample: $4.00. Back issues: $4.00. Discounts: 33⅓% to bookstores, etc. 300pp plus; 9X6; †of. Reporting time: 1-3 months. Payment: copies plus offprints. Publisher copyrights unless otherwise negotiated. Pub's reviews: 10 in 1979. §modern and contemporary literature, critical theory, film. Ads: $65/$40. CCLM, COSMEP.

Bourne Press (see SELF AND SOCIETY)

BOX 749, The Printable Arts Society, Inc., David Ferguson, Editor In Chief; P. Raymond Marunas, Art Editor; Thomas Garber, Music Editor; Mary Maud Ferguson, Lester Afflick, Brian Padol, Amy H. Gateff, Julia McCartney, Box 749, Old Chelsea Station, New York, NY 10011. 1972. Poetry, fiction, art, photos, cartoons, satire, music, parts-of-novels, long-poems, collages, plays. "*BOX 749* is a magazine of the printable arts—open to all kinds of writing, graphic art and music. We have no particular stylistic or ideological bias. We will consider—and have serialized—long fiction; we have published one-act plays and will consider plays that are full length. (We have also printed the first two poems, with art work, of a six-part broadside series.)" circ. 3,000. 1/yr. Expects 1 issue 1980, 1 issue 1981. sub. price: $7.00/4 issues; per copy: Vol 2, double issue, numbers 2&3, $2.50 ($3.25 mail); sample: $2.00 ($3.25 for mail orders). Back issues: $5 each ($5.75 for mail orders). Discounts: 4-issue subscription is $6 to libraries. No discounts for single copies. 100pp; 8½X11; of. Reporting time: 1-3 months. Payment: copies. Copyrighted, reverts to author. no ads. CCLM, COSMEP, NESPA.

BOXCAR, Mothra Press, Leslie Brody, PO Box 14337, San Francisco, CA 94114. 1977. Poetry, fiction, articles, photos, cartoons, satire, parts-of-novels, collages, plays. "Prefer short journals, short fiction, one-act plays. *Boxcar* wants to blur the distinction between fiction and travel. Some contributors: Laura Beausoleil, John Digby, Jenifer Shepherd." circ. 3000. quarterly. Pub'd 2 issues 1979; expects 4 issues 1980, 4 issues 1981. sub. price: $5.00; per copy: 50¢ + postage; sample: 50¢ + postage. Back issues: $1.00 plus postage. Discounts: will exchange with other mags. 8pp (tabloid); 17X11½; of. Reporting time: 2 months. Payment: none yet; soon. Copyrighted, reverts to author.

The Boxwood Press, Dr Ralph Buchsbaum, 183 Ocean View Blvd, Pacific Grove, CA 93950, 408-375-9110. 1952. "*Books:* science & natural history, misc." avg. press run 1,000. Pub'd 8 titles 1979; expects 8 titles 1980. avg. price, cloth: $10.00; paper: $4.95. Discounts: 20% on texts;/40% trade. 200pp; 5½X8½; of. Reporting time: 30 days. Payment: 10% royalty. Copyrights for author.

Boyd & Fraser Publishing Company, Jack Taylor, Frederick Mitchell, 3627 Sacramento St., San

Francisco, CA 94118, 415-346-0686. 1970. "Publish college level text books only." avg. press run 3,000 - 5,000. Pub'd 6 titles 1979; expects 10 titles 1980, 10 titles 1981. avg. price, cloth: $15.00; paper: $6.95. Discounts: Text short discount. 400pp; 6X9; of. Reporting time: as soon as possible. Payment varies. We own copyright.

Bradley David Associates, Ltd., Janet Scudder, Box 5279, 909 Third Avenue, New York, NY 10150, (212) 246-1114. 1978. Art, photos, cartoons, collages, news items. Expects 1 title 1980, 5 titles 1981. avg. price, paper: $2.50. Discounts: 50% wholesaler, 40% trade. 4¼X7; of. Reporting time: 1 year. Payment: Percentage after expenses (no advances). Copyrights for author.

Bradt Enterprises, George Bradt, 409 Beacon Street, Boston, MA 02115, (617) 536-5976. 1978. Articles, photos. "First person backpacking hikes, trips, in South America and 3rd world. Self-catering, North America much trekking material used. 2,000-4,000 words, with maps and photos. Must be concise and logical with natural history, geology, etc." avg. press run 5,000. Pub'd 2 titles 1979; expects 2 titles 1980, 2 titles 1981. avg. price, paper: $5.95. Discounts: 20%-60%. 130pp; 4½X7; of. Reporting time: 2 weeks. Payment: on agreement when material is accepted. COSMEP.

BRAIN/MIND BULLETIN, Interface Press, Marilyn Ferguson, P O Box 42211, Los Angeles, CA 90042. 1975. Articles, interviews, reviews, news items. circ. 7,000. 17/yr. Pub'd 24 issues 1979; expects 24 issues 1980, 17 issues 1981. sub. price: $15.00; per copy: $.75 (minimum of 2); sample: free. Back issues: $15 for 24 in sequence — otherwise $.75 each. Discounts: none except bulk classroom, inquire. 4pp; 8½X11; of. Payment: none. Copyrighted. Pub's reviews: 50+ in 1979. §Psychology, psychiatry, altered states of consciousness, learning, human potential, growth, etc. no ads.

BRAINWAIFS, Leslie A. Richardson, Arts Centre, Micrlegate, York, England, United Kingdom, 795219. 1977. Poetry. "Usually short poems, say 3-/40 lines. Local poets." circ. 250. 1/yr. Pub'd 1 issue 1979; expects 1 issue 1980, 1 issue 1981. price per copy: 50p; sample: 50p and postage. Back issues: none available. 60pp; †mi. Reporting time: 3 months. Payment: none. Not copyrighted.

BRANCHING OUT, Sharon Batt, Editor, Box 4098, Edmonton, Alberta T6E 4S8, Canada. 1973. Poetry, fiction, articles, art, photos, cartoons, interviews, satire, reviews. "Material by Canadian women writers only. We review unsolicited manuscripts from Canadian women only." circ. 4,000. 4/yr. Pub'd 4 issues 1979; expects 4 issues 1980, 4 issues 1981. sub. price: $6.00 Canada; $7.00 US; $8.00 anywhere else; $10.00 institutions ($11.00 & $12.00 outside of Canada); per copy: $1.75; sample: $1.75 in Canadian funds. Back issues: '73-'76 $1.75 each in Canadian funds. 48pp; 8½X11; of. Reporting time: 2-3 months. Payment: $5-20.00. Copyrighted, reverts to author. Pub's reviews: 30 in 1979. §We do not accept unsolicited book reviews. Ads: $220.00/$125.00/50¢. New Women's Magazine Society.

Brason-Sargar Publications, Sondra Anice Barnes, Publisher, PO Box 842, Reseda, CA 91335, (213) 851-1229. 1978. Poetry, art. "Must express psychological truths. Must use as few words as possible." avg. press run 1,000. Pub'd 1 title 1979; expects 1 title 1980, 1 title 1981. 1 title listed in the *Small Press Record of Books in Print* (9th Edition, 1980). avg. price, paper: $3.95. Discounts: 40% Bookstores, 50% Distributers, 25% Libraries. 84pp; 5½X8½; of. Reporting time: 30 days. Payment: To be negotiated. Copyrights for author.

Brattle Publications, Christine Anderson, 4 Brattle Street, Suite 306, Cambridge, MA 02138, (617) 661-7467. 1977. "We are publishing a series of books on job hunting throughout the U.S.A. The first, *The Job Hunter's Guide to Eight Great American Cities,* was published in June. A second title, *The Job Hunter's Guide to The Sunbelt,* will be published in early 1979" avg. press run 2,500. Expects 1 title 1980, 2 titles 1981. 3 titles listed in the *Small Press Record of Books in Print* (9th Edition, 1980). avg. price, other: $12.50 (8½ X 11). Discounts: 1 copy, 20%; 2 copies, 25%; 3 or more copies 30%. Add 5% to each discount for prepaid orders. 156pp; 8½X11; of. Copyrights for author.

BRAVO, King and Cowen (New York), Jose Garcia Villa, 1081 Trafalgar Street, Teaneck, NJ 07666, (201) 836-5922. 1980. Poetry. "Jose Garcia Villa, Editor, 780 Greenwich Street, New York, NY 10014. BRAVO believes that 1. poetry must have formal excellence; 2. poetry must be lyrical. Recent contributors: Hugh Connor, John Cowen, Gloria Guy, Robert King, George Wagner, Robert Levine" circ. 500. 2/yr. Expects 2 issues 1980. price per copy: $2.00. Discounts: 15%. 48pp; 6X9; of. Reporting time: 2 weeks to 1 month. Payment: none. Copyrighted, reverts to author. Ads: $150/$75. NYSSPA.

Breakwater Books Limited, 277 Duckworth Street, St. John's, Newfoundland A1C 1G9, Canada, (709) 722-6680. 1973. Poetry, fiction, photos, satire, parts-of-novels, plays. avg. press run 6,000. Pub'd 6 titles 1979; expects 12 titles 1980, 20 titles 1981. avg. price, cloth: $10.95; paper: $5.95. Discounts: Depends on quantity of order. 150pp; 5½X8; of. Reporting time: varies. Payment: confidential. Copyrights for author. ACP, APA, CBIC, CBA.

THE BREATH OF THE PEOPLE, Susan Moon, Zea Morvitz, Nancy Clement, 1631 Grant Street, Berkeley, CA 94703, 415-548-2208. 1977. Poetry, fiction, articles, art, cartoons, interviews, satire, reviews, letters. "Humor, by and for both children and adults." circ. 300. 3/yr. Pub'd 2 issues 1979; expects 3 issues 1980, 3 issues 1981. sub. price: $3.00; sample: free. 12pp; 11X17; of. Reporting time: 1 month. Copyrighted, reverts to author. COSMEP.

BREATHINGSPACE (see Watershed Intermedia)

Breitenbush Publications, Inc., James Anderson, Publisher & Executive Editor; James Mooney, Managing Editor, P.O. Box 02137, Portland, OR 97202. 1977. Poetry. "Length - open; Biases? We want to publish poetry that is wellwritten by poets who have published in magazines but who have been unable to publish in book form. Ex. Peter Sears, Mary Barnard, Naomi Shihab Nye." avg. press run 1,000. Pub'd 1 title 1979; expects 1 title 1980, 2 titles 1981. 4 titles listed in the *Small Press Record of Books in Print* (9th Edition, 1980). avg. price, cloth: $14.95; paper: $5.95. Discounts: Standard to bookstores. 75pp; 5½X8½; of. Reporting time: 3 months. Payment: Varies, depending upon author. Copyrights for author. PNWBPA.

BRIARPATCH, Briarpatch Press, Moreland Hogan, Box 2482, Davidson, NC 28036, (704) 892-7644. 1979. Poetry, fiction, articles. "A 'publisher's magazine' with a broader interest in private presses in the eastern part of the country, regional literature and history, and smallness and independence in general." circ. 1,000. 6/yr. Pub'd 5 issues 1979. sub. price: $7.50; per copy: $1.50. 32pp; 7½X11; of. Copyrighted, reverts to author.

Briarpatch Press (see also BRIARPATCH), Moreland Hogan, Box 2482, Davidson, NC 28036, (704) 892-7644. 1973. Poetry, fiction. avg. press run 250. Pub'd 4 titles 1979; expects 4 titles 1980, 4 titles 1981. avg. price, cloth: $15.00; paper: $4.00. Discounts: 1-4 copies, 20%; 5 or more, 40%. 32-64pp; size varies. Payment: varies. Copyrights for author.

BRIARPATCH REVIEW: A Journal of Right Livelihood and Simple Living, Portola Institute, Michael Phillips, Kristin Anundsen, 330 Ellis Street, San Francisco, CA 94102. 1973. circ. 2,000. 4/yr. sub. price: $5.00; per copy: $1.00; sample: $1.00. Discounts: 50%. 40pp; 8½X7; of. Pub's reviews. §business, living on less, simple living, sharing resources. Ads: we pay our advertisers $25.00 an ad.

BRICK: A Journal Of Reviews, Brick/Nairn, Stan Dragland, Jean McKay, Box 219, Ilderton, Ontario N0M 2AO, Canada, (519) 666-0283. 1976. Articles, criticism, reviews. "The review finds its own length. Experiment with form, according to what the book requires: consider, for instance, the visual. No book is unreviewable." circ. 500. 3/yr. Pub'd 3 issues 1979; expects 3 issues 1980. sub. price: $5.50, $15.00/3 yrs; per copy: $2.00; sample: $2.00. Back issues: *Brick* 1: $3.50 (some copies left). Discounts: see Brick/Nairn. 70pp; 8½X11; of. Reporting time: 21 days. Payment: one copy of the issue concerned. Copyrighted, reverts to author. Pub's reviews: 75 in 1979. §all. no ads.

Brick House Publishing, Co., Jack D. Howell, Publisher, 3 Main Street, Andover, MA 01810, (617) 475-9568. 1976. "Brick Publisher devoted to alternative life styles especially alternative energy. Also general trade books in consumer credited health, medicine and nutrition, leisure activities, how-to, and documentary studies of 'how men and women deal with the things of this world'. A informative young publishing company in solar energy." avg. press run 5,000. Pub'd 4 titles 1979; expects 8 titles 1980, 8 titles 1981. avg. price, cloth: $12.95; paper: $7.95. Discounts: Trade 40-46%; Jobber 40-50%. 280pp; 8½X11; lp. Reporting time: 1 month. Payment: Royalty paid 6 months from pub date. List royalty. Copyrights for author.

Brick/Nairn (see also BRICK: A Journal Of Reviews), Stan Dragland, Don McKay, Box 219, Ilderton, Ontario N0M 2AO, Canada, (519) 666-0283. 1972. Poetry, fiction. "Brick/Nairn isn't looking for unsolicited manuscripts." avg. press run 500. Expects 3 titles 1980. 11 titles listed in the *Small Press Record of Books in Print* (9th Edition, 1980). avg. price, paper: $2.50. Discounts: 40% trade, no other discount except 20% on 15 or more copies. 30pp; size varies; of/lp. Reporting time: 2 months. Payment: copies.

BRIDGE MAGAZINE, Asian American Perspectives Inc., Priscilla Chung, C.N. Lee, Merle Motooka, Bill Wong, N.T Yung, P.O. Box 477, New York, NY 10013, (212) 233-2154. 1971. Poetry, fiction, articles, art, photos, cartoons, interviews, criticism, reviews, letters, plays, parts-of-novels. "Contents: articles on social, political and cultural interest, regular features: news, dance, editorial, film, and book reviews, letters from the readers. Additional information: publish new writers as well as established. Some contributors: David Wand, Noam Chomsky, Diana Chang, Frank Chin, Frank Ching." circ. 5,000. 4/yr. Expects 4 issues 1980. sub. price: $5.00; per copy: $1.50; sample: free. Back issues: $1.50. Discounts: none. 55pp; 8½X11; of. Reporting time: if requested. Pub's reviews: 20 in 1979. §Asian Americans Related Issues. Ads: $300/$150.

"BRILLIANT CORNERS": A Magazine of The Arts, Art Lange, 7600 N Sheridan #104, Chicago, IL 60626, 312-761-3702. 1975. Poetry, fiction, articles, art, photos, cartoons, interviews, satire, criticism, reviews, music, letters, parts-of-novels, long-poems, collages, plays, concrete art. "The magazine prints large selection (10-20 pages) of poetry per poet. Essays & reviews 600-3,000 words. Recent contributors include: Ted Berrigan, Alice Notley, Richard Kostelanetz, Peter Kostakis, Frank O'Hara, Charles Henri Ford, Ned Rorem, Kenward Emslie, Tony Towle, Philip Whalen, Anthony Braxton, John Cage, Anselm Hollo, Fielding Dawson, Gunter Hampel, Jack Kerouac, Ron Padgett, Stan Brakhage, Studs Terkel. With this current issue, number 10, *Brilliant Corners* is temporarily suspending publication. *No new manuscripts are being considered, so please don't send any.* Nor are new subscriptions being accepted. Current subscriptions will be fulfilled with available back issues. Other inquiries about the availability of certain individual back issues (or the complete set) are welcome." circ. 500. sample price: $2.00 or 3 issues for $5.00. Back issues: Complete set (#1-10) costs $100.00. Discounts: 60-40 percent. 100pp; 8½X7; of. No new submissions are being considered at this time. Payment: 2 copies. Copyrighted, reverts to author. Pub's reviews: 4 in 1979. §poetry, fiction, music, painting, etc. CCLM.

THE BRITISH ALTERNATIVE PRESS INDEX, John L. Noyce, PO Box 450, Brighton, Sussex BN1 8GR, United Kingdom. 1976. "Subject index to articles in alternative magazine/periodicals published in Britain." circ. 3-500. Pub'd 4 issues 1979; expects 4 issues 1980, 4 issues 1981. sub. price: Indiv. $10.00, Libr. $15.00; sample: Indiv. $3.00, Libr. $5.00. Discounts: Trade: 10%. of. Copyrighted. Ads: Exchange ads welcome.

BRITISH BOOK NEWS, Gillian Dickinson, 65 Davies St., London W1Y 2AA, United Kingdom, 01-499-8011. 1940. Articles, reviews. circ. 9,000. 12/yr. sub. price: UK £12, overseas £15.60, US $36, Can $40. Discounts: 5% on 6-12 ads with 12 months. 100pp; 260mm x 185mm; of. Payment: £4 per review. Copyrighted. Pub's reviews: 3,000 in 1979. §most. Ads: £180/£95/£50.

BRITISH COLUMBIA HISTORICAL NEWS, Patricia E. Roy Dr., Terrance M. Eastwood, G.P.O. Box 1738, Victoria, BC V8W 2Y3, Canada, (604) 387-6671. 1968. Art, reviews, articles, photos. "Strictly relating to history of British Columbia." circ. 1,300. 4/yr. Pub'd 4 issues 1979. sub. price: $5.00 Indiv., $10.00 Instit.; per copy: $1.25; sample: $1.25. 40pp; 8½X11; of. Payment: none. Pub's reviews: 12 in 1979. §British Columbia history only.

BRITISH JOURNAL OF AESTHETICS, Oxford University Press, Dr. T.J. Diffey, The univ. of Sussex, Sch. of Cultural & Comm. Studies, Arts Building, Falmer, Brighton, Sussex BN1 9QN, United Kingdom. 1960. Articles, reviews, letters. "For ad rates write Oxford University Press, Oxford Journals, Press Road, Neasden, London NW10 60DD, United Kingdom." 4/yr. Pub'd 4 issues 1979; expects 4 issues 1980. sub. price: $25.00; per copy: $7.00; sample: free. 96pp; 234X155mm; of. Reporting time: normally 3 months. Payment: 20 free offprints. Copyrighted. Pub's reviews: 19 in 1979. §aesthetics, philosophy of art, theory of art, theory of art and literary criticism; reviews are commissioned; unsolicited reviews not accepted. Ads: rates available on request.

BRITISH JOURNAL OF IN-SERVICE EDUCATION, Studies in Education Ltd., Malcolm Lee, David Johnston, Bob Gough, British Journal of In-Service Education, Doncaster Metropolitan Institue of Higher Education, High Melton, Doncaster DN5 7SZ, United Kingdom. 1974. Articles, reviews, interviews, news items. "Prints articles on new development and practice of in-service education for teacher and other professional workers." circ. 2,000. 3/yr. sub. price: £3.50; per copy: £1.50; sample: £1.50. Back issues: as above. Discounts: 10% on ads. 80pp; 25cm x 18cm; of. Reporting time: 1 month. Payment: none. Ads: £50.

BRITISH NATURALISTS' ASSOCIATION (PUBLISHERS), Roger Tabor, 6 Chancery Place, The Green, Writtle, Essex, England CM1 3D4, United Kingdom, Chelmsford 420756. 1905. Articles. "Occasional publications in paperback form—prices 15p-80p—on all aspects of wild life. List on request." irregular. 11 titles listed in the *Small Press Record of Books in Print* (9th Edition, 1980). price per copy: 24p plus p.p. Discounts: 10% to booksellers. 16pp; 14X22; lp. Reporting time: varies. Payment: none. Copyrighted, reverts to author. §Natural history generally, also countryside topics generally.

British Science Fiction Assoc. Ltd. (see also VECTOR; MATRIX; FOCUS), Mike Dickinson, (Vector); John Harvey, (Matrix); Robert Holdstock, (Focus); Chris Evans, (Focus), 269 Wykeham Road, Reading RG6 1PL, United Kingdom, 0734-666142. 1958. Poetry, fiction, articles, art, photos, cartoons, interviews, satire, criticism, reviews, letters, news items. "Membership address: 18 Gordon Terrace, Blantyre G72 9NA, United Kingdom. *Vector* is the official journal of British SF Association.

Serious critical journal. Contibutions by many leading science fiction writers. *Matrix* is the 'club' magazine, and *Focus* is fiction plus information and articles aimed at the new writer." avg. press run 900. Pub'd 6 titles 1979; expects 6 titles 1980. 1 title listed in the *Small Press Record of Books in Print* (9th Edition, 1980). avg. price, paper: 75p. Discounts: 33⅓ to dealers. 32pp; size A4 (Matrix, Focus), A5 (Vector); of. Reporting time: 3-6 weeks. No payment. Copyrights for author.

BRITISH THEATRE INSTITUTE NEWSLETTER & REPORT, BTI, c/o 125 Markyate Road, Dagenham, Essex RM8 2LB, United Kingdom. 1974. Articles, reviews, interviews, criticism, news items. "To establish a theatre institute in the United Kingdom." 6/yr. sub. price: £12-50; per copy: £1. Back issues: 33⅓. Discounts: 33⅓%. 10pp; size A4. Payment: copies. Ads: £30.

BROADSHEET, Broadsheet Collective, P.O. Box 5799, Wellesley St. P.O., Auckland, New Zealand. 1972. Poetry, fiction, articles, art, photos, cartoons, interviews, satire, criticism, reviews, music, letters, news items. "New Zealand's only feminist magazine covering the women's movement. Comment on current events mainly in New Zealand, theoretical articles on feminism, fiction and poetry. Trying to get a mass of women as well as feminists so present attractively with good graphics and photos." circ. 3,500. 10/yr. Pub'd 10 issues 1979; expects 10 issues 1980. sub. price: $13.00 NZ Overseas/$9.50 NZ Inland; per copy: $.90 N.Z.; sample: $.90 N.Z. Back issues: complete set $20.00 N.Z. plus postage. Discounts: 10%. 40pp; 20½cm x 26½cm; of. Reporting time: 2 months. Payment: none. Pub's reviews: 27 in 1979. §women, feminism, abortion, women's art-culture, novels by women, poetry, children's books. Ads: $100.00/$55.00/$1.66.

Broadside Press (see THE BLACK POSITION)

Broken Whisker Studio, Joan H. Lee, PO Box 1303, (5D), Chicago, IL 60690. 1976. Poetry, fiction, art. "Short fiction, juveniles, poetry, miscellany (cards, poemcards, — whatever of interest). Limited edition paperbacks, some perfectbound. Offset printing is done outside; letterpress printing is done in-house. Contributors must use SASE." avg. press run 300 plus/minus. 7 titles listed in the *Small Press Record of Books in Print* (9th Edition, 1980). avg. price, paper: $3.50. Discounts: 40% booksellers on 5+ copies, 20% libraries. 64pp; †of/lp. Reporting time: 1 month. Payment: arrangement. copyrights by arrangement. COSMEP, CBC (Chicago Book Clinic).

Brown Rabbit Press, Helen Williams, V.T. Abercrombie, Box 19111, Houston, TX 77024, (713) 622-1844; 465-1168. 1979. Poetry. "Guide books, short fiction and prose poetry. We are a regional press publishing, so far, guide books, and anthologies by Texas writers." avg. press run 2,000-5,000. Pub'd 1 title 1979; expects 2 titles 1980, 2 titles 1981. avg. price, paper: $4.50-$6.00. Discounts: 40% to trade, 50% to jobber, 5% to book rep. 100-200pp; 5½X8; of. Reporting time: 3 months. Payment: 1 copy. Copyrights for author.

BROWNING SOCIETY NOTES, J Woolford, Fitzwilliam College, Cambridge, England, United Kingdom, 0223 458657, ext 63. 1970. Articles, reviews, criticism. "Articles should be about 10-15 double-spaced typed pages in length, though slightly longer acceptable if merit warrants, and shorter is often necessary if subject requires (we don't want extra padding to make articles longer than they need be.) Notes published. Reports of work in progress desired. Original bias was biographical, but at present we are running concurrent critical series, one on the poems of Elizabeth Barrett Browning, one Robert Browning's Asolando Volume, one on the *Parleyings* and one on textual matters. We hope to begin one on vocabulary studies in the near future.. This does not exclude continued interest in biographical, bibliographical and social material connected with these two poets. Persons wishing to act as reviewers should contact review editor, Dr. Ian Small, Univ. of Birmingham. Recent contributors: Philip Drew, W. David Shaw, James F. Loucks, Barbara Melchiori, Park Honan." circ. 250. 3/yr. Pub'd 3 issues 1979; expects 3 issues 1980. sub. price: £1.75/sub; £2/sub instit; per copy: £1. Back issues: £1.75 vol, 70p single copy. Discounts: 10 percent for advertising in series of 3 issues. 20 percent if camera-ready copy supplied. 20pp; 8X10; †lo. Reporting time: 1-3 wks. Payment: 1 copy of journal; offprints if available. Pub's reviews: 2 in 1979. §Robert and Elizabeth Barrett Browning: life, works, contemporaries. Ads: £30/£16.

Brux Am Books, B.F. Emmer, PO Box 4052, Clifton, NJ 07012, (201) 667-4895. 1979. "Published *Europe's Finest: Belgian Cooking Today* (a cookbook). Does not accept unsolicited mss. at this time." avg. press run 2,000. Pub'd 1 title 1979. avg. price, paper: $8.50. Discounts: varies. 256pp; 5½X8½; of. COSMEP.

BTI (see also BRITISH THEATRE INSTITUTE NEWSLETTER & REPORT), c/o 125 Markyate Road, Dagenham, Essex, England RM8 2LB, United Kingdom. Articles, reviews, interviews, criticism, news items. 10pp; size A4.

BUCKLE, Bernhard Frank, State Univ College/1300 Elmwood Av, English Dept., Buffalo, NY 14222,

716-886-7033. 1977. Poetry, art, photos, long-poems. "Excellence only criteria for poetry. Minority poetry (Black, Indian, Gay, Women's) welcome, but not propaganda. No xeroxes, carbons or multiple submissions, please. SASE required." circ. 1,000. 2/yr. Pub'd 2 issues 1979; expects 2 issues 1980, 2 issues 1981. sub. price: $1.50; per copy: $1.00; sample: $1.00. Back issues: $1.00. Discounts: 40% to bookstores. 50pp; 5½X8½; of. Reporting time: 2 wks. Payment: contributor copies. Copyrighted, reverts to author.

BUCKNELL REVIEW, Harry R. Garvin, Bucknell University, Lewisburg, PA 17837. 1941. Articles, criticism. "Each issue is devoted to a major theme or movement in humanities or sciences." 2/yr. Pub'd 2 issues 1979; expects 2 issues 1980, 2 issues 1981. sub. price: $18.00; per copy: $12.00; sample: $12.00. Back issues: $2.50. 185pp; 6X9. Reporting time: 4-8 weeks. Payment: 1 complimentary copy of issue, contributor may xerox the essay. Copyrighted. Ads: No ads.

Buddhist Text Translation Society (see also VAJRA BODHI SEA), Sino American Buddhist Assn., 1731 15th Street, Gold Mountain Monastery, San Francisco, CA 94103, 415-861-9672. 1968. Poetry, fiction, articles, art, photos, non-fiction. "The Buddhist Text Translation Society began publishing in 1972 with the goal of making the principles of Buddhist wisdom available to the American reader in a form that can be put directly into practice. BTTS translators are not only scholars but are practicing Buddhists who encounter every day the living meaning of the works they translate. Each translation is accompanied by a contemporary commentary. On the publishing list are standard Buddhist classics such as the *Shurangama Sutra,* the *Lotus Sutra,* and the *Vajra Sutra;* esoteric works such as the *Earth Store Bodhisattva Sutra* and the *Great Compassion Dharani Sutra;* books of informal instruction in meditation; and books, including fiction, that have grown out of the American Buddhist experience. Beginning in 1979 the Society will be publishing translations of Buddhist Scriptures bi-lingually (Chinese and English). Some of the works which are scheduled to be available this year bi-lingually include chapters from the *Avatamsaka Sutra, The Heart Sutra,* & *The Song of Enlightenment.* Extensive commentaries accompany each of these works in both languages. The Society also plans to publish works in other languages in the future. This year, 1980 the Society published two translation works into Spanish." avg. press run 4,000. Pub'd 10 titles 1979; expects 10 titles 1980, 10-15 titles 1981. 30 titles listed in the *Small Press Record of Books in Print* (9th Edition, 1980). avg. price, paper: $6.95. Discounts: on orders of one book, no discount; 2-4 books, 20 percent; 5-9 books, 30 percent; 40 percent thereafter; domestic only (overseas: maximum 30% on orders of ten or more). 200pp; 5½X8½; of. Payment: none-non profit org. Copyrights for author.

Bull Publishing Co., David C. Bull, P O Box 208, Palo Alto, CA 94302, 415-322-2855. 1974. "Texts in health sciences; books in nutrition and health and cancer patient education." avg. press run 7,000. Pub'd 3 titles 1979; expects 6 titles 1980, 6 titles 1981. 18 titles listed in the *Small Press Record of Books in Print* (9th Edition, 1980). avg. price, cloth: $7.00; paper: $5.00. Discounts: Trade: 1-3 30 percent, 4-9 40 percent, 10-49 42 percent, 50 plus 44 percent, jobber: 1-3 30 percent, 4 plus 50 percent, text 20 percent, bulk 10-49 10 percent 50 plus 20 percent. 200pp. Reporting time: 1 week. Copyrights for author. COSMEP.

BULLETIN OF HISPANIC STUDIES, Liverpool University Press, H.B. Hall, School Of Hispanic Studies, The University, PO Box 147, Liverpool L69 3BX, United Kingdom. 1923. Articles, reviews. "Specialist articles on the language and literatures of Spain, Portugal and Latin America, in English, Spanish, Portuguese and Catalan." circ. 1,000. 4/yr. sub. price: Inland (UK & Eire) indiv. £9; instit. £12.50; overseas indiv. £10/US $21; instit. £15/US $32; per copy: £3. Discounts: as before. 380pp. No payment. Pub's reviews.

BULLETIN OF THE BOARD OF CELTIC STUDIES, University Of Wales Press, D. Ellis Evans, J. Beverley Smith, R. G. Livens, Univ. of Wales Press, 6 Gwennyth Street, Cathays, Cardiff CF2 4YD, United Kingdom. Articles. "Articles on Language and Literature, History and Law, Archealogy and Art." circ. 450. 2 parts/yr. Pub'd 2 issues 1979; expects 2 issues 1980, 2 issues 1981. sub. price: £4 per annum; per copy: £2. Discounts: 33⅓ %. 187pp; lp.

THE BULWER LYTTON CHRONICLE, High Orchard Press, Howard Cooper-Brown, Eric Ford, High Orchard, 125 Markyate Rd, Dagenham, Essex RM8 2LB, United Kingdom. 1973. Poetry, articles, art, photos, cartoons, interviews, satire, criticism, reviews, music, letters, plays, news items. "Dissemination of works, life, times, contemporaries, influences on and from, upon and about Bulwer Lytton and his family. Bulwer Lytton British Author (1803-1873) Statesman, Dramatist and Poet." circ. 100. 1/yr. sub. price: £2; per copy: £1; sample: £1. Back issues: bulk issues 20% list. Discounts: 20%. 40pp; size A5; of/dupl. Reporting time: 6 mos. Payment: copies. Copyrighted. Pub's reviews. Ads: £15/pro rata. COSMEP.

Burning Deck Press, Keith Waldrop, Rosmarie Waldrop, 71 Elmgrove Ave., Providence, RI 02906.

1962. Poetry. "Submissions by invitation." avg. press run 350-1,000. Pub'd 8 titles 1979. 67 titles listed in the *Small Press Record of Books in Print* (9th Edition, 1980). avg. price, cloth: $12.50; paper: $3.50; other: $2.50. Discounts: 1 copy net; 2-4, 30%; 5, 40%. 20-80pp; 6X9; †lp. Submissions by invitation. Payment: 10% of edition (copies).

BUZZ, Peter Meadows, Publishing Editor; Susan Fry, Art Editor; Lindsay Tuffin, Editor; Chris Gander, Art Director, 51 Haydons Road, South Wimbledon, London SW19 1HG, United Kingdom, 01-542 7661. Articles, poetry, art, cartoons, photos, satire, reviews, news items, interviews, criticism, music, letters. 12/yr. sub. price: £3.54 ($7.00 surface, $12.00 air); per copy: 40p. Discounts: over 25 copies 17p each post free, over 20 copies 30p. 40pp; size A4; of. Ads: 22p a word, £4 minimum.

Byron Press, John Lucas, Allan Rodway, George Parfitt, The English Dept., Univ. Park, Nottingham, United Kingdom. Poetry. Discounts: 33% trade. lp.

C

C.S.P. WORLD NEWS, Edition Stencil, Guy F. Claude Hamel, Editor & Publisher, P.O. Box 2608, Station D. Ottawa K1P5W7, Canada, (613) 741-8675. 1962. Poetry, satire, reviews. "Recent Contributors: Hundreds of poets. Best Book of the Year (1977) Contest: Wm. B. Eerdmans, publishers; Poet of the Year (1977) Teresa Peirinska, televised series *Poetry Ottawa* by Hamel Theatre Productions. C.S.P. World News Poet of the Year: 1975, Alexandre L. Amprimoz, Winnipeg, Man.; 1976, Lynda Rostad, Toronto, Ont.; 1977, Teresinka Pereira, Boulder, CO.; 1978, Sheila Sommer, Toronto, Ont.; 1979, Marilyn Carmen, Mechanicsburg, PA.; Book of the Year Contest Winners: 1977, Wm. B. Eerdmans, Grand Rapids, MI.; 1978, Rasheed Mohammed, New York, NY. Poet of the Year 1980: Bluebell S. Phillips, Dorval, P. Que." circ. 2,000. 12/yr. Pub'd 12 issues 1979. sub. price: $10.00; per copy: $1.00; sample: $1.00. Back issues: $1 per copy. Discounts: 10%. 12pp; 8X14; †of. Reporting time: 2 weeks. Payment: $1 per typewritten page. Copyrighted. Pub's reviews: 312 in 1979. §all types books and LP's and tapes. Ads: $25/$15/$.02.

The Cabbagehead Press, John L. Risseeuw, 214 E Main Street, Vermillion, SD 57069, (605) 624-8828. 1972. Poetry, art, plays, concrete art. "The Cabbagehead Press is a private press dealing in limited edition works of fine printing utilizing letterpress (handset and hand printed on a Vandercook proof press) and other printmaking techniques for the production of books, broadsides, and prints as works of fine art. We have small production, limited funds, and do not consider unsolicited manuscripts of any kind." avg. press run 25-50. Pub'd 5 titles 1979; expects 12 titles 1980. 3 titles listed in the *Small Press Record of Books in Print* (9th Edition, 1980). avg. price, paper: $10; other: $15-$30. Discounts: none as yet. 24-32pp; 7X9; †lp. Payment: individual. Copyrights for author. CBA (Center for Book Arts), STA (Society of Typographic Arts).

Cadenza Press (Tadpole Press), Theodora M. Link, 3922 Arthur Street, N.E., Columbia Heights, MN 55421, (612) 788-0455. 1978. "Only 2 pieces have been published so far: *With Typewriter and T-Square: Guide for the Novice Editor* deals with producing a newsletter and has step-by-step instructions for setting up budget, staff, goals, how to distribute, mailing instructions, etc. Illustrated. Paperback, spiral binding...$2.50 (55 pages) 5½ x 8½. *Melissa's Morning* Children's Color-It-Yourself Book. Text is in poetry, large illustrations, 11 pages, paperback, $1.50, 8½ x 11. Both written by Theodora M. Link; both have been copyrighted." Expects 2 titles 1980, 3 titles 1981. 2 titles listed in the *Small Press Record of Books in Print* (9th Edition, 1980). avg. price, paper: $2.00. 50pp; 5½X8½; of.

CADERNOS DO TERCEIRO MUNDO, Tricontinental Editora Ltda., Neiva Moreira, Editor-in-Chief; Altair L. Campos, Editor, Calcada de Combro 10-1, Lisbon 1200, Portugal. 1978. Articles, photos, cartoons, interviews, news items, letters. "'A magazine on the Third World made by Third World journalists.' The Portuguese edition of *Cuadernos del Tercer Mundo,* an international magazine published in three languages (Spanish, English and Portuguese) by an independent, nonprofit association of militant professional journalists from over 40 countries. It basically aims to provide alternative information on the Third World, promote awareness on the causes of underdevelopment and the means to overcome it, and support cooperation among progressive sectors throughtout the world. It circulates mainly in Portuguese-speaking African countries and Brazil." circ. 45,000. 12/yr. Pub'd 9 issues 1979; expects 10 issues 1980. sub. price: $17.00; per copy: $1.50; sample: free. Back issues: $2.00 (prices apply throughout the world, including air mail). Discounts: 40%. 128pp; 6X9; of. Reporting time: 2 weeks. Payment: occasional. Copyrighted. Ads: $750.00/$375.00.

Cadmus Editions, Jeffrey Miller, PO Box 4725, Santa Barbara, CA 93103. 1979. Poetry, fiction, letters, parts-of-novels. "Recent Contributors: Gavin Lambert, Paul Bowles, Mohamed Choukri, Tom Clark, Clayton Eshleman, William Burroughs, Kenneth Rexroth." avg. press run 1,500. Pub'd 1 title 1979; expects 4 titles 1980, 5 titles 1981. 2 titles listed in the *Small Press Record of Books in Print* (9th Edition, 1980). avg. price, paper: $5.00; other: $15.00 signed/ltd. Discounts: 1-4 copies, 20%; 5-49 copies, 40%; 50-99 copies, 42%; 100 or more 45%. Terms to qualified wholesalers upon request. 90pp; 5X8; lp, of. Reporting time: 30 days. Payment: 10% paid semi-annually. Copyrights for author.

CAFE SOLO, Solo Press, Glenna Luschei, Publisher, 7975 San Marcos, Atascadero, CA 93422. 1969. Poetry, fiction, articles, art, photos, interviews, criticism, letters, collages, concrete art. "We have closed out the old *Cafe Solo* with issue 10. Our second series is now available. One/two & 2/3 are a double issues of graphics, photography and poetry. Regrettably, new material will be accepted on a request basis only. We are working towards an English-Spanish quarterly." circ. 750. Pub'd 1 issue 1979. sub. price: $7.00; per copy: $5.00; sample: $2.00. Back issues: $2.00 (6, 7 and 9). Discounts: 40% orders over 5. 44pp; 8X11; of. Copyrighted, reverts to author. Pub's reviews: 4 in 1979. §Spanish literature. CCLM, COSMEP.

CAFETERIA, Rick Robbins, Gordon Preston, PO Box 4104, Modesto, CA 95352. 1970. Poetry, articles, reviews, letters. "Recent Contributors: Douglas Blazek, Stuart Dybek, Colette Inez, Thomas Johnson, Marina Rivera, Dennis Saleh, Peter Wild. Secondary address: PO Box 8781, Missoula, MT 59807." circ. 300+. 1-2/yr. Pub'd 1 issue 1979; expects 1 issue 1980. sub. price: $3.00/yr; per copy: $1.50; sample: free if back copies available. Back issues: $1.50 if available. Discounts: none. 60-80pp; 6X9; of. Reporting time: soon. Payment: copies. Copyrighted, does not revert to author. Pub's reviews. §books of poetry & little magazines. Ads: none. CCLM.

CAHIER, Jozef Peeters, Lobergenbos 27, B 3200 Leuven, Belgium. 1970. Fiction, articles, art, photos, criticism, reviews. "Focus: science fiction, horror, fantasy, mystery and detection novels in The Netherlands and Belgium. Articles devoted to the Flemish writer Jean Ray-John Flanders. Languages used in text: Dutch, French, English." circ. 600. 1/yr. Pub'd 1 issue 1979. 100pp. Copyrighted. Pub's reviews: 50 in 1979. §Science fiction, horror, fantasy.

Calamus Books, Larry Mitchell, Box 689, Cooper Station, New York, NY 10003. 1977. Poetry, fiction, photos, interviews, plays. "We publish only works by or about lesbians & gay men. We are concerned that the material be politically progressive." avg. press run 2,000. Pub'd 2 titles 1979; expects 3 titles 1980, 4 titles 1981. 1 title listed in the *Small Press Record of Books in Print* (9th Edition, 1980). avg. price, cloth: $10.00; paper: $5.00. Discounts: 40% bookstores, 20% college bookstores. 100pp; of. Reporting time: 2 months. Payment: negotiable. Copyrights for author.

CALIBAN: A Journal of New World Thought & Writing, Roberto Marquez, Box 797, Amherst, MA 01002. 1975. Poetry, fiction, articles, art, interviews, criticism, parts-of-novels. circ. 500-600. 2/yr. Pub'd 2 issues 1979; expects 2 issues 1980. sub. price: $5.00; per copy: $2.50; sample: $2.50. Back issues: $3.00. Discounts: Bookstore rate $1.75 per issue. 94-100pp; 6X9; lp. Reporting time: 4 weeks usually. Payment: copies of issue in which piece appears. Copyrighted, reverts to author. Ads: $100.-00/$50.00. CCLM.

California Contemporary Craftspeople Publications, Dea Rackley, Louise Caraco, 1560 Beverly Place, Berkeley, CA 94706, (415) 525-5254. 1978. Photos, interviews. "PO Box 836, Carmel Valley, CA 93924. This is a annual biography of craftspeople." avg. press run 10,000. Pub'd 1 title 1979; expects 2 titles 1980. avg. price, paper: $5.95. Discounts: 40% wholesalers, 55% jobbers. 188pp; 8X10; †lp. COSMEP, AAPN.

California Living Books (Examiner Special Projects), Hal Silverman, Director; Janet Leonard, Managing Editor, 223 Hearst Building, Third & Market Streets, San Francisco, CA 94103, (415) 543-5981. 1975. Fiction, articles, art, photos, cartoons, music. "Some of our California Living Books are regional in appeal; others are of national or international interest. They all stem from the west coast experience, highlighting its unique quality of life in their texts, photographs and illustrations." avg. press run 10,000. Pub'd 6 titles 1979; expects 6 titles 1980, 12 titles 1981. avg. price, cloth: $17.50; paper: $7.95. Discounts: 1-4, 20%; 5-24, 40%; 25-49, 41%; 5-99, 42%; 100-249, 43%; 250 or more, 45%. 150pp; 8½X11; of. Reporting time: 1 month more or less. Payment: Flexible, usually 6-10% royalties with $500.00-$1,000.00 advance. Copyrights for author. NCBPA, WPA.

THE CALIFORNIA QUARTERLY, Elliot Gilbert, Sandra Gilbert, Diane Johnson, 100 Sproul Hall, Univ of Calif, Davis, CA 95616. 1971. Poetry, fiction, art, photos, interviews, parts-of-novels, long-poems. "Stories should not exceed 5,000 words, though we make exceptions. We like 'California material' however you care to define that, but don't insist on it. We publish whatever we think is good and recommend that authors glance at past issues. Recent contributors include Charles Simic, Robert

Kelly, Karl Shapiro, James Bertolino, Marjorie Grene, Jerry Bumpus, Sandra Gilbert, Rosellen Brown, Ann Stanford, Joyce Carol Oates, Ruth Stone, Flossie Lewis." circ. 600. 2-4/yr. Pub'd 1 dbl issues 1979; expects 1 dbl, 1 single issues 1980. sub. price: $5.00; per copy: $1.50; sample: $1.50. Back issues: #1 $2.00; #2-10 $1.50; #11-12 & #13-14 $2.50. 83pp; 8½X5½; lp. Reporting time: 6 weeks to 2 months. Payment: $3/page poetry & graphics; $2/page prose. Copyrighted, reverts to author. Ads: $40 page/$25 1/2. CCLM, COSMEP.

California Street, Ariel Fragment, Managing Editor, 723 Dwight Way, Berkeley, CA 94710, (415) 548-8273. 1974. Poetry, fiction, photos, cartoons, interviews, satire. "Standard varies from project to project" avg. press run 3,000. Pub'd 3 titles 1979; expects 3 titles 1980. 6 titles listed in the *Small Press Record of Books in Print* (9th Edition, 1980). avg. price, paper: $6.95. Discounts: 20% for school, library; other rates standard. 96pp; 7X9; †of. Reporting time: We do not accept submissions of any kind. Payment: 5-10%, advance equal to roylty on first printing. Copyrights for author.

California Tomorrow (see CRY CALIFORNIA)

THE CALL/EL CLARIN, Call Publications, Dan Burstein, Box 5597, Chicago, IL 60680. 1972. News items. "Published weekly with a section in Spanish." circ. 20,000. 50/yr. Pub'd 50 issues 1979; expects 50 issues 1980. sub. price: $12.00; per copy: $.25; sample: free. Discounts: bulk discount-40% off. 28pp; 11¼X14½; lp/of. Pub's reviews: 11 in 1979. §politics/international news/mass movements. Ads: $5.00 per col inch.

Call Publications (see also THE CALL/EL CLARIN), Box 5597, Chicago, IL 60680. 8 titles listed in the *Small Press Record of Books in Print* (9th Edition, 1980).

CALLALOO, Charles H. Rowell, Editor-in-Chief; Tom Dent, Co-Editor; Jerry W. Ward Jr., Co-Editor, Department of English, University of Kentucky, Lexington, KY 40506, (606) 257-2614. 1976. Poetry, fiction, articles, art, photos, interviews, criticism, reviews, parts-of-novels, plays, news items. "Short one act plays" circ. 450. 3/yr. Expects 3 issues 1980, 3 issues 1981. sub. price: $6.00/yr; per copy: $3.00. 140pp; 5½X8½; of. Reporting time: 1 month. Payment: 2 copies. Copyrighted, reverts to author. Pub's reviews: 10 in 1979. §Creative literature by Black writers and critical works about Black literature. Ads: $100.00/$50.00.

CALLIOPE, Ampersand Press, Martha Christina, Editor, Creative Writing Program, Roger Williams College, Bristol, RI 02809. 1977. Poetry, fiction, art, photos, interviews, reviews, parts-of-novels, long-poems, plays. "Interested in good new writers as well as established ones. We are open to a wide variety of form and content but look for work that shows a good knowledge of craft. Some recent contributors: Jim Hall, George E. Murphy Jr., Lucien Stryk, James Bertolino, Ted Kooser, Joan Colby." circ. 400. 2/yr. Pub'd 2 issues 1979; expects 2 issues 1980, 2 issues 1981. sub. price: $1.50; per copy: $1.00; sample: $1.00. Back issues: Vol 1 & Vol 2/1 unavailable; others $1.00 while they last. Discounts: 40% bookstores. 40pp; 5½X8½; of. Reporting time: immediately to 3 months. Payment: 2 copies. Copyrighted, reverts to author. Pub's reviews: 18 in 1979. §Little magazines. CCLM, COSMEP.

Calliope Press (see also THE PAWN REVIEW), 1162 Lincoln Ave #227, Walnut Creek, CA 94596. 1977. Poetry, long-poems. "Chapbooks by contemporary authors who have not previously published a book of poems; *Waiting For Water* by Si Dunn (1977); *Poems* by James P. White (1978); *The Heart's Geographer* by Janet Samuelson (1979). *Sleepyhead* by Stephen Harrigan (1979)." avg. press run 400. Pub'd 1 title 1979; expects 1 title 1980, 1 title 1981. 1 title listed in the *Small Press Record of Books in Print* (9th Edition, 1980). avg. price, paper: $3.00. Discounts: Trade bookstores (on consignment): 40%; University bookstores, 5-19, 25%; 20-49, 30%; 50+, 40% plus shipping via Insured library rate or better, no returns. 36pp; 5½X8½; of. Reporting time: query first. Payment: 10% of print run. Copyrights for author. COSMEP, COSMEP/South, Texas Circuit.

Calliope Publishing Inc. (see also PAID MY DUES: JOURNAL OF WOMEN AND MUSIC), Karen Corti, Kathryn Gohl, P.O. Box 6517, Chicago, IL 60680, (312) 929-5592. 1974. Articles, art, photos, cartoons, interviews, criticism, reviews, music, letters, news items. "We have a definite feminist perspective." avg. press run 2,500. Pub'd 4 titles 1979; expects 3 titles 1980, 3 titles 1981. avg. price, paper: $2.50; other: $2.25; $10.00 yearly subscription; $11.50 Canada & Mexico, $13.00 elsewhere; $15.00 institutions. Discounts: 30% on bulk orders of 5 or more; 20% to subscription services for institutions. 44pp; 8X11; of. Reporting time: 3 months. Payment: $5.00-$10.00 per thousand words for articles; no payment is made for music printed; $4.00 per shoto used. Copyrights for author.

Calliopea Press, Carol Denison, 701 Longstaff, Missoula, MT 59801, 406-549-6945. 1976. Poetry, fiction, art, parts-of-novels, long-poems, plays. "1976. David Ernst. Poetry, *Windy Road, Narrow Bridges* 4 vo. 40 pgs. Handmade paper. Illustrated by Deborah Padrick. $10.00 hardbound. (out of print) 1977. Lynn Watson. Fiction, *Rehearse & The Grandmother Story.* 4 vo. 14 pgs. Hardbound $3.50; softbound $2.00. 300 copies, 1978. Fox, Siv Cedering. Poetry broadsides (Poemfolio). *Color Poems* 27 broadsides in a portfolio, illustrated by 16 artists from four countries. $25.00. 500 copies." avg. press run 300-500. Pub'd 5 titles 1979. 1 title listed in the *Small Press Record of Books in Print* (9th Edition, 1980). avg. price, cloth: varies; paper: varies. Discounts: 35 percent to bookstores or by special arrangements. pp varies depending on book; size varies; †lp. Reporting time: 3 months. Payment: individual arrangements with each author. Copyrights for author. COSMEP.

CALYX: A Journal of Art and Literature by Women, Linda Morgan, Karen Ratte, Vickie Shuck, Val Eames, Barbara Baldwin, Margarita Donnelly, Meredith Jenkins, PO Box B, Corvallis, OR 97330, 503-753-9384. 1975. Poetry, fiction, art, photos, criticism, parts-of-novels. "Prose no more than 5,000 words. Poetry. Art work suitable for reproduction in black and white. Submit 35 mm slides or 8 x 10 black and white glossy photo. *Calyx* is a journal of art and literature by women. Recent contibutors publihed: Olga Broumas, Sharon Olds, Marge Piercy, Ingrid Wendt, Carol Jane Bangs, Betty La Duke, Myrna Shiras, Eleanor Wilner." circ. 1,000 subscribers-100 bookstores. 3/yr. Pub'd 3 issues 1979; expects 3 issues 1980. sub. price: $10.00; per copy: $3.50 + postage; sample: $3.50 + postage. Back issues: limited supply, please inquire. Discounts: Trade 40 percent, we do our own distribution. 64pp; 8X7; of. Reporting time: 8-10 weeks. Payment: free copy to each contributor accepted. Copyrighted, reverts to author. Ads: none. CCLM.

Camas Press (see THE ARCHER)

CAMBRIC POETRY PROJECT, Cambric Press, Joel Rudinger, 912 Strowbridge Drive, Huron, OH 44839, 419-433-4221. 1978. Poetry, art, long-poems. "query w/SASE first" circ. varies. annual. Expects 1 issue 1980, 1 issue 1981. sub. price: $6.95; per copy: $6.95; sample: $6.95. Back issues: $6.95, when there are back issues. Discounts: 40%, 3 or more copies. 80-120pp; 7¼X4½; of. Reporting time: 2 weeks. Payment: co-op sharing. Copyrighted. §Good poetry, any length, any style; no doggeral.

Cambric Press (see also FIRELANDS ARTS REVIEW; CAMBRIC POETRY PROJECT), Joel Rudinger, Publisher, 912 Strowbridge Dr., Huron, OH 44839, 419-433-4221. 1975. avg. press run 1,000. Pub'd 2 titles 1979; expects 3 titles 1980. 7 titles listed in the *Small Press Record of Books in Print* (9th Edition, 1980). avg. price, paper: $3.00. Discounts: 30 percent on bulk orders over 10;. 80pp; 5½X8½; of. Reporting time: 4-8 weeks. Payment: FIRELANDS ARTS REVIEW copies only. Copyrights for author.

CAMERA OBSCURA: A Journal of Feminism and Film Theory, Janet Bergstrom, Elisabeth Lyon, Constance Penley, PO Box 4517, Berkeley, CA 94704. 1976. Articles, photos, interviews, criticism, reviews, letters. circ. 3,000. 3/yr. Pub'd 3 issues 1979; expects 3 issues 1980. sub. price: $9.00 Indiv.; $18.00 Instit.; per copy: $3.00; sample: $3.00. Back issues: $3.00. Discounts: 30% bookstores. 150pp; 5½X8½; of. Reporting time: 2 weeks. Payment: Possibly in the fiscal year 1979-80. Copyrighted, does not revert to author. Pub's reviews: 4 in 1979. §Film, feminist theory, political theory, psychoanalysis, photography. Ads: $200.00/$100.00.

Camera Work Gallery, Les Sattinger, Deborah Cowder, PO Box 32, Frostburg, MD 21532, (301) 689-5666. 1978. Poetry, photos. "Camera Work Gallery was conceived for the purpose of self-publication. The editors are also the authors." avg. press run 500. Expects 1 title 1980. avg. price, paper: $6.50. Discounts: Trade: 40%. 65pp; 8X9; †of. Payment: Indefinite at present time.

Campanile Press (see PACIFIC POETRY AND FICTION REVIEW)

Canada Publishing Co. (see also ART & LITERARY DIGEST), Roy Cadwell, Tweed, Ont K0K 3J0, Canada. 1969. 1 title listed in the *Small Press Record of Books in Print* (9th Edition, 1980).

CANADIAN AUTHOR & BOOKMAN, 24 Ryerson Ave, Toronto, Ontario M5T 2P3, Canada, (416) 868-6916. 1921. Poetry, articles, criticism, reviews. "Want Canadian literary doings-writing craft articles from any writer." circ. 5,000. 4/yr. Pub'd 4 issues 1979; expects 4 issues 1980. sub. price: $6.00; per copy: $1.50; sample: $1.00. Back issues: $1.50. Discounts: 15 percent. 32pp; 8½X11; of. Reporting time: up to 2 months. Payment: 1 cent a word and up. Copyrighted. Pub's reviews: 50 in 1979. §all areas. Ads: $180.00/$110.00/$0.25 word.

CANADIAN CHILDREN'S LITERATURE, Mary Rubio, Elizabeth Waterston, P.O. Box 335, Guelph, Ontario N1H 6K5, Canada. 1975. Articles, interviews, criticism, reviews. "CCL publishes critical articles and in-depth reviews of books written for Canadian children and adolescents." circ. 1,500. 4/yr. Pub'd 4 issues 1979. 2 titles listed in the *Small Press Record of Books in Print* (9th Edition, 1980). sub. price: $11.00 (plus $2.00 postage outside Canada); per copy: $3.50; sample: $3.00 (plus 50¢ postage outside Canada). Back Issues: Prices available upon request. Discounts: 10% to agencies.

80pp; 6X9; of. Reporting time: 2 mos. Copyrighted. Pub's reviews. §books written for Canadian children and adolescents. Ads: $75/$45. CPPA.

CANADIAN DIMENSION, Editorial Board, 801-44 Princess, Winnipeg, Manitoba R3B 1K2, Canada, 957-1519. 1965. Articles, art, photos, cartoons, criticism, reviews, music. circ. 8,000. 8/yr. Pub'd 8 issues 1979; expects 8 issues 1980, 8 issues 1981. sub. price: 8 issues $10.00/pensioners and students 8 issues for $7.00/for libraries, organizations and institutions 8 issues for $15.00; per copy: $1.50; sample: free. Back issues: 75¢ per issue. Discounts: 25% discount to bookstores 1/3 discount to distributors. 56pp; 8½X11; of. Pub's reviews. §politics/economics/contemp. topics. Ads: $250/$150.

CANADIAN FICTION MAGAZINE, Geoffrey Hancock, PO Box 946, Station F, Toronto, Ontario M4Y 2N9, Canada, (416) 534-1259. 1971. Fiction, interviews, criticism, reviews, parts-of-novels. "We publish only the work of writers and artists resident in Canada and Canadians living abroad. No restriction on length, subject matter or style though we tend to prefer fiction that astonishes both through technique & meaning. We offer an annual $250.00 contributors prize. Recent contributors include Derk Wynand, Michel Tremblay, Jacques Ferron, Felix Leclerc, George Woodcock, Matt Cohen, Rikki, Joyce Marshall, Leon Rooke, Hugh Hood, Robert Harlow, Jane Rule, John Metcalf, Yves Theriault, Robert Kroetsch, Robertson Davies, Mavis Gallant, Susan Musgrave." circ. 1,800. 4/yr. Pub'd 4 issues 1979; expects 4 issues 1980. sub. price: $20.00 Canada, $22.00 USA; per copy: $5.00; sample: $5.35 in Canadian funds (inc. postage for current issue). Back issues: price on request; average price $3.85 (inc. postage). Discounts: 5% agent, 40% consignment to stores. 148pp; 6X9; of. Reporting time: 4-6 weeks. Payment: $10.00 per printed page on publication. buys first North American serial rights. Pub's reviews: 35 in 1979. §Surrealism & magic realism in short fiction; also Canadian short stories & novellas, French-Canadian writers in translation; interviews, forums of future of fiction. Ads: $100/$65. CPPA.

THE CANADIAN FORUM, Sam Solecki, Editor; Susan Glover, Mans. Editor, 70 The Esplanade, Third Floor, Toronto, Ontario M5E 1R2, Canada, 416-364-2431. 1920. Poetry, fiction, articles, art, photos, cartoons, interviews, satire, criticism, reviews, music, letters. circ. 10,000. 10/yr. Pub'd 10 issues 1979; expects 10 issues 1980. sub. price: $15.00; per copy: $1.50; sample: $2.00. 44pp; 8½X11; of. Reporting time: 2 mo. Payment: $75-article $10-review. Copyrighted. Pub's reviews: 120 in 1979. Ads: $600/$400/$.20. CPPA.

CANADIAN JOURNAL OF COMMUNICATION, Earle Beattie, Editor, Box 272, Station R, Toronto, Ontario M4G 3T0, Canada, 425-6756. 1974. Articles, reviews. "3,000 words on communication and mass media" circ. 1,000. 4/yr. Pub'd 4 issues 1979. sub. price: $8.00/Canada; $10.00/Foreign; per copy: $2.00/Canada; $2.50/Foreign; sample: $2.00/Canada; $2.50/Foreign. Back issues: $2.00/Canada; $2.50/Foreign. Discounts: 10%. 60pp; 8½X11; of. Reporting time: 2 months. Copyrighted, reverts to author. Pub's reviews: 4 in 1979. §as above. Ads: $80.00/$50.-00/$0.50 word, $5.00 minimum. Can Periodical Publishers Association.

CANADIAN LITERATURE, W.H. New, University of British Columbia, 2021 West Mall, Vancouver, B.C. V6T 1W5, Canada, (604) 228-2780. 1959. Poetry, criticism, reviews. "Only criticism and reviews relating to Canadian writers are used." circ. 2,500. 4/yr (March, June, September, December). sub. price: $18.00 Canada/$21.00 abroad; per copy: $5.00; sample: $5.00. Back issues: May be obtained from Kraus Reprint Co., Millwood, New York 10546. Discounts: $1.00 for agencies. 145pp; 6¾X9¾; lp. Reporting time: 1 month. Payment: $5.00 a page. Copyrighted. Pub's reviews: 50+ in 1979. §Canadian writers and writing. Ads: $150.00/$90.00/$50.00/$30.00. CPPA.

CANADIAN PUBLIC POLICY- Analyse de Politiques, J. Vanderkamp, Arts Building, University of Guelph, Guelph, Ontario N1G2W1, Canada. 1975. Articles, reviews. "A journal for the discussion of social and economic policy. Recent contributors include: S. Ostry, J.E. Pesando, J. Lukasiewicz, N.B. Ridler, D.G. Hartle, K. Kernaghan, D.J. Daly, A.E. Safarian, C. Castonguay, D. Usher, D.V. Smiley, J.F. Helliwell, M. Gunderson." circ. 2,500. 4/yr. Pub'd 4 issues 1979; expects 5 issues 1980, 4 issues 1981. sub. price: $15.00/individual; $13.00/members of sponsoring associations; $10.00/students; $20.00/institutions; per copy: $6.00; sample: $6.00. Back issues: regular rates. Discounts: can be arranged. 150pp; 6½X9¾; of. Reporting time: 35 days. Not copyrighted. Pub's reviews: 88 in 1979. §public policy. Ads: $250.00/$150.00.

Canadian Review of Books Ltd. (see BOOKS IN CANADA: A National Review Of Books)

CANADIAN SLAVONIC PAPERS, R.D.B. Thomson, Centre for Russian & East European Studies, University of Toronto, Toronto, Ontario M5S 1A1, Canada. 1956. Articles, reviews. "We publish scholarly articles in all disciplines of Russian, Soviet & East European studies. Manuscripts-no longer than 30 typewritten double spaced pages. Directory" circ. 1,000. 4/yr. Pub'd 4 issues 1979; expects 4 issues 1980. 1 title listed in the *Small Press Record of Books in Print* (9th Edition, 1980). sub. price:

$17.00; per copy: $5.00. Back issues: $5.00. Discounts: none. 150pp; 6X9; of. Reporting time: 3 mos. Payment: none. copyrighted, rights remain with journal. Pub's reviews: 145 in 1979. §in Russian & East European studies. Ads: $75/$40/outside back cover $100.

CANADIAN THEATRE REVIEW, CTR Publications, Don Rubin, Alan Richardson, 4700 Keele Street, Downsview, Ontario M3J1P3, Canada, 416-667-3768. 1973. Articles, plays, photos, interviews, criticism, reviews, letters. "Documents & analysis of professional theatre with emphasis on Canadian Theatre. A full-length playscript is published in each issue. An international journal." circ. 3,500. 4/yr. Pub'd 4 issues 1979; expects 4 issues 1980. 8 titles listed in the *Small Press Record of Books in Print* (9th Edition, 1980). sub. price: $12.00, Libraries $15.00 (Add $1.75 per year postage from USA, $2.50 Overseas); per copy: $3.50; sample: $3.50. Back issues: $3.50 each. Discounts: 25% Agencies; 40% Bookstores. 144pp; 6X9; of. Reporting time: 3 weeks. Payment varies. Not copyrighted. Pub's reviews: 20-25 in 1979. §drama. Ads: $400.00/$240.00. CPPA.

Canadian Women's Educational Press, 280 Bloor St. W. Suite 313, Toronto, Ontario, Canada, (416) 922-9447. 1971. Fiction, articles, photos, interviews. "Book publisher. Plans on ms for books on social & political issues. US distribution through Bookpeople, 2940 Seventh Street, Berkeley, CA 94710; Canadian & US distribution University of Toronto Press, 5201 Dufferin Street, Downsview, Ont, M3H 5T8, Canada. U.S. distribution from University of Toronto Press shipped from Buffalo, New York." avg. press run 5,000. Pub'd 4 titles 1979; expects 7 titles 1980, 5 titles 1981. 27 titles listed in the *Small Press Record of Books in Print* (9th Edition, 1980). avg. price, cloth: $8.20-$15.30; paper: $3.-60-$6.50. Discounts: 40% trade, 20% educational. size varies; of. Reporting time: Varies. Payment: Varies. ACP, CBIC, CBA.

CANDELABRUM POETRY MAGAZINE, CANDELABRUM POETRY MAGAZINE, Dale Gunthord, M.L. McCarthy, 19 South Hill Park, London NW3 2ST, United Kingdom. 1970. Poetry. "Provides an outlet for poets using traditional verse. The founders believe that the purpose of poetry is to delight and exalt through the pattern of language & the beauty of imagery. As the English language is heavily accented, English poetry has developed as metrical verse; it is the belief of the founders that the disciplines imposed by the structure & accentuation of the language must be observed for sustained artistry to be possible in poetry." 2/yr. sub. price: 55p £1/2 yr £1.40/3 yr; sample: 20p (60¢). 36pp.

CANTO Review of the Arts, Pat Goodheart, Diane Kent, Robert Kent, Jan Schreiber, Carol Shloss, David Van Vactor, Canto, Inc., 9 Bartlet Street, Andover, MA 01810, 617-475-3971. 1976. Poetry, fiction, articles, art, interviews, criticism, reviews, letters, parts-of-novels, long-poems, plays. "In the format of a handsomely designed paperback, CANTO prints original fiction, poems, essays, and reviews, and often longer fiction and plays—the work of writers from all parts of the United States and several foreign countries. CANTO publishes well established writers as well as new talent in search of an audience" circ. 1,000. 3/yr. Pub'd 3 issues 1979; expects 3 issues 1980, 3 issues 1981. sub. price: Four Issues $15.00 USA; $17.00 Foreign; $18.00 Institutions USA; $20.00 Institutions Foreign; per copy: $4.50 ppd USA; $5.00 Foreign; sample: $4.50 ppd USA; $5.00 Foreign. Back issues: no special price. Discounts: Trade, 40%; bulk, none; classroom, none; agent, negotiable. 200pp; 6X8¼; of. Reporting time: 6 weeks minimum. Payment: Negotiable cash payment + 2 complimentary copies. Copyrighted, reverts to author. Pub's reviews: 15 in 1979. §Literature, philosophy, art, social commentary, music, translations, politics. Ads: $120.00/15%. CCLM.

CANVASS, R. Kay Hejny, 1714 Tabor, Houston, TX 77009, (713) 861-2337. 1979. Poetry, art. "We prefer poems of 30 lines or less. We are brand new and expect to have our first issue out in October 1979. This is a quarterly poetry publication. We get all of our material from our subscribers only. We are open minded and accept poems of all types, however, we do prefer poems with imagination and good word usage." circ. 150. 4/yr. Pub'd 1 issue 1979. sub. price: $6.50; per copy: $2.00; sample: $2.00. Back issues: $2.00. 40pp; 5½X8½; †of. Reporting time: 1-2 weeks. Payment: pay is seeing your writing in print. Copyrighted, reverts to author. Ads: $25.00/$12.50/$0.50 a word with 15 word min.

Cape Cod Writers Inc (see also SANDSCRIPT), Barbara Renkens Dunning, Editor, Box 333, Cummaquid, MA 02637.

THE CAPE ROCK, R. A. Burns, English Dept, Southeast Missouri State, Cape Girardeau, MO 63701, 314-651-2151. 1964. Poetry, photos. "We consider poems of any style on almost any subject. Our criterion for selection is the quality of the poetry. We like to feature the work of a single photographer in each issue; submit 30 thematically organized 8 x 10 B & W glossies, or send five pix with query. We favor poems under 70 lines. SASE required for return of submissions. Submissions should bear authors' names and complete addresses in the upper right-hand corner of each page." circ. 1,000. 2/yr. Pub'd 2 issues 1979; expects 2 issues 1980. sub. price: $1.50; per copy: $1.00; sample: $1.00.

Back issues: $1.00 per copy. Discounts: 25% off on orders of 20 or more (our cost plus postage). 64pp; 5½X8¾; †of. Reporting time: 1-4 mos. Payment: copies only. magazine is copyrighted. Rights to contents released to authors and artists upon request, subject only to their giving credit to *The Cape Rock* whenever and wherever else the work is placed. *The Cape Rock* retains reprint rights. no ads. CCLM, COSMEP, NESPA.

Capemead Ltd. (see HEALTHY LIVING)

THE CAPILANO REVIEW, Bill Schermbrucker, 2055 Purcell Way, North Vancouver, B.C. V7J3H5, Canada, 604-986-1911. 1972. Poetry, fiction, art, photos, interviews, criticism, reviews, music, parts-of-novels, long-poems, collages, plays, concrete art. "*The Capilano Review* is a quarterly literary and visual art magazine, publishing only what its editors consider to be the very best work being produced. The magazine is published at considerable cost and the editors collectively put in a great deal of energy in order to give writers and other artists the best possible presentation and circulation of their work. Sample issues are available at the regular $3.00 per single copy cost. The most intelligent way of seeing if your material is likely to interest us is to read the magazine. (it is also available in over 100 major libraries in Canada, the U.S., and other countries.) We are most interested in publishing artists whose work has not yet received the attention it deserves. We are not interested in imitative, derivative, or unfinished work. We have no format exclusions." circ. 1,000-1,500. 4/yr. Pub'd 2 issues 1979; expects 4 issues 1980. sub. price: $9.00 individual/$10.00 libraries/add $1.00 postage for U.S. & overseas.; per copy: $3.00; sample: $3.00. Back issues: $5.00 per copy. Discounts: 40 percent to bookstores. 120pp; 8X5½ (approx); of. Reporting time: up to 4 months. Payment: $10.00-$40.00. Copyrighted, reverts to author. Ads: exchange ads only.

Capra Press, Noel Young, P.O. Box 2068, Santa Barbara, CA 93120, 805-966-4590. 1969. Fiction, interviews, satire, criticism, art, photos, letters. "Eclectic booklist, a independent press in the broadest sense of the word." avg. press run 5,000. Pub'd 12 titles 1979; expects 12 titles 1980. 8 titles listed in the *Small Press Record of Books in Print* (9th Edition, 1980). avg. price, cloth: $10.00; paper: $5.00. Discounts: 1-4, 20 percent; 5-49, 40 percent; 50-99, 42 percent; distributors, 50 percent. 96-256pp; 6X9; of/lp. Reporting time: 6 weeks average. Payment: royalties negotiated. copyright in author's name. COSMEP.

Caratzas Brothers, Publishers, Aristide Caratzas, Marybeth Sollins, Assistant, PO Box 210, 481 Main Street, New Rochelle, NY 10802, (914) 632-8487. 1975. Fiction, art, photos, music. "We are interested specifically in greek-related topics - we have recently begun a 'Modern Greek History' Series. We also have a line of college classical textbooks." avg. press run 3,000. Pub'd 20 titles 1979; expects 15 titles 1980. 6 titles listed in the *Small Press Record of Books in Print* (9th Edition, 1980). avg. price, cloth: $12.00; other: $50.00 (artbooks). Discounts: trade and short (for artbooks). 300pp; size varies; of. Reporting time: 3 months. Payment: varies. Copyrights for author.

Carcanet Press (see also POETRY NATION REVIEW), 330 Corn Exchange Buildings, Manchester, England M4 3BG, United Kingdom, (06l) 834-8730. 1969. Poetry, interviews, criticism, reviews. avg. press run 1,500. Pub'd 40 titles 1979; expects 40 titles 1980, 40 titles 1981. avg. price, cloth: £5.90; paper: £2.95. Discounts: 35% trade. 250pp; size demi; of. Copyrights for author.

Cardinal Press, Inc., Mary McAnally, 76 N Yorktown, Tulsa, OK 74110, (918) 583-3651. 1978. Poetry, art, photos, long-poems. "Bias for Midwest (Southwest poets, for women, prisoners, minorities). Will not publish any racist or sexist material. Socialist/humanist orientation." avg. press run 300. Expects 1 title 1980, 2-4 titles 1981. 2 titles listed in the *Small Press Record of Books in Print* (9th Edition, 1980). avg. price, paper: $3.00. 48pp; 6X9; of. Reporting time: 1-3 months. Payment: Arbitrary/varies. Does not copyright for author.

CARLETON MISCELLANY, Keith Harrison, Editor; Donald Schier, Associate Editor; Carolyn Soule, Managing Editor, Carleton College, Northfield, MN 55057. 1960. Poetry, fiction, articles, interviews, satire, criticism, reviews, letters, parts-of-novels, long-poems, plays. "On request we assign copyrights to authors without charge. Reprint requests are routinely granted on request." circ. 700. Irregular at the moment. 3 issues per volume with the issues coming out at irregular intervals. Pub'd 1 issue 1979; expects 2 issues 1980. sub. price: $5.50 per volume; per copy: $2.00; sample: $2.00. Back issues: Most back issues of the *Miscellany* are available. In good condition. Discounts: 50% for bookstores; 20% for magazine agencies. 150pp; 6X9. Reporting time: 2 weeks or as long as 4 to 5 months. Payment: $10.00 a page for poetry/$8.00 a page for prose. Copyrighted. Pub's reviews: 45 in 1979. §Primarily the humanities. CCLM.

Carma Press, Florence Nelson, Box 12633, St Paul, MN 55112, 612-631-3120. 1976. Articles, art. "We are looking for material in one area only: *Help For The Teacher of Adults.* We deal with techniques, problem situations, how to construct and use teaching materials, etc. We would like to see various

70

subject areas (i.e., How to teach Real Estate, Astrology, Writing, Crafts...anything!). Our recent publication, YES YOU CAN TEACH! deals with teaching in general. Now we'd like to get more specific. Length: from 20 to 60 pages." avg. press run varies. Pub'd 3 titles 1979; expects 3 titles 1980, 3 titles 1981. 5 titles listed in the *Small Press Record of Books in Print* (9th Edition, 1980). avg. price, paper: $3.50. Discounts: Standard. 25pp; 8½X11, 8½X5½; of. Reporting time: query first-immed. reply. Outright payment. Copyrights for author. COSMEP, NCEA.

CARN (a link between the Celtic nations), Blackrock Printers, Cathal O Luain, Celtic League, 9 Br Cnoc Sion, Ath Cliath 9, Republic of Ireland, Dublin 373957. 1973. Articles, reviews, criticism, news items, poetry, interviews, letters. "500-1M words per article, 2000 for one or two in each issue. -1/3 to -1/4 of the material in Celtic languages, rest in English, CARN is the organ of the Celtic League which fosters co-operation & solidarity between the Celtic nations." circ. 2M. 4/yr. Pub'd 4 issues 1979; expects 4 issues 1980. sub. price: £3.00 (Ireland, Gt. Britain), $7.50 USA and other non-European countries.; per copy: 40p; sample: 20p. Back issues: 35p per copy. Discounts: 20-25 percent bookshops. 24pp; 8½X10½; of. Reporting time: up to 3 months. No payment. Copyrighted, remains with CARN. Pub's reviews: 13 in 1979. §History of the Celtic nations; history of the Celtic languages; movements for national freedom and language restoration; bilingual education. Ads: £4.00 column inch.

CAROLINA QUARTERLY, Dorothy Hill, Greenlaw Hall 066-A, Univ of N. Carolina, Chapel Hill, NC 27514, (9l9) 933-0244. 1948. Poetry, fiction, art, photos, reviews, parts-of-novels, long-poems. "'Looking for the well-crafted poem or story, with an emphasis on original language use'. Recent contributors: John Tagliabue, Judith Moffett, D.W. Baker, Greg Kuzma, Lee Smith, William Harmon, John Hollander, Arthur Vogelsang, Douglas Blazek, Paul Smyth, Graham Petrie, Fred Chappell, Jessie Schell, Albert Goldbarth, James Seay, Christopher Brookhouse, T.C. Boyle, Richard Dokey, Allen Wier, Kevin O'Neill, Rosanne Coggeshall, Reynolds Price, Kate Jennings, Diane Ackerman, W. S. Doxey, Leon Driskell." circ. 1,000. 3/yr. Pub'd 3 issues 1979; expects 3 issues 1980. sub. price: $6.00; per copy: $2.00; sample: $3.00. Back issues: $3.00. Discounts: 20% local stores; 40% out of state; agent, 10%. 120pp; 6X9; of. Reporting time: 3-4 months. Payment: $3/page; $5/poem. Copyrighted, reverts to author. Pub's reviews: 3 in 1979. §Short stories, poems, novels. Ads: $80/$50. CCLM, COSMEP.

The Carolina Wren Press (see also HYPERION A Poetry Journal), Judy Hogan, 300 Barclay Road, Chapel Hill, NC 27514, 919-967-8666. 1976. Poetry, fiction, plays. "I am primarily publishing new North Carolina writers. Bias toward writing capable of bringing about cultural change but I evaluate it as writing (poetry or whatever). Among early titles; *Chrome Grass* (Liner); *Milky Way Poems* (Rigsby); *American Peasant* (Herron); *dead on Arrival* (Jaki Shelton). *Eat Your Natchos:* Texas COSMEP Anthology (Hogan, Ed.). *Forcehymm* Huey; *Rituals of Our Time* Herron; *Poems in One Part Harmony* Reddy; *Brinktown* Ramirez." avg. press run 750 for poetry; 1,000 for novels. Pub'd 3 titles 1979; expects 6 titles 1980, 9 titles 1981. 7 titles listed in the *Small Press Record of Books in Print* (9th Edition, 1980). avg. price, cloth: $8.00 (novels); paper: $3.00. Discounts: 40 percent to bookstores. 75-150pp; 5½X8½; 6X9; of. Reporting time: 6 months to 1 year. Payment: l0% of printrun or equivalent in cash. Copyrights for author. COSMEP, COSMEP-SOUTH.

Caroline House Publishers, Jameson G. Jr. Campaigne, PO Box 738, Ottawa, IL 61350, (815) 434-7905. 1974. "Editorial affairs are handled by Mr. Campaigne at: Caroline House Publishers, PO Box 738, Ottawa, Illinois 61350, 815-434-7905. We publish our own titles and distribute to the book trade for some twenty-five other publishers." avg. press run varies. Pub'd 25 titles 1979; expects 50 titles 1980, 100 titles 1981. of. Reporting time: varies. Payment: varies. ABA, COSMEP, AAP.

Carolyn Bean Publishing, Ltd., Lawrence M. Barnett, John C.W. Carroll, 120 2nd Street, San Francisco, CA 94105, 415-957-9574. 1976. Art, photos. "We publish books and notecards. Our direction in publishing seems to be to publish books and cards that deal, in a visual way, with problems in the Human Condition. Our first book, *Smile in a Mad Dog's i,* by Richard Stine, and our subsequent books depict cliches, conundra, and stereotypes of our contemporary life. We seek works of 'Heart'." avg. press run Varies. Pub'd 1 title 1979. avg. price, cloth: varies; paper: varies; other: varies. Discounts: trade, 40 percent: agents, 55 percent: jobbers, 50-65 percent. pp varies; size varies; of. Reporting time: later. Payment varies. Copyrights for author. AIGA, GAA.

CAROUSEL, Jane Fox, Editor, The Writer's Center, Glen Echo Park, Glen Echo, MD 20768. 1976. Articles, letters, news items. "We are staff produced (and sometimes by invitation). We will publish manuscript needs, and news of interest in the small press world, i.e. contests, new magazines, defunct mags, anything of use to the literary community." circ. 800. 10/yr. Pub'd 10 issues 1979. sub. price: $10.00; per copy: $1.00; sample: $1.00. Back issues: They are out of print almost immediately. 4pp; 8½X11; †of. Reporting time: 30 days. Copyrighted. Ads: $40.00/$20.00/$12.50/.

71

Carousel Press, Carole Terwilliger Meyers, Editor-in-Chief; Gene Howard Meyers, Editor, P.O. Box 6061, Albany, CA 94706, 415-527-5849. 1976. Art, photos, cartoons. "We are interested in books on parenting, including family travel guides. 100-150 pages." avg. press run 2,500. Pub'd 1 title 1979; expects 1 title 1980, 1 title 1981. 4 titles listed in the *Small Press Record of Books in Print* (9th Edition, 1980). avg. price, cloth: $8.95; paper: $4.95. Discounts: trade, bulk, jobber; 40 percent for five or more books, libraries 10 percent. 150pp; 5½X8½; of. Reporting time: 6 weeks, include return postage. Payment: Royalties and flat payments. Copyrights for author.

Carpenter Press, Bob Fox, Susan Fox, Route 4, Pomeroy, OH 45769, 614-992-7520. 1973. Poetry, fiction, art, photos. "Full-length fiction and poetry, chapbooks, S-F. Interested in vision more than style. Publish traditional as well as experimental fiction. Recent full-length fiction by Daniel Lusk, Brian Swam, and Matthew Paris. I'm always backlogged but will look at new material if queried first. I will not read xeroxed queries and will not return material without SASE." avg. press run 500-1,500. Pub'd 3 titles 1979; expects 3 titles 1980. 7 titles listed in the *Small Press Record of Books in Print* (9th Edition, 1980). avg. price, paper: $5.00; other: $1.50 - Chapbooks. Discounts: Trade. 6X9; of/lp. Reporting time: several months. Payment: by contract. Copyrights for author. COSMEP, NESPA.

CARTA ABIERTA, Juan Rodriguez, Center for Mexican American Studies, Student Services Building 307, Texas Univ, Austin, TX 78712, (512) 471-4557. 1975. Articles, interviews, criticism, reviews, letters, news items. "News about the Chicano literary world." circ. 1,000. 4/yr. Pub'd 4 issues 1979; expects 4 issues 1980, 4 issues 1981. sub. price: $10.00 institutions-$20.00; per copy: $2.50; sample: $3.00. 12pp; 8X11½; †of. Reporting time: immediate. Copyrighted, reverts to author. Pub's reviews: 250 in 1979. §Chicano literature in particular, but will review third world literature also.

Casa del Sensitive (see LOST AND FOUND TIMES)

CASE ANALYSIS, Progresiv Publishr, Kenneth H. Ives, 401 E 32nd, #1002, Chicago, IL 60616, (312) 225-9181. 1977. Articles, reviews. "Retain non-exclusive reprint rights, sharing resulting royalties." circ. 100. 2/yr. sub. price: Vol 1: $10.00 indiv., $15.00 instit; Vol 2: $12.00, $18.00; per copy: $3.50 indiv.; $5.00 instit.; sample: Vol 1: $3.50 indiv., $5.00 instit. 80-100pp; 7X8½; of. Reporting time: 1-3 months. Payment: 1 copy of issue plus 10 reprints. Copyrighted. Pub's reviews: 2 in 1979.

CASINO & SPORTS, GBC Press, Howard Schwartz, Editor, 630 S. 11th St., Box 4115, Las Vegas, NV 89106, (702)382-7555. 1977. Interviews, reviews, news items. "This publication is an off-shoot of *Systems & Methods,* which covered all gambling systems in volumes #1 thru #18. Starting with #19 *S&M* covers pari-mutuel events, and this one, *Casino & Sports,* will cover reviews of casino play and sports betting." circ. 2,000. 6/yr. Pub'd 2 issues 1979; expects 6 issues 1980, 6 issues 1981. sub. price: $15.00; per copy: $3.00. Back issues: $2.00 each. Discounts: Trade, 50%; Jobber, 62%;. 64pp; 5¼X8¼; †of. Reporting time: 30 days. Payment: depends on type and length. Copyrighted, reverts to author. Pub's reviews: 15 in 1979. §Casino & sports betting. no ads accepted. BPASC/ABA Affiliate.

Cassandra Publications (see also NOE VALLEY POETS WORKSHOP), Stephanie Mines, 7397 Boris Court #9, Rohnert Park, CA 94928, 239-1253. 1972. Poetry. avg. press run 500. 3 titles listed in the *Small Press Record of Books in Print* (9th Edition, 1980). avg. price, paper: $3.00. Discounts: 60/40. 50-150pp; 6X9; of/lp. Payment: very loose. Copyrights for author. COSMEP.

'THE CASSETTE GAZETTE', Handshake Editions, Jim Haynes, Jack Henry Moore, Atelier A2, 83 rue de la Tombe-Issoire, Paris 75014, France, 327-1767. 1971. Poetry, interviews, music, long-poems, collages, plays. "'*The Cassette Gazette*' is an audio 'magazine' - two hours in length - and contains contributions from Germaine Greer, Lawrence Ferlinghetti, Charles Bukowski, Grandma Haynes, Heathcote Williams, Charles de Gaulle, Shawn Phillips, Tuli Kupferberg, Hyde Manhattan, etc etc. Cheques to be paid to: Jim Haynes." circ. 250. sub. price: 4 issues/$40.00. Payment: copies. Copyrighted, reverts to author.

Cat Anna Press, Helen Prescott, Lou Robinson, c/o Prescott, 328-D E. Whitcomb, Madison Hgts., MI 48071, (313) 588-6486. 1977. Poetry, fiction, art. "This year we are working on a book about ways of transforming consciousness to understand and work within our quickly changing realities. We'll be including fiction and articles on psychic development, astrological and historical perspectives, prophecies,and clues from other realms and other cultures." avg. press run 500 copies. Pub'd 1 title 1979. 1 title listed in the *Small Press Record of Books in Print* (9th Edition, 1980). avg. price, paper: $2.50. Discounts: 40% for orders of 10 or more; 25% for orders of 5 up and to libraries. 25-100 pp.; 4½X6, 8X10; †of. Please query first with idea. Payment: no arrangements yet-to be worked out. the authors hold all copyrights.

Catalyst, Ian Young, 315 Blantyre Ave., Scarborough, Ontario M1N2S6, Canada. 1967. Poetry, fiction, long-poems, plays. "We are a non-profit co-operative with emphasis on gay writing and

Canadian writing. We have recently published books by: Ian Young, Graham Jackson, Gavin Dillard, Oswell Blakeston, Wayne McNeill, Tom Meyer, E.A. Lacey, Dennis Cooper." avg. press run 1,000. Pub'd 4 titles 1979; expects 4 titles 1980, 4 titles 1981. 22 titles listed in the *Small Press Record of Books in Print* (9th Edition, 1980). avg. price, cloth: $10.00; paper: $3.95. Discounts: 40% (less than 10 items, 30%). of. Reporting time: within one week. Payment: 10% royalty. IPA.

Catex Press, Jack Clifton, 1150 Spruce St, Berkeley, CA 94707. 1975. "Children's literature, fiction, non-fiction, poetry. Things of interest to children of all ages" Expects 2 titles 1980. 7X8½; of. Reporting time: 1 week. Does not copyright for author.

Cat's Pajamas Press (see also MOJO NAVIGATOR(E)), John Jacob, 527 Lyman, Oak Park, IL 60304. 1968. Poetry, fiction, criticism, parts-of-novels, long-poems. "Our most recent titles include *Hojo Supreme* by Bernie Bever and *Scar Mirror* by Derek Pell, the first a short book of violent poems, the second a Robbe-Grilletain fantasy narrative. Our books by Ken Smith, John Oliver Simon, Tom Montag, Eric Felderman, and Thomas Michael Fisher are still in-print. We have maintained our broadside series with the most recent publication of poems by Sara Plath. The broadside series soon will be available as a set. We plan to publish a title or two per year and lean toward extremely short, unified manuscripts, whether poetry or prose. We will also publish very limited print runs, usually between 100 and 250. We don't like a lot of what we read and we want to retain validity as a true alternative to mainstream material. The press is a guerrilla press that will use whatever means available to suit our aesthetic ends, whether cheap xerography or cloth bindings and expensive papers." avg. press run 100-1,000. Pub'd 1 title 1979. 8 titles listed in the *Small Press Record of Books in Print* (9th Edition, 1980). avg. price, cloth: $2.50; paper: $1.00; other: $5.00. Discounts: 40% on multiples. 8-32pp; 5X8; 8X11; mi/of/lp. Reporting time: 4-6 weeks. Payment: min. 20% print run. Copyrights for author.

Cliff Catton Press, Cliff Catton, 195 Ridge Street #7, Glensfalls, NY 12801. 1974. Poetry, articles, art, photos, cartoons. "Secondary address: Catton, P.O. Box 341, Cairo, NY 12413. Poetry accenting positive side of life. Religious poetry and articles. *Again (Why Not), Selected Poems* Cliff Catton; *From My Heart, Selected Poems* Cliff Catton; *Maranatha* Cliff Catton." avg. press run 300. Pub'd 7 titles 1979. 6 titles listed in the *Small Press Record of Books in Print* (9th Edition, 1980). avg. price, paper: $2.00; other: $0.25 postcards. Discounts: 15% on 10 or more copies. pp varies; 8½X11; †mi/of. Reporting time: one to two weeks. Payment: negotiable. Copyrights for author.

The Cauldron Press, Howard Schwartz, Dept of English, Univ. of Missouri, 8001 Natural Bridge Road, St. Louis, MO 63121, (314) 453-5541. 1976. Poetry, fiction. "Books to date by Yehuda Amichai, Shlomo Vinner, Aaron Sussaman, Howard Schwartz, Mojmir Drvota, Gabriel Preil and others. Primarily interested in books of poetry translated from the Hebrew and writings of Missouri poets and short story writers. Submission only at the publisher's request. The general format is 48 pages, occasionally longer." avg. press run 400. Pub'd 4 titles 1979; expects 4 titles 1980. avg. price, paper: $4.00. Discounts: 40%. 48pp; 5½X8½; of. Not open to general submissions; only at publisher's request. Payment: By arrangement. Copyrights for author.

Caxton Press (see NEW ZEALAND MONTHLY REVIEW)

Cedar Creek Press, John G. Henry, PO Box 801, Dekalb, IL 60115. 1966. Poetry. avg. press run 500. Pub'd 5 titles 1979; expects 6 titles 1980. 2 titles listed in the *Small Press Record of Books in Print* (9th Edition, 1980). avg. price, cloth: $5.00; paper: $2.00. Discounts: 20 percent on orders for more than 5 copies. 32-48pp; 6X9; †lp. Reporting time: 3-4 weeks max. Payment: 10 percent of press run. Copyrights for author.

Cedar Creek Publishers, Phyllis Robb, 2310 Sawmill Road, Fort Wayne, IN 46825, 637-3856. 1980. "1980 title: *Cooking for Hyperactive and Allergic Children.* Wanted: material on food allergies and other special diet problems, specifically recipe books." avg. press run 2,200. avg. price, cloth: $9.95; paper: $5.95. Discounts: 1-4, 20%; 5 or more, 40%. 6X9; of. Reporting time: 2 weeks. Payment: no advance, 12% of retail. Copyrights for author.

Cedar House Enterprises, Janet Wherry, PO Box 70, El Granada, CA 94018, 415-726-4096. 1976. Fiction. "I prefer things that do well at trade fairs like cookbooks, coloring books, books with local interest appeal." avg. press run 300. Pub'd 1 title 1979; expects 1 title 1980, 1 title 1981. 5 titles listed in the *Small Press Record of Books in Print* (9th Edition, 1980). avg. price, paper: $2.00. Discounts: classroom. 20 to 250pp; 8½X11; †mi. Reporting time: 2 weeks. Payment: author receives percent of profit by check in mail bimonthly. Copyrights for author. COSMEP.

CEDAR ROCK, Cedar Rock Press, David C. Yates, Pat Ellis Taylor, Fiction Editor; Naomi Shihab Nye, 1121 Madeline, New Braunfels, TX 78130, 512-625-6002. 1975. Fiction, satire, criticism, news items, poetry, articles, art, photos, reviews, long-poems. "Emphasis on readable poetry and fiction-although any form-conventional or free verse-considered. Recent contributors include: Judson Jerome, Diane Wakoski, Peter Wild, Karl Kopp, Clayton Eshleman. Fiction editor address: PO Box 370, Edgewood, TX 75117." circ. 2000. 4/yr. Pub'd 4 issues 1979; expects 4 issues 1980. sub. price: $5.00; per copy: $1.50; sample: $1.50. Back issues: $1.50 per issue. Discounts: $3.50 per student. 28pp; size tabloid; of. Reporting time: 2 wks to 3 weeks. Pays $2 to $100 for material, on acceptance, plus 1 contributor's copy. Copyrighted, reverts to author. Pub's reviews: 18 in 1979. §poetry. Ads: $200/$115. COSMEP, CCLM.

Cedar Rock Press (see also CEDAR ROCK), David C. Yates, Publisher, 1121 Madeline, New Braunfels, TX 78130. 1975. Poetry, long-poems. "Published 2 chapbooks in 78, expects 3 more in 79 and 80." avg. press run 1,000. Pub'd 3 titles 1979; expects 1 title 1980, 1 title 1981. 5 titles listed in the *Small Press Record of Books in Print* (9th Edition, 1980). avg. price, cloth: $5.50; paper: $2.50. 36pp; 5½X8½; of. Books by invitation only. Payment: varies. Copyrights for author.

Celebrating Women Productions, Buckwheat Turner, PO Box 251, Warrensburg, NY 12885. 1978. Articles. "120 page book on book collections concerning women *Bibliotees Femina: A Herstory of Book Collections Concerning Women*" avg. press run 2,000. Expects 1 title 1980. avg. price, cloth: $5.00. Discounts: 40% Bookstores. 120pp; 5X7½. Reporting time: i. Self publish. Copyrights for author.

CELEBRATION, Wm. J. Sullivan, 2707 Lawina Road, Baltimore, MD 21216. 1975. "All styles, we hope to be as unbiased as contributors will permit. Recent contributors: Karen Donnelly, Lora Dunetz, Don Harrold, Michael R. Pashall." circ. 300. occasional. price per copy: $1.00; sample: $1.25. Back issues: $1.25. 30pp; 5½X8½; of. Reporting time: 8 weeks. Payment: copies. COSMEP.

Celestial Arts, David Morris, Senior Editor; Joycelyn Moulton, 231 Adrian Rd., Millbrae, CA 94030. 1969. "Publishes quality paperback originals. Query first with outline and sample chapters. Include descriptions and examples of artwork and photos. SASE. Philosophy-subjects of unique interest or unique approach to subject of general interest, non-fiction, health, sports." avg. press run 7m. Pub'd 28 titles 1979; expects 28 titles 1980. avg. price, paper: $6.95. Reporting time: 3 months. Payment: standard royalty contract. Copyrights for author.

Celestial Otter (see also MAGIC CHANGES), Donald Bullen, Cheryl Joy, John Sennett, 1923 Finchley Ct, Schaumburg, IL 60194, (312) 884-6425. 1978. Poetry, fiction, art, photos, interviews, satire, music, long-poems, plays, criticism, reviews. "Send wild poetical journals! Query first." avg. press run 400. Expects 2 titles 1981. avg. price, paper: $3.00. Discounts: Inquire. 48pp; †lp. Reporting time: 2 months. Payment: Negotiable. Copyrights for author.

Celestial Gifts, Ron Dalrymple, Box 175, Rockville, MD 20850. 1976. Fiction, satire. "Presently publishing own works, including (1.) *Richard the Liar-Hearted* (political satire, 1st edition, 40 pages, cover illustration, saddle stitch binding, $2.50 retail, published June 14, 1979), a scorching Nixon expose, guaranteed to make you laugh, and (2.) *Are You a Genius?* (metaphysical, 1st edition, 15 pages, saddle stitch binding, $1.00 retail, published July 1978), a new theory of mind based on Einsteinian physics and modern psychology." avg. press run 1,000. Pub'd 1 title 1979; expects 2 titles 1980. 1 title listed in the *Small Press Record of Books in Print* (9th Edition, 1980). avg. price, paper: $2.00. Discounts: standard industry. 40pp; 5X8; †of. Reporting time: not presently accepting unsolicited manuscripts. Copyrights for author.

Celo Press, Jim Best, Nancy Wood, Route #5, Burnsville, NY 28714, (702) 675-4925. 1962. Poetry, articles, art, letters. "We publish books that have a social-concerns orientation, promote appalachian culture, spiritual emphasis, are community-oriented. Primary emphasis to date: death & dying education." avg. press run 2,000. Pub'd 2 titles 1979; expects 3 titles 1980, 2 titles 1981. avg. price, cloth: $8.00; paper: $6.00. Discounts: 40% bookstores more than 1 copy, 33% libraries, 50% jobber. 289pp; 5½X8½; †of. Reporting time: 1-2 months. Copyrights for author.

THE CENTENNIAL REVIEW, David Mead, 110 Morrill Hall, Mich. State Univ., E. Lansing, MI 48824, 517-355-1905. 1955. Poetry, articles. "Topics cover English literature, soc. sci, sciences, humanities, 3,000 words, double-spaced. Contributors:Joseph Needham, Susan Fromberg Schaeffer" circ. 1,000. 4/yr. sub. price: $3.00; per copy: $1.00; sample: $1.00. Back issues: $1 copy. 100pp; 6X9; of. Reporting time: 3-6 months. Payment: year's free subscription. Copyrighted, reverts to author.

CENTER, Carol Berge, P.O. Box 7494, Old Albuquerque Station, Albuquerque, NM 87194, (505) 247-9337. 1970. Fiction, articles, satire, criticism, reviews, letters, parts-of-novels, non-fiction. " *Innovative prose only.* No poetry. From short sections to longer prose 'chapbooks'. New writers *must* query before submitting, *and must have read current issue.* Enclose SASE. If in doubt, query Poets and Writers for current address." circ. 2,000. 2/yr. Pub'd 2 issues 1979; expects 2 issues 1980. sub. price: No subscriptions issued; per copy: $2.00 & SSAE to individuals, $2.50 to libraries.; sample: $2.00 & SSAE. Back issues: First 3 issues, $50.00 to libraries; negotiable to writers. Other back issues: $4.00 each, (when available), plus SASE and 59¢ postage. 76pp; 8½X11; of. Reporting time: 2 wks. Payment: $3.00-$4.50 pg. Copyrighted, revert to authors 6 mos. after pubn. Pub's reviews. §Innovative prose & fiction; science fiction. no ads. CCLM, SFRA, Popular Culture Assn, NEA, NVSCA (New York State Council on Arts), RGWA (Rio Grande Writers Assn).

Center for the Art of Living, Gary Michael Durst, 2203 N Sheffield, Chicago, IL 60614, (312) 871-5681. 1979. Poetry. "Book length mss, philosophical, psychological topics" circ. 2,000. Pub'd 1 issue 1979. 1 title listed in the *Small Press Record of Books in Print* (9th Edition, 1980). price per copy: $4.95. Discounts: 40% to trade, 50% to wholesalers (45% for advance payment on trade orders). 230pp; 6X8½; of. Payment: no arrangement yet made.

The Center For Book Arts (see BOOK ARTS)

Center For Contemporary Poetry, John Judson, Murphy Library, Univ of Wisconsin, La Crosse, WI 54601, 608-785-8511. 1971. Poetry, articles, interviews. "We publish an annual volume under the title *Voyages To The Inland Sea;* emphasis is on midwestern poetry. Each volume includes two or three poets, with representative poems and an essay by each. Prices for Vols 3-6, $6.00 reg & $10.00 signed. For 1977 & after are $8.00 reg ed & $15.00 signed. Vol VII features poets Hale Chatfield & Wm. Kloefkorn. Vol I and II are O.O.P. MSS. are not solicited. Vol VIII features poets James Hazard & Felix Stefanile." avg. press run 500 vols. Pub'd 1 title 1979; expects 1 title 1980. 2 titles listed in the *Small Press Record of Books in Print* (9th Edition, 1980). avg. price, cloth: $8.00; other: $15.00 signed. Discounts: 20% to dealers, jobbers. 65pp; 8½X5½; of. mss not solicited. Payment: one-time fee to authors. Copyrights for author.

Center for Science in the Public Interest (see also NUTRITION ACTION), Charles Stahler, Marketing Director, 1755 'S' Street, N.W., Washington, DC 20009, (202) 332-9110. 1971. "and a limited amount of free-lance material.Food, health and nutrition from an activist, public interest, consumer-oriented point of view. Watchdog on government and private industry. Educational materials from this point of view for schools, parents, individuals, food activists, concerned citizens, etc. 1978 published *The Changing American Diet,* on how food consumption has changed since the early 1900's, and *Midget Encyclopedia of Food & Nutrition,* five brochures on how to survive in the modern food situation. So far we've only published our own, internally-generated stuff or things from our Board members and a limited amount of free-lance material." avg. press run 2000 to 50,000. Pub'd 3 titles 1979; expects 5 titles 1980, 5 titles 1981. 3 titles listed in the *Small Press Record of Books in Print* (9th Edition, 1980). avg. price, cloth: $12.95; paper: $4.50; other: posters $2.00. 100pp; size varies; of. Payment: negotiable.

Center for Southern Folklore (see also CENTER FOR SOUTHERN FOLKLORE MAGAZINE), Kini Kedigh, Editor; Ruth Amy, Assistant Editor, PO Box 40105, 1216 Peabody Avenue, Memphis, TN 38104, (901) 726-4205. 1972. Interviews. avg. press run 3,000-5,000. Pub'd 3 titles 1979; expects 1 title 1980. avg. price, paper: $7.50. Discounts: 40% on orders of 5 or more copies of each book. 50-100pp; 8½X11; of. Reporting time: ASAP. Copyrights for author.

CENTER FOR SOUTHERN FOLKLORE MAGAZINE, Center for Southern Folklore, Kini Kedigh, Editor, PO Box 40105, 1216 Peabody Avenue, Memphis, TN 38104, (901) 726-4205. 1978. Articles, art, photos, reviews, letters, news items. "500 words; 4,000 words feature articles; double spaced; yped on 60 space line; photgraphs welcome." circ. 4,000. 2/yr. Pub'd 2 issues 1979; expects 2 issues 1980. sub. price: $5.00; per copy: $2.00; sample: free. Back issues: $2.00 or free depending on which issue. Discounts: 40% on orders of 10 & above. 24pp; 11¼X16¾; of. Reporting time: ASAP. Copyrighted, reverts to author. Pub's reviews. §History, photography, folklore, art & crafts, music. Ads: No ads. COSMEP.

The Center For Study of Multiple Gestation, Donald M. Keith, Louis G. Keith, Suite 463-5, 333 East Superior St., Chicago, IL 60611, (312) 266-9093. 1977. Articles, news items. "Use ONLY material associated with the phenomenon of multiple birth, twin care, con-joined twins, triplets, etc." avg. press run 5-50,000. Pub'd 1 title 1979; expects 2 titles 1980, 2 titles 1981. 1 title listed in the *Small Press Record of Books in Print* (9th Edition, 1980). avg. price, cloth: $12.95; paper: $6.75. Discounts: standard trade. 128pp; 4X7; lp. Reporting time: 4 weeks. Payment: sliding depending on total sales, 10% minimum, 15% maximum. Copyrights for author.

Center for Women's Studies & Services (CWSS) (see also FEMINIST BULLETIN), Carol Rowell, Shelley Savren, P.O. Box 350, San Diego, CA 92101, 714-233-8984. 1971. Articles. avg. press run 3M. Pub'd 6 titles 1979. 4pp; 7X8½; of. Reporting time: 2 months. Payment: none. Copyrights for

author. COSMEP.

Center Press (see also JOURNAL OF BIOLOGICAL EXPERIENCE), Ian J. Grand, General Editor, 2045 Francisco Street, Berkeley, CA 94709, (415) 526-8373. 1979. "Center Press publishes books and monographs concerned with the life of the body. Currently it has published *Somatic Reality* and *Your Body Speaks Its Mind* by Stanley Keleman and *The Journal of Biological Experience*." avg. press run 5,000. Pub'd 2 titles 1979; expects 5 titles 1980. avg. price, cloth: $9.00; paper: $5.00. Discounts: 1 copy, 20%; 2-4, 30%; 5 & more, 40%. 150pp; 5½X8½; †of. Reporting time: 6 months. Payment: usual trade. Copyrights for author.

Center Publications, Taizan Maezumi, Tetsugen Glassman, 905 S Normandie Ave., Los Angeles, CA 90006, 213-387-2356. 1976. Poetry, articles, art, photos. "Zen practice is a living experience, as at home in twentieth century America as in ancient Japan. To bring the practice of Zen home to Western readers and to further the current dialogue between Zen and modern American culture is the reason for Center Publications and the Zen writings series. Books cover a broad range of topics from translations of classical texts, to meditation guides, to the expression of Zen in the arts." avg. press run 10,000. Pub'd 2 titles 1979; expects 6 titles 1980, 8 titles 1981. 13 titles listed in the *Small Press Record of Books in Print* (9th Edition, 1980). avg. price, cloth: $10.00; paper: $6.00. Discounts: included. 150pp; size varies; of. Reporting time: 30 days. Payment: differs from book to book. Copyrights for author. COSMEP.

‡**CENTERGRAM, Centergram Press**, Terry Gross, 109 E. Main Street, Middletown, NY 10940. 1977. Poetry. "Not accepting anything but books to review." circ. 100. 4/yr. Expects 4 issues 1980. sub. price: $12.00, price includes two books and two issues of magazine. 40-80pp; 5X8; †lp. Reporting time: Immediate. Payment: copies. Copyrighted, reverts to author. Pub's reviews. §Poetry, fiction. Ads: none.

‡**Centergram Press (see also CENTERGRAM)**, Terry Gross, 109 E. Main Street, Middletown, NY 10940. 1977. Poetry. "In a temporary (we hope) holding pattern." avg. press run varies. avg. price, paper: $6.00. pp varies; 5X8; †lp. Reporting time: 1 month. Payment: copies. Copyrights for author.

CENTERING: A Magazine of Poetry, Years Press, F. Richard Thomas, ATL EBH, Michigan State University, E. Lansing, MI 48824. 1973. Poetry. "Unlike many little magazines, *CENTERING* contains at least 10 pages of each poet's work. Because of limitations of time and money, I rarely accept unsolicited material." circ. 300-400. 1/yr. Pub'd 1 issue 1979; expects 1 issue 1980. sub. price: $1.50; per copy: $1.50; sample: $1.50. Back issues: #2, $2.50; #3, $2.00; #4, $1.50. 48-64pp; 7X8½; of. mss. solicited. Payment: 5 copies. Copyrighted, reverts to author. Ads: No ads. COSMEP, CCLM.

CENTRAL PARK, Stephen-Paul Martin, Richard Royal, 410 West End Ave., Apt 1E, New York, NY 10024. 1979. Poetry, fiction, articles, art, photos, interviews, satire, criticism, reviews, parts-of-novels, long-poems, plays. "We are interested in material that takes a fresh approach, but also displays familiarity with the traditions it emerges from. All forms are welcome, although we are suspicious of experimental approaches when they do not reveal at least an internal coherence and command of language. Work that is *overtly* autobiographical or relies too heavily on the element of shock will get little sympathy here. We prefer writing that locates an imaginative self which is at the same time rooted in the socio-political tensions of the time. We are an urban journal, desirous of reflecting the multi-racial, international texture of the city." circ. 500. 4/yr. Pub'd 1 issue 1979. sub. price: $6.00; per copy: $2.00; sample: $1.50. 80pp; 5X8; of. Reporting time: 6 weeks. Payment: 1 copy. Copyrighted, reverts to author. Pub's reviews. §Poetry, fiction, socio-political commentary, criticism.

Century Three Press, John E. Rosenow, Gerreld L. Pulsipher, 411 So 13th Street, Suite 315, Lincoln, NB 68508, (402) 474-6345. 1979. Pub'd 1 title 1979. 1 title listed in the *Small Press Record of Books in Print* (9th Edition, 1980). avg. price, cloth: $17.95. 257pp; 7X10; †of.

Ceolfrith Press, Tony Knipe, Editor; Catherine Hepworth, Administrator, 27 Stockton Road, Sunderland, Tyne & Wear SR27DF, United Kingdom, 0783-41214. 1970. Poetry, art. "Ceolfrith Press is not a commercial enterprise but a 'small press' financed by grant aid. Its policy is to promote, extend and preserve, through publishing, the content of selected exhibitions and activities organised by Ceolfrith arts, sunderland arts centre, and the works of national andd international poets, writers and musicians associated with the centre, or living and working in the northern arts region. Publications include visual poetry, poetry, print folders, fine art exhibition catalogues, and books published on the occasion of specific 'popular' exhibitions e.g. science fiction and football. A printed brochure of publications is available on request. (Authors of recent publications include Norman Nicholson, Jon Silkin, Glyn Hughes and Pete Morgan. A major publication of 1975 was on the visual world of Gerard Manley Hopkins.) Authors of recent publications include R.S. Thomas. Also recently published is the first major study of the artist Jack Smith and his work and major exhibition catalogues on Finnish glass

76

and London artist Nigel Hall" avg. press run Varies: 750-2,000. Pub'd 7 titles 1979; expects 5 titles 1980, 5 titles 1981. avg. price, paper: Most poetry £2.00, art titles vary.; other: Signed limited editions (av. run 50-75) price usually £5.00. Discounts: 33⅓ percent trade discount to recognised booksellers. Poetry 28-80 pp, art varies too much to specify.; size Varies: Most poetry titles 8¼X6, most art books A4-11½X8¼; of. Copyrights for author.

Clo Chailleann, 9 Taybridge Road, Aberfeldy PH15 2BH, Scotland. 1979. Poetry, fiction. "This press is concerned only with the publication of material in or concerning Scottish Galtic." avg. press run 1,000-1,500. Pub'd 3 titles 1979. 3 titles listed in the *Small Press Record of Books in Print* (9th Edition, 1980). avg. price, paper: £2.00. Discounts: Trade 33⅓%. 75pp; of, lp. Payment: 10%. Copyrights for author.

The Chair, Stan Wells, 161 Stokesley Crescent, Billingham, Cleveland TS23 1NQ, United Kingdom. 1977. Poetry. "*Moods* by A. K. Whitehouse (BB2). *Torn No* by Stan Wells (BB1)." avg. press run 200. Expects 2 titles 1980. avg. price, paper: 5p. Discounts: 2/3's of face value. 16pp; size A10. Reporting time: 1 month where possible. Payment: 25 free copies. ALP, ALM.

THE CHAIR, Stan Wells, 161 Stokesly Crescent, Billingham, Cleveland TS23 1NQ, United Kingdom. 1977. Poetry, fiction, art, criticism, reviews, music, news items. circ. 200. 4/yr. Pub'd 4 issues 1979; expects 4 issues 1980, 4 issues 1981. sub. price: 75p; per copy: 20p; sample: 20p + postage. Back issues: 20p + postage. Discounts: 2/3's of face value. 24pp; size A5. Reporting time: 1 month where possible. Payment: unfortunately not. Not copyrighted. Pub's reviews: 30 in 1979. §Poetry. Ads: £20/£10. ALP, ALM.

CHAIRMAN'S CHAT, Dominion Press, A. Stuart Otto, P O Box 696, San Marcos, CA 92069, 714-746-9430. 1975. Articles, reviews, letters, news items. "All material staff written. Publication is official Journal of the Committee for Elimination of Death." circ. 1,000 to 1,500. 4/yr. sub. price: $10.00; per copy: $4.00; sample: free. Back issues: Regular sub rate (includes binding). Discounts: 1/3 to anyone in quantities. 4pp; 8½X11; of. not accepting mss. Pub's reviews: 1 in 1979. §Immortalism/futurism (not to be confused with 'hereafter' immortality). Ads: No ads.

Chalardpro Books, D. E. Smith, 802 Sixth Avenue, Coraopolis, PA 15108, 264-2236. 1979. Poetry. "Editor in Thailand, Nong Chalardpro, 779-2 Soi Luechal, Pahonyotin Road, Bangkok, Thailand" avg. press run 500. Pub'd 3 titles 1979. 1 title listed in the *Small Press Record of Books in Print* (9th Edition, 1980). avg. price, paper: $2.00. Discounts: Undecided. 60pp; 6X10; †mi. Reporting time: 1 month. Payment: negotiable. Copyrights for author.

Champoeg Press, PO Box 92, Forest Grove, OR 97116. 3 titles listed in the *Small Press Record of Books in Print* (9th Edition, 1980).

Chandler & Sharp Publishers, Inc., Jonathan Sharp, Howard Chandler, 11A Commercial Blvd., Novato, CA 94947, 415-883-2353. 1972. "We are strictly book publishers-Adult non fiction trade books and college textbooks in the social sciences and humanities." avg. press run 4,000. Pub'd 4 titles 1979; expects 6 titles 1980, 6 titles 1981. 24 titles listed in the *Small Press Record of Books in Print* (9th Edition, 1980). avg. price, cloth: $12.00; paper: $5.00. Discounts: Trade books: 40 percent; textbooks: 20 percent; wholesalers: 50 percent. 192pp; 6X9; of. Reporting time: 2-6 weeks. Payment: royalties. copyrights for author on request. COSMEP, AAA.

Chandonnet, Ann, PO Box A, Chugiak, AK 99567. 1977. Poetry. avg. press run 200-350. Pub'd 2 titles 1979; expects 1 title 1980. 3 titles listed in the *Small Press Record of Books in Print* (9th Edition, 1980). avg. price, paper: $2.00-$4.25. Discounts: 40% to bookstores and libraries. 48pp; 5½X8½; of. Reporting time: I print only my own work: poetry and local history. Copyrights for author.

CHANDRABHAGA, Jayanta Mahapatra, Tinkonia Bagicha, Cuttack 753 001, Orissa, India, 20-566. 1979. Poetry, fiction, interviews, criticism, reviews. "The magazine is international in scope. Although emphasis is on Indian writing (in English and other Indian Languages), recent contributors include Frank Allen (USA), Sapardi Djoko Damono (Indonesia), Bruce King (New Zealand), Kazuko Shiraishi (Japan); and Indian poets/scholars such as V. Y. Kantak, Brijraj Singh, Ayyappa Paniker, and Hinki novelist Krishna Baldev Vaid (now in residence in US)." circ. 1,000. 2/yr. Pub'd 2 issues 1979; expects 2 issues 1980. sub. price: In India, Rupees Fifteen, Foreign Countries, Dollars Ten (US); per copy: $5.00; sample: First issue free, subsequent issues at single copy rate. 88pp; 12cm x 24cm; lp. Reporting time: 3-4 weeks. Payment: 2 copies of the magazine & 10 offprints of work. The work, as it appears in *Chandrabhaga,* is copyright for that issue only. Subsequent publication of the work (in anthology or book) must be with written permission of the editor. Ads: Rupees One Thousand (India), $500.00/Rupees Five Hundred (India), $250.00.

THE CHANEY CHRONICAL, London Northwest, David H Schlottmann, 929 South Bay Rd,

Olympia, WA 98506, (206) 352-8622. 1972. "Devoted to study of William H. Chaney (1821-1903) who is generally believed to be father of author Jack London. A companion paper to WHAT'S NEW ABOUT LONDON, JACK? Future items will include articles written by Chaney on spiritualism, astrology, etc, a horoscope cast for a Salem, Oregon resident, and bibliographies." circ. 30. irreg. Pub'd 1 issue 1979; expects 1 issue 1980. price per copy: $.50; sample: $0.50. Back issues: xerox available. 10pp; 8½X11; †mi. Payment: none. Pub's reviews. §Wm. H. Chaney. Ads: 1 cent/wd classified.

CHANGE, Synergistic Press, Art Coulter, 1825 North Lake Shore Dr, Chapel Hill, NC 27514, 919-942-2994. 1954. Articles, criticism, reviews, letters. "Synergetics is the art and science of evoking synergy in the human mind, in small groups, and in other complex systems." circ. 200. 5/yr. Pub'd 5 issues 1979; expects 5 issues 1980. sub. price: $5.00; per copy: $1.00; sample: $1.00. 25pp; 8½X11; †of. Reporting time: 30 days. Payment: copies only. Not copyrighted. Pub's reviews: 5 in 1979.

THE CHARIOTEER, Parnassos, Andonis Decavalles, Bebe Spanos Ikaris, PO Box 2928, Grand Central Station, New York, NY 10017. 1960. Criticism, reviews. "We are a review of modern Greek culture and 75 percent to 80 percent of each issue consists of translations from modern Greek authors." circ. 1,500. 1/yr. Pub'd 1 issue 1979; expects 1 issue 1980, 1 issue 1981. sub. price: $5.00; per copy: $5.00; sample: $5.00. Back issues: $4.00 regular issues; $6.00 double-issues. Discounts on multiple issues. Discounts: 10 percent for recognized agencies provided check accompanies order. 100pp; 5½X8½; lp. Reporting time: 3 months. Payment: none. Copyrighted, reverts by arrangement. Pub's reviews: 12 in 1979. §Greek culture, especially modern. Ads: $150.00/$100/none. CCLM, COSMEP.

Charisma Press (see also CHARISMA PRESS REVIEW), Lucius Annese, Director & Editor; Gregory Palma, Poetry Editor; Leonard Bacigalupo, History Editor, PO Box 263, St. Francis Seminary, Andover, MA 01810, (617) 851-7910. 1978. Poetry, articles, criticism, interviews, reviews. "Approximately 120-150 pages. No biases - but some specialty in philosophical political & religious orientations. Recent contributor (first), Lucius Annese, Gregory Palma, Leonard Bacigalupo." avg. press run 500-1,000. Pub'd 1 title 1979; expects 2 titles 1980, 12 titles 1981. 8 titles listed in the *Small Press Record of Books in Print* (9th Edition, 1980). avg. price, cloth: $10.00-$15.00; paper: $5.00-$7.00. Discounts: 10% to 35%. 120-150pp; 5½X8½; †of. Reporting time: soon as possible by arrangement.

CHARISMA PRESS REVIEW, Charisma Press, Fr. Lucius Annese, PO Box 263, Andover, MA 01810, 617-851-7910. 1980. Poetry, articles, criticism, reviews. "Usually single page (5½ x 8½) long. No biases but spectral and middle of road. Contributors: Fr. Lucius Annese, Gregory J. Palma, Leonard Bacigalupo, Mary Ellen Verville, Patricia T. Sullivan." circ. 3,000-5,000. 12/yr. Pub'd 12 issues 1979. sub. price: $6.00; per copy: $0.50. Discounts: by inquiry. 5½X8½; †of. Copyrighted. Pub's reviews. §Philosophy, theology, religion, political science, texts, poetry, how-to, eductional. Ads: $50.00/$25.00/$15.00.

CHARITON REVIEW, Chariton Review Press, Jim Barnes, Northeast Missouri State University, Kirksville, MO 63501, 816-665-5121 ext 2156. 1975. Poetry, fiction, art, photos, reviews. "We try to keep open minds, but admit a bias to work that relies more on strong imagery than talkiness. We are very interested in translation, particularly translations of modern poets and especially those from languages other than French or Spanish though we have used numerous translations from those two languages. Recent contributors include Richard Hugo, John Haines, Phil Levine, Maura Stanton, David Ray, Madeline Defrees, James Tate, Tess Gallagher, Raymond Carver, Quinton Duval, James Welch, Paul Zimmer, Dennis Schmitz, Russel Edson; translations of Supervielle, Lorca, Rozewicz. No xerox or carbons!" circ. 650+. 2/yr. Pub'd 2 issues 1979; expects 2 issues 1980. 2 titles listed in the *Small Press Record of Books in Print* (9th Edition, 1980). sub. price: $4.00/yr ($7.00 2/yr); per copy: $2.00; sample: $2.00. Back issues: Vol. 1 No. 1 $20.00; Vol. 2 No. 1 $10.00; others, $2.00. Discounts: on request. 104pp; 6X9; lp. Reporting time: 1 month or less. Payment: $5.00 page up to $50.00 and 2 copies. Copyrighted, returned to author on request. Pub's reviews: 4 in 1979. §Modern poetry, fiction, translation. Ads: $100.00/$50.00. CCLM.

Chariton Review Press, CHARITON REVIEW, Jim Barnes, Northeast Missouri State University, Kirksville, MO 63501, 816-665-5121 ext 2156. Poetry. "Submitters should query before sending manuscripts. We like our books to run between 100 and 125 pages. We have absolutely no desire to print chapbooks. Our first full length collection of poetry—*The Tramp's Cup,* by David Ray — won the 1979 William Carlos Williams Award from The Poetry Society of America, which allowed us to go into a second edition with a print run of 1,200 copies. Funds permitting, we plan to do one book per year. We are interested only in solid contemporary poetry of first rank. We pay 10% royalty, or a flat rate (usually between 300 and 500 dollars)." circ. 700. Pub'd 1 issue 1979; expects 1 issue 1980. price per copy: $3.00. Discounts: 40%. 125pp; 6X9; of, lp. Reporting time: 1 week to 1 month (submitter

78

mut query first). Payment: 10% or flat rate. Copyrighted. CCLM.

Charles H. Kerr Publishing Company, Burton Rosen, Fred Thompson, 600 W Jackson Blvd, Suite 413, Chicago, IL 60606, (312) 454-0363. 1886. "Charles H. Kerr is a non-profit organization, publishing in the field of American Labor History, Women's History and Socialism. At present, there is no paid staff, and all office work is done by volunteers. All production is contracted to outside commercial shops. Additional address: PO Box 914, Chicago IL 60690. The Kerr company acts as distributor of the publications of the Illinois Labor History Society, and of other similar organizations. Kerr publishes for educational purposes and is not engaged in any profit-making or political activities. Most of Kerr's sales are to schools and libraries." avg. press run 10,000. Pub'd 2 titles 1979; expects 2-3 titles 1980, 3-4 titles 1981. 18 titles listed in the *Small Press Record of Books in Print* (9th Edition, 1980). avg. price, cloth: $10.00; paper: $4.50. Discounts: Trade 40%, Text 25%, special discounts on bulk orders of pamphlets, by negotiation. 20% text on itjems with list price under $2.00. 250pp; 5X8, 6X9; of. Reporting time: 2 months. Payment: varies. Copyrights for author.

Charles River Books, Inc., Leslie Zheutlin, Editor; Mark Rosenblatt, Editor, 59 Commercial Wharf, Boston, MA 02110, 617-742-9493. 1976. Poetry, fiction, art, music. "We publish, import, and distribute a variety of titles: poetry, reprints, sports, theology, social work, do-it-yourself series, etc." avg. press run 5,000. Pub'd 5 titles 1979; expects 10 titles 1980, 50 titles 1981. 16 titles listed in the *Small Press Record of Books in Print* (9th Edition, 1980). avg. price, cloth: $6.95; paper: $2.95. Discounts: Wholesalers, 50% for 10 or more; Trade, up to 46% for 100 (40% 5-29 books). Poetry books, average 40pp; reprints average 200.pp; of/lp. Reporting time: varies. Payment: 8%. Copyrights for author. COSMEP.

The Charles Street Press (see also COMMON WORD), Phillip McCaffrey, P.O. Box 4692, Baltimore, MD 21212. 1978. Poetry, fiction. "In the spring of 1979 we are initiating two series of chapbooks. *University Prize* books will be selected in a national competition among college and university students. Annual deadline: February 1. Manuscripts of poetry should be 20-24 pages. Winning author will receive $100 cash prize and 100 copies. Remaining 400 copies will be distributed free of charge to subscribers, schools, editors, and libraries. Each manuscript must be accompanied by a $1 reading fee. *Folio* books will be chapbooks of 24-36 pages, poetry or fiction, by new and established authors. Editions of 500 and 1000. Retail $2, but available to subscribers at half price: 4 for $5.00, 10 for $10. We are actively soliciting poetry manuscripts for this series, beginning in June, 1978. Each manuscript must be accompanied by a $1 reading fee." avg. press run 500 or 1000. Expects 3 titles 1980, 4 titles 1981. avg. price, paper: $2.00; other: subscriptions at half price. Discounts: trade, 50%; orders of 5 or more, same title or mixed, 50%. 28pp; 5½X8; of. Reporting time: 3 weeks, occasionally longer for acceptances. Payment: University Prize: $100 and 100 copies; Folio: 10 copies. Copyrights for author.

Charnel House, Crad Kilodney, c/o Crad Kilodney, 134 Haddington Avenue, Toronto, Ontario M5M 2P6, Canada, (416) 482-1341. 1979. Fiction, art, collages. "Private imprint. No mss wanted. Limited need for b & w drawings, photos, and collages. Artists and photographers may send non-returnable samples to be kept on file. I will notify potential contributors of my requirements for each new book. Current title in print, *World Under Anaesthesia,* $2.00 postpaid. New title expected Spring 1980." avg. press run 1,000. Pub'd 1 title 1979; expects 1 title 1980. 1 title listed in the *Small Press Record of Books in Print* (9th Edition, 1980). avg. price, paper: $2.00. Discounts: query. 40pp; 6X9; of. Reporting time: no report on samples, for art work I solicit, report within 2-3 months. Payment: copies. Copyrights for author.

CHASQUI, Kenneth W. Massey, Dept of Modern Languages, Swarthmore College, Swarthmore, PA 19081, (215) 447-7145. 1971. Poetry, fiction, articles, interviews, criticism, reviews, parts-of-novels. "*Chasqui* accepts creative writing written in Spanish or Portuguese. All other material may be in either English, Spanish or Portuguese. Subscription information should be directed to Howard Fraser, Dept of Modern Language, College of William and Mary, Williamsburg, Virginia 23185." circ. 500. 3/yr. Pub'd 3 issues 1979; expects 3 issues 1980, 3 issues 1981. sub. price: $9.00; per copy: $4.00; sample: $4.00. Back issues: $5.00. 130pp; 8½X11; of. Reporting time: 3 months, maximum. Pub's reviews: 50 in 1979. §Brazilian and Spanish American literature, literary criticism, theory. Ads: $50.00/$35.00. CCLM.

CHAWED RAWZIN, Chawed Rawzin Press, Charles Behlen, 225 W. Crosby, Slaton, TX 79364. 1974. Poetry, long-poems. "There is no limit to the length of the submission being considered. The focus is on Southwest poets, but not exclusively. Recent contributors: Mike Anderson, Dave Oliphant, Tom McGroth, Gene Frumkin, Del Marie Rogers, Noome Shihob." circ. 300-500. 1/yr. Pub'd 1 issue 1979; expects 1 issue 1980, 1 issue 1981. price per copy: $0.50; sample: $0.50. 30pp; 5½X8½; †of. Reporting time: 2-3 weeks. Payment: approx, 5 copies of mag. Copyrighted, reverts to author. Ads: $25.00/$15.00.

Chawed Rawzin Press (see also CHAWED RAWZIN), Charles Behlen, 225 W. Crosby, Slaton, TX 79364. 1974. Poetry, long-poems. Pub'd 1 title 1979; expects 1 title 1980. avg. price, paper: $0.-60-$4.50. 23-64pp; 5½X8½; †of. Reporting time: 2-3 weeks. Payment: 50-100 copies of book.

Cheat Mountain Press (see also BACKCOUNTRY), Michael Mazzolini, Box 390, Elkins, WV 26241, (304) 636-6236. 1977. Poetry, fiction, art, cartoons, satire, long-poems, collages, plays. "To date we have published only one chapbook of poetry, *Hot Knives, Greasy Spoons, and All Night Diners,* by Michael Mazzolini which retails for $3.50 (includes postage). We are just beginning and are sort of a cooperative press, each author pays for their own publication. We would handle promotional, distribution, and reviews on a cooperative basis." avg. press run 500. Pub'd 1 title 1979. 1 title listed in the *Small Press Record of Books in Print* (9th Edition, 1980). avg. price, paper: $3.50. Payment: 10% of retail cost would go towards press for distribution purposes. COSMEP.

CHECKLIST OF HUMAN RIGHTS DOCUMENTS, Earl M Coleman Enterprises, Inc, Guido F. Olivera, Editor, PO Box 143, Pine Plains, NY 12567, (518) 398-7193. 1975. "A monthly compilation of bibliographic entries for print materials which concern international human rights." 12/yr. Pub'd 12 issues 1979; expects 12 issues 1980, 12 issues 1981. sub. price: $75.00; sample: free. Back issues: vols 1-3 (1976-78) @ $75.00 complete. Discounts: 10% to jobbers and agents, for others contact publisher. 40pp; 8½X11; of. Copyrighted. Ads: $200.00.

CHELSEA, Sonia Raiziss, Editor; Alfredo de Palchi, Brian Swann, Associate Editors; Richard Foerster, Barbara A. Penn, Assistant Editors, Box 5880, Grand Central Station, New York, NY 10017. 1958. Poetry, fiction, articles, art, interviews, criticism, parts-of-novels, long-poems, plays, concrete art. "Stress on quality, originality, style, variety...(superior translations). No special biases, no requirements on length (according to suitability). Attitudes, eclectic material. Recent contributors: Laura (Riding) Jackson, Fernando Arrabal, Joseph Bruchac, Gene Frumkin, Christine L. Hewitt, Jonathan Holden, Jascha Kessler, McKeel McBride, John Morgan, Tom O'Horgan, David Posner, Susan Fromberg Schaeffer, William V. Spanos, John Tagliabue, Maria Thomas, Frances Whyatt." circ. 1,100. 1-2/yr. Pub'd 1 issue 1979; expects 2 issues 1980. 1 title listed in the *Small Press Record of Books in Print* (9th Edition, 1980). sub. price: $6.00/2 consecutive issues as published; per copy: $3.50; sample: $2.00 or more. Back issues: prices range from $3.00 to $15.00 if rare. Discounts: agency discount: 40%; bookstores : 30%. 200pp; 5½X8½; of. Reporting time: 2 mos. Payment: copies, or token fee. Copyrighted. Ads: only exchange ads with other literary mags. CCLM.

THE CHELSEA JOURNAL, A. de Valk, Editor; Daniel Callan, Associate Editor, 1437 College Drive, Saskatoon, Saskatchewan S7N0W6, Canada, 306-343-4561. 1975. Poetry, fiction, articles, interviews, reviews, letters, plays, news items, non-fiction. circ. 1,800. 6/yr. Pub'd 6 issues 1979; expects 6 issues 1980. sub. price: $10.00 Canada/$12.00 U.S. & Foreign; per copy: $1.75; sample: $1.75. Back issues: $1.75 each. Discounts: consignment sales-30%. 48pp; 8X11. Reporting time: 6 to 8 weeks. Payment: $.02 per word. Copyrighted. Pub's reviews: 36 in 1979. §Current affairs, literature, spirituality. Ads: $100/$60. CPPA.

Cherry Valley Editions (see also NORTHEAST RISING SUN), Pamela Beach Plymell, Charles Plymell, Joshua Norton, Box 303, Cherry Valley, NY 13320, 607-264-3204. 1974. "1977 saw the publication of 6 books including ROD MCKUEN reads *IN MEMORY OF MY FATHER* by CHARLES PLYMELL (a record of the poem is included in the back of the chapbook), it is also a selection of the SMALL PRESS BOOK CLUB. In 1978 we will publish a wide variety of writers, John Gierach, Ray Bremser, Kirk Robertson, Allen Ginsberg, Charles Henri Ford, Mary Beach, Joyce Mansour, Janine Pommy Vega, Joshua Norton. 1980 will see publication of Herbert E. Huncke's *The Evening Sun Turned Crimson* and Geoffrey Cook's translation of *The Miscellanea of Venantius Fortunatus.* We look for good writing of an unusual nature frequently experimental. Looking for photography books. Charles Henri Ford's *Om Krishna II.*" avg. press run 1,000. Pub'd 8 titles 1979. 21 titles listed in the *Small Press Record of Books in Print* (9th Edition, 1980). avg. price, cloth: $15.00; paper: $3.00; other: Signed $25.00. Discounts: 1-4: 20 percent; 5-19: 40 percent; 20 plus: 50 percent. 64-80pp; 5½X8½; of. Reporting time: A.S.A.P. Payment: 10 percent royalty, for books only. Copyrights for author. COSMEP-EAST, NYSSPA.

Cheshire Books, Michael Riordan, Linda Goodman, 514 Bryant Street, Palo Alto, CA 94301, 415-854-0393. 1976. "We are presently publishing material we create ourselves or solicit specifically for our own books. Starting in 1979, we will be publishing material from the writing public at large, and authors are invited to submit manuscripts in fields of art, architecture, energy & the environment, and science. Accepting non-fiction only. Most recent book is *A Golden Thread.* Two others in the works." avg. press run 15,000. Pub'd 1 title 1979; expects 2 titles 1980, 3 titles 1981. 3 titles listed in the *Small Press Record of Books in Print* (9th Edition, 1980). avg. price, cloth: $14.95; paper: $9.50. Discounts: Trade distribution through wholesale jobbers, including Bookpeople, Ingram, and Baker & Taylor.

Offer 50-52% discount to wholesalers; cash orders from retailers will receive 42% discount on 20 or more books. 304pp; size varies; of. Reporting time: two months. Payment: 7-10% of list price, small advance payable on delivery. Copyrights for author.

Chicago New Art Association (see also NEW ART EXAMINER), Jane Allen, Editor; Derek Guthrie, Associate Editor, 230 E. Ohio, RM. 207, Chicago, IL 60611, 312-642-6236. 1973. Articles, art, photos, cartoons, interviews, criticism, reviews, letters, news items. "Commentary on and analysis of the exhibition and making of art, film, photographs, inlcuding humor, occasional cartoons, Jack Burnham, Joshua Kind." avg. press run 7,000. Pub'd 10 titles 1979; expects 10 titles 1980, 10 titles 1981. avg. price, paper: $1.75. Discounts: 3x, 5x plus 10x rates, 1 yr sub (10 titles) $15.00. 28pp; 11½X17; of. Payment: $10.00, 350 word reviews, $75.00 article. Copyrights for author.

CHICAGO REVIEW, Bill Monroe, University of Chicago, 5700 S. Ingleside Box C, Chicago, IL 60637, 212-753-3571. 1946. Poetry, fiction, articles, art, photos, interviews, criticism, reviews, parts-of-novels, letters, plays. "*CR* has an international readership; submissions from unknown writers are welcome. *CR* looks for poems and fictions which participate in and test the bounds of their respective traditions. It seeks essays, reviews and interviews which address contemporary literary and cultural questions and problems. Recent numbers include the poetry of Nobel Laureate Odysseus Elytis, Lisel Mueller, Sandra McPherson, and Alvin Greenberg; interviews with Jorge Luis Borges and Richard Stern; and fiction by Stephen Dixon and D.C. Muecke. SASE expected (including subs. from agents)." circ. 2,000. 4/yr. Pub'd 4 issues 1979; expects 4 issues 1980, 4 issues 1981. sub. price: $10.00; per copy: $3.00; sample: $3.00. Back issues: Yes, on inquiry. Discounts: agency-10 percent subscription, classroom orders — $2.50/copy. 140-160pp; 6X9; of. Reporting time: 3 months. Payment: primarily in contributors copies. Copyrighted, rights revert only on request. Pub's reviews: 14 in 1979. §literature & the arts. Ads: $120.00/$70.00. CCLM, COSMEP.

Chicano Studies Research Center Publications (see also AZTLAN: International Journal of Chicano Studies), University of California-Los Angeles, 405 Hilgard Avenue, Los Angeles, CA 90025, 213-825-2642. 16 titles listed in the *Small Press Record of Books in Print* (9th Edition, 1980).

Children's Art Foundation, Inc. (see also STONE SOUP, The Magazine By Children), Gerry Mandel, William Rubel, Box 83, Santa Cruz, CA 95063, (408) 426-5557. 1973. Poetry, fiction, art, photos, reviews, letters, parts-of-novels, long-poems, plays. "All material written and drawn by children ages 3-13." avg. press run 7,000. Pub'd 5 titles 1979. 9 titles listed in the *Small Press Record of Books in Print* (9th Edition, 1980). avg. price, paper: $2.50. Discounts: available upon request. 48pp; 6X8¾; of. Reporting time: 3 weeks. Payment: copies. Copyrights for author. CCLM.

Children's Book Press/Imprenta de Libros Infantiles, Harriet Rohmer, Roger I Reyes, Robin Cherin, 1461 9th Ave., San Francisco, CA 94122, 415-664-8500. 1975. "We publish myths, legends, folklore and conteemporary stories of the different peoples who live in America today. Most of our books are bilingual in Spanish, Chinese, Tagalog (Pilipino), Korean or Vietnamese." avg. press run 5,000. Pub'd 5 titles 1979; expects 5 titles 1980, 5 titles 1981. 21 titles listed in the *Small Press Record of Books in Print* (9th Edition, 1980). avg. price, paper: $3.95. Discounts: 40 percent trade discount, other rates on request. 24pp; 9X9½; of. We do not solicit manuscripts. Payment: yes. Copyrights for author.

CHIMERA-A Complete Theater Piece, HS Press, Harry William Saffren, 5538 Morris Street, Philadelphia, PA 19144. 1976. Fiction, plays. "CHIMERA is a complete theater piece, including: the theater, sets, characters, and script; to cutout, put together and perform. Issue No. 1 (April 1976) contains Kenneth Marcus Lipman's *This Is Money-A Story Told To An Audience Of Two.* Issue No. 2 (Dec. 1976) contains Edgar Allan Poe's *The Cask Of Amontillado.* Issue No. 3 (due June 1978) will be *The Jeniper Tree* from Grimms' Tales." circ. 1,000. 1/yr. Expects 1 issue 1980, 1 issue 1981. sub. price: £7.00; per copy: $3.95. Back issues: $3.95. Discounts: 20% on 2-4 issues, 40% 5 or more. 8½X11; of.

CHINA QUARTERLY, Dick Wilson, School of Oriental & African Studies, Malet St., London WC1E 7HP, United Kingdom. 1960. Articles, reviews. "About 7000 words." circ. 5,500. 4/yr. sub. price: £6; per copy: £1.50. 200pp. Reporting time: 3 months. Payment: none. Ads: £45.

CHOCK, Chock Publications, Ian C. Durant, Rutherford College, Kent University, Canterbury, Kent CT27NX, United Kingdom, CHISLET 388. 1978. Poetry, fiction, articles, art, cartoons, photos, reviews, letters. "Will consider unpublished material. Recent (poetry) contributors include: Pereira, Sneyd, Daugherty, W. Stafford, A. Ginsberg, etc. First issue out in March '78. McDowell, Brown, Bartlett, Nations, Toczek, Guest, Oandasan, Ditsky, Bruchac." circ. 600. 2-3/yr. Expects 4 issues 1980. sub. price: $8.00/2 issue; per copy: $4.00 or 75p. Back issues: Issue 2 & 3, $5.00 or £1. 34pp; 15cm x 21cm; of. Reporting time: 3 weeks. Payment: complimentary copies. Copyrighted, reverts to author. Pub's reviews: 12 in 1979. §poetry. Ads: $50.00/$20.00. ALP.

Chock Publications (see also CHOCK), Ian C. Durant, Rutherford College, Kent University, Canterbury, Kent CT27NX, United Kingdom, CHISLET 388. 1978. Poetry, fiction, articles, art, interviews, parts-of-novels, plays. "*At the Sign of the Black Manikin, Village Voice,* both now out of print. *Chock Freesheet* numbers 1 & 2 now out of print." avg. press run 200. Expects 2-3 titles 1980. Reporting time: 2-3 weeks. Copyrights for author.

CHOOMIA (A literary review), Yarrow Press, Ann Guido, Jay Barwell, P.O. Box 40322, Tucson, AZ 85719. 1975. Poetry, fiction, articles, art, interviews, criticism, reviews, parts-of-novels, long-poems. "We are open-minded. Recent contributors: Philip Booth, Ruth Whitman, Ruth Stone, James Schevill, John Engels, May Sarton, Alan Feldman, C.E. Poverman, Jane Shore, Patricia Hampl, Steve Orlen." circ. 500. 2/yr. Pub'd 2 issues 1979; expects 2 issues 1980. sub. price: 3 consecutive issues for $7.00; per copy: $2.50; sample: $2.50. Back issues: $1.00 for Nos. 2, 3, & 6; $2.00 special New England issue 100 pp. Discounts: 40 percent to bookstores in bulk orders over 10 copies; 40 percent to classes over 10 copies. 100pp; 5X8; of. Reporting time: 1 to 2 months. Payment: usually 2 copies. Copyrighted, reverts to author. Pub's reviews: 2 in 1979. §poetry/fiction. Ads: $55.00/$30.00. CCLM.

CHOUTEAU REVIEW, David Perkins, Editor, Box 10016, Kansas City, MO 64111, (816) 561-3086. 1975. Poetry, fiction, articles, art, photos, cartoons, interviews, satire, criticism, reviews, music, parts-of-novels, long-poems, concrete art. "Prefer poems 1 or 2 pages, no more than 5; stories from 5-20 pages (our pages). Catholic taste; we want clarity, excitement, intelligence, novel forms. Contributors include: Bly, Anderson, Codrescu, A.S. Hamilton, Barry Lopez, R. Kostelanetz, S. Dunn, A. Salkey, T. Veitch, C. Coolidge, J. Tate, A. Feldman, Ascher/Straus, Tom Whalen, Steve Dixon. *Chouteau Review* is published by Chouteau Arts, Inc." circ. 2,000. 2/yr. Pub'd 2 issues 1979; expects 2 issues 1980, 2 issues 1981. sub. price: $12.00 two years; per copy: $3.00; sample: $3.00. Discounts: none estbl. 116pp; 6X9; of. Reporting time: 1 week—1 month. Payment varies. Copyrighted, does not revert to author. Pub's reviews: 3 in 1979. §Poetry, film, novels, interviews, musical scores, graphics, photography. Ads: $100.00/$60.00.

Chowder Chapbooks (see also THE CHOWDER REVIEW), Ron Slate, Editor, PO Box 33, Wollaston, MA 02170. 1977. Poetry, long-poems. "We are reading unsolicited manuscripts for our third and fourth series (eight additional titles). Send for style and guide sheet before submitting. Recent books: *Rough Edges* by Floyd Skloot, *Men At Table* by Philip Dacey, *A Change in Weather,* by Mekeel McBride." avg. press run 400. Pub'd 3 titles 1979; expects 3 titles 1980. 8 titles listed in the *Small Press Record of Books in Print* (9th Edition, 1980). avg. price, paper: $2.00. Discounts: 40% to retail. 32-36pp; 8½X5½; of. Reporting time: 6-8 weeks. Payment: copies. Copyrights for author.

THE CHOWDER REVIEW, Chowder Chapbooks, Ron Slate, Editor; Floyd Skloot, Assoc Editor, PO Box 33, Wollaston, MA 02170. 1973. Poetry, articles, interviews, criticism, reviews, long-poems. "We publish poems that show the delicate balance between intention and flow, poems that give as much as they demand. Translations; special features. A chapbook review section. Richard Shelton, Carolyn Forche, David Wagoner, Brendan Galvin, Stephen Dunn." circ. 800. 2/yr. Pub'd 2 issues 1979; expects 2 issues 1980. sub. price: $7.00/3 issues; $9.00 institutions; per copy: $2.50; sample: $2.50. Back issues: Nos. 1, 4-6, 8, 12, 13: $2.00 Double issue 10/11: $3.00. Discounts: 40% stores. 100pp; 8½X5½; of. Reporting time: 3 weeks. Payment: copies or subscription, payment when funds available. Copyrighted, does not revert to author. Pub's reviews: 40 in 1979. §poetry/poetics/review maps. Ads: $40.00/$25.00. CCLM/PDS (Plains Distribution Service).

Christopher Davies Publishers Ltd. (see also POETRY WALES), J. P. Ward, Cary Archard, Reviews Editor, 52 Mansel Street, Swansea SA1 5EL, United Kingdom, 0792 41933. 1949. Poetry, fiction, criticism. avg. press run varies greatly. Pub'd 16 titles 1979; expects 18 titles 1980, 24 titles 1981. avg. price, cloth: $5.95. Discounts: 35% UK, 40% export. 200-250pp; size varies; of. Reporting time: up to 6 weeks. Payment: by contract.

Christopher's Books, Melissa Mytinger, 850 Talbot Avenue, Berkeley, CA 94706, (415) 482-2198. 1969. Poetry, fiction, criticism, letters, parts-of-novels, long-poems. "Recent contributors: Kenneth Rexroth, Barry Gifford, Laura Chester, James Den Boer, Gloria Frym, Frederick Turner, Albert Goldbarth, Howard McCord." avg. press run 1,200. Pub'd 6 titles 1979; expects 9 titles 1980, 10 titles 1981. 18 titles listed in the *Small Press Record of Books in Print* (9th Edition, 1980). avg. price, cloth: $15.00; paper: $5.00. Discounts: 2-4 copies, 20%; 5 plus copies, 40%; wholesalers, rates upon request. 50-200pp; 6X9; lp, of. Reporting time: 2 months. Payment: varies. Copyrights for author.

Chronicle Books/Prism Editions, Richard Schuettge, Editor & Publisher; Jane Vandenburgh, Senior Editor; Susan Harper, Editor, 870 Market Street Suite 915, San Francisco, CA 94102, 415-777-7240. 1968. Art, photos. "Chronicle Books continues to publish regional outdoor and western guidebooks, with a broadened scope that includes travel and other non-fiction books of national interest. Prism Editions, our new imprint, features visual books focusing on lifestyle, popular fine arts, and photography." avg. press run 7,500 (Chronicle Books), 20,000 (Prism Editions). Pub'd 30 titles 1979. avg. price, cloth: $25.00; paper: $5.95(Chron), $9.95(Prism); other: Cloth ltd (Prism): $25.00. Discounts: 1-4, 33%; 5-24, 40%; 25-49, 41%; 50-249, 42%; 250-499, 43%; 500-999, 44%; 1,000 plus, 45%. l60pp; 8X9; 10X13; of, lp. Reporting time: one month. Payment: 8 percent paid twice yearly. Copyrights for author.

CHRYSALIS: A Magazine of Women's Culture, Kirsten Grimstad, Deborah Marrow, Arlene Raven, Susan Rennie, 1052 W. 6th Street, #330, Los Angeles, CA 90017, (213) 482-5120. 1977. Poetry, fiction, articles, art, photos, interviews, satire, criticism, reviews, letters, parts-of-novels, long-poems, collages, plays. "*Chrysalis* is a magazine of women's culture." circ. 30M. 4/yr. Pub'd 4 issues 1979; expects 4 issues 1980, 4 issues 1981. sub. price: $15.00; per copy: $4.50; sample: $4.50. Back issues: varies. 128pp; 7¾X11; of. Reporting time: 2 months. Payment: $50.00/I.O.U. Copyrighted, reverts to author. Pub's reviews: 8 in 1979. §All culture related to women. Ads: $600.00/$510.00/$0.75.

Chthon Press/Nonesuch Publications, Paul J.J. Payack, 77 Mark Vincent Drive, Westford, MA 01886. 1973. Poetry, fiction. "By invitation only. (Metafiction)" avg. press run 1,000. Pub'd 4 titles 1979; expects 4 titles 1980. 17 titles listed in the *Small Press Record of Books in Print* (9th Edition, 1980). avg. price, paper: $2.50. Discounts: 40% standard. 20-40pp; 5½X8½; of. Copyrights for author. COSMEP.

THE CHUNGA REVIEW, Michael Felten, Box 158, Felch, MI 49831, (906) 246-3562. 1978. Poetry, fiction, long-poems, plays. "Emphasis on poetry. A maximum of 2-3 mainstream/humorous short story/experimental prose/play per issue. Need short fiction works. 1980 poetry contest w/cash awards & publishing or winning entries. Send for details. All ad's must be photo-ready no reducing provided." circ. 250. 4/yr. Pub'd 1 issue 1979; expects 4 issues 1980, 4 issues 1981. sub. price: $6.00; per copy: $1.50; sample: $1.25. Back issues: $1.25. Discounts: 40% to bookstores, 25% to libraries. 40pp; 5½X8½; of. Reporting time: 6 weeks maximum. Payment: one contributor copy. Copyrighted, reverts to author. Ads: $24.00/$15.00.

Cibola Press, Nash Candelaria, Editor, P.O. Box 1495, Palo Alto, CA 94302. 1977. Fiction. "This is a self-publishing press started to publish novels by the editor and founder." avg. press run 2,000. Pub'd 1 title 1979; expects 1 title 1981. 1 title listed in the *Small Press Record of Books in Print* (9th Edition, 1980). avg. price, cloth: $8.95; paper: $3.95. Discounts: Bookstores, distributors, jobbers: 1-4 copies 20%; 5-24 copies 40%; 25-49 copies 43%; 50-99 copies 46%; 100 or more 50%. 192pp; 5½X8½; of. no submissions accepted. Copyrights for author. COSMEP, COSMEP WEST.

CICADA, Eric Amann, 627 Broadview Ave., Toronto, Ontario M4K 2N9, Canada. 1977. Poetry, articles, criticism, reviews. "Haiku or Haiku-related poems, reviews, articles." circ. 800. 4/yr. Pub'd 4 issues 1979; expects 4 issues 1980, 4 issues 1981. sub. price: $10.00; per copy: $3.00; sample: $3.00. Back issues: $3.00. Discounts: 20%. 52pp; 5½X8½; †of. Reporting time: 1 week. Payment: 1 complimentary copy, $50.00 for best contribution to each issue. Copyrighted, reverts to author. Pub's reviews: 4 in 1979. §Books of or about haiku. Ads: no ads.

Cider Barrel Press, Charles D. Ertle, Snake Road, S Newbury, VT 05066, (802) 866-5516. 1976. Poetry, fiction, art, photos, cartoons, satire, long-poems, plays, concrete art. avg. press run 1,000. Pub'd 5 titles 1979. avg. price, paper: $3.50. 80pp; 5½X8½; †of. Copyrights for author.

Cider Mill Press, P O Box 211, Stratford, CT 06497. 1966. Poetry. "*Hope Farm: New & Selected Poems,* H.R. coursen, Ed by Napoleon St. Cyr c. 1979, paper, $2.50, ISBN 0-910380-03-1" avg. press run 500. Pub'd 1 title 1979. 3 titles listed in the *Small Press Record of Books in Print* (9th Edition, 1980). avg. price, cloth: $3.50. Discounts: inquire. 64-72pp; 5¼X8½; of. by solicitation only. Payment: yes. Copyrights for author.

Cienfuegos Press (see also ANARCHIST REVIEW), Stuart Christie, Over the Water, Sanday, Orkney KW17 2BL, United Kingdom. 1974. Poetry, fiction, articles, satire. avg. press run 2,500-3,000. Pub'd 3 titles 1979; expects 5 titles 1980, 8 titles 1981. avg. price, paper: £2.95. of. Reporting time: 1 month. Copyrights for author.

CIMARRON REVIEW, Oklahoma State University Press, Neil J. Hackett, Ed-in-Chief; Jeanne Adams Wray, Managing Editor, Oklahoma State University, Stillwater, OK 74074, (405) 624-6573. 1967. Poetry, fiction, articles, art, interviews. circ. 500. 4/yr. Pub'd 4 issues 1979; expects 4 issues 1980, 4 issues 1981. sub. price: $10; per copy: $4; sample: free. Back issues: half-price. 64-72pp; 6X9; †of. Reporting time: 2-4 weeks. Payment in copies, usually, in process, through grants. Copyrighted, does not revert to author. Ads: No ads.

83

Cin Publications, Clifford Cannon Cin, PO Box 11277, San Francisco, CA 94101, 861-5018. 1978. Articles, art, long-poems, news items. "Cin Publications are 'tight', i.e. concentrated, succinctly informative, because they are mainly for people who hate tomes, who live fast, who read only to make life decisions, who appreaciate expert (out capsulated) info. Present titles include: *Welcome, Hot Plate!* (ways to live thriftily); *The Vitamin Guide; Natural Living Book; Alpha Shorthand: 3-Hour Self-Instructor* ; *How to I-N-C-R-E-A-S-E Gas Mileage; Rejuvevate Thyself; Unusual Original Salads; Naturopathic Formulary* (natural cures & therapies). Writers should inquire before submitting mss, as our material is prepared in-house as a rule. A book may be 2 pages to 64 pages-we like it tight. Cin Pubs. Get around by work of mouth. We sell books, print broadsides to give free. We have yet to publish for profit, editor as outside job." avg. press run varies. Pub'd 3 titles 1979; expects 3 titles 1980, 3 titles 1981. 6 titles listed in the *Small Press Record of Books in Print* (9th Edition, 1980). avg. price, cloth: $10.00; paper: $2.00-$3.00. 2-64pp; †of/lp. Reporting time: In ten days, if ms was requested. Payment in books only at this time. Other arrangements possible.

Cincinnati Chess Federation (see also J'ADOUBE!), David Moeser, Publisher, PO Box 30072, Cincinnati, OH 45230, (513) 232-3204. 1972. "Occasional publishing of books a possibility." Pub'd 1 title 1979; expects 1 title 1980.

CINCINNATI POETRY REVIEW, Dallas Wiebe, James Bertolino, Dept of English, University of Cincinnati, Cincinnati, OH 45221, 513-475-4484. 1975. Poetry. "*CPR* is electic. Takes all kinds of poetry. Each issue features on writer or a group of writers. Send $1.00 for sample copy." circ. 600. 2/yr. Pub'd 2 issues 1979; expects 2 issues 1980, 2 issues 1981. sub. price: $3.50; per copy: $2.00; sample: $1.00. Back issues: Complete set (six issues) $12.00. Discounts: 40% on consignment. 64-72pp; 6X9; of. Reporting time: 2-4 months. Payment: 2 copies of issue. Copyrighted.

CINEASTE MAGAZINE, Gary Crowdus, Dan Georgakas, Lenny Rubenstein, 419 Park Avenue South, New York, NY 10016. 1967. Articles, photos, interviews, satire, criticism, reviews, letters. "Offers a social & political perspective on the cinema—everything from the latest hollywood flicks & the American independent scene to political thrillers from Europe and revolutionary cinema from the Third World." circ. 7M. 4/yr. Pub'd 4 issues 1979; expects 4 issues 1980, 4 issues 1981. sub. price: $6.00 ($9.00 institutions); per copy: $1.75; sample: $1.00. Back issues: $1.75 to subscribers/$2.25 to others. Discounts: 25%. 64pp; 8½X11; of. Reporting time: 2-3 wks. Payment: reviews, $5.00; articles, $10.$15. Copyrighted. Pub's reviews: 48 in 1979. §Social, political perspective on all aspects of movies. Ads: $175.00/$100.00.

CINEMA/QUEBEC, Jean-Pierre Tadros, c.p. 309, Station Outremont, Montreal, Quebec H2V 4N1, Canada, 514-272-1058. 1971. Articles, photos, interviews. 10/yr. sub. price: $10.00 normal; $8.50 student; $15.00 company, library, institution & foreign; per copy: $1.25; sample: free. Discounts: 20%. 54pp; 7X10; †of. §cinema. Ads: $275/$150.

CINEMAGIC, David Hutchison, 475 Park Ave, South, New York, NY 10016, (212) 689-2830. 1979. Articles, photos, news items. circ. 20,000. 6/yr. Pub'd 6 issues 1979. sub. price: $8.98; per copy: $1.75; sample: $1.75. 36pp; 8½X11; of. Reporting time: 6 weeks. Payment: negotiated. Copyrighted. Pub's reviews: 6 in 1979. §Filmmaking. Ads: $500.00/$275.00.

Circinatum Press, Ron Trimble, Fiction& Poetry, PO Box 99309, Tacoma, WA 98499, (206) 627-4816. 1978. Poetry, fiction. avg. press run 1,000. Pub'd 2 titles 1979; expects 4 titles 1980. 2 titles listed in the *Small Press Record of Books in Print* (9th Edition, 1980). avg. price, paper: $4.75. Discounts: 1, 25%; 2-50, 40%; 51+, 50%. 88pp; 5½X8½; of. Reporting time: 5-6 weeks. Payment by arrangement with individual author. Copyrights for author.

THE CIRCLE, 105 S Huntington Avenue, Jamaica Plain, MA 02130, (617) 232-0343. 1974. Poetry, fiction, articles, art, photos, cartoons, interviews, news items. "Analysis of current situation with native American and energy developement. Reviews contemporary literature by and about native Americans. Recent contributors: Jack Hayes, Winona La Duke, Lorne Simon, Regina White, Louise Erdrich." circ. 3,500. 6-8/yr. Pub'd 7 issues 1979; expects 8 issues 1980, 8 issues 1981. sub. price: $3.00; per copy: $0.25; sample: $0.50. Back issues: $3.00 complete back issue sample. 16pp; 12X14; of. Reporting time: 2 weeks. Payment: copies. Pub's reviews: 6 in 1979. §Native American, politics, fiction, poetry. Ads: $150.00/$85.00/$0.10.

CIRCLE, Circle Forum, J.M. Gates, P.O. Box 176, Portland, OR 97207. 1973. Poetry, long-poems. "*CIRCLE* IS NOW A BIENNIAL PUBLICATION SUPPLEMENTED BY AN OCCASIONAL NEWSLETTER *CIRCLETS*. CIRCLE is exclusively dedicated to first-time publication of reversible poetry. Long poems, which are reversible, are particularly welcome. A bibliography of reversible poetry is in progress. 'Circlets' Newsletter is provided gratis to Circle purchasers; for others, a self addressed stamped envelope is required. Query please; sufficient backlog now. Defer manuscript submissions.

84

Subscriptions discontinued (Institutions invoiced after mailing). Reserve for *Circle* Issue #9 by July 1, 1981." circ. 200. Biennial. Expects 1 issue 1980, 1 issue 1981. price per copy: $4.00 effective 1980. Back issues: $2 each when available (for issues prior to 1980); other issues $4.00 each. 40pp biennial; 5½X8½; of. Reporting time: 4 months. Payment: 1 contributor's copy. Copyrighted. no advertising. COSMEP.

Circle Forum (see also CIRCLE), J.M. Gates, Editor, P.O. Box 176, Portland, OR 97207. 1973. Poetry, long-poems. "Circle is exclusively dedicated to reversible poetry. A biennial publication supplemented by an occasional newsletter (Circlets). 'Circlets' Newsletter is provided gratis to Circle purchasers; for others SASE is required. Defer manuscript submissions. Query." avg. press run 200. Pub'd 1 title 1979. 4 titles listed in the *Small Press Record of Books in Print* (9th Edition, 1980). 5½X8½; of. Reporting time: 4 months. Payment: 1 contributor's copy. Copyrights for author. COSMEP.

Citrus House Ltd, 1335 N Citrus Ave, Los Angeles, CA 90028, (213) 469-7234. 1978. "Combination diary, appointment calendar, telephone book & guide to cities" avg. press run 15,000. Pub'd 2 titles 1979; expects 3 titles 1980, 6 titles 1981. avg. price, cloth: $19.95. Discounts: 50%. 288pp; 7X10; of. Payment: no authors.

City Lights Books (see also CITY LIGHTS JOURNAL), Lawrence Ferlinghetti, Nancy J. Peters, 261 Columbus Ave., San Francisco, CA 94133, (415) 362-8193. 1955. Poetry, fiction, articles, non-fiction. avg. press run 3,000. Pub'd 5 titles 1979; expects 5 titles 1980. 79 titles listed in the *Small Press Record of Books in Print* (9th Edition, 1980). avg. price, paper: $4.00. 100pp; size varies; of. Reporting time: 2 weeks. Copyrights for author. COSMEP.

CITY LIGHTS JOURNAL, City Lights Books, Lawrence Ferlinghetti, Nancy J. Peters, 261 Columbus Avenue, San Francisco, CA 94133, (415) 362-8193. "1 issue every 2 years, infrequent." sub. price: No subscriptions available.

CITY MINER, Michael Helm, P.O. Box 176, Berkeley, CA 94701, 415-524-1162. 1976. Poetry, fiction, articles, photos, cartoons, interviews, satire, letters. "Northern California and Bay area focus. Ideal length of articles is 1,500-3,000 words. Bias toward decentralism, experimentation, community, and poetry. Gary Snyder, Alta, Robert Anton Wilson, Ishmael Reed, Lenore Kandel, Ernest Callenbach, Bob Callahan, Malcolm Margolin, Edward Field, Terry Kennedy, Jennifer Stone, Peter Berg, and Frank Polite. Looking for good line drawings, short fiction with urban flavor." circ. 5,000. 3-4/yr. Pub'd 3 issues 1979; expects 3 issues 1980. sub. price: $4.00; per copy: $1.00; sample: $1.00. Back issues: Complete set $100.00. Individual copies of Vol 8-14 (except #10, which is $5.00) are $1.00 each. Discounts: 40% trade, 40% bulk, 40% classroom. 48pp; 7⅛X10¼; of. Reporting time: 2—3 weeks. Payment: 1 cent word for articles and prose. Copyrighted. Pub's reviews: 20 in 1979. §Community, poetry, ecology, cities. Ads: $150.00/$85.00, -1/4 page $45.00, -1/8 page $30.00/25% dis—2 issues.

CLAIMANTS NEWSPAPER (Claimants Unite), Co-operative, NFCU Publications (International), 134 Villa Rd, Birmingham, England B191NN, United Kingdom. 1970. Articles, news items, letters, plays, photos, satire, reviews. "No subscriptions. Current list on request (stamped addressed envelope). (IPRC) Pamphlets also published. Copyright issue lodged with British library. ISSN: 0309-5576" circ. 1,000. 4/yr. Pub'd 3 issues 1979; expects 4 issues 1980. 4 titles listed in the *Small Press Record of Books in Print* (9th Edition, 1980). price per copy: 15p plus 15p postage; sample: 15p plus 15p postage. Back issues: Issues 1-16 published to date 30/3/79. Discounts: usual. 8pp; size A4; of. Payment: None. Copyrighted. Pub's reviews. §Social security, welfare rights. Ads: rates on application.

Clamshell Press, D.L. Emblen, Suzanne Carlson, 160 California Avenue, Santa Rosa, CA 95405. 1973. avg. press run 250-500. Pub'd 1 title 1979; expects 2 titles 1980, 2 titles 1981. 1 title listed in the *Small Press Record of Books in Print* (9th Edition, 1980). avg. price, paper: $3.50. 48pp; 5½X8½; †lp. Reporting time: we do not read unsolicited mss. Copyrights for author.

CLARITY, J.M. Sprague, 3 Greenway, Berkhamsted, Herts HP4 3JD, United Kingdom. 1968. Articles, poetry, criticism, letters. "Length of material approx. 750-2500 words. Aimed at intelligent non-specialist who is interested in Christianity; interdenominational, covering a broad spectrum of views & attitudes. CLARITY is the house magazine of the MENSA Christian Group, for MENSA members who are interested in Christianity. Contributors are mainly group members, but outside contributors & subscribers are welcome." circ. 100 plus. 6/yr. Pub'd 6 issues 1979; expects 6 issues 1980. sub. price: £1.50 UK, $3.00 US surface mail; $5.25 US air mail. 20-24pp; size -1/2 flscp; †dupl. Copyrighted. Pub's reviews: 2 in 1979. §religious, social science, psychology. MCG

CLASSIC FILM/VIDEO IMAGES, Samuel K. Rubin, PO Box 4079, Davenport, IA 52808. 1962.

Articles, art, photos, cartoons, interviews, criticism, reviews, letters, news items. "No standard." circ. 2,500. 6/yr. Pub'd 6 issues 1979. sub. price: $10.00; per copy: $2.25; sample: $1.00. Back issues: $2.25 each. 64pp; 11X14; of. Copyrighted. Pub's reviews. §film. Ads: $100.00/$55.00/$0.15.

CLASSIC IMAGES REVIEW, Samuel K. Rubin, PO Box 4079, Davenport, IA 52808, (319) 323-9738. 1979. Articles, art, photos, cartoons, interviews, criticism, reviews, news items. "Advertising address: P.O.Box 809, Muscatine, Iowa 52761. Length of material varies" circ. 25,000. 4/yr. Expects 1 issue 1980. sub. price: free. 52pp; 11X14. Payment: none. Copyrighted, return of copyright varies. Pub's reviews: 0 in 1979. §Film. Ads: $600/$335.

Clatworthy Colorvues, Mike Mandel, Larry Sultan, 111½ Riverview St, Santa Cruz, CA 95062, 408-426-6401. 1973. Photos. "We do not solicit contributors. We are artists and publish our own work. We have at present five titles published. Much of the work has been supported by grants from the National Endowment for the Arts. We also have designed four billboard (non-commercial) exhibitions in San Francisco since 1973." avg. press run 1,000 copies. Pub'd 1 title 1979. 6 titles listed in the *Small Press Record of Books in Print* (9th Edition, 1980). avg. price, cloth: $12.95; paper: $3.00. Discounts: 40 percent to retailer. 5½X8½; of. Copyrights for author.

CLAUDEL STUDIES, Moses M. Nagy, University of Dallas Station, Irving, TX 75061. 1972. Criticism. "Our journal dedicates itself to the promotion of the writings of Paul Claudel (playwright and prose writer), and we accept articles, papers in English or in French. Some of our contributors in 1975: Edwin Marie Landau (Switzerland). Jacques Cassar (France), Ann Bugliani (Chicago), Elsie M. Wiedner (Rutgers), Moses M. Nagy (Dallas), Georgia H. Shurr (Idaho). Some of our contributors in 1977: Jean-Claude Renard (France), Catharine S. Brosman (Tulane), Vinio Rossi (Oberlin), Stuart Barr (Birmingham, England), Alfred Cismaru (Texas Tech), Jacques Cotnam (York Univ. Canada), Moses M. Nagy (Univ. of Dallas)." circ. 500. 2/yr. Pub'd 2 issues 1979; expects 2 issues 1980. sub. price: $10.00; per copy: $6.00; sample: free. Back issues: $6.00. 80-100pp; 4.5 by 7 inches; of. Reporting time: 2 months. Payment: none. Not copyrighted. Pub's reviews: 7 in 1979. §Books concerning Paul Claudel's works or books on theater. no ads.

Clean Energy Press, Howard C. Wiig, 3593-a Alani Dr, Honolulu, HI 96822, 808-988-4155. 1975. Articles. "Editor is now seeking material on alternative energy sources, and on energy-saving original material. Emphasis is on clean-energy vehicles." avg. press run 2,000. 1 title listed in the *Small Press Record of Books in Print* (9th Edition, 1980). avg. price, paper: $1.65. Discounts: $1.00 per copy to dealers. 176pp; 7X4¼; of. Reporting time: 2 weeks. Payment: 5 cents per word. COSMEPA, COSMEP-WEST.

CLEARWATER NAVIGATOR, Thomas Whyatt, 112 Market Street, Poughkeepsie, NY 12601, (914) 454-7673. 1969. Articles, photos, letters, news items. "Our publication is mainly an environmental newsletter centered on the issues facing the Hudson River Valley and eastern New York State. We are also concerned with problems facing estuaries, such as the Hudson, fishery research and natural resource management. Subscriptions are mainly through membership in our parent organization, the Hudson River Sloop Clearwater, Inc., an educational environmental organization whose main objective is to defend and restore the Hudson River. We do this by maintaining a 106 ft. replica of 18th century wooden sloop and by giving educational sails aboard it." circ. 5,000. 11/yr. Pub'd 11 issues 1979; expects 11 issues 1980, 11 issues 1981. sub. price: $3.00; per copy: free, if available; sample: free. Back issues: free, if available. 8-16pp; 7X11; of. Reporting time: varies widely.

Cleis Press, Frederique Delacoste, Felice Newman, 3141 Pleasant Avenue, South, Minneapolis, MN 55408, (612) 825-8872. 1980. Poetry, fiction, articles, art, photos. "Full-length book manuscripts only. Please include SASE w/complete ms. or sample chapter(s). Welcome manuscripts or query letters from feminist writers/artists. Cleis Press is committed to publishing woman-identified literature." avg. press run 3,000. Pub'd 3 titles 1979. avg. price, paper: $5.00. Discounts: standard bookstore & distributor, please write for terms. 50-200pp; of. Reporting time: 1-2 months. Copyrights for author.

Cleveland State Univ. Poetry Center, Alberta Turner, Leonard Trawick, Dept English, Cleveland State Univ, Cleveland, OH 44115, 216-687-3986. 1962. Poetry, concrete art. "1 local poetry series —25 published since 1969—32 pp-50. 1 national series; 1 vol. per year; have already published Stuart Friebert, Thomas Lux, Stratis Haviaris, David Young, Jan Haagensen, and Mark Jarman. Query before submitting. About 50-100 pp." avg. press run 500 local series; 1,500 national series. Pub'd 5 titles 1979; expects 4 titles 1980, 4 titles 1981. 12 titles listed in the *Small Press Record of Books in Print* (9th Edition, 1980). avg. price, paper: $3.50. Discounts: 50 percent for bulk orders. National series distributed by National Association of College Stores, Oberlin, Ohio 44074 and *Field,* Oberlin College, Oberlin, Ohio, 44074. 32-100pp; size varies; †of. Reporting time: 4-8 weeks. Payment: 10

percent national series; 100 copies local series. Copyrights for author.

Clover Press (see also GREEN'S MAGAZINE), David Green, Box 313, Detroit, MI 48231. 1975. "Capable of limited-run production; type by compositor; no reduction capability; noncoated stock. Will not undertake distribution except in conjunction with GREEN'S MAGAZINE. Mail, art extra." avg. press run 1,000. Pub'd 1 title 1979; expects 1 title 1980, 1 title 1981. 4 titles listed in the *Small Press Record of Books in Print* (9th Edition, 1980). avg. price, paper: $2.00 per 100 page 5¼ x 8½ - staple binding. size up to 11X14 (full sheet); †of. Reporting time: 6 weeks. Copyrights for author.

CLOWN WAR, Bob Heman, P.O. Box 1093, Brooklyn, NY 11202. 1971. Poetry, art, long-poems, concrete art. "CLOWN WAR has doubled its press run & is now distributed free in bookstores & galleries. We are especially interested in experimental poetry & prose, in prosepoems, & in works that touch the 'sense of wonder.' Also very interested in pen & ink drawings that do the same. We like to have sections of three or four writers per issue, but special issues are always a possibility. Recent contributors include Lyn Hejinian, Ray Dipalma, David Gitin, John Jacob, A.F. Caldiero." circ. 500-1,000. 4-8/yr. Pub'd 6 issues 1979; expects 8 issues 1980. No back issues available. 24-28pp; 5X7; †of. Reporting time: 1 week - 3 months. Payment: copies. §Poetry, experimental prose, narrative graphics. CCLM.

Coach House Press (see also RUNE), Stan Bevington, David Young, Frank Davey, Clifford James, B.P. Nichol, Michael Ondaatje, Linda McCartney, Sarah Sheard, Dennis Reid, 401 Huron St. (Rear), Toronto, Ontario M5S 2G5, Canada, (416) 979-2217. Poetry, fiction, art, photos, satire, parts-of-novels, long-poems, collages, plays. avg. press run 1,000. Pub'd 18 titles 1979. 62 titles listed in the *Small Press Record of Books in Print* (9th Edition, 1980). avg. price, cloth: $15.00; paper: $4.50. Discounts: Bookstores & the trade 1-4, 20%; 5-49, 40%; 50 plus, 50%; Libraries and institutions: 20%. 175pp; 6X9; †of. Reporting time: 8 weeks. Payment: 10% normally. Copyrights for author. ACP, COSMEP, LPG.

Coast to Coast Books, Mark Beach, 2934 NE 16th, Portland, OR 97212, (503) 282-5891. 1979. Photos. avg. press run 5,000. Pub'd 2 titles 1979. 3 titles listed in the *Small Press Record of Books in Print* (9th Edition, 1980). avg. price, paper: $5.00. 100pp; of.

Cobbers, Jean Martensen, 22725 Orchard Lake Road, Farmington, MI 48024, (313) 478-3322. 1979. Fiction, articles, parts-of-novels. "We do only material with an Australian theme or from Australian authors or reprints of books first published in Australia. We will consider criticisms, interviews, reviews, articles, parts of novels, etc., by American authors if the content dilineates Australia, or Australians. Thus far we have published a book of humorous essays about Australian bushcooking, are in the midst of publishing the first in a small series of children's books about a koala bear and are negotiating for rights for a detective series and a book of short stories: in short, we seek a development of a list that will be a good general cross-section of Australian literature." avg. press run 2,000. Pub'd 2 titles 1979; expects 2 titles 1980, 4 titles 1981. avg. price, cloth: $7.95; paper: $5.00. Discounts: Trade 40%; Dist. & Jobber 50%; Libraries 10%. 120-250pp; 4½X7; of. Reporting time: 1 month. Payment: Advance plus 8-10% (8% to 10,000 and 10% over) or 10-12% in lieu of advance. Copyrights for author.

Cobblesmith, Gene H. Boyington, General; Gerald Hausman, Juvenile Poetry, Box 191, RFD 1, Freeport, ME 04032, 207-865-6495. 1974. "We are a general non-fiction publisher. The thread that runs through all our publications is personal growth & a greater responsibility of each individual for him/herself & for others in the human community. If each of us is personally fulfilled and nearly self-sufficient, each will be able to contribute more of himself to the betterment of the community as a whole." avg. press run 2,000. Pub'd 3 titles 1979; expects 5 titles 1980. 12 titles listed in the *Small Press Record of Books in Print* (9th Edition, 1980). avg. price, cloth: $12.00; paper: $4.00. Discounts: on request. 120pp; 8½X11; of/lp. Reporting time: 1 week to 6 months. Copyrights for author. COSMEP.

COBBLESTONE: The History Magazine for Children, Frances Nankin, 28 Main Street, Peterborough, NH 03458, (603) 924-7209. 1980. Poetry, fiction, articles, art, photos, cartoons, reviews, music, plays. "Material must be written for children in grades 4-6, not in a style which talks down to children, most articles do not exceed 500 words, send to Editor for guidelines as we focus each issue on a particular theme." circ. 8,500. 12/yr. Pub'd 12 issues 1979; expects 12 issues 1980. sub. price: $15.00; per copy: $1.50; sample: $1.50. Back issues: currently $1.50; subject to change. Discounts: 10% to agency only. 48pp; 7X9; of. Reporting time: within 30 days. Payment: within 30 days. Copyrighted. Pub's reviews. §History books for children, ages 8-12. Ads: $400.00/$208.00.

‡COBBLESTONE, Fragments/The Valentine Press, Phil Yeh, Editor; Janet Valentine, Editor; Don DeContreras, Editor, P.O. Box 1128, Los Alamitos, CA 90720. 1975. Poetry, fiction, articles, art, photos, cartoons, interviews, satire, criticism, reviews, music letters. "We like articles about 2-15 pages (2-spaced) on science fiction & fantasy topics. Recent contributor Ray Bradbury." circ. 5,-000-15,000. 4/yr. sub. price: $7.50; per copy: $1.50; sample: $2.00. Back issues: usually $1.00 each. Discounts: 1-50 $.90 each, 51-199 $.75 each, 200-999 $.60 each, 1,000 & up $.45 each, retail $1.50. 56pp; 8½X11; of. Reporting time: 2 weeks. Payment: none (at least not yet). Copyrighted, reverts to author. Pub's reviews. §Fantasy, art, science fiction, non-fiction, literature relating to artists. Ads: $100.00/$50.00.

CODA: Poets & Writers Newsletter, Poets & Writers, Inc., Poets & Writers, Inc., 201 West 54th St., New York, NY 10019, 212-757-1766. 1973. Articles, photos, news items. "*Coda* publishes factual articles of interest to writers, editors, publishers, and all others interested in contemporary American literature. Most articles are researched and written by the staff of Poets & Writers, Inc. However, *Coda* welcomes all news readers might think of interest to the writing community and encourages them to send information in. A *Letters* column has recently been established. Recent articles have included taxes and the writer, copyright information, small press distribution, writing for television, manuscript submission, poetry in prisons programs. Regular columns include grants and awards, publishing opportunities, and book fairs and festivals." circ. 6,500. 5/yr. Pub'd 5 issues 1979; expects 5 issues 1980. sub. price: $7.00/1yr; $12.00/2yrs; per copy: $1.50; sample: $1.50. Back issues: $1.50. Discounts: $5.50/yr to authors listed with Poets & Writers; to bookstores, min. 5 copies, 40 percent; to distributors, min. 20 copies, 50 percent; to teachers, for bulk subscriptions, min. 5, 20 percent. 32-36pp; 8½X11; of. Copyrighted, does not revert to author. Pub's reviews: 14 in 1979. §technical or practical books, we do not review poetry or fiction. Only writer's market guides and other technical works. Ads: $320/$175/$100/$60. COSMEP, CCLM, NYSSPA.

CODA: The Jazz Magazine, Bill Smith, David Lee, Box 87 Stn. J., Toronto, Ont. M4J4X8, Canada. 1958. Photos, interviews, criticism, reviews, articles, news items. "Our emphasis is on the art rather than the commerce of the music (i.e. we concentrate on non-commercialism) and we cover jazz of all styles and areas." circ. 5,000. 6/yr. Pub'd 6 issues 1979. sub. price: $9.00 Canada/$9.00 U.S. other countries for 6 issues; per copy: $1.50; sample: free. Back issues: $1.50. Discounts: agency discount (subscriptions only) 25%. 40pp; 8¼X11¼; of. Reporting time: 1 month to 2 years. Payment: none. Pub's reviews. §jazz, blues. Ads: $150.00/$80.00/$0.25 (min. $5.00).

Coda Press, Inc (see also SOCIAL TEXT), S. Aronowitz, J. Brenkman, F. Jameson, 700 West Badger Road, Suite 101, Madison, WI 53713, (608) 251-9662. 1977. Criticism. "Recent Authors: Raymond Federman, Maurice Roche, Henry Sussman. Primarily interested in publishing cultural studies of a theoretical and critical nature. We prefer single author titles, but will consider collections of essays which have not been previously published." avg. press run 2,000. Pub'd 3 titles 1979; expects 2 titles 1980. 5 titles listed in the *Small Press Record of Books in Print* (9th Edition, 1980). avg. price, cloth: $13.50; paper: $6.00. Discounts: 25% consignment; 40% outright sale. 200pp; 6X9; of. Reporting time: 3 months approx. Payment: varies widely. Copyrights for author. COSMEP.

COEVOLUTION QUARTERLY, Stewart Brand, Box 428, Sausalito, CA 94965, 415-332-1716. 1974. Poetry, fiction, articles, art, photos, cartoons, interviews, reviews, parts-of-novels, plays. circ. 50,000. 4/yr. Pub'd 4 issues 1979; expects 4 issues 1980. sub. price: $12.00; per copy: $3.50. Back issues: $3.00 back issue price. Issues 1,3,4,5,6,7,8,9,12,13 are out of print. Discounts: 50% to distributors. 144pp; 6X9; of. Reporting time: 1 month. Payment: Ranges from $10 for suggestions and letters to $250 for a major article. Copyrighted, reverts to author. Pub's reviews: 300-400 in 1979. §Soft tech., craft, architecture, sports & travel, educational mat'ls. We do not accept advertising. ABA.

COFFEE BREAK, Coffee Break Press, Dolores Nicolai, Editor; Helen L. Ross, Non-fiction; Paula Craig, Juvenile; James A. Hanf, Poetry, P.O. Box 103, Burley, WA 98322, 857-4329. 1977. Poetry, fiction, articles, art, photos, cartoons, interviews, satire, long-poems. "*Coffee Break* publishes mss. directed toward juveniles and adults. Photos are seldom printed but sketches are sometimes made from them. Humor is preferred to all else. Our flexible editorial policy is easily swayed by freshness and quality. Our editors work with writers when they feel mss. are worth salvaging for *Coffee Break*. Mss. under 1,500 words are preferred but additional space is always allotted to longer well written works. But, if you got a ms. about a writer that got sparkling and twinkling eyes when he/she got an idea to drown his/her spouse in a pool of coffee during the coffee break they got from the Coffee Cake Bakery, *We Got No Room For It!* Most of our illustration is pen and ink. We will consider new ideas for cover design. We also need artwork for yearly calendar design. Please send SASE, with *sufficient* return postage, with all mss. and comuniques. Send SASE for free writers guidelines." circ. 5,000. 4/yr. Pub'd 2 issues 1979; expects 4 issues 1980, 4 issues 1981. sub. price: $6.00; per copy: $1.50; sample: $1.00. Back issues: $3.00 (when available). Discounts: Usually 40% (negotiable). 80pp; 5¼X8¼; †of. Reporting time: 6-8 weeks. Payment: $5.00-$25.00 or copies. Copyrighted, reverts to

author. COSMEP.

Coffee Break Press (see also COFFEE BREAK), Dolores Nicolai, PO Box 103, Burley, WA 98322, 857-4329. 1978. Fiction, articles, art, photos, cartoons, satire, letters, long-poems, collages, plays. "There is neither a minimum nor maximum ms. length. *Coffee Break* offers 3 types of contracts, all negotiated individually with each ms.: 1. Royalty publishing, 2. Cooperative publishing, 3. Self-publishing. Presently all mss. over 200 pp. fall into method 2 or 3. All self-published books, bearing the Coffee Break Press trademark, will receive the same promotion as Royalty Books. Mss. not accepted as *Coffee Break* books will simply be printed and turned over to the author. This will be clearly stated, in writing, before any book is published. Rarely will we accept a poetry mss. on a royalty basis. We will publish children's books as well as adult mss. There are virtually no restrictions on self-published books. Quality is the essential ingredient in *Coffee Break* books. Last year we published a juvenile fantasy, a poetry collection and a non-fiction book. We hope to publish, at least, six titles this year. So far we are committed to: *Pocketful of Smiles,* cartoons by Earle Engleman; *Men of Courage,* Helen L. Ross, Congressional Medal of Honor stories; 2 cookbooks and 1 anthology. There is no restriction on page size. Most *Coffee Break* books are 5¼ x 8¼ to fit our racks." avg. press run 1,000. Expects 3 titles 1980, 6 titles 1981. avg. price, cloth: $8.00; paper: $3.50. Discounts: Usually 40% (negotiable). 64pp; 5¼X8¼; of. Reporting time: 6-8 weeks (up to 14 weeks on mss. over 200 pages). Payment: Lenient and negotiable. Copyrights for author. COSMEP.

THE COFFEEHOUSE, Wire Press, Dino Siotis, 3448 19th Street, San Francisco, CA 94110. 1975. Poetry, fiction, articles, art, photos, music, collages, plays. "Contemporary Greek Arts & Letters" circ. 1,000. 2/yr. Pub'd 2 issues 1979; expects 2 issues 1980. sub. price: $5.00; per copy: $2.00; sample: $2.00. Back issues: $4.00 each. Discounts: 40 percent for bookstores. 70pp; 7X8½; †of. Payment: no. Not copyrighted. Pub's reviews. §Books translated from Greek or written in English and deal with Greek topics. Ads: $20.00/$12.00. CCLM.

Coker Books, Editorial Board, Box 395, 3530 Timmons, Houston, TX 77027. 1970. Fiction, satire. avg. press run 5,000. Pub'd 6-10 titles 1979; expects 6-10 titles 1980, 6-10 titles 1981. 5 titles listed in the *Small Press Record of Books in Print* (9th Edition, 1980). avg. price, cloth: $10.95; paper: $4.95. Discounts: 25% to retailers, 50% to jobbers. 150pp; 5½X8½. Reporting time: 2-4 weeks. Payment: negotiable.

Cold Mountain Press, Ryan Petty, Editor, c/o Provision House, PO Box 5487, Austin, TX 78763. 1973. Poetry, fiction. "Cold Mountain Press is the literary imprint of Provision House (see 'Provision House' listing in this directory). We have published collections by Wendell Berry, Joseph Bruchac, Laura Chester, Michael Delp, Samuel Green, Michael Hogan, Ted Kooger, Stephen Leggett, and David Ray. Many of our publications are available in fine letterpress editions, with copies numbered and signed by the authors. Our most recent publication is representative: *The Ice-Hearts* by Joseph Bruchac was published, via letterpress, in a handsewn pamphlet, limited to 300 copies, numbered & signed by both the poet and by the printer, David Holman. It sells for $12.00. Write for our free catlogue." Pub'd 1 title 1979; expects 1 title 1980, 1 title 1981. 8 titles listed in the *Small Press Record of Books in Print* (9th Edition, 1980). lp. Reporting time: no unsolicited submissions. Payment: negotiated with the author.

Earl M Coleman Enterprises, Inc (see also UNIVERSAL HUMAN RIGHTS; COMMUNICA-TIONS AND THE LAW; CHECKLIST OF HUMAN RIGHTS DOCUMENTS; JOURNAL OF SOCIAL RECONSTRUCTION), Ellen Coleman, PO Box 143, Pine Plains, NY 12567, (518) 398-7193. 1977. Articles, reviews. "Publisher of original books in the social sciences, political science, human rights, and reprints in the fields of horticulture, maritime affairs, indian legal materials, and schorarly journals." avg. press run varies. Pub'd 10 titles 1979; expects 30 titles 1980. 33 titles listed in the *Small Press Record of Books in Print* (9th Edition, 1980). avg. price, cloth: varies. Discounts: contact publisher. variespp; size varies; of. Reporting time: 2-6 weeks. Payment: varies depending upon type of book.

COLLABORATION, Matagiri, Eric Hughes, Matagiri Sri Aurobindo Center, Inc., Mt. Tremper, NY 12457, (914) 679-8322. 1974. Poetry, articles, art, photos, reviews, letters, news items. "*COLLABORATION* is devoted to the philosophy of Sri Aurobindo, with extracts from his works and relevant material by others. Also includes news of the city of Auroville and Sri Aurobindo centers around the world." circ. 1,000. 4/yr. Pub'd 4 issues 1979; expects 4 issues 1980. sub. price: by contribution (any amount; suggested: $2.00); per copy: 50¢; sample: free. Back issues: Some available. 24pp; 8¾X11¼; of. Reporting time: 2 weeks. Copyrighted, reverts to author. Pub's reviews: 3 in 1979. §relevant to Sri Aurobindo and his philosophy, and Auroville; futurology. Ads: No ads. COSMEP.

COLLECTOR'S ITEM, Padre Productions, Lachlan P. MacDonald, PO Box 1275, San Luis Obispo,

CA 93406, 805-543-5404. 1979. "*Collector's Item* is national and international coverage of collectibles and antiques as an industry, investment, phenomena—an insider's report with much forecasting." circ. 500. 6/yr. Pub'd 6 issues 1979. sub. price: $18.00; sample: charter issue only, on request. Back issues: per year rate. Discounts: Subscription rate for 12 monthly issues, $18.00 each title. 8pp; 8½X11; of. Reporting time: 10 days—2 weeks. Payment: by arrangement. Copyrighted, reverts on req. Pub's reviews. §Antiques/collectibles/trends. Ads: none available. COSMEP.

COLLEGE ENGLISH, National Council of Teachers of English, Donald Gray, Editor, Dept of English, Indiana University, Bloomington, IN 47401, 812-337-8183. 1939. Poetry, articles, cartoons, satire, criticism, reviews. circ. 12,000. 8/yr. Pub'd 8 issues 1979; expects 8 issues 1980. sub. price: $20.00; per copy: $2.50. Back issues: $2.50. 112pp; 7½X9½; of. Reporting time: up to 3 mos. Payment: copies only. Copyrighted. Pub's reviews: 8-10 in 1979. §Literary theory, linguistic theory, theory of learning and pedagogy, history of English studies. Ads: $340/$225.

College V, UCSC (see also QUARRY WEST), Lou Mathews, David Swanger, Advisory; Eric Bolt, Suzanne Dunn, Eileen Drew, Rosy Liggett, Carter Young, College Five, UCSC, Santa Cruz, CA 95064. 1972. Poetry, fiction, articles, art, criticism. avg. press run 1,000. Pub'd 3 titles 1979. 1 title listed in the *Small Press Record of Books in Print* (9th Edition, 1980). avg. price, cloth: $2.50. 96pp; 8X7; of. Reporting time: 8 weeks. Payment: 2 copies, 1 poster. Copyrights for author.

Cologne Press, Vincent J. Luciani, PO Box 682, Cologne, NJ 08213, (609) 965-5163. 1979. "Not yet prepared to accept mss, but will consider American historical, folklore." avg. press run 1,000. Pub'd 1 title 1979; expects 1-2 titles 1980. avg. price, paper: $4.95. Discounts: on request. 100pp; 5X8. Reporting time: 2 weeks.

COLONNADES, Dr. Andrew J. Angyal, Faculty Advisor, Box 2245, Elon College, NC 27244. 1937. Poetry, fiction, articles, art, photos, satire, criticism, parts-of-novels, long-poems, plays. "*Colonnades* accepts poetry, short stories, essays reviews, critical articles, graphics, fine arts, and photography. The editors will also consider occasional excerpts from longer fictional works. Submissions should be clearly labeled with name and address on the back of each page. A self-addressed, stamped envelope should accompany each submission." circ. 2,500. 1/yr. Pub'd 1 issue 1979. sub. price: Free to students, faculty and alumni of Elm College; per copy: free to contributors; sample: free upon request if copies are available. 50-90pp; 6X9; of. Reporting time: 4 months. Payment: none except for contest winners. Ads: No ads. CCLM.

COLORADO-NORTH REVIEW, Ron Parro, University Center, Greeley, CO 80639, 303-351-4347. 1964. Poetry, fiction, articles, art, photos, reviews, long-poems, collages, plays. "Preference toward original intaglio. On written request of author copyright is reassigned." circ. 5,000. 3/yr. Pub'd 3 issues 1979; expects 3 issues 1980, 3 issues 1981. sub. price: $5.00; per copy: $2.00; sample: $2.00. Back issues: $2.00. Discounts: none. 80pp; 5½X8½; of. Reporting time: two to ten weeks. Payment: copies. Copyrighted, reverts to author. COSMEP.

COLORADO STATE REVIEW, Colorado State Review Press, Bill Tremblay, Poetry; Wayne Ude, Fiction; Mary Crow, Translations, 322 Eddy, English Department, Colorado State University, Fort Collins, CO 80523, (303) 491-6428. 1955. Poetry, fiction, articles, interviews, criticism, reviews, parts-of-novels, long-poems. "Two issues each year, one all fiction, the other all poetry. 1/5 of each devoted to translations. Fiction reading period each Aug-Dec, poetry each Jan-May. do not submit at other times. Allow until end of reading period for reply." circ. 500. 2/yr. Pub'd 2 issues 1979; expects 2 issues 1980, 2 issues 1981. sub. price: $4.00; per copy: $2.00; sample: $2.00. Back issues: Spring 1978 special Cuban poetry issue $5.00, all others $2.00. Discounts: 50% to distributors, 40% to bookstores, classes, other orders of 10 or more copies. 80pp; 5½X8½; of. Reporting time: 3 months. Payment: 2 copies plus one free subscription. Copyrighted, reverts to author. Pub's reviews: 6 in 1979. §Contemporary fiction & poetry. CCLM.

Colorado State Review Press (see also COLORADO STATE REVIEW), Bill Tremblay, Poetry; Wayne Ude, Fiction; Mary Crow, Translations, 322 Eddy, English Department, Colorado State University, Fort Collins, CO 80523, (303) 491-6428. 1978. Poetry, fiction. "Colorado State Review Press publishes one volume each year in its *poetry series* and one in its *fiction series. Estos Cantos Habitados/These Living Songs* 15 new Cuban poets, trans. & ed. by Margaret Randall, and *Skin and Bones,* short fiction by Robert Abel, were the 1978 selections, submission of manuscripts by invitation only. Queries welcomed. Copyright: Do not copyright for author, but we assign copyright for material to author on request. We wish to keep rights to individual book as an entity, while leaving writer free to reprint *all* material from book within other volumes later." avg. press run 500-1,000. Pub'd 2 titles 1979; expects 2 titles 1981. avg. price, paper: $4.00. Discounts: 50% to distributors, 40% to bookstores, classes, other orders of 10 or more copies. 100pp; 5½X8½; of. Reporting time: 3 months. Payment:

Author receives 10% of each print run; book will be kept in print. CCLM.

DE COLORES: Journal of Emerging Raza Philosophy, Pajarito Publications, Jose Armas, Managing Editor; Helena Quintana, Linda Morales Armas, P O Box 7264, Albuquerque, NM 87104, (505) 242-2839. 1973. Poetry, fiction, articles, art, photos, criticism, interviews, satire, reviews, music, letters, long-poems, collages, plays, concrete art. "We are currently one of two independent quarterlies in the country publishing limited editions of the best in Chicano expression and thought. We publish both known and new Raza talent and have strived to fill a large void publishing art as well as scholarly work which contribute to Chicano-self-awareness and affirmation. Recent contributors: Octavio Paz, Jose Armas, Bernice Zamola, Rolando Hinojosa, Angela de Hoyos." circ. 2,000. 4/yr. Pub'd 4 issues 1979; expects 4 issues 1980, 4 issues 1981. sub. price: individuals $10.00; institutions $18.00; per copy: $3.00/individual; $5.00/instit.; sample: $3.00. Back issues: $3.00 per issue/individual; $5.00/institution. Discounts: 40% discount on multiple orders (5 or more); Library 10%. 88pp; 9X6; of. Reporting time: 4 months. Payment: in copies. Copyrighted, reverts to author. Pub's reviews: 10 in 1979. §Socio/Political, Mexican American Education, Chicano Lit & Poetry, Chicano Politics, etc. Ads: $400.00/$200.00. CCLM, RAYAS.

COLUMBIA: A MAGAZINE OF POETRY AND PROSE, Bonnie Zobell, Nancy Schoenberger, 404 Dodge, Columbia University, New York, NY 10027, 280-4391. 1976. Poetry, fiction, interviews. "Fiction under 5,000 words. Joyce Carol Oates, Norman Dubie, Carol Muske, Frederick Busch, Nicholas Del banco, Joseph Brodsky, George Seferis." circ. 1000. 2/yr. Pub'd 1 issue 1979; expects 2 issues 1980, 2 issues 1981. sub. price: $6.00 ($7.00 library sub); per copy: $3.00 ($3.50 library sub); sample: $3.00. Back issues: $2.50. Discounts: 40%. 100pp; 5½X8¼; of. Reporting time: 2 months. Payment: 2 copies. Copyrighted, reverts to author. Ads: $100.00/$60.00/.

COLUMBUS FREE PRESS, Libby Gregory, Box 3162, Columbus, OH 43210, 294-2062. 1970. Articles, art, photos, cartoons, interviews, satire, criticism, reviews, music, letters, collages, news items. "The shorter the better. We prefer articles which refer to facts, as opposed to 'true answer' articles. Nothing which might offend on the basis of race or sex. Loosely left perspective, anti religious, okay." circ. 8,000. 12/yr. Pub'd 12 issues 1979; expects 12 issues 1980, 12 issues 1981. sub. price: $5.00; per copy: $0.20; sample: $0.20 plus postage. Back issues: Free to prisoners, $0.20 each plus postage. Discounts: We exchange freely with other periodicals. 12-16pp; 10½X14; of. Reporting time: 1 week. Pub's reviews: 4 in 1979. §All non-fiction. Ads: $175.00/$100.00.

COMBINATIONS, A JOURNAL OF PHOTOGRAPHY, Mary Ann Lynch, Middle Grove Road, Greenfield Center, NY 12833, 518-584-4612. 1976. Poetry, fiction, articles, photos, interviews, criticism, reviews, letters. "Issue I: Jacqueline Livingston, Roger Williams, Ted Orland, Sue Robinson, Merry Moor Winnett, Margaretta Mitchell, Dave Read, Ron Rosenstock (photographs) poetry by Joseph Bruchac, Margaretta Mitchell, (Duane Niatum—issue 2) interview with Clarence John Laughlin by John Messina (issue 2). Issue 3—Photography: A.J. Meek, Laima Druskis, Monte Gerlach, Lois Lord, Robin Brown; Interview with Ruth Bernhard, Suzanne Camp Crosby, Kenneth Shorr. We accept work during specific times only. $4.00 consideration fee & SASE reqd. Next accepting period, June 1-July 15, 1979." circ. 700-1,000. 4/yr. Pub'd 1 issue 1979; expects 4 issues 1980, 4 issues 1981. sub. price: $12.00 overseas, $17.00 Europe-airmail; per copy: $4.00 plus 50¢ postage; sample: $4.00 plus 50¢ postage. Discounts to contributors, galleries, bookstores, inquire. 44-48pp; size Varies; of. Reporting time: 2-4 weeks past deadline. Payment: copies. Copyrighted, reverts to author. Pub's reviews: 1 in 1979. §photographic/ photography/small press publishing in photography. Ads: $100.-00/$50.00.

Come! Unity Press (see also ANARCHISM: The Feminist Connection), 13 E 17th Street, New York, NY 10003. 1972. "Non-commercial radical information." †of.

COME-ALL-YE, Legacy Books (formerly Folklore Associates), Richard Burns, Editor; Lillian Krelove, Asst. Ed., P.O. Box 494, Hatboro, PA 19040, (215) 675-6762. 1977. Poetry, art, music, parts-of-novels, news items. "' . . . contains reviews and book selection news of publications in the fields of folklore/folklife, social history, studies investigating the culture, fabric and spirit of people in communities. The journal seeks to provide a reference , selection and advisory guide to inform professionals, faculty, scholars, students and the general interested public of significant current publications.' — from the masthead" circ. 2,000-3,000. 5/yr. Pub'd 2 issues 1979; expects 4 issues 1980, 4 issues 1981. sub. price: $5.00; per copy: $2.00; sample: free. Back issues: $2.00. Discounts: none. 12-16pp; 8¼X11; of. Reporting time: 1 month. Payment: none. Copyrighted, reverts to author. Pub's reviews: 100-200 in 1979. §folklore, social history, local history, regional surveys, music (all but classical), american culture, black studies, anthropology, ethnic culture, music and studies. Ads: $50.00/$25.-00/$15.00. COSMEP/ABA.

Commen Cents, Paul T. Aunger, P.O. Box 3282, Station D, Willowdale, Ontario M2R 3G6, Canada. 1979. Articles, photos, cartoons, interviews, reviews, letters, news items. "Under 1,000 words; interests: saving/managing money. Send completed manuscript." circ. 10,000. 6/yr. Pub'd 3 issues 1979; expects 6 issues 1980, 6 issues 1981. sub. price: $6.95; per copy: $1.25; sample: $1.25. Back issues: $1.25. Discounts: negotiable. 52pp; 8½X11; of. Payment: negotiable. Copyrighted, reverts to author. Pub's reviews. §Free books on any subject and money saving/managing books. Ads: $300.-00/$197.00. COSMEP, CPPA.

The Common Table, Hugh Miller, 216 Crown Street, Room 506, New Haven, CT 06510. 1979. Poetry, art, long-poems. "We have published only Bert Meyers' *Windowsills* to date. We are interested in poets who have learned their craft and know how to use it, who write poems that are vital and, in Charles Reznikoff's words, who write 'not for a seat upon the dias/but at the common table'." avg. press run 500. Pub'd 1 title 1979; expects 1-3 titles 1980, 1-3 titles 1981. 1 title listed in the *Small Press Record of Books in Print* (9th Edition, 1980). avg. price, cloth: $7.95; paper: $3.95. Discounts: To the trade: paper 5 copies, 40%; cloth 5 copies 20%, may be asorted. 40pp; 4X7; of. Reporting time: 2 months. Payment: will vary with each book. Copyrights for author.

COMMON WORD, The Charles Street Press, Phillip McCaffrey, P.O. Box 4692, Baltimore, MD 21212. 1978. Interviews, criticism, reviews, plays. "A local newsletter for writers. We are interested in small press news, reviews (of poetry primarily), interviews, especially with authors in the Baltimore-Washington area, and critical features. Length: 400-1000 words. Reviews will be available as separate offprints to authors and publishers, to help them publicize their work." circ. 500. quarterly. Expects 2 issues 1980, 4 issues 1981. sub. price: $2.00/yr; per copy: 50¢; sample: 14¢ postage. Discounts: Five copies to same address, $5 subscription (4 issues). 6pp; 8½X11; of. Reporting time: 2-4 weeks. Payment: copies. Copyrighted, reverts to author. Pub's reviews. §poetry, literary fiction, criticism and aesthetics. Ads: $20/$12/free.

Commonsense Books, Ann Law, Box 287, Bedford, MA 01730. 1 title listed in the *Small Press Record of Books in Print* (9th Edition, 1980).

Communicate Press, Rodney G. Miller, PO Box 132, Toowong, Queensland 4066, Australia, (07) 370 1298. 1978. Articles, photos, cartoons, interviews, satire, criticism, reviews, news items. "Communicate Press publishes books and monographs of academic and serious popular level on human communication. The bias is towards international material of lasting importance and interest and towards Australian and Pacific communication studies. Recent Titles include: *Communication and Language in Australia: Papers on Public Communication; Australians Speak: A New Anthology of Speeches by Prominent Australians; Freedom of Information: A Bibliography*." avg. press run 500-1,000. Pub'd 2 titles 1979; expects 2 titles 1980, 3 titles 1981. avg. price, paper: $7.00-$15.00. Discounts: 40% off recommended retail (plus handling and postage charges), apply only to trade or bulk orders (20 or more). 70pp; 7X10; of. Reporting time: 4 months from receipt of material. Payment: by individual contract. Copyrights for author. ABPA.

Communication Creativity, Deborah Frost, 5644 La Jolla Blvd., La Jolla, CA 92037, (714) 459-4489. 1977. Non-fiction. "Communication Creativity Books are designed to be both entertaining and informational. They deal primarily with subjects in the fields of leisure and business." avg. press run 5,000. Pub'd 3 titles 1979; expects 26 titles 1980, 40 titles 1981. 4 titles listed in the *Small Press Record of Books in Print* (9th Edition, 1980). avg. price, cloth: $9.95; paper: $4.95. Discounts: From 20 percent to 50 percent. 144pp; 5½X8½, 6X9, 8½X11; of. Not soliciting submissions. Payment: Negotiable. Copyrights for author. COSMEP, BPSC (Book Publicists of Southern California).

The Communication Press, Randall Harrison, P O Box 22541, San Francisco, CA 94122, 415-566-3921. 1977. Cartoons. "Our focus is on humorous how-to, such as our *How To Cut Your Water Use — and Still Stay Sane and Sanitary.* We also are interested in art, psychology and communication. We're probably a poor market for free lancers as we already have as many projects as we can handle for the next few years; and we hope to stay small and quality oriented." avg. press run 5,000. Pub'd 1-2 titles 1979. 2 titles listed in the *Small Press Record of Books in Print* (9th Edition, 1980). avg. price, cloth: $7.50; paper: $3.50. Discounts: 40 percent trade. 96 to 128pp; 5X8; of. Reporting time: 6 to 8 weeks. Payment variable. Copyrights for author. COSMEP.

COMMUNICATIONS AND THE LAW, Earl M Coleman Enterprises, Inc, Theodore R. Kupferman, PO Box 143, Pine Plains, NY 12567. 1979. Articles, reviews. "Expanding technologies, aggressive use of media by business, censorship, public opinion formation by government: these and scores of communication issues have daily impact upon legislative, judicial, and legal affairs. Communications and the Law is devoted to the study and discussion of such issues." 4/yr. Pub'd 4 issues 1979. sub. price: Institution $39.50, Individual $19.50; per copy: $12.50; sample: free. Back issues: $12.50.

Discounts: 10% agentss & jobbers, for other rates contact publisher. 96pp; 6X9; of. Reporting time: one month. Copyrighted. Pub's reviews: 6 in 1979. §Relating communictions law. Ads: $200.00.

COMMUNICATOR, Bob Eby, P.O. Box 2140, Springhill, Nova Scotia BOM IXO, Canada. 1972. Poetry, fiction, articles, cartoons, interviews, satire, criticism, news items. "Prison magazine. Material should relate to some perspective of the prison experience, solitude, social injustice, although abstractions which could be interpreted as relevant will be considered." circ. 1,000. 6/yr. Pub'd 6 issues 1979; expects 6 issues 1980, 6 issues 1981. sub. price: $6.00; per copy: $1.50; sample: free. Back issues: $0.75. Discounts: Exchange with anyone, cheaper to convicts, jobbers, free year to contributors. 46pp; 8½X14; †mi. Reporting time: immediately. Payment: Subscription/copies only. Copyrighted. Pub's reviews: 3 in 1979. §Prison, prison poetry, criminology, etc. Ads: $200.00/$0.10/freee to anyone giving something away to prisoners. COSMEP.

COMMUNITY ACTION, Collective, P.O. Box 665, London SW1X 8DZ, United Kingdom. 1972. Articles, news items. circ. 4,750. 6/yr. Pub'd 6 issues 1979; expects 6 issues 1980. sub. price: £1.80 (£3.50 libraries etc.); per copy: 30p plus 15p post; sample: 30p plus 15p post. Back issues: reduced rates for various packages. 40pp; size A4; of. Payment: No. Pub's reviews: 100 in 1979. Ads: No charge for ads but we have strict policy on which ones we do put in.

Community Collaborators, Virginia A. Decker, Managing Editor, PO Box 5429, Charlottesville, VA 22905, 804-977-1126. 1977. Articles. "*The Funding Process: Grantsmanship & Proposal Development* 6 x 9, H.C., 120 pages. *The Basic Steps of Planning* 6 x 9, paper, 24 pages. *Creating Interagency Projects: School & Community Agencies* 8½ x 11½, paper, 56 pages. *Community Involvement For Classroom Teachers* 8½ x 11½, paper, 63 pages. *Managing Federalism: Evolution and Development of the Grant-In-Aid System* 6 x 9, H.C., 320 pages. *A Directory of Publishing Opportunities For Teachers of Writing* 6 x 9, paper, 52 pages. *Foundations of Community Education* 8½ x 11, paper, 69 pages." avg. press run 5,000. Pub'd 2 titles 1979; expects 3 titles 1980, 3 titles 1981. 5 titles listed in the *Small Press Record of Books in Print* (9th Edition, 1980). avg. price, cloth: $11.50; paper: $3.00. Discounts: Bulk 10+, 20%; 25+ copies, 30%. 100pp; 6X9, 8½X11½; of. Reporting time: two weeks. Payment: range 10 to 15%. Copyrights for author. COSMEP.

COMMUNITY DEVELOPMENT JOURNAL, B.K. Taylor, Community Development Journal, Social Administration, The New University of Ulester, Coleraine NI, United Kingdom. 1966. Articles, reviews, news items. "Articles (should be sent) to Editorial address above. For subs, advertising, back nos., write Journal Manager, Oxford Univ. Press, Press road, Neasden, London NW10. Copyright held by Oxford University Press." circ. 2,000. 3/yr. Pub'd 3 issues 1979; expects 3 issues 1980, 3 issues 1981. sub. price: £9 (U.S. $19.50); per copy: £3.00 (U.S. $7.00). Discounts: on request for more than 20 copies. 75pp. Pub's reviews: 45 in 1979. §Community problems, politics, policy making, planning, programming, participation, action. Ads: £60/£35.

COMMUNITY SERVICE NEWSLETTER, Jane Morgan, Director, Box 243, Yellow Springs, OH 45387, 513-767-2161. 1940. Articles, reviews, letters. circ. 800. 6/yr. Pub'd 6 issues 1979; expects 6 issues 1980, 6 issues 1981. 30 titles listed in the *Small Press Record of Books in Print* (9th Edition, 1980). sub. price: $10.00; per copy: $1.00, varies with size; sample: free. Back Issues: list for indiv. newsletters free on request. Discounts: none. 12pp; 7X8½; of. Reporting time: two weeks. Payment: copies. Not copyrighted. Pub's reviews: 8 in 1979. §community, alternatives in community, society, economy, education, governance, technology, land and land reform. Ads: exchange ads.

COMPASS, Chris Mansell, Dane Thwaites, 11 Baker Street, Enfield, NSW 2136, Australia, (02) 7471592. 1978. Poetry, fiction, photos, cartoons, interviews, criticism, reviews, parts-of-novels, long-poems. "Biased toward exciting contemporary Australian writing. Recent contributors range from the very well-known to the never before published. Hope to continue to have wide appeal and to pursue an eclectic editorial policy." circ. 500. 4/yr. Pub'd 4 issues 1979; expects 4 issues 1980, 4 issues 1981. sub. price: $6.00; $20.00/institutions (plus postage if overseas); per copy: $1.50, $5.00/institutions (plus postage if overseas); sample: $1.50 plus postage. Discounts: Negotiable. 64pp; 6½X9½; of. Reporting time: 1 month. Payment: minimum $5.00 page. Copyrighted, reverts to author. Pub's reviews: 15 in 1979. §Poetry and creative prose. Ads: $100.00/$60.00. ASMA.

COMPUTER MUSIC JOURNAL, The Mit Press, Curtis Roads, Editor, 28 Carleton Street, Cambridge, MA 02142, 617-253-5646. 1977. Articles, photos, reviews, music. "We cover a broad range of musical and computational subjects" circ. 3,500. 4/yr. Pub'd 4 issues 1979; expects 4 issues 1980. sub. price: $20.00 US, $28.00 elsewhere mailed airmail, $30.00 institutional rate, $38.00 institutional rate overseas; per copy: $5.00; sample: $5.00. Back issues: $5.00 if in stock, $9.00 if out-of-stock (xerox form). Discounts to resellers and subscription agencies. 64pp; 8½X11; of. Reporting time: 6 weeks. Payment: none. Copyrighted, reverts to author. Pub's reviews: 10 in 1979. §computer music, acoustics of musical instruments, music theory, psychoacoustics, computer design, electronics, composition, recording. Ads: $300.00/$175.00/$90.00.

CONCEPTIONS SOUTHWEST, Gayle M. Krueger, Robert C. Masterson, Box 20, UNM Post Office, Albuquerque, NM 87131, (505) 277-5656. 1977. Poetry, fiction, art, photos, plays. "We accept material *only* from artists/writers/creators from the University of New Mexico community. We request manuscripts be typed, double-spaced and submitted in duplicate, SASE enclosed for return. For art, photography & visuals: 8 x 10 black & white prints." circ. 1,000. 1/yr. Expects 1 issue 1980, 1 issue 1981. sub. price: $2.00; per copy: $2.00; sample: $2.00. Back issues: $1.00 plus postage. 75pp; †of. Reporting time: 60 days. Copyrighted.

CONCERNING POETRY, Ellwood Johnson, Editor; Robert Huff, Poetry Editor, English Department, Western Wash. University, Bellingham, WA 98225. 1968. Poetry, articles, criticism, reviews. "Articles not over about 10-12 type-written, double-spaced pages. Poems rarely longer than two type-written pages." circ. 400. 2/yr. Pub'd 2 issues 1979. 1 title listed in the *Small Press Record of Books in Print* (9th Edition, 1980). sub. price: $4.00; per copy: $2.00; sample: $2.00. Back issues: $2.00 per copy. Discounts: none: agents may add 20 percent to our base prices. 85pp; 9X6; of. Reporting time: 2-3 months. Payment: copies only. Copyrighted, reverts to author. Pub's reviews: 8 in 1979. §poetry books; books about poetry (criticism). Ads: $40/$20.

CONCH MAGAZINE, Conch Magazine Ltd. (Publishers), Dr. S.O. Anozie, 102 Normal Avenue, Buffalo, NY 14213, 716-885-3686. 1969. Articles, criticism. "Unsolicited articles are not acceptable for publication in the CONCH journal." circ. 2½M. 2/yr. Pub'd 2 issues 1979; expects 2 issues 1980. sub. price: Ind $10.00, library $12.00, foreign add $2.00. Back issues: 50¢ for catalogue. Discounts: details available upon request. 100pp; 5½X8½; of. Payment: copies only. Copyrighted. Ads: General adv. $300.00/$200.00/$0.50; Pub rate $200.00/$150.00. COSMEP.

Conch Magazine Ltd. (Publishers) (see also CONCH MAGAZINE; CONCH REVIEW OF BOOKS; Trado-Medic Books), Dr. S. O. Anozie, General Editor, 102 Normal Avenue, (Symphony Circle), Buffalo, NY 14213, 716-885-3686. 1972. Articles, interviews, criticism, non-fiction. "Law, medicine, semiotics, linguistics, sociology, history, children's literature, politics, anthropology, structuralism. Conch Magazine, Ltd. is an indigenous African publisher of scholarly monographs and periodicals. Our editorial interest, reflected in our program of independent series of studies, is to present authentic African viewpoint through an original analysis and interpretation of current and significant issues in Africa." avg. press run 2M. Pub'd 5 titles 1979; expects 6 titles 1980. 14 titles listed in the *Small Press Record of Books in Print* (9th Edition, 1980). avg. price, cloth: $8.00; paper: $5.00. Discounts: Quantity discounts available upon request. 150pp; 6X9; of. Reporting time: 30-60 days. Payment: Terms negotiable. Copyrights for author. COSMEP.

CONCH REVIEW OF BOOKS, Conch Magazine Ltd. (Publishers), Dr. S.O. Anozie, 102 Normal Ave., Buffalo, NY 14213, 716-885-3686. 1973. Reviews. "Writers may submit book reviews, film reviews, music reviews for possible publication in CONCH REVIEW OF BOOKS: A Literary Supplement on Africa. We request that authors comply with the MLA style sheet, and that a review does not exceed 1000 words. It is desirable that prospective contributors contact the editor before making a submission." circ. 2M. 4/yr. Pub'd 7 issues 1979; expects 4 issues 1980. sub. price: $10.00 (Indiv); $15.00 (Lib); Foreign add $2.00. Back issues: 50¢ for catalogue. Discounts: Details available upon request. 50pp; 6½X9½; of. Reporting time: 30 days. Payment: copies only. Copyrighted. Pub's reviews. §African studies, incl all areas of books (children's lit, history, literature, etc.). Ads: General adv. $300.00/$200.00/$0.50; Publishers $200.00/$150.00. COSMEP.

CONDITIONS, Elly Bulkin, Jan Clausen, Irena Klepfisz, Rima Shore, PO Box 56, Van Brunt Sta., Brooklyn, NY 11215, 212-857-5351/768-2453. 1976. Poetry, fiction, articles, interviews, criticism, reviews, parts-of-novels, long-poems, plays, letters. "*Conditions* is a magazine of women's writing with an emphasis on writing by lesbians." circ. 3,000. 2/yr. Pub'd 2 issues 1979; expects 2 issues 1980, 2 issues 1981. sub. price: $8.00, $15.00 instit.; per copy: $3.00; sample: $3.00. Discounts: 40 percent discount on bookstore orders of 5 or more. 180pp; 5½X8½; of. Reporting time: up to 6 months. Payment: 2 copies. Copyrighted, reverts to author. Pub's reviews: 14 in 1979. §special bias in favor of women's & lesbian press. Ads: $100.00/$50.00/$25.00/$0.25 per word, 20 word minimum. CCLM.

CONFEDERATE CALENDAR WORKS, Lawrence T. Jones III, PO Box 5404, Austin, TX 78763. 1975. Photos. "Original photos (tintypes, ambrotypes, etc.) of Confederate soldiers published & featured for each month of year. Daily listing of historical events during the civil war." circ. 5,000. 1/yr. sub. price: $5.95. Back issues: $4.95. Discounts: 40% to dealers. 14pp; 8½X11; of. Copyrighted. COSMEP.

Confluence Press, Inc. (see also THE SLACKWATER REVIEW), M.K. Browning, Spalding Hall,

Lewis-Clark State College, Lewiston, ID 83501. 1976. Poetry, fiction, articles, art, photos, cartoons, interviews, satire, criticism, reviews, music. avg. press run 500. Pub'd 2 titles 1979; expects 2 titles 1980, 2 titles 1981. 18 titles listed in the *Small Press Record of Books in Print* (9th Edition, 1980). avg. price, paper: $2.50. Discounts: 40% to retailer, 50% to wholesaler. 100pp; 5½X8½; of. Reporting time: 2-3 months. Payment: poetry $0.35 a line; prose $0.05 a word; photos & pictures by arrangement, when funds allow, otherwise complimentary copies. CCLM.

LA CONFLUENCIA, Patricia D'Andrea, Susan Dewitt, Karl C. Kopp, P.O. Box 409, Albuquerque, NM 87103. 1976. Poetry, fiction, articles, art, photos, interviews, reviews, letters, news items. "Query before sending ms. of more than 5,000 words. Prints English, Spanish, S.W. Indian languages. Interviews, teacher's observations, and community case studies." circ. 1,000. 4/yr. Pub'd 3 issues 1979; expects 4 issues 1980. 1 title listed in the *Small Press Record of Books in Print* (9th Edition, 1980). sub. price: 4 issues $8.00; per copy: $2.50, $4.00, $5.00. Back issues: Vols. 1 & 2 @ $6.00/set. Discounts: classroom (teachers, students) $6.00 per volume (4 issues). 50pp; 8½X11; of. Reporting time: 1 month. Payment: In copies only. Copyrighted, reverts to author. Pub's reviews: 16 in 1979. §southwest...anthropology, history, folklore, teaching. COSMEP.

CONFRONTATION, Martin Tucker, English Dept., Long Island University, Brooklyn, NY 11201. 1968. Poetry, fiction, articles, interviews, parts-of-novels, long-poems, plays. circ. 2,000. 2/yr. Pub'd 2 issues 1979. sub. price: $5.00; per copy: $3.00; sample: $1.50. Back issues: $2.00. 160-190pp; 5X9; lp. Reporting time: 6 weeks. Payment: $20-$50 stories, $5-25 poetry. Copyrighted, reverts to author. §fiction, poetry. COSMEP.

CONNECTICUT FIRESIDE, Fireside Press, Albert Callan, P.O. Box 5293, Hamden, CT 06518, 203-248-1023. 1972. Poetry, fiction, articles, art, photos, cartoons, satire, criticism, reviews, letters, parts-of-novels. "Fireside is becoming more literary and less general. We will have more fiction and fewer articles. Prefer articles on literary subjects, as piece on HP Lovecraft and Raymond Chandler piece in Fireside #6." circ. 500. 4/yr. Pub'd 1 issue 1979; expects 3 issues 1980, 4 issues 1981. 1 title listed in the *Small Press Record of Books in Print* (9th Edition, 1980). sub. price: 4 issues-$4.00/6 issues-$6.00; per copy: $1.50; sample: $1.50. Back issues: cover price when available. Discounts: none. 100pp; 7X9½; †of. Reporting time: 2 weeks. Payment: copies. Copyrighted, reverts to author. Pub's reviews: 100+ in 1979. §literary, politics, esoteric. Ads: none. CCLM.

CONNECTICUT QUARTERLY, Fred Sokol, Associate Editor; Carol Haber, Editor; Judy Shaffer, Associate Editor; F.D. Reeve, Contributing Editor; Henry Van Dyke, Contributing Editor; James Miller, Contributing Editor; Katherine Green, Managing Editor, Box 68, Enfield, CT 06082, (203) 745-1603. 1979. Poetry, fiction, articles, art, photos, cartoons, interviews, satire, criticism, reviews, letters, parts-of-novels, long-poems, collages. "Becoming a highly academic, esoteric literary journal is what we want to avoid. We will strive to find literature that is of high quality, but can appeal to the general community as well as scholars. We look for the exciting and meaningful, whether expressed in *formal language* or *street language.*" circ. 500. 4/yr. Pub'd 4 issues 1979. sub. price: $7.50; per copy: $2.00; sample: free. Back issues: $2.00. Discounts: Agent or jobber, 40%. 75pp; 6X9. Reporting time: 2 months. Payment: 1 year subscription. Copyrighted, reverts to author. Pub's reviews. §New 'serious' literature.

CONNECTION NEWS RELEASE, Collective, c/o Release Publications Ltd., 1, Elgin Avenue, London W9, United Kingdom. 1972. Reviews, news items. "We don't want poetry or anything else 'creative'!" circ. 2,000. 4/yr. sub. price: £4; per copy: 35p; sample: 35p. Back issues: 30p. Discounts: 1/3. 24pp; size A4; of. Reporting time: variable. Copyrighted. Pub's reviews. §Relevant to areas of work. Ads: £100.

Connection Press, Molly M. Willett Ph. D., P.O. Box 689, Mill Valley, CA 94941, 415-383-9163. 1976. Photos, interviews. "Two books: 1) *The Self Connection,* a book on growing self loving, includes 40-page catalogue of resources. 2) *Channeling* a process guide to inner light, calligraphed, 30 illustrations." avg. press run 2,000. Pub'd 2 titles 1979. 2 titles listed in the *Small Press Record of Books in Print* (9th Edition, 1980). avg. price, paper: $6.95. Discounts: 30 percent trade. 72-250pp; 5X7; 7¼X9¾; †of. Reporting time: 3 months. Copyrights for author.

CONNECTIONS MAGAZINE, Toni Ortner-Zimmerman, Bell Hollow Road, Putnam Valley, NY 10579. 1971. Poetry. "Modern (free verse) poetry. Nothing rhymed or sentimental." circ. 600. 1/yr. Expects 1 issue 1980, 1 issue 1981. sub. price: $3.50/yr; per copy: $3.50; sample: $3.50. Back issues: $3.50. 70pp; 5½X8½. Reporting time: immediately. Payment: copies. Copyrighted, reverts to author.

Connections Press, Robert Merideth, Director, PO Box 454, Bolinas, CA 94924, (415) 868-1753. 1978. "One way to describe Connections Press is to say I and my firends and connections use it to publish our work. This way we can do it our way. We pay for it ourselves. Most of it we do physically, except for the press run. Thus the chief early books of the Press are scheduled to be: Robert Merideth's *Transformations: A Dictionary of Contemporary Changes* (ISBN 0-930474-00-7, 1979, 246 pp., 6 x 9¼, $6.00); Jay Mechling, Robert Merideth, and David Wilson's *Morning Work: A Trialogue on Issues of Knowledge and Freedom in Doing American Culture Studies* (ISBN 0-930474-01-5, 1979, 200+ pp., 8½ x 11, about $8.00); John Norton's volume of poems, as yet untitled (ISBN 0-930474-05-8, 1979, 32 pp., 5½ x 8½, about $2.50); Jack Gurian's poetry parodies, *I Hear American Studies Singing* (ISBN 0-930474-06-6, 1979, 24 pp., 5½ x 8½, about $2.00); and so on. Another way to describe the Press in its early stage is to say it grows historically out of the activities of the radical caucus of the American Studies Association. Anarchist in politics, gestalt in psychology, ecumenical in religion, the Press takes as its aim helping the world save itself from itself. It publishes signs and blueprints of a new society. Decentralize. Change it yourself. Liberation books on liberation themes. Low cost, high consciousness. People's pamphlets. Posters, post cards, calendars, cassette (and maybe video) tapes. The thought is that these re-visions will be immersed in scholarship, knowledge, and understanding (e.g., all the authors so far have Ph. D.s), but these are means to the ends of beauty, truth, and massive changes in this soft, sick social system we suffer" avg. press run 1,000. Expects 1 title 1980, 4 titles 1981. avg. price, paper: $5.00. Discounts: Standard. 150pp; 6X9¼; of. I do not solicit submissions, and thus do not report. Copyrights for author.

CONNEXIONS, Canadian Information Sharing Service, 121 Avenue Road, Toronto, Ontario M5R 2G3, Canada, 960-3903. 1976. Articles, art, photos, cartoons, interviews, criticism, reviews, news items. "We are an abstract service linking groups working for social justice-we are interested in documents for limited distribution that include reflection, analysis, report on action—always with a *Canadian* Focus." circ. 600. 5/yr. Pub'd 6 issues 1979; expects 5 issues 1980, 5 issues 1981. sub. price: $12.00 indiv., $25.00 instit.; per copy: $2.50; sample: $2.50. Back issues: $2.50. Discounts: Negotiable. 36pp; 8½X11; of. Reporting time: 3 months maximum. Payment: none. Not copyrighted. Pub's reviews: 46 in 1979. §Social justice struggles/analysis. Ads: none.

Conococheague Associates, Inc. (see also ANIMA), 1053 Wilson Ave, Chambersburg, PA 17201. 10 titles listed in the *Small Press Record of Books in Print* (9th Edition, 1980). Copyrights for author.

CONRADIANA, David Leon Higdon, Dept. of English, Box 4530, Texas Tech University, Lubbock, TX 79409. 1968. Articles, photos, interviews, criticism, reviews, news items. circ. 750. 3/yr. Pub'd 3 issues 1979; expects 3 issues 1980. sub. price: $7.50; per copy: $2.50; sample: $2.00. Back issues: Available. Discounts: None. 95pp; 6X9; †lp. Reporting time: 60 days. Payment: 20 offprints. Copyrighted. Pub's reviews. §books related to Joseph Conrad. Ads: $100.00/$50.00. CCLM, COSMEP.

CONSPIRACIES UNLIMITED, Robert S. Hertz, P O Box 3085, St Paul, MN 55165. 1978. Articles, letters, news items. "Intended to serve as an informal clearing-house for conspiracy research of many kinds. Expecially: religious & occult conspiracies, overall economic strategies, assassinations. But no anti-semitism or racism." circ. 250. 4/yr. Expects 4 issues 1980, 4 issues 1981. 1 title listed in the *Small Press Record of Books in Print* (9th Edition, 1980). sub. price: $2.00; per copy: $.50; sample: free. Back issues: $1.00 each. Discounts: 40% discount to trade. 12pp; 5X8; of. Reporting time: 3 weeks. §general occult & conspiracy.

CONSTELLATIONS, Harold M. Brown, Francine Kimmel, Don Emblen, PO Box 4378, Santa Rosa, CA 95402, (707) 526-6020. 1980. "*Constellations* is a new literary journal. Our goal is to provide a vehicle of publication to talented writers previously published or unpublished. All rights reserved; rights reassigned to author upon request." 2/yr. sub. price: $5.00; per copy: $3.00; sample: $3.00. 50-100pp; 8½X11. Payment: 2 copies. Ads: No ads.

CONSTRUCTIVE ACTION FOR GOOD HEALTH, The American Conference of Therapeutic Selfhelp/Selfhealth/Social Clubs, Sr. Shirley Burghard, R.N., A.A.S., B.A., O.S.L., D.S.H., B 1104 Ross Towers, 710 Lodi St., Syracuse, NY 13203, 315-471-4644. 1960. "We prefer material that shows people how they can help themselves to new and better lives via the use of selfhelp poetry therapy, selfhelp art therapy, selfhelp creative writing therapy, selfhelp pet therapy, selfhelp horticulture therapy, selfhealth natural food recipe therapy, selfhealth supplemental vitamin and mineral therapy etc. We are primarily constructive in nature, but we are against the therapeutic state, the new gods known as psychiatrists, the great mental illness-mental health rip off of the psychoquackiatrists, the psychofrauds and the mental health racketeers. We are against state mental institutions because of the abuse, assaults, atrocities committed in them by the staff against the patient. We believe not only in the right to treatment but the right to refuse treatment when it consists of brain cell destroying electric convulsive shock treatment and over tranquilization to a zombie state and brain surgery." circ. 500. 12/yr. Pub'd 12 issues 1979; expects 12 issues 1980, 12 issues 1981. sub. price: $6.00; per copy: $1.00; sample: $1.00. Back issues: no back issues available. Discounts: none. 20pp; 8½X14; †mi. Reporting time: about 3 weeks. Payment: copy. Not copyrighted. Pub's reviews: 3 in 1979. §Selfhelp-

/Selfhealth or the fucking over of little people by the big psychiatric profession. Ads: 5¢/word, $5.00 extra for line drawing illustrations. North American Conference on Human Rights and Psychiatric Oppressions.

CONTACT/11: A Bimonthly Poetry Review Magazine, Strawberry Press, Maurice Kenny, J. G. Gosciak, PO Box 451, Bowling Green Station, New York, NY 10004, 212-425-5979. 1976. Poetry, articles, art, photos, cartoons, interviews, satire, criticism, reviews, letters, news items, non-fiction. " *CONTACT/11: A Bimonthly Poetry Review* gives voice in magazine format to poetry and poets regardless of region, school, or subject matter. We try to be as open-minded and fair as humanly possible with all comers. We try to limit material (other than poems) to a 2-page spread. Poems are poems and we do not edit. We are always interested in reviews, criticism, articles on poetry. Recent contributors include: Barbara A. Holland, Rochelle Rattner, Patricia Wilcox, Phyllis Holliday, Lyn Lifshin, Siv Cedering, Richard Longchamps, John Brandi, Kirby Congdon, James Purdy, Duane Niatum, Wendy Rose, Theodore Enslin, Keith Wilson, Joseph Bruchac, Joe Johnson, William Packard, Robert Peters, Norman Russell, Tom Montag, George Hitchcock, Mei-Mei Berssenbrugge, Morgan Gibson, John Yau, Miguel Algarin, Carol Lee Sanchez, Olga Cabral, Jerome Rothenberg, Ted Joans." circ. 750-1,000. 6/yr. Pub'd 6 issues 1979; expects 6 issues 1980. sub. price: $6.00/$12.00 Institutions; per copy: $2.50; sample: $3.00. Back issues: $3.50 each where available. Discounts: 40%. 32pp; 8½X11; of. Reporting time: 6 weeks. Payment: in copies. Copyrighted, reverts to author. Pub's reviews: 27 in 1979. §poets/poetry/works by or about poets. Ads: $100.00/$50.00/$25.00. CCLM, NYSCA, NEA.

Contact II: Publications (see also CONTACT/11: A Bimonthly Poetry Review Magazine), Maurice Kenny, J.G. Gesciak, PO Box 451, Bowling Green Station, New York, NY 10004, 212-522-3227. 1976. Poetry. "*Nuke Chromicles,* a brief anthology of poems by Allen Ginsberg, Joseph Bruchac, Tuli Kupferberg, Carter Revard, Ron MacFarland, Ed Sanders. *Toll Bridge,* a new collection of poems by Wilma Elizabeth McDaniel." avg. press run 500. Pub'd 1 title 1979. avg. price, paper: $2.50. Discounts: standard. 32pp; 5½X8½; of. Reporting time: 2 months. Payment: copies. Copyrights for author. CCLM, NYSCA, NEA.

CONTEMPORARY ART/SOUTHEAST, John English, 3317 Piedmont Road NE #15, Atlanta, GA 30305. 1976. Articles, art, photos, interviews, criticism, reviews, letters. "First issue was published in April/May 1977. The magazine is concerned with the visual arts, from the traditional media through more experimental art forms. It's to have a regional focus & will deal with issues & problems in the total visual art system, using the Southeastern U.S. as a model for examining those problems. We will encourage the development of substantive critical writing on the visual arts and provide a medium for the exchange of information in the arts." circ. 10,000. 6/yr. Pub'd 6 issues 1979; expects 6 issues 1980. sub. price: Individual $9.00-yr; Institutional $12.00-yr; per copy: $3.00; sample: $2.00-$3.00. Back issues: $3.00. 64pp; 8½X11; of. Reporting time: 2 months. Copyrighted. Pub's reviews: 3 in 1979. §visual arts (including video & experimental film, performance art), art & culture. Ads: $300.-00/$165.00.

Contemporary Curriculums, PO Box 83, Oak Lawn, IL 60453. 1973. "Creativity lessons for elementary grades (Ideabooks)" avg. press run 1,000. Pub'd 1 title 1979; expects 1 title 1980, 1 title 1981. 5 titles listed in the *Small Press Record of Books in Print* (9th Edition, 1980). avg. price, paper: $5.00. Discounts: 30%. 75pp; 8½X11; of. Reporting time: 6 weeks. Payment: varies. Copyrights for author. COSMEP.

THE CONTEMPORARY LITERARY SCENE, Salem Press, Inc., Walton Beacham, Dept. of English, Va. Commonwealth Univ., Richmond, VA 23284. 1973. 1/yr. price per copy: $8.95. 300pp. Reporting time: 1 month. Payment: $1.00 per article.

CONTEMPORARY LITERATURE, University of Wisconsin Press, L.S. Dembo, 7141 Helen C. White Hall, University of Wisconsin, Madison, WI 53706. 1960. Criticism, reviews. "Scholarly literary criticism" circ. 2,000 plus. 4/yr. sub. price: individuals $10.00/yr; institutions $20.00; per copy: varies. Back issues: write for details. Discounts: 5% subscription agency. 136pp; 6X9; of. Payment: none. Pub's reviews. Ads: $150/$80.

CONTEMPORARY POETRY: A Journal of Criticism, Thomas H. Jackson, Selwyn Kittridge, Contemporary Poetry, Bryn Mawr College, Bryn Mawr, PA 19010, (215) LA5-1000. 1973. Articles, interviews, criticism. "*CP* was formerly published at Fairleigh Dickinson Univesity in New Jersey. After an inactive period, the journal has begun to appear once again from Bryn Mawr & we are planning for its growth in many ways." circ. 200-300. 4/yr. Pub'd 2 issues 1979; expects 4 issues 1980, 4 issues 1981. sub. price: $5.00 Individuals, $6.00 Institutions; per copy: $1.75; sample: $1.75. Back issues: $1.75. 70+pp; 6X8½; †of. Reporting time: 2-3 weeks. Payment: copies. Copyrighted, reverts to author. Ads: no ads. CCLM.

CONTRABAND MAGAZINE, Contraband Press, Kilgore, Holsapple, Empfield, P.O. Box 4073, Sta. A, Portland, ME 04101. 1971. Poetry, fiction, articles, art, photos, cartoons, interviews, satire, criticism, reviews, music, letters, parts-of-novels, long-poems, collages, plays, concrete art, news items. "Modern and experimental literature and art." circ. 500. 1/yr. Pub'd 1 issue 1979; expects 1 issue 1980, 1 issue 1981. sub. price: $4.00 for 4 issues; per copy: $1.00; sample: $1.00. Back issues: $100.00 for the set, #1 thru #14. Discounts: 40%. 80pp; 7X8½; of. Reporting time: 3 weeks at the most. Payment: 2 to 10 copies. Copyrighted, reverts to author on publication. Pub's reviews: 2 in 1979. §Any area. Ads: none. CCLM, MWPA.

Contraband Press (see also CONTRABAND MAGAZINE), Kilgore, Holsapple, Empfield, P.O. Box 4073, Sta A, Portland, ME 04101. 1971. Poetry, fiction, articles, art, photos, cartoons, interviews, satire, criticism, reviews, music, letters, parts-of-novels, long-poems, collages, plays, concrete art, news items. "Modern and experimental literature and art." avg. press run 500. Pub'd 2 titles 1979; expects 2 titles 1980, 2 titles 1981. 10 titles listed in the *Small Press Record of Books in Print* (9th Edition, 1980). avg. price, paper: $1.50. Discounts: 40 percent. 80pp; 5½X8; of/lp. Reporting time: 3 weeks. Payment: 100 copies. copyrights, not Library of Congress. MWPA.

CONTRACULTURA, David Grinberg, C C Central 1332, Buenos Aires 1000, Argentina. 1970. Articles. "Spanish language and translations." circ. 2,000. 2/yr. Pub'd 3 issues 1979; expects 2 issues 1980, 2 issues 1981. sub. price: No subscriptions; per copy: $1.00; sample: free. Back issues: Free. Discounts: none. 16pp; 13 cm x 18 cm; lp. Reporting time: immediate. Payment: none. Not copyrighted. Pub's reviews: 4 in 1979. §Counterculture. no ads. APS, NS (Nueva Sincronia).

CONTRAST, changes yearly, Western Maryland College, Westminster, MD 21157. 1960. Poetry, fiction, photos, concrete art. "Looking for good fire-driven poetry and fiction. Fiction should be no longer than 1,200 words. Avoid academic poetry and seek imagery bound non-sentimental poems. Recent contributors: Jesse Glass, Leo Connelian, Jeff Whittaker, Keith Slifer, Joe Gainer." 3/yr. Pub'd 3 issues 1979; expects 3 issues 1980, 3 issues 1981. sub. price: $3.00; per copy: $1.00. 20pp; 4X5½; mi. Reporting time: 3 months at most. Payment: in copies. Copyrighted, reverts to author.

CONTRIBUTORS BULLETIN (also FREELANCE WRITING), Freelance Press Services, Arthur Waite, FREELANCE WRITING; S.E. Williams, CONTRIBUTORS BULLETIN, 5/9 Bexley Square, Salford, Manchester, England M3 6DB, United Kingdom, 061-832 5079. 1962. Articles, photos, letters. circ. CB 800, FLW 3,000. 4/yr (FLW) 12/yr (CB). sub. price: £2.50 FLW; £8.75 CB; per copy: 60p. 12 pp CB, 32 pp FLW; 13X8, FLW 8½X6; †of. Reporting time: 2 weeks. Payment: £7.00 per 1,000. Copyrighted. Ads: £25.00/10p word.

CO-OP: The Harbinger of Economic Democracy, North American Students of Cooperation, Margaret Lamb, Editor, Box 7293, Ann Arbor, MI 48107, 313-663-0889. 1971. Articles, cartoons, interviews, satire, reviews, letters. "1,000-4,000 words. Articles should be related to cooperatives, esp. consumer co-ops, or similar efforts at social change." circ. 3,100. 6/yr. Pub'd 4 issues 1979; expects 5 issues 1980, 6 issues 1981. sub. price: $10.50; per copy: $1.75; sample: $1.00. Back issues: Write for free list. Discounts: 40 percent. 48pp; 6X9; of. Reporting time: two weeks. Payment: Usually none, occasionally some. Copyrighted, does not revert to author. Pub's reviews: 8 in 1979. §co-ops; social change; economic democracy. Ads: $100.00/$70.00/$0.10. COSMEP.

Co-op Books Ltd. (see also THE MONGREL FOX), Neil Jordan, Dermot Moran, Ronan Sheehan, Leland Bardwell, Steve McDonough, 50 Merrion Sq., Dublin 2, Ireland. 1975. Fiction, plays. "The Irish Writers' Cooperative was formed in 1975 to provide new outlets for fiction in Ireland (*not* restricted to Irish authors) and publishes novels, collections of stories, and recently, plays which have been premiered in Ireland. No length is specified though to date, no novel longer than 200 pages has been published. Neil Jordan *Night in Junisia* (1976), Des Hogan *The Ikon-Maker* (1976), Leland Bardwell *Girl on a Bicycle* (1977), James Brennan *Seaman* (1978) and Ronan Sheehan *Tennis - Players* (1977) are among the novels published to date. Bias is towards new creative fiction, avoiding 'popular' and boring conventionality. Desire is to publish quality fiction with contemporary appeal. It is supported by grants from the Arts Council of Ireland." avg. press run 3,000. Pub'd 4 titles 1979; expects 9 titles 1980, 10 titles 1981. avg. price, paper: $3.00. Discounts: Trade discount 35%, publication agent is Steve MacDonogh, 9 Beaver Row, Donnybrook, Dublin 4, Ireland. 100-200pp; 5X7 1/4; of. Reporting time: 1 month. Payment: 10% royalty. Tax free in republic of Ireland. Paid quarterly from publication. Copyrights for author. CLE (Irish Publishers Organisation).

THE CO-OP OBSERVER, Carol J. Ott, 241 W 23rd Street, New York, NY 10011, (212) 675-7226. 1980. Articles, art, photos, interviews, news items. "A monthly newsletter for people living in and investing in New York cooperatives. *The Co-Op Observer* will begin publication in the summer of 1980."

98

12/yr. sub. price: $12.00; per copy: $1.00; sample: free. 11X14; of. Reporting time: 6-8 weeks. Payment: $0.10 per word. Copyrighted. Pub's reviews. §Anything pertaining to NYC real estate, cooperative living, design, etc. Ads: No ads.

Copley Books, Richard F. Pourade, General Editor; Jean I. Bradford, Office Manager, 7776 Ivanhoe Avenue, P O Box 957, La Jolla, CA 92038, 714-454-1842. 1959. "We want submissions *only* in our publishing area. We publish no poetry, childrens stories, or non-fiction. Specialty authentic (non-fictional) history of California, the Southwest, and Mexico." avg. press run 3,000-5,000. Pub'd 1-2 titles 1979. 20 titles listed in the *Small Press Record of Books in Print* (9th Edition, 1980). avg. price, cloth: $12.50; paper: $6.50. Discounts: Booksellers 40 percent; libraries 20 percent. 200-300pp; 8½X11; of. Payment: As arranged. copyright per arrangement with author.

Copper Beech Press, Edwin Honig, James Schevill, David Cloutier, Box 1852 Brown Univ., Providence, RI 02912, 401-863-2393. 1973. Poetry, fiction, long-poems. "Distributed exclusively by Serendipity Small Press Distribution, 1636 Ocean View Ave., Kensington, CA 94707." avg. press run varies between 350 and 1,000. Pub'd 3 titles 1979; expects 8-10 titles 1980, 10-12 titles 1981. 29 titles listed in the *Small Press Record of Books in Print* (9th Edition, 1980). avg. price, paper: $2.50 - $7.50. Poetry 40-75pp, fiction 150-275.pp; size varies; of. Reporting time: ASAP, usually within 3 months. Payment: copies. Does not copyright for author.

Copper Canyon Press/Copperhead, Sam Hamill, Tree Swenson, P.O. Box 271, Port Townsend, WA 98368. 1973. Poetry, long-poems. "We publish book-length manuscripts of poetry. Authors should query before sending unsolicited mss. We expect our authors to have read our books and to have studied the (Ta Hsio) of Kung-fu tzu. No SASE, no reply. We are not interested in arm-chair or academic poetry. Our poets are rooted and write out of a strong sense of place." avg. press run 1,000. Pub'd 8 titles 1979; expects 8 titles 1980, 8 titles 1981. 38 titles listed in the *Small Press Record of Books in Print* (9th Edition, 1980). avg. price, cloth: $14.00; paper: $3.50. Discounts: Standard 40%, returnable. 64pp; size varies (6X10); †of/lp. Reporting time: 1 month. Payment: 10% of edition. Copyrights for author.

CO-OP MAGAZINE, Margaret C. Lamb, Box 7293, Ann Arbor, MI 48107, (313) 663-0889. 1972. Articles, art, photos, cartoons, interviews, satire, reviews, letters. circ. 3,000. 6/yr. Pub'd 6 issues 1979; expects 6 issues 1980, 6 issues 1981. sub. price: $10.50; per copy: $1.75; sample: $1.00. Back issues: $0.50-$1.50. Discounts: Bulk: 10-25 subs, $7.50 ea; 26-50, $7.00; 51-100, $6.50. 48pp; 6X9. Reporting time: 30 days. Payment: $5.00-$25.00. Copyrighted. Pub's reviews: 4 in 1979. §Co-operatives. Ads: $100.00/$70.00/$0.10. COSMEP.

COPULA, James Bradford, Sharon Byrum, W1114 Indiana Street, Spokane, WA 99205, 325-2985. 1980. Poetry, articles, art, interviews, satire, reviews. "First issue anticipated in May. Surrealism, experimental poetry, humor, myth, fantasy, minority poetry; poetry as lightning between the unknown and the unconscious; synapse between the world to come and the world that's gone; and between the objective world and the mind, not a mirror, but cathexis." circ. 500. 4/yr. sub. price: $4.00; per copy: $1.00. 50pp; 5½X8½; of. Reporting time: 2 weeks to 1 month. Payment: copies. Copyrighted, reverts to author. Pub's reviews. §Poetry.

COPY CORNUCOPIA, The Direct Marketing Creative Guild, Lee Marc Stein, Editor-in-Chief; Richard Sachinis, Managing Editor, 516 Fifth Avenue, New York, NY 10036. 1964. Poetry, fiction, articles, cartoons, interviews, criticism, reviews, letters. "The Guild is the only nonprofit group devoted to the interests of the direct response (freelance and employed by others). Mostly staff written because we can't find enough good material on effective direct response advertising (the major thrust of the newsletter)." circ. 200-610. monthly. Pub'd 12 issues 1979; expects 12 issues 1980, 12 issues 1981. sub. price: $28.00; per copy: $4.00; sample: free. Back issues: $5.50. Discounts: none. 8pp; 8½X11; of. Reporting time: 3 weeks. Payment: none. Copyrighted. Pub's reviews: 4 in 1979. §Techniques of effective advertising, especially in the direct response business. Ads: $25.00.

‡**Corinth Books Inc.,** 228 Everit St., New Haven, CT 06511. 33 titles listed in the *Small Press Record of Books in Print* (9th Edition, 1980).

Cornerstone Press (see also IMAGE MAGAZINE), Anthony J. Summers, P.O. Box 28048, St. Louis, MO 63119, 314-487-4303. 1974. Poetry, fiction, art, cartoons, plays, articles, interviews, reviews, collages, concrete art, news items. "We have published 6 books to date. We are looking for works of art no matter how they are produced. Submit only things that will stand on their own. We will not publish any books until further notice or 1981, whichever comes first." avg. press run 500-600. Pub'd 2 titles 1979; expects 1 title 1980. 6 titles listed in the *Small Press Record of Books in Print* (9th Edition, 1980). avg. price, cloth: $4-5.00; paper: $1.00 - $3.00. Discounts: one free to any prisoner requesting. 48-72pp; 5X11; of. Reporting time: 2 weeks to 6 months *not seeking any submissions until further notice*

. Payment: money and copies to be arranged. Copyrights for author. CCLM, COSMEP, COSMEP-SOUTH.

CORNFIELD REVIEW, David Citino, The Ohio State University Marion Campus, 1465 Mt. Vernon Avenue, Marion, OH 43302, (614) 389-2361. 1974. Poetry, fiction, articles, art, photos, criticism. "Much of the material we use from 'outside' is solicited. Recent contributors: Paul Bennett, Grace Butcher, Robert Flanagan, Peter Cooley, Wayne Dodd, John Ditsky, Emilie Glen, Menke Katz, Jack Matthews, William Stafford, Hollis Summers, Alberta Turner, Ronald Wallace, etc. We've published a special issue, *73 Ohio Poets,* an anthology supported by the Ohio Arts Council." circ. 550-600. 1-2/yr. Pub'd 2 issues 1979; expects 1 issue 1980, 1 issue 1981. 1 title listed in the *Small Press Record of Books in Print* (9th Edition, 1980). sub. price: $1.00/yr; per copy: $1.00 for regular issues; sample: $1.00. Back issues: $1.00 for 1-5, $3.95 for special isssue *73 Ohio Poets.* Discounts: 40% to stores. 6X9; of. Reporting time: 2 months maximum. Payment: 2 copies. Copyrighted, on written request.

COSMEP NEWSLETTER, Richard Morris, PO Box 703, San Francisco, CA 94101, (415) 922-9490. 1968. "Published for COSMEP members. Membership is $35 per year." 12/yr. Pub'd 12 issues 1979; expects 12 issues 1980. sub. price: $35.00; sample: free. 8pp; 8½X11. Reporting time: 1 week. Payment: $25.00 for articles, query first. Pub's reviews: 10 in 1979. §Books of interest to publishers. Ads: No ads.

THE COSMEP PRISON PROJECT NEWSLETTER, Joseph Bruchac III, Editor; Carol W. Bruchac, Editor, C/O The Greenfield Review, Greenfield Center, NY 12833. 1976. Articles, letters, reviews. "Free to inmates and to writers conducting workshops in prisons.The *Cosmep Prison Project Newsletter* prints letters, very short prose and poetry, from prison inmates who are receiving literary materials from us. We also publish articles relating to creative writing and poetry workshops in prison, reviews of work by inmate writers, etc. Aguila, Hogan, Natkie, Petaccia, Mary McAnally, Janet Lembke." circ. 1,000. 2/yr. Pub'd 2 issues 1979; expects 2 issues 1980, 2 issues 1981. sub. price: $5.00 Indiv., $10.00 Libraries, free to inmates; per copy: $2.00; sample: $2.00. Back issues: none available. 28-32pp; 8½X11; of. Reporting time: 1 to 2 weeks. Payment: $2.00/page minimum, plus copies. Copyrighted, reverts to author. Pub's reviews: 6 in 1979. §Only those relating directly to writers in prison. no ads. COSMEP.

Cosmic Brain Trust (see also COSMIC CIRCUS), Rey King, Editor, 414 So 41st Street, Richmond, CA 94804, (415) 658-0233. 1974. Poetry, fiction, articles, art, photos, cartoons, interviews, satire, reviews, collages, plays. avg. press run 1,500. Pub'd 2 titles 1979; expects 3 titles 1980, 3 titles 1981. avg. price, paper: $2.00. 40pp; 8X10, 4X8; †of. Reporting time: 1 month. Payment: on publication. Copyrights for author. CCLM.

COSMIC CIRCUS, Cosmic Brain Trust, Rey King, 414 So 41st Street, Richmond, CA 94804, 415-658-0233. 1972. Poetry, fiction, articles, art, photos, cartoons, interviews, satire, reviews, collages, plays. "We publish as follows: 50 percent underground comixs, 25 percent short stories, 10 percent poetry, 10 percent photos. This publication presents material which may be considered strange or 'beyond human comprehension.' Subscription includes membership. Submissions by members are given primary consideration but others are welcomed to try. Also available are hour long tapes." circ. 500-1,500. 2-3/yr. Pub'd 2 issues 1979; expects 3 issues 1980, 3 issues 1981. sub. price: $5.00; per copy: $2.00; sample: $2.00 plus $0.50 postage and handling. Back issues: Issues 1-4, $2.50; tapes or records (soundsheets) $1.00. 40pp; 8½X10; †of. Reporting time: 1 month to 6 weeks. Payment: in books or $10 per page (artwork), $5 per page (poetry). Copyrighted. Pub's reviews: 2 in 1979. §Occult, comics, science fiction, film, poetry, sexuality. Ads: $50.00/$25.00/$0.15. CCLM.

COSMOPOLITAN CONTACT, Pantheon Press, Romulus Rexner, Editor-in-Chief; Irene Anders, Managing Editor, P. O. Box 1566, Fontana, CA 92335. 1962. Articles, cartoons, interviews, criticism, reviews, letters. "*Cosmopolitan Contact*-a polyglot magazine, promotes intercultural understanding & intellectual growth as means toward the reduction of intergroup and international tension and conflict. Worldwide, friendly exchange of letters, hobbies, gifts, ideas, hospitality, information and other mutual travel or trade assistance among members. As a result of listings in this directory, in Writers' Markets, etc. more and better literary material is being contributed and more space will be allocated to literary material relevant to the philosophy and objectives of Planetary Legion for Peace (P.L.P.) and Planetary Universalism. It is the publication's object to have as universal appeal as possible — students, graduates and others interested in international affairs, cooperation, contacts, travel, friendships, trade, exchanges, self-improvement and widening of mental horizons through multicultural interaction. This publication has world wide distribution and participation, including the Communist countries. We need material designed to promote across all frontiers bonds of spiritual unity, intellectual understanding and sincere friendship among people by means of correspondence, meetings, publishing activities, tapes, records, exchange of hospitality, books, periodicals in various languages, hobbies and other contacts. Most of the material is not written by experts to enlighten or to amuse the readers, but it is written by the readers who also are freelance writers. The material is didactic, provocative, pragmatic — not art-for-art's sake — and tries to answer the reader's question: 'What can I do about it?' (Not what our leaders should do about the problem or need.) If a writer wants us to be interested in him, he/she should also be interested in our aims. Many writers are mainly preoccupied with their own self-aggrandisement and not interested in participating continuously in our work. The addresses of all contributors are published in order to facilitate global contacts among our contributors, editors and readers/members. Instead of writing e.g. about Lincoln or history, it is better to be an emancipator and to make history by promoting high ideals of mankind. Consequently, the material submitted to us should not be only descriptive, but it should be analytical, creative, action and future-oriented. Expose, preferably concentrating on government, education, etc., informational, inspiration, personal experience, travel, opinion. 'Silence is not always golden; sometimes it is yellow'. However, an average individual who wants to express publicly his own views or experiences finds out that the means of communication are controlled either by indoctrinated government officials, or by profit-seeking businessmen. The pages of 'Cosmopolitan Contact' are open to its readers who are invited to write regarding matters of general interest. These letters and articles will be published as far as space permits. Maximum 500 words. We are not interested in any contribution containing vulgar language, extreme, intolerant, pro-Soviet or anti-American opinions." circ. 1,500. 2-3/yr. Pub'd 2-3 issues 1979; expects 2-3 issues 1980. sub. price: $2.00; per copy: $1.00; sample: $1.00. Back issues: 8 back issues $2.00. Discounts: 40%. Reporting time: 4 wks.

J. DuHadway Craig, J. DuHadway Craig, PO Box 42, Pebble Beach, CA 93953, (408) 624-0354. 1976. "Only the work of J. DuHadway Craig is published. This consists of 'The Antiquated American' (c., 1976), a book of essays on government, and 'Luis & Les Deus Coins' (copyright, 1976), a book of two short novels. 'Luis & Les Deux Coins' will be distributed by J. DuHadway Craig in 1979, although it is presently being distributed by another publisher." avg. press run varies. Expects 2 titles 1981. 2 titles listed in the *Small Press Record of Books in Print* (9th Edition, 1980). avg. price, cloth: $5.95; paper: $4.50. 180pp; 5½X8½; of/lp. No submissions are accepted.

CRAWL OUT YOUR WINDOW, Crawl Out Your Window Press, Melvyn Freilicher, Eleanor Bluestein, 704 Nob Ave, Del Mar, CA 92014, 714-755-1258. 1975. Fiction, art, photos, music, parts-of-novels, long-poems, collages. "Try to give 10 pages to all contributors." circ. 500. 1/yr. price per copy: $2.00. 150pp; 8½X11; of. Payment: Several issues of magazine. Copyrighted, reverts to author. §New fiction, visual art. COSMEP.

Crawl Out Your Window Press (see also CRAWL OUT YOUR WINDOW), Melvyn Freilicher, 704 Nob Ave, Del Mar, CA 92014, 714-755-1258. 1975. Fiction, art, photos, parts-of-novels, long-poems, collages. "Mostly interested in Southern California avant'-garde' art. Intermedia and collaborative works especially." avg. press run 350-500. Pub'd 2 titles 1979; expects 3 titles 1980. size varies widely; of.

CRAZY HORSE, Delbert E. Wylder, Managing Editor; Edith P. Wylder, Managing Editor; Jorie Graham, Poetry Editor; Joe Ashby Porter, Fiction Editor, Murray State University, College of Humanistic Studies, Dept of English, Murray, KY 42071, (502) 762-2401. 1967. Poetry, fiction. "On special occasion (assigned) criticism, reviews." circ. 250. 2/yr. Pub'd 2 issues 1979; expects 2 issues 1980, 2 issues 1981. sub. price: $8.00; per copy: $4.00; sample: $2.00. Back issues: $2.00-$4.00. Discounts: Agencies, 40%; Bookstores, 40%. 100pp; 6X9; of. Reporting time: 2-4 weeks. Payment: none. Copyrighted. Ads: $125.00/$75.00. CCLM.

CRCS Publications, Joan M. Case, PO Drawer 4307, Vancouver, WA 98662, (206) 256-8979. 1975. Art. "We are specializing in the production of high-quality, aesthetically-pleasing astrological books, with a psychological and spiritual slant." avg. press run 5,000. Pub'd 2 titles 1979; expects 3 titles 1980. 7 titles listed in the *Small Press Record of Books in Print* (9th Edition, 1980). avg. price, cloth: $8.95-$10.95; paper: $4.95 - $7.95. Discounts: 40 percent off on orders of 5 or more books to dealers; 40 percent off on all pre-paid orders from dealers, in any quantity; 10 percent disc. to libraries if requested. 200 pluspp; size Varies; of. Reporting time: 8 weeks. Payment: Royalties plus large discounts on books. Copyrights for author. COSMEP.

CREACION, Editorial Creacion, Cirilo Toro-Vargas, Hector J. Martell-Morales, Apartado 111, Estacion 6, Ponce, PR 00731. 1975. Poetry, fiction, articles, art, photos, cartoons, interviews, criticism, reviews, letters. "Objectives: (1) to establish a link of communication; mutual understanding and acceptance between creators and the people. (2) to work towards the individual and collective improvement of the creators by means of the *APPAC*. (3) to help cultural workers (both graphic and literary) be known, especially those who remain anonymous because no help is given to them. Printed in Spanish, but works in other languages may be submitted." circ. 1,000. 1/yr. Pub'd 1 issue 1979;

expects 1 issue 1980. sub. price: $4.00 (P.R. and U.S.; $7.00 other countries); per copy: $4.00 (plus $0.35 mail charges in P.R. and U.S.; other countries add up the proper mail charges). Back issues: $1.00 per copy (1975-78 issues). Discounts: 20 percent for trade. 32-60pp; 4X7; of. Reporting time: One to six months, depending on our time available since we manage to work on the magazine on our leisure time. Payment: in copies. Copyrighted, copyright reverts to author upon publication. Pub's reviews. §art and literature (especially from and about Latin America). Ads: $100.00/$50.00. CCLM.

CREAM CITY REVIEW, Henri Cole, P O Box 413, English Dept, Curtin Hall, Univ of Wisconsin, Milwaukee, WI 53201. 1975. Poetry, fiction, articles, art, photos, interviews, satire, criticism, reviews, letters, parts-of-novels, long-poems, plays. "No biases except quality. Fiction up to 10 typed pages. Poetry no length limit. Recent contributors: James Liddy, David Steingass, William Harrold, George Chambers, John Judson, Richard Eberhart, Robert Siegel, Peter Klappert, Philip Dacey, Ihab Hassan, Raymond Federman." circ. 800. 2/yr. Pub'd 2 issues 1979; expects 2 issues 1980, 2 issues 1981. sub. price: $6.00; per copy: $3.00; sample: $3.00. Back issues: $2.00. 100-120pp; 5½X8½; of. Reporting time: 4-8 weeks. Payment: copies. Copyrighted, reverts to author. Pub's reviews: 4 in 1979. §Current fiction and poetry. Ads: $100.00/$50.00. CCLM, COSMEP.

CREAMANIA, James Kelly, PO Box 92, Boston, MA 02199. 1980. Articles, reviews, letters. "*Creamania* is devoted exclusively to the sinister *Dr. Thomas Neill Cream,* the most amazing creature in the annals of criminology. We publish everything pertaining to the abominable history of the venemous *Dr. Cream,* practitioner of murder. Though unable to welcome new manuscripts at this time, we certainly welcome all correspondence concerning the notorious doctor." circ. 500. 6/yr. Pub'd 4 issues 1979; expects 6 issues 1980. sub. price: $18.00; per copy: $3.00; sample: $3.00 postpaid. Back issues: $3.00 postpaid. 16-24pp; 5½X8½; of. Copyrighted, reverts to author. Pub's reviews. §True crime, Victorian crime, medical jurisprudence, toxicology, forensic medicine.

Creative Arts Book Company, Don Ellis, 833 Bancroft Way, Berkeley, CA 94710, 415-848-4777. 1976. Fiction, articles, art, photos, interviews, criticism, letters, non-fiction. "We publish mainly non-fiction material, but remain open to anything. Recent and forthcoming works include: *Obituaries* by William Saroyan; *Pharos & Pharillon* by E.M. Forster; *Working With Arthritis* by Isabel Hanson; *Port Tropique* by Barry Gifford; *Homage to Frank O'Hara* ed. by Bill Berkson." avg. press run 2,500-10,000. Pub'd 7 titles 1979; expects 6 titles 1980. 19 titles listed in the *Small Press Record of Books in Print* (9th Edition, 1980). avg. price, cloth: $10.95; paper: $4.95. Discounts: Single copies 10%. 2-4, 20 percent; 5+, 40 percent. Distrib. to the trade by Bookpeople; McBride & Broadley (UK & Europe); Wild & Woolley (Australia). pp varies; 5½X8½; †of. Reporting time: 1 week to 3 months. Payment varies. Copyrights for author. AAP.

Creative Book Company, Sol H. Marshall, 8210 Varna Ave., Van Nuys, CA 91402, 213-988-2334. 1965. Articles. "Our general fields are those of community organization and education. Agency and school fund-raising and public relations. Personal and professional development for people in those fields. Cookbooks." avg. press run first run 300 copies. After that 1,000 or 2,000. Pub'd 20 titles 1979; expects 20 titles 1980, 12-20 titles 1981. 46 titles listed in the *Small Press Record of Books in Print* (9th Edition, 1980). avg. price, cloth: $8.80; paper: $2.20-$6.60; other: Folios & Reports, $1.00. Discounts: 20 percent on 1 to 4 copies, mixed titles okay. 40 percent on 5 or more copies; mixed titles okay. Additional 10 percent for annotated listings in catalogs. 32 to 48pp; 8X10½; 5¼X8¼; of. Reporting time: 2 weeks. Payment: flat fee. copyright for Creative Book Company.

CREATIVE COMPUTING, Creative Computing Press, David H. Ahl, Publisher; Theodor Nelson, Editor, P.O. Box 789-M, Morristown, NJ 07960, 201-540-0445. 1974. Poetry, fiction, articles, art, photos, cartoons, interviews, satire, reviews, letters. "Magazine is for hobbyists, educators, small business computer users, students, and anyone curious about computers. Articles and stories about the effect of the computer on society, privacy, art, science, etc. Human interest side of computers. Lots of practical applications, classroom activities, games, with complete program listings and microcomputer profiles. Fiction: stories about runaway computers, robots, computers gaining human intelligence, etc. Book reviews, cartoon, humor, sf, fantasy, some poetry." circ. 80,000. 12/yr. Pub'd 12 issues 1979; expects 12 issues 1980, 12 issues 1981. 4 titles listed in the *Small Press Record of Books in Print* (9th Edition, 1980). sub. price: $15.00; per copy: $2.00; sample: $2.00. Back issues: Available: $2.00 each, 3 for $5.00, 10 for $15.00; not all back issues are available. Discounts: agent:10%, bulk: up to 50%. 192pp; 8½X11; of. Reporting time: 4-6 weeks. Payment: Fiction: 3¢/word—Cartoons: $15. Copyrighted, reverts, but we hold rights to anthologize. Pub's reviews: 50 in 1979. §Computers, technology, sf, microcomputer kits and equipment. Ads: $1,400.00/$900.00/$80.00 inch.

Creative Computing Press (see also CREATIVE COMPUTING), David H. Ahl, Publisher; Burchenal Green, Managing Editor, PO Box 789-M, Morristown, NJ 07960, 201-540-0445. 1974. Poetry, fiction, articles, art, photos, cartoons, interviews, satire, reviews, letters. "Publish books about how to understand and use a micro computer, innovative, fun, programs for a micro computer, computer fiction and cartoons, with emphasis on computers in the home and the effect that will cause in society." avg. press run 10,000. Pub'd 5 titles 1979; expects 8 titles 1980, 8 titles 1981. 5 titles listed in the *Small Press Record of Books in Print* (9th Edition, 1980). avg. price, cloth: $10.00; paper: $8.95. Discounts: Bulk & bookstores-from 40 to 50 percent. 336pp; 8½X11; of. Reporting time: 4-6 weeks. Payment: varies. Copyrights for author.

Creative Editions & Capitol Enquiry, Kathleen Anderson, Alan Pritchard, PO Box 22246, Sacramento, CA 95822. 1973. "Types of material: government & politics only. Capitol Enquiry publishes an annual pocket directory of the California legislature and Capitol Quarterly, a digest of government information. Creative Editions has published *Getting Her Elected*: a political woman's handbook, *California Before 1776,* and a preschool-kindergarten-primary developmental assessment manual." avg. press run 2,500-5,000. Pub'd 3 titles 1979; expects 2 titles 1980, 4 titles 1981. 12 titles listed in the *Small Press Record of Books in Print* (9th Edition, 1980). avg. price, paper: $4.50. Discounts: 10% to 40%. 60pp; 4X6, 5½X8; of. Reporting time: 2 months. Payment: 10%. Copyrights for author. NCBPA, WBPA.

Creative Eye Press, John Mercer, Patricia Mercer, P.O. Box 620, Sonoma, CA 95476, (707) 996-4377. 1975. Photos. "Submissions by invitation only!!!" avg. press run 2,500. Pub'd 1 title 1979; expects 1 title 1981. 1 title listed in the *Small Press Record of Books in Print* (9th Edition, 1980). avg. price, paper: $5.00. Discounts: 40%/trade. 35pp; 5X8; of. Payment: none. Copyrights for author.

CREATIVE PITTSBURGH, G. Ulrich Musinsky, H. Kermit Jackson, Michael O'Connor, Joe McFadden, PO Box 7346, Pittsburgh, PA 15137, (412) 624-5934. 1976. Poetry, fiction, art, parts-of-novels, long-poems. "While we will not reject a piece because of length, a very long piece, particularly of poetry, will have a harder time making our magazine than a short one." circ. 800+. 3/yr. Pub'd 2 issues 1979; expects 3 issues 1980. sub. price: $5.50; per copy: $2.75; sample: $2.75. Back issues: $2.75 for issue 1 or 2. Discounts: 20% over 10 issues. 56pp; 6X9; of, lp. Reporting time: 1 to 6 months. Payment: contributor copy, plus discount on extras. Copyrighted. Ads: $75.00/$40.00. CCLM.

Creative With Words Publications (CWW), Brigitta Geltrich, Senior Editor, 8259 Fountain Avenue #5, West Hollywood, CA 90046, (213) 656-5358. 1975. Poetry, fiction, articles, art, cartoons, satire, plays. "Length: brevity is the key word. Submittals must be by children or senior citizens, *and/or for children and senior citizens. Query is a *must.*" avg. press run varies. Pub'd 5 titles 1979; expects 3 titles 1980, 3 titles 1981. 2 titles listed in the *Small Press Record of Books in Print* (9th Edition, 1980). avg. price, paper: must inquire; other: must inquire. Discounts: participants, schools, libraries, and senior citizens receive rates, inquire. 60pp; 5½X8½; mi. Reporting time: 2 weeks to 1 month. Payment: 25-30% reduction of regular cost to participants. Copyrights for author. SCBW.

THE CREATIVE WOMAN, Helen E. Hughes, Governors State University, Park Forest South, IL 60466, (312) 534-5000, Ext. 2524. 1977. Poetry, fiction, articles, art, photos, cartoons, interviews, satire, criticism, reviews, music, letters, long-poems, news items. 4/yr. Pub'd 2 issues 1979; expects 4 issues 1980, 4 issues 1981. sub. price: $5.00; per copy: $1.50. Back issues: $1.50. Discounts: 40%. 24pp; 8½X11; †of. Copyrighted, reverts to author. Pub's reviews: 2 in 1979. §Women's involvement in creative endeavors, any aspect of creativity in any field applied to women or studies of brain function are invited. Ads: no ads.

CREDENCES: A Journal of Twentieth Century Poetry and Poetics, Robert Bertholf, Capen Hall, New York State University, c/o Poetry Collection, Buffalo, NY 14260, (716) 673-2917. 1975. Poetry, fiction, articles, art, photos, interviews, criticism, reviews, letters, parts-of-novels, long-poems, collages, plays. "We are interested in poems which project 'the fictive voice' in the poem. Long poems are welcome. We are also interested in reviews, articles and documents on and about twentieth century poetry and special collections librarianship. Robert Duncan, Michael Rumaker, Richard Blevins, David Bromige, Michael Palmer, Nathaniel Tarn, Kenneth Irby, William Bronk, James Broughton, Helen Adam." circ. 750. 3/yr. Pub'd 1 issue 1979; expects 3 issues 1980, 3 issues 1981. sub. price: $10.00 institutions; $8.00 individuals; per copy: $3.00. Back issues: No. 1 $8.00. Discounts: less 40% to the trade, special orders with special agreements. 110pp; 7X8½; of. Reporting time: 2-3 weeks. Payment: money and issues. Copyrighted, reverts to author. Pub's reviews: 5 in 1979. §long poems, single issues on a single author. CCLM.

Creekwood Press, Charles Ghigna, Box 11191, Birmingham, AL 35202, (205) 870-4261. 1975. Poetry, art, long-poems. "Chapbooks (18 poems or less)/Authors please inquiry first with SASE." avg. press run 500. Pub'd 1 title 1979; expects 1 title 1980, 2 titles 1981. 1 title listed in the *Small Press Record of Books in Print* (9th Edition, 1980). avg. price, paper: $2.00. 20pp; 5½X8½; of/lp. Reporting time: 2 weeks to a month. Payment: Negotiable.

CRIME AND SOCIAL JUSTICE: ISSUES IN CRIMINOLOGY., Crime and Social Justice Asso-

ciates, Inc., Greg Shank, Paul Takagi, Tony Platt, P.O. Box 4373, Berkeley, CA 94704. 1974. Poetry, articles, art, photos, cartoons, interviews, criticism, reviews. "30pp. Manuscript maximum-bias-marxist and radical perspectives." circ. 1,500. 2/yr. Pub'd 2 issues 1979; expects 2 issues 1980. sub. price: $7.00 indiv., $13.00 instit.; per copy: $4.00; sample: $4.00. Discounts: 40% off to bookstores. 72-100pp; 8¼X10½; of. Reporting time: 1 month. Payment: 50% of reprinting fee if that occurs. Copyrighted, does not revert to author. Pub's reviews: 8 in 1979. §Criminology, Occupational Health and Safety. Ads: available upon request.

Crime and Social Justice Associates, Inc. (see also CRIME AND SOCIAL JUSTICE: ISSUES IN CRIMINOLOGY.), 131 Townsend Street, San Francisco, CA 94107, (415) 543-2079. 1977. avg. price, paper: $8.00. Discounts: 40%. 200pp; 8¼X10½.

CRISS-CROSS ART COMMUNICATIONS, Richard Kallweit, Clark Richert, Fred Worden, Charles DiJulio, PO Box 2022, Boulder, CO 80306, (303) 443-0244. 1975. Art, criticism, reviews. "Criss-Cross seeks out and supports new work and encourages cross-communication among artists—in the remote areas as well as the population centers. We emphasize the straight forward presentation of art rather than critical analysis. Interviews, articles, essays and original work. Emphasis as criss-cross as portable exhibition space in magazine format. Color pages." circ. 3,000. 3/yr. Pub'd 3 issues 1979. sub. price: $15.00; per copy: $4.00; sample: free. Back issues: $15.00. Discounts: $3.00 ea. $4.00 retail. 60pp; 8¾X8; of/perfect bound. Payment: not yet. Not copyrighted. §contemporary art.

THE CRITICAL REVIEW, S. L. Goldberg, Editor; T. B. Tomlinson, Managing Editor, History of Ideas Unit, Australian National University, P.O. Box 4, Canberra, A.C.T. 2600, Australia. 1958. Criticism. "c. 7,000-8,000 words or less. No footnotes or notes at end. Critical articles on English literature and related topics; also review articles, commentaries, etc." circ. 1,600. 1/yr. sub. price: $3.00 U.S.; per copy: $3.00. Discounts: 10%. 100pp; size A5; lp. Reporting time: 2 months. Payment: 6 off prints of article. Copyrighted, reverts to author. §English literature. Ads: No ads.

CRITIQUE: Studies in Modern Fiction, James Dean Young, Dept. of English, Georgia Tech, Atlanta, GA 30332. 1956. Criticism. "Particular consideration will be given to critical essays on the fiction of writers from any country who are alive and without great reputations." circ. 1,500. 3/yr. Pub'd 3 issues 1979; expects 3 issues 1980. sub. price: $7.50 individuals; $9.00 libraries; per copy: $3.00. Back issues: $3.00 per issue (from Vol. 17 only). Discounts: 10 percent. 112pp; 9X6; of. Reporting time: 4 to 6 mos. Payment: 25 offprints; 5 copies of issue. copyrighted by editor.

‡Critiques Livres, Rosalind Boehlinger, Jean Claude Salomon, 173 avenue de la Dhuys, Bagnolet 93170, France, 360 56 90. 1976. "So far, all research and editorial work has been done by the above founders/editors. Basically, we work from publishers' catalogues since our bibliographies include only available works in all fields, except scientific/medical/technical, in English, French, German, and Italian. (We welcome cooperation from publishers, adding us to their mailing lists.) We have attempted to use a Marxist approach to the organisation and presentation of books ideologically in a bibliography." avg. press run 3,000. Pub'd 1 title 1979. 2 titles listed in the *Small Press Record of Books in Print* (9th Edition, 1980). avg. price, paper: $4.00. Discounts: 1-3 copies, 25 percent; 3-10 copies, 33 percent; 10 plus copies, 40 percent; 50 copies or more, 50 percent. 88pp; 8½X11; of.

Croissant & Company, Duane Schneider, P.O. Box 282, Athens, OH 45701, 614-593-8339. 1968. Poetry, criticism. "Usually not able to handle unsolicited material, at least not in the near future, because of commitments through 1982." avg. press run 300-400 copies. Pub'd 3 titles 1979; expects 3 titles 1980, 3 titles 1981. 10 titles listed in the *Small Press Record of Books in Print* (9th Edition, 1980). avg. price, cloth: $10/$25; paper: $3.00. Discounts: trade disc 40 percent. 10pp; 5½X8; of. Reporting time: variable. Payment: negotiable. Copyrights for author. COSMEP.

CROP DUST, Crop Dust Press, Edward C. Lynskey, Wayne Kline, Cameron W. Yeatts, Route 2, Box 392, Bealeton, VA 22712, (703) 439-2140. 1979. Poetry, fiction, articles, interviews, reviews, long-poems, plays, satire, criticism, letters. "*Crop Dust* has no biases or special requirements in the material we publish, only what turns us on. We are receptive to known as well as unknown writers. Send us your best cave works and try us. No. 1 featured William Heyen, Peter Klappert, Patrick Bizzaro, Lyn Lifshin, and others." circ. 300. 2/yr. Pub'd 2 issues 1979; expects 4 issues 1980, 4 issues 1981. sub. price: $4.50; per copy: $2.50; sample: $1.50. Back issues: $1.50 as long as they last. Discounts: negotiate. 40-50pp; 8½X11; of. Reporting time: 2 months. Payment: 2 contributor copies. Copyrighted, reverts to author. Pub's reviews: 15 in 1979. §We are interested in small press publications, chapbooks, etc. Ads: $10.00 page, willing to exchange ads with other mags.

Crop Dust Press (see also CROP DUST), Edward C. Lynskey, Route 2, Box 392, Bealeton, VA 22712, 703-439-2140. 1979. Poetry. "By invitation only. Interested in putting together concept chapbook-length publications." avg. press run 250. avg. price, paper: $2.50. Discounts: will negotiate. 25pp;

5X8; of. Reporting time: 6 months when start chapbook series. Payment: author will receive 100 copies and 20%. Copyrights for author.

Crosley Inc, Clyde Crosley, 1515 Kitchen, Jonesboro, AR 72401, (501) 935-3928. 1979. "Book length, nonfiction with emphasis on prison conditions during the 1930's. Not seeking ms. founded to publish editor's works." avg. press run 2,000. Pub'd 1 title 1979. 1 title listed in the *Small Press Record of Books in Print* (9th Edition, 1980). avg. price, cloth: $10.75. Discounts: 1 copy, 20&; 2-4, 30%; 5-10, 40%; over 10 copies, 45%. Prepaid shipping charges. 100% payment must accompany order, return policy, 60 days on salable copies. 225pp; 6X9. Reporting time: not seeking mss.

Cross Country Press, Ltd. (see also CROSSCOUNTRY), Jim Mele, Ken Norris, PO Box 21081, Woodhaven, NY 11421, 212-896-7648. 1975. Poetry, concrete art. "We publish Canadian & U.S. poetry. Our Canadian address is 5572 Clark Street Montreal, P.Q. H2T 2V4. We will publish six new titles in 1980 and cannot consider new manuscripts at this time." avg. press run 500. Pub'd 5 titles 1979; expects 6 titles 1980, 3 titles 1981. 17 titles listed in the *Small Press Record of Books in Print* (9th Edition, 1980). avg. price, cloth: $10.95; paper: $1.50/$3.50. Discounts: 50 percent bulk & 40 percent trade. 24-72pp; 5½X8½; of. Reporting time: 6 months. Payment: by arrangement with individual author. Copyrights for author. CCLM, NYSSPA.

CROSSCOUNTRY, Cross Country Press, Ltd., Jim Mele, Ken Norris, PO Box 21081, Woodhaven, NY 11421, 212-896-7648. 1975. Poetry, art, photos, criticism, reviews, letters, interviews. "CC is a magazine of Canadian-U.S. poetry. Recent contributors have included Terry Stokes, David McFadden, William Bronk, Tom Clark, bp Nichol, Margaret Atwood, George Bowering and Gerard Malanga. We are only able to accept a small number of unsolicited manuscripts each year. CC's Canadian address is 5572 Clark St., Montreal, P.Q. H2B 2V4." circ. 500. 3/yr. Pub'd 3 issues 1979; expects 3 issues 1980. sub. price: $6.00 Indiv.; $7.50 Instit. & Libr.; per copy: $3.00; sample: $1.00. Back issues: No. 1-$10.00, No. 2-$1.00. Discounts: 50 percent bulk, 40 percent trade, 25 percent subscription agency. 72pp; 5½X8¼; of. Reporting time: 6 to 12 weeks. Payment: 2 copies. Copyrighted, reverts to author. Pub's reviews: 3 in 1979. §poetry, both Canadian & U.S. CCLM.

CROSSCURRENTS, Greenwich-Meridian, Bob Fink, 516 Ave K South, Saskatoon, Saskatchewan, Canada. 1975. Satire, criticism, music, news items. "Crosscurrents themes are interdisciplinary. They deal with concrete events, but also with lasting or universal aspects surrounding any event. Issues include one on inflation, on modern Art Galleries, Population, you name it. I see no reason why a serious sheet can't be made about science, anthropology, art, music, ecology—a kind of 'leaflet-college' aimed at everyone, and always aimed at a theme of freedom. I don't pretend to be an expert on anything, but I do intend to speak out anyway. Crosscurrents even prints free musical scores (like Greensleeves)—put a little music in your life. Greenwich-Meridian press has published two books (by myself). One is *Continuum—The Evolution of Matter into Humankind.* A left-wing, cross-discipline approach to art, science, ecology and current social issues, It should be read by the old and new left. It's 400 pages, 7" x 10", 2-colors, limited numbered edition, illustrated, hand insets on cover, and a special fold-out section of precise hand-illustrations on architecture. H.C., Black and Gold, index, $35. Another section is on the modern 'cultural revolution' now going on in the West. The other book is *The University of Music* (on the origin of music) $5 & $10. Write for brochures and review comments. Do small books and printing at very low cost. May become a community newspaper." circ. 500 to 5,000. occasional. sub. price: $10.00 for 12 issues; per copy: $.25 plus postage (25¢). Back issues: $5 for 9 from 1975. 1pp; 8½X11 or 14; †mi/of. Reporting time: sometimes forever. Payment: copies. Copyrighted, reverts to author.

Crosscut Saw Press, Randy Fingland, Tom Plante, Managing Editor, 2940 Seventh Street, Berkeley, CA 94710. 1971. Poetry, fiction, art, photos, long-poems, collages. avg. press run 500. Pub'd 4 titles 1979; expects 6 titles 1980, 5 titles 1981. 8 titles listed in the *Small Press Record of Books in Print* (9th Edition, 1980). avg. price, paper: $2.50. Discounts: Trade: 10% 2-4 copies; 30% 5-9 copies; 40% 10 or more. 50pp; 5X8; of. Reporting time: 3-4 weeks. Payment: By agreement. Copyrights for author.

The Crossing Press, John Gill, Elaine Gill, 17 W Main Street, Trumansburg, NY 14886, 607-387-6217. 1966. Poetry, fiction. avg. press run 1,000-5,000. Pub'd 8-10 titles 1979; expects 8-10 titles 1980. 15 titles listed in the *Small Press Record of Books in Print* (9th Edition, 1980). avg. price, cloth: $8.95; paper: $4.95. Discounts: 1-4 books, 25 percent: 5 or more titles 40 percent: wholesale-jobbers negociable. 64-300pp; 8½X5½, 6X9; of. Reporting time: 4-6 wks. Payment: percent of run or royalties. copyrights all material. CCLM, COSMEP, NESPA.

CROTON REVIEW, Lawrence Alson, Ruth Lisa Schechter, Dan B. Thomas, Editors; Patrick J. Criscia, Theresa Stengle, Associate Editors; Elsa Colligan, Editorial Assistant, P.O. Box 277, Croton on Hudson, NY 10520, (914) 271-3144. 1978. Poetry, fiction, interviews. "Short-short stories; poetry

(40 to 75 lines). We seek quality, diversity . . . original, unpublished work of known and unknown writers in our area and elsewhere in the U.S. SASE must be included with submissions. Contributors (Vol. 1): Marge Piercy, Clarence Major, T. Alan Broughton, Yvonne, Carol Emshwiller, T. Coraghessan Boyle, Harold Witt, Olga Cabral, Kathleen Collins, Alfred Gillespie, Stephen Dixon, Mary Cheever, Virginia Brady Young. , Susan Fromberg Schaeffer, Robert Phillips, David Evonier." circ. 2000. annual. Pub'd 1 issue 1979; expects 1 issue 1980, 1 issue 1981. sub. price: $3.00/3 years sponsor: $10; patron: $25; per copy: $1.00 (each); sample: 60¢. Back issues: 60¢. Discounts: standard. 16 or 20pp; 11½X20; of. Reporting time: 4-6 weeks. Payment: 2 copies. Copyrighted, reverts to author. Ads: $100/$50/10¢/word. COSMEP.

Crow, Darrell Forney, 5430 Del Rio Rd, Sacramento, CA 95822, (916) 441-5358. 1972. Art, photos, collages. "Specific themes as announced." avg. press run 500-4,000. Pub'd 1 title 1979; expects 2 titles 1981. 1 title listed in the *Small Press Record of Books in Print* (9th Edition, 1980). avg. price, paper: $4.00; other: $0.30 postcard. Discounts: 60/40. 100pp; 5½X8½; of. Payment: copies trade. Copyrights for author.

Crowfoot Press, J. Wilson Powers, Editor; Richard E. McMullen, Warren Jay Hecht, Poetry Editor, PO Box 7631, Liberty Station, Ann Arbor, MI 48107, (313) 482-5394. 1972. Poetry, fiction, letters. "We are interested in publishing collections of letters, memoirs, reminiscences by older adults." avg. press run 500. Pub'd 3 titles 1979; expects 7 titles 1980, 10 titles 1981. 5 titles listed in the *Small Press Record of Books in Print* (9th Edition, 1980). avg. price, paper: $3.95. Discounts: 2-5 30%; 6-20 40%; 21-34 42%; over 35 45%. 64pp; 6X9; of. Reporting time: 3-4 weeks. Payment: arrangement with authors. Copyrights for author. COSMEP, COSMEP MIDWEST.

The Crow's Mark Press, Hayden Carruth, 851 Maryland Avenue, Syracuse, NY 13210. 1967. Poetry, art, criticism, long-poems, collages, plays. "Very irregular publication of limited edition books and booklets. No unsolicited mss accepted.Book titles: 1977 - *The Chain Saw Dance,* poems by David Budbill; 1978 - *Tour of Duty,* poems by David Huddle; cassette tape:*The Chain Saw Dance.*" avg. press run 1000. Pub'd 1 title 1979; expects 1 title 1980, 2 titles 1981. 1 title listed in the *Small Press Record of Books in Print* (9th Edition, 1980). avg. price, paper: $2.50; other: $5.00(cassette tapes). Discounts: 40%/wholesale; 48% to distributors & jobbers. 32-64pp; 6X9; of/lp. Copyrights for author.

CRUSADE, Thirty Press, Ltd., Derek Williams, 19 Draycott Place, London SW3 2SJ, United Kingdom. 1955. Articles, art, photos, interviews, reviews, letters, news items. circ. 16,334. 12/yr. sub. price: £6.95; per copy: 40p; sample: free. Discounts: negotiable. 74pp; size A4; of. Payment: yes. Copyrighted. Pub's reviews. §Christian doctrine, biography, living. Ads: £156/£83/14p (word).

CRY CALIFORNIA, California Tomorrow, Richard A. Grant, Walt Anderson, 681 Market Street, Room 1059, San Francisco, CA 94105, 415-391-7544. 1965. Articles, photos, cartoons. "Walt Anderson is Editor of *Cry California* Annual Review; Richard A. Grant is Executive Secretary, and Editor of *Cry California Reports.* Southern California office: 650 South Grand Ave.,, Room 911, Los Angeles, CA 90017. Tel. 213-627-5624" circ. 3,500. 4/yr. Pub'd 4 issues 1979; expects 4 issues 1980, 4 issues 1981. sub. price: $20.00/yr membership; $12.00/students and retired persons; $12.00 library subscription; per copy: $1.00 to members/$2.00 to non-members; sample: $2.00. Back issues: inquire. Discounts: 20%/campus bookstores. 20-80pp; 7X10; of. Payment: negotiated. Copyrighted, does not revert to author.

CRYPTOC: The Crypt of Comics, Michael Lail, 1001 Harvey Road, Seminole, OK 74868, (405) 382-3354. 1977. Poetry, fiction, articles, art, photos, cartoons, interviews, satire, criticism, reviews, letters, parts-of-novels, long-poems, collages, plays, news items. "Our goal is to encourage communiction in *all* genres by becoming a publication for new, inexperienced artists and writers and by becoming a market place for experimental material from professionals." circ. 600. 3/yr. Pub'd 3 issues 1979; expects 3 issues 1980, 3 issues 1981. sub. price: $2.50; per copy: $0.80; sample: $0.80. Back issues: #1, $0.30; #2, $0.40; #3, $0.50; #4, $0.65; #5 & 6, $0.75; #7 & 8, $0.80. Discounts: $0.37 per copy, all copies are now coverpriced at $0.80 each for issues #7 on. 48pp; 6½X9½; †of. Reporting time: 2 weeks. Payment: by reader vote, $5.00 each issue to best poem, fiction, non-fiction, artist. Copyrighted, reverts to author. Pub's reviews: 15 in 1979. §All areas. Ads: $7.20/$4.80/$0.05 per work.

CS JOURNAL, R.S.H. Publications Worldwide, R. Sublett Hawkins, Publisher and Promoter, P.O. Box 512-B, Silver Spring, MD 20907, 301-588-7896. 1975. "All subjects considered for our publication, except smut. Audience is christian and potential christian people of all ages. Material must drill into the bone of human problems and tell how to solve them from a christian standpoint. Length: open. Is a market for christian and potential christian writers. Publication is designed to promote the anointed writers of GOD who, for circumstances and lack of recognition, cannot do what they know

GOD has called them to do. Simultaneous submissions are taboo. Recent contributors are Rev. Oral Roberts, Rev. R.W. Schambach, John Tissot, O.J. Robertson, Gertrude Katz, a syndicated columnist for the Tribune Newspaper, and many more well-known writers and ministers, but we are primarily looking for writers who need an outlet for their creative ideas. *CS JOURNAL* has a sister companion, *CS GLOBE REPORTER NEWSPAPER.* Query first. Special assignments are offered to freelancers interested in news coverage of Christian events taken place in the area of Washington, D.C. for the CS Globe Reporter. Query always, first." 12/yr. sub. price: $10.00; per copy: $2.00; sample: $2.00. Back issues: $1.00 and $0.50 to help defray postage rates. 56pp; 8½X11; †of/lp. Reporting time: 4 to 6 weeks, sometimes longer. Payment varies with author. Copyrighted. Pub's reviews. §Christianity, especially mags. All areas, no smut please!. Ads: write for info. COSMEP.

CTHULHU, Spectre Press, Jon M Harvey, 61 Abbey Road, Heathfield, Fareham, Hampshire, United Kingdom. 1976. Poetry, fiction, art, long-poems, satire. "Fantasy-orientated material in the Cthulhu mythos genre (re. the stories of H.P. Lovecraft). However, I am not looking for or printing the usually dull rehash of the old mythos stories, but am interested in new, off-beat ideas. Recent contributors: Glen Singer, Andrew Darlington, Brian Mooney, Brian Lumley, and David A. Sutton." circ. 750. infrequent. Pub'd 1 issue 1979; expects 1 issue 1981. price per copy: 50p($1.00); sample: 50p($1.00). Discounts: agent, 50 percent; bulk, 40 percent for 10-49 copies; 50 percent, for 50 or more copies. 24pp; 5½X8¼; of. Reporting time: 1-2 mos. Payment: copies only. buys first U.K. rights only. no ads.

CTR Publications (see also CANADIAN THEATRE REVIEW), Don Rubin, Alan Richardson, York University, Downsview, Ontario M3J1P3, Canada. 1973. Articles, plays, reviews. avg. press run 3,500. Pub'd 4 titles 1979; expects 4 titles 1980. 12 titles listed in the *Small Press Record of Books in Print* (9th Edition, 1980). avg. price, paper: $3.00. Discounts: 40 percent to bookstores. 144pp; 6X9; †of. Reporting time: 3 weeks. Payment varies. Copyrights for author. CPPA.

CUADERNOS DEL TERCER MUNDO, Third World Journalists/Periodistas del Tercer Mundo, Neiva Moreira, Editor-in-Chief; Pablo Piacentini, International Editor; Beatriz Bissio, International Editor; Roberto Remo, Managing Editor; Geronimo Cardozo, General Manager, Apartado 20-572, Mexico 20 DF, Mexico, 559-30-13. 1974. Articles, photos, cartoons, interviews, news items, letters. "'A magazine on the Third World made by Third World journalists.' The magazine is published in three languages (Spanish, Portuguese and English) by an independent, nonprofit association of militant professional journalists, and basically aims to provide alternative information on the Third World, promote awareness on the causes of underdevelopment and means to overrcome it, and support cooperation among progressive sectors throughout the world." circ. 15,000. 12/yr. Pub'd 8 issues 1979; expects 8 issues 1980, 12 issues 1981. sub. price: $25.00; per copy: $1.85; sample: free upon request. Back issues: $2.30 (prices apply for US, including air mail). Discounts: 40%. 96pp; 6½X9; of. Reporting time: 2 weeks. Copyrighted. Ads: $750.00/$375.00.

CULTURAL WATCHDOG NEWSLETTER, Louis Ehrenkrantz, Eleanor Ehrenkrantz, 6 Winslow Road, White Plains, NY 10606, (212) 986-7152. 1977. Articles, interviews, criticism, reviews. "I cover material ignored by the mass media. The regular feature 'Reviewing the Reviewers' evaluates the practice of reviewing and literary criticism." circ. 498. 12/yr. Pub'd 1 issue 1979; expects 12 issues 1980, 12 issues 1981. 1 title listed in the *Small Press Record of Books in Print* (9th Edition, 1980). sub. price: $12.00; per copy: $1.00; sample: $1.00. Back issues: $.50. Discounts: 40%. 5pp; 8½X11; of. No outside contributors of an unsolicited nature. Payment: in copies. Copyrighted, reverts to author. Pub's reviews: 11 in 1979. §Literature and philosophy or pychology. Ads: $75.00/$40.00/$0.10.

CUMBERLAND JOURNAL, George Myers Jr., P.O. Box 2648, Harrisburg, PA 17105. 1976. Interviews, criticism, reviews, music, letters, parts-of-novels. "Recent contributors: Charles Olson, Ezra Pound, Edmund Wilson, William Burroughs, Mary Oppen, Dick Higgins, Richard Kostelanetz, Joseph Napora, Paul Hindemith, Kenneth Burke, Chinua Achebe, Jerzy Kosinski, George Sand, Carolee Schneeman, Gretchen Johnsen, Ted Berrigan, Frank O'Hara, Serge Gavronsky, Warren C. Miller, Henry Miller, Octavio Paz, Richard Grayson. Pesons disinterested in CJ's survival should not submit material. Thematic issues announced. Music, geography/place, nurturing issues still available for $3.00. Letters, journals, loose talk, for the possibility of autonomy in art." circ. 300. 3/yr. Pub'd 4 issues 1979; expects 3 issues 1980, 3 issues 1981. 5 titles listed in the *Small Press Record of Books in Print* (9th Edition, 1980). sub. price: $8.00 for 4 consecutive issues; per copy: $3.00; sample: $3.00. Back issues: $3.00. 80pp; 5X8; of. Reporting time: 1-2 weeks usually. Payment: copy. Copyrighted, reverts to author. Pub's reviews: 30 in 1979. §Unintelligible fiction, art books, biography, criticism, poetry. Ads: $30.00/$20.00. COSMEP, CCLM.

CUMBERLANDS, Pikeville College Press, Dr. Leonard Roberts, Dr. Harold Branam, Sandy Branam, Art, College Box 2, Pikeville, KY 41501, 432-9227. 1965. Poetry, fiction, articles, interviews, criticism, parts-of-novels. "Poetry-40 lines; stories-3,000 words; No biases. Guy Owen, David Axelrod, Emilie Glen, Irene Wanner, James Stuart." circ. under 500. 2/yr. Pub'd 1 issue 1979; expects 1 issue 1980, 3 issues 1981. sub. price: $5.00; per copy: $2.50; sample: $1.50. Back issues: as issued, varies from $1.00 to $5.00. Discounts: Contributors-50 percent—jobbers-20 percent—sub services-20 percent. 36-40pp; 8½X10; of. Reporting time: 6 weeks. Payment: copies, awards of $25.00. Copyrighted, reverts on request. Pub's reviews: 1 in 1979. §writers, lit, poetry. Ads: none. CCLM, COSMEP.

La Cumbre Publishing Co., Gary R. Bencar, 1761 Calle Poniente, Santa Barbara, CA 93101, (805) 966-5534. 1979. "1 book is in final development. Expected publishing date is early in 1980. No other detailed printing data has been resolved." Pub'd 1 title 1979.

Cupola Productions (see ROCKINGCHAIR)

Curbstone Press, Alexander Taylor, 321 Jackson Street, Willimantic, CT 06226, 423-9190. 1973. "For the most part we publish short books (32—48pp) of poetry and translations of poetry. We have a bias toward poetry of the left that rises above political invective. We also have a Danish series. American poets we have published include James Scully, Richard Schaaf, Margaret Gibson and Marion Metivier. Danish: Ole Sarvig & Klaus Rifbjerg. We have done some broadsides & will do more this year, as well as poetry postcards. Writers scheduled for cards and broadsides are: Victor Contoski, James Scully, Roberta Metz, Phil Paradis, and George Butterick." avg. press run 850. Pub'd 5 titles 1979; expects 5 titles 1980. 16 titles listed in the *Small Press Record of Books in Print* (9th Edition, 1980). avg. price, cloth: $5.00-$10.00; paper: $2.50-$6.50; other: Signed, limited $10.00-$15.00. Discounts: 40% off to bookstores; 50% off to distributors; no library discount. 32-84pp—usually we expect about 48pp; 6X9; †of. We do not ask for unsolicited ms. If they come in, it may take 2—3 months to respond. Payment: We lose money on the books & do not pay a royalty, except in copies. The author retains all rights. Copyrights for author.

The Curlew Press (see also POETRY QUARTERLY (previously CURLEW)), P.J. Precious, Hare Cott, Kettlesing, Harrogate, Yorkshire, United Kingdom, Harrogate 770686. 1975. Poetry, fiction, articles, art, photos, cartoons, interviews, satire, criticism, reviews, letters, parts-of-novels, long-poems, collages, plays, concrete art, news items, non-fiction. "One poet collections: Booklets, broadsheets, poemcards. Further details on request. Poets published by the press include: Nigel Gray, Colin Simms, Barry Edgar Pilcher, Steve Sneyd, Max Noiprox, Paul St. Vincent, E.A. Markham. (U.K.) Merritt Clifton, Arthur Winfield Knight (U.S.A.). To avoid contravening U.K. law, monies payable are deemed to be voluntary contributions." avg. press run Variable. up to 500. Pub'd 8 titles 1979; expects 4 titles 1980. 8 titles listed in the *Small Press Record of Books in Print* (9th Edition, 1980). avg. price, paper: £1.75/$3.50. pp variable. up to 100; size varies; of/Xerox. Reporting time: By return of post when possible. Payment: None. Copyrights for author.

CURRENT (a reprint magazine), Grant S. McClellan, Editor, Editorial Office, R.D. #1, Barre, VT 05641, 802-476-4000. 1960. "Reprints articles and book excerpts on social-political affairs. Current magazine is published by Helen Dwight Reid Educational Foundation, (HELDREF), 4000 Albemarle St., N.W., Washington, DC 20016, telephone 202-362-6445." circ. 6,700. 10/yr (combined March/April & July/August). Pub'd 10 issues 1979; expects 10 issues 1980, 10 issues 1981. sub. price: $12.00 Indiv.; $20.00 Instit.; per copy: $2.50; sample: free. Back issues: $1.50-$2.00. 60pp; 7X10. Payment: We pay reprint fees. Copyrighted. §political-eco-social affairs.

Current Issues Publications, Sabina J. Stock, 2707 Walker Street, Berkeley, CA 94705, (415) 549-1451. 1979. "History, historical essays" avg. press run 500-1000. Pub'd 1 title 1979; expects 2 titles 1980, 5 titles 1981. 1 title listed in the *Small Press Record of Books in Print* (9th Edition, 1980). avg. price, paper: $7.95. Discounts: 2-4, 20%; 5-9, 30%; 10-24, 40%; 25-100, 44%; 101-199, 48%; over 200, 50%. 112pp; 8½X11; of. Copyrights for author.

CURTAINS, Pressed Curtains, Paul Buck, 4 Bower Street, Maidstone, Kent ME16 8SD, United Kingdom, 0622-63681. 1971. Poetry, fiction, articles, art, interviews, criticism, music, parts-of-novels, long-poems, photos, reviews. "Presents mainly French writings in translation. Blanchot, Bataille, Noel, Faye. Though English & American poetry also strongly featured." circ. 450. 1/yr. Pub'd 1 issue 1979; expects 1 issue 1980. price per copy: $7.00. 200pp; size A4; of/colored inks. Reporting time: days. Payment: copies. Copyrighted. Pub's reviews: 4 in 1979. §same as content material. Ads: none. ALMS, Set International.

Curvd H&Z, J.W. Curry, c/o 60 Fenley Drive, Weston, Ontario, Canada. 1977. Poetry, fiction, articles, art, photos, cartoons, interviews, satire, criticism, reviews, music, letters, parts-of-novels, long-poems, collages, plays, concrete art. "Curvy H&Z has abondand its old series & startd fresh, doing as much as evrything as i can. are divided up into many series: Th Wrecking Ballzark, concrete; Sticky Lights, street poster essays; Th Mini Mlart, graphics; Industrial Sabotage, magazine; Pomez A

Penny, a 1¢ poetry series; & a cataloguing series. would like to see anything that anybody believes in. more concrete would be appreciatd. still just using rubbrstamp but photocopying & linocuts spread th reaching distance. have done 53 #s since Septembr uv '79, but we're slowing down ' doing better more presentable leaflets now. send a buck orso fr a sample sampling. titles by Greg Andley; dave beach; jwcurry; Randall Brock; Don Garner; RDHanson; Bob Lee; Peggy lefler; Ray Salter; jasmine silverwind. above address is mailing address only. would like to see more submissions. we need them as we can't, or, prefer not to, survive on just our own materials. i for one *know* there are people who write out there. need more fiction & art especially. would like to see more concrete as well." avg. press run 24 - 100. Pub'd 39 titles 1979; expects 34 titles 1980. avg. price, cloth: $1.75 signd, $1.00 un; paper: from 1¢ to $10.00; other: $7.50. Discounts: th more yu get, th more yu pay. 1-16pp; 1½X1½; 8½X11; †rubbrstamp, photocopy, linocut. Reporting time: fast. Payment: author gets 1/4 th press run. this w/ books. fr a pennypome, 10 copies, submissions to the mag, depends.

CUTBANK, SmokeRoot, Dan Schoyield, Sara Miller, English Dept., U. of Montana, Missoula, MT 59812. 1973. Poetry, fiction, articles, art, photos, interviews, criticism, reviews, parts-of-novels, long-poems. "Jim Heynen, Tess Gallagher, William Stafford, Richard Hugo, Raymond Carver, Roberta Hill, John Haines, Madeline DeFrees, Ira Sadoff, Robert Hedin, Albert Goldbarth." circ. 600. 2/yr. Pub'd 2 issues 1979; expects 2 issues 1980, 2 issues 1981. 2 titles listed in the *Small Press Record of Books in Print* (9th Edition, 1980). sub. price: $4.00; per copy: $2.50; sample: $2.50. Back issues: Full set Nos. 1-14, $16.00. Discounts: trade rates for bulk orders. 120pp; 5½X8½; of. Reporting time: 4 weeks. Payment: copies. Copyrighted. Pub's reviews: 10 in 1979. §poetry/fiction/criticism/translations. Ads: $50.00/$30.00. CCLM.

The * CWS Group Press, C.W. Staley, PO Box 543, 807 West 15th Street, Vinton, IA 52349, 319-472-3552. 1 title listed in the *Small Press Record of Books in Print* (9th Edition, 1980).

Cykx Books, R. Buttigieg, S. Buttigieg, PO Box 299, Lenox Hill Station, New York, NY 10021, (212) 876-6577. 1977. "Cykx Books Publishes (Division of Cykx Inc) ISMP (International Society of Modern Poets) *Awards & Prizes Receiving from all over the World,* yearly in *Mayday* we announce the ISMP Awards & Prizes for the best poem and lyric of the year, for the best poetic and lyrical achievements. Offering $1,000.00. Poems and lyrics for the awards and prizes; *any style, any length, any subject:* contemporary, modern, experimental, avand garde, nature, social, technological, spiritual, space, science, folk, religious, future, electronic, fictional, comic, creative ideas, etc. etc. These themes apply also for poems & lyrics for the Modern Poetry Anthologies 'American Anthology' & 'Poets of the World'." Expects 3 titles 1980, 5 titles 1981. 1 title listed in the *Small Press Record of Books in Print* (9th Edition, 1980). avg. price, cloth: $9.95; paper: $4.99. 150pp; 5 1/2X8. Reporting time: 2 weeks to 30 days. Payment: $300.00 advance for book manuscript, concepts. Query first please. Copyrights for author.

D

D.& E. Career Publishing Co., 5146 W Imperial, Los Angeles, CA 90045, (213) 374-7486. 1972. "All materials in vocational education for students, teachers, counselors, and administrators for use in career classes, libraries, career centers, and work experience programs." avg. press run 2,000. Pub'd 9 titles 1979; expects 10 titles 1980, 20 titles 1981. 8 titles listed in the *Small Press Record of Books in Print* (9th Edition, 1980). avg. price, paper: $5.50. Discounts: classroom: 15% (25-50); 20% (50+); jobber: 40%; agent: 30%. 100pp; of. Reporting time: one week. Payment: 5-10% of net sales. Copyrights for author.

D.D.B. Press (see also APALACHEE QUARTERLY), P.V. LeForge, David Morrill, Richard Johnson, Len Schweitzer, Monica Faeth, P O Box 20106, Tallahasaee, FL 32304, 904-224-0478. 1972. Poetry, fiction, articles, satire, criticism, long-poems, plays. "We are not accepting manuscripts for publication at the present time. Because of funding problems, we are limited to local work and *The Apalachee Quarterly.*" avg. press run varies. Pub'd 2 titles 1979. 15 titles listed in the *Small Press Record of Books in Print* (9th Edition, 1980). avg. price, paper: $2.50. 100pp; 6X8; of. We are not reading manuscripts at this time. Payment: to be discussed. Copyrights for author. CCLM.

DACOTAH TERRITORY, Territorial Press, Mark Vinz, Ed.; Grayce Ray, Assoc. Ed., P.O. Box 775, Moorhead, MN 56560. 1971. Poetry. "Yearly thematic anthology of poetry. No. 16 (1979) *Hotels and Cafes;* No. 17 (1980) *Fathers.*" circ. 1M. 1/yr. Pub'd 2 issues 1979; expects 1 issue 1980, 1 issue 1981. sub. price: $2.50; per copy: $2.50; sample: $2.50. Back issues: Issues 14-15 available at $1.50 each. Discounts: 20-40%. 96pp; 7X8½; of. Reporting time: 1 week to 2 months, read mss only in summers, each annual issue theme oriented/Not reading mss. in 1980. Payment: 2 copies. Copyrighted, reverts to author. no ads. CCLM, Plains Distribution Service Magazine Committee.

Dada Center Publications, 2319 West Dry Creek Road, Healdsburg, CA 95448, 707 433-2161. 1977. Poetry, articles, art, photos, interviews. avg. press run 5000. Expects 1 title 1981. 1 title listed in the *Small Press Record of Books in Print* (9th Edition, 1980). avg. price, paper: $3.95. Discounts: 40% bookstore, 50% distributor. 100pp; 6X9; of.

DAEDALUS, Journal of the American Academy of Arts and Sciences, American Academy of Arts and Sciences, Stephen R. Graubard, Editor; William Brubeck, Managing Editor, 7 Linden Street, Cambridge, MA 02138, (617) 495-4431, 4482. 1958. Articles. "Subscriptions: American Academy of Arts and Sciences, 165 Allandale Street, Jamaica Plain Station, Boston, MA 02130" circ. 35,000. 4/yr. Pub'd 4 issues 1979; expects 4 issues 1980, 4 issues 1981. sub. price: $14.00; per copy: $4.00; sample: $4.00. Back issues: $4.00. 224pp; 6¾X9¾; of. Reporting time: 1 month. Copyrighted, does not revert to author. Ads: No ads.

DAIMON, House of Keys, Norman Finkelstein, Terrill Shepard Soules, Phillip DePoy, P O Box 7952, Atlanta, GA 30357, 404-873-3820. 1976. Poetry. "We open each submission hoping to read the permanent poem. The sample issue we will send you in exchange for a stamp will show you what approximates our idea of the genuine article. *Daimon* is a quarterly broadside that each issue publishes four (rarely five) poets, together with the work of one visual artist. We do not have mailing list; but a subscription is only a dollar. The big panel each poet's work appears on show cases that poet's work in a way very few magazines can. Our publication looks good,our editing is scrupulous (long-distance calls about commas are not unheard of), and our payment, by current standards, generous. We do not discriminate against the unknown poet. We are proud of the poems—by, for example, Helen Adam, Nat Anderson, Barbara McGahee Brown, James Cervantes, Gay Clifford, Jerry Cullum, Phillip DePoy, Kay Leigh Hagan, Tom Hansen, David B. Hopes, Gita Maritzer Smith, Roger Mitchell, Peter Mladnic, Melinda Mueller, Brad Stark, Henry Weinfield, Scott Wilson, Norman Finkelstein and Terrill Shepard Soules—that we have published." circ. 1,500. 4/yr. Pub'd 4 issues 1979; expects 4 issues 1980, 4 issues 1981. sub. price: $1.00; per copy: send $0.15 stamp for single copy; sample: send $0.15 stamp for sample. Back issues: Issues 4 to current available for postage. Discounts: Distributed for free. 1pp; 17¼X21¾; of. Reporting time: 1 month. Payment: $10.00 per appearance. Copyrighted, reverts to author. no ads. CCLM.

Daisy Press, Marilyn Ross, PO Box 883, La Mesa, CA 92041. 1979. Cartoons. avg. press run 2,000. Pub'd 1 title 1979. avg. price, paper: $3.95. Discounts: standard. 96pp; 5½X8½; of. Reporting time: not seeking submissions at this time.

Dakota Press, John R. Milton, Swes, University of South Dakota, Vermillion, SD 57069, 605-677-5281. 1968. Poetry, fiction, articles, photos, criticism, reviews. avg. press run 1,000. Pub'd 2 titles 1979; expects 3 titles 1980. 24 titles listed in the *Small Press Record of Books in Print* (9th Edition, 1980). avg. price, cloth: $9.00; paper: $5.95. Discounts: 1-5 copies 20%; 6-9 copies 30%; 10+ copies 40%. 50-400pp; size varies; lp/of. Reporting time: 1 month. Payment: varies. Copyrights for author.

THE DALHOUSIE REVIEW, Dr. Alan Kennedy, Editor; Dr. J. Crowley, Assistant Editor, Killam Library, Dalhousie University Press Ltd, Attn: Helen L. Gorman, Bus. Mgr., 4413 Halifax, Nova Scotia B3H4H8, Canada. 1921. "Authors change with each issue." circ. 1,100. 4/yr. sub. price: $10.00; per copy: $3.00 plus handling. Back issues: Vary from $3 to $10 plus handling. Discounts: none. 200pp; 9X6½; lp. Reporting time: varies. Payment: $1 per page (honorarium only) $3 for each poem used. Copyrighted, permission from both. Pub's reviews: 30-40 in 1979. §all areas would be examined. Ads: $50.00/$25.00/$18.00/$10.00.

Dan River Press, Robert Olmsted, Elaine Olmsted, PO Box 249, Stafford, VA 22554. 7 titles listed in the *Small Press Record of Books in Print* (9th Edition, 1980).

Danbury Press, Eli Chappe, Marilyn Silverman, PO Box 613, Suffern, NY 10901, (914) 357-0420. 1979. "Government business books. Sell via mail only." avg. press run 1,000. Pub'd 1 title 1979. avg. price, other: $24.95. 120pp; 8½X11; †of. Reporting time: 4 months. Payment: follow trade custom. Copyrights for author.

DANCE BOOK FORUM, Dance Motion Press, D'lela Zuck, 22 West 77th Street #62, New York, NY 10024, 212-362-9921. 1980. Reviews, news items. "We accept for reviewing any material that the author believes is related to the field of dance. We hold the right to edit material as well as to reject it and return it to the author. Non-profit organization." circ. 15,000. 4/yr. sub. price: $6.00; per copy: $1.50; sample: free. Discounts: self distribution. 24pp; 8½X11; of. Reporting time: 3 months. Pub's reviews. §Dance and dance related areas. Ads: $500.00/$225.00/$25.00 per inch (rates vary from 2

110

to 4 issues).

DANCE HERALD, William Moore, 243 West 63st, New York, NY 10023. 1975. Articles, art, photos, cartoons, interviews, criticism, reviews, letters. "Due to length of publication everything must be very *short.*" circ. 300. 4/yr. sub. price: $3.00; per copy: $.75; sample: $.75. 6pp; 8½X12; of. Reporting time: 4 months. Payment: none. Pub's reviews. §black dance/black music/art. Ads: One ad rate: $25 for 1 x 5¼.

DANCE IN CANADA, Michael Crabb, Editor, 100 Richmond Street, E. Suite 325, Toronto, ON M5C 2P9, Canada. 1973. Articles, photos, interviews, criticism, reviews, music, letters. "Canada's only national bilingual dance magazine. Exclusive coverage of ideas, events, personalities and criticism from coast to coast." circ. 2,000. 4/yr. Pub'd 4 issues 1979; expects 4 issues 1980, 4 issues 1981. sub. price: $7.50; per copy: $2.00; sample: $2.00. Back issues: $2.00. Discounts: 40% on consignment. 40pp; 8½X11; of. Reporting time: 8 weeks. Payment: $25-$50. Copyrighted, reverts to author. Pub's reviews: 20 in 1979. §dance/performing arts. Ads: $350.00/$225.00/$5.00 per line.

Dance Motion Press (see also DANCE BOOK FORUM), D'lela Zuck, 22 West 77th Street #62, New York, NY 10024, 212-362-9921. 1978. "We accept any material for reviewing and will consult and direct the authors as to our position taken on this material." avg. press run 5,000. Pub'd 1 title 1979; expects 1 title 1980. avg. price, paper: $8.00-$14.50. Discounts: 40% stores, 50% distributors. 80-224pp; 6½X9½, 8½X7¾; of. Payment: in accordance with contract arrangements.

DANCE SCOPE, American Dance Guild Inc, Richard Lorber, 1133 Broadway #1427, New York, NY 10010, (212) 691-4564. 1965. Poetry, fiction, cartoons, satire, criticism, reviews, letters. circ. 7,000. 4/yr. Pub'd 3-4 issues 1979. sub. price: $10.00; per copy: $2.50 (double issue $4.00); sample: $2.50 postpaid. Back issues: $2.50 postpaid. Discounts: 30-40%. 80pp; 6X9; †of. Reporting time: 3 mos. Payment: $45.00. Pub's reviews: 6 in 1979. §dance, theatre, music, film, video, etc. Ads: $175.-00/$95.00. CCLM.

THE DANDELION, Michael E Coughlin, 1985 Selby Ave, St Paul, MN 55104, 612-646-8917. 1977. Articles, cartoons, satire, criticism, reviews, letters. "*The Dandelion* is a quarterly journal of philosophical anarchism which welcomes a wide variety of articles, poems, cartoons, reviews, satire, criticism and news items. Prefers shorter articles, but will consider major pieces if appropriate. A sample copy is available at no cost to prospective authors." circ. about 400. 4/yr. Pub'd 3 issues 1979; expects 4 issues 1980, 4 issues 1981. 1 title listed in the *Small Press Record of Books in Print* (9th Edition, 1980). sub. price: $4.50; per copy: $1.00; sample: free. Back issues: $1.50. Discounts: 25 percent off listed price for bulk orders. 28pp; 5½X8½; of. Reporting time: one month. Payment in copies of the magazine. Not copyrighted. Pub's reviews: 1 in 1979. §Anarchist/libertarian history, biographies, philosophy. Ads: $15.00/$10.00.

Daniel Stokes, Publisher (see also EAST RIVER REVIEW), Daniel M.J. Stokes, 128 E 4th Street, New York, NY 10003. 1974. "q" avg. press run 500. Pub'd 2 titles 1979; expects 2 titles 1980, 3 titles 1981. avg. price, paper: $0.75-$1.50. Discounts: 40%, 10 copies +. 32pp; 5½X8½; of. Reporting time: 6 months. Payment: 10% print run. Copyrights for author. CCLM.

Daran Inc. (see also HUERFANO), Vicki Thompson, Editor, 5730 N Via Elena, Tucson, AZ 85718. 1974. Poetry. "Annual Daran Award of $50.00." avg. press run 200. Pub'd 2 titles 1979. avg. price, paper: $1.00. 40pp; 5½X8½; of. Reporting time: 2 months. Payment: Copies only. Does not copyright for author. CCLM.

DARK FANTASY, Shadow Press, Howard Gene Day, Con. Editor; C. R. Saunders, Gale Jack, Box 207, Gananoque, Ontario K7G2T7, Canada, 613-382-2794. 1973. Poetry, fiction, art. "Generally tales of fast moving adventure, S-F & S&S or horror. No heavy sex—very light in that aspect. 3,000 words preferred but always willing to compromise. Recent contributors: R.E.Howard. Neal Adams." circ. 500-600. 4-6/yr. Pub'd 5-6 issues 1979. sub. price: $5.00 for 5 issues; per copy: $1.00; sample: $1.00. Back issues: usually $1.25. Discounts: 40 percent flat discount on orders over 10. 40-52pp; 5½X8½; of. Reporting time: 4-6 weeks. Payment: -1/2 cent per word, $1.00 per poem, $5.00 for art use. Copyrighted, reverts to author. Ads: $8.00/$5.00/none.

DARK HORSE, Margery Cuyler, Managing Editor, Box 36, Newton Lower Falls, MA 02166, (617) 964-0192. 1974. Poetry, fiction, articles, art, photos, interviews, criticism, reviews, long-poems, collages, news items. "Welcome submissions of poetry, fiction, reviews of small press, drawings, photography, literary articles, interviews. Publish column of literary news primarily of Boston/New England area. All submissions must be accompanied by SASE and brief bio note. Selection of material based on literary excellence, without prejudice toward any group, and without favoring previously published authors. Poetry, fiction and art selected by different staff or guest editors for each fissue. Read sample copy before submitting ($2.00)." circ. 2,000. 4/yr. Pub'd 4 issues 1979; expects 4 issues 1980, 4 issues 1981. sub. price: $5.00 indiv., $10.00 instit.; per copy: $1.50 or $2.00 thru mail; sample: $1.50 or $2.00 through mail. Back issues: $0.75. Discounts: 40% bookstores or classroom orders of 20 or more; free to prisoners. 20-24pp; 11½X17 (tabloid); of. Reporting time: 1 - 12 weeks. Payment: 4 copies. Copyrighted, reverts to author. Pub's reviews: 10 in 1979. §Poetry, fiction, small press. Ads: write for rates. CCLM.

Dark House Press, Nancy Rodgers, Jack Ramey, Box 184, Fountain, FL 32438, (904) 722-4840. 1979. Poetry. "Publishes *Genesis Poetry Series,* Recent titles include *Eurydice's Kiss,* 1979, and *The Future Past* by Jack Ramey, 1980. Accepting poems about war for 1981 publication. 1 title per year." avg. press run 1,000. Pub'd 1 title 1979; expects 1 title 1980. avg. price, paper: $3.00. Discounts: 40% trade. 90pp; 5X8; of. Reporting time: 1 month. Payment: copies and royalties.

Daughters Publishing Co., Inc., Parke Bowman, June Arnold, M5590 PO Box 42999, Houston, TX 77042. 1972. Fiction. "Full-length finished (completed) novel manuscripts with passionate feminist content. Letter of query first." avg. press run 5,000. Pub'd 5 titles 1979; expects 5 titles 1980. 19 titles listed in the *Small Press Record of Books in Print* (9th Edition, 1980). avg. price, paper: $4.25. Discounts: 50% distributors; 40% to bookstores (10 copy mixed); 25% libraries, feminist studies teachers. 300pp; 5¼X8½; of. Reporting time: 6 weeks. Payment: 10% on cover price with advances. Copyrights for author. COSMEP, AAP.

DAVINCI MAGAZINE, Vehicule Press, Allan Bealy, General Editor and Founder; Si Dardick, Literary Editor; Guy Lavoie, Contributing Editor; Dave Vessey, M. Dufresne, W. Wood, P.O. Box 125, Station LA CITE, Montreal, P.Q. H2X 3M0, Canada. 1973. Poetry, fiction, art, photos, parts-of-novels, collages, concrete art. "*Davinci Magazine* attempts to present, in a manner that is not so offensively 'magazine' oriented, new works in avant-garde poetry, art & photography by artists who have not already been heavily produced in other, more commercial formats. Contributors have included Maurizio Nannucci, George Bowering, Dick Higgins, Allan Bealy, Clark Blaise, Tim Mancusi, Bob McGee, Opal L. Nations, Richard Kostelanetz, Insurrection art Co, Douglas Blazek, Ante Vukov, John Heward, David McFadden, Daddaland, John McAuley, Ken Norris, Guy Lavoie, Comet Nirvanno et al." circ. 350. irregular. Pub'd 1 issue 1979. sub. price: $6.00/3 issues, individuals; $8.00/3 issues, institutions; per copy: $2.00; sample: $2.00. Back issues: All six issues $10.00. Discounts: 40% trade, 20% distributors. 44-104pp; 5¼X7½; †of. Reporting time: sixty days. Payment: copies. Copyrighted, reverts to author.

DAWN, Collective, 168 Rathgar Road, Belfast 7 6, Northern Ireland. 1974. Articles, art, photos, cartoons, interviews, reviews, letters, news items. "Dawn exists to explore relevance of nonviolence to struggle for peace & justice in Ireland, and to promote concrete nonviolent actions. Nonviolent action, civil liberties and movements for change. Also use address of 63 Haypark Avenue, Belfast 7." circ. 1,000. 10/yr. Pub'd 8 issues 1979; expects 10-11 issues 1980, 10-11 issues 1981. 2 titles listed in the *Small Press Record of Books in Print* (9th Edition, 1980). sub. price: £2.50 surface, £4.00 airmail; per copy: 15p; sample: 15p plus postage. Back issues: 10p a copy surface mail for 3 or more copies. 12pp; size A4; of. Reporting time: usually 1 month. Payment: none. Pub's reviews: 35 in 1979. §nonviolence, pacifism, community action, ecology, sexual politics, anarchism, mutual aid, third world, Irish history, affiliated organisation of Irish Campaign for Nuclear Disarmament. Ads: £30/£15/40 pence per cm. APS, Also associate publication, War Resisters International Sponsor of CAAT.

The Dawn Horse Press (see also VISION MOUND: The Journal of the Religious and Spiritual Teaching of Bubba Free John), Saniel Bonder, David Todd, PO Box 3680, Clearlake Highlands, CA 95422, 994-9497, 994-9498. 1976. "Returns only are sent to Publisher's Services, Box 3914, San Rafael, CA 94902." avg. press run 10,000. Pub'd 4 titles 1979; expects 6 titles 1980. avg. price, cloth: $10.95; paper: $5.95. Discounts: 5-25 copies 40%/26-50 copies 41%/50-100 copies 42%/100 up copies 43%. 350pp; 5¼X8½; 9X6; of. Reporting time: 2-3 weeks. Payment: royalties 10 percent. Copyrights for author.

Dawn Valley Press, Nancy E. James, Box 58, New Wilmington, PA 16142. 1976. Poetry, fiction, articles. "Dawn Valley Press has broadened its subject area to include, along with poetry and fiction, material of local interest to the New Wilmington area. The latter includes a new magazine, *Just Reminiscing,* which is New Wilmington's answer to *Foxfire.* At present manuscripts are read by invitation only. Queries are not encouraged and are likely to be answered only after lengthy procrastination." avg. press run 1,000. Pub'd 2 titles 1979; expects 2-3 titles 1980, 2-3 titles 1981. 8 titles listed in the *Small Press Record of Books in Print* (9th Edition, 1980). avg. price, paper: $3.00-$4.00. Discounts: Retail: 1 copy, 20 percent; 2-5, 25 percent; 6-25, 40 percent; 26 or more, 50 percent. Wholesale: 1 copy, 25 percent; 2-5, 40 percent; 6 or more, 50 percent. 60pp; 5X8; of. Payment: Individually arranged.

Copyrights for author. COSMEP.

de la Ree Publications, Gerry de la Ree, Helen de la Ree, 7 Cedarwood Lane, Saddle River, NJ 07458. 1972. "We publish hard-cover books of science fiction and fantasy art by illustrators established in the field. No fiction" avg. press run 1,300. Pub'd 4 titles 1979. 15 titles listed in the *Small Press Record of Books in Print* (9th Edition, 1980). avg. price, cloth: $15.50. Discounts: 40 percent on 10 or more copies. 128pp; 8½X11; of. Reporting time: Immediate. Payment: Varies. Copyrights for author.

DECEMBER MAGAZINE, December Press, Curt Johnson, Robert Wilson, 6232 N Hoyne #1C, Chicago, IL 60659, (312) 973-7360. 1958. Poetry, fiction, articles, art, photos, interviews, satire, criticism, reviews. circ. 1,000. irregular. Pub'd 4 issues 1979; expects 4 issues 1980, 4 issues 1981. sub. price: 4-issues $12.50; per copy: $4.00; sample: $2.00. Back issues: twice over cover price. Discounts: 20% 10 or more-agency 20%. 228pp; 5½X8½; of. Reporting time: 6-8 weeks. Payment: free copies. Copyrighted, does not revert to author. Pub's reviews: 1 in 1979. §fiction. Ads: $100/$60. CCLM, COSMEP.

December Press (see also DECEMBER MAGAZINE), Curt Johnson, Robert Wilson, 6232 N Hoyne, 1C, Chicago, IL 60659, (312) 973-7360. 1958. Poetry, fiction, articles, art, photos, cartoons, interviews, satire, criticism, reviews. avg. press run 1000. Pub'd 4 titles 1979; expects 4 titles 1980, 2 titles 1981. 11 titles listed in the *Small Press Record of Books in Print* (9th Edition, 1980). avg. price, paper: $5.00. Discounts: 40%. 224pp; 5½X8½; of. Reporting time: 6-10 weeks. Payment: copies and cash. Copyrights for author. COSMEP, CCLM.

Deciduous (see also Everyman), Christopher Franke, 1456 West 54th Street, Cleveland, OH 44102, (216) 651-7725. 1970. Poetry, art, photos, cartoons, collages, concrete art. "*Up Against The Wall,* 15 poems by Christopher Franke on a 20' x 26' broadside, is available for $1.00. Various poem-collage leaflets are available for a S.A.S. envelope. *Deciduous* is dormant in the winter and estivates in the summer. As for spring and fall, ?. *Everyman* '77 was a broadside subtitled poster available for $2.00. *S.,* by Christopher Franke, a group of 17 love poems, chapbook, $0.71. Everyman '79, $1.50." Pub'd 2 titles 1979. 2 titles listed in the *Small Press Record of Books in Print* (9th Edition, 1980). 1pp plus; size varies. Reporting time: varies. Payment: copies. CCLM.

Deinotation 7 Press, Albert A. M. Stella, Box 194, Susquehanna, PA 18847, (717) 853-3050. 1978. Plays. "Deinotation 7 exists solely to publish the wit and wisdom and whims of one: Albert A. M. Stella - expecially his play: 'Crystal Star'." avg. press run 500. Expects 1 title 1980. 1 title listed in the *Small Press Record of Books in Print* (9th Edition, 1980). avg. price, paper: $3.00. Discounts: Whatever's fair. 85pp; 5½X8½; of. Reporting time: Forever.

THE DEKALB LITERARY ARTS JOURNAL, William S. Newman, 555 N. Indian Creek Dr, Clarkston, GA 30021. 1966. Poetry, fiction, articles, art, photos, criticism, reviews, music, plays. circ. 1M. 4/yr. Pub'd 4 issues 1979; expects 4 issues 1980. sub. price: $6.00; per copy: $1.75; sample: $2.00. Back issues: upon request. 80pp; 6X9; of. Reporting time: 8-10 wks. Payment: copies only. Copyrighted, reverts to author. Pub's reviews. §The arts. no ads. CCLM, COSMEP.

DELAWARE TODAY, John Taylor, Editor; Rolf Rykken, Asst Editor, 2401 Pennsylvania Avenue, Wilmington, DE 19806, (302) 655-1571. 1961. Fiction, articles, satire, letters. "Fiction size: 1,500 to 3,000 words, contemporary stories with interesting characters and some semblance of plot; we have eclectic tastes and will consider everything, no regional bias as to setting. Articles: 3,000 word size, must be Delaware story, query letter necessary for news and news feature marticles. Recent fiction writers: James Hines, Virgil Rupp, Shelia Matin, Rolf Rykken." circ. 12,000. 12/yr. Pub'd 12 issues 1979; expects 12 issues 1980, 12 issues 1981. sub. price: $10.00; per copy: $1.50; sample: free. Discounts: regular commercial rate, others negotiable. 64pp; 8½X11. Reporting time: 1 month. Payment: Fiction: $75.00 to $150.00; News Articles: $100.00 to $200.00. Copyrighted, reverts to author. Ads: $675.00/$430.00/$0.40.

Delicious Desserts For Diabetics & Their Sugar Free Friends, Janet W. Herringshaw, 747 Towne Drive, Freeport, IL 61032, (815) 232-6695. 1979. "This book is filled with sugar and chemical free recipes and tips for sugar free people. It includes calories & exchanges for each recipe. Contains about 50 recipes solely sweetened by fruit. Have been selling most copies through the mail. It's been written up in local newspapers (Journal Standard, Freeport, Rockford Register Star) and nationally in the Detroit Free Press, Arizona Daily Star and Sun Times from Sun City, Arizona. It's also been mentioned in the quarterly *Alternatives,* local stores are carrying it and the Freeport Hospital Gift Shop carries it. I'm listed in the vertical index and have answered orders to many libraries. Prevention magazine will be mentioning it in the near future." avg. press run 500. Pub'd 1 title 1979. avg. price, paper: $4.95. Discounts: $3.50 per dozen. 42pp; 5X8; of. Payment: I am the author.

113

DELIRIUM, Libra Press, Jim Mc Curry, PO Box 341, Wataga, IL 61488. 1975. Poetry, fiction, articles, art, photos, cartoons, criticism, reviews, letters, parts-of-novels, long-poems, collages, plays. "No biases in a restrictive sense. Recent contributors include Guy Beining, Carol Cardozo, Larry Eigner, Bruce Andrews, Douglas Blazek, Sandra Case, David Cope, Melissa Cummings, Thomas Michael Fisher, Hugh Fox, Marilyn Krysl, Lyn Lifshin, Lewis MacAdams, Christopher Middleton, David Plante, Charles Plymell, Stephen Ruffus, Arlene Zekowski & Stanley Berne.Issue 4/5 due April '78. Filled thru no. 8. Issue 8, filled, is devoted to language-centered writers. After issue 8, title changes to *Parole*. Issue 6/7, tacitly dedicated to Jack Kerouac, will be delayed until summer 1981, while I am finishing up Ph.D. dissertation on Charles Olson. I am not reading anything until then." circ. 500. 1/yr. Pub'd 1 issue 1979; expects 1 issue 1981. sub. price: $4.00/4 issues; $10.00/4 issues, institutions; per copy: $1.50; $3.00 double issue; sample: #3, 4, 5 while they last, in return for a 9 x 12 envelope with 75¢ postage. Back issues: #3, 4, 5 while they last, in return for a 9 x 12 envelope with 75¢ postage (You can't beat that!). Discounts: 10% agencies; 40% libraries & classrooms on orders of 10 or more. 100pp; 5½X8½; of. Reporting time: 1-2 weeks. Payment: 1 copy plus lifetime subscription. Copyrighted, reverts to author. Pub's reviews. §poetry, prosepoems, fiction. Ads: exchange ads. CCLM, COSMEP.

THE DELPHYS FORUM, S. M. Schneble, Editor-Publisher, P.O. Box 677, Pacific Palisades, CA 90272, 213-395-7787. Fiction, art, criticism, letters, concrete art, news items. "Articles, interviews, reviews, (black and white photos), occasionally poetry (cetacean related). Our subject matter is scholarly and scientific—anything having to do with whales, dolphins and propoises for an international audience comprised of academics, scientists, marine biologists, environmentalists, and government institutions, etc. Query best bet. Include S.A.S.E. for prompt return." circ. 5M to 10M. 6/yr. sub. price: $35.00; per copy: $3.00. Back issues: none. Discounts: sub agent, $25.00/yr; bkstr., $2.00/copy. $25/year for colleges and universities. 4pp; 8½X11; of. Reporting time: 2 weeks. Payment: Negotiable. Copyrighted, reverts to author. Pub's reviews: 1 in 1979. §cetacean related. Ads: $95.00 for -1/6th of page only.

DELTA Literary Review, Michael Launchbury, Geoffrey Pawling, 2 Bridge House Cottages, Finches Lane, Twyford, Winchester S021 1QF, United Kingdom. 1953. Poetry, fiction, reviews, criticism. circ. 1,000. 3/yr. sub. price: £2.70 or $9.00 for three issues; per copy: 70p or $3.00. Back issues: £1.50. 44pp; 8½X5½; of. Payment: by negotiation. Copyrighted. Pub's reviews. §contemp. literature. Ads: £25/£15/£8 1/4.

DEMOCRATIC LEFT, Michael Harrington, Editor; Maxine Phillips, Man. Editor, 853 Broadway, Suite 801, New York, NY 10003, (212) 260-3270. 1972. Articles, photos, cartoons, interviews, criticism, letters, news items. "Almost all of the articles are written from a democratic socialist perspective." circ. 5,000. 10/yr. Pub'd 10 issues 1979; expects 10 issues 1980, 10 issues 1981. sub. price: $5.00/$10.00 in 1981; per copy: $1.00; sample: $0.25. Back issues: $1.50. Discounts: 40% to bookstores for order of 20 or more, prepaid. 16pp; 8½X11; of. Reporting time: one month lead time. Pub's reviews: 6 in 1979. §Political science, socialist stragies, history. Ads: $50.00 col inch/$2.00 line.

DENTAL FLOSS MAGAZINE, Toothpaste Press, Allan Kornblum, P.O. Box 546, 626 E. Main, West Branch, IA 52358, 319-643-2604. 1975. Poetry. "Unsolicited manuscripts will not be considered. Recent contributors: Josephine Clare, Bob Perelman & Brad Harvey." circ. 375. 1/yr. Pub'd 1 issue 1979; expects 2 issues 1980, 2 issues 1981. sub. price: $5.00/Vol.; per copy: $3.00; sample: $3.00. Discounts: 1-4 copies-25%,5 & over 40%. 24pp; 6¼X9; †lp. Reporting time: 6-8 weeks. Payment: 2 copies. COSMEP.

DENVER QUARTERLY, Leland H Chambers, Editor; Robert D RichardsonJr, Book Review Editor, University of Denver, Denver, CO 80208, 303-753-2869. 1966. Poetry, fiction, articles, criticism, reviews, parts-of-novels. "Essays: Rene Girard, Maurince Blanchot, Luis Leal, Jean Starobinski, Donald Sutherland/Fiction: Carlos Fuentes, Jose Agustin, Salvador Elizondo, Damian Sharp, Deborah Tall/Poems: Jonathan Holden, Octavio Paz, Marco Antonio Montes de Oca, Peter Huchel, Rosemarie Waldrop, Dagmar Nick." circ. 1,000. 4/yr. Pub'd 4 issues 1979; expects 4 issues 1980, 4 issues 1981. sub. price: $8.00; per copy: $2.00; sample: $2.00. Back issues: $3.00 copy over one year old. 125-160pp; 6X9; of. Reporting time: 6 wks. Payment: fiction and essays $5.00 page poetry $10.00 page. Copyrighted, reverts to author. Pub's reviews: 20 in 1979. §literary & philosophic culture of last 100 years. Ads: $100.00/$60.00. CCLM, COSMEP.

DEPARTURES: Contemporary Arts Review, Michael Tucker, Sharyn Jeanne Skeeter, 140 N. Main Street, Concord, NH 03301. 1979. Fiction, art, photos, interviews, satire, criticism, reviews, music, letters, parts-of-novels, plays. "*Departures* is publishing what is new, vital, and enduring in the arts. Contributors to recent issues; Jerome Klinkowitz, Clarence Major, Phillip Lopate, Andrei Codrescu, Stephen Dixon, M.D. Elevitch, William S. Burroughs. We want to see short fiction, art/photographs, interviews, and review-essays. Fiction: up to 3,000 words; non-traditional, satire, fantasy, ethnic; self-contained novel and play excerpts; translations; can contain black and white graphics. Art: portfolios up to ten graphics; cover; black and white photographs, general subjects and of contemporary artists and writers; line art that can be reproduced in black and white. Interviews: of important and/well-known writers and artists; query first. Review-essays: important books of contemporary fiction; also reviews of theater, film, dance, fine/graphic arts; open, but prefer reviewers working in the arts—especially interested in reviews by fiction writers. Submissions must contain SASE for reply." circ. 1,000. 4/yr. Expects 3 issues 1980, 4 issues 1981. sub. price: $11.00 Indiv., $12.00 Instit.; per copy: $3.00; sample: $3.00. Discounts: Booksellers, 40%; other, query. 96pp; 5½X8½; of. Reporting time: 3 weeks. Payment: 2 copies. Copyrighted, reverts to author. Pub's reviews. §Fiction, fine/graphic arts, photography, film, theater, dance, music, literary/arts criticism. Ads: $50.00/$30.-00/$15.00/$10.00. COSMEP.

Dervy, A. J., PO Box 874, Santa Monica, CA 90406, 213 395-6020. 1 title listed in the *Small Press Record of Books in Print* (9th Edition, 1980). avg. price, paper: $4.50. Discounts: 40% of retail. 200pp; 6X9; of.

Derwyddon Press (see also LODGISTIKS), Lodge North, Box 7694, Station A, Edmonton, Alta T5J 2X8, Canada. 1972. Poetry, fiction, articles, art. avg. press run 100. Pub'd 2 titles 1979; expects 2 titles 1980. 4 titles listed in the *Small Press Record of Books in Print* (9th Edition, 1980). avg. price, paper: $5.00. Discounts: Trade: 1-9 copies, 20%; 10 or more, 30%. Libraries (direct order only): 10%. 60pp; size Varies.; of/mi. Reporting time: 6-8 weeks. Payment: 2 author's copies, option to buy copies at cost. Copyrights for author.

DESCANT, Texas Christian University Press, Betsy Feagan Colquitt, English Department, TCU, Fort Worth, TX 76129. 1955. Poetry, fiction, articles. circ. 650. 4/yr. sub. price: $5.00; per copy: $1.50; sample: $1.50. 48pp; 6X9; of. Reporting time: about six weeks. Payment: in copies. Copyrighted.

DESCANT, Karen Mulhallen, P.O. Box 314 Station P, Toronto, Ontario M5S 2S8, Canada. 1970. Poetry, fiction, articles, art, photos, cartoons, interviews, satire, music, parts-of-novels, long-poems, collages, plays, concrete art. circ. 1,000. 3/yr. Pub'd 3 issues 1979; expects 4 issues 1980. sub. price: $8.00 - $16.00; per copy: $3.50; sample: $1.00. 110pp; 6X8; of. Reporting time: 4-6 months. Payment varies. Copyrighted, does not revert to author. Ads: None. COSMEP, CPPA.

Design Enterprises of San Francisco, Donald McCunn, Editor, P.O. Box 27677, San Francisco, CA 94127. 1977. "How-to-Books related to clothing design and programing personal computers. Also books on Asia." avg. press run 5000. Pub'd 2 titles 1979. 3 titles listed in the *Small Press Record of Books in Print* (9th Edition, 1980). avg. price, paper: $6.95. Discounts: Single copy 10%, 2 to 4 copies 20%, 5 to 9 copies 30%, 10 or more copies 40%. 200pp; 8½X11; of. Send letters of inquiry only.

Desserco Publishing, Roquita French, P.O. Box 2433, Culver City, CA 90230. 1975. Articles, criticism, reviews, collages. "Recently published book: 'God Rejected.'" avg. press run 2,000. 1 title listed in the *Small Press Record of Books in Print* (9th Edition, 1980). avg. price, cloth: $4.95; paper: $2.95. Discounts: various up to 54%. 128pp; 5½X8½; of. Payment: none—author published. Copyrights for author.

DEUTSCHHEFT (see Verlag Pohl'n'Mayer)

THE DEVELOPING COUNTRY COURIER, Allan F. Matthews, P.O.Box 239, McLean, VA 22101, (703) 356-7561. 1978. Reviews, news items. "At present, all written in-house by editor" 6/yr. Pub'd 6 issues 1979; expects 6 issues 1980, 6 issues 1981. sub. price: $9.00 N. America, $15.00 airmail outside N. America; per copy: $1.50; sample: $.50. Back issues: $1.50. Discounts: 40%. 12pp; 8½X11; of. Pub's reviews: 5 in 1979. §Relations between Third World and Industrial Countries.

THE DEVIL'S MILLHOPPER, Stephen Corey, Lola Haskins, c/o Lola Haskins, Box 178, LaCrosse, FL 32658, (904) 462-3117. 1976. Poetry. "Prefer poems of 100 lines or less. Poets published include Stephen Spender, K. Eberhart, R. Dana." circ. 400. 2/yr. Pub'd 1 issue 1979; expects 1 issue 1980, 2 issues 1981. sub. price: $3.50/yr; per copy: $2.00; sample: $2.00. Back issues: $1.00. 32pp; 5½X8½; of. Reporting time: 1 month. Payment: 2 copies. Not copyrighted. CCLM.

Dharma Publishing (see also GESAR- Buddhist Perspectives), Merrill Peterson, Managing Editor; Kimberley Bacon, Director of Promotion, 2425 Hillside Avenue, Berkeley, CA 94704. 1972. Articles, art, photos, interviews, reviews, news items. "43 titles currently in print; over 50 Tibetan reproductions in full color. Sepcializes in books on Buddhism. We have our own photo-typesetting and offset printing facilities. 6 titles forthcoming for 1980." avg. press run 5,000. Pub'd 11 titles 1979; expects 6 titles 1980, 10 titles 1981. 8 titles listed in the *Small Press Record of Books in Print* (9th Edition, 1980).

avg. price, cloth: $12.95; paper: $5.95; other: $1.95 Gesar, $3.50 Thankas. Discounts: Bookstores, libraries, distributors: 1 book, 0%; 2-4, 20%; 5-25, 40%; 26-49, 42%; 50-99, 45%; 100-250, 48%; 250+, 50%. 200pp; 5½X8½; †of. Reporting time: 2 months. Payment: Subject to individual arrangement. ABA.

Diablo Western Press, PO Box 766, Alamo, CA 94507, (415) 820-6338.

DIAL-A-POEM POETS LP'S, Giorno Poetry Systems Records, John Giorno, 222 Bowery, New York, NY 10012, 212-925-6372. 1969. Poetry. "LP records of over 100 poets reading their work." circ. 2,000. 4 LPs/yr. Pub'd 4 issues 1979; expects 4 issues 1980. price per copy: $5.98 single album/$8.98 double album. Discounts: 40% for book and record stores. Payment: $50.00 to each poet. CCLM, COSMEP.

DIALOGUE, Steven Bennish, Amy Lustig, Albert Geiser, Ronald Day, Bard College, PO Box 95, Annanandale-on-Hudson, NY 12504, (914) 758-8506. 1978. Poetry, fiction, articles, art, interviews, satire, criticism, reviews, parts-of-novels, long-poems, plays. "We are interested in publishing high quality fiction and poetry regardless of genre. Length is negotiable. We have a preference for essays on contemporary fiction." circ. 500. 2/yr. Pub'd 2 issues 1979; expects 2 issues 1980. sub. price: $2.50; per copy: $1.25; sample: free. Back issues: $1.25. 64pp; 5¾X8½; of. Reporting time: 2-3 weeks. Payment: in copies. Copyrighted, reverts to author. Pub's reviews. §LIterature, poetry, essays on fiction. Ads: $75.00/$50.00.

Diana Press, Inc, Coletta Reid, Casey Czarnik, 4400 Market St, Oakland, CA 94608, (415) 658-5558. 1972. Non-fiction. "We publish feminist books by women, for women." avg. press run 5,000. Pub'd 5 titles 1979; expects 1 title 1980, 2 titles 1981. 15 titles listed in the *Small Press Record of Books in Print* (9th Edition, 1980). avg. price, cloth: $8.75; paper: $5.00. Discounts: trade 40%, library 25%, college course with unlimited return 20%. 224pp; 5½X8½. Reporting time: 6 mos. Payment: 7½% retail price or 50% net profit. Copyrights for author. WIP, COSMEP.

DIANA'S ALMANAC, Diana's Bimonthly Press, Tom Ahern, 71 Elmgrove Ave., Providence, RI 02906. 1972. Poetry, fiction, art, photos. "The first almanac includes: 3 short fictions by German author Helmut Heissenbuttel in translation; *Florida,* a long fiction by Kathy Acker; the early work of Hannah Weiner, *The Code Poems*; and the single extant piece of writing of the obscure, but praised, modernist movement Bibisme: Bibi-la-bibiste, by Raymonde Linossier, translated from the French for the first time. The second almanac contains: 2 major sequences of poems by Harrison Fisher; translations from French and of Uruguayan novelist, Armonia Somers; illustrated narratives by World Imitation Products and Jaimy Gordon; and the last poems of Ray Ragosta." circ. 1,000. 1/yr. sub. price: $4.50; per copy: $4.95; sample: $4.95. Back issues: $20 for complete Vol 1/$20 for Vol 2/$25 for Vol 3, $50 for vol 4. Discounts: 40% to dealers on orders of 5 or more. 100pp; 5½X8½; of/lp/silkscreen. Reporting time: 1 week. Payment: 15% of press run or negotiable. Copyrighted, reverts to author. CCLM, CRISP.

Diana's Bimonthly Press (see also DIANA'S ALMANAC), Tom Ahern, 71 Elmgrove Avenue, Providence, RI 02906, (401) 274-5417. 1978. Poetry, fiction, art, photos. "4 titles are currently in-print: *Occupant X,* by Gary Panter; *I've Been Had!!,* by Dennis Hlynsky; *Self-Portraits,* by Tom Ahern; and *Equilibrium and the Rotary Disc,* by Robert Cumming. All of these are illustrated narratives." avg. press run 1,000. Pub'd 2 titles 1979; expects 4 titles 1980, 6 titles 1981. 14 titles listed in the *Small Press Record of Books in Print* (9th Edition, 1980). avg. price, paper: $4.95. Discounts: 40% to dealers on orders of 5 or more. 40pp; size varies; of. Reporting time: 1 week. Payment: negotiated. Copyrights for author.

The Dickens Fellowship (see also THE DICKENSIAN), Andrew Sanders Dr., 48 Doughty Street, London WC1 2LF, United Kingdom. 1905. Articles, criticism. avg. press run 2,000. Pub'd 3 titles 1979; expects 3 titles 1980. avg. price, paper: £1.50. 64pp. Reporting time: 1 month. Copyrights for author.

THE DICKENSIAN, The Dickens Fellowship, Andrew Sanders Dr., 48 Doughty St., London WC1N 2LF, United Kingdom. 1905. Articles, criticism. "Specialist journal referring to Dickens, his life & works, with Victorian background information and book reviews, reports on Fellowship (International) activities and strong critical and academic articles." circ. 2,000 plus. 3/yr. Pub'd 3 issues 1979; expects 3 issues 1980. sub. price: £3.50 UK; £4.00 overseas; per copy: £1.00. 64pp; 8½X5⅝; lp. Reporting time: 1 month. Payment: nil. Copyrighted. Pub's reviews: 15 in 1979. §Books on Dickens and his circle. Books on nineteenth-century fiction. Ads: £40.00/£45.00(overseas) pro rata.

DICKINSON STUDIES, Higginson Press, Frederick L. Morey, Editor & Publisher, 4508 38th St., Brentwood, MD 20722, 301-864-8527. 1968. Articles, criticism, reviews. "4000 word maximum; MLA style sheet; contributors: Jay Leyda, Lawrence Perrine, William White, George Monteiro (all professors). Also academics from Finland, Japan, and India. Publish reviews usually on Emily Dickinson only." circ. 250. 2/yr. Pub'd 2 issues 1979; expects 2 issues 1980, 2 issues 1981. sub. price: $5.00 individuals $10.00 libraries; per copy: $3.00; sample: $3.00. Back issues: $10/yr $160 for 40 currently in print. Discounts: 10%. 50pp; 5X8; of. Reporting time: 2 weeks. Payment: 1 copy only. Not copyrighted. Pub's reviews: 5 in 1979. §Criticism, biography, etc. for Dickinson. Book rates, sales, rare, paper, of her books. Ads: $90/$50.

DICO, Cheryl M. Armour, PO Box 6204, Postal Station C, Victoria, B.C. V8P 4G0, Canada, 477-9654. 1978. Poetry, cartoons. "Poems dealing with emotional topics - love, anger, happiness or sadness. Must be powerful and moving. Hard-hitting but understandable! All styles considered. Emphasis on poems with strong initial impact not on intellectual, 'clubby' type poetry. Cartoons revealing discrepancies in modern society." 4/yr. Expects 1 issue 1980, 4 issues 1981. sub. price: $3.50; per copy: $0.95; sample: $.50. Back issues: $1.00. Discounts: $3.00 per year. 26pp; 5X8; mi, of. Reporting time: 4 weeks. Payment: 2 copies. Copyrighted, reverts to author.

DIGNITY, Jim Highland, 1500 Massachusetts Ave., NW, Suite 11, Washington, DC 20005, 202-861-0017. 1969. Interviews, letters, news items, articles, photos, cartoons. "Recent contributors: Gregory Baum, Bob Nugent, Bill Roberts, John McNeill, Norman Pittenger, Jeannine Gramick, Thomas Oddo, Paul Diederich, Bob Fournier, Peg Barry, Paul Weidig." circ. 5,000 plus per issue. monthly. Pub'd 12 issues 1979; expects 12 issues 1980, 12 issues 1981. 3 titles listed in the *Small Press Record of Books in Print* (9th Edition, 1980). sub. price: $11.00; sample: free. Back issues: negotiable. 6pp; 8½X11; of. Copyrighted. Pub's reviews: 4 in 1979. §gay Catholic experience.

DIMENSION, A. Leslie Willson, Editor, Box 7032, Austin, TX 78712, 512-471-4314. 1968. Poetry, fiction, art, parts-of-novels, long-poems, plays. "Contributions in German with English translations." circ. 1,200. 3/yr. Pub'd 3 issues 1979; expects 3 issues 1980, 3 issues 1981. sub. price: $12.00 indiv; $15.00 instit; per copy: $6.00; sample: $6.00. Discounts: 20% to agencies and bookdealers. 150-200pp; 6X9; lp/of. Reporting time: 3 months to 6 months. Payment: yes (not to translators). Copyrighted, reverts to author. CCLM.

Dimensionist Press, Arnold Arias, 5931 Stanton Avenue, Highland, CA 92346, 862-4521. 1978. Poetry. "This publication represents a new movement in the arts called 'Dimensionism'. A dimensionist strives to describe or evoke supernatural, mystical, imaginary, heavenly, extraterrestrial, or ultra-dimensional worlds in word, image, or sound. (Published 1 book of poetry, *The Iridescent Dimension* by Arnold Arias.)" avg. press run 500-1,000. Expects 1 title 1981. 1 title listed in the *Small Press Record of Books in Print* (9th Edition, 1980). avg. price, paper: $2.50. Discounts: 40%. 85pp; 4¼X7¼; of. Reporting time: 1 month, SASE. Payment: copies. Copyrights for author.

The Direct Marketing Creative Guild (see also COPY CORNUCOPIA), Lee Marc Stein, Editor-in-Chief; Richard Sachinis, Managing Editor, 516 5th Avenue, New York, NY 10036. 1964. Poetry, fiction, articles, cartoons, interviews, criticism, reviews, letters. avg. price, other: $4.00. 8pp; 8½X11; of. Reporting time: 3 weeks.

Distant Thunder Press, Jeffrey Winke, Carol Winke, 1224 E Clarke Street, Milwaukee, WI 53212. 1979. Poetry, art, photos, collages, concrete art. "Brief collections and small press runs are the rule. Prefer poetry collections that capture a particular event, experience, or mind set of the writer. For example, recently published *Mountain Talk* by Jusan Atnarko. *Mountain Talk* is a collection of wilderness visions, winter chants, and cabin poems, written over a two year period while the author was living as an illegal alien in the coast mountains of western British Columbia. Also publish poetry postcards, foldsheets, and broadsides. Please inquire before submitting." avg. press run 150. Pub'd 2 titles 1979. 2 titles listed in the *Small Press Record of Books in Print* (9th Edition, 1980). avg. price, paper: $3.50. 20pp; †of. Reporting time: 3 weeks. Payment: pay with copies. Copyrights for author.

The Distributors (see and books)

Do It Now Foundation (see also DRUG SURVIVAL NEWS), Dario McDarby, Editor, P.O. Box 5115, Phoenix, AZ 85010, 602-257-0797. 1968. Articles, news items, photos, art. "Write to editor for guidelines before sending material. It must be substance abuse related." avg. press run 20,000. Pub'd 66 titles 1979; expects 68 titles 1980. avg. price, paper: $0.15 per pamphlet; 40-50¢ per booklet, $1.25-$1.50 larger booklets. Discounts: quantity. 3-25pp; size varies; †of. Reporting time: Varies, 2 weeks to 2 months. Payment: Available, but not often; must be special material. Copyrights for author.

Do-It-Yourself Publications, Co., Benji Anosike, Executive Editor, 150 Fifth Ave., New York, NY 10011, (212) 242-2840. 1978. avg. press run 1,200. Pub'd 1 title 1979; expects 5 titles 1980, 5 titles 1981. avg. price, cloth: $6.95. Discounts: Bookstores, 40%; Libraries, 25%. 100pp; 8½X11,

117

5½X8½; of. Reporting time: 4 weeks. Payment: 15%. Copyrights for author.

DR. DOBB'S JOURNAL OF COMPUTER CALISTHENICS & ORTHODONTIA, People's Computer Co., Suzanne M. Rodriquez, 1263 El Camino, P. O. Box E, Menlo Park, CA 94025, 415-323-3111. 1976. Articles, interviews, criticism, reviews, letters. "Considered the source of software for personal and home computing." circ. 11,000 copies sold per issue. 10/yr. Pub'd 10 issues 1979; expects 10 issues 1980. sub. price: $15.00; per copy: $2.00; sample: $2.00. Back issues: $15.00 for all of 1976 (Volume 1). Discounts to resellers and subscription agencies. 48 to 64pp; 8½X11; of. Reporting time: Quickly. Payment: none. Copyrighted. Pub's reviews. §computers & computer software. Ads: $500.00/$300.00/$170.00.

Doctor Jazz, A.J. Wright, PO Box 1043, Auburn, AL 36830, (205) 887-5066. 1979. Poetry, art. "In 1979 DJ Press began issuing the first of its poetry broadsides, many of which will also feature original drawings. Coming in the future are postcard poems, a yearly anthology called *Solar Wind* and chapbooks featuring one or more poets. At this time money and correspondance are welcome, but submissions would be wasted. I have enough material on hand for more than a year. DJ Press is committed to the idea that real poetry lies in the vast middle ground between half-baked sentiment and half-baked experiment. Anything else goes. Until next time, this is Doctor Jazz singing off." avg. press run 100. Pub'd 2 titles 1979; expects 10 titles 1980. 2 titles listed in the *Small Press Record of Books in Print* (9th Edition, 1980). avg. price, other: $2.50, 3 broadsides. 1pp; 8½X11; of. Reporting time: less than a month. Payment: 25 copies. Copyrights for author.

The Dog Ear Press, Mark Melnicove, PO Box 155, Hulls Cove, ME 04644. 1977. Poetry, art, photos, cartoons, music, collages, concrete art, news items. "Looking to publish anything likely to be dog-eared for years to come. Now available: *The Maine Poets Festival Book 1979,* $4.00. *Brotherly, and Other Loves* by Kala Ladenheim $3.50. Upcoming: *Poets on Photography,* an international anthology of poems about photography. Always willing to receive experimental poetry, photography and typography. Interested in work that'll change the world or something close to it." avg. press run 500-2,000. Pub'd 1 title 1979; expects 4 titles 1980. avg. price, paper: $4.00. Discounts: write for info. 64pp; 6X9, 8X9; †of, lp. Reporting time: immediately, month. Payment: variable. Copyrights for author. MPW.

Doggeral Press (see also FOUR DOGS MOUNTAIN SONGS), A. Karle, P. Katoff, 417 Sea View Road, Santa Barbara, CA 93108, (805) 966-9966, 969-2500. 1971. Poetry, fiction, art, long-poems. "Our aim is to publish literature & art of the best quality we can find in the bet manner that we are capable of. Recent contributors: John Wilson, John Brandi, Barbara Szerlip, C. K. Lord Haines, Thor, Tina Wolfe and Calhoun." avg. press run 160-275. Pub'd 2 titles 1979. †lp. Reporting time: 1 month. Payment: 10% combination books & copies.

Dollar of Soul Press, Owen Davis, Jeremy Hilton, 15 Argyle Road, Swanage, Dorset, United Kingdom. 1975. Poetry. avg. press run 200. Pub'd 4 titles 1979. 7 titles listed in the *Small Press Record of Books in Print* (9th Edition, 1980). avg. price, paper: 45p. Discounts: 33⅓ percent trade. 30pp; size A5; of. no unsolicited mss. Payment: nil. copyright by author.

Dolly Varden Publications, Thomas S. Terrill, Box 2017, Oceanside, CA 92054, (714) 729-1736. 1979. Articles. avg. press run 1,000. Pub'd 1 title 1979. avg. price, paper: $8.95. Discounts: Trade, 50%; Classroom, 15/30%; Libraries, 25%. 125pp; 8½X11; of. Reporting time: 2 weeks. Payment: varies.

Dominion Press (see also CHAIRMAN'S CHAT; THEOLOGIA 21; MASTER THOUGHTS), A. Stuart Otto, P O Box 37, San Marcos, CA 92069, 714-746-9430. 1966. "*Theologia 21* is religious (Alternative Christianity). No outside contributors. Published quarterly. Our books are also in the same field." avg. press run 1,000-1,500. 6 titles listed in the *Small Press Record of Books in Print* (9th Edition, 1980). avg. price, cloth: $15.00; paper: $5.00. Discounts: 40% to dealers in quantities. 50-200pp; 8½X11; of. No mss accepted. Payment: none. non-profit organization, staff on salary.

Donnelly & Sons Publishing Co., Warren L. Donnelly, PO Box 7880, Colorado Springs, CO 80933, (303) 593-8025. 1972. "Non-Fiction *Traveling With a Radio* is a new 360-page guide to 8,096 AM and FM radio stations in 3,323 cities and towns in the United States. The book lists, in adition to dial settings, the maximum broadcast power, program formats, and network affiliation of the stations. It also covers CB, WR (weather radio), TIS (Travelers Information Station), and much more." avg. press run 5,000. Pub'd 1 title 1979. avg. price, paper: $4.95. Discounts: 40% in quantities over 10. 360pp; 5¼X9; of.

The Donning Company / Publishers, Robert S. Friedman, 5041 Admiral Wright Road, Virginia Beach, VA 23462, (804) 499-0589. 1974. Fiction. avg. press run 5000. Pub'd 18 titles 1979; expects 20 titles 1980, 25 titles 1981. avg. price, cloth: $14.95; paper: $5.95. Discounts: inquire. 208pp; of.

118

Reporting time: four weeks. Pays royalties semi-annually. Copyrights for author.

The Doodly-Squat Press (see also THE HOT SPRINGS GAZETTE), Eric Irving, Editor, P.O. Box 40124, Albuquerque, NM 87106. 1976. Poetry, fiction, articles, art, photos, cartoons, interviews, satire, criticism, reviews, letters, news items. "All material must concern hot springs" avg. press run 1,000. Pub'd 3 titles 1979. 3 titles listed in the *Small Press Record of Books in Print* (9th Edition, 1980). avg. price, paper: $2.00. Discounts: $1.00 over 10. 30pp; 6X8; †of.

DOUBLE HARNESS, Avalon Editions, Andrew Cozens, 9 Bradmore Road, Oxford OX2 6QN, United Kingdom. 1978. Poetry, fiction, articles, art, reviews, letters, long-poems, photos, cartoons, interviews, criticism, music, news items. "*Double Harness* is a magazine combining modern literature, poetry, music, reviews, etc. with social/community issues, particularly lifestyle dicisions. All genuine letters receive personal attention" circ. 500-1,000. irregular. Pub'd 2-3 issues 1979. sub. price: 4 issues, £3.00 UK, £3.50 USA, I.M.O.S. preferred; per copy: 50p; sample: postage. Back issues: free for postage. Discounts: by arrangement. 64pp; 8X5; †lo. Reporting time: varies but immediate acowledgement. Payment: none as yet. Not copyrighted. Pub's reviews: 10 in 1979. §Poetry, contemporary fiction, literary criticism, records, lefestyle, social/community issues. Ads: All by arrangement. ALP, ALMS.

Dovetail Press Ltd (see also HOUSESMITHS JOURNAL), Roger Jordan, Senior Editor; Robert Morehouse, Managing Editor, Box 1496, Boulder, CO 80306. "Title of Book: *Timber Frame Raising* by Stewart Elliott." avg. press run 5,000. Pub'd 1 title 1979; expects 1 title 1980, 1 title 1981. avg. price, paper: $9.95. Discounts: 1-4, 25%; 5-24, 40%; 25-49, 42%; 50-99, 45%; 100+, 50%. 133pp; 8½X11. Copyrights for author.

Down There Press + (My Mama's Press), Joani Blank, PO Box 2086, Burlingame, CA 94010, 415-342-9867. 1975. "Probably the only small press in the country publishing exclusively six education & sexual self-awareness books. The Original *Playbooks (for men and women) about sex* are still very popular. New titles in 1980 are *The Playbook for Kids About Sex, Men Loving Themselves,* and the *Sensuous Coloring Book.*" avg. press run 4,000. Pub'd 2 titles 1979. 5 titles listed in the *Small Press Record of Books in Print* (9th Edition, 1980). avg. price, paper: $5.00, $1.85. Discounts: 30%-40% to booksellers, average 25-30% for 5 or more copies of one title. 48-86pp; 8½X11; 5½X8½; of. Payment: varies. COSMEP.

Downtown Poets Co-op (X Press Press), David Gershator, Phillis Gershator, G.P.O. Box 1720, Brooklyn, NY 11202. 1976. Poetry, long-poems. "Interested in quality, energy, talent. Chapbooks by Enid Dame, Irving Stettner, Fritz Hamilton, Jack Alchemy, David Gershator, Ivan Arguelles, Althea Romeo, Don Lev, and others. So far, cooperative publication by invitation." avg. press run 750. Pub'd 2 titles 1979; expects 6 titles 1980, 6 titles 1981. 6 titles listed in the *Small Press Record of Books in Print* (9th Edition, 1980). avg. price, paper: $2.00. Discounts: 40% trade, jobber. 56pp; 5½X8½; of. Reporting time: 1 month. NYSSPA.

DRAGONFLY:A Quarterly Of Haiku, J&C Transcripts, Lorraine Ellis Harr, Assoc; Carl F. Harr, Kametaro Yagi, (Japan); Kazuo Sato, (Japan), 4102 N.E. 130th Pl., Portland, OR 97230. 1967. Poetry. "Classical/traditional Haiku only. 300 word articles on pertinent subjects. Forum page: 300 word (or less) Articles on points of Haiku writing. Must be concise. Carl F. Harr, Kazuo Sato, Prof. K. Yagi, Oliver Statler, Alan Watts, Richard Hansen, Robert Draper, Paul O. Williams, Richard Crist, Dorothy G. Neher, Helen C. Acton, Lorraine Ellis Harr." circ. over 500. 4/yr. Pub'd 4 issues 1979. 6 titles listed in the *Small Press Record of Books in Print* (9th Edition, 1980). sub. price: $10.00, Foreign $15.00, Canada $12.00; per copy: $2.50; sample: $2.50. Back issues: $2.50. Discounts: 10 percent off yearly sub. 68pp; 5½X8½; lp. Reporting time: usually by return mail within 30 days. Payment: Many cash & book prizes, awards. n.p. Copyrighted. Pub's reviews: 12-24 in 1979. §Oriental poetry, anything relating to Haiku-Senryu-Haibun, Zen/Am. Indian, etc. no ads. WWHS.

Dragon's Teeth Press, Cornel Lengyel, Adams Acres, El Dorado Nat. Forest, Georgetown, CA 95634. 1970. Poetry, music, long-poems, plays. avg. press run 1,000. Pub'd 4 titles 1979. 15 titles listed in the *Small Press Record of Books in Print* (9th Edition, 1980). avg. price, paper: $3.50. Discounts: 30-40%. 64-128pp; 5½X8½ or 8½X11; of. Reporting time: 6 wks. Payment: 10% royalty. Copyrights for author.

Dragonsbreath Press, Fred Johnson, Rt. #1, Sister Bay, WI 54234, (414) 854-2742. 1973. Poetry, fiction, art, photos, satire, long-poems. "The press moved into its own building last year so finally has a permanent home. Unfortunately work on the building has taken precedence over press work so far. I'm still hoping to get at least 2 books out this year. One being a biography on the artist F.V. Poole. I'm mainly interested in limited edition handmade books. Working mainly with handset type and illustrated with original artwork. The subject matter is completely open, but more partial to short stories than poetry. Prices depend on the book. I am still offering memberships in the press, write for information." Pub'd 2 titles 1979; expects 3-4 titles 1980. 4 titles listed in the *Small Press Record of Books in Print* (9th Edition, 1980). †lp. Reporting time: 1 to 3 weeks, should write before sending ms. include SASE. Copyrights for author.

THE DRAMA REVIEW, Michael Kirby, Editor; Terry Helbing, Managing Editor, 51 West 4th St. Room 300, New York, NY 10012, 212-598-2597. 1955. Articles, photos, plays. "TDR documents new trends in contemporary avant-garde performance. (plays are published only as partial documentation of historically significant productions). TDR is interested in performance analysis, not dramatic evaluation, interpretation or criticism." circ. 10,000. 4/yr. Pub'd 4 issues 1979; expects 4 issues 1980, 4 issues 1981. sub. price: $14.00; per copy: $4.00; sample: $4.00. Back issues: $3.50-$6.00, depending on no. of copies still in print & available. Discounts: 40 percent bookstores; 10 percent subscription agencies. 144pp; 7X10; of. Reporting time: 2 weeks. Payment: 2 cents a word; $10.00/photo. Copyrighted, reverts to author. Pub's reviews: 20 in 1979. §Theatre, drama, art performance, avant-garde performance indigenous drama. Ads: $330.00/$197.80. CCLM, COSMEP, ASME, CELJ.

DRAMATIKA, Dramatika Press, John Pyros, Andrea Pyros, 429 Hope Street, Tarpon Springs, FL 33589. 1968. Plays. "Performable pieces only (plays, songs, etc.)" 2/yr. 1 title listed in the *Small Press Record of Books in Print* (9th Edition, 1980). sub. price: $10.00; per copy: $5.00. Back issues: $5.00. 50pp; 8X11. Reporting time: 2 mos. Payment: copies only. CCLM, COSMEP.

Dramatika Press (see also DRAMATIKA), John Pyros, Andrea Pyros, 429 Hope Street, Tarpon Springs, FL 33589. 1968. Photos, long-poems, plays, concrete art. "Solicit biographies of performing arts, avant-garde figures, especially from previously unpublished M.A. or PH.D. theses-also off-beat novella length pieces." Expects 2 titles 1980. 3 titles listed in the *Small Press Record of Books in Print* (9th Edition, 1980). 50pp; 8X11; of.

Dream Place Publications, David Bain, PO Box 9416, Stanford, CA 94305, (415) 494-6083. 1977. Poetry, articles, art, photos, interviews, music, news items. "We publish books in the area of show business and the arts. We are interested in innovative material in areas in which little has been previously published. We currently are looking for topics dealing with Middle Eastern culture, particularly dance orientale or 'belly dancing'." avg. press run 2,000. Pub'd 1 title 1979; expects 1 title 1980. avg. price, cloth: $14.95; paper: $9.95. Discounts: 40% on 5 or more copies. 200pp; 8½X11; of. Reporting time: 3 weeks. Payment: standard royalty. Copyrights for author. COSMEP.

DREAMS, Steve Haggard, W.L. Gertz, 76 Beaver Street, Suite 400, New York, NY 10005, (212) 996-0812. 1977. Poetry, fiction, articles, art, photos, interviews, criticism, reviews, music, letters. "Fiction must be short (1,500 word max.). Reviews & criticism are usually provacative, i.e., strongly pro or con. Editorials & regular manifestos propound our zealously pro-art, anti-commercial movement: gob-o-realism!" circ. 1,500. 6/yr. Pub'd 2 issues 1979; expects 6 issues 1980, 6 issues 1981. sub. price: $8.00; per copy: $1.00; sample: $1.00. Back issues: $1.25 each. 32pp; 5½X8½; of. Reporting time: 3 weeks. Payment: No money - 5 copies. Copyrighted, reverts to author. §Music, film, art, history, philosophy. Ads: $75.00/$40.00.

DRUG SURVIVAL NEWS, Do It Now Foundation, Dario McDarby, Editor, P.O. Box 5115, Phoenix, AZ 85010, 602-257-0797. 1976. Articles, interviews, news items, reviews. "All items MUST be drug and alcohol related." circ. 20M. 6/yr. Pub'd 6 issues 1979; expects 6 issues 1980, 6 issues 1981. sub. price: $4.00 U.S.; $4.50 Canada & Mexico; $5.00 other foreign; per copy: $0.67 U.S.; $0.75 Canada & Mexico; $0.83 other foreign; sample: free. Discounts: none. 16-18pp; 11X13¼; of. Reporting time: 1-2 weeks. Payment: 25¢/col. in. for news clippings; 50¢/col. in. for original material. Copyrighted. Pub's reviews. §Substance abuse field only. Ads: $250.00/$140.00.

Druid Books, Jon Reilly, Ephraim, WI 54211. 1969. Poetry, fiction, photos. avg. press run 1,500. Pub'd 1 title 1979; expects 3 titles 1980, 3 titles 1981. 7 titles listed in the *Small Press Record of Books in Print* (9th Edition, 1980). avg. price, paper: $3.00. Discounts: 40% book retail, 50% book distributors. 50pp; 5½X8½ usually; of. Reporting time: ASAP. Payment: Author's royalties 10% of retail price, plus copies.

Druid Heights Books, 685 Camino Del Canyon, Muir Woods, Mill Valley, CA 94941. 1969. 3 titles listed in the *Small Press Record of Books in Print* (9th Edition, 1980). Discounts: orders for 5 copies or more for resale, 40%.

Dryad Press, PO Box 29161, Presidio, San Francisco, CA 94129. 1969. 17 titles listed in the *Small Press Record of Books in Print* (9th Edition, 1980). avg. price, cloth: $12.00; paper: $4.00. 60pp; 5½X8½, 6X9. Copyrights for author. CCLM.

Duck Down Press (see also SCREE), Kirk Robertson, Nila Northsun, PO Box 1047, Fallon, NV

89406, (702) 423-2220. 1973. Poetry, fiction, art, collages, concrete art, photos. "Titles in print: *Chase* - Gerald Locklin; *Red Work Black Widow* - Steve Richmond; *Men Under Fire* - Ronald Koertge; *The Kid Comes Home* - Leo Mailman; *The Man In The Black Chevrolet* - Todd Moore; *Diet Pepsi & Nacho Cheese* - Nila Northsun; *Whiplash On The Couch* - John Bennett; *Asylum Picnic* - Robert Matte, Jr. Titles in prepartion include: *The Wages of Sin* stories by Gerald Haslam; *None Such Creek* new & selected poems by A. Masarik and others." avg. press run 500-750. Pub'd 2 titles 1979; expects 2-4 titles 1980. 13 titles listed in the *Small Press Record of Books in Print* (9th Edition, 1980). avg. price, paper: $2.00 - $4.95; other: Signed lettered editions - $25.00 (no discount). Discounts: 5 or more, 40 percent. 24-120pp; size varies; of. Reporting time: Fast. Payment: Copies plus share of money above expenses. Copyrights for author. CCLM.

DUCK SOUP, David England, Adviser, 2000 Walnut Hill Lane, Irving, TX 75062, (214) 659-5279. 1978. Poetry, fiction, articles, art, photos, cartoons, interviews, satire, criticism, reviews, letters, collages, plays, concrete art. "College literary magazine open to limited number of submissions from outside the college." circ. 3,000. 1/yr. Pub'd 1 issue 1979; expects 1 issue 1980. sample price: Free upon request and availability. Back issues: free upon request and availability. 64pp; 8½X11; of. Reporting time: 1 to 3 months, depending on time of year. Late fall quickest; late spring longest. Payment: 2 copies. Copyrighted, reverts to author.

Duende Press, Larry Goodell, Box 571, Placitas, NM 87043. 1964. Poetry, fiction, art, photos, cartoons, interviews, satire, reviews, music, letters, parts-of-novels, long-poems, collages, plays, news items. "Post avant garde song. Unworthy submissions will be burned. Judson Crews' *The Noose, A Retrospective, Three Decades* is now available, $4.00." avg. press run 500. Pub'd 1 title 1979; expects 1 title 1980, 1 title 1981. 1 title listed in the *Small Press Record of Books in Print* (9th Edition, 1980). avg. price, paper: $4.00. Discounts: 40% plus mailing, minimum order: 4 copies. 120pp; size standard; †of. Reporting time: Eternity or before. Copyrights for author. RGWA, CCLM.

Duir Press, Ellen Cooney, 919 Sutter #9, San Francisco, CA 94109, (415) 441-8354. 1979. Poetry, art, photos, long-poems. "Have only done one book, by myself, *The Silver Rose.* Financing will determine future direction of the press. Would like to do several other of my own books, then take it from there. Very interested in long myths. Interested in high quality visual appeal as well." avg. press run 1,000. Pub'd 1 title 1979. 1 title listed in the *Small Press Record of Books in Print* (9th Edition, 1980). avg. price, paper: $5.95. Discounts: Bookstores, 40%. of, lp.

Duke University Press (see also AMERICAN LITERATURE), Ashbel G. Brice, Director, Box 6697 College Station, Durham, NC 27708, (919) 684-2173. 1921. Poetry, art, satire, music, letters, parts-of-novels, plays. "Scholarly publications." avg. press run 1,500. Pub'd 15 titles 1979; expects 19 titles 1980, 20 titles 1981. avg. price, cloth: $14.00; paper: $7.00. Discounts: Available on request. 275pp; 6⅛X9¼; 5½X8½; of/lp. Reporting time: From 1 week to 9 months. Payment: Variable. Request copyright assignment to Duke Press.

DUMP HEAP (Diverse Unsung Miracle Plants for Healthy Evolution Among People), Jamie Jobb, 2950 Walnut Blvd., Walnut Creek, CA 94598. 1978. "Write publisher for manuscript details." circ. 1,500. 4/yr. Pub'd 4 issues 1979; expects 4 issues 1980, 4 issues 1981. sub. price: $6.00; per copy: $1.75; sample: $1.75. Back issues: $2.00. 16pp; 7X8½; †of. Reporting time: 2 months. Copyrighted, does not revert to author. Pub's reviews: 12 in 1979. §Wild edge horticulture, tree crops, permanent agriculture, solar energy, app. technology, uncommon economic plants, heritage varieties of food plants. Ads: no ads.

Dundee Publishing, David Bellin, Kristen Banfield, Edmund Pardo, Box 202, Dundee, NY 14837, (607) 243-5559. 1979. Fiction. "Fiction with political basis and scholarly political-science." avg. press run 2,000. Pub'd 3 titles 1979. avg. price, cloth: $10.95; paper: $4.95. Discounts: customary. 200pp; 5½X8½; of. Payment: negotiated. Copyrights for author. COSMEP.

DURAK: An International Magazine of Poetry, Robert Lloyd, D. S. Hoffman, RD 1, Box 352, Joe Green Road, Erin, NY 14838. 1978. Poetry, interviews. "Contributors include Charles Simic, Mark Strand, James Tate, Charles Wright, James Wright, Russell Edson. Translations of Papa, Ritsos, Holub, Bialoszewski, Krolow." circ. 1,000. 2/yr. Pub'd 2 issues 1979; expects 2 issues 1980, 2 issues 1981. sub. price: $3.00; per copy: $1.50; sample: $1.00. Discounts: Bookstores, agencies 40%. 64pp; 5¼X8½; of. Reporting time: 1-2 weeks. Copyrighted, reverts to author. Ads: $50.00/$30.00. CCLM.

THE DURHAM UNIVERSITY JOURNAL, J.M.J. Rogister, 43 North Bailey, Durham DH1 3EX, United Kingdom. 1876. Criticism. "Mss. and books for review should be sent to the editor, 43 N. Bailey, Durham, England. All correspondence on other matters relating to the journal should be sent to the chief clerk, Univ. Office, Old Shire Hall, Durham. Subscriptions should be made payable to University of Durham." circ. 800. 2/yr. Pub'd 2 issues 1979; expects 2 issues 1980. sub. price:

£3.50 plus 35p (postage); per copy: £1.75 plus 15p (postage). 250-300pp; 7¼X4; of. Reporting time: 3 mos. No payment. Copyrighted, does not revert to author. Pub's reviews: 80 in 1979. §Literature, history, philosophy, classical studies, theology, poetry. Ads: £50.00/£30.00/£4.00 -1/4 page.

Dustbooks (see also THE SMALL PRESS REVIEW), Len Fulton, Ellen Ferber, Box 100, Paradise, CA 95969, 916-877-6110. 1963. "We have a small general trade list: poetry, novels, anthologies, non-fiction prose, how-to, etc. But it should be remembered that our real expertise & commitment is small press-mag info. On January 1st of every year we face a full year of publishing without looking at one new manuscript. We do three annuals: this Directory you're holding which takes 5 months from start to finish; its companion volume, the *Directory of Small Magazine/Press Editors and Publishers,* and the *Small Press Record of Books in Print*(latest edition - 550 pp). We do one monthly, the *Small Press Review* (see separate listing), which also includes the Small Press Book Club. We've done a nice string of general trade books (see ads) and will do many more, but our capacity is severely modified by our mainstay titles above. In 1975 Dustbooks initiated The 'American Dust' Series, which seeks to chronicle the geographical, stylistic, ethnic, and genre diversity and richness of writing in the Contemporary Americas. Best to query before sending anything. NOTE: Canadian and foreign please remit in US funds only when ordering." avg. press run 1-2 M. Pub'd 8 titles 1979; expects 5 titles 1980, 8 titles 1981. 41 titles listed in the *Small Press Record of Books in Print* (9th Edition, 1980). avg. price, cloth: $8.95; paper: $2.95. Discounts: 2-10, 25 percent; 11-25, 40 percent; 26 plus, 50 percent (bookstores), distributors by arrangement, jobbers 20-25 percent. Returns only after six months but before one year; returns are for credit ONLY. 100-300pp; 5½X8½, 6X9; of. Reporting time: 3-6 months. Payment: royalty (15%). Copyrights for author.

E

E & E Enterprises, Edmond Knowles, P.O. Box 405, Howell, NJ 07731, 201-364-1398. 1974. "Recent book: DYNAMICS OF THE FAMILY UNIT, by Edmond Knowles." avg. press run 5,000. Pub'd 1 title 1979; expects 1 title 1980. 3 titles listed in the *Small Press Record of Books in Print* (9th Edition, 1980). avg. price, cloth: $4.00; paper: $3.00. Discounts: yes, 50%. 124pp; 5¾X9. Payment: standard 10%. Copyrights for author.

Eads Street Press, Mort Castle, 402 Stanton Lane, Crete, IL 60417. 1975. Poetry, fiction. "In 1975 and 1976, Eads Street published 4 good poetry chapbooks; sales were underwhelming. Look, nobody's in small press to get rich, but...Anyhoo, didn't publish thing one in '77, though came across a half dozen manuscripts that belonged in print. See, it takes $$$ to make books happen; don't want bookstore sales in the millions, don't want big federal funding, just want people besides my relatives to glom onto what we're doing. Find it especially irritating when an author, pseudo-author, or semi-skilled typist hits me with a manuscript that plainly reveals she has never seen one of our books and has no idea if Eads publishes high class poetics or low class porno. When possible, hope it's by fall of '78, want to get out some new titles, but this does not mean we are actively considering manuscripts at this time. Query first, telling me about your self/work. Don't bother if you don't know your craft, think Harold Robbins and Rod McKuen represent the epitome of American letters, or if you believe there'll be a Woodstock II to wig us into the far-out, whacked-out, peace-love-dope ozone. 1979 update: Does anyone really buy small press stuff or are we all kidding ourselves, huh!" avg. press run 300-500. 4 titles listed in the *Small Press Record of Books in Print* (9th Edition, 1980). avg. price, paper: $0.75, but may go to a buck to make some big profits!. Discounts: 40 percent bookstores agents. pp varies; 8½X5½; of. Reporting time: faster than fast, usually, but I'm getting old and starting to slow down. Payment: generous batch of copies. Copyrights for author.

EAR MAGAZINE, Richard Hayman, Michael Cooper, David Feldman, Charlie Morrow, Peter Wetzler, Stuart Leigh, David Garland, Nigel Rollings, 365 West End Avenue, New York, NY 10024, 212-475-8223. 1973. Fiction, articles, art, photos, cartoons, interviews, satire, criticism, reviews, music, letters, parts-of-novels, collages, concrete art. "Short is best. Avant-garde bias. Contributors: Nam June Paik, Anna Lockwood, Alison Knowles, Dick Higgins, John Cage." circ. 1,500. 5/yr. Pub'd 5 issues 1979. sub. price: $10.00; per copy: $1.00; sample: $1.00. Back issues: Price varies (approx $2 each). Discounts: 50 cents each. 12pp; 16X11½; of. Reporting time: 4 mos. Payment: none available. Copyrighted. Pub's reviews: 4 in 1979. §Events. Ads: $100/$50/$1.

EARTH'S DAUGHTERS, Kastle Brill, Marion Perry, Robin Willoughby, P O Box 41, Station H, Buffalo, NY 14214. 1971. Poetry, fiction, art, photos, parts-of-novels, long-poems, plays, satire, music, collages. "We are a feminist arts periodical." circ. 1,000. 2-4/yr. Pub'd 1 issue 1979; expects 3 issues 1980, 4 issues 1981. sub. price: 4 issues: $5.00; 8 issues, $9.00. Instit. $15.00/4 issues; per copy: varies; sample: $2.00. Back issues: Collector sets available upon inquiry. Discounts: trade 30-35%; bulk 35%; jobber-straight rates. pp varies; size Varies; of. Reporting time: very slow - mucho backlog!. Payment: 4 issues complimentary and reduced prices on further copies. Copyrighted, reverts to author. §Work by women or in feminist themes. CCLM, NYSSPA, NEW (Niagara Erie Writers).

EARTHWISE: A Journal of Poetry, Earthwise Publications, PO Box 680-536, Miami, FL 33168.

EARTHWISE NEWSLETTER, Earthwise Publications, Barbara Holley, Sally Newhouse, PO Box 680-536, Miami, FL 33168, 305-688-8558. 1979. Poetry, articles, art, interviews, criticism, reviews, letters, concrete art, news items. "Newsletter comes out bimonthly, sells for $1.00 per copy. Some back issues available. Subscription is $4.60 for quarterly to subscribers only. Sample copies are mailed out quarterly minus some subscriber features. Sscr. fee includes postage." circ. 3,000. 6/yr. Pub'd 6 issues 1979. sub. price: $4.60; per copy: $1.00; sample: $0.50. Back issues: $0.50 where available. Discounts: negotiable. 4-8pp; 8½X11½; of. Reporting time: 30-60 days. Payment: sometimes small fee paid, always in contributors copies. Copyrighted, reverts to author. Pub's reviews. §Poetry, fiction, ecology, crafts. Ads: $10.00/$5.00/$0.50. COSMEP, CODA.

Earthwise Publications (see also EARTHWISE: A Journal of Poetry; EARTHWISE NEWSLETTER; TEMPEST: Avant-Garde Poetry), Barbara Holley, Herman Gold, PO Box 680-536, Miami, FL 33168, (305) 688-8558. 1979. Poetry, fiction, articles, art, interviews, satire, criticism, reviews, letters, long-poems, collages, concrete art, news items. "We will consider anything related to poets, poetry, reviews of poetry books, cameos on poets, interviews, short stories, black and white, woodcuts, etc. This journal, as opposed to our other, *Earthwise*, is considered 'avant-garde' primarily because it concerns itself with issues, topics which may not be totally acceptable to general audiences. We do *not* accept pornography, however; try to remain within the realm of good taste. Thanks." avg. press run 200-300. avg. price, paper: $3.00 + postage. Discounts: on consignment, $1.50 per. 46-50pp; 5½X8½; of. Reporting time: 3 months. Payment: $2.00 each for poems, $5.00 for interviews, articles, short stories, $10.00 for cover art, $2.00 each for blk and whites, woodcuts a bit more. Copyrights for author. COSMEP, CODA.

East African Publishing House, Richard C. Ntiru, Paul Ngige Njoroge, D. Nyoike Waiyaki, PO Box 30571, Nairobi, Kenya, Africa, 557417 & 555694. 1965. avg. press run 7,500. Pub'd 25 titles 1979; expects 35 titles 1980, 35 titles 1981. avg. price, cloth: Ksh. 60.00; paper: Ksh. 30.00. Discounts: 20 percent, 25 percent, 30 percent, 35 percent. size A4, A5; lp/of.

EAST EUROPEAN QUARTERLY, Stephen Fischer-Galati, Box 29 Regent Hall, University of Colorado, Boulder, CO 80309, (303) 492-6157. 1967. Articles. "Articles ranging from 8 to 48 printed pages; reviews. All articles dealing with Eastern European problems in historical perspective. Cointributors from US and foreign academic institutions" circ. 800. 4/yr. Pub'd 4 issues 1979; expects 4 issues 1980, 4 issues 1981. sub. price: $12.00/yr; per copy: $3.00; sample: free. Back issues: Same as regular rates. Discounts: Agencies 12.5%; all others 12.5%. 128pp; 5 1/2X8 1/2; of. Reporting time: 6-8 weeks. Payment: none. Not copyrighted. Pub's reviews: 32 in 1979. §East European history, civilization, economics, society, politics. Ads: $100.00/$50.00.

East River Anthology, Jan Barry, W. D. Ehrhart, 75 Gates Ave, Montclair, NJ 07042. 1975. Poetry, fiction, art, photos. "Currently distributing *Demilitarized ZONES: Veterans After Vietnam*, East River Anthology, 1976; 100 contributors, 177pp, $2.95; and *WINNING HEARTS AND MINDS: War Poems by Vietnam Veterans*, 1st Casualty Press (now defunct), 1972; 33 contributors, 108pp, $1.95. Seeking new material; our orientation: anti-war; peace and freedom through non-violent social action. Recent contributors: Philip Appleman, John Balaban, Jan Barry, D.C. Berry, Steven Ford Brown, Michael Casey, Merritt Clifton, Horace Coleman, W.D. Ehrhart, George Knowlton, Gerald McCarthy, Stephen Sossaman, Bruce Weigl and 120 others." avg. press run 5,000. Pub'd 1 title 1979. 2 titles listed in the *Small Press Record of Books in Print* (9th Edition, 1980). avg. price, paper: $2.45. Discounts: Bulk orders of 10 or more: 50% plus shipping; bookstores: 40% plus shipping; jobbers: 20% plus shipping. 5¼X8; of. Reporting time: varies, as soon as possible. Payment: contributors copies, reprint fees. Copyright to East River Anthology, but place no restrictions on future use by individual authors. COSMEP.

EAST RIVER REVIEW, Daniel Stokes, Publisher, Daniel M. J. Stokes, 128 E 4th St, New York, NY 10003. 1974. Poetry, fiction, plays. "No Biases. Recent contributors: William Packard, Amiri Baraka, Doug Blazek, etc., etc.." circ. 500. irreg. Pub'd 2 issues 1979; expects 3 issues 1980, 4 issues 1981. sub. price: $5.00 for 3 issues; per copy: $1.00; sample: $1.00. Discounts: 10 plus 40%. 18-48pp; 5½X8½; of. Reporting time: 2 months. Payment: 2 copies plus $1.00 to $10.00 per poem. Copyrighted, reverts to author. Ads: $100.00/$50.00. CCLM.

The East Woods Press, Sally Hill McMillan, 820 East Boulevard, Charlotte, NC 28203, (704) 334-0897. 1977. "RETURNS POLICY: No permission required. Books must be in saleable condition with no markings or stickers. All returns are credited at maximum discount unless invoice numbers are supplied. Please allow at least three months shelf time before returning books. Please return books to our warehouse: 620 W. Morehead, Charlotte, NC 28208. TERMS: 2% 10, net 30 days. No discount allowed after ten days. FREIGHT: Prepaid in all 50 states on orders of 25+ per ship-to. NEW ACCOUNTS: Prepayment of first order assures promt shipment. For consideration for open account status, please furnish D&B, trade and banking references. STOP: Single Title Order Plan @35%. WHOLESALERS: 50%, 100+books; LIBRARIES & INDIVIDUALS: No discount. OTHER PUBLISHERS: 20% courtesy discount." avg. press run 8,000. Pub'd 10 titles 1979; expects 10 titles 1980, 10 titles 1981. avg. price, cloth: $12.95; paper: $6.95; other: $10.95. Discounts: 1-4, 20%; 5-9, 34%; 10-49, 40%; 50-99, 41%; 100-199, 42%; 200-299, 43%; 300-499, 44%; 500+, 45%; max on library bindings is 20%. 192pp; 5½X8½; of. Reporting time: 2-3 months. Payment: 5-10% retail price, pay 2 times per year. Copyrights for author. ABA, WICI.

Ecart Publications (see also THE GENEVA POND BUBBLES), John M. Armleder, Patrick Lucchini, 6, Rue Plantamour, PO Box 253, Geneva CH -1211-1, Switzerland, 022-32.67.94/022-45.73.95. (1969) 1973. Poetry, art, photos, interviews, music, letters, collages, concrete art. "Fluxus, post fluxus, intermedia, mail-art, rubber-stamp. Recent publications by: Endre Tot, Herve Fischer, Paul-Armand Gette, Dan Graham, Genesis P. Orridge/Coum, Robert Filliou, Tamas Sentjoy, Al Souza, James W. Felter. Planning 2 mags in 1978-79. Recent publications by: Michael Harvey, Lawrence Weiner, Braco Dimitrijevio, Sol Lewitt, Fluxus, Maurizio Nannucci, Ben Vautier, Barry McCallion, Rene Schmid, Taka iimura, Anthony MACCALL." avg. press run 500. Pub'd 10 titles 1979; expects 10 titles 1980, 10 titles 1981. 42 titles listed in the *Small Press Record of Books in Print* (9th Edition, 1980). avg. price, cloth: $5.00-$10.00; paper: $2.50-$8.00; other: $2.50-$8.00. Discounts: trade: 33⅓%, 50% on mass-orders and distribution services. 30/100pp; size din A5-A4; †of. Reporting time: slow. Payment: no standards. copyright to the author, usually. AAP (Assoc. Art Publishers).

The Ecco Press (see also ANTAEUS), Daniel Halpern, Susan Dwyer, 1 West 30th St, New York City, NY 10001, (212) 736-2599. 1971. Poetry, fiction, criticism. avg. press run 4,000. Pub'd 11 titles 1979; expects 8 titles 1980, 10 titles 1981. 41 titles listed in the *Small Press Record of Books in Print* (9th Edition, 1980). avg. price, cloth: $7.95; paper: $4.95. Discounts: Distributed by Viking - their discount schedule. pp varies; size Varies. Reporting time: 1 month. Payment: advance and royalties. Copyrights for author.

ECHOS, Robert W. Thurber, 391 Union Ave #D, Campbell, CA 95008, (408) 377-2505. 1979. Poetry, articles. "Length: 20 lines maximum. No sex poems, poems with four-letter words, intellectual snobbery, (poems that no reader could understand unless he/she were a Rhodes scholar,) no poems of violence or anything 'far-out' as we see it, all of these areas are off-limits with us. We do have a special feeling for Haiku, would like to see much of that. Some recent poets: Laurel Speer, Cassie Edwards, Robert Whisler, James Magorian, Patricia Lieb, Eugene Botelho, Ruth Wildes Schuler. Articles should be historical pertaining to writers of the past. We are new, 1st issue just came out. We hope to grow in the future" circ. 130-150. 4/yr. Pub'd 3 issues 1979; expects 4 issues 1980, 4 issues 1981. sub. price: $6.00; per copy: $1.75; sample: $1.75. Back issues: $1.75. Discounts: none. 52-55pp; 5½X8½; of. Reporting time: 10-12 days. Payment: None at present. $5.00 cash award for best poem of each issue. Copyrighted, reverts to author. Pub's reviews: 1 in 1979. §Poetry. Ads: no advertising carried. none.

ECLIPSE, Jan Figurski, D. J. Paul, 456 Piccadilly Street, London, Ontario N5Y 3G3, Canada, (519) 438-1526. 1979. Poetry, articles, art, interviews, criticism, reviews. "Length usually 1 page at most 2. Regularly features poetry in translation." circ. 150. 3/yr. Pub'd 1 issue 1979; expects 3 issues 1980, 3 issues 1981. sub. price: $4.00; per copy: $1.50; sample: $1.50. 40pp; 6X9; of. Reporting time: 2-6 weeks. Payment: copy. Pub's reviews. §Poetry.

ECO CONTEMPORANEO, Eco Contemporaneo Press, Miguel Grinberg, C C Central 1933, 1000 Buenos Aires, Argentina. 1961. Poetry, articles. "Magazine printed on letterpress/poetry supplements are mimeographed." circ. 1,000. Quarterly. Pub'd 4 issues 1979; expects 4 issues 1980, 8 issues 1981. price per copy: $1.00; sample: Free. Back issues: free. Discounts: None. 24pp; 20 cm x 15 cm; †mi/lp. Reporting time: Immediate. Payment: None. Copyrighted. Pub's reviews. §New consciousness. no ads. APS.

Eco Contemporaneo Press (see also ECO CONTEMPORANEO), Miguel Grinberg, C C Central 1933, 1000 Buenos Aires, Argentina. 1961. Poetry, articles. "Magazine printed on letterpress/poetry supplements are mimeographed." avg. press run 1,000. Pub'd 4 titles 1979; expects 4 titles 1980, 8 titles 1981. avg. price, paper: $1.00. 24pp; size varies; †mi/lp. Reporting time: Immediate. Payment: nothing. Copyrights for author. APS.

ECOSYSTEMS, THE NEW ECOLOGIST, Edward Goldsmith, Editor, 73 Molesworth St., Wadebridge, Cornwall PL27 7DS, United Kingdom, 2996-7. 1978. Articles, photos, criticism, reviews, letters. "Articles up to 6M words on the philosophical, scientific, ideological implications of the post industrial society." circ. 5,000 plus. 4/yr. sub. price: £4.00 (Sterling) ($9.00); per copy: £1.00; sample: free. Discounts: agents 20%. 80pp; size A5; of. Payment: £10.00 per thousand words. Copyrighted, does not revert to author. Pub's reviews: 3 in 1979. §Ecologial philosophy, future planning. Ads: £60.00 ($12.00)/£30.00 ($60.00).

ECW Press (see also ESSAYS ON CANADIAN WRITING), Jack David, Robert Lecker, 357 Stong College, York University, Downsview, ON M3J 1P3, Canada, (416) 667-3055. 1978. Poetry, articles, criticism. "We specialize in books of literary criticism, especially of Canadian writers and issues. We also specialize in bibliographs, including the *Bibliography of Canadian Literature*" avg. press run 1,000. Pub'd 2 titles 1979; expects 7 titles 1980, 10 titles 1981. avg. price, cloth: $15.00; paper: $8.00. Discounts: Varies. 240pp; 6X9; of. Reporting time: 1 month. Payment: 10% paid yearly. Copyrights for author. ACP, CPPA.

Ed-U Press, Inc., Kathleen Ph. D. Everly, Box 583, Fayetteville, NY 13066. 1973. "Books, pamphlets, audio-visual materials in the area of family life education. Primarily distribute to state agencies, libraries, schools, and bookstores." avg. press run 10,000. Pub'd 3 titles 1979. 3 titles listed in the *Small Press Record of Books in Print* (9th Edition, 1980). avg. price, paper: $3.50. Discounts: 20% library; 20-40% bookstores; 40% jobbers. 48pp; 6X9. Copyrights for author.

Edgepress (Evaluation News), Michael Scriven, Box 64, Point Reyes, CA 94956, 415-663-1511. 1975. "Usually only consider articles and book length manuscripts in evaluation of the philosophy of science, practical logic, contemporary moral issues. Check before sending. Will evaluate, also publish in all fields at author's expense." avg. press run 2,000. Pub'd 2 titles 1979; expects 2 titles 1980. avg. price, cloth: $12.50; paper: $8.50. Discounts: trade 25 percent/bulk 20 percent/classroom 25 percent-/agent 35 percent/jobber 35 percent. 300pp; 5½X8½; of. Reporting time: preliminary within a few days. Payment: either straight 15 percent or 25 percent of profits. Copyrights for author. COSMEP.

Edition Stencil (see also C.S.P. WORLD NEWS), Guy F Claude Hamel, Editor, PO Box 2608, Station D, Ottawa, Ontario K1P 5W7, Canada, 741-9220. 1973. Fiction, criticism, long-poems, collages, plays, concrete art. avg. press run 100. Pub'd 5 titles 1979; expects 5 titles 1980, 5 titles 1981. 18 titles listed in the *Small Press Record of Books in Print* (9th Edition, 1980). avg. price, paper: $7.95. Discounts: 10%. 160pp; 8½X11; †mi/lp. Reporting time: by return mail/one month. Payment: negociable. Copyrights for author. COSMEP.

Editorial Creacion (see also CREACION), Cirilo Toro-Vargas, Hector J. Martel-Morales, Apartado 111, Estacion 6, Ponce, PR 00731. 1977. Poetry, fiction, art, criticism. "We prefer not to be submitted. We realize the first contact." avg. press run 1,000. Pub'd 1 title 1979; expects 1 title 1980. 3 titles listed in the *Small Press Record of Books in Print* (9th Edition, 1980). avg. price, paper: $1.00. 50pp; size varies; of. Payment: varies. Does not copyright for author.

Editorial Experts, Inc (see also EDITORIAL EYE), Barbara Hughes, Coordinating Author, 5905 Pratt Street, Alexandria, VA 22310, 971-7350. 1979. "The booklet is a manual for production typists. It includes information on style, consistency, punctuation, corrections, and supplies. Among the sections are ones on corrections for camera-ready copy, statistical material, word processing, and proofreading." avg. press run 200. Pub'd 3 titles 1979. avg. price, paper: $15.00. Discounts: 1-2 copies, $15.00; 3-10 copies, $11.00; 11-24 copies, $8.00; 25 or more, $5.00. 27pp; 8½X11; of. Copyrights for author.

EDITORIAL EYE, Editorial Experts, Inc, Peggy Smith, 5905 Pratt Street, Alexandria, VA 22310. 1978. Articles, reviews. "*The Editorial Eye* focuses on editorial standards and practices. Its purpose is by providing to help its readers produce high quality publications information on content, usage, style and language. We also cover meetings and lectures on editorial subjects as well as list a calendar of such events." circ. 750. 15-20/yr. Pub'd 19 issues 1979; expects 17 issues 1980, 15 issues 1981. sub. price: $45.00 for 20 issues; per copy: $3.00; sample: free. Back issues: $3.00. Discounts: 10% to subscription agencies. 4-8pp; 8½X11; of. Reporting time: do not accept unsolicited mss, articles are assigned. Copyrighted, does not revert to author. Pub's reviews: 4 in 1979. §Editorial matters, style guides, typing production, proofreading, editing. NAGC, IABC, STC, ASBPE, ASI, ASAE.

Editorial Justa Publications, Inc., Herminio Rios, Editor-in-Chief; Rudy Espinoza, Executive Editor,

125

P. O. Box 2131-C, Berkeley, CA 94702, 415 848-3628. 1975. Poetry, fiction, criticism, plays. "Bilingual materials for elementary school." avg. press run 3,000-5,000. Pub'd 5 titles 1979; expects 7 titles 1980, 9 titles 1981. 2 titles listed in the *Small Press Record of Books in Print* (9th Edition, 1980). avg. price, cloth: $7.50; paper: $4.50. Discounts: 25%-40%. 200pp; 5½X8½, 6X9; of. Reporting time: 3 months. Payment: negotiated. Copyrights for author.

Editorial Research Service (see also JOURNAL OF SUPERSTITION AND MAGICAL THINKING), Laird M. Wilcox, P.O.Box 1832, Kansas City, MO 54141, (913) 342-6768. 1978. Articles, interviews, reviews, letters, news items. "Publications include: *Directory of the American Right,* 1980, 2160 listings; *Directory of the American Left* 1980, 1,755 listings; *Directory of the Occult and Paranormal* 1980, 685 listings; *Bibliography on the American Right* 1980, 400 entries; *Bibliography on the American Left* 1980, 400 entries" avg. press run 500. Pub'd 3 titles 1979; expects 8 titles 1980. avg. price, paper: $9.95. Discounts: 10% single copies, 40% 5 or more copies; prepayment required. 32pp; 5½X8½; of.

Editorial Services Co., Jacqueline Thompson, 1140 Avenue of the Americas, New York, NY 10036, (212) 354-5025. 1978. Satire. avg. press run 3,000. avg. price, paper: $17.50. 96pp; 6X9; of.

EDUCATIONAL CONSIDERATIONS, K-State Press, Charles Litz, William Sparkman, College of Education, K.S.U., Manhattan, KS 66506, 913-532-6367. 1973. Articles. "Current issues in educational theory, practice and administration. Also moral issues in education. Creighton Peden Illich's Omnicopetent Individual: A process Perspective." circ. 1,000. 3/yr. sub. price: $4.00; per copy: $1.50; sample: free. Back issues: $2.00 if we have them. Discounts: Fifty cents off $4.00 p.a. subscription for institutions if requested. 28-32pp; 21½cm x 28cm; †of. Reporting time: 4-8 weeks. No payment. Not copyrighted. Pub's reviews: 5 in 1979. §see 11. Ads: no ads.

EDWARDIAN STUDIES, Edwardian Studies Association, Eric Ford, High Orchard, 125 Markyate Road, Dagenham, Essex RM8 2LB, United Kingdom. 1976. Poetry, articles, art, photos, cartoons, interviews, satire, criticism, reviews, music, letters, plays, news items. "Promote interest in Edwardian drama & literature and arts." 1/yr. sub. price: £3; per copy: £3; sample: £3. Discounts: 20%. size A5; of/dupl. Reporting time: 6 months. Payment: copies. Copyrighted. Pub's reviews. Ads: £15/pro rata (new journal check rates, please).

Edwardian Studies Association (see EDWARDIAN STUDIES)

EFRYDIAU ATHRONYDDOL, University Of Wales Press, T.A. Roberts, Professor, 6 Gwennyth St., Cathays, Cardiff, Wales, United Kingdom, Cardiff 31919. Articles. "Philosphical material." circ. 100. 1/yr. Pub'd 1 issue 1979; expects 1 issue 1980, 1 issue 1981. sub. price: £1.00; per copy: £1.00; sample: £1.00. Back issues: 50p up to Vol 41. Discounts: trade 33⅓%. 80pp; 9½X6; lp. Payment: none. Copyrighted, does not revert to author. Pub's reviews: 1 in 1979. §philosphical.

Eggplant Press, Pat Wagner, Chocolate Waters, directors, P.O. Box 18641, Denver, CO 80218, 303 841-1442. 1975. Poetry, fiction, art, photos. "We work with groups and individuals, particularly women, who wish to publish themselves. No submissions, but glad to assist folks in Colorado with their projects. Books include: *Bones, Seeds, Dragons (1978), Take Me Like a Photograph, Charting New Waters* and postcard series. Authors include: Pat Wagner, Chocolate Waters, Terra, etc. Send self-addressed stamped envelope for catalog and information." avg. press run 500-4000. Pub'd 1 title 1979; expects 6 titles 1980, 4 titles 1981. 2 titles listed in the *Small Press Record of Books in Print* (9th Edition, 1980). avg. price, paper: $2.00 - $5.50. Discounts: 40% prepaid on orders of 5 or more; 30% consignment on orders of 5 or more; 50% distributors - orders of 25 or more; All 12% for postage. 36 to 96pp; 5X8; of. no submissions. Payment: Separate for each author. Copyrights for author. COSMEP.

Eight Miles High Press (see also LUDD'S MILL), Andrew Darlington, 44 Spa Croft Road, Teall Street, Ossett, W. Yorks WF5 0HE, United Kingdom. 1971.

Either/Or Publications (see ALPHA)

†ELAN POETIQUE LITTERAIRE ET PACIFISTE, Louis Lippens, 31 Rue Foch, Linselles 59126, France, (20)78.30.68. 1955. "Poesie et temoignages au service du pacifisme integral, de la non-violence active et de l'objection de conscience permanente." circ. 2,000 exemplaires. trimestriel. 2 titles listed in the *Small Press Record of Books in Print* (9th Edition, 1980). sub. price: abonnement annuel: 20 francs (soit 4 dollars environ); sample: specimen gratuit. 12pp; of. Not copyrighted. §Pacifisme. APS.

Electronic Music Enterprises (see also XENHARMONIC BULLETIN), Ivor Darreg, 349 1/2 W. California Ave, Glendale, CA 91203, (213) 243-3477. 1966. Articles, interviews, reviews, music, letters. avg. press run 100. Pub'd 1 title 1979. 4 titles listed in the *Small Press Record of Books in Print* (9th Edition, 1980). avg. price, paper: $2.00. 25pp; 8½X11; of. Reporting time: 6 weeks.

EL FUEGO DE AZTLAN, Oscar Trevino, Maria Orozco, 3408 Dwinelle Hall, Univ of Calif, Berkeley, CA 94720. 1976. "Short stories no longer than 7 typewritten pages; Poems should reflect the Chicano experience in US, if not by Chicano poets/writers." 4/yr. 2 titles listed in the *Small Press Record of Books in Print* (9th Edition, 1980). sub. price: $3.50 indiv.; per copy: $8.00 instit.; sample: varies. Discounts: none. pp varies; size varies. Reporting time: 4-6 weeks. Payment: contributor's copies. Not copyrighted. Pub's reviews. §Chicano and Ethnic Studies, art, lit, etc.

The Elizabeth Press, James L Weil, Editor & Publisher; Carroll Arnett, Associate Editor; Simon Perchik, Associate Editor, 103 Van Etten Blvd, New Rochelle, NY 10804. 1961. Poetry. "Mss. by solicitation only." avg. press run 400. Pub'd 6 titles 1979; expects 6 titles 1980, 5 titles 1981. avg. price, cloth: $16.00; paper: $8.00. Discounts: Trade only: single, 10%; 2-4 assorted titles, 20%; 5-assorted, 40%. No consignment, no returns. 64pp; 6X9; lp. Reporting time: 4 weeks. Payment: private. Copyrights for author.

Ellen's Old Alchemical Press (see also HARD PRESSED), Ellen Rosser, Editor; Ronald Alexander, Jim Normington, Contributing editors, P.O. Box 161915, Sacramento, CA 95816, 916-455-9984. 1975. Poetry, art. "Linoleum block or wood block art work. Each poem on a separate page suitable for display." avg. press run 500. Pub'd 2 titles 1979. avg. price, paper: $2.00. Discounts: 40%. 24pp; 8½X11; †lp. Reporting time: 4 weeks. Payment: 2 copies. Copyrights for author. COSMEP.

Elpenor Books, Djordje Nikolic, Editor; Mary Kinzie, Poetry Editor; Donna Mills, Associate Editor, P O Box 3152, Merchandise Mart Plaza, Chicago, IL 60654, (312) 935-1343. 1974. Poetry. avg. press run 300. Pub'd 1 title 1979; expects 3 titles 1980, 3 titles 1981. avg. price, cloth: $7.95; paper: $3.00. Discounts: 10-40%. 64pp; 6X9; of. Reporting time: 6 weeks. Payment: 12 percent of press run. Copyrights for author.

ELVIS THE RECORD, Wimmer Brothers Books, Billy Smith, Marty Lacker, Bill Davis, Janine Buford, PO Box 18408, Memphis, TN 38118, (901) 362-8906. 1979. Interviews, news items. "Magazine centered around personal rememberances of Elvis Presley by those close to him. Stories about Elvis from the 1950's, 60's, and 70's by Billy Smith, his first cousin, Marty Lacker, best man at Elvis' wedding and Bill Davis, another close friend. Stories for reader response. A magazine for the true Elvis fan." circ. 5,000. 9/yr. Pub'd 7 issues 1979. sub. price: $19.00; per copy: $3.00; sample: $3.00. Back issues: 1 for $3.00, 2 for $5.50, 3 for $8.00, 4 for $10.00. Discounts: 25 to 99 copies, 40%; 100-199 copies, 50%; 200-499 copies, 55%; 500 or more, 60%. 28pp; 8½X11; of. Reporting time: staff written. Payment: gratis. Copyrighted. Pub's reviews. §Books about Elvis Presley. Ads: $515.-25/$174.50/$1.00 (10 words minimum).

Embee Press, Mark Baczynsky, 82 Pine Grove Avenue, Kingston, NY 12401, (914) 338-2226. 1977. "Photocrafts guides deal with antique camera restorations, also adaptation of various vintage photographic apparatus to modern equipment. Basically these publications are *how-to* materials which will be gradually compiled into *Photocrafts Book of Guides* (publication date: December 1978). All material is written and edited by Mark Baczynsky. *Photocrafts Book of Guides,* $29.95" avg. press run 1,000. Pub'd 7 titles 1979; expects 14 titles 1980, 16 titles 1981. 1 title listed in the *Small Press Record of Books in Print* (9th Edition, 1980). avg. price, paper: $3.50; other: $29.95. Discounts: 40%. 32pp; 5X7; †of.

Embers Publications, c/o Maude Meehan, 2150 Portola Drive, Santa Cruz, CA 95062, 408-476-6164. 1975. Poetry, fiction, long-poems. "Anthologies of Santa Cruz women poets *published bi-yearly.*" avg. press run 1,000. Pub'd 1 title 1979. avg. price, paper: $3.00; other: $3.50 for coming anthology. 120pp; 5½X8¾; of. Payment: we are a collective and use money from books to publish future issues. Copyrights for author.

Emerald City Press (see YELLOW BRICK ROAD)

EMERGENCY LIBRARIAN, Carol-Ann Haycock, Ken Haycock, PO Box 46258, Station G, Vancouver VGR 460, Canada, 487-8365. 1973. Articles, art, criticism, reviews, letters, news items. "About 1,200 words with emphasis on service to children and young adults." circ. 1600. 6/yr. Pub'd 6 issues 1979. sub. price: $15.00; per copy: $3.00; sample: $2.00. Back issues: $3.00. Discounts: none. 24pp; 8½X11; of. Reporting time: 1 month. Payment: $25.00/article. Copyrighted, does not revert to author. Pub's reviews: 72 in 1979. §Professional materials for librarians, magazines for young people, books for liberated kids, new paperbacks for children, new paperbacks for young adults. Ads: $150/$80. CPPA.

EMPIRE: For the SF Writer, Mark J. McGarry, Editor & Publisher, Box 967, New Haven, CT 06511, 777-6952. 1974. Articles, art, cartoons, interviews, criticism, reviews, letters, news items.

"*Empire* SF is geared towards helping the SF writer however possible. We publish market reports, profiles of younger writers, first-person accounts... the litmus test is: would this piece help someone to become a better writer? We have no length limits, though we rarely receive anything longer than 5,000 words. Recent contributors (from 1/78 through 6/80) include Gene Wolfe, George R.R. Martin, Ben Bova, Pamela Sargent, Steve Goldin, Diane Duane, Ed Bryant, Barry Longyear, Barry Malzberg, Orson Scott Card, Charles Sheffield, Steve Spruill, Robert Silverberg, and Samuel R. Delany." circ. 500. 4/yr. Pub'd 4 issues 1979; expects 4 issues 1980, 4 issues 1981. sub. price: $6.00; per copy: $1.50; sample: $1.50. Back issues: $2.00 apiece or 3 for $5.00. Discounts: 40% to bookstores, bulk purchasers. 24pp; 8½X11; of. Reporting time: 2 to 4 weeks. Payment: one-year subscription & 2 extra copies of issue in which article appears. Copyrighted, reverts to author. Pub's reviews: 3 in 1979. §Science & technology for layfolk, SF, new authors, how-to books on writing. Ads: $40.-00/$25.00.

EN PASSANT/POETRY, James A. Costello, 1906 Brant Rd, Wilmington, DE 19810. 1975. Poetry, art, reviews. "Poetry, including translations; poetry book reviews; artwork. All submissions are carefully and promptly considered and comments are offered where they might be of help. The artwork is selected with the same care and attention as the poetry. Book reviews must be well-conceived, well-reasoned, and well-written" circ. 500. 2/yr. Pub'd 2 issues 1979; expects 2 issues 1980, 2 issues 1981. sub. price: $6.00, 4 issue; per copy: $1.75; sample: $1.50. 40pp; 5½X8½; of. Reporting time: 1 to 3 weeks. Payment: 2 copies, book reviews are paid for at the rate of $10.00 per printed page. takes first rights, shares remaining rights with author. §Books of poetry especially those published by small presses/Query first. Ads: none.

‡ENCRES VIVES, Castillon 09800, France.

Endurance, Rory Donaldson, Box 2382, Santa Barbara, CA 93120, (805) 962-2034. 1978. Interviews, criticism, news items. "Manuals focusing on specific areas of fitness, health, exercise: *Gentle Jogging* ; *Exercise and Heart Disease; Jogging Through Pregnancy; Don't Exercise;* more - average length 20 pages." avg. press run 5,000. Pub'd 2 titles 1979; expects 6 titles 1980. 8 titles listed in the *Small Press Record of Books in Print* (9th Edition, 1980). avg. price, paper: $2.95. 20pp; 5½X8½; of. Reporting time: open. Payment: 5-15%. Copyrights for author.

Energy Earth Communications, Inc. (see also HOO-DOO BlackSeries; IN ORBIT: A Journal of Earth Literature; SYNERGY), A. Zu-Bolton, J. Ward, H. Mullen, R.X. Nelson, PO Box 1141, Galveston, TX 77553. 1973. Poetry, fiction, articles, interviews, criticism, reviews. avg. press run 1,300. Pub'd 2 titles 1979; expects 5 titles 1980. 8 titles listed in the *Small Press Record of Books in Print* (9th Edition, 1980). avg. price, paper: $3.00. Discounts: 40% bookstores. size varies; of.

ENERGY EFFICIENT HOMES, Natural Dynamics, Inc., Wendy Priesnitz, Box 640, Jarvis, Ontario N0A 1J0, Canada. 1980. Articles, art, photos, cartoons, interviews, letters. "Renewable energy technologies with direct application to personal housing; inspirational, how-to." circ. 5,000. 4/yr. sub. price: $10.00; per copy: $2.50. Discounts: over 5 copies, 40% plus shipping. 86pp; 7X10.

Energy Publishing Company, Franklin Attkisson, 1412 Ave H S W, Winter Haven, FL 33880, 813-293-2576. 1977. Articles, art. avg. press run 1,000. 1 title listed in the *Small Press Record of Books in Print* (9th Edition, 1980). avg. price, cloth: $5.95; paper: $5.95. Discounts: 40%. 124pp; 8½X11; of. Reporting time: 2 weeks. Copyrights for author.

Engendra Press Ltd., Ronald Rosenthall, Box 235, Westmount Station, Montreal, Quebec H3Z 2T2, Canada, 514 933-1282. 1975. Poetry, fiction, satire, criticism, parts-of-novels, plays. "It should be noted that we are a small press (proceeding one volume at a time) that does 'big press' books. Our area of specialization is the translation into English of important modern European writing. Ideas for books tend to originate in house; we will not consider unsolicited manuscripts. Given the costs of purchasing English-language rights from foreign publishers, translators/editors are rarely remunerated unless special funds are made available for the purpose by some outside body. Indeed, the point has been reached where publication of a book has become financially impracticable unless the translator/editor (invariably an academic) can obtain a grant from his or her university, or again, if sufficient funds are made available by some other establishment or agency." avg. press run 1,500 - 2,000 copies. Pub'd 2 titles 1979. 5 titles listed in the *Small Press Record of Books in Print* (9th Edition, 1980). avg. price, cloth: $14.50. Discounts: Trade and wholesalers' discounts on request; institutional discount, 10 percent; discount to individuals, nil. 230pp; size varies; of. Reporting time: queries answered within 3 weeks. Copyrights for author.

ENGLISH DANCE AND SONG, Dave Arthur, Cecil Sharp House, 2 Regents Park Rd, London NW1 7AY, United Kingdom. 1936. Articles, cartoons, photos, criticism, music, letters, reviews. circ. 12,000. 3/yr. Pub'd 3 issues 1979; expects 3 issues 1980, 3 issues 1981. sub. price: £5.50; per copy: 40p. Back issues: 40p. Discounts: agency 10%. 40pp; size A4; of. Payment: £5 per printed page. Copyrighted. Pub's reviews: 50 in 1979. §English folk music, dance, or customs. Ads: £60.00/£35.00/5p.

English Language Literature Association (see LINQ)

ENGLISH STUDIES IN AFRICA-A Journal of the Humanities, Witwatersrand University Press, Professor B.D. Cheadle, Witwatersrand University Press, 1 Jan Smuts Ave., Johannesburg 2001, South Africa, (011) 39-4011 Ext. 794. 1958. Criticism, reviews. circ. 500. 2/yr. sub. price: R. 6.00 (indiv), R 9.00 (instit); per copy: R. 4.00; sample: free. Back issues: available on request. Discounts: 10% discount for agents. 56pp; 19.5X13 cm; lp. Reporting time: 3 months. §African & South African literature only. Ads: R. 25/R. 15.

Enitharmon Press, Alan Clodd, 22 Huntingdon Rd, East Finchley, London N2 9DU, United Kingdom, 01 883 8764. 1969. Poetry, criticism. avg. press run 400. Pub'd 8 titles 1979. 27 titles listed in the *Small Press Record of Books in Print* (9th Edition, 1980). avg. price, cloth: £3.50; paper: £2.00; other: £7.50 signed, numbered issue. Discounts: 33% on wrapped and hardbound issues, 25% on signed, numbered. 8V0; lp/of. Reporting time: 2 mos. Payment: royalty.

Entwhistle Books, Paul Williams, Editor, Box 611, Glen Ellen, CA 95442. 1968. Fiction, articles, letters. "Prefer queries to manuscripts; include postage with manuscripts. Current and forthcoming books include essays, novels, journals and uncategorizable material; authors include Philip K. Dick, Chester Anderson, Laura Kwong, John Valentine, and Paul Williams. Poorly capitalized and under-staffed, we publish books we love by authors we like, and then only if we believe we can market the book effectively." avg. press run 500 to 10,000. Pub'd 1 title 1979; expects 2 titles 1980, 4 titles 1981. 10 titles listed in the *Small Press Record of Books in Print* (9th Edition, 1980). avg. price, cloth: $9.95; paper: $5.95. Discounts: Single copies 20%, 5 or more 40%, most titles available through Bookpeople. 50-300pp; 5½X8½; of. Reporting time: 2 months. Payment: Share profits or 7.5/10% royalties. Copyrights for author.

ENVOI, J.C. Meredith Scott, Lagan Nam Bann, Ballachulish, Argyll, Scotland, United Kingdom. 1956. Poetry, reviews. "ENVOI indicates: poetry, brief, traditional not barred. Non-political and not noticeably erotic." 3/yr. sub. price: £1; per copy: 33p. 22pp; 6X8. Payment: by arrangement.

L'Epervier Press, Bob McNamara, Bridget McNamara, 762 Hayes #15, Seattle, WA 98109. 1977. Poetry. "Full length books only. Books by: Paul Nelson, Lynn Strongin, Pamela Stewart, Jack Myers, Bob Herz, Michael Burkard, Christopher Howell, Carolyn Maisel, Robert Morgan, Bruce Renner, Sam Pereira, Robert Lietz, Paul Jenkins, David Lenson, Barry Seiler, Mary Burritt, Bill Nelson." avg. press run 500. Pub'd 9 titles 1979; expects 10 titles 1980, 10 titles 1981. 19 titles listed in the *Small Press Record of Books in Print* (9th Edition, 1980). avg. price, cloth: $6.95; paper: $3.75. Discounts: Distributed by SBD: Small Press Distribution. 64pp; 5½X8½; of. Reporting time: Varies. We try for 2-3 months. Unsolicited mss.: up to 6 months. Must send query first. Payment: copies (10% of press run). Copyrights for author.

Epic, Peter Fraterdeus, 1024 Judson Avenue, Evanston, IL 60202, (312) 475-8517. 1979. Poetry, art. "We anticipate a format which integrates calligraphic design and original pen-writing which varied letterpress typographies. Hoping to include silkscreen, offset, etching, etc. in multi-media original broadsides and small edition bound work." avg. press run 200. Pub'd 1 title 1979. †of/lp. EFPC.

EPOCH, C.S. Giscombe, Managing Editor; James McConkey, Editor; Walter Slatoff, Editor, 245 Goldwin Smith Hall, Cornell Univ., Ithaca, NY 14853, (607) 256-3385. 1947. Poetry, fiction, reviews. "We are interested in the work of both new and established writers." circ. 1,000. 3/yr. Pub'd 3 issues 1979; expects 3 issues 1980, 3 issues 1981. sub. price: $5.00; per copy: $2.00; sample: $2.00. Back issues: $2.00. Discounts: 40% dealers, bookstores, etc. 100pp; 6X9; of. Reporting time: 2 months. Payment: copies. Copyrighted, does not revert to author. Pub's reviews: 2 in 1979. §Fiction, poetry, biography, autobiogrphy, essays. Ads: $150/$80. CCLM.

EPoCH, William Gummer, 2a Lebanon Rd, Croydon, Surrey CR0 6UR, United Kingdom. 1972. "All material relating to environmental health. Environmental health." 4/yr. Pub'd 4 issues 1979. sub. price: £5.00; sample: free. Back issues: at published price/inquire. 28pp; lp. Payment: yes. Copyrighted, does not revert to author. Pub's reviews. §Environmental health. Ads: inquire.

Equal Time Press, Hugh Seidman, Frances Whyatt, 463 West St. Apt H 960, New York, NY 10014. 1972. "Our only publication to date is *Equal Time,* an anthology of poetry. It is still available." 1 title listed in the *Small Press Record of Books in Print* (9th Edition, 1980). NESPA.

Erin Hills Publishers, Dean Trembly, 1390 Fairway Dr, San Luis Obispo, CA 93401, (805) 543-3050. 1974. avg. press run 10,000. 1 title listed in the *Small Press Record of Books in Print* (9th Edition, 1980).

avg. price, cloth: $5.95; paper: $3.95. Discounts: 30%. 128pp; 5½X8½; of.

Erewon Press, Peter Hjersman, P.O. Box 4253, Berkeley, CA 94704. 1975. Poetry, concrete art, non-fiction. avg. press run 1,000-5,000. Pub'd 2 titles 1979. 2 titles listed in the *Small Press Record of Books in Print* (9th Edition, 1980). avg. price, cloth: $5.00-$10.00; paper: $1.00 - $7.50. Discounts: retail through publisher; distributors 50 percent. 8-300pp; 8½X11; †of/lp. nothing sought at this time. Payment: as appropriate. Copyrights for author. WIP.

ESE California (see ACADEMY AWARDS OSCAR ANNUAL)

ESSAYS ON CANADIAN WRITING, ECW Press, Jack David, Robert Lecker, 357 Stong College, York University, Downsview, ON M3J1P3, Canada, (416) 667-3055. 1974. Articles, art, photos, interviews, criticism, reviews, letters. "We prefer intelligent, well-written criticism of Canadian writing from any period or genre. We lean towards formalist criticism, and specialize in bibliographies, small press reviews, and French-Canadian literature. Recent contributors: Margaret Atwood, Doug Jones, Stephen Scobie" circ. 1,300. 4/yr. Pub'd 4 issues 1979; expects 4 issues 1980, 4 issues 1981. sub. price: $18.00 Libraries, $9.00 Indiv.; per copy: $3.00; sample: $3.00. Back issues: $5.00. Discounts: 40% trade. 250pp; 5X7½; of. Reporting time: 1 month. Payment: Depends on need. Copyrighted, reverts to author. Pub's reviews: 50 in 1979. §Canadian writing or criticism. Ads: $200.00/$110.00. CPPA.

ETC Publications, Richard W. Hostrop Dr., P.O. Drawer 1627-A, Palm Springs, CA 92263, 714-325-5352. 1972. "Considers timely topics in all non-fiction areas." avg. press run 3,500. Pub'd 12 titles 1979; expects 15 titles 1980. avg. price, cloth: $10.00; paper: $7.00. Discounts: usual trade. 256pp; 6X9; of. Reporting time: 4 weeks. Payment: standard book royalties. Copyrights for author. COSMEP.

THE ETHNODISC JOURNAL OF RECORDED SOUND, Pachart Publishing House, Dr. J.M. Pacholczyk, Box 35549, Tucson, AZ 85740, (602) 297-4797. 1973. Music. "Original recordings of music of various cultures accompanied by historical, critical and analytical notes and by song texts & their English translations." Pub'd 10 issues 1979. sub. price: $50.00 (five vols cassettes); per copy: $12.50. Discounts: 20% prepaid, us invoiceing (Agents). Copyrighted.

Eurail Guide Annual, 27540 Pacific Coast, Malibu, CA 90265, (213) 457-7286. 1971. "Annually revised travel book, co-authors: Marvin L. Saltzman andKathryn Saltzman Muileman" Pub'd 1 title 1979; expects 1 title 1980, 1 title 1981. avg. price, paper: $9.95. Discounts: available for bookstores and jobbers, write for rates. 816pp; of.

EURAIL GUIDE ANNUAL, 27540 Pacific Coast Hwy, Malibu, CA 90265. 1 title listed in the *Small Press Record of Books in Print* (9th Edition, 1980).

EUREKA REVIEW, Orion Press, Roger Ladd Memmott, 90 Harrison Avenue, New Canaan, CT 06840. 1975. Poetry, fiction, articles, art, photos, reviews, parts-of-novels. "*Eureka Review* is published by Orion Press, an independent organization devoted to furthering the literary arts. The magazine publishes fiction primarily, some poetry, artwork, photographs, articles, and reviews. It is receptive to both established as well as previously unpublished and relatively unknown writers of worth. Editorial policy is eclectic. Although word count alone will never be responsible for a manuscript's rejection, stories beyond 7,500 words may run into problems of space. Material must be well-written, honest, and 'literarily sound,' whether conventional or avant-garde. The best literature achieves a balance of content and form. *No* sentimentality, academicism, or work with a cheap metaphysical slant. Recent contributors: Raymond Carver, Raymond Federman, Richard Kostelanetz, Leonard Michaels, Lyn Lifshin, James Bertolino, Greg Kuzma, Ron Silliman." circ. 1,000. 2-3/yr. Pub'd 1 issue 1979; expects 1 issue 1980, 2 issues 1981. sub. price: $7.00/4 issues; per copy: $2.00; sample: $1.50. Back issues: $2.00. Discounts: 25-50%. 112pp; 5½X8½; of. Reporting time: 1-6 weeks. Payment: 2-3 copies. Rights revert to author on request. Pub's reviews: 2 in 1979. §fiction & poetry. Ads: $40/$20. CCLM, COSMEP, OAC.

EUTERPE, The New York Literary Press, Stephen H. Martin, Kira Laura Ferrand, John Bashian, Margaret Leong, 419 W. 56th Street, New York, NY 10019. 1977. Poetry, fiction, articles, art, photos, interviews, criticism, reviews, parts-of-novels, plays. "No bias, except that a longer poem must sustain the line-for-line intensity of a small one. Contributors: Barbara Holland, Barry Wallenstein, Steven Cohen, Daniel Gabriel, Richard Royal, John Burrows, Scott Ellis." circ. 500. 2/yr. Pub'd 2 issues 1979. sub. price: No subscriptions; per copy: $2.00; sample: $1.50. 64pp; 5½X8; of. Reporting time: 3 months (must include SASE). Payment: 1 copy. Copyrighted, reverts to author. Ads: no ads.

Evaluation News (see Edgepress)

Evans Publications, Robert L. Evans, 133 S. Main, P.O.Box 520, Perkins, OK 74059, (405) 547-2882. 1969. "Up until recently have been publishers of specialized monthly tab newspapers, such as *Horse Country, Motor Sports Forum,* etc., to local and area readership/ Are now entering the book publishing field with one historical, *Cimarron Family Legends,* one reprint, *Pistol Pete — Veteran of the Old West,* a second reprint, *Formulas and Recipes, Methods and Secret P rocesses,* readt for the press; work underway on a Micro-Wave Cooking and Recipe book; working on a manuscript relating to a historical novel. We are looking for a half-dozen to ten good manuscripts a year relating to'How To' subjects, historical fiction, nostalgia, biography, rural and small town fiction, etc. We are small so might suggest submitting a query to see if we're interested. Manuscripts are permissable if desired, with SASE for return. We would not consider anything less than 150 pages." avg. press run 1,000-5,000. Expects 1 title 1980, 5 titles 1981. avg. price, cloth: $14.95; paper: $8.95. Discounts: 30% to 40% off list or cover price. 300pp; of. Reporting time: 30-60 days. Payment: we will pay royalty or purchase all rights. Does not copyright for author.

THE EVENER, Elizabeth Jones, Putney, VT 05346, (802) 387-4243. 1976. Poetry, fiction, articles, art, photos, cartoons, interviews, reviews, letters, news items. circ. 9,000. 6/yr. Pub'd 11 issues 1979; expects 6 issues 1980, 6 issues 1981. sub. price: $8.50; per copy: $2.00; sample: $2.00. Back issues: $2.00. Discounts: none. 54pp; 10X7; of. Reporting time: one month. Payment: $25.00. Copyrighted, does not revert to author. Pub's reviews: 10 in 1979. §farming, logging, working with draft animals. Ads: $250/$150/35¢/word. COSMEP.

EVENT, John Levin, Douglas College, P.O. Box 2503, New Westminster, B.C. V3L5B2, Canada. 1970. Poetry, fiction, articles, art, photos, reviews, parts-of-novels, long-poems, plays, interviews. "George Woodcock, Bill T. O'Brien, Charles Bukowski, Alden Nowlan, Pat Lowther, Gordon Pinsent, Harvey Shapiro, Cynthia Ozick, George Bowering, John Newlove, Earle Birney." circ. 700. Bi-annual Spring, Winter. Pub'd 2 issues 1979; expects 2 issues 1980, 2 issues 1981. sub. price: $5.00, $9.00/2 yrs; per copy: $2.50; sample: $2.50. Back issues: $2.50. Discounts: 20%. 180pp; 6X9; of. Reporting time: 4 months. Payment: $5.00-$30.00. Pub's reviews. §Poetry, fiction, photography, drama. Ads: $100/$50. COSMEP, CPPA.

Everyman (see also Deciduous), 1456 West 54th Street, Cleveland, OH 44102.

EXCHANGE: A Journal of Opinion for the Ferforming Arts, David L. Jorns, 129 Fine Arts Center, Missouri University, Columbia, MO 65211, (314) 882-2021. 1975. "*Exchange* is a journal designed to give the author an opportunity for expression free of editorial flat. Creative work, notes, letters, reviews, comment or criticism concerning any of the performing arts are acceptable." 3/yr. Pub'd 3 issues 1979; expects 2 issues 1980, 2 issues 1981. price per copy: $1.00; sample: $1.00. Back issues: $1.00. 70pp; 8½X11. Reporting time: 90 days. Copyrighted. Pub's reviews: 1 in 1979. §Dramatic arts. COSMEP.

EXILE, Exile Editions Ltd, Barry Callaghan, Box 546, Downsview, Ontario, Canada, 416-9679391/6673892. 1972. Poetry, fiction, art, photos, parts-of-novels, long-poems, collages, plays, concrete art. "Any length — Seamus Heaney, Ted Hughes, Marie-Claire Blais, John Montague, numerous Canadians, Joyce Carol Oates, Jerzy Kosinski, etc." circ. 1200-1800. 4/yr. Pub'd 4 issues 1979; expects 4 issues 1980, 4 issues 1981. sub. price: $10/yr; per copy: $3. Back issues: Vol. 1 No. 1 — $10.00; Vol. 1 No. 2 — $6.00; Vol. 1 No. 3 — $5.00; all others except double issues, $2.00. Discounts: none. 140pp; of. Reporting time: 3 weeks to a month. Payment: varies. Copyrighted, reverts to author. no ads.

Exile Editions Ltd (see also EXILE), Barry Callaghan, 20 Dale Ave, Toronto, Canada, 416-667-3892. 1976. "Novels, poetry, memoirs, special editions, fine quality, signed limited, drawings, engravings, musical scores, plays. Don't read submissions." avg. press run 750-1000. Pub'd 4 titles 1979; expects 12 titles 1980. avg. price, cloth: $6.00 - $90.00; paper: $6.95; other: $25.00. pp varies; size varies. Payment: standard. Copyrights for author.

EXIT, Rochester Routes/Creative Arts Projects, Robert Johnson, Frank Judge, Stanley Duke, Gregory FitzGerald, 50 Inglewood Dr, Rochester, NY 14619. 1976. Poetry, fiction, art, photos, interviews. "*Exit* publishes poetry, fiction, translations, interviews, and art work. We are interested primarily in *quality* and prefer shorter pieces. Past numbers have included Feldman, Rimanelli, FitzGerald, Cimatti, Bonazzi, Lifshin, Rastaman, Nepo, Salzmann, Williams. Please *furnish brief biobibliographical blurb* for use with accepted material." circ. 600. 3/yr. Pub'd 3 issues 1979. sub. price: $7.00/3 issues; per copy: $2.00. Back issues: $2.50. 48pp; 5½X8½; of/xerox. Reporting time: 2 months. Payment: 3 copies. Copyrighted, reverts to author. Ads: $30.00. COSMEP.

Expanded Media Editions (see also SOFT NEED), Pociao, Herwarthstr. 27, Bonn 5300, W-Germany, 02221/655 887. 1969. Poetry, fiction, art, photos, interviews, criticism, music, collages. "Recent contributors: W. S. Burroughs, Jurgen Ploog, Claude Pelieu-Washburn, Allen Ginsberg, Gerard Malanga." avg. press run 2,000. Pub'd 3 titles 1979; expects 2 titles 1980, 4 titles 1981. 13 titles listed in the *Small Press Record of Books in Print* (9th Edition, 1980). avg. price, paper: DM 10.-. Discounts: 1 to 5 copies, 25%; 6 to 20 copies, 30%; 21 to 50 copies, 40%; more than 50 copies, 50%. 100pp; 21X14; lp. Payment: 10% per sold book. Copyrights for author.

EXPANDING HORIZONS, Sylvia Baron, 93-05 68th Avenue, Forest Hills, NY 11375, (212) LI4-9807. 1977. Poetry, fiction, articles, art, satire, reviews. "Recent contributors: Jim Walker, Margaret Cusick, Sylvia Baron, Alice Peden, Lee Walker, Alice Corman. Written by older people for all people. (Try to limit to 1,000 words for articles and fiction)." circ. 1,000-2,000. 4/yr. Pub'd 4 issues 1979. sub. price: $4.00; per copy: $1.00; sample: $1.00. 32pp; 8½X11; of. Reporting time: 2 weeks to 1 month. Payment: In copies. Copyrighted, reverts to author. Pub's reviews: 3 in 1979. §Anything hopeful of interest to active older people. Ads: $100 - issue/$60 - issue.

Expedition Press, Bruce White, 420 Davis, Kalamazoo, MI 49007. 1978. Poetry. "Chapbooks" avg. press run 200. Pub'd 2 titles 1979; expects 3 titles 1980. 4 titles listed in the *Small Press Record of Books in Print* (9th Edition, 1980). avg. price, paper: $2.00. 20-30pp; 5½X8½; of. Reporting time: one month. Payment: open. Copyrights for author.

Exponent Ltd., Jack R. Lander, 2243 First Street, La Verne, CA 91750, (714) 595-3418. 1977. "Books only; 'how-to' only; especially those dealing with self help in career & health." avg. press run 3,000. Pub'd 3 titles 1979; expects 1 title 1980. 1 title listed in the *Small Press Record of Books in Print* (9th Edition, 1980). avg. price, paper: $4.00; other: $12.00 cassette. 100pp; 8½X11; of. Reporting time: 2 weeks. Payment: conventional or better. Copyrights for author. COSMEP.

EXPRESSION, Ontario Library Association, Lawrence A. Moore, 73 Richmond Street, W., Suite 402, Toronto, Ontario M5H 1Z4, Canada, 416-762-7232. 1976. Articles, photos, interviews. circ. 2,500. 2/yr. Expects 2 issues 1980. sub. price: $5.00; per copy: $3.00; sample: free. Back issues: as above. Discounts: agent, jobber 20 percent. 48pp; 8½X11; of. Payment: none. Copyrighted, reverts to author. Ads: $150.00/$80.00.

F

FAG RAG, Fag Rag Collective, Box 331, Kenmore Station, Boston, MA 02215, 617-426-4469. 1970. Poetry, fiction, articles, art, photos, cartoons, interviews, satire, criticism, reviews, music, letters, parts-of-novels, long-poems, collages, plays, concrete art. "prefer short contributions; need new b & w art always" circ. 5,000. 4/yr. Pub'd 4 issues 1979; expects 4 issues 1980, 4 issues 1981. 6 titles listed in the *Small Press Record of Books in Print* (9th Edition, 1980). sub. price: $8.00 8 issues; per copy: $1.99; sample: $2.50. Back issues: $2.00. Discounts: $1.50 retail; 40 percent disc. to retailers, 50 percent to distributors. 32pp tabloidpp; 11X17; of. Reporting time: max. 3 months. Payment: copies. Copyrighted, reverts to author. §politics, gay lit., poetry, essays, culture. no ads. CCLM, COSMEP, NESPA.

FAIRFAX FOLIO, Marc Steven Dworkin, Editor; Mark Henke, Assoc. Editor, 3039 Shasta Circle South, Los Angeles, CA 90065. 1979. Poetry. "We are open to all forms and styles of poetry. Having grown out of a grass roots beginning, we encourage the unpublished as well as the more experienced poet to submit work. The unpretentious poem that goes beyond an imitation of structure or rhythm is something we seek after. Please keep poems to a maximum of thirty lines." circ. 250. 2/yr. Pub'd 1 issue 1979. sub. price: $4.00; per copy: $2.00; sample: $1.50. 20pp; 5½X8½; of. Reporting time: 1 month. Payment: copies. Copyrighted, reverts to author.

Falconiforme Press Ltd., Box 4047, Saskatoon, Saskatchewan S7K3T1, Canada. 1974. Fiction, art, photos. "Books on Falconry and Birds of Prey." avg. press run 1000. Pub'd 2 titles 1979; expects 2 titles 1980. avg. price, cloth: $15.00; paper: $2.25. Discounts: trade 40%, library 15-25%, agent 50%. 300pp; 5½X7½; of. Copyrights for author.

Falkynor Books, Michael Blate, P O Box 8060, Hollywood, FL 33024, 305-581-4950. 1976. avg. press run 2,000-5,000. Expects 2 titles 1980, 2 titles 1981. 1 title listed in the *Small Press Record of Books in Print* (9th Edition, 1980). avg. price, paper: $7.95. Discounts: up to 50%. At the present time, we are publishing only in-house work. COSMEP.

Fallen Angel, Leonard Kniffel, 1981 West McNichols C-1, Highland Park, MI 48203, 313-864-0982. 1975. Poetry. "No restrictions, just want to put good poetry in print. Authors: Margaret Kaminski,

A. D. Winans, Lynn Strongin, Helen Duberstein, Guy Veryzer, Melba Boyd, E. G. Burrows, Lee Upton. Two titles yearly. Unsolicited manuscripts in December only, please" avg. press run 500. Pub'd 2 titles 1979; expects 2 titles 1980, 2 titles 1981. 7 titles listed in the *Small Press Record of Books in Print* (9th Edition, 1980). avg. price, paper: $2.00. Discounts: 40% to bookstores and distributors on orders of 5 or more. 25pp; 5½X8½; of. Reporting time: 2 month. Payment: copies. Does not copyright for author. Poetry Resource Center of Michigan (PRC/M).

FAMILY THERAPY, Libra Publishers, Inc., 391 Willets Road, Roslyn Heights, L.I., NY 11577, (516) 484-4950. 1960. Articles. circ. 1,500. 3/yr. Pub'd 3 issues 1979; expects 3 issues 1980, 3 issues 1981. sub. price: $25.00 instit., $20.00 indiv.; per copy: $7.00; sample: $7.00. Back issues: $7.50. Discounts: 10% to subscriber agents. 112pp; 6X9; of. Reporting time: 3 weeks. Copyrighted. Pub's reviews: 60 in 1979. §Behavioral sciences. Ads: $150/$85.

FANTASY EXPRESS, Publishing Associates, Mark French, 159 Ralston Street, San Francisco, CA 94132, (415) 586-2209. 1979. Poetry. "This magazine publishes short prose, puzzles, riddles, crosswords and other items of interest to children. However, this magazine is primarily a poetry magazine." circ. 1,000. 4/yr. Pub'd 1 issue 1979. sub. price: $8.50; per copy: $1.75; sample: no samples. 32pp; 5½X8½; of. Reporting time: 10 days. Payment: 2 copies. Copyrighted. Pub's reviews. §Poetry, short stories, novels, etc that would interest children. Ads: $75.00/$50.00/$0.50 per word.

FANZINE DIRECTORY, Allan Beatty, PO Box 1040, Ames, IA 50010. 1976. "Overseas prices: Australia $1.00, Canada $1.15, 60p, or 5 international reply coupons. Also available for trade with other fanzines. Unused postage stamps in any of the above currencies accepted." circ. 400. Expects 2 issues 1980, 1 issue 1981. price per copy: $1.00. Back issues: inquire. Discounts: 20%, 5 or more to same US address. 20pp; 8½X11; of. Copyrighted. Ads: Inquire.

Far Out West Publications, Cliff MacGillivray, PO Box 953, South Pasadena, CA 91030, (213) 799-3754. 1979. "Mostly we are interested in 'how-to' books, written with humor in mind. We do not like dull, drab highly technical how to books. We could consider sports and activity books." avg. press run 3,500. Pub'd 1 title 1979; expects 2 titles 1980, 4 titles 1981. 1 title listed in the *Small Press Record of Books in Print* (9th Edition, 1980). avg. price, paper: $4.95. Discounts: Trade, 40%; Library, 20%; Jobber, 50%. 104pp; 7X8½; 6X9. Reporting time: 2 weeks to 2 months. Payment: negotiable. Copyrights for author. COSMEP.

FARMING UNCLE, Louis Toro, Editor, Box 91, Liberty, NY 12754. 1977. Poetry, articles, art, photos, criticism, reviews, letters, collages. "Mother/nature, earth, gardening, etc." circ. 2000. 4/yr. Pub'd 4 issues 1979; expects 4 issues 1980, 4 issues 1981. sub. price: $6.00, $25.00/5 yrs.; per copy: $1.50 plus postage; sample: $1.50 plus postage. Back issues: $1.50 plus postage. Discounts: In multiple of ten subscriptions or more 20%. 44-50pp; 8X11½; of. Reporting time: immediate. We pay (minimal). Pub's reviews: 5 in 1979. §Earth, nature, animals, small stock, health, poultry, etc. Ads: $100.00/$55.00/$.15.

Fashion Imprints Associates, Thelma H. Shirley, 3523 Merchandise Mart, Chicago, IL 60654, 821-5922. 1978. Interviews, reviews, news items. "Success guide is 151 page publication describing the fashion industry, the 'how-to' of production of fashion shows, how to save and make money, and many sample shows that can be produced. It includes quotes, accounts of and interviews with fashion personalities. Quotes from Bernadine Morris, N.Y. Times; a student's thesis entitled *Fashion and the Pill* by Alice Sullivan. (I am a self-publisher)" avg. press run 5,000. Expects 1 title 1980. 1 title listed in the *Small Press Record of Books in Print* (9th Edition, 1980). avg. price, cloth: $14.95; paper: $12.50. Discounts: 10%, 10-49; 20%, 50; 40%. 150pp; 7X10; lp. Copyrights for author.

THE FAULT, The Fault Press, Terrence McMahon, 33513 6th St., Union City, CA 94587. 1971. Poetry, fiction, art, photos, parts-of-novels, long-poems, collages, plays, concrete art, satire. "Each issue is a balanced format of fiction, poetry, drama & art." circ. 500. 2/yr. Pub'd 1 issue 1979; expects 2 issues 1980, 1 issue 1981. price per copy: $2.25; sample: $2.25. Back issues: $2.25. Discounts: 50% 5 copies or more. 150pp; 8½X5½; †of,lp. Reporting time: 2-4 weeks. Payment: 3 copies. Copyrighted.

The Fault Press (see also THE FAULT), Terrence McMahon, 33513 6th St, Union City, CA 94587, 415-489-8561. 1971. Poetry, fiction, art, photos, cartoons, satire, parts-of-novels, long-poems, collages, plays, concrete art. "We specialize in dada mail art and all non-traditional irratic visual experience. Open exchange policy." avg. press run 500. Pub'd 1 title 1979; expects 4 titles 1980. 24 titles listed in the *Small Press Record of Books in Print* (9th Edition, 1980). avg. price, paper: $2.25. Discounts: 50% orders of five or more. Mag. 100pp, Chapbooks 60pp; 7X8½; †of/lp. Reporting time: 4 weeks. Pay in copies for chapbooks and magazines. usually copyrights for author.

FEDERAL NOTES, Wallace E. Breitman, PO Box 986, Saratoga, CA 95070, 408-356-4667. 1973.

Articles, reviews, news items. "*Federal Notes* provides a biweekly summary of activities affecting education, science, and biomedical funding sources. Dealing predominantly with Federal funding, it covers new and forthcoming grant/contract programs; upcoming deadlines; legislation; proposed and final regulations; budgets and appropriations. Occasionally, it reviews publications of interest to individuals involved in grant/contract development and administration, and prints short articles related to the grant/contract development and administration process." circ. 800. 24/yr. Pub'd 24 issues 1979; expects 24 issues 1980, 24 issues 1981. sub. price: $72.00; per copy: $2.50; sample: free. Back issues: All back issues at single copy price if available. Discounts: $110.00 for 2 years; $155.00 for 3 years. 8pp; 8½X11; of. Reporting time: 3 days to 2 weeks. Payment: none at the moment. Not copyrighted. Pub's reviews: 4 in 1979. §Grant/contracts, proposal development, Federal funding and policies, foundations.

National Federation Of Claimants Unions Publications (see also CLAIMANTS NEWSPAPER (Claimants Unite)), 134 Villa Rd, Birmingham B19 1NN, United Kingdom. 1970. 4 titles listed in the *Small Press Record of Books in Print* (9th Edition, 1980).

Fels and Firn Press, John M. Montgomery, Editor and Publisher, 1843 Vassar Ave., Mountain View, CA 94043, 415-965-4291. 1961. Criticism, letters. "I published (1977) my own essay about Kerouac whom I knew. This is a more than doubling of a 1970 pamphlet of mine published elsewhere. 2,500 - 2,600 copies. Distribution in U.K., Europe & Australasia as well" Pub'd 1 title 1979; expects 1 title 1980, 1 title 1981. 3 titles listed in the *Small Press Record of Books in Print* (9th Edition, 1980). Discounts: Trade 30-40 percent, bulk 50 percent, jobber various. 50pp; 5½X9½; of. Reporting time: 30 days. Payment: Conventional. Copyrights for author.

FEMINARY, Susan Ballinger, Deborah Giddens, Minnie Bruce Pratt, Mab Segrest, Cris South, P.O.Box 954, Chapel Hill, NC 27514. 1971. Poetry, fiction, articles, art, photos, interviews, criticism, reviews, letters, parts-of-novels, long-poems, plays, news items. "80 pages. Lesbian and feminist journal for the South." circ. 600. 3/yr. Pub'd 3 issues 1979; expects 3 issues 1980, 3 issues 1981. sub. price: $6.50 for 3 issues individual/ $13 inst; per copy: $2.50 + 50¢ postage; sample: sample copies free to bookstores and institutions. Back issues: $2.50 + 50¢ postage. Discounts: to bookstores, min order 5 and 30% disc, order of 15+ 40%, no returns. 80pp; 6X8; †lp. Reporting time: 3 months. Payment: 3 copies or year's sub. Copyrighted, reverts to author. Pub's reviews: 9 in 1979. §books: blacks, women, feminists, lesbians, Southern culture and history. Ads: $40.00/$25.00/free up to 40 words.

FEMINIST, Ikuko Atsumi, 6-5-8 Todoroki, Setagaya-ku, Tokyo 158, Japan, (03) 402-4028, 702-0289. 1977. Poetry, fiction, articles, art, photos, cartoons, interviews, satire, criticism, reviews, letters, news items. "We formed a supportive group for our cause, called All-Japan-Feminist-Association. While inviting Ms. Adrienne Rich, feminist poet to Japan we are trying to spread feminist idea in Japan by means of publication of *Feminist.*" circ. 9,000. 6/yr. Pub'd 6 issues 1979; expects 7 issues 1980, 7 issues 1981. sub. price: 3500 yen; per copy: 550 yen. Back issues: 390 yen. 100pp; of. Reporting time: 2 months, depends on contents. Payments are equally made. Copyrighted, reverts to author. Pub's reviews: 20 in 1979. §Women, working as well as women in mass-media, women's movement too. Ads: $400.

FEMINIST BULLETIN, Center for Women's Studies & Services (CWSS), Carol Rowell, Shelley Sarren, Associate Editor, P.O. Box 350, San Diego, CA 92101, 714-233-8984. 1971. Articles. "This is the newsletter/newspaper of a radical feminist organization: the Center for Women's Studies & Services. Material submitted should ave at least a women's liberation oriented viewpoint and should be no longer than 1000 words." circ. 800. 6/yr. Pub'd 6 issues 1979; expects 6 issues 1980, 6 issues 1981. sub. price: $3.00; per copy: free; sample: free. 4pp; 7X8½; of. Reporting time: 2 months. Copyrighted, reverts to author. COSMEP.

The Feminist Poetry & Graphics Center (see also THE GREATER GOLDEN HILL POETRY EXPRESS), 3040 Clairemont Drive, San Diego, CA 92117, 714-239-3664. 1976.

The Feminist Press (see also WOMEN'S STUDIES NEWSLETTER), Elizabeth Phillips, Box 334, Old Westbury, NY 11568. 1970. "The Feminist Press is a non-profit, tax-exempt publishing house, engaged in educational change. We publish reprints of neglected women's writing, biographies, & materials for nonsexist curriculum at every educational level." avg. press run 3,000-5,000. Pub'd 4 titles 1979; expects 6 titles 1980. 36 titles listed in the *Small Press Record of Books in Print* (9th Edition, 1980). avg. price, cloth: $6.95; paper: $1.95-$7.95. Discounts: inquire. lp. Payment: small royalty.

Feminist Publishing Alliance, Inc. (see PLEXUS, Bay Area Women's Newspaper)

FEMINIST STUDIES, Claire Moses, Managing Editor, c/o Women's Studies Program, Univ of MD,

College Park, MD 20742, 301-454-2363. 1972. Poetry, fiction, articles, art, photos, cartoons, interviews, criticism, reviews. "*Feminist Studies* is a journal which publishes articles contributing to feminist scholarship, theory, analysis and debate. Some articles in Volume 5, number 1 include: Mary P. Ryan, *The Power of Women's Networks*; John P. Gillis, *Servants, Sexual Relations and the Risks of Illegitimacy in London, 1801-1900*; Leonore Davidoff, *Sex and Class in Victorian England*; Barbara Taylor, *Socialism, Feminism, and Sexual Antagonism in the London Tailoring Trade in the Early 1830's*; Joan Kelly, *The Doubled Vision of Feminist Theory*." circ. 3,000. 3/yr. Expects 3 issues 1980, 3 issues 1981. sub. price: $16.00 institutions; $10.00 individuals; per copy: $6.00; sample: $4.00. Back issues: $5.50 individuals; $8.50 institutions. 175pp; 6X9; of. Reporting time: 3 months. Copyrighted. Pub's reviews. §In all fields of women's studies, on feminism, on sexuality, on family, on human relations, on psychology, significant works by women authors. Ads: $200.00/$100.00.

F. Fergeson Productions, David Jeffrey Fletcher MD, Box 433, Lake Bluff, IL 60044, 312-864-7696. 1979. Articles, art, photos, reviews, music. avg. press run 5,000. Pub'd 1 title 1979; expects 2 titles 1980. avg. price, paper: $10.00. Discounts: Standard 40% trade. 300pp; 8½X11; of. COSMEP.

Festival Publications, Alan Gadney, Editor, P.O. Box 10180, Glendale, CA 91209. 1976. "Current book is *Gadney's Guide to 1,800 International Contests, Festivals, and Grants in Film and Video, Photography, TV-Radio Broadcasting, Writing, Poetry, Playwriting and Journalism* awarded 'Outstanding Reference Book of the Year' by the American Library Association (5½ x 8½, 610 pages, $15.95 for softbound, $21.95 for hardbound, plus $1.75 each postage & handling). (Are intersted in book-length manuscripts or proposals in above listed subject areas; primarily reference works in film, video, photography, TV-radio broadcasting, script and playwriting)." avg. press run 5,000. Pub'd 1 title 1979; expects 3 titles 1980, 5 titles 1981. 1 title listed in the *Small Press Record of Books in Print* (9th Edition, 1980). avg. price, cloth: $21.95; paper: $15.95. Discounts: Bookstore, 1 copy, 20%; 2 copies, 25%; 3 copies, 30%; 4 copies, 35%; 5 or more copies, 40%. 500pp; 5½X8½. Reporting time: 6 weeks. Payment: Trade standard. Copyrights for author. COSMEP.

FICTION, Mark Mirsky, c/o Dept. of English, City College, 138th Street & Convent Ave., New York, NY 10031. 1972. Fiction, art, photos, parts-of-novels, collages, concrete art. "We tend slightly towards the so-called 'experimental', though do not limit ourselves to that. Recent contributors have included: Donald Barthelme, Manuel Puig, Ann Beattie, Grace Paley, Ishmael Reed, Julio Cortazar, as well as their emerging (less known) counterparts." circ. 5,000. 2/yr. Pub'd 1 issue 1979; expects 2 issues 1980, 2 issues 1981. sub. price: $8.00; per copy: $4.00. Back issues: vol 1 #2 - vol 3 #1, $1.50/ vol 3 2/3 - vol 5 2/3 $3/ vol 6 #1 $4. Discounts: 40 percent discount to bookstores; 50 percent to distributors, 10 percent to teachers (bulk). 180pp; 9X6; of. Reporting time: as much as six months, we do accept mss May through Sept. Payment: neither our editors nor our contributors receive payment; translators we pay 2 cents per word. Copyrighted, reverts if requested. CCLM.

Fiction Collective, Inc., c/o George Braziller, Inc., One Park Avenue, New York, NY 10016. 1974. Fiction. "Novels and collections of short stories. Members are authors we have published or are about to publish. Distribution through George Braziller, Inc., One Park Avenue, New York, NY 10016. Manuscript queries to Fiction Collective Manuscript Central, Padelford Hall GN-30, University of Washington, Seattle, WA 98195." avg. press run 2,200. Pub'd 6 titles 1979. 31 titles listed in the *Small Press Record of Books in Print* (9th Edition, 1980). avg. price, cloth: $8.95; paper: $3.95. Discounts: 40%. 200pp; 5½X8½; of. Reporting time: 6 months to 1 year. Payment: Authors make profits only on subsidiary-rights sales. Copyrights for author.

FICTION INTERNATIONAL, Joe David Bellamy, St. Lawrence Univ., Canton, NY 13617, (315) 379-5961. 1973. Fiction, articles, interviews, criticism, reviews, parts-of-novels. "Recent issues have been collections of stories by one author published simultaneously in book editions. Forthcoming issues will return to an anthology format. Mss are to be considered only from Sept thru Dec of each year. *Fiction International* also sponsors: the St. Lawrence Award for Fiction, a $1,000.00 prize given for an outstanding first collection of short fiction published in North America, and the annual fiction international/St. Lawrence University Writers' Conference." circ. 5M. 1/yr. Pub'd 1 issue 1979; expects 1 issue 1980, 1 issue 1981. sub. price: $5.00; per copy: $8.00 instit.; sample: $5.00. Back issues: Nos. 2-3, 4-5, 6-7, $3.50 each; Nos. 8-9, 10-11, $5.00 each. Discounts: standard rates. 200pp; 5½X8½; of. Reporting time: 1-3 mos. Payment: $0-$100.00. Copyrighted, reverts to author. Pub's reviews: 30+ in 1979. §Fiction primarily with special interest in story collections; also non-fiction books on literary subjects. Ads: $100/$65. CCLM.

THE FIDDLEHEAD, Roger Ploude, Managing Editor; Robert Gibbs, Poetry Editor; Ted Colson, Fiction Editor, The Observatory, Univ. New Brunswick, Fredericton, NB E3B 5A3, Canada, 506-454-3591. 1945. Poetry, fiction, art, reviews, parts-of-novels, long-poems, plays. circ. 1,050. 4/yr. Pub'd 4 issues 1979. sub. price: $10.00 Canada $11.00 U.S.; per copy: $2.50 Can, $2.75 US; sample:

$2.50 Can, $2.75 US. Back issues: $3.00. Discounts: 10% on purchases of 10 copies or more; Bookstores 33⅓%. 150pp; 5¼X8½; of. Reporting time: 4-6 wks. Payment: $5 printed page. Copyrighted. Pub's reviews: 47 in 1979. §Canlit. Ads: $50/$26. CPPA.

FIELD, David Young, Stuart Friebert, Rice Hall, Oberlin College, Oberlin, OH 44074. 1969. Poetry, long-poems. "Also essays on poetry and translations of poetry." circ. 2,000. 2/yr. Pub'd 2 issues 1979; expects 2 issues 1980. sub. price: $5.00, $8.00/2 yrs.; per copy: $2.50; sample: $2.50. Back issues: $10.00, all backs. Discounts: bookstores: 40%, agencies: 30%. 100pp; 5¼X8½. Reporting time: 1-2 wks. Payment: $25 a page. Copyrighted, reverts to author. Ads: No ads. CCLM, COSMEP.

THE FIFTH HORSEMAN, The Scopcraeft Press, Antony Oldknow, General Editor and Publisher; Hadrian Manske, Associate Editor, 3200 Ellis Street #16, Stevens Point, WI 54481, (715) 345-0865. 1967. Poetry, criticism, reviews. "This magazine will publish only poems of exceptional excellence, ones that touch the quick. The length of an issue will depend upon the supply of poems that fit our criteria" circ. 200. 4/yr. sub. price: $7.50; per copy: $2.00; sample: $2.00. 8X5; †mi/of. Reporting time: varies. Payment: 2 copies and reduced rates of purchase. Pub's reviews. §poetry only.

FIFTH SUN, Max Benavidez, Editor, 1134-B Chelsea Ave, Santa Monica, CA 90403, (213) 828-2918. 1977. Poetry, fiction, articles, art, photos, interviews, satire, criticism, reviews, letters, parts-of-novels, long-poems, collages, plays, concrete art. "A chronicle of rage and anger assumes a new attitudebest referred to (as of June 1980) as a *punkitude*. This means a revolt against the sexist, racist, clitist assumptions of the American art world. At a time when an electronic technocracy is entrenching itself across the land in our schools, industry and government we ask our contributors to probe for seeds of discontent, to stare up at the asshole of death. We are looking for rough expressions of hope, anger and pain. Street art and agit-poems wanted. Also: political poster art. Brecht: where are you now? Past contributors include: Sudeka X. Harrison, Rita Rosenfeld, Richard Grayson, B. Traven, Muhammad Al-Amrikani, Yolanda Lopez, Kathleen Vozoff, Pancho Aguila, Blakeslee Stevens,Merrit Clifton, Steve Kagan, Ianthe Thomas, T. M. Luna, and Liu Cheh-Teh" circ. 500-650. 2/yr. Expects 2 issues 1980. sub. price: $7.00; per copy: $1.00; sample: $1.00. Back issues: $2.00 per copy. 50pp; 8½X11; of. Reporting time: 2 months. Payment: copies. Copyrighted, reverts to author. Pub's reviews. §Art, poetry, fiction, plays, minority/women, film, social commentary, photography, literature. Ads: $25.00/$15.00/$.05.

FIGHTING WOMAN NEWS, Valerie Eads, P.O. Box 1459, Grand Central Station, New York, NY 10017, 212-228-0900. 1975. Articles, art, photos, cartoons, interviews, reviews, letters, news items, non-fiction. "We need articles to 2,000 words, with photos, on martial arts, self defense & combative sports. Our readership is knowledgeable & critical. Also feminist. We have published men including artists Rick Bryant, Val Mayerik & Sergio Aragones." circ. 7,000. 4/yr. Pub'd 4 issues 1979; expects 4 issues 1980, 4 issues 1981. 2 titles listed in the *Small Press Record of Books in Print* (9th Edition, 1980). sub. price: $6.00 individuals; $10.00 institutional; per copy: $1.50; sample: $2.00 set of 3 (incl. post). Discounts: delivered by Carrier Pigeon, 40% consignment. 24-32pp; 8½X11; of. Reporting time: asap. Payment: From contributors' copies to honorarium (rarely), cover photo $10.00. Copyrighted, reverts to author. Pub's reviews: 10 in 1979. §martial arts, self defense, combative sports, women's history in these areas, women's adventure fiction. Ads: local: $125/$65/20¢, national: $250/$130/40¢.

The Figures, Laura Chester, Geoffrey Young, 2016 Cedar, Berkeley, CA 94709, 415-843-3120. 1975. Poetry, fiction. "Summer Brenner, prose, THE SOFT ROOM; Tom Raworth, a long poem, ACE; Christopher Dewdney, prose, SPRING TRANCES IN THE CONTROL EMERALD NIGHT; Laura Chester, a novella, WATERMARK; Bob Perelman, 7 WORKS; Rae Armantrout, poems, EXTREMITIES; Barbara Einzig, prose, DISAPPEARING WORK, a recounting; Stephen Rodefer, poems, THE BELL CLERK'S TEARS KEEP FLOWING; Kit Robinson, poems, DOWN AND BACK; Lyn Hejinian, poetry, WRITING IS AN AID TO MEMORY; Steve Benson, poems, AS IS; John Brandi, DIARY FROM A JOURNEY TO THE CENTER OF THE WORLD;Alan Bernheimer, poems CAFE ISOTOPE; David Bromige, prose & poems MY POETRY; Laura Chester, poems MY PLEASURE; Kathleen Fraser,prose EACH NEXT; Geoffrey Young, poems & prose SUBJECT TO FITS." avg. press run 750. Pub'd 5 titles 1979; expects 5 titles 1980, 5 titles 1981. 23 titles listed in the *Small Press Record of Books in Print* (9th Edition, 1980). avg. price, cloth: $10.00; paper: $3.50. 75pp; 5½X8½; of. Reporting time: 1 month. Payment: 10 percent edition, 40 percent off on extra sales. Copyrights for author.

FILE MAG, Art Official Inc., 217 Richmond Street West, Toronto, ON M5V 1W2, Canada, (416) 977-1685. 1972. Art, photos, interviews, reviews. "We do not usually publish unsolicited material." circ. 3,000. 1-2/yr. Pub'd 1 issue 1979; expects 2 issues 1980. sub. price: $10.00 for 4 issues; per copy: $3.00; sample: $3.00. Back issues: on request. Discounts: bulk orders-35 percent. 64+pp;

136

10¾X14; of. Reporting time: varies. Payment varies. Copyrighted, reverts to author. Ads: $400.-00/$200.00.

FILM, Peter Cargin, 81 Dean St., London W1V6AA, United Kingdom, 01 437 4355. 1954. Articles, photos, interviews, criticism, news items. "Film news, criticisms, etc. advertising managers: address, 81 Dean St. London W1A6AA" circ. 3,000. 12/yr. Pub'd 12 issues 1979; expects 12 issues 1980. sub. price: $25.00-yr £12.00; per copy: 40p; sample: free. 12pp; size A4; of. Reporting time: 2 wks. Payment: by arrangement. Copyrighted, reverts to author. Pub's reviews: 40 in 1979. §cinema, television, video, social and critical uses of film. Ads: £60/£32.

FILM CULTURE, Film Culture Non-Profit, Inc., Jonas Mekas, P. Adams Sitney, G. P. O. Box 1499, New York, NY 10001. 1955. Poetry, articles, photos, letters. "We are a magazine devoted to avant-garde cinema and classical cinema. Recent contributors have been James Broughton, John G. Hanhardt, Richard Foreman, P. Adams Sitney, Regina Cornwall, etc. The next three issues will be devoted to the LEGEND OF MAYA DEREN, a documentary biography in three volumes, edited by VeVe Clark, Millicent Hodson and Catrina Neiman." circ. 4,500. 4/yr. Pub'd 2 issues 1979; expects 4 issues 1980, 4 issues 1981. 8 titles listed in the *Small Press Record of Books in Print* (9th Edition, 1980). sub. price: $12.00 in U.S., $14.00 Foreign; per copy: $2.00-$6.00; sample: $1.00. Back issues: inquire. Discounts: We give 25 percent to 40 percent discount to bookstores. 90-200pp; 5½X8; of. Payment: At present articles are submitted without payment. Copyrighted, reverts to author. Pub's reviews. §Cinema, poetry. Ads: $300.00/$150.00/none. CCLM.

Film Culture Non-Profit, Inc. (see also FILM CULTURE), Jonas Mekas, P. Adams Sitney, G. P. O. Box 1499, New York, NY 10001. 1955. Poetry, fiction, articles, photos, letters. "Film Culture publishes anything that it deams important to avantgarde cinema—journals, poetry, fiction, prose, articles on film, etc." avg. press run 5,000. avg. price, cloth: varies; paper: varies. Discounts: 25-40 percent discount to bookstores. other discounts must be negotiated individually. pp varies; size varies; of. Reporting time: Varies. Payment: Negotiated individually after production costs are paid. Copyrights for author. CCLM.

FILM LIBRARY QUARTERLY, William Sloan, Ron Rollet, Box 348, Radio City Station, New York, NY 10019. 1967. "Articles and reviews on noncommercial cinema-documentary, avant-garde, childrens, and on video." circ. 1,900. 4/yr. Pub'd 4 issues 1979; expects 4 issues 1980, 4 issues 1981. sub. price: $10.00; per copy: $2.50; sample: free. Back issues: $2.00 per issue. 56pp; 6X9 inches; of. Reporting time: 10 days. Payment: copies. Copyrighted, reverts to author. Pub's reviews: 9 in 1979. §cinema, video. Ads: $200.00/$100.00.

FILM QUARTERLY, University of California Press, Ernest Callenbach, University of California Press, Berkeley, CA 94720. 1945. Interviews, criticism, reviews. circ. 7M. 4/yr. Pub'd 4 issues 1979. sub. price: $7.00; per copy: $1.75; sample: gratis. Back issues: $1.75 and $3.00. Discounts: 10% for subscription agents, 25% for stores. 62pp; 6¾X8⅜; of. Reporting time: 2-3 weeks. Payment: 3¢ per word. Copyrighted, does not revert to author. Pub's reviews: about 100 in 1979. §Film. Ads: $250.-00/$150.00.

Findhorn Publications (see also ONEARTH IMAGE), Roy McVicar, Denis Evanson, Jeremy Slocombe, Findhorn Foundation, The Park, Forres, Morayshire 1V360TZ, Scotland, 030-93-2582. 1966. Articles, art, photos, cartoons, interviews, reviews. "Mostly books by people connected with the Findhorn Community. Spiritual Metaphysical and New Age themes, especially related to living in spiritual communities, and man's cooperation with nature. Recently published *My LIfe-My Trees* by Richard St. Barbe Baker. We are interested in soliciting suitable material from new contributors who should be familiar with our work; book length or magazine article length." avg. press run 6,000. Pub'd 6 titles 1979; expects 7 titles 1980, 9 titles 1981. 20 titles listed in the *Small Press Record of Books in Print* (9th Edition, 1980). avg. price, cloth: £3.00, $7.50; paper: £2.25, $6.30. Discounts: UK 1-2 items, 25%; 3 or more, 35%. Overseas: 1-2 items, 25%; 3-9 items, 33⅓%; 10 or more items, 40%. 140pp; 5¾X8½; of. Reporting time: 1-2 months. Payment: By arrangement, competitive with normal trade practice. IPG, SGPA.

FINE PRINT: A Review for the Arts of the Book, Sandra Kirshenbaum, Linnea Gentry, Assoc. Editor; Susan Spring Wilson, Assoc. Editor, P O Box 7741, San Francisco, CA 94120, 415-776-1530. 1975. Articles, interviews, criticism, reviews. "The first review medium devoted to the finely printed limited editions of private and specialized presses, giving full biblographic description and comments. Plus newsnotes, trade reviews and feature articles on typography, papermaking, calligraphy, handbookbinding, book-illustration and the history of the book. Send all mail to: P.O. Box 7741, San Francisco, California 94120." circ. 1,800. 4/yr. Pub'd 4 issues 1979; expects 4 issues 1980. sub. price: $20.00 indiv., $25.00 instit.; per copy: $5.00; sample: $5.00. Back issues: Inquire as to issues currently available. Stock changes quickly. Discounts: Bookstores may subscribe for three issues. In multiples of 3 (3, 6, 9, 12 etc) at 20% per sub or issues. Payment in advance. No returns. $2.00 off institutional orders from agents. 32pp; 8X11; 9X12; lp. Reporting time: 3-4 weeks. Payment: author's copies. Copyrighted, under new laws. Pub's reviews. §Book arts, history, printing, calligraphy, binding, typography. Ads: $400.00/$175.00/$0.20.

Fintzenberg Publishers, D. Altabe, J. Altabe, Art Editor, Box 301, Long Beach, NY 11561. 1978. Poetry. "Books Published: Altabe, David, F. trans. *Symphony of Love: Las Rimas* of Gustavo Adolfo Becquer, Long Beach, NY: Regina Publising House 1974. *bilingual edition - illustrateed) 224 pp. Altabe, David F. Chapter and Verse,* Long Beach, NY, Fintzenberg Publ., 1978. (with illustrations) 92 pp." avg. press run 1,000. Pub'd 1 title 1979. avg. price, cloth: $6.50; paper: $4.00. Discounts: Trade 40%; Library 33⅓%. 200pp. Reporting time: 2 weeks. Payment: so far, we have published only our own poetry. Copyrights for author.

Firefly Press, Carl Kay, 26 Hingham Street, Cambridge, MA 02138, (617) 661-9784. 1978. Poetry, fiction, art, long-poems, concrete art, letters, parts-of-novels. "Poetry rooted in the body; creative translation. We're interested in any work that genuinely moves, covers ground, even one step if its hard-earned and deeply felt. New England Indians, Buddhism. All work till now produced by hand, will continue this while expanding to include longer offset books. Works by Waldman, Ginsberg, Judy Katz-Levine, W. E. Butts, Bly, Elsa Dorfman. *Poets Get Outa Your Heads!*" avg. press run 400. Pub'd 3 titles 1979; expects 6 titles 1980, 12 titles 1981. 3 titles listed in the *Small Press Record of Books in Print* (9th Edition, 1980). avg. price, cloth: $35.00; paper: $3.00. Discounts: 40% trade, 45% on large orders. 24pp; 6X9; †lp. Reporting time: 90 days. Payment: copies or 10% of cover price in some cases. Copyrights for author. NESPA.

FIRELANDS ARTS REVIEW, Cambric Press, Joel Rudinger, Firelands Campus, Huron, OH 44839, 419-433-4221. 1972. Poetry, fiction, photos. circ. 1M. annual. Pub'd 1 issue 1979; expects 1 issue 1980. sub. price: $3.00; per copy: $3.00; sample: $2.50. Back issues: 1972 $1.50; 1973 $1.50; 1974 $1.80; 1975 $2.30; 1976 $2.30; 1977-78 $3.00. Discounts: 30 percent over 10 copies. 96pp; 8½X5½; of. Reporting time: 4-8 wks. Payment: copies. Copyrighted. Pub's reviews: 1 in 1979. §Humorous good fiction; serious poetry and fiction (not escapist). CCLM.

Fireside Press (see also CONNECTICUT FIRESIDE), Albert Callan, Editor, P.O. Box 5293, Hamden, CT 06518. 1972. "Poetry chapbooks and *Connecticut Fireside*. Please see listing under *Connecticue Fireside* additional details." avg. press run 200. Pub'd 1 title 1979; expects 2 titles 1980. 2 titles listed in the *Small Press Record of Books in Print* (9th Edition, 1980). avg. price, paper: $2.00. 60-70pp; 5½X8½; †of. Reporting time: 2 weeks. Payment: by arrangement. Copyrights for author. CCLM.

Firestein Books, Sabra Firestein, 11959 Barrel Cooper Court, Reston, VA 22091, (703) 860-1637. 1979. Fiction, plays. "Books of literary quality that do not fall into a readily identifiable market category. Up to 500 pages." avg. press run 1,000. Pub'd 1 title 1979. avg. price, paper: $6.95. Discounts: 40% trade; 20% libraries. 250pp; 5½X8½; of. Reporting time: 30 days. Payment: 10% royalty. Copyrights for author.

W.D. Firestone Press, W. D. Firestone, 1313 South Jefferson Avenue, Springfield, MO 65807, (417) 866-5141. 1979. "All material submitted must be accompanied by SASE or it will not be retuned. This applies to all letters of inquiry regarding submissions. This is the Missouri Ozarks — all material sent through the mail done at the writer's own risk! At present, manuscripts must be under twenty-five pages in length. Preference is given to short-short fiction especially — fiction that is 200 to 250 words maximum length. All submitted material must be typed. Material accepted for publication will be published at the editor's earliest date. Payment will be in copies only, and the copyright will be in the author's own name. Four titles to be published per year; this is the tentative plan, subject to change. Will consider poetry collections." avg. press run varies. 2 titles listed in the *Small Press Record of Books in Print* (9th Edition, 1980). avg. price, cloth: varies; paper: varies. Discounts: 'short'. varies per publicationpp; 4X4; 6X9; †of. Reporting time: 2 months. Payment: in copies only.

The First Haiku Press (see also AMOSKEAG: A Magazine of Haiku), Matsuo Allard, 113 Comeau Street, Manchester, NH 03102. 1978. Poetry. "The only haiku press to publish a major series of chapbooks and full length books of haiku, either English originals or in translation. We print all forms of the Japanese one-line verse known as the haiku (no 'western' haiku of 3 or so lines). Also, we publish one-line poems (Ichigyoshi) distinct from haiku. At this writing, several chapbooks are in the process of being released, with several others on the way. Potential writers should send large selections of their work to enable us to select only their quintesential best for publication. Current chapbooks: *No More Questions No More Answers,* Eric Amann; *Landscapes* Hitoshi Funaki (Onsey Nakagawa, tr.); *Up a Distant Ridge,* John Wills; *Winter Haiku,* Mutsuo Takahashi (Hiroaki Sato, tr.); others coming, by

Duane Ackerson, Marlene Wills, Frank Short, Larry Gates, Tsutomu Fukuda, Frank Sauers & many more." avg. press run 200-1,000. Pub'd 1 title 1979; expects 8 titles 1980, 4 titles 1981. avg. price, paper: $1.00-$2.00. Discounts: 2-10, 25%; 10 and up, 40%. 10-400pp; 8½X2⅓; †mi/of. Reporting time: within 3 months on full length book mss, sooner on chapbooks. Payment: 25% plus 10-25 copies. Copyrights for author.

First Impressions, John W. Davenport, PO Box 9073, Madison, WI 53715, (608) 238-6254.

The First Ozark Press (see TOTAL LIFESTYLE- The Magazine of Natural Living; REBUTTAL! The Bicentennial Newsletter of Truth)

FIT, Brent Spencer, Cathrine Spencer, 263 S Franklin Street, Apt E, Wilkes-Barre, PA 18701, (717) 825-5142. 1977. Poetry, reviews, news items. "Besides printing the best poetry we receive, we also serve Pennsylvania, New York, and New Jersey by listing upcoming readings in the tri-state area and reviewing them. We solicit information and reviews of such readings in addition to the needs listed above." circ. 300. sporadic. Pub'd 1 issue 1979; expects 2 issues 1980. sub. price: 4 SASE = 4 issues; per copy: SASE; sample: SASE. Back issues: SASE. Discounts: none. 4pp; 17X11; of. Reporting time: 3 weeks - 2 months. Payment: 2 copies. Copyrighted, reverts to author. Pub's reviews: 2 in 1979. §Poetry, poetry readings. Ads: No ads.

Five Arches Press (see THE ANGLO-WELSH REVIEW)

Five Trees Press, Cheryl Miller, Kathy Walkup, PO Box 327, Palo Alto, CA 94302. 1973. Poetry, fiction, parts-of-novels, long-poems, collages. avg. press run 500. Pub'd 8-10 titles 1979. 4 titles listed in the *Small Press Record of Books in Print* (9th Edition, 1980). avg. price, cloth: $25.00; paper: $5.00. Discounts: 1-4 copies, 20% off; 5 or more, 40% off. 48pp; †lp. Reporting time: 4-6 weeks. Payment: 10% royalty on gross sales. Does not copyright for author.

Fred A. Fleet II, 151 N Lincoln St, Washington, PA 15301, (412) 228-5061. 1978. Articles. "This book is my first one, but not my last. 28 pages long." avg. press run 500. Expects 3 titles 1981. 1 title listed in the *Small Press Record of Books in Print* (9th Edition, 1980). avg. price, paper: $4.95. Discounts: Through mail order distributors direct to jobbers, and some direct to bookstores. 32pp; 8½X5½; of. Reporting time: less than 30 days. At the present time I write all my own material. Copyrights for author. COSMEP.

FLOATING ISLAND, Floating Island Publications, Michael Sykes, Floating Island Publications, P.O. Box 516, Point Reyes Station, CA 94956. 1976. Poetry, fiction, articles, art, photos, cartoons, parts-of-novels, long-poems, collages. "Floating Island pubs. 1 every 2 years approx.8½ x 11, 160pp, perfectbound cover in color, text B&W, 24pp of photographs (full-page) on coated stock, approx. 50 percent of text is poetry, 25 percent fiction & prose, 25 percent graphics-poetry fiction & prose is frequently illustrated, engravings, woodblocks, pen & pencil etc.-some artwork halftoned to retain fidelity, most is line-shot-contributors include well-known poets & writers as well as previous unpublished artists. Editorial policy is determined solely by whim and is akin to a celebration which various persons have been invited to attend in the Seliep they may enjoy one another's company and perhaps find a small and appreciative audience as well." circ. 500. 1 every 2 years. Expects 1 issue 1980. sub. price: standing orders only - full price; per copy: $6.95 I & II, $8.95 for III; sample: $5.00 for I & II, $6.00 for III. Back issues: $5.00 for I & II, $6.00 for III. Discounts: 50% to dist.; 40% to retail outlets. 160pp; 8½X11; of. Reporting time: 2-4 weeks. Payment: Copies. Copyrighted, all rights revert to authors upon request. no ads.

Floating Island Publications (see also FLOATING ISLAND), Michael Sykes, PO Box 516, Pt Reyes Sta, CA 94956. 1976. Poetry, fiction, articles, art, photos, parts-of-novels, long-poems. "I'll do 1 or 2 books a year, more if possible. I'm interested as much in the design and production of a book as its content and choose to work with manuscripts that offer me an interesting possibility of balancing these two areas of concern. Consequently the work is slow and deliberate. Authors must be patient. *Sleeping With The Enemy* by Christine Zawadiwsky, *Barn Fires* by Peter Wild." avg. press run 500. Expects 1 title 1980, 1 title 1981. 7 titles listed in the *Small Press Record of Books in Print* (9th Edition, 1980). avg. price, paper: $4.00. Discounts: 50% jobbers, 40% bookstores. 40pp; 5X9; of. Reporting time: 6-8 weeks. Payment: 10% of the press run. Does not copyright for author.

FLORAL UNDERAWL GAZETTE, Kxe6s Verein R Press, Steven Buntin, PO Box 2066 or 2204, Chapel Hill, NC 27514. 1977. Poetry, fiction, articles, art, cartoons, interviews, satire, criticism, reviews, music, letters, parts-of-novels, long-poems. "Heavily orientd toward reporting freedom of press violations, public interest pieces and informational stories." 12/yr. sub. price: $20.00; per copy: $1.50; sample: $1.00. Back issues: $1.00 each. Discounts: we are our own agents. 20+pp; 5½X8½; †mi/of. submissions used as needed. Payment: case by case, most work done by staff.

Copyrighted. Pub's reviews. §Copyright law, journalism, press, music, science. Ads: $100.00/$55.-00/$0.75. COSMEP, COSMEP/SOUTH, COSMEP/EAST.

Florida Arts Gazette, Kirt M. Dressler, Managing Editor; Judith Ortiz Cofer, Poetry Editor, P.O. Box 397, Ft. Lauderdale, FL 33302, (305) 463-6891. 1977. Poetry, articles, art, photos, interviews, satire, reviews, concrete art, criticism, news items, fiction, cartoons. *"The Florida Arts Gazette* is Florida's arts newsmagazine. Articles and other submissions should relate to the visual arts, crafts, music, literature/poetry, media, dance or theatre in the state of Florida or be of national significance to artists or arts organizations (legislation, funding, conferences, etc.) No rock pieces or longpoems. Please include sample(s) of your work with query letter." circ. 12,000. monthly. Pub'd 12 issues 1979; expects 12 issues 1980, 12 issues 1981. sub. price: $10.00 indiv., $12.00 lib/inst.; per copy: $1.00; sample: $1.00. Back issues: send SASE for list. Discounts: bulk copies available to arts organizations in Florida (inquire). 20pp; 11½X17½; of. Reporting time: 6 weeks or less. Payment: query. Copyrighted, reverts to author. Pub's reviews: 3 in 1979. §The arts, any kind of books by Florida authors. Ads: $640.-00/$320.00/$0.20. COSMEP.

Flower Press, Mary Appelhof, 121 E Van Hoesen, Kalamazoo, MI 49002, 616-343-3809. 1976. "Flower Press came into being in order to present to people information and ideas which otherwise might never have the opportunity to be expressed in print form. We have published a volume of poetry by Susie Clemens, a How-To book which is 'the first of a series designed to help people regain control over their own lives', and a directory of feminist businesses. We believe that by developing skills, sharing knowledge, and working cooperatively, we can accomplish together what none of us could do alone. *Nomad Shelves* (how-to), paper, 22 pp, $3.00, author Mary Appelhof; *Ms. Fortune 500 Directory* coast-to-coast listing, ed. Mary Appelhof of feminist businesses. Paper, 88 pp, 4¼ x 6¼, spiral binding, $3.00 plus $0.50 postage & handling, 1978. *Finding Back Your Family* (genealogy) paper, 102 pp, 8½ x 11, private edition, authors Gilbert and Hilda Appelhof, 1979." avg. press run 500. Expects 2 titles 1981. 3 titles listed in the *Small Press Record of Books in Print* (9th Edition, 1980). avg. price, paper: $3.00. Discounts: 40% to sellers. 40pp; 5¼X8¼; †of. Payment: Author defrays publishing cost. Copyrights for author.

FLY BY NIGHT, Old Pages Books Co, Gary Nargi, PO Box 921, Huntington, NY 11743. 1980. Poetry, fiction, criticism, reviews, letters, parts-of-novels, long-poems. "We would like to proceed in some kind of experimental/philosophical tradition, if you can call that a tradition. Interested in ideas and theories as much as fiction or poetry-we *love* corresponding, so if you think you have something to say, or just feel like writing, drop us aline-but please enclose SASE." circ. 500. Discounts: 40% trade, barter w/other presses. mi, of. Reporting time: immediate, receipt acknowledged if much longer. Payment: copies. Copyrighted, reverts to author. Pub's reviews. §Experimental prose, collage, critical or theoretical writing.

Flying Buttress Publications, Terry Nantier, PO Box 254, Endicott, NY 13760, (607) 785-5423. 1976. Cartoons. "We publish *graphic novels* a concept imported from Europe of high-quality *comics* in book form." avg. press run 3,000. Pub'd 1 title 1979; expects 2 titles 1980, 5-7 titles 1981. 3 titles listed in the *Small Press Record of Books in Print* (9th Edition, 1980). avg. price, cloth: $4.95; paper: $2.45. Discounts: Those of our distributor Caroline House. 52pp; 8½X11; of. Payment: 10% of sales (retail). Copyrights for author. COSMEP.

Flying Diamond Books, Francie M. Berg, RR2, Box D301, Hettinger, ND 58639, (701) 567-2646. 3 titles listed in the *Small Press Record of Books in Print* (9th Edition, 1980).

THE FOC'SLE, James Chapman, PO Box 21355, Concord, CA 94521, (415) 687-5673. 1980. Poetry, fiction, articles, art, cartoons, interviews, reviews, letters, long-poems. "No limit on length, we reserve the right to edit all material. No politically oriented material. To date all material has been written by our staff. No material returned unless accompanied by SASE." circ. 2,500. 6/yr. sub. price: $9.00; sample: $1.50. Back issues: $1.50. Discounts: 25%. 30pp; 8½X11; of. Reporting time: 1 month prifor to deadlines, 1st of every other month beginning Jan. Payment: $0.03 per word. Pub's reviews. §Maritime history, the maritime industry today, almost anything except political material. Ads: $120.-00/$60.00/$0.25.

FOCUS, British Science Fiction Assoc. Ltd., Robert Holdstock, Chris Evans, 269 Wykeham Road, Reading RG6 1PL, United Kingdom. 1979. Fiction, articles, art, cartoons, interviews, letters, news items. "*Focus* is the magazine of the British Science Fiction Association aimed at helping new writers." circ. 1,000. 2/yr. Pub'd 1 issue 1979; expects 2 issues 1980, 2 issues 1981. sub. price: Free to members; per copy: 75p; sample: 60p. Back issues: 75p. Discounts: 33⅓ to dealers. 32pp; size A4; of. Reporting time: 3-6 weeks. Payment: none. Copyrighted, reverts to author. Ads: £100/£50.

FOCUS: A Journal For Lesbians, 1151 Mass. Avenue, Cambridge, MA 02138. 1970. Poetry, fiction, cartoons, reviews, articles, art, satire, criticism, parts-of-novels, long-poems, letters. "Drawings must be in pen and ink." circ. 300. 6/yr. Pub'd 12 issues 1979; expects 6 issues 1980, 6 issues 1981. sub. price: $8.00/yr; per copy: $1.35; sample: $1.35. Back issues: 60¢. 30pp; 7X8½; of. Reporting time: 2-3 months. Payment: copies. Copyrighted, reverts to author. Pub's reviews: 14 in 1979. §matters of direct concern to lesbians and/or feminists. Ads: $50.00/$30.00/$0.10.

FOCUS/ MIDWEST, Focus/Midwest Publishing Co., Inc., Charles Klotzer, Editor & Publisher; Dan Jaffe, Poetry Editor, 928a N. McKnight, St. Louis, MO 63132, 314-991-1698. 1962. Poetry, articles, interviews, satire, criticism, letters, reviews, news items. circ. 5,500. bi-monthly. Pub'd 6 issues 1979; expects 6 issues 1980, 6 issues 1981. sub. price: $7.00; per copy: $1.25; sample: $1.25. Back issues: $2.00. Discounts: sub./agencies: 20%; retail outlets/stores, 40%. 32-48pp; 8½X11; of. Reporting time: 4-8 weeks. Payment: upon publication. Copyrighted, does not revert to author. Pub's reviews. §politics, social, literary, urban, cultural. Ads: $350.00/$185.00/$.16.

Focus/Midwest Publishing Co., Inc. (see FOCUS/ MIDWEST; ST. LOUIS JOURNALISM REVIEW)

Folder Editions, Daisy Aldan, 10326 68th Road, #A63, Forest Hills, NY 11375, 212-275-3839. 1959. Poetry, plays, fiction. "West Coast address: Hermes Press: 451½ N Spaulding Ave, Los Angeles, California 90036. Recent Publications: *I Wanted to See Something Flying* poems by Harriet Zinnes, *The Fall of Antichrist* play in verse by Swiss poet, Albert Steffen translated from German by Dora Baxer, *The Breaking Which Brings Us Anew* poems by Charles Taylor, *Stones* by Daisy Aldan, *Verses For the Zodiac* by Daisy Aldan. *Between High Tides* poems by Daisy Aldan, *A Golden Story* novel, (pub. with NEA grant). Distributorm, last two titles: Caroline House: 2 Ellis Place, Ossining, New York 10562." avg. press run 800. Pub'd 2 titles 1979; expects 3 titles 1980. 3 titles listed in the *Small Press Record of Books in Print* (9th Edition, 1980). avg. price, cloth: $5.95; paper: $4.50; other: $12.50 limited, signed. Discounts: 40% for 5 copies or more to bookstores, dealers. 65pp; 6X9; of/lp. no unsolicited ms.

FOLIO, John Letts, 202 Great Suffolk Street, London SE1 1PR, United Kingdom. 1947. Articles, photos, reviews. circ. 30,000. 4/yr. sub. price: £1; per copy: 25p. 36pp; 8X5; of. Ads: £140 full page; £75 1/2 page.

FOLIO, Richard Wolinsky, Editor; Daniel Ziegler, Art Director, 2207 Shattuck Ave., Berkeley, CA 94704. 1949. Poetry, fiction, articles, art, photos, cartoons, satire, criticism, reviews, letters, collages. "This is basically a program guide. However, each issue contains articles that are program-related: for example, in recent months we have had special programming related to science fiction, and had articles and fiction by authors such as Fritz Leiber and Richard Lupoff, another issue focussed on Three Mile Island, and contained articles on news coverage on the event, as well as the future of the anti-nuclear movement. Other issues have focussed on South Africa, live music vs recorded music, and gay liberation. Future issues are planned on the relationship of the left and the new age folks, black literature, etc." circ. 22,000. 11/yr. Pub'd 11 issues 1979; expects 11 issues 1980, 11 issues 1981. sub. price: $30.00; sample: free. 24-32pp; 15X11¾; of. Pub's reviews. §politics, social criticism, 3rd world authors, science fiction, environment, film. Ads: $291.00/$156.00/$1.50 per line.

‡FOLLIES, L/A House, Kenneth J. Atchity, Editor; Bonnie Fraser, Art Director, PO Box 41110, Los Angeles, CA 90041, (213) 254-4455. 1975. Poetry, articles, art, photos, cartoons, interviews, criticism, reviews, letters, collages, concrete art, news items. "A community journal of arts and opinion. Heavy on criticism and reviews of films, art, rock and jazz record reviews. Small amount of poetry and cartoons, 'Door to Door', Focus: 'Art is the Playhouse of the Mind'." circ. 10,000 - 12,000. 12/yr. Pub'd 12 issues 1979; expects 12 issues 1980, 12 issues 1981. sub. price: $12.00; per copy: free; sample: free. Back issues: Will mail special back issues for postage. 12pp; 10X16; of. Reporting time: 1-2 weeks. No payment at this time. Copyrighted, reverts to author. Pub's reviews: 20 in 1979. §Any small press publications. Ads: $250.00/$150.00. WIP, CCLM.

Food For Thought Publications, Dick McLeester, PO Box 331, Amherst, MA 01004, 413-256-6158. 1976. "Special focus: Dreams." 4 titles listed in the *Small Press Record of Books in Print* (9th Edition, 1980). avg. price, paper: $3.00 plus 75¢ postage. Discounts: trade 3-4 copies—30 percent; 5 or more copies—40 percent. 30 day billing. 124 pp; 7X8½; of. COSMEP.

Foolproof Press, Meryl Natchez, Maureen Solomon, PO Box 647, Berkeley, CA 94701. 1979. Poetry, art, photos, cartoons, collages, news items. "*Women oriented calendr: The Whole Woman Calendar* uses cartoons, photos (b & w and color). Additional address: PO Box 215, Monson, MA 01057. *The Notebook* is essentially a blank page spiral bound notebook with photos, quotes, & practical information oriented towards women." avg. press run 10,000. avg. price, paper: $2.75; other: Calendar $4.95. Discounts: 50% purchase, 40% consignment. 12-192pp; 5X7¾, 11X14; of/lp. Reporting time: 6 months. Payment: $20.00 - $100.00 photograph per printing of 10,000 price depends on size and

141

placement. Copyrights for author. ABA.

Footnotes, F. Randolph Swartz, S. Finkelstein, 1300 Arch Street, Philadelphia, PA 19107. 1974. Interviews, criticism, reviews. avg. press run 300,000. 1 title listed in the *Small Press Record of Books in Print* (9th Edition, 1980). Discounts: Free. 96pp; 8½X11; of.

FOOTPRINT MAGAZINE, Nicholas Kolumban, Editor, 150 West Summit St, Somerville, NJ 08876. 1978. Poetry, interviews, reviews. "Open to any style and subject matter. Main concern is with quality. There is a section of poems that deal with the lives and ways of immigrants in America and with Americans living abroad; there is also a section of translations. Recent contributors: Russell Edson, Civ C. Fox, Brian Swann, Dave Kelly, Thomas Lux, William Jay Smith, Ira Sadoff, Edmund Keeley, Kimon Friar, Peter Klappert. We also interviewed Paula Fox, Thomas Lux, Patricia Hampl, Thomas Johnson and James Moore." circ. 400. 2/yr. Pub'd 2 issues 1979; expects 2 issues 1980. sub. price: $5.50; per copy: $3.00; sample: $2.50. 60pp; 9X6; lo. Reporting time: 4 weeks. Payment: 2 copies. Copyrighted. Pub's reviews: 2 in 1979. §Poetry. CCLM.

Forbidden Additions (see also sun rise fall down artpress), Meikal And, 838a Wisconsin St, Oshkosh, WI 54901. 1980. Poetry, fiction, articles, art, photos, cartoons, interviews, satire, criticism, music, letters, parts-of-novels, long-poems, collages, plays, concrete art. "Forbidden Additions is a limited edition pamphlet series (100 copies) that will be produced in the writer/artist's own typescript. Prospective contributors are encouraged to send a draft of the work for consideration. There will be a special emphasis on lnguage oriented writing. The first four are: *8 Poems* by Simon Perchik, *Born Out* by Martin J Rosenblum, *Through Birds Through Fire But Not through Glass* by Miekal And, & an unnamed volume by Cedar." avg. press run 100. Expects 4 titles 1980, 4 titles 1981. avg. price, paper: $1.00; other: $5 signed & illuminated. Discounts: none. 12-20pp; 5½X8½; †of. Reporting time: couple of weeks. Payment: 10% of the run. Does not copyright for author. COSMEP Midwest.

FOREIGN POETS AND AUTHORS REVIEW, Le Beacon Presse, Keith Gormezano, 621 Holt, Iowa City, IA 52240, 319-354-5447. 1980. Poetry, fiction, articles, art, photos, cartoons, interviews, satire, criticism, reviews, music, letters, parts-of-novels, long-poems, collages, plays, concrete art, news items. "Good informative, thought provoking writing by foreign poets and authors. Our purpose is to expose American editors, publishers, libraries, to the creative works by foreign authors. We prefer English translations. Please use a PICA typewriter and send good, clean, clear, fairly dark photocopied submissions along with your brief (less than 150 word) resume. Only non-American authors can be published." circ. 200. 6/yr. sub. price: $8.00/2 yrs; per copy: $2.00; sample: $1.95. 60-80pp; 5X8. Reporting time: up to a year. Pub's reviews: 20 in 1979. §Must be written by non-American authors, we will review *all* books and magazines received. Ads: $5.00/$3.00/$0.05 20 word minimum, will exchange. COSMEP.

FORESIGHT MAGAZINE, John W.B. Barklam, J. Barklam, 29 Beaufort Av., Hodge Hill, Birmingham, England B346AD, United Kingdom, 021-783-0587. 1970. Articles, reviews, letters, news items. "Articles of approx 1000 words welcomed. A bias towards philsophy as related to life. Dealing also in mysticism, occultism, U.F.O.S and allied subjects. Aims are to help create peace and encourage spiritual awareness and evolution in the world." circ. 1500. 6/yr. Pub'd 6 issues 1979; expects 6 issues 1980, 6 issues 1981. sub. price: £2.20 - $4.50; per copy: 40p, $0.75; sample: 40p, $0.75. Back issues: 22p approx, $0.50. Discounts: none. 20pp; 5¾X8¼; †dupl. Reporting time: immediately. Pub's reviews: 17 in 1979. §Health, philosophy, psychic phenomena, UFOs, prediction, allied fiction. Ads: £9 ($16.25)/£5 ($9.00)/2p ($0.03).

The Forest Library Edentata, PO Box 349, Redway, CA 95560. 1 title listed in the *Small Press Record of Books in Print* (9th Edition, 1980).

Forest Primeval Press, J. T. Ledbetter, 1335 Norman, Thousand Oaks, CA 91360. 1979. Poetry. avg. press run 500. Pub'd 1 title 1979. 2 titles listed in the *Small Press Record of Books in Print* (9th Edition, 1980). avg. price, other: free. 1pp; 8½X11; of. Reporting time: 2 week. Payment: copies.

FORGE, Christopher W. Parker, Editor, 47 Murray Street, New York, NY 10007, (212) 349-8788. 1978. Poetry, photos, criticism, reviews. "Submit manuscripts of three to five poems and include a SASE. We will publish mainstream poetry of high literary standards, also seeking poetry with a new contemporary voice. Expect special sections on the experimental, the avant-garde." circ. 500-1,000. 4/yr. Expects 4 issues 1981. 1 title listed in the *Small Press Record of Books in Print* (9th Edition, 1980). sub. price: $9.00; per copy: $2.50; sample: $2.50. Back issues: $3.00. Discounts: Write for arrangement. 30pp; 6X9; †of. Reporting time: 2 months. Payment: In contributors copies. Copyrighted, reverts to author. Pub's reviews. §Poetry, chapbooks, broadsheets, books, fine presses. Ads: $35.-00/$20.00. COSMEP.

FORMAT, Seven Oaks Press, C. L. Morrison, 405 S. 7th Street, St. Charles, IL 60174, (312) 584-0187. 1978. Poetry, articles, art, interviews, criticism, letters, parts-of-novels, long-poems, concrete art, news items. "Nonfiction up to 3,000 words. *Investing in Art—Bad Practice and Damn Near Impossible,* by Tom Bowie; *Chicago-New York Connection,* by C. L. Morrison; *Variations on a Theme by Stevie Wonder,* by Alfred L. Woods." circ. 1,000. 12/yr. Pub'd 12 issues 1979. sub. price: $6.00; per copy: $.80; sample: free. Back issues: $1.50. Discounts: none. 20 - 32pp; 7½X10; †of. Reporting time: 2 weeks to one month. Payment: $1.50-$30.00. Copyrighted, reverts to author. Pub's reviews. §Art, psychology, sociology, literature. Ads: $100.00/$50.00/$0.10.

FORMS: A Magazine of Poetry and Fine Art, Ken Fifer, Betsy Fifter, Michael Ņattersley, Len Roberts, Rieardo Viera, Rosalind Pace, 1724 Maple Street, Bethlehem, PA 18017. 1978. Poetry, art, photos, criticism. "*Forms* seeks excellence in poetry and visual art. We are particularly interested in new, original, and unrecognized work. Recent contributors include: Bob Behr, Liz Stout, Larry Fink, Bill Firschein, Michael Carey, Francisco Mendez-Diez, and others. Please enclose a SASE with all correspondence" circ. 500. 3/yr. Expects 1 issue 1980, 3 issues 1981. sub. price: $5.00; per copy: $2.00. Discounts: Negotiable. 16pp; 11X15; of. Reporting time: 2 weeks to 4 months. Payment: one year's subscription. Ads: $200.00/$100.00.

Four Corners Press, Victor Lipton, 463 West Street, New York, NY 10014, (212) 989-1284. 1978. Poetry, fiction, parts-of-novels, long-poems, plays. "Poetry as externalized dialogue, monologue. Drama that fuses poetry, time & place, utilizes musical forms and dance." avg. press run 1,000. Pub'd 1 title 1979; expects 2 titles 1980. 1 title listed in the *Small Press Record of Books in Print* (9th Edition, 1980). avg. price, paper: $2.50. Discounts: 40%. 60pp; 5X7; †of/lp. Reporting time: 2 months. Payment: individually negotiated.

FOUR DOGS MOUNTAIN SONGS, Doggeral Press, Peter Katoff, Alice Karle, Toby Juan, 417 Sea View Road, Santa Barbara, CA 93108. 1971. Poetry, fiction, art, satire, parts-of-novels, long-poems. "Not really a mag, but an anthology." price per copy: $25.00. Back issues: $20.00 for Four Dogs 1971. 60pp; 6⅛X9⅛; †lp. Reporting time: 2 months. Payment: copies.

FOUR QUARTERS, John C. Kleis, LaSalle College, Philadelphia, PA 19141. 1951. Poetry, fiction, articles. circ. 700. 4/yr. sub. price: $4.00; per copy: $1.00; sample: $1.00. Back issues: $1. 48pp; 6X9; lp. Reporting time: 6 wks. Payment: $5 poem; story, article up to $25 + 3 copies. CCLM.

‡Four Seasons Foundation, PO Box 159, Bolinas, CA 94924.

THE FOUR ZOAS JOURNAL OF POETRY & LETTERS, The Four Zoas Press, M. Gordon, P. Daniels, H. Ehrenfeld, Box 461, Ware, MA 01082. 1971. Poetry, letters, long-poems. "We are a limited edition press, printing our books by hand, often using rag papers. The *Journal* is a *Contemporary* magazine and has published Jon Silkin, Gary Gach, Ken Smith, Alicia Ostriker, John Stevens Wade, Jack Hirschman, Diane Stevenson, among the many. And we believe what Oscar Wilde said, that 'a beautiful thing helps us by being what it is.'" circ. 1,000. 2 or 3 issues/year. Pub'd 4 issues 1979. sub. price: $7.50; per copy: $3.00; sample: $2.00. Back issues: issue 1 & 2 (amnesty) $10. Discounts: 10 or more-50% disc cash basis. 50pp; 9X6; †le. Reporting time: 3-6 weeks. Payment: 2 copies. Not copyrighted. Pub's reviews: 2 in 1979. §contemporary poetry magazines, books of poems, letterpress pub. Ads: $50 or exchange/$25. CCLM, COSMEP, NESPA.

The Four Zoas Press (see also THE FOUR ZOAS JOURNAL OF POETRY & LETTERS), Box 461, Ware, MA 01082. 1971. "We practice the whole art of language" avg. press run 300. 19 titles listed in the *Small Press Record of Books in Print* (9th Edition, 1980). avg. price, cloth: $25.00; paper: $4.00; other: $3.00. Discounts: bookstores write for schedule. 25 - 40pp; 5½X8; †lp. Reporting time: 2 - 8 weeks. Payment: 2 copies. Does not copyright for author. CCLM, NESPA.

FOURTH DIMENSION, P.J. Kemp, Editor; Noreen Ledoux, Contributing Editor, Box 10, Brigham, Quebec JOE 1JO, Canada. 1979. Fiction, articles, art, reviews, news items, interviews, criticism. "*Fourth Dimension* is a magazine of science and scientific inquiry to offset dry, pedantic 'scientism'. Articles wanted on how the peripheral subjects of parapsychology, religion and philosophy tie in with established scientific theory. Speculative articles, no matter how far-fetched or unusual, are welcome, but must have solid background of scientific reasoning and facts, rather than being mere flights of fancy. ALL material must be to the purpose of expanding useful knowledge rather than merely adding information bits to an already disorderly and chaotic collection. Emphasis is on how to incorporate such knowledge into daily life and practical application. USA contributors submit to Box 231, Richford, VT 05476." circ. 200. 3-4/yr. Pub'd 3 issues 1979; expects 3-4 issues 1980, 3-4 issues 1981. sub. price: $5.00; per copy: $1.50. 20-30pp; 8½X11; †of. Reporting time: two weeks. Payment: up to 5 complimentary copies. Copyrighted, reverts to author. Pub's reviews: 27 in 1979. §scientific discovery, religion, philosophy, parapsychology.

Fragments/The Valentine Press (see also COBBLESTONE), Phil Yeh, Janet Valentine, Don De-Contreras, P.O. Box 1128, Los Alamitos, CA 90720. 1974. Poetry, fiction, articles, art, photos, cartoons, interviews, satire, criticism, reviews, music, letters. "Basically Fragments West publishes *art* — we are a company dedicated to young artists. By *art* we include all aspects of the arts (film, plays, drawings, cartoons, novels, etc.)—-Recent contributors: Ray Bradbury, Robert Illes, Don DeContr-eras, Gregg Rickman." avg. press run 5,000. 3 titles listed in the *Small Press Record of Books in Print* (9th Edition, 1980). avg. price, paper: $1.50. Discounts: 40% discount on most orders. 60pp; 8½X11; of. Reporting time: 2 weeks. Payment: yes. Copyrights for author.

The Chas. Franklin Press, Linda D. Meyer, 18409 90th Avenue W, Edmonds, WA 98020, (206) 774-6979. 1979. "This press was formed for the specific purpose of publishing *The Cesarean (R)evolution,* a handbook for parents and childbirth educators. There is a possibility of publishing 2 more books in the next few years." avg. press run 5,000. Pub'd 1 title 1979. avg. price, paper: $4.95. Discounts: 40% to regular bookstores. 143pp; 5½X8.

Franklin Publishing Company (see also BOOK BUYER'S GUIDE/MARKETPLACE), Kevin K. Kopec, PO Box 208, East Millstone, NJ 08873, 201-873-2156. 1975. Articles. "Consumer orientation material. Source directories." avg. press run 10,000. 1 title listed in the *Small Press Record of Books in Print* (9th Edition, 1980). avg. price, paper: $3.95. Discounts: 50 percent. 50-100pp; 8½X11; of. Reporting time: 3 months. Payment: 25 percent. Copyrights for author. COSMEP.

Franson Publications (see also NOTES FROM THE UNDERGROUND), Robert Wilfred Franson, Michael J. Dunn, Notes from Underground, 4291 Van Dyke Place, San Diego, CA 92116. 1975. Parts-of-novels, long-poems. Discounts: 40% on minimum 5 copies mixed. of. Reporting time: 3 weeks. Payment: varies, usually 20%. Copyrights for author.

Free People Press (see BOTH SIDES NOW)

FREE VENICE BEACHHEAD, PO Box 504, Venice, CA 90291, 823-5092. 1968. Poetry, articles, art, photos, cartoons, interviews, satire, criticism, reviews, letters, collages, news items. circ. 10,000. 12/yr. Pub'd 12 issues 1979; expects 12 issues 1980, 12 issues 1981. sub. price: $5.00; per copy: free; sample: free. Back issues: $1.00 per issue, if available. 16pp; 11X17; of. Payment: none. Pub's reviews: 2 in 1979. Ads: $150.00/$90.00/$5.00 col inch. APS, LNS.

FREEDOM, Freedom Press, Collective, In Angel Alley, 84B Whitechapel High St, London E1, United Kingdom, 01 247 9249. 1886. Articles, cartoons, reviews, news items, criticism, letters. circ. 1,500. fortnightly. Pub'd 25 issues 1979; expects 25 issues 1980. 7 titles listed in the *Small Press Record of Books in Print* (9th Edition, 1980). sub. price: £7.00 ($15.00) airmail, rates on request, seasonal; per copy: 25p; sample: SAE. Back issues: available at price of current issue (or of sub. for year sets). Discounts: 25% to indiv/bulk order, 33% to shops. 16pp; 12X8½; of. Reporting time: normally by return. Payment: none. Copyrighted, reverts to author. Pub's reviews: 30-35 in 1979. §anarchism. Ads: none.

Freedom Press (see also FREEDOM), Collective, In Angel Alley, 84B Whitechapel High St, London E1, United Kingdom, 01-247-9249. 1886. avg. press run 2,000. Pub'd 2 titles 1979; expects 2 titles 1980. 8 titles listed in the *Small Press Record of Books in Print* (9th Edition, 1980). avg. price, cloth: £4.00; paper: £1.00. Discounts: 33⅓% plus postage. 150pp; 8X5; li. Reporting time: by return. Payment: by negociation. copyrights for author if required.

FREEDOMWAYS, Esther Jackson, Managing Editor; John Henrik Clarke, Associate Editor; J. H. O'Dell, Associate Editor; Ernest Kaiser, Associate Editor, Freedomways Associates, Inc., 799 Broadway Suite 542, New York, NY 10003. 1961. Poetry, articles, cartoons, reviews. circ. 7,000. 4/yr. Pub'd 4 issues 1979; expects 4 issues 1980. sub. price: $4.50 (US)/$6.00 (outside US); per copy: $1.25; sample: free. Back issues: $2.00 except for special back issues @ $2.50 each. Discounts: 30% discount-bulk, agent only. 96pp; 4½X7¼; of. Reporting time: several months. No payment. Copyrighted, does not revert to author. Pub's reviews: 40 in 1979. §Black culture, economics. Ads: $150.00/$75.00.

FREELANCE, Frelance Publishing Co., Simon Sinclair, 204 W 20th St, New York, NY 10011. 1979. Articles, art, photos, interviews, news items. "Payment is made upon publishing of creative works. Payments range from $15 and up. Articles of 1500 word or less are preferred. Articles about periodical publishing, magazine editing and writing, public relations, advertising, grant proposal writing, fund-raising, and relative subjects appeal to the interests of the editors." circ. 5000. 12/yr. sub. price: $40; per copy: $4; sample: $4. Discounts: agencies: 2/3rds subsc rate. 8pp; 8½X11; of. Reporting time: 2 weeks or less. Payment: $15 and up. Copyrighted. Pub's reviews. §see above. Ads: $250/$150/40¢. FRA, MAAA, DMMA, NPNY.

Freelance Press Services (see CONTRIBUTORS BULLETIN (also FREELANCE WRITING))

Freelance Publications, M. Simony, Box 8, Bayport, NY 11705, (516) 472-1799. 1978. "230 McConnell Avenue, Bayport, NY 11705. 1st and only title thus far: *Travel Agency* A How-To-Do-It Manual for Starting One Of Your Own by Anne Stenholm. LC 78-67643, ISBN 0960205004." avg. press run 1,000. Pub'd 3 titles 1979. avg. price, paper: $8.95. Discounts: 2-4 20%; 5-9 30%; 10-24 40%; 25 and up 45%; 64 (box) 50%. 123pp; 7¼X9½; of. Payment: none. Copyrights for author. COSMEP.

Frelance Publishing Co. (see also FREELANCE), Simon Sinclair, 204 West 20th St., New York, NY 10011. 1979. Articles, art, photos, interviews, news items. "Freelnce writers and authors can get ssistance with an advisor on publishing their works." avg. press run 5000. Expects 2 titles 1980. avg. price, cloth: negotiable. of. Reporting time: 2 weeks or less. Copyrights for author. FRA, MAAA, DMMA, NPNY.

Freestone Publishing Collective, Jeannine Paruati Baker, Frederich Vishnu Dass Baker, Tamara Slayton Glenn, 10001 E Zayante Road, Felton, CA 95018, (408) 335-3714. 1973. "At this point, both of our publications deal with women's health and reproductive concerns. Additional address: Freestone North, Tamara Slayton Glenn - Advertising Manager, 1547 Rose Avenue, Santa Rosa, Calif 95401. *Pre-Natal Yoga & Natural Childbirth* 5,000 (38,000 total) ; *Hygieia, A Woman's Herbal* 10,000 (20,000 total)." avg. press run 5,000 to 10,000. Pub'd 1 title 1979; expects 1 title 1980. avg. price, paper: $3.50, $9.00. 64, 276pp; 8½X11; 9X9. Payment: all royalties, minus 20% which goes to collective fund, go directly to authors. Copyrights for author. COSMEP.

Fresh Press, Sharon Elliot, 774 Allen Court, Palo Alto, CA 94303, (415) 493-3596. 1977. Art. "Tasty, creative, natural foods recipes. *The Busy People's Fast Foodbook* a 'fast-foods' approach to more healthful eating. *Tofu Goes West* tofu in American style main dishes, breads and desserts *Tofu at Center Stage.*" avg. press run 20,000. Pub'd 1 title 1979; expects 1 title 1980, 1 title 1981. 2 titles listed in the *Small Press Record of Books in Print* (9th Edition, 1980). avg. price, paper: $4.95. Discounts: Jobbers: 50%; Trade: 10-50%, depending on number of books purchased. 120pp; 8X8; of. Reporting time: Immediate reply on receipt; one month determination time. Payment: standard royalty. Copyrights for author. WBPA.

FRIENDS & FELONS, David Kronenwetter, 2115 Esplanade Avenue, New Orleans, LA 70119, 504-943-7041.

FRIENDS OF POETRY, Ron Ellis, Dept of English, University of Wisconsin, Whitewater, WI 53190, (414) 472-1036. 1979. Poetry, art, photos. "We are interested in short, intense, highly crafted work in any form. Longer poems will also be considered." circ. 400. 2/yr. Pub'd 1 issue 1979; expects 2 issues 1980, 2 issues 1981. sub. price: $5.00; per copy: $3.00; sample: $3.00. 40 - 50pp; 5½X8½; of. Reporting time: 2-4 weeks. Payment: 3 copies. Copyrighted.

Friends of the Earth (see also NOT MAN APART), Bruce Colman, 124 Spear, San Francisco, CA 94105, 415-495-4770. 1969. "We don't accept unsolicited manuscripts." avg. press run 8,500. Pub'd 8 titles 1979; expects 6 titles 1980, 8 titles 1981. 17 titles listed in the *Small Press Record of Books in Print* (9th Edition, 1980). avg. price, cloth: $15.00; paper: $6.95. Discounts: 1-4, 20%; 5-49, 40%; 50-99, 42%; 100+, 45%. 250pp; 6X9. Copyrights for author. WBPA.

Frog in the Well, Susan Hester, 430 Oakdale Road, East Palo Alto, CA 94303, 415-323-1237. 1980. Fiction. avg. press run 2,000. avg. price, paper: $4.50. Discounts: 40% on 5 or more trade; Bulk, jobber 50%. 150pp; 5½X8½; of. Reporting time: 3 months. Payment: 50% minus production costs. Copyrights for author.

From Here Press (see also XTRAS), William J. Higginson, Penny Harter, Box 219, Fanwood, NJ 07023. 1975. Poetry, fiction, parts-of-novels, long-poems, plays, criticism. "In addition to *XTRAS* we publish broadsides, regional (NJ) anthologies, and miniatures. (No submissions until 1981, please)." avg. press run 500 - 1000. Expects 3 titles 1980, 5 titles 1981. 26 titles listed in the *Small Press Record of Books in Print* (9th Edition, 1980). avg. price, paper: 10¢ - $10.00. Discounts: 40% to trade (5 mixed titles). 1 - 100pp; size varies; of. Reporting time: Immediate. Payment: varies. Copyrights for author. COSMEP.

FROM THE CENTER: A FOLIO, Maurice Kenny, PO Box 451, Bowling Green Station, New York, NY 10004, (212) 522-3227. 1978. Poetry, fiction, art. "*From the Center,* a folio of poems, brief fiction and art on broadsides, the work of many of the most important Native American poets and artists of this time. Some contributors: Paula Gunn Allen, Peter Blue Cloud, Joy Harjo, Geary Hobson, Duane Niatum, Mary Tall Mountain, Wendy Rose, Joseph Bruchac, Simon J. Ortiz." circ. 500-1,000. irregular. Pub'd 2 issues 1979. price per copy: $7.50; sample: $7.50. Back issues: $15.00. Discounts: 40%. of. Reporting time: 6 weeks. Payment: small payment and copies. Copyrighted, reverts to author. CCLM, NYSCA.

C J Frompovich Publications, Catherine J. Frompovich, RD 1, Chestnut Road, Coopersburg, PA 18036, (215) 346-8461. 1978. avg. press run 5,000-10,000. Pub'd 5 titles 1979; expects 4 titles 1980. 9 titles listed in the *Small Press Record of Books in Print* (9th Edition, 1980). avg. price, paper: $0.-69-$2.50; other: $2.95-$3.95. Discounts: 50%. 32-160pp; †of. Reporting time: varies, usually 30 days. Copyrights for author. COSMEP.

THE FRONT, The Front Press, Jim Smith, P.O. Box 1355, Kingston, Ontario K7L5C6, Canada. 1974. Poetry, fiction, articles, art, photos, cartoons, interviews, satire, criticism, reviews, letters, parts-of-novels, long-poems, collages, plays, concrete art. "Bias towards post-modernist & experimental, exploratory work (slight). Length no matter (as long as contributors understand that longer pieces might be broken into 2 or more numbers). Open to any style. Recent contributors: Stuart MacKinnon, Jim Smith, David McFadden, Wayne Clifford, B P Nichol, Joan Harcourt, Ken Norris, Jim Joyce, Montreal poets." circ. 500. 4/yr. Pub'd 4 issues 1979; expects 5 issues 1980, 5 issues 1981. sub. price: $10.00; per copy: $2.00; sample: $2.00. Back issues: $10.00. Discounts: 40 percent, 5 copies or more, also by barter. 50 - 80pp; 8½X11; 5½X8½; †mi/of. Reporting time: 2 weeks. Payment: Copies (5). buys first serial publication only. Pub's reviews: 5 in 1979. §poetry/fiction/avant -garde & experimental arts. Ads: Free/exchange. $25.00 for full-page.

The Front Press (see also THE FRONT), Jim Smith, Editor, P.O. Box 1355, Kingston, ON K7L5C6, Canada. 1974. Poetry, fiction, articles, art, photos, cartoons, interviews, satire, criticism, reviews, music, letters, parts-of-novels, long-poems, collages, plays, concrete art, news items. "2 chapbooks a year (36 pg) beginning March 1979. Write for catalog" avg. press run 300 - 500. Expects 3 titles 1980, 3 titles 1981. 4 titles listed in the *Small Press Record of Books in Print* (9th Edition, 1980). avg. price, cloth: $5.00 US; paper: $3.50 US; other: varies. Discounts: 40% over ten copies, 90 day return, with permission. 36 - 100pp; size varies. Reporting time: 1 month or less. Payment: TBA. Copyrights for author.

FRONT STREET TROLLEY, Molly McIntosh, 2125 Acklen Ave., Nashville, TN 37212, 615-297-2977. 1974. Poetry, fiction, articles, art, cartoons, interviews, satire, criticism, reviews. "Short fiction (maximum 2,500), short articles, etc., poetry (any length)-works of a satirical nature especially welcome, preparance given to Southern writers." circ. 300-500. 2/yr. Pub'd 2 issues 1979; expects 2 issues 1980. sub. price: $3.00; per copy: $1.50; sample: $0.50 or free. Back issues: $0.50. Discounts: none. 32pp; 8½X11; of. Reporting time: one to three months. Payment: copies. Copyrighted. Pub's reviews. §Poetry, films, books. no ads, except of the announcement nature. COSMEP, CCLM.

FRONTIERS: A Journal of Women Studies, George, Managing Editor; Parker, Renton, c/o Women Studies, University of Colorado, Boulder, CO 80309, 303-492-5065. 1975. Poetry, fiction, articles, art, photos, cartoons, interviews, satire, criticism, reviews, letters, parts-of-novels, long-poems, plays, news items. "*FRONTIERS* bridges the gap between academic and community women by publishing a journal which is exciting and accessible to all women. We seek both traditional and innovative work, collaborative and interdisciplinary manuscripts. Each issue has a theme, and articles are published around it from different viewpoints; also in each issue are a variety of other articles on non-theme topics. We have no 'political bias' except feminism — in all its manifestations. We prefer to consider manuscripts under 20 pages. We also consider poetry, short stories, photographs, and graphics." circ. 2,500. 3/yr. Pub'd 3 issues 1979; expects 3 issues 1980, 3 issues 1981. sub. price: $11.00 indiv., $18.00 instit.; per copy: $3.75 indiv., $6.00 instit.; sample: $3.75. Back issues: (same as single copy, but Volume I and parts of Volume II & Volume III are now completely out of print). Discounts: Bookstores: 40%; consignment orders accepted. Bulk rate: 10% discount if 10 (ten) or more copies of the same issue are purchased/ordered together. (No other discounts.). 88pp; 8½X11; of. Reporting time: Articles: 3-6 months; poetry: 2-4 months. Payment: None (If published, 2 free copies of the issue are sent.). Copyrighted, reverts if requested by author in advance. Pub's reviews: 10 in 1979. §All books of interest to women, on all subjects. Ads: $110.00/$75.00. COSMEP.

Frontier Press, Harvey Brown, Elizabeth Warner, P O Box 5023, Santa Rosa, CA 95402, 707-544-5174. 1964. Poetry. avg. press run 2,000. Pub'd 3 titles 1979; expects 2 titles 1980. 16 titles listed in the *Small Press Record of Books in Print* (9th Edition, 1980). avg. price, cloth: $8.00; paper: $2.00. Discounts: 40 percent. 100pp; 6X8; lp/of. Copyrights for author. COSMEP.

FRONTLINES, Robert Poole Jr., Marty Zupan, Box 40105, Santa Barbara, CA 93101, 805-963-5993. 1978. Articles, news items. "Mostly staff written. All material deals with the libertarian movement." circ. 1,800. 11/yr. Pub'd 4 issues 1979; expects 11 issues 1980. sub. price: $15.00; per copy: $1.25; sample: $1.25. Back issues: cover price. 8pp; 8½X11; of. Reporting time: 45 days. Payment: $10.-00-$25.00. Copyrighted. Ads: $180.00/$100.00/$0.20.

FROZEN WAFFLES, Pitjon Press/BackBack Media, Backpack Media, Bro. Dimitrios, David Wade,

3215 Sec Ave West, Bradenton, FL 33505. 1976. Poetry, fiction, articles, art, interviews, reviews, collages, concrete art. "Want poems using the magic of the banal, subreal, 'everyday' (cf Prevert, Zen poetry, Brautigan at his best, D. Wade & Richard Gombar's poems in *Stoney Lonesomes* No. 4 & 5, Spike Jones writing about Stravinsky's shoes squeaking, etc.) or the magic of the 'meta-real' (cf Breton, Neruda, Bly when he's not bull shitting, the school of Duane Locke at it's best, etc.) Frags from diaries (names changed to protect the guilty), anectotes, weird observations, fresh interviews, art work (India ink only!) will also be appreciated. Ditto: book & mag reviews (short!). Due to various delays, we'll be coming out (Nos. 1-3) in late '80 and/or early '81. Would like black India ink sketches of poets accepted by us. Preferably self-portraits: or by fellow-artists of poets. This last requirement is a must! We're weird about wanting pictures *or black & white photos* of the poet. Don't send us anything unless you wish to meet our last requirement. We have been delayed until funding problems stabilize. *Zen Events, Banal Episodes* has been superseded by *Hungry Horse in a Blank Field: Zen-Centered Poems* by Dimitrios/Wade. It is being published before *Frozen Waffles* (Anthology) goes to press. We have one more big 'crisis' (economic, of course) to go through before *FW* #1 is published, *but looks like we're clear to get Hungry Horse off the ground in a few days.* Two or three copies of *Death of a Chinese Paratrooper* by David Wade are still available at the rare (unsalable) price of $30.00 each. *Hungry Horse*, though on a limited scale (around 200 copies), may be our best thing since *Four New Poets* Lp of 1966. Three deaths in our family in a short time period, plus probate of estate has slowed us down further! But we continue to work toward publication. Plan to print special issues of a single poet, also. Actually, *Frozen Waffles* is the *anthology* of poetry and art work and short fiction, etc. which will appear irregularly until funding permits us to function on an annual basis." circ. 200-400. 2-3/yr. sub. price: not set. But figure about $4.50 per copy.; per copy: about $4.50 to rise to the occasion each year as inflation nibbles away; sample: $6.00. Back issues: $6.00 each (after 2 years: $10.00 each). Discounts: 10% off five or more. 36-80pp; size varies; of. Reporting time: 2 weeks-2 months; if no reply, you had no SASE, or material was lost in the mail. Payment: 1 copy. Copyrighted. Pub's reviews. §poetry, poetics, bios of poets. no ads: not yet, anyway.

EL FUEGO DE AZTLAN, Oscar Trevino, 3408 Dwinelle Hall, Univ of Calif, Berkeley, CA 94720. 1976. Poetry, fiction, articles, art, photos, cartoons, interviews, satire, criticism, reviews, parts-of-novels, long-poems, plays. "Short stories over 10 doublespaced typewritten pages have little chance of being considered. Looking for unusual, original Chicano material. Free to prisoners (as long as we can afford it)." 4/yr. Pub'd 4 issues 1979; expects 4 issues 1980. sub. price: $8.00 institution-$3.50; per copy: $1.50. Discounts: 10 or more, 25 percent off. 32pp; of. Reporting time: 6 weeks. Payment: contributor's copies. Copyrighted, reverts to author. Pub's reviews. §Chicano/Mexican American. CCLM.

Fulcourte Press, Lyn Deardorff, PO Box 1961, Decatur, GA 30031, (404) 378-5750. 1978. Art, cartoons, satire. "Our first book, *The Taxpayer's Coloring Book,* is a humorous, cartoon interpretation of Senator William Proxmire's Golden Fleece Awards. It is offset printing in paperback, 56 pages, with black & white cartoons, original copy. We hope to continue in the humorous, interpretative vein, but will not be limited to this only." avg. press run 5,000. Expects 1 title 1980, 4 titles 1981. 1 title listed in the *Small Press Record of Books in Print* (9th Edition, 1980). avg. price, paper: $3.00. Discounts: Standard. 56pp; 8½X11; of. Copyrights for author.

Full Count Press, Betty Shipley, Nina Langley, 223 N. Broadway, Edmond, OK 73034, 341-8497. 1979. Poetry, long-poems. "Anthology, new poems, anti-nuke movement. Contributors include: William Pitt Root, Charles Fishman, Laurel Speer." avg. press run 1,000. Pub'd 1 title 1979. avg. price, paper: $3.95. Discounts: 40% off, over 5 more than 1, 10%. 64pp; 6X8½; of. Reporting time: 3 weeks. Payment: copies. Copyrights for author.

Full Court Press (see also THE GOODFELLOW REVIEW OF CRAFTS), Christopher Weills, Sarah Satterlee, Box 4520, Berkeley, CA 94704, 415-845-7645. 1973. Art, articles, photos, interviews, reviews, concrete art, news items. avg. press run 15,000. Pub'd 6 titles 1979; expects 6 titles 1980. 2 titles listed in the *Small Press Record of Books in Print* (9th Edition, 1980). avg. price, other: $1.00. Discounts: 50 percent. 24pp; 14X10; of. Reporting time: 3 weeks. Payment: Negotiated. Copyrights for author. COSMEP.

Full Court Press, Inc., Ron Padgett, Joan Simon, Anne Waldman, 15 Laight Street, New York, NY 10017. 1974. Poetry, fiction, plays. "Recent books by Frank O'Hara, Larry Fagin & Tom Veitch." avg. press run 2,000. Expects 3 titles 1980. avg. price, cloth: $9.95; paper: $3.50. Discounts: 40% trade. 150pp; 5½X7½; of. Reporting time: Varies. Payment: yes. Copyrights for author.

Full Track Press (see also UNMENDABLY INTEGRAL: an audiocassette quarterly of the arts), Joe Cuomo, Editorial Director, PO Box 55, Planetarium Station, New York, NY 10024. 1978. Poetry, fiction, interviews, long-poems. "Full Track Press produces professionally directed and expertly engineered audio programs (many Full Track Press tapes have been broadcast on Pacifica radio WBAI-FM in New York), which are published on high quality cassette. Broadcast quality open reel (7½ips) copies are also available to radio stations & individuals (inquire: Broadcast Dept, Full Track Press). We publish *Unmendably Integral*: an audiocassette quarterly of the arts (issue #1: Meridel Le Sueur; #2: Roman Vishniac; #3: James Purdy; as well as 'books' of poetry read by authors such as Marie Ponsot and Fred Buell. We also publish a Documentary Arts Series, the first program of which is *The Illigal Alien*: the plight of the undocumental worker in the United States. Almost all Full Track Press programs are 90 minutes long and cost $10.00 each." Pub'd 4 titles 1979; expects 7 titles 1980, 6 titles 1981. avg. price, other: audiocassette: $10.00. Discounts: 15% to agents, quarterly. 90 minutes. Reporting time: 2 months. Copyrights for author.

Funch Press (see also PAN AMERICAN REVIEW), Seth Wade, 1101 Tori Lane, Edinburg, TX 78539, (512) 383-7893. 1969. "No plans to do anything but the PAN AMERICAN REVIEW at present" of. Reporting time: 1-4 weeks. Payment: copies. Copyrights for author. COSMEP.

FUNNYWORLD - The Magazine of Animation and Comic Art, Mike Borrier, PO Box 1633, New York, NY 10001, (212) 544-0120. Articles, art, photos, cartoons, interviews, reviews, letters, criticism. "Reviews & histories of Disney, Warners, MGM & foreign animation studios & contemporary animation work; reviews & histories of comic strips & their creators, also underground comix. Fairly scholarly. Uses stills and rare photos." circ. 7,000. 4/yr. Expects 3 issues 1980, 4 issues 1981. sub. price: $12.00; per copy: $3.50; sample: $3.50. Back issues: $3.50. Discounts: 40%, 10+ copies: 50%, 150+ copies. 52pp; 8½X11; of. Reporting time: Varies. Copyrighted, rights do not revert. Pub's reviews: 12 in 1979. §Animation and/or Comic Art. Ads: On request. ASIFA.

Futile (see also BANGE DAGEN), Ric Blok, PO Box 812, Rotterdam 3000AV, Holland. 1971. Poetry, fiction, articles, art, photos, cartoons, interviews, satire, criticism, reviews, letters, parts-of-novels, long-poems, collages, news items. avg. press run 1,000-3,000. Pub'd 6 titles 1979; expects 8 titles 1980, 12 titles 1981. 17 titles listed in the *Small Press Record of Books in Print* (9th Edition, 1980). avg. price, paper: dfl 15. Discounts: over 10 copies, 60%. 120 - 160pp; 140X120 mm; †of. Payment: yes. Copyrights for author.

The Future Press, Richard Kostelanetz, P.O. Box 73, Canal St., New York, NY 10013. 1976. Poetry, fiction, articles, art, music, parts-of-novels, long-poems, concrete art. "Committed exclusively to radically alternative materials for books and radically alternative forms of books. Have so far done a ladderbook, a cut-out book, a collection of cards containing numerals, a looseleaf book, a fold-out book, a book entirely of numbers, the same verbal text in two radically different book formats. What we can do depends, alas, largely on grants; and since U.S. funding agencies have been notoriously ungenerous toward experimental work and its practitioners, *The Future Press* is scarcely sanguine. The artists are there; the audience is there; the trouble lies in the middle." avg. press run 600-1,000. Pub'd 2 titles 1979; expects 4 titles 1980. 10 titles listed in the *Small Press Record of Books in Print* (9th Edition, 1980). avg. price, cloth: $10.00; paper: $3.00. Discounts: 40% discount to legitimate retailers paying in advance, and including postage. 1-48pp; size varies; of. We can't encourage submissions until the funding jam is busted. Payment: generous percentage of edition. Copyrights for author.

Future Publishing Co., Carol Cubberley, Jump Off Road, St Andrews, TN 37372, (615) 598-5320. 1979. avg. press run 1,000. Pub'd 1 title 1979. 1 title listed in the *Small Press Record of Books in Print* (9th Edition, 1980). avg. price, paper: $10.00. Discounts: 40% to distributors, 10% jobbers & libraries. of. Reporting time: 1 month. Payment: negotiable. Copyrights for author.

FUTURE STUDIES CENTRE NEWSLETTER, Roland Chaplain, 15 Kelso Road, Leeds, W Yorks LS2 9PR, United Kingdom, Leeds 459865. 1973. Reviews, news items. "Bias ecological etc. The format is 1/3 'introduction' news of wht the *Future Studies Centre* is currently doing etc. 1/3 reviews of books and periodicals, and contacts names and addresses. 1/3 diary of events worldwide. It's written by anyone around at the time. Reviews are up to 350 words each." circ. 1,400. 6/yr. Pub'd 6 issues 1979; expects 6 issues 1980, 6 issues 1981. sub. price: £5; sample: free usually. Back issues: nobody's ever asked. Probably free. 10pp; size A4. Reporting time: 16 days before expected publication date. Pub's reviews. §Future studies, environment, community, energy, collectives, agriculture, recycling. Ads: no ads.

148

G

G F E BOOK SHEET, G. F. Edwards, Box 1461, Lawton, OK 73502, (405) 248-6870. 1978. "An ad sheet of books & paper items. Doesn't have articles, ads only of paper and ink items wanted and/or for sale." circ. 500. 12/yr. Pub'd 12 issues 1979; expects 12 issues 1980, 12 issues 1981. sub. price: $3.75; per copy: $0.40; sample: $0.40. Back issues: none available. 12pp; 8½X11; †of. Not copyrighted. Ads: 10¢ per line less appropriate discounts.

Gabbro Press, D. Borkowski, P. Robinson, G. Noble, I. Ainsworth, 73 Marion Street, Toronto, Ontario M6R 1E6, Canada, 536-7235. 1979. Poetry. "Any length. We have no obvious bias except, of course, excellence." avg. press run 200. Pub'd 1 title 1979; expects 4 titles 1980. 2 titles listed in the *Small Press Record of Books in Print* (9th Edition, 1980). avg. price, paper: $3.95. Discounts: 40%. 48pp; 5X8½; †lp. Reporting time: 2-4 weeks. Payment: 10% of profit. Copyrights for author.

GAIRM, Gairm Publications, Derick S. Thomson, 29 Waterloo St., Glasgow, Scotland G2, United Kingdom. 1952. Articles, poetry, fiction, cartoons, photos, reviews, interviews, criticism. "All matter printed is in Gaelic" circ. 2,000. 4/yr. Pub'd 4 issues 1979; expects 4 issues 1980. sub. price: $5.00; per copy: $1.25. Back issues: available in most cases. size c. 8vo.; lp. Payment: nominal. Pub's reviews: 14 in 1979. §Scottish, Irish, poetry. Ads: £40/£25.

Gairm Publications (see also GAIRM), Derick S. Thomson, 29 Waterloo St, Glasgow, Scotland G2, United Kingdom. 1952. Poetry, fiction, articles, cartoons, interviews, criticism, reviews. "All publications are in Scottish, Gaelic" avg. press run 1,000. Expects 6 titles 1981. 8 titles listed in the *Small Press Record of Books in Print* (9th Edition, 1980). Payment: 10%.

GALILEO, Ave Victor Hugo Publishing, Charles C. Ryan, Editor, 339 Newbury Street, Boston, MA 02115. 1976. Poetry, fiction, articles, interviews, criticism, reviews, parts-of-novels, plays. "Science fiction and fantasy magazine." circ. 50 m. 6/yr. Pub'd 4 issues 1979; expects 6 issues 1980. sub. price: $7.50; per copy: $1.95; sample: $1.95. Back issues: Numbers 1 & 2, $6.00; Number 3, $4.50. Discounts: 40%. 96pp; 8½X11. Reporting time: 2 months. Payment: 2-7¢ a word. Copyrighted, reverts to author. Pub's reviews: 24 in 1979. §Books of fiction and non-fiction related to science and science fiction, also poetry and art. Ads: $1,000.00/$512.00/$0.50.

GALLERY SERIES/POETS, Harper Square Press, Phyllis Ford-Choyke, Arthur Choyke, 401 W. Ontario St., c/o Artcrest Products, Chicago, IL 60610. 1967. "*Gallery Series Five/Poets-To An Aging Nation (with occult overtones)* is last of present series. No unsolited material." circ. 1,000 plus. Irreg. sub. price: $2.25 each; per copy: $2.25. Back issues: GS I, $1.25; GS II, $1.50; GS III, $1.75; GS IV, $2.00. 104pp; 4¼X11; of. No ms. solicited. Payment: yes. Copyrighted. CCLM, COSMEP.

Galloping Dog Press, Peter Hodgkiss, 32 The Promenade, Swansea, West Glamorgan SA1 6EN, United Kingdom. 1976. Poetry, fiction, long-poems, non-fiction, criticism. "GDP is an *unsubsidised* press operated completely separately from poetry information. Publications. Jim Burns-*Playing It Cool*; David Tipton-*A Graph of Love*. Publications 1977-8 (Until Spring 1978): Colin Simms *Parfleche*; Phil Maillard *Grazing the Octave*; Clayton Eshleman *On Mules Sent From Chavin*; John Freeman *A Landscape Out of Focus*; Kenneth White *The Life-Technique of John Cowper Powys*. Do own printing, mimeo only. 1979 titles so far published: Opal L. Nations *A Pen, Some Paper, Many Dreams & Other Eye Movements* ; Phil Maillard *Quartz: A Winter Book*; Alan Halsey *Yearspace*; Chris Hall *Long Time Sun Shining Down*." avg. press run 300-750. Pub'd 3 titles 1979; expects 3 titles 1980. 7 titles listed in the *Small Press Record of Books in Print* (9th Edition, 1980). avg. price, cloth: varies; paper: from 50p to £1.50, $1.50-$3.50; other: varies. Discounts: 25 percent or 33⅓ cash sale. 30-40pp; size A5/A4 (mimeo); †of/mi. Payment: Copies. Copyrights for author. ALP.

Gamma Books, Donald Smith, 307 Willow Ave, Ithaca, NY 14850, 607 539-7698. 1979. Fiction, art. "Lead-off book: *Goobersville Breakdown* an illustrated novel by Robert Lieberman (author of best-selling *Paradise Rezoned*" avg. press run 10,000. Pub'd 1 title 1979; expects 3 titles 1980, 4 titles 1981. 1 title listed in the *Small Press Record of Books in Print* (9th Edition, 1980). avg. price, cloth: $10.95; paper: $4.95. Discounts: 40% to bookstores. 200pp; 5½X8½; of. No submissions without prior query. Payment: confidential. Copyrights for author.

THE GAR, Gar Publishing Co., Hal Wylie, Carolyn Wylie, Box 4793, Austin, TX 78765, (512) 453-2556. 1971. Poetry, fiction, articles, art, photos, cartoons, criticism, reviews, letters. "*Short* poetry & fiction, feature articles will be considered. Emphasis varies-several issues have been primarily focused on African literature, others more general. Decocratic socialist political leanings. Recent contributors: Dennis Brutus, James Matthews, Wayne Kamin, Wally Serote, Lynette Brimble, Charlotte Bruner, Rene Depestre." circ. 2,000. 1-2/yr. Pub'd 1 issue 1979; expects 2 issues 1980, 2 issues 1981. sub. price: $3.00; per copy: $.50; sample: $1.00. Back issues: $1.00 per issue. 32pp; 8½X11; of. Reporting time: 3 months. No payment except free copies of issue in which work appears. Copyrighted, reverts to author. Pub's reviews: 3 in 1979. §African literature, democratic socialism. Ads: $70, $40, 25¢ a word prepaid. APS.

Gar Publishing Co. (see also THE GAR), Hal Wylie, Carolyn Wylie, PO Box 4793, Austin, TX 78765, (512) 453-2556. 1971. Poetry, photos. "We have published only 2 books so far, both poetry, with photos in addition to the poems: *Beat Street Poetry,* by Jim Ryan, $1.00, 16pp. (magazine format), published 1975, still in print. Printed offset. *Jumpsongs,* poems by Norman Moser, photos by Hal Wylie, 65pp. (paperback book), out of print (price was $3.00). Mimeographed. We hope to do more books in future-no definite plans right now." avg. press run 500. of. Reporting time: 3 months (send letter of inquiry, not ms.). Copyrights for author. APS.

Garage #3, Fred Merkel, Mary Chan, PO Box 1118, Stanwood, WA 98292.

Garamond Press (see TYPE & PRESS)

GARCIA LORCA REVIEW, Dr. Grace Alvarez-Altman, State Univ. of N.Y., Brockport, NY 14220. 1973. Poetry, articles, interviews, criticism, reviews, music, plays. "Musical composition with words of poem 'verde que te quiero verde' comments and photos of Garcia Lorca in Vermont never published before." circ. 200. 1/yr. sub. price: $4.50; per copy: $4.50; sample: $4.50. Back issues: $5.00. Discounts: none. 200pp; 6X9; of. Reporting time: 3 months. Payment: none. Copyrighted, reverts to author. Pub's reviews: 1 in 1979. §Garcia Lorca's life, works, memorabelia, cont spanish theatre. Ads: $50.00/$25.00.

Garcia River Press, Art Sussman, Louie Frazier, PO Box 527, Pt. Arena, CA 95468, (707) 882-9956. 1978. avg. press run 10,000. Expects 1 title 1980. 1 title listed in the *Small Press Record of Books in Print* (9th Edition, 1980). avg. price, paper: $4.95. Discounts: 40 to 56% off. 100pp; 7X8.

Garden Way Publishing Company, Jack Williamson, Publisher; Roger Griffith, Editor, Charlotte, VT 05445, (802) 425-2171. 1971. "How-to books for self-sufficient living in the areas of energy conservation, home construction, gardening, food preparation, livestock care and country living." Pub'd 15 titles 1979; expects 15 titles 1980, 15 titles 1981. avg. price, cloth: $12.95; paper: $6.95.

GARGOYLE, Jeffrey Kelly, Claudia Buckholts, 40 St John St 2F, Jamaica Plain, MA 02130. 1975. Poetry, art. "We prefer poems with craft and vision. We are receptive to new writers." circ. 400. 2/yr. Pub'd 2 issues 1979; expects 2 issues 1980, 2 issues 1981. sub. price: $3.50, $5.00 to libraries and institutions; per copy: $1.50; sample: $1.50. Back issues: No. 1-5 and 9 sold out. Nos. 6, 7, 8, 10 $1.50 each. Discounts: 40% to trade. 48pp; 5½X8½; of. Reporting time: deadlines March 1 and Sept. 1— report up to 3 mo. Payment: copies. Copyrighted, reverts to author but if material republished prefer note that it first appeared in Gargoyle. NESPA, CCLM.

GARGOYLE, Paycock Press, Richard Myers Peabody Jr, Editor & Publisher; Gretchen Johnsen, Poetry Editor, PO Box 57206, Washington, DC 20037, 202 333-1544. 1976. Poetry, fiction, art, photos, satire, reviews, long-poems, interviews, collages, parts-of-novels, articles. "We are anglophiles. First 14 issues have featured many British poets and writers; interviews with Chandler Brossard, Allen Ginsberg, Denis Boyles, Janine Pommy Vega, Michael Horovitz, John Gardner, Ted White, Michael M. Mooney; Poetry by Terry Stokes, Harrison Fisher, James Maher, Pete Brown, Jesse Glass, Jr., Steven Ford Brown, David Childers, Diana Vance, Larry Eigner, Adelaide Blomfield, Linda McCloud, Ron Androla, Diane DeVaul, David McAleavey, Susan Hankla; Fiction by D.E. Steward, Richard Grayson, Albert Drake, John Bennett, Curt Johnson, Rochelle Holt Dubois, Mary Clearman, Shirley Cochrane, Colin David Webb, Frank Gatling, and Kevin Urick; Autobiography by Herbert Huncke and Charles Plymell; Continuing columns by Eric Baizer, John Elsberg and George Myers, Jr./We print full-page graphics. Open to interviewers and reviewers. Query first. Open to exchange ads and subscriptions with interested presses." circ. 700 - 1,000. 3/yr. Pub'd 3 issues 1979; expects 3 issues 1980, 3 issues 1981. sub. price: $5.00; per copy: $2.50; sample: $2.50. Back issues: inquire/limited. 60pp; 8½X11; of. Reporting time: 1-2 month. Payment: 1 copy. Copyrighted, reverts to author. Pub's reviews: 20 in 1979. §Fiction, poetry, rock-jazz, exotic, avant-garde. Ads: $30.00/$15.00.

The Garlic Press, Max Lent, Tina Lent, PO Box 24799, Los Angeles, CA 90024. 1978. Pub'd 1 title 1979; expects 2 titles 1980, 3 titles 1981. 1 title listed in the *Small Press Record of Books in Print* (9th Edition, 1980). avg. price, cloth: $17.95; paper: $12.00. Discounts: 5+, 40%; 30% libraries. 150pp; 9X12; of, lp. Reporting time: no submissions accepted without query first. Copyrights for author.

GARLIC TIMES, Lovers Of The Stinking Rose/Aris Books, L. John Harris, 526 Santa Barbara

Road, Berkeley, CA 94707, 527-1958. 1976. Poetry, articles, art, photos, cartoons, interviews, satire, reviews, letters, collages, news items. "We celebrate the cuisine, folklore, herbalism cultivation and humor of garlic & onions. We use recipes, remedies, interviews with herbalism, chefs, medical doctors, etc. Members keep us informed of various media attention payed to garlic. Jeanne Rose, the popular herbalist, writes a column in each issue, our approach is light-hearted, but our information is quite serious." circ. 5,000. 1/yr. Pub'd 1 issue 1979. sub. price: $12.00 membership (yearly dues varies); per copy: $1.50. Back issues: $1.00. Discounts: trade, 40 percent; bulk, 50-55 percent; wholesale, 50-60 percent. 16pp; 7X8; of. Reporting time: 6 weeks. Payment varies. Copyrighted. Pub's reviews: 3 in 1979. §cookbooks, herbal books, natural history: garlic & onion related. Ads: $200.00/$100.-00/$50.00.

Garrett Park Press, Willis L. Johnson, Garrett Park, MD 20766. 1968. avg. press run 4,000. Pub'd 3 titles 1979; expects 4 titles 1980, 4 titles 1981. 11 titles listed in the *Small Press Record of Books in Print* (9th Edition, 1980). avg. price, paper: $15.00. Discounts: 30 percent. 400pp; 8½X11; of. Reporting time: 1 month. Payment: 10 percent. Copyrights for author.

A GAY BIBLIOGRAPHY, Gay Task Force, American Library Association, Barbara Gittings, P.O. Box 2383, Philadelphia, PA 19103, (215) 382-3222. 1971. "*A Gay Bibliography* is a non-fiction list of books, pamphlets, articles, periodicals, directories, and audiovisuals." circ. 30,000. 1 every 3 - 4 years. price per copy: $1.00. Discounts: inquire for bulk rates. 16pp; 8½X11; of. §gay/lesbian material.

GAY COMMUNITY NEWS, National Gay News, Inc., Richard Burns, Managing Editor; Amy Hoffman, Features Editor; Denise Sudell, News Editor, 22 Bromfield St., Boston, MA 02108, 617-426-4469. 1973. Articles, art, photos, interviews, satire, criticism, reviews, music, letters, cartoons, news items. "Also includes weekly news of and about gay people including news commentaries." circ. 10,000. 50/yr. Pub'd 50 issues 1979; expects 50 issues 1980. sub. price: $17.50; per copy: $.50; sample: $0.50. 20pp; 10¼X15½; of. Reporting time: 1 week. Payment: In copies. Copyrighted, does not revert to author. Pub's reviews: 200 in 1979. §gay, sexual, feminist. Ads: $300.00/$175.00/$4.00 for 4 lines. COSMEP, NEPA, RCFP (Reporter's Committe for the Freedom of the Press).

GAY INSURGENT, Daniel Tsang, PO Box 2337, Philadelphia, PA 19103. 1977. Articles, art, photos, cartoons, interviews, criticism, reviews, letters, news items. "Want gay socialist material. Recent contributors: Gayle Rubin, Louie Crew, Don Mager, Joan Nestle. Also want gay research material." circ. 2,000. 3/yr. Pub'd 1 issue 1979; expects 3 issues 1980, 3 issues 1981. sub. price: $5.00; per copy: $2.00; sample: $2.00. Discounts: 30%. 48pp; 8½X11; of. Reporting time: 30 days. Payment: Copy of issue. Copyrighted, reverts to author. Pub's reviews: 10 in 1979. §Gay liberation, history, research, fiction, socialism, feminism. Ads: $50.00/$25.00. COSMEP, APS.

THE GAY LUTHERAN, Howard Erickson, Editor, Lutherans Concerned, Box 19114A, Los Angeles, CA 90019, (213) 663-7816. 1974. Articles. "We provide concise, comprehensive news reporting on gay-church relations in all mainline Christian churches, and the views and opinions of gay Lutheran and other women and men. Recently: Rev. Charles Lewis, Fr. Malcolm Boyd, Martin Marty, Diane Fraser, Cathy Spooner, Kris Warmoth, Dr. Ralph Blair, Dr. W. Norman Pittenger, et al." circ. 1,600. 10/yr. Pub'd 10 issues 1979; expects 10 issues 1980, 10 issues 1981. sub. price: $8.50; per copy: $.85; sample: $.85. Back issues: Rates for complete file of all back issues available on request. Discounts: Bulk rate for church agencies, etc., $12 for 10 issues (of 2 to 4 copies mailed in same envelope). 6 to 8pp; 8½X11; of. Payment: copies. Not copyrighted. Pub's reviews: 12 in 1979. §Only gay-church questions, or gay-general books of use to churchfolk seeking understanding, or feminist/church concerns. Ads: $30.00 1/2 page.

GAY SUNSHINE: A Journal of Gay Liberation, Gay Sunshine Press, Inc., Winston Leyland, P.O. Box 40397, San Francisco, CA 94140. 1970. Poetry, fiction, articles, art, photos, cartoons, interviews, satire, criticism, reviews, letters, parts-of-novels. "'Gay Sunshine' is a cultural gay liberation journal. We concentrate on poetry, interviews, political literary articles, graphics, photos. We need good material. Manuscripts should be double spaced, typed & less than 15 pages. Recent contributors include Jonathan Williams, Allen Ginsberg, Gore Vidal, John Wieners, James Broughton." circ. 5000. 3/yr. Pub'd 4 issues 1979; expects 3 issues 1980, 3 issues 1981. sub. price: $15.00/8 issues; per copy: $2.00; sample: $2.50 postpaid. Back issues: $15 for packet #1 (13 issues). Discounts: 35% off cover, postpaid, for 10 or more copies. 36pp; 17½X11¼; of. Reporting time: 1 month. Payment: copies/free subs. Copyrighted, reverts to author. Pub's reviews: 20 in 1979. §poetry, some fiction, literary essays, biog. Ads: please write for rates. CCLM, COSMEP.

Gay Sunshine Press, Inc. (see also GAY SUNSHINE: A Journal of Gay Liberation), Winston Leyland, P.O. Box 40397, San Francisco, CA 94140. 1970. Poetry, fiction, interviews, criticism, letters. "*Gay Sunshine Press* was founded in 1970 to publish cultural, literary, political material by Gay people.

During the first five years of its existence it published only the tabloid cultural journal, *Gay Sunshine*. Since 1975 it has been publishing chapbooks and books. It was incorporated as non-profit in 1976." avg. press run 3,000. Pub'd 3 titles 1979; expects 3 titles 1980, 3 titles 1981. 11 titles listed in the *Small Press Record of Books in Print* (9th Edition, 1980). avg. price, cloth: $15.00; paper: $5.95; other: $2.50. Discounts: distributors to the Book Trade: Book People Distributors (at 40 percent discount) No discounts to individuals or libraries. Discounts to book jobbers & specialty shops. 250pp; 6X9, 5½X8½. Reporting time: 1 month. Payment: royalties. Copyrights for author.

Gay Task Force, American Library Association (see also A GAY BIBLIOGRAPHY), Barbara Gittings, Coordinator, PO Box 2383, Philadelphia, PA 19103, (215) 382-3222. 1970. 2 titles listed in the *Small Press Record of Books in Print* (9th Edition, 1980).

Gazelle Publications, T. E. Jr. Wade, 106 Hodges Lane, Takoma Park, MD 20012, (301) 585-8393. 1976. Poetry. "We consider junenile material that is not fantasy, material suitable for classroom use, or how-to material. Brochure available showing current titles." avg. press run 5,000. Pub'd 2 titles 1979; expects 2 titles 1980, 2 titles 1981. 2 titles listed in the *Small Press Record of Books in Print* (9th Edition, 1980). avg. price, paper: $1.00. Discounts: 40% trade, 50 to 55% distributors. 48pp; 5½X7½; of. Reporting time: 1 week. Payment: Open, depends on market potential. Copyrights for author.

GAZUNDA, Rob Earl, 73 Ware Street, Bearsted, Maidstone, Kent ME14 4PG, England, (0622) 36436. 1975. Poetry, art, cartoons, satire, collages. "There are no rules. Slugs and the samples have outlived their usefulness after 3 issues each (both as). The Uncle Nasty series features belligerent or unusual art & poetry, all A5, poems short and art monochrome. A little satire as well. *Gazunda* is A4 and extravagant, prints inviting poetry (short/medium length stuff) and cartoons. I don't fish for famous names. i only print stuff if I like it. Costs rising - please send 5 to 10 I.R.C.'s if *Gazunda* #3 is required from U.S.A." circ. 100-200. 3-4/yr. Pub'd 2 issues 1979; expects 3 issues 1980, 4 issues 1981. sub. price: free; per copy: free; sample: free. Back issues: Free if available. 20-40pp; size A4, A5, A6; †of. Reporting time: for USA a couple of months, for UK a couple of weeks. Payment: free copy. Copyrighted, reverts to author.

GBC Press (see also CASINO & SPORTS; SYSTEMS & METHODS), John Luckman, Howard Schwartz, Editors, Gambler's Book Club, 630 S. 11th St., Box 4115, Las Vegas, NV 89106, (702)-382-7555. 1964. avg. press run 3,000-5,000. Pub'd 24 titles 1979; expects 24 titles 1980, 24 titles 1981. 81 titles listed in the *Small Press Record of Books in Print* (9th Edition, 1980). avg. price, paper: $2.00. Discounts: Trade fact series 60%; Gambler's book shelf series 50%; Standards 40%; Jobbers 62% all. 64pp; 5¼X8¼; †of. Reporting time: 30 days approx. Payment: 10% sales. Copyrights for author. BPASC/ABA Affiliate.

Gearhead Press, 835 9th NW, Grand Rapids, MI 49504, 459-7861. 1975. Poetry, long-poems. "Our favorite poet right now is Bruce Rizzon. Write for free list of our titles." avg. press run 10,000. Pub'd 3 titles 1979; expects 5 titles 1980, 5 titles 1981. avg. price, paper: $2.50; other: $1.00. 26-60pp; 5½X8½; of. Copyrights for author.

GEGENSCHEIN, Eric B. Lindsay, 6 Hillcrest Ave., Falconbridge, New South Wales 2776, Australia. 1971. Reviews, criticism, letters, art, cartoons. "Editor written. No outside contributors except art, cartoons." circ. 250. 4/yr. Pub'd 5 issues 1979; expects 4 issues 1980. sample price: $1.00. Back issues: Soon available in X24 microfiche at $2.00 for 3 issues. 40pp; 8X10; †mi. Copyrighted. Pub's reviews: 100 in 1979. §Science fiction. no ads.

GEGENSCHEIN, NeoNeo DoDo, Phil Smith, Phil Demise, Bitty O'Sullivan-Smith, 111 Third Ave. #12C, New York, NY 10003, (212) 473-1883. 1971. Poetry, fiction, art, music, long-poems, collages, plays, concrete art. "*Gegenschein* announces the first series of Gegenschein Presse - Notbook Editions: *Maninfested* by Phil Demise, *Ice Rescue Station* by Guy Beining, *From the Desk of Dr. Know* by Henry Korn, and *White Rushes* by Phil Smith. *Gegenschein* (the magazine) will change to one thematic anthology per year. 1980 will be a Rock 'n Roll issue. For possible inclusion in the *Gegenschein Yearbooks* please please write to us for details but please be aware that our personal tastes lean heavily towards experimental and highly individual forms of expression. *Gegenschein also announces the formal issuance of The Placenter Tapes* (tapes of live performances at the *Gegenschein Vaudeville Placenter* 1976-1978) and includes readings and performances by Dick Higgins, Opal Nations, Jackson MacLow, Phil Demise, Ray DiPalma-Michael Lally-Bruce Andrews, William Packard, Henry Korn, Charles Bernstein, N. DoDo Band and more. C-60 cassettes are $7, C-90 cassettes are $10." circ. 300-600. 1-2/yr. Pub'd 1 issue 1979; expects 1 issue 1980. Back issues: GQ #'s 1-18, $250.00. Discounts: 40% consign, 50% cash. 100-200pp; 8½X11; of. Reporting time: 2 wks-1 month. Payment: copies. §any areas. CCLM.

Gem Guides Book Co., Alfred Mayerski, 5409 Lenvale, Whittier, CA 90601, 213-692-5492. 1964.

Articles, photos. avg. press run 500. avg. price, paper: $2.95. Discounts: trade-40 percent wholesale only. 100pp; 5½X8½; of. Payment: semi/annual percentage. Copyrights for author.

Gemini (see MADRONA)

Gemini Press, J. Michael Anuskiewicz, Editor-in-Chief, 625 Pennsylvania Avenue, Oakmont, PA 15139, 412-828-3315. 1978. Fiction, articles. "Gemini Press' emphasis is upon tersely written (75,000 words and under) quality books of fiction and non-fiction with an element of popular appeal. The scholarly academic work has no place here. Poetry, short stories, drama and literary criticism will not be considered. How to books, occult, occult fiction, science fiction, psychology, travel, selected fiction and non-fiction titles will be considered at a later date." avg. press run 1,000. Pub'd 1 title 1979; expects 1 title 1980, 2 titles 1981. 1 title listed in the *Small Press Record of Books in Print* (9th Edition, 1980). avg. price, paper: $4.95. Discounts: 40% to bookstores, 25% to libraries. 175pp; 5½X8½; of. not accepting submissions at this time.

General Hall, Inc., Ravi Mehra, 23-45 Corporal Kennedy Street, Bayside, NY 11360, (212) 423-9397. 1975. "College texts" avg. press run 3,500. Pub'd 3 titles 1979; expects 3 titles 1980, 3-5 titles 1981. 5 titles listed in the *Small Press Record of Books in Print* (9th Edition, 1980). avg. price, cloth: $17.95; paper: $6.95. Discounts: 20%. 200-250pp; 5¼X8¼; of. Reporting time: 4-8 weeks. Payment: 10%.

The Generalist Assn., Inc. (see PULPSMITH)

THE GENEVA POND BUBBLES, Leathern Wing Scribble Press, Ecart Publications, John M. Armleder, 6 Rue Plantamour, PO Box 253, Geneve CH-1211-1, Switzerland, 022-32-6794 & 022-45.73.95. 1977. Poetry, art, photos, music, collages, concrete art. "A paper in tabloid format , mostly hand-made, variable edition, miscellaneous material selected by the publisher, or guest editor of special issues. One or more post-fluxus hick-ups. Frequency is not predictable, but 5 issues a year is possible average planned. No subscriptions to all issues planned (some issues are small editions), price for 5 issues produced over 100 copies: Sfr. 25,- Normal issues: 6,- Sfr. Others: 10,-/100,- Sfr." 5/yr. Expects 5 issues 1980, 5 issues 1981. Back issues: On request. Discounts: 33⅓ on normal issues; 50% on bulk orders (normal issues). 8-16 pp, or double 42 pp.; 50X70cm sheets, folded; †mi/of/lp. Reporting time: slow. Payment: fair number of copies of publ. Ads: no standard.

Genny Smith Books, Genny Smith, 1304 Pitman Avenue, Palo Alto, CA 94301, 415-321-7247. 1976. Articles, photos. "All my publications are distributed by Wm. Kaufmann Inc., One First Street, Los Altos, CA 94022. I specialize on publications on the Eastern Sierra region of California — to date, guidebooks and sets of historic postcards. My guidebooks (I edit and co-author them) to this mountain-and desert vacation area includes chapters on roads, trails, natural history and history. Best known localities in this region are Owens Valley and Mammoth Lakes. These guidebooks are for sightseers, campers, hikers, fishermen, nature lovers and history buffs. The new edition of *DEEPEST VALLEY* includes material of interest to those with environmental concerns. It has thirty pages of new material on one of the most significant environmental disputes of our time: the lawsuit filed by Inyo County against the City of Los Angeles over the fundamental question, 'How much more Owens Valley water shall go to Los Angeles?'" avg. press run 7,000. Pub'd 1 title 1979; expects 1 title 1980. 5 titles listed in the *Small Press Record of Books in Print* (9th Edition, 1980). avg. price, paper: $7.95. Discounts: 40%. 224pp; 6X9; of. Payment: Varies from sharing of royalties to flat payment for material.

Genotype, J.A. Kroth, 15042 Montebello Road, Cupertino, CA 95014, (408) 867-6860. 1980. Poetry, photos. "Not currently accepting submissions. General interests are in metapsychology." avg. press run 1,000. Pub'd 1 title 1979. avg. price, paper: $12.50. Discounts: 40% trade, bulk, classroom, libraries. 290pp; 6X9. Reporting time: 6 months. COSMEP.

GEORGE SPELVIN'S THEATRE BOOK, Proscenium Press, Gordon Henderson, PO Box 361, Newark, NJ 19711, (215) 255-4083. 1978. Poetry, fiction, articles, art, photos, cartoons, interviews, satire, criticism, reviews, music, letters, plays, news items. "The policy of the magazine is broad and eclectic. We are interested in all theatrical periods and all theatrical media" circ. 700. 3/yr. Pub'd 3 issues 1979; expects 3 issues 1980, 3 issues 1981. sub. price: $12.00, $15.00 Instit.; per copy: $4.00; sample: $4.00. Back issues: $5.00. Discounts: 20%. 150-200pp; 5½X8½; lp. Reporting time: 1 to 3 months. Payment: Usually only in copies. Copyrighted, reverts to author. Pub's reviews. §Books related to dramatic literature. Ads: $200.00/$100.00.

George Sroda, Publisher, George Sroda, Amherst Jct., WI 54407. Articles. "Has published one book, *Facts About Nightcrawlers.*" avg. press run 30,000. Pub'd 1 title 1979; expects 1 title 1980. 2 titles listed in the *Small Press Record of Books in Print* (9th Edition, 1980). avg. price, paper: $3.95. Discounts: Distributors, 40%. 8¼X5½.

THE GEORGIA REVIEW, Stanley W. Lindberg, Univ. of Georgia, Athens, GA 30602, 404-542-3481. 1947. Poetry, fiction, articles, art, photos, interviews, criticism, reviews. "Contributors range from previously unpublished writers to some of America's most honored artists: Robert Penn Warren, Joyce Carol Oates, Malcom Cowley, Howard Nemerov, Eudora Welty, Rene Wellek, Jack Mathews, David Wagoner, Robert Bly. During the months of July and August unsolicited manuscripts are not considered (and will be returned unread)." circ. 3,600. 4/yr. Pub'd 4 issues 1979; expects 4 issues 1980. sub. price: $6.00; per copy: $3.00; sample: $3.00. Back issues: $3.00. Discounts: agency sub. 20% ads 15%. 240pp; 7X10; lp. Reporting time: 1-2 mos. Payment: $10.00 minimum page prose; $1.00 line poetry; plus copies. copyrighted by University of Georgia, who reassigns upon request. Pub's reviews: 61 in 1979. §General humanities, poetry, fiction, the South. Ads: $120.00/$70.00.

Geraventure Corp. (see also LIVING OFF THE LAND, Subtropic Newsletter), Marian Van Atta, Kathleen Wilcox, PO Box 2131, Melbourne, FL 32901, (305) 723-5554. 1973. "So far has published only 'Living off the Land', subtropic handbook by Marian Van Atta. 1st edition 1972, 2nd 1974, and 3rd 1977. No plans at present for publishing other authors - but may be able to in the future." avg. press run 5,000. Pub'd 1 title 1979; expects 1 title 1980, 2 titles 1981. 1 title listed in the *Small Press Record of Books in Print* (9th Edition, 1980). avg. price, paper: $2.00. Discounts: 40%. 60pp; 8X5 1/2. Copyrights for author. COSMEP.

Gerber Publications, Frederick H. Gerber, Juanita G. Gerber, PO Box 1355, Ormond Beach, FL 32074, (905) 677-9283. 1977. Art. "Specialized studies, in-depth, of various natural dyes, their history, use and modern day craft applications. Botanical clarifications and the anthropoligical implications of the antiquity and world wide distribution since pre-historic times. Average publication length is 80 pages, black and white photos, line drawings, Bilbligraphy and indexed." avg. press run 2,000. Pub'd 1 title 1979; expects 2 titles 1980, 2 titles 1981. avg. price, paper: $4.75-$6.75. Discounts: In amounts of six of one title or six divided among the three (present) titles we extend 40% to the retail trade or bulk lot buyer for classes, guilds and others. 80pp; 5½X8½; of.

GESAR- Buddhist Perspectives, Dharma Publishing, Sylvia Derman, Managing Editor, 5856 Doyle St., Emeryville, CA 94608, 415-655-1025. 1973. Poetry, art, photos, interviews, reviews, news items. "News from Buddhist organizations accepted." circ. 3,500. 4/yr. Pub'd 4 issues 1979; expects 4 issues 1980, 4 issues 1981. sub. price: $7.00; per copy: $1.95; sample: $1.00. Back issues: $1.50/copy. Discounts: 40%. 64pp; 7X9¼; †of. Reporting time: 2 months. Payment: none. Copyrighted, does not revert to author. Pub's reviews: 10 in 1979. §Buddhist, self-growth. Ads: $250.00/$125.00. LPS.

Ghost Dance: THE INTERNATIONAL QUARTERLY OF EXPERIMENTAL POETRY, Ghost Dance Press, Hugh Fox, Paul Ferlazzo, N.W. Werner, 6009 W 101st Place, Shawnee Mission, KS 66207, 351-5977. 1968. Poetry. "Recent contributors: Richard Morris, Helen Duberstein, Bill Costley. Looking for new forms, new ideas, *really* new. *Not* looking for warmed-over Concretism, Dadaism, Futurism, etc." circ. 300. 4/yr. sub. price: $3.00; per copy: $1.00; sample: $1.00. Back issues: $1.00. Discounts: none. 32pp; 5½X8½; †of. Reporting time: 1 hour. Payment: copies. Not copyrighted. Ads: none. CCLM, COSMEP.

Ghost Dance Press (see also Ghost Dance: THE INTERNATIONAL QUARTERLY OF EXPERI-MENTAL POETRY), Hugh Fox, N.W. Werner, Paul Ferlazzo, 6009 W 101st Pl, Shawnee Mission, KS 66207. 1968. Poetry. "Anything breaking new formal ground. We want to stay the forever-about-to-break newest wave you can ride into *Nirvana.*" avg. press run 200-500. Expects 4-5 titles 1981. 15 titles listed in the *Small Press Record of Books in Print* (9th Edition, 1980). avg. price, paper: $1.00; other: $1.00. Discounts: 50 percent to trade. 32-36pp; 5½X8½; †of. Reporting time: 1 day. Payment: copies. common law copyright. CCLM, COSMEP.

Gibbous Press (see also HODMANDOD), M. Cimperman, S. Kremsky, K. White, 150 10th Avenue, San Francisco, CA 94118, 415-752-5898. 1977. Poetry, fiction, interviews, criticism, parts-of-novels, long-poems. "Starting sometime summer '79, our first project will be monthly publication of broadsides, each with original art work. They'll be completely hand set and hand printed on out 1906 platen press. Authors will include Kathleen Fraser and Milton Kessler. Interested in longpoems, fiction-possibly interesting critical works, interviews. Also open to translations." avg. press run 150. Expects 5 titles 1980, 12-15 titles 1981. avg. price, other: $2.50. Discounts: inquire. †lp. Reporting time: 6 weeks. Payment: to be discussed with each other. Copyrights for author.

Gibson-Hiller, M. Reed, Editor, P O Box 22, Dayton, OH 45406, 513-277-2427. 1976. avg. press run 1,000. 1 title listed in the *Small Press Record of Books in Print* (9th Edition, 1980). avg. price, cloth: $4.95; paper: $2.95. Discounts: custom. 80pp; 5X7; of. Reporting time: 90 days. Payment: custom. Copyrights for author.

Giddyup Press, 4812 1/2 Del Mar, San Diego, CA 92107. 1979. Poetry, fiction, articles, art, photos, letters. "Recent Contributor: Stephanie Mood *Gold in Them Hills* (poetry & fiction). Query first." avg. press run 300. Pub'd 1 title 1979; expects 1 title 1980, 2 titles 1981. avg. price, paper: $2.00. Discounts: 40% trade. 40pp. Payment: arranged. Copyrights for author.

Gilgamesh Press Ltd., K. A. Mooradian, V. A. Mooradian, 1059 W Ardmore Avenue (literary division), Chicago, IL 60660, (312) 334-0327. 1978. Art, photos, interviews, criticism, reviews, letters. "(marketing division) 1644-D W. Robinson Street, Norman OK 73069 (405) 321-7539" avg. press run 5,000. Pub'd 2 titles 1979; expects 2 titles 1980. avg. price, cloth: $33.00; paper: $9.95. Discounts: Universal Schedule. 300pp; 6X9; †of. Reporting time: query first (one-month). Payment: 15% net profit.

GILTEDGE: New Series, Madeline DeFrees, Carol Ann Russell, Elizabeth Weber, PO Box 8081, Missoula, MT 59807. 1975. Poetry, fiction, articles, art, photos, interviews, criticism, reviews. circ. 500. 1/yr. Pub'd 1 issue 1979; expects 1 issue 1980, 1 issue 1981. sub. price: $3.50/yr; per copy: $3.50; sample: $3.50. 122pp; 8½X10; of. Reporting time: 2 months. Payment: copies. Copyrighted, reverts to author. Pub's reviews: 3 in 1979. §Poetry, fiction.

Ginseng Press, Glenn P. Joyner, Rt 2, Box 1105, Franklin, NC 28734, 704-369-9735. 1978. "My wife and I are operating this business fulltime. We write and publish primarily 'how-to' and self-help books. Titles this year: *How to Save Thousands When You Sell Your Home,* and *Parents' Guide to Football Safety, or How to Keep Your Son From Becoming a Statistic!*" avg. press run 1,000-5,000. Pub'd 2 titles 1979; expects 3 titles 1980. 2 titles listed in the *Small Press Record of Books in Print* (9th Edition, 1980). avg. price, paper: $8.00. Discounts: Available on request. 50pp; 8½X11; of. Reporting time: 1 week. Payment: Policy not established as yet. Copyrights for author.

Giorno Poetry Systems Records (see also DIAL-A-POEM POETS LP'S), John Giorno, 222 Bowery, New York City, NY 10012. 1969. avg. press run 2,000. Pub'd 4 titles 1979. 6 titles listed in the *Small Press Record of Books in Print* (9th Edition, 1980). avg. price, cloth: $8.98 double album. Discounts: 40% to book & record stores. Payment: $50.00 to each poet. Copyrights for author.

Glad Hag Books, Joan E. Biren, PO Box 2934, Washington, DC 20013, (202) 399-0117. 1979. Photos. "Only one title to date *Eye to Eye: Portraits of Lesbians,* photographs by Jeb." avg. press run 3,000. Pub'd 1 title 1979. avg. price, paper: $8.95. Discounts: 40%-60%. 80pp; 8½X11; of. Reporting time: 1 month.

Glass Bell Press, Margaret Kaminski, 5053 Commonwealth, Detroit, MI 48208, 313-898-7972. 1974. Poetry. "Glass Bell is named after a book by Anais Nin, who printed her work in the 40's. For 1975, International Women's Year, Glass Bell was awarded a grant from Mich. Council for the Arts to print poems by Mich. women poets; this project is now out of print. *Sisters And Other Selves,* by Judith McCombs, was the press's 1976 project, an offset production with cover art by Catherine Claytor-Becker. 1974 poets included Ellen Bass, Audre Lorde, Susan Fromberg Schaeffer, Toni Ortner Zimmerman, Lili Bita, Gloria Dyc, Gail Steslick, and Judith McCombs. These hand-set broadsides are still in print for $0.10 each plus $0.50 postage. (1 pp., 8½ x 11). 1977 Project: *Journal Of A Woman Almost* 30, by Gloria Dyc - $2.00, pap." avg. press run 300. 2 titles listed in the *Small Press Record of Books in Print* (9th Edition, 1980). avg. price, paper: $2.00. Discounts: Bookstores & distributors, classroom: 50%. 50pp; 8½X11 or 5⅜X8¼; of/lp. Reporting time: 1 to 4 weeks. Payment: copies only. Does not copyright for author.

GLASSWORKS, Betty Bressi, Estelle Visconti, Managing Editor, PO Box 163, Rosebank sta, Staten Island, NY 10305. 1975. Poetry, art, concrete art, long-poems, collages, photos. "Established and new writers/artists. Recent contributors: Colette Inez, Richard Shelton, Brian Swann, Helen Saslow, Alfred Starr Hamilton, Natale S. Polly, Peter Wild, Rochelle Ratner, Mary Ferrari, Maurice Kenny." circ. 500. 3 issues yr. sub. price: Volume 3, 1977-78, $4.50 includes set of 12 poetry/art postcards. Magazine only: $3.00; postcards only $2.00; per copy: $1.50; sample: $1.50. Back issues: $1.50 from Vol 1 or Vol 2. Discounts: libraries, subscription $6.00, single copy $2.00. 110pp; 5½X8½; of. Reporting time: 4 weeks. Payment: 2 copies. Copyrighted, reverts to author. Ads: $30/$15. CCLM, NESPA, NYSSPA.

Glenbow-Alberta Institute, 9th Avenue & 1st Street, SE, Calgary, AB T2G 0P3, Canada. 1955. avg. press run 1,000. Pub'd 4 titles 1979; expects 4 titles 1980. 1 title listed in the *Small Press Record of Books in Print* (9th Edition, 1980). avg. price, paper: $4 to $12. Discounts: 1/3rd. of.

GLENIFFER NEWS, Gleniffer Press, Ian MacDonald, 11 Low Road, Castlehead, Paisley PA2 6AQ, United Kingdom. 1977. "A newsheet about miniature books. Annual." circ. 500. 1/yr. Pub'd 1 issue 1979; expects 1 issue 1980. sub. price: free on stamp; per copy: free on stamp; sample: free on stamp. Back issues: free on stamp. 1pp; size A4; †of. Reporting time: 1 month. Copyrighted, reverts to author.

Pub's reviews: 10 in 1979. §Miniature books only. Ads: No ads. BPS (British Printing Society), SGPA (Scottish General Publishers Association).

Gleniffer Press (see also GLENIFFER NEWS), Ian Macdonald, 11 Low Road, Castlehead, Paisley PA2 6AQ, United Kingdom, 041-889-9579. 1968. Poetry, art, photos, letters, long-poems, plays. "Specialist in miniature books, limited editions. Mailing list of private buyers now established. Recently published 'Smallest Book In The World'. Elected 'printer of the year 1976" by British Printing Society." avg. press run 250-1,000. Pub'd 2 titles 1979; expects 2 titles 1980, 2 titles 1981. 3 titles listed in the Small Press Record of Books in Print (9th Edition, 1980). avg. price, cloth: varies; paper: varies; other: Varies. Discounts: 33⅓%. 20pp; size up to quarto; †lp/of. Reporting time: 2 wks. Payment: Single fees. Copyrights for author. BPS, SGPA, PLA.

GLOBAL TAPESTRY JOURNAL, BB Books, Dave Cunliffe, 1 Spring Bank, Salesbury, Blackburn, Lancs, England BB1 9EU, United Kingdom, 0254 49128. 1971. Poetry, fiction, articles, art, interviews, reviews, letters, parts-of-novels, long-poems, collages, concrete art. "Mainly concerned with creative poetry & prose. Also those energy communications networks which liberate human animal beast mind. Be it psychedelics, mutant vampires or dead history memory recall. PM Newsletter is now incorporated, printing reviews, notices and listings." circ. 1,000. 4/yr. Pub'd 4 issues 1979; expects 4 issues 1980, 4 issues 1981. sub. price: $6.84/4 issues; per copy: $1.20 (+ 52¢ pfp); sample: £1.00. Back issues: $1.00. Discounts: one third trade. 60pp; 8X6½; †of. Reporting time: soon. Payment: one copy. Pub's reviews: 80 in 1979. §Poetry, creative prose. Ads: none.

The Globe Pequot Press, Robert Wilkerson, President; Linda Kennedy, Publications Director, Old Chester Road, Chester, CT 06412, (203) 526-9572. 1947. Art, photos. "We publish New England Americana and guide books. No poetry, fiction or children's stories. We prefer a letter query, but a standard submission consists of one sample chapter, a table of contents, a one-page precis detailing the book and its sales appeal, and a cover letter with some information about the author. We are looking for books for the six-state New England market. Recent titles include A Century of New England in News Photos, the fifth edition of Guide to the Recommended Country Inns of New England, the fourth edition of Factory Store Guide to all New England, and The New England Indians. We specialize in original paperbacks. Other subject areas include cook books, city guide books, camping handbooks, crafts books, homeowners' guides. We extend few advances , usually for expenses only." avg. press run 5,000. Pub'd 20 titles 1979; expects 21 titles 1980, 20 titles 1981. avg. price, cloth: $14.95; paper: $5.95. Discounts: Trade: 40% and ascending. Contingent upon quantity. 192pp; 5½X9; of. Reporting time: 2 weeks. Payment: 7½% - 12½% on retail price of book. Copyrights for author.

Glouchester Press (Music Publ), William R. Tudor, PO Box 1044, Fairmont, WV 26554, 304-366-3758. 1971. Music. "So far we publish only College Music text books and serious music." avg. press run 1,000. Pub'd 1 title 1979; expects 1 title 1980, 1 title 1981. 1 title listed in the Small Press Record of Books in Print (9th Edition, 1980). avg. price, cloth: $17.50 (notebook style). Discounts: 40 percent (trade, agent & jobber) 20 percent (classroom). 200pp; 8½X11; of. Reporting time: 1 month. Payment: 10 percent annual. Copyrights for author. ASCAP.

Gluxlit Press, Bud Long, P O Box 11165, Dallas, TX 75223. 1977. Fiction, parts-of-novels. "Novels and novelettes by deaf authors — does not publish books by authors with normal hearing." avg. press run 1,000. Pub'd 2 titles 1979; expects 2 titles 1980, 2 titles 1981. 5 titles listed in the Small Press Record of Books in Print (9th Edition, 1980). avg. price, paper: $2.25. Discounts: 20% library discount, wholesale rates available on request. 30pp; size varies; of. Reporting time: 30-90 days. Payment: 10% of gross income on book. We offer our deaf authors three publishing plans to choose from as below. No deaf author is ever rejected!!! Plan A. Straight royality, author receives 10% royality from gross, and Gluxlit markets the books. Plan B. Outright purchase, author receives a one-time check. Gluxlit owns the copyright. Plan C. Self-publishing, Gluxlit produces the books for a price which author pays, author markets the books. Copyrights for author.

GNOME BAKER, Madeleine Burnside, Andrew Kelly, Bo 337, Great River, NY 11739, (516) 277-3777. 1975. Art, music, long-poems. "Recent contributors: Barbara Einzig, Karen Shaw, Lyn Hejinian, Charles Bernstein, Douglas Huebler, Geoff Young, David Bromige, Robert Wilson. Each author/artist gets 10-30 pages." circ. 750. 2/yr. Pub'd 1 issue 1979; expects 2 issues 1980, 2 issues 1981. sub. price: $10.00; per copy: $3.00; sample: $3.00. Back issues: #1, $6.00; #2-4, $4.00; #5-6, $3.00. Discounts: 40%. 112pp; 5½X8¼; of. Reporting time: 3 months unless submitted to schedule. Payment: share of author fund-approx $20.00. Copyrighted. Ads: $45.00/$25.00. CCLM.

GNOSIS, Arkady Rovner, Earl Hall Center, Columbia University, New York, NY 10027, (212) 280-5113. 1977. Poetry, fiction, articles, criticism, reviews. "Additional Address: 527 Riverside Drive, Box 86, New York, NY 10027. Bilingual journal in English and Russian. Gnosis encourages research in religion philosophy, literature and the arts. The journal is entirely apolitical and rather takes a major interest in the metaphysical elements of literature. It is one of the few journals in America featuring translations of Russian poetry and prose into English and vice versa. The journal does not represent one position and attempts to provide a forum for mutual understanding and rapport between American and Russian cultures." circ. 400. 2/yr. Pub'd 4 issues 1979; expects 2 issues 1980, 4 issues 1981. sub. price: Instit. $20.00; Indiv. $12.00; per copy: $6.00; sample: $3.00. Back issues: Vol. 1 & 2, $4.00 each, Vols 3 -6, $6.00 each, double vols III-IV,V-VI $6.00 each. Discounts: Distributors 25%. 205pp; 5½X8; of. Payment: for those in need $25.00. Copyrighted, reverts to author. Pub's reviews: 6 in 1979. §Poetry, prose, short stories, religious and philosophical essays. Ads: Free on exchange basis.

Gododdin Publishing, PO Box 5242, Everett, WA 98206, (206) 334-6120. 1979. Poetry, fiction. "Because of our financial position at this time, we can offer only assistance, counsel or co-operation in collective or self-publishing ventures, and editorial assistance. This year we published Michael de Angelo's *Cyr Myrddin, The Coming of Age of Merlin.* Correspondence is welcome." avg. press run 2,000. Pub'd 1 title 1979. 1 title listed in the *Small Press Record of Books in Print* (9th Edition, 1980). avg. price, cloth: $12.95. Discounts: 30% limited fine edition, first printing. 40% second edition. 200pp; 5X8; of. Reporting time: not currently accepting submissions.

GOLDEN GATE REVIEW, Publishing Associates, Renee French, 159 Ralston Street, San Francisco, CA 94132, (415) 586-2209. 1979. Poetry, art. "A contemporary magazine for serious poets who consider their work to be not only deeply perceptive of our times but also a work of art." circ. 1,000. 4/yr. Pub'd 1 issue 1979. sub. price: $7.00; per copy: $1.50; sample: no samples. 32pp; 5½X8½; of. Reporting time: 10 days. Payment: 2 copies. Copyrighted. Pub's reviews. §Poetry. Ads: $75.00/$50.-00/$0.50.

Golden Quill Publishers Inc, Doug Mellars, PO Box 1278, Colton, CA 92324, (714) 783-0119. 1977. "We publish book & booklets in the Holistic Health field and hope to publish recipe books and 'how to' books soon. Our booklets are from 10 to 56 pages in length. Our books range from 100 to 200 pages. The scope of the books range from a lay audience to a scientist/doctor exploring the areas of preventive medicine and holistic health." avg. press run 10,000. Pub'd 2 titles 1979; expects 3 titles 1980, 5 titles 1981. 2 titles listed in the *Small Press Record of Books in Print* (9th Edition, 1980). avg. price, cloth: $29.50; paper: $3.95. Discounts: Due to the nature of our market & publications, rates vary with each publications and type of market. 175pp; 6X9. Reporting time: 2 weeks-2 months. Payment: 6-10%. Copyrights for author. COSMEP.

Golden West Books, Donald Duke, PO Box 8136, San Marino, CA 91108, 213-283-3446. 1963. Fiction, photos. avg. press run 5,000. Pub'd 8 titles 1979; expects 8 titles 1980. avg. price, cloth: $10.00-$27.95; paper: $5.95. Discounts: 40 percent. 265pp; 8½X11; of. Reporting time: 3 weeks. Payment: Royalties. Copyrights for author.

Golden West Historical Publications, William O'Shaunnessay, Dir of Publ; Albert Cummings, PO Box 1906, Ventura, CA 93002. 1977. Articles. "Generally between fifty to eighty pages in length in monograph set - only real bias is for historical/politically scientific accurate analyses - revisionist historian Daniel Patrick Brown *Woodrow Wilson and The Treaty of Versailles: The German Leftist Press' Response*; Daniel Patrick Brown's *The Tragedy of Libby & Andersonville Prison Camps*; & political analyst Bruce Jennings *The Brest-Litovsk Controversy* (an examination of the Russian surrender to Wilhelmine Germany in November-December, 1917), et al." avg. press run 3,500-5,000. Pub'd 2 titles 1979; expects 2 titles 1980, 3 titles 1981. 4 titles listed in the *Small Press Record of Books in Print* (9th Edition, 1980). avg. price, paper: $2.95. Discounts: In multiples of ten, 10%, for classroom, college bookstore purchases (regardless of quantity) $2.75@. 55-60pp; 6X9; of. Reporting time: 2 months. Payment: Due to the fact that this firm is principally an outgrowth of the Valley Historical Alliance, only 3% per book. Copyrights for author.

Golden West Publishers, Hal Mitchell, 4113 N. Longview, Phoenix, AZ 85014. 1973. "ARIZONA COOK BOOK, Al Fischer and Mildred Fischer; MEXICO'S WEST COAST BEACHES, Al Fischer and Mildred Fischer. *California Cook Book* edited by Al Fischer & Mildred Fischer; *Citrus Cook Book* compiled by Glenda McGillis; *Chili-Lovers' Cook Book* edited by Al Fischer & Mildred Fischer; *Greater Phoenix Street Map* (book 96 pages)" avg. press run 10,000. Pub'd 1 title 1979; expects 3 titles 1980, 5 titles 1981. 6 titles listed in the *Small Press Record of Books in Print* (9th Edition, 1980). avg. price, paper: $3.00. Discounts: 5-99, 40%; 100 or more, 50%. 144pp; 5½X8½; of. Payment: buy mscp. outright. AAA.

Goldermood Rainbow Press (see also "NITTY GRITTY"), Bill Wilkins, Editor, 331 W. Bonneville, Pasco, WA 99301, 509-547-5525. 1974. Poetry, fiction, articles, art, photos, cartoons, interviews, satire, criticism, reviews, letters, concrete art. "Articles, commentary, fiction, maximum 10,000. Poetry-mostly short. Reviews-short-maximum 500 words. Cartoons-humor-photos." avg. press run 2,-000-3,000. Pub'd 1 title 1979; expects 2 titles 1980, 2 titles 1981. 3 titles listed in the *Small Press Record of Books in Print* (9th Edition, 1980). avg. price, paper: $6.00; other: $6.00. Discounts: trade 40 percent. 250pp; 8½X11; †of. Reporting time: 120-180 days. Payment: fiction $15.00, poetry & photos $2.00, cartoons & art work $5.00, commentary-personal experience-reviews-articles $10.00. Copyrights for author. COSMEP, CCLM.

Gomer Press (see TRIVIUM)

THE GOODFELLOW REVIEW OF CRAFTS, Full Court Press, Christopher Weills, Sarah Satterlee, PO Box 4520, Berkeley, CA 94704, 415-845-7645. 1973. Art, articles, photos, interviews, reviews, concrete art, news items. "Articles covering traditional & contemporary crafts." circ. 15,000 (printed). 6/yr. Pub'd 6 issues 1979; expects 6 issues 1980. sub. price: $10.00; per copy: $1.00; sample: Free. Back issues: $1.00. Discounts: 50 percent. 24pp; 10X14; of. Reporting time: 3 weeks. Payment: Negotiated. Copyrighted, reverts to author. Pub's reviews: 28 in 1979. §Arts & crafts. Ads: $250.-00/$150.00/$0.15 a word. COSMEP.

Gordon Publishing Co., Inc., Jennifer J Rodgers Gordon, 1302 N 5th Street, Salina, KS 67401, (913) 827-0569. 1978. Poetry. avg. press run 1,000. Pub'd 2 titles 1979. avg. price, other: $4.50. Discounts: 30% all retailers. 50pp; 8½X11; of. Reporting time: not accepting any mss at this time.

GOTHIC, Gothic Press, Gary William Crawford, 4998 Perkins Road, Baton Rouge, LA 70808, (504) 766-2906. 1979. Poetry, fiction, articles, reviews. "Criticism, fiction, and poetry devoted to or derived from the tradition of the eighteenth-century Gothic novel. Macabre tales in the tradition of Poe, Sheridan LeFanu, M. R. James, and H. P. Lovecraft." circ. 1,000. 2/yr. Pub'd 2 issues 1979. sub. price: $6.00; per copy: $3.25; sample: $3.25. Back issues: $4.00. Discounts: $1.95 per copy. 36pp; 8½X11; lp. Reporting time: two to three months. Payment: Fiction: 1 cent a word, higher for authors with agents; criticism, book reviews: in copies; poetry: 50 cents per line. Copyrighted, reverts to author. Pub's reviews: 7 in 1979. §Criticism, fiction devoted to or deriving from the Gothic in literature. Ads: No ads.

Gothic Press (see GOTHIC)

Gotuit Enterprises, Fairfax Stephenson, Editor & Owner, PO Box 2568, 1300 Golden Rain #9-C, Seal Beach, CA 90740, (213) 430-5198. 1977. "I publish for myself only, my own books. Four titles so far, three averaging 100 pages each; a fourth, a well-bound booklet of 30 pages." avg. press run 1,500. Pub'd 1 title 1979; expects 2 titles 1980, 2 titles 1981. 4 titles listed in the *Small Press Record of Books in Print* (9th Edition, 1980). avg. price, paper: $4.60. Discounts: 2-5 copies, 10%; 6-10, 15%. Libraries & Bookstores, 30%. 80pp; 5½X8½; of. Copyrights for author. COSMEP.

GPU NEWS, Liberation Publications, Inc., Eldon E. Murray, PO Box 92203, Milwaukee, WI 53202, 414-276-0612. 1971. Poetry, fiction, articles, art, photos, cartoons, interviews, satire, criticism, reviews, music, letters, plays, news items. circ. 3,000. monthly. Pub'd 12 issues 1979; expects 12 issues 1980, 12 issues 1981. sub. price: $10.00($11.00 foreign); per copy: $1.00; sample: $1.00. Back issues: $.75 each in lots of five or more. Discounts: To retailers only. 52pp; 8½X11; of. Reporting time: 1 month. Payment: By arrangement only, style sheet on request. Copyrighted, does not revert to author. Pub's reviews: 47 in 1979. §Must be of interest to gay readers. Ads: $60.00/$40.00/$0.20.

THE GRACKLE: Improvised Music In Transition, Ron Welburn, Edit. Director; Roger Riggins, Jim Stewart, Victor Rosa, Box 244 Vanderveer Station, Brookly, NY 11210. 1976. Articles, interviews, criticism, music, photos. "Interviews w/ Marion Brown, Steve Lacy, David Murray, Ronnie Boykins, Ralph Ellison, Harriet Bluiett, James Newton, Jerome Cooper, Anthony Davis, Hilton Ruiz. We lean more toward 'free improvisational jazz' but of course are interested in all. Interested in discography, bibliography, international jazz. Moving toward black music/jazz scholarship." circ. 1,000. irreg. Pub'd 1 issue 1979; expects 1 issue 1980, 1 issue 1981. price per copy: $1.50 ($2.25 Foreign). sample: $1.50 ($2.25 Foreign). Back issues: Only No. 3 and 4 available $2.00 ($3.50). 28-50pp; 8½X11; of. no unsolicited ms. Payment: copies. Copyrighted. Pub's reviews. §Music-jazz, R&B, 20th C. internat'l.

GRAHAM HOUSE REVIEW, Peter Balakian, Bruce Smith, Bishop North, Phillips Academy, Andover, MA 01810. 1976. Poetry. "Our aim is to publish good poetry wherever we find it, poetry from the unknown and the well-established. We believe the best poetry struggles with language for music, image, and voice; is well made and attached with integrity to experience. Some recent contributors include: Hugo, Goldbarth, Soto, Wheatcroft, Stern, Blessing, Pierson, Broughton, E. Knight and others." circ. 500. 2/yr. Pub'd 2 issues 1979; expects 2 issues 1980. sub. price: $3.50; per copy: $1.75; sample: $1.75. Discounts: trade discount 20-40 percent, negotiable. 40-50pp; 5½X8½; of. Reporting time: 2-4 wks. Payment: copies only. Copyrighted, reverts to author. CCLM, COSMEP.

158

The Grail (see IN TOUCH)

THE GRAMERCY REVIEW, Dennis Bartel, Mark Heyman, Ann Markum, Associate, P.O. Box 15362, Los Angeles, CA 90015. 1977. Poetry, fiction, articles, criticism, reviews, parts-of-novels. "Much that we publish is from established writers but new writers are encouraged and some work by a previously unpublished writer is nearly always included in each issue. Also, when we publish the work of an unknown writer we try to be extravagant in our support, which reduces the number of unknowns we publish. Special issue in past years include Los Angeles Women Writers (Robin Johnson, guest editor), and two issues of Arizona Writers featuring work by Peter Wild, Norman Dubie, Richard Shelton and Steve Orlen. Other recent contributors: Mark Harris, X.J. Kennedy, William Dickey, David Waggoner, Paul Smyth, Josephine Miles, Ann Stanford, Lawrence Spingarn, Jascha Kessler and interviews with Christopher Isherwood and Eugene Ionesco. Upcoming special issue on formalism, edited by Henri Coulette. Our regular commentators include John Weston and Jascha Kessler but other reviews and critical works are published. For reviews: send copy of your work and we will commission you to write a review." circ. 1,200. 4/yr. Expects 4 issues 1980. sub. price: $7.00; per copy: $1.50; sample: free to mags & institutions. Back issues: $2.50. 85-100pp; 5½X8½; of. Reporting time: 1 month. Payment: varies. Copyrighted, does not revert to author. Pub's reviews: 15 in 1979. §Poetry and fiction (novels and collections of short stories). no ads. COSMEP, CCLM.

GRAND RIVER REVIEW/CAPITOL CITY MOON, Gary R. Andrews, PO Box 15052, Lansing, MI 48901. 1972. "Preferred length less than 2500 words, most any topic considered, mostly into historical or relevant local area material." circ. 500 to 5,000. irreg. price per copy: $1.00; sample: $1.00. Back issues: $1.00 each for Nos. 1, 2, 3, 4. 24pp plus; size little to tabloid; †of. Reporting time: 3 months. Payment: none. Copyrighted, reverts to author. Pub's reviews.

Granny Soot Publications, Colin Browne, 1871 East Pender Street, Vancouver, BC V5L 1W6, Canada. 1970. Poetry, long-poems. avg. press run 300. avg. price, paper: $2.50. Discounts: over 5 copies 40%. of. Reporting time: 2 wks.

The Grapevine Press, Inc. (see also THE GRAPEVINE WEEKLY), Karl Kayser, Richard P. Clarke, 114 West State Street, Ithaca, NY 14850, (607) 272-3470. 1974. Poetry, photos, long-poems. "We have published three different books by upstate New Yorkers in the past few years and plan to continue publishing one or two books each year in the future. Past titles are *Letters to Tiohero* by Peter Fortunato, a longpoem; *The Halloween Book* by Jon Reis, photographs; and *The Rudy Baga Garden Book* by Dennis Kolva. We also published the *Supernormal Ithaca History Calendar 1978* by Paul Glover." avg. press run 300-1,000. Pub'd 2 titles 1979; expects 1 title 1981. avg. price, paper: $3.50. Discounts: Rates available upon request. 20-300pp; of. Reporting time: worked out with author. Payment: negotiated percentage. Copyrights for author.

THE GRAPEVINE WEEKLY, The Grapevine Press, Inc., George Sheldon, Features Editor; Anne Treichler, Managing Editor, 114 West State Street, Ithaca, NY 14850, (607) 272-3470. 1974. Poetry, fiction, articles, art, photos, cartoons, interviews, reviews, letters, parts-of-novels, long-poems. "We offer coverage of topical area issues such as nuclear waste disposal, articles on community personalities and organizations, reviews of books and the arts, how-to advice from local experts on a range of subjects, as well as poetry, fiction, photographs, cartoons, and puzzles by upstate New Yorkers." circ. 23,000. weekly. Pub'd 49 issues 1979; expects 49 issues 1980, 49 issues 1981. sub. price: $10.00; per copy: free; sample: $0.50. Back issues: $1.00 if available. Discounts: rates available on request. 32pp; 10X13; of. Copyrighted, reverts to author. Pub's reviews: 25 in 1979. §Any other weekly community magazines. Ads: $270.00/$135.00/$0.20, $2.00 minimum.

Grass-Hooper Press, Robert E. Knittel, 4030 Connecticut Street, St Louis, MO 63116, (314) 772-8164. 1978. Fiction, art, plays. "Grass-Hooper Press is a self-publishing venture with one book published, Dec. 16, 1978. The book is titled *Walking In Tower Grove Park* and is distributed through Paperback Supply, St. Louis, and through the author. The book has been selected for distribution to its customers by Tower Grove Bank, St. Louis. Although the book is locality oriented, its descriptions of the park may have wider appeal. Tower Grove Park is a national historic landmark. Two additional books by the author-publisher, Robert E. Knittel, are planned for 1979. *Walking In Tower Grove Park* by Robert E. Knittel, illustrations by Daniel J. Weismann. 98 pages, 11 pen and ink drawings, three maps, foreward, preface. Retail $5.95 paperback. ISBN No. 0-93303-800-3, CIP No. 78-71312." avg. press run 1,000. Expects 1 title 1980, 2 titles 1981. 1 title listed in the *Small Press Record of Books in Print* (9th Edition, 1980). avg. price, paper: $6.00. Discounts: One schedule, 1-4 copies, 20%; 5-24 copies, 40%; 25-49 copies, 43%; 50-99 copies, 46%; 100 or more copies, 50%. 100-150pp; 6X9; of. Not reading manuscripts at this time. Copyrights for author. COSMEP.

GRASS ROOTS, David Miller, Meg Miller, Box 900, Shepparton, Victoria 3630, Australia. 1973.

Articles, photos, letters. "Similar to *Mother Earth News*" circ. 10,000. 4 issues/yr. Pub'd 4 issues 1979; expects 4 issues 1980, 4 issues 1981. sub. price: $a9 yr for overseas subs. $8.00 local sub; per copy: $2.00; sample: $2.00. Back issues: $a 2.00. 90pp; size quarto; of. Reporting time: 3 months. Payment: $10 per page. Copyrighted, does not revert to author. Pub's reviews: 80 in 1979. §alternatives, gardening, technology, horticulture, agriculture, craft, food, community, health, natural lifestyles. Ads: $200.00/$120.00/$2 per classified ad. no word rate Australian.

GRAVIDA, Lynne Savitt, Box 118, Bayville, NY 11709, (516) 628-3356. 1973. Poetry, reviews, interviews. "Our bias is excellence of craft, fresh imagery. Diane Wakoski, Andre Codrescu, Colette Inez, Michael McMahon, A.D. Winans, etc. etc. Bukowski, Ignatow, Sam Hamill, Malanga, Stainton etc. etc." circ. 500-1,000. 1/yr. Pub'd 1 issue 1979; expects 1 issue 1980, 1 issue 1981. sub. price: $3.50; per copy: $3.50. 64-68pp; 5½X8½; of. Reporting time: 6 weeks. Payment: copies only. Copyrighted, reverts to author. Pub's reviews: 2 in 1979. §poety. CCLM, COSMEP.

Gray Beard Publishing, Ben Dennis, Publisher; Jane Bailey, Editor, 107 W. John Street, Seattle, WA 98119, (206) 285-3171. 1978. Art, photos. "Gray Beard publishes illustrated historical books, well-researched and containing commissioned art, photographs and period art. Gordon Newell, Robert Wing are contributors. At present we concentrate on Northwest history." avg. press run 5,000. Expects 2 titles 1980, 2 titles 1981. avg. price, cloth: $20.00; paper: $9.95. Discounts: Retail: 1, 25%; 2-4, 33⅓%; 5-24, 40%; 25-49, 41%. Distributor: 2-4, 33⅓%; 5-9, 40%; 10-99, 46%; 100+, 50%. 128pp; 9X11; of. Reporting time: 6 weeks. Payment: Standard royalty.

Gray Flannel Press, Adrian C. Louis, Publisher; Alice C. Parker, Editor, P.O. Box 9181, Providence, RI 02940. 1974. Poetry, fiction. "Looking for electric,intellectually angry, non-third world poetry, query first." Pub'd 2 titles 1979; expects 2 titles 1980, 3 titles 1981. 3 titles listed in the *Small Press Record of Books in Print* (9th Edition, 1980). avg. price, paper: varies. Discounts: usual. variespp; of. Reporting time: 4 wks. CRISP.

The Graywolf Press, Scott Walker, P.O. Box 142, Port Townsend, WA 98368, 206-385-1160. 1974. Poetry, fiction, art, photos, criticism, long-poems. "Queries or mss without SASE will not be answered" avg. press run 200-2,000+. Pub'd 5-7 titles 1979. 9 titles listed in the *Small Press Record of Books in Print* (9th Edition, 1980). avg. price, cloth: $8.00; paper: $4.00. Discounts: 1 copy, 10 percent; 2 copies, 20 percent; 3-5 copies, 30 percent; 6 or more 40 percent. 20-40 percent on cloth. 10 percent on handbound in boards. pp varies, 12-86; size varies; †of/lp. Reporting time: 1 wk to 4 wks. Payment: Negotiable. Usually 10 percent of edition in copies. Copyrights for author.

Great Basin Press, Eric N. Moody, Senior Editor; Lee Mortensen, Senior Editor; Phillip I. Earl, Chris Peto, Lynn E. Williamson, Box 11162, Reno, NV 89510, (702) 826-7729. 1976. "Interested, primarily, in history and literary criticism pertaining to Great Basin region." avg. press run 1000 copies. Pub'd 3 titles 1979; expects 3 titles 1980, 4 titles 1981. avg. price, paper: $5.00. Discounts: 40 percent to retailers, (5-99 copies); 20% (1-4 copies). 100pp; 5½X8½; of. Reporting time: 1-2 months. Payment: percentage of sales. Copyrights for author.

GREAT CIRCUMPOLAR BEAR CULT, Bear Cult Press, Rick Penn, David Kubach, Box 468, Ashland, WI 54806. 1976. Poetry, fiction, articles, art, interviews, criticism, reviews, long-poems. "Published one anthology in 1979" circ. 500. 1/yr. Pub'd 1 issue 1979; expects 1 issue 1980. sub. price: $3.00; per copy: $2.00. Back issues: #1 $2.50. Discounts: 60/40. 64pp; 7X8½; of. Reporting time: 2 weeks-2 months. Payment: 2 issues. Copyrighted. Pub's reviews: 5 in 1979. §poety.

Great Eastern Book Company, Samuel Bercholz, Editor-in-Chief; Larry Mermelstein, Editorial Asst, PO Box 271, Boulder, CO 80306, (303) 449-6113. 1978. Poetry, art, photos, music. "Note: Great Eastern Book Company is a wholly-owned subsidiary of Shambhala Publications, Inc." avg. press run 2,000. Pub'd 20 titles 1979; expects 20 titles 1980, 20 titles 1981. 31 titles listed in the *Small Press Record of Books in Print* (9th Edition, 1980). avg. price, cloth: $17.50; paper: $7.95. Discounts: 1-4, 20%; 5 and up, 40%. pp varies; size varies; of/lp. Reporting time: 4-6 weeks. Payment: Standard. Copyrights for author. ABA.

Great Lakes Publishing, Stan Zeyorich, 2674 7th Street, Cuyahoga Falls, OH 44221, (216) 655-2996. 1978. Cartoons, satire. avg. press run 1,000. Expects 1 title 1980, 1 title 1981. avg. price, paper: $2.50. Discounts: Standard. 50pp; 6X4. Reporting time: 6 weeks. Payment: Negotiable. Copyrights for author.

The Great Outdoors Trading Company, Les Taylor, 24759 Shoreline Highway, Marshall, CA 94940, (707) 878-2811. 1972. "We are publishing a series of source books for back-to-nature sports. Non-fiction, photos." avg. press run 10,000. Pub'd 1 title 1979; expects 2 titles 1980, 3 titles 1981. 1 title listed in the *Small Press Record of Books in Print* (9th Edition, 1980). avg. price, cloth: $12.95; paper:

$6.95. Discounts: standard trade. 208pp; 8½X11; of. Reporting time: 90 days. Payment: varies. Copyrights for author.

Great Raven Press, Paul Martin, Editor, P.O. Box 813, Ft Kent, ME 04743, 834-6447. 1976. Poetry, long-poems. "*Great Raven Review* is published as chapbooks featuring individual poets. So far, *Circles* Ted Enslin, *Traces/Fire* Winslow Durgin, *Risky Business* Michael Hogan, *Songs Visions Traditions of Northwest Indian Tribes* Paul Martin, *Dark Moon/White Pine* Gary Lawless & S. Fox, *Desert Cenote* Keith Wilson, *Divisions/One* Martin Rosenblum, *Poems From Four Corners* John Brandi, *Andiamo* James Koller, Franco Beltrametti & Harry Hoogstraten, *Death in Lobsterland* Leo Connellan; and forthcoming: *Poems for Pemaquid* Kendall Merriam, *Bear Dancing on the Hill* Gunnar Hansen, *An Introduction to the Geography of Iowa* M.R. Doty, *The Floating World Cycle Poems* Paul Martin, and as-yet untitled chapbook from Drummond Hadley. I publish translations poems, long-poems/prose-poems preferred. Querybefore making submissions. 'Regional/ethnopoetics' touch me most . . . looking to hear from new as well as established poets.*Great Raven Review* nos. 1 thru 12 are available at $3 & $4 each, $6 signed." avg. press run Limited editions 200 to 500 copies-4 books published per set. Pub'd 8 titles 1979; expects 8-12 titles 1980. 19 titles listed in the *Small Press Record of Books in Print* (9th Edition, 1980). avg. price, paper: $2.50 to $4, $6 signed; other: $6.00 signed. Discounts: 40 percent to trade. 24-36 pp-photo of poet along with bio information; 6X9; 5½X8½; of. Reporting time: 1 month. Payment in copies. Does not copyright for author. MWPA, NESPA.

GREAT RIVER REVIEW, Jean Ervin, Fiction Editor; Chet Corey, Poetry & Book Review Editor; Heidi Schwabacher, Art Editor, PO Box 14805, Minneapolis, MN 55414, 612-378-9076. 1977. "Poetry, fiction, articles on Midwestern writers, particularly contemporary authors. Articles up to 4,000 words. Spot drawings welcome. We are esp interested in material from and bout the Upper Midwest, but will accept submissions of quality from any part of the country." circ. 400. 2/yr. Pub'd 2 issues 1979; expects 2 issues 1980. sub. price: $8.00. per copy: $3.00. Back issues: $2.50. 140pp; 6X8; of. Reporting time: 1-4 months. Copyrighted. Pub's reviews. §Arts, humanities, poetry, fiction.

Great Society Press, Angelo De Luca, 451 Heckman St. Apt. 308, Phillipsburg, NJ 08865, 201-859-6134. 1960. Poetry. "no unsolicited mss" avg. press run 500. Pub'd 1 title 1979; expects 1 title 1980, 1 title 1981. 25 titles listed in the *Small Press Record of Books in Print* (9th Edition, 1980). avg. price, paper: $0.50. Discounts: 40%. 17pp; 5X7; lp/of.

GREAT WORKS, Great Works Editions, Peter Philpott, 25 Portland Road, Bishops Stortford, Hertfordshire, United Kingdom. 1973. Poetry, fiction, articles, art, criticism, reviews, letters, long-poems. "No. 7 includes: David Chaloner, Michael Haslam, Rod Mengham, David Miller, Peter Riley, Nigel Wheale, John Wilkinson." circ. 200. 2-3/yr. Pub'd 2 issues 1979; expects 3 issues 1980. sub. price: £2.00 ($6.00); per copy: 75p ($2.40); sample: 75p ($2.40). Back issues: 1 60p. Discounts: 1/3 for trade. 80pp; size A4; †duplicated. Reporting time: 1 month. Payment: none. copyright to author. Pub's reviews: 0 in 1979. §contemporary writing. Ads: negotiable. ALP.

Great Works Editions (see also GREAT WORKS), Peter Philpott, 25 Portland Rd., Bishops Stortford, Herts, United Kingdom. 1973. Poetry, fiction, parts-of-novels, long-poems, criticism. "Could publish anything but prefers to publish contemporary English writing. Current publisher Andrew Crozier: *Pleats,* Neil Oram: *The Golden Forgotten,* Lorand Caspar: *Ground Absolute* (trans. Peter Riley), Allen Fisher: *Docking,* John Hall: *Couch Grass,* Louis Patler: *Eloisa.*" avg. press run 200 or more. Pub'd 8 titles 1979. 11 titles listed in the *Small Press Record of Books in Print* (9th Edition, 1980). avg. price, paper: 75p. Discounts: 1/3 trade sale or return accepted. 30pp; size A4 usually; †mi/of. Reporting time: 1 month. Payment: 50 percent any profits. copyright to author. ALP.

THE GREATER GOLDEN HILL POETRY EXPRESS, The Feminist Poetry & Graphics Center, Joyce Nower, Shelley Savren, Mary Montgomery, 2829 Broadway, San Diego, CA 92102, 714-239-3664. 1975. Poetry. "Recent contributors: Sharon Olds, Kathy Kozachenko, Kathleen Fraser, Joyce Nower, Shelley Savren, Deena Metzger, Margaret Kaminski. Manuscripts being solicited." circ. 400. 3-4/yr. Pub'd 3 issues 1979; expects 3 issues 1980, 3 issues 1981. price per copy: $1.50 out of town. Back issues: Summer 1976-National issue $2.00. 45pp; 7X8½; of. Reporting time: up to 3 mo. Payment: Free copy. Copyrighted, reverts to author. Ads: none.

Greatland Publishing Co., William C. Gilmore, Vice President; Robert J. Traister, Senior Editor, 7 South Street, Front Royal, VA 22630, (703) 635-7180. 1978. Fiction. "We primarily publish self-help and some how-to books. However, our current list contains a historical-sightseeing book on the Shenandoah Valley, a novel and an opportunity book on making money in rural land. Upcoming are books on cartoons, cooking and Bible self-help." avg. press run 5,000-10,000. Pub'd 1 title 1979; expects 2 titles 1980, 4 titles 1981. 3 titles listed in the *Small Press Record of Books in Print* (9th Edition, 1980). avg. price, cloth: $9.95; paper: $4.95; other: $19.95 special. Discounts: 40-50%. 250pp;

5½X8½; of/lp. Reporting time: 2-3 months. Payment: 10%. Copyrights for author. COSMEP.

Green Eagle Press, C. Adler, P. Murphy, 241 W 97th Street, New York, NY 10025, 212-663-2167. 1973. *"Ecological Fantasies, The Queer Dutchman"* avg. press run 1,500. Pub'd 1 title 1979; expects 2 titles 1980. 4 titles listed in the *Small Press Record of Books in Print* (9th Edition, 1980). avg. price, cloth: $11.95; paper: $4.50. 250pp; 5X8½; of. Reporting time: 2 months. Payment: open. Copyrights for author.

GREEN FEATHER, Quality Publications, Inc., Gary S. Skeens, Editor, PO Box 2633, Lakewood, OH 44107. 1978. Poetry, fiction, articles. "Length of material: Stories (2,000 to 3,500 words), Poetry (from Haiku to 40 lines). Pay: For now in a contributor's copy. Subject matter is open/though one theme that might be aimed at is that of America, American life; the people, locations, history, etc. No material of an obscene or explicit nature. Tends to have a western slant. Some recent contributor's: June Ward, Eliza Gatewood Warren, Betty Streib, Robert L. McCalvin, William Rainey. Our special desire is for strong plotting and characterization in stories through a subtle blending of conflicts. And above all a high degree of quality, and a high standard of craftsmanship and creativity must exist. Manuscripts should be submitted typed and double-spaced on one side of 8½ x 11 white typing paper (and be sure to always enclose a SASE with submissions)." circ. 150. 4/yr. Pub'd 2 issues 1979. sub. price: $4.00; per copy: $1.25; sample: $0.75. Back issues: $0.50. Discounts: 25-50%. 50pp; 5½X8½. Reporting time: 4-6 weeks. Payment: copy of issue work appears in (for the present). Copyrighted, reverts to author. Pub's reviews. §open. COSMEP.

Green Horse Press, William Greenwood, 471 Carr Avenue, Aromas, CA 95004, (408) 724-6863. 1972. Poetry. "Green Horse is devoted to the discovery and translation of outstanding collections of poems not yet available in English. Dual-language titles include: *The Dog of Hearts* Rene Char; *Peace Has Yet to be Won* Arqueles Morales; *Destruction or Love* Vicente Aleixandre (o.p.). First publications by North Americans are chapbooks: *Into the Center of America* Wm. Greenwood; *Flame People* Gregory Hall." avg. press run 1,000. Pub'd 1 title 1979. 4 titles listed in the *Small Press Record of Books in Print* (9th Edition, 1980). avg. price, paper: $3.00. Discounts: 40% discount on bookstore/jobber orders of more than 3 copies. 60pp; of/lp. Reporting time: 3-6 weeks.

The Green Hut Press, Janet Wullner Faiss, Publisher & Editor, 24051 Rotunda Rd, Valencia Hills, CA 91355, 805-259-5290. 1972. Poetry, fiction, art. "As our contribution to humanism and the unification of art and science, we publish the writing and artistic work of Fritz Faiss. We are also happy to consider the writing of others when it can suitably accompany Faiss art work. Limited editions. Thus far we work by mail order only, except for a few selected bookstores. Enquiries welcome. We have prices ranging between $4.00 and, for a hand-colored-by-artist edition, $125.00." avg. press run 200 copies. Pub'd 2 titles 1979; expects 2 titles 1980, 2 titles 1981. 6 titles listed in the *Small Press Record of Books in Print* (9th Edition, 1980). Discounts: Libraries 10%; Booksellers 40% on minimum order of 6, 20% on deluxe editions. 75pp; size varies; †of. We do not accept manuscripts, unless they are suitable for Faiss artwork. Reports: 6 weeks. Include postage please. Payment: Individual contract arrangements through Heacock Literary Agency (Venice, CA). Copyrights for author.

Green Knight Press, Ritchie Darling, 45 Hillcrest Place, Amherst, MA 01002. 1965. Poetry, fiction, satire, criticism. "Francis Golffing. The press is dormant at the moment." avg. press run 1,000. avg. price, paper: $2.00. Discounts: bookstores, 40%; bulk orders, 10%. 40pp; 8½X5½ or 9X6; of. Reporting time: 6 months. Payment: $10 per poem; prose by arrangement. Copyrights for author. COSMEP, NESPA.

THE GREEN REVOLUTION, The School of Living, Rarihokwats, Mildred J. Loomis, Editor Emeritus, P O Box 3233, York, PA 17402. 1940. Poetry, articles, art, photos, interviews, reviews, letters, news items. "Voice of decentralization and balanced living; interested in back-to-the-land whys & hows" circ. 2,500. 10/yr. Pub'd 10 issues 1979; expects 10 issues 1980, 10 issues 1981. sub. price: $8.00 or donation; per copy: $1.00; sample: $1.00 free by special request. Back issues: $2.00, 35 No. 1 community directory. Discounts: Bulk 40% Agents 20%. 48pp; 8½X11; of. Reporting time: Rapid. Payment: usually none. Not copyrighted. Pub's reviews: 15 in 1979. §See type of material. Ads: No paid advertising. APS.

GREEN'S MAGAZINE, Clover Press, David Green, Box 313, Detroit, MI 48231. 1972. Poetry, fiction. "Stories to approx 3,500 poems to 40 lines. Want deep characterization in complex conflicts. Prefer to avoid profanity, explicit sexuality. Recents: Stanley Field, Timothy Wade Black, Warren C. Miller, Wayne Barton, Lyn Lifshin, Gary Fincke, Terry Kennedy. No carbons or photostats please." circ. 700. 4/yr. Pub'd 4 issues 1979; expects 4 issues 1980. sub. price: $7.50; per copy: $2.00; sample: $2.00. Discounts: negotiable. 100pp; 5¼X8½; †of. Reporting time: 8 wks. Payment: up to $25.00. Copyrighted, will reassign rights. Pub's reviews: 4 in 1979. §general. Ads: $100/$60. CCLM, COS-

MEP.

Lorna Greene, Lorna Greene, 1240 1/2 North Havenhurst Drive, Los Angeles, CA 90046, (213) 654-2482. 1978. Poetry, art, photos, collages. "Concept is 'today'. Book, visual, easy to read, designed for the today people, distracted almost to a level of stress, to soothe, entertain, relax, almost in the vogue of a poetic newspaper. Most people pick it up, read it, and finish it, before letting go" avg. press run 3,000. 2 titles listed in the *Small Press Record of Books in Print* (9th Edition, 1980). avg. price, paper: $7.95. Discounts: 40%-60%. 64pp; 8½X11½; of.

THE GREENFIELD REVIEW, The Greenfield Review Press, Joseph Bruchac, Carol Bruchac, Ossie Enekwe, P.O. Box 80, Greenfield Center, NY 12833, 518-584-1728. 1968. Poetry, reviews. "Open to both new and established poets. Some of our special features in past and forthcoming issues include a special prison writing issue, Modern African poetry, Asian-American poets. Contributors include Michael Hogan, Joan Colby, Gayl Jones, Alvin Aubert, Christine Zawadisky, Colette Inez, Ross Talarico, Freya Manfred, Mary Feeney, Geraldine Kudaka, Michael McMahon, Thomas Johnson, Victor Hernandez Cruz, Alan Chong Lau, Leslie Silko, John L. Natkie, Jeanne Finley, Peter Wild, Ted Kooser, Paul Corrigan, Catherine Clark, Eugenie Eersel." circ. 750. 2 double issues/yr. Pub'd 2 issues 1979; expects 2 issues 1980. sub. price: $6.00; per copy: $3.00; sample: $2.50. Back issues: Issue #1-$20. Discounts: standard discounts. 200pp; 5½X8½; of. Reporting time: 1 wk-6 wks. Payment: Copies. Copyrighted, reverts to author after first printing. Pub's reviews: 12 in 1979. §poetry. Ads: $50.00/$25.00/None. CCLM, COSMEP, NESPA.

The Greenfield Review Press (see also THE GREENFIELD REVIEW), Joseph Bruchac III, Editor; Carol Worthen Bruchac, Editor, P.O. Box 80, Greenfield Center, NY 12833. 1970. Poetry. "Our main interest is contemporary poetry in general. Although we have been particularly open to work by writers not usually published by American small presses — writers from the '3rd World'women, prison writers. Some of our recent publications include books of poetry by Kofi Awoonor, Janet Campbell, Geraldine Kudaka, Gary Kizer, Ron Welburn, Judy Ray, Linda Hogan, Carolyn Baxter, Peter Cummings, Kofi Anydoho, Kwesi Brew and Osmond Enekwe..as well as a major anthology of poetry in English from Africa, Asia and the Caribbean: Aftermath. The length of the books we publish ranges from small chapbooks of 24 pages to full-size volumes. We are often overstocked, so it is always best to query before sending a manuscript." avg. press run 500. Pub'd 4 titles 1979; expects 4 titles 1980, 4 titles 1981. 34 titles listed in the *Small Press Record of Books in Print* (9th Edition, 1980). avg. price, paper: $2.00-$3.00. Discounts: Trade: 1-5 copies, 25%; 5 or more copies, 40%. 40pp; 5½X8½; of. Reporting time: 2 weeks to 2 months. Payment: 10 copies plus 10% retail price on each copy sold. Copyrights for author. CCLM, COSMEP, NESPA.

GREENHOUSE REVIEW, Greenhouse Review Press, Gary Young, 126 Escalona Dr., Santa Cruz, CA 95060, 408-426-4355. 1975. Poetry, fiction, long-poems. "Recent work by Charles Wright, Diane Wakoski, James McMichael, Russell Edson, D.J. Waldie and others. Due to backlog of material we are no longer accepting unsolicited mss." circ. 500. 2/yr. Pub'd 2 issues 1979; expects 2 issues 1980. sub. price: $2.00; per copy: $1.00; sample: $1.00. Discounts: 40% to bookstores. 40pp; 5½X8½; †of. Reporting time: 4 weeks. Payment: copies. Copyrighted. §poetry.

Greenhouse Review Press (see also GREENHOUSE REVIEW), Gary Young, 126 Escalona Dr., Santa Cruz, CA 95060, 408-426-4355. 1975. Poetry, parts-of-novels, long-poems. "Greenhouse Review Press publishes a chapbook and broadside series. We are interested in manuscripts of up to 20 pages. Titles: *The Fugitive Vowels* by D.J. Waldie; *The Dreams of Mercurius* by John Hall; *House Fires* by Peter Wild; *Thirteen Ways of Deranging An Angel* by Stephen Kessler; *Looking Up* by Christopher Budkley; *Any Minute* by Laurel Blossom; *Yes* by Timothy Sheehan; *By Me By Any Can and Can't Be Done* by Killarney Clary." avg. press run 350. Pub'd 3 titles 1979; expects 4 titles 1980. 11 titles listed in the *Small Press Record of Books in Print* (9th Edition, 1980). avg. price, cloth: $10.00; paper: $3.00. Discounts: 40% to bookstores. 16-32pp; †lp. Reporting time: 4 weeks. Payment: copies. Copyrights for author.

Greenleaf Press, D. Roediger, B. Pelz, PO Box 471, Evanston, IL 60204, 465-6156. Articles. "Joseph Weydemeyer, articles on the eight hour movement, edited by David R. Roediger" avg. press run 2,000. Pub'd 1 title 1979; expects 5 titles 1980, 5 titles 1981. 2 titles listed in the *Small Press Record of Books in Print* (9th Edition, 1980). avg. price, paper: $.50. 20pp; 7X8½; of. Reporting time: 2 months. Copyrights for author. GLP.

GREENPEACE (London) Newsletter, c/o 6 Endsleigh St., London WC1, United Kingdom. Articles, reviews, news items. "Environmental/pacifistLibertarian/Anarchist." circ. 500-1000. Bimonthly. Pub'd 6 issues 1979; expects 6 issues 1980. sub. price: £1.00 minimum; per copy: stamped addressed envelope; sample: Stamped addressed envelope. 6-8pp; size A4; †mi. Payment: Never. Not copyrighted. Pub's reviews: 6 in 1979. §Energy, Nonviolence/anti-militarism, environmental problems. Ads: No ads. APS.

GREENSBORO REVIEW, Lee Zacharias, Dept English, North Carolina University — Greensboro, Greensboro, NC 27412. 1966. Poetry, fiction. "*THE GREENSBORO REVIEW* publishes the best of the unsolicited material it receives as well as the best work by students in the University of North Carolina at Greensboro's M.F.A. students. No restrictions on length or material, but please note that we accept mss. only in October and February. Contributors are asked not to submit from March through August." circ. 1,000. 2/yr. Pub'd 2 issues 1979; expects 2 issues 1980, 2 issues 1981. sub. price: $3.00; per copy: $1.50; sample: $1.50. Back issues: $1.50. Discounts: none. 100pp; 6X9; lp. Reporting time: We report on submissions in October and February. While some material may be returned as it is read, all material being considered must be held until those months. Payment: copies. Copyrighted, reverts upon request.

Greenwich-Meridian (see also CROSSCURRENTS), Bob Fink, 516 Ave K So, Saskatoon, Sask, Canada. 1970. Expects 1 title 1980. 5 titles listed in the *Small Press Record of Books in Print* (9th Edition, 1980).

Greenwood Press, Inc., James Sabin, 51 Riverside Avenue, Westport, CT 06880, (203) 226-3571. 1968. Articles, interviews, criticism. avg. press run 5,000. Pub'd 127 titles 1979; expects 150 titles 1980, 175 titles 1981. avg. price, cloth: $20.00; paper: $5.00. Discounts: Inquiries should be addressed to Marketing Department. 320pp; 6⅛X9¼; 5½X8¼ both; of. Reporting time: 3 months. Payment: Varies. Copyrights for author. CBPA, PPA, PLPG, DMA, ABA, IIA.

THE GREYLEDGE REVIEW, Laurence J. Sasso Jr., Box 481, Greenville, RI 02828, (401) 231-2076. 1979. Poetry, fiction, articles, photos, interviews, satire, criticism, reviews, letters, parts-of-novels, long-poems, plays. "We will consider work of almost any length in most any *genre. The Greyledge Review* is a magazine of experience and ideas. We aim to put literature and experience side by side in our pages, relating the world to art and art to the world. Our intention is to relate the way experience contributes to the intellectual attitudes we assume. William Carlos Williams said: 'No ideas but in things'. We believe that experience is the connection between things and ideas." 2/yr. Pub'd 1 issue 1979; expects 2 issues 1980, 2 issues 1981. sub. price: $7.00; per copy: $4.00; sample: $4.00. Back issues: $3.00 when available. Discounts: 20 copies and over, 35%. 76pp; 6X9; of. Reporting time: 4 to 6 weeks. Payment: None at this time. Prizes will be awarded. Copyrighted, reverts to author. Pub's reviews: 1 in 1979. §Poetry, fiction, essays. Ads: $100.00/$50.00. COSMEP,NESPA.

Gridgraffiti Press, 3814 Maple Avenue, Brooklyn, NY 11224. 3 titles listed in the *Small Press Record of Books in Print* (9th Edition, 1980).

Griffin Books, Inc., Margaret K. Jones, 50 Penn Place - Suite 380, Oklahoma City, OK 73118, (405) 842-0398. avg. press run 2,200. Pub'd 1 title 1979; expects 3 titles 1980, 3 titles 1981. 1 title listed in the *Small Press Record of Books in Print* (9th Edition, 1980). avg. price, cloth: $15.95. Discounts: 25% Library; 40% Bookstore. 160pp; 7¾X10¼; of. Reporting time: 4 weeks. Copyrights for author.

Griffon House Publications, Anne Paolucci, Henry Paolucci, PO Box 81, Whitestone, NY 11357. "Newsletter of the Bagehot Council, Pres. Henry Paolucci; Exec. Dir. Larry Franklin. *State of the Nation* (monthly-except August) Ed. Henry Paolucci. *Review of National Literatures* (annual volume); publication of the Council on National Literatures (Exec. Dir. Anne Paolucci) Ed. Anne Paolucci. *Council on National Literatures Quarterly World Report* (quarterly) Ed. Anne Paolucci. Other books: fiction, poetry, translation, politics and government, etc." avg. press run 1,000. Pub'd 2 titles 1979; expects 5 titles 1980, 2-5 titles 1981. 8 titles listed in the *Small Press Record of Books in Print* (9th Edition, 1980). avg. price, paper: $2.50-$8.00. Discounts: 10% for all agencies. 160-200pp; 5½X8½; †of. Copyrights for author.

Grilled Flowers Press, Frank Graziano, PO Box 3254, Durango, CO 81301. 1976. Poetry, long-poems. "Looking for good translations of contemporary foreign authors. Queries always welcome — unsolicited/uninvited mss will be returned unread. Most recent publication: *A World Rich IN Anniversaries,* prose poems by Jean Follain, tr. Mary Feeney and William Matthews." avg. press run 400-500. Pub'd 2 titles 1979; expects 4 titles 1980, 4 titles 1981. 7 titles listed in the *Small Press Record of Books in Print* (9th Edition, 1980). avg. price, paper: $4.00. Discounts: 40% trade; others arranged. pp varies; 5¼X8; of. Reporting time: 1-2 weeks. Payment: in copies. Copyrights for author. CCLM.

Ground Under Press, Tobey Kaplan, A. Dibz, 2913 Shattuck Avenue, Berkeley, CA 94705. 1978. Poetry, fiction, articles, art, cartoons, interviews, satire, reviews, parts-of-novels, collages, plays, concrete art. "Ground Under Press is dedicated to producing the work of established, new, and under published poets who are interested in surfacing with books that they had a hand in making thru design and distribution, as well as financially supporting (hopefully).Forthcoming: novels in progress, experimental/visual poems, poems on poetry, broadsides. Also will consult with other publishers and co-publish." avg. press run 1,000. Pub'd 2 titles 1979; expects 3 titles 1980, 3 titles 1981. 3 titles listed in the *Small Press Record of Books in Print* (9th Edition, 1980). avg. price, paper: $2.50. Discounts: 40% for bookstores, 20% libraries. 30pp; 5½X8½; †of. Reporting time: send inquiry first/varies. Payment: varies, copies only for now. Copyrights for author. COSMEP.

THE GROVE, Naturist Foundation, Editorial Committee, Naturist Headquarters, Sheepcote, Orpington, Kent BR5 4ET, United Kingdom, Orpington 71200. 1950. Articles, cartoons, photos, news items, letters, non-fiction. "House journal of Naturist Foundation & Sun Societies, circulating internationally to naturists. Contributions on subjects of interest to naturists welcome-with or without illustrations. But no payment offered!" circ. 800. 3/yr. Pub'd 3 issues 1979; expects 3 issues 1980. sub. price: £5.00 ($12.00); per copy: £1.75 ($5.00); sample: £1.75 ($5.00). Back issues: $2.00. 16pp; 9½X7½; lp. Payment: none. Copyrighted. Ads: £40.00 ($90.00)/£20.00 ($45.00).

Growing Room Collective (see also ROOM OF ONE'S OWN), Janice Pentland-Smith, Gayl Reid, Gail VanVarseveld, Eleanor Wachtel, Jean Wilson, Box 46160, Station G, Vancouver, BC V6R 4G5, Canada, (604) 733-3529. 1974. Poetry, fiction, art, photos, cartoons, interviews, criticism, reviews, parts-of-novels, long-poems, plays. "Good quality literary material by & about women, written from a feminist perspective" avg. press run 1,500. Pub'd 4 titles 1979. 1 title listed in the *Small Press Record of Books in Print* (9th Edition, 1980). avg. price, paper: $2.50. Discounts: 30% retail, trade; bulk negotiable; agent 15% off institutional orders only. 80pp; 5½X8½; of. Reporting time: 6 weeks to 3 months. Payment: $3.50 per printed page. Copyrights for author. CPPA.

GROWING WITHOUT SCHOOLING, Holt Associates, Inc., John Holt, Editor; Peg Durkee, Managing Editor; Donna Richoux, Assoc Editor, 308 Boylston Street, Boston, MA 02116, 617-261-3920. 1977. Articles, letters, news items. "Dialogue between editor and readers; mostly letter form." circ. 1,500. 6/yr. Pub'd 6 issues 1979; expects 6 issues 1980, 6 issues 1981. sub. price: $10.00; per copy: $2.00; sample: $2.00. Back issues: $2.00/each; 5 or more, $1.00 each; 10 or more $0.50 each. Discounts: $18.00 for two-year sub; $24.00 for 3 year sub, etc. $2.00 per additional subs. In 'group subs' (per year) So a 2X subs.=$12.00, a 3X=$14.00, etc. all subs in a group sub go to one address. 16pp; 8½X11; of. Copyrighted, does not revert to author. Pub's reviews: 12 in 1979. §Teaching at home, respecting children, books for children to read (or be read to children).

GRUB STREET, Alan Ball, Patricia Russell, PO Box 1, Winterhill Branch, Somerville, MA 02145. 1969. Poetry, fiction, art, photos. "Since we publish an average of only 15 pages of fiction per year, shorter pieces - from 200 to 1200 words - generally have a much better chance with us. We are particularly interested in fiction dealing with aspects of survival as it pertains to jobs, work and other economic facets of our lives. Eighty percent of *Grub Street* is comprised of poetry (including prose poems) of diverse styles and subjects. We prefer concrete images and effects and are less enthusiastic about abstract philosophizing and obscure symbolism. Unsolicited submissions are limited to one 8-page maximum piece or group per writer in a six-month period. Care should therefore be taken to submit material that is representative of the writer's strongest work. Perusal of at least one issue before submitting is strongly encouraged.u" circ. 1,000. 2/yr. Pub'd 2 issues 1979; expects 2 issues 1980. 1 title listed in the *Small Press Record of Books in Print* (9th Edition, 1980). sub. price: $3.25; per copy: $1.75; sample: $1.50. Back issues: $1.75. Discounts: 40 percent on 5 or more copies to same address. 40 percent to bookstores in any quantity. Will accept consignment orders from bookstores. Distributor discounts by arrangement. 44-56pp; 5½X8½; of. Reporting time: 1 week to 4 months. Payment: 1 to 3 copies; one featured poet in each issue receives cash & copies. Copyrighted, reverts to author. CCLM.

GRYPHON, Dr. Hans Juergensen, College of Arts & Letters, Room 370, Department of Humanities, Univ of South Florida, Tampa, FL 33620. 1975. Poetry, fiction, satire, criticism, parts-of-novels, long-poems, plays. "We publish one-act plays, original and translations; also poetry translations. Short stories up to 20 pp. Feature poets as many as 5 pp. Eclectic policy-but welcome experimental as well as humorous work. Contributors from America and alroad. William Stafford, Richard Eberbart, Charles Guenther, Anne Marx, Hans Juergensen." 4/yr. Pub'd 4 issues 1979; expects 4 issues 1980, 4 issues 1981. sub. price: $4.00; per copy: $1.00; sample: $1.00. Discounts: 20% to bookstores. 35-50pp; 8X11; †mi. Reporting time: 1 month - 3 months. Payment: in copies. Copyrighted, reverts to author. Ads: No ads.

GRYPHON: A Culture's Critic, Lion Enterprises, Jr. Robert Villegas, RR 3, Box 127, Walkerton, IN 46574, 219-369-9394. 1975. Poetry, fiction, articles, interviews, criticism, reviews, letters. "Published by Students of Objectivism. Only those who agree with Ayn Rand's philosophy, Objectivism need submit. Recently published Jesse F. Knight,Ernie Ross and Edward Cline." circ. 75. 4/yr. Pub'd

4 issues 1979; expects 4 issues 1980, 4 issues 1981. sub. price: $8.00; per copy: $2.50; sample: $2.50. Back issues: Inquire about catalog. Discounts: We discount to bookstores and anyone interested in displaying our magazine. 13pp; 5½X8½; of. Reporting time: 2 weeks. Payment: $.02 per page per issue printed. Copyrighted, reverts to author. Pub's reviews: 4 in 1979. §Philosophy, economics, art, politics. no ads.

GUARDIAN, Institute for Independent Social Journalism, Inc., Jack Smith, Editor; Barbara Miner, Managing Editor, 33 W 17th St, New York, NY 10011, 212-691-0404. 1948. Articles, photos, cartoons, interviews, criticism, reviews, letters, news items. circ. 25,000. 50/yr. Pub'd 50 issues 1979; expects 50 issues 1980. sub. price: $17.00; per copy: $0.50; sample: free. Back issues: $0.65. Discounts: 40% for resale. 24pp; 10¼X15; of. Reporting time: up to 1 month. Payment: yes. Pub's reviews: 50 in 1979. §Politics, history, current events, social trends, international affairs. Ads: $450.-00/$250.00/$.25 a word.

Guernica Editions (see also THE GUERNICA REVIEW), Antonio D'Alfonso, PO Box 633, Station N.D.G., Montreal, Quebec H4A 3R1, Canada, (514) 254-2917. 1978. Poetry, fiction, criticism, long-poems, plays. "Guernica Editions is a non-profit publishing house which handles its own distribution. We publish any fine work dealing with literature, criticism or politics. We will also attempt at having pamphlets dealing with certain filmmakers. Children books are more than welcomed. What we desire is serious thinking from conscientious persons. To date we have published two poetry collections *Instants* by Marco Fraticelli and *Queror* by Antonio D'Alfonso. A third volume *Conceptions* by Jane Dick will be published by fall '80. Forthcoming: *Rish of Wings* by Alex Soestmeyer, *Sirventi* by Filippo Salvatore, and *Black Tongue* by Antonio D'Alfonso; a children's and adult's comic book, *Animots,* by Richard Bouchoux" avg. press run 500. Pub'd 2 titles 1979. 2 titles listed in the *Small Press Record of Books in Print* (9th Edition, 1980). avg. price, cloth: $12.00; paper: $4.00. 1-4 no discount, 5 and over, 50%. 70pp; 5½X8½; of. Reporting time: We usually take some two months before answering. Payment: Authors keep copyrights. They receive about 20-25 copies. Money made goes to reprinting or publishing other authors. Copyrights for author.

THE GUERNICA REVIEW, Guernica Editions, Antonio D'Alfonso, Editor, P.O. Box 633, Sta N.D.G., Montreal, Quebec H4A 3R1, Canada. 1980. Poetry, fiction, articles, art, photos, cartoons, interviews, satire, criticism, reviews, music, letters, news items. circ. 1000. 4/yr. Expects 4 issues 1981. sub. price: $7.00/individuals; $8.00/institutions; per copy: $2.00; sample: free. 16pp; 8X10; of. Reporting time: 2 months. Payment: in copies, and, in future, in cash. Author and Review keep rights. Pub's reviews. §Books, music, art. Ads: $40.00/$25.00.

Jean Guenot, Jean Guenot, 85, rue des Tennerolles, Saint-Cloud 92210, France, 771-79-63. 1973. Fiction, satire, criticism. "I publish only my own books (novels and short stories mostly). I print 1,000 numbered copies of each of my fiction titles *La tour de papier, Comestibles, Jalmince,* etc. My best-selling titles (up to 4,000 copies) are a critical study of Louis-Ferdinand Celine's style and guide book for writers *Ecrire.* I write and publish only in French and only my own stuff." avg. press run 1,500. Pub'd 2 titles 1979; expects 1 title 1980, 2 titles 1981. 224pp; 14cm x 19cm; of. Reporting time: no submissions, I publish only my own books.

The Guide to Small Press Publishing (see also Peradam Publishing House), Arnold Wolman, Ted Wolter, Art Editor; Andre Duval, French Editor, PO Box 85, Urbana, IL 61801, (217) 352-5476. 1971. "We are especially interested in books on mushrooms, and in children's books. We publish the following people: Arnold Wolman, Ted Wolter, Bruce Sanders, James Magorian, Keith Hitchcock, Carole Bersin, James Kleinhans, K.T. Moore, Elvan, Kay Prickett, Susan Metz, Doris Ball, Andre Duval. We are distributed nationally and internationally. We are distributed nationally via: The Distributors of South Bend, Ind., Peradam Publishing House Book Distribution Division, and Curt Nelson Book Distributors of Broomfield, Colorado. And we are distributed internationally via Peradam Publishing House of Illinois, and Peradam Publishing House of Xalapa, Mexico and LeMans, France (beginning in May 1979)" avg. press run 250-10,000. Pub'd 8 titles 1979; expects 5 titles 1980. avg. price, cloth: $2.95; paper: $2.95; other: $2.50-$9.95. Discounts: 30%, 40%, 50%, 60%. 34-36pp; size varies; of. Reporting time: Usually we report within 3 months. Sometimes immediately. It depends. Payment: Very unique. 5-15% but sometimes more. Normally we work out each royalty payment with each author separately. COSMEP, MPP (Midwest Poetry Publishers).

Guildford Poets Press (see also WEYFARERS), John Emuss, Margaret George, Margaret Pain, Susan James, 10 Ashcroft, Shalford, Guildford, Surrey, United Kingdom. 1972. Poetry. Pub'd 3 titles 1979. 8 titles listed in the *Small Press Record of Books in Print* (9th Edition, 1980). avg. price, paper: 50p. 32pp; 8X6; of. Reporting time: 3 months. Payment: None. Does not copyright for author.

GUSTO, Gusto, M. Karl Kulikowski, PO Box 1009, Bronx, NY 10465, (212) 931-8964. 1978. Poetry, articles, art, satire, criticism, reviews, letters, long-poems, news items. "Our aim to publish poems that deserve to be published & poets who deserve to be published. No limit on length of poetry. Seeking high quality—with *Gusto*. As to biases, each poem will be judged on its merits. We do not sell ads, but we have given full page and more to contests and other announcements" circ. 500. 6/yr. Pub'd 4 issues 1979; expects 6 issues 1980, 6 issues 1981. sub. price: $10.00 for 6 issues; per copy: $2.00; sample: $2.00. Back issues: $2.00. Discounts: 40%. 92pp; 5½X8½; †mi. Reporting time: 2 weeks or less. No payment. Copyrighted, reverts to author. Pub's reviews: 11 in 1979. §Poetry, haiku, literary themes. COSMEP, CCLM.

Gusto (see also GUSTO), M. Karl Kulikowski, PO Box 1009, Bronx, NY 10465, (212) 931-8964. 1978. Poetry, articles, art, satire, criticism, reviews, letters, long-poems, news items. "We publish books of poetry primarily, but we are also publishing books of short stories as well - and although we have printed books more than 160pp our best working range is 120pp and under. This year, 1979-80 we tried something new - if long enough, book length, we try commercial presses if the work warrants it. We have succeeded placing two writers with two different commercial presses. One of these books, *Bucket*, will come out in hardcover this fall. We try to help the writers who submit material to us." avg. press run 350. Pub'd 10 titles 1979; expects 10 titles 1980, 10 titles 1981. 11 titles listed in the *Small Press Record of Books in Print* (9th Edition, 1980). avg. price, paper: $3.50. Discounts: 40%. 60+pp; 5½X8½; †mi. Reporting time: 2 weeks or less. Payment: 20% royalty paid Jan. 1 and July 1. Copyrights for author. CCLM, COSMEP.

GUTS AND GRACE, D. B. McCoy, Box 529, Massillon, OH 44648. 1979. Poetry. "Like poetry under 24 lines." circ. 200. 2/yr. Pub'd 1 issue 1979; expects 2 issues 1980. sub. price: $2.50; per copy: $1.25; sample: free. 24pp; 4X7; of. Reporting time: up to three months. Payment: copies. Copyrighted.

THE GYPSY SCHOLAR: A Graduate Forum for Literary Criticism, Judy Funston, Managing Editor, Dept. of English, Michigan State U., East Lansing, MI 48824, 517-355-7578. 1973. Criticism. "Manuscripts should not exceed 30 typed pages and conform to the *MLA Style Sheet.* 'The editors invite any graduate students to submit manuscripts which employ venturesome, speculative, inquiring, or controversial approaches to the study of literature. Brief forum articles dealing with the problems and professional concerns of English graduate students are also encouraged.' We also publish an *Annual Bibliography of Doctoral Dissertations in British, American and Canadian Literature.*" circ. 750. 3/yr. Pub'd 3 issues 1979; expects 3 issues 1980, 3 issues 1981. sub. price: Stud: $3.00/Fac: $5.00/Lib: $7.00; per copy: $3.50; sample: free. Back issues: $3.50. Discounts: Agents: 20%. 55-60pp; 9 by 6; lp. Reporting time: 4-6 weeks. Payment: two complimentary copies. Copyrighted, reverts to author. Pub's reviews: none last year; 3-5 this year in 1979. §Texts on the teaching of writing; reading methodology; anthologies for use in the classroom. no advertising.

H

H.E.L.P. Books Inc., Hershel Thornburg, Editor, 1201 E. Calle Elena, Tucson, AZ 85718. 1977. "Thornburg, Ellen*President" avg. press run 10,000. Pub'd 2 titles 1979; expects 3 titles 1980, 5 titles 1981. 3 titles listed in the *Small Press Record of Books in Print* (9th Edition, 1980). avg. price, cloth: $6.95; paper: $5.95. Discounts: 1 copy 20%, 2-4 copies 33%, 5 or more copies 40%, 50% to jobbers. 132-156pp; 6X9; lp. Copyrights for author.

Haifa Publications (see also VOICES - ISRAEL), 29 Bar Kokhba Street, Tel Aviv, Israel. 1 title listed in the *Small Press Record of Books in Print* (9th Edition, 1980).

Haiku Society of America, Inc. (see HSA FROGPOND)

Clarence H. Hall, Clarence H. Hall, 3409 Altvater Road, Avon Park, IL 33825. 1 title listed in the *Small Press Record of Books in Print* (9th Edition, 1980).

Halls of Ivy Press, Edmand J. Gross, Publisher & President, 13050 Raymer Street, North Hollywood, CA 91605, (213) 875-3050. 1968. avg. press run 3M. Pub'd 1 title 1979; expects 1 title 1980, 2 titles 1981. avg. price, paper: $10.00. Discounts: Trade varies to 40%, schools 20%, jobbers 20%-40%. 120pp; 8½X11; †of. Payment: 10% of net sales. Copyrights for author.

Halty Ferguson Publishing Co., William Ferguson, Raquel Ferguson, 376 Harvard Street, Cambridge, MA 02138, 617-868-6190. 1970. Poetry, fiction. "We do not encourage unsolicited material at the moment. To date we have published Jorge Guillen (in Spanish), James Tate (two titles), Tim

Reynolds, William Ferguson, Peter Davison, Mark Strand, and John Updike." avg. press run 500-1,000. Expects 3 titles 1980, 2 titles 1981. avg. price, cloth: $25.00; paper: $4.00. Discounts: 40 percent on trade books, 30 percent on luxury signed editions. 60-100pp; 6X9; †lp. Reporting time: asap. Payment: 10 percent of list. Copyrights for author.

THE HAMPDEN-SYDNEY POETRY REVIEW, Tom O'Grady, P.O. Box 126, Hampden-Sydney, VA 23943, 804-223-4381. 1975. Poetry, criticism. "W. D. Snodgrass, David Ignatow, Peter Viereck, Louis Simpson, Howard Moss, William Stafford, Josephine Jacobsen, Kenneth Rexroth, Denise Levertov." circ. 500. 2/yr. Pub'd 2 issues 1979. sub. price: $5.00; per copy: $3.00; sample: $2.00. Discounts: none. 52pp; 9X5; †of/lp. Reporting time: 6 weeks. Payment: copies. Copyrighted. §essays on poetics. Ads: none. CCLM.

Hancock House Publishers, Barbara Herringer, 10 Orwell Street, N Vancouver, B.C. V7J 3K1, Canada, 604-980-4113. 1972. Articles, art, photos. "No unsolicited material. Inquire in advance before submitting. SASE. Canadian and Northwest material preferred. Eskimo and Indian art and culture. Current resource books on mining, trucking, logging and fishing. All our books use professional-quality photographs and art-work. 50,000 to 60,000 words. Authors include Zoe Landale, *Harvest of Salmon*; Ed Gould, *Logging and Oil*; John Magor, *UFO Report*; Paul St. Pierre. Wish more wildlife and plant guides." circ. 5,000. Pub'd 20 issues 1979; expects 28 issues 1980, 30 issues 1981. 21 titles listed in the *Small Press Record of Books in Print* (9th Edition, 1980). Discounts: Under 5 titles, 30%; 5 or more titles, 37%; 50-99 titles, 38%; 100-199 assorted titles, 39%; 200-499 assorted, 40%; 500 or more assorted, 41%. 200pp; 5½X8½; of. Reporting time: 90 days. Payment: yes. Copyrighted. COSMEP, ACP, BCPG.

HAND BOOK, Susan Mernit, Rochelle Ratner, 50 Spring Street, Apt. #2, New York, NY 10012. 1976. Poetry, fiction, articles, art, letters, parts-of-novels, long-poems, collages, photos, music. "A large collection of the energy. *Handbook* as catalyst and place for shared concerns. Issues are thematic: #4 (current) is a special issue of Collaboration/Fusion of the arts and sciences. Contributors include Jerome Rothenberg, Nathan Whiting, Charlie Morrow, Marc Kaminsky. Back issues: Prayer (#1) and Silene (#2). Contributors include: DiPrima, Stafford, Appleton, Isnatow, McCord, Grossinger. #4 will be a special issue on collaboration and cross discipline. Unsolicited manuscripts are okay, but *be familar* with the magazine-we will sell you a sample issue," circ. 1,000. 1-2/yr. Pub'd 1 issue 1979; expects 2 issues 1980. sub. price: Indiv. $8.00, Lib. $12.00 (2 issues); per copy: $4.00; sample: $3.00. Back issues: No. 1 Spring 1977 Prayer $4.00 #2 Silence 1978 $4.00, #3 1979 The Spiritual Sword. Discounts: 20-40% off. We are handled by Faxon, Ebsco and most small press distributors. 224pp; 7X9; of. Reporting time: 1 week to 3 months. Payment: contrib. copies. Copyrighted, reverts to author. Pub's reviews. §poetry, social sci., religion. Query for ad rates. NYSPA.

Handshake Editions (see also 'THE CASSETTE GAZETTE'), Jim Haynes, Atelier A2, 83 rue de la Tombe-Issoire, Paris 75014, France, 327-1767. 1971. Poetry, fiction, articles, photos, cartoons, parts-of-novels. "Handshake mainly publishes Paris-based writers. Small print-runs, but we attempt to keep everything in print (ie frequent re-prints). Libertarian bias. Writers recently published include Ted Joans, Sarah Bean, Michael Zwerin, Robert Cordier, Jim Haynes, and Jill Diamond." avg. press run 100. avg. price, paper: $7.00. Discounts: 1/3 prepaid; all cheques payable to Jim Haynes. 90pp. Reporting time: only personal face-to-face submissions solicited. Payment: by copies of the book. Copyrights for author.

HANGING LOOSE, Hanging Loose Press, Robert Hershon, Emmett Jarrett, Dick Lourie, Ron Schreiber, Denise Levertov, Contrib. Ed., 231 Wyckoff St, Brooklyn, NY 11217. 1966. Poetry, fiction. "Emphasis remains on the work of new writers-and when we find people we like, we stay with them. Among recent contributors: Harley Elliott, Jacqueline Lapidus, Helen Adam, Frances Phillips, Carol Cox, William Lane, Sam Kashner, Jack Anderson, Karen Brodine, Donna Brook, Rochelle Ratner, Eric Torgersen. We welcome submissions to the magazine, but artwork & book mss. are by invitation only." circ. 1,200. 4/yr. Pub'd 4 issues 1979; expects 4 issues 1980. sub. price: $5.50-4 issues (to individuals); per copy: $2.00; sample: $2.00. Back issues: Prices on request, including complete sets. Discounts: 40% to bookstores, 20% to jobbers. 72pp; 7X8½; of. Reporting time: 2-3 Months. Payment: 3 copies. Copyrighted. Pub's reviews. §poetry. no ads. CCLM, COSMEP.

Hanging Loose Press (see also HANGING LOOSE), 231 Wyckoff St, Brooklyn, NY 11217. 1966. Poetry, fiction. "Book mss by invitation only" avg. press run 1000. Pub'd 5 titles 1979; expects 5 titles 1980, 5 titles 1981. 20 titles listed in the *Small Press Record of Books in Print* (9th Edition, 1980). avg. price, paper: $3.00. Discounts: Bookstores, 40% (more than 4 copies); 20%, 1-4 copies. Jobbers, 20%. 72pp; 5½X8½; of. By invitation only. Payment: 10% of cover price. Copyrights for author. CCLM, COSMEP, NYSSPA.

168

Hans Zell Publishers Ltd. (see also THE AFRICAN BOOK PUBLISHING RECORD), P O Box 56, Oxford OX1 3EL, United Kingdom. 1 title listed in the *Small Press Record of Books in Print* (9th Edition, 1980).

HAPPINESS HOLDING TANK, Stone Press, Albert Drake, 1790 Grand River, Okemos, MI 48864. 1970. Poetry, articles, criticism, reviews, letters, news items. "We've emphasized poetry, information, printing processes, & people. Any information of a literary nature will be passed along. The current issue (No. 19) lists dozens of new mags, dead mags, contests, etc. (in addition to poetry, commentary, essays, etc.) only $1.25. Still doing posters, post cards, pamphlets, books. A poetry pack brings a lot ($4.00). Philip Whalen, Earle Birney, Wm. Matthews, Wm. Stafford, Anselm Hollo, and more than 300 known/unknown poets. No mss during summer." circ. 300-500. 1-2/yr. Pub'd 1 issue 1979; expects 1 issue 1980, 2 issues 1981. sub. price: $3.50; per copy: $1.00-$1.25; sample: $1.00. Back issues: Limited sets: 1-19 for $50.00 to libraries. Discounts: 40%. 50pp; 8½X11; †mi/of. Reporting time: 1-3 weeks. Payment: copies. Copyrighted. Pub's reviews: 20 in 1979. §poetry & fiction. Ads: $15/$8. CCLM.

The Happy Press (see also POETRY COMICS), Dave Morice, Box 585, Iowa City, IA 52244, (319) 338-0084. 1970. "The press was originally founded to publish *GUM Magazine* (1970-1974). It is a very small & erratic publisher of booklets in mimeo or multilith form. At present it publishes *Poetry Comics,* and there is really no time for anything else." Pub'd 1 title 1979; expects 4 titles 1980. avg. price, paper: $1.50. Discounts: write for info on back issues of Gum, Matchbook, and Poetry Comics. 50pp; 8½X11; mi, of. Reporting time: 1 month.

Harbour Publishing (see also RAINCOAST CHRONICLES), Howard White, P.O. Box 119, Madeira Park, BC V0N 2H0, Canada, (604) 883-2730. 1972. avg. press run 5,000. Pub'd 6 titles 1979; expects 6 titles 1980. avg. price, paper: $3.95. Discounts: 40%, bookstores over 10; 35% under; 20% libraries; 50% distribu-tors. 48pp; 6X8; of. Reporting time: 4 weeks. Payment: 10% of cover.

HARD CRABS, Paul Bartlett, Ben Reynolds, Md. Writers Council, 1110 St. Paul Street, Baltimore, MD 21202, (301) 685-5239. 1978. Poetry, articles, art, photos, interviews, criticism, reviews, letters, news items. "Generally 50 word limit for body copy. We are an 'asssembling' sort of mag. We will insert and distribute 1000 flyers (either 8½ X 11 or 11 X 17) any month for $20.00. Our mailing list is primarily Baltimore/Washington" circ. 1000+. Monthly. Pub'd 11 issues 1979; expects 10 issues 1980, 11 issues 1981. sub. price: $4.00/yr; per copy: 50¢; sample: free. Back issues: 50¢. Payment: none. Not copyrighted. Pub's reviews: 49 in 1979. §mid-atlantic region. Ads: 3 x 2 camera ready $7.50.

THE HARDHITTING INTERMITTENT NORTH IDAHO NEWS, Mole Publishing Co., Mike Oehler, Rt. 1, Box 618, Bonners Ferry, ID 83805. 1977. Satire, criticism. "An environmental, underground sheet dedicated to exposing the 'establishment' of Bonners Ferry Idaho and other northern Idaho towns. Do not use outside material. Two high school boys staying the summer at editors land, Josh Walden and Dave Eskin have done material for the sheet." circ. 150. Pub'd 4 issues 1979; expects 1 issue 1980, 3 issues 1981. sub. price: free; per copy: free. Back issues: Are collector items and can only be individually negotiated. 3pp; 8½X11; †mi.

Hard Press, Jeff Wright, 340 East Eleventh Street, New York, NY 10003, (212) 673-1152. 1976. Poetry, art, photos, cartoons, music, letters, collages. "To date Hard Press has published 64 different *post cards,* generally poetry of two to twenty lines, sometimes accompanied by art-work, but sometimes just original art work, cartoons, collages, photos, by themselves. Contributors include: Ted Berrigan, Robert Creeley, Anselm Hollo, Jack Hirschman, Alice Notley, Maureen Owen, Paul Violi, Allen Ginsburg, Amiri Baraka, Anne Waldman, Jayne Anne Phillips, and others." avg. press run 500. Pub'd 20 titles 1979; expects 24 titles 1980, 24 titles 1981. 9 titles listed in the *Small Press Record of Books in Print* (9th Edition, 1980). avg. price, paper: $0.25; other: postage. Discounts: 40% or $0.10 per card. 1pp; 5½X4¼; of. Reporting time: 6 weeks. Payment: Dependant on CCLM grant pending/10% of copy. Copyrights for author. CCLM.

HARD PRESSED, Ellen's Old Alchemical Press, Ellen Rosser, Donald Alexander, Jim Normington, Contributing Editors, P.O. Box 161915, Sacramento, CA 95816, 916-455-9984. 1975. Poetry, art. "Portfolio format. Each poem (40 lines or fewer) on a separate page suitable for display. Recent contributors: Marge Piercy, Mary MacKey, William Everson, Joan Colby, Quincy Troupe, William Harrold, Robert Stern, Kenneth Rexroth, Ling Chung, Lyn Lifshin." circ. 500. 2/yr. Pub'd 2 issues 1979; expects 2 issues 1980. sub. price: Indiv. $4.00; Instit. $8.00; per copy: $2.00; sample: $2.00. Back issues: Ind. $8.00; inst. $16.00. Discounts: 40%. 24pp; 8½X11; †lp. Reporting time: 4 weeks. Payment: 2 copies. Copyrighted. COSMEP.

Harden Publications, Dorothy E. Harden, 5332 E 26th Street, Tulsa, OK 74114, (918) 936-8846. 1979. Fiction. "Harden Publications writes and publishes children's picture books for ages 8 thru 12.

We use one color pictures printed on newsprint.. a high quality product and an inexpensive package. By using this method of production we make our books affordable to everyone. Payment: inasmuch as we have never worked with other authors, this phase of our operations is incomplete. However, I'm sure we'll use a standard contract for R & P." avg. press run 1,000. Pub'd 1 title 1979. 2 titles listed in the *Small Press Record of Books in Print* (9th Edition, 1980). avg. price, paper: $2.95. Discounts: A blanket 20% with orders of 15 copies or more. 21pp; 8½X10½; †of. Reporting time: 6 weeks. Payment: standard authors contract. Copyrights for author.

Harian Creative Press, Harry Barba, Publisher, 47 Hyde Blvd, Ballston SPA, NY 12020, 518-885-7397. 1967. Poetry, fiction, articles, parts-of-novels, plays. "1) Booklength fiction, collection of poems, general tradebooks 2) monographs on education, literature, art and culture 3) Harry Barba, Harold Bond, Leo Hamalian & others 4) exceptional how-to books 5) Harian Creative Award socially functional fiction, 3,000-20,000 words" avg. press run 2,000-3,000. Pub'd 3 titles 1979; expects 3-5 titles 1980. 12 titles listed in the *Small Press Record of Books in Print* (9th Edition, 1980). avg. price, cloth: $7.95; paper: $3.95; other: $0.95-$1.25 (offprints). Discounts: trade 40 percent cash, 30 percent consignment; bulk 50 percent; classroom 20 percent; jobber 50 percent. 200pp; 8½X5½; of/lp. Reporting time: 2-3 months, longer in special cases but will communicate with author for permission. Payment: by arrangement. copyright, if individual book. COSMEP, ALP, COSMEPA, NESPA, PWI, AWP, PEN, MLA, CEA.

Harlo Press, L. W. Mueller, 50 Victor, Detroit, MI 48203. 1946. "We are primarily book printers although we publish a few titles" avg. press run 2 - 5000. Pub'd 3-4 titles 1979. 11 titles listed in the *Small Press Record of Books in Print* (9th Edition, 1980). avg. price, cloth: $9.00; paper: $6.00. Discounts: 1-4, 20%; 5-24, 40%; 25-49, 43%; 50-99, 46%; 100 or more, 50%. 200pp; 5½X8½; †lp/of. Payment: yes. Copyrights for author.

Harper Square Press (see also GALLERY SERIES/POETS), c/o Artcrest Products Co., Inc., 401 W Ontario Street, Chicago, IL 60610, (312) 751-1650. 1967. Poetry. avg. press run 1,000. Pub'd 1 title 1979. 1 title listed in the *Small Press Record of Books in Print* (9th Edition, 1980). Discounts: To be arranged. 104pp; 5½X8½. No ms solicited. Copyrights for author. COSMEP.

HARPOON, Steven C. Levi, Joanne Townsend, PO Box 2581, Anchorage, AK 99510, 276-1279. 1979. Poetry, fiction, articles, art, satire, criticism. "*Harpoon* is a literary journal dedicated to quality. We have no specific point of view and will consider poetry and short fiction in all its forms. We have printed poets such as Ann Chandonnet, Shelia Nickerson, Ruben Gaines, Margaret Mielke and John Haines. We are also interested in art work as well as criticism. Of the three issues printed each year, one issue is open to a guest critic." circ. 100. 3/yr. Pub'd 3 issues 1979; expects 3 issues 1980, 3 issues 1981. 4 titles listed in the *Small Press Record of Books in Print* (9th Edition, 1980). sub. price: $7.00; per copy: $2.75; sample: $2.75. Back issues: $2.75 per issue. 40pp; 5½X8½; of. Reporting time: about 6 weeks. Payment: Contributors copy. Copyrighted, reverts to author. Pub's reviews: 4 in 1979. §Poetry, short fiction, satire.

Hartmus Press, 23 Lomita Drive, Mill Valley, CA 94941. 1957. Poetry. avg. press run 400-700. Expects 1 title 1980. 10 titles listed in the *Small Press Record of Books in Print* (9th Edition, 1980). avg. price, paper: $4.00. Discounts: 40% trade. 70pp; 6X9; †of. Payment: copies of title & discount. Copyrights for author.

THE HARVARD ADVOCATE, Charles Gerard, President, 21 South St., Cambridge, MA 02138, 617-495-7820. 1866. Poetry, fiction, articles, art, photos, interviews, criticism, reviews, parts-of-novels, long-poems, plays. "THE HARVARD ADVOCATE publishes work from Harvard affiliates and alumni. We regret that we cannot read manuscripts from other sources." circ. 20,000. 4/yr. Pub'd 4 issues 1979; expects 4 issues 1980, 4 issues 1981. sub. price: $7.50 Indiv.; $10.00 for Institutions (for 4 issues); per copy: $3.00; sample: $1.00. Back issues: Price varies. Discounts: none. 32pp; 8½X11; of. Reporting time: 3/4 weeks. Payment: none. Copyrighted, does not revert to author. Pub's reviews: 8 in 1979. §literature and art. Ads: $200.00/$120.00.

HARVEST, Robert T. Casey, Maryland Lincoln, Antonia Van-Loon, P.O. Box 78, Farmington, CT 06032. 1974. Poetry, fiction, articles, art, satire, parts-of-novels. "Submitters must be members of Connecticut writers league. Membership open to all. Dues $10.00/year." circ. 500. 1/yr. Pub'd 1 issue 1979; expects 1 issue 1980, 1 issue 1981. sub. price: $3.00; per copy: $3.00. Back issues: $2.00. Discounts: 20% to stores. 40pp; 8½X11; of. Reporting time: 2 months. Payment: none. Copyrighted, reverts to author. Ads: none. CWL.

Harvest Press, Patty Dunks, Thom Dunks, P.O. Box 1265, Santa Cruz, CA 95061, 415-335-5015. 1976. "One title at this time-*Gardening With Children*." avg. press run 5,000. 1 title listed in the *Small Press Record of Books in Print* (9th Edition, 1980). avg. price, paper: $4.95. Discounts: 40 percent trade,

45-50 percent bulk. 176pp; 8½X5½. Copyrights for author.

Harvest Publishers (see also HARVEST QUARTERLY), Ann Baxandall Krooth, Editorial Board; Richard Krooth, Editorial Board; Jackie Greenberg, 907 Santa Barbara Street, Santa Barbara, CA 93101. 1975. Poetry, articles, art, photos, cartoons, interviews, criticism, reviews, letters, long-poems, concrete art, plays. "Coming soon *The Great Homestead Strike of 1892,* a new analysis of the most importnat strike in the 19th century. 4 classic titles are available: *Poets & Players,* including an interview '*Simone de Beauvoir Questions Jean-Paul Sartre'; A Classic Poem About Alaska's Historical Conquest* by Richard Dauenhauer; and *Afro-American Poetry* by Nandi Jordan. *Empire: A Bicentennial Appraisal,* by Richard Krooth, covering the historical roots of the U.S. empire. *Japan: Five Stages Of Development,* a short & concise history of Japan & its place in the world today. *Arms and Empire: Imperial Patterns Before World War II,* by Richard Krooth." avg. press run 3,500-4,000. Pub'd 4 titles 1979; expects 4 titles 1980, 4 titles 1981. 8 titles listed in the *Small Press Record of Books in Print* (9th Edition, 1980). avg. price, paper: $2.50-$6.75; other: $1.75. Discounts: Jobber discounts on trade, terms for books in bulk. 75pp; of. Reporting time: 30-90 days. Payment: no longer possible. Copyrights for author. Alternative Press Index.

HARVEST QUARTERLY, Harvest Publishers, Ann Baxandall Krooth, Editorial Board; Richard Krooth, 907 Santa Barbara Street, Santa Barbara, CA 93101. 1976. Poetry, articles, art, photos, cartoons, interviews, criticism, reviews, letters, long-poems, concrete art, plays. "HARVEST QUARTERLY: Classic studies of society and social movements. Outstanding features in Quarterly No. 1, *Essays On Movement Projects;* Quarterly No. 2, *Classics On The Division Of Labor;* Quarterly Nos. 3-4, *Oral History & Women In Struggle;* Quarterly No. 5, *Questions About The Social Order;* Quarterly No. 6, *Alternative Institutions & Classic Radical Essays;* Quarterly No. 7, (Fall 1977) Features Flora Tristan: *Socialist Feminist Of 1840 On The Emancipation Of Women;* Quarterly No. 8-9, (Winter-Spring 1977-80) Features *Arms and Empire: Imperial Patterns Before World War II.*" circ. 1,000-1,500. 4/yr. Pub'd 4 issues 1979; expects 4 issues 1980. sub. price: $6.00 U.S. & $7.00 Canada, $8.00 elsewhere; per copy: $1.75; sample: $1.75. Back issues: Same as original price. Discounts: 30% 10 or more for resale, organizations, study-groups or classrooms. 160pp; 5½X11; of. Reporting time: 2 or 3 months. Payment: 3 copies of edition in which author's work appears. Copyright right to reprint by permission of HARVEST Quarterly. Pub's reviews. §Political economy, literary radicalism, philosophical notes, socialist feminist history to labor struggles. Ads: $120.00/$60.00/$2.00 for ten words. Alternative Press Index.

Harvestman and Associates, Maria Marcias, Sales Director, PO Box 271, Menlo Park, CA 94025, (415) 969-0125. 1978. Photos. "Pictorial essay of road rider/touring motorcyclists with their families at a 'Party Run'." avg. press run 5,000. Expects 1 title 1980. 1 title listed in the *Small Press Record of Books in Print* (9th Edition, 1980). avg. price, paper: $6.25. Discounts: 60/40. 92pp; 8½X8; of. Copyrights for author.

Haskell House Publishers, Ltd., H. Smith, Box FF, Brooklyn, NY 11219, 212-435-0500. 1964. "Interested in many subjects." avg. press run 200. avg. price, cloth: $20.00. Discounts: inquire. 300pp. Payment: 10%. Copyrights for author.

HAWAII LITERARY ARTS COUNCIL NEWSLETTER, Pat Matsueda, PO Box 11213, Moiliili Station, Honolulu, HI 96814. 1975. Poetry, fiction, articles, interviews, satire, criticism, reviews, letters, news items. "Hawaii's literary arts scene is extremely active right now. Recent articles include reviews of readings given by Robert Stone, Marvin Bell, Charles Wright, Galway Kinnell, Frank Chin. Recent contributors include Leon Edel, Mark Lofstrom, Phyllis Hoge Thompson, Frank Stewart, Norman Hindley, Tony Quagliano, Vickie Nelson." circ. 350. 10/yr. Pub'd 10 issues 1979; expects 10 issues 1980, 10 issues 1981. sub. price: $4.00, $2.00 for students; per copy: free; sample: free. 6pp; 8½X11; of. Reporting time: 4 weeks usually. Payment: contributor's copy. Copyrighted, reverts to author. Pub's reviews. Ads: $50.00/$25.00.

HAWK PRESS Hawk Press, Alan Loney, 30 Miro Street, Eastbourne, New Zealand, Wellington 628-648. 1975. Poetry. "All work—design, handsetting type, printing on a treadle platen, & binding —is done by the sole owner of the press. General aim—to produce poetry in limited editions, & have the labour of the book appropriate to the poetry. I can take mss up to 50 pages or so, & I have no desire to print only New Zealand work. Poets printed so far, are: Ian Wedde, Stephen Oliver, Alan Loney, Alan Brunton, Graham Lindsay, and Robert Creeley, Rhys Pasley, Russell Haley, David Miller, Anne Donovan. Joanna Paul, Murray Edmond" avg. press run 300 copies limited editions. Pub'd 3 titles 1979; expects 5 titles 1980, 3 titles 1981. 5 titles listed in the *Small Press Record of Books in Print* (9th Edition, 1980). avg. price, paper: $5.00. Discounts: Trade 33⅓%, Libraries 10%, Trade Standing Orders 40%, Libraries Standing Orders 20%. 36 to 40pp; 6½X9¼; †lp. Reporting time: 1 month. Payment: Some have waived payment, but else, 10 percent monthly. Copyrights for author.

HAWK-WIND, Pentagram Press, Michael Tarachow, Box 379, Markesan, WI 53946. 1979. Poetry, fiction, articles, criticism, reviews, parts-of-novels, news items. "*Hawk-Wind* #s 1&2 appeared in 1979, a mixst bag of poetry, prose, & commentary/review. Starting in 1980, chances are excellent the focus will be all commentary/review——there's so much being done in the way of writing & so little critical attention paid to it. Generally, essays will look at the opus of a writer's work, rather than a single volume; the overall list of a given press, rather than one book; a 'kind' of poetry, rather than given author. Tho of course, where need be, *anything*'s possible. Those interested in writing for *HW* are welcome to query with ideas for essays. *Otherwise, no unsolicited mss wanted.*" circ. 225. 2/yr. Pub'd 2 issues 1979; expects 2 issues 1980, 2 issues 1981. sub. price: $5.00 indiv., $7.50 instit.; per copy: $3.00 plus postage; sample: $3.00 plus postage. Back issues: $5.00 each. 64-72pp; 5X8; †mi. Reporting time: Contributions mainly solicited, then quick response. Payment: Copies. Copyrighted, reverts to author. Pub's reviews. §Poetry, prose, essays, books that explore combinations of those, books on publishing, typography. Ads: No ads.

Hays, Rolfes & Associates, Helen S. Hays, Ellen R. Rolfes, PO Box 11465, Memphis, TN 38111, (901) 682-8128. 1978. News items. "*The Collection: Classic Community Cookbooks* is the first annual directory of quality, regional cookbooks across the country. It offers pertinent ordering information, discount schedules, cross-index, and a fifty word promotional description written by ninety-nine community cookbooks (published by non-profit groups: museums, historical societies, spymphony leagues, churches, junior leagues, and others). Since these publications are among the top sellers in the cookbook catagory, but have never traditionally used any 'book listing source', *The Collection* is a complete reference for the retailer or food page editor to locate a requested cookbook (for a customer or book review) or increase inventory with trusted buying direction." Expects 1 title 1981. 1 title listed in the *Small Press Record of Books in Print* (9th Edition, 1980). avg. price, paper: $6.95; other: $7.50 post paid. Discounts: Marked only to retail, bookseller, food editor. 10% given to bookseller who orders 10 or more copies. 50pp; 6X9; of. Reporting time: 10 months. Payment: self-published. ABA.

HEALTH SCIENCE, Natural Hygiene Press, Jack Dunn Trop, 1920 Irving Park Road, Chicago, IL 60613, (312) 929-7420. 1978. Articles, photos, interviews, reviews, letters, news items. "The editor favors creative articles on the innumerable underappreciated habits and environmental conditions (besides diet) which affect our physical and mental wellbeing. Articles should contain practical suges-tions for improving the quality of one's life. Length of material: 1,200-3,600 words for feature articles; 750-2,500 words for column articles." circ. 6000. 6/yr. Pub'd 6 issues 1979. sub. price: $15.00; per copy: $2.50; sample: $2.00. Back issues: $1.50. Discounts: 1-4 copies, $1.50; 5 and over, $1.00 each. 32pp; 8X10½; of. Reporting time: 2 months. Payment: varies. Copyrighted, reverts to author. Pub's reviews: 4 in 1979. §Nutrition, exercise, rest & sleep, natural healing, organic gardening, ecology, self-discipline & development, parenthood & child care, dental hygiene. Ads: /$167.13. COSMEP.

HEALTHY LIVING, Capemead Ltd., Helene Hodge, 16 Ennismore Ave, London W4 1SF, United Kingdom, 01-994-1314. 1966. Articles, photos, cartoons, interviews, satire, criticism, reviews, letters, news items. "up to 1,000 words, natural health bias" circ. 25,000. monthly. Pub'd 12 issues 1979; expects 12 issues 1980, 12 issues 1981. sub. price: £5.70, $12.00 US; per copy: 45p; sample: free. Discounts: on application. 72pp; 8X10¾; of. Reporting time: 3 months prior to publication. Payment: £15/thousand words. Copyrighted, does not revert to author. Pub's reviews: 70 in 1979. §health, food, ecology, esoteric sciences, gardening. Ads: £158/£84/£.10/word (min £2.00).

Hearthstone Press (see also ATTENTION PLEASE), Harold Leland Johnson, 708 Inglewood Drive, Broderick, CA 95605, 916-372-0250. 1975. Poetry. "Book production limited 2-3 annually." avg. press run 200-500. Pub'd 3 titles 1979; expects 2 titles 1980. 1 title listed in the *Small Press Record of Books in Print* (9th Edition, 1980). avg. price, cloth: $3.50/$10.00; paper: $1.00/$3.50. Discounts: 40 percent trade. 65pp; 5½X8½; †mi, lp, of. Reporting time: 2-3 weeks. Payment: By agreement. Copy-rights for author. COSMEP.

Heavy Evidence Press, Irwin M. Prohlo, E.T. Caldwell, P.O. Box 92893, Milwaukee, WI 53202. 1938. Poetry, fiction, art, satire, collages, concrete art. "Publishers of *Heavy Evidence; Science Fiction Dreams; Dada Gun.* DADA/satire welcome." avg. press run 200. Expects 4 titles 1980. 5 titles listed in the *Small Press Record of Books in Print* (9th Edition, 1980). avg. price, paper: $1.00. Discounts: none. 12pp; 8½X11; of. Reporting time: 2 weeks. Payment: copies. Copyrights for author.

HECATE, Carole Ferrier, Editor; Jane Sunderland, Associate Editor, G.P.O. Box 99, St. Lucia, Queensland 4067, Australia. 1975. Poetry, fiction, criticism, art, plays, articles. "Articles on historical, sociological, literary, etc. Aspects of women's oppression. Some interviews and reviews. Some creative writing." circ. 2,500. 2/yr. Pub'd 2 issues 1979; expects 2 issues 1980, 2 issues 1981. sub. price: $4.00/yr; per copy: $2.50; sample: $2.50. Back issues: $4.00 volume. Discounts: 33% for bookshops.

172

112pp; 4X6½; of. Reporting time: varies. Payment: $3-4 page. Copyrighted. Pub's reviews: 3 in 1979. §Socialist, feminist. Ads: negotiable/exchange.

Heidelberg Graphics (see also PHANTASM), Larry S. Jackson, P.O. Box 3606D, Chico, CA 95927, 916-342-6582. 1972. "Heidelberg Graphics reads unsolicited manuscripts for nonfiction books only. We do not publish books of unsolicited poetry or fiction. Please send poetry, fiction and other literary material to our bimonthly magazine, *Phantasm*. Recent titles include *The Middle Aged Princess and the Frog* (Alison Zier), *Focus 101* (LaVerne Harrell Clark), *The Face of Poetry* (ed. by Clark and Mary MacArthur), *Back in Town* (ed. by Susan Bent), *After the War* by H.R. Coursen and our annual *Year of the Native American* calendar." avg. press run 600-6,000. Pub'd 5 titles 1979; expects 4 titles 1980, 5 titles 1981. 7 titles listed in the *Small Press Record of Books in Print* (9th Edition, 1980). Discounts: Write for prices, wholesale, retail, distributor's. 6X9; †of/lp. Reporting time: 4 to 12 weeks. Payment: Negotiable. Copyrights for author. COSMEP, CCLM, SCCIPHC.

Heinemann (see AFRICAN LITERATURE TODAY)

Heinemann Publisher's (NZ) Ltd, David Ling, Graham McEwan, Box 36064, Auckland, New Zealand, 489154. 1969. "Principally high school books" avg. press run 3,500. Pub'd 21 titles 1979; expects 20 titles 1980, 20 titles 1981. 13 titles listed in the *Small Press Record of Books in Print* (9th Edition, 1980). avg. price, paper: $4.00. Discounts: 35%. 64pp; 8X10; of. Reporting time: 2 weeks. Payment: 15% price received. Copyrights for author. BPANZ.

HEIRS, Heirs Press, Alfred Durand Garcia, Publisher; Jill Immerman, Ernest J. Oswald, 657 Mission St., San Francisco, CA 94105, (415) 824-8604. 1968. Poetry, fiction, articles, art, photos, interviews, criticism, reviews, music, parts-of-novels, long-poems, collages, plays, concrete art. "Quality and variety is the major focus—translations encouraged—essays dealing with art and humanism encouraged. Major articles on artists, etc. appear in English, Spanish, and Chinese. Contributors include: John Morita, Bruce Hutchinson, Dan Georgakas, Kenneth Lee, Luciano Mezzetta, Dadaland, Lorraine Tong, Andrei Codrescu, Sandra Case, Buriel Clay II, Jessica Hagedorn, et. al.." circ. 4,000. 2/yr. Pub'd 1 issue 1979. sub. price: $8.00/2 issues; per copy: $4.00; sample: $4.00. Back issues: #9-$5, #8-$3, #6,7-$3, #5-$2, #4-$2, #1-$5, #2,3-$7. Discounts: 50% to distributors; 30% to bookstores 5 or more copies. 80pp; 8½X11; of. Reporting time: 6-8 wks. Payment: copies & token $ if available. Copyrighted. Pub's reviews. §visual art/plays/fiction. Ads: $300.00/$200.00/$100.00. CCLM, COSMEP/WIP.

Heirs Press (see also HEIRS), Jill Immerman, Alfred Garcia, 657 Mission St, San Francisco, CA 94105. 1972. Poetry, fiction, plays. avg. press run 700. Pub'd 5 titles 1979. 6 titles listed in the *Small Press Record of Books in Print* (9th Edition, 1980). avg. price, paper: $4.00; other: $10.00. Discounts: 30% ten or more copies; 40% bookstores; 50% agents. 60pp; 5½X8½; of. Reporting time: 6 weeks maximum. Payment: Varies, usually 10%. WIP.

Helaine Victoria Press, Nancy Victoria Poore, Jocelyn Helaine Cohen, 4080 Dynasty Lane, Martinsville, IN 46151, (317) 537-2868. 1973. Photos, cartoons, news items. "We are printers of historical documents on women's history, including labor, suffrage, civil rights, ecology, arts & ideas, lifestyles, and particularly interesting individuals. By far most of our printing takes the form of picture postcards on these themes, with descriptive &/or biographical captions on the backs. We also do some political/-historical notecards and broadsides. Our work is often used by schools, libraries, small groups, etc., as a convenient, effective learning aid in place of books, or to complement them. It is also excellent for wall displays.. Currently we offer depictions of about 100 women and events. A new catalog is availalbe for 30¢ in stamps or coins. Most of our printing is done on our antique Chandler & Price cast-iron, handfed platen press. Very often we work with foundry type, piece borders, and old engravings rescued from the melting pots and antique dealers. Historians, feminists, and fine printing buffs number large among our most loyal customers. Mostly mail order; dealer & fundraiser inquiries invited." avg. press run 1,500-2,000. Pub'd 15 titles 1979; expects 6 titles 1980, 5 titles 1981. Discounts: varies with size of order: about 50% on orders over $50.00; details on request. 1pp; 3½X5½; 4¼X6; 5½X7¼; †lp.

THE HELEN REVIEW, Tiresias Press, Dorothy Friedman, Carol Polcovar, Lillian Von Binder, 389 Union Street, Brooklyn, NY 11231, (212) 875-2168. 1978. Poetry, fiction, articles, art, photos, interviews, satire, criticism, reviews, letters, parts-of-novels. "We try to print quality poetry & fiction that has as editor Dorothy Friedman puts it, 'All the energy of people eating sauerkraut..color, coliseums, flashes of your life as you lie dreaming'. Fiction pieces should be no longer than 10 pages. Query first as to our needs, each issue is built around a theme. We also accept interviews & articles. Recent interviews: Woody Allen, Allen Ginsberg, Gerard Malanga. Recent contributors: Edward Field, William Packard, Daisy Aldan, Judith Johnson Sherwin, Rochelle Owens, Yvonne, Daniela Glosffi, Susan

Fromberg Schaeffer." circ. 1,000. 2/yr. Pub'd 1 issue 1979; expects 1 issue 1980. sub. price: $7.00; per copy: $2.75; sample: $2.00. Back issues: $1.50. Discounts: 40% on orders of 10 or more. 8X6; of. Reporting time: 3-6 months. Payment: copy. Copyrighted. Pub's reviews: 6 in 1979. §New poetry, experimental fiction, critical literary thought. Ads: $100.00/$60.00/$5.00.

The Helen Vale Foundation (see also JOURNAL OF THE HELEN VALE FOUNDATION), Shri Vijayadev Yogendra, 12 Chapel Street, St Kilda, Victoria 3182, Australia. 1970. Articles. avg. press run 5,000-10,000. Pub'd 2 titles 1979; expects 3 titles 1980, 4 titles 1981. avg. price, cloth: A$8; paper: A$2.95. Discounts: 40% retailer; 55% wholesaler. 200pp; 5½X8½; †of. Reporting time: 4 weeks. Payment: Negotiated. AIPA.

Helikon Press, Robin Prising, William Leo Coakley, 120 West 71st Street, New York City, NY 10023. 1972. Poetry, art, long-poems. "We try to publish the most vital contemporary poetry in the tradition of English verse—using the work of the finest artists, designers, and printers and the best materials possible. We cannot now encourage submissions—we read a wide variety of magazines and ask poets to build a collection around particular poems we have selected. We hope to continue without government subsidy. Poets: Helen Adam, George Barker, John Heath-Stubbs, and Michael Miller." avg. press run 100 for limited editions; 500 for 1st printing of trade ed. Pub'd 1 title 1979. 4 titles listed in the *Small Press Record of Books in Print* (9th Edition, 1980). avg. price, cloth: $7.00-$12.00; other: limited eds. $5.00 or $10.00. Discount to the book trade: 30% for limited editions and 1-4 of trade edition; 40% for 5 or more of trade edition. 16 pages limited editions, 60 pages trade edition; size No standard size: each book is designed to suit the particular poems & poet; of/lp. Reporting time: 2 weeks. Payment: yes. Copyrights for author.

HELIX, Les Harrop, 119 Maltravers Road, Ivanhoe, Victoria 3079, Australia, 03-497-1741. 1977. Poetry, fiction, articles, art, photos, cartoons, interviews, satire, criticism, reviews, music, letters, parts-of-novels, long-poems, collages, plays, concrete art. "*Helix* is an international review of literature and the arts, and especially welcomes contributions from outside Australia. Emphasis on poetry, and in its first 3 issues it has published work by Kinnell, Strand, Redgrove, Atwood, McPherson, Lowell, D. M. Thomas, R. S. Thomas, Ted Hughes, McWhirter,Montale , Vyshnia, Akhmatova, Murray, Harwood and many others." circ. 2,000. 2/yr. Pub'd 2 issues 1979; expects 2 issues 1980, 2 issues 1981. sub. price: $6.00; per copy: $3.00; sample: $3.00. Back issues: No. 1, $10.00 each; No. 2, $5.00 each. Discounts: $2.25 per copy (minimum 4 copies). 64pp; 8½X10½. Reporting time: 1 month maximum. Payment: All contributors are paid; rates are variable but $10.00 a page minimum. Copyrighted, reverts to author. Pub's reviews: 11 in 1979. §Poetry, fiction, drama, visual arts, litarary biography, letters, travel. Ads: $100.00/$60.00/$30.00. ASMA (Australian Small Magazines Association).

Helix House, Ken Kuhlken, Charles Brashers, PO Box 1595, La Mesa, CA 92041, 714-460-4107. 1974. Poetry, fiction, long-poems. "We are not actively seeking manuscripts at this time. Little chance with poetry this year. Please query for fiction." avg. press run 1,000 first printing. 4 titles listed in the *Small Press Record of Books in Print* (9th Edition, 1980). avg. price, cloth: $7.95; paper: $2.95. Discounts: 40% to bookstores, 50% to distributors. 50 pp for poetry. 125 pp for fiction.; 8X5; of. Reporting time: 1-2 months. Payment: By arrangement. Copyrights for author.

‡HELLCOAL ANNUAL, Hellcoal Press, Ann Dunnington, Box 4 SAO, Brown University, Providence, RI 02912. 1965. Poetry, fiction, parts-of-novels, long-poems, plays, art, satire, criticism. circ. 400. irregular. Pub'd 1 issue 1979; expects 4 issues 1980, 4 issues 1981. sub. price: $8.00; per copy: $4.00/$2.50; varies; sample: $2.00. Back issues: Negotiable. 200pp; 6X9; lp. Reporting time: 2-3 months. Payment: 2-10 copies, depends on sales. Copyrighted, reverts to author.

‡Hellcoal Press (see also HELLCOAL ANNUAL), Ann Dunnington, Box SAO, Brown Univ., Providence, RI 02912. 1965. Poetry, fiction, parts-of-novels, long-poems, plays, art, satire, criticism. avg. press run varies. Pub'd 1 title 1979; expects 4 titles 1980, 4 titles 1981. 18 titles listed in the *Small Press Record of Books in Print* (9th Edition, 1980). avg. price, paper: varies, from $2.50 to $4.00. pp varies; 6X9; of/lp. Reporting time: 2-3 months. Payment: copy. Copyrights for author.

HENNEPIN COUNTY LIBRARY CATALOGING BULLETIN, Hennepin County Library, Technical Services Division, 7009 York Ave. S., Secretary, Technical Services Division,Hennepin Co. Library, Edina, MN 55435, 612-830-4980. 1973. "Purpose of publication: To announce changes in the Hennepin County Library Catalog (e.g., new or altered cross-reference, DDC-numbers, and subject descriptors, citing authorities, precedents, & applications), Indexes: No. 1-10 ($3.00), No. 11-20 ($5.00), No. 21-30 ($5.00), No. 31-40 ($5.00)." circ. 400. 6/yr. Pub'd 6 issues 1979; expects 6 issues 1980. sub. price: Individuals $6.00; Institutions $12.00; per copy: $1.50 (Including all back-issues); sample: free. Back Issues: all back issues available each $1.50 indexes: #1-10 $3, #11-20 $5.00, 21-30 $5.00,

$31-40 ($5.00). Discounts: none. 30pp; 8½X11; †of. Reporting time: 1 week. Payment: 2 copies. Not copyrighted. Ads: None. COSMEP.

HER Publishing Co., Betty L. Morrison, Editor, P.O. Box 1168, Oakwood Shopping Center, Gretna, LA 70053. 1977. Poetry, fiction. "200-300 page books, 24-50 page booklets" avg. press run 1,-000-3,500 books, 500 booklets. avg. price, cloth: $15.00; paper: $4.95; other: $3.95. Discounts: 40%. 200-300pp hard cover, 60pp paper; of. Reporting time: 6 weeks to 3 months. Payment: 15%; Poetry 1% and copies. Copyrights for author. COSMEP.

HERESIES: A FEMINIST PUBLICATION ON ART AND POLITICS, Collectively edited, Box 766, Canal St Sta, New York, NY 10013, 212-431-9060. 1976. Poetry, fiction, articles, art, photos, cartoons, interviews, satire, criticism, music, letters, parts-of-novels, long-poems, collages, plays, concrete art. "First issue: Feminism, Art, & Politics; second issue: Patterns of Communication and Space Among Women; third issue: Lesbian Art and Artists; fourth issue: Women's Traditional Art and Artmaking: The Politics of Aesthetics. Send for brochure and/or guidelines to contributors; check backs of current issues for lists of themes of upcoming issues. *All issues are thematic. Submissions are welcome but always returned unless marked specifically for a certain issue.*." circ. 2,000. 4/yr. Expects 4 issues 1980. sub. price: $15.00 individuals; $24.00 institutions; add $2.00 for o'seas subs; per copy: $5.00. Back issues: No back issues available (except for #7, 8). Discounts: none. 96pp; 8½X11; of. Reporting time: depends on process for individual issues. Payment: $5-$25 so far. Copyrighted, reverts to author. Ads: on request.

Heresy Press, George Beahm, 713 Paul Street, Newport News, VA 23605, (804) 827-2631. 1975. "Checklists on current fantasy artists. The first of these, *The Vaughn Bode Index,* appeared in 1975 and is still in print, just barely. The second, *Kirk's Works,* on the artist Tim Kirk, should go to press in a few weeks. A third, on artist Richard Corben, is in preparation. These books are done in cooperation with, and annotated by, the artist involved; they are extensively illustrated, with an original color cover and photos of the artist besides examples of his work." avg. press run 2,000. avg. price, cloth: $20.00; paper: $9.00. Discounts: wholesale 40% for 10 or more, 50% for 100 or more. 90pp; 8½X11. Copyrights for author.

Heritage Books Inc., Laird C. Towle, Editor, 3602 Maureen, Bowie, MD 20715, 301-464-1159. 1977. "We publish books, original or reprints. Current titles: *Genealogical Periodical Annual Index,* vol. 16, 1977 $12.50 cloth, back issues available: vols 13, 14, 15 $9.50 each. *Colonial Era History of Dover, N.H., 1923,* reprint, $27.50, cloth. *Vital Records of Dover, N.H., 1894,* reprint, $17.50, cloth. *History of Amesbury and Merrimac, Mass., 1880,* reprint, $27.50, cloth. *Reminiscences of a Newburyport Nonagenarian, 1879,* reprint, $20.50, cloth. *Gardening from the Merrimack to the Kennebec, 1978* 2nd ed, $6.95, paper. *History of the Town of Exeter, NH, 1888* reprint, $35.00, cloth. *Exeter and Hampton, NH, 1908: Census and Business Directory, 1908,* reprint, $12.50, clothcloth. *New England Annals: History and Genealogy 1980,* $20.00, cloth.. *Newspaper Genealogical Column Directory, 1979,* $8.00, cl. *Provincetown Massachusetts Cemetery Inscriptions, 1980,* $15.00," avg. press run 500-1500. Pub'd 6 titles 1979; expects 8 titles 1980, 10 titles 1981. avg. price, cloth: $18.00; paper: $10.00. Discounts: 40% on six or more assorted titles. 50-1000pp; 6X9; 5½X8½; 8X10; 9X12; of. Reporting time: 30 days or less. Payment: by arrangement. Copyrights for author. ABA.

Heritage Press, Wilbert L. Walker, PO Box 18625, Baltimore, MD 21216, (301) 383-9330. 1979. Fiction. "Interested in fiction and non-fiction on the black experience in America." avg. press run 3,000. Pub'd 2 titles 1979; expects 1 title 1980. avg. price, cloth: $9.00. Discounts: Trade 40%; Jobber 46%; Librries 30%. 175pp; 5½X8½; lp. Reporting time: two months. Payment: no advance, 30% royalty. Copyrights for author.

The Heron Press, B. Chandler, M. Weiss, 36 Bromfield St., Boston, MA 02108. 1968. Poetry, art, satire, long-poems, plays. "Most recent books: Jon Silkin, *The Peaceable Kingdom,* 1975 and Armand Schwerner, *The Tablets XVI-XVII,* 1976. John Wellman *Opera Brevis* 1977. Jerred Metz *Angels in the House* 1978. *Occasions of Grace* David Glotzer (1979)." avg. press run 300. Pub'd 2 titles 1979; expects 2 titles 1980. 6 titles listed in the *Small Press Record of Books in Print* (9th Edition, 1980). avg. price, cloth: $65.00; paper: $5.00. Discounts: 20-30 percent. 24-48pp; size varies; †lp. Reporting time: 1 mo-4 mos. Payment: copies. author must copyright.

Hesperidian Press, E. Halpern, 105 Riverside Drive, c/o Halpern, New York, NY 10024, 362-2831. Poetry, long-poems. "Allen Katzman: *Paracelsus' Walk*" avg. press run 250-500. Expects 1 title 1980, 2 titles 1981. 2 titles listed in the *Small Press Record of Books in Print* (9th Edition, 1980). avg. price, paper: $3.00. Discounts: 40%. 45pp; 5X4⅜; of. Reporting time: 1 month. Copyrights for author.

Hexagon Press (see also WESTERN CITY SUBTOPIAN TIMES), Ken Rolph, Editor, P.O. Box 269, Greenacre, N.S.W. 2190, Australia, (02) 724-4444. 1977. Poetry, fiction, art, photos, cartoons. "I am interested in publishing material on the intersection of the Christian faith and the modern world, esp. the search for a new, alternative, sustainable (etc etc) lifestyle. This includes works of imagination (science fiction & fantasy) as well as works of reason. In general I search for the items I want, but be happy to read manuscripts and discuss items from anyone.u" avg. press run 750. Pub'd 1 title 1979; expects 4 titles 1980, 5 titles 1981. 1 title listed in the *Small Press Record of Books in Print* (9th Edition, 1980). avg. price, paper: A$2.50. Discounts: Bookshops 35-40%, others by negotiation, will deal sale or return in Sydney only. †of. Reporting time: 1-2 months. Payment: 10% paid June-December. Copyrights for author.

HEY LADY, Morgan Press, Edwin H. Burton, 1819 N. Oakland Avenue, Milwaukee, WI 53202, (414) 272-3256. 1968. Poetry, fiction, art, photos, parts-of-novels, long-poems, plays. "No biases we're aware of. Lifshin, Blazek, Hillebrand, Gibson, Sorcic, Gibbons" circ. 500. 4/yr. Pub'd 3 issues 1979; expects 5 issues 1980, 3 issues 1981. sub. price: free; per copy: free; sample: free. Back issues: free. 20-50pp; †of, lp. Reporting time: quickly. Payment: copies. Copyrighted.

Heyday Books, Malcolm Margolin, Box 9145, Berkeley, CA 94709, (415) 849-1438. 1974. "We specialize in books about California natural history, history, and ethnology — especially books about the San Francisco Bay Area." avg. press run 7,000. Expects 2 titles 1980, 3 titles 1981. 2 titles listed in the *Small Press Record of Books in Print* (9th Edition, 1980). avg. price, cloth: $8.95; paper: $4.95. Discounts: 40% trade on orders of 5 copies or more. 175pp; 6X9; of. Reporting time: 1 month. Payment: Comparable to what's offered by major publishers, in fact modeled on their contracts. Copyrights for author.

The Heyeck Press, Robin Heyeck, 25 Patrol Ct., Woodside, CA 94062. 1976. Poetry. "cloth edition handmade paper" avg. press run 500. Pub'd 3 titles 1979; expects 3 titles 1980, 3 titles 1981. 4 titles listed in the *Small Press Record of Books in Print* (9th Edition, 1980). avg. price, cloth: $100.00; paper: $8.00. 60pp; †lp. Reporting time: as soon as possible. Copyrights for author.

Hibiscus Press (see also IN A NUTSHELL), Margaret Wensrich, Fiction; Joyce Odam, Poetry, P.O. Box 22248, Sacramento, CA 95822. 1972. Poetry, fiction, cartoons, art. "Write before sending a manuscript" avg. press run 2m. Pub'd 1 title 1979; expects 2 titles 1980. 6 titles listed in the *Small Press Record of Books in Print* (9th Edition, 1980). avg. price, paper: $3.00. Write for discount. 36pp; 5½X8½; of. Reporting time: 2-4 weeks. Payment: -1/2 cent fiction/$2 min poetry/$5 min cartoons. CCLM, COSMEP.

Hidden People Press (see JUST PULP: The Magazine of Popular Fiction)

Hidden Valley Press, 7051 Poole Jones Road, Frederick, MD 21701, (301) 662-6745. 1979. "An independent press publishing books on health, psychology, and spiritual subjects." avg. press run 1,000-100,000. Pub'd 1 title 1979; expects 2 titles 1980. 1 title listed in the *Small Press Record of Books in Print* (9th Edition, 1980). avg. price, cloth: $10.95; paper: $5.00. 200pp; 5½X8½; of. Reporting time: 4-12 weeks. Payment: negotiable. COSMEP.

Hiddigeigei Books, R. A. Wolf, P.O. Box 5031, San Francisco, CA 94103. 1976. "Hiddigeigei does not solicit any materials (Ms. or other) at this time" 8 titles listed in the *Small Press Record of Books in Print* (9th Edition, 1980). avg. price, paper: $2.50. Discounts: 40% retail/50% wholesale. 56pp; 8X10. COSMEP.

HIGGINSON JOURNAL, Higginson Press, Frederick L. Morey, Editor & Publisher, 4508 38th St., Brentwood, MD 20722, 301-864-8527. 1971. Poetry, articles, art, criticism, reviews. "4,000 words, popular middle style (chiefly Emily Dickinson overflow from EDB), contemporary poets considered if crafted, recently George Monteiro, Howard Meyer, C.G. Jung and US literature issue, Rebecca Patterson issue." circ. 200. 2/yr. Pub'd 3 issues 1979; expects 3 issues 1980, 2 issues 1981. sub. price: $10.00 libraries (invoiced)/$5.00 individuals; per copy: $3.00; sample: $3.00. Back issues: $40.00 for the fourteen in print. Discounts: 10% to any agent. 50pp; 8½X5½; of. Reporting time: 2 weeks. Payment: 1 copy. Not copyrighted. Pub's reviews: 12 in 1979. §E. Dickinson and poetry in general also Carl Jung psychology, gay liberation. Contemporary poets: 50 published yearly. Ads: $90.-00/$50.00.

Higginson Press (see also DICKINSON STUDIES; HIGGINSON JOURNAL), Frederick L. Morey, Editor & Publisher, 4508 38th Street, Brentwood, MD 20722, (301) 864-8527. 1968. Poetry, articles, art, photos, cartoons, interviews, criticism, reviews, letters, news items. avg. press run 500. Pub'd 3 titles 1979; expects 3 titles 1980, 2 titles 1981. avg. price, paper: $3.00; other: $5.00 back issue. Discounts: 10% to agents only. 50pp; 5½X8½; of. Reporting time: 2 weeks. Payment: One copy only. Does not copyright for author. COSMEP.

High Country Communications Ltd. (see WHISTLER ANSWER)

HIGH COUNTRY NEWS, Geoffrey O'Gara, Editor; Joan Nice, Associate Editor, Box K, 331 Main St., Lander, WY 82520, 332-4877 (307). 1969. Articles, art, photos, cartoons, interviews, criticism, reviews, letters, news items. "We're after hard-hitting, environmental journalism with a regional slant. We cover Montana, Wyoming, Colorado, Utah, Idaho and, occasionally, the Dakotas and Arizona and New Mexico." circ. 4000. 25/yr. sub. price: $15.00; per copy: $0.75; sample: free. Back issues: 60¢ single copy; bulk rates available on request. Discounts: sell in bulk to schools, libraries, organizations. 16pp; 10X14; of. Reporting time: 2 weeks. Payment: two to five cents per word, $4.00 to $10.00 per published B & W photo. Not copyrighted. Pub's reviews: 50 in 1979. §Conservation, wildlife, energy, land use, and other natural resources issues. Ads: $218.40/$112.00/$0.10, $1.00 min.

High Orchard Press (see also THE BULWER LYTTON CHRONICLE; SHAVIAN—JOURNAL OF BERNARD SHAW; WELLSIANA, The World Of H.G. Wells), Eric Ford, Exec; Rayston King, Howard Cooper-Brown, Robert Clare, 125 Markyate Road, Dagenham, Essex, England RM8 2LB, United Kingdom. 1948.

HIGH PERFORMANCE, Astro Artz, Linda Frye Burnham, 240 S. Broadway, 5th Floor, Los Angeles, CA 90012, (213) 687-7362. 1977. Articles, art, photos, interviews, news items. "*High Performance* is a documentary magazine about performance art ('happenings'). Primarily, we publish photos and descriptions of live art works, submitted by the artists who perform them. We do not publish material about dance, theater or music performances. Interviews with performance artists, please query. Scope: international. Recent contributors: Barbara Smith, Moira Roth, Suzanne Lacy, Paul McCarthy, Richard Newton, Nancy Buchanan, Kipper Kids, Chris Burden, Eleanor Antin, Bob + Bob, Carolee Schneemann, Les Levine, Peter Frank, Dick Higgins, Anna Banana, Jerry Dreva." circ. 5,000. quarterly. Expects 4 issues 1980, 4 issues 1981. sub. price: $8.00 USA, $10.00 Canada, Mexico, $12.00 other countries ($22.00 air mail); per copy: $2.50 including postage; sample: $2.50 including postage. Back issues: $3.00. Discounts: 25% bookstores, 40-50% distributors. 64pp; 8½X11; of. Reporting time: three months. Payment: two copies. Copyrighted, reverts to author. Ads: $200/$125/10¢/word($2.00 min.). COSMEP, AAP.

HIGH/COO: A Quarterly of Short Poetry, High/Coo Press, Randy Brooks, Shirley Brooks, Route 1, Battleground, IN 47920. 1976. Poetry, reviews, concrete art. "We are interested in short poetry —13 lines or less. Especially interested in haiku, haibun, renga, short series, short sequences, senryu, tanka, epigrams with a rockbed of images. Recent contributors include Sanford Goldstein, Lee Perron, Raymond Roseliep, John Judson, Elizabeth Searle Lamb, Bill Pauly, Gary Hines, and Larry Eigner." circ. 250. 4/yr. Pub'd 4 issues 1979; expects 4 issues 1980, 4 issues 1981. sub. price: $5.00 (includes 2 chapbooks); per copy: $1.00; sample: $1.00. Back issues: $2.00. Discounts: 40 percent discount to bookstores and schools, 20% on consignment. 24-40pp; 4¼X5½; of. Reporting time: 1 month. Payment: 2 copies. Copyrighted, reverts to author. Pub's reviews: 5 in 1979. §haiku, tanka, short lyric books, concretes.

High/Coo Press (see also HIGH/COO: A Quarterly of Short Poetry), Randy Brooks, Shirley Brooks, Route 1, Battleground, IN 47920. 1976. Poetry, reviews, concrete art. "We publish a chapbook and a mini-chapbook every six months which are distributed with our quarterly. Our chapbook titles: *Sun In His Belly* by Raymond Roseliep, *Wind the Clock by Bittersweet* by Bill Pauly, *Rain in Her Voice* by Lawrence Fitzgerald and *Bird Day Afternoon* by R. Clarence Matsuo-Allard. Mini-chapbooks are to be submitted before March 31 each year. We also publish a poemcard with each issue of *High/Coo.*" avg. press run 350. Pub'd 6 titles 1979; expects 6 titles 1980, 6 titles 1981. 15 titles listed in the *Small Press Record of Books in Print* (9th Edition, 1980). avg. price, paper: $1.50 (chapbooks); other: $1.00 (mini-chapbooks). Discounts: 40 percent bookstores and author, 20% on consignment. 40-48pp; 4¼X5½; of. Reporting time: 1 month. Payment: copies and 15 percent after costs are met. Does not copyright for author.

Highway Book Shop (see also LIFELINE), Lee Hobbs, Cobalt, Ontario P0J1C0, Canada. 1957. Poetry, fiction. "Primarily publishing Northern Ontario authors." avg. press run 1,000. Pub'd 34 titles 1979; expects 35 titles 1980. avg. price, cloth: $12.00; paper: $3.00. Discounts: 40% to retail, 20% educational & library. 5X8, 7X8; †of. Reporting time: 2 months. Payment: 10% royalty. Copyrights for author. ACP.

HILLS, Bob Perelman, 36 Clyde, San Francisco, CA 94107. 1971. Poetry. "Comes out irregularly. Price varies with issue size." circ. 450. 1/yr. Pub'd 1 issue 1979; expects 1 issue 1980, 1 issue 1981. sub. price: $5.00; per copy: $5.00; sample: $2.00. Back issues: No. 1 $25.00; No. 2 $5.00; No. 3 $25.00; No. 4 $5.00. Discounts: Complete set 1-4 $50.00. 100pp; 5½X8; of. Reporting time: 1 week to 2 months. Payment: if grants permit. §Poetry, prose.

Himalayan Institute Publishers and Distributors, Robert Hughes, Sales & Publicity Director, RD 1,

Box 88, Honesdale, PA 18431, (717) 253-5551. 1971. "Seven years ago, the Himalayan Institute recognized the dearth of authoritative literature in the combined disciplines of Eastern philosophy and Western science. As a result, the Institute's staff of physicians, psychologists and philosophers were prompted to offer it expertise to the larger public. Thus a pioneer printing venture grew into an efficient publishing operation, the Himalayan Institute Publishers and Distributors. We now specialize in educational books on practical philosophy, psychology and health sciences, attracting a broad range of Eastern scholars and Western scientists as collaborating authors. Our unique titles are among the most knowledgeable and useful in their field and are now widely sought after by conscientious readers throughout the country." avg. press run 10,000. Pub'd 13 titles 1979; expects 10 titles 1980, 12 titles 1981. avg. price, cloth: $11.95; paper: $3.95. Discounts: Conventional trade. 250pp; †of. Reporting time: 6 months. Copyrights for author.

Hippopotamus Press, Roland John, B.A. Martin, Business Manager, 26 Cedar Road, Sutton, Surrey SM25DG, United Kingdom, 01-643-1970. 1974. Poetry, long-poems. "Size, number of pages, cost will vary with the material. Against: concrete, typewriter, neo-surrealism and experimental work. For: competent poetry in recognisable English, a knowledge of syntax and construction, finished work and not glimpses into the workshop, also translations. Recent pamphlets and books include G.S. Sharat Chandra (U.S.A.), David Summers (Canada), Stan Trevor (S. Africa) Shaun McCarthy, Neil McNeil, Peter Dale, William Bedford, Humphrey Clucas, William Cookson, Peter Dent." avg. press run 1,000. Pub'd 3 titles 1979. 14 titles listed in the *Small Press Record of Books in Print* (9th Edition, 1980). avg. price, paper: £1.75, $4.00. Discounts: 33⅓ off singles, 40 percent off bulk orders. 40pp; size variable; lp. Reporting time: 1 month. Payment: by arrangement/royalty. Standard UK copyright. Remaining with author. ALP.

HIRAM POETRY REVIEW, David Fratus, Carol Donley, Box 162, Hiram, OH 44234, 216-569-3211. 1967. Poetry, fiction, articles, art, photos, interviews, satire, criticism, reviews, letters, parts-of-novels, long-poems, collages, plays, concrete art. "Reviews, essays, art, photos, etc. Only by invitation. Poetry is 95 percent of what we accept. We have also re-instituted the Supplement series — short pamphlets of work by one author. By invitation only." circ. 500. 2/yr. Pub'd 2 issues 1979; expects 2 issues 1980, 2 issues 1981. sub. price: $2.00; per copy: $1.00; sample: free. Back issues: No. 1 unavail.; others vary; send for info. Discounts: 50-50 to subscription agencies; 60-40 to retail bookstores. 40pp; 9X6; of. Reporting time: 6-8 wks. Payment: 2 copies plus yr's. subscription. Copyrighted, reverts by request. Pub's reviews: 6 in 1979. §Poetry, books, some little magazines. no ads. CCLM, COSMEP.

Historical Society of Alberta (see also ALBERTA HISTORY), Hugh A. Dempsey, 95 Holmwood Ave. NW, Calgary, Alberta T2K 2G7, Canada. 1907. avg. press run 3000. Pub'd 1 title 1979; expects 1 title 1980, 1 title 1981. avg. price, cloth: $20.00. Discounts: 33%. 400pp; 6X9; of. Reporting time: 3 months. Payment: flat fee. Does not copyright for author.

THE HISTORY BOOK DIGEST, Edward Lukes, PO Box 18383, Tampa, FL 33679, (813) 837-0250. 1979. "*The History Book Digest* is a periodical which contains condensed versions of the finer works of historical merit." 3/yr. sub. price: $18.00. Back issues: limited by first printing supply, $6.00. Discounts: 10-15% (depending on size of order) to libries and bookstores. 300pp; 5½X8½; of. Copyrighted.

HOB-NOB, Mildred K. Henderson, 715 Dorsea Road, Lancaster, PA 17601. 1969. Poetry, fiction, articles, art, cartoons, satire, criticism, reviews, letters, parts-of-novels, long-poems, news items. "Prose, poetry, crafts, puzzles. No new material accepted between 3/1/80 and 1/1/81 pending decision on a 2nd issue in 1980." circ. 100+. annual. Pub'd 1 issue 1979; expects 1 or 2 issues 1980, ? issues 1981. sub. price: $1.40; per copy: 50/(1978); $1 + 40¢ postage. Back issues: 40/. 40pp; 8½X11; of. Reporting time: 2 weeks for rejections, longer for acceptances. Payment: free copy, first appearance only. Copyrighted, reverts to author. Pub's reviews: 5-6 in 1979. Ads: $1/paragraph.

Hobbit House Press, Marlys Mayfield, 5920 Dimm Way, Richmond, CA 94805, 415-232-3428.

Hobby Horse Publishing, R. L. Jr. Anderson, 10091 Hobby Horse Lane, Box 54, Mentor, OH 44060, (216) 255-3434. 1979. Fiction. "This is an author-owned press, publishing books by R. L. Anderson, Jr. only. These books are to be a series of juvenile science-fiction adventures, for ages 10-14 approx. The first in this series, *The Abominable Spaceman,* was released Oct. 11, 1979. This book is 182 pages, fully illustrated by the author, quality oversized paper back. (13 illustrations)" Pub'd 1 title 1979. 1 title listed in the *Small Press Record of Books in Print* (9th Edition, 1980). avg. price, paper: $5.95. Discounts: 30% for wholesale, other rates may be negotiated. 182pp; 5½X8½; of.

Hoddypoll Press, Denise Kastan, 3841-B 24th Street, San Francisco, CA 94114. 1968. Poetry. "Poetry chapbooks." avg. press run 500. Pub'd 3 titles 1979; expects 4 titles 1980. 7 titles listed in the

Small Press Record of Books in Print (9th Edition, 1980). avg. price, paper: $3.50; other: $3.00. 50pp; 5½X8½; of. Reporting time: 1 mo. Copyrights for author.

HODMANDOD, Gibbous Press, S. Kremsky, K. White, M Cimperman, 150 10th Avenue, San Francisco, CA 94118, 415-752-5898. 1977. Poetry. "Open to any submissions, we are 3 editors with varied tastes. Magazine will be hand-set and printed." circ. 500. 4/yr. Expects 3 issues 1980, 4 issues 1981. sub. price: $5.00; per copy: $1.50; sample: $1.50. Discounts: inquire. 30pp; 5½X7; †lp. Reporting time: 6 weeks. Payment: 1 copy. Copyrighted, reverts to author. Ads: inquire.

THE HOLLINS CRITIC, John Rees Moore, Editor, P.O. Box 9538, Hollins College, VA 24020. 1964. Poetry, criticism, reviews. "Essay on particular work of one author; several poems. Essay approximately 5000 words, no footnotes. No unsolicited essay mss. Short poems are published in almost every issue. Other features are a front picture of the author under discussion, a checklist of his writing and a brief sketch of career, plus book reviews." circ. 850. 5/yr. Pub'd 5 issues 1979. sub. price: $4.00 U.S.; ($5.00 elsewhere); per copy: $1.25 U.S.; ($1.60 elsewhere); sample: $1.25 U.S.; ($1.60 elsewhere). Back issues: $1.25 U.S.; ($1.60 elsewhere). 20pp; 7½X10; lp. Reporting time: 1 month. Payment: $20 for poems. Copyrighted, does not revert to author. Pub's reviews: 28 in 1979. §mainly current fiction and poetry. CCLM, COSMEP.

HOLLOW SPRING REVIEW OF POETRY, Alex Harvey, RD 1, Bancroft Road, Chester, MA 01011. 1975. Poetry, articles, art, interviews, satire, criticism, reviews, long-poems, news items. "Open to new writers of poetry as well as established poets. Open to all subjects and poetic forms. Recent contributors: Ron Atkinson, Duane Niatum, Judith Leet, Robert Morgan, Edward Field, John Stevens Wade, Kurt Heinzelman, Susan Snively, Guy Davenport, Joan Colby, Ron Wallace, Louis Phillips, Melvin Dixon, William DeVoti, Leo Connellan, Robert Pack, William Packard, Donald Junkins, Peter Wild, Mark Vinz, Fred Chappell, Ronald Wallace, Dean Phelps, Harry Smith, Robert Sargent and Lennart Bruce." circ. 1,200. 2/yr. Pub'd 2 issues 1979; expects 2 issues 1980, 2 issues 1981. sub. price: $6.00 indiv., $8.00 libraries; per copy: $3.00; sample: $3.00. Back issues: Vol. 1 No. 1 unavailable, back copies. Discounts: 40% bookstores. 96-144pp; 8½X5½; †of, lp. Reporting time: 2-6 weeks, not accepting unsolicited material for 81-82. Payment: copies, pays $25.00 for poems accepted. Copyrighted, reverts to author. Pub's reviews. §Poetry, criticism, chapbooks. Ads: $100.00/$60.00. COSMEP, CCLM, NESPA.

Hollywood Film Archive, D. Richard Baer, Editor, 8344 Melrose Ave., Hollywood, CA 90069, (213) 933-3345. 1972. "HFA compiles and publishes film reference information. In addition to our own books, we are interested in high-quality comprehensive reference information on film or television. Please inquire before submitting material. Those submitting unsolicited material must include a self-addressed stamped envelope in order to have it returned. Our Cinema Book Society book club considers books of other publishers for sale to members, libraries, the film and TV industries, and the general public." avg. press run 5,000. 1 title listed in the *Small Press Record of Books in Print* (9th Edition, 1980). avg. price, cloth: $25.00; paper: $10.00. Discounts: 1 to 4 copies, 20% discount to bona fide booksellers, wholesalers, jobbers, etc. 5 or more 40%; large quantities, inquire. 8½X11; of. Reporting time: 3 to 4 weeks.

Holmgangers Press, Gary Elder, Editor; Jeane Elder, Editor, 22 Ardith Lane, Alamo, CA 94507. 1974. Poetry, fiction, art, photos, long-poems, collages, plays, concrete art. avg. press run 500. Pub'd 3 titles 1979; expects 3 titles 1980, 3 titles 1981. 29 titles listed in the *Small Press Record of Books in Print* (9th Edition, 1980). avg. price, paper: $3.00. Discounts: 20% off 4 or less; 40% off 5 or more. 90pp; 5½X8½; of. Reporting time: 1-4 weeks. Payment: 10 percent net-after recovery. Copyrights for author.

Holt Associates, Inc. (see GROWING WITHOUT SCHOOLING)

HOLY BEGGARS' GAZETTE, Judaic Book Service, Steven L. Maimes, Elana Rappaport, 3726 Virden Ave., Oakland, CA 94619. 1971. Poetry, articles, art, photos. "We are a journal of Chassidic Judaism. Our issues have contained teachings from Rabbi Shlomo Carlebach & Rabbi Zalman Schachter, stories from Chassidic Rebbes, Jewish mysticism and poetry." circ. 1,000. Irregular. Pub'd 1 issue 1979. price per copy: $2.50 appx.; sample: $2.00. Back issues: $1.25 each. Discounts: trade —40%. 24+pp; 7X10; of. Reporting time: 2 weeks. Payment: copies only. Copyrighted.

Holy Cow! Press, James Perlman, P O Box 618, Minneapolis, MN 55440. 1977. Poetry, fiction, parts-of-novels, long-poems, articles. "HOLY COW! Press is a new Midwestern small press publisher that features fresh work by both well-known and younger writers. Besides poetry collections, we try to tastefully assemble anthologies centered around important ideas. Our first five books are: *At the Barre* by Candyce Clayton, *Letters to Tomasito* by Thomas McGrath, *Brother Songs: A Male Anthology of Poetry* edited by Jim Perlman, *Chicken and in Love,* by Natalie Logue and Lawrence Sutin. Forthcoming collections include a collection of essays about the continuing influence of Walt Whitman featuring work by: Meridel LeSueur, Patricia Hampl, Joseph Bruchac, Anselm Hollo, Thomas McGrath, Philip Dacey, Alvaro Cardona-Hine, and others. We are particularly supportive of first books by younger writers; please query before submitting manuscripts." avg. press run 750. Pub'd 1 title 1979; expects 2 titles 1980, 3 titles 1981. 4 titles listed in the *Small Press Record of Books in Print* (9th Edition, 1980). avg. price, cloth: $7.95; paper: $2.50; other: $2.50. Discounts: 40% off to classrooms, bulk, institutions, bookstores. 64pp; 5½X8½; of. Reporting time: 2 to 3 months. Payment: negotiable with each author. Copyrights for author.

HOME PLANET NEWS, Home Planet Publications, Enid Dame, Donald Lev, P.O. Box 415 Stuyvesant Station, New York, NY 10009, (212) 534-2372. 1979. Poetry, fiction, articles, art, photos, cartoons, interviews, criticism, reviews, parts-of-novels, letters. "We like lively work of all types and schools. Poetry should run about a page. (Need shorter ones right now.) For articles, reviews, etc., please query first. Some recent contributors include: Daniela Gioseffi, Edward Butscher, Eunice Wolfgram, Alison Colbert, Steve and Gloria Tropp, Martin Mitchell, Irving Stettner, Lynne Savitt, John Payne, Robertoh Faber, Miguel Algarin." circ. 3,000. 4/yr. Pub'd 4 issues 1979; expects 4 issues 1980, 4 issues 1981. sub. price: $5.00; per copy: $1.25; sample: $1.25. Discounts: 40% consignment, 50% cash, 25% agents. 20pp; 10X15; of. Reporting time: 2-3 months. Payment: copies & 1 yr gift subscription. Copyrighted, reverts to author. Pub's reviews: 12 in 1979. §poetry, fiction, theater. Ads: $200.00/$100.00. COSMEP.

Home Planet Publications (see also HOME PLANET NEWS), Donald Lev, Enid Dame, P.O. Box 415 Stuyvesant Station, New York, NY 10009, (212) 534-2372. 1971. Poetry. "Home Planet Publications publishes occasional books of poetry, but does not consider unsolicited manuscripts. For our magazine, *Home Planet News,* see listing above." avg. press run 400. Expects 1 title 1980, 3 titles 1981. 5 titles listed in the *Small Press Record of Books in Print* (9th Edition, 1980). avg. price, paper: $1.50. Discounts: 50% cash to stores; 40% consignment; 25% agents. 60pp; 5X8; of. Payment: negotiable. Copyrights for author. COSMEP.

Homosexual Information Center Inc, Don Slater, Joseph Hansen, 6715 Hollywood Blvd 210, Hollywood, CA 90028. 1965. "*Seeds of the American Sexual Revolution,* discussions of the studies of Alfred Kinsey, $3.00; *Reader at Large,* (Tangents reprint, discussions of the books on homosexuality of the early 1960's), $.35; *Lesbian Paperbakc,* reviews reprinted from *Tangents,* $.35; *Directory of Homosexual Organizations & Publications,* 1979 ed., $3.00; HIC Newsletter (irreg.), no charge; *Selected Bibliography of Homosexuality,* $.35. Prostitution is legal." avg. press run 3,000. Pub'd 3 titles 1979. 5 titles listed in the *Small Press Record of Books in Print* (9th Edition, 1980). 6X9.

HOO-DOO BlackSeries, Energy Earth Communications, Inc., Ahmos Zu-Bolton, Jerry Ward, PO Box 1141, Galveston, TX 77553. 1973. Poetry, fiction, articles, art, photos, cartoons, interviews, satire, criticism, reviews, music, letters, parts-of-novels, long-poems, collages, plays, concrete art. "Black works aimed at Southern lore." circ. 2,000. 1/yr. Pub'd 2 issues 1979; expects 2 issues 1980. sub. price: $13.00 for No. 7 - No. 13 (13 is exit & emerging No. in *HOO-DOO* rituals - completes the series).; per copy: $3.50; sample: $3.50. Back issues: vol. one valued at $26.00/#4 - $4.00/#5 - $3.00/#6½ - $3.00. Discounts: 40% to bookstores. 100pp; size varies; of. Reporting time: 2 weeks to 2 months. Payment: copies. copyrights for contributors. Pub's reviews. §Black, third-world, spiritual, open workings. Ads: $100.00. CCLM.

Horizons, PO Box 35008, Phoenix, AZ 85069. "Not accepting mss. at this time." 1 title listed in the *Small Press Record of Books in Print* (9th Edition, 1980).

The Hosanna Press, Cathie Ruggie, 1230 Parkside Ave, Park Ridge, IL 60068, (312) 823-0401. 1974. Poetry, fiction, art, concrete art. "Still in process: *Flown* (a chapbook of Gerald Lange's poetry with an original serigraph by Cathie Ruggie). Limited edition fine printings from foundry type on rag & unique handmade papers, w/ original graphics. Innovative concepts of book, paper, and print pursued." avg. press run 25-100. Pub'd 1 title 1979; expects 2 titles 1980, 2 titles 1981. 11 titles listed in the *Small Press Record of Books in Print* (9th Edition, 1980). avg. price, cloth: prices on request. size varies; †lp. Reporting time: 3-6 weeks. Payment: 10% of edition. Copyrights for author. APHA.

HOT LOGARITHON, Julius Votali, George Schaub, 301 Maple Avenue, Sea Cliff, NY 11579. 1980. Poetry, fiction, articles, art, photos, cartoons, interviews, collages. "Exploitation and advancement of international puddle photography competition. Sakrete-art, ihore-tite photography, delineation of the daily angst collage, eggistential word-montage. Recent articles, 'Barnarticles', chicken reality (eggs over easy street), architecture subjected to the laws of smiling. Possible folio signed editions. All submissions unless mail art must be SASE." circ. 250. 1/yr. Pub'd 1 issue 1979. sub. price: $4.00; per copy: $4.00; sample: $4.00. Back issues: $4.00. Discounts: 20% to liraries, agents and anybody that orders more than 1. 25-30pp; 8X10; of. Reporting time: 30 days or as soon as possible. Payment: copy. Pub's reviews. §Photo, art, dada/surrealism, poetry, fiction. Ads: $100.00/$60.00/$0.25.

THE HOT SPRINGS GAZETTE, The Doodly-Squat Press, Eric Irving, Editor, P.O. Box 40124, Albuquerque, NM 87106, 505-243-4272. 1977. Articles, art. "Directions, statistics and description of thermal springs. Skinny dipping articles, drawings." circ. 1000. 4/yr. price per copy: $2.00; sample: $2.00. Back issues: $2.00. Discounts: $1.00 over ten. 30pp; 6X8; †of. Reporting time: 2 weeks. Payment: subscription. Copyrighted, reverts to author. Pub's reviews: 1 in 1979. §Hot springs.

HOT WATER REVIEW, Hotwater, Joel Colten, Peter Bushyeager, PO Box 8396, Philadelphia, PA 19101. 1976. Poetry, art, photos. circ. 1,000. 1/yr. Pub'd 1 issue 1979. price per copy: $3.00; sample: $3.00. Back issues: $3.00. Discounts: 60/40. 88pp; 8½X5½; of. Reporting time: 2-3 months. Payment: copies. Copyrighted. Ads: $90/$50.

Hotwater (see also HOT WATER REVIEW), Peter Bushyeager, Joel Colten, PO Box 8396, Philadelphia, PA 19101. "See *HOT WATER REVIEW*." 3 titles listed in the *Small Press Record of Books in Print* (9th Edition, 1980).

House of Anansi Press Limited/Publishing Co., Ann Wall, Publisher; James Polk, Editorial Director, 35 Britain St., Toronto M5A1R7, Canada, 416-363-5444. 1967. Poetry, fiction, criticism. "*Anansi* is a small, Canadian, literary publisher. We will consider non-fiction manuscripts that have contemporary, social criticism themes. We publish only Canadian authors. We now have a distributor in the States: all our titles are shipped from there, the address is: c/o University of Toronto Press, 33 East Tupper Street, Buffalo, New York 14203." avg. press run 1,000-20,000. Pub'd 8 titles 1979; expects 7 titles 1980. 47 titles listed in the *Small Press Record of Books in Print* (9th Edition, 1980). avg. price, cloth: $18.00; paper: $6.00. Discounts: Set by our distributor; usual industry discounts. 60-200pp; 5¼X8½; of. Reporting time: 4-6 weeks. Payment varies; advance plus royalties. Copyrights for author. ACP, LPG.

House of Keys (see also DAIMON), Norman Finkelstein, Terrill Shepard Soules, Phillip DePoy, P O Box 7952, Atlanta, GA 30357, 404-873-3820. 1977. Poetry. "In 1980, House of Keys will publish two books of poems: *A Grade School Grammar* by Bradford Stark, and *In the Sweetness of the New Time* by Henry Weinfield. Also available: *The Objects In YOur Life* by Norman Finkelstein, *My Hand My Only Map* by Nat Anderson, and *Messages From Beyond* by Phillip Depoy with photographs by Michael Goodman. We ask poets with manuscripts to submit poems to Daimon before inquiring about publication by House of Keys." avg. press run 500 copies. Pub'd 1 title 1979; expects 2 titles 1980, 1 title 1981. 4 titles listed in the *Small Press Record of Books in Print* (9th Edition, 1980). avg. price, cloth: $10.00; paper: $4.00. Discounts: 40% bookstores. 34pp; 5½X8½; of/lp. Reporting time: 6 weeks. Payment: 50 copies to author. Copyrights for author.

House of White Shell Woman, Janith Aust-Schminke, Hunter Hutchison, Carmelita Moffat, Pam Stevenson, Box 1344, Brea, CA 92621. 1978. Poetry, art. "Dedicated to publishing material by women who come to or are part of House of White Shell Woman (Laguna Beach, CA)." avg. press run 250. Pub'd 1 title 1979; expects 1 title 1980. avg. price, paper: $3.99. 112pp; 5X8½; of. Reporting time: 6 months. Payment: contribution. Copyrights for author.

HOUSESMITHS JOURNAL, Dovetail Press Ltd, Box 1496, Boulder, CO 80306, (303) 449-2681. Articles, photos, interviews, reviews, letters. "Forum for owner-builders, timber-framing." 4/yr. Pub'd 1 issue 1979. sub. price: $6.00; per copy: $1.50. Discounts: 50% to retail outlets. 16-24pp; 8½X11. Copyrighted.

HOUSMAN SOCIETY JOURNAL, Richard Perceval Graves, Penybryn House, Boot Street, Whittington, Oswestry, Salop SY11 4DG, United Kingdom, 069162313. Poetry, articles, art, photos, interviews, criticism, reviews. "Must all be directly related to A.E. Housman, or his brothers, sisters, or parents." circ. 500. 1/yr. Pub'd 1 issue 1979; expects 1 issue 1980, 1 issue 1981. Discounts: by special agreement. 50pp; 8½X6; of. Reporting time: one month. Payment: none. Pub's reviews. §Books relating to the life or work of the Housmans.

Houston Writers Workshop (see also TOUCHSTONE), Guida Jackson, Managing Editor; Marge Baron, Senior Editor; Pat Kochera, Editor, Drawer 42331, Houston, TX 77042, (713) 461-6201. 1976. Poetry, fiction, articles, art, cartoons, interviews, satire, criticism, reviews, music, letters. avg. press run varies. Pub'd 4 titles 1979; expects 4 titles 1980. avg. price, paper: $1.75. Discounts: 45 percent-20 or more copies. 32pp; 7X8½; of. Reporting time: 6 weeks. no payment. copyright assigned to author on request.

How to Tutor Your Child in Reading, How-to, box 504, Exton, PA 19341, (215) 692-5358.

HOWL, H.S.A. Committee, PO Box 19, Tonbridge, Kent, England, United Kingdom. 1963. Articles, photos, cartoons, letters, news items. "Biased towards animal rights (*not* conservation) with particular emphasis on bloodsports (hunting with hounds). Direct action group." circ. 3,500. 3-4/yr. Pub'd 3 issues 1979; expects 3 issues 1980, 3 issues 1981. sub. price: Free to members, membership £1 per yr or $5.00; per copy: 5p (UK), $0.50; sample: nothing in England, $0.50 USA. Discounts: by arrangement (depends mostly on whatever the postage would come to). 4pp; 12X16. Reporting time: 1 month. Payment: nil. Ads: No ads.

HS Press (see also CHIMERA-A Complete Theater Piece), Harry Wm. Saltron, 5538 Morris Street, Philadelphia, PA 19144. 1976. 4 titles listed in the *Small Press Record of Books in Print* (9th Edition, 1980).

HSA FROGPOND, Haiku Society of America, Inc., Lilli Tanzer, Editor; Mildred Fineberg, Editorial Assistant, RD 7 Box 265, Hopewell Junction, NY 12533, (914) 226-7117. 1968. Poetry, articles, news items. "HSA (Haiku Society of America, Inc. recognized as non-profit & tax exempt). Mailing address, 333 East 47 Street, N.Y.C., NY 10017. The HSA is an organization of poets and others interested in the unique nature of haiku as written in Japanese and other languages. HSA is interested in exploring the nature of the classic form as well as the contemporary developments of the genre in Japan. These are discussed at meetings open to the public, and in the HSA magazine *Frogpond*. Being the voice of the Haiku Society of America, HSA Frogpond is particularly interested in haiku as written in English, although it does include translations/derivations section with a panel working from the original Japanese. *Frogpond* is by and for its contributors, and membership in HSA is open to anyone in the world. Only sub/mem haiku are included, except when haiku appear in articles. Haiku are unscreened. It is our policy to print whatever is, while it is. Before submitting articles or essays, non-member/subscribers please query editor at editiorial address. HSA conducts an annual Harold G. Henderson memorial contest, open to all. General information, and *Frogpond* submission information, is available upon receipt of SASE. HSA meets annually and conducts open mettings free to the public, throughout the year. The 1980 president is Hiroaki Sato." circ. 250. quarterly. Pub'd 4 issues 1979; expects 4 issues 1980, 4 issues 1981. sub. price: combined subscription/membership (Jan calendar yr) $10.00 domestic, $15.00 overseas surface, $18.00 overseas air. Specify; per copy: $2.75; sample: $2.75. Back issues: $2.50 for late subscribers. Discounts: none. 48pp; 5½X8½; of. submissions are held for future use - may be recalled, SASE before deadline. Payment: none. Copyrighted, reverts on publication. Ads: none.

THE HUDSON REVIEW, Paula Deitz, Co-editor; Frederick Morgan, Co-editor, 65 East 55th St., New York City, NY 10022, 212-755-9040. 1948. Poetry, fiction, articles, criticism, reviews, parts-of-novels, long-poems. "Although we have developed a recognizable group of contributors who are identified with the magazine, we are always open to new writers and publish them in every issue. We have no university affiliation and are not committed to any narrow academic aim; nor to any particular political perspective." circ. 3,500. 4/yr. Pub'd 4 issues 1979; expects 4 issues 1980, 4 issues 1981. 2 titles listed in the *Small Press Record of Books in Print* (9th Edition, 1980). sub. price: $12.00; per copy: $3.50; sample: $3.50. Back issues: varies. Discounts: bulk rates and discount schedules on request. 160pp; 4½X7½; of. Reporting time: 12 weeks maximum. Payment: 2½ cents per word for prose; 50 cents per line for poetry. Copyrighted, policy under new 1978 law on request. Pub's reviews: 80 in 1979. §Literature, fine and performing arts, sociology and cultural anthropology. Ads: $225.-00/$125.00. CCLM, COSMEP.

HUERFANO, Daran Inc., Randell Shutt, Editor; Vicki Thompson, Poetry Editor, 5730 N. Via Elena, Tucson, AZ 85718. 1974. Poetry. "Annual Daran Award of $50.00" circ. 200. 2/yr. Pub'd 2 issues 1979. sub. price: $2.00; per copy: $1.00; sample: $1.00. Back issues: $1.00. Discounts: 60/40 for bookstores. 30-40pp; 5½X8½; of. Reporting time: 2-3 weeks. Payment: copies only. Copyrighted, reverts to author. Pub's reviews: 1 in 1979. §Poetry. Ads: $10.00/$5.00. CCLM.

The Huffman Press, Katherine Gekker Huffman, 311 Madison St, Alexandria, VA 22314, 703-836-7160. 1974. Poetry, fiction, art, photos, music, parts-of-novels, long-poems. "Send inquiries first." avg. press run 100 copies. Pub'd 2 titles 1979; expects 2 titles 1980. 3 titles listed in the *Small Press Record of Books in Print* (9th Edition, 1980). avg. price, cloth: $15.00; paper: $3.00. Discounts: standard. 12pp; 7½X6; †lp, of. Reporting time: 2-4 weeks. Payment: open. Copyrights for author.

Human Kinetics Pub. Inc. (see also JOURNAL OF SPORT PSYCHOLOGY; QUEST), Rainer Martons, Box 5076, Champaign, IL 61820, 217-351-5076. 1975. "Scholarly books in sport and physical education." avg. press run 3,000. Pub'd 2 titles 1979; expects 3 titles 1980, 6 titles 1981. avg. price, cloth: $15.00; paper: $7.95. Discounts: Text 20%, Trade 40%. 300pp; 5½X8½; of. Reporting time: 1 month. Payment: negotiable (10-18%). Copyrights for author.

THE HUMANIST, Lloyd L. Morain, 7 Harwood Drive, Amherst, NY 14426, 716-839-5080. 1940.

Articles, art, photos, cartoons, interviews, criticism, reviews. circ. 28,500. 6/yr. Pub'd 6 issues 1979; expects 6 issues 1980. sub. price: $12.00; per copy: $2.00; sample: Free. Back issues: $2.50. Discounts: 40% bulk discount. 64pp; 8½X11; of, lp. Reporting time: 1-2 months. Payment: depends on piece. Copyrighted, reverts to author. Pub's reviews: 18 in 1979. §Philosophy, Psychology, Social Science, & Religion. Ads: $495.00/$265.00/$.45.

HUMANIST IN CANADA, Pacific Northwest Humanist Publications, Rod Dr. Symington, P.O. Box 157, Victoria, B.C. V8W2M6, Canada, 604-388-5323. 1967. Poetry, articles, photos, criticism, reviews, letters. "The magazine explains and advocates the humanist philosophy." circ. 1,800. 4/yr. Pub'd 4 issues 1979; expects 4 issues 1980. sub. price: $4.00; per copy: $1.00; sample: $1.00. Back issues: $1. Discounts: 33%. 48pp; 8X11; web of. Reporting time: 1 month maximum. Payment: nil. Not copyrighted. Pub's reviews: 20 in 1979. §Philosophy, ethics, politics, social issues. Ads: $100.-00/$60.00/$35.00/$0.25 word. CPPA.

Humble Hills Press, PO Box 7, Kalamazoo, MI 49004. 1 title listed in the *Small Press Record of Books in Print* (9th Edition, 1980).

THE HUNGRY YEARS, Les Brown, PO Box 7213, Newport Beach, CA 92660, 548-3324. 1978. Poetry, fiction, art, cartoons, reviews. "Short stories, poetry, pen & ink art compositions (no color), sketches, block prints, abstracts." circ. 1,000. 4/yr. Pub'd 2 issues 1979; expects 4 issues 1980. sub. price: $2.50; per copy: $0.50; sample: $0.50. Back issues: single issue price. 42pp; 5½X8½. Reporting time: 3 months. Payment: contributors copies. Copyrighted, reverts to author. Pub's reviews. §All areas concerning mag material requested. COSMEP.

Hunter Publishing, Co., Diane Thomas, P.O. Box 9533, Phoenix, AZ 85068, 602-944-1022. 1975. "We publish creative Ojo books—4 separate titles now. Interested in undertaking publishing venture for good craft oriented ideas-resale to craft & hobby shops, book stores, museum gift stores, etc. Also 2 books pub. on Japanese silk flower making. *The Southwestern Indian Detours,* paperback, ISBN 0-918126-11-8, $5.95; *The Southwestern Indian Detours,* handcover, ISBN 0-918126-12-6, $8.95. The above book will encompass some 300+ pages, together with some 50 pages of photographs of the original Fred Harvey Co. & The Atchison, Topeka, and Santa Fe R.R. files of the tourist trips run in the Southwest, mainly in New Mexico, Arizona, Colorado, and California. To be published in the Fall of 1978." avg. press run 10m-20m plus. Pub'd 2 titles 1979. 10 titles listed in the *Small Press Record of Books in Print* (9th Edition, 1980). avg. price, paper: $1.50-$2.95. Discounts: 40-50 percent retail. Higher disc. to distributors. 24-52pp; 8½X11. Reporting time: 1-2 weeks. Copyrights for author.

Huntsville Literary Association (see also POEM), Robert L. Welker, Editor, PO Box 1247, Huntsville, AL 35807. 1967. Poetry. avg. press run 500. Pub'd 3 titles 1979; expects 3 titles 1980, 3 titles 1981. 70pp; 4½X7⅓; lp. Reporting time: 30 days. Payment: copies. Copyrights for author. CCLM.

The Hurricane Company, Mark Raney, PO Box 426, Jacksonville, NC 28540, 919-353-4201. 1972. Poetry, fiction. "For the near future I will only publish my own books." avg. press run 2,000. Pub'd 1 title 1979; expects 1 title 1980, 1 title 1981. 2 titles listed in the *Small Press Record of Books in Print* (9th Edition, 1980). avg. price, cloth: $10.00. Discounts: The standard 40%, or better with quantity. 250pp. No submissions please.

Hurtig Publishers, Sarah A. Reid, Editor-in-Chief, 10560-105st, Edmonton, Alberta T5H2W7, Canada, 403-426-2359. 1956. Art, photos, cartoons, satire, criticism. "Canadian interest only." avg. press run 7,500. Pub'd 12 titles 1979; expects 12 titles 1980, 15 titles 1981. 18 titles listed in the *Small Press Record of Books in Print* (9th Edition, 1980). avg. price, cloth: $12.95; paper: $4.95. Discounts: on request. 200pp; size varies; of. Reporting time: 6 weeks. Payment: varies. Copyrights for author. ACP, APA.

Hwong Publishing Company, Dr. Hilmi Ibrahim, Editor-in-Chief; Sara H. Keating, Managing Editor; Barbara Van Hoven, Dr. Joseph Collier, 10353 Los Alamitos Blvd., Los Alamitos, CA 90720, (213) 598-2428. 1972. Poetry, fiction. "Book length material. Recent publications: *Forces in the Shaping of American Culture,* Joseph Collier, Editor; *The Complete Travel Guideto China* by Dr. Hilliard Saunders; *Mexican American Leaders and Movements* by Carlos Larralde; *The Complete Book on Disco and Ballroom Dancing* by Ann Kilbride and Angelo Algoso. *White Winds* by Joe Wilcox. *Leisure: A Psychological Approach* Hilmi Ibrahim, editor." avg. press run 3,000. Pub'd 18 titles 1979; expects 20 titles 1980, 26 titles 1981. avg. price, cloth: $10.00; paper: $4.00. Discounts: Trade books: 1-4 copies 20%; 5 & over, 40%; college texts: 20%. 200pp; 5⅜X8⅜; †of. Reporting time: varies from 2-3 weeks to 6 weeks. Payment: royalties are set by contract as is the payment arrangement. Copyrights for author. IPG.

Hyde Park Socialist, J. Hughes, 21 Brightling Road, London SE4 1SQ, United Kingdom. 1968. Articles, poetry, reviews, news items, interviews, criticism, letters. "800-1000 words. Non-party, non-sectarian, libertarian, socialist. F.A. Ridley & Denis Cobell." circ. 500. 4/yr. Pub'd 4 issues 1979. sub. price: 68p; per copy: 7p; sample: free. Discounts: 33% 6 copies plus. 8pp; size A4; xerox. Reporting time: 3 wks. Payment: copies. Pub's reviews: 10 in 1979. §Socialism.

HYPERION A Poetry Journal, Thorp Springs Press, Paul Foreman, Judy Hogan, Foster Robertson, c/o Hogan/300 Barclay Road, Chapel Hill, NC 27514. 1969. Poetry, criticism, reviews, long-poems. "Would like to see essays on poetics, esp concerned with American tradition. Reprint rights available on request." circ. 2,000. 2-3/yr. Pub'd 1 issue 1979; expects 1 issue 1980, 1 issue 1981. sub. price: $5.00, individ.; $10.00, institu.; $12.00, overseas institu.; per copy: combined issues $5.00; sample: $5.00. Back issues: One & two $25.00 each, 3-10 $5.00 each, 11 & 12 & 13 $10.00 each. Discounts: bookstore 40%, jobbers 10% 1-10 copies, 20% 11-50 copies. 200pp; 6X9; of. Reporting time: 2-6 mos. Payment: copies only. Copyrighted. Pub's reviews. §Poetry, literature, languages, Asian literature, Greek literature, modern poetry. CCLM, COSMEP.

I

Icarus Press, Margaret Diorio, P.O. Box 8, Riderwood, MD 21139, 301-821-7807. 1973. "Poetry chapbooks. 24-50 pages. No biases. Reporting time 1-2 months. 1st book *Homecoming* by John Stevens Wade, poems, 1978; 2nd book *Spokes for Memory* by Paul Alexander Bartlett, poems, 1979; 3rd book *The Great Horned Owl* by Maggie Anderson, poems, 1979; 4th book *Bringing in the Plants* by Margaret Toarello Diorio, poems, 1980." avg. press run 500. Pub'd 2 titles 1979. 4 titles listed in the *Small Press Record of Books in Print* (9th Edition, 1980). avg. price, paper: $2.50-$3.00. Discounts: 30% off 5-20; 40% off 21 or more. 40-50pp; 5½X8½; †of. Reporting time: 1-2 months. Payment: 10 copies of book, discounts for author. copyright by author. COSMEP.

I.D.H.H.B., Inc, E. J. Gold, Editor, Box 370, Nevada City, CA 95959. 1972. "Length-varied, spiritual, new age bias. E.J. Gold, Zalman Shalomi, Reshad Feild." avg. press run 5,000-10,000. Pub'd 1 title 1979; expects 6 titles 1980. 9 titles listed in the *Small Press Record of Books in Print* (9th Edition, 1980). avg. price, paper: $4.95. Discounts: 40% Trade, 50% wholesalers (negotiable). 200pp; 5½X8½; of. Reporting time: 3 months maximum. Payment: negotiable.

IDO-LETRO, International Language (IDO) Society of Great Britain, Tom Lang, International Language (IDO) Society of Gt. Britain, 14 Stray Towers, Victoria Road, Harrogate, N. Yorkshire HG2 0LJ, United Kingdom. 1930. Articles, poetry, fiction, reviews, news items, letters. "Official bulletin of International Language (IDO) Society. Informal style, non-commercial, international outlook, circulates world-wide." circ. 150. 4/yr. Pub'd 4 issues 1979; expects 4 issues 1980, 4 issues 1981. sub. price: $2.50; per copy: $0.70; sample: $0.70. Back issues: not available. Discounts: bulk orders. 4pp; size A4; duplication. Pub's reviews: 3 in 1979. §Languages, interlinguistics. Ads: No ads.

IF LIFE, THEN ONE AMONG AT LEAST FOUR, Horace G. Oliver Jr., P.O. Box 282, Palisades Park, NJ 07650. 1975. "Monthly magazine of Epistemology." circ. 100. 12/yr. Expects 8 issues 1980. sub. price: $10.00; per copy: $2.00; sample: free. Back issues: $3.00 each. Discounts: None. 16pp; 4½X7¼; †of. Reporting time: 1 month. Payment: Open. Copyrighted, reverts to author. Ads: No ads.

Ilkon Press, Ilse Bing, 210 Riverside Drive No. 6G, New York, NY 10025, 212-663-2579. 1975. Poetry, art, concrete art. avg. press run 1,000 books. 2 titles listed in the *Small Press Record of Books in Print* (9th Edition, 1980). avg. price, cloth: $10.00; paper: $7.00. Discounts: Libraries 20 percent; bookstores 40 percent; jobbers 50 percent when ordering 5 books minimum - otherwise 40 percent. 180pp; 12X9; of. Copyrights for author. NESPA, COSMEP.

Illuminati (see also ORPHEUS), P. Schneidre, 1147 So. Robertson Blvd., Los Angeles, CA 90035, (213) 273-8372. 1978. Poetry, art, photos, cartoons, long-poems, plays. "Interested in seeing submissions of all kinds. Include return postage." avg. press run 1,000. Pub'd 4 titles 1979; expects 11 titles 1980, 15 titles 1981. avg. price, cloth: $10.00; paper: $4.00. Discounts: On request. 64pp; 5X8; †of/lp. Reporting time: 2 weeks. Payment: by arrangement. Copyrights for author. CCLM, COSMEP.

ILLUMINATIONS, Illuminations Press, N. Moser, 1321-L Dwight Way, Berkeley, CA 94702, 415-849-2102. 1965. Poetry, fiction, articles, art, photos, reviews, letters, long-poems, collages, plays. "Fiction not usually over approx. 10 pp., plays not over 20 pp., reviews and short articles not over 7-8 pp. No biases, entirely eclectic. Contributors: Wakoski, J. Hays, F. Alexander, W. Witherup, Bukowski, Blazek, P. Wild, Ginsberg, etc. Plan 1-2 issues more if NEA grant comes thru." circ. varies, 500-2,000. 1/yr. Pub'd 1 issue 1979; expects 1 issue 1980, 1 issue 1981. sub. price: Indiv. $20.00 -

Instit. $30.00; per copy: $2.50; sample: $2.50. Back issues: $100.00 complete set minus No. 1; $75.00 beginning No. 3. Discounts: -1/3 discount to retail outlets. No other discounts. 30-60pp; 8X11; of. Reporting time: 3-6 months. Payment: copies, occasional prizes to 'best poem,' etc. Copyrighted, reverts to author. Pub's reviews. §books, arts; sometimes other matters. Ads: $75.00/$40.00/$15.-00/$8.00. CCLM.

Illuminations Press (see also ILLUMINATIONS), N. Moser, 1321-L Dwight Way, Berkeley, CA 94702, 415-849-2102. 1965. Poetry, fiction, long-poems, plays. "Via CCLM funds, and sales of mag., etc, 1 or more titles. Big on planning boards is a 300 pp. *ILLUMINATIONS* Reader antholgoy. ($5.00 paperback; $10.00 cloth)." avg. press run 1,000 - 2,000. Expects 1 title 1980, 1 title 1981. avg. price, paper: $1.50. Discounts: -1/3 discount to retail outlets. No other discounts. 30-40pp; 8X11 or larger; of. Reporting time: 3-6 months. Payment: Agreed percentage. Copyrights for author. CCLM.

Image and Idea, Inc., Richard Dyer MacCann, Box 1991, Iowa City, IA 52240. 1978. "Trying to set precedent for publication of unproduced student screenplays. Humor book by Donald Kaul (Des Moines Register Columnist) helps pay for that, we hope. Also into film production." Pub'd 1 title 1979; expects 3 titles 1980. avg. price, paper: $3.00-$5.00. Discounts: 40% to trade. 150pp; 5X7; of. Reporting time: not really soliciting submissions. Copyrights for author.

IMAGE MAGAZINE, Cornerstone Press, Anthony J. Summers, P.O. Box 28048, St. Louis, MO 63119, 314-487-4303. 1972. Poetry, fiction, articles, art, photos, cartoons, interviews, satire, reviews, letters, parts-of-novels, long-poems, plays, concrete art. "We want stuff that will make us scream or otherwise perform unnatural acts. It must be good, and daring. Some recent contributors: check back issues. No sloppy attempts at creativity. No SASE results in letter bomb back to sender. Submissions must be tight, well-written. You gotta be good to get in. We are always in need of good artwork and photography." circ. 400-600. 3/yr. Pub'd 3 issues 1979; expects 3 issues 1980. sub. price: $4.50; per copy: $1.50; sample: $1.50. Back issues: $5.00 per copy if I can find them. They are collectors items. Discounts: 1 free copy to any prisoner requesting. 40-60pp; 5X11; of. Reporting time: 2 weeks to infinity. Payment: 2 copies to author. plus $10.00 for best poem/s. story per issue. Copyrighted, reverts to author. Pub's reviews: 2 in 1979. §anything. no ads. CCLM, COSMEP, COSMEP-SOUTH.

IMAGES, Gary Pacernick, Bruce Pilgrim, English Dept, Wright State Univ., Dayton, OH 45435. 1974. Poetry. "Recent cont's: B.Z. Niditch, Carol Berge, Chris Bursk, Joan Colby, Mordecai Marcus, Betsy Adams, David Kherdian, Martin Robbins, Ada Aharoni, Millen Brand, Robert Peters, Peter Cooley, Daniel Langton, Arlene Stone, Josephine Jacobsen, Lyn Lifshin, Milton Kessler, Opal Nations, Peter Wild, William Virgil Davis." circ. 1000. 3/yr. Pub'd 3 issues 1979. sub. price: $1.50; per copy: $.50; sample: $0.50. Back issues: $0.50. 12pp; 16 (L) x 11½ (W); of. Reporting time: 1 month. Payment: copies. CCLM, COSMEP.

Images Press, Robert Leverant, David Bratman, P.O. Box 9444, Berkeley, CA 94709, 415-843-8834. 1968. Art, photos, non-fiction. avg. press run 2,000. Pub'd 2 titles 1979; expects 3 titles 1980. 4 titles listed in the *Small Press Record of Books in Print* (9th Edition, 1980). avg. price, paper: $3.50. Discounts: 40 percent 5 books or more. 64pp; size varies; of. Reporting time: 2 weeks. Payment: 10%. Copyrights for author. COSMEP, COSMEP-WEST, WIPS.

The Imaginary Press, Peter Payack, Box 193, Cambridge, MA 02141. 1978. "The Imaginary Press also publishes many environmental poetry projects which are designed to make poetry more visible by taking it out of books and putting it into living spaces. These include, STAR-POEMS where short celestial poems are flashed on a grid of high intensity lightbulbs beneath the wings of an airplane; POETRY WINDOWS, & business people where thematic poems are painted with glass wax and food colorings on store windows; and POETRY BALLOONS, where short uplifting poems are stuffed into helium balloones and distributed in an effort to show that poetry doesn't have to be weighty, obtuse, and inaccessible, but can be light, approachable, and far reaching! Short poems are always needed for these and future environmental poetry projects." of. Payment: copies.

IMAGINE, Gorman Bechard, Sandy Skiarnulis, Box 2715, Waterbury, CT 06720, (203) 753-2167. 1978. Articles, photos, interviews, criticism, reviews, music, letters, news items. "All articles must be music related. Record reviews, interviews, feature stories. Reviews should be 200 - 400 words in length, major articles 1,000 - 5,000 words." circ. 25,000. 6/yr. Expects 5 issues 1980, 12 issues 1981. sub. price: $10.00; per copy: $1.25; sample: $1.25. Back issues: #2 & #3, $3.00 each. Discounts: Purchase 20 or more year subscriptions at the same time, mailed to the same address, cost $8.00 per year sub. 52pp; 13½X15. Reporting time: 1 week to 2 months. Payment: none. Copyrighted, does not revert to author. Pub's reviews: 12 in 1979. §Anything that has to do with the world of music. Ads: $225.00/$125.00/30¢.

Imp Press, Ruth Geller, PO Box 93, Buffalo, NY 14213, (716) 881-5391. 1979. Fiction.

IMPACT, An International Publication of Contemporary Literature & the Arts, TLM Press, Gary Lagier, Editor; Thomas Piekarski, Associate Editor; Vange Peterson, Art Editor, 1070 Noriega, Sunnyvale, CA 94086, (408) 733-9615. 1975. Poetry, fiction. "We publish when we have enough material of first rate quality. *Impact* is given free to subscribers of *The Literary Monitor,* and does not maintain a separate subscription list." circ. 3,080. 1/yr. Pub'd 1 issue 1979. price per copy: $5.95 + SASE (8 x 10, 59¢). 300-500pp; 6X9; of. Reporting time: 2 weeks. Payment: One copy of *Impact.* Copyrighted, does not revert to author. CCLM, AWP.

Impact Publishers, Inc. (see also ASSERT NEWSLETTER), Robert E. Alberti, President, PO Box 1094, San Luis Obispo, CA 93406, 805-543-5911. 1970. Photos, cartoons, non-fiction. "Personal development/social change/health." avg. press run 5,000-10,000. Pub'd 3 titles 1979; expects 5 titles 1980, 3 titles 1981. 18 titles listed in the *Small Press Record of Books in Print* (9th Edition, 1980). avg. price, cloth: $8.95; paper: $4.95. Discounts: Bookstores & wholesale distributors: up to 4 copies, 20 percent; 5-99 copies 40 percent; 100 plus copies, contact Impact re terms. Libraries paper 10 percent; cloth 15 percent. 200-300pp; 5¼X8; of. Reporting time: 4-6 weeks. Payment: standard royalty contract. Copyrights for author.

IMPEGNO 70, Sicilian Antigruppo, Rolando Certa, Nat Scammacca, Via Argentaria Km.4, 91100 Trapani, Sicily. 1975. Poetry, articles, interviews, satire, criticism, reviews, letters, collages, concrete art. "3 to 5 typewritten pages, cultural in every field. Recent contributors: Enrico Crespolti, Guiseppe Zagarrio, Nicolo DAlessandro, Nat Scammacca, Francesco Carbone, Gianni Diecedue, Franco DiMarco, *only* Italian." circ. 1,250. 3/yr. sub. price: $5.00; per copy: $2.00; sample: $1.50. Back issues: $2.00. Discounts: 33 percent. 64pp; 5X8; of. Reporting time: 1 month. Payment: none. Copyrighted, reverts to author. Pub's reviews. §all areas. Ads: $100.00/$50.00/0.

IMPETUS MAGAZINE, Kenneth Ansell, 68 Hillfield Avenue, Hornsey, London N8 7DN, United Kingdom, 01-348-2927. 1976. Articles, photos, interviews, criticism, reviews, music. "*Impetus* is devoted to the experimental and exploratory areas of rock, jazz and contemporary classical music. The primary format is artist/composer profiles, generally based on interviews. Articles are allowed to run to the length neccessary to convey all relevant information without padding." circ. 4,000. 6/yr. Pub'd 2 issues 1979; expects 6 issues 1980, 6 issues 1981. sub. price: £3.30; per copy: 60p; sample: 60p. Back issues: #1, 40p; #5 & 6, 45p each; #8 & 9, 60p each (all including postage). Discounts: 33⅓% (overses postge added at cost). 48pp; size A4; of. Reporting time: varies. Copyrighted. Pub's reviews: 40 in 1979. §General range of subject magazines, music books. Ads: £60/£30/8p.

Impress Inc. (see PRIMIPARA)

IMPULSE, Eldon Garnet, Eldon Garnet, Editor; Shelagh Alexnder, Editor, Box 901, Station Q, Toronto, Ontario, Canada. 1971. Fiction, articles, art, photos, cartoons, interviews, news items. "Bias for the innovator—Les Levine, Mark Prent, Joe Hall, Michael Snow. An eclectic literary/arts magazine constantly changing formats. V 5/2 - an lp album by singer Joe Hall, V 5/3 - a magazine,V 5/4-6/1 - monograph of photos by levine, V 6/2 - news photos (in conjunction with *Impressions Magazine*) & finally, our most latest, post-idiocyncracy - V 6/3 - on cinefiche!Standardized magazine format release 3 times yearly, supplimented by 2 Impulse Editons which expand upon experimental focus of magazine. In 1979: Michael Snow's High School and Eldon Garnet's Spiralling/JFM 232." circ. 10,000. 3/yr. 10 titles listed in the *Small Press Record of Books in Print* (9th Edition, 1980). sub. price: $10.00; per copy: $2.00; sample: $2.00. Back issues: normal prices except for those which are limited. Discounts: 40 percent. 64pp; 11X11. Reporting time: 1 month. Payment: negotiable. §experimental. Ads: $400.00/$225.00. CPPA.

IN A NUTSHELL, Hibiscus Press, Margaret Wensrich, Fiction; Joyce Odam, Poetry, P.O. Box 22248, Sacramento, CA 95822. 1975. Poetry, fiction, art, cartoons. "Poetry: No line or subject limit. Fiction, 1,500-2,500 words. Payment on publication. Send SASE with all submissions. Closes Oct. 31. Send SASE for rules & entry form." circ. 5M. 4/yr. Pub'd 4 issues 1979; expects 4 issues 1980. sub. price: $8.00; per copy: $2.50; sample: $2.50. Back issues: $2.50. Write for discount. Order must be for 5 or more copies of the same issue. 20-24pp; 8½X11; of. Reporting time: 3-4 wks. Payment: -1/2 cent fiction/$2 minimum poetry/$5 minimum cartoons. Copyrighted, right reverts to author upon publication. no ads. CCLM, COSMEP.

In Between Books, Margaret Karla Andersdatter, Box T, Sausalito, CA 94965, 388-8048. 1974. Poetry, non-fiction. avg. press run depends. Pub'd 1 title 1979. 4 titles listed in the *Small Press Record of Books in Print* (9th Edition, 1980). Discounts: 20 percent to libraries; 40 percent to bookstores; 50-55 percent to distributors. 100pp; 5X8; of. query first. Copyrights for author. CCLM, COSMEP.

IN BUSINESS, The JG Press, Inc., Jerome Goldstein, Box 323, Emmaus, PA 18049, (215) 967-4135. 1978. Articles, art, photos, reviews. circ. 10,000. 6/yr. Pub'd 4 issues 1979; expects 6 issues 1980,

6 issues 1981. sub. price: $14.00; per copy: $2.50; sample: $2.50. Discounts: Available on request. 56pp; 8½X11; of. Reporting time: 2 weeks. Payment: $150.00-$200.00. Copyrighted. Pub's reviews: 20 in 1979. §Business fields, self-employment, social/economic small-scale ideology. Ads: $650.-00/$335.00/$0.15.

IN THE LIGHT, Jim Hanson, 1249 W Loyola #207, Chicago, IL 60626. 1975. Poetry. "Anselm Hollo, Allan Kornblum, David Cope, Alice Notley, Dave Morice, Shelley Kraut, Jeff Wright, Josephine Clare, Elizabeth Zima, Steve Toth, Andrew Carrigan, Elizabeth Eddy, John Sjoberg, Walter Hall, Sheila Heldenbrand, Art Lange, Maxine Chernoff & more.Generally, I select the poems I want for the magazine from works I hear when poets read their work in public. Under most circumstances I publish only solicited manuscripts. I do not look favorably on unsolicited manuscripts from people who have never seen my magazine." circ. 250. 1/yr. Pub'd 1 issue 1979; expects 1 issue 1980, 1 issue 1981. price per copy: $2.50. Back issues: varies. 90pp; 8½X11; mi. Copyrighted, reverts to author. CCLM, COSMEP-Midwest.

IN ORBIT: A Journal of Earth Literature, Energy Earth Communications, Inc., Rava X. Nelson, PO Box 1141, Galveston, TX 77553. 1977. Poetry, fiction, articles, interviews, criticism, reviews. "Science fiction plus." circ. 2,000. 1/yr. Reporting time: 2 weeks to 2 months. Copyrighted, reverts to author. Pub's reviews. §Science future fiction poetry.

IN STRIDE, David Eastland, Publisher; Dan Logan, Editor, 28570 Marguerite Parkway, Suite 103, Mission Viejo, CA 92692, (714) 831-0464. 1979. Poetry, fiction, articles, art, photos, cartoons, interviews, satire, reviews, letters. "Southern California & Southwestern U.S. magazine for participant athletes, particularley runners. Fiction need not have regional slant." circ. 10,000. 12/yr. Pub'd 2 issues 1979. sub. price: $12.00; per copy: $1.50; sample: $2.00. Discounts: 40% trade. 56pp; 8⅜X10⅞; of. Reporting time: 2 months. Payment: $15.00-$50.00 for 1,000-4,500 words, photos: $10.00-$15.00 interior color or b & w; $50.00 cover. Copyrighted, reverts to author. Pub's reviews. §Sports, health, outdoors. Ads: $540.00/$304.00/$0.36, $12.00 min. COSMEP.

IN TOUCH, The Grail, Jackie Rolo, The Grail, 125 Waxwell Lane, Pinner, Middx HA5 3ER, United Kingdom. 1969. Articles, poetry, photos, reviews, news items, interviews. "1,000-1,500 words. Personal & immediate-human interest, educational, spiritual-housewives, business men, professional men/women, young people, volunteers, clergy, religious. Ad rates: A market place page for: sale, wanted, exchange, information. 2p per word" circ. 1,200. 4/yr. Pub'd 4 issues 1979; expects 4 issues 1980, 4 issues 1981. sub. price: £1.50 UK, £2.00 abroad; per copy: 40p; sample: 20p. Back issues: 10p each. Discounts: Special circumstances only and sorted out at the time. 12pp; size A4; of. Payment: nominal. we do not copyright, but we do expect acknowledgement if articles are used. Pub's reviews: 6 in 1979. §Educational and religious.

INC., Just Buffalo Press, Bud Navero, Debora Daley, John Daley, 111 Elmwood Avenue, Buffalo, NY 14201, (716) 885-6400. 1975. Poetry, fiction, photos, interviews, parts-of-novels. "Recent contributors: Anselm Hollo, Bobbie Louise Hawkins, Anne Waldman, Jerome Rothenberg, Sonia Sanchez, Amiri Baraka, Simon Ortiz, Allen DeLoach, Fielding Dawson, Ray Federman, Rudy Burckhardt, Alice Hotley, Josie Clare, Ed Sanders, Maureen Owen and more. Magazine format, 8½ x 5½, 48 pps." 2-3/yr. Pub'd 3 issues 1979. price per copy: $2.00. Discounts: 40% to the trade. 48pp; 5½X8½; of. Reporting time: varies. Payment: when possible. Copyrighted, reverts to author.

Incunabula Collection Press, Paul Meinhardt, Lela Meinhardt, 277 Hillside Ave, Nutley, NJ 07110. 1977. Articles. "Title published Dec. 22, '77, *Cinderella's Housework Dialectics* by Lela Meinhardt & Paul Meinhardt. Kirk & Erik Meinhardt (illustrations & caligraphy). A radical analysis of housework, household and family. Materials used: feminist, anthropology, archaeology." avg. press run 3,000. Pub'd 1 title 1979. avg. price, paper: $5.00. Discounts: library and classroom-teaching less 20 percent; trade (bookstores) $2.72 on 10 or more copies; $3.00, 5-9 copies; $3.50, 2-4 copies. 300pp; 5½X8½; †of. COSMEP.

Independence Unlimited, Julia Atkinson, 27 Gardner Street, Portsmouth, NH 03801, (603) 431-6530. 1974. Fiction. "Independence Unlimited is a one-person operation. I published my novel *Emergence* in 1974 (page size 8 x 8) and *Seeing is Perceiving* in 1978 (page size 5 1/2 x 8 1/2 and both books are 'whole books' in that not only have I written them, but also designed both their form and format—with the exception of graphic artwork for their covers. For *Emergence,* I typeset and did the layout. For *Seeing is Perceiving* I also chose the type face, and did the layout but had it professionally typeset and printed, bound. Both novels have been distributed by direct mail most effectively, although small press outlets and commercial ones have also been used." avg. press run 500. Expects 1 title 1980. 3 titles listed in the *Small Press Record of Books in Print* (9th Edition, 1980). avg. price, paper: $5.00. No discount on less than three copies. $8.00 per copy for *Emergence.* $5.50 for *Seeing is Perceiving*

. For bookstores, 40% on consignment of ninety days. 279pp; of. Copyrights for author.

THE INDEPENDENT JOURNAL OF PHILOSOPHY, The Independent Philosophy Press, George Elliott Tucker, Cobenzlgasse 13/4, A-1190 Vienna, Austria. 1977. Articles, criticism, reviews, letters, news items. "We are attempting to forge and further a 'third force' in philosophy, beyond analyticism and existentialism/Marxism. Articles in German or English of 20 to 30 double-spaced typewritten pages, as well as short notices and replies, are welcomed. Prospective book-reviewers should consult the editor first. Issues for 1977-78: *'What Is Philosophy',* 'Leo Strauss—*Essays On The Issues And Themes Of His Life-Work',.* For 1979: *Hegel Today"* circ. 1,000. 1/yr. Pub'd 1 issue 1979; expects 1 issue 1980. sub. price: $8.50 students; $12.00 individuals; $18.00 institutions; sample: $8.50 students; $12.00 indiv.; $18.00 insti. Back issues: Same as subscription. Discounts: By arrangement. 140-160pp; 11⅝X8¼; of. Reporting time: 3-6 months. Payment: 50 offprints. Copyrighted, does not revert to author. Pub's reviews: 12 in 1979. §Philosophy, relevant books from other disciples, political, science, classics, education. Ads: $100.00/$60.00/.

The Independent Philosophy Press (see also THE INDEPENDENT JOURNAL OF PHILOSOPHY), George Elliott Tucker, Cobenzlgasse 13/4, A-1190 Vienna, Austria. 1977. Articles, criticism. "We are attempting to forge and further a 'third force' in philosophy, beyond analyticism and existentialism/marxism. We are interested in translations, scholarly reprints (basic texts and monographs) as well as first rate contemporary work. Authors should send a detailed outline before submitting manuscripts." Discounts: by arrangement. of. Reporting time: 3-6 months. Payment: by arrangement. Copyrights for author.

Independent Press Distribution, Administrator: Heidi Armbruster, c/o 12 Stevenage Road, London SW6 6ES, United Kingdom. 1 title listed in the *Small Press Record of Books in Print* (9th Edition, 1980).

Independent Publishing Fund of the Americas (see also IPFA NEWS), circa 25 advisory editors, 119 S Cuyler, Oak Park, IL 60302. 1977. Fiction, interviews, plays. "The I.P.F.A. is a new organization dedicated to the promotion, sponsorship and distribution of good new books of a popular nature— fiction or non-fiction—which treat issues of current social significance. The I.P.F.A. screens and selects manuscripts for sponsorship and funds their publication by various affiliated small presses. Original fundraising and organizational formation is still underway (March 1979)." Reporting time: 1 to 3 months.

INDEX ON CENSORSHIP, Michael Scammell, George Theiner, 21 Russell St., Covent Garden, London WC2B 5HP, United Kingdom, 01-836-0024. 1972. Articles, poetry, fiction, cartoons, satire, news items, interviews, criticism, letters, parts-of-novels, plays, reviews, non-fiction. "US sub price includes air-surface postage. Magazine is an outlet for manuscripts by authors who cannot be published in their own countries; and publishes reports on threats to freedom of expression-such as the censorship or persecution or torture of writers, scholars, journalists, artists, film-makers etc. Also publishes interviews, discussions and questionnaires. Scope is international-West and East. Contributors include: Viktor Nekrasov, A. Tverdokhlebov, Ludvik Vaculik, Vaclav Havel, V. Fainberg, Kim Chi-ha, George Mangakis, Reza Baraheni, Amnesty International, Arthur Miller, Robert Birley, James Michener, Nadine Gordimer. Rodolfo Walsh, Eduardo Galeano, Julio Cortazar, Ernesto Cardenal, Pyotr Grigorenko, Roy Medvedev, Georgi Vladimov, Sipho Sepamla, Don Mattera, Mario Varga Llosa. US address: Room 1303, 205 E 42nd Street, New York, NY 10017" circ. 4,500. 6/yr. Pub'd 6 issues 1979; expects 6 issues 1980. 16 titles listed in the *Small Press Record of Books in Print* (9th Edition, 1980). sub. price: $18.00; £9.00; per copy: $3.00; £1.50; sample: free. Back issues: $3.50; £1.75. Discounts: [Publishers 20 percent, non profit 40 percent. These discounts apply only to advertisements placed in INDEX.] Agent 10 percent. Bookshops variable (supplied via Random House). 80pp; 24X17cms; lp. Reporting time: variable. Payment: £30 per thou to authors. authors' copyrights by arrangement. Pub's reviews: 29 in 1979. §Censorship, human rights. Ads: £75.00 ($150.00)/£40.00 ($80.00).

Indian Academy of Letters (see also INDIAN Literature), Keshav Malik, 35 Feroze Shah Road, New Delhi 110001, India. 1958. Poetry, fiction, articles, criticism, reviews, parts-of-novels, long-poems. Pub'd 60 titles 1979. 1 title listed in the *Small Press Record of Books in Print* (9th Edition, 1980). avg. price, paper: RS 2.00; other: RS 2.00. 200pp. Reporting time: 1 year.

INDIAN ARIZONA NEWS, Janice Brunson, 1777 W. Camelback Road A-108, Phoenix, AZ 85015, (602) 248-0184. 1978. Articles, art, photos, interviews, news items. circ. 20,000. 12/yr. Pub'd 12 issues 1979; expects 12 issues 1980, 12 issues 1981. sub. price: $12.00; per copy: $1.00; sample: free. Back issues: $1.00 if available per copy. Discounts: 50 to 1 address, $10.00 per month. 32pp; 11½X15; of. Reporting time: 1 month. Copyrighted. Ads: $240.00/$120.00/$4.30.

INDIAN HOUSE, Tony Isaacs, Ida Isaacs, Box 472, Taos, NM 87571, (505) 776-2953. 1966. Photos, music. "We specialize in recordings of traditional American Indian music, published in LP Phonodisc, Cassette, and 8-track formats." 6/yr. price per copy: $7.98 list. Discounts: wholesale to record stores, 46.1% off list. of.

INDIAN Literature, Indian Academy of Letters, Keshav Malik, Rabindra Bhavan, 35 Feroze Shah Road, New Delhi 110001, India. 1958. Poetry, fiction, articles, criticism, reviews, parts-of-novels, long-poems. "Articles about 5,000 words maximum." circ. 1,500. 6/yr. Pub'd 6 issues 1979; expects 6 issues 1980, 6 issues 1981. sub. price: Rs.12.00, $6.00; per copy: Rs.2; sample: RS. 2.00. Back issues: RS. 2.00. 150pp; 21cm x 13½cm; lp. Reporting time: 1 year. Payment: RS. 100 — per article. Pub's reviews: 60 in 1979. §literary/poetry. Ads: RS. 300 — per page.

Indian Publications, Paul Weldon, Garrett Springer, 1869 2nd Avenue, New York, NY 10467. 1979. Poetry, fiction, plays. "*Saga of Chief Crazy Horse* by Garrett Springer, $5.00." avg. press run 1,000. Pub'd 2 titles 1979. 1 title listed in the *Small Press Record of Books in Print* (9th Edition, 1980). avg. price, cloth: $7.00; paper: $5.00. Discounts: 40%, 120 days. 70pp; 6X9. Reporting time: 1 week. Payment: varies. Copyrights for author.

Indian Tree Press (see also ABSINTHE), Lela Crystal Neuburger, Editor, Barryville, NY 12719, 914-557-8141. 1977. Poetry, fiction, art. "Founded as an 'alternative' press for children's literatue (ages 3-12). We like a *natural living* slant. No limit on length. What we really *dislike* is stuff written *down* to children!" avg. press run 500. Pub'd 1 title 1979; expects 1-2 titles 1980. 1 title listed in the *Small Press Record of Books in Print* (9th Edition, 1980). avg. price, paper: $2.00-$3.50. Discount on bulk purchase for resale: 10% off 6-10 copies, 18% off 11 copies or more. 25-50pp; 5½X8½; of. Reporting time: ASAP, about 2 weeks. Payment: 10% of sales. Copyrights for author.

INDIAN TRUTH, Ann T. Laquer, 1505 Race St., Philadelphia, PA 19102, 215-563-8349. 1924. Articles, photos, reviews, poetry, art, news items. circ. 2,000. 6/yr. Pub'd 6 issues 1979; expects 8 issues 1980, 8 issues 1981. sub. price: $15.00; per copy: free; sample: Free. Back issues: $0.25. 6pp; 8½X11; of. Reporting time: 30 days. Pub's reviews: 2 in 1979. §Native American and affairs, history, literature. no ads.

THE INDIAN VOICE, Donna Doss, 102-423 West Broadway, Vancouver, British Columbia V5Y1R4, Canada, 604-112-876-0944. 1969. Poetry, articles, art, photos, interviews, reviews, letters, collages. "THE INDIAN VOICE newspaper was founded to serve as a communications vehicle for native Indians of the North American continent. Because we are funded by the Secretary of State we ask our contributing writers to do the work gratis. We have, at other times, given a nominal fee which varies according to the money in the bank." circ. 3,000. 12/yr. Pub'd 13 issues 1979; expects 12 issues 1980, 12 issues 1981. sub. price: Canadian $5.00/overseas and U.S. $5.50; per copy: $.50; sample: no charge. Back issues: 50¢. Discounts: (Can) $4.80 (Foreign) $5.30. 12-24pp; 15 inch tabloid; of. Pub's reviews: 6 in 1979. §all areas affecting the native Indian. Ads: $300/$150/$4.00 per col. inch.

INDIANA WRITES, T. Richey, Editor; D. Paulson, Bus. Coord; A. Campbell, Associate Editor, 110 Morgan Hall, IU, Bloomington, IN 47401, (812) 337-3439. 1975. Poetry, fiction, articles, art, photos, interviews, criticism, reviews, letters, parts-of-novels, long-poems, plays, news items. "We publish a wide variety of genres, writing oriented mainly to a Midwestern audience, and writing from schoolchildren grades kindergarten through 12. Contributors: Brian O'Neill, Sonia Gernes, Roger Pfingston." circ. 1,500 (readership 4,000+). 4/yr. Pub'd 4 issues 1979. sub. price: $8.00; per copy: $2.25; sample: $2.00. Back issues: $2.50 for bicentennial double issue. Discounts: Trade: 60/40 percent split; classroom $1.50 a copy. 80pp; 9X6; of. Reporting time: 2 months. Payment: 2 copies. Copyrighted, reverts to author. Pub's reviews: 0 in 1979. §Teaching writing, poetry, fiction, small press books. CCLM, COSMEP, COSMEP-MIDWEST.

INDUSTRIAL WORKER, Editorial Collective, 3435 N Sheffield Rm 202, Chicago, IL 60657, 312-549-5045. 1912. Articles, art, photos, cartoons, interviews, reviews, letters. "Report on and analyse news events from a working class perspective." circ. 2,500. 12/yr. Pub'd 12 issues 1979; expects 12 issues 1980, 12 issues 1981. 13 titles listed in the *Small Press Record of Books in Print* (9th Edition, 1980). sub. price: $7.50 insti.; $4.00 indiv.; per copy: $0.25; sample: free. Back issues: 50 cents 1 copy. Discount 60 percent of cover price for 5 or more copies. 8pp; 8½X17; of. Not copyrighted. Pub's reviews. §labor, labor history, economics. Ads: no paid or commercial ads ever accepted. APS.

Information Alternative, Kelly Warnken, Box 657, Woodstock, NY 12498. 1977. "We publish the *DIRECTORY OF FEE-BASED INFORMATION SERVICES,* an annual directory of free lance librarians, information brokers and others. *The Journal of Fee-Based Information Services* is a bimonthly, for freelance librarians, information brokers and others in the field. The directory is $6.95, the journal is $9.00 to individuals and $11.00 to institutions per year" Pub'd 1 title 1979. 1 title listed in the *Small Press Record of Books in Print* (9th Edition, 1980). avg. price, paper: $6.95.

INFORMATION MOSCOW, Wendy Earl, Editor, 970 San Antonio Road, Palo Alto, CA 94303, (415) 493-1885. 1977. "*Information Moscow* is a biannually updated reference handbook on the city of Moscow. It does not contain articles, but rather information most generally available to the average traveller (business or pleasure) to the USSR. We refer to it as a periodical because it is published twice a year in volume form." circ. 5,300. 2/yr. Pub'd 1 issue 1979; expects 1 issue 1980, 2 issues 1981. sub. price: $24.00 US; $26.00 International; per copy: $13.50 postpaid. Back issues: $5.00 each. Discounts: 25 copies or less, 40%; 26-50 copies, 45%; 50 or more copies, 50%. 375pp; 5X7; of. No unsolicited manuscripts accepted. Payment: Arranged individually. Copyrighted, does not revert to author. Ads: $950.00/$500.00. COSMEP.

Ink Blot Press (see also RAINBOW'S END), Earl Blanchard, 6340 Mission Street, Daly City, CA 94014, (415) 992-1750. 1975. avg. press run 150. Pub'd 10 titles 1979; expects 50 titles 1980, 100 titles 1981. avg. price, paper: $1.50. Discounts: 33⅓%. 16pp; 4X7. Reporting time: 1 week. Copyrights for author.

Ink Links Ltd., J. Weal, 271 Kentish Town Road, London NW5 2JS, United Kingdom, 01-267-0661. 1977. Articles, criticism. avg. press run 3,000. Pub'd 1 title 1979; expects 2 titles 1980, 7 titles 1981. avg. price, cloth: $18.00; paper: $8.00. Discounts: 33⅓% trade, 25% single. 127-500pp; 5¼X8¾; of. Reporting time: 2-3 months. Payment: negotiable. Copyrights for author.

INKLINGS, Mudborn Press, Judyl Mudfoot, 209 West De la Guerra, Santa Barbara, CA 93101, (805) 962-9996. 1979. Poetry, long-poems. "*Inklings* is now formally launched, as a series of bilingual chapbooks 24-32pp of quality authors (not necessarily contemporary) and selections not otherwise available in English. Our first three *Inklings* are Portuguese (Jorge de Sena), Nahuatl (Aztec birth poems), and Latvian (Astrid Ivask). We are looking for the uncommon and the uncommonly translated; *Inklings* is intended to be semi-scholarly; production done letterpress in Mudborn's own shop." circ. 800. irregular. Pub'd 2 issues 1979; expects 3 issues 1980, 3 issues 1981. price per copy: varies; sample: $3.00. Discounts: trade buyers, write for terms, info. 28pp; 7X10; †lp. Reporting time: one month. Payment: 10% total royalty; advance varies. Copyrighted, reverts to author. Ads: no ads. ALTA.

INKY TRAILS and TIME TO PAUSE, Inky Trails Publications, Pearl L. Kirk, Inky Trails Publications, P.O.Box 345, Middleton, ID 83644. 1967. Poetry, articles, art, photos, cartoons, reviews, long-poems. "*Time to Pause* use the longer material 17 lines to 50. Devotional nature on poems and articles, plus cartoons and art work. Please send art in india ink or dark outline easy to have published. $6.50 a year, 2 issues a year. Need material and support here to continue. *Inky Trails* policy since editor's return from surgury. Payments to contributors: A sure winner, pet peeve; and monthly poetry 'subject' contest winners $2.00 off toward their subscriptions. Send SASE for information. Also Inky Trails 'poem of the year' poetry contest this offer cash awards, certificates and gifts. Inky Trails accepts material 16 lines or less on any subject or style (good clean material); original and unpublished; one poem per page, typewritten on one side, and one side only with their name and address and zip code, at botton of page, please. Must be a subscriber to receive yearly awards such as poet of the year, writer of the year, artist of the year and poet laureate. A special at this time is both Inky Trails and Time To Pause for $15.00 a year a savings of $3.50, or you, may send SASE for information. Be sure and send SASE for details for poem of the year contest, deadline is September 1, 1980. Pathways: Inky Trails Publication new magazine for children send SASE for information. Both adults and children may write. Their is a special on at this time for all 3 publications $3.50 for Pathways or special: $18.50 for all 3 publications for 1 year." circ. 200. 3/yr. Pub'd 3 issues 1979; expects 3 issues 1980, 3 issues 1981. sub. price: $12.00; per copy: $5.00; sample: $2.50 to sub. to non-sub is $4.00. Back issues: $2.00 plus postage 39 cents. 50-70pp; 8X11; †mi. Reporting time: 2-4 weeks. Payment: A sure winner pays $2.00 toward subscription. Copyrighted, reverts to author. Pub's reviews: 20-25 in 1979. §Poetry, history, religious, (anything of interested subjects - good clean material). Ads: $15.00/$10.00/$.10.

Inky Trails Publications (see also INKY TRAILS and TIME TO PAUSE), Pearl L. Kirk, PO Box 345, Middleton, ID 83644. 1967. Poetry, fiction, articles, art, reviews, long-poems. "*Time to Pause* devotional type, religious, nature, humor or just restful also take articles and art work; *Pathways* for the children, if adults write write for the children, from ages 0 to 19 years old.. so must be good quality and clean material. *Inky Trails* 16 lines or less, art, articles, short stories not over 1,500 words, good quality and clean material, markets, books review (send book for review) contest, Poem of the Year (4-cash awards); pet peeves pay $2.00; Sure Winner pay $2.00 and more to offer. Always looking for that special person to receive the 'civic' awards." †mi.

INPRINT, Writers' Center Press, Jim Powell, 6360 N. Guilford Ave, Indianapolis, IN 46220, (317) 253-3733. 1978. Poetry, fiction, articles, art, interviews, criticism, reviews, letters, plays, concrete art, news items, parts-of-novels, long-poems. "A continuation of the *Indianapolis Broadsheet*, we have no restrictions on subject, style, etc., but do have something of a bias toward Indiana writers. With work of comparable quality (and we don't claim infallibility there) we'll take the work of an Indiana author over another writer. Mainly we serve as a cohesive link for serious Indiana writers, but try to avoid insulation from the world at large. Length: poems generally to 50 lines; prose to 4,000 words; news as short as possible. Richard Pflum, Elizabeth Cohen, Darryl Garnett, Gloria Still." circ. 1,000-2,000. 6/yr. Pub'd 3 issues 1979; expects 6 issues 1980, 6 issues 1981. sub. price: $4.00; per copy: $0.75; sample: $1.00. Back issues: Complete Broadsheet set $10.00, inprints $1.00, if available. Discounts: trade, classroom 40%. 20pp; 8½X11; of. Reporting time: 8-12 weeks (SASE required). Payment: 2 copies + discount on add'l copies. Copyrighted, reverts to author. Pub's reviews: 6 in 1979. §Midwestern small press and authors, subjects receive high priority; others also of interest. Ads: $70.00/$40.-00/$0.10.

THE INQUIRER, Fred M. Ryde, 1-6 Essex Street, London WC2R 3HY, United Kingdom. 1842. Articles, poetry, cartoons. 26/yr. sub. price: £4.10; per copy: 10p; sample: free. 4pp; of. Payment: £5 per author above 1,000 wds. Copyrighted. Pub's reviews: 30 in 1979. §religion, social matters. Ads: 75p cm.

INQUIRY MAGAZINE, Williamson M. Evers, 747 Front Street, San Francisco, CA 94111, (415) 433-4319. 1977. Poetry, articles, art, interviews, criticism, reviews, music, letters, news items. "Political semimonthly, with art reviews, including books, film, dance, music. Recent contributors, Nat Hertoff, Nicholas von Hoffman, Barry Lynn, George Kennan, Thomas Szasz, Anthony Burgess." circ. 12,000. 20/yr. sub. price: $15.00; per copy: $1.25; sample: free. Discounts: 50% newsstand distributors, 40% bookstore. 32pp; of. Payment: 10¢ word. Copyrighted, reverts to author. Pub's reviews: 100 in 1979. Ads: $300.00/$190.00/$0.25.

Inquiry Press, 4925 Jefferson Ave, Midland, MI 48640, 517-631-3350. 1975. 2 titles listed in the *Small Press Record of Books in Print* (9th Edition, 1980). avg. price, cloth: $15.00; paper: $7.95. Discounts: 40% trade/20% textbook. 450pp; 6X9; of/lp. Reporting time: 30 days.

INS & OUTS, Ins & Outs Press, Edward Woods, PO Box 3759, Amsterdam, Netherlands, 278483/276868. 1978. Poetry, fiction, articles, art, photos, cartoons, interviews, satire, criticism, reviews, music, letters, parts-of-novels, long-poems, collages, plays, concrete art, news items. "*Ins & Outs* is an English-language magazine published in Amsterdam & distributed internationally. Its mood is anarchist, its flavor magical, its bent literary. Our only position is total eclecticism, in form-style-subject matter. There are no taboos. Even our ideas concerning artistic excellence are varied. Our main game is awareness, on whatever level.. you choose the approach. We accept contributions from anywhere, incl. translations & previously published material that deserves more attention. We have printed plays by Mel Clay & Heathcote Williams, articles by Woodstock Jones, Simon Vinkenoog & William Levy, fiction by Rachel Pollack & Hans Plomp, pornography, comix, the aphorisms of Ganesh Baba, photos by Marc Morrel & the poems of Ira Cohen, Allen Ginsberg, Patti Smith, Piero Heliczer, Lewis MacAdams, Harold Norse, Brion Gysin & Joe Nobodyetknows. Interesting mss, especially short tough prose from women writers, always welcome, but be advised that we now receive more material than we can handle and are particularly overloaded w/poetry." circ. 2,500. irregular. Pub'd 3 issues 1979; expects 1 issue 1980, 3 issues 1981. sub. price: $20.00 airmail; per copy: $2.50; sample: $1.00. Discounts: 35% retailers, 50% distributors. 60pp; 6½X9½; of. Reporting time: between now & never, average 3 months. Payment: whatever we can afford, copies certainly. Copyrighted, reverts to author. Pub's reviews: 6 in 1979. §Almost anything from war to peace, sublime to ridiculous, sacred to profane, fact, fiction, poetry, literature, far out topics dealt with in original ways. Ads: $250.00/$150.00/small ads free unless you're selling something, then 10¢ a word. APS, COSMEP.

Ins & Outs Press (see also INS & OUTS), Edward Woods, PO Box 3759, Amsterdam, Holland. 1979. Poetry, photos, long-poems. "The press, apart from the magazine, is new & moving ahead slowly. This year we published only one small longpoem book *Manifesto: Cosa Nostra di Poesia by Ronald Sauer,* a critical broadsheet *Other World Poetry Newsletter* and a series of postcards. For 1980 we plan at least two poetry books (one of which, *Bhutto & Other Love Poems* by Eddie Woods), more postcards & other material not yet decided upon—in addition to the magazine, of course. For the present we are *not* much interested in unsolicited book MSS though authors who feel they have something truly unique which they would like us to publish are welcome to write a letter & tell us what they have. As for the magazine, interesting MSS are always welcome. And we now have our own Ins & Outs International Bookstore at O.Z. Achterburgwal 169, Amsterdam, which is rapidly becoming a major literary meeting place." avg. press run 500-1,000. Pub'd 1 title 1979; expects 2 titles 1980. avg. price, paper: $7.00. Discounts: 30% to retailers, 50% to distributors. 100pp; of. Reporting time: 3-6 months. Payment: negotiable. Copyrights for author. APS, COSMEP.

THE INSIDE TRACK, Sam Breck, 306 Westwood, Ann Arbor, MI 48103, (313) 668-7703. 1970.

Articles, reviews, news items. "Feature articles dealing with railroad history and operations may run as much as 5-6,000 words. Covers railroads and railroading in the Great Lakes and s.w. Ontario regions almost exclusively." circ. 550. 5/yr. Pub'd 5 issues 1979; expects 5 issues 1980, 5 issues 1981. sub. price: $5.00; sample: $2.00 if available. Back issues: produced by xerography only, details in each issue. 28pp; 8½X11; †of. Reporting time: 3-4 weeks. Payment: none; all material voluntarily submitted. Pub's reviews: 5 in 1979. §Railroad history and current operations. Ads: No ads.

INSIDE/OUT, TIME CAPSULE, INC., Matthew Hejna, Editor, GPO Box 1185, New York, NY 10001, (212) 595-8448. 1980. Poetry, fiction, art, reviews, letters. "Fiction, 3,000 words—poetry, 100 lines, max. Type (if possible) on 60 space margin. We only publish incarcerated writers." circ. 2,000. 4/yr. Expects 4 issues 1980, 4 issues 1981. sub. price: $5.00; per copy: $1.50; sample: $1.00. Back issues: $1.00. Discounts: Single issues $1.00 apiece with purchase of 100 or more. 12pp; 11½X17; of. Reporting time: 6 weeks. Payment: $20.00 each published poem or short story. Copyrighted, reverts to author. Pub's reviews. §Literature. Ads: $700.00/$350.00.

INSIGHT: A Quarterly of LESBIAN/GAY CHRISTIAN OPINION, Edward Prucha, Gabriel Lanci, Jeannine Gramick, P.O. Box 5110,, Grand Central Station, New York, NY 10017. 1976. Poetry, articles, art, photos, cartoons, interviews, satire, criticism, reviews, news items. "Sexuality, homosexuality, and the Christian churches. 500 word length. Recent contributors: John McNeill, SJ; Patricia Nell Warren; Jeannine Gramick, SND; Jean O'Leary; Brian McNaught; Thomas Sweetin; Paris Baldacci; Louie Crew; Peter Fink, S.J." circ. 6M. 4/yr. Pub'd 4 issues 1979; expects 4 issues 1980, 4 issues 1981. sub. price: $8.00/yr; per copy: $2.00. Back issues: Vol 1 (1976-77) $3.00 each. Discounts: Bulk rate on orders of 25 copies or more 40% discount. 28pp; 8½X11; lp. Reporting time: one month. Payment: none. Copyrighted, reverts six months after publication. Pub's reviews: 6 in 1979. §Homosexuality & religion; gay issues & religion. Ads: $100/. COSMEP.

Institute for Contemporary Studies (see also TAXING & SPENDING), A. Laurence Chickering, 260 California Street, Suite 811, San Francisco, CA 94111, (415) 398-3010. 1972. Articles, news items. "Books on public policy issues. Each author contributes a chapter in the area of his or her expertise. Contributors include: Milton Friedman, David Broder, Seymour Martin Lipset, James R. Schlesinger, Ben Wattenburg, S. I. Hayakawa." avg. press run 5,000. Pub'd 3 titles 1979; expects 4-5 titles 1980, 4-5 titles 1981. avg. price, cloth: $10.00; paper: $6.95; other: $2.00 summary booklets. Discounts: 20% discount to libraries, bookstores, wholesalers on orders of 10 or more books. 300pp; 5¼X8½; of. Reporting time: 1-3 months. Payment: Institute holds copyrights. Payment on approval $600.00 - $3,000.00. COSMEP.

Institute for Independent Social Journalism, Inc. (see also GUARDIAN), Jack A. Smith, Editor; Barbara Miner, Managing Editor, 33 W 17th St, New York, NY 10011, (212) 691-0404. 1948. Articles, photos, cartoons, interviews, criticism, reviews, letters, news items. avg. press run 5,000. Pub'd 3 titles 1979; expects 4 titles 1981. avg. price, paper: $4.95; other: $1.50 pamphlet. Discounts: 10 or more 40%. of.

Institute for Local Self-Reliance (see also SELF-RELIANCE), 1717 18th St NW, Washington, DC 20009. 1974. Articles, interviews, criticism, reviews, news items. avg. press run 2,500. Pub'd 6 titles 1979. 9 titles listed in the *Small Press Record of Books in Print* (9th Edition, 1980). avg. price, paper: $3.00. Discounts: 40% on orders of ten or more. 16pp; of. Reporting time: 2 weeks. Payment: yes. Copyrights for author.

Institute for Polynesian Studies, Robert D. Craig, Editor, Brigham Young University, Laie, HI 96762. 1977. Articles, reviews. avg. press run 1,000. 6 titles listed in the *Small Press Record of Books in Print* (9th Edition, 1980). avg. price, paper: $2.50, Sub $5.00 yr. 100-125pp; 6X9. Payment: yes.

Institute for Southern Studies (see also SOUTHERN EXPOSURE), P.O. Box 230, Chapel Hill, NC 27514. 9 titles listed in the *Small Press Record of Books in Print* (9th Edition, 1980).

Institute for the Study of Human Issues (ISHI), Betty C. Jutkowitz, 3401 Market Street, Suite 252, Philadelphia, PA 19104, (215) 387-9002. 1975. "ISHI publishes scholarly books in such fields as anthropology, political science, sociology, folklore, and history. Special subjects of interest are Latin American politics and the trade and use of narcotics. New and recent books include: *Revolutionary Cuba in the World Arena,* edited by Martin Weinstein; *Jews in the Eyes of the Germans,* by Alfred D. Low; *Cannabis in Costa Rica,* edited by William E. Carter; and *Caste: The Emergence of the South Asian Social System,* by Morton Klass." avg. press run 1,500. Pub'd 12 titles 1979; expects 16 titles 1980, 16 titles 1981. avg. price, cloth: $15.00; paper: $8.00. Discounts: Generally short, but varies according to title. 250pp; 6⅛X9¼; of. Reporting time: 3 months. Payment: 10-12% royalty on net receipts.

Institute of Pyramidology (see also PYRAMIDOLOGY MAGAZINE), James Rutheford, Editor, 31

Station Road, Harpenden, Herts AL5 4XB, United Kingdom, Harpenden 64510. 1940. Photos. "20,000-150,000 words. Religious bias. Recent contributor: Dr. Adam Rutherford." avg. press run 5M-10M. Pub'd 5 titles 1979; expects 1 title 1980, 1 title 1981. 5 titles listed in the *Small Press Record of Books in Print* (9th Edition, 1980). avg. price, cloth: $10.00 - $30.00; paper: $3.00/$5.00. Discounts: 1-4 books, 30% plus shipping; 40% on 5 or more copies, plus shipping. 100-600pp; 5½X8½; of. Reporting time: 2 months. Payment: negotiable. Copyrights for author.

THE INSURGENT SOCIOLOGIST, The Insurgent Sociologist Collective, c/o Department of Sociology, Univ. of Oregon, Eugene, OR 97403. 1969. Poetry, articles, art, criticism, letters, reviews. "Have a comprehensive back index available." circ. 3,000. 4/yr. Pub'd 4 issues 1979. sub. price: indiv. $12.00; low income $8.00; sustaining, $25.00; institutions $20.00; per copy: $4.00; sample: free. Back issues: $6.00 Vol. 8 #2&3, Vol. 1 $5.00, Vol. 9 #2, 3 $6.00. Discounts: 40% booksellers with standing orders. 100pp; 7½X10⅜; of. Reporting time: 90 days. No payment. Copyrighted, does not revert to author. Pub's reviews: 20 in 1979. §politics/history/sociology, philosophy. Ads: $150/$80.

INTERCOM, Manor Press, Dwight L. Musser, Editor, Box 305, Ridge Manor, FL 33525, 904-583-2343. 1977. Articles. "*Intercom* encourages alternative economy, recycling, barter, co-operation, and printing as a hand craft." circ. 500. 4/yr. Pub'd 4 issues 1979; expects 4 issues 1980. sub. price: barter. Back issues: postage only. 4pp; 4X6; †lp. Reporting time: none. Payment: copies. Not copyrighted.

INTERCONTINENTAL PRESS/INPRECOR, Mary-Alice Waters, 410 West Street, New York, NY 10014. 1963. News items. "Contributors: Ernest Mandel, George Novack, Livio Maitan, Pierre Frank." circ. 4,500. 49/yr. Pub'd 49 issues 1979; expects 49 issues 1980. sub. price: $30.00; per copy: $0.85; sample: free. Back issues: $1.00. 32pp; 8½X11; of. Reporting time: 2 weeks. Copyrighted. Pub's reviews: 17 books, 92 magazines in 1979. §politics/ecology. no ads.

INTERFACE: THE COMPUTER EDUCATION QUARTERLY, David Kroenke, Harold Stone, Gordon Davis, Joyce Little, Robert Aiken, 116 Royal Oak, Santa Cruz, CA 95066, (408) 438-5018. 1979. Articles, photos, cartoons, interviews. "For computer teachers at the secondary and post-secondary level, and for industrial training in computers and word processing. Features six regular columns by well-known professionals, extensive book reviews, special articles and case studies." circ. 2,000. 4/yr. Pub'd 4 issues 1979. sub. price: $26.00; per copy: $7.00; sample: free. Discounts: $9.00 rate for individual college or high school instructors. 20% to agents & jobbers. 84pp; 8½X11; of. Reporting time: 30 days. Copyrighted, reverts to author. Pub's reviews: 30 in 1979. §Introductory level books on computers, computer programming, business data processing. Ads: $400.00/$250.-00/$5.00.

INTERFACE JOURNAL: Alternatives in Higher Education, Carl Ginsburg, 505 Fruit Ave NW, Albuquerque, NM 87102. 1975. Articles, interviews, reviews. "We accept articles from people engaged in projects for change in post-secondary education. Special issue 3-4 was devoted to alternative concepts of the learning process. Some authors published include, Carol Berge, Lewis Hyde, Bill Romey and David Zeller. SASE for return of unused material." circ. 300. 2/yr. Pub'd 1 issue 1979; expects 2 issues 1980. sub. price: $8.00/4 issues, $10.00 institutions; per copy: $2.00/$4.00 double issue. Discounts: 25%. 56pp; 8½X11; of. Reporting time: 2 mo. Payment: copies. Pub's reviews. §education/innovative education. Ads: $65/$40.

Interface Press (see also BRAIN/MIND BULLETIN), Marilyn Ferguson, Harris Ph.D. Brotman, P.O. Box 42211, Los Angeles, CA 90042, 213 257-2500. 1975. Articles, interviews, reviews, news items. avg. press run 10,000. Pub'd 1 title 1979; expects 2 titles 1980, 2 titles 1981. avg. price, other: .75¢. Discounts: inquire. 4pp; 8½X11; of. Payment: none.

Interim Books, Kirby Congdon, Box 35, Village Station, New York, NY 10014. 1962. Poetry. "Doing broadsides until money is forthcoming for next issue. Next year: no schedule; dislike being programmed. All correspondence is attentively read; usually courteously answered. Interim's ambitions are slothful, distribution lousy. You would be much happier with someone else." Payment: Copies.

Interim Press, Peter Dent, 3 Thornton Close, Budleigh Salterton, Devon EX9 6PJ, United Kingdom. 1975. Poetry, art, criticism, letters, plays. "Collections in print from: Daud Kamal, Alasdair Paterson & Roland John. A verse play by John Gurney." avg. press run 250 copies. Pub'd 4 titles 1979. 8 titles listed in the *Small Press Record of Books in Print* (9th Edition, 1980). avg. price, paper: £0.65. Discounts: 33 percent to trade. 16-32pp; 8½X6; of. Reporting time: 2 wks. Payment: copies only. all material copyrighted for author (translators also).

INTERMEDIA, Harley W. Lond, Blair H. Allen, D.L. Klauck, P O Box 31-464, San Francisco, CA 94131. 1974. Poetry, fiction, articles, art, photos, satire, criticism, reviews, music, collages, plays, concrete art. "Publishing experimental literary issues, visual art chapbooks, art broadsides, as well as art magazine. Issue #5 is a tabloid 'Entropy' issue, each page functioning as a pull-out poster of words and images. #6 is a boxed 'arti-fact' issue, with posters, broadsides, manifestoes, postcards, photographs, etc. #7 is an American literary issue of experimental works. #8 is a dada/krazy art/mail art issue. #9 is a special Latin American/European visual and literary issue. #5, #6, and #7 now available. No longer accepting material as we are booked solid until 1981. In addition, publishing *Divine Nations* by Opal Nations; as well as a special series of art broadsides, 17 x 22 posters of art works — currently available — *Analogical Aesthetics* by Lew Thomas, and *1285 18CLN Futura Bold — Press Poem* by Lionell Glaze; $1.00 each plus $0.25 postage. In addition, we are also publishing the Intermedia Arts and Communication Resource Newsletter, a bi-monthly offset 12 page resource guide to art groups, publications, video and cinema groups, dance, theatre and musician organizations, and social change and alternative groups. The Newsletter is a spin-off from the very successful Resource Section yellow Pages of Intermedia Magazine. Subscriptions are $12.00 a year for 6 issues, institutions $8.00." circ. 3,000. irregular. Pub'd 1 issue 1979; expects 3 issues 1980, 3 issues 1981. 5 titles listed in the *Small Press Record of Books in Print* (9th Edition, 1980). sub. price: $7.50; sample: Single copy copy. Back issues: Issue #5, $2.00; #6, $3.50; #7, $2.00. Discounts: 40% trade, bulk institutions: $8.00. 60pp; 8½X11; of. Reporting time: max-1½ mo. Payment: contrib. copies. Copyrighted, reverts to author. §experimental literature/art. Ads: none.

Intermedia Press, Box 3294, Vancouver, BC V6B 3X9, Canada. 1972. Poetry, fiction, long-poems. avg. press run 1,000. Pub'd 4 titles 1979; expects 6 titles 1980, 8 titles 1981. 25 titles listed in the *Small Press Record of Books in Print* (9th Edition, 1980). avg. price, cloth: $12.95; paper: $6.95. Discounts: 5 and over, 40%. 72pp; 5½X8½; †of. Reporting time: 3 weeks. Payment: 10% of printed edition. Copyrights for author. COSMEP, LPG, BCPG.

Intermundial Research, Box 518, Inverness, CA 94937. 2 titles listed in the *Small Press Record of Books in Print* (9th Edition, 1980).

International Childbirth Education Association, Inc., Doreen Shanteau, Director of Publications, PO Box 20048, Minneapolis, MN 55420. 1960. avg. press run 1,000-15,000. Pub'd 4 titles 1979; expects 2 titles 1980, 26 titles 1981. 1 title listed in the *Small Press Record of Books in Print* (9th Edition, 1980). avg. price, paper: $4.00. Discounts: 40%. 100pp; 8½X11; of. Payment: all authors contribute, no royalties. we hold.

THE INTERNATIONAL FICTION REVIEW, Dr. Saad Elkhadem, Dept. of German & Russian, UNB, Fredericton, nb, Canada. 1973. "The *IFR* is a biannual periodical devoted to international fiction. Mss are accepted in English and should be prepared in conformity with the *York Press Style Manual*; articles: 10-20 typewritten pages; reviews: 2-6 pp.; spelling, hyphenation, and capitalization according to *Webster*" circ. 600. 2/yr. Pub'd 2 issues 1979; expects 2 issues 1980. sub. price: $10.00 for institutions/$8.00 for individuals; per copy: $5.00; sample: $5.00. Back issues: the same rate. Discounts: 20% for agents and jobbers. 90pp; 6X9; of. Reporting time: 6 weeks. Payment: none. Not copyrighted. Pub's reviews: 35 in 1979. §Fiction and scholarly works on fiction. Ads: $60/$40. IFA.

International General, P.O. Box 350, New York, NY 10013. "Left studies on all aspects of communication and culture." Pub'd 3 titles 1979; expects 4 titles 1980. 9 titles listed in the *Small Press Record of Books in Print* (9th Edition, 1980). Discounts: 1-4, 25%; 5-9, 33⅓%; 10+, 40%.

International Human Systems Institute, Barbara J. Owen, General Manager, 3136 Dundas Street West, Toronto, Ontario M6P 2A1, Canada, (416) 762-1363. 1979. "Publish behavioral science books." avg. press run 5,000. Pub'd 1 title 1979. avg. price, cloth: $14.95; paper: $9.95. Discounts: 25% bookstore; 40% jobber. 200pp; 5¼X8¼. Reporting time: not interested in unsolicited manuscripts. COSMEP.

International Marine Publishing Co. (see also NATIONAL FISHERMAN), Kathleen Brandes, Managing Editor; Bruce White, Editor, 21 Elm Street, Camden, ME 04843, 207-236-4342. 1969. "We publish non-fiction marine books." avg. press run 5,000. Pub'd 13 titles 1979; expects 15 titles 1980, 15 titles 1981. 55 titles listed in the *Small Press Record of Books in Print* (9th Edition, 1980). avg. price, cloth: $15.00; paper: $9.95. Discounts: trade 40 percent; wholesale 46 percent. 225pp; 6X9; 7X10; 8½X11; of. Reporting time: 6 weeks. Payment: 10 percent of list price. Copyrights for author. AAP.

International Language (IDO) Society of Great Britain (see also IDO-LETRO), Tom Lang, 18 Lane Head Rise, Staincross Common, Mapplewell, Barnsley S75 6NQ, United Kingdom. 1930. "We publish Ido books and leaflets from time to time as needed." 1 title listed in the *Small Press Record of Books in Print* (9th Edition, 1980).

INTERNATIONAL P.E.N. BULLETIN of SELECTED BOOKS, Kathleen Nott, International PEN, 7 Dilke Street, London SW3 4JE, United Kingdom. 1950. Articles, reviews. "A bilingual (English-French) guide, backed by U.N.E.S.C.O. to notable books belonging to literatures of lesser currency. Most numbers contain articles and reviews from several countries, but there have also been eleven special numbers devoted to one country, the most recent being on Bulgarian literature. A new series devoted to particular themes has been projected; the first two to Criticism and International Children's Books." circ. 2,500. 4/yr. sub. price: 68p; per copy: 17p; sample: free. Back issues: 17p per copy. Discounts: to agents cost 50p. 30pp; 8. Reporting time: short. Payment: £5.00 for article, £3-4 for review.

INTERNATIONAL POETRY REVIEW, Evalyn P. Gill, Raymond Tyner, Clare Rosen, Associate Editor, Box 2047, Greensboro, NC 27402. 1974. Poetry, art, photos, long-poems. "Primary interest in translations from contemporary foreign language poetry. Section of poetry in English, Bilingual publication. SVSC Box 56, University Center, Mich 48710 is an additional address, for subscriptions, not for manuscripts. Translators should include xerox of originals with source (book, date, publisher), and short biographical statement on original poet and translator." circ. 350. 2/yr. sub. price: $6.00, 2 yrs $11.00, 3 yrs $16.00; per copy: $3.00; sample: $3.00. Back issues: $5.00 per copy. Discounts: 20 percent to agents and jobbers. 136pp; 6X9; of. Reporting time: 2-3 months. Payment: in copies. Copyrighted, reverts to author. Ads: $100.00/$50.00. CCLM.

INTERNATIONAL PORTLAND REVIEW, Cindy Ragland, Editor; Dan Pedersen, Assoc. Editor, P.O. Box 751, Portland, OR 97207. 1953. Poetry, fiction, articles, long-poems, parts-of-novels. "1980 issue is original language poetry printed with corresponding English translations representing 57 countries and 41 languages." circ. 4M. 1/yr. Pub'd 1 issue 1979; expects 1 issue 1980, 1 issue 1981. sub. price: $5.95; per copy: $5.95; sample: $3.95. Back issues: $1.50 (2 years prior). 504pp; 6X9; of. Reporting time: 1-3 months. Payment: copies only. Copyrighted, reverts to author. Pub's reviews. §Translation. Ads: no ads. CCLM.

THE INTERNATIONAL UNIVERSITY POETRY QUARTERLY, The International University Press, John Wayne Johnston, Editor, 1301 S. Noland Rd., Independence, MO 64055. 1974. Poetry, criticism, reviews. "We prefer short, personal poetry, constructive criticism, and sprightly reviews. Emphasis is at all times upon creativity and insightfulness." circ. 250. 4/yr. Pub'd 4 issues 1979. sub. price: $3.00; per copy: $1.00; sample: $1.00. Back issues: $1.00 per issue. 6pp; 8½X11; †mi. Reporting time: 2-4 weeks. Payment: copies. Copyrighted, reverts to author. Pub's reviews. Ads: $25.00/$15.-00/$0.30. COSMEP.

The International University Press (see also THE INTERNATIONAL UNIVERSITY POETRY QUARTERLY), John Wayne Johnston, Editor, 1301 S. Noland Rd., Independence, MO 64055. 1973. Poetry, criticism, reviews. "In addition to The International University Poetry Quarterly, TIU Press also prints TIU Annual Report, TIU Newsletter, and TIU Collegiate Sports Report. We print several academic books with a growing list of such works each year." avg. press run 250. Pub'd 20 titles 1979. 4 titles listed in the *Small Press Record of Books in Print* (9th Edition, 1980). avg. price, paper: $5.00. 150pp; 8½X11; †mi. Reporting time: 2-4 weeks. Payment: copies. Copyrights for author. COSMEP.

INTERRACIAL BOOKS FOR CHILDREN BULLETIN, Bradford Chambers, 1841 Broadway, New York, NY 10023, 212-757-5339. 1967. Articles, art, photos, cartoons, reviews. circ. 10,000. 8/yr. Expects 6 issues 1981. 10 titles listed in the *Small Press Record of Books in Print* (9th Edition, 1980). sub. price: indiv. $10.00, instit. $15.00; per copy: $2.00 single issue, $3.00 double issue; sample: $2.00 single issue, $3.00 double issue. Back issues: $2.00 single issue, $3.00 double issue. Discounts: single issues: $1.75 each for 10 or more; double issue: $2.00 each for 10 or more. 24pp; 8½X11; of. Reporting time: 2 months. Payment: minimal. Copyrighted, does not revert to author. Pub's reviews: 100 in 1979. §Children's books 1-11 yrs. Educational-Human value/Anti-racism/Anti-sexism. Third World, Feminist, Children's Books, school textbooks. Ads: no ads. COSMEP, LPS.

Intersection Inc., 756 Union St., San Francisco, CA 94133.

INTERSTATE, Noumenon Press, Loris Essary, Mark Loeffler, P.O. Box 7068, U.T. Sta., Austin, TX 78712. 1974. Poetry, fiction, art, reviews, music, parts-of-novels, long-poems, collages, plays, concrete art. "Experimental. Recent contributors: Bruce Andrews, Ascher/Straus, Stanley Berne, Charles Bernstein, Carl D. Clark, Robert Coover, Peter Finch, Peter Mayer, Klaus Groh, Gabortoth, Siri Valoch, Keith Waldrop, Rosmarie Waldrop, Brian Eno, Allen Fisher, Michael Gibbs, Dick Higgins, Karl Kempton, Richard Kostelanetz, David Miller, Bern Porter, Dan Raphael, Ron Silliman, Arlene Zekowski. Special emphasis on visual and performance pieces." circ. 500. 1-2/yr. Pub'd 1 issue 1979; expects 2 issues 1980, 1 issue 1981. sub. price: $6.00/4 issues; sample: $3.00. Back issues: By arrangement. Discounts: 40% to bookstores. 108pp; 8.5X5.5; of. Reporting time: As soon as possible.

Payment: copies. Copyrighted. Pub's reviews. §all genres of the arts. Ads: none. COSMEP/CCLM.

INTREPID, Intrepid Press, Allen De Loach, P.O. Box 1423, Buffalo, NY 14214. 1964. Poetry, fiction, articles, art, photos, cartoons, interviews, satire, criticism, letters, parts-of-novels, long-poems, collages, plays, concrete art. "Contributors indexed in #23/24 include Ginsberg, Blackburn, Mottram, Wantling, Bremser, DeLoach, Shaetter, di Prima, Rothenberg." circ. 1M. irreg. sub. price: $6.00/4 issues; per copy: $2.00; sample: $2.00. Back issues: Available. 200pp; 5½X8; of. Reporting time: 3 mos. Payment: copies only. CCLM, Niagara-Erie Writers, COSMEP.

Intrepid Press (see also BEAU FLEUVE SERIES; INTREPID; 23 CLUB SERIES), DeLoach, Allen, P O Box 1423, Buffalo, NY 14214. 1964. 10 titles listed in the *Small Press Record of Books in Print* (9th Edition, 1980). Reporting time: 3 months. Payment: complimentary copies to 10%, varies. Copyrights for author. CCLM, Niagara-Erie Writers, COSMEP.

INTRINSIC: An International Magazine of Poetry & Poetics, Absolute O Kelvin (AOK) Press, Michael Zizis, Mary Ellen Kappler, Box 485, Station P, Toronto, Ontario M5S 2T1, Canada, (416) 534-0139. 1977. Poetry, art, photos, interviews, criticism, reviews, letters, long-poems. "We are devoted poetry, (not religious, please) of every length. We want to encourage the longpoem, if that is the artist choice. We love receiving artwork in any form. Among our recent contributors are Eugenio Montale, Margaret Atwood, and Diane Wakoski." circ. 1,000. 4/yr. Pub'd 6 issues 1979; expects 4 issues 1980, 4 issues 1981. sub. price: $10.00; sample: gratis. Back issues: #1, $10.00; #2, $6.00; we publish double issues at $6.00 each. Discounts: 40%. 200pp; 6X9; of. Reporting time: at least four months. Payment: 1 free contributors copy. Copyrighted. Pub's reviews: 4 in 1979. §Poetry, poetry overviews.

INVISIBLE CITY, Red Hill Press, Los Angeles & Fairfax, John McBride, Paul Vangelisti, 6 San Gabriel Drive, Fairfax, CA 94930. 1971. Poetry, articles, photos, criticism, reviews, letters. "The tabloid Invisible City #26 features 1980, a collection of current poetry (and its extensions - visuals welcome) as well as a report on aspects of the European avant-garde. Later this year, we will begin, parallel to the tabloid, a series of Invisible City in the book format. #1, the first 25, features work from the first 25 issues of the magazine (est. 1971); #2, All Things Considered, is a manual of Italian avant-garde poetry (both linear & visual) of the years 1960-1980, edited by Adriano Spatola and Paul Vangelisti. Details on these volumes soon. The tabloid continues." circ. 2,000. 1-2/yr. Pub'd 1-2 issues 1979; expects 2+ issues 1980. sub. price: $5.00; per copy: $2.00; sample: $2.00 ppd. Back issues: Sampler: $3.00/3 ppd. Bound sets available shortly (with index). 32pp; 11X17; of. Reporting time: 2-3 months at worst. Payment: copies for sure. authors, translators retain rights. Pub's reviews: 5 in 1979. §translation, criticism, poetry. CCLM, COSMEP.

Inwood Press, c/o Teachers & Writers, 84 Fifth Avenue, New York, NY 10011. 1974. Poetry, fiction. "*Dreamline Express* by Yvette Mintzer; *A New House* by Marc Kaminsky; *Chain Hearings* by Aaron Fogel; *Lies & Stories* by Glenda Adams; *Nonrequiem* by Steven Schrader; *Nonrequiem* by Mel Konner; *New Listings* by Allan Appel; *Thaw* by Simone Press." avg. press run 1,000. avg. price, paper: $2.50. of. Copyrights for author.

Io (named after moon of Jupiter), North Atlantic Books, Richard Grossinger, 635 Amador Street, Richmond, CA 94805, 415-236-1197. 1964. "All issues are thematic. Recent ones have been on ecology, baseball, alchemy, and astrology. In the near future, there will be ones on basketball, baseball, dreams, star/music, and perhaps stars.u" circ. 1500. irregular. Pub'd 2 issues 1979; expects 2 issues 1980, 2 issues 1981. sub. price: $17.50 for 4 consecutive issues; per copy: $2.00 to $11.95; sample: $4.00 if No. unspecified. Back issues: All back issues still available, most at original prices (current issue is 27) full set is $173.30 (thru 27). The following are scarce: 4, 6, 7, 8, 10, 11, 14, 20, 21. Discounts: 3 or more, 60& retail; 50 or more, 55% retail; 100 or more, 50% retail. 250pp; 6X9; 8½X11; of. Reporting time: Immediate—but do not want unsolicited submissions. Payment: yes. Copyrighted, reverts to author. Ads: no ads. CCLM.

ION, Peter Nordlinger, Dept of English, University of Victoria, Victoria, B.C., Canada, (604) 477-6911. 1978. Poetry, fiction, articles, interviews, satire, criticism, reviews, music, parts-of-novels, long-poems, plays. "Shorter (2-3,000 words) items given preference." circ. 1,000. 4/yr. Pub'd 1 issue 1979; expects 3-4 issues 1980. sub. price: $5.00; per copy: $1.25; sample: free. Back issues: $1.25. Discounts: 15%. 60pp; 5X6. Reporting time: 2 months. Copyrighted, reverts to author. Pub's reviews. §All areas.

IOWA CITY BEACON LITERARY REVIEW, Le Beacon Presse, Keith Gormezano, 621 Holt Avenue, Iowa City, IA 52244, (319) 354-5447. 1979. Poetry, fiction, articles, art, photos, cartoons, interviews, satire, criticism, reviews, music, letters, parts-of-novels, long-poems, collages, plays, concrete art, news items. "Only for those who have not been published before. We prefer unknown authors. We will review *everything* mags/books sent to us usually a line or paragraph." circ. 200. 12/yr.

Pub'd 4 issues 1979. sub. price: $10.00; per copy: $1.00; sample: $0.50 w/SASE. Discounts: Trade lil; 50% postpaid; 40% billed to agent, jobbers, etc. 50% to libraries. 40pp; 5½X8; multilith. Reporting time: 30 days /w SASE. Copyrighted, reverts to author. Pub's reviews. §We will only review books by new authors (i.e. their first or second book) all magazines accepted. Ads: $5.00/$3.00/$0.05. COSMEP.

IOWA REVIEW, David Hamilton, Editor; Fredrick Woodard, Editor, 308 EPB, Univ. Of Iowa, Iowa City, IA 52242, (319) 353-6048. 1970. Fiction, poetry, criticism. "We are considering *the essay* as an independent art form we will gladly consider for publication." circ. 750. Quarterly. Pub'd 4 issues 1979; expects 4 issues 1980. sub. price: Instit. $8.00 ($9.50 outside US); Indiv. $7.00 ($8.50 outside US); per copy: $2.00 postpaid; sample: $2.00. Back issues: All available still. Discounts: 30% to bookstores. 128pp; 6X9; of. Reporting time: 4 wks 3 months. Payment: Fiction & criticism $10.00/pg; poetry $2.00/line on publication. Copyrighted. Pub's reviews. §Reviews of recent poetry, fiction, translations as well as books in related fields. Ads: $100.00/$60.00.

Iowa State University Press (see POET & CRITIC)

IOWA WOMAN, Valerie Staats, Route 3, Box 202C, Iowa City, IA 52240, (319) 683-2659. 1979. Poetry, fiction, articles, art, photos, interviews, letters, long-poems, news items. "Material length is flexible; whatever it takes to say what needs to be said. Some recent articles have been 'Political Priorities for 1980' for women in Iowa; communal kitchens; massage, the healing art; the 'Women's Standard,' a turn-of-the-century feminist paper from Iowa; hunting for wild mushrooms; a woman's letter-press and how she runs it; and Iowa independent dance companies. The magazine features history, education, opinion essay, fiction, a regular photography portfolio, letters, graphics,; *Iowa Woman* is a feature-oriented journal for women. PAYMENT: Contributors' copies (3), biographical note in issue (also, applying for grants and then will pay for articles)." circ. 1,000. 6/yr. sub. price: Indiv. $6.00; Lib & Inst. $12.00; per copy: $1.25; sample: $1.25. Discounts: Bulk to bookstores on consignment basis—retailer gets 40%, publisher gets 60%. 40pp; 8X10; of. Reporting time: 6-8 weeks. Copyrighted, reverts to author. Ads: No ads. COSMEP.

IPFA NEWS, Independent Publishing Fund of the Americas, John B. Foster, Editor, 119 S Cuyler, Oak Park, IL 60302, 35695. 1977. Articles, interviews, criticism, reviews. "*IPFA NEWS* is the newsletter/journal of the Independent Publishing Fund of the Americas. IPFA NEWS contains news and feature articles of interest to those involved in publishing and communications for social change, as well as reviews and announcements of new social-change books." circ. 3,000. 4/yr. sub. price: $10.00; sample: free. Back issues: free on request. 8-24pp; 8½X11; of. Reporting time: approximately 1 month. Payment: contributions are unpaid. Pub's reviews. §Popular fiction or non-fiction, on issues of current social importance.

Iris Press, Patricia Wilcox, 27 Chestnut St., Binghamton, NY 13905, 607-722-6739. 1975. Poetry, fiction. "Iris Press publishes books of poetry, broadsides, short story collections and novels. We always have more we'd like to do than we can handle, so authors should write ahead of sending manuscripts, including SASE. Our goal is to bring out significant and readable literature in handsome editions." avg. press run 1,000. Pub'd 2 titles 1979. 6 titles listed in the *Small Press Record of Books in Print* (9th Edition, 1980). avg. price, cloth: $7.00; paper: $4.00. Discounts: 40 percent on 5-50 copies. Book services will be given 20 percent on any order. 85pp; 6X9; of. Reporting time: 1 month. Payment: negotiated individually. Copyrights for author. COSMEP, NYSSPA.

IRON, Iron Press, Peter Mortimer, Editor; Pete Swan, Art Editor, 5 Marden Terrace, Cullercoats, North Shields, Tyne & Wear NE30 4PD, United Kingdom, 0632-531901. 1973. Poetry, fiction, art, letters, long-poems, plays. "*Iron,* by the end of 1979 will have passed the 25 edition mark, and will have featured more than 500 writers from five continents, as well as displaying the work of many graphic artists and photographers. It is an active encourager of new poetry, but also - just as important - the short story, a form it can publish up to 6,000 words. All material submitted gets an honest hearing, even if not accepted. Rejection slips form no part of *Iron's* philosophy." circ. 900. 4/yr. Pub'd 4 issues 1979; expects 4 issues 1980, 4 issues 1981. sub. price: $6.00, £2.00; per copy: $1.50, 50p; sample: for postage. Back issues: 35p ($1.00 cents) post free. Discounts: trade discount 33 percent. bulk discount negotiable. 52pp; size A4; of. Reporting time: 2 weeks. Payments rare. rights remain with author. Pub's reviews: 28 in 1979. §poetry, all small press publ. Ads: $50.00 (£25.00)/$30.00 (£14.00). ALP, ASM.

Iron Mountain Press, Robert Denham, Editor and Publisher, Box D, Emory, VA 24327, 703-944-5363. 1975. "I publish chapbooks of excellent poetry. All printing is done from handset type using high quality paper. The Iron Mountain Press Poetry Chapbooks average 28 pages in length, and include the poetry of Ann Deagon, Kate Jennings, Mike Martin, Robert Cluett, Elizabeth Fisher, and

197

Geoffrey Hartman. I also publish poetry post cards, illustrated with linocuts. All printing is done by hand on a C & P letterpress. Bindings are handsewn." avg. press run 400 copies. Pub'd 2 titles 1979; expects 2 titles 1980. 6 titles listed in the *Small Press Record of Books in Print* (9th Edition, 1980). avg. price, paper: $4.00. 28pp; 5½X8½; †lp. Reporting time: 1 week. Payment: Author receives a portion of the copies. I keep the remainder. Does not copyright for author.

Iron Press (see also IRON), Peter Mortimer, Art Editor, Editor; Pete Swan, Reviews Editor; Yann Lovelock, 5 Marden Terrace, Cullercoats, Northumberland, United Kingdom. 1973. Poetry, fiction, art, letters, long-poems, reviews. avg. press run 900. Pub'd 4 titles 1979; expects 4 titles 1980, 4 titles 1981. 10 titles listed in the *Small Press Record of Books in Print* (9th Edition, 1980). avg. price, paper: 50p, $1.50 plus postage. Discounts: Trade 33%, bulk on negotiation. 52pp; size A4; of. Reporting time: 2 weeks. Payment: rare. Does not copyright for author. ASM.

IRONWOOD, Ironwood Press, Michael Cuddihy, P.O.Box 40907, Tucson, AZ 85717. 1972. Poetry, articles, art, photos, interviews, criticism, reviews, letters, long-poems. "Michael Cuddihy, editor. Prints poetry, including long poem, poetry reviews, interviews, translations, essays, and memoirs. Every 3rd or 4th issue is a special issue on a single poet or aspect of poetry. Special issues so far: Oppen, James Wright, Transtromer. Linda Gregg/Vallejo. IRONWOOD stresses quality in materials, design, and content." circ. 750. 2/yr. Pub'd 2 issues 1979; expects 2 issues 1980, 2 issues 1981. sub. price: $5.00, indiv.; $5.50, insti.; per copy: $2.50; sample: $2.50. Back issues: List available on request. Discounts: 40% to bookstores. 132pp; 6X9; of. Reporting time: 2 to 7 weeks. Payment: $10.00 per page for poems (often less for longer poems). Pub's reviews: 5 in 1979. §Poetry, criticism, books of essays, autobiographies. Ads: $50.00/$30.00/$20.00 2 inches high camera ready. CCLM.

Ironwood Press (see also IRONWOOD), Michael Cuddihy, PO Box 40907, Tucson, AZ 85717. 1971. Poetry, articles, art, photos, interviews, criticism, reviews, music, long-poems. "We also print translations and special issues on single poets." avg. press run 500. Pub'd 3 titles 1979; expects 1 title 1980. 8 titles listed in the *Small Press Record of Books in Print* (9th Edition, 1980). avg. price, paper: $2.-50/$3.50. Discounts: 40% off for bookstores who order 5 or more. 32pp; 6X9; of. Reporting time: 2 to 7 weeks magazine/2-6 months books. Payment: 10% of press run to author. Copyrights for author. CCLM.

Iroquois House, Publishers, Lorette Zirker, Box 15, Sunspot, NM 88349, (505) 437-2807. 1977. Fiction, non-fiction. "Fiction, aviation only. All lengths. Non-fiction, ecumenical religious studies. Book length." avg. press run 3,500-5,000. Pub'd 1 title 1979. 1 title listed in the *Small Press Record of Books in Print* (9th Edition, 1980). avg. price, cloth: $12.00; paper: $5.95. Discounts: 2-9, 40%; 10-24, 50%; all customers, all editions. 200-350pp; of. Reporting time: 2-4 weeks. Payment: standard royalties. Copyrights for author.

Ishtar Press, Inc. (see also PAINTBRUSH: A Journal of Poetry, Translations & Letters), Ben Bennani, Dept of English, Northeastern University, 360 Huntington Avenue, Boston, MA 02115. 1974. Poetry. "New address effective September, 1978: Department of English, Riyadh University, P.O. Box 2456 Riyadh, Saudi Arabia. Richard Eberhart, Denise Levertov, David Ignatow, George Keithley, Joseph Bruchac, Douglas Blazek, Charles Levendosky, Sam Hamill, G. Wilson Knight, and others." avg. press run 500. Pub'd 1 title 1979. avg. price, paper: $5.00. Discounts: 20-40 percent. 65pp; 5½X8½; of/lp. Reporting time: 1-2 weeks. Payment: 10 percent of sales. copyright is author's. CCLM, COSMEP, Associated Writing Programs.

Island Press - A Division of Round Valley Agrarian Institute, Barbara Dean, Star Route 1, Box 38, Covelo, CA 95428. 1978. Fiction. "We publish trade paperback books and are especially interested in the environment and human experience." avg. press run 5,000. Pub'd 4 titles 1979; expects 6 titles 1980. avg. price, cloth: $10.00; paper: $6.00. Discounts: Introductory schedule: 1-2 books, 30%; 3-9 books, 40%; 10-49 books, 45%; 50 plus books, 50%. of. Reporting time: 3 months. Payment: 10% until break even point; 15% thereafter, payment semi-annually. Copyrights for author. COSMEP.

Islands (see also ISLANDS, A New Zealand Quarterly of Arts & Letters), Robin Dudding, 4 Sealy Road, Torbay, Auckland 10, New Zealand, 4039007. 1972. Poetry, fiction. "Book publishing only an occasional offshoot. *ISLANDS* quarterly main function." avg. press run 2,000. Pub'd 1 title 1979; expects 1 title 1980. 2 titles listed in the *Small Press Record of Books in Print* (9th Edition, 1980). avg. price, cloth: $6.00; paper: $3.50. Discounts: 33⅓%, 2 or more; 25% single copies to retailers. 112pp; of/lp. Reporting time: ASAP. Payment: by arrangement. Copyrights for author.

ISLANDS, A New Zealand Quarterly of Arts & Letters, Islands, Robin Dudding, 4 Sealy Road, Torbay, Auckland 10, New Zealand, 4039007. 1972. Poetry, fiction, articles, art, photos, cartoons, interviews, satire, criticism, reviews, music, letters, parts-of-novels, long-poems, collages, plays, concrete art. "Basically New Zealand-related material. Copyrights revert to author but acknowledgement for future printings required, and notification." circ. 2,000. 4/yr. Pub'd 4 issues 1979; expects 4 issues 1980. sub. price: $12.00 (NZ)-$15.00 (NZ) overseas; per copy: $3.50 (NZ)- $4.00 (NZ) overseas; sample: $3.50 NZ); $4.00 (NZ) overseas. Back issues: First 5 vols available, at subscription price. Discounts: 33⅓% trade 2 or more copies 25% single copies, 20% on gross price for subsc. agencies. 112pp; 8½X6; of/lp. Reporting time: A.S.A.P. Payment: No set rate. Copyrighted, reverts to author. Pub's reviews: 26 in 1979. §Basically NZ fiction, verse, criticism. Ads: $60(NZ)/$38(NZ).

ISRAEL HORIZONS, Richard Yaffe, Editor; Yosef Gotlieb, Associate Editor; Arieh Lebowitz, Managing Editor, 150 Fifth Avenue, Room 1002, New York, NY 10011, (212) 255-8760. 1952. Poetry, articles, interviews, reviews, letters, news items. "Most of our articles are about 1,000 - 1,500 words in length. The magazine is a progressive/socialist Zionist monthly, dealing with: progressive forces in Israel, specifically MAPAM and the Kibbutz Artzi federation — but not *exclusively* these groups — and general articles about Israeli life and culture. We also deal with problems facing the world Jewish community, from a progressive/socialist Zionist perspective. Finally, we are also interested in bringing our readers general info that wouldn't make space in 'non-progressive' Jewish weekly and monthly periodicals." circ. 2,500. 10/yr. Pub'd 9 issues 1979; expects 10 issues 1980, 10 issues 1981. sub. price: $10.00; per copy: $1.25; sample: free. Back issues: $1.25, depending on availability. Discounts: ten subs for $80.00, student/limited income reduced rates; inquire. 32pp; 5¾X8¼; of. Payment: occasionally, up to $30.00; generally done *gratis* for exposure and experience. Pub's reviews: 10 in 1979. §Judaica, Middle Eastern Affairs, Socialist and other progressive political stuff, poetry, fiction, and other like material. Ads: $250.00/$150.00.

Ithaca House, Baxter Hathaway, Ilga Semeiks, John Latta, Lou Robinson, 108 N. Plain St, Ithaca, NY 14850, 607-272-1233. 1970. Poetry, fiction. "High-quality work, no trend or style or philosophy excluded. Books published under Ithaca House name." avg. press run 500. Pub'd 8 titles 1979; expects 4 titles 1980, 4 titles 1981. 76 titles listed in the *Small Press Record of Books in Print* (9th Edition, 1980). avg. price, paper: $4.00. Discounts: 1, 10 percent; 2-4, 20 percent; 5 or more, 40 percent. 64pp; 6X8½; †of/lp. Reporting time: 3 months. Payment: 10 copies. COSMEP.

Ithaca Press, Charles E. Jarvis, Paul Jarvis, P.O. Box 853, Lowell, MA 01853. 1974. Fiction, criticism. "*Visions of Kerouac; The Life of Jack Kerouac,* by Charles E. Jarvis. *Zeus Has Two Urns,* by Charles E. Jarvis. *The Tyrants* by Charles E. Jarvis, 1977, fiction, 5¼ x 8, 161 pp, SQPA, $2.95, The book is a socio-political novel of the United States in the era of the Great Depression" avg. press run 5,000. Pub'd 1 title 1979. 3 titles listed in the *Small Press Record of Books in Print* (9th Edition, 1980). avg. price, cloth: $7.95; paper: $3.45. Discounts: 40%. 220pp; 5½X8½; of. Copyrights for author. COSMEP, NESPA.

J

J&C Transcripts (see also DRAGONFLY:A Quarterly Of Haiku), L.E. Harr, Box 15, Kanona, NY 14856, 607-776-3709. 1963. Poetry, articles, reviews, letters. "Publishes *Jean's Journal* (Jean Calkins, Ed.), *Orphic Lute* (Viola Gardner, Ed.), and *Parnassus* (Monica Boyce, Ed.). L.E. Harr is Ed. of *Dragonfly* ." avg. press run 200. Pub'd 25 titles 1979; expects 25 titles 1980, 25 titles 1981. 37 titles listed in the *Small Press Record of Books in Print* (9th Edition, 1980). avg. price, paper: $2.00. 50pp; 5½X8½; †mi. Reporting time: 2 weeks. Payment: none. Copyrights for author.

J&J Publishing, John Taylor, Joy Taylor, PO Box 1105, Reseda, CA 91335, (213) 345-3797. 1980. Poetry, fiction, reviews, music. "Health, occult, children's" avg. press run 1,000. Pub'd 1 title 1979; expects 2 titles 1980, 5 titles 1981. 1 title listed in the *Small Press Record of Books in Print* (9th Edition, 1980). avg. price, paper: $5.95. Discounts: Bookstores, healthfood stores, librries, groups and organizations, trade, bulk. 180pp; 5½X8½; †of. Reporting time: 30 days. Payment: negotiated at time of acceptance. Copyrights for author. COSMEP.

The JG Press, Inc. (see also IN BUSINESS), James Ridgeway, Box 351, Emmaus, PA 18049, (215) 967-4135. 1979. avg. press run 5,000. Pub'd 1 title 1979; expects 1 title 1980. 1 title listed in the *Small Press Record of Books in Print* (9th Edition, 1980). avg. price, cloth: $14.95; paper: $9.95. 225pp; of.

JH Press, Terry Helbing, PO Box 294, Village Station, New York, NY 10014, 255-4713. 1979. Plays. "JH Press is a gay theatre publishing company, specializing in acting editions of gay plays. JH Press also handles the leasing rights for amateur productions of the plays. We have already published the *Gay Theatre Alliance Directory of Gay Plays,* compiled and edited and with an introduction by Terry

Helbing and over the coming months will be publishing play scripts by Doric Wilson, Arch Brown and other playwrights." avg. press run 1,000-2,000. Pub'd 1 title 1979; expects 2 titles 1980, 2 titles 1981. avg. price, paper: $3.00-$6.00. Discounts: 40% trade, 5 or more copies mixed titles. 144pp; 6X9; of. Reporting time: 2 weeks. Payment: % of retail sales to be negotiated. Copyrights for author. GPNY.

J and J Press, Jeffrey R. Brosbe, Julia M. Lueken, 2441 Montgomery Avenue, Cardiff-by-the-Sea, CA 92007, (714) 753-2053. 1978. Poetry, fiction. "New press dedicated to publishing previously undiscovered writers." avg. press run 1,000-2,000. Pub'd 1 title 1979. 1 title listed in the *Small Press Record of Books in Print* (9th Edition, 1980). avg. price, paper: $3.95. 75pp; 6X9; of, lp. Reporting time: 2-4 weeks. Copyrights for author.

The Jacek Publishing Company, Mike F. Holodnak, Author, 38 Morris Lane, Milford, CT 06460, 203-874-4544. 1976. Articles. "Has pub'd a selection of some of Holodnak's best *Brass Tacks* columns published in modern times from 1971 to 1976. Novel: *We Ain't Going Back No More, Nohow* by Mike F. Holodnak, 247 pages, $7.95, perfect bound, issued: 1977, 1,000 copies." avg. press run 1,000. Pub'd 1 title 1979. 2 titles listed in the *Small Press Record of Books in Print* (9th Edition, 1980). avg. price, cloth: $1.50; paper: $1.50. Discounts: 40 percent bulk, jobber, classroom. 47pp; 6X9; of. Copyrights for author. COSMEP, ASW (am. society of writers).

The Jackpine Press, A.R. Ammons, Gen. Ed.; Emily Wilson, Isabel Zuber, Betty Leighton, Ed. Board, 1878 Meadowbrook Drive, Winston-Salem, NC 27106. 1975. Poetry, fiction. "1st book: *Balancing On Stones,* poems by Emily Wilson. 2nd book: *Out In The Country, Back Home,* poems by Jeff Daniel Marion. *Orion,* poem by Jerald Bullis. *Sidetracks,* poems by Clint McCown. *A Walk With Raschid and Other Stories* by Josephine Jacobsen." avg. press run 1,000-1,500. Pub'd 1 title 1979; expects 1 title 1980. 5 titles listed in the *Small Press Record of Books in Print* (9th Edition, 1980). avg. price, cloth: $6.95; paper: $3.95. 70pp; 6X9; of. Reporting time: 2-3 months. Payment: separate arrangements with each author. copyright by author. COSMEP.

JACKSONVILLE POETRY QUARTERLY, Arcane Order, Dell Lebo, General Editor; William H. Cohen, Poetry Editor, 2904 Rosemary Lane, Falls Church, VA 22042. 1950. Poetry, art. "We publish only material by members: Virginia Cathey, Ed Crusoe IV, Evelyn Bell, Lorraine M. Albert, Lillian Johann, Jon Darling, etc." circ. over 1,010 members. 2-4/yr. Pub'd 2 issues 1979; expects 2-4 issues 1980, 2-4 issues 1981. sub. price: available to members only, gratis; per copy: $1.00-$2.00, members only; sample: $1.00-$2.00 members only. Back issues: Available to members at $1.00 to $2.00. Discounts: Distributed gratis to members. 2-10pp; 8½X11; †mi/of. We publish only material by members. No payment. Not copyrighted. §Poetry, satire. no advertising.

J'ADOUBE!, Cincinnati Chess Federation, David Moeser, Editor; Thomas Bender, Art Editor; Mark Peilen, Dan Doernberg, Fred Cramer, Contributing Editors, P O Box 30072, Cincinnati, OH 45230, 513-232-3204. 1972. Poetry, articles, art, photos, cartoons, interviews, satire, criticism, reviews, letters, news items. "ISSN number 0146-2202" circ. 300. 6/yr. Pub'd 8 issues 1979; expects 7 issues 1980, 8 issues 1981. sub. price: $4.00; per copy: $1.00; sample: $1.00. Back issues: $1.50 per issue if available. Discounts: none. 30pp; 8½X11; †mi. Reporting time: Variable. Payment: none-generally. Copyrighted, reverts to author. Pub's reviews: 10+ in 1979. §Chess. Ads: $9.00/$5.00/$0.03. COSMEP.

Jaffe Books, Santhamma Punnoose, Aymanathuparampil House, Kurichy P.O., Kottayam, Kerala, India. 1979. avg. press run 1,100. Pub'd 4 titles 1979. avg. price, cloth: $10.00. Discounts: 40%. lp. Reporting time: 3 months. Payment: 10 to 15%. Copyrights for author.

Jaks Publishing Co., James A. Kohl, PO Box 5625, 1106 N Washington Street, Helena, MT 59601, (406) 442-5486. 1979. Articles. avg. press run 3,000. 1 title listed in the *Small Press Record of Books in Print* (9th Edition, 1980). avg. price, paper: $10.00; other: $5.00. Discounts: 2-10, 25%; 10-49, 40%; 50-75, 45%; 76-199, 48%; 200 +, 50%. 88pp; 8½X11. Reporting time: 4 weeks. Payment: standard. Copyrights for author.

Jakubowsky, Frank Jakubowsky, Box 209, Oakland, CA 94604, (415) 763-4324. 1978. "Do not accept manuscripts. Published first book *Creation* in 1978. It is the story of the world written in poetry. I plan to publish my own books, but may consider on a cooperative basis titles on religion or astrology." avg. press run 1,000. Expects 1 title 1980, 2 titles 1981. 2 titles listed in the *Small Press Record of Books in Print* (9th Edition, 1980). avg. price, paper: $3.95. Discounts: 40% bookstores; 25% library. 100pp; 4X7; of. Do not accept manuscripts. Payment: Author financed. COSMEP, NAIRD.

Jalmar Press, Inc., Alvyn M. Freed, President; Margaret Freed, Vice-President, 6501 Elvas Ave, Sacramento, CA 95819, 916-451-2897. 1973. "Primarily interested in works in the humanistic area of psychology and books of general how-to interest.Have two series: *Transactional Analysis For Every-body, Warm Fuzzy Series* vol. 1. Claude Steiner, *A Warm Fuzzy Tale;* Dennis Look, *Joy Of Backpacking: People's Guide To The Wilderness;* Margaret DeHaan Freed, *A Time To Teach, A Time To Dance.* Vol. 1 Warm Fuzzy Series for children - average length, 60 pages with illustrations. Titles in *TA for Everybody Series* : Freed, Alvyn M. *TA for Tots* (and other prinzes); Freed, Alvyn & Margaret *TA for Kids* (and Grown-ups, too) 3rd edition newly revised and illustrated. Freed, Alvyn M. *TA for Teens* (and other important people); Novey, Theodore *TA for Management;* Freed, Alvyn M. *TA for Tots Coloring Book.*" avg. press run 10,000-25,000. Pub'd 4 titles 1979; expects 8 titles 1980. 19 titles listed in the *Small Press Record of Books in Print* (9th Edition, 1980). avg. price, cloth: $9.00; paper: $5.00. Discounts: yes. 200pp; 8X11; of. Reporting time: 2½ weeks. Payment: 4 percent - 15 percent. Copyrights for author. COS-MEP, WPA, NACM, ABA, NSSEA.

JAM TO-DAY, Don Stanford, Judith Stanford, Floyd Stuart, P.O. Box 249, Northfield, VT 05663. 1973. Poetry, fiction, art, photos, long-poems. "Interested in any style of poetry from traditional to avant garde. Also looking for high-quality fiction and will publish 1 fiction piece per issue if quality of submissions allows." circ. 400. 1-2/yr. Pub'd 1 issue 1979; expects 1 issue 1980, 1 issue 1981. sub. price: $4.75/2 issues; per copy: $2.50; sample: $2.50. Back issues: issues 1-4, $5.00 each; 5-6 $2.00 each; 7, $2.50. Discounts: 40% to bookstores. 64pp; 5½X8½; of. Reporting time: 3-6 weeks. Payment: $5.00/poem plus 2 copies of mag. Fiction rate $5.00 per printed page plus 2 copies of mag. Graphics and photos, $10.00 per page. Copyrighted, rights revert if requested. Pub's reviews: 1 in 1979. §poetry. Ads: $30.00/$20.00. CCLM, NESPA.

Jama Books, J. Magee Dugan, PO Box 30751, Santa Barbara, CA 93105, (805) 687-9325. 1979. Art, photos. avg. press run 5,000. Pub'd 1 title 1979. avg. price, cloth: $9.95; paper: $3.95. Discounts: Trade 40%; Bulk up to 50%; Library 20%. 60pp; 9X6; of.

JAMES JOYCE QUARTERLY, Academic Publications, Thomas F. Staley, University of Tulsa, 600 S. College, Tulsa, OK 74104. 1963. Articles, criticism, reviews. "Academic criticism of Joyce's works and of his critics; book reviews, notes, bibliographies; material relating to Joyce and Irish Renaissance and Joyce's relationship to other writers of his time. Articles should not normally exceed 20 pp. Notes should not excceed 6 pp. Please consult MLA *Style Sheet* and 'Special Note to Contributors' which appears on p.2 of each issue of the *JJQ* regarding style & preparation of manuscript." circ. 1,200. 4/yr. Pub'd 4 issues 1979; expects 4 issues 1980, 4 issues 1981. sub. price: $10.00 U.S.; $11.00 institutions and foreign; per copy: $3.00-U.S., $3.50-Foreign; sample: $3.00. Back issues: $2.25. 120pp; 6X9; of. Reporting time: 6-12 weeks. Payment: contributors' copies & offprints. Copyrighted. Pub's reviews: 11 in 1979. §Joyce studies. Ads: $100.00 ($135 includes copy of *JJQ* subscription list on set of self-adhesive address labels)/$60.00.

JANUS, Jeanne Gomoll, Janice Bogstad, PO Boxx 1624, Madison, WI 53701, 267-7483; 241-8445. 1975. Poetry, fiction, articles, art, photos, cartoons, interviews, satire, criticism, reviews, letters, collages. "5-10 double-spaced typed pages, articles, rviews, non-sexist, sf/feminist-oriented material. Twice nominated for international award: *hugo* for best amateur publication: 1978, 1979." circ. 1,000. 4/yr. Pub'd 3 issues 1979; expects 4 issues 1980, 4 issues 1981. sub. price: $6.00; per copy: $1.50; sample: $1.50. Back issues: $2.00 for available issues. Discounts: trade one-for-one. 40pp; 8½X11; of. Reporting time: 3 weeks. Payment: copy of issue contributor is printed. Copyrighted, reverts to author. Pub's reviews: 20 in 1979. §Science fiction, feminism, related.

Janus Press, Claire Van Vliet, Rt #2, West Burke, VT 05871. 1954. Art, poetry, fiction. "No unsolic-ited manuscripts please." avg. press run 75-300. Pub'd 7 titles 1979; expects 7 titles 1980, 5 titles 1981. 3 titles listed in the *Small Press Record of Books in Print* (9th Edition, 1980). avg. price, cloth: $30.00; paper: $15.00; other: Artists books 100-450. Discounts: Standing order 30%; Trade 20%; 5 copies 30%; 10 copies 40%. 32pp; 7X10; †lp. Payment: 10%. Copyrights for author.

Jawbone Press, Samuel Green, Editor; Sara Birtch, Assistant Editor, 17023 5th Avenue NE, Seattle, WA 98155. 1975. Poetry. "New Chapbooks and pamphlets by Mark Halperin, Howard Aaron, David Brewster, and Robert Hedin. Our first full-length book published in November '79, by Melinda Mueller. Current commitments and available funds make it necessary to continue manuscript-by-solicitation-only policy. This is absolute." avg. press run 500/1,000. Pub'd 5 titles 1979; expects 2 titles 1980, 2 titles 1981. 18 titles listed in the *Small Press Record of Books in Print* (9th Edition, 1980). avg. price, cloth: $10.00; paper: $3.00-$4.00. Discounts: None. 36/54pp; size varies; of. solicitation only. Payment: copies, 10% of run. Copyrights for author. None.

JAZZ, Jazz Press, George Fuller, 3650 W Pico, Los Angeles, CA 90019. 1974. Poetry, fiction, articles, art, photos, parts-of-novels, long-poems, collages, plays, concrete art. "*Jazz* is a 'multi-lingual' journal, printing both the original tongue of a piece, and an English translation. We also print a wide selection of work originally in English. Recent contributors: Vicente Aleixandre/Stephen Kessler (tr.); Jean Genet/Jeremy Reed (tr.); George Hitchcock; Colette Inez; Ann Lauterbach; Shelley Spencer (graphics)-" circ. 1,000. 2/yr. Pub'd 2 issues 1979; expects 2 issues 1980, 2 issues 1981. sub. price: $6.00; per copy: $3.00; sample: inquire. Back issues: inquire. Discounts: 60/40 to bookstores, dealers; $11.00 two year subscription rate. 80pp; 7X10; †of. Reporting time: 2 to 4 weeks. Payment: copies (2). Copyrighted, reverts to author. Ads: no ads. CCLM, CAC.

Jazz Press (see also JAZZ), George Fuller, Shelley Spencer, 3650 W Pico, Los Angeles, CA 90019, (213) 821-2889. 1976. Poetry, fiction, art, photos, long-poems, collages, plays. avg. press run 500-1,000. Pub'd 2 titles 1979; expects 2 titles 1980, 2 titles 1981. 1 title listed in the *Small Press Record of Books in Print* (9th Edition, 1980). avg. price, paper: $3.00. Discounts: 60/40 to bookstores, dealers; others inquire. 64-100pp; 7X10; †of. Reporting time: 2 weeks to 1 month. Payment: Inquire. Copyrights for author. CCLM.

JC/DC Cartoons Ink, Jack Corbett, Dawn Corbett, 5536 Fruitland Rd NE, Salem, OR 97301, 585-6161. 1979. Cartoons. "We are currently looking at cartoon *gags*." avg. press run 3,000. Expects 1 title 1981. avg. price, paper: $3.95. Discounts: 5-9 books (20%), 10-24 books (30%), 25-49 books (40%), 50-99 books (46%), 100 or more (50%). 127pp; 5½X8½; †of. Payment: 25% of price paid for cartoon when sold. COSMEP.

Jelm Mountain Publications, Jean R. Jones, Editor & Owner, 304 So. 3rd Street, Laramie, WY 82070, 307-742-8053. 1977. Poetry, fiction, art, photos, plays. "A prime interest is Western, especially Rocky Mt. area, history and folktales or 1st person accounts of early day life. Will look at anything-in any classification or category. Critique and advise potential market for materials we can't use-for a small fee." avg. press run 500-1,000. Pub'd 3 titles 1979; expects 3-5 titles 1980, 3-5 titles 1981. 13 titles listed in the *Small Press Record of Books in Print* (9th Edition, 1980). avg. price, cloth: $6.00-$8.00; paper: $3.00-$5.00. Discounts: 30% to agents and bookstores for quantities. 80-100pp; 5X8, 8½X11; of/lp. Reporting time: 2 to 3 weeks. Payment: variable. Does not copyright for author. COSMEP.

JEOPARDY, Western Washington University, Western Washington University, Humanities 350, WWU, Bellingham, WA 98225. 1966. Poetry, fiction, art, photos, long-poems, plays. "1) prefer poetry of no more than 3 single spaced, legal-paper pages in length. 2) prefer stories of no more than 10 single spaced, legal-paper pages in length. 3) open to nearly any style, with the possible bias against Haiku. 4) recent well known contributors: William Stafford, James Bertolino, Ron Bayes, Daniel Halpern, Joyce Odam, Madeline DeFrees, Richard Hugo, R.H.W. Dillard, Al Young, Beth Bentley, Annie Dillard." circ. 2,500. 1/yr. sub. price: $1.00; per copy: $1.00; sample: $1.00. Back issues: $1.00. 120pp; size varies; of. Reporting time: as long as 4 months. Payment: none. CCLM, COSMEP.

Jewel Publications, Jerome A. Welch, 2417 Hazelwood Ave., Fort Wayne, IN 46805, 219-483-6625. 1977. "Publishes one book: *CATHOLICISM TODAY*" avg. press run 1,000. Pub'd 1 title 1979. 1 title listed in the *Small Press Record of Books in Print* (9th Edition, 1980). avg. price, cloth: $7.95; paper: $6.95. Discounts: 2-4 books, 20%; 5-24, 40%; 25-49, 43%; 50 or more, 46%. 316pp; 5½X8½; of.

JOE SOAP'S CANOE, Syntaxophone Publications, Martin Stannard, 298 High Road, Trimley St. Martin, Ipswich, Suff, England. 1978. Poetry, fiction, articles, art, photos, criticism, reviews, letters, parts-of-novels, long-poems. "Poetry of any length considered. Non-academic bias. Recent Contributors include: Breton, Reverdy, Jim Burns, Cory Harding, Dersley, Mallin,Grubb, Ian McMillan, Lovelock, Bay." circ. 400. 2/yr. Pub'd 2 issues 1979; expects 2 issues 1980, 2 issues 1981. sub. price: £2.00 for 3 issues (USA $6.00); per copy: 50p plus postage; sample: 50p plus postage. Back issues: issue 3 - 30p plus postage. Discounts: 40% on 5 copies or more. 48pp; size A5; of. Reporting time: 3 to 6 weeks. Payment: copies only at present. Copyrighted. Pub's reviews. §Any. Ads: £20/£10/negotiable. ALP.

John Muir Publications, Inc., Ken Luboff, Eve Muir, Paul Abrams, P.O. Box 613, Santa Fe, NM 87501, 505-982-4078. 1969. "non-fiction" avg. press run 5,000-10,000. Pub'd 4 titles 1979; expects 6 titles 1980, 6 titles 1981. 13 titles listed in the *Small Press Record of Books in Print* (9th Edition, 1980). avg. price, cloth: $8.00; paper: $6.00. Discounts: 40-50 percent. 300pp; 8½X11, 6X9; of. Reporting time: 4-6 weeks. Payment: by individual contract. Does not copyright for author. COSMEP, ABA.

"JOINT" CONFERENCE, King Publications, Kathryn E. King, Editor and Publisher, P.O. Box 19332, Washington, DC 20036, 202-234-1681. 1974. Poetry, fiction, articles, art, cartoons. "This is an inmate-written literary magazine and I accept material *ONLY* from inmates. I'd like to receive more work by women. There will be a short story contest again in 1980. Recent contributors: David L. Rice, Carl L. Harp, Michael Hogan, Daniel L. Klauck, John P. Minarik, and John L. Natkie." circ. 250. irregular. Pub'd 1 issue 1979; expects 2 issues 1980, 2 issues 1981. sub. price: $6.00, $3.00 for inmates; per copy: $2.00; sample: $2.00. Back issues: $2.00. Discounts: 40% to libraries and bookstores. 60-64pp; 6X9; of. Reporting time: variable. Payment: $3.00-$30.00 plus copy. Copyrighted, reverts to author upon request. Pub's reviews: 14 in 1979. §Books by inmates and anthologies of inmate work. Ads: $30.00/$15.00. CCLM, COSMEP, COSMEP-SOUTH.

Journal Books (see also THE NEW JOURNAL), Richard A. Bodien, Editor,Publisher, 704 Baylor Street, Austin, TX 78703. 1976. avg. press run 200. Pub'd 1 title 1979; expects 1 title 1980, 1 title 1981. avg. price, paper: $3.00. Discounts: customary. pp varies; size varies.

JOURNAL OF ALTERNATIVE HUMAN SERVICES, Lincoln Cushing, Community Congress of S.D., 1172 Morena Blvd, San Diego, CA 92110, (714) 275-1700. 1974. Poetry, articles, interviews, reviews, letters. "Articles 10-20 double spaced, typewritten pages. Orientation toward program description and training in human services (drug rehabilitation, counselling, battered women, etc.) though do accept analytic/theoretical pieces" circ. 2,000. Quarterly. Pub'd 4 issues 1979; expects 4 issues 1980, 4 issues 1981. sub. price: $10/yr students & low income, $12/yr indiv, $18/yr instit; per copy: $3.00; sample: $2.50. Back issues: $2.50. Discounts: on request. 36pp; 8½X11; †of. Reporting time: short. Payment: none. Not copyrighted. Pub's reviews: 50 in 1979. §human services, counseling, community development. Ads: on request.

JOURNAL OF BIOLOGICAL EXPERIENCE, Center Press, Ian J. Grand, General Editor, 2045 Francisco Street, Berkeley, CA 94709, (415) 526-8373. 1978. Poetry, articles, interviews, reviews. " *The Journal* is devoted to the understanding and appreciation of the bodily life. It publishes Studies that address our emotional, intellectual, and aesthetic experience, social interaction, and the sense of the sacred. *The Journal* is primarily concerned with the development of a language of biological process, thought, and educational practices that embrace the diversity of our bodily experience. Some recent contributors: Stanley Keleman, Alexander Lowen, Robert Duncan, Michael McClure." circ. 1,000. 2/yr. Pub'd 1 issue 1979; expects 2 issues 1980, 2 issues 1981. sub. price: $9.00; per copy: $5.00. Back issues: $5.00. Discounts: 30%. 80-100pp; 6X9; †of. Reporting time: 2 months. Copyrighted. Pub's reviews. §Somatic studies, psychology and the body, psychophyiology, literature related to biological experience.

JOURNAL OF BORDERLAND RESEARCH, Borderland Sciences Research Foundation, Riley Hansard Crabb, P.O. Box 549, Vista, CA 92083, 724-2043. 1945. Articles, photos, reviews, news items. "Metaphysical and occult interpretation of the news, science and religion in articles two to five pages long, by the Associates and from the news and magazine articles sent in as relevant to our search for truth. Our journal is supported entirely by membership/subscriptions, donations and sales of literature and lecture tapes. No advertising." circ. 500. published every two months. Pub'd 6 issues 1979; expects 6 issues 1980, 6 issues 1981. sub. price: $10.00; per copy: $2.00; sample: $2.00. Back issues: $2.00 each. Discounts: none. 36pp; 8½X11; †of. Reporting time: a few days. Payment: none. Not copyrighted. Pub's reviews: 10 in 1979. §occult, flying saucers, parapsychology.

JOURNAL OF CALIFORNIA AND GREAT BASIN ANTHROPOLOGY, Malki Museum Press, Philip Wilke, Editor; Harry W. Lawton, Managing Editor; James Swenson, Assistant Editor, Department of Anthroplogy, University of California, Riverside, CA 92521, 714-787-3885. 1974. Articles. "Papers on ethnology, ethnohistory, archaeology, and linquistics of the Native Americans ofthe Great Basin and California and Baja California. Editorial offices for manuscripts is in care of the Department of Anthropology, University of California, Riverside, California 92521. If you can only use one address use this one. The business address above is for the publisher, Malki Museum, Inc., a non-profit educational institution on the Morongo Indian Reservation. The journal is published by Malki Museum Press in cooperation with the Department of Anthropology at the University of California, Riverside. Renewals or new subscriptions by individuals after July 1 of any year are billed at 2 rate of $17.00." circ. 900. 2/yr. Pub'd 2 issues 1979; expects 2 issues 1980. sub. price: $12.00 Individual - $15.00 Institutions up to July 1.; per copy: $6.50; sample: $5.00. Back issues: $5.00 plus postage. Discounts: None. 160pp; 8X10½; of. Reporting time: 2 months. Payment: none. Copyrighted, rights revert to author where authorized by the Editorial Board. Pub's reviews: 26 in 1979. §only books on California Indians (or mags). Ads: $90.00/$50.00.

JOURNAL OF CANADIAN FICTION, Bellrock Press, John R. Sorfleet, Managing Ed., 2050 Mackay Street, Montreal, Quebec H3G 2J1, Canada. 1972. Fiction, criticism, reviews. "*Primary* focus is *Canadian* fiction & criticism & reviews thereof." circ. 1,500. 4/yr. Pub'd 4 issues 1979; expects 4 issues 1980. sub. price: $12.00 plus $2.00 postage outside Canada; per copy: $4.00 plus $0.50 postage outside Canada; sample: $4.00 plus $0.50 postage outside Canada. Discounts: 10% to agencies. 175pp; 5X8; of. Reporting time: 3-6 months. Payment: $100.00/stories, $10.00/reviews. Copyrighted, reverts to author. Pub's reviews: 30 in 1979. §Fiction, criticism of fiction writers. Ads: $75/$50. CPPA.

JOURNAL OF CANADIAN POETRY, Frank M. Tierney, W. Glenn Clever, PO Box 5147, Station

F, Ottawa K2C 3H4, Canada, (613) 224-6837. 1976. Criticism, reviews. "Concerned solely with criticism and reviews of Canadian poetry. Does *not* publish poetry per se." circ. 500. 2/yr. Pub'd 1 issue 1979; expects 2 issues 1980, 2 issues 1981. sub. price: $7.50; per copy: $4.50; sample: $2.00. Back issues: $4.00. Discounts: Book wholesalers 20%. 75pp; 5 1/2X8 1/2; †of. Reporting time: 4 months. Copyrighted, reverts to author.

JOURNAL of CANADIAN STUDIES/Revue d'etudes canadiennes, Trent University, Ralph R. Heintzman, Trent Univ., Peterborough, Ont., Canada. 1966. Articles, criticism, reviews. circ. 1,600. 4/yr. Pub'd 4 issues 1979. sub. price: $10.00, individuals/yr; $20.00, institution; per copy: $4.-00/$6.00. Back issues: $3.00 prior to 1977 — $6.00 after. Discounts: 15%. 120pp; 7½X10; of. Pub's reviews: 3 in 1979. Ads: $200.00/$125.00.

THE JOURNAL OF COMMONWEALTH LITERATURE, Prof A.J. Gurr, School of English, Univ. of Leeds, Leeds LS2 9JT, United Kingdom. 1965. Articles, reviews, interviews. "Maximum length for articles: 4000 words. Oxford style. Published by: Hans Zell Publishers Ltd., 14 a St. Giles, PO Box 56, Oxford, OX1 3EL, England, United Kingdom" circ. 1M. 3/yr. sub. price: £3.50/sub; £1.70/third bibliographic issue; per copy: 95p. Discounts: agents 10%. 100pp; 5½X8½; lp. Reporting time: 2-3 mos. Payment: £4/100 words, articles; £3/100 words, reviews.

JOURNAL OF THE HELEN VALE FOUNDATION, The Helen Vale Foundation, Shri Vijayadev Yogendra, 12 Chapel Street, St Kilda, Victoria 3182, Australia, (03) 51-9861. 1977. Articles, interviews, reviews. circ. 2,500. 4/yr. Pub'd 2 issues 1979; expects 2 issues 1980, 2 issues 1981. sub. price: A$8; per copy: A$4. Back issues: A$1.50. Discounts: 40% wholesaler. 56pp; 5½X8½; †of. Reporting time: 2 weeks. Copyrighted. AIPA.

JOURNAL OF THE HELLENIC DIASPORA, Pella Publ. Co, D Georgakas, P Kitromilides, P Pappas, Y Roubatis, P Craig, 461 Eighth Ave, New York, NY 10001, 212-279-9586. 1974. Poetry, fiction, articles, art, photos, cartoons, interviews, satire, criticism, reviews, music, parts-of-novels, long-poems, collages, plays. "The magazine is concerned with the entire spectrum of scholarly, critical, and artistic work that is based on contemporary Greece. It is now under new editorial direction and has a new and expanded format." circ. 300-500. 4/yr. Pub'd 4 issues 1979; expects 4 issues 1980, 4 issues 1981. sub. price: $8.00; per copy: $2.50; sample: $2.50. Back issues: $3.00. 96-112pp; 5½X8; †lp. Reporting time: 4 weeks. Payment: 25 offprints for articles. Copyrighted, reverts to author. Pub's reviews: 10 in 1979. §Modern Greek studies and affairs. Ads: $100.00/$50.00. COSMEP.

JOURNAL OF IRISH LITERATURE, Proscenium Press, Robert Hogan, P O Box 361, Newark, DE 19711, (215) 255-4083. 1972. Poetry, fiction, articles, art, photos, cartoons, interviews, satire, criticism, reviews, letters, parts-of-novels, long-poems, plays. "Obviously work by or about Irish or Irish-American writers." circ. 750. 3/yr. Pub'd 3 issues 1979; expects 3 issues 1980, 3 issues 1981. sub. price: $10.00; per copy: $3.50; sample: $3.50. Back issues: $5.00. Discounts: 20%. 150-200pp; 5½X8½; lp. Reporting time: 1 month or more, sometimes much more. Payment: none. Copyrighted, reverts to author. Pub's reviews: 31 in 1979. §Irish writing. Ads: $200.00/$100.00.

JOURNAL OF MODERN LITERATURE, Maurice Beebe, Editor-in-Chief, Temple Univ., Philadelphia, PA 19122. 1970. Articles, interviews, criticism, reviews. circ. 2,200. 4/yr. Pub'd 4 issues 1979; expects 4 issues 1980, 4 issues 1981. sub. price: $10.00 individuals; $12.00 institutions; per copy: $3.00 reg, $4.00 annual review bibliography; sample: free. Back issues: $3.00 regular; $4.00 annual review. Discounts: 10% for agencies. 160pp; 7X10; of. Reporting time: 6 wks. Payment: $100 articles; $50 short notes. Copyrighted, does not revert to author. Pub's reviews. §critical and scholarly works only. no ads. COSMEP.

JOURNAL OF NARRATIVE TECHNIQUE, George Perkins, Barbara Perkins, English Dept, Eastern Michigan University, Ypsilanti, MI 48197, (313) 487-0151. 1970. Criticism. "JNT is a scholarly magazine with international circulation. Essays run generally from 15 to 30 typed pages. Contributors should follow MLA style." circ. 550. 3/yr. Pub'd 3 issues 1979; expects 3 issues 1980, 3 issues 1981. sub. price: $6.00; per copy: $2.00; sample: free. Back issues: $2.00. 75pp; 6X9; of. Reporting time: 1-4 mos. Payment: copies only. Copyrighted, reverts to author.

JOURNAL OF NEW JERSEY POETS, A. Decavalles, V. Halpert, Managing Editor; M. Keyishian, W Zander, Fairleigh Dickinson Univ., English Dept., 285 Madison Avenue, Madison, NJ 07940, 01-377-4700. 1976. Poetry, reviews. "Open to submission of poetry from present and past residents of New Jersey; no biases concerning style or subject. Review of books by New Jersey poets." circ. 300. 2/yr. Pub'd 2 issues 1979; expects 2 issues 1980. 2 titles listed in the *Small Press Record of Books in Print* (9th Edition, 1980). sub. price: $3.00; per copy: $1.50; sample: $1.00. Back issues: $1.00. Discounts: 40 percent. 40pp; 8½X11; †of. Reporting time: 1-4 months. Payment: 2 copies. Copyrighted, reverts to author. Pub's reviews: 2 in 1979. §Poetry, books about poetry.

JOURNAL OF PSYCHEDELIC DRUGS, Stash, Inc., Marsha Bishop, E. Leif Zerkin, M.D. David E. Smith, 118 South Bedford Street, Madison, WI 53703, 608-251-4200. 1967. Articles, art, photos. "The *Journal of Psychedelic Drugs* is a cooperative effort of Stash and the Haight-Ashbury Free Medical Clinic. Designed as a multidisciplinary forum for the study of drugs and the drug culture, every issue features a variety of articles by noted researchers and theorists (e.g., Andrew Weil, Howard Becker)." circ. 3,000. 4/yr. Pub'd 4 issues 1979; expects 4 issues 1980, 4 issues 1981. sub. price: $30-40; per copy: $5.00; sample: $5.00. Back issues: $5.00 each while supply lasts. 100pp; 8½X11; of. Reporting time: 60-90 days on articles; 30 days on art for cover or book reviews. Copyrighted, does not revert to author. Pub's reviews: 4 in 1979. §Drug-related topics. Ads: $210.00/$120.00.

THE JOURNAL of PSYCHOHISTORY, Psychohistory Press, David Beisel, Editor, 2315 Broadway, NY, NY 10024, 212-873-3760. 1973. Articles, reviews. "Psychohistory of individuals and groups, history of childhood and family." circ. 3000. 4/yr. Pub'd 4 issues 1979. sub. price: $18.00/individual $28.00 organization; per copy: $4.50; sample: $4.50. Back issues: $6.00. Discounts: 10% agency. 150pp; 7X9; of. Reporting time: 2 weeks. Payment: none. Copyrighted, does not revert to author. Pub's reviews: 40 in 1979. §psychology & history. Ads: $150/$90.

THE JOURNAL OF PSYCHOLOGICAL ANTHROPOLOGY, Psychohistory Press, Arthur Hippler, Editor, 2315 Broadway, New York, NY 10024, 212-873-3760. 1978. Articles, reviews, news items. circ. 2,000. 4/yr. Pub'd 4 issues 1979; expects 4 issues 1980, 4 issues 1981. sub. price: $18/indiv, $28/instit; per copy: $4.50; sample: $4.50. Back issues: $6.00. Discounts: 10%. 100pp; 7X9; of. Reporting time: 2 weeks. Copyrighted, does not revert to author. §psychiatry, anthropology. Ads: $150/$90.

JOURNAL OF SOCIAL RECONSTRUCTION, Earl M Coleman Enterprises, Inc, Marcus Raskin, PO Box 143, Pine Plains, NY 12067. 1980. Articles, reviews. "A bewildering crisis of knowledge, politics, and social organization grips the world. *The Journal of Social Reconstruction* is a tiny searchlight in the effort to understand this crisis." 4/yr. sub. price: Instit. $39.50; Indiv. $19.50; per copy: $12.50; sample: free. Back issues: $12.50. Discounts: 10% agents & jobbers, for others contact publisher. 100pp; 6X9; of. Reporting time: 4 weeks. Payment: none. Copyrighted, does not revert to author. Pub's reviews. Ads: $200.00.

JOURNAL OF SOUTH ASIAN LITERATURE, Asian Studies Center, Carlo Coppola, Surjit Dulai, Mich State Univ, Asian Studies Ctr., E. Lansing, MI 48823, 517-353-1680. 1964. Poetry, fiction, articles, interviews, satire, criticism, reviews, parts-of-novels, long-poems, plays. circ. 300. 2/yr. Pub'd 2 issues 1979. sub. price: $14.00-$20.00; per copy: $7.00-$10.00. Back issues: $2.50-$7.00. Discounts: none. 200-400pp; 6X9; of. Reporting time: 2 wks. Copyrighted. Pub's reviews. §South Asian. CCLM.

JOURNAL OF SPORT PSYCHOLOGY, Human Kinetics Pub. Inc., Daniel M. Landers, Box 5076, Champaign, IL 61820, 217-351-5076. 1975. Articles, reviews. "Scholarly journals." circ. 850. 4/yr. Pub'd 4 issues 1979. sub. price: $16.00; per copy: $5.00; sample: free. Back issues: $5.00. Discounts: 5%. 96pp; 6X9; of. Reporting time: 2 months. Copyrighted. Pub's reviews. §Sport, sport science, physical education. Ads: $150.00/$90.00.

JOURNAL OF SUPERSTITION AND MAGICAL THINKING, Editorial Research Service, Laird M. Wilcox, P.O.Box 1832, Kansas City, MO 64141, (913) 342-6768. 1978. Articles, interviews, reviews, letters, news items. "Dedicated to critical and rational examination of the claims of spokesmen and prcatitioners of the occult and paranormal. Emphasis on debunking and expose of fraudulent and unproven claims" circ. 285. 2/yr. Pub'd 2 issues 1979; expects 2 issues 1980, 2 issues 1981. sub. price: $12.00; per copy: $6.00. Back issues: $6.00 per issue. 48pp; 8½X11; of. Reporting time: 30 days. Payment: yes. Copyrighted, reverts to author. Pub's reviews: 0 in 1979. §Occult, paranormal, superstition, magical thinking, parapsychology, ESP, UFO's.

JOURNAL OF THE WEST, Sunflower University Press, Robin Higham, Editor & President, Box 1009, Manhattan, KS 66502, (913) 532-6733 or (913) 539-3668. 1962. Articles, reviews. "We solicit our own articles and reviews, but will consider articles submitted from outside." circ. 4,500. 4/yr. Pub'd 4 issues 1979; expects 4 issues 1980, 4 issues 1981. sub. price: $22.00-$27.00; per copy: $8.00; sample: Free. Back issues: Handled by Kraus. Discounts: 25% on a no-returns basis and we pay shipping. 120pp; 7⅜X9¾; †of. Reporting time: 3 months. Payment: 10 copies of issue. Copyrighted, does not revert to author. Pub's reviews: 160 in 1979. §The West, all angles. Ads: $250.00/$150.00/Fillers $30.00.

Journalism Laboratory Press (see SHENANDOAH)

Journey Publications, Kent Babcock, PO Box 3567, Santa Rosa, CA 95402, 707-539-1659. 1976. avg. press run 3,000-5,000. Pub'd 2 titles 1979; expects 4 titles 1980, 1 title 1981. avg. price, cloth: $8.95;

paper: $3.95. 125pp; 5½X8½; †of. Payment: contract. Copyrights for author. COSMEP.

Joy Woods Press, Andrea Granahan, PO Box 25, Bodega, CA 94922, (707) 874-3064.

JOYCEAN LIVELY ARTS GUILD REVIEW, Pakka Press, Elaine Sughrue, Jack Sughrue, Box 459, East Douglas, MA 01516, (617) 476-7630. 1972. Poetry, reviews. "All poetry must be contained on single sheets (typed or xeroxed), batches of 3, reprints are perfectly acceptable (Give credits!); we do own reviews; line drawings smaller than 5 x 7 acceptable (We can't reduce.) reprints or xerox." circ. 600-1,000. 4/yr. Pub'd 4 issues 1979; expects 4 issues 1980, 4 issues 1981. sub. price: $3.00; per copy: $0.75; sample: $1.00. Back issues: all our back issues given to libraries, workshops, etc. Discounts: 25 copies or more $0.50 @, plus 4th-class postage. 40pp; 5X7; †of. Reporting time: 3 months. Payment: issue in which work appears. Copyrighted, reverts to author. Pub's reviews: 43 in 1979. §Poetry, fiction, all small-press stuff. COSMEP, NESPA, SPRIL.

Joyful Press (formerly: T. I Opportunities), Joyce Groscop, Tom Groscop, 9013 Long Point Road, Houston, TX 77055, (713) 467-4711; 465-3131. 1978. Articles, satire, plays. "1st book: Dec. 1978 — title: *Dining With Joy* by Joyce and Tom Groscop now in second printing." avg. press run 1,000. Pub'd 1 title 1979; expects 1 title 1980. avg. price, paper: $3.00. Discounts: Retailer 40%, Distributor 60%. 34pp; 5½X8½; of. Reporting time: 3 months. Payment: negotiable.

Judaic Book Service (see HOLY BEGGARS' GAZETTE; TZADDIKIM)

JUICE, Stephen Morse, Judy Brekke, 1015 Rose Avenue, Oakland, CA 94611, 415-532-5621. 1970. Poetry, fiction, art, photos, cartoons, interviews, satire, criticism, reviews, music, parts-of-novels, long-poems, plays. "No length limits. Recent issues have been primarily poetry & fiction, but we're open. Tend to like poetry as written and influenced by R. Creeley, R. Bly, James Tate, W. S. Merwin, T. Roethke, C. Simic, etc., mostly contemporary and suspicious of verse. Recent contributors: Emilie Glen, Susan Fromberg Schaeffer, Hugh Fox, Nellie Hill, Jared Smith, Dadda Dadio, Steve Richmond, Peter Payack, Nila NorthSun, Tony Moffeit. Looking for poetry with energy, not overly fond of doom/gloom political poems, though quality anything has a good chance at Juice. New people welcome—We don't even look at the name 'til we've read the submission." circ. 900. 2/yr. Pub'd 2 issues 1979; expects 2 issues 1980. sub. price: $5.00; per copy: $3.00; sample: $2.00. Back issues: $3.00 except Juice 1, 1975 which is $5.00. Discounts: 40% classrooms or orders of 10 or more. 48pp; size varies; of. Reporting time: 4 weeks. Payment: 2 copies. Copyrighted. Pub's reviews. §Poetry, fiction, art. CCLM.

Jules Verne Circle (see also JULES VERNE VOYAGER), F. James, Editor, 125 Markyate Road, Dagenham, Essex RM82LB, England. 1977/78. Poetry, fiction, articles, art, photos, cartoons, interviews, satire, criticism, reviews, music, letters, parts-of-novels, long-poems, collages, plays, concrete art, news items, non-fiction. "Research and scholarship on and about Jules Verne and pioneers of SF." avg. press run 100. avg. price, paper: $5.00. Discounts: Agents 20 percent. 10pp; size A5; †of. Reporting time: 6 months. Pays in copies. Copyrights for author.

JULES VERNE VOYAGER, Jules Verne Circle, F. James, Editor, 125 Markyate Road, Dagenham, Essex RM82LB, England. 1977/78. Poetry, fiction, articles, art, photos, cartoons, interviews, satire, criticism, reviews, music, letters, parts-of-novels, long-poems, collages, plays, concrete art, news items, non-fiction. "Research and scholarship on and about Verne and his life works, times, contemporaries, influences, inc SF." circ. 100. sub. price: $5.00 pa. Discounts: Agents 20 percent. 10pp; size A5 upright; †of. Reporting time: 6 months. Pays in copies. Copyrighted. Pub's reviews. Ads: $15.00 pro rata.

JUMP CUT, A Review of Contemporary Cinema, John Hess, Chuck Kleinhans, Julia Lesage, P.O. Box 865, Berkeley, CA 94701, 415-548-1507. 1974. Articles, art, photos, cartoons, interviews, criticism, reviews, letters. "Interested in commercial and independent film since 1970. Length as needed to make points, but shorter preferred; we strive for clarity in style. Biased to radical criticism, esp. Marxist and feminist. No cute and superficial reviews. Strongly suggest reading an issue before submission. Send sase for 'Notice to Writers'." circ. 4,000. irreg. Pub'd 2 issues 1979; expects 3 issues 1980. sub. price: $6.00-Canada & abroad $8.00; $9.00 & $ll.00 insti.; per copy: $1.25; Canada & abroad $1.50; sample: $1.25; Canada & abroad $1.50. Back issues: Nos. 1 & 2,6,7,8 sold out. $1.50 ($1.25 with a sub); Canada & abroad $1.75 ($1.50 with sub). Also they are available from [Xerox International Microfilm]. Discounts: Institutional rate is $9.00; Canada & abroad $ll.00; Agency discount is 10 percent. 36-40pp; 16½X10¼; of. Reporting time: 3 wks-3 mos. Payment: copies. contributor may retain c-right. Pub's reviews: 6 in 1979. §On the subjects of film and marxist culture and criticism. Ads: $250/$125. COSMEP.

Jump River Press, Inc. (see also JUMP RIVER REVIEW), Mark Bruner, 819 Single Avenue, Wausau, WI 54401, (715) 842-8243. 1979. Poetry, fiction, satire, criticism, long-poems, plays, concrete art. "All thematic concerns and stylistic forms are welcome. We are especially interested in myth, legend, folklore, folklife, ritualism, heritage, although these are not exclusive interests. We will be doing chapbooks, broadsides and post cards. Query if specifically interested in either of these projects. We answer promptly and *try* to give individual criticism on manuscripts submitted." avg. press run 200-500. Pub'd 4 titles 1979. 1 title listed in the *Small Press Record of Books in Print* (9th Edition, 1980). avg. price, paper: $1.00. Discounts: negotiable. 24pp; 5½X8½; †of. Reporting time: 1 week. Payment: copies (and in some instances 10% after costs are met. Copyrights for author.

JUMP RIVER REVIEW, Jump River Press, Inc., Mark Bruner, 819 Single Avenue, Wausau, WI 54401, (715)842-8243. 1979. Poetry, fiction, articles, art, interviews, satire, criticism, reviews, long-poems, plays, concrete art. "All thematic concerns and stylistic forms are welcome. We are especially interested in myth, legend, folklore, folklife, and ritualism, although these are not exclusive interests. Our objective is to reflect, through quality written art, the richness, complexity, and potency of both our heritage and our contemporary culture. We are a forum for both new and established writers. A portion of each issue will be devoted to our greatest cultural resource, high school and elementay aged writers. We try to respond promptly and with individual feedback." circ. 600. 4/yr. Pub'd 4 issues 1979. sub. price: $10.00; per copy: $2.50; sample: exchange or $2.50. Back issues: $2.50. Discounts: negotiable. 60pp; 5½X8½; †of. Reporting time: immediately to 2 weeks. Payment: copies and occassional cash awards. Copyrighted, reverts to author. Pub's reviews: 50 in 1979. §Poetry, myth, folklore, fiction, essays, criticism, drama, language games.

Jungle Garden Press, Marie C. Dern, 47 Oak Rd, Fairfax, CA 94930. 1973. Poetry, art. "Susan Efros, *Two-Way Streets*; Jana Harris, *This House That Rocks With Every Truck on the Road*; Russell Hill, *Letters From the Mines.* Jana Harris, *Pin Money*; Phyllis Koestenbaum, *Hunger Food.*" avg. press run 500. Pub'd 1 title 1979; expects 2 titles 1981. 2 titles listed in the *Small Press Record of Books in Print* (9th Edition, 1980). avg. price, paper: $4.00. 30-40pp; †lp. COSMEP.

Juniper Press (see also NORTHEAST/JUNIPER BOOKS), 1310 Shorewood Dr, La Crosse, WI 54601. Pub'd 8 titles 1979; expects 12 titles 1980. 46 titles listed in the *Small Press Record of Books in Print* (9th Edition, 1980). avg. price, cloth: $9.00; paper: $2.50-$4.00; other: $16.00. pp varies; size Varies; †lp/of. No submissions accepted without query first. Copyrights for author. None.

Just Buffalo Press (see also INC.), Bud Navero, Debora Daley, John Daley, 111 Elmwood Avenue, Buffalo, NY 14201, (716) 885-6400. 1975. Fiction, photos, interviews, parts-of-novels. "Just Buffalo Press publishes books by individuals, *Inc.*, a magazine of the literary arts, and limited edition silk-screened broadsides. Broadside writers include: Jerome Rothenberg, John Weiners, Ed Dorn, Maureen Owen, Alice Notley, Diane diPrima, Josephine Clare, John Daley, Ed Sanders, Anselm Hollo, Tom Clark, Joanne Kyger. Signed and unsigned sets and singles available." avg. press run 500. Pub'd 2 titles 1979. avg. price, paper: $2.00; other: $15 broadsides signed, unsigned $5. Discounts: 40% to the trade. 60pp; 5½X8½; of. Reporting time: varies. Payment: 10% of the print run to authors. Copyrights for author.

JUST PULP: The Magazine of Popular Fiction, Hidden People Press, Thomas R. Rankin, Ed-in-Chief; Stephen Strang, Fiction; Pat Leitch, Poetry, PO Box 243, Narragansett, RI 02882. 1976. Poetry, fiction, parts-of-novels, long-poems. "*Just Pulp* is devoted primarily to 'popular' and mainstream fiction by un or little known writers who will soom be 'breaking in' to the mass markets. Fiction limit: 15,000 words. Poetry limit: none. Bias: we expect clear, vibrant writing, well thought out plots and well told stories. In poetry we are looking for lucid and clear images/thoughts/concepts. Recent contributors: Jay Boyer, first publication, excerpt from detective novel to be published by Doubleday this year. Steve Vance, 2nd publication credit, 2 S.F. novels out now. Joe Schifino, first credit, house writer for *Fantasy Tales* (London) now." circ. 600. 4/yr. Pub'd 3 issues 1979; expects 2 issues 1980, 4 issues 1981. sub. price: $5.00; per copy: $1.50 + $0.50 postage; sample: $1.50 + $0.50 postage. Back issues: $1.00 each through Vol II #2, $1.50 each for subsequent issues. Discounts: 40% consignment, 50% 30 days net (no return). 92-100pp; 5¼X7½; †of. Reporting time: 1 week to 3 months. Payment: 1/4¢/wd for fiction, $5.00/poem. Copyrighted, reverts to author. Ads: open for exchange. NESPA, NESPD, COSMEP.

K

K-State Press (see EDUCATIONAL CONSIDERATIONS)

KALDRON, Karl Kempton, 441 North 6th St., Grover City, CA 93433, 805-481-2360. 1976. Poetry. "KALDRON is an international journal of visual poetry and language publishing ancient, middle ages and contemporary work, submissions are welcome but for a response must include self-addressed and stamped (correct postage) envelope." circ. 1,000. Pub'd 2 issues 1979; expects 3 issues 1980, 4 issues 1981. sub. price: donations taken; per copy: cost of postage-north am $.28; elsewhere $1.24; sample: North America $.28 stamp; elsewhere $1.24 stamp. 12-16pp; 11X18. Reporting time: 2 weeks to a month. Payment: 4 copies. copyright belongs to contributor. Pub's reviews: several in 1979. §Visual poetry, language art publications, line poetry. CCLM.

KALLIOPE, A Journal of Women's Art, Betty Bedell, Editor; Peggy Friedmann, Associate Editor, 101 W. State Street, Jacksonville, FL 32202, 904-633-8340. 1979. Poetry, fiction, articles, art, photos, interviews, criticism, reviews, music. "*Kalliope* celebrates women in the arts by publishing their work and providing a medium of communication through which they may share ideas and opinions. Our issues to date have included interviews with poets Denise Levertov and Tess Gallagher; photographs by Judith Gefter; sculpture by Margaret Koscielny; drawings by Louise Brown; the craft work of Memphis Wood; poems by Paula Rankin, Ruth Moon Kempher, and Naomi Shihab Nye; and fiction by Janice Eidus, and others. Our summer 1980 issue features an interview with poet Gwendolyn Brooks and an interview with and photographs by Evon Streetman." circ. 1,000. 3-4/yr. Pub'd 3 issues 1979; expects 3u issues 1980. sub. price: $7.50; per copy: $2.50; sample: $2.50. Back issues: $2.50 no specials. 72-80pp; 6X9; of. Reporting time: 2 months. Payment: copies. Copyrighted, reverts to author. Pub's reviews. §Women in the arts. COSMEP.

Kangam, David M. Carson, PO Box 3354, Kansas City, KS 66103, (816) 931-1344. 1979. Fiction, cartoons, satire. "Science fiction is preferred." avg. press run 250. Pub'd 2 titles 1979. avg. price, paper: $3.00. Discounts: 40% bulk. 110pp; 5X7; of. Reporting time: 1 month. Payment: monthly payment, royalty negotiable. Copyrights for author. COSMEP.

KANSAS QUARTERLY, Harold W. Schneider, Ben Nyberg, W.R. Moses, Denison Hall, Kansas St. Univ., Manhattan, KS 66506, 913-532-6716. 1968. Poetry, fiction, art, criticism. "We prefer excellent fiction and poetry, aimed at an adult audience. We have no preference between the traditional or experimental, but we have no interest in either for its own sake. We do special numbers in literary criticism, art, and history, but contributors should note special announced topics before submitting. Recent contributors: Joyce Carol Oates, Greg Kuzma, Stephen Dixon, Dan Curzon, Robert Day, Brian Swann, Rolaine Hockstein, Mary Morris, Natalie L.M. Petesch, H.E. Francis, Paula Rankin, Kim Robert Stafford." circ. 1,000-1,300. 4/yr. Pub'd 4 issues 1979; expects 4 issues 1980, 4 issues 1981. sub. price: $9.00; per copy: $2.50; sample: $2.50. Back issues: $2.50 each. Discounts: 10 percent to subscription agencies, 40 percent to bookstores with regular accounts (on consignment). 128pp; 5X8; of. Reporting time: 2 to 4 months. Payment: 2 subscription copies-and yearly awards to short fiction & poetry. Fic.: $250.00/$150.00/$100.00. P.: $150.00/$100.00/$50.00/$25. Copyrighted, reverts to author. Ads: $125/$100/$55. CCLM, KAC.

Kanthaka Press, Alex Jack, Ann Fawcett, P.O. Box 696, Brookline Village, MA 02147, 617-734-8146. 1973. "Publishers of *The Adamantine Sherlock Holmes: The Adventures in Tibet & India* by Hapi, *Shanti, the Game of Lasting Peace*." avg. press run 1,000. Pub'd 1 title 1979; expects 1 title 1980. 2 titles listed in the *Small Press Record of Books in Print* (9th Edition, 1980). Discounts: 40 percent. of.

KARAKI, Ken Fernstrom, Ed.; Rick Stevenson, Associate Editor, 831 Kelvin Street, Coquitlam, B.C., Canada, 604-931-5417. 1971. Poetry, fiction, articles, art, cartoons, satire, reviews, letters, parts-of-novels, plays, interviews, concrete art. "We are slow. If you have submitted the same material to other mags than don't bother to submit it to us as we don't want to get into silly copyright problems. We don't care about length but we do mind having 35 or 100 poems sent to us. And no xerox. Would like to see plays (preferably produced), short stories and translations. As far as biases i guess we go for surrealism and wit coupled with intelligence. If you're impotent, had a bad love affair or a bad trip of any sort we don't particularly want to hear about it. Read editorial in #5. Recent contributors: Bryan Wade, Colin Partridge, Marco Fraticelli, Eugene McNamara, Leslie Fernstrom, Christopher Heide, etc." circ. 250. irreg. Pub'd 2 issues 1979; expects 2 issues 1980. price per copy: $2.95 (#6), $1.50 (#5); sample: $1.50 min. Back issues: negotiable. 52pp; 8½X5½; of. Reporting time: Long. Payment: 2 copies. Copyrighted. Pub's reviews. §The usual arty regions, but most especially collections of short stories or plays. Ads: Exchange.

KARAMU, Bruce Guernsey, Editor, English Dept, Eastern Illinois Univ., Charleston, IL 61920, 217-581-5013. 1967. Poetry, fiction, criticism, parts-of-novels, reviews. "Prefer criticism on very contemporary literature (after 1960). Traditional or experimental fiction (2,000-8,000 words). Prefer poems that are a fresh act of language, that have a strong sense of place and speaker" circ. 500. 1/yr. Pub'd 1-2 issues 1979; expects 1 issue 1980. sub. price: $1.50; per copy: $1.50; sample: $1.50. Back issues: $1.00. 76pp; 9X6; of. Reporting time: 2-3 weeks, poetry; 1-2 months, fiction. Payment: 2 copies. Copyrighted, reverts to author. Pub's reviews. §Contemporary poetry & fiction.

Karl Bern Publishers, George K. Lovgren, Editor, 9939 Riviera Drive, Sun City, AZ 85351. 1977. Art, concrete art. "*The Art of Inner Seeing* by George K. Lovgren." avg. press run 1,000. Expects 1 title 1980, 1 title 1981. avg. price, cloth: $7.95; paper: $4.95. 140pp; 6X9; of. Copyrights for author.

Karmic Revenge Laundry Shop Press, Rita Karman, Box 14, Guttenberg, NJ 07093, 201-868-8106. 1972. Poetry, fiction, interviews, satire, reviews, parts-of-novels, long-poems, plays. "Originality and ability in expression looked for. Recent contributor: Anna May Xerox *Dyke Tracy*, Rita Karman *I Wandered Lonely As A Cow* (Poetry in Public Places)." avg. press run 200-300. Pub'd 2 titles 1979; expects 2 titles 1980. 6 titles listed in the *Small Press Record of Books in Print* (9th Edition, 1980). avg. price, paper: $2.00. Discounts: usual 1/3. 40pp; of/lp. Reporting time: Variable. Payment: Variable. Copyrights for author.

William Kaufmann, Inc., William Kaufmann, One First Street, Los Altos, CA 94022, 415-948-5810. "General trade publishers." avg. press run 5,000. Pub'd 8 titles 1979; expects 15 titles 1980. avg. price, cloth: $13.00; paper: $7.00. 6X9, 8½X11; of. Reporting time: varies with our interest in the project. Payment: differs book to book. AAP,NCBPA,WBPA.

Kawabata Press (see also SEPIA), Colin David Webb, Editor, Knill Cross House, Higher Anderton Road, Millbrook, Nr Torpoint, Cornwall, United Kingdom. 1977. Poetry, fiction, articles. "At present booklets (about 30 pages each) by invitation, but would in an exceptional case publish from unsolicited work. Length about 10,000 words maximum in prose, poems maximum 900 words. Recent booklets, Cobin Webb *Novella 1959-60*; forthcoming George A Moore *Days and Months* poetry April 1978." avg. press run 100. Pub'd 2 titles 1979; expects 4 titles 1980, 4 titles 1981. 15 titles listed in the *Small Press Record of Books in Print* (9th Edition, 1980). avg. price, paper: 25p. 35pp; 6X8½; †mi. Reporting time: 14 days. Copyrights for author.

KAYAK, Kayak Press, George Hitchcock, 325 Ocean View, Santa Cruz, CA 95062. 1964. Poetry, criticism. circ. 1,400. 3-4/yr. sub. price: $5.00; per copy: $1.00; sample: $1.00. Back issues: $2.00 ea. Discounts: 40% 5 or more, 33⅓% less than 5 to bookdealers. 70pp; 5½X8½; †of. Reporting time: 2 wks. Pub's reviews. Ads: $40/$20. CCLM.

Kayak Press (see also KAYAK), 325 Ocean View, Santa Cruz, CA 95062. 7 titles listed in the *Small Press Record of Books in Print* (9th Edition, 1980).

KEEPSAKE POEMS, Keepsake Press, R. Lewis, S. Toulson, 26 Sydney Road, Richmond, Surrey TW9 UEB, United Kingdom, 01 940 9364. 1957. Poetry, art, cartoons, satire, long-poems, plays. "We publish books rather than a magazine. KEEPSAKE POEMS are a series of single poems but are only one of our interests." circ. 200-300. irreg. Pub'd 6 issues 1979. 14 titles listed in the *Small Press Record of Books in Print* (9th Edition, 1980). sub. price: varies; per copy: $1.00; sample: $1.00. Back issues: when available. Discounts: 33% to bookseller. 4-50pp; 9X14; †various methods of production. Reporting time: 3 weeks. Payment: by agreement if any. buys first serial rights. ALP.

Keepsake Press (see KEEPSAKE POEMS)

KELLNER'S MONEYGRAM, H. T. Kellner, Editor & Publisher, 1768 Rockville Drive, Baldwin, NY 11510, (516) 868-3177. 1977. Articles, photos, cartoons, interviews. "400-450 word pieces on photo marketing. Sherry Morris, Ed Carlin, Chris Niedenthal, Cheryl May. *MG* is a newsletter for the photo marketing industry." circ. 2,000. 11/yr. Pub'd 11 issues 1979; expects 11 issues 1980, 11 issues 1981. sub. price: $56.00; per copy: $8.00; sample: $8.00. Back issues: $8.00. Discounts: write for information. 16pp; 8½X11; of. Reporting time: 2 weeks. Payment: varies with quality of the piece. Copyrighted, reverts to author. Pub's reviews: 11 in 1979. §Photography, photo marketing, photo writing.

Kelsey St. Press, Patricia Dienstfrey, Kit Duane, Rena Rosenwasser, Marina LaPalma, Lila Dargahi, 2824 Kelsey St., Berkeley, CA 94705, 841-2044. 1975. Poetry, fiction, art. avg. press run 350 letterpress, 750 offset. Pub'd 2 titles 1979; expects 5 titles 1980, 4 titles 1981. 6 titles listed in the *Small Press Record of Books in Print* (9th Edition, 1980). avg. price, paper: $4.50. 48pp; 5½X8½; of/lp. Reporting time: we are not soliciting mss this year. Payment: In copies. copyright retained by author unless otherwise agreed.

Kenmore Press, Meryl Chayt, Steven Chayt, Arthur Lane, 3317 Thornhill Road SW, Winter Haven, FL 33880. 1977. Poetry, fiction, art, letters, concrete art. "Dedicated to pursuing the craft of fine printing. The press will also be engaged in papermaking and type founding." avg. press run 100-400. 2 titles listed in the *Small Press Record of Books in Print* (9th Edition, 1980). avg. price, cloth: $15.00; paper: $6.50; other: $25.00 (manuscript). Discounts: 60/40. 35pp; 6X9; †lp. Payment: open.

Kensington Press, Box 16412, San Diego, CA 92116, (714) 284-4424. 1979. avg. press run 1,000. Pub'd 1 title 1979. 1 title listed in the *Small Press Record of Books in Print* (9th Edition, 1980). avg. price, paper: $3.95. Discounts: 1-5, 20%; 6+, 40%. 75pp; 8½X5½; of.

Kent Popular Press (see also LEFTWORKS), John Logue, Bob Howard, Box 715, Kent, OH 44240, (216) 678-9355. 1978. Articles, art, interviews, criticism, news items. avg. press run 500-1,000. Pub'd 2 titles 1979; expects 3 titles 1980, 4-5 titles 1981. 5 titles listed in the *Small Press Record of Books in Print* (9th Edition, 1980). avg. price, paper: $2.95. Discounts: 40% Trade, 60% Distributor. 100pp; 5½X8½; of. Reporting time: open, depends on submission.

Kent Publications (see also SAN FERNANDO POETRY JOURNAL), Richard Cloke, General Manager; Lori C. Smith, Editor-in-Chief; Shirley J. Rodecker, Novels, 18301 Halsted St, Northridge, CA 91324, 213-349-5088; 349-2080. 1976. Poetry, fiction. "Richard Cloke-Mister Pistol-John; Vector-Lee; My Pal Al; Jerry the Put; Yvar, Prince of Rus. Interested in San Fernando Valley authors, even if not part of staff." avg. press run 1,000. Pub'd 2 titles 1979; expects 2 titles 1980, 2 titles 1981. 6 titles listed in the *Small Press Record of Books in Print* (9th Edition, 1980). avg. price, paper: $2.50-$3.25. Discounts: jobber-30 percent; trade-20 percent; lib., libraries-20 percent. 200pp; 5½X8½; 6X9; of. Payment: 50 percent to author as received. Copyrights for author. COSMEP.

Kenyon Hill Publications (see NEW ENGLAND REVIEW)

THE KENYON REVIEW, Ronald Sharp, Frederick Turner, Kenyon College, Gambier, OH 43022, (614) 427-3339. 1978. Poetry, fiction, articles, satire, criticism, parts-of-novels, long-poems, plays, music. "Vladimir Nabokov, Joyce Carol Oates, Samuel Beckett, James Merrill, Ursula Le Guin, George Steiner, Robert Haas, William Gass, Joseph Brodsky, Linda Gregg, Galway Kinnell, Julio Cortazar, E.L. Doctorow, Guy Davenport, Harold Bloom, Aleksandr Solhenitsyn, Kenneth Burke, Woody Allen, and Wayne Booth." circ. 20,000. 4/yr. Pub'd 4 issues 1979; expects 4 issues 1980, 4 issues 1981. sub. price: $15/yr; per copy: $5.00; sample: $6.00. Back issues: $6.00. Discounts: agency discount 25%. 144pp; 7X10; of. Reporting time: 3 months. Payment: $10 prose, $15 poetry (per page) $15 minimum per poem. Copyrighted, reverts to author. Ads: $450.00/$275.00. COSMEP, CCLM.

Kids Can Press, Priscilla Carrier, Co-Director; Valerie Hussey, Co-Director, 585½ Bloor Street W, Toronto, Ontario M6G 1K5, Canada. 1974. avg. press run 5M. Pub'd 6 titles 1979; expects 8 titles 1980, 8 titles 1981. 5 titles listed in the *Small Press Record of Books in Print* (9th Edition, 1980). avg. price, cloth: $6.95; paper: $2.95. Discounts: 40%/trade. pp varies; 7X7. Reporting time: 2 months. Payment: 10% split author/illustrator. Copyrights for author. ACP, CBIC.

King and Cowen (New York) (see also BRAVO), Jose Garcia Villa, 1081 Trafalgar Street (John Cowen), Teaneck, NJ 07666, 201-836-5922. 1977. "299 Park Avenue, 32nd Floor, New York, NY 10017 (Robert L. King) Biases: (1) Poetry must have formal excellence, (2) Poetry must be lyrical. Books Published: *Introducing Mr. Vanderborg* poems by Arthur Vanderberg; *Appassionata: Poems in Praise of Love,* Jose Garcia Villa; (forthcoming) *The Collected Poems of Jose Garcia Villa* by Jose Garcia Villa." avg. press run 1,500. Pub'd 1 title 1979; expects 1 title 1980, 1 title 1981. avg. price, cloth: $10.00; paper: $4.95. Discounts: 40%. 96pp; 6¼X9½; lp. Reporting time: mss by invitation. Payment: by arrangement with author. Copyrights for author. NYSSPA.

King Publications (see also "JOINT" CONFERENCE), Kathryn E. King, Editor and Publisher, P O Box 19332, Washington, DC 20036, 202-234-1681. 1974. Poetry, art, photos. "Poetry books by inmates." avg. press run 100. Pub'd 3 titles 1979; expects 2 titles 1980, 2 titles 1981. 12 titles listed in the *Small Press Record of Books in Print* (9th Edition, 1980). avg. price, paper: $2.00. Discounts: 40%. 28-32pp; 5½X8½; of. Reporting time: varies. Payment: After I recover printing costs I split sales with the author. Copyrights for author. COSMEP, COSMEP/SOUTH, CCLM.

THE KIPLING JOURNAL, G.H. Webb, 18 Northumberland Ave., London WC2N 5BJ, United Kingdom. 1927. Articles, letters. "Not more than 2,500 words. Published quarterly in March, June, September & December. Please make cheques payable to The Kipling Society (Journal a/c)." circ. 900. 4/yr. Pub'd 4 issues 1979. sub. price: £4.00; sample: £1.00. Back issues: £2.00. Discounts: 20% is allowed on advance payments, made in Sterling, for one year (4 issues). 30pp; 5½X8½. Pub's reviews: 6 in 1979. Ads: £60/£55/£50/£27.50/£25/£12.50.

210

Kitchen Harvest, Sue Anderson Gross, Sidney A. Gross, 3N 681 Bittersweet Drive, St. Charles, IL 60174, 312-584-4084. 1973. "Cookbooklets: Sourdough Rye and Other Good Breads; The Honey Book; Holiday Baking; Bagels, Bagels, Bagels; The Early Spring Garden Book; Fruit Flavored Yogurt & More; The Roll Basket; Old World Breads; Danish to Donuts. Pizza to Your Taste; Homemade Mixes; Crazy About Croutons, Beekeeping Books: Honey Marketing; Tips for the Small Producer" avg. press run 500. Pub'd 3 titles 1979; expects 4 titles 1980. 13 titles listed in the *Small Press Record of Books in Print* (9th Edition, 1980). avg. price, paper: $2.95. Discounts: 1-4 copies, 20 percent; 5 or more copies, 40 percent. 16-52pp; 5⅛X8½; †of. All material copyrighted.

Kitchen Sink Enterprises (see also WEIRD TRIPS; SNARF), Denis Kitchen, Box 7, Princeton, WI 54968, 414-295-3972. 1973. Articles, art, cartoons, interviews, letters, news items. "Uses non-fiction only. *Weird Trips* copyrights, but often only first rights. Actually covers virtually any subject. The above have been covered in previous issues. Looking for the off-beat, the unusual; personal experiences; *Weird Trips,* but all *true.* Photos also welcomed & illustrations. Best to view a sample copy before submitting an article or query." avg. press run 10,000. Expects 1 title 1980. 47 titles listed in the *Small Press Record of Books in Print* (9th Edition, 1980). avg. price, paper: $1.00; other: $1.00. Discounts: 40% off to stores, 60% off to distributors. 36-48pp; 7X10; of. Reporting time: Often same day. Two weeks at outside. Payment: Royalty basis. From $20 to $200 per article. Copyrights for author.

KITE LINES, Valerie Govig, 7106 Campfield Road, Baltimore, MD 21207, (301) 484-6287. 1977. Articles, photos, interviews, reviews, letters, news items. "All material is about *kites.* Do rights revert: rights limited to reprint in magazine; all other rights revert to author." circ. 5,000. 4/yr. Pub'd 4 issues 1979. sub. price: $9.00; per copy: $2.50; sample: $2.50. Back issues: $2.50 each, 4 for $9.00. Discounts: To kite shops, 5 copies minimum, $1.70 each for resale. 56pp; 8½X11; of. Reporting time: 2 weeks to 3 months (varies with workload). Payment: in copies, photo expenses covered in some cases. Copyrighted. Pub's reviews: 4 in 1979. §Kites. Ads: $324.00/$185.00/$0.20.

Dr. Albert R. Klinski, Dr. Albert R. Klinski, Lynn J. Falkenthal, 3928 N. St. Louis, Chicago, IL 60618, KE9-6159. 1979. Poetry, fiction, photos, satire, criticism, music. "*Animal School* is a 96 page sequel to George Orwell's *Animal Farm* that utilizes all of the items circled, and brilliantly attacks the medical-educational complex that has presently a death grip on our colleges and their students. More accurately the Catholic Universities and the people who run them over their students." avg. press run 52,000. Expects 1 title 1980, 2 titles 1981. avg. price, cloth: $7.95; paper: $2.95. Discounts: 10%. 100pp; 8X5; of. Reporting time: 2 weeks. Payment: 12% on hardbound and 4-6% on softcovers. Copyrights for author.

Klutz Enterprises, John Cassidy, PO Box 2992, Stanford, CA 94306, (415) 327-3808. 1977. "Have published one title, *Juggling for the Complete Klutz.* Interested in publishing humorous how-to books." avg. press run 25,000. Expects 1 title 1980, 1 title 1981. avg. price, paper: $6.95. 75pp; 5X8½. Reporting time: 60 days. Payment: negotiable. Copyrights for author.

Knollwood Publishing Company, Box 735, Willmar, MN 56201, 612-235-4950. 1973. "Currently a one-book, one-record publishing house—'*Silver Spurs', Santa's Smallest Brightest Elf.* Record, sheet music, 4 full color posters (scenes from book), t-shirt stencil (5 x 8-full color)." 1 title listed in the *Small Press Record of Books in Print* (9th Edition, 1980). avg. price, cloth: $3.95; other: Record $2.00. Discounts: libraries, schools, bookstores-30 to 40 percent; fund raisers & distributors-50 percent. 39pp; 8½X11.

Know, Inc., Phyllis Wetherby, P.O. Box 86031, Pittsburgh, PA 15221. 1969. Poetry, articles, reviews. "Know, Inc. is a small but growing feminist publishing company. We were founded in 1969 and currently publish both hard and soft cover books, pamphlets, a newsletter for members (6/yr) and a poetry series. Our list is very broad, covering subjects in all areas of the women's movement." †of. COSMEP.

KOMPOST, Werner Pieper, 6941 Lohrbach, Western Germany. 1971. "If material is too long to publish in the magazine, we have an additional paper *Der Grone Zweig* to publish long works...contributors: from all over the world..." circ. 10,000-40,000. 4/yr. Pub'd 4 issues 1979; expects 4 issues 1980, 4 issues 1981. sub. price: DM 30.00; sample: 5 for 20.00 DM. Back issues: special list. Discounts: 30-50%. 100pp; 29cm x 19cm; of. Payment: 10 copies per printed page. Copyrighted. Pub's reviews: 30 in 1979. Ads: 1000 DM/500 DM.

KONGLOMERATI, Konglomerati Press, Richard Mathews, Barbara Russ, PO Box 5001, Gulfport, FL 33737, 813-323-0386. 1972. Poetry, fiction, art, cartoons, collages, concrete art. "Recent contributors include F.A. Nettelbeck, Jim Hall, Adelle Aldridge, Peter Meinke, David Shevin, Jerred Metz. We look for clear, original, innovative voices." circ. 300-500. 4/yr. Pub'd 4 issues 1979; expects 4 issues 1980. sub. price: $20.00; per copy: $7.50; sample: No special rate for sample copies. Back issues: No.

1 *Faces* $5.00/No. 2 *Concrete* I-$25.00 (only five copies remain). Others-rates on request. Discounts: 1-4 copies, 20 percent; 5 or more copies, 40 percent to bookstores. 45-60pp; 7X10; †lp. Reporting time: 1 month-6 weeks. Payment: copy. Copyrighted, reprint rights by permission. Pub's reviews. §Literary, poetry, avant garde, fine printing. Ads: $60.00/$35.00. WMS, PHS, CCLM.

Konglomerati Press (see also KONGLOMERATI), Richard Mathews, Barbara Russ, PO Box 5001, Gulfport, FL 33737, 813-323-0386. 1971. Poetry, fiction, art, cartoons, collages, concrete art. "Exploring visual poetry, letterpress typography and the hand made book. Books (limited editions) chapbooks with illustrations, handsewn binding, letterpress-printed, some hand-made papers. Two-Bit Bird Sheets (single poems), post cards and notecards." avg. press run 1,000. Pub'd 4 titles 1979; expects 4 titles 1980. 20 titles listed in the *Small Press Record of Books in Print* (9th Edition, 1980). avg. price, cloth: $15.00; paper: $5.00. Discounts: 1-4 copies, 20 percent; 5 or more 40 percent to bookstores. 60pp; 6X7; †lp. Reporting time: 1 month - 6 weeks. Payment: up to 10% of the edition plus 40% disc on add. copies; or up to 8% royalties. Copyrights for author. WMS, PHS.

Konocti Books (see also SIPAPU), Noel Peattie, Route 1, Box 216, Winters, CA 95694. 1973. Poetry. "We have done 2 poetry books and 4 broadsides. We will be doing mostly broadsides in future. No new books are planned at this time under this imprint. However, we are now issuing broadsides under the imprint of Cannonade Press, using a 6 x 10 Kelsey." avg. press run 500. Pub'd 1 title 1979; expects 1 title 1980. 6 titles listed in the *Small Press Record of Books in Print* (9th Edition, 1980). avg. price, paper: $2.00; other: broadsides are free. Discounts: 40 percent booksellers. 40pp; lp. Reporting time: 3 weeks. Payment: author's copies only. Copyrights for author. COSMEP, APS.

Kontexts Publications (see also ARTZIEN), Michael Gibbs, Eerste Van Der Helststraat 55, Amsterdam, Nthlnd, (020) 768556. 1969. Poetry, articles, art, interviews, criticism, reviews, letters, concrete art, photos, collages. "Concerned with visual/experimental poetry and language arts. The magazine has now folded. Last number 9/10 Winter 76/77, but Kontexts Publications will be continuing with the production of books and book-objects by individual writers/artists. Recent books: *6 Plays* by Ulises Carrion; *Pages* by Michael Gibbs; *Limits* by Michael Gibbs; Kontextsound — compilation of sound poetry activity ed. M. Gibbs. *Deciphering America* ed. M. Gibbs" avg. press run 400. Pub'd 3 titles 1979; expects 3 titles 1980, 3 titles 1981. 8 titles listed in the *Small Press Record of Books in Print* (9th Edition, 1980). avg. price, paper: $3.00; other: average book price: $3.00. Discounts: 33⅓% on 6 or more. †mi/of/lp. Copyrights for author.

KOSMOS, Kosmos, Kosrof Chantikian, 2580 Polk Street, San Francisco, CA 94109, 415-928-4332. 1975. Poetry, articles, interviews, criticism, reviews, letters, long-poems. "*Kosmos* a journal of poetry is reborn twice yearly and welcomes your inventive work. For us poetry is the invitation to go to the *Ching*, the *Well*, the necessary & inexhaustible source of nourishment, to the very foundations of life. Manuscripts must be original and unpublished. When English translations are being sent please include a copy of the original language text. And except in this case where foreign language manuscripts are included, no photocopies are ever wanted. Permission to publish translations of poetry from the poet or authorized agent must accompany manuscript. Bring or send your work in the original with a self-addressed, stamped envelope to the address above. *Kosmos* number 4 is a special translation issue and includes Spanish, German, French, Greek, Hungarian, Italian, Russian and Japanese poetry. The first four issues of *Kosmos* have included: Joan Murray, Rochelle Owens, Ruth Lisa Schechter, Colette Inez, Alfred Starr Hamilton, Larry Tucker, Rafael Alberti, Bertolo Cattafi, Sandor Csoori, Mohammed Dib, Daphne Andronikou-Dimitriou, Hans Magnus Enzensberger, Attila Jozsef, Nicholas Kolumban, Velemir Khlebnikov, Hugo Lindo, Amado Nervo, Nellie Sachs, Giorgos Seferis, Arthur Rimbaud, Shuntaro Tanikawa and Rainer Maria Rilke. Issues five & six are a special double edition devoted to Octavio Paz. It is highly recommended that a recent issue of *Kosmos* be read before submitting your work. In the case of articles and reviews, query before sending (enclosing the usual self-addressed & stamped envelope)" circ. 1,000. 2/yr. Pub'd 2 issues 1979. 2 titles listed in the *Small Press Record of Books in Print* (9th Edition, 1980). sub. price: $8.00; $15.00, 2 years; Libraries: $12.00; $23.00, 2 years; per copy: $4.00 + 65¢ for mailing; sample: $4.00 + 65¢ for mailing; Libraries: $6.00 + 65¢ for mailing. Back issues: $4.00 + 65¢ for mailing; Libraries: $6.00 + 65¢ for mailing. Discounts: 40% trade. 100pp; 6X9; of. Reporting time: 7-9 weeks. Payment: 2-3 copies, Cash when available: $3.00-$5.00 manuscript page in *Kosmos*. Copyrighted, does not revert to author. Pub's reviews. §Poetry, also literary works on a specific or general poetic idea or person. Ads: $100.-00/$65.00. CCLM.

Kosmos (see also KOSMOS), Kosrof Chantikian, 2580 Polk Street, San Francisco, CA 94109, (415) 928-4332. 1974. Poetry. "Kosmos has inaugurated a 'Modern Poets Series' with the publication in 1978 of *Prophecies & Transformations* by Kosrof Chantikian; 88 pps, sewn, 6 x 9. We plan to publish three more volumes in this series in 1980. We are also very much interested in publishing contemporary works by poets from outside of the United States and to this end have begun our second series of books called: 'Modern Poets in Translation.' We are interested in reading MSS. from all languages. Our first book in the 'Modern Poets in Translation' Series (each of which are to be bi-lingual editions) is by Rafael Alberti. The Modern Poets Series and Modern Poets in Translation Series have been established to publish poets deserving further recognition and to introduce poets of other parts of this planet to the reading public in the United States. A letter of inquiry (along with a self-addressed, stamped envelope) stating particulars and giving an outline of the proposed project should be sent to the editor before the submission of any MSS followed by *Transparent God* by Claude Esteban and *The Reaches of Thule* by Jean Laude." avg. press run 1,000. Pub'd 2 titles 1979. avg. price, cloth: $10.00; paper: $3.95. Discounts: 40% trade only. 88pp; 6X9; of. Reporting time: 7 weeks. Payment: standard. Copyrights for author.

KRAX, Andy Robson, 63 Dixon Lane, Leeds, Yorkshire LS12 4RR, United Kingdom. 1971. Articles, poetry, fiction, art, interviews, cartoons. "Favour younger writers and fantasy art" 2/yr. Pub'd 1 issue 1979; expects 2 issues 1980, 3 issues 1981. 2 titles listed in the *Small Press Record of Books in Print* (9th Edition, 1980). sub. price: £1.50 ($4.00) inclusive; per copy: 75p incl. post. Back issues: On request. 48pp; size A5; of. Reporting time: 1-2 weeks. Payment: cover design only-£2. Copyrighted, reverts to author. Ads: £8/£4.50.

KROKLOK, Writers Forum, Don Silvester Houedard, Bob Cobbing, Peter Mayer, 262 Randolph Ave, London W9, United Kingdom. 1971. Articles, poetry, concrete art. "An anthology of concrete-/sound poetry to be completed in 21 issues." circ. 500 plus. irreg. Expects 1 issue 1980. price per copy: 50p; sample: 50p plus postage. Discounts: trade 33%. 32pp; size A4; †mi/of. Reporting time: 3 weeks. Payment: copies. Not copyrighted. ALP.

Kropotkin's Lighthouse Publications, Jas Huggon, c/o Housmans Bookshop, 5 Caledonian Rd., London N19DX, United Kingdom. 1969. Poetry, fiction, art, non-fiction. "We do not require unsolicited mss. Recent publication incl. postcards (4), calendars (2), poetry, anthologies, bibliography, fiction, pamphlets, posters." avg. press run 500. Pub'd 1 title 1979; expects 1 title 1980. 10 titles listed in the *Small Press Record of Books in Print* (9th Edition, 1980). avg. price, paper: £0.40 (sterling): $0.80 US. Discounts: 33⅓% plus postage. 25pp; size varies; †of/lp/mi. Reporting time: by return. Payment: none. if required. ALP.

KT Did Productions, Thomas Fitzsimmons, Karen Fitzsimmons, c/o English Dept, Oakland University, Rochester, MI 48063.

KTQ:KITTY TORTURE QUARTERLY, S & S Press, PO Box 5931, Austin, TX 78763. 4/yr. sub. price: $4.00.

KUDOS, Graham Sykes, 78 Easterly Road, Leeds LS8 3AN, England. 1979. Poetry, fiction, articles, art, photos, cartoons, interviews, satire, criticism, reviews, music, parts-of-novels, long-poems, collages, concrete art. "No length limit, no biases, seeks to present the best available work from both new and established writers, crossing as many barriers as possible. Amongst the better known contributors are Douglas Blazek, Jim Burns, Theodore Enslin, Clayton Eshleman, John Heath-Stubbs, Alexis Lykiard, Adrian Mitchell, Edwin Morgan, Peter Redgrove, Alan Sillitoe, DM Thomas etc." circ. 500-1,000. 3/yr. Pub'd 3 issues 1979. sub. price: £1.80/$5.00 US including postage; per copy: 60p plus postage; sample: 60p plus postage. Back issues: 50p. Discounts: 1/3 trade. 60pp; size A5; of. Reporting time: 3 weeks usually. Payment: copies. Copyrighted, reverts to author. Pub's reviews: 150 in 1979. §Poetry, novels, short stories, criticism, graphic work. Ads: £20.00/£10.00.

KUDZU, Stephen Gardner, Andrew N. Williams, 166 Cokesdale Road, Columbia, SC 29210. 1977. Poetry, art. "Art - black & white line drawings (cover & back); poetry - 100 line limit; recent contributors: Christine Zawadiwsky, Peter Wild, Greg Kuzma, David Citino, Lyn Lifshin, Alvin Aubert, Joseph Bruchac." circ. 500. 4/yr. Pub'd 2 issues 1979; expects 3 issues 1980, 2 issues 1981. sub. price: $4.00/yr; per copy: $1.00; sample: $1.00. Back issues: $1.00. Discounts: inquire. 24pp; 5½X8½; of. Reporting time: 2 weeks. Payment: 3 copies. Copyrighted, reverts to author.

KUKSU: Journal of Backcountry Writing, Dale Pendell, Box 980 Alleghany Star Rt., Nevada City, CA 95959. 1972. Poetry, fiction, articles, art, photos, interviews, criticism, reviews, parts-of-novels. "Please see an issue before submitting material." circ. 1,500. 1-2/yr. sub. price: $5.00/2 issues; per copy: $2.50; sample: $2.50. Discounts: 40%-trade, bulk. 140pp; 5X8; of. Reporting time: 1-3 mos. Payment: copies. Copyrighted. Pub's reviews. §poetry/anthropology/western American/counter culture. CCLM.

Kulchur Foundation, Lita Hornick, 888 Park Ave., New York, NY 10021, 988-5193. 1970. Poetry. avg. press run 1,000. Pub'd 2 titles 1979. 1 title listed in the *Small Press Record of Books in Print* (9th

Edition, 1980). avg. price, cloth: $7.00; paper: $3.50. Discounts: 40 percent to bookstores, 20 percent to libraries. 128pp; 7½X10; of. We do not consider unsolicited manuscripts. Payment: $500.00 a book. Copyrights for author.

Kurios Press, Barbie Engstrom, Publisher, Box 946, Bryn Mawr, PA 19010, 215-527-4635. 1974. "We have begun a "To See and Enjoy" series of travel guides. The first PARIS to SEE AND ENJOY, a 5,000 run is sold out. The next KENYA SAFARI, has just been published. We only publish travel books now. We do not solicit manuscripts, as all our titles are done on assignment." avg. press run 5,000 to 10,000 but it has been as low as 500 to begin with. Pub'd 2 titles 1979. 5 titles listed in the *Small Press Record of Books in Print* (9th Edition, 1980). avg. price, paper: $10.00-$15.00. Discounts: Standard except when special offers are given. 100+pp; size varies; of. Payment: none. Copyrights for author.

KXE6S VEREIN R NEWSLETTER, Kxe6s Verein R Press, Steven Buntin, PO Box 2066 or 2204, Chapel Hill, NC 27514. 1975. Poetry, fiction, articles, art, photos, cartoons, interviews, satire, criticism, reviews, letters, parts-of-novels, collages, plays. "Prefer materials on chess or literary nature, player biographies, profiles, organization, book reviews, etc." circ. 500+. 6/yr. sub. price: $5.00; per copy: $1.00; sample: $0.50. Back issues: $0.75 each. 20-24pp; 5½X8½; of. Reporting time: ASAP, national stories have priority. Payment: case by case, most work by staff. Copyrighted, reverts to author. Pub's reviews. §Chess, board games, freedom of the press. Ads: $12.00/$6.50/$0.10 ($1.50 min.). CCLM, COSMEP, COSMEP/EAST.

Kxe6s Verein R Press (see also KXE6S VEREIN R NEWSLETTER; FLORAL UNDERAWL GAZETTE; ADVISORY BOARD RECORD; NEWS RELEASE FROM THE CHESS PRESS SYNDICATE), Steven Buntin, PO Box 2066 or 2204, Chapel Hill, NC 27514. 1974. Poetry, fiction, articles, art, photos, cartoons, interviews, satire, criticism, reviews, letters, parts-of-novels, collages, plays. "Prefer materials of chessic nature (our bailiwick) but can and will print all types of materials: poetry, novels, short stories, music, postcards, business cards, etc." Discounts: by job only. †mi/of. Payment: negotiable. Copyrights for author. CCLM, COSMEP, COSMEP/SOUTH, COSMEP/EAST.

L

L.W.M. Publications (see also THE LITTLE WORD MACHINE), Nick Toczek, Philip Nanton, Yann Lovelock, 5 Beech Terrace, Undercliffe, Bradford, West Yorkshire, England BD3 0PY, United Kingdom. 1977. Poetry, fiction, articles, art, photos, cartoons, criticism, reviews, parts-of-novels, collages, concrete art. avg. press run 1000. Pub'd 2 titles 1979. 5 titles listed in the *Small Press Record of Books in Print* (9th Edition, 1980). avg. price, cloth: £2.50(UK), £3.50(overseas); paper: £1.50(UK), £2.50(overseas). Discounts: 1/3rd off for 6+ copies. 200pp; 21X15cm; of. Reporting time: 3 months. Payment: varies. Copyrights for author.

L/A House (see FOLLIES)

La Reina Press (see also LIVE WRITERS! LOCAL ON TAP), Lupe A. Gonzalez, Karen Feinberg, Donna D. Vitucci, PO Box 8182, Cincinnati, OH 45208, (513) 579-8798.

Labor Arts Books, Emanuel Fried, 1064 Amherst St., Buffalo, NY 14216, 716-873-4131. 1975. "For the moment not seeking submissions. Still working on distribution of present publications: *The Dodo Bird, Drop Hammer.*" avg. press run 5,000. 2 titles listed in the *Small Press Record of Books in Print* (9th Edition, 1980). avg. price, paper: $1.50-$2.50. Discounts: write for information. 72-128pp; 4¼X7, 4½X7; Print Press. Payment: individual arrangement. COSMEP.

LABOUR LEADER, 49 Top Moor Side, Leeds LS11 9LW, United Kingdom. price per copy: 5p. APS.

LAD (see SOURCE)

THE LADDER, The Ladder Press, Gene Damon, 7800 Westside Drive, Weatherby Lake, MO 64152. 1956. Poetry, fiction, articles, art, photos, cartoons, interviews, satire, criticism, reviews, music, letters, parts-of-novels, long-poems, plays. "Material must pertain to women, with primary emphasis on lesbians. Recent works by poets: Lyn Strongin, Rita Mae Brown, Martha Shelley, Rochelle Holt. Recent fiction by: Jane Rule, F. Ellen Isaacs, Rochelle Holt. Art column by: Sarah Whitworth. Art by: Georgia O'Keeffe, Romaine Brooks, Audrey Flack, etc-The press has available the book THE LESBIAN IN LITERATURE by Gene Damon, Jan Watson and Robin Jordan, 2nd Ed., 1975 at $10.00. Also, THE INDEX, (to 16 years of THE LADDER magazine) for $10." circ. 1,750. 6/yr. sub. price:

$7.50; per copy: $1.25. 56pp; 5¼X8¼; of. Reporting time: 15 days. Payment: copies only. Ads: $80/$45.

The Ladder Press (see also THE LADDER), 7800 Westside Drive, Weatherby Lake, MO 64152. 2 titles listed in the *Small Press Record of Books in Print* (9th Edition, 1980).

LADY-UNIQUE-INCLINATION-OF-THE-NIGHT, Kay F. Turner, Editor, Box 803, New Brunswick, NJ 08903. 1975. Poetry, fiction, articles, art, photos, interviews, criticism, reviews, music, concrete art. "We primarily seek in-depth research on the history and meaning of the goddesses, women and religion, women's folklore, women's mythological heritage, etc. but some poetry and fiction is always included." circ. 1,500. 1/yr. Pub'd 1 issue 1979; expects 1 issue 1980, 1 issue 1981. price per copy: $3.00 + $.75 postage. Back issues: Cycles 2 & 3 $3.00 + $0.50 postage each. Discounts: Bookstores, 3-10 copies at 25%; 11 or more at 40%; Distributors, 50%. 80pp; 7X8½; of. Reporting time: within 1 month. Payment: None at this time except free copy of the journal. Copyrighted, reverts to author. Pub's reviews. §All women's creative, political and spiritual material. Ads: $90.00/$50.-00/$35.00/$25.00.

LAKE STREET REVIEW, Kevin FitzPatrick, Editor; David Moore, Associate Editor, c/o CD/DM Books, Box 7188, Powderhorn Station, Minneapolis, MN 55407. 1975. Poetry, fiction, articles, art, interviews, satire, criticism, reviews, music, parts-of-novels, long-poems, plays, concrete art. "The *Lake Street Review* is a general literary magazine focusing on poets and writers who live or have lived in the Mpls-St Paul MN area. Fiction: 500-4,000 words; drawings: black and white, 7 x 8½; songs: with musical notation. Recent contributors: Dan Brennan, Margaret Hasse, Will Fisher, Beryl Williams, James Naiden, Jonathan Sisson, Waneta Eddy, Ethna McKiernan, Thomas Dillon Redshaw, Michael Kincaid and Richard Grossman." circ. 500. 2/yr. Pub'd 2 issues 1979; expects 2 issues 1980, 2 issues 1981. sub. price: $5.00 for 4 issues (2 years); per copy: $1.25; sample: $1.25. Back issues: $1.25. Discounts: $1.00 each for orders of 10 or more. 40pp; 7X8½; of. Reporting time: 1 month. Payment: 2 copies. Copyrighted, reverts to author. Pub's reviews. §general literature; poetry, fiction. Ads: No ads. CCLM.

Lakes & Prairies Press, Edward Haggard, Constance Leininger, 28 Elmwood Street (Rear), West Somerville, MA 02144. 1980. Fiction, parts-of-novels. "Lakes & Prairies Press is a spinoff activity from the now discontinued *Lakes & Prairies: A Journal of Writings*. First volume, expected Summer/Fall 1980, will be *Discovering the Mandala* by Angela Peckenpaugh." avg. press run 500. Expects 2 titles 1980, 3 titles 1981. Discounts: 40% (5, 10 or 25 copies). of. Reporting time: 8-12 weeks. Payment: negotiable in percentage of profits, plus 3 complimentary copies (single author volumes only). Contributors to anthologies receive 2 complimentary copies as total payment. Copyrights for author.

Lakstun Press, Lawrence F. M.D. Berley, Po Box 429, Bensalem, PA 19020, (215) 639-7261.

Lame Johnny Press, L. M. Hasselstrom, Box 66, Hermosa, SD 57744, 605-255-4228. 1971. Poetry, fiction. "No limits; lean toward Great Plains writers, fiction, poetry." avg. press run 1,500. Pub'd 2 titles 1979; expects 5 titles 1980. 8 titles listed in the *Small Press Record of Books in Print* (9th Edition, 1980). avg. price, cloth: $5.50 postpaid; paper: $3.50 postpaid; other: $1.95 (chapbooks). Discounts: 1-5 books, no discount; 6-24 40%; discounts to bookstores and distributors only if account paid within 30 days. *Returns:* Books in saleable condition may be returned not less than 90 days nor more than 9 months after date of publisher's invoice. If returned with copy of invoice, 100% of invoice price, minus postage, will be credited; otherwise no discount will be assumed. 32-120pp; 8X8; 5½X8½; of. Reporting time: 3-10 weeks. LJP is a cooperative subsidy press; brochure on request with SASE; payment varies, is percentage of sale price. copyright rests with author. COSMEP.

LAMISHPAHA, Elchanan Indelman, 1841 Broadway, New York, NY 10023, (212) 581-5151. 1963. circ. 7,000. 10/yr. Pub'd 10 issues 1979; expects 10 issues 1980, 10 issues 1981. sub. price: $7.00; per copy: $0.70; sample: $0.70. Back issues: $0.70. Discounts: Agents 30%. 16pp; 8½X11; of. Reporting time: 1 month. Payment: editor's discretion. Pub's reviews. Ads: $500.00/$250.00.

Lamm-Morada Publishing Co., Box 7607, Stockton, CA 95207, (209) 931-1056. 2 titles listed in the *Small Press Record of Books in Print* (9th Edition, 1980).

Lamplighters Roadway Press, J.B. Grant, 1162 W Sexton Road, Sebastopol, CA 95472. 1972. Poetry, fiction, articles, art, photos, interviews, criticism, reviews. avg. press run 2,500. 2 titles listed in the *Small Press Record of Books in Print* (9th Edition, 1980). avg. price, paper: $3.00. Discounts: trade. 100pp; size varies; of. ms. not solicited. Copyrights for author. COSMEP.

Lancaster - Miller Publishers, Alan Rinzler, Janet King, Max Knight, 3165 Adeline Street, Berkeley, CA 94703, (415) 845-3782. 1977. Art, photos, letters. "Varied titles in Asian Humanities (including art books, philosophical and religious texts, literature). Trade books including *The Joy of Automobile*

Repair, The Love Poems of Honniker Winkley (poetry), *America the Beautiful* (prose), and others. Cookbook: *The Original Blue Danube Cookbook.* Lancaster-Miller art series of full-color, hardcover books, including *Buttons: Art in Miniature,* Dragons & Other Creatures, *Mel Ramos: Watercolors, Colored Reading,* and *California Murals.*" avg. press run 5,000. Pub'd 12 titles 1979; expects 19 titles 1980, 25 titles 1981. 9 titles listed in the *Small Press Record of Books in Print* (9th Edition, 1980). avg. price, cloth: $20.00 art books/$8.95 trade; paper: $5.95. Discounts: Bookstores: 25% for 1-4; 40% for 5-9; 43% on 10-49; 45% for 50+. Jobbers: 1-4 books, 10%; 5-24 books, 40%; 25 or more, 50%. 6X9; 7½X8; of. Reporting time: 2 weeks. Payment: negotiable. Copyrights for author.

Lancer Militaria, PO Box 35188, Houston, TX 77035, (713) 522-7036. 1978. "Specialize in reference type material for military collectors/historians." avg. press run 3,000. Pub'd 1 title 1979; expects 2 titles 1980. avg. price, paper: $10.00. Discounts: 40-50% depending on quantity. 112pp; 8½X11. Copyrights for author.

Land Educational Associates Foundation, Inc., Gertrude Dixon, 3368 Oak Avenue, Stevens Point, WI 54481, (715) 344-6158.

LANDSCAPE, Blair Boyd, Editor; Bonnie Loyd, Managing Editor, PO Box 7107, Berkeley, CA 94707, (415) 549-3233. 1951. Articles, photos, reviews. "A scholarly journal addressed to cultural geography, architecture, planning, environmental design, landscape architecture." circ. 1,500. 3/yr. Pub'd 3 issues 1979; expects 3 issues 1980, 3 issues 1981. sub. price: $12.00 Indiv. US; $14.00 Foreign Indiv.; $20.00 all institutions; per copy: $4.50; sample: $4.50. Back issues: On request. Discounts: 40%. 48pp; 8 1/2X11; of. Reporting time: 8-10 weeks. Payment: 2 year subscription. Copyrighted, does not revert to author. Pub's reviews: 6 in 1979. §Geography, architecture, landscape architecture, planning.

L=A=N=G=U=A=G=E, Charles Bernstein, Bruce Andrews, 464 Amsterdam Avenue, New York, NY 10024, 212-799-4475. 1978. Criticism, reviews, letters. "A newsletter for discussion and interchange emphasizing that spectrum of poetry writing that places its attention in some primary way on process, shape, vocabulary, grammar, syntax, subject matter — as ways of generating meaning." circ. 600. 6/yr. Expects 6 issues 1980. sub. price: $4.00/3 issues; per copy: $2.00; sample: $2.00. Back issues: Vol 1 168 page bound reprint $6.00. 60pp; 5¼X8; of. Reporting time: 6 weeks. Copyrighted. Pub's reviews.

The Language Press, Warren Shibles, P.O.Box 342, Whitewater, WI 53190, (414) 473-2767. 1971. Articles, criticism. "The Language Press is basically a non profit press established for the purpose of promoting inquiry. The books published must be contemporary, critical and attempt to solve practical human problems. The approach is honest, open, informed inquiry. It is objectively humanistic." avg. press run 1000. Expects 6 titles 1981. 12 titles listed in the *Small Press Record of Books in Print* (9th Edition, 1980). avg. price, cloth: $5.00 to $10.00; paper: $3.25 to $8.00. Discounts: 20% bookstores; 40% if order three or more of same title. 80 to 580pp; 6X9; of. Reporting time: 2 weeks. Payment: 10 to 15%. Copyrights for author.

LAOMEDON REVIEW, Erindale College, 3359 Mississauga Road, Mississauga, Ontario L5L1C6, Canada. 1974. Poetry, fiction, articles, art, photos, cartoons, satire, criticism, long-poems, plays, interviews, reviews, parts-of-novels. circ. 2,500. 1-2/yr. Pub'd 1 issue 1979; expects 1 issue 1980. sub. price: $5.00; per copy: $3.00. Back issues: $5.00. 112pp; 6X9; of. Reporting time: 3 months. Payment: none. Copyrighted, reverts to author. Pub's reviews. §literary/cultural/educational. Ads: $150/$80.

LAPIS, Lapis Educational Association, Inc., Karen Degenhart, 18225 Gottschalk, Homewood, IL 60430, (312) 798-5648. 1977. Poetry, fiction, articles, art, interviews, criticism, reviews, letters, long-poems. "Especially interested in Jungian psychology articles and short papers. Literature and psychology, poetry, new age spiritual studies, mythology interpretations like Joseph Campbell's. Depth psychology, archetypal studies, religion and cultural studies." circ. 200. 2/yr. Pub'd 2 issues 1979; expects 2 issues 1980, 2 issues 1981. sub. price: $6.00; per copy: $3.50; sample: $1.50. Back issues: $3.50 for any 2 issues of back issues, (not counting the most recent issue). Discounts: 5-10 copies, $1.75 each; 11-25, $1.50 each; more than 25 copies, if available, $1.00 each; plus possible small charge for postage. 64pp; 5X8; of. Reporting time: 2 months or less. Copyrighted, reverts to author. Pub's reviews. §Jungian psychology, theories of psychotherapy, some poetry. Ads: $20.00/$10.00/35 words for $6.00.

Lapis Educational Association, Inc. (see also LAPIS), Karen Degenhart, 18225 Gottschalk, Homewood, IL 60430, (312) 798-5648. 1978. Poetry, fiction, articles, art, interviews, criticism, reviews, letters, long-poems, news items. "*Jungian Psychology,* depth psychology, archetypal studies, literature and psychology, poetry, esoteric and spiritual articles, short stories, (occasionally), criticism, art therapy, poetry therapy, Joseph Campbell type material, new age spiritual development. Dreams, inner life growth experiences. Right now we only print *Lapis,* but other works are being planned for production or distribution. Contributors must become members to be published, if their manuscript is accepted." avg. press run 200. Pub'd 2 titles 1979; expects 2 titles 1980, 2 titles 1981. 1 title listed in the *Small Press Record of Books in Print* (9th Edition, 1980). avg. price, paper: $3.50. 2 issue subscriptions are $6.00 for periodicals. Discounts for larger orders, (10 or more). 65pp; 5X8; of. Reporting time: 2 months or less. Payment: We are a non-profit organization, and as a rule do not usually pay any kind of royalties. copyright to be negociated, for publications other than *Lapis.*

‡**Larkspur Press,** Rt. 3 Severn Creek, Monterey, Owenton, KY 40359. 3 titles listed in the *Small Press Record of Books in Print* (9th Edition, 1980).

LATIN AMERICAN PERSPECTIVES, Ronald H. Chilcote, Managing Editor, PO Box 5703, Riverside, CA 92517, (714) 787-5508. 1974. Articles, art, photos, reviews, interviews. circ. 2,000. 4/yr. Pub'd 4 issues 1979; expects 4 issues 1980, 4 issues 1981. sub. price: $14.00; per copy: $3.95. Back issues: Issues 1-11, $7.00; Issues 12-23, $4.00. Discounts: 20%, 10 or more copies; 30% commercial bookstores; 20% classroom & university bookstores. 144pp; 6X9; of. Reporting time: 6 months. Copyrighted. Pub's reviews: 8 in 1979. §Latin America, radical theory. Ads: $150.00/$85.00.

LATITUDES, Martin Jr. Willitts, 405 N. Highland Ave, E Syracuse, NY 13057, (315) 437-5994. 1978. Poetry, long-poems. "Will accept only poems with 38 letter/space lines (or less). Interested in new poets (and local). Published: William Pillin, Susan Mernit, Martin Willitts, A.J. Wright, Pat Mooney, Donna Davis, etc." circ. 150. 1/yr. Pub'd 1 issue 1979; expects 1 issue 1980. sub. price: $1.00; per copy: $1.00; sample: $1.00. Back issues: $0.80. Discounts: 50% discount to stores. 24-36pp; †lp. Reporting time: 3 months. Payment: 2 copies. Copyrighted, reverts to author.

The Latona Press, Marion K. Stocking, David M. Stocking, RFD 2, Box 154, Lamoine, ME 04605. 1978. "Firt book: Chandler Richmond's *Beyond the Spring: Cordelia Stanwood of Birdsacre.* We are not looking for further manuscripts at the present time." avg. press run 1,500. Expects 1 title 1980. 1 title listed in the *Small Press Record of Books in Print* (9th Edition, 1980). avg. price, cloth: $15.00; paper: $8.00. Discounts: To bookstores and wholesalers: 1-4 copies 20%, 5 or more 40%. Postage and shipping extra. No discount on orders not paid for in 30 days. 200pp; 6X9; of. No submissions solicited at the present. Payment: Pays royalties. Copyrights for author.

LAUGHING BEAR, Laughing Bear Press, Tom Person, Editor, Box 14, Woodinville, WA 98072, 206-524-2314. 1976. Poetry, fiction, articles, interviews, reviews, letters, long-poems, plays, concrete art, criticism, news items. "Recent contributors include Roberta Metz, Hugh Fox, James Magorian, Albert Drake, Paul J.J. Payack" circ. 1,000. irregular. Pub'd 1 issue 1979; expects 4 issues 1980, 4 issues 1981. sub. price: $10.00 for 4 issues; per copy: $2.50; sample: free. Back issues: No special prices. Discounts: 40% trade. 64pp; 6X9; †mi. Reporting time: 1 day to 6 weeks. Payment: copies. buys all rights, but will negotiate. Pub's reviews: 4 in 1979. §Experimental literature, nonfiction on about anything; traditional poetry, fiction, drama; reference material. Ads: $100.00/$60.00. COSMEP, CCLM.

Laughing Bear Press (see also LAUGHING BEAR), Tom Person, Editor, Box 14, Woodinville, WA 98072, 206-524-2314. 1976. Poetry. "By invitation only." avg. press run 1,000. Expects 6 titles 1980, 4 titles 1981. 9 titles listed in the *Small Press Record of Books in Print* (9th Edition, 1980). avg. price, paper: $2.00. Discounts: Trade 40%. 64pp; 6X9; †mi. Reporting time: 1 day to 6 months. Payment: percentage of run. Copyrights for author. COSMEP, CCLM.

LAUGHING UNICORN, Publishing Associates, Earl Blanchard, 432 Heathcliff Drive, Pacifica, CA 94044, (415) 355-3630. 1979. Poetry, news items. "Poetry and short prose, black and white graphics." circ. 500. 4-5/yr. Pub'd 3 issues 1979. sub. price: $7.00; per copy: $1.50; sample: $1.00. Back issues: over 5 copies, $1.00. Discounts: 33⅓%. 32pp; 5½X8; of. Reporting time: 10 days. Payment: copies. Copyrighted, reverts to author. Ads: $25.00/$15.00/$0.10, $1.00 min.

THE LAUREL REVIEW, Mark De Foe, Margaret Keating, Jeanne DeFoe, West Virginia Wesleyan College, Buckhannon, WV 26201, 303-473-8006. 1960. Poetry, fiction, articles, interviews, parts-of-novels, plays, reviews, long-poems. "While we seek to encourage writers in Appalachia, THE LAUREL REVIEW is not a 'spit and whittle' magazine. We will purblish anything by anyone if it strikes our fancy, from the avant garde to the traditional. We are interested in intelligent, lucid, provocative writing-craftmanship and meaning do count! Although the *Laurel Review* does encourage writers from Appalachia, we do publish work from writers all across America, Canada and abroad. We do not drop names. We are interested in fine writing—not reputations! Lastly, we will send xerox submissions back unread!" circ. 500. 2-3/yr. Pub'd 2 issues 1979; expects 2 issues 1980, 2 issues 1981. sub. price: $3.00; per copy: $1.50; sample: $1.50. 60pp; 5½X8; lp. Reporting time: 1 week to 3 months. Payment: 2 copies. Copyrighted. Pub's reviews. §Poetry, books on Appalachian subjects, fiction. Ads: $80/$40/$.-

Laurentian Valley Press, Elizabeth St. Jacques, 406 Elizabeth Street, Sault Ste. Marie, Ontario P6B 3H4, Canada, (705) 254-1285. 1977. Poetry, art. "Poems up to 30 lines; any subject so long as handled with dignity and respect. Welcomes haiku and short poems. Guidelines available for SASE; American postage accepted. Illustrated, black india ink sketches. Buys first rights, copyrighted; rights return to author upon publication. (We appreciate credit line for CPAF reprints.) Recent contributors: John Kinsella, Sheila R. Jensen, C.M. Buckaway, Vietta Wines, Sheila Martindale. In hand deadline: Sept 1 but we begin working on next edition immediately after publication so suggest poets submit *well ahead* of deadline. Back copies available for $4.00 per copy: (1977 edition sold out). Beginning with 1980 edition, accepting ads: $0.10 word." avg. press run 200. Pub'd 1 title 1979; expects 1 title 1980, 1 title 1981. avg. price, paper: $4.00. 96pp; 5½X8½; of. Reporting time: immediately. Payment: none; illustrators, however, receive one copy. Copyrights for author.

Lawrence Hill & Company, Publishers, Inc., Lawrence Hill, 520 Riverside Ave., Westport, CT 06880, 203-226-9392. 1972. Poetry, fiction, art, cartoons, interviews, satire, music, letters. "Have strong Black Studies list but are equally interested in other materials." avg. press run 5,000. Pub'd 6-8 titles 1979. avg. price, cloth: $12.95; paper: $5.95. Discounts: See ABA handbook; 10 percent discount to teachers and professors with prepayment; also SCOP 40 percent. Textbook 20%. 256pp; 5½X8½; of. Reporting time: 2-3 weeks. Payment: standard royalty arrangements. Copyrights for author. AAP, CBPA.

Lawson Books, Jean M. Lawson, PO Box 487, Seneca Falls, NY 13148. 1978. "Expect to begin a newsletter in 1980 dealing with the problems of individuals and families in managing their money more successfully - probably late fall '80. In 1978 we pub'd *The Double Key,* how to manage your money using the simple successful methods of business." avg. press run 1,000. Expects 1 title 1980, 1 title 1981. 1 title listed in the *Small Press Record of Books in Print* (9th Edition, 1980). avg. price, paper: $3.95. Discounts: library 35%, dealers 40%. 50pp; 6X9; of.

Lawton Press, Susan Lawton, Editor, 673 Pelham Road, Apt 16E, New Rochelle, NY 10805, 914-636-3852. 1976. Poetry, art, photos. "Lawton Press has changed in the last year. Since my access to a printing press has become very limited, I can no longer consider unsolisited manuscripts. Please don't consider this an R.I.P., still printing *Stone Country, Cumberland Journal* (formally *X, A Journal of the Arts*) and a few individual familiar faces, like my own. Hoping to someday come back strong. Will let you know in next years directory which way the winds have blown." avg. press run 200-1,000 copies. Pub'd 14 titles 1979; expects 10 titles 1980, 6 titles 1981. avg. price, paper: $3.00. 40-100pp; 5½X8½; 7X8½; of. Payment: Author/editor subsidized only. Copyrights for author.

League Books (see POETS' LEAGUE of GREATER CLEVELAND NEWSLETTER)

Leathern Wing Scribble Press (see also THE GENEVA POND BUBBLES), John M. Armleder, 6 Rue Plantamour p.o.b. 253, Geneve CH-l2ll-l, Switzerland, 022-32-6794, 022 45.73.95. 1948. Poetry, art, photos, music, collages, concrete art. "The complete works of John M. Armleder, hand-script-books, mail-activity, collective-books, exchanges, objects, ephemeralia, ready-mades and rubbish. Recent Publications: Ecart's 1977 cooperative works. Fluxus Container, a tribute to George Maciunas by over 25 fluxartists." avg. press run 1,500. Pub'd 9 titles 1979; expects 12 titles 1980, 20 titles 1981. 9 titles listed in the *Small Press Record of Books in Print* (9th Edition, 1980). avg. price, cloth: $10-100 (according to edition); paper: $1-100 (id.); other: free to infinite. Discounts: 33⅓. 12pp; †mi/of/lp. Reporting time: sometimes years. Payment: cups of tea.

Leaves of Grass Press, Stephen Gerstman, PO Box 3914, San Rafael, CA 94902. 1974. avg. press run 5,000. 3 titles listed in the *Small Press Record of Books in Print* (9th Edition, 1980). of.

Leete's Island Books, Peter Neill, Michelle Press, Box 1131, New Haven, CT 06505, (203) 481-2536. 1977. "Fiction, essays, interesting reprints; for the moment, because of time, no unsolicited manuscripts accepted" avg. press run 2500-5000. Pub'd 2 titles 1979; expects 3 titles 1980, 5 titles 1981. 7 titles listed in the *Small Press Record of Books in Print* (9th Edition, 1980). avg. price, paper: $3.95. Discounts: 40%. 5½X8½; of. Payment: varies with title. Copyrights for author.

LEFT CURVE, Left Curve Publications, Csaba Polony, Elliot Ross, Susan Schwartzenberg, 1230 Grant St. Box 302, San Francisco, CA 94133. 1974. Poetry, fiction, articles, art, photos, cartoons, interviews, criticism, reviews, music, letters, long-poems, collages, concrete art. "*LEFT CURVE* focuses on theoretical & practical issues concerning art & revolution. Average length of main articles, 8 pages. All styles from avant -garde to traditional. Recent contributors: E. San Juan, Jr., Willis H. Truitt, Ian Burn, Margaret Randall, Eva Cockcroft. Including editors, Csaba Polony." circ. 1,500. Irregular. sub. price: $7.00 indiv/$14.00 institutions; per copy: $2.50; sample: $2.50. Back issues:

$2.50. Discounts: 1/3 trade. 100pp; 8½X11; of. Reporting time: max. 3 months. Payment: 5 copies. Copyrighted. Pub's reviews: 1 in 1979. §Contemporary art, poetry, cultural politics. Ads: $100/$50.

Left Curve Publications (see also LEFT CURVE), Csaba Polony, Susan Schwartzenberg, Elliot Ross, 1230 Grant St, Box 302, San Francisco, CA 94133. 1974. Poetry, fiction, articles, art, photos, cartoons, interviews, satire, criticism, reviews, music, letters, parts-of-novels, long-poems, collages, concrete art. avg. press run 1,500. Expects 3 titles 1980. 1 title listed in the *Small Press Record of Books in Print* (9th Edition, 1980). avg. price, paper: $2.50. Discounts: 1/3 trade. 100pp; 8½X11; of. Reporting time: 3 months. Payment: 5 copies of issue. Copyrights for author.

LEFTWORKS, Kent Popular Press, John Logue, Bob Howard, John Hennig, Box 715, Kent, OH 44240, (216) 678-9355. 1976. Articles, art, interviews, criticism, news items. "From a non-sectarian, non-dogmatic point of view examines current & recurrent popular issues. #6: Sociology & Science Fiction, 37pp. #7: Language of the American Ultra-Left, 33pp." circ. 50-100. Pub'd 2 issues 1979; expects 3 issues 1980, 2 issues 1981. sub. price: $5.00; per copy: $0.50; sample: $0.50. Back issues: $0.50. Discounts: Library & Institutional rate $10.00/10 issues or $1.00 a copy. 35pp; 5X7. Reporting time: 1 month.

Legacy Books (formerly Folklore Associates) (see also COME-ALL-YE), Richard K. Burns, Lillian Krelove, P.O. Box 494, Hatboro, PA 19040, (215) 675-6762. 1970. "We consider booklength mss in the areas of ethnic music, folklore, social history. Additionally, we import (England, Australia, Wales, etc.) a number of book and pamphlet materials and serve as U.S. distributor. Our latest publishing effort is *The Broadside Ballad* by Leslie Shepard; pub date Aug 16, 1978. We have a regional history (VA) in the works, as well as large compendium of Irish fiddle music." avg. press run 4500. Expects 2 titles 1980, 4 titles 1981. 24 titles listed in the *Small Press Record of Books in Print* (9th Edition, 1980). avg. price, cloth: $9.95; paper: $4.95. Discounts: standard discounts. 205pp; 6X9; lp. Reporting time: 4 months. Payment: 10% on actual (adjusted for discounts) gross income. COSMEP/ABA.

Legal Publications, Inc., Alvin B. Baranov, PO Box 3723, Van Nuys, CA 91407, (213) 782-6545; 873-4939. 1975. "We publish how-to-do it yourself legal books. *How To Evict a Tenant* $7.95; *Incorporation Made Easy* $8.50; *Divorces California Style* $5.95; *What Every Husband & Wife Should Know Before Its Too Late,* a legal, financial and emotional book on marriage, $2.95." avg. press run 5,000. Pub'd 2 titles 1979; expects 1 title 1980, 1 title 1981. 4 titles listed in the *Small Press Record of Books in Print* (9th Edition, 1980). Discounts: 40% to retailers, 55% distributors. 175pp; 8½X11; lp. Reporting time: we publish our own books.

Leland Mellott Books, Leland Mellott, 1461 Page Street, San Francisco, CA 94117, 431-2407. 1977. Poetry, fiction. "Daniel Curzon, Leland Mellott" avg. press run 700. Pub'd 1 title 1979; expects 1 title 1980. Discounts: 40%/trade. of. Reporting time: one month. WIP.

THE LESBIAN TIDE, Tide Publications, Jeanne Cordova, Sharon McDonald, 8706 Cadillac Ave., Los Angeles, CA 90034. 1971. Poetry, fiction, articles, art, photos, cartoons, interviews, satire, criticism, reviews, letters, parts-of-novels, long-poems, plays. "Oldest and largest lesbian publication in the U.S., we present material by and for the international lesbian, feminist, and gay communities. Submissions sought from 1 to 5 pages (double-spaced), with exceptions for special materials. Radical feminist perspectives especially encouraged, but all women's view points welcomed. No male contributors." circ. 10,500. 6 issues/yr. Pub'd 6 issues 1979; expects 6 issues 1980. sub. price: $7.50; per copy: $1.00; sample: $l.50. Back issues: $1.00. Discounts: bulk (10 copies min.) 25% off; institutions $10.00; overseas $8.00. 40pp; 8½X11. Reporting time: Bimonthly. Payment: $5.00-$25.00. Copyrighted, reverts to author. Pub's reviews: 17 in 1979. §lesbians/feminists/women/gay movement. Ads: $80.00/$40.00/$3.00 col. inch.

LESBIAN VOICES, Rosalie Nichols, Editor; Johnie Staggs, Associate Editor, 330 South Third Suite B, San Jose, CA 95112, 408-289-1088. 1973. Poetry, fiction, articles, photos, interviews, reviews, parts-of-novels, long-poems, plays, non-fiction. "All views expressed in this publication are the ideas and opinions of the individual contributor. Favorable treatment of any idea, ideology, product, etc. in *LESBIAN VOICES* does not constitute an endorsement by this magazine, its editors or publisher. We welcome differing points of view on controversial issues, but request that ideas be expressed clearly and rationally and in a tone and style compatible with *LESBIAN VOICES.* We attempt to present a dignified format and a positive, constructive sense of life, in keeping with our belief that lesbianism (and indeed life itself) can be and should be good, wholesome, fulfilling and joyful. We reject the view of lesbianism as material for psychiatric study, religious censure, or pornography..all of which treat lesbianism as sick, sinful or salicious. We reject this view of lesbianism whether it is promulgated by straight society, voyerristic men, or by lesbians themselves." circ. 5,000. 4/yr. Pub'd 4 issues 1979; expects 4 issues 1980. sub. price: $7.00; per copy: $2.00; sample: $1.50. Send for list of back issues.

Discounts: 40 percent on orders of five or more. 100pp; 5½X8½; †of. Reporting time: 2 weeks. Payment: copies. Copyrighted, reverts to author. Pub's reviews. §women's history/lesbian novels. Ads: $75.00/$45.00/$30.00. COSMEP.

LETTERS, Mainespring Press, G. F. Bush, Publisher; Helen Nash, Editor, Box 82, Stonington, ME 04681, 207-367-2484. 1964. Poetry, fiction. "For readers of general literary interests. Quality, (no ethical submissions invited) with SASE for submissions and sample copy." circ. 6500. quarterly. Pub'd 4 issues 1979; expects 4 issues 1980, 4 issues 1981. sub. price: $4.00; per copy: $1.00; sample: Free with SASE. Back issues: available on request. Discounts: none. 4 pp minimum; 8½X11; †of. Reporting time: one month. Payment: moderate; some payment always made. Copyrighted, buys all rights (write for details). Pub's reviews: 1 in 1979. §any, including technical. Ads: $300/$165/none.

LETTERS MAGAZINE, Carole Bovoso, Editor; James Lecesne, Co-editor, P.O. Box 786, New York, NY 10008. 1974. Poetry, fiction, articles, art, photos, cartoons, interviews, satire, music, letters, parts-of-novels, long-poems, collages, plays, concrete art. circ. 1,000. 2/yr. sub. price: $10.00; per copy: $3.00; sample: $4.00. Back issues: Please query. 65pp; 5½X8½; of. Reporting time: 1 mo-3 months. Payment: 3 copies. CCLM, COSMEP.

Levenson Press, P.O.B. 19606, Los Angeles, CA 90019. 1972. "Staff written only, doesn't accept outside ms. Press publishes books only." Expects 1 title 1980. 3 titles listed in the *Small Press Record of Books in Print* (9th Edition, 1980). avg. price, paper: $12.50. Discounts: 23 percent wholesalers. pp varies.; 8½X11; of. Copyrights for author. WNBA, BPSC.

Samuel P. Levine, Samuel P. Levine, PO Box 174, Canoga Park, CA 91305, (213) 343-0550. 1979. "Published *Ham—Kosher Style!* Samuel P. Levine, author and publisher, publication date 9/1/79. ISBN 960290-613 HC $9.95, ISBN 960290-605 PB $5.95. Non-fiction biography of the 'little man' in show business." avg. press run 5,000. Pub'd 1 title 1979. avg. price, cloth: $9.95; paper: $5.95. Discounts: 20% libraries, 40% booksellers, 50% jobbers. 128pp; 5½X8½; lp.

THE LEY HUNTER: The Magazine Of Earth Mysteries, Paul Devereux, PO Box 152, London, England N10 2EF, United Kingdom, 01-883-3949. 1969. Articles, reviews, interviews. "A magazine of earth mysteries: leys; folklore; prehistoric earthworks and megaliths; terrestival zodiacs; ancient earth markings; UFO'S etc. Articles of 500 words upwards on these and related topics of alernative archaeology and ancient cosmology and science. Recent contributors have included Janet Bord, John Michell and John Wilcock, Dr. E.C. Krupp, Prof. Lyle Borst, Fritjof Capra, etc." circ. 2000. 4/yr. Pub'd 4 issues 1979; expects 4 issues 1980, 4 issues 1981. sub. price: £3.60 (U.K.)/£4.50 Europe/£5.45 rest of world ($11.50); per copy: 90p; sample: 90p. Back issues: 50p. Discounts: 33%. 28-36pp; size A5; litho. Reporting time: 2 months. No payment. Copyrighted. Pub's reviews. §Ancient mysteries/Dowsins/fringe science. Ads: £30.00/£16.00/3p.

LIB ED, Collective, 6 Beaconsfield Road, Leicester, England, United Kingdom, 0533-21866. 1966. Poetry, articles, photos, cartoons, interviews, reviews, letters. circ. 1,350. 3/yr. Pub'd 3 issues 1979; expects 3 issues 1980, 3 issues 1981. sub. price: £1; per copy: 40p; sample: 40p. Discounts: 25% to the trade. 20pp; 7X10; of. Reporting time: 1 month. Payment: nil. Pub's reviews: 15 in 1979. §Anarchism, libatarian and raddical education. UAPS (E).

LIBERAL NEWS, Terence Wynn, 1 Whitehall Place, London SW1A2HE, United Kingdom, 01 839 3658. 1946. Articles, photos, news items. "Newspaper" circ. 8,500. 52/yr. Pub'd 51 issues 1979; expects 51 issues 1980. sub. price: $20.00; per copy: 16p. Back issues: not available. Discounts: 6 for price of 5 on advertisements. 15 percent agency commission on advertisements. 8pp; 17X11; of. Payment: nil. Pub's reviews. §political. Ads: £150/£90/5p.

Liberation Publications, Inc. (see also GPU NEWS), Eldon E. Murray, Box 92203, Milwaukee, WI 53202, (414) 276-0612. 1971. avg. press run 3,500.

THE LIBERATOR, Nick Ripperger, P.O. Box 189, Forest Lake, MN 55025. 1975. circ. 2,000. 12/yr. sub. price: $7.50; per copy: $.25; sample: free to distributors. Back issues: 25¢ ea. Discounts: 10% to agents. 10pp; 8½X11; of. Reporting time: 30 days. Pub's reviews. §law/men's lib/women's lib/-divorce. Ads: $10-column inch.

Liberator Press, Douglas Rae, director, P.O. Box 7128, Chicago, IL 60680, 312-663-4329. 1975. News items, photos. "We publish books and pamphlets, generally nonfiction, with an emphasis on subjects that relate to current events." avg. press run 5,000. Pub'd 3 titles 1979; expects 5 titles 1980, 10 titles 1981. 12 titles listed in the *Small Press Record of Books in Print* (9th Edition, 1980). avg. price, cloth: $12.00; paper: $4.00. Discounts: 40 percent bookstores, 25 percent individuals ordering 10 or more, special distributor discounts available. 325pp; 5½X8½; †of. Reporting time: 3 months. Payment: varies-usually, advance then per-centage of gross. Copyrights for author.

LIBERO INTERNATIONAL, Editorial Committee, c/o Tohyama, 3-13-5, Shojaku, Settsu, Osaka, 564 Japan. 1975. Articles, cartoons, news items. "We published five issues between 1975 and 1979. Due to pressure of movement commitments, issue #6, ready in Feb-March 1980, will be the last. We intend to concentrate on producing a book-length history of the anarchist movement in Korea." circ. 500. price per copy: $1.50; sample: $1.50. Back issues: $1.50. 48-54pp; 8X8; of. Payment: none. Not copyrighted.

Liberty Publishing Company, Inc., 50 Scott Adam Road, Cockeysville, MD 21030. 1977. "Nonfiction, consumer and children's books." Pub'd 7 titles 1979. 4 titles listed in the *Small Press Record of Books in Print* (9th Edition, 1980).

Libra Press (see also DELIRIUM), Jim McCurry, PO Box 341, Wataga, IL 61488. 1975. Poetry, fiction, art, photos, cartoons, letters, parts-of-novels, long-poems, collages. "No length restrictions, although I like to edit prose: no biases. Recent contributors: Hugh Fox, Stanley Berne, Linda Bohe, Jack Collom, David Cope, Thomas Michael Fisher, John Giorno, Christy Kyckelhahn, Lyn Lifshin, Christopher Middleton, Toby Olson, Sandra Case, Melissa Cummings, Stephen Ruffus, David Plante, Ron Silliman, Dan Raphael, Bruce Andrews, Paul Vangelisti, Charles Plymell, Marc Weber, Arlene Zekowski & others. Two books out, 1980: Melissa Cummings' *Difficult to Sleep in the Quiet World,* and Rawdon Tomlinson's *Touching the Dead* (both poetry collections)." avg. press run 650. Expects 2 titles 1980. 2 titles listed in the *Small Press Record of Books in Print* (9th Edition, 1980). avg. price, paper: $2.00. Discounts: 10% agencies; 40% classrooms & libraries on orders of 10 or more. 60pp; 5½X8½; of. Reporting time: immediately to 2 weeks. Payment: individual terms (inquire). power of copyright reverts to author. CCLM, COSMEP.

Libra Publishers, Inc. (see also ADOLESCENCE; FAMILY THERAPY), William Kroll, President, 391 Willets Road, Roslyn Heights, L.I., NY 11577, (516) 484-4950. 1960. Poetry, fiction, articles, art, photos, cartoons, interviews, satire, criticism, reviews, music, letters, parts-of-novels, long-poems, collages, plays, concrete art, news items. "Most interested in books in the behavioral sciences." avg. press run 3,000. Pub'd 15 titles 1979; expects 20 titles 1980, 22 titles 1981. avg. price, cloth: $7.95; paper: $4.95. Discounts: 1-4 copies, 33⅓%; 5 or more, 40%. 160pp; 5½X8½; of. Reporting time: 4 weeks. Payment: 10% of retail price. Copyrights for author.

Librairie Droz S.A. (see BIBLIOTHEQUE D'HUMANISME ET RENAISSANCE)

LIBRARIANS FOR SOCIAL CHANGE, John L Noyce, Publisher, John L. Noyce, PO Box 450, Brighton, Sussex BN1 8GR, United Kingdom. 1972. Articles, poetry, fiction, art, cartoons, satire, news items, interviews, photos. "Anything on librarianship and social change; sexism, racism, workers' control in librarianship and related areas such as info work, publishing, etc." circ. 400. 3/yr. Pub'd 3 issues 1979; expects 3 issues 1980, 3 issues 1981. sub. price: libraries £8/$18; individuals £3.00/$8.00; per copy: £3.50 libraries (£1.00 individuals); sample: £3.00 libraries (£1.00 individuals). Back issues: £3.00 libraries (£1.00 individuals). Discounts: 10 percent to trade. 32pp; size A4; of. Reporting time: we try. Payment: free copy. Pub's reviews: 24 in 1979. §libraries, social change, alternative society/work/ideas. Ads: on application. U/APS (EUROPE)

THE LIBRARY IMAGINATION PAPER!, Carol Bryan, 1000 Byus Drive, Charleston, WV 25311, (304) 345-2378. 1979. Articles, art, photos, cartoons, interviews, satire, reviews, concrete art, news items. "Each issue features ready-to-go, reproducible art, copy and ideas for all types of library programs and promotions. Also included are in-depth articles dealing with Library PR subjects - some written by illustrious guest specialists - and tips on dealing with printers, papers, people, and promotion. Issues contain an abundance of tried and tested tips for practical librarians, and adventurous ideas for brave librarians. Valuable source listings for obtaining related help and materials are also featured. One issue featured 14 ready-to-go library activity sketches; another had 18 ready-to-go bookmark ideas." circ. 1,500. 4/yr. Pub'd 4 issues 1979. sub. price: $12.00; per copy: $3.00; sample: $0.25. Back issues: $3.00 per back issue. Discounts: Baker's Dozen Special of 13 subscriptions for the price of 12 when bulk mailed to a single address. 4pp; 11X17; of. Reporting time: depends. Payment: usually a free subscription. Copyrighted, depends.

Library Research Associates, Matilda A. Gocek, RD #5, Box 41, Dunderberg Road, Monroe, NY 10950, 914-783-1144. 1968. "I attempt to give authors of non-fiction local history (N.Y.) a chance to be published." avg. press run 2,500. Pub'd 4 titles 1979; expects 3 titles 1980. 9 titles listed in the *Small Press Record of Books in Print* (9th Edition, 1980). avg. price, cloth: $9.00; paper: $3.00. Discounts: 40% to book sellers. 150pp; 5½X8½; of/lp. Reporting time: 1 month. Payment: 10 percent royalties. Copyrights for author.

LIBRARY REVIEW, J. D. Hendry, G. Jones, 30 Clydeholm Road, Glasgow G14 OBJ, United Kingdom. 1927. Articles, interviews, reviews. 4/yr. Pub'd 4 issues 1979. sub. price: £11.00. Discounts:

16⅔% to agents. 72pp; lp. Reporting time: 1 month. Payment: by arrangement. Copyrighted, does not revert to author. Ads: £50/£30/.

Libre Press (see also THE METRO), John J. White, Publisher; Joseph Skorupa, Managing Editor, 529-530 Connell Bldg, Scranton, PA 18503. 1978. Poetry, fiction, articles, art, photos, cartoons, interviews, satire, criticism, reviews, long-poems, news items. "Return envelop necessary with postage." avg. press run 10,000. Pub'd 10 titles 1979; expects 10 titles 1980, 22 titles 1981. avg. price, paper: $0.50. 16-32pp; of. Reporting time: 3 months. Payment: depends on article $5.00 to $150.00. Copyrights for author. APS.

Lidiraven Books: A Division of Biogeocosmological Press, Gladys Goldfin, Chuck Gordon, Managing Editor, Box 5567, Sherman Oaks, CA 91413, (213) 892-0059. 1979. Satire, criticism. "We are interested in books that attack and expose chicanery and deceit, such as: UFOs, colonic irrigation, space aliens, science fiction, the flat earth society, dolphin intelligence, the turin shroud, charms and miraculous cures, exorcism, ghosts, clairvoyance, levitation, chariots of the gods, encounterers of the third kind, pet rocks, star trekkies, star wariors, the ballot box, or geodesic domes. We are looking for books that consider scientific and technical solutions to man's problems-solutions that would point the way toward an abundant, long, and fruitful life for every human, whatever his color or shape. Latest title: *Is There Intelligent Life On Earth?* by Jack Catran." avg. press run 10,000-20,000. Pub'd 3 titles 1979. 1 title listed in the *Small Press Record of Books in Print* (9th Edition, 1980). avg. price, cloth: $8.95. Discounts: 45% to booksellers, books must be kept at least 9 months. 250pp; 5½X8¼; of. Reporting time: 3 weeks. Payment: negotiable, and generous. Copyrights for author.

Lieb/Schott Publications (see PTERANODON)

LIFELINE, Highway Book Shop, Douglas C. Pollard, Cobalt, Ontario P0J1C0, Canada. 1974. Articles. "Always interested in short articles (500 words or less) on any aspect of writing and/or publishing." circ. 700. 24/yr. Pub'd 24 issues 1979. sub. price: $15.00; per copy: $1.00; sample: $1.00. 16pp; 8½X11; †of. Reporting time: 1 week. Payment: 1 year sub. Pub's reviews. §Writing and/or publishing. Ads: $.10. COSMEP, CPPA.

LIGHT: A Poetry Review, Roberta C. Gould, Lora M. Eckert, Assistant Editor, P.O. Box 1298D Stuyvesant PO, New York City, NY 10009. 1973. Poetry, photos, collages, concrete art. "An eclectic selection in terms of both content & form. We feature translations. Open to political statements but the poem must make it as a poem. Also looking for concrete or visual poems. Line drawings & photographs should be camera ready, 4 x 5. Plan reviews. Would like more submissions by women. Contributors: Ree Dragonette, Daisy Aldan, Robert Stock, Barbara Holland, Rosario Castellanos, Brian Swann, Victoria Theodhorou, Eve Triem, Olga Cabral, John Tagliabue, Donald Walsh, Roberta Gould, No. 3 & 5 special translation issues, Greek, Turkish, Mexican women poets, etc. No xerox. Large manilla envelope submissions not accepted. It is strongly suggested that potential contributors read the magazine before submitting work. All correspondence should include SASE" circ. 700. 1/yr. Pub'd 1 issue 1979; expects 1 issue 1980. sub. price: $5.50 - 4 issues; per copy: $1.50; sample: $1.50. Back issues: $1.50 except No. 1 - $5.00. Discounts: $6/4 issues to libraries; 40% off to bkstrs (Cash only.). 64pp; 8½X5½; of. Reporting time: 2 months/6 months. Payment: copies. Copyrighted, reverts to author. Pub's reviews. §Poetry. Ads: exchange/interested in exchange ads only. CCLM, COSMEP.

Light Living Library (see also MESSAGE POST), Hank Schultz, PO Box 190, Philomath, OR 97370. 1979. Articles. "Home-camp tools & techniques, portable shelters, wildcrafting, hoboing (*not* farming, permanent buildings, ecology)." Pub'd 7 titles 1979. avg. price, other: $0.60 unbound. 4pp; 8½X11; of. Reporting time: away summers. Payment: 20% after 20.

Lightbooks, Paul Castle, Senior Editor, Box 425, Marlton, NJ 08053, (609) 983-5978. 1973. Photos. "We publish for photographers who want to make money (or *more* money) with their cameras. Our books tell them new and better ways to do it. Recent titles tell it all *How to Produce and Mass-Market Your Creative Photography; Outdoor Photography: How to Shoot It, How to Sell It; How to Produce and Market Your Limited Edition Photography; $25,000 a Year With Color Postcards and Brochures.* We want mss any length or style, with or w/o pix that fit that format. Please! *No books of pretty pictures for the coffee-table ! We don't do those.*" avg. press run 2-3,000. Pub'd 2 titles 1979; expects 4 titles 1980, 4 titles 1981. 5 titles listed in the *Small Press Record of Books in Print* (9th Edition, 1980). avg. price, cloth: $15.00; paper: $12.50; other: Also put out 32 page paper-covered pamphlets at $3-5. 190pp; 6X9; of. Reporting time: very quick, usually, 2-3 weeks. Payment: 5-15% depending on material & re-writing needed. Copyrights for author. COSMEP.

The Lightning Tree, Jetta C. Lyon, Jene Lyon, PO Box 1837, Santa Fe, NM 87501, (505) 983-7434. 1973. "We publish general trade books, including, but not limited to, history, poetry, folk lore, ecology, science, cook books, etc." avg. press run 1,500-3,000. Pub'd 7 titles 1979; expects 6 titles

1980, 9 titles 1981. avg. price, cloth: $9.95; paper: $4.95; other: $2.00 (posters). Discounts: Regular trade discounts to retailers (same for jobbers), special discounts for libraries and institutions. 128pp; 5¼X7; 8½X11; †of/lp. Reporting time: Very long. Payment: Royalty based on list price & quantity; starts at 10%. Copyrights for author. RMBPA (Rocky Mountain Book Publishers Association).

LILITH, Susan W. Schneider, Exec Editor; Aviva Cantor, Acq Editor; Amy Stone, Senior Editor; Reena Sigman Freedman, News Editor, 250 W 57th, Suite 1328, New York, NY 10019, (212) 757-0818. 1976. Poetry, fiction, articles, art, photos, cartoons, interviews, satire, criticism, reviews, letters, parts-of-novels, plays, news items. "The 'Jewish Woman's Quarterly" circ. 10,000. 4/yr. Pub'd 2 issues 1979; expects 4 issues 1980, 4 issues 1981. sub. price: $8.00 for 4 issues; per copy: $2.50 prepaid; sample: $2.50 prepaid. Back issues: $2.50 prepaid, issues 1, 2, 3 are out of print. 50pp; 8½X11; of. Reporting time: Several months. Payment: Nachas and kovod and small honorarium (under $50.00 usually). Copyrighted, rights revert to authors if they want. Pub's reviews: 10 in 1979. §Jewish women. Ads: $250.00/$150.00/$0.40.

THE LIMBERLOST REVIEW, Richard Ardinger, 704 S. Arthur Street, Pocatello, ID 83201. 1976. Poetry, fiction, interviews, reviews. "THE LIMBERLOST REVIEW is an independent small press of poetry. Known contributors include John Clellon Holmes, Ed Dorn, Eugene McCarthy, Greg Kuzma, Harald Wyndham, Jim Doyle, Walter McDonald, Charles Bukowski, others. No restrictions on style or form. We're primarily a poetry magazine, though we would like to have interviews with poets and novelists. TLR is not merely a regional publicaiton. Alternate issues are devoted to the work of one poet in the form of a chapbook. No. 8 was devoted to a chapbook of poems by John Clellon Holmes entitled *Death Drag: Selected Poems 1948-1979.*" circ. 300. 2-3/yr. Pub'd 3 issues 1979; expects 3 issues 1980, 3-4 issues 1981. sub. price: $5.50; per copy: $1.50; sample: $1.50. Back issues: $2.50. Discounts: 30% 10 or more. 45pp; 5½X8½; of/lp. Reporting time: 1-2 months. Payment: in copies. Copyrighted, reverts to author. §Poetry. Ads: $25.00/$12.50. CCLM.

LIMIT! (The National Newsletter Of The Libertarian Republican Alliance), Joseph L. Gentili, Publisher; Elliott Capon, Editor, 1149 E 32nd Street, Brooklyn, NY 11210. 1974. "750-1,500 words preferable, non-pedantic style. Topic should be politically oriented. Slant should appeal to Libertarians, Conservatives, Republicans (or any combination thereof). Recent contributors: Tibor R. Machan, Rep. Ronald E. Paul*M.D., Sid Greenberg, Sam Wells, Jack R. Patterson, James Robert Riis, J. Keen Holland, Dean Allen Sr., Fred Stein, George Steven Swan." circ. 300. 12/yr. Pub'd 12 issues 1979; expects 12 issues 1980. sub. price: $5.00; per copy: $0.50; sample: free. 6pp; 8½X11; of. Reporting time: 1-2 weeks. Pay in copies. Not copyrighted. Pub's reviews: 6 in 1979. §Politics with a libertarian, Conservative, Republican slant, individualistic sci. fi. Ads: $25.00/$15.00/$10.00 1/4 page.

LINES REVIEW, M. Macdonald, William Montgomerie, Macdonald, Edgefield Rd, Loanhead, Midlothian EH20 9SY, United Kingdom. 1952. Articles, poetry, reviews, long-poems. circ. 850. 4/yr. sub. price: £2.08; per copy: 40p. Back issues: 40p. 48pp; 8½X5½; †lp. Reporting time: by return. Payment: approx £4.00 per page. Pub's reviews: 12 in 1979. §literature, poetry. Ads: £16/£10/£6 1/4 page.

LINQ, English Language Literature Association, Cheryl Frost, Coordinating Editor, English Dept., James Cook University of North Queensland, Townsville 4811, Australia. 1971. Poetry, fiction, articles, interviews, criticism, reviews, parts-of-novels, long-poems, plays. "Critical articles about 3000 words. Reviews 1000 words." circ. 150. 3/yr. Pub'd 3 issues 1979. sub. price: $7.00 indiv; $10.00 instit plus postage, Australian; per copy: $2.00, Australian; sample: $a1-00. Back issues: $a0-50. 80pp; 5½X8½; of. Reporting time: 2 mo. Payment: dependent on subsidy. Copyrighted. Pub's reviews: 20 in 1979. §any area of contemporary interest, political, sociological, literary.

Lintel, Bonnie E. Nelson, Box 34, St. George, NY 10301. 1978. Poetry, fiction, art, long-poems. "We have gotten some good back-cover blurbs from Kurt Vonnequt, David Ignatow, Anthony Burgess, et al. We finance a book through advance subscriptions." avg. press run 1,000. Expects 3 titles 1980, 3 titles 1981. 7 titles listed in the *Small Press Record of Books in Print* (9th Edition, 1980). avg. price, cloth: $9.00; paper: $4.95. Discounts: 40% to Bookstores and Libraries. 80pp; 5¾X9; of. Reporting time: 2 months. Payment: Author gets 100 copies on publication, and shares in the profits, if any. Each contract is worked out individually. Copyrights for author. COSMEP, NYSSPA.

Lion Enterprises (see also GRYPHON: A Culture's Critic), Jr Robert Villegas, RR 3, Box 127, Walkerton, IN 46574, 219-369-9394. 1975. Poetry, fiction, articles, criticism, plays. "Primarily interested in elevating Romantic Art and in developing interest in it. Will publish high quality books, novels, plays, poetry if it is consistent with Romanticism. Any prospective author should read and fully understand Ayn Rand's book *The Romantic Manifesto* before submitting." avg. press run 500. Pub'd 1 title 1979; expects 4 titles 1980, 3 titles 1981. 2 titles listed in the *Small Press Record of Books in Print* (9th Edition, 1980). avg. price, cloth: $8.00; paper: $4.00. Discounts: Lists available upon request. Discounts competitive with other publishers. 50pp; 5½X8½; of. Reporting time: 2 weeks to 1 month. Payment: negotiable. Copyrights for author.

Lionhead Publishing, Martin J. Rosenblum, Editor, 2521 East Stratford Court, Shorewood, WI 53211, 414-332-7474. 1970. Poetry, long-poems. "We only publish sporadically and want no submissions. We publish experimental poetry only." avg. press run 200. Pub'd 2 titles 1979. 5 titles listed in the *Small Press Record of Books in Print* (9th Edition, 1980). avg. price, paper: $7.00. Discounts: none. 100pp; size varies considerably; of. We do not solicit any submissions at this time at all. Payment: varies, usually copies. Copyrights for author.

Literary Herald Press, Daniel McLaughlin, 408 Oak Street, Danville, IL 61832, (213) 446-5740.

LITERARY MARKET REVIEW, Kunnuparampil P. Punnoose, 73-47 255th Street, Glen Oaks, NY 11004, (212) 343-7285. 1975. Articles, reviews, news items. "*Literary Market Review* is an international journal promoting the export of American books and journals to Asian countries. Editorial office: 6/77 WEA Ajmalkhan Road, New Delhi 110 005, India" circ. 2,000. 4/yr. Pub'd 4 issues 1979; expects 4 issues 1980, 4 issues 1981. sub. price: $5.00; per copy: $1.25; sample: free. Discounts: 15%. 32pp; 9X11; lp. Reporting time: 1 month. Payment: depends on every piece. Pub's reviews. §All subjects of human interest. Ads: $150.00/$80.00.

LITERARY MONITOR: The Voice of Contemporary Literature, TLM Press, Gary Lagier, Editor; Thomas Piekarski, Associate Editor; Gordon Bubar, Legal Columnist; Jim Wortham, Distribution Columnist, 1070 Noriega, Sunnyvale, CA 94086. 1977. Poetry, fiction, articles, photos, interviews, satire, criticism, reviews, letters, news items, long-poems. "*LM* is actively seeking: reviews, small press profiles (interviews with leading small press editors, publishers and writers with particular emphasis on exposing them to their potential contributors), new publication listings, photographs (books, magazines, writers, editors, events, conventions, etc.), articles (how-to and field-wide surveys), manuscripts wanted, contests/awards listings, interviews (in-depth), resources, personality profiles, news (of the contemporary literature scene), special focus articles (third world, women, native American, Black, etc.), and is also interested in letters for our letter column. Our legal column answers letters on legal problems writers & publishers encounter. We've added a poetry and fiction (under 2,000 words) section." circ. 14,000. 6/yr. Pub'd 6 issues 1979; expects 6 issues 1980. sub. price: $12.00; $15.00 Instit.; per copy: $2.50 + 9 x 12 SASE with 59¢ postage; sample: $2.50 + 9 x 12 SASE with 59¢ postage. 64-96pp; 8½X11; of. Reporting time: 2-4 weeks. Payment: One copy of *TLM* in which item appears. Copyrighted, does not revert to author. Pub's reviews: Several hundred in 1979. §All literature (poetry, fiction, criticism) plus how-to & articles for writers/publishers. Ads: Write for them, with SASE. CCLM, AWP.

LITERARY RESEARCH NEWSLETTER, Vincent L. Tollers, Editor; Mary Ann O'Donnell, Assoc Editor; Robert F. Kiernan, Assoc Editor, Department of English and World Literature, Manhattan College, Bronx, NY 10471, (212) 548-1400 Ext. 118. 1976. Articles, reviews, news items. "Oriented toward information on literary research projects and the teaching of courses in literary research." circ. 350. quarterly. Pub'd 4 issues 1979; expects 4 issues 1980, 4 issues 1981. sub. price: $4.00; per copy: $1.50; sample: free. Back issues: $1.50. Discounts: none. 48pp; 5½X8½; †of. Reporting time: 4 months. Payment: none. Copyrighted, does not revert to author. Pub's reviews: 14 in 1979. §bibliography, research guides, studies of the literary research course. Ads: none.

THE LITERARY REVIEW, Martin Green, Harry Keyishian, Fairleigh Dickinson University, 285 Madison Avenue, Madison, NJ 07940, 201 377-4050. 1957. Poetry, fiction, articles, interviews, criticism, reviews, long-poems, plays. "We consider fiction and poetry submissions of any type and of any length (within reason) from new and established writers. We welcome critical articles on any aspect of American and international literature and are anxious to have submissions of essays that are written for a general literary audience and not aimed at the academic quarterly market. We are preparing some special issues on the following themes and particularly welcome essays on these topics: *The Great Depression* and *Its Literary Impact;* the modern practice of tragedy in fiction, drama, and film; popular genres in the U.S. and abroad. *TLR* has always had a special emphasis on contemporary writing abroad (in translation) and we welcome submissions from overseas, and new translations of contemporary foreign literature. We are particularly interested in receiving translations of and essays on ethnic writing abroad. Our pattern of publication is fall (fiction issue); winter (international issue); spring (poetry issue); summer (special issue)." circ. 1,000-1,200. 4/yr. Pub'd 4 issues 1979; expects 4 issues 1980, 4 issues 1981. sub. price: $9.00 U.S., $10.00 foreign; per copy: $3.50 U.S., $4.00 foreign; sample: selected back issues, $2.00; recent issues, $3.50. Back issues: price varies. 128-150pp; 6X9; of. Reporting time: 2-3 months. Payment: 2 free copies, additional copies at discount. Copyrighted, does not revert to author. Pub's reviews: 5 in 1979. §Contemporary fiction, poetry, literary theory, US and world literature (contemporary). CCLM.

224

LITERARY SKETCHES, Mary Lewis Chapman, Box 711, Williamsburg, VA 23185, 804-229-2901. 1961. Articles, interviews, reviews, letters. "1,000 word maximum" circ. 500. 11/yr. Pub'd 11 issues 1979. 1 title listed in the *Small Press Record of Books in Print* (9th Edition, 1980). sub. price: $2.50; per copy: $.25; sample: $.25. Back issues: $0.25. 4pp; 11X8½; of. Reporting time: month. Payment: 1/2 cent per word. Not copyrighted. Pub's reviews: 15-20 in 1979. §Literary Biographies only, books on books. Ads: $2.00 per inch.

LITERATURE OF LIBERTY, Suzanne Woods, Leonard Liggio, John V. Cody, 1177 University Drive, Menlo Park, CA 94025, 415-323-6933. 1978. "Scholarly articles, social sciences, humanities, law, etc., political philosophy." circ. 1,100. 4/yr. Pub'd 4 issues 1979; expects 4 issues 1980. sub. price: $12.00; per copy: $4.00; sample: $4.00. Back issues: $4.00 each. Discounts: 60/40%. 96pp; 7X10; of. Copyrighted. Pub's reviews. §Historical, philosophical, scholarly, research. Ads: $60.-00/$30.00.

LITERATUREGATE (see White Murray Press)

Litmus, Inc., Charles Potts, Editor, 525 Bryant, Walla Walla, WA 99362. 1966. Poetry, photos, long-poems, plays. "Charles Bukowski, Mike Finley, Edward Smith, Karen Waring. Inquire before submitting." 16 titles listed in the *Small Press Record of Books in Print* (9th Edition, 1980). avg. price, paper: $5.00. Discounts: 40 percent on 5 or more, mixed titles OK. 64pp; 5½X8½; †of/lp. Reporting time: 6 months. Payment: 10%. Copyrights for author.

THE LITTLE AROUND JOURNAL, Around Publishing, Janos Szebedinszky, Patricia Walsh, PO Box 541, Mentone, IN 46539. 1975. Poetry, fiction, articles, art, photos, cartoons, interviews, satire, criticism, reviews, music, letters, parts-of-novels, long-poems, collages, plays, concrete art, news items. "Length of material determines size of publication. Biases are toward less 'down' information, more toward intertainment, and access to things." circ. 2,000 to 5,000. 6/yr. sub. price: $5.00; per copy: $0.50; sample: free. Back issues: $1.00 each. Discounts: general 25-35 percent discount. 16-28pp; size tab; †of. Reporting time: 2-5 weeks. Payment: Promissory notes, and an occasional check. Copyrighted, reverts to author. Pub's reviews. §Ecology, philosophy, anthropology, sci-fi, poetry, science, homemaking, humor, and all other good things. Ads: $200.00/$100.00/$0.15.

LITTLE CAESAR, Little Caesar Press, Dennis Cooper, 3373 Overland Ave., #2, Los Angeles, CA 90034, 213-837-8255. 1976. Poetry, fiction, art, photos, cartoons, interviews. "We like work that's on fire. Originality catches our eyes. We want to reach everyone from poetry fans to rock'n'rollers to the Dodgers, so keep that in mind. We hope our biases are against dullness and didacticism, and pro-energy. Recent contributors: Tom Clark, Gerard Malanga, Joe Brainard, Edmund White, Allen Ginsberg, Lou Reed, Michael Lally." circ. 1,000. 3-4/yr. Pub'd 3 issues 1979; expects 3 issues 1980, 4 issues 1981. sub. price: $4.00; per copy: $1.50; sample: $1.50. Back issues: $1.50 per issue. Discounts: 40 percent discount for trade, libraries, schools, etc. 130pp; 5½X8½; of. Reporting time: 6 weeks to 6 months. Payment: 3 copies. Copyrighted, reverts to author. Pub's reviews: 1 in 1979. §Literature publications chiefly, also films, art and music. Ads: $1.00.

Little Caesar Press (see also LITTLE CAESAR), Dennis Cooper, Editor, 3373 Overland Ave #2, Los Angeles, CA 90034, (213) 837-8255. 1977. "Cooper, Dennis, *Tiger Beat*, Little Caesar Press, 1978, 5½ x 8½; 20 pp.; saddle/ $1.00; Poet's second chapbook. Rimbaud, Arthur (translated by Bell, Scott), *Travels In Abyssinia And The Harar*, Little Caesar Press, 1979, 5½ x 8½; 40 pp.; paper/ $3.00; The first English language edition of Rimbaud's final work. Dlugos, Tim *Je Suis Ein Americano*, Little Caesar Press, 1979, 5½ x 8½; 36 pp.; paper/$2.00; First big book by popular New Yorker. Malange, Gerard, *100 Years Have Passed*, Little Caesar Press, 1978, 4 x 5; 46 pp; paper/$2.00; Great poet's final section of Benedetta poems. Koertge, Ron, *Sex Object*, Little Caesar Press, 1979, 5½ x 8½; 64 pp.; paper/$3.00; New edition of Country Press classic, revised by poet. Cooper, Dennis and McNeill, Wayne, *Time Machine*, Little Caesar Press, 1979, 5½ x 8½; 48 pp; paper/$2.00; Collaborative 'future' work by the popular young poets" avg. press run 800. Pub'd 2 titles 1979; expects 4 titles 1980. 9 titles listed in the *Small Press Record of Books in Print* (9th Edition, 1980). avg. price, paper: $2.00. Discounts: 40% to bookstores. of. Reporting time: 6 weeks to 6 months. Copyrights for author.

Little Dinosaur Press, Gary Burnett, Kathleen Burnett, 1222 Solano Avenue, Albany, CA 94706. 1980. Poetry. "Two titles from 1980: Michael Davidson *Discovering Motion,* Michael Palmer *Transparency of the Mirror.* We do not accept unsolicited manuscripts" avg. press run 250, 25 numbered, signed. avg. price, paper: $3.50. Discounts: 1 copy 10%, 2-4 copies 20%, 5 or more 40%. 24pp; 5½X8½; of. Payment: copies. Copyrights for author.

LITTLE FREE PRESS, Larry F. Johnson, Mike Takefreedom, 715 E. 14th St., Minneapolis, MN 55404. 1969. "Anything logical utopian. Information for dropping out of Rat Race." circ. 5000. 9/yr. Pub'd 9 issues 1979; expects 9 issues 1980, 9 issues 1981. 2 titles listed in the *Small Press Record of*

Books in Print (9th Edition, 1980). sub. price: free; per copy: free; sample: free. Back issues: free. Discounts: none. 8pp; 3½X8½; of. Payment: gratis only. Not copyrighted. no ads.

THE LITTLE MAGAZINE, Felicity Thoet, Managing Editor, Box 207 Cathedral Station, New York, NY 10025. 1965. Poetry, fiction, satire, parts-of-novels, long-poems. "No bias-just the best. Recent special issues: Women's Issue, Fiction Issue, Formal Poetry Issue" circ. 1,000. 4/yr. Pub'd 3 issues 1979; expects 4 issues 1980. sub. price: $7.00; per copy: $2.00; sample: $2.00. 64pp; 5½X8½; of. Reporting time: 1 month. Payment: 2 copies. Copyrighted, reverts to author. Ads: none. CCLM.

Little Red Hen, Inc., T. J. MD. McDevitt, PO Box 4260, Pocatello, ID 83201, (208) 233-3755. 1978. Fiction. avg. press run 1,000. Expects 1 title 1980, 1 title 1981. 1 title listed in the *Small Press Record of Books in Print* (9th Edition, 1980). avg. price, cloth: $8.95. Discounts: Usual. of.

THE LITTLE REVIEW, John McKernan, Marshall University, Box 205, Huntington, WV 25701. 1968. "Modern poetry & translations." circ. 1,000. 2/yr. Pub'd 2 issues 1979; expects 2 issues 1980, 2 issues 1981. sub. price: $4.00; per copy: $2.00; sample: $2.00. Back issues: inquire. Discounts: 40% to bookstores. 24-32pp; 8½X11; of. Reporting time: 2 mos. (not reviewing mss. until Feb. 1981). Payment: copies. Copyrighted, reverts to author. Pub's reviews. §poetry. Ads: none. CCLM.

Little River Press, Ronald Edwards, 10 Lowell Avenue, Westfield, MA 01085, (413) 568-5598. 1976. Poetry. "Little River Press does not read or return unsolicited mss. We do limited editions of poetry. *Anonyms,* prose poems by Stephen Sossaman (1978) is available from an edition of 25 signed and 75 other copies at $5 and $2 respectively, postpaid. *Arrangements and Transformations in 18 pt. Century Oldstyle Bold* concrete poetry by R. Edwards, $1.50. *Tenerife Haiku, Islas Canarias* by Cliff Edwards, $5.00; *Messages* concrete poetry by R. Edwards, $2.50." avg. press run 50-100. Pub'd 3 titles 1979; expects 2 titles 1980, 3 titles 1981. 4 titles listed in the *Small Press Record of Books in Print* (9th Edition, 1980). avg. price, paper: $2.00. 16-20pp; 7½X6¼; †lp. Copyrights for author.

Little Wing Publishing, Gloria J. Leitner, General Delivery, Lund, B.C. V0N 2G0, Canada. 1975. Poetry, fiction, articles. "Two books: *Poems of Song & Passion,* a collection (1975) $2.50; and *Lovebud: Expectations of the Heart,* a poetically-told tale (1978) $4.50. Only publish editor's own work" avg. press run 1,000. Pub'd 1 title 1979. 2 titles listed in the *Small Press Record of Books in Print* (9th Edition, 1980). avg. price, paper: $4.00. Discounts: 40%. 60pp; 6X8; lp.

THE LITTLE WORD MACHINE, L.W.M. Publications, Nick Toczek, Editor; Yann Lovelock, Assistant Editor, 5 Beech Terrace, Undercliffe, Bradford, West Yorkshire, England BD3 0PY, United Kingdom. 1972. Articles, poetry, fiction, art, reviews, criticism, concrete art. "Includes known & unknown writers & a wide variety of styles & forms of contemporary writing. Recent contributors include Seamus Heaney, Edward Lucie-Smith, Peter Redgrove, Michael & Frances Horovitz, F.G. Lorca (tr), Andrew Salkey, Gavin Ewart, etc." circ. 1,000. 4/yr. Expects 4 issues 1980, 4 issues 1981. sub. price: £2.00(UK), £4.00(overseas); per copy: 60p(UK), £1.20(overseas); sample: 60p(UK), £1.20(overseas). Discounts: 33⅓ to shops on order of 6 or more. 88-100pp; 21X15cm; of. Reporting time: 3 mos. Payment: none. Copyrighted, reverts to author. Pub's reviews: 20 in 1979. §mags/books (mostly small press), records, cassettes, writers reference books, etc. Ads: £12/£8/£5 1/4.

LIVE WRITERS! LOCAL ON TAP, La Reina Press, Lupe A. Gonzalez, Karen Feinberg, Donna D. Vitucci, PO Box 8182, Cincinnati, OH 45208, (513) 579-8798. 1979. Poetry, fiction, art, photos. "Poetry can be any length; Fiction limited to approx. 1,000 words; line drawings approx. 4½ x 7 or reduced to that size & must be camera-ready, B/W preferably; photos approx. 4½ x 7. We are a Cinti-based small press with future plans for a monthly periodical, books on women's lit., Third World lit., children's books, and a writers' conference in Sept. each year. Our literary mag is our first publication, giving the southwestern area of OH a local outlet for their work. This area includes Indiana, Kentucky. Distribution of ALL La Reina Press publications will include Cleveland, Columbus, Cinti, Chicago, Los Angeles, San Francisco, Eugene, Ore." circ. 1,000. 4/yr. sub. price: $10.00; per copy: $2.25; sample: $2.25. Back issues: $2.50 plus postage $0.50. Discounts: 40% Trade. 75pp; 5½X8½; of. Reporting time: 4-6 weeks. Payment: copies. Copyrighted, reverts to author. Ads: $125.-00/$65.00. COSMEP.

Live-Oak Press, J. Lawrence Lembo, PO Box 99444, San Francisco, CA 94109, (415) 771-4992. 1980. Poetry, articles. "Only poetry & articles for the betterment of mankind. No restrictions on length, etc." avg. press run 1,000. 1 title listed in the *Small Press Record of Books in Print* (9th Edition, 1980). avg. price, paper: $5.00. Discounts: 40% bookseller's. 65-100pp; 5½X8½; of. Reporting time: 2 weeks.

Liverpool University Press (see also BULLETIN OF HISPANIC STUDIES), H.B. Hall, School of Hispanic Studies, The Univ., P.O. Box 147, Liverpool L69 3BX, United Kingdom. Articles, reviews. "Specialist articles on the languages and literatures of Spain, Portugal and Latin America, in English,

Spanish, Portuguese, and Catalan.".

LIVING BLUES, Jim O'Neal, Amy O'Neal, 2615 N. Wilton, Chicago, IL 60614. 1970. Articles, photos, interviews, reviews, music. circ. 3,500. Pub'd 4 issues 1979; expects 4 issues 1980, 6 issues 1981. sub. price: $6.00; per copy: $1.50; sample: $1.50. Back issues: $1.50. Discounts: 40%. 50pp; 8X10 1/2; of. Reporting time: 2 months. Copyrighted, reverts to author. Pub's reviews: 4 in 1979. §Blues only. Ads: $200.00/$100.00/$.20 each (20 word min).

LIVING OFF THE LAND, Subtropic Newsletter, Geraventure Corp., Marian Van Atta, Kathleen Wilcox, PO Box 2131, Melbourne, FL 32901, (305) 723-5554. 1975. Articles, letters. "Publishes short articles (500) words on edibles of the subtropics. *The Surinam Cherry* by Dr. George Webster. *Red Bay, The Southland's Edible Aristocrat* by Donald Ray Patterson. Has a seed exchange" circ. 500. 6/yr. Pub'd 6 issues 1979; expects 6 issues 1980, 6 issues 1981. sub. price: $6.00 (U.S.)/$7.50 overseas; per copy: $1.00; sample: free. Back issues: $1.00. Discounts: none. 6pp; 8 1/2X11; of. Reporting time: 60 days. Payment: yes. Not copyrighted. Pub's reviews: 8 in 1979. §Subtropic gardening, foraging. Ads: $10.00 per ad. COSMEP.

LLEN CYMRU (Board of Celtic Studies), University Of Wales Press, A.O.H. Jarman, 6 Gwennyth Sr., Cathays, Cardiff, Wales, United Kingdom. "Journal of various aspects of Welsh literature, printed in the Welsh language" circ. 300. 4 parts per volume. sub. price: £1.50 per double issue. Discounts: 33⅓ %. 143pp.

Llewellyn Publications (see also ASTROLOGY NOW), Carl L. Weschcke, PO Box 43383, St Paul, MN 55164, (612) 291-1970. 1975. Articles, photos, cartoons, interviews, reviews, letters, parts-of-novels, news items. "Covers all occult and metaphysical subjects. We also publish astrology titles" avg. press run 5,000-10,000. Pub'd 10 titles 1979; expects 10 titles 1980, 10 titles 1981. 2 titles listed in the *Small Press Record of Books in Print* (9th Edition, 1980). avg. price, cloth: $10.00; paper: $4.95; other: $2.00. Discounts: Bookstores, 40%; Chains, 43%; Distributors, 50%. 250pp. Reporting time: 3 months. Payment: Varied. ABA.

LOCAL DRIZZLE, Henn Haus, Ed-n-Chef; E. Rodriquez, Art Ed., PO Box 388, Carnation, WA 98014, (206) 333-4980. 1978. Poetry, articles, art, photos, cartoons, interviews, satire, criticism, reviews, music, letters, long-poems, collages, news items. "*LD* interested in expression and the exchange of young and old, whether the editorial is edible, poetic, philosophical, prosaic, earthly, graphic, political or comic or cozmic, or none of the above. Recent contribe: rellim, ralph marion coates, denny redman, oberHaus, ken saville, james magorian, l.e. cornelison, a.d. kraile, evalynS, danKersten, norman cousins, carolVrba, LVO, julieJ, ernest Mann, john fogg, stevie daniels, pawel petasz I, joeLee, carl Smool, jasdoulong, venNess-adams, jake kilpatrick, christineO, hayden, andrewP, signeS and rudolph the Red." circ. 3,300. 2-3/yr. Pub'd 1 issue 1979; expects 2 issues 1980. sub. price: $5.00; per copy: $1.50; sample: $1.75. Back issues: $2.00. Discounts: 30-40%. 16pp; 17½X22½; lp/of. Reporting time: 2 weeks to 2 years. Payment: $5.00 to $50.00 depending on subject/inquire. Copyrighted, reverts to author. Pub's reviews: 1 in 1979. §Contemporary as pertinent to historicals and the perspective entertainment. Ads: $500.00/$275.00/35 words $5.00.

LOCUS: The Newspaper of the Science Fiction Field, Charles N. Brown, Editor & Publisher; Mariam Rodstein, Managing Editor; Rachel Holmen, Editorial Assistant, Box 3938, San Francisco, CA 94119, 415-339-9196. 1968. Articles, photos, interviews, criticism, reviews, letters, news items. "News stories, reports on SF events." circ. 5,500. 12/yr. Pub'd 11 issues 1979; expects 12 issues 1980, 12 issues 1981. sub. price: $12.00, individual/yr; $13.50, institution; per copy: $1.25; sample: $1.25. Back issues: $1.25. Discounts: 40% plus postage on 10 or more. 24pp; 8½X11; of. Payment: yes. Copyrighted. Pub's reviews: 1,300 in 1979. §only S.F. Ads: $180.00/$100.00/$1.25 per line.

LODGISTIKS, Derwyddon Press, David Uu, Lodge North, Box 7694, Station A, Edmonton, Alta T5J 2X8, Canada. 1972. Poetry, fiction, articles, art, photos, parts-of-novels, long-poems, collages, plays, non-fiction. "No restrictions on length. Inclined towards language experimentation (visual poetry, etc.) surrealism and fantastic art. Particularly interested in philosophy and occult philosophy (alchemy, etc.) expressed through the arts. Past contributors include: Bill Bissett, Jack Wise, Alan Neil, Paul de Vree, Gerry Gilbert, Ivo Vroom, Gary Lee-Nova, Edwin Varney, etc." circ. 100-500. irreg. sub. price: $10.00/4 issues; per copy: Varies. Back issues: Prices available on request. Discounts: 1-5 20%/6-10 27%/over 10 33⅓%. 40pp; 8½X11; †of/mi. Reporting time: 6 weeks. Payment: 2 copies. Copyrighted, reverts to author. DOL.

Loggeerhead (see also SWIM LITE NEWS (newsletter)), Gretchen Schreiber, PO Box 7231, Shawnee Mission, KS 66207, 816-566-2174. 1978. Articles, interviews, news items. "Rt 1, Box 178A, Bates City, Missouri 64011." avg. press run 1,000. Pub'd 1 title 1979; expects 2 titles 1980. 2 titles listed in the *Small Press Record of Books in Print* (9th Edition, 1980). avg. price, paper: $5.00. Discounts:

20-40%. 100pp; 5½X8½; †of. Copyrights for author.

LOL, Elwyn Ioan, Robat Gruffudd, Lolfa, Y, Talybont, Dyfed, Wales SY24 5ER, United Kingdom. 1965. Art, cartoons, satire, photos. "Satire, cartoons, nudes, Twll Tin Pob Sais." 1/yr. sub. price: 30p. 28pp; 15X10. No payment. Ads: £30. ALP.

Lollipop Power, Inc., P O Box 1171, Chapel Hill, NC 27514, 919-929-4857. 1970. Fiction. "We publish only non-sexist, non-racist books for children. Priority is on manuscripts with strong female protagonists, especially Black, Native-American and Latino." avg. press run 4,000. Pub'd 1 title 1979; expects 2 titles 1981. 15 titles listed in the *Small Press Record of Books in Print* (9th Edition, 1980). avg. price, cloth: $6.50; paper: $2.15. Discounts: 20% libraries & schools; 40% bookstores 30+ copies, 30% — 30 copies. 32pp; size varies greatly; †of. Reporting time: 6-8 weeks. Payment: $200.00 flat fee on paperbacks. Copyrights for author. COSMEP.

The Lomond Press, R.L. Cook, 4 Whitecraigs, Kinnesswood, Kinross KY13 7JN, Scotland, 059 284 301. 1978. Poetry, long-poems. "Publications scheduled for 1980/81 include: *Selected Poems of Anne Bulley, Collected Poems of Iris Birtwistle, Geordie Tough's Squeel* a Scots poem written in 1881 by John Walker Ritchie. Also *Selected Poems* of Henry King and Richard Crashaw: this will be the first of a projected series of new selections from minor poets from the 16th to the 20th centuries. All or most of the foregoing will be limited editions - as will most of the future titles to be published. Almost all our material is solicited." avg. press run 300. Expects 3 titles 1980, 4 titles 1981. 1 title listed in the *Small Press Record of Books in Print* (9th Edition, 1980). avg. price, paper: £1.00 ($2.00). Discounts: 33 1/3 % booksellers; others by arrangement. 36pp; 5 1/2X8 1/2; lp. Copyrights for author. ALP.

THE LONDON COLLECTOR, Wolf House Books, Richard Weiderman, Dennis E. Hensley, P.O. Box 209, Cedar Springs, MI 49319. 1970. Poetry, articles, art, photos, cartoons, interviews, criticism, reviews, letters. "THE LONDON COLLECTOR publishes articles of interest to fans and students of Jack London. One topic is discussed each issue. Wolf House Books reprints rare ephemera & other scarce London material. Future plans call for further reprinting of desirable material as well as a series of monographs by contemporary London scholars." circ. 130. irreg. sub. price: $2.00; per copy: $2.00. Back issues: $2.00. Discounts: 40% five or more. 20pp; 5½X8½; of. Reporting time: immediate. Payment: 12 copies.

LONDON MYSTERY MAGAZINE, Norman Kark, 268-270 Vauxhall Bridge Rd., London SW1 1BB, United Kingdom. 1949. "Macabre, ghosts, and whodunits up to 4000 words. Must be strong and novel in plot." 4/yr. sub. price: 35p. Payment: by arrangement.

London Northwest (see also THE CHANEY CHRONICAL; WHAT'S NEW ABOUT LONDON, JACK?), David H. Schlottmann, 929 So Bay Rd, Olympia, WA 98506. 2 titles listed in the *Small Press Record of Books in Print* (9th Edition, 1980).

Lonely Planet Publications, Tony Wheeler, P.O. Box 88, South Yarra, Victoria 3141, Australia, 03 429-5268. 1972. "Travel guides for the low budget traveler-& to exotic, unusual countries." avg. press run 10,000. Pub'd 5 titles 1979; expects 8 titles 1980. 13 titles listed in the *Small Press Record of Books in Print* (9th Edition, 1980). avg. price, paper: $5.95. Discounts: generally 55 percent to my overseas accounts. 192pp; 5X7¼; of. Copyrights for author. ABPA.

Long Haul Press, Jan Clausen, Box 592 Van Brunt Station, Brooklyn, NY 11215, (212) 857-5351. 1978. Poetry. "LHP is my own self-publishing effort, created to publish *Waking At The Bottom Of The Dark* and to distribute *After Touch*. I may publish others in the future, but it seems unlikely." avg. press run 2,000. Pub'd 1 title 1979. 2 titles listed in the *Small Press Record of Books in Print* (9th Edition, 1980). avg. price, paper: $3.00. Discounts: 40%/bookstores; 50%/distributors. 80pp; 8½X5½; of.

LONG ISLAND CHILDBIRTH ALTERNATIVES QUARTERLY, Janet Isaacs Ashford, 15 Brewster Lane, East Setauket, NY 11733, (516) 689-8229. 1979. Poetry, articles, art, photos, interviews, criticism, reviews, letters, news items. "*LICA Quarterly* is a publication of Long Island Childbirth Alternatives, a non-profit organization which promotes home birth, alternative hospital birth and maternal health care consumerism. We carry some local news but our major focus is national, as part of the network of publications serving the alternative childbirth movement. We welcome submissions of articles (2,000 words or less) and news items on the following: midwifery, home birth, alterntive birth programs, maternal health legislation, reports on health conferences, personal birth accounts, regulation of drugs and medical procedures, nutrition, pregnancy, efforts of the medical establishment to suppress birth alternatives, etc. We also welcome original drawings, poems, and photographs of births, calendar items, book reviews, and information on useful organizations, products and services." circ. 1,000. 4/yr. Pub'd 1 issue 1979; expects 4 issues 1980, 4 issues 1981. sub. price: $5.00; per copy: $0.50; sample: $0.50. Back issues: $0.50. Discounts: $30.00 per hundred. 16pp;

8½X11; of. Reporting time: 1 month or less. Payment: copies and gratitude. Pub's reviews: 1 in 1979. §Pregnancy and childbirth, home birth, women and medicine, midwifery, etc. Ads: $60.00/$30.00.

Long Island Poetry Collective, Inc. (see also NEWSLETTER), PO Box 773, Huntington, NY 11743. 2 titles listed in the *Small Press Record of Books in Print* (9th Edition, 1980).

Long Measure Press (see also PONTCHARTRAIN REVIEW; THE NEW LAUREL REVIEW), James E. Morris, P O BOX 1618, Meraux, LA 70075, 241-7454. 1975. Poetry, fiction, articles, art, photos, cartoons, interviews, satire, criticism, reviews, music, letters, parts-of-novels, long-poems, collages, plays, concrete art. "We are a profit/non-profit press doing (1), standard publishing (at our expense, with a royalty to author), (2), co-operative publishing (author and the press share the expenses, with a proportional royalty), and (3), subsidized publishing (author assumes most of the expenses, the press only a small percentage; author receives a proportional amount of return). It's our philosophy that no book should be published entirely at either the press's or the author's expense. Distribution is handled by the press, or in conjunction with the author. We are creative people interested in good/great writing, and believe that such writing should be housed in a well crafted book. If we think a work is good, we will publish it at our expense if funds are available; if we can't bear the full expense ourselves, perhaps one of the other plans would be suitable. Submissions must include SASE." avg. press run 1,000. Pub'd 10 titles 1979; expects 14 titles 1980. avg. price, cloth: $9.00; paper: $3.50; other: as appropriate. Discounts: yes. 6X9; †of/lp. Copyrights for author.

LONG POND REVIEW, Russell Steinke, William O'Brien, Anthony DiFranco, English Dept, Suffolk Community College, Selden Long Island, NY 11784. 1974. Poetry, fiction, art, photos, interviews, satire, criticism, reviews, parts-of-novels. "LONG POND REVIEW prints what's best in contemporary poetry, fiction, art, photos, and criticism. Some recent contributors: May Swenson, David Ignatow, John Hall Wheelock, William Heyen, Aaron Kramer, Allen Planz, Robert DeMaria, Greg Kuzma, Tom Snapp, John Haines, Fred Chappell, Harold Witt, Linda Pastan, Jim Barnes, Paul Ramsey, Lyn Lifshin, Joseph Bruchac, Dave Etter, Jerald Bullis, John Colby, Gary Youree, Colette Inez, William Virgil Davis, Ora Lerman. LPR is listed as an outstanding small press in *The Pushcart Prize* II and IV. Note: Send ms. to the Editors." circ. 1M. 2/yr. sub. price: $4.00; per copy: $2.00; sample: $1.50. Back issues: LPR #2: $2.00. Discounts: none. 60-72pp; 6X9; of. Reporting time: 2-6 months. Payment: copies only. Copyrighted, reverts to author. Pub's reviews: 2 in 1979. §Fiction, poetry, science-fiction, in-depth reviews of books on political, philosophical, cultural issues, art, nature. Ads: $100.00/$60.-00. NYSPA.

THE LONGEST REVOLUTION, Lisa Cobbs, Carol Rowell, Center for Women's Studies and Services, P.O.Box 350, San Diego, CA 92101, (714) 233-8984. 1977. Articles, art, photos, interviews, criticism, reviews. "This is the newspaper of a radical feminist organization: the Center for Women's Studies and Services. Material submitted should have at least a women's liberation/feminist oriented viewpoint and should be no longer than 2000 words" circ. 5,000. 6/yr. Pub'd 6 issues 1979; expects 6 issues 1980, 6 issues 1981. sub. price: $6.00; per copy: $0.50; sample: free. Back issues: free. Discounts: Free to prisoners and women in mental institutions. 20pp; 17 1/2X11; of. Reporting time: 2 months. Payment: none. Copyrighted. Pub's reviews: 6 in 1979. §Women's issues, gay issues, liberation, health, sports, history, feminist perspectives on any issues or areas, art and culture. Ads: $5.00/column inch. Classifieds: $.10/word. COSMEP ISBN.

LONGHOUSE, Longhouse, Bob Arnold, Green River R.F.D., Brattleboro, VT 05301. 1974. Poetry, long-poems. "*Longhouse* takes on no grants, funding or subscription - rather supports itself thru the good hearts of poets & readers of the journal. We're a homespun publication on the lookout for poems from the serious working poet. Any region/any style. Recent contributors: Hayden Carruth, Barbara Moraff, David Budbill, William Witherup, James Koller, Janine Pommy Vega." circ. 200. 1/yr. Pub'd 1 issue 1979; expects 1 issue 1980, 1 issue 1981. sub. price: donation; sample: $2.00. 30pp; 8X9; †mi, of. Reporting time: 48 hours. Payment: one-copy per contributor. Pub's reviews: 10 in 1979. §Poetry, literary history, rural essays.

Longhouse (see also LONGHOUSE), Bob Arnold, Green River R.F.D., Brattleboro, VT 05301. 1974. Poetry, long-poems, concrete art. "Under the *Longhouse* imprint we have published 2 books of poetry: *3* (letterpress): poems by Bob Arnold, John Levy and David Giannini, and *shims,* poems by Bob Arnold. *The Poets Who Sleep* imprint has published 17 folders of one-poet's work. Poets range from: Theodore Enslin, Mark Mendel, Robert Morgan, John Brandi, Lee Sharkey, Jack Hirschman, Barbara Moraff, Hayden Carruth, Steve Lewandowski, Marguerite Swift." avg. press run 100-500. Pub'd 2 titles 1979; expects 3 titles 1980, 3 titles 1981. avg. price, paper: $1.00-$3.00. 5-30pp; 8X11; †mi, of, lp. Reporting time: strictly solicited. Payment: copies. Copyrights for author.

Longship Press, William Vorm, Crooked Lane, Nantucket, MA 02554, (207) 722-3344. 1976. Fiction.

"We have so far concentrated on European works and their release in this country." avg. press run 2,000. Pub'd 3 titles 1979; expects 5 titles 1980. 7 titles listed in the *Small Press Record of Books in Print* (9th Edition, 1980). avg. price, cloth: $9.50. Discounts: contact publisher. 200pp; size varies; of. Reporting time: 60 days. Payment: varies. COSMEP.

LOOK QUICK, Quick Books, Robbie Rubinstein, Joel Scherzer, P.O. Box 222, Pueblo, CO 81002. 1975. Poetry, fiction, music. "We seek material with a feel for the bizarre and the erotic. Original use of language is a top priority. Much of what we publish has urban themes, often with an eye to the cinema. We can relate to writing with strange and even unwholesome undercurrents. Among other things, we're devotees of the hard-boiled school of American fiction and its modern derivatives. Blues lyrics are always welcome, as are imaginative line drawings. Recent contributors include: Guy R. Beining, Judson Crews, Stuart Dybek, Arthur Winfield Knight, Lyn Lifshin, Errol Miller, Philip Whalen, Wanda Coleman, Charles Alymell, Richard Kostelanetz, and Tony Moffeit." circ. 500. 2/yr. Pub'd 2 issues 1979; expects 2 issues 1980, 2 issues 1981. sub. price: $2.50 - 4 issues.; per copy: $.75; sample: $0.75. Back issues: $.75. 24pp; 5½X8½; †of. Reporting time: As soon as possible up to two months. Payment: copies. Copyrighted, reverts to author. Pub's reviews: none in 1979. §Poetry. no ads. COSMEP, CCLM.

Loompanics Unlimited, Michael Hoy, PO Box 264, Mason, MI 48854, (517) 694-2240. 1973. Articles, photos, satire, reviews, news items. "Recent titles: *Exotic Weapons: An Access Book*; *The Code Book: All About Unbreakable Codes & How To Use Them*; *Uninhabited Pacific Islands*; *Principia Discordia*; *The Strategy And Tactics Of Black Market Operations*; *How to Start Your Own Country*; *Close Shaves: The Complete Book of Razor Fighting*; *The Last Frontiers On Earth*." avg. press run 1,000. Pub'd 5 titles 1979; expects 10 titles 1980, 15 titles 1981. 17 titles listed in the *Small Press Record of Books in Print* (9th Edition, 1980). avg. price, paper: $6.00. Discounts: 5 copies, 40%. 80pp; 5½X8½; of. Reporting time: 3 months. Payment: negotiable. Copyrights for author.

LoonBooks, Gunnar Hansen, PO Box 901, Northeast Harbor, ME 04662, (207) 276-3693. 1979. Poetry, parts-of-novels. "Our first two books are just coming out—both poetry. One, however, is a translation of poems by an Icelandic novelist. In the next couple of years LoonBooks will become more involved with translations, especially of Scandinavian works. We are still interested in seeing American work, especially poetry and some short fiction." avg. press run 300-500. Expects 2 titles 1980, 2 titles 1981. 2 titles listed in the *Small Press Record of Books in Print* (9th Edition, 1980). avg. price, cloth: $12.00; paper: $9.00. Discounts: 40% to bookstores ordering at least 5 copies. 70pp; 5½X8½; of. Reporting time: 6 weeks. Payment: 10% of printing, no cash. Copyrights for author. NWPA.

LOONFEATHER: Minnesota North Country Art, William Elliott, Regional Editor; Ted Fiskewold, Campus Editor, Box 48, Hagg-Sauer Hall, Bemidji, MN 56601, (218) 755-2813. 1979. Poetry, fiction, photos. "Short poems and fiction (1,500 words), 90% Minnesota writers, primarily north central. *Query* before submitting." circ. 2,000. 3/yr. sub. price: $5.00; per copy: $2.00; sample: $2.00. Back issues: $1.50. 36pp; 8X10; †of. Reporting time: 1-2 months. Payment: 2 copies. Copyrighted, reverts to author. Pub's reviews. §Upper Midwest, poetry, fiction, non-fiction. Ads: $100.00/$50.00.

LOOT, Spectacular Diseases, Paul Green, 83(b) London Road, Peterborough, Cambs, United Kingdom. 1979. Long-poems. "*Loot* is a mimeo supplement to spectacular diseases magazine. Each issue is devoted to the work of one author only. Material usually solicited. Inquire before sending." circ. 200. Pub'd 2 issues 1979. price per copy: 30p; sample: post. Discounts: Trade 33⅓%. 12pp; 13X8; mi. Reporting time: almost immediate. Payment: copies, 10% of total run. Copyrighted, reverts to author. ALP.

LORE AND LANGUAGE, J.D.A. Widdowson Dr., The Centre for English Cultural Tradition and Language, The University, Sheffield S10 2TN, United Kingdom, Sheffield 78555 ext 4211. 1969. Articles, reviews. "Articles and items for those interested in language, folklore, cultural tradition and oral history." circ. 1,000. 2/yr. Pub'd 2 issues 1979; expects 2 issues 1980. sub. price: £2; per copy: £1. Back issues: Vol. 1 25p each, Vol 2 50p each. Discounts: none. 54pp; 15X21cm; lo. Reporting time: 3 wks. Payment: none. Copyrighted. Pub's reviews: 284 in 1979. §Language, folklore, cultural tradition, oral history. Ads: none. CECTAL.

Lorien House, David A. Wilson, PO Box 1112, Black Mountain, NC 28711, 704 669-9992. 1969. Poetry, fiction. "Basically publishing the works of 2-3 people. Am looking for works from others if I find it 'exciting' in literary quality. I will produce books on a 'you pay' basis." avg. press run 200-2,000. Pub'd 1 title 1979; expects 2 titles 1980, 4 titles 1981. 4 titles listed in the *Small Press Record of Books in Print* (9th Edition, 1980). avg. price, paper: $1.50-$5.00. Discounts: 5 copies, 40%. 56pp; 8X10; 5½X8½; of. Reporting time: 1 week to 1 month. Payment: Individual. Copyrights for author.

LOST AND FOUND TIMES, Luna Bisonte Prods, John M. Bennett, 137 Leland Ave, Columbus, OH 43214. 1975. Poetry, fiction, articles, art, photos, cartoons, satire, reviews, letters, parts-of-novels, long-poems, collages, concrete art. "The co-founder of *L&FT,* Douglas C. Landies, died suddenly in Jan. 1978. The magazine will continue; the format and content for each issue will vary considerably. I am interested in the experimental and the primitive, and in anything new or unusual. See Luna Bisonte Prods for further information." circ. 300. irreg. Pub'd 1 issue 1979; expects 2 issues 1980, 2 issues 1981. sub. price: $5.00 for 5 issues; per copy: $1.50; sample: $1.00 for sample packet. Discounts: 40% for resale. 15-20pp; size varies; of. Reporting time: 2 wks. Payment: copies. Copyrighted, reverts to author. Pub's reviews. §Literature, Art, Reviews. COSMEP.

LOST GENERATION JOURNAL, Dr. Thomas W. Wood Jr., Deloris Wood, Route 5, Box 134, Salem, MO 65560, (314) 729-5669: (501) 568-6241. 1973. Poetry, fiction, articles, art, photos, cartoons, interviews, criticism, reviews, letters, news items. "*LGJ* topics deal with Americans in Europe, chiefly Paris, between 1919 and 1939. Primary emphasis is placed on Americans who began making a name for themselves in literature, graphic and performing arts such as Pound, Stein and Hemingway. Article length can vary, but we prefer pieces between 800 and 2,500 words. Poetry should be 20 lines or less. Good photographs and art should relate to the theme in time and place as should the articles and poetry. Scholars must document their work with footnotes and bibliography. Lost Generation people (those who started in Paris) must state when they were abroad and supply evidence on their qualifications or cite references for confirmation. Authors should supply a passport size photograph of themselves and a 200-word biographical blurb. Recent contributors: Stanley Kimmel, R.P. Harris, Lansing Warren, Ernest B. Speck, Townsing Ludington, David Shi." circ. 400. 3/yr. Pub'd 1 issue 1979; expects 2 issues 1980, 3 issues 1981. sub. price: $7.50; per copy: $3.00; sample: $3.00. Back issues: $4.00. Discounts: $7.00 per year to subscription agency. 32pp; 8½X11; of. Reporting time: 6 weeks, SASE earlier. Payment: 3 copies of issue article appears. Copyrighted. Pub's reviews: 7 in 1979. §Twentieth Century literature, bibliography, biography, Americans in Paris, Hemingway, Pound, Stein, Shirer. Ads: $150.00/$125.00/$85.00/$5.00 an inch.

LOST GLOVE, Ellen Kahaner, c/o Kahaner, 161 W 86th Street, Apt 6A, New York, NY 10024. 1977. Poetry, fiction, articles, art, interviews, satire, criticism, reviews, letters, parts-of-novels. circ. 200. 2/yr. Pub'd 1 issue 1979; expects 2 issues 1980, 2 issues 1981. sub. price: $5.00; per copy: $1.25; sample: $1.25. Discounts: 40%/bookstores. 50pp; 5X8; lp. Reporting time: 1 month. Payment: 2 issues plus free subscription. Copyrighted, reverts to author. Pub's reviews: none in 1979. §Any poetry, fiction, anti-nuke, anti-war. Ads: $60/$30/free.

LOST PAPER (see Station Hill Press)

Lost Roads Publishers, C. D. Wright, Editor, PO Box 11143, San Francisco, CA 94101. 1977. Poetry, fiction, photos, long-poems. "If funded adequately we will publish 3 books of narrative drawings and poetry in 1980. Covors feature local, regional, & national photographers. Special editions are silkscreened (cover). Published *The Battlefield Where The Moon Says I Love You,* a 542 page poem by Frank Stanford in 1978 in conjunction with MIll Mountain Press under a grant for experimental lit awarded by the NEA." avg. press run 750-1,000. Pub'd 6 titles 1979; expects 4 titles 1980, 4 titles 1981. 13 titles listed in the *Small Press Record of Books in Print* (9th Edition, 1980). avg. price, paper: $3.00-$4.00; other: Long poem special limited edition $9.00 by FS. Discounts: Usually 40% off, 60-90 day terms. 50pp; 6X9; of, lp. Reporting time: 1 month. Payment: $200.00 author's payment, 50 copies. Editor send copyright forms to author-to copyright in their name.

Lothlorien, Joy M. Hendry, S2 Bath Street, Edinburg EH 15 1 HF, Scotland, 031 669 9332. 1969. Poetry, fiction, art, criticism, long-poems. avg. press run 1200. Expects 3 titles 1980. 5 titles listed in the *Small Press Record of Books in Print* (9th Edition, 1980). avg. price, paper: 60p. Discounts: by arrangement. 60pp; 7X9; of. Reporting time: 1 month. Payment: £2.00/page (magazine). copyright negotiated.

Louisiana Entertains, Hope J. Norman, Louise A. Simon, Rapides Symphony Guild, Box 4172, Alexandria, LA 71301, (318) 443-7786. 1978. "This is a 'classic' community menu cookbook and entertainment guide. It includes original and favorite recipes of successful Louisiana hostesses. It has a thorough index of the carefully tested recipes." avg. press run 20,000. Pub'd 1 title 1979. 1 title listed in the *Small Press Record of Books in Print* (9th Edition, 1980). avg. price, paper: $7.95. Discounts: 40% wholesale, STOP plan available, $6.00 each for orders of 50 or more retail. 300pp; 6½X9; of. Payment: all proceeds go to Rapides Symphony Guild. Copyrights for author.

THE LOUISVILLE REVIEW, Sena Jeter Naslund, Faculty Editor, University of Louisville, Louisville, KY 40208, (502) 588-5921. 1976. Poetry, fiction, parts-of-novels, long-poems, plays. "Some recent contributors: James Bertolino, William Borden,P. C. Irving Halperin, Lawrence Kearney,D. M.

Thomas McAfee, Jonnathan Penner, Natalie L. M. Petesch, Susan Fromberg Schaeffer, Hollis Summers, Ruth Whitman, Peter Cooley, David Madden." circ. 1,000. 2/yr. Pub'd 2 issues 1979; expects 2 issues 1980, 2 issues 1981. sub. price: $3.50 (postpaid); per copy: $2.00 (postpaid); sample: $2.00 (post paid: add $.25 per issue). Back issues: $2.25 each (postpaid). 96pp; 6X9; lp. Reporting time: 2 - 8 weeks. Payment: 2 compl copies plus 1 year subscription. Copyrighted, reverts to author.

LOVE, Pat Warren, Bob Love, Box 9, Prospect Hill, NC 27314, (919) 562-3380. 1977. Poetry, fiction, articles, art, cartoons, interviews, satire, criticism, reviews, letters, long-poems, plays, news items. "Accepts no mss." circ. 450. 6/yr. Pub'd 6 issues 1979; expects 8 issues 1980, 8 issues 1981. sub. price: Free; per copy: free; sample: free. Back issues: free, as available. 40pp; 6X8; †mi. Copyrighted, reverts to author. Pub's reviews. §Religion, science, psychology.

Love Street Books, Judie Rice, 2176 Allison Lane #13, Jeffersonville, IN 47130. 1969. Poetry, plays. "Send inquiry before sending manuscript. Enclose SASE. We are looking for extra sales reps to carry our line." avg. press run 5,000. Pub'd 6 titles 1979; expects 6 titles 1980. 17 titles listed in the *Small Press Record of Books in Print* (9th Edition, 1980). avg. price, cloth: $6.95; paper: $2.50. Discounts: 40% to trade. 64pp; 5½X8½; of/lp. Reporting time: 2 weeks. Payment: 10% royalty. copyright in author's name. COSMEP.

The Lovejoy Press, Nathaniel Polster, 2128 Wyoming Avenue, Washington, DC 20008. 1975. Poetry, fiction, articles. "We publish poetry to which we add line drawings in writer/artist co-authorship. We publish articles on freedom of the press history. Recent contributors: Patricia McCarthey, James Pines, Jacqueline M.G. Polster." avg. press run 2,000. Pub'd 3 titles 1979; expects 3 titles 1980. avg. price, paper: $5.00. Discounts: 4 copies to trade 33%, 12 or more copies to trade 50%. 24pp; 8½X11, 4X7, 8X5½; †lp. Reporting time: 1 week. Payment: 50% after covering costs. Copyrights for author.

Lovers Of The Stinking Rose/Aris Books (see GARLIC TIMES)

Loving Publishers, Alma E. Blanton, Gene Woodward, Editor, 4576 Alla Road, Los Angeles, CA 90066, (213) 822-7413. 1979. Poetry, articles, photos, reviews, letters, plays. "Prefer non-sectarian Biblical interpretation that has a specialty whether it be the number of trees in Genesis or the number of ways that Salvation is presented. Especially interested in up-beat approaches to the use of women in presenting the over-all themes of the Bible. If you think that women represent evil please don't write or call — see someone for phyciatric help. Looking for teaching-training helps on same subject. If you have following, we will help you put together material into saleable form. Small profit is nice but not manditory. Like small chapbooks in print-ready condition." avg. press run 1,000. Pub'd 3 titles 1979. 2 titles listed in the *Small Press Record of Books in Print* (9th Edition, 1980). avg. price, paper: $5.00; other: chapbooks must be $2.50 or less. Discounts: 40%. 120pp; 5½X8½; photo-copy large press. Reporting time: 6 weeks. Payment: depends on author and need. Copyrights for author. COSMEP.

LOWLANDS REVIEW, Tom Whalen, Nancy Harris, 6048 Perrier, New Orleans, LA 70118. 1974. Poetry, fiction, art, interviews, reviews, parts-of-novels, long-poems. "We like the experimental/surreal, but are not averse to good work in any vein. Recent contributors include George Garrett, Stuart Dybek, Brian Swann, Julia Randall, Christopher Middleton, Robert Walser, William Harrison, Dino Buzzati, Henri Michaux, JoAnn Monks, etc. Would like to see more translations." circ. 400. 2/yr. Pub'd 2 issues 1979; expects 2 issues 1980. sub. price: $4.00; per copy: $2.00; sample: $2.00. Back issues: 1-8 $2.00 each. 48pp; 6X9; of. Reporting time: 2 wks to 2 mos. Payment: 2 copies. Copyrighted, reverts to author. Pub's reviews: none in 1979. §fiction, poetry (contemporary).

Lowy Publishing, David C. Lowy, President, 5047 Wigton, Houston, TX 77096, (713) 723-3209. 1979. Fiction, art, cartoons, satire, letters, plays. "Our only published work so far is *Pencil Drawings by David X.* published August 10, 1979 a collection of pencil drawings of *pencils* ranging from humorous to entertaining to artistic. By David C. Lowy." avg. press run 2,000. Pub'd 1 title 1979. avg. price, paper: $3.25. 112pp; 7⅛X5¼; of. Reporting time: not reading mss. presently. Copyrights for author.

LP Publications (see also THE SEEKER NEWSLETTER), Diane Kennedy Pike, Arleen Lorrance, (The Love Project), PO Box 7601, San Diego, CA 92107, (714) 225-0133. 1972. Poetry, articles, photos, cartoons, letters. avg. press run 2,000. Pub'd 2 titles 1979; expects 2 titles 1980, 2 titles 1981. 6 titles listed in the *Small Press Record of Books in Print* (9th Edition, 1980). avg. price, paper: $3.00. Discounts: 40% for retail outlets; 10 for the price of 9 for all others. 120pp; size varies; of. Reporting time: 1 month. Copyrights for author.

LSM Information Center, LSM Press, P.O. Box 2077, Oakland, CA 94604, 635-4863. 1970. Articles, art, photos, interviews, criticism, reviews. "Edited by LSM Information Center. We publish our own material on the national Liberation Struggles in Southern Africa. Recent publications are *The People In Power* documenting - from first-hand experience - the recent conflict in Angola, *Sowing the First*

Harvest, Guinea-Bissau, Namibia: SWAPO Fights for Freedom and *Zimbabwe: The Final Advance.*" avg. press run 3,000. 38 titles listed in the *Small Press Record of Books in Print* (9th Edition, 1980). avg. price, paper: $2.95. Discounts: Bookstores only-40% add 10% postage & handling. 50-125pp; 5¼X8¼. Payment: none. copyright sometimes.

LUCKY HEART BOOKS, Salt Lick Press, James Haining, Box 1064, Quincy, IL 62301. 1939. Poetry, fiction, articles, art, photos, cartoons, interviews, satire, criticism, reviews, music, letters, parts-of-novels, long-poems, collages, plays, concrete art. "Letters to Obscure Men. Verse by Gerald Burns. Catch My Breath. Verse, prose, and fiction by Michael Lally. George Washington Trammell. Verse by Robert Trammell. Two Kids & The Three Bears. Prose narrative by John Dennis Brown. A Quincy History. Verse, journal record by James Haining. Three titles in 1979: *Next Services,* poetry by Michalea Moore. *Book of Spells* (first third), poetry by Gerald Burns. *A Quincy History* poetry, journal record by James Haining. Magazine issue also scheduled. *Newicons* verse by Peggy Davis; *Next Services* verse by Michalea Moore; *A Book of Spells* (first third) verse by Gerald Burns; *Lovers/Killers* verse by Gerald Burns." circ. 1,500 mag, 500 books. irreg. Pub'd 1 issue 1979; expects 4 issues 1980, 3 issues 1981. sub. price: $5.00 mag, $3.00 books, $1.00 samplers; sample: $2.00. Back issues: write for information. Discounts: 65%-35%. 68pp; 8X10½; 9X6; †of/lp. Reporting time: 10 days. Payment: copies and $ if available. Magazine copyrighted and rights released. Books copyrighted by press. Pub's reviews. §Open. Ads: none. CCLM, COSMEP.

LUDD'S MILL, Eight Miles High Press, Andrew Darlington, 44 Spa Croft Road, Teall Street, Ossett, West Yorkshire WF50HE, United Kingdom, Ossett 275814. 1971. Articles, poetry, fiction, art, cartoons, reviews, music. "Bizarre, dada, psychedelic, anarchist, punk, science fiction, erotic, Tuli Kupferberg Mike Horovitz, Barrington J. Bayley, Jeff Nuttall, M.J. Harrison, surreal, left-political, Brian Stableford, Charles Plymell, jazz, bebop, rock 'n roll, bizarre, collage's." circ. 1,000. 9 monthly. Pub'd 2 issues 1979; expects 1 issue 1980, 2 issues 1981. sub. price: $1.00; per copy: $1.00; sample: $1.00. Back issues: sold out. Discounts: 1/3 indiv orders 6 copies or more, bookshops. 36pp; size A4; of. Reporting time: varies, 1 month. Payment: Free copy. Rights remain with contributor. Pub's reviews: 100+ in 1979. §Anything within the areas specified in comments. (emphasis on poetry, alternative arts, rock/jazz, science fiction). Ads: $30.00/$15.00.

LUMBEE NATION TIMES, Dr. M.L. Webber, Editor; Dr. E.M. Reed, Co-editor, PO Box 911, Exeter, CA 93221, (209) 592-3327. 1977. Poetry, articles, cartoons, photos, interviews, letters, news items. "We accept only Native American Indian material." circ. 5,000. 4/yr. Pub'd 5 issues 1979; expects 3 issues 1980. sub. price: $2.00; per copy: $0.50; sample: $0.50. Back issues: $1.00. Discounts: 50% to schools, libraries, etc. 8pp; 17X22; of. Copyrighted. Pub's reviews. §Worldwide, California. Ads: $104.00/$60.00/$0.10.

LUMEN/AVENUE A, James Graham, PO Box 412, Stuyvesant Station, New York, NY 10009. 1979. Poetry, fiction, art, photos, interviews, criticism, reviews, long-poems, plays. "*Lumen/Avenue A* appeared once in 79; in the future we hope to publish twice a year. There's no bias as to material genre. Poetry *is* the basis, and outward from there. Hopefully we can always broaden. *Lumen* would also like to expand and upgrade its *visuals,* so non-literary work is certainly welcomed. And if it were at all possible *Lumen* would love to run pieces political in nature. Contributors to the first issue include Allen Ginsberg, Armand Schwerner, David Unger; Robert Kelly in #2. I am in need of a distributor for the Midwest and the West Coast. *Lumen/Avenue A* is, as the first issue demonstrated, very interested in translations, generally works that have not been translated before. In #1, we ran a letter from Pier Paolo Pasolini to Allen Ginsberg, a poem by Luis Cernuda (both of which had never been translated before) a poem by Apollinaire that is hard to find in English, and part of a new translation of the *Philoctetes* of Sophocles. So that remains a vital interest of the magazine." 2/yr. Pub'd 2 issues 1979; expects 1 issue 1980. sub. price: $8.00; per copy: $3.00; sample: gratis. Back issues: $1.00 each. Discounts: Most bookstores work the usual 60/40 percentage. I have no other distributor than thru individual bookstores. 50pp; 7½X10; of. Reporting time: I try to respond quickly. Copyrighted. Pub's reviews. §Poetry, politics, anthropology, energy, etc. Ads: we don't run ads.

Luna Bisonte Prods (see also LOST AND FOUND TIMES), John M. Bennett, 137 Leland Ave, Columbus, OH 43214, (614) 846-4126. 1974. Poetry, art, cartoons, satire, letters, collages, concrete art. "Mostly dedicated to the work of JMB, but continue to expand. Interested in exchanges. We print broadsides and labels, chapbooks, poetry products. Have published work by Richard Kostelaneta, Douglas Landies, Lyle Lee, Kirk Robertson, T. M. Fisher, S. Hitchcock, G. Myers, Nick L. Nips, Bruce Andrews, Robin Crozier, Keith Rahmmings, Dan Raphael, Karl Kempton, Peter Frank, and many others. See *Lost & Found Times* for further info." avg. press run 400. Pub'd 3 titles 1979; expects 4 titles 1980, 5 titles 1981. 17 titles listed in the *Small Press Record of Books in Print* (9th Edition, 1980). avg. price, paper: $2.00. Discounts: 40% for resale. 20pp; size varies; of/rubber stamps. Reporting time: 2 wks. Payment: copies. author must do own registering for copyright. COSMEP.

LUNCH, Robert J. Quatrone, Chief Editor, 220 Montross Ave, Rutherford, NJ 07070. 1975. Poetry, fiction, articles, art, cartoons, interviews, satire, criticism, letters, parts-of-novels, long-poems, plays, concrete art, reviews. "Long works are subject to editing because of space. Emphasis on contemporary poetry and prose. Have published Lyn Lifshin, Barbara Holland, Paul Violi, Martin Steingessen, Robert Laguardia, Michael Andre, Max Greenberg, Karla Hammond." circ. 500. 4/yr. Pub'd 4 issues 1979; expects 4 issues 1980, 4 issues 1981. sub. price: $6.00; per copy: $1.50. 100pp; 8X11; †mi. Reporting time: one month. Payment: copies. Copyrighted, reverts to author. Pub's reviews: one in 1979. §poetry, fiction. Ads: $25/$12.50.

Lycabettus Press, John Chapple, P.O. Box 3391, Kolonaki, Athens, Greece, 363-5567. 1970. "Lycabettus Press publishes material of Greek interest. Of particular interest are *Greek Dances* and a series of archaeological guide books on parts of Greece such as Delphi, Mani, Vergina and Lefkadia and such islands as Aegina, Kos, Naxos, Paros, Poros, and Spetsai. Recent titles: *Hydra* and *Nauplion*. Also publish Greek literature and poetry in translation, including a new translation of *Mythistorima and Gymnopaidia* by George Seferis. Lycabettus Press is distributed in England by the Oxus Press, 16 Haslemere Road, London N8" avg. press run 5,000. Pub'd 3 titles 1979; expects 3 titles 1980, 4 titles 1981. 10 titles listed in the *Small Press Record of Books in Print* (9th Edition, 1980). avg. price, cloth: $14.00; paper: $5.00. Discounts: 35%. 130pp; 7¾X5½; of. Reporting time: prompt. Payment: 10% of income received.

LYNN VOICES, BLT Press (Bates, Lear, and Tulp), Peter Bates, Bill Costley, Arnold Trachtman, 72 Lowell Street, Peabody, MA 01960, (617) 531-7348. 1977. Poetry, fiction, art, photos, satire, letters. "We are a radical tabloid, based in Lynn, MA, zeroing in on the grit of daily life. Although we are socialists, we welcome all types of critical realism. We abhor racism, sexism, along with all attempts to ramanticize, sterotype, or otherwise moan about the plight of the working stiff. We believe every artist has a moral and political duty to be at least 40% satirist, hopefully more, for 'there are so many things left to kill' (Patchen) and so few willing to risk it. Recent contributors are the above listed editors, but we are open to more." circ. 5,000. 1/yr. Expects 1 issue 1981. price per copy: $.25; sample: $.25. Discounts: Free bundles of ten to any library, community group, or publication. 8pp; 11X16; of. Reporting time: 1 month. Payment: 1 copy.

Lynx House Press, Robert Abel, Christopher Howell, David Lyon, Managing Editor, PO Box 800, Amherst, MA 01004, (413) 773-7988. 1971. Poetry, fiction. "We publish poetry and fiction of excellent quality; these are primarily first books by 'young' writers with substantial magazine/journal publication whose first book is long overdue. We have published Floyce Alexander, Ray Amorosi, Tomas O'Leary, Wayne Ude, Hal Stowell, Valerie Martin, Robert Hahn, Don Hendrie Jr., Bill Tremblay, David Lenson, Margaret Robison, Joyce Thompson, Robbie Gordon, Adam Hammer, Yusef Komunyakaa and Patricia Goedicke, among others. We also have a chapbook series. *Lynx,* a journal of poetry and the arts, is published by the same editors from the same address but is not technically part of Lynx House Press" avg. press run 500-1000. Pub'd 7 titles 1979; expects 12 titles 1980, 8 titles 1981. 20 titles listed in the *Small Press Record of Books in Print* (9th Edition, 1980). avg. price, cloth: $7.95; paper: $3.50. Discounts: 40%. 64pp; 5.5X8.5 or 6X9; of/lp. Reporting time: 1-3 months. Payment: 10 percent of press run. we copyright for author.

M

M. N. Publishers, Ruby A. Newman, Route 2, Box 55, Bonnerdale, AR 71933, (501) 991-3815. 1977. Fiction. "160 page, softcover, size 5½ x 8½, Christian fiction for teen and older persons reading. Two novels *Tour For Seven* by Ruby A. Newman, *Rebel Preacher* by Ruby A. Newman." avg. press run 600-1,000. Pub'd 1 title 1979; expects 2 titles 1980, 2 titles 1981. 2 titles listed in the *Small Press Record of Books in Print* (9th Edition, 1980). avg. price, paper: $3.50; other: $3.50. Discounts: 40% on 10 to 24 books, 43% on 25 to 49 books, 46% on 50 to 99 books, 50% on 100 or more books. 160pp; 5½X8½; of. Reporting time: we are a new company publishing only our own work so far. Therefore no royalty arrangement until later. Copyrights for author.

M.O. Publishing Company (see also MODUS OPERANDI), Sheila R. Jensen, 14332 Howard Road, Dayton, MD 21036, (301) 774-2900. 1970. Poetry. "We publish four poetry anthologies each year; each has a different title, different foreword author and different illustrator. Poets are invited to send #10 SASE for Guideline. Postage due mail is automatically refused and returned to sender. Manuscripts not accompanied by self-addressed, stamped envelope are tossed into wastebasket. We are only interested in original, unpublished poetry; we do not read xerox or carbon copies. Only one poem may be typed on 8½ x 11 white paper; number of lines counted and listed in upper right corner of manuscript. Of course we expect the poet's name and full mailing address to be typed in upper left corner of each manuscript. If you must rely on profanity to express yourself, don't waste your postage by sending your work to us." avg. press run 500. Pub'd 4 titles 1979; expects 4 titles 1980, 4 titles 1981. 25 titles listed in the *Small Press Record of Books in Print* (9th Edition, 1980). avg. price, paper: $3.00; other: Subscription price: US $6.00 yr; $11.00/2 yrs; Foreign $8.00 yr; $15.00/2 yrs. 60pp; 8½X11; †mi/of. Reporting time: turn around mail. COSMEP, CCLM.

M.O.P. Press (see also TIOTIS POETRY NEWS), Shirley Aycock, Rt 24, Box 53C, Fort Myers, FL 33908, (813) 482-0802. 1978. Poetry, long-poems. "Basic purpose of press, self-publishing and quarterly. Booklets printed containing others work will be infrequent, by special cooperative arrangement. Considering plans for other periodical publications in the future, such as newsletter, reviews; also possible special theme poetry collections." avg. press run 320. Pub'd 2 titles 1979; expects 2 titles 1980, 2 titles 1981. 6 titles listed in the *Small Press Record of Books in Print* (9th Edition, 1980). avg. price, paper: $2.25; other: SL (smaller/long) 4¼ x 7; or 3½ x 8½; = $1.25 + postage. Discounts: 30%-40%. 24pp; 7X8½; †mi. Reporting time: 2 weeks. Payment: Special cooperative arrangement. Copyrights for author. COSMEP, UAPAA.

M. Macdonald (see LINES REVIEW)

Mad River Press, Inc., David L. Largent, RT 2, Box 151B, Eureka, CA 95501, (707) 443-2947. 1973. avg. press run 1,500. Pub'd 4 titles 1979; expects 6 titles 1980, 4 titles 1981. avg. price, paper: $5.50. Discounts: Trade: 0-10, 10%; 11-25, 20%; 26-50, 30%; 50 and over, 40%. Textbook 20%. 140pp; 5X7; of. Reporting time: 1 year. Payment: 50% of the profits after all expenses. Copyrights for author. MRP.

THE MADISON REVIEW, Jay Clayton, Executive Editor; Ron Wallace, Advisory Editor, Dept. of English, University of Wisconsin, Madison, WI 53706, (608) 263-3705. 1979. Poetry, fiction, articles, interviews, reviews. "About half of the contributors are University of Wisconsin students. Half are professional writers. Recent contributors include May Sarton, Stephen Dunn, Lisel Mueller, Philip Dacey, John Woods, Peter Wild, John Allman, Felix Pollak, Conrad Hilberry, Dave Etter, David Steingass, Kelly Cherry. Editorial staff composed of creative writing majors in the Department of English." circ. 500. 2/yr. Pub'd 1 issue 1979; expects 2 issues 1980, 2 issues 1981. sub. price: $4.00; per copy: $2.00; sample: $1.50. 60-100pp; 5½X8½; of. Reporting time: 4 weeks. Payment: 1 contributor's copy. Copyrighted. Pub's reviews. §Contemporary poetry and fiction, criticism of contemporary lit.

MADOC (see Speed Limit Press)

MADNESS NETWORK NEWS, PO Box 684, San Francisco, CA 94101, (415) 548-2980. 1972. Poetry, fiction, articles, art, photos, cartoons, interviews, satire, criticism, reviews, letters, parts-of-novels, long-poems, news items. "We publish information on psychotropic drugs, mental health advocacy, patients/inmates; rights groups. Bias against involuntary committments." circ. 3,000. 4/yr. Pub'd 3 issues 1979; expects 3 issues 1980, 3 issues 1981. sub. price: $5.00; per copy: $0.75; sample: $0.75, 1 free on request. Back issues: Some early issues $0.50 each. Discounts: 6 issues subscription free to former mental patients & current mental patients; $1.00 to prisoners. 20-36pp; 11½X17½; of. Reporting time: varies. Pub's reviews. §Rights of psychiatric patients, experiences with 'madness'. Ads: No ads.

MADRONA, Gemini, Charles Webb, Editor; Jeff Powers, Managing Editor; Gretchen Wigton, J. K. Osborne, Vasselis Zambaras, John Levy, Associate Editors, 505 S Wilton Pl #203, Los Angeles, CA 90020. 1971. Poetry, fiction, art, photos, interviews, satire, letters, long-poems. "For comments, biases see under Gemini." circ. 500. irregular-published when we get enough material for a good issue. Pub'd 2 issues 1979; expects 2 issues 1980. 1 title listed in the *Small Press Record of Books in Print* (9th Edition, 1980). sub. price: $5.00/volume; per copy: $2.50; sample: $2.00 + SASE. Back issues: query. Discounts: 40% dealers, 40% classrooms. 75 per double issuepp; 7X8; of. Reporting time: 1 wk-3 months-longer when we're out of town. Payment: copies. Copyrighted. Pub's reviews: 10 in 1979. §poetry, fiction. Ads: $40.00/$20.00/none. CCLM.

Maelstrom Press (see also MAELSTROM REVIEW), P O Box 4261, Long Beach, CA 90804. 1972. Poetry, fiction, art, photos, cartoons, criticism, reviews, long-poems, plays. "Generally publish 2 books per year." avg. press run 500-700. Pub'd 2 titles 1979; expects 2 titles 1980, 2 titles 1981. 6 titles listed in the *Small Press Record of Books in Print* (9th Edition, 1980). avg. price, paper: $2.00. Discounts: 40% on two or more copies. 68pp; 5½X8½; †of. Reporting time: 4-8 weeks. Payment: 25

copies plus half price on add'l copies. Copyrights for author. WIP/LPSC.

MAELSTROM REVIEW, Maelstrom Press, Leo Mailman, Gerald Locklin, Associate Editor; Ray Zepeda, Associate Editor, P.O. Box 4261, Long Beach, CA 90804. 1972. Poetry, fiction, art, photos, cartoons, criticism, reviews, long-poems, plays. "I tend toward poetry with a minimum of poetic diction, and that is socially relevant and/or humorous: the epitome of this style would be the poetry of Edward Field. Recent contributors: Gerald Locklin, Ronald Koertge, Edward Field, Kirk Robertson, William Olsen, Billy Collins, Steve Richmond, Charles Webb, Fritz Hamilton, David Barker & Joan Smith." circ. 400. 2-3/yr. Pub'd 2 issues 1979; expects 2 issues 1980, 2 issues 1981. sub. price: $5.00 (4 iss)/indiv.; $5.00 (institutions, 2 iss); per copy: $2.00; sample: $2.00. Back issues: *Nausea* #1-11: (ltd offer): $15.00. Discounts: 40% to bookstores (2 or more copies). 48pp; 7X8½; †of. Reporting time: 4-8 wks. Payment: 2 copies and awards ($15.00 each for best poem and best short story per calender year). Copyrighted, reverts to author. Pub's reviews: 12 in 1979. §po/fi/small press efforts. CCLM.

Mafdet Press, W.D. Firestone, 1313 South Jefferson Avenue, Springfield, MO 65807, (417) 866-5141. 1974. Poetry, fiction. "Specializing in poetry and short fiction. Most recent publication was the novelette, *Goodbye, Lon Chaney, Jr., Goodbye,* by H.L. Prosser. (Have a preference for fantasy & poetry)." avg. press run varies per publiction. Pub'd 1 title 1979. 3 titles listed in the *Small Press Record of Books in Print* (9th Edition, 1980). Discounts: short. variespp; 6X9; †of. Reporting time: 2 months. Payment: in copies only. Yes.

MAG CITY, Gregory Masters, Michael Scholnick, Gary Lenhart, 437 East 12 St. No. 26, New York, NY 10009. 1977. Poetry, art, cartoons, long-poems. "Last issue, #8, included Rene Ricard, Helena Hughes, Alice Notley, Elinor Naven, Ted Berrigan and others." circ. 300. 3/yr. Pub'd 3 issues 1979; expects 3 issues 1980, 3 issues 1981. sub. price: $6.00/yr; per copy: $2.00; sample: $2.00. Back issues: No. 1 unavailable, all others $3.00. 70pp; 8½X11; †of/mi. Reporting time: 2 weeks to 2 months. Payment: none. Copyrighted, reverts to author.

MAGIC CHANGES, Celestial Otter, John Sennett, Donald Bullen, Cheryl Joy, 1923 Finchley Ct, Schaumburg, IL 60194, (312) 884-6425. 1978. Poetry, fiction, art, photos, cartoons, interviews, satire, music, long-poems, plays, criticism, reviews. "Towards a new, experimental American culture. We herald an arts renaisance and are intelligent, strong & fun. Naturally, our material is likewise. We love writing cogniscent of environment (be it the mintcream Missouri splashing moonlight or skyscraper visions)." circ. 3,000. 4/yr. Expects 2 issues 1980, 4 issues 1981. sub. price: $12.00; per copy: $4.00; sample: $3.00. Back issues: $3.00. Discounts: Inquire. 107pp; 8½X11; †lp. Reporting time: 3-6 weeks. Payment: 1 or 2 issues. Copyrighted, reverts to author. Pub's reviews: 20 in 1979. §Poetry, rock n roll, short fiction, photography, all music. Ads: $60.00/$30.00/$0.10.

Magic Circle Press, Valerie Harms, 10 Hyde Ridge Rd, Weston, CT 06883. 1972. Fiction, art, photos, criticism, concrete art. "Recent contributors are children's authors Ann McGovern and Ruth Krauss; Diarist and novelist Anais Nin, Erika Duncan, Susan Thompson, Sas Colby. Also have done special projects such as poetry of women from prison. Not soliciting any new material." avg. press run 2,000. Pub'd 3 titles 1979; expects 6 titles 1980. 7 titles listed in the *Small Press Record of Books in Print* (9th Edition, 1980). avg. price, cloth: $8.00; paper: $5.00. Discounts: 40% trade, 15% library. 150pp; 6X9; of. Reporting time: 2 mos. Payment: depends. Copyrights for author. COSMEP, NESPA, PEN.

MAGIC SAM, "Absolutely Furious" Productions, Ken Bolton, Sal Brereton, Box 164 Wentworth Building, Darlington, N.S.W. 2008, Australia. 1975. Poetry, fiction, art, photos, cartoons, interviews, reviews, parts-of-novels, long-poems. "We take work (outside Australia by solicitation only) written conscious of the assumptions on which it works, i.e. formally &/or intellectually self-aware — each piece defining & exploring its limits as a style & as a range of possibility." circ. 300-400. 1/yr. Pub'd 2 issues 1979; expects 2 issues 1980. price per copy: $3.00 (Australian); sample: $3.00 (Australian). Back issues: $3.00 a. Discounts: none. 180pp; size quarto; †mi and silkscreen. Reporting time: 6-8 weeks, or less. Payment: none. Copyrighted. Pub's reviews: 30 in 1979. §avant-garde writing. Ads: none.

MAGICAL BLEND, Magical Blend, Katherine Zunic, Michael Peter Langeuin, PO Box 11303, San Francisco, CA 94101. 1980. Poetry, fiction, articles, art, photos, interviews, reviews. "Dane Rudhyar/Michael Moorcock/Justin Green. Length approx 1,500 words average. Bias we print material which is of a positive, uplifting, psychic or spitutual nature. We hope to make our readers feel better about themselves & the world and help them get a better grasp of their destiny." circ. 10,000. 4/yr. sub. price: $8.00; per copy: $2.00; sample: $2.00. Back issues: $2.00. Discounts: 100 or more, 60% retail. 60pp; 8½X11; of. Reporting time: 1 month. Payment: copies. Copyrighted, reverts to author.

Magical Blend (see also MAGICAL BLEND), Katherine Zunic, Michael Langevil, PO Box 11303, San

Francisco, CA 94101. 1980. Fiction, articles, art, photos, interviews, reviews, letters, parts-of-novels. avg. press run 6,000. avg. price, paper: $2.00. Discounts: 50% & shipping. 60pp; 8½X11; of. Reporting time: 1 month. Payment: copies. Copyrights for author.

The Maguey Press, Rolly Kent, Ray Quintanar, Lisa Cooper, Nancy Mairs, Box 3395, Tucson, AZ 85722, 602-623-9711. 1976. Poetry, fiction, art, photos, letters, parts-of-novels, long-poems. "The Maguey Press is looking for good publishing projects using as context or reference point the culture and/or geography of U.S. Southwest & Latin America. The present project is a poetry chapbook series featuring poets of the above region: Rolly Kent, W. A. Roecker, Greg Pape, Keith Wilson, Pamela Stewart, Nancy Mairs, Leo Romero, Jefferson Carter. Mss. of poetry should be 25-30 typescript. SASE." avg. press run 1,000. Pub'd 1 title 1979. 8 titles listed in the *Small Press Record of Books in Print* (9th Edition, 1980). avg. price, paper: $2.50. Discounts: Trade 40% discount; poets & writers listed professionals 40% off; others by arrangement. 32pp; 5X7½; of. Reporting time: 6 weeks. Payment: copies (10% of run). Does not copyright for author.

Main Track Publications, Bob Vincent, 12435 Ventura Court, Studio City, CA 91604, (213) 506-0151. 1979. Music. "One book out, *Show Business is Two Worlds*" avg. press run 5,000. Pub'd 1 title 1979. avg. price, cloth: $12.50. Discounts: Libraries, colleges 30%; agents 40%; jobbers 50%.

MAIN TREND, Editorial Committee, PO Box 344 Cooper Station, New York, NY 10003. 1978. Poetry, fiction, articles, art, photos, cartoons, interviews, satire, criticism, reviews, music, letters, parts-of-novels, long-poems, collages, plays, news items. "*Main Trend* has two basic functions: the first is to publish examples of the revolutionary culture that is growing out of the anti-imperialist movement; the second is to criticize bourgeois culture, especially the mass media. It is aimed at the broad masses of working and oppressed peoples and every effort is made to get out of the usual audience for cultural publications. Articles and other material should be short and written in a 'mass style'. Recent contributors include: Amiri Baraka, Nathan Heard, Gary Allan Kizer, Sylvia Jones, Joel Cohyen, Jose Figeroa." circ. 3,000. 3 or more/yr. Expects 3 issues 1980, 4 issues 1981. sub. price: $4.00; per copy: $.75; sample: $1.00. Discounts: 40% on 5 or more; consignment basis. 32pp; 8 1/2X11; †of. Reporting time: 1 month. Payment: None as yet. Copyrighted, reverts to author. Pub's reviews. §Revolutionary culture, Marxist analysis of cultural/political problems. Ads: $40.00/$20.-00/$.10.

Mainespring Press (see also LETTERS), G. F. Bush, Publisher; Helen Nash, Editor, Box 82, Stonington, ME 04681, 207-367-2484. 1965. "E.B. White, George Garret, Carlos Baker, G.F. Bush, Charles Black, R. Buckminster Fuller, S.F. Morse, Kay Boyle,typical authors." avg. press run 4,500 min. Pub'd 1 title 1979; expects 2 titles 1980, 3 titles 1981. 1 title listed in the *Small Press Record of Books in Print* (9th Edition, 1980). avg. price, cloth: $6.95; paper: $3.00. 50 pp minimum; size varies; †of. Reporting time: one month. Payment: usual. we retain all rights only; details available. ALP, COS-MEPA.

THE MAINSTREETER, The Scopcraeft Press, Antony Oldknow, 3200 Ellis Street #16, St Point, WI 54481. 1971. Poetry, fiction, art, photos, reviews, parts-of-novels, long-poems. "Wish to print regular-meter poems as often as possible; welcome translations (but must see original text); recent contributors: Mark Vinz. Richard Lyons, William Virgil Davis, Tom McKeown, Tom McGrath, Richard Behm, Stephen Liu, Arthur Knight, Lyn Lifshin, Dan Eades, Clyde Fixmer." circ. 400. irreg. Pub'd 1 issue 1979; expects 1 issue 1980, 1 issue 1981. price per copy: $2.00; sample: $1.50. Discounts: bulk, classroom-both 15% off face value. 64pp; 8X5; of. Reporting time: varies. Payment: 2 copies. Copyrighted, reverts to author. Pub's reviews: 2 in 1979. §modern poetry, fiction, criticism, books on movies, modern poetry. Ads: $50/$25. CCLM.

MAIZE, Maize Press, Alurista, Xelina, Box 8251, San Diego, CA 92102, 714-235-6135/714-455-1128. 1977. Poetry, fiction, art, photos, cartoons, satire, criticism, parts-of-novels, long-poems, plays, concrete art. "Chicano, Indian, Latin American Preferences" circ. 500. 4/yr. Expects 4 issues 1980. sub. price: $5.00; per copy: $2.00; sample: $2.00. Back issues: $10.00 for 4 issues/ $2.00 per issue. Discounts: 40%/20 issues — libraries/bookstores. 64pp; 5½X8½; of/lp. Reporting time: 2 months. Payment: none yet. §Chicano, Indian, Latin American literature and art. CCLM.

Maize Press (see also MAIZE), Alurista, Xelina, P.O. Box 8251, San Diego, CA 92102, 714-235-6135. 1977. Poetry, fiction, art, photos, cartoons, interviews, satire, criticism, music, letters, parts-of-novels, long-poems, collages, plays, concrete art. "We print black, indian, asian, Latin American and northamerican work pertinent to continental reality." avg. press run 1000. Expects 4 titles 1980. 5 titles listed in the *Small Press Record of Books in Print* (9th Edition, 1980). avg. price, paper: $2.00. Discounts: 40% on 20+ copies. 64pp; 5½X8½; lp. Reporting time: 3 months. Payment: copies. Copyrights for author. CCLM.

MAJORITY REPORT, Nancy Borman, Joanne Steele, 74 Grove St, New York, NY 10014, 212-691-4950. 1971. Articles, interviews, criticism, reviews. "Newspaper, tabloid, in two colors. National international and local coverage of feminist events and women's issues. Habits of rapists. Calendar of feminist events. Subversive medical information. Feminist reviews of books, poetry, drama, film, media. Galleries listing. Women's business listing." circ. 25,000. 26/yr. Pub'd 26 issues 1979; expects 26 issues 1980. sub. price: $5.00 indiv./$10.00 institutions; per copy: $.25; sample: $.50. Back Issues: Jan-Dec 72 (as available) $15.00/Jan-Dec 73, $15.00/Jan-Dec 74 $12.50/Jan-Dec 75 $10.00. Discounts: bulk, 40%; agent subscriptions, 20%. 20pp; 11X17; of. Reporting time: immed/4 wks. Payment: none. buys one-time rights. Pub's reviews. §feminist/women's/lesbian etc. Ads: $745.00/$380.-00/$0.50 ($7.50 min). COSMEP.

THE MALAHAT REVIEW, Robin Skelton, Editor; William David Thomas, Asst. Editor, P.O. Box 1700, Victoria, British Columbia V8W 2Y2, Canada. 1967. Poetry, fiction, articles, art, photos, interviews, satire, criticism, letters, parts-of-novels, long-poems, collages, plays, concrete art. "Short works preferred. Index available 1967-1977, $3.95; $4.95 overseas" circ. 900. 4/yr. Pub'd 4 issues 1979. sub. price: $10.00, $12.00 Overseas; per copy: $3.00, special issues $5.00; sample: $2.50. Back issues: $3.00. Discounts: 33⅓%, agents and bookstores only, no returns policy. 150pp; 9X6; of. Reporting time: 8 to 10 weeks. Payment: $10.00 per poem page, $25.00 per thousand words-prose. Copyrighted. Pub's reviews: 55 in 1979. §Poetry, biographies, art, fiction, mystery. Ads: $100.00.

MALEDICTA: The International Journal of Verbal Aggression, Maledicta Press, Reinhold A. Aman, Editor & Publisher, 331 S. Greenfield Ave., Waukesha, WI 53186, 414-542-5853. 1975. Articles. "See any issue. 'Style Sheet' available." circ. 2,000. 2/yr. Pub'd 2 issues 1979; expects 2 issues 1980, 2 issues 1981. sub. price: $15.00, Institutions $20.00; sample: No sample copies available. Back issues: same as current. Discounts: Members: 20%; Booksellers: Varies; Jobbers: varies. 160pp; 5½X8½; of. Reporting time: 1 week. Payment: 20 free offprints. Copyrighted, does not revert to author. Pub's reviews: 83 in 1979. §Verbal Aggression (insults, curses, slang, etc.).

Maledicta Press (see also MALEDICTA: The International Journal of Verbal Aggression), Reinhold A. Aman, Editor & Publisher, 331 S. Greenfield Ave., Waukesha, WI 53186, 414-542-5853. 1975. Articles. "Material of 100 pp typed minimum for books, and 25 pp maximum for articles; must deal with verbal aggression. Glossaries monolingual or bilingual, are preferred to other material. Backlog of 2 years. No cloth binding available" avg. press run 2,000. Pub'd 1 title 1979; expects 2 titles 1980, 3 titles 1981. 6 titles listed in the *Small Press Record of Books in Print* (9th Edition, 1980). avg. price, paper: $10.00. Discounts: Members: 20%; Booksellers: Varies; Jobbers: varies. 160pp; 5½X8½; of. Reporting time: 1 week. Payment: 10% paid annually. No advance. Copyrights for author.

Malki Museum Press (see also JOURNAL OF CALIFORNIA AND GREAT BASIN ANTHROPOLOGY), Katherine Siva Saubel, President of Malki Museum, Inc. and Chairman of Editorial Board; William Bright, Editorial Director; Harry W. Lawton, Managing Director, Malki Museum Press, 11-795 Fields Road, Morongo Indian Reservation, Banning, CA 92220, 714-849-7289. 1965. "Books and phamphets of a scholarly or popular nature on the Native American peoples of California. Malki Museum Press has published 120 books, including Carobeth Laird's best-selling *Encounter With An Angry God,* and numerous booklets." avg. press run 1,500-2,000. Pub'd 2 titles 1979; expects 3 titles 1980. 9 titles listed in the *Small Press Record of Books in Print* (9th Edition, 1980). avg. price, cloth: $10.00; paper: $6.50; other: $1.50. Dealer discounts of 40 percent. pp varies.; size varies; of. Reporting time: 3 months. Payment: 10 percent royalties to authors. Copyrights for author.

Malpelo, Lee Mallory, 1916 Court Avenue, Newport Beach, CA 92663. 1969. Poetry. "Latest offering is a broadside series featuring known and unknown writers. A majority of broadsides in each edition are numbered and signed by the poet. Recent contributors include: Thomas Kerrigan, Mike Finley, Lyn Lifshin, and Gordon Preston. All copies of this initial series are free. No unsolicited manuscripts." 2 titles listed in the *Small Press Record of Books in Print* (9th Edition, 1980). of.

MAMASHEE, Sydenham Press, Margaret Drage, R R 1, Inwood, Ontario NON1KO, Canada, (519)-844-2805. Poetry, fiction, art, reviews, news items. "Short fiction - up to 2,000 words (usually one or two per issue)short essays or guest editorials dealing with literary subjects. Poetry - up to two-page length - no porno stuff - but won't reject quality work because of strong language. Recent contributor-sinclude Robert Whisler, Maryland, Len Gasparini, Toronto, Alex Amprimoz, Windsor, Ont." circ. 150. quarterly. Pub'd 4 issues 1979; expects 4 issues 1980, 4 issues 1981. sub. price: $5.00; per copy: $1.50; sample: $1.50. Back issues: inquire. Discounts: none. 48pp; 8½X11; †dupl. Reporting time: 2 months. Payment: copies. Copyrighted, reverts to author. Pub's reviews: 5-6 in 1979. §poetry or critical works. Ads: none.

MAN AT ARMS, Mowbray Company Publishers, E. Andrew Mowbray, Editor & Publisher; Richard

238

Alan Dow, Exec. Editor, 222 West Exchange Street, Providence, RI 02903, (401) 861-1000. 1979. "A magazine for collectors, investors, and enthusiasts of arms, armor, uniforms, accoutrements — from all countries and all periods. Heavily illustrated with extensive use of color. Highest quality materials used throughout." circ. 10,000. 6/yr. Pub'd 6 issues 1979. sub. price: $15.00; per copy: $3.00; sample: $3.00. Back issues: $3.00 (subscriptions from first issue available while supplies last). Discounts: usual. 68pp; 8¼X10¾. Reporting time: 2-3 weeks. Payment: $100.00-$200.00. Copyrighted, reverts to author. Pub's reviews. §Arms, armor. Ads: $900.00-$425.00/$500.00-$250.00.

MANASSAS REVIEW: ESSAYS ON CONTEMPORARY AMERICAN POETRY, Patrick Bizzaro, Communications Division, Northern Virginia Community College, Manassas, VA 22110. 1977. Articles, interviews, criticism. "We are presently focusing on essays about one poet each issue. Our first three issues have dealt with Stokes, Heyen, and Simic, respectively. We print self-interview, essays by people in touch with the contemporary poetic scene, new poems. The articles are intended to make poets accessible to the academic community *before* the poets die." circ. 500. 2-3/yr. Pub'd 3 issues 1979. sample price: free. Discounts: Presently (for first 3 issues) funded by a college grant that makes sale of the journal impossible. Copies are sent free to college libraries, Engl. deptments and those asking for a copy. 72pp; 5¼X8½; of. Reporting time: 6-8 weeks, query first. Payment: 2 copies (for the time being). Copyrighted, reverts to author. Pub's reviews: 2 in 1979. §Poetry: equally interested in Small Presses & Big Houses. As a rule, our subjects for each issue will participate in both worlds.

The Mandeville Press, Peter Scupham, John Mole, The Mandeville Press, 2 Taylor's Hill, Hitchin, Hertfordshire SG49AD, United Kingdom. 1974. Poetry. "The Mandeville Press publishes pamphlet collections of poets both new and established, in runs of approximately 250. The pamphlets are printed in letterpress, by hand, and sewn into card-covers. Recent collections by John Mole, Patric Dickinson, Lawrence Sail, and anthologies of contemporary verse." avg. press run 200-250. Pub'd 5 titles 1979. 9 titles listed in the *Small Press Record of Books in Print* (9th Edition, 1980). avg. price, paper: 50p. Discounts: 33⅓% to trade. 16pp; 8⅝X5½; †lp. Reporting time: 2-3 wks. Payment: copies. Copyrights for author.

Mandarin Press, William M. Plank, Editor, 210 Fifth Avenue, New York, NY 10010. 1977. "Mandarin Press currently publishes books in science and psychology, but we are thinking about diversifying our subject matter. Unfortunately, at the present time, we are not ready to accept unsolicited manuscripts." avg. press run 1,000 copies for first printing. Pub'd 1 title 1979; expects 1 title 1981. 1 title listed in the *Small Press Record of Books in Print* (9th Edition, 1980). avg. price, cloth: $8.50; paper: $3.50. Discounts: Trade 40%; Libraries 40%; Wholesalers 50%. 150-200pp; 5½X8½; lp. Payment: No advances. Author gets 50% of profits. Copyrights for author.

Mandorla Publications, John James, R.M.B. 917, Dooralong, N.S.W. 2259, Australia, (043) 551219. 1978. Art, criticism. "We publish scholarly works on medieval art and architecture for the authors who pay printing costs. Distribution in conjunction with Croom Helm of London. As copies are sold author is repaid plus 10%. *The James Ratio Hunter* 36 pp, 7 x 6½, $5.70, paper cover; *The Contractors of Chartres,* vol 1 248 pp, 7½ x 11½, hard cover, $42.00 including postage. Signed edition, limited to 500 copies. *The Builders of Durham,* 140 pp, 9½ x 7, hard cover, $35.00." avg. press run 500-1000. Pub'd 2 titles 1979; expects 2 titles 1980, 3 titles 1981. 5 titles listed in the *Small Press Record of Books in Print* (9th Edition, 1980). avg. price, cloth: $40; paper: $5-$14. Discounts: 33% trade, 50% wholesaler. 300pp; 7½X11½; lp. Reporting time: estimates within one month. Payment: Printing costs plus 10% from sales, made monthly. Copyrights for author.

MANGO, Lorna Dee Cervantes, Orlando Ramirez, Adrian Rocha, PO Box 28546, San Jose, CA 95159. 1976. Poetry, fiction, art, cartoons, interviews, satire, criticism, reviews, parts-of-novels, long-poems. "Chicano litmag by emphasis—multi-cultural in actuality, unsolicited Anglos rarely, but we read *all* material & answer all in the form of personal correspondence—publishes grahics, bilingual. Editors are serious & dedicated Chicano writers who expect the same from contributors. We're partial to young Chicanos. Recent contributors include: Jose Montoya, Omar Salinas, Jose Antonio Burciaga, Victor Martinez, Bernice Zamora, Wendy Rose, Jose Saldivar, Gary Soto, Leonard Adame, Richardo Sanchez, Pancho Aguila, Noaomi Clark, Geraldine Kudaka, Max Martinez & Victor Hernandez Cruz." circ. 1,000. Irregular. Pub'd 1 issue 1979; expects 4 issues 1980, 2 issues 1981. sub. price: $5.00; per copy: $2.00; sample: $2.00. Back issues: (Ano I, Num. 3,4) $2.00. 100pp; 5½X8½; †of/lp. Reporting time: 3 months immediate acknowledgement on request. Payment: copies. Copyrighted, reverts to author. Pub's reviews: 4 in 1979. §Chicano literature. Ads: $15.00/$7.50/none.

THE MANHATTAN REVIEW, Philip Fried, c/o P. Fried, 304 Third Avenue, 4A, New York, NY 10010. 1980. Poetry, articles, criticism, long-poems. "'My only prejudice is against those who lack ambition, believing there is no more to writing than purveying superficial ironies, jokes, or shared sentiments; or those who dedicate themselves to the proposition that poetry of a word, by a word and for a word shall not perish from this earth. A poem is not purely a verbal artifact. It must speak to and for human concerns. I welcome experiments, but poetry must ultimately communicate to an audience. It is not an unobserved wave in the vast ocean of language.' (quoted from preface to 1st issue)" circ. 500. 2/yr. price per copy: $1.50; sample: $1.50. 32pp; 5½X8½; of. Reporting time: 6-8 weeks. Payment: 2 copies. Copyrighted, reverts to author. Ads: $150.00/$75.00.

Manhole Publications, 5641 San Luis Ct, Pleasanton, CA 94566. 2 titles listed in the *Small Press Record of Books in Print* (9th Edition, 1980).

MANITOBA NATURE (formerly ZOOLOG), Robert E. Wrigley, Manitoba Museum of Man and Nature, 190 Rupert Ave., Winnipeg, Manitoba R3B0N2, Canada. 1966. Poetry, articles, art, photos, cartoons, satire, letters. "Mostly local content so do not seek submissions." circ. 3,000. 4/yr. sub. price: $6.00 Canada-USA, other $9.00; per copy: $1.75 Can-USA, foreign $2.00; sample: free. Back issues: $1.75 Can-USA, other $2.00. 32pp; 8½X11. Payment: none. Not copyrighted. Pub's reviews. §Any area of natural history, particularly northern US and Canada. Ads: $350/$210.

Jim Mann & Associates (see also MEDIA MANAGEMENT MONOGRAPHS), Jim Mann, 7 Biscayne Drive, Ramsey, NJ 07446, (201) 327-8492. 1974.

MANNA, Nina A. Wicker, Route 8, Box 368, Sanford, NC 27330. 1978. Poetry. "Good clean poetry, prose, inspirational poems-short, homespun-farm poems, humorous poems - if it's good, we'll consider it - if it's good and humorous, we'll publish it. All material will be read, but none returned unless accompanied by self-addressed envelope." circ. 500. 2/yr. Expects 1 issue 1980, 2 issues 1981. sub. price: $5.00; per copy: $2.50; sample: $2.50. 50pp; 5½X8½. Reporting time: fast. Payment: prizes. Copyrighted, reverts to author.

Manor Press (see also INTERCOM), Dwight L. Musser, Editor, Box 305, Ridge Manor, FL 33525. 1960. Articles. "Have published pamphlets on crafts and hobbies: *World Paper Money Collectors Guide, World Coin and Currency Handbook, Notgeld Newsletter, World Paper Money Journal.* Additionally interested in alternate economy and printing as a hand craft." avg. press run 500. avg. price, paper: $1.00. Discounts: Private distribution only. 20pp; 8½X11; †mi/lp.

MANROOT, Manroot Books, Paul Mariah, Richard Tagett, Box 982, South San Francisco, CA 94080. 1969. "Send self addressed stamped envelope for complete catalog listing and free poems that are available. We've published Robert Peters' THE POET AS ICESKATER, Helen Luster's YEAR OF THE HARE POEMS, Paul Mariah's Selected Poems 1960-1975,Jack Micheline's Selected Poems 1954-1975." circ. 1,000. 1-2/yr. Pub'd 1 issue 1979. sub. price: $5.00; per copy: $2.50; sample: $2.50. Back issues: MR #6/7 $5.00; MR #5,8,9 $3.00; others inquire. Discounts: 40% bookstores & bulk available for classroom. 120pp; 8½X5½; of. Reporting time: 3 months. Payment varies. Copyrighted. Pub's reviews: 1 in 1979. §poetry/gay/prison/theatre. Ads: None. CCLM, COSMEP.

Manroot Books (see also MANROOT), Paul Mariah, Richard Tagett, Box 982, So San Francisco, CA 94080. 1969. Poetry, long-poems. "We solicit. *Please* do not send mss without inquiring first. Primary interest. *Poetics* not poems." avg. press run 1,000. Pub'd 5 titles 1979; expects 3 titles 1980. 20 titles listed in the *Small Press Record of Books in Print* (9th Edition, 1980). avg. price, cloth: $15.00; paper: $2.95-$5.95; other: Handset items higher as well as signed items. Discounts: 40% to stores. 10-200pp; 5½X8½; of. Reporting time: 3 months. Payment: yes. Copyrights for author.

The Many Press (see also VANESSA POETRY MAGAZINE), John Welch, 15 Norcott Road, London N16 7BJ, United Kingdom. 1976. Poetry, criticism, reviews. "87" avg. press run 200. Pub'd 8 titles 1979; expects 7 titles 1980. 21 titles listed in the *Small Press Record of Books in Print* (9th Edition, 1980). avg. price, paper: $1.50. Discounts: Trade terms one third. 28pp; size A5; of. Reporting time: 2 months. Payment in copies. Copyrights for author. ALP, ALMS.

MANY SMOKES, Bear Tribe, Wabun, SunBear, Nimimosha, Art Director, P.O. Box 9167, Spokane, WA 99209. 1966. Poetry, articles, art, interviews, reviews, fiction, photos, cartoons, satire, criticism, music, letters. "Short stuff-Native American religions emphasis, and earth awareness. Must be constructive in attitude. Not scholarly, but accurate." circ. 5,000. 2/yr. Pub'd 4 issues 1979; expects 2 issues 1980, 2 issues 1981. sub. price: $1.00 (US); $1.50 (other countries); per copy: $1.00. Back issues: $1.50. Discounts: 30 percent agent, 50 percent jobber. 32-40pp; 8½X11; of. Reporting time: 1 month to 6 weeks. Payment: none. Copyrighted. Pub's reviews: 31 in 1979. §American Indian religion, history, environment, new age. Ads: $300/$150/$.25. CCLM.

Manzanita Press, Florence Strange, P.O.Box 4027, San Raphael, CA 94903, (415) 479-9636. 1977. Fiction, art. "We are organized for the primary purpose of self-publishing picture books for young children. Our current publications are *Rock-A-Bye Whale,* a full color picture book about the birth of a Humpback whale; and *Brown Pelican at the Pond,* an ecology story. At present we have no plans to

240

publish books by other authors." avg. press run 2M-5M. Pub'd 1 title 1979; expects 1 title 1981. 2 titles listed in the *Small Press Record of Books in Print* (9th Edition, 1980). avg. price, cloth: $7.95. Discounts: on request. 32pp; 8½X11; lo.

Manzano Press, Reed Cooper, 85 Ardmore Rd, Kensington, CA 94707, (415) 526-6980. 1978. Music. avg. press run 200. Pub'd 1 title 1979. avg. price, paper: $2.95. Discounts: 1-4 copies, $2.95; 5-9 copies, $2.00; 10 or more copies, $1.80. 8½X11; lp. Copyrights for author.

THE MARGARINE MAYPOLE ORANGOUTANG EXPRESS, Anonymous Owl Press, Carl Mayfield, Editor; Morrow Baker, Editorial Consultant, 3209 Wellesley, NE 1, Albuquerque, NM 87107. 1973. Poetry. "Interested in all poems, poetic or otherwise. Space permits only the shorter pieces of a person's work. Recent contributors: William Stafford, Gene Frumkin, Lyn Lifshin, Joy Walsh, Robert Spiegel" circ. 50-100. 6/yr. sub. price: $1.00; per copy: $.50; sample: $.50. Back issues: First issue: $10.00 most back issues: $1.00. Discounts: none. 1pp; 5½X8½; of. Reporting time: 2 weeks. Payment: 3 free copies. Not copyrighted. CCLM.

Abraham Marinoff Publications, Abraham Marinoff, 400 Argyle Road, Brooklyn, NY 11218.

MARK TWAIN JOURNAL, Cyril Clemens, Mark Twain Journal, Kirkwood, MO 63122. 1936. sub. price: $3.00; per copy: $1.00; sample: $1.00. Back issues: all $1 a copy. 21pp; 10X8. Reporting time: 10 days. §literary/biography/criticism. Ads: $100.

Maro Verlag, Benno Kaesmayr, Christiane Kaesmayr, Bismarckstr, 7½, D-8900 Augsburg, West Germany, 0821-577131. 1969. Poetry, fiction. "We are one of the 'German Alternative-Presses'. We are editing young German poets, and important American writers: William S. Burroughs, Charles Bukowski, Jack Kerouac, Jack Micheline, Harald Norse and Al Masarik). Every two years we arrange a complete catalogue of German Small Presses and Little Magazines. *Turpentine On The Rocks* is called a new anthology presenting the best poems out of US small presses 1966 — 1977, edited by Bukowski and Weissner." avg. press run 2,000-25,000. Pub'd 4 titles 1979; expects 4 titles 1980. avg. price, paper: dm 10.00 to dm 15.00. Discounts: 35-50 percent. 150pp; 20.5X13.5 cm; †of. Reporting time: 6 months. Payment: 10-15 percent of retail prize. Copyrights for author. AGAV.

Maryland Historical Press, Vera F. Rollo, 9205 Tuckerman St, Lanham, MD 20801, (301)577-2436 and 557-5308. 1965. "We publish material for schools in Maryland on free-lance basis. History, Govt., Geog., Biography, and Black History. Our books are mostly set in type, printed via off-set process, illustrated, and about 50 percent are casebound, 50 percent paperback" avg. press run 2,000 copies on paperbacks, 5,000 on casebound. Pub'd 1 title 1979; expects 1 title 1980, 1 title 1981. 8 titles listed in the *Small Press Record of Books in Print* (9th Edition, 1980). avg. price, cloth: $6.00-$8.00; paper: $3.00 - $5.00. Discounts: 33 percent to jobbers/dealers. 100-400pp; 8½X11; of. We buy almost nothing, sorry. Payment: None. Author is partner. Copyright in name of Vera Rollo or in one case Md H'l Press. Washington Book Publisher's Association.

MARXIST PERSPECTIVES, Eugene D. Genovese, Editor; Jacques Marchand, Publisher, 420 West End Avenue, New York, NY 10024, (212) 242-7777. 1978. Poetry, articles, criticism, reviews. "Some recent articles: Marxism & Psychoanalysis, Black Religion & Resistance on Lovis Althusser, on nationalism, The Museum of Modern Art, The Soviet Dissidents, Marxism & Darwinism, on Virginia Woolf, on U.S. Naipul, film criticism, poetry." circ. 8,000. 4/yr. Pub'd 4 issues 1979; expects 4 issues 1980. sub. price: Individual $18.00; Institutional $30.00; per copy: $4.95; sample: $4.95. Back issues: $4.95. Discounts: correspond with publisher. 176pp; 6X9; of. Reporting time: 3 months. Copyrighted. Pub's reviews: 5 in 1979. §History, cultural criticism, politics, economy, Marxism, arts & letters, science. Ads: $350.00-$250.00/$150.00.

THE MASSACHUSETTS REVIEW, John Hicks, Lee Edwards, Robert Tucker, Memorial Hall, Univ. of Mass, Amherst, MA 01003, 413-545-2689. 1959. Poetry, fiction, articles, art, photos, interviews, satire, criticism, reviews, letters, long-poems, plays. circ. 2M plus. 4/yr. Pub'd 4 issues 1979; expects 4 issues 1980. sub. price: $10.00; per copy: $3.00; sample: $3.00 and $.50 postage. Back issues: $4 & $5. Discounts: 15 percent discount on ads for univ. presses, adv. agencies, small presses; 40 percent bookstores. 200pp; 6X9; lp. Reporting time: 4-6 wks. Payment: $50 stories $10 min poetry. Ads: $125/$75/$50 1/4. CCLM.

Master Key Publications, John Marino, Dianne Marino, PO Box 519, Bonita, CA 92002, (714) 475-6060. 1979. Articles, news items. "Interested in pieces dealing with real estate, investments, sales, 'how-to'." avg. press run 5,000. Pub'd 1 title 1979. 1 title listed in the *Small Press Record of Books in Print* (9th Edition, 1980). avg. price, paper: $8.00. Discounts: 1-3, $8.00; 4-9, $7.00; 10 or more, $6.00. 180pp; 5½X8½; of. Reporting time: 3 weeks. Payment: negotiable.

MASTER THOUGHTS, Dominion Press, Friend Stuart, Editor, PO Box 37, San Marcos, CA 92069,

(714) 746-9430. 1972. Articles. "Advanced Christian metaphysics. Not recommended for beginners. Weekly, but published periodically for several weeks ahead. Mailed 4-6 times per year" circ. 200. Pub'd 52 issues 1979. sub. price: $6.00. Back issues: 1972-76 complete, bound $22.00; 1977-79 complete, bound $14.00. Discounts: 30% (dealers and agencies only). 2pp; 5½X8½; of. No ms. accepted.

Masters Publications, James I. Masters, Box 1332, Brooklyn, NY 11201, (212) 596-1598. 1976. "We publish under three imprints. Blue Claw Press. Guidebooks, maps, informational materials on Long Island and Cape Cod. Outdoor recreation is the focus—fishing, camping, boating. Transition Books. Activity books for children ages 6-9. Subjects are major events in the lives of children, such as moving, new sibling, mother goes to work, starting school, visit to the doctor, dentist. Real Life Books. Story books about children who have mental or physical disabilities. Introductions provide factual information for teachers. Copyright Assistance Service. For a fee, Masters helps other small publishers file their Copyright Registration forms. He will help you sort out your 'work made for hire' agreements and permissions. Send a SASE for his brochure." avg. press run 5,000-100,000. Pub'd 1 title 1979; expects 3 titles 1980, 6 titles 1981. 5 titles listed in the *Small Press Record of Books in Print* (9th Edition, 1980). avg. price, cloth: $6.95; paper: $4.95. Discounts: Standard discounts; 40% on orders of ten or more. Activity Books 64pp; Guidebooks 354pp; 6X9; 8½X11; of. Reporting time: 4-6 months. Payment: Low advance, usually under $100.00. Excellent royalties on childrens books. Copyrights for author. Publisher's Alliance.

Matagiri (see also COLLABORATION), Matagiri Sri Aurobindo Center, Mt. Tremper, NY 12457, (914) 679-8322. 1971. "Primarily a distributor; published 1 title. Rarely use unsolicited material".

MATHEMATICAL SPECTRUM, Applied Probability Trust, D.W. Sharpe, Dept of Pure Mathematics, The University, Sheffield S3 7RH, United Kingdom. 1968. Articles, reviews, letters. circ. 2,500. 3/yr. Pub'd 3 issues 1979; expects 3 issues 1980, 3 issues 1981. sub. price: £4.00 ($9.00 U.S.). Back issues: on request. 32pp. Payment: none. Copyrighted, does not revert to author. Pub's reviews. §books on mathematics suitable for senior student's in schools and beginning undergraduates in colleges and universities.

Mathom Publishing Co, Lewis Turco, Editor, 68 East Mohawk St, Oswego, NY 13126, 315-343-3035. 1977. Poetry, fiction, photos. "Regional material or authors only. Wesli Court, Charlie Davis, Olga Clark. Note: We are primarily interested in New York State regionals. Our regional market is good for about 1,500 copies in the paperback price range $3.95-6.95 and hard cover $8.95-12.00." avg. press run 500-1,000. Pub'd 2 titles 1979; expects 1 title 1980, 1 title 1981. 4 titles listed in the *Small Press Record of Books in Print* (9th Edition, 1980). avg. price, cloth: $7.95; paper: $4.95; other: $12.00 signed hardcover. Discounts: 40% to bookstores ordering 12 copies; 22% libraries ordering 5 copies. 100pp; 6X9; of. Reporting time: 1 month. Payment: 10%. Copyrights for author. COSMEP.

MATI, Ommation Press, Effie Mihopoulos, 5548 N. Sawyer, Chicago, IL 60625. 1975. Poetry, articles, art, photos, interviews, reviews, letters, long-poems. "Very open to experimental poetry and especially poems by women. The magazine was established to provide another source where new poets can see their work in print. The work doesn't have to be perfect, but show potential. MATI wants to encourage young poets to see as much of their work in print as possible. Open to exchange (magazines and ads) with other magazines. *Mati* will also be doing a series of poem postcards as special issues (both letterpress and offset, $1.00 a set) for which short poems are welcome to be submitted for consideration. Recent contributors: Anne Waldman, Alice Notley, Ron Padgett, Ted Berrigan, Opal L. Nations, John Tagliabue, Faye Kicknosway, Richard Kostelanetz, Lyn Lifshin." circ. 500. 4/yr. Pub'd 4 issues 1979; expects 4 issues 1980. sub. price: $4.50; per copy: $1.50; sample: $1.50. Back issues: No. 1, $10.00; No. 2, $20.00; No. 3, $10.00; No. 6, $2.00. Discounts: 40%. 40pp; 8½X11; of. Reporting time: Immediately - 2 weeks. Payment: 1 copy. Copyrighted, reverts to author. Ads: $80/$40/$15. CCLM, COSMEP-Midwest.

MATRIX, Phil Lanthier, Box 510, Lennoxville, Quebec J1M 1Z6, Canada, (819) 563-6881. 1975. Poetry, fiction, articles, satire, criticism, reviews, parts-of-novels. "Recent contributors: Earle Birney, Russell Banks, Jerald Bullis, David Solway, W. P. Kinsella, Merritt Clifton, Lyn Lifshin, Eldon Garnet, Ralph Gustafson, D. G. Jones, Jon Whyte, Irving Layton, Bernard Epps" circ. 1,000. 2/yr. Pub'd 2 issues 1979; expects 2 issues 1980, 2 issues 1981. sub. price: $4.00; per copy: $2.00; sample: $2.00. Discounts: On request. 84pp; 7X10; of. Reporting time: 8 weeks. Payment: $7.00 - $10.00 per page. Pub's reviews: 20 in 1979. §Recent poetry, fiction, criticism, children's literature and science fiction. CPPA.

MATRIX, British Science Fiction Assoc. Ltd., John Harvey, 269 Wykeham Road, Reading RG6 1PL, United Kingdom. Articles, art, cartoons, interviews, satire, criticism, letters, news items. "The news-

242

letter of the British SF Association." circ. 800. 6/yr. Pub'd 6 issues 1979; expects 6 issues 1980, 6 issues 1981. sub. price: Free to members; sample: 35p. Back issues: Few held; write for information. 32pp; size A4; †mi. Payment: Nil. Copyrighted, reverts to author.

Matrix Press, Kathleen A. Walkup, PO Box 327, Palo Alto, CA 94302. 1979. Poetry, fiction, collages. "Formerly with Five Trees Press, now embarking on what I hope will be multi-faceted printing & publishing with a continuing emphasis on letterpress work." avg. press run 500. Pub'd 3 titles 1979. avg. price, cloth: $25.00; paper: $5.00. Discounts: Trade 1-4 copies, 20%; 5 or more, 40%; smaller rates on limited editions. †lp. Reporting time: 1 month. Payment: 10% on net.

MATTOID, Wendy Morgan, c/o School of Humanities, Deakin University, Victoria 3217, Australia. 1978. Poetry, fiction, art, photos, interviews. circ. 400. 3/yr. Pub'd 2 issues 1979. sub. price: $5.00 for 3 isssues; per copy: $2.00. Back issues: $1.00. Discounts: $1.50. 44-48pp; 6X8¼; of. Reporting time: 3-6 months. Copyrighted, reverts to author.

MAW: A MAGAZINE OF APPALACHIAN WOMEN, PO Box 490, Mars Hill, NC 28754. 1977. Poetry, fiction, articles, art, photos, cartoons, interviews, reviews, letters. "Lillie D. Chaffin (KY. poet) in Nov.-Dec. '77. Articles of up to 5,000 words." circ. 2,000. 4/yr. Pub'd 2 issues 1979; expects 4 issues 1980. sub. price: $5.00 indiv. $10.00 library; per copy: $1.00; sample: $1.00. Back issues: $1.00 a copy. Discounts: 40% off to bookstores, 50% off to distributors. 40pp; 8½X11; of. Reporting time: 2-3 weeks. Payment: 3 copies of issue. Copyrighted, does not revert to author. Pub's reviews: 5 in 1979. §Women, Appalachia, Art. Ads: $100.00/$55.00/$0.10 a word. COSMEP.

MAXY'S JOURNAL, Truedog Press, Inc., Mac Bennett, Craig Chambers, 216 West Academy Street, Lonoke, AR 72086, (501) 676-2467. 1977. Poetry, fiction, photos, cartoons, satire, reviews, parts-of-novels, long-poems, plays. "Play, one-acts only. Traditional forms are admired here. (In poems, expecially)" circ. 500+. 3/yr. Expects 2 issues 1980, 3 issues 1981. sub. price: $5.00; per copy: $2.00; sample: $2.00. Back issues: $2.00. Discounts: Will distribute to bookstores on consignment. 50pp; 6X9; of. Reporting time: 2 months. Payment: 1 copy. Copyrighted, reverts to author. Pub's reviews: 2 in 1979. §Poetry, plays, fiction, novels. Ads: $40.00/$25.00. COSMEP.

May-Murdock Publications, Jayne May, Dick Murdock, PO Box 343, 90 Glenwood, Ross, CA 94957, (415) 454-1771. 1976. Poetry, letters. "*Love Lines* is in its 4th printing. It's 126 pages. Two booklets, *Walnut Creek's Unique Old Station* and *Port Costa,* 1879-1941, A saga of sails, sacks & rails. *How Fighting Can Enhance Your Marriage,* just released" avg. press run 1,000-3,000. Pub'd 2 titles 1979; expects 1 title 1980, 2-3 titles 1981. 6 titles listed in the *Small Press Record of Books in Print* (9th Edition, 1980). avg. price, paper: $2.00-$5.00. We will discount 40% to any type wholesaler, but our business is primarily mail order. 126pp; 5½X8½; †of. We do all our own writing. Copyrights for author.

Mayapple Press, Judith Kerman, PO Box 7508, Liberty Station, Ann Arbor, MI 48107, (313) 971-2223. 1978. Poetry, fiction, art, parts-of-novels, long-poems. "We have a special interest in regional writing, particularly from the Great Lakes area, as well as contemporary poetry, art/crafts, and feminist literature. We are generally interested only in *chapbook* length poetry or fiction. Our first book was a how-to crafts book (soft sculpture); our first poetry chapbook was by Toni Ortner-Zimmerman; forthcoming chapbook is by Judith Minty (1980)," avg. press run 500-1,000. Pub'd 1 title 1979; expects 1 title 1980, 1-2 titles 1981. 3 titles listed in the *Small Press Record of Books in Print* (9th Edition, 1980). avg. price, paper: $2.00-$7.00. Discounts: 1-5 copies to bookstores, jobbers & libraries 20%; 6 or more (mixed or same title) 30% consignment; 40% cash/returns; 50% no returns. 16-24pp; 5½X8½, 7X8, 8½X11; of. Reporting time: up to 2 months. Payment: for poetry/fiction, 6 copies plus generous discount on purchase of copies; for other, negotiable. Copyrights for author. COSMEP.

Mayer Press (see PIVOT)

McBooks Press, Alexander G. Skutt, 106 North Aurora Street, Ithaca, NY 14850, (607) 272-6602. 1979. "We can accept *no* unsolicited manuscripts. Letters of inquiry are welcome. We publish a very few books and we make the decision to publish on the basis of both commercial potential and artistic merit. Although we have no rule against fiction, we are mostly interested in purposeful, well-written non-fiction. Our first two books were *Vegetarian Baby* by Sharon Yntema & *Rapunzel, Rapunzel:* poetry, prose and photgraphs by women on the subject of hair edited by Katharyn Machan Aal." avg. press run 3,250. Pub'd 2 titles 1979; expects 2 titles 1980. avg. price, cloth: $10.95; paper: $5.95. Discounts: Standard terms are available to bookstores, wholesalers, etc. through our exclusive distributor, The Crossing Press, Trumansburg, NY 14886. 176pp; of. Reporting time: 1 month on query letters, no unsolicited manuscripts. Payment: paid on usual basis, sometimes with an advance. Copyrights for author.

McFarland & Company, Inc., Publishers, Robert Franklin, President, Box 611, Jefferson, NC 28640,

(919) 246-4460. 1979. "We want book-length manuscripts (at least 200-225 pp. double spaced) of scholarly or reference books on film, literature, women's studies, political affairs, music, theatre/-drama, parapsychology (not 'occult'), chess, science, etc., etc. No fiction, poetry, children's books, memoirs, etc." avg. press run 750. Expects 15-20 titles 1980, 15-20 titles 1981. 14 titles listed in the *Small Press Record of Books in Print* (9th Edition, 1980). avg. price, cloth: $12.00; paper: $9.00. Discounts: Short discount to wholesalers and by special arrangement. No trade bookstore sales. 225pp; 6X9; of. Reporting time: 3 to 10 days. Payment: Usually 10% of gross income from sales on first 1,000 sold; 15% thereafter. Copyrights for author. AAP, COSMEP, ALA.

McNally & Loftin, West, Janice Timbrook, W.J. McNally III, Box 1316, Santa Barbara, CA 93101, (805) 964-7079. 1956. "Specialize in Santa Barbara Channel Islands; agricultural and environmental history" avg. press run 2,500. Pub'd 4 titles 1979; expects 6 titles 1980, 4 titles 1981. avg. price, cloth: $15.00; paper: $6.50. Discounts: Trade 40%, college text 20%. 275pp; 6X9; †lp. Reporting time: 4 weeks. Payment: 10% net. Copyrights for author. COSMEP.

Meanings Press, Stephen Alan Saft, 902 Maryland Ave NE, Washington, DC 20002. 1975. 1 title listed in the *Small Press Record of Books in Print* (9th Edition, 1980). of. Reporting time: one month plus.

MEANJIN QUARTERLY, J.H. Davidson, Judith Rodriguez, Poetry, University of Melbourne, Parkville, Victoria 3052, Australia, 341-6950. 1940. Poetry, fiction, articles, criticism, reviews, parts-of-novels, long-poems, plays. circ. 3,000. 4/yr. Pub'd 4 issues 1979; expects 4 issues 1980, 4 issues 1981. sub. price: $14.00 Ausl.; per copy: $3.50 Austl.; sample: $3.50 Austl. 144pp; 8½X5; lp. Reporting time: 2 months. Payment: for articles from $75. Copyrighted, reverts to author. Pub's reviews: 40 in 1979. §cultural politics. Ads: $220/$120.

MEDIA HISTORY DIGEST, Hiley H. Ph. D. Ward, PO Box 867, William Penn Station, Philadelphia, PA 19105, (215) 787-9121. 1979. Articles, interviews, criticism, reviews, news items. "This will be a quarterly 'digest' of material on media history, using original manuscripts only. Ms will be original, but digest (brief) format will be followed. Articles should not exceed 2,500. First issue — Summer 1980" circ. 10,000. 4/yr. Expects 2 issues 1980, 4 issues 1981. sub. price: $5.00; per copy: $1.50; sample: $1.50. Back issues: $2.00. Discounts: to be determined. 64pp; 5½X8½; of. Reporting time: 3-4 months. Payment: in copies; other payment to be determined. Copyrighted. Pub's reviews: Beginning 1980 in 1979. §Newspaper, broadcast, film, magazine, book history. Ads: $525.00/$315.-00.

MEDIA MANAGEMENT MONOGRAPHS, Jim Mann & Associates, Jim Mann, 7 Biscayne Drive, Ramsey, NJ 07446, (201) 327-8492. 1978. Interviews. "Outside contributions not accepted. Each issue deals with a single subject or aspect of periodical management." circ. 150. 12/yr. Pub'd 12 issues 1979; expects 12 issues 1980, 12 issues 1981. sub. price: $97.00; per copy: $10.00; sample: $10.00. Back issues: $10.00. Discounts: Write for information, recognized subscription agencies may take 5% provided check accompanies order. 16pp; 5½X8-5/16; of. Copyrighted. Ads: No ads.

MEDIA REPORT TO WOMEN, Women's Institute for Freedom of the Press, Donna Allen, Editor; Martha Leslie Allen, Associate Editor, 3306 Ross Pl. N.W., Washington, DC 20008, 202-363-0812. 1972. News items. "We publish annually an annotated, cumulative index of all past volumes of MEDIA REPORT TO WOMEN and a directory of women's media [periodicals, presses, publishers, news service, media columns, radio/tv groups and regular programs, video and cable groups, film, multi-media, art/graphic/theater groups, music (groups, recording companies, etc)] speakers bureaus, media courses, media organizations/media change/guidelines, distributors, bookstores and mail order, special library collections, selected directories and catalogs. Also includes directory of media women and media-concerned women. Descriptions of women or groups in their words, with address, phone, contact people and other vital information. Brochure available." circ. 1,500. 12/yr. Pub'd 12 issues 1979; expects 12 issues 1980, 12 issues 1981. sub. price: $20.00; per copy: $1.50; sample: $1.50. Back issues: $1.50 and $20.00 per spiral bound volume (on calendar year basis). Discounts: bulk-40% on 3 or more. 12-16pp; 8½X11; of. Reporting time: 2 weeks. Payment: none. Not copyrighted. Pub's reviews: 30-50 in 1979. §media/women. Ads: $0.75 per word.

Medic Publishing Co., Murray A. Swanson, PO Box O, Issaquah, WA 98027, 392-5665. 1974. "Patient education booklets for the medical professions" avg. press run 40,000. Expects 2 titles 1980, 3 titles 1981. avg. price, paper: $1.00. Discounts: Typical bulk price: $0.40 each. 24pp; 5½X8½; †of. Payment: Varies with collaboration arrangement.

MEDICAL HISTORY, W.F. Bynum, V. Nutton, Wellcome Institute for the History of Medicine, 183 Euston Rd., London NW1 2BP, United Kingdom. 1957. Articles, reviews, news items. circ. 1,300. 4/yr. Pub'd 4 issues 1979; expects 4 issues 1980. sub. price: £12.00 ($30.00); per copy: £3.00; sample: £3.00. Back issues: £3.50 if available. Discounts: 10% for four consecutive issues. 128pp; 5X8; of.

Reporting time: 2 wks. No payment. Not copyrighted. Pub's reviews: 290 in 1979. §All aspects of history of medicine and allied sciences. Ads: £40//25.

MEDICAL SELF-CARE, Tom Ferguson, MD; Roger Hoffmann, Publisher, Boxx 718, Inverness, CA 94937, (415) 663-1403. 1976. Articles, interviews, reviews, news items. circ. 20,000. 4/yr. Pub'd 4 issues 1979; expects 4 issues 1980, 4 issues 1981. sub. price: $10.00; per copy: $2.50; sample: $3.00. Back issues: $3.00 each. Discounts: 40%-50%. 64pp; 7-1/16X10; †of. Reporting time: 90 days. Payment: varies. Copyrighted. Pub's reviews: 120 in 1979. §Medical self-care. Ads: $1,200.00/$660.-00/$1.00.

Membrane Press, Karl Young, Publisher, P.O. Box 11601-Shorewood, Milwaukee, WI 53211. "Not looking for unsolicited material at this time. Books currently available by: Toby Olson, Martin J. Rosenblum, Kathleen Wiegner, Hilary Ayer, John Shannon, Tenney Nathanson, Barbara Einzig, Jerome Rothenberg, Nathaniel Tarn, Harris Lenowitz, Jackson MacLow, Karl Young, B.P. Nichol, Steve McCaffery, Dick Higgins, Robert Filliou, George Brecht, Dieter Roth. Membrane Press post cards (sample pack of at least 8 cards-50 cents)." avg. press run 700. Pub'd 6 titles 1979. 26 titles listed in the *Small Press Record of Books in Print* (9th Edition, 1980). avg. price, paper: $2.50. Discounts: 40 percent trade. 80pp; size varies; †of. Payment varies.

MEN'S, Richard Doyle, P.O. Box 189, Forest Lake, MN 55025. 1975. Articles, reviews, news items. circ. 2,000. 12/yr. Pub'd 12 issues 1979; expects 12 issues 1980, 12 issues 1981. 1 title listed in the *Small Press Record of Books in Print* (9th Edition, 1980). sub. price: $10.00 (to non-members); per copy: $1.00; sample: Free to distributors. Back issues: $1.00 each. Discounts: 10 percent to agents. 14pp; 7X8½; of. Reporting time: 30 days. Payment: no. Not copyrighted. Pub's reviews: 24 in 1979. §Law, men's lib, women's lib, divorce. Ads: $10.00-column inch.

The Menard Press, Anthony Rudolf, 23 Fitzwarren Gardens, London N19, United Kingdom. 1971. Poetry. "1) poetry, poetics, translated poetry. 2)4 books were published in 1979. 3) the press's books are distributed in the USA by Small Press Distribution Inc., Kensington, CA" avg. press run 750. Pub'd 4 titles 1979; expects 11 titles 1980, 5 titles 1981. 28 titles listed in the *Small Press Record of Books in Print* (9th Edition, 1980). avg. price, paper: $4.00. 56pp; size demi octavo; of/lp. no new manuscripts can be considered for time being. ALP.

Mercantine Press, Reba M. Kuklin, 4351 Washington Street, Lincoln, NB 68506, (402) 489-2626. 1979. "Material is book length, non-fiction, dealing with business, economics, investments, stock market. All manuscripts are preplanned and solicited by the publisher." avg. press run 2,000. Pub'd 1 title 1979. avg. price, cloth: $12.95; paper: $6.95. Discounts: 1-5 copies, 20%; 6-20 copies, 40%; over 20, 46%. 230pp; 6X9; †of.

Mercer House Press, Henry G. III La Brie, Director, P.O. Box 681, Kennebunkport, ME 04046, 207-282-7116. 1971. avg. press run 1,500. Pub'd 1 title 1979; expects 2 titles 1980, 2 titles 1981. 1 title listed in the *Small Press Record of Books in Print* (9th Edition, 1980). avg. price, cloth: $10.00; paper: $4.00. Discounts: 40% to wholesalers. 140pp; 6X9; of. Reporting time: 2 weeks. Payment: 10-15%. Copyrights for author.

Merganzer Press, Nicholas A. Ganzer, 659 Northmoor Road, Lake Forest, IL 60045, (312) 234-7208. 1979. "70 page book on fishing *How to Prepare, Rig, and Fish Natural Baits For Great Lakes Salmon and Trout*" avg. press run 5,000. Pub'd 1 title 1979. 1 title listed in the *Small Press Record of Books in Print* (9th Edition, 1980). avg. price, paper: $4.50. Discounts: varies with quantity of order, query first. 5½X8½; of. Reporting time: 1 month. Copyrights for author. AAP.

Merging Media (see also VALHALLA), Diane C. Erdmann, Rochelle H. DuBois, 59 Sandra Circle A-3, Westfield, NJ 07090, 232-7224. 1978. Poetry, fiction, articles, art, photos, cartoons, interviews, criticism, reviews, letters, news items. "VALHALLA 6 Lifespan '80, dedicated to Henry Miller. VALHALLA 5 Anais Nin issue '77, $3.00. Other titles: *Mysteries Poems* by Rochelle Ratner; *Yellow Pears Smooth as Silk* 45 rpm record by R. Holt; *Night Rained Her* by Isel Revero; *Wind Songs* by R. Zaller; *A Legend in His Time* Navajo adolescent novella ($2.50); *Pangs* by R. Dubois, a novel ($5.00). Additional address* 5111 N. 42nd Avenue, Phoenix, AZ 85019" avg. press run 300-500. 26 titles listed in the *Small Press Record of Books in Print* (9th Edition, 1980). avg. price, cloth: $3.00; paper: $2.50 plus 50¢ postage; other: $2.00. Discounts: 40% no consignment. 50pp; 6X9; of. Reporting time: 1 month. Payment: Contributors copies. Copyrights for author. CCLM, WIFT, AWP, IWWG.

MERIP REPORTS, Lynne Barbee, Peter Johnson, Philip Khoury, Joan Mandell, Jim Paul, Joe Stork, Judith Tucker, P.O. Box 3122, Columbia Heights Station, Washington, DC 20010, (202) 667-1188. 1971. Articles, art, photos, cartoons, interviews, reviews, letters, news items. circ. 3,000. 9/yr. Pub'd 10 issues 1979; expects 9 issues 1980, 9 issues 1981. sub. price: $12.00; per copy: $1.65; sample: $2.35

(incl. postage). Back issues: $2.00. Discounts: 40% for dealers with standing orders, 20% for orders of 5 or more from dealers without standing orders; 20% for non-trade bulk orders of 25 or more. 32pp; 8½X11; of. Reporting time: 4-8 weeks. Payment: $100.00 maximum. Copyrighted. Pub's reviews: 16 in 1979. §middle east politics, economics, international economics, oil. Ads: $100.00/$55.-00. APS, COSMEP.

Merlin Engine Works, V. M. Greene, Box 169, Milbrae, CA 94040. 1958. "2 books non-fiction published *Underwater Prospecting Techniques* $2.50; *The Gold Diver's Handbook* $7.50; and *Astronauts of Ancient Japan* $7.50. Distributed by Charles E. Tuttle Publishers, Putney, VT" avg. press run 5,000 per year each. Pub'd 1 title 1979; expects 1 title 1980, 1 title 1981. 2 titles listed in the *Small Press Record of Books in Print* (9th Edition, 1980). of/lp. Does not copyright for author.

‡MERLIN PAPERS, Merlin Press, Milton Loventhal, Jennifer McDowell, PO Box 5602, San Jose, CA 95150. 1969. Poetry, fiction, art, photos, reviews, music, parts-of-novels, plays. "Prose pieces should not exceed 10 pages. Two to 6 poems per submission is preferred. Enclose SASE. Recent contributors: Julia Vinograd, George Kauffman, Nancy Gaugier." circ. 1,000. Irregular. Pub'd 1 issue 1979; expects 1 issue 1980. sub. price: 5 issues $4.00-institutions; 5 issues $5.00; per copy: $1.00; sample: no sample copies. Back issues: Issues 1-6 $3.00, each others $1.00 each. Discounts: One-third off. 8pp; 19X11; of. Reporting time: 6 months. Payment: Copies. Copyrighted, reverts to author. Pub's reviews. Ads: $50.00/$25.00/$10.00 for 2" x 2". CCLM.

Merlin Press (see also MERLIN PAPERS), Jennifer McDowell, Milton Loventhal, P. O. Box 5602, San Jose, CA 95150. 1973. Poetry, music, non-fiction. avg. press run 1,000. Pub'd 1 title 1979; expects 1 title 1981. 2 titles listed in the *Small Press Record of Books in Print* (9th Edition, 1980). avg. price, cloth: $9.95; paper: $7.95. Discounts: 1-10 copies, 10 percent; 11-20 copies, 20 percent; above 20, 30 percent. of. Reporting time: 6 months. Copyrights for author. CCLM.

Robert L. Merriam, Newhall Road, Conway, MA 01341, 413-369-4052. 1960. "These are miniature books, usually with material written by editor. Robert L. Merriam, publisher of miniatures and some other pamphlets. Miniatures under 3 inches in height are: *Pleasant Beth, The Darling Twins, John Carson, Moses Armstrong* and *C.J.Hamilton Rose.* Each limited to 1,000 copies, bound in heavy cover stock and contained within a slipcase. Each $1.75. Each is illustrated. *The Bibliography of the Redeemed Captive,* limited to 350 signed and numbered copies. Miniature. Illustrated. Other pamphlets: *A Christmas Legend, The Ancient Art of Skating, Santa's Snack, Abigail Challenges the Telephone Company, The Energy Crisis.*" avg. press run 1000. Pub'd 2 titles 1979; expects 1 title 1980, 2 titles 1981. 12 titles listed in the *Small Press Record of Books in Print* (9th Edition, 1980). Discounts: 40% over 5 copies. 32pp; 2X3; of.

THE MERVYN PEAKE REVIEW, Mervyn Peake Society Publications, G. Peter Winnington, Les 3 Chasseurs, 1411 Orzens, Vaud, Switzerland. 1975. Poetry, articles, art, interviews, criticism, reviews, letters. "Concentrates on Mervyn Peake's work as novelist, poet, illustrator and painter. Contains original work by Mervyn Peake; prints reviews and articles on his work; reviews other books relevant to Mervyn Peake and lists current work/in/progress on Mervyn Peake. ISSN 0309-1309" circ. 300. 2/yr. Pub'd 2 issues 1979; expects 2 issues 1980, 2 issues 1981. sub. price: $14.00; sample: free. 44pp; 5¾X8⅓; of. Reporting time: Usually within 30 days. Payment: None; contributors receive 5 free copies. Copyrighted, reverts to author. Pub's reviews: 6 in 1979. §Publications containing discussion of any aspect of Mervyn Peake's work, or reproducing any of his art work. Ads: $40.00/$22.00.

Mervyn Peake Society Publications (see also THE MERVYN PEAKE REVIEW), G. Peter Winnington, Les 3 Chasseurs, 1411 Orzens, Vaud, Switzerland. 1978. Poetry, articles, art, criticism. "Publication of out-of-print Peake material, works illustrated by Peake, critical studies on Peake, and other items of direct relevance to Peake studies." avg. press run 1,000. Expects 1 title 1980. 1 title listed in the *Small Press Record of Books in Print* (9th Edition, 1980). avg. price, paper: $5.50. of. Copyrights for author.

THE MESSAGE, Sufi Order Publications, Graham Munir, Route 15, Box 270, Tucson, AZ 85715, 602-299-4597. 1975. Poetry, fiction, articles, interviews, reviews, parts-of-novels, art, photos, long-poems. "*The Message* is the monthly publication of the Sufi Order in the West. It presents with scope and depth teachings particularly relevant to the spiritual trends of our time, emphasising the unity of religions and dedicated to the ideals of love, harmony, and beauty. Covering a wide range of themes, *The Message* seeks to promote the new, holistic consciousness of humanity that is emerging in the world today." circ. 1300. monthly. Pub'd 12 issues 1979; expects 12 issues 1980, 12 issues 1981. sub. price: $12.00; per copy: $1.25; sample: $1.25. Back issues: $1.25. 24-32pp; 6X9; †of. Reporting time: 3 months. Payment: none. Copyrighted, reverts to author. Pub's reviews: 3 in 1979. §Spiritual, esp. science and spirituality and unity of religions. Ads: no ads.

246

MESSAGE POST, Light Living Library, Hank Schultz, PO Box 190, Philomath, OR 97370. 1980. Reviews, letters. circ. 600. 4/yr. sub. price: $2.00. Discounts: presently free to outdoor centers & earth bookstores. 12pp; 5½X8½; of. Payment: subscriptions or ads. Pub's reviews. §Long-period camping, portable dwellings, wildcrafting. Ads: $20.00/$0.10.

METAMORFOSIS, Erasmo Gamboa, Center for Chicano Studies, GN-09, Washington University, Seattle, WA 98018, (206) 543-9080. 1977. Poetry, fiction, articles, interviews, criticism, reviews, parts-of-novels, collages, plays. "Recent contributors: Ruben Sierra, Tomas F. Ybarra, Yvonne Yarbro-Bejarano" circ. 1,000. 2/yr. sub. price: $5.00 indiv., $10.00 instit.; per copy: $3.00; sample: free. Back issues: price back issue (same). Discounts: institution rate. 40pp; 8X11½; lp. Reporting time: 60 days. Payment: in form of isues of Metamorfosis. Copyrighted, reverts to author. Pub's reviews: 1 in 1979. §Chicano literature, poetry, prose.

Metatron Press, Jay C. Livingston, 2447 N. 59th Street, Milwaukee, WI 53210, (414) 444-6266. 1977. Poetry, fiction, art, photos, long-poems, plays. "So far, we have specialized in first works (of poetry) but are interested in tackling anything of artistic merit or practical usefulness. A primary focus is not 'over-editing' an author's work. A staff of artists, designers and photographers work closely to actuate the *author's* needs. Quality work, and shoulder-to-the-grindstone types of writers are our bias. We welcome the work of authorss who consider their art, also a responsibility which requires nothing less than unflagging dedication. Usually those with that characteristic end up as prime creators. We'd like to stimulate a renaissance of 19th Century stylism in verse and the medium of the novel. The coming together of the visual and written arts is of great concern to this press. The editor would like to see more sonnets by capable practitioners of the form; also, other 'antiquated' modes — for preservation's sake. Actual numerical average: 900 units; most run: 500 units. Direct retail discount: 40%, library: full price, quantity sales: negotiated, wholesale/jobber: 70%." Pub'd 2 titles 1979; expects 3 titles 1980, 2 titles 1981. avg. price, cloth: $5.95; paper: $3.50. 60pp; 5½X8½; of. Reporting time: 2-3 weeks for poetry; up to six for fullbody text mss. Payment: we suggest some self-marketing, but apply the standard 10-15% when *we* do. Copyrights for author. NYSSPA, NESPA.

Fran Metcalf Books, Fran Metcalf, 734 Millard Ave, Conneaut, OH 44030, (216) 599-7972. 1979. Criticism, letters. "This is my first book; which I have self-published and edited on my own. It is hard cover and 178 pages long. It is political, controversial and truthful. It should be on the shelf of every library in the schools all over the USA. Those in government have expressed that they are very impressed with my book. It teaches proper dissent, how to become elected to office and the way our government works on the local level. It, also, encourages participation in government. My book, also, points out several major problems of our society today along with the solutions to these problems. Plus, it is the story of a three year fight with city hall, telling of my personal experiences in doing so in an interesting manner. *How to Fight City Hall, Any City USA*" avg. press run 1,000. Pub'd 1 title 1979. avg. price, cloth: $6.95. Discounts: 22%. 178pp; 5X7; lp.

Metis Press, Arny Christine Straayer, Christine Leslie Johnson, Janet Soule, PO Box 25187, Chicago, IL 60657. 1976. Poetry, fiction, art, photos, cartoons, long-poems. "Feminist Publishing Collective. New books out: *Wild Women Don't Get the Blues,* short stories by Barbara Emrys ($3.00), *Shedevils,* short stories by Barbara Sheen ($3.50). Mss of booklength sought; women only. *Guide to Self Publishing,* Straayer & Johnson; *The Rock & Me Immediately,* Chris Straayer, children's stories, $5.00; *The Secret Witch,* Linda Stem, children's story, $4.00; *Hurtin & Healin & Talkin It Over,* Chris Straayer, short stories, $5.00" Pub'd 1 title 1979; expects 4 titles 1980, 4 titles 1981. 6 titles listed in the *Small Press Record of Books in Print* (9th Edition, 1980). avg. price, paper: $4.00-$5.00. Discounts: 40% on bulk. 120pp; 5½X8½, 8¼X11; †of. Reporting time: 4 months. Payment: Contracts vary with authors participation.

Metloc (see THE BARD)

THE METRO, Libre Press, John J. White, Publisher; Joseph Skorupa, Managing Editor, The Metro, Suite 529-530 Connell Bldg., Scranton, PA 18503, (717) 348-1010. 1976. Poetry, fiction, articles, art, photos, cartoons, interviews, satire, criticism, reviews, long-poems, news items. "Return envelope necessary with postage." circ. 10,000. 12/yr. sub. price: $6.00; per copy: $0.50; sample: $0.50. Back issues: $1.00. 28pp; 17X28; of. Reporting time: 3 months. Payment: $5.00 to $150.00 depends on article. Copyrighted, reverts to author. Pub's reviews: 24 in 1979. §Theatre, Satire, Political Reviews. Ads: $500.00/$250.00/$135.00/$75.00. CCLM, APS.

MEUSE, Grant Caldwell, Geoff Aldridge, Les Wicks, Box 61, Wentworth Bldg., Sydney University, NSW 2006, Australia. 1977. Poetry, fiction, art, photos, cartoons, parts-of-novels, long-poems. "Tend to favour prose over poetry. Wide range of contributors both local and from UK/US. Issues united thematically around various aspects of social dissent. Equal emphasis given to artwork & writing." circ.

247

3,000. 3-6/yr. Pub'd 3 issues 1979; expects 3 issues 1980, 3 issues 1981. sub. price: $7.00 US; per copy: $2.50 US. Back issues: varies: $2.00 to $10.50 US. 50-65pp; 8X10; of. Reporting time: 3-6 weeks. Payment: $5.50 US, per page. Copyrighted, reverts to author. ASMA.

MEXICO WEST, Baja Trail Publications, Inc., Shirley Miller, Editor; Victor Cook, Managing Editor; Tom Miller, Consulting Editor, P.O. Box 6088, Huntington Beach, CA 92646, 714-536-8081. 1975. Articles, news items. "500-750 words. Current travel and recreational information on Baja and west coast of Mexico-story style." circ. 1,500. 6/yr. Pub'd 6 issues 1979; expects 6 issues 1980. sub. price: $8.00, $15.00 2 yrs; per copy: $1.25; sample: $1.00. Back issues: $1.00 each. Discounts: none. 12pp; 8X10½; of. Reporting time: 2 weeks before 1st of Feb., Apr., June, Aug., Oct., Dec. Payment: $20. Copyrighted, reverts to author. Pub's reviews: 3 in 1979. §Mexico/travel/Baja. Ads: classified 40¢ per word. COSMEP.

MFRC Publishing, John Fisher, 287 MacPherson Avenue, Toronto, Ontario M4V 1A4, Canada, (416) 961-0381. 1977. Cartoons, news items. "Subject matter #95 Management & fund Raising" avg. press run 5,000. Pub'd 1 title 1979. 1 title listed in the *Small Press Record of Books in Print* (9th Edition, 1980). avg. price, paper: $8.95. Discounts: Trade discount for bookstores=10% on orders of 6 or more. 213pp; 5¾X8¾. Payment: yes. Copyrights for author. CBIC.

M'GODOLIM, Le Beacon Presse, Shabatai Gormezano, 621 Holt Avenue, Iowa City, IA 52240, 319-354-5447. 1979. Poetry, fiction, articles, art, photos, cartoons, interviews, satire, criticism, reviews, music, letters, parts-of-novels, long-poems, collages, plays, concrete art, news items. "We are committed towards publishing creative works of Jewish authors. We are interested in good, solid, thought-provoking writing along with your resume. Submissions should be typed with a PICA typewriter and single spaced as we reduce your work 74% as it is for multilithing. We prefer submissions to be 'single spaced' but if your manuscript is double, send it anyway. Clean, clear, fairly dark photocopies are okay. We currently have a policy of reviewing *all* books and magazines received, usually a paragraph or two if we think highly of it. Recent contributions have discussed the Kaddish as an art form to a humorous look at Judaic-Christian realtions along with poetry, fiction, cartoons, etc." circ. 200. 4/yr. Pub'd 4 issues 1979. sub. price: $3.00; per copy: $0.95. 32-40pp; 5½X8. Reporting time: 1-6 months. Pub's reviews: 20 in 1979. §Poetry, fiction, should be judaic interest or by individuals of judaic background. Ads: $5.00/$3.00/$0.05 20 word minimum. COSMEP.

MIAMI INTERNATIONAL, Toni Silver, Exc. Editor; Richard Jay, Editor, 2951 S. Bayshore Drive, Miami, FL 33133, (305) 443-5251. 1971. Interviews, reviews, music, letters. "Submit art and interviews to: Toni Silver, Executive Editor, 2951 South Bayshore Drive, Miami, FL 33133." circ. 10,000. 12/yr. Pub'd 12 issues 1979; expects 12 issues 1980, 12 issues 1981. sub. price: $15.00; per copy: $2.00; sample: $2.00. Back issues: no back issues. 64pp; 8½X11; †of. Reporting time: 1 month. Payment: 5 contributor copies. Copyrighted, reverts to author. Pub's reviews: 72 in 1979. Ads: write for rate card.

Micah Publications, Robert Kalechofsky, Roberta Kalechofsky, 255 Humphrey St, Marblehead, MA 01945. 1975. Fiction, articles, criticism. "Micah Publications publishes prose: scholarly, fictional, lyrical; a prose that addresses itself to issues without offending esthetic sensibilities, a prose that is aware of the esthetics of language without succumbing to esthetic solipsism. Two books a year. No unsolicited mss." avg. press run 600 books. Pub'd 2 titles 1979. 7 titles listed in the *Small Press Record of Books in Print* (9th Edition, 1980). avg. price, paper: $4.50. Discounts: 1-5 books 30%/6-50 books 40%/51 books and up 50%. 200pp; 5½X8½. Reporting time: 3 months. Payment: 40% to authors; they undertake some responsibility for selling and advertising of book. Copyrights for author. COSMEP, NESPA.

Michael Joseph Phillips Editions, Michael Joseph Phillips, 430 E Wylie, Bloomington, IN 47401, 317-255-2555. 1978. Poetry, concrete art. "Due to the unimaginative, rotten taste in this nuclear democracy in poetry, and around the world I have been forced to publish my own poetry in book form. Our universities continue to decline - for the mot part telling people bad poetry is good poetry. I accept the fact that it might be my own poetry that is bad and not everybody else's, but I don't really think so after a 20 year long haul at educating myself in pst and present literature. Recent titles include *31 Erotic Concrete Sonnets for ?Samantha* ($1.00), *4 Visual Waka* ($1.00), *21 Erotic Haiku for Samantha* ($2.00), *Beginnings of Samantha* ($1.00) and *Movie Star Poems* ($2.00). I have recently come to believe that a sort of combination of Jesus Christ and Robert Herrick is the way - with these two people one can do one's best to resist what Yeats has called the 'filthy modern tide'. The politics of my press are as follows 'A woman should be required by law to make love five or more times a week after she is fourteen. Also, any woman who says no to a man sexually or marriage wise after she is twenty-one should be put in a bordello'." avg. press run 100. Pub'd 4 titles 1979. 20 titles listed in the *Small Press Record of Books in Print* (9th Edition, 1980). avg. price, paper: $2.00. Discounts: 40% to bookstores.

24pp; 5½X8½. Reporting time: not looking for poetry by other people at present. Payment in 1-2 the copies printed only. Does not copyright for author.

MICHIGAN OCCASIONAL PAPERS IN WOMEN'S STUDIES, Women's Studies Editorial Collective, 1058 LSA Building, The University of Michigan, Ann Arbor, MI 48109, (313) 763-2047. 1974. Articles, criticism. "Individual papers, published on an irregular basis, approx 12-25 per year. Back issues of U-M Papers in Women's Studies, Vols. I, II (4 issues to each volume). Price per Vol: $20.00 Institutions, $12.00 Individuals, $8.50 Students. For Mich. Occasional Papers: 10% off on orders of more than $10.00." circ. 300. Irreg. Pub'd 9 issues 1979; expects 15 issues 1980, 15 issues 1981. sub. price: approx $30.00; per copy: $1.50-$3.00; sample: $2.50. Back issues: $3.00 each. Discounts: 10% on orders over $10.00. 35pp; 8½X11; of. Reporting time: 6 months. Payment: Contributors receive offprints of their paper. Copyrighted, reverts to author. Ads: no ads.

MICHIGAN QUARTERLY REVIEW, Laurence Goldstein, 3032 Rackham Bldg., University of Michigan, Ann Arbor, MI 48109, (313)764-9265. 1962. Poetry, fiction, articles, art, interviews, criticism, reviews, letters, parts-of-novels, long-poems. "We are no longer solely a literary magazine. In addition to poetry, fiction, and reviews, we now include essays on a variety of topics including philosophy, history, religion, rhetoric, technology, art, and law. We are also featuring graphic work in each issue. Our recent and forthcoming contributors include Joyce Carol Oates, Tom Wolfe, Karl Popper, Richard Howard, Walker Percy, Harvey Cox, Joan Didion, and others." circ. 2,000. quarterly. Pub'd 4 issues 1979; expects 4 issues 1980, 4 issues 1981. sub. price: $12.00; per copy: $3.50; sample: $2.50. Back issues: $2.00. Discounts: Agency rates - $14.00 for institution subscription; 15% for agent. 160pp; 6X9; lp. Reporting time: 6 weeks. Payment: $10/page of poetry; $5-$8/page essays. Copyrighted, does not revert to author. Pub's reviews: 12 in 1979. §poetry, fiction, history, politics, the arts. Ads: $50/$25.

THE MICKLE STREET REVIEW, Geoffrey M. Sill, Frank McQuilken, 46 Centre Street, Haddonfield, NJ 08033, (609) 795-7887. 1976. Poetry, fiction, articles, art, photos, interviews. "A journal dedicated to preserving and furthering the influence of Walt Whitman on American poetry, published from Whitman's last residence." 1/yr. Pub'd 1 issue 1979. sub. price: $3.00; per copy: $3.00. Reporting time: 2 months. Payment: 2 copies. Copyrighted. COSMEP.

MID-ATLANTIC NEWS, Ken Bossong, 1110 Sixth Streeet, N.W., Washington, DC 20001, 202-387-8998. 1978. Reviews, news items. "Usually each issue is 14 pages" circ. 1,000. 4/yr. Pub'd 3 issues 1979; expects 4 issues 1980, 4 issues 1981. sub. price: free; per copy: free; sample: free. Back issues: not available. 4pp; 8½X11; of. Reporting time: one month. Not copyrighted. Pub's reviews: 20+ in 1979. §Alternative energy, health care, housing, agriculture, transportation. Ads: no ads.

THE MIDATLANTIC REVIEW, Stephen Baily, Walter Blanco, Billy Collins, P O Box 398, Baldwin Place, NY 10505. 1975. Poetry, fiction. "In poetry we favor clean-edged images and language that's up to something; in fiction, particularity grounded in dramatic narrative. Recent contributors: Charles Bukowski, Robert Peters, Ramon Sender, Ruth Jespersen." circ. 1,000. 4/yr. Pub'd 3 issues 1979; expects 4 issues 1980, 4 issues 1981. sub. price: $6.00; per copy: $1.50; sample: $1.50. Back issues: Prices vary. Discounts: 40 percent. 96pp; 5½X8½; †of. Reporting time: 3-5 weeks. Payment: Two copies on publication. Copyrighted, reverts to author. §Poetry and fiction. Ads: $50.00/$25.00/none. CCLM.

The Middle Atlantic Press, Karen Waldauer, Publisher, Box 263, Wallingford, PA 19086, 215-565-2445. 1968. "We are a trade book and educational materials publisher. Our material is oriented to the Middle Atlantic region, but all of our books are sold nation-wide." avg. press run varies with title. Pub'd 3 titles 1979; expects 3 titles 1980, 3 titles 1981. 7 titles listed in the *Small Press Record of Books in Print* (9th Edition, 1980). avg. price, cloth: varies with title; paper: varies with title; other: Varies with title. Discounts: 40% for 5 plus copies. pp varies with title; size varies with title; of. Reporting time: 2 months. Payment: 10 percent royalty to author. Copyrights for author.

Midmarch Associates (see also WOMEN ARTISTS NEWS), Cynthia Navaretta, Editor, 3304 Grand Central Sta, New York City, NY 10017, 212-666-6990. 1975. Articles, art, photos, interviews, news items. "Title pub'd to date: *Guide to Women's Art Organizations, Voices of Women: 3 Critics on 3 Poets on 3 Heroines.*" avg. press run 1500-2000. Pub'd 1-2 titles 1979. avg. price, paper: $5.00. Discounts: Student or group (5 or more) $4.00, Institutional $5.00, Jobber $3.75. 5½X8½; of. Copyrights for author. CCLM, COSMEP.

MIDWEST ALLIANCE, John Crawford, PO Box 4642, Kansas City, MO 64109, (816) 753-4587. 1979. Poetry, fiction, articles, art, photos, cartoons, interviews, criticism, reviews, music, letters, news items. "Left-wing politics with communist or populist bias; both rural and urban interest; people's art, culture, news, reviews. Strongly mid-western, western onientation." circ. 100. 1/yr. Pub'd 1 issue

1979. sub. price: $1.50; per copy: $1.50; sample: $1.50. Back issues: Vol 1 #1 discounted to $1.50. Discounts: All: 40% over 5 copies; bookstores for resale; 40% any number, consignment. 36pp; 8½X11; of. Reporting time: 3 months. Payment: copies (3). Copyrighted, reverts to author. Pub's reviews. §Politics, literature, populism, midwest. Ads: $50.00/$25.00/$15.00. COSMEP, CCLM.

MIDWEST CHAPARRAL, Marguerite Kingman, 5508 Osage, Kansas City, KS 66106. 1942. Poetry. "Haiku (3 lines) to 20 lines free, blank or rhymed. 4-8 line light verse-no juvenile verse." circ. 250. 3/yr. Pub'd 3 issues 1979. sub. price: $3.00; per copy: $1.00; sample: $.75. Back issues: $.50. 28-32pp; 6X9; lp. Reporting time: wk-10 days. Not copyrighted.

THE MIDWEST QUARTERLY, V.J. Emmett Jr., Editor; Michael Heffernan, Poetry, Pittsburg State University, Pittsburg, KS 66762, 316-231-7000. 1959. Poetry, articles, criticism, reviews. "Scholarly articles on history, literature, the social sciences (especially political), art, music, the natural sciences (in non-technical language). Most articles run 4,000 to 5,000 words. Can use a brief note of 1,000 to 2,000 words once in a while. Chief bias is an aversion to jargon and pedantry. Instead of footnotes we use a minimum of parenthetical documentation. Reviews are assigned. We use only solicited verse. Contributors: Kuzma, Dave Smith, Turner, Pinsker, Bosmajian, Etter, O'leary, Ruark, Gallagher, Oliver." circ. 1,000. 4/yr. Pub'd 4 issues 1979; expects 4 issues 1980. sub. price: $4.00; per copy: $1.50; sample: $1.50. Back issues: $1.50. Discounts: 10% to agencies. 110pp; 6X9; of. Reporting time: 3-6 months. Payment: copies only. Copyrighted, reverts to author. Pub's reviews: 6 in 1979. §poetry, non-fiction, fiction by authors we have published. no ads.

Miles & Weir, Ltd., Stanley Weir, Robert Miles, Editor, Box 1906, San Pedro, CA 90733, 213-831-2012. 1977. Fiction, articles. "Currently soliciting fiction, articles and biography dealing with work, written by those not primarily authors; up to 25,000 words, shorter material preferred." avg. press run 1,000-1,500. Pub'd 3 titles 1979; expects 7 titles 1980, 10 titles 1981. 1 title listed in the *Small Press Record of Books in Print* (9th Edition, 1980). avg. price, cloth: $10.00; paper: $2.95. Discounts: Normal trade, distributor, jobber, etc. discounts. 64pp; 5½X8½; of. Reporting time: 8 weeks. Payment: small advance against 10% royalty. Copyrights for author. COSMEP.

R. & E. Miles, Elaine Miles, Robert Miles, PO Box 1906, San Pedro, CA 90733, (213) 833-8856. 1979. "First four titles will deal with some aspect of American quilts and quilting." avg. press run 3,200. Expects 2 titles 1981. 2 titles listed in the *Small Press Record of Books in Print* (9th Edition, 1980). avg. price, cloth: $7.95; paper: $4.95. Discounts: Normal trade. 168pp; of. Reporting time: 8 weeks. Payment: Small advance against 10% royalty. Copyrights for author.

THE MILITANT, Steve Clark, Editor; Andy Rose, Assoc Editor; Cindy Jaquith, Assoc Editor, 14 Charles Lane, New York, NY 10014, 212-243-6392. 1928. circ. 30,000. 52/yr. Pub'd 48 issues 1979; expects 48 issues 1980. sub. price: $20.00; per copy: $0.50; sample: free. Back issues: $.50. Discounts: Bulk $0.35 copy, Agent $0.25. 28pp; 11½X18; of. Pub's reviews: 70 in 1979. §politics, economics, black studies, women's studies. Ads: $400.00/$250.00/$0.75.

MILITARY IMAGES MAGAZINE, Harry Roach, PO Box 300, Alburtis, PA 18011. 1979. Articles, photos, interviews, reviews. "Up to 5,000 words. Emphasis on American military history, 1839-1939, with heavy use of period photos (50 to 75 per issue). Some recent contributors: (all military historians) Michael J. McAfee, Philip Katcher, John Stacey, George C. Hart, Dale Biever, Joseph G. Bilby, Jacques N. Jacobsen, Jr., William Gladstone, William Frassanito." circ. 2,000. 6/yr. Pub'd 3 issues 1979; expects 6 issues 1980. sub. price: $12.00; per copy: $2.00; sample: $2.50. Discounts: $1.00 per copy to retailers in lots of 20 or more. 20% to jobbers. 32pp; 8½X11; of. Reporting time: 2-4 weeks. Payment: currently $0.02 word; will be raised in near future. Copyrighted, reverts to author. Pub's reviews: 10-12 in 1979. §American military history, 1839-1939. Ads: $75.00/$40.00/$0.50. COSMEP.

MILK QUARTERLY, The Yellow Press, Richard Friedman, Peter Kostakis, Darlene Pearlstein, 2394 Blue Island Ave, Chicago, IL 60608. 1972. Poetry, fiction, art, photos, cartoons, music, long-poems, collages, plays. "The magazine has evolved more toward the concept of 'theme project' issues: e.g. 'Chicago Poets' and 'The Hat Issue'. Contributors include Claes Oldenburg, Erica Jong, Robert Creeley, Bill Knott, Alice Notley, Jayzey Lynch, composer Marion Brown, John Wieners, David Henderson, Gwendolyn Brooks, Paul Metcalf and Thomas McGuane." circ. 2,000. irreg. Pub'd 1 issue 1979; expects 1 issue 1980. price per copy: $3.00 (Hat Issue #11, 12); sample: $1.00 (Milk Quarterly #8). Discounts: bulk only. 95pp; 8½X11, to 5½X8½; of. no new submissions please. Payment: varying. Copyrighted, reverts to author. no ads. CCLM, SBD (Small Press Distribution).

MILKWEED CHRONICLE, Emilie Buchwald, Editor; Randall W. Scholes, Art Director, Box 24303, Edina, MN 55424, (612) 941-5993. 1979. Poetry, art, photos, cartoons, letters, long-poems, collages, concrete art. "*Milkweed Chronicle* is a journal of poetry and graphics. We will have several guest columns on issues pertinent to poets and artists and encourage collaboration between poets and artists in every way possible. No regular reviews." circ. 5,000. 3/yr. Pub'd 3 issues 1979; expects 3 issues 1980. sub. price: $6.00; per copy: $3.00; sample: $2.50. Back issues: $2.00. 28pp; 11½X17⅜; of. Reporting time: 1 month. Payment: $25.00 on essays, word or picture, usually commissioned; $5.00 poem. Copyrighted, reverts to author. Ads: $425.00/$295.00/$0.30.

THE MILL, The White Ewe Press, Kevin Urick, Editor, Box 996, Adelphi, MD 20783. 1976. Poetry, fiction, art, cartoons, satire, parts-of-novels, long-poems. "Prefer short fiction (3,000 words or less). Would like to see more satire. Recent contributors: Poets E. Ethelbert Miller, Walter Kerr, Arlene Stone, Pat O'Neill; fiction by Albert Drake. Michael McMahon, Opal Nations, George Myers, Jr., Richard Peabody Jr., Donna Kaulkin, Meribeth Talbert." circ. minute. 1-2/yr. Pub'd 2 issues 1979; expects 2 issues 1980. sub. price: Indiv. $6.50, libraries $9.00.; per copy: $2.00; sample: $1.50. Back issues: inquire. Discounts: negotiable. 40-60pp; size varies; of. Reporting time: 2 days to 1 month. Payment: copies only. Copyrighted, reverts to author. Pub's reviews: 3-8 in 1979. §Fiction, poetry. Ads: negotiable.

MIME JOURNAL, Thomas Leabhart, Performing Arts Center, Grand Valley State Colleges, Allendale, MI 49401. 1974. Articles, art, photos, interviews, criticism, reviews. "MIME JOURNAL publishes articles relating to mime and movement for theatre in the broadest sense. Articles of 1,500 words and up, illustrated with photographs and drawings." circ. 350. 2/yr. Pub'd 2 issues 1979; expects 2 issues 1980, 2 issues 1981. sub. price: Libraries & Inst. $16.00, Indv. $8.00; per copy: varies. Back issues: Decroux 80th birthday issue, Instit. $16.00, Indiv. $8.00. Jacques Copeau's School for Actors, $16, $8. Discounts: 30 percent to Booksellers and Subscription services. 36 - 80pp; 7X8½; of. Reporting time: Immediate. Payment: none. Copyrighted. Pub's reviews. §Mime and movement for the theatre. Ads: no ads.

MINAS TIRITH EVENING-STAR, Philip Helms, Marciu Helms, PO Box 277, Union Lake, MI 48085. 1975. Poetry, fiction, articles, art, cartoons, interviews, criticism, reviews, letters, long-poems, news items. "All material in the magazine relates to the life and/or works of Prof J.R.R. Tolkien, author of *The Hobbit, The Lord of the Rings, The Silmarillion* and others." circ. 400. 12/yr. Pub'd 12 issues 1979; expects 12 issues 1980, 12 issues 1981. sub. price: $5.00; per copy: $1.00; sample: $1.00. Discounts: 20% on 10+ copies. 20pp; 8½X11; of. Reporting time: up to 3 weeks. Payment: one copy. Copyrighted, reverts to author. Pub's reviews: 23 in 1979. §books concerned in whole or in part with the life of Tolkien. Ads: $50/$25.

MINI-TAUR SERIES, Taurean Horn Press, Bill Vartnaw, 601 Leavenworth #45, San Francisco, CA 94109. 1977. Poetry, art, cartoons. "Includes: Carol Lee Sanchez, Tim Jacobs, Bill Vartnaw, Gary A. Blackman, Poetry For The People (SFCC group), Robert Matte Jr. Each edition features one author or group" circ. 100. Irreg. price per copy: $0.25-$1.00; sample: $0.25. 12-24pp; 8½X7; †mi. No unsolicited ms. Payment: 50% of copies. Copyrighted, reverts to author. WIP.

Minicomputer Press, Charles Moore, Box 1, Richboro, PA 18954, 215-355-6084. 1977. Articles, reviews, letters, news items. "Hobby computing." avg. press run 500 copies. Pub'd 1 title 1979; expects 3 titles 1980, 5 titles 1981. avg. price, cloth: $15.00; paper: $7.00. Discounts: Universal. 200pp; 5X7, 7X10; †of. Reporting time: 2 weeks. Payment: depends. Copyrights for author. COSMEP.

THE MINNESOTA REVIEW, Roger Mitchell, Editor; Lyman Andrews, Paul Buhle, Victor Contoski, Fredric Jameson, David Peck, M.L. Raina, Scott Sanders, Assoc. Eds., Box 211, Bloomington, IN 47401. 1960. Poetry, fiction, articles, art, photos, cartoons, interviews, satire, criticism, reviews, letters, parts-of-novels, long-poems, plays. "Interested in committed writing. Recent contributors include: LIVING NEWSPAPER, Jon Silkin, Walter Benjamin, Heiner Muller, Graham Good, James Hazard, James Scully, John Williams, Stanley Arondwitz, Roy Fuller, Marge Piercy, Tom Wayman, Lola Haskins, Albert Goldbarth, Antler, Darko Suvin, Fredric Jameson, David Peck, Victor Contoski, Dave Wagner, Donald Wesling, Carol Papenhausen, Barry Pritchard, Margaret Randall, David Craig, Kathleen Wiegner, Bart Friedman, Yannos Ritsos, Scott Sanders, Terry Eagleton, David Bathrick, Shiela Delaney, Ed Ochester, Roger Howard, Lee Baxandall, Gaylord Leroy, Thomas McGrath, Frederic Will, many more. Starting with NS14 (Sprint 1980), the magazine also becomes a press - Minnesota Review Press - and our 1st book is *May Day,* a book of poems by James Scully. Essentially, *MR* will now, in alternate isues, be both a magazine and a press." circ. 1,200. 2/yr. Pub'd 2 issues 1979; expects 2 issues 1980. sub. price: $6.00; per copy: $3.00; sample: $3.00. Back issues: Available; price $1.00 more than single copy price. Discounts: 40%. 150pp; 8½X5½; of. Reporting time: 1-3 mos. Payment: copies. Copyrighted, reverts to author. Pub's reviews: 20 in 1979. §poetry, fiction, drama, very interested in marxist literary & cultural criticism. Ads: $40/$20. CCLM.

Minnesota Scholarly Press, Inc., Marcia La Sota, Ralph Gabriel, PO Box 224, Manbato, MN 56001, (507) 387-4964. 1977. Fiction, articles, reviews. avg. press run 1,000. Pub'd 3 titles 1979; expects 8 titles 1980, 15 titles 1981. avg. price, cloth: $12.00; paper: $6.95. Discounts: available on request. 250pp; 6X9; of/lp. Reporting time: 4 weeks. Payment: varies.

Minnesota Writers' Publishing House, Louis Jenkins, Keith Gunderson, Cary Waterman, RR #1, Box 148, Kasota, MN 56050, (507) 931-4120. 1972. Poetry. "A writers' co-operative press publishing short manuscripts of exceptionally good verse by both new and established writers. Each writer invited to join (on the basis of acceptance of a manuscript by a committee of previously published writers). Contributes $300 to help pay the initial cost of an edition of 1,000 copies. This money is gradually returned to the writers in the form of royalties. Most of our booklets have gone into 2nd or 3rd printings. Recent contributors: Mark McKeon, Mike Finley, Kate Green, Charles Waterman, Cary Waterman." avg. press run 1,000. Pub'd 2 titles 1979; expects 2 titles 1980, 1-4 titles 1981. 14 titles listed in the *Small Press Record of Books in Print* (9th Edition, 1980). avg. price, paper: $1.50. Discounts: 40% to bookstores; 50% to large quantity wholesalers; 20% to libraries; 20% on consignment. 32pp; 5¾X9; †of. Reporting time: Slow: 1 to 6 months. Copyrights for author.

MINORITY RIGHTS GROUP REPORTS, MRG Press, B. Whitaker, MRG, 36 Craven St., London WC2N5NG, United Kingdom, 01-586-0439. 1970. "Specially commissioned reports only. Reports already published include those on Refugees, the Basques, Mexican-Americans, Zimbabwe, What future for the Amerinidians of South America, The Two Irelands, Namibians of S.W. Africa, Arab Women etc. for complete list please contact M.R.G. or California Branch: MGR; c/o A/Prof. Dinah Shelton, Law Dept., Univ. of Santa Clara, Caif., CA 95053" circ. 2,000. 5/yr. 37 titles listed in the *Small Press Record of Books in Print* (9th Edition, 1980). sub. price: $7.00 (£3.50); per copy: 75p. Discounts: for bulk orders. 30pp; size A4. Copyrighted, does not revert to author.

Miocene Press, Roland Neave, 634 Tunstall Cres., Kamloops, BC V2C 3J1, Canada, 604-374-5644. 1974. "We publish only books, non-fiction dealing with regions and in travelogue style. Minimum book length is 40,000 words. No mss being considered in 1980." avg. press run 5,000 but depends on book content. avg. price, paper: $5.00. Discounts: 35% retailer, 55% distributor, 20% library. 200pp. Reporting time: acknowledge immed. report 1 month. Payment: 9% royalty on retail price. Copyrights for author.

MIORITA, Norman Simms, Charles Carlton, Dept of F.L.L.L., Univ of Rochester, PO Box 13-049, Rochester, NY 14627. 1973. Criticism, reviews, non-fiction. "Scholarly." circ. 300. 2/yr. Pub'd 2 issues 1979; expects 2 issues 1980. sub. price: $8.00 individuals; $15.00 institutions; per copy: $5.00; sample: $5.00. Discounts: 1/3 to retail; 10 percent sub agents. 60-100pp; size A4; mi. Reporting time: 2 months. Payment: copies. Copyrighted. Pub's reviews: 20 in 1979. §Romania and related fields. Ads: $100/$60.

MISSISSIPPI MUD, Mud Press, Joel Weinstein, 3125 S.E. Van Water, Portland, OR 97222. 1973. Poetry, fiction, art, photos, cartoons, interviews, satire, criticism, reviews, parts-of-novels, collages, plays. "*Mississippi Mud* is a post-bohemian journal of the Pacific Northwest, featuring poetry, prose and graphics of the region and elsewhere. Contributions are welcome, with return postage, and should not exceed 5,000 words." circ. 500. 4/yr. Pub'd 3 issues 1979; expects 4 issues 1980, 4 issues 1981. 1 title listed in the *Small Press Record of Books in Print* (9th Edition, 1980). sub. price: $5.00; per copy: $1.75; sample: $0.85. Back issues: $.60 per copy vol 2 #6 & 7, vol 3 #1 & #2, #15, #16-#18. 48pp; 7X8½; of. Reporting time: 1-2 mos. Payment: copies. Copyrighted. Pub's reviews. §arts & politics.

MISSISSIPPI REVIEW, Frederick Barthelme, Editor; Kim A. Herzinger, Elizabeth Inness Brown, Asociate Editors, Box 5144, Southern Station, Hattiesburg, MS 39401. 1971. Poetry, fiction, interviews, satire, criticism, letters, parts-of-novels, long-poems, art, plays, photos, reviews. circ. 2,000. 3/yr. Pub'd 3 issues 1979; expects 2 issues 1980, 3 issues 1981. sub. price: $8.00; per copy: $3.00; sample: $3.00. Back issues: $2.50 and as offered. Discounts: none. 125-200pp; 5⅞X8⅝; †of. Reporting time: 8 to 10 weeks. Payment: copies. Copyrighted, reverts to author. Pub's reviews. §Contemporary lit & criticism. Ads: $100.00/$50.00/ Will consider trade-out. CCLM, COSMEP.

MISSISSIPPI VALLEY REVIEW, Forrest Robinson, Editor; Loren Logsdon, Fiction; John Mann, Poetry, Dept. of English, Western Ill. University, Macomb, IL 61455, 309-298-1514. 1971. Poetry, fiction. "Little, if any, ms. reading during summer. No long poems and no novella-length stories. MVR has published work by Jack Matthews, Howard Nemerov, Lucien Stryk, Laurence Lieberman, Daniel Curley, Ralph Mills, Jr., James Ballowe, John Judson, Lester Goldberg, Paul Bartlett, Winston Weathers, & John Craig Stewart. We prefer that poets submit no more than five poems at one time; fiction writers: one story at a time. We usually solicit our reviews. We will not return submissions not including a SASE" circ. 400. 2/yr. Pub'd 2 issues 1979; expects 2 issues 1980, 2 issues 1981. sub. price: $4.00; per copy: $2.00; sample: $2.00 plus postage. 64pp; 6X9; lp. Reporting time: 3 months. Payment: 2 copies of issue in which work appears plus 1 copy of succeeding 2 issues. Copyrighted, reverts to author. Pub's reviews: 2 in 1979. §We solicit our own. CCLM, COSMEP.

THE MISSOURI REVIEW, Marcia Southwick, Larry Levis, Eric Staley, Managing Editor, Dept. of English, 231 Arts & Science, University of Missouri-Columbia, Columbia, MO 65211. 1978. Poetry, fiction, articles. "Poetry by: Robert Bly, Patricia Goedicke, Daniel Halpern, Philip Levine, Lisel Mueller, Joyce Carol Oates, Louis Simpson, Russel Edson, Nancy Willard, Naomireplansky, David St. John, William Stafford, Gerald Stern, James Tate, Diane Wakoski, Michael Waters, Charles Wright, David Young. Fiction by R.V. Cassill, James B. Hall. Criticism by M.L. Rosenthal, Philip Stevick, Ian Watt." circ. 750. 3/yr. Pub'd 3 issues 1979; expects 3 issues 1980, 3 issues 1981. sub. price: 1 yr (3 issues), $7.00; 2 yrs (6 issues), $12.00; yearly foreign countries, $8.00; per copy: $2.50; sample: free until January, 1981. Discounts: 40% bookstores, 10% library. 104pp; 6X9; of. Reporting time: 6 weeks maximum. Payment: $5.00 per page. Copyrighted, author can reprint material without charge if author acknowledges mag. Pub's reviews. §Omnibus reviews of poetry and fiction. Ads: $50.00/$25.-00/ or exchange. CCLM, COSMEP.

MR. COGITO, Robert A. Davies, John M. Gogol, Box 627, Pacific Univ., Forest Grove, OR 97116. 1973. Poetry, art, long-poems. "We will publish the best poetry from the most varied schools of poetry. We are particularly interested in good translations of foreign poetry, both modern and ancient. Among recent poets in our pages were Norman Russell, Peter Wild, Walt Curtis, Ursula LeGuin, Patrick Gray, Kenneth O. Hanson & Zbigniew Herbert." circ. 500. 2/yr. Expects 2-3 issues 1981. 2 titles listed in the *Small Press Record of Books in Print* (9th Edition, 1980). sub. price: $3.00; per copy: $1.00; sample: $0.50. Back issues: varies. Discounts: 40%. 24pp; 4½X11; †of. Reporting time: 2 wks to 3 mos. Payment: copies only. Copyrighted. Ads: 1 pg @$75.00. CCLM.

The Mit Press (see COMPUTER MUSIC JOURNAL)

Mixed Breed, Jack Saunders, Box 42, Delray Beach, FL 33444, (305) 276-8611. 1976. Poetry, fiction, articles, art, photos, cartoons, interviews, satire, criticism, reviews, music, letters, parts-of-novels, long-poems, collages, plays, concrete art, news items. "Two-man operation: Jack Saunders, Box 42, Delray Beach, Fl 33444; and Larry Schluefer, 1834 Robert Street, New Orleans, LA 70115. Currently publishing screed in 5-sheet installments. Each sheet 4 pages. Price $1.00 per installment. Availability varies. Inquire. Back list includes pamphlets, chapbooks. Inquire." avg. press run 1,000. 4 titles listed in the *Small Press Record of Books in Print* (9th Edition, 1980). Discounts: Free to prisons, mental hospitals, acloholism treatment facilities. 8½X11; of. Reporting time: no plans to publish other writers.

MJG Company, Mary J. Goodwin, Lemuel R. Goodwin, P.O. Box 7743, Midland, TX 79703, 915-682-3184. 1978. Poetry, fiction, art, photos, reviews. "At present we are not receiving material from outside. We will make an announcement when we do. We hyave a book for children coming out in October, another scheduled for 1979 and some material for a how-to book. Books vary in length depending on materials, photos, art, etc. The first book is 25,000 words with seven illustrations and is paperback. We are planning on 100 of 1000 copies to be hardback. We print & publish birthday and photo-art cards. *The Mystery of the Baroque Pearl* by Mary J. Goodwin; illustrator: G.W. Greenwood. Art work to illustrate book is paid for either outright or on a 10% royalty basis - contract for artist gives choice." avg. press run 1,000. Expects 1 title 1980, 1 title 1981. 9 titles listed in the *Small Press Record of Books in Print* (9th Edition, 1980). avg. price, paper: $3.95. Discounts: Agent, 20%; bookstore, 5 copies 30%, over 5 40%; review copy avail. on request. 72pp; 5½X8½; mi/of.

Mockingbird Press, Tuli Kupferberg, 160 6th Avenue, New York, NY 10013, (212) 925-3823. 1973. "Will do pamphlets up to 96pp; have satirical & libertarian bias." avg. press run 5M. 2 titles listed in the *Small Press Record of Books in Print* (9th Edition, 1980). avg. price, paper: $1.00 or less. Discounts: 40%. 64pp; size varies; of. Reporting time: quick. Payment: author receives all — above costs. Does not copyright for author.

MODERN HAIKU, Robert Spiess, PO Box 1752, Madison, WI 53701, (608) 255-2660. 1969. Poetry, articles, reviews, news items. "Twice recipient of National Endowment for the Arts grant-awards. International circulation. Good university and public library subscription list. Publishes haiku only, plus related book reviews and articles. No restrictions on article length. Contributors should enclose self-addressed, stamped return envelope." circ. 500. 3/yr. Pub'd 3 issues 1979; expects 3 issues 1980, 3 issues 1981. sub. price: $7.00; per copy: $2.60; sample: $2.40. Back issues: $2.60. 60pp; 5½X8½; of. Reporting time: 4 weeks. Payment: cash & other prizes for best work, $110.00 an issue. Copyrighted, reverts to author. Pub's reviews: 30 in 1979. §Haiku only. Ads: No ads. CCLM.

MODERN IMAGES, Antonio Giraudien, Box 912, Mattoon, IL 61920. Poetry, art, satire. circ. 500. 4/yr. Pub'd 4 issues 1979; expects 4 issues 1980, 4 issues 1981. sub. price: $7.95; per copy: $2.00;

sample: $2.00. Back issues: $2.00. 32pp; 5½X8; †of. Reporting time: 2 weeks. Copyrighted, reverts to author.

THE MODERN LANGUAGE JOURNAL, David P. Benseler, Editor, 314 Cunz Hall, Ohio State University, Columbus, OH 43210, 614-422-6985. 1916. Articles, reviews, news items. "David P. Benseler, Editor, *The Modern Language Journal* (1980-82) Address of Editor: Department of German, The Ohio State University, Columbus, OH 43210" circ. 7,000. 4/yr. Pub'd 6 issues 1979; expects 4 issues 1980, 4 issues 1981. sub. price: $12.00; per copy: $3.50; sample: $3.50. 150pp; 7½X10. Reporting time: 1 to 3 months. Payment: 2 copies of issue in which article appears. Copyrighted, does not revert to author. Pub's reviews: 210 in 1979. §Subjects of interest to language teachers. Ads: $250.00/$200.00/$110.00.

MODERN LANGUAGE QUARTERLY, William H. Matchett, 4045 Brooklyn Ave. N.E., Seattle, WA 98105. 1940. Criticism, reviews. "No unsolicited reviews. Literary criticism by and for scholars." circ. 1,975. 4/yr. Pub'd 4 issues 1979. sub. price: $8.00 domestic, $9.50 foreign; per copy: $2.25 domestic, $2.50 foreign; sample: $2.25. Discounts: 10%. 112pp; 6⅝X9⅝; of. Reporting time: 1 to 3 mos. Payment: none. Copyrighted, does not revert to author. Pub's reviews: 32 in 1979. §only literary criticism. Ads: no ads.

MODERN LITURGY, Resource Publications, William Burns, Editor; Jake SJ Empereur, Editor-in-Chief; C.P. Mudd, Poetry Editor, Box 444, Saratoga, CA 95070. 1973. Poetry, fiction, articles, art, photos, cartoons, criticism, reviews, music, letters, plays, concrete art. circ. 16,000. 8/yr. Pub'd 8 issues 1979; expects 8 issues 1980, 8 issues 1981. sub. price: $19.00; per copy: $2.50; sample: $2.50. Back issues: $3.00. Discounts: 40 percent trade & bulk, $0.50 per subscr. 40pp; 8½X11; of. Reporting time: 6 weeks. Payment: $1.00 to $100.00. Copyrighted, does not revert to author. Pub's reviews: 187 in 1979. §Religious arts, music, religious education. Ads: $647.00/$472.00/$0.50. COSMEP, CPA, WIP.

MODERN POETRY STUDIES, Jerry L. McGuire, Robert Miklitsch, 207 Delaware Avenue, Buffalo, NY 14202, (716) 847-2555. 1970. Poetry, articles, interviews, criticism, reviews, long-poems. "*Modern Poetry Studies* is a journal of English language verse as well as poems in translation, criticism of contemporary and modernist poetry by writers of both established and modest reputation, reviews of currently-issued books, and interviews with poets. Publishing three issues yearly, the magazine devotes at least one in every volume to a special presentation, often focusing acclaim and critical attention upon the work of a single American poet or foreign nation's poetry. It has offered more creative writing and analytical essays by and regarding women than any periodical not advertising itself as feminist explicitly. Forthcoming contributors include Jonathan Holden, Susan van Dyne, Eugenio Andrade Irving, Feldman, et al. Written permission necessary before republication of *MPS* material (copyright)." circ. 500. 3/yr. Pub'd 3 issues 1979; expects 3 issues 1980, 6 issues 1981. sub. price: $7.50 indiv., $9.00 instit.; per copy: $2.50 indiv., $3.00 instit.; sample: free to institutions. Discounts: 10% to subscription companies. 85pp; 5⅜X8½; of. Reporting time: three months when we are on normal ownership patterns. Payment: 2 complimentary copies of issue. Copyrighted. Pub's reviews: 1 in 1979. §Contemporary English language poetry or volumes of poetry in translation.

THE MODULARIST REVIEW, Wooden Needle Press, R.C. Morse, 53 18 68th Street, Maspeth, NY 11378, (212) 672-9449. 1972. Poetry, fiction, articles, art, photos, interviews, criticism, reviews, letters, parts-of-novels, long-poems. circ. 1,000. 1/yr. Pub'd 1 issue 1979; expects 1 issue 1980. sub. price: $3.00; per copy: $3.00; sample: $3.00. Back issues: $2.00 (if available). Discounts: trade-40%. 96pp; 5X8; of. Reporting time: 1-2 months. Payment: copies, subscription. Copyrighted. Pub's reviews. §poetry, prose, art, architecture, sculpture, etc. Ads: ad rate card sent upon request. CCLM, NESPA.

MODUS OPERANDI, M.O. Publishing Company, Sheila R. Jensen, 14332 Howard Road, Dayton, MD 21036, 301-774-2900. 1970. Poetry, fiction, articles, art, satire, criticism, letters, cartoons. "We welcome manuscripts from known and unknown writers, *but they should send #10 SASE for Guideline for Writers and $2.00 for sample copy before submitting manuscripts or artwork.* We like editorials, fiction and true life humorous stories 500 to 1,500 words; we expect carefully typed manuscripts with number of words counted and listed in upper right corner of manuscript. We assume every writer knows to type his name and full mailing address in the upper left corner of the manuscript. We do not stand in line at the post office to accept 'postage due' mail; it is automatically refused and returned to the sender. Manuscripts not accompanied by SASE (self-addressed, stamped envelope) are tossed into wastebasket. We do not read xerox or carbon copies. We will not accept any manuscript containing profanity; a writer worthy of the name has an adequate vocabulary to express himself without resorting to profanity. We sponsor three or four contests for subscribers each year and give $25.00 checks to the winners." circ. 600. 12/yr. Pub'd 12 issues 1979; expects 12 issues 1980, 6 issues 1981. sub. price:

254

$9.00 US; $11.00 Foreign (money order for US funds); sample: $2.00 US; $2.50 Foreign (US funds). Back issues: Only by annual volume $20.00. Discounts: Bookstores, 40%. 40-60pp; 8½X11; †mi/Electronic Stencils/Silk Screen. Reporting time: Fast!. No monetary payment or contributor copy. Copyrighted, reverts to author. Pub's reviews: 100 in 1979. §Any small press magazine. Ads: $0.10 word. CCLM, COSMEP.

Mojave Books, Judith R. Bazol, Sr. Editor; Ruth B. Franklin, 7040 Darby Ave., Reseda, CA 91335, 213-342-3403. 1969. Poetry, fiction, plays, non-fiction. "We are book publishers-general subjects, poetry, political science, etc." Pub'd 60 titles 1979. 73 titles listed in the *Small Press Record of Books in Print* (9th Edition, 1980). Discounts: 10-40 percent paperback; 25-40 percent hard back, based on quantities purchased. 5½X8½; of. Reporting time: 3 weeks. Copyrights for author. COSMEP.

MOJO NAVIGATOR(E), Cat's Pajamas Press, John Jacob, Martha Jacob, Fiction, 527 Lyman, Oak Park, IL 60304. "Magazine is *Defunct*. We will accept orders for issue #4 ($1.00) and triple-issue #5 ($2.50). We cannot consider new material.".

Mole Publishing Co. (see also THE HARDHITTING INTERMITTENT NORTH IDAHO NEWS), Mike Oehler, Rt 1, Box 618, Bonners Ferry, ID 83805. 1978. "Have one book in print, *The $50 & Up Underground House Book*. All about underground architecture, design and building." avg. press run 5,000. Expects 1 title 1980. 1 title listed in the *Small Press Record of Books in Print* (9th Edition, 1980). avg. price, paper: $6.00. 1, list; 2-4, 10%; 5-9, 30%; 10 & up, 40%; special discounts for distributors are negotiated. 113pp; 8½X11; of. Not looking for material at this time.

Molly Yes Press, David O'Connor, Virginia O'Connor, R.D. 3, Box 70-B, New Berlin, NY 13411, 607-847-8070. 1977. Fiction, articles. "We publish books (histories, novels, etc.) that have a regional (central New York) interest." avg. press run 500. Pub'd 3 titles 1979; expects 4 titles 1980, 4 titles 1981. 3 titles listed in the *Small Press Record of Books in Print* (9th Edition, 1980). Discounts: 30% (paid in advance) bookstores. †of. Reporting time: 4-8 weeks. Payment: small advance plus royalty. Copyrights for author.

Momentum Press, William Mohr, Editor, 512 Hill Street #4, Santa Monica, CA 90405. 1975. "Momentum Press will have published sixteen books of poetry and prose by the end of 1979, including a major collection of work by Los Angeles poets, *The Streets Inside: 10 Los Angeles Poets*. Titles for 1980 include: *Tiresias I:9:B Great Slave Lake Suite* by Leland Hickman; *Beyond the Straits* by Marine Robert Warden; *The Mother/Child Papers* by Alicia Ostriker; and major collections of work by Michael C. Ford, Dick Barnes, and Len Roberts." avg. press run 500. Pub'd 4 titles 1979; expects 4 titles 1980. 16 titles listed in the *Small Press Record of Books in Print* (9th Edition, 1980). avg. price, paper: $3.00. Discounts: 40 percent. 60pp; size varies; of. Reporting time: 1-3 months. Payment: Copies. Copyrights for author.

Momo's Press (see also SHOCKS), PO Box 14061, San Francisco, CA 94114. 7 titles listed in the *Small Press Record of Books in Print* (9th Edition, 1980).

MONCHANIN JOURNAL, Jacques Langlais, Associate Editor; Mary Stark, Associate Editor, Centre Monchanin, 4917 St-Urbain, Montreal, Quebec H2T 2W1, Canada, (514) 288-7229. 1968. Articles. "*Language*: Bilingual journal - French/English *Length of Material*: 7,000 - 10,000 words average (each issue devoted to a particular theme) *Material*: cross-cultural understanding - themes include* Education, Medicine, Spirituality, Communication, Politics and Law in an intercultural perspective. *Recent Titles*: *Intercultural Health*; *Intercultural Education*; *Inner Harmony*; *The Meeting of Cultures*; *Political Self-Determination of Native Peoples*; *Law, Politics, Cultures*; *Budhist-Christian Dialogue*. *Recent Contributors*: Raimundo Panikkar, Paul Younger, Kalpana Das, Dom Le Saux, Ka Ien Ta Ron Kwen, Robert Vachon." circ. 500. 4/yr. Pub'd 4 issues 1979; expects 4 issues 1980, 4 issues 1981. sub. price: $6.00 U.S./outside Canada; $7.00; per copy: $2.00 U.S./outside Canada; $2.25. Back issues: #50, 55-$2.50, each; #62, #64, $2.50. Discounts: $1.00 discount on sale price to agents. 40pp; 7X8½; of. Reporting time: 3 months. Copyrighted.

THE MONGREL FOX, Co-op Books Ltd., Ronan Sheehan, 50 Merrion Square, Dublin 2, Ireland. 1977. Poetry, fiction, interviews, criticism, reviews, parts-of-novels. "A journal of Irish arts, letters and politics. No party-line but diversity encouraged. Seeks to provide a critical voice in Irish society. Biassed towards Irish affairs but will review novels etc. from all countries." circ. 1,500. 4/yr. Pub'd 2 issues 1979; expects 4 issues 1981. sub. price: $4.00; per copy: $1.00; sample: free. Discounts: Trade direct mail order. 50pp; 7 1/2X11 1/2; of. Reporting time: 1 month. Payment: 40 dollars for story/article of medium length (4,000 words). Copyrighted, reverts to author. Pub's reviews: 6 in 1979. §Literature, politics, criticism. Ads: $150.00/$75.00. CLE (Ireland).

‡Montana Books, Publishers, Inc., 3426 Wallingford Ave. North, Box 30017, Seattle, WA 98103.

THE MONTANA REVIEW, Owl Creek Press, Rich Ives, Laurie Blauner, 520 S Second W, Missoula, MT 59801, (406) 728-0479. 1979. Poetry, fiction, articles, criticism, parts-of-novels, long-poems. "We are interested in quality translations in both poetry and fiction. Each issue includes quest-edited comments on new and neglected books and a critical article on a small press or magazine." circ. 500. 2/yr. Pub'd 1 issue 1979. sub. price: $5.00; per copy: $3.00; sample: $3.00. Discounts: standard. 100pp; 5½X8½; †lp. Reporting time: 1-2 weeks. Payment: 3 copies and a year's subscription. Copyrighted. Pub's reviews. §Poetry, fiction, translations and non-fiction. Ads: $30.00/$20.00. CCLM.

MONTEMORA, Eliot Weinberger, The Montemora Foundation Inc., Box 336, Cooper Station, New York, NY 10003, 212-255-2733. 1975. Poetry, art, criticism, reviews, letters, long-poems, interviews. "In our first six issues we've published interviews with Reznikoff, Bunting, Jabes, Montale, MacDiarmid and George & Mary Oppen; poetry or prose by all of the above, as well as Paz, Bronk, Baraka, Corman, Rakosi, Cesaire, Niedecker, Miyazawa, Omar Pound, Tarn, Huidobro, Eshleman, Rothenberg and a wide variety of lesser-known poets, some appearing in print for the first time. Each issue also presents work by British writers who are generally little-known in the U.S.; extensive translations from the Chinese and Japanese by Burton Watson, Hiroaki Sato, A.C., Graham and Jonathan Chaves; and first or new translations of Medieval & Renaissance texts. And there's a great deal of critical comment: articles on Zukofsky, Croce, Eliade, Rexroth, Vallejo, Blackburn, to name only a few. Longer poems or selections are stressed. Unsolicited manuscripts from *Montemora readers,* accompanied by the usual SASE, are welcome. We only publish translations that have received authorization from the foreign poet, publisher or estate. We like to hear from barely, rather than widely, published poets; and we always ignore the chronically unsolicited, whose knowledge of the magazine is limited to this notice. Four Montemora Supplements are also currently available at $3.00 each: first collections of poetry by Rachel Blau DuPlessis, Mark Kirschen, Mary Oppen, and Gustaf Sobin." circ. 1,000. 2/yr. Pub'd 2 issues 1979; expects 2 issues 1980. sub. price: $12.00/3 issues, institutions; $10.00/3 issues, individuals; per copy: $4.00; sample: $4.00. Back issues: $4.00. Discounts: 40% trade. 200-300pp; 9X6; of. Reporting time: immediate. Payment: When possible. Copyrighted. Pub's reviews: 15 in 1979. §poetry/literary/criticism. Ads: $100.00/$50.00. CCLM, NYSSPA.

Montessori Learning Center, PO Box 767, Altoona, PA 16602, (814) 946-5213. 1975. "Publishes only books by Aline D. Wolf. There is no average size or price. Specifics for each publication are as follows: *Tutoring Is Caring — You Can Help Someone To Read* 8 1/2 x 11, 215 pages, $12.50 plus $1.00 shipping; *A Parents' Guide To The Montessori Classroom* 5 1/2 x 8 1/2, 58 pages, $3.50 plus $1.00 shipping; *Look At The Child* 6 x 8 1/2, 64 pages, $4.00 plus $1.00 shipping." avg. press run 4,000-45,000. Expects 1 title 1980, 1 title 1981. 5 titles listed in the *Small Press Record of Books in Print* (9th Edition, 1980). Discounts: Quantity prices for classrooms, trade, bulk, jobber. of, lp. Reporting time: We do not consider manuscripts of other authors.

Montreal Poems (see also Sunken Forum Press), Keitha K. MacIntosh, Dewittville JOS 1CO, Canada, 514-264-2866. 1974. "Unsolicited material accepted." avg. press run 1000. Pub'd 8 titles 1979. avg. price, paper: $3.00. Discounts: 25%. 50pp; 8X10; of. Payment: none. Copyrights for author.

MONUMENT IN CANTOS AND ESSAYS, Victor Myers, 4508 Mexico Gravel Road, Columbia, MO 65201. 1968. Poetry, fiction, articles, photos, parts-of-novels. "5 poems each submission, 1 fiction piece (max. 12 typed pages), require SASE. Prefer poetry with vivid imagery, carefully chosen language, concise, strong particularity. Only interested in fiction of similar character with impact." circ. 300. irreg. sub. price: $1.00 individual/$2.00 institutional; per copy: $1.00; sample: $1.00. Back issues: $2.00. 50pp; 5½X8½; of. Reporting time: 3 months. Payment: 2 copies. §poetry as described above, esp dealing with nature, Zen perceptions, American Indian, monistic philosophical inclinations.

Moody Street Irregulars (see also MOODY STREET IRREGULARS), Joy Walsh, P.O. Box 157, Clarence Center, NY 14032, (716) 741-3393. 1977. Poetry, articles, art, photos, cartoons, interviews, criticism, reviews, letters, news items. "Moody Street Irregulars will print poetry, and material pertaining to Kerouac and the Beats." avg. press run 1,000-2,500. Pub'd 4 titles 1979; expects 4 titles 1980, 4 titles 1981. 2 titles listed in the *Small Press Record of Books in Print* (9th Edition, 1980). avg. price, other: $1.50, $4.00 yr, $5.00 libraries. Discounts: 40% to bookstores. 12-24pp; 8½X11; of. Reporting time: one month. Payment: copies. Copyrights for author. NEW, COSMEP.

MOODY STREET IRREGULARS, Moody Street Irregulars, Joy Walsh, P.O. Box 157, Clarence Center, NY 14032, (716) 741-3393. 1977. Poetry, articles, art, photos, cartoons, interviews, criticism, reviews, letters, news items. "*Moody Street Irregulars* is a Kerouac newsletter. We are looking for material on Kerouac and other Beat writers. The magazine will always retain the spirit of Jack Kerouac. Recent contributors: George Dardess, Joy Walsh, Ted Joans, John Elellon Holmes, Tetsus Nakagami, Gerld Nicosia, Dennis McNally, Janet Kerouac, Jack Kerouac." circ. 500-1000. 4/yr. Pub'd 4 issues

1979; expects 4 issues 1980, 4 issues 1981. sub. price: $4.00; per copy: $1.50; sample: $1.50. Back issues: $1.50. Discounts: 40% to bookstores. 12-24pp; 8½X11; of. Reporting time: one month. Payment: copies. Copyrighted, reverts to author. Pub's reviews: 3 in 1979. §books on Kerouac and the Beats. Ads: No ads. Will accept contributions. NEW, COSMEP.

Moon Books, Anne Kent Rush, Anica Vesel Mander, P. O. Box 9223, Berkeley, CA 94709, 415-444-0465. 1974. Fiction, art. avg. press run 10,000. avg. price, paper: $5.95. Discounts: 40 percent. 250pp; 5¼X8½; of. Reporting time: 2 to 6 weeks. Payment: 7.5 percent on paper and 10 percent on cloth. Copyrights for author. COSMEP, FLG.

Moon Publications, Bill Dalton, Founder; Joe Bisignani, David Stanley, PO Box 1696, 133 W Lindo, Chico, CA 95927, (916) 345-5473. 1973. Art, photos, criticism, letters. "We specialize on budget guidebooks on the Pacific and Asian regions, particularly meant for the adventurous. *Indonesia Handbook* is a backpacker's guide through over 40 smaller archipelagos of the immense Indonesian Archipelago, and *South Pacific Handbook* surveys the low-cost, best value way to enjoy, learn from and travel through 15 South Pacific island nations. We also distribute an Indonesian language phasebook. 133 W Lindo, Chico, CA 95926." avg. press run 5,000-10,000. Pub'd 1 title 1979; expects 1 title 1980, 1 title 1981. 2 titles listed in the *Small Press Record of Books in Print* (9th Edition, 1980). avg. price, paper: $8.50. Discounts: Trade: 40%; Distributors: 50%; Libraries: 20%; Bulk: 65%; Advance Sales: 72½%. 425pp; 5⅛X7⅜; of. Reporting time: we accept travel manuscripts, writers must contact us first before submitting ms's. Payment: usually 10% to writer upon submission of completed ms with maps pre-drawn, writers must be briefed first by us. Copyrights for author. COSMEP.

Moonfire Press (see also THIRD COAST ARCHIVES), Eddee Daniel, Lynn Kapitan, 3061 N Newhall Street, Milwaukee, WI 53211, 414-964-0173. 1976. Poetry, art, long-poems, concrete art. "We do *Third Coast Archives* quarterly, also small chapbooks, 'foldsheets,' and poetic postcards.It is our goal to present contemporary poetry—including haiku—in a creative format through the use of illustrations and graphic design." avg. press run 150-250. Pub'd 1 title 1979; expects 2 titles 1980. avg. price, paper: $1.50; other: $1.00 for 8 poetic postcards. Discounts: 40% plus postage on 5 or more. 40-60pp; 5½X8½; of. Reporting time: 2 weeks to 2 months not actively seeking manuscripts at this time. Payment: copies. Copyrights for author.

Moonlight Publications, Fred Laughter, Jan Lundy, Mary McAnally, Elizabeth Pearson, PO Drawer 2850, La Jolla, CA 92038. 1975. Poetry, fiction, art, photos, satire, parts-of-novels, long-poems, plays. "Moonlight Publications annually produces a 200-page anthology of art, poetry, and short fiction, as well as books (50 to 80 pp.) by individual poets and guest editors. *Contents Under Pressure* (1980, $10.00) is a collection of satire, joy, and experimental form; our first anthology, *Serpent's Egg* (1979, $10.00), dealt with sorrow and pain, and the human response of transmutation. We are currently seeking art and literature on the broad topics of Work and Boredom for a boxed set of two volumes to be published in 1981. Recent books include Guy Beining's *Backroads & Artism,* Richard Behm's *The Book of Moonlight,* and an anthology of Oklahoma prison poetry entitled *Warning: Hitchhikers May be Escaping Convicts.*" avg. press run 700. Pub'd 2 titles 1979; expects 4 titles 1980. avg. price, paper: $5.00. Discounts: 30%/10 or more. 100pp; 5½X8½; of. Reporting time: varies. Payment: publication-specific arrangements. Copyrights for author.

THE MOONSHINE REVIEW, Tom Liner, Lewis Miller, Moonshine Cooperative, Rt. 2 Box 488, Flowery Branch, GA 30542, (404) 967-3326. 1978. Poetry, fiction, articles, art, cartoons, interviews, satire, criticism, reviews, letters, parts-of-novels, long-poems, plays, concrete art. "We are interested primarily in the new writer, but we print whatever turns us on. No biases, no prejudices. Any submission will get a careful (and kind) reading. We like it strange, raunchy, sweet — what you will. You haven't heard of our recent contributors — but you will. (SASE, of course)" circ. 300. 1/yr. Expects 1 issue 1980, 1 issue 1981. sub. price: $2.00; per copy: $2.00; sample: $2.00. Back issues: $1.00. Discounts: Write us. If we like you we'll send you a schedule. 50-100pp; 7X8½; †of. Reporting time: 1 month and longer. Payment: copies. Copyrighted, reverts to author. Pub's reviews: 1 in 1979. §poetry, fiction, most anything that is off-the-wall. Ads: None normally, but if it's a good cause, we'll print it free.

Moonsquilt Press, Michael Hettich, Karen Osborne, 2312 10th Street, Denver, CO 80211, 458-1070. 1979. Poetry, long-poems, fiction, interviews, criticism, reviews, music. "We are interested in poetry that comes out of an awareness of *tradition* but is not necessarily *traditional.* We like craft but not craftiness or excessive sheen. We want to be moved. Mss 25 plus pages w/SASE." avg. press run 500-750. Pub'd 3 titles 1979; expects 2-3 titles 1980. avg. price, paper: $2.00. Discounts: Free to schools, libraries. 30pp; 5½X8½; of. Reporting time: 3-4 weeks. Payment: copies. Copyrights for author. CCLM, COSMEP.

Moore Publishing Company (see also WAYS & MEANS), Eugene V. Grace, PO Box 3036, Durham, NC 27705, (919) 286-2250. 1968. Poetry, fiction. avg. press run 1,000. Pub'd 12 titles 1979. avg. price, cloth: $7.95; paper: $4.50. Discounts: Wholesalers & jobbers - 48% on 1-4 copies, 50% on 5 or more copies; Libraries and colleges - 20%; Bookdealers - 1-4 copies, 33⅓%, 5-24 copies, 42%, 25-49 copies, 43%, 50-99 copies, 44%, over 99 copies, 46%. 200pp; 6X9; of. Reporting time: 6-8 weeks. Payment: 10% of net sales paid once a year.

THE MOOSEHEAD REVIEW, Robert Allen, Jan Draper, Stephen Luxton, Hugh Dow, Box 169, Ayer's Cliff, Quebec, Canada, 819-838-5921, 819-838-4801. 1977. Poetry, fiction, articles, art, photos, cartoons, satire, criticism, reviews, parts-of-novels, long-poems, plays. "This is a new magazine, its fourth and fifth issues due in 1980. We will consider anything, regardless of length, but are especially interested in long poems, parts of novels, political articles (especially Marxist Literary Theory). Moosehead Press will begin to publish books of poetry, fiction and criticism, beginning in 1980. Our first book is *Late Romantics,* a collaborative book & poems by Robert Allen, Stephen Luxton and Mark Teicher, 64 pp $4.50" circ. 500. 2/yr. Pub'd 1 issue 1979; expects 2 issues 1980, 2 issues 1981. sub. price: $5.50; per copy: $3.00; sample: $3.00. Back issues: $2.00. Discounts: 40% to bookstores. 80pp; 5X8; of. Reporting time: 6-8 weeks. Payment: copies. Copyrighted, reverts to author. Pub's reviews: 4 in 1979. §poetry, fiction, political. Ads: $50.00/$30.00.

Morgan Press (see also HEY LADY), Edwin H. Burton, 1819 N. Oakland Avenue, Milwaukee, WI 53202, (414) 272-3256. 1967. Poetry, fiction, art, photos, parts-of-novels, long-poems, plays. "No biases & no problem with long works. Hikaru Hida, Keiko Gibson, Robert Hillebrand, Tetsuya Taguchi, Lyn Lifshin." avg. press run 500-1,000. Pub'd 3 titles 1979; expects 3 titles 1980, 5 titles 1981. avg. price, cloth: free; other: free. 30-200pp; 5X8 TO 24X36; †of, lp. Reporting time: fairly quickly. Payment: copies. Copyrights for author.

Morning Glory Press, 6595 San Haroldo Way, Buena Park, CA 90620. 5 titles listed in the *Small Press Record of Books in Print* (9th Edition, 1980).

Morning Star Press (see also THE PHOENIX; WESTBERE REVIEW), James Cooney, Poplar Hill Road, RFD, Haydenville, MA 01039, 413-665-4754. 1970. Poetry, letters, parts-of-novels, long-poems, plays, non-fiction. "Best to write for full details on our American Poets Co-Operative Publications & American Novelists Co-Operative Publications." avg. press run 500-5,000. 2 titles listed in the *Small Press Record of Books in Print* (9th Edition, 1980). †lp. Reporting time: 2-4 weeks.

El Moro Publications, Jane H. Bailey, P.O. Box 965, Morro Bay, CA 93442, (805) 772-3514. 1978. "Interested in natural history." avg. press run 3,000. Pub'd 1 title 1979; expects 1 title 1980, 1 title 1981. 1 title listed in the *Small Press Record of Books in Print* (9th Edition, 1980). avg. price, paper: $5.50. Discounts: 40% bookstores, 30% other shops, 505 chains etc. Will negotiate. 176pp; 5X8; of. Reporting time: one month. Payment: will negotiate. Copyrights for author.

Mosaic Press/Valley Editions, S. Mayne, H. Aster, M. Walsh, P. Potichnyj, PO Box 1032, Oakville, Ontario L6J 5E9, Canada. 1975. Poetry, fiction, criticism. avg. press run 2500. Expects 13 titles 1980, 15 titles 1981. 21 titles listed in the *Small Press Record of Books in Print* (9th Edition, 1980). avg. price, cloth: $10.95; paper: $5.95. Discounts: 40% to bookstores. 250pp; 6X9. Reporting time: 3-6 months. Payment: 10% of list. Copyrights for author. ACP.

Mosaic Press, Miriam Owen Irwin, 358 Oliver Road, Dept. 11, Cincinnati, OH 45215, (513) 761-5977. 1977. Poetry, fiction, satire. "We publish fine, hard-bound miniature books on any subject we find fascinating. Details are available for writers for $3.00 in our writer's manual, '*How to Write Miniature Books for Mosaic Press*'. We also publish a free miniature book catalog." avg. press run 2,000. Pub'd 7 titles 1979; expects 24 titles 1980, 24 titles 1981. 15 titles listed in the *Small Press Record of Books in Print* (9th Edition, 1980). avg. price, cloth: $16.00. Discounts: 40% on prepaid orders of 10 or more, any combination of titles. 64pp; size -3/4X1; of. Reporting time: 2 weeks. Payment: $50.00 & 5 copies of book. Copyrights for author. COSMEP.

Mota Press (see MUSEUM OF TEMPORARY ART (MOTA) MAGAZINE)

Motheroot Journal, Motheroot Publications, Anne Pride, Paulette Balogh, Felice Newman, Pat McElligot, 214 Dewey Street, Pittsburgh, PA 15218, (412)731-4453. 1978. Criticism, reviews. "We will rview books from the small presses by, published by, of special interest to or about women." circ. 2,000. quarterly. Pub'd 1 issue 1979; expects 4 issues 1980, 4 issues 1981. sub. price: $5.00; per copy: $1.25; sample: $1.25. Back issues: $1.25. Discounts: 40% Bookstores; 50% Distributors. 16pp; size tabloid; of. Reporting time: 6 weeks. Payment: copies. Copyrighted, reverts to author. Pub's reviews: 16 in 1979. §Books by, for, or about women. Ads: $100.00/$100.00/$50.00/$25.00. COS-MEP/CCLM.

Motheroot Publications (see also Motheroot Journal), Anne Pride, Paulette Balogh, Felice Newman, Pat McElligott, 214 Dewey St., Pittsburgh, PA 15218. 1977. Poetry, fiction, articles, long-poems, plays. "We are a women's press — our first chapbook by Adrienne Rich published in July 1977. 2nd book May 1978. Material for/about women. Five books to date." avg. press run 1,000. Pub'd 2 titles 1979; expects 3 titles 1980, 3 titles 1981. 3 titles listed in the *Small Press Record of Books in Print* (9th Edition, 1980). avg. price, paper: $3.00. Discounts: 40% bookstores, 50% distributors. 25pp; 8½X5½; of. Reporting time: 6 weeks. Payment: 25% after costs. Copyrights for author. COSMEP/CCLM.

Mothra Press (see also BOXCAR), Leslie Brody, 1001-B Guerrero, San Francisco, CA 94110. 1977. Poetry, fiction, articles, photos, cartoons, satire, parts-of-novels, collages, plays. "Prefer short fiction, short journals, one act plays" avg. press run 3,000. Discounts: Will exchange. 8pp; 17X11½. Reporting time: 2 months. Payment: Copies.

Mountain Press Publishing Co., David Flaccus, 283 W Front, PO Box 2399, Missoula, MT 59806, (406) 728-1900. 1948. "Mountain Press publishes books on environmental conservation, hunting, fishing and the outdoors. We also publish a series of roadside geology and western Americana books. We started as a printing company. We then began to publish medical text books and have since sold the printing plant and evolved into the publishing categories mentioned above." avg. press run 5,000. Pub'd 6 titles 1979; expects 7 titles 1980, 8 titles 1981. 7 titles listed in the *Small Press Record of Books in Print* (9th Edition, 1980). avg. price, cloth: $12.95; paper: $6.95. Discounts: Normal trade 40%, classroom 20%, wholesale 50-55%. 250pp; 6X9; of. Reporting time: varies, depending on type of submission. Payment: usually 10-15%. Pacific Northwest Book Publishers Assn.

MOUNTAIN REVIEW, Betty Edwards, Renee Stamper, Box 660, Whitesburg, KY 41858. 1974. Poetry, fiction, articles, art, photos, cartoons, interviews, criticism, reviews, music, letters, satire, parts-of-novels, plays. "Fiction, non-fiction: 1000-3000 wds. Poetry: printable on one page or less. Material must be related to life in Southern Appalachians." circ. 2,000. 4/yr. Pub'd 4 issues 1979; expects 4 issues 1980, 4 issues 1981. sub. price: $7.50; per copy: $2.00; sample: free. Back issues: $2.00. Discounts: wholesale price:-40%- $1.20 per copy. 48pp; 8½X11; of. Reporting time: 6 months. Payment: complimentary copy of magazine. Copyrighted, reverts on request. Pub's reviews: 8 in 1979. §Southern Appalachians. Ads: $175.00/$85.00/75¢. CCLM, COSMEP.

Mountain Union Books, Bob Snyder, c/o Bob Snyder, 1511 Jackson Street, Apt AB, Charleston, WV 25311. 1974. Poetry, fiction. avg. press run 500. Pub'd 2 titles 1979. 1 title listed in the *Small Press Record of Books in Print* (9th Edition, 1980). avg. price, paper: $3.50. Discounts: 20% to bookstores. 80pp; 6X8; of. Reporting time: 2 months. COSMEP.

The Mountaineers Books, John Pollock, Director, 719-B Pike Street, Seattle, WA 98101, (206) 682-4636. 1960. "We have over 70 titles in print, all having to do with mountains - how to, where to, history-climbing, hiking, skiing, snowshoeing, bicycling, mountaineering & expeditions." avg. press run 5,000. Pub'd 22 titles 1979; expects 15 titles 1980, 15 titles 1981. avg. price, cloth: $20.00; paper: $7.00. Discounts: 50% to wholesalers, 20-44% to stores depending on quantity. 224pp; 5½X8½; of. Reporting time: 2-3 months. Payment: 10% of gross, 17½% of net, all negotiable. Copyrights for author.

MOUTH OF THE DRAGON, Andrew Bifrost, Editor, Box 957, c/o Bifrost, New York, NY 10009. 1974. Poetry, criticism. circ. 1,000. Pub'd 3 issues 1979; expects 2 issues 1980, 3 issues 1981. sub. price: $13.00 Indiv.; $18.00 Instit. (based on a 5 issue subscription); per copy: $3.00. 7X11; of. Reporting time: 4 to 8 weeks. Payment: 2 copies per issue of appearance of work. Copyrighted, reverts to author. CCLM.

MOVEMENT, Nationalist, Scop Publications, Inc., Mary Condren, SCM Publications, 168 Rathgar Road, Dublin 6, Ireland, Dublin 970975. 1971. Articles, cartoons, reviews, news items, letters, interviews, satire, criticism. "Av. length 2,500 words, each issue carries 30,000 word 'in depth' study; theology & gay liberation; theology & sexual politics; feminist theology; christianity & mental health care; the christian church & its revolutionary role (in Cuba, Ireland, S. Korea, Namibia, USA especially). Liberation theology, the rise of fascism, materialist, reading of Bible, christian marxism. Biases-radical christian ideas & actions. Contributors include: Daniel Berrigan, Thomas Szasz, Rosemary Ruether, Mary Daly, Bruce Kent, Rictor Norton, Walter Hollenweger, Des Wilson, Gustavo Gutierrez, Helder Camara, etc." circ. 10,000. 5/yr. Pub'd 5 issues 1979. sub. price: Britain & Ireland £3/overseas £3.25 (airmail £6.50); per copy: 35p; sample: 35p. Back issues: upon enquiry. Discounts: on request-/negotiation. 48pp; size A4; of. Reporting time: 4 weeks. Payments very rare. We usually hold copyright unless author requests reversion. Pub's reviews. §radical christianity/marxism/fascism/alternative society/peace movements/gays. Ads: £54/£30/3p a word. APS, LNS, WSCF, SPC, USI, NUS, EPS, IFOR, CNOE.

MOVING OUT: Feminist Literary & Arts Journal, Gloria Dyc, Margaret Kaminski, 4866 Third & Warren, Wayne State University, Detroit, MI 48202, 313 898-7972/313 833-9156. 1970. Poetry, fiction, articles, art, photos, interviews, criticism, reviews, parts-of-novels, long-poems, plays. "We publish quality work by women. LIBRARY JOURNAL recently described our journal as one with a 'well-defined aesthetic sense which considers all facets of women's lives and literature. . .first choice for librarians who must make such a choice.' Please do not double submit or send work which has been published elsewhere. Enclose SASE. Plan 2 issues each for 1980 + 1981." circ. 2500. 2/yr. Pub'd 2 issues 1979; expects 2 issues 1980. sub. price: $4.50; per copy: $2.50 back issues; $3.50 current issue; $3.00 double issue; sample: $2.50 back issues; $3.50 current issue; $3.00 double issue. Back issues: $2.50 back issues; $3.50 current issue; $3.00 double issue. Discounts: none. 48-100pp; 8½X11; of. Reporting time: 6 to 12 months. Payment: none, copy only. Copyrighted. Pub's reviews: 2 in 1979. §women's writings. Ads: $200.00/$100.00. COSMEP.

Mowbray Company Publishers (see also MAN AT ARMS), E. Andrew Mowbray, Editor & Publisher; Richard Alan Dow, Exec. Editor, 222 W Exchange Street, Providence, RI 02903, (401) 861-1000. 1967. "Limited edition books in the arts-history field. We also publish for organizations - both books and magazines." avg. press run 5,000. Pub'd 3 titles 1979; expects 4 titles 1980, 4 titles 1981. Discounts: usual. Reporting time: 4-5 weeks. Payment: standard. Copyrights for author.

THE MRB NETWORK, James A. Cox, Hank Luttrell, 1121 University Avenue, Madison, WI 53715, (608) 256-1946. 1979. Poetry, articles, art, reviews. "Primarily a newsletter of the MRB book review and public affairs programming for radio and television as well as print media review activities." circ. 1,000. 6/yr. Pub'd 6 issues 1979. sub. price: $10.00; sample: stamped envelope, $1.00. Discounts: bulk rate six for $6.00. 6pp; 8X11; of. Reporting time: 4 to 6 weeks. Payment: No. Copyrighted, reverts to author. Pub's reviews: 3 in 1979. §Small press, university press, poetry, philosophy, alternative life style, political, how-to. Ads: $50/$30/10¢.

M-R-K Publishing, Rural Route #6, Petaluma, CA 94952, (707) 763-0056. 1977. avg. press run 5,000. Pub'd 1 title 1979; expects 1 title 1980. 2 titles listed in the *Small Press Record of Books in Print* (9th Edition, 1980). avg. price, cloth: $10.95; paper: $5.90. Discounts: Distributors, 50%; Jobbers, 40%; Libraries & Schools, 20% (2 or more copies-post paid, with remmitance). 200pp; 6X9; of. Copyrights for author. COSMEP, WIP, NABD.

MRG Press (see MINORITY RIGHTS GROUP REPORTS)

Mu Publications, G. Dunbar Moomaw, Publisher, Box 612, Dahlgren, VA 22448. 1976. "Mu Publications presently operates for advancing the works of poet-G. Dunbar Moomaw. Thru books, posters, bookmarks, etc. Published in '77 were: (Books) *Thoughts of Innocence.* Cloth $3.25, Paper $1.30; *The Dawn: Poetics of Deep Thought,* Cloth $3.50, Paper $1.50. (Posters) 5½ x 8½ *Spirit Love,* $1.50; *Certificate of Romance,* $1.00; *The Eternal One,* $1.50; *Sanctuary,* $1.00; 8½ x 11, *Proclamation of Success: Power to Abundant Riches,* $2.00. Tentatively scheduled for release sometime in '78 is: *The Mu Journal of Contemplative Thought* which will probably be published irregularly, with hopes of becoming quarterly. Complete details yet to be finalized. Mu Publications now operates for the publishing and marketing the works of one Poet-Philosopher G. Dunbar Moomaw. Also sells other books and items of interest from other publishers, etc. The Mu Journal of Contemplative Thought has been temporarily cancelled. MU Publications presently operates for advancing the work of Poet-Philosopher—G. Dunbar Moomaw. Thru books, posters, etc. Some titles published in '78 were: *The Ten Commandments of Romance, The Ten Commandments of Equality, The One Cosmic Force That Makes Us As Gods.* '79 were: *The Ten Commandments of Positive Thinking,* and *Romance Recipe For Happy Lovin'.* and in 1980: *Woman* and *Man.*" avg. press run 200. Pub'd 5 titles 1979; expects 2 titles 1980, 2 titles 1981. 39 titles listed in the *Small Press Record of Books in Print* (9th Edition, 1980). avg. price, cloth: $3.00; paper: $1.25; other: $1.50 posters. Discounts: 40 percent for: bookstores, libraries. 26pp; 4¼X7; 3X4½; mi/of. COSMEP.

Mud Press (see MISSISSIPPI MUD)

Mudborn Press (see also ROCKBOTTOM; INKLINGS), Sasha Newborn, Judyl Mudfoot, 209 W. De la Guerra, Santa Barbara, CA 93101, 805-962-9996. 1975. Poetry, fiction, interviews, music, letters, parts-of-novels, plays, articles. "For 1980 we are looking at translations or translation anthologies primarily, particularly in languages not commonly translated—this year we are doing Portuguese, Latvian, Spanish, German, possibly Flemish and Thai. We also do contemporary American prose and poetry but are full up right now. *The Village Idiot* is not accepting any new material." avg. press run 1,000. Pub'd 7 titles 1979; expects 10 titles 1980, 10 titles 1981. 25 titles listed in the *Small Press Record of Books in Print* (9th Edition, 1980). avg. price, cloth: $12.00; paper: $3.50. Discounts: Trade buyers write for terms and information. 80pp; size octavo; †lp. Reporting time: 1 month. Payment: 5 percent cash or 10 percent press run, books only. Copyrights for author. CCLM.

MUNDUS ARTIUM: A Journal of International Literature & Art, Rainer Schulte, Box 688, Richardson, TX 75080. 1967. Poetry, fiction, art, photos, criticism, parts-of-novels, long-poems, plays. "Foreign poetry in bi-lingual format. Interdisciplinary focus on contemporary arts. Interested in translation of younger international writers. Conceptual rather than representational." circ. 1,000-1,200. 2/yr. 2 titles listed in the *Small Press Record of Books in Print* (9th Edition, 1980). sub. price: $10.00 Inst; $8.00 indiv.; per copy: $4.50; sample: $4.00. Back Issues: vol 1&2 rare $20 ea, single issues $3.50, volumes $6.00 each; Arabic issue $6.00. 180pp; 6X9; lp. Reporting time: 1-2 months. Payment varies. Pub's reviews. §International art scene, translations. Ads: $100/$60. CCLM, COSMEP.

Michael F. Murphy Ph. D., Michael F. Murphy, Dept of Microbiology, Univ Az College of Medicine, Tucson, AZ 85724, (714) 222-7254. 1978. "Most recent book; *Gorillas Are Vanishing Intriguing Primates* population statistics; social behavior; diseases." avg. press run 5,000. Expects 1 title 1980, 2 titles 1981. 1 title listed in the *Small Press Record of Books in Print* (9th Edition, 1980). avg. price, other: $5.95. Discounts: 40% wholesale for resale. 96pp; 6X9. Copyrights for author.

Museum of New Mexico Press (see also EL PALACIO), Richard Polese, Editor, PO Box 2087, Santa Fe, NM 87503. 1913. Articles, art, photos, reviews. avg. press run 2,000. Pub'd 5 titles 1979; expects 8 titles 1980, 10 titles 1981. 66 titles listed in the *Small Press Record of Books in Print* (9th Edition, 1980). Discounts: 1 to 5, 30%; 5 and up 40%. Reporting time: 4 weeks.

MUSEUM OF TEMPORARY ART (MOTA) MAGAZINE, Mota Press, Janet Schmuckal, PO Box 28385, Washington, DC 20005, 202-638-3400. 1975. Poetry, fiction, articles, art, photos, cartoons, interviews, satire, criticism, reviews, music, letters, collages, concrete art. "We are backlogged with poetry and fiction. No unsolicited mss will be considered until 1982." circ. 200-1500. 1/yr. Pub'd 1 issue 1979; expects 1 issue 1980. sub. price: No subscription rate; per copy: varies; sample: $2.00 issue #16; $1.50 issue #17. Back issues: *Mota* 16, $2.00. Discounts: none. 32-96pp; 5½X8½; †of. Reporting time: 6 months. Copyrighted, reverts to author. Ads: Write for information.

MUSIC AND LETTERS, Oxford University Press, Denis Arnold, Edward Olleson, 32 Holywell, Oxford, United Kingdom. 1920. Articles, reviews, music, letters. "Not specialized in scope, being open to the discussion of anything from primitive music to the latest experiments in the laboratory. But preference is given to contributors who can write, who have a respect for the English language and are willing to take the trouble to use it effectively." circ. 2,000. 4/yr. Pub'd 4 issues 1979; expects 4 issues 1980, 4 issues 1981. sub. price: £7.00 ($18.00); per copy: £2.00 ($5.00); sample: free. 120pp; 6X9¾; of. Payment: £1.00 per printed page. Copyrighted, reverts to author. Pub's reviews: 79 books, 95 pieces of music in 1979. §Music, musical criticism, musical history, etc. Ads: £40.00 & pro rata/£23.00.

MUSICAL OPINION, Laurence Swinyard, Spring Road, Barn & Mouth, United Kingdom. 1877. Articles. "500-2000 words of general musical interest, organ & church matters. No verse." 12/yr. price per copy: 25p.

MYTHLORE, Gracia Fay Ellwood, Lee Speth, PO Box 4671, Whittier, CA 90607. 1967. Poetry, articles, art, criticism, reviews, letters, news items. "Orders dept c/o Lee Speth" circ. 500-1,000. 4/yr. Pub'd 1 issue 1979; expects 4 issues 1980, 4 issues 1981. sub. price: $10.00; per copy: $3.00; sample: free. Back issues: varies depending on supply & size of issue. Discounts: 40%. 48pp; 8½X11; of. Reporting time: 5 weeks. Payment: free copies. Copyrighted, reverts to author. Pub's reviews: 25 in 1979. §Children's & adult fantasy, scholarly studies on JRR Tolkien, Ls Lewis & Chas Williams. Ads: $24.00/$14.00/$0.10.

N

Nada (see also BIG SCREAM), David Cope, Susan Cope, 2782 Dixie, SW, Grandville, MI 49418, 616-531-1442. 1974. Poetry, fiction, art. avg. press run 100. avg. price, paper: $1.00. Discounts: 5-10 copies 25 percent; more than 10 40 percent. 30pp; 8X8½; †mi. Reporting time: 1 week - 1 month. Payment: 3 copies.

EL NAHUATZEN, Lowell L. Jaeger, PO Box 2134, Iowa City, IA 52244, (319) 353-7170. 1978. Poetry, articles. "Emphasis on poetry by Chicano and Native Americans, but will consider 'quality' manuscripts from any interested poet. Each issue of *El Nahuatzen* will feature an unpublished Chicano or Native American poet, and a poem or open letter from a prison inmate. Beyond that our only bias is for literary 'quality.'" circ. 200. 2/yr. Expects 1 issue 1980, 2 issues 1981. sub. price: $6.00; per copy: $3.00; sample: $2.00. Back issues: $2.00. 48pp; 5½X8; of. Reporting time: 3 months. Payment: 2 copies. Copyrighted, reverts to author. Ads: $50/$25/. COSMEP.

The Naiad Press, Inc., Barbara Grier, 7800 Westside Drive, Weatherby Lake, MO 64152, 816-741-2283. 1973. Fiction, poetry. "Small press publishing material by and for women. Publishes only Lesbian/Feminist novels and poetry. 16 titles to date. We are expanding, and will be publishing 4 other titles in the next 9 months. Writers of Lesbian/Feminist novels are invited to inquire. We have expanded to include lesbian non-fiction with literary tie-ins in 1980." avg. press run 3,000 copies. Pub'd 4 titles 1979; expects 4 titles 1980, 6 titles 1981. 12 titles listed in the *Small Press Record of Books in Print* (9th Edition, 1980). avg. price, paper: $5.50. Discounts: 40 percent dealers - 5 or more copies. of. Reporting time: 4 weeks. Payment: 50 percent. varies. Copyrights for author. COSMEP.

NAMAZU, Namazu Collective, 2-12-2 Asahimachi, Abeno, Osaka, Japan. 1978. Articles, cartoons, news items. "Publication is sporadic due to the involvement of the editors in local activities." circ. 500. Pub'd 3 issues 1979; expects 1 issue 1980. sub. price: Contribution; per copy: Contribution. 16-48pp; of.

Nanny Goat Productions, Joyce Farmer, Chin Lyvely, Box 845, Laguna Beach, CA 92652, (714) 494-7930. 1972. Cartoons, satire. "*Tits & Clits, Abortion Eve,* & *Pandora's Box* are comic books dealing primarily with female sexuality in a humorous way. *Tits & Clits* is a series of 5 books, #5 was published by Last Gasp in San Francisco in 1979." avg. press run 90,000. avg. price, paper: $1.25. 32pp; 7X10; of. Payment: 10% of cover price per page. Copyrights for author. COSMEP.

NANTUCKET REVIEW, Richard Cumbie, Richard Burns, P.O. Box 1234, Nantucket, MA 02554. 1974. Poetry, fiction, articles, art, satire, criticism, reviews, parts-of-novels, long-poems. "Send all review copies and exchange copies to PO box 825, Leverett, MA 01054" circ. 700. 3/yr. Pub'd 3 issues 1979; expects 3 issues 1980, 3 issues 1981. 1 title listed in the *Small Press Record of Books in Print* (9th Edition, 1980). sub. price: $5.00; per copy: $2.00; sample: $1.50. Back issues: $1.50. Discounts: 40%. 60-70pp; 5½X8½; of. Reporting time: 2 mos. Payment: copies, cash occasionally. Copyrighted, reverts to author. Pub's reviews: 3 in 1979. §Fiction, poetry. Ads: $50/$25. COSMEP, CCLM.

Narbulla Agency, Alfred Lubran, 4 Stradella Rd., Herne Hill, London, England SE24 9HA, United Kingdom. "Belles lettres-miniature books-typographical ephmerea-limited editions." 11 titles listed in the *Small Press Record of Books in Print* (9th Edition, 1980).

Natalie Slohm Associates, Inc., Natalie Slohm, 49 West Main Street, Cambridge, NY 12816, (518) 677-3040. 1975. Poetry, fiction, long-poems. "Lyn Lifshin, Viveca Lindfors" avg. press run 2000. Pub'd 1 title 1979; expects 1 title 1980, 2 titles 1981. 2 titles listed in the *Small Press Record of Books in Print* (9th Edition, 1980). avg. price, paper: $2.95. Discounts: Trade, 40%. 80pp; 5½X8; †of. Payment: advance against royalty/per book sold. Copyrights for author.

National Council of Teachers of English (see COLLEGE ENGLISH)

National Financial Publications, PO Box 50173, Palo Alto, CA 94303. 1974. "Publish books on small business; how to earn money at home, etc. Books were written to order. Only thing we might possibly be interested in are books along this line, or closely related. Books are designed to sell well by mail." 3 titles listed in the *Small Press Record of Books in Print* (9th Edition, 1980). avg. price, cloth: $9.95; paper: $5.95. Discounts: write us. 8¼X10¾; of. Reporting time: 1 week. Payment: arranged individually.

NATIONAL FISHERMAN, David R. Getchell, 21 Elm St., Camden, ME 04843, 207-236-4342. 1946. Articles, art, photos. "journal of the American fishing industry (commercial) and custom boat building." circ. 67,000. 13/yr. Pub'd 13 issues 1979; expects 13 issues 1980, 13 issues 1981. sub. price: $15.00; per copy: $1.50; sample: $0.00. Back issues: $1.50. Discounts: none. 120pp; 10X15; †of. Reporting time: 4-6 weeks. Payment: $0.05 per word, $10.00 per photograph. Copyrighted, reverts to author. Pub's reviews: 21 in 1979. §marine non-fiction. Ads: $1,700/$1,185/$0.50. ABP.

National Gay News, Inc. (see also GAY COMMUNITY NEWS), Richard D. Burns, Managing Editor, 22 Bromfield St, Boston, MA 02108, 617-426-4469. 1973. Articles, art, photos, cartoons, interviews, satire, criticism, reviews, music, letters, news items. avg. press run 10,000. Pub'd 50 titles 1979; expects 50 titles 1980. avg. price, cloth: $17.50; other: $0.50. 10¼X15¾; of. Reporting time: 1 week. Payment: copies. Does not copyright for author. New England Press Association, COSMEP.

Nationalist (see MOVEMENT)

Natural Dynamics, Inc. (see also ENERGY EFFICIENT HOMES; NATURAL LIFE), Wendy Priesnitz, Box 640, Jarvis, Ont. N0A 1J0, Canada. 1976. Articles, art, photos, cartoons, interviews, letters, reviews, news items. "Access to alternatives in food, energy, lifestyle." avg. press run 50M. Pub'd 6 titles 1979; expects 6 titles 1980, 6 titles 1981. 1 title listed in the *Small Press Record of Books in*

Print (9th Edition, 1980). avg. price, other: $1.25. Discounts: retail: 40% - 5 to 49; 50% - 50 to 99; 60% - 100+; plus 5¢/copy p/h. 80pp; 7X10; of. Reporting time: 2 weeks. Payment: varies. Copyrights for author. CPPA.

Natural Hygiene Press (see also HEALTH SCIENCE), Jack Dunn Trop, 1920 Irving Park Road, Chicago, IL 60613, (312) 929-7420. 1964. Articles. "Research writers knowledgeable in the area of natural, healthful, ecological living are hired for specific projects assigned by the publisher. Enquiries and resumes welcome." avg. press run 10,000-15,000. Expects 3 titles 1980, 3 titles 1981. 15 titles listed in the *Small Press Record of Books in Print* (9th Edition, 1980). avg. price, paper: $2.25. Discounts: 2-24 copies 30%; 400 or more 42%. 300pp; 4X7; of/lp. Reporting time: 4 months. Payment: 5% minimum; for anthologies edited by publisher, NHP negotiates purchase of rights. Copyrights for author. COSMEP.

NATURAL LIFE, Natural Dynamics, Inc., Wendy Priesnitz, Box 640, Jarvis, Ont N0A 1J0, Canada. 1976. Articles, art, photos, cartoons, interviews, letters. "Down-to-earth, how-to-do-it, self-sufficiency oriented articles. Access to alternatives." circ. 50,000. 6/yr. Pub'd 6 issues 1979. sub. price: $8.00; per copy: $1.50; sample: $1.50 + 50¢ postage. Back issues: $1.50 + 50¢ postage each. Discounts: retail: 5-49 - 40% plus 5¢/copy p/h. 80pp; 7X10; of. Reporting time: 2 wks. Payment: 2 to 5 cents/wd. approx-varies per article. Copyrighted, reverts to author. Pub's reviews: 50 in 1979. §self-sufficiency, alternate energy, natural foods, cookery, health, vegetarianism. Ads: $500.00/$300.00/$0.50. CPPA.

Naturegraph Publishers, Inc., David L. Moore, Editor, P. O. Box 1075, Happy Camp, CA 96039, 916-496-5353. 1946. "Our list includes, natural history, Native American studies, gardening, health, and new age publications. Now looking at mss. on holistic learning." avg. press run 4,000. Pub'd 3 titles 1979; expects 6 titles 1980, 6 titles 1981. 67 titles listed in the *Small Press Record of Books in Print* (9th Edition, 1980). avg. price, cloth: varies; paper: varies. Discounts: 1-4, 20%; 5-49, 40%; 50-99, 42%; 100 and up, 44%. 160pp; size varies; †of. Reporting time: 1-8 weeks. Payment: Royalties. Copyrights for author. COSMEP.

Naturist Foundation (see THE GROVE)

NAZUNAH, Marey Maddock, Keir Mondstrahl, PO Box 1662, Bloomington, IN 47402, (812) 336-0572. 1979. Poetry, art, photos. "*Nazunah* usually reserves its pages for poetry under 100 lines. The editors are pleased to view manuscripts of original poetry or poetry-in-translation, as well as original artwork." 2/yr. Pub'd 2 issues 1979; expects 2 issues 1980. sub. price: $4.00; per copy: $2.00; sample: $2.00. Back issues: $2.00. Discounts: 40%. 50pp; 5½X8½; †Platen press. Reporting time: varies according to how close to deadlines that manuscripts are submitted. Payment: copies. Copyrighted, reverts to author. Ads: No ads. COSMEP.

NEBULA, Ken Stange, Ed; Ursula Stange, Associate Editor; Gil McElroy, Associate Editor, 970 Copeland, North Bay, Ontario P1B3E4, Canada. 1974. Poetry, fiction, articles, art, photos, cartoons, interviews, satire, criticism, reviews, music, letters, parts-of-novels, long-poems, collages, plays, concrete art. "We are interested in formal innovation: the carefully crafted but originally structured work is always of interest to us. We do thematic issues, so a would-be contributor is advised to send a buck for a sample of latest issue, wherein he/she will find a statement of our immediate thematic interests. (And those dollars will help keep us alive). Our contributors range from the very established to the totally unknown. Some names, Robert Kroetsch, Michael McMahon, Martin Booth, Charles Plymell, Garcia Lorca, Glen Sorestad, Allan Brown, Len Gasparini, Opal Nations, Brian Shein, David McFadden, George Amabile, Andy Suknaski, Earle Birney, Tom Wayman, Al Moritz." circ. 750. 4/yr. Pub'd 4 issues 1979; expects 4 issues 1980, 4 issues 1981. sub. price: $8.00-1 yr, institutions $15.00-1 yr; per copy: $2.00; sample: $2.00. Back issues: Nos. 1, 4, and 9 sold out; others $2.00. Discounts: 40%. 88pp; 5½X8½; of. Reporting time: 1-2 months. Payment: contributor copies. Copyrighted, reverts to author. Pub's reviews. §extremely eclectic. Ads: $50.00/$25.00. COSMEP, CPPA.

Ted Nelson, Publisher, c/o the distributors, 702 So. Michigan, South Bend, IN 46618. 1974. Articles, art, photos, cartoons, music, collages, news items. "motto: 'The World's Most Unusual Books'" avg. press run 5,000. Pub'd 2 titles 1979; expects 3 titles 1980, 4 titles 1981. 2 titles listed in the *Small Press Record of Books in Print* (9th Edition, 1980). avg. price, paper: $2.00-$7.00. Discounts: 15 copies assorted 40%, 2-14 copies assorted 30%, 1 copy net. 250pp; size variable; of/lp. Reporting time: 1 year. Copyrights for author.

NETHULA JOURNAL OF CONTEMPORARY LITERATURE, Kathy Elaine Anderson, Editor; Keith Jones, Asst. Editor; Essex C. Hemphill, Publisher; Cynthia L. Williams, Art Editor, PO Box 50368, Washington, DC 20004. 1978. Poetry, fiction, articles, art, photos, interviews, reviews, parts-of-novels. circ. 1,000-1,250. 2/yr. Pub'd 2 issues 1979; expects 2 issues 1980, 2 issues 1981. sub. price: $6.00; per copy: $3.50; sample: free to reviewers. 60-80pp; 6X9. Reporting time: 3-5 weeks. Payment:

2 copies of the issue accepted work appears in. Copyrighted, reverts to author. Pub's reviews: 2 in 1979. §Third World Literature. Ads: $60.50/$30.00.

Nevada Publications, Stanley W. Paher, Box 15444, Las Vegas, NV 89114, 702-871-1800. 1970. Poetry, articles, art, photos, cartoons. "We publish books on Nevada, California and Arizona, mostly guides to scenic areas and ghost towns. All are lavishly illustrated and are solidly based in orginal research and are well edited." avg. press run 11,000. Pub'd 5 titles 1979; expects 5 titles 1980. 2 titles listed in the *Small Press Record of Books in Print* (9th Edition, 1980). avg. price, cloth: $7.50; paper: $2.95. Discounts: 1, 25%; 2 plus, 40%. 48pp; 9X12; of. We generally seek out the author, and do not solicit manuscripts. Payment: 10% 1st edition; subsequent editions negotiable. Does not copyright for author.

New-Age Foods Publications, William Shurtleff, PO Box 234, Lafayette, CA 94549. 1975. "We publish books about production of foods made from soybeans. The volume I of each set is published by a large publisher (such as Harper & Row or Autumn Press) with nationwide distribution." avg. press run 2,000. Pub'd 1 title 1979; expects 1 title 1980, 1 title 1981. 3 titles listed in the *Small Press Record of Books in Print* (9th Edition, 1980). avg. price, cloth: $16.95; paper: $12.95. Discounts: 20% on 2 to 5 copies; 30% on 6 or more: prepaid orders *only*. 192pp; 8½X11; of. Reporting time: we write all our own material. Copyrights for author.

NEW AMERICA, Humanities Room 324, University of New Mexico, Albuquerque, NM 87131, (505) 277-3929. 1974. Poetry, fiction, articles, photos, criticism, reviews, letters, parts-of-novels. "*New America* is sponsored by the Graduate Student Association and is not a function of the University. We take a broadly humanistic approach toward American Studies with emphasis on the Southwest. Each issue is usually thematically oriented, for example, 'Women's Issue,' 'Native American Issue,' 'Photographs of the Southwest Issue,' 'Southwest Regionalism Issue,' 'Chicano Anthology.' We sometimes involve guest editors on specific thematic issues. We also have a high visual orientation (graphics and photographs). Recent contributors include Raymond Johnson, Meridel LeSueur, Lee H. Marmon, Henry Roth, Leslie Silko. We are interested in innovative scholarship as well as creative work, and welcome submissions from beginning writers and artists." circ. 750. 3/yr. Pub'd 2 issues 1979; expects 4 issues 1980, 3 issues 1981. sub. price: $8.00/yrindividual; $15.00/yr institution; per copy: $3.50; sample: $1.00. Back issues: not available. Discounts: 40% to bookstores and distributors; 10% to individuals for bulk purchases. 80pp; 8½X11; †of. Reporting time: 1 to 3 months. Payment: copies. Copyrighted, reverts to author. Pub's reviews: §Generally, American Studies, specifically, Southwest oriented. CCLM, COSMEP.

NEW ART EXAMINER, Chicago New Art Association, Jane Addams Allen, Derek Guthrie, Associate Editor, 230 E. Ohio, Chicago, IL 60611, 312-642-6236. 1973. Art, articles, interviews, criticism, reviews, letters, news items. "Commentary on and analysis of the exhibtion and making of art, film, photographs, including humor, occasional cartoons, Jack Burnham, Joshua Kind." circ. 7,000. 10/yr. Pub'd 10 issues 1979; expects 10 issues 1980, 10 issues 1981. sub. price: $15.00, $25.00 for 2 years; per copy: $1.75; sample: free. Back issues: Volume 1, $2.50 each; Volume 2, $2.25 each; Volume 3, $2.00 each; Volume 4, $1.75 each; Volume 5, $1.50 each, volume 6, $1.25 each. Discounts: 3x, 5x plus 10x rates. 28pp; size tabloid 11; of. Reporting time: three months. Payment: $10 word reviews/$35-$75 article. Copyrighted, does not revert to author. Pub's reviews: 20 in 1979. §visual art/film photography/architecture. Ads: $450.00/$240.00/$0.15.

THE NEW AUTHOR, Fremont Johnson, Ed Sanders, Route 1-Box 745, Aransas Pass, TX 78336. 1976. Poetry, fiction, parts-of-novels. 4/yr. sub. price: $3.00; per copy: $1.00; sample: $.75. 64pp; 5½X8½; †of. Payment: copies. Pub's reviews: §literary works. Ads: $40/$20/$.10-word. COSMEP.

New Bedford Press, Saul Burnstein, Editorial Director; Susan Goldman, Assoc Editor, 5800 W Century Blvd., Suite 91502, Los Angeles, CA 90009, 837-2961. 1977. Fiction. "Will debut paperback division in July 1979 under *Bedpress Books* banner." avg. press run 5,000. Expects 3 titles 1980, 6 titles 1981. 2 titles listed in the *Small Press Record of Books in Print* (9th Edition, 1980). avg. price, cloth: $10.00; paper: $1.50. Discounts: 40% up to 24 copies; over 25 copies 50%. 230pp; 5½X8; of/lp. Reporting time: 4-6 weeks. Payment: 10% flat, 12% 2nd edition, 15% 3rd edition. Copyrights for author.

NEW BOSTON REVIEW, Boston Critic, Inc., Gail Pool, J.M. Alonso, Lorna Condon, Angela Gerst, 77 Sacramento St., Somerville, MA 02143. 1975. Poetry, fiction, articles, interviews, criticism, reviews, parts-of-novels. "Essays—2,000-4,000 words covering art, literature, music, film, photography, theater. Contributors range from Geoffrey Barraclough, Glenn Gould, Octavio Paz to free-lance writers." circ. 11,000. 6/yr. Pub'd 4 issues 1979; expects 6 issues 1980. sub. price: $4.50; per copy: $0.85; sample: $0.85. Back issues: $1.00. Discounts: bookstores 50%. 28-32pp; 11¼X15¼; of. Reporting time: 2 months. Payment: none. Copyrighted, rights revert if requested. Pub's reviews: 40 in 1979. §poetry/fiction/criticism/all the arts. Ads: $300.00/$175.00. COSMEP, NESPA, CCLM.

NEW COLLAGE MAGAZINE, A. McA. Miller, 5700 North Trail, Sarasota, FL 33580, 315-355-7671, Ex 203. 1970. Poetry. "We want poetry with clear focus and strong imagery. Would like to see fresh free verse and contemporary slants on traditional prosodies. Issues are often thematic; so query before sending poems." circ. 1,000. 3/yr. Pub'd 3 issues 1979; expects 3 issues 1980. 2 titles listed in the *Small Press Record of Books in Print* (9th Edition, 1980). sub. price: $6.00; per copy: $2.00; sample: $2.00. Back issues: All available, 8 volumes at $1/issue or $3.00 per volume. Recent volumes. $2.00/issue, or $6.00 volume. Discounts: 60%/40% to dealers. 32pp; 5½X8½; of. Reporting time: 3 weeks. Payment: copies or token payment cash. Copyrighted, reverts to author. Pub's reviews: 2 in 1979. §Poetry, some interviews. Ads: none. CCLM, COSMEP, COSMEP-SOUTH, NESPA, FSWC.

NEW DEPARTURES, Michael Horovitz, Piedmont, Bisley, Stroud, Glos., England GL6 7BU, United Kingdom. 1959. Articles, poetry, art, cartoons, photos, reviews, music, plays, collages, concrete art. "A new issue of the magazine has always been an event readers found worth waiting for. Current issue a bumper celebration double #7 & #8—containing poetry, drawings, photos, collages, music & prose by: David Hockney, Gregory Corso, Ivor Cutler, Heathcote Williams, Samuel Beckett, R. D. Laing, Ted Hughes, Roger McGough, John Cage, Michael Hamburger, Thom Gunn & many more." circ. 5,000. irreg. sub. price: £2; per copy: 40p; sample: 40p. Back issues: 6 & 9 only, 36p + post. Discounts: 1/3 to booksellers, agents, distributors. 60pp; 9½X6; of. Reporting time: varies. Payment: by arrangement. Ads: £50/pro rata. ALP.

NEW DIRECTIONS FOR WOMEN, Vivian J. Scheinmark, Managing Editor, 223 Old Hook Road, Westwood, NJ 07675, 201-666-4677. 1971. Articles, art, photos, cartoons, interviews, satire, criticism, reviews, letters, poetry, fiction, collages, news items. "Maximum length 1,000 words. Must be from a feminist perspective or to help women." circ. 30,000. 6/yr. Pub'd 5 issues 1979; expects 6 issues 1980, 6 issues 1981. sub. price: $6.00 indiv; $10.00 instit; sample: free. Back issues: $1.00 each. Discounts: $0.90 2-25 copies; $0.75 each over 25 copies. 20pp; 10X16; of. Reporting time: 3 months. Payment: none-free copies. Not copyrighted. Pub's reviews: 75 in 1979. §By, for and about women & feminism. Ads: $500.00/$280.00/$0.40. COSMEP.

THE NEW ECOLOGIST, ECOSYSTEMS, Nicholas Hildyard, Joint Editor; Ruth Lumley-Smith, Joint Editor, 73 Molesworth Street, Wadebridge, Cornwall PL27 7DS, United Kingdom, 2996-7. 1978. Articles, photos, cartoons, interviews, criticism, reviews, letters, news items. "Articles of a serious and well researched type from 1000 to 3000 words. Shorter reports. Journal should be studied for style and content." circ. 10M. 6/yr. sub. price: £4.00 ($9.00); per copy: 60p; sample: free. size A4; of. Reporting time: 2 to 3 weeks. Payment: £10.00 per thousand words or by arrangement. Copyrighted, does not revert to author. Pub's reviews: 90 in 1979. §Mostly books on environmental subjects nuclear power, transport, pollution, alternative lifestyles, future planning. Not fiction. Ads: £90.00($180.00)/£45.00($90.00)/£40.00($80.00)/10p($0.10) minimum £3.00($6.00).

NEW EDINBURGH REVIEW, James Campbell, 1 Buccleuch Place, Edinburgh, Scotland EH8 9LW, United Kingdom. 1969. Articles, poetry, art, photos, reviews, interviews, criticism, long-poems, fiction. "Member of Scottish Assocn of Magazine Publishers. Contributors, recent & future include: J. P. Mackintosh M. P., I. MacCormick M. P., Prof. L. A. Gunn; Murray Grigor, Sorley MacLean." circ. 2,500. 4/yr. Pub'd 4 issues 1979. sub. price: UK £2.50 o/seas £2.50; per copy: 50p. Back issues: list available on application. Discounts: 33⅓% to trade. 40pp; size A4; of. Reporting time: 1 month. Payment: by negotiation. Copyrighted. Pub's reviews. §Arts, ecology, history, politics, general. Ads: £75/£45. SGPA.

THE NEW ENGLAND CONSERVATIONIST, Jerry Angel, John McLoughlin, Box 112A, Canaan, ME 04924, (207) 474-9125. 1978. Articles, art, photos, cartoons, interviews, criticism, reviews, letters, news items. circ. 5,000. 4/yr. sub. price: $3.50; per copy: $.95. 40pp; 8 1/2X11; of. Reporting time: varies. Payment: varies. Pub's reviews. §Environmental. Ads: $125.00/$75.00/$10.00 for 30 words.

New England Press, Gerald Dorset, 45 Tudor City #1903, New York, NY 10117. 1976. Poetry, fiction, criticism, plays. "Poetry, prose, plays, literary criticism. Two poetry books in 1977, two in 1978, *How to Write Love Letters* and *Video Tapes*; two in 1979, *Trips Through Time, Inscriptions and Appelations* . Plans 3 titles in 1980. MSS by invitations only. Poets invited: Mike Finley, Erica Jong, Ronald Koertge. *The Mystery of Mr. Poe*, essays, under print. Paper, from $1.50 to $4.95. Discount 30% on 5 or more. 6 x 9. Press run 1,000." avg. press run 500-1,000. Pub'd 2 titles 1979; expects 2 titles 1980, 2 titles 1981. 3 titles listed in the *Small Press Record of Books in Print* (9th Edition, 1980). avg. price, paper: $3.00. Discounts: 30%. 96pp; 6X9; lp. Reporting time: not inviting submission, by invitation only. Payment: 20% royalty paid Jan 1 and July 1. Copyrights for author. CCLM, COSMEP.

NEW ENGLAND REVIEW, Kenyon Hill Publications, Sydney Lea, Editor; M. Robin Barone, Managing Editor, Box 170, Hanover, NH 03755, (802) 649-1005. 1978. Poetry, fiction, articles, interviews, criticism, reviews, long-poems. circ. 2,500. 4/yr. Pub'd 4 issues 1979; expects 4 issues 1980, 4 issues 1981. sub. price: $12.00; per copy: $3.00; sample: $3.00. Back issues: Undecided. Discounts: 2 years, $22.00; 3 years, $30.00. 160pp; 6X9; of. Reporting time: 6 weeks. Payment: competitive. Copyrighted. Pub's reviews: 14 in 1979. §Contemporary fiction, poetry, biography, autiobiography, non-fiction. Ads: $320.00/$175.00/$100.00 quarter page. COSMEP.

NEW ENGLAND SAMPLER, Seacoast Press, Virginia M. Rimm, Editor; Arnold Perrin, Poetry Editor; Ruth Grierson, Assistant Editor; Henry Briggs, Contributing Editor, RFD #1, Box M119, Brooks, ME 04921, (207) 525-3575. 1980. Poetry, fiction, articles, photos, cartoons, reviews, interviews. "We're a family-oriented publication with strong emphasis on traditional values and heritage of New England. Are looking for upbeat material of professional calibre. Use one adult fiction per issue, average 2,500 words—humor, mystery, suspense, historical, adventure, etc. New England slant. Non-fiction: 3,000 word maximum including human interest, interview, inspirational, humor, personality pieces. Short items on lesser known but interesting places to visit for 'Off the Beaten Path'. Historical features, folklore, unusual occupations, etc. etc. also welcome. No objection to articles on famous New Englanders, but we like most to feature the every-day sort of person who doesn't make the headlines but is leading a courageous, heroic, challenging, unique or inspiring life. Profanity, obscenity are taboo! Black & white photos: scenics, humor, human interest. We type all material directly, take to printer for offset printing." 12/yr. Pub'd 6 issues 1979; expects 12 issues 1980. sub. price: $7.50; per copy: $0.75; sample: $1.00 (includes mailing costs). Back issues: $1.00. 48pp; 6X9. Reporting time: 4-6 weeks maximum. Payment: copies. Copyrighted, reverts to author. Pub's reviews. §Poetry, New England historical or fiction or biographical. Ads: $15.00/$10.00/$0.10, $2.00 minimum.

NEW GERMAN STUDIES, Alan Best, Derek Attwood, Dept Of German, Univ. Hull, Hull HU6 7RX, United Kingdom, 0482 46311 (extn 7652). 1973. Articles. "Up to 4,000 words on German language, literature, culture." circ. 250. 3/yr. Pub'd 3 issues 1979; expects 3 issues 1980. sub. price: £3.50 (indiv) £4.50 (institution); per copy: £1.50; sample: £1.50. Back issues: £2.50 (indiv) £3.50 (institution) vols 5-7. Discounts: 15 percent. 60 - 70pp; size A5; of. Reporting time: 1-2 months. Payment: nil. copyrights with editors. Pub's reviews: 40 in 1979. §German language, literature, culture. Ads: £10/page.

New Glide Publ., 330 Ellis Street, San Francisco, CA 94102. 1977. Articles, art, criticism, news items. "All materials published in book form only." avg. press run 5,000. Pub'd 5 titles 1979; expects 7 titles 1980, 9 titles 1981. 25 titles listed in the *Small Press Record of Books in Print* (9th Edition, 1980). avg. price, cloth: $10.00; paper: $5.95. Discounts: 20% one copy, 35% 2-9 copies, 40% 10 copies and up. 40% STOP and SCOP orders, 50% distributors. 200pp; of. Reporting time: 2-3 months. Copyrights for author.

NEW GUARD, Richard F. Lamountain, Woodland Rd, Sterling, VA 22170, 703-450-5162. 1961. Articles, photos, cartoons, interviews, reviews, letters, news items. "Official magazine of Young Americans for Freedom, the nation's largest conservative youth organization. Most articls 2000-2500 words." circ. 6000. 12/yr. Pub'd 12 issues 1979; expects 12 issues 1980, 12 issues 1981. sub. price: $3; per copy: $1; sample: $1. 48pp; 8½X11; of. Reporting time: 2 weeks. Payment: $40; $25 for short pieces or reviews. Copyrighted, does not revert to author. Pub's reviews: 24 in 1979. §world affairs. Ads: $175/$100/$25-5 lines or less. YAF.

NEW HUMANIST, Rationalist Press Association, Nicolas Walter, 88 Islington High St, London N1 8EW, United Kingdom. 1885. Articles, cartoons, interviews, satire, criticism, reviews, letters, news items. "Humanism, Religion" circ. 2,500. 6/yr. Pub'd 6 issues 1979; expects 6 issues 1980, 6 issues 1981. sub. price: £5.00; per copy: 50p; sample: free. Back issues: 50p. Discounts: Publishers 10%. 36pp; size A4; lp. Reporting time: 1 month. Payment: £10/1000 words. Copyrighted, reverts to author. Pub's reviews: 40 in 1979. Ads: £60/page & pro rata.

NIR/NEW INFINITY REVIEW, James R. Pack, Editor; Ron Houchin, Manuscript Editor; Ariyan, Art Editor, PO Box 804, Ironton, OH 45638. 1974. Poetry, fiction, articles, art, photos, cartoons, satire, criticism, reviews, letters, parts-of-novels, long-poems, concrete art. "*Fiction:* 2,000 to 4,000 words-we seek stories that are mentally exciting and germinal with ideas. Science fiction, fantasy and mystery find an eager eye. *Poetry:* no length limit—we try to feature at least one poet every issue. *The New Infinity Review* is dedicated to the new and unknown writer." circ. 500. 4/yr. Pub'd 4 issues 1979; expects 4 issues 1980. sub. price: $3.50; per copy: $1.00; sample: $0.75. Back issues: $1.25. Discounts: subscription agency discount: subscription-$3.00 per year. 60pp; 5½X8½; of. Reporting time: 6-8 weeks. Payment: two copies, art $5.00 up. Copyrighted, rights assigned on request. Pub's reviews: 2

in 1979. §poetry, short stories, fantasy of any length. CCLM.

NEW JERSEY POETRY MONTHLY, George W. Cooke, Elliot Braha, James A. Harrington, Art, P.O. Box 824, Saddle Brook, NJ 07662, 201-445-9436. 1977. Poetry. "We prefer 4 to 5 short poems of high quality submitted at one time. ISSN 0146-1087" circ. 500. 4/yr. Pub'd 5 issues 1979; expects 4 issues 1980, 4 issues 1981. sub. price: $12.00; per copy: $1.50; sample: $1.50. Back issues: $1.50. Discounts: none. 42pp; 5½X8½; of. Reporting time: 4 weeks. Payment in copies. Copyrighted, does not revert to author. COSMEP, CCLM.

THE NEW JOURNAL, Journal Books, Richard A. Bodien, Editor & Publisher, 704 Baylor Street, Austin, TX 78703. 1976. "*The New Journal* is an annual journal of new poetry and poetry translation. *The New Journal* No. 3, 1978, features poetry by Michael Lally, Jerome Sala, Richard Bodien, Jim Feast, Robie Liscomb, Jim Haining, Robert Trammell, Simon Schuchat, Gyla McFarland, David Gene Fowler, and an interview with Carolyn Cassady" circ. 200. annual. Pub'd 1 issue 1979; expects 1 issue 1980, 1 issue 1981. sub. price: $3.00; per copy: $3.00; sample: $3.00. Back issues: limited copies of *Journal II* at $3.00, *Journal I* o.p. Discounts: customary. pp varies; size varies. Payment: copies.

THE NEW LAUREL REVIEW, Long Measure Press, Alice Moser Claudel, Editor; Dr. Calvin A. Claudel, Assistant Editor for Translations, PO Box 1083, Chalmette, LA 70044, 504-271-4209. 1971. "Biased only toward work which seems to us to be *alive.* We have the usual antipathies, I think: against vague abstractions, too much personal confession, smart-alec scholarship (as opposed to sound research and ideas); nature for decoration's sake; etc. Tom O'Grady, James P. White, Lyn Lifshin, Jesse Stuart, Joshua Norton, Michael Anderson, Laurence Perrine, Herb Francis, Lee M. Grue, Gail Peck." circ. 500. 2/yr. Pub'd 2 issues 1979; expects 2 issues 1980, 2 issues 1981. sub. price: $4.- 00-$4.50 for libraries & institutions; per copy: $2.00; sample: $1.50. Back issues: $4.00 for back numbers; $3.00 for more recent numbers; that is, 1974,75,& 76. 60pp; 6X9; of. Reporting time: Varies-longer time for interesting work. Somewhat crowded with poetry (about 3 weeks). Payment: two copies of the magazine in which their work appears. Copyrighted. Pub's reviews: 2 in 1979. §poetry and books about poets and related matter. CCLM.

NEW LETTERS, David Ray, University of Missouri, Kansas City, MO 64110, 816-276-1168. 1971 (Predecessor, *University Review,* 1934). Poetry, fiction, articles, parts-of-novels, long-poems, art, photos, satire, reviews. "The best in contemporary fiction, poetry, personal essay, art, and photography. Contributors include Bly, Ignatow, Stafford, Gildner, Mayo, Colter, Levertov, Kumin. Special issue on Paul Goodman." 4/yr. Pub'd 4 issues 1979; expects 4 issues 1980. 2 titles listed in the *Small Press Record of Books in Print* (9th Edition, 1980). sub. price: $8.00; per copy: $2.50; sample: $2.50. Back issues: $5. Discounts: 14% agencies, 2% 10 days, 25% disc. on contract of 4 ads. 128pp; 6X9; of. Reporting time: 2 wks to 2 mos. Payment: small, upon pub. Copyrighted, reverts to author. Pub's reviews: 30 in 1979. §Lit, art. Ads: $100/$60/$.25. CCLM, COSMEP.

NEW LITERATURE & IDEOLOGY, People's Canada Publishing House, Norman Bethune Institute, Publ.; Canadian Cultural Workers Committee, Ed., PO Box 727, Adelaide Station, Toronto, Ontario, Canada. 1968. Poetry, fiction, articles, art, photos, cartoons, interviews, satire, criticism, reviews, music, letters, parts-of-novels, long-poems, plays. "*New Literature and Ideology* is available in both English and French from issue No. 21 on. Subscriptions are based on 4 issues for $5 (rather than on a yearly rate)." 4/yr. Pub'd 2 issues 1979; expects 4 issues 1980, 4 issues 1981. 3 titles listed in the *Small Press Record of Books in Print* (9th Edition, 1980). price per copy: $1.25; sample: free. Back issues: $1.25. 130pp; 5X8. Reporting time: 2 months. Payment: none. Not copyrighted. Pub's reviews: 1 in 1979. §Culture, politics, labour.

New London Press, Cameron Northouse, Editor; Donna Northouse, Anne Dickson, Tom Landess, Lynn Canty, Donna Bagwell, Hank Coleman, Mary Zingleman, Box 7458, Dallas, TX 75209, 214- 742-9037. 1976. Poetry, fiction, articles, art, photos, interviews, criticism, reviews, music, letters, parts-of-novels, long-poems, collages, plays, concrete art. "Publications: *Articles on English Literature: A Comprehensive Bib. 1900-1975; Directory of Business and Economics Journals; Business and Economics Book Review Index;* New London Interviews; *Selected Essays* by Andrew Lytle; *Two Plays* by James Purdy; *Frankenstein* by John Gardner." avg. press run varies. 13 titles listed in the *Small Press Record of Books in Print* (9th Edition, 1980). avg. price, cloth: varies. Discounts: Trade 40%; Classroom 20%; Jobber 50%;. 100pp; 5½X8½; of/lp. Reporting time: varies. Payment: negotiated. Copyrights for author.

NEW MAGAZINE REVIEW, Bill Ludwig, PO Box 3699, N Las Vegas, NV 89030, (702) 734-6730. 1978. Reviews. "We review the New Magazine as they become available, for librarians, organizations & businesses needing this information." circ. 1725. 12/yr. Pub'd 1 issue 1979; expects 5 issues 1980. sub. price: $42.00; sample: free. Back issues: We are very low on back issues as many of the subscribing libraries want all of Vol 1. Discounts: Starting in July we are offering a 15% to mag subscription agents but we haven't considered the others because the occassion hasn't arizen. 8pp; 8½X11; of. Reporting time: no submissions, staff written. Copyrighted, reverts to author. Pub's reviews: 240 in 1979. §Magazines (any kind) as long as they are still within their first year of publishing. Ads: no ads.

NEW MEXICO HUMANITIES REVIEW, John Rothfork, Jerry Bradley, Jim Corey, Box A, New Mexico Tech, Socorro, NM 87801, (505) 835-5445. 1978. Poetry, fiction, articles, art, photos, criticism, reviews, parts-of-novels. "A Southwest regional journal with broad interests. Recent essays on Pablo Neruda, Paul Horgan, Walt Whitman and ecology, movies; photo-essays on Albuquerque of the 1920's, H.H. Richardson's library; fiction by George Garrett, Fred Chappell, William Peden, Joe Nicholson, Frederic Will, Suhail Hanna, David Ohle; poetry by Peter Wild, E.G. Burrows, Walt McDonald, Peter Klappert. We encourage submissions from and about the Southwest, including Native American and Chicano material. We are also interested in essays on science/technology and society written for a general readership." circ. 800. 3/yr. Pub'd 3 issues 1979; expects 3 issues 1980, 3 issues 1981. sub. price: $5.00; per copy: $2.00; sample: $2.00. Back issues: $2.00 except for #1. 90pp; 6X9; of. Reporting time: 4-6 weeks. Payment: one year's subscription + $3.00/page. Copyrighted, reverts to author. Pub's reviews: 40 in 1979. §Southwest regional, small press, Native American. Ads: $30.00/$15.00. CCLM, RGWA.

New Oregon Publishers, Inc. (see also OREGON TIMES MAGAZINE), 208 SW Stark, Suite 500, Portland, OR 97204. 1 title listed in the *Small Press Record of Books in Print* (9th Edition, 1980).

NEW OREGON REVIEW, Nor Publications, Steven Dimeo, Ph.D., Editor-in-Chief, 537 N.E. Lincoln St., Hillsboro, OR 97123, (503)640-1375. 1976. Poetry, fiction, articles, art, photos, cartoons, interviews, satire, criticism, reviews, letters. "We generally have a surfeit of poetry, prefer to see intelligent prose of 2,000 - 4,000 words, particularly satire, psychological horror, SF/fantasy, mainstream." circ. 300. 2/yr. Expects 1 issue 1980. sub. price: $2.50/2 issues; per copy: $1.25; sample: $1.00. Back issues: Issue #1, $2.00; Issue #2, $1.00. Must mention *Dustbooks* in request. Discounts: Discontinued. 20pp; 5X8½; of. Reporting time: 2-3 months. Payment: $25.00/story; $10/poem, photo or artwork. 'Name' authors paid double, annual contest $100.00 for best short story. Copyrighted, reverts to author. Pub's reviews: 13 in 1979. §popular psychology, science, occult, popular fiction. Ads: $75/$50/$1/word (min. 15 words). CCLM, COSMEP.

NEW ORLEANS REVIEW, Leisa Reinecke Flynn, Managing Editor; John Biguenet, Loyola University, New Orleans, LA 70118, 504-865-2294. 1968. Poetry, fiction, articles, art, photos, interviews, criticism, reviews, plays. "Walker Percy, Susan Fromberg Schaeffer, Peter Wild, Christopher Isherwood, David Madden, Annie Dillard, Rosemary Daniell, Natalie Petesch, Doris Betts, Larry Rubin, Greg Kuzma, Harry Taylor, John William Corrington. We like to see high quality material in all aspects of human endeavor and culture." circ. 1,500. 3/yr. Pub'd 3 issues 1979; expects 3 issues 1980, 3 issues 1981. sub. price: 3 issues, $7.00: 6 issues, $13.00: 9 issues, $19.00; per copy: $2.50; sample: $2.50. Back issues: Vol 2-Vol 3, No. 1-$1.25 each issue, Vol 3-Vol 4 $1.50 each issue. Discounts: Sub agencies: 3 issues, $6.00: 6 isues, $11.00: 9 issues, $16.00. 112pp; 8½X11; of. Reporting time: 2 wks-2 mos. Payment: $50.00 fiction/articles; $10.00 poetry/art work. copyright release available on request. Pub's reviews: 35-40 in 1979. §all areas. Ads: Available upon request. CCLM, COSMEP.

NEW PAGES, New Pages Press, Casey Hill, Marjorie Wentworth, 4426 South Belsay Rd., Grand Blanc, MI 48439. 1979. Articles, art, photos, cartoons, satire, criticism, reviews, news items. "News and reviews of the progressive book trade. Access to informational tools. We are concerned with the growth & survival of an independent, progressive book trade and will be an alternative voice in an information sharing network. Pub'd bimonthly going monthly ASAP. 1st 3 issues of 1980 controlled circulation. 2,000 each." 6/yr. Pub'd 1 issue 1979; expects 5 issues 1980, 6 issues 1981. sub. price: $10/yr; per copy: $2.00; sample: $1.00. 32pp; 8½X11; of. Reporting time: 3-4 weeks. Copyrighted, reverts to author. Pub's reviews. §consider all materials rec'd. Ads: $150/$85/$50.

New Pages Press (see NEW PAGES)

NEW POETRY, The Poetry Society of Australia, Prism Books, Robert Adamson, Editor; Debra Adamson, Associate Editor, Box N110 Grosvenor St Post Office, Sydney, N.S.W. 2000, Australia. 1954. Poetry, fiction, articles, art, photos, interviews, criticism, reviews, long-poems. "NEW POETRY is at the centre of Australian poetry. We are primarily interested in contemporary poetry with a bias to the Black Mountain/post-Black Mountain influences, but we do publish a fairly extensive range of poetry and would like to extend our publication of criticism and reviews. NEW POETRY has published the most important new poets working in Australia alongside the established poets. Recent contributors include Robert Duncan, Michael McClure, Donald Davie, Charles Tomlinson, Robert Adamson, Jennifer Maiden, Charles Bukowski, Sylvia Kantarizis, Max Williams, Thom Gunn, Ribeyro, Tate, Strand, Michael Wilding. Although the magazine has been around for a while now, it is continually changing and growing, with the rest of Australian art. It is internationally significant. Essentially. Have a look for $2.00 (sample). Essential before submitting material to look at an issue." circ. 2,000. 4/yr. Pub'd 4 issues 1979. sub. price: $20.00(Australian) includes postage to institutions. $18.00 (Aust.) to individuals.; per copy: $4.50 (incl. post); sample: $2.00 (Aust.). Back issues: Pre 1972 are rare & about $5-$10 post 1972-$3.00/copy. Discounts: trade 40%; bulk 25%. 80pp; 22 cm x 14½ cm; of/lp. Reporting time: 6 weeks. Payment: min. $10.00 up to $200.00. Copyrighted, reverts to author. Pub's reviews: 22 in 1979. §Black Mountain & Post Black Mountain-Olson, Duncan, Pound, Creeley—et al. Ads: $50/$25. AIPA.

The New Poets Series, Clarinda Harriss Lott, Editor-in-Chief, 541 Piccadilly Rd., Baltimore, MD 21204, 301-828-8783. 1970. Poetry. "NPS chapbooks contain enough poems (or poems plus graphics) to make about 42 pp. of type. Editorial bias in favor of excellent material in an original voice. Most recent issue: *The Vinegar Year,* poems by Lynne Dowell. Next-to-last issue, *Blind Leading The Blind,* has been nominated by novelist Anne Tyler for The Pushcart Prize, a national small-press book award." avg. press run 1,000. Pub'd 3 titles 1979. 6 titles listed in the *Small Press Record of Books in Print* (9th Edition, 1980). avg. price, paper: $2.95. Discounts: $2.25 to bookstores; $2.95 retail; $2.50 to mail subscribers. 50pp; 5½X8½; of. Reporting time: 6 mos. Payment: none: all revenue from sales goes to publish the next issue. author holds own copyright. CCLM, COSMEP, Maryland Writers Council, Maryland Arts Council.

THE NEW RENAISSANCE, An International Magazine of Ideas & Opinions, Emphasizing Literature & The Arts, Louise T. Reynolds, Harry Jackel, Editor; Louise E. Reynolds, Manager; Stanwood Bolton, Poetry, 9 Heath Road, Arlington, MA 02174. 1968. Poetry, fiction, articles, art, photos, interviews, satire, criticism, reviews, music, letters, parts-of-novels, collages, plays. "*NO QUERIES W/O SASE.* Our only prejudice is toward writing which has something to say, says it w/some style, grace and speaks in a personal voice. We're not biased toward any age group (17 or 70, it makes no difference); sex; ethnic background; colour; or political stance, etc. We're prejudiced vs sloppy, careless writing, can't phrases or attitudes, & progaganda of any political or sociological set; we also object to writing which calls attention to itself or which emphasizes the superiority of the writer; we also do not want to see writing that is self-indulgent or self-consciously 'literary'. We have international interests and are interested in writing from all over the world. Beginning with January 1979, we are asking all writers who haven't bought an issue of *TNR* in 3 yrs. Submit to *TNR* to buy a back issue @ $1.90 US, Canada, $2.15 other, which is strong in their area or a current issue (TNR #9) at $2.75 US, Canada, $3.00 other, (fiction or poetry); *TNR #10* at $3.00 US (non-fiction or poetry). Recent contributors include: Allen Hoey, Charles Ghigna, John Hanley, Ruth Moose, John Kenny Crane, G.P. Vimal, Jane Somerville, Joan Colby, Larry Bailey, Tambuzi, James Hearst, Mary Engel, Ruth Good, Louis Ehrenkranz, Kathleen Susan Winkler, Eleanor Ehrenkranz, Beth Griffin, James E. A. Woodbury, Stanwood Bolton, Tom Wallace Lyons, Jane Mayhall, Barbara Holland, Wm. Aiken, Steve Carter, Melvin Martin, Gerald Flshrty, Kathleen Henry; Artists: Wm. Christopher, Sam Kirszencwajg, Nona Hatay, George Tooker." circ. 1,500. 2/yr. Pub'd 2 issues 1979; expects 2 issues 1980. sub. price: $7.00/3 issues, USA: $7.20/3 issues, Canada & Mexico; Europe, $8.00/3 issues; All others, $8.30; per copy: $3.50 USA; $3.60 Canada & Mexico; $3.75, Europe; $3.90, All others; sample: $1.90 (back issues). Back issues: Nos. 2-7, $1.90; No. 8-$2.40. Discounts: Agents, etc.: 22½%, 20 copies or more or classroom use: 20%; 50 or more copies, 30%. 104-120pp; 6X9; of. Reporting time: 10-30 weeks. Payment: $7.00 - $20.00 poems; $15.00 to $50.00 fiction; $35.00 to $75.00 non-fiction; $18.50 to $38.50 essay/reviews; $6.00 per drawing and/or visual art. Copyrighted, does not revert to author. Pub's reviews: 4 in 1979. §Do not want unsolicited books or magazines. Ads: $150/$85. CCLM.

New Rivers Press, Inc., C. W. Truesdale, 1602 Selby Avenue, St. Paul, MN 55104. 1968. Poetry, art, photos, long-poems, concrete art, fiction. "We publish new writing of merit and distinction, mostly poetry, some combinations of prose & poetry, & a fair number of translations. We like to use graphics in as many books as possible. We also do postcards, usually keyed to books we have published." avg. press run 750. Pub'd 12 titles 1979; expects 12 titles 1980. 10 titles listed in the *Small Press Record of Books in Print* (9th Edition, 1980). avg. price, cloth: $10.00; paper: $3.00; other: $2.00. Discounts: 40% trade discount; 25% discount to subscribers to all our publications. 48-96pp; size variable; of. Reporting time: 1-6 months. Payment: 100 copies of book to author, commissions (variable for art work). Copyrights for author. COSMEP, CCLM, PC.

NEW ROOTS, Rob Okun, News; Ellen Perley Frank, Features; Mitch Anthony, Patricia Greene, Resource, Box 548, Greenfield, MA 01301, (413) 774-2257/774-2258. 1978. Poetry, articles, art, photos, cartoons, interviews, satire, reviews, music, letters, collages, news items. circ. 50,000. 8/yr. Pub'd 6 issues 1979; expects 8 issues 1980. sub. price: $10.00; per copy: $1.50; sample: $1.50. Back issues: $1.50. 84pp; 8¼X10¾; of. Reporting time: 4 - 6 weeks. Payment: minimum 5¢ a word. Copyrighted, reverts to author. Pub's reviews: 25 in 1979. §Solar and renewable energy, community, culture, the Northeast, agriculture, environment, anti-nuke, cooperatives, spiritual arts, theatre, writing, photgraphy, health, nutrition, humor, health, how-to, children/family. Ads: $500.00/$360.-00/$0.50.

New Seed Press, We are a feminist collective & make decisions together, P.O. Box 3016, Stanford, CA 94305. 1972. Fiction, art. "We are a small feminist collective commited to publishing non-sexist, non-racist stories for children which actively confront issues of sexism, racism, classism. We are currently soliciting manuscripts by and about Third World women and children or stories by and about children of lesbians (or lesbian living situations). Manuscripts should be typed and sent with return stamped envelope. We will consider any length ms. though our budget usually forces us to limit the size of those we accept." avg. press run 2,000. Pub'd 2 titles 1979; expects 2 titles 1980, 2 titles 1981. avg. price, paper: $1.50; $2.00. Discounts: 40 percent to bookstores and distributors. Pay in advance including 15 percent postage. pp varies; size varies; †of. Reporting time: 2 months. Payment: varies. Copyrights for author.

The New South Company, Nancy Stone, 924 Westwood Blvd., Suite 935, Los Angeles, CA 90024, 213 477-2061. 1976. Fiction, art. avg. press run 2,000. Pub'd 2 titles 1979; expects 2 titles 1980, 2 titles 1981. 4 titles listed in the *Small Press Record of Books in Print* (9th Edition, 1980). avg. price, cloth: $10.00; paper: $6.00. Discounts: Furnished upon request. lp. Reporting time: 3 to 4 weeks. Payment: Varies. Copyrights for author.

NEW TIMES, Margaret Moran, 1000 21st Street, Rock Island, IL 61201, 309 786-6944. 1969. Poetry, articles, art, photos, cartoons, interviews, reviews, music, letters, news items. "Even though we only publish once a month we call *New Times* a newspaper and are members of Alternative Press Syndicate." circ. 2,300. 11/yr. Pub'd 12 issues 1979; expects 11 issues 1980, 11 issues 1981. sub. price: $4.00; per copy: $0.25; sample: free. Back issues: $0.30. Discounts: Agent keeps $0.20. 8pp; 10¾X16; of. Payment: none. Copyrighted. Pub's reviews: 4 in 1979. §Trial justice, jazz, peace, anti nuke. Ads: $158.40/$79.20/$1.50 per 10 words. APS.

New Traditions, Stephen Sossaman, Allen Coit Road, Norwich Hill, Huntington, MA 01050. 1979. Poetry, fiction. "With a Kelsey Star platen press, we plan an assortment of chapbooks, broadsides, postcards, and booklets. Our intention is to produce beautifully crafted hand-set editions of truly excellent writing, with paper, type, size, and press run selected to fit each work rather than to comply with a standard format. Because of our limited time, we absolutely will not read or consider unsolicited manuscripts. The data below represents our expectations as we begin." avg. press run 100-500. Expects 1 title 1980, 2-3 titles 1981. avg. price, paper: $1.00-$10.00. Discounts: 40% to bookstores. 1-16pp; †lp. Copyrights for author. NESPA.

NEW UNIONIST, Jeff Miller, Greg Cecil, 621 West Lake Street, Rm 301, Minneapolis, MN 55408, (612) 823-2593. 1975. Articles, cartoons, news items, photos, reviews, letters. circ. 1,400. 12/yr. Pub'd 11 issues 1979; expects 12 issues 1980, 12 issues 1981. sub. price: $2.00; per copy: $0.20; sample: free. Discounts: $0.10 each. 6pp; 8½X11; of. No outside manuscripts. Payment: copies only. Pub's reviews. §Socialism, labor, politics, current affairs.

New Victoria Publishers, Claudia Lamperti, 7 Bank St., Lebanon, NH 03766, (603) 448-2264. 1977. Poetry, fiction, art, photos. "There are two companies: New Victoria Publishers, and a printing shop, New Victoria Printers. Non-profit" avg. press run 1000. Pub'd 1 title 1979; expects 2 titles 1980, 3 titles 1981. 3 titles listed in the *Small Press Record of Books in Print* (9th Edition, 1980). avg. price, paper: $3.00. 50pp; 5½X8½; 8½X11; of. Reporting time: 2 weeks. Payment: in copies. Copyrights for author. COSMEP, NESPA.

NEW VIRGINIA REVIEW, Editorial Board, PO Box 415, Norfolk, VA 23501, (804) 622-1991. 1978. Poetry, fiction, articles, art, photos, interviews, parts-of-novels, long-poems. "We are primarily interested in first-rate work by Virginia residents: poetry; fiction; articles on the arts in Virginia; interviews with notable writers. We also reproduce art and photography. In adddition to works by Virginians, we also consider material from notable visitors to the state, such as guest writers and artists at Virginia universities. We do *not* publish criticism or reviews. We strive for a balance between well-established contributors and promising newcomers. We try to encourage openness and diversity by appointing new fiction, poetry, articles, and art editors each year." circ. 1,500. 1/yr. Pub'd 1 issue 1979. sub. price: $12.00; per copy: $12.00; sample: $12.00. Back issues: $15.00. Discounts: cost to bookstores is $6.00. 250pp; 7X10⅞; of. Reporting time: 3 to 6 months. Payment: upon publication. Copyrighted, rights held jointly by author and publisher. Ads: No ads.

New Visions Press, Herbert Mertz Jr., PO Box 2025, Gaithersburg, MD 20760, (301) 869-1888. 1979. "Publishers of *Workers' Capitalism.*" Pub'd 1 title 1979. avg. price, paper: $3.95. Discounts: 40% to bookstores. 215pp; 5½X8½; of.

270

NEW VOICES, Don Fried, P. O. Box 308, Clintondale, NY 12515. 1972. Poetry, fiction, satire, parts-of-novels, long-poems, plays. "NV is dedicated to airing the work of unpublished or little known writers. Although some photographs and graphics are used, only those which can be clearly reproduced by offset should be submitted." circ. 500 plus. 1/yr. sub. price: $3.50; per copy: $3.50; sample: $3.50. Back issues: $2.00. 300pp; 5½X8½; of. Reporting time: 1 month. Payment: copy. Copyrighted, reverts to author. CCLM, COSMEP.

NEW VOICES, Lorraine Moreau Laverriere, 24 Edgewood Ter, Methuen, MA 01844, (617) 688-1669. 1980. Poetry. "Prefer personal poetry that reflects sensitivity of thoughts & ideas. Any style. Like short poems (45 lines or less). New and umpublished poets encouraged to submit. All mss will be read carefully. I don't believe in formal rejection slips. Would rather accept one poem to provide space for more voices." circ. 200. 4/yr. Pub'd 4 issues 1979. sub. price: $7.50; per copy: $2.00; sample: $2.00. Back issues: $1.00 (when available). Discounts: standard. 40pp; 5½X8½; of. Reporting time: 2 weeks or ASAP. Payment: 1 copy. Copyrighted, reverts to author.

New Woman Press, Jean Mountaingrove, Ruth Mountaingrove, Box 56, Wolf Creek, OR 97497. 1975. Poetry, music, photos, art, long-poems. "Book Published: *Turned-On Woman Songbook,* 34 pages, 27 original songs, feminist bent, photos and drawings. 1975, $3.00 tapes available: 12 songs-custom-$6.50; 18 songs-pre-chosed $5.00. Book Published: *For Those Who Cannot Sleep,* by Ruth Ikeler/Mountaingrove, 82 pages, 13 illustrations by Chrystos, Introduction, 63 page poem. 1977 $3.50. Tape available: reading of poem by author, $5.50." Pub'd 2 titles 1979. 3 titles listed in the *Small Press Record of Books in Print* (9th Edition, 1980). of. Payment: royalties/15% on songbook, 15% on poetry. COSMEP.

NEW WOMEN'S TIMES & NEW WOMEN'S TIMES FEMINIST REVIEW, Martha Brown, Karen Hagberg, Maxine Sobel, 804 Meigs Street, Rochester, NY 14620. 1975. Articles, art, photos, cartoons, interviews, satire, criticism, reviews, music, letters, news items. "*The New Women's Times* bi-weekly newspaper includes feature length articles, no more than 700-1,000 words (2½ - 3 typed double spaced pages) on health, politics, ed., legal etc. All with feminist perspective. *The New Women's Times Feminist Review,* a bi-monthly supplement reviews feminist writings, art, music, poetry, etc." circ. 15,000-20,000. 24/yr. Pub'd 24 issues 1979; expects 24 issues 1980, 24 issues 1981. sub. price: $12.00 individuals/$24.00 institutions; per copy: $.50; sample: $.50. Back issues: $1.00 includes newspaper & review supplement. Discounts: Special agreements available upon request. 16-20pp; 10½X14½; of. Reporting time: 3 month max. Payment: Complimentary subscription, copies of article. Copyrighted, reverts to author. Pub's reviews: 125 in 1979. §All books pertinent to feminist & women's issues. Ads: $675.00/$337.50/$.50. COSMEP.

‡**NEW WORLD JOURNAL, Turtle Island Foundation,** Bob Callahan, 2845 Buena Vista Way, Berkeley, CA 94708. 1975. Poetry, fiction, articles, art. "New world history and literature: Anderson, Barlow, Callahan, Cardenal, Dorn, Dawson, DeAngulo, DiPrima, HD, Irey, Metcalf, Olson, Sauer, Tarn." circ. 1,000. 2/yr. price per copy: $3.00; sample: $3.00. Discounts: 40% trade. 64-96pp; 5½X8½; †lp. §New World Letters. CCLM, COSMEP.

New Worlds Unlimited, Sal St. John Buttaci, Susan Linda Gerstle, PO Box 556, Saddle Brook, NJ 07662. 1974. Poetry. "We seek previously unpublished poems (length 2-14 lines) rich in imagery, poems that show intelligent treatment of universal themes and reveal the poet's understanding, even limiteed of the poetry craft. We use about 400 poems per annual hardcover anthology. Writer's guidelines for SASE. Annual poetry contest dealines April 15. Recent contributors: Barbara Holland (NY), Beverly Giambrese (NJ), Arnold Perrin (Maine), Esther Leiper (NH)." avg. press run 700. Pub'd 1 title 1979; expects 1 title 1980, 1 title 1981. avg. price, cloth: $10.95. Discounts: cost to libraries, bookdealers, schools in quantity copies, $7.95. 130pp; 7X10; of. Reporting time: from immediately to 6 months. Copyrights for author. COSMEP, NAPA.

NEW YORK ARTS JOURNAL, Richard Burgin, 560 Riverside Drive, New York, NY 10027. 1976. Poetry, fiction, articles, art, photos, cartoons, interviews, satire, criticism, reviews, music, letters, parts-of-novels, long-poems, collages, concrete art. "NEW YORK ARTS JOURNAL tries to achieve a balance between worthwhile creative achievement and critical reflection in dealing with the major art forms. As such it is open to different styles of work. Contributors in our first issue included: John Cage, Alain Robbe-Grillet, Duane Michals, David Shapiro, Robert Bly, John Updike, Jonathan Baumbach and George Stude." circ. 25,000. 25/yr. sub. price: $4.00; per copy: $1.00; sample: $1.00. Back issues: $2.00 plus postage. Discounts: classroom-institutions 15%/ad agencies 15%. 44pp; 11½X15½; of. Reporting time: maximum 1 month. Payment: poetry $1.00-line/prose $3.00-page. Pub's reviews: 25 in 1979. §criticism, fiction, poetry, music, art. Ads: $300.00/$160.00.

The New York Literary Press (see also EUTERPE), Margaret Leong, Scott Ellis Leong, Editors, 419

West 56th St., New York, NY 10019. 1977. Poetry, fiction, art, photos, parts-of-novels, plays. "*The New York Literary Press* has, at present published four books of poetry and two collections of children's verse (in addition to *Euterpe*)." avg. press run 500. Pub'd 3 titles 1979; expects 3 titles 1980, 3 titles 1981. 4 titles listed in the *Small Press Record of Books in Print* (9th Edition, 1980). avg. price, cloth: $2.50; paper: $2.50; other: $2.50. 5½X8; of. Reporting time: 3 months (all manuscripts are solicited). Copyrights for author.

NEW YORK QUARTERLY, William Packard, Editor; Marjorie Finnell, Senior Editor, PO Box 2415 G Central Stn., New York, NY 10017, 212-242-9876. 1969. Poetry, articles, photos, interviews, letters, long-poems. "Poetry, articles (on the craft of writing poetry — usually staff-produced), photos(staff-produced), craft interviews with outstanding poets on the subject of writing poetry (staff-produced only), letters of interest to poets on the craft of poetry, longpoems rarely. Read 'How to Submit Manuscripts' in *NYQ* #13 for description of *NYQ* screenng procedures. One issue per year 1974-1977. Back on a quarterly schedule effective 1978." circ. 2-5M. 4/yr. Pub'd 1 issue 1979; expects 4 issues 1980, 4 issues 1981. sub. price: $17 (libraries), $11 (individuals), Foreign: add $2 for mailing; per copy: $3.00; sample: $3.00. Back issues: $4.00. Discounts: negotiable. 100+pp; 6X9; of. Reporting time: 1-3 months. Payment: copies; two awards of $100 each per issue. Copyrighted. Ads: $350/$200/$3.75-line. CCLM.

NEW ZEALAND MONTHLY REVIEW, Caxton Press, Box 345, Christchurch, New Zealand. 1959. circ. 2,100. 11/yr. sub. price: $6.00; per copy: $0.60. Back issues: difficult. 24pp; size crown; lp. Payment: nil. copyright: ours. Pub's reviews: 20 in 1979. §Political, social, poetry. Ads: $50.00/$25.00.

NEWORLD, Fred Beauford, 6331 Hollywood Blvd #624, Los Angeles, CA 90028, 465-1560. 1974. Poetry, fiction, articles, art, photos, interviews, criticism, reviews, letters, parts-of-novels. circ. 10,000. 6/yr. Pub'd 6 issues 1979; expects 6 issues 1980, 6 issues 1981. sub. price: $7.50, $12.00/2 yrs.; per copy: $1.25; sample: $1.25. Back issues: $3.00 each. 56pp; 8½X11; of. Reporting time: 1 month. Payment: $50.00 article. Copyrighted. Pub's reviews. §The arts. Ads: $500/$350.

NEWS AND LETTERS, News and Letters Press, Charles Denby, Editor; Felix Martin, Co-Editor; O. Domanski, Managing Editor, 2832 E Grand Blvd, Detroit, MI 48211, 313 873-8969. 1955. Articles, photos, cartoons, interviews, criticism, reviews, letters, news items. circ. 7,000. 10/yr. Pub'd 10 issues 1979; expects 10 issues 1980, 10 issues 1981. sub. price: $1.00; per copy: $.10; sample: free. Back issues: $.10 each; bound volumes available, prices on request. Discounts: Bulk order of five or more copies $.06 each. 8-12pp; 11½X14½; of. Reporting time: no limit. Not copyrighted. Pub's reviews: 22 in 1979. §Labor movement, Marxism, Black struggle, history, women's movement, philosophy, the Third World, economics, Hispanic, Native, and Asian American movements, anti-war, youth movement, revolution, anti-nuclear movement. Ads: No ads.

News and Letters Press (see also NEWS AND LETTERS), Charles Denby, 2832 East Grand Blvd. Rm 316, Detroit, MI 48211. 1955. Articles, photos, cartoons, interviews, criticism, reviews, letters, news items. "*News & Letters* was founded in 1955, the year of the Detroit wildcats against Automation and the Montgomery, Ala. Bus Boycott against segregation — activities which signalled new movements *from practice*, which were themselves a form of theory. *News & Letters* was created so that the voices from below could be heard, and the unity of worker and intellectual could be worked out for our age. A Black production worker, *Charles Denby,* is the editor. The paper is the monthly publication of News and Letters Committees, an organization of Marxist-Humanists that stands for the abolition of capitalism, whether in its private form as in the U.S., or in its state form calling itself Communist, as in Russia and China. The National Chairwoman, *Raya Dunayevskaya,* is the author of *Philosophy and Revolution* and *Marxism and Freedom* which spell out the philosophic ground of Marx's Humanism for our age internationally, as *American Civilization on Trial* concretizes it on the American scene. In opposing this capitalistic, exploitative, racist, sexist society, we participate in all freedom struggles and do not separate the mass activities of workers, Blacks, women and youth from the activity of thinking. We invite you to join with us both in the freedom struggle and in working out a theory of liberation for our age." avg. press run 7,000. 32 titles listed in the *Small Press Record of Books in Print* (9th Edition, 1980). Discounts: 20% trade discount. mi/of.

THE NEWS CIRCLE, ARAB AMERICAN ALMANAC, Joseph Haiek, PO Box 74637, Los Angeles, CA 90004, (213) 483-5111. 1972. Articles, photos, cartoons, interviews. "On Arab Americans community affairs." circ. 5,000. 12/yr. Pub'd 12 issues 1979; expects 12 issues 1980, 12 issues 1981. sub. price: $10.00; per copy: $1.00; sample: $0.50. Back issues: $2.00. Discounts: 40% more or less. 16pp; 12X17; of. Reporting time: 2 weeks. Payment: 5¢ per word. Pub's reviews: 12 in 1979. §On Arab Americans, Arab World & Middle East affairs. Ads: $294.00/$176.00/$10.00 col in.

NEWS FROM NEASDEN, 12 Fleet Road, London NW3 2QS, United Kingdom. 1975. "Mailed free to bookshops (120 in Australia and New Zealand, 50 in Europe, 400 in North America, 300 in UK). *NFN* lists new radical publications. We charge publishers for entries. We have added a 20-page-section of 'real' reviews which has helped bookshop sales and subscriptions." circ. 3,000. 3/yr. sub. price: £2.50/$6.00 Libraries £5.00/$10.00 (includes annual index & address list); per copy: 80p/$2.00; sample: free to libraries. 80pp; 5X8¼; of. Pub's reviews. §Left and radical. Ads: £30/$60.00 per title for commercial publishers, £20/$40.00 for non-commercial publishers, £10/$20.00 for a title selling at £1/$2.00 for less. Exchange ads welcomed with periodicals. APS.

NEWS RELEASE FROM THE CHESS PRESS SYNDICATE, Kxe6s Verein R Press, Steven Buntin, PO Box 2204, Chapel Hill, NC 27514. 1977. Poetry, fiction, articles, art, photos, cartoons, interviews, satire, criticism, reviews, letters, parts-of-novels, collages, plays. "News service and redactor for Chess Press Syndicate." Discounts: None. We are our own agents. 2+pp; 8½X14; †mi/of. Not copyrighted. Pub's reviews. §Chess, board games, freedom of press. COSMEP, CCLM, COSMEP/EAST.

THE NEWSCRIBES, Vincent Campo, Greg Collins, Len Rysdyk, Harriet Brown, 1223 Newkirk Avenue, Brooklyn, NY 11230, (212) 282-8461. 1976. Poetry, fiction, articles, art, satire, criticism, letters, parts-of-novels, long-poems. "Length depends on the quality of material submitted. *Jestful of Ashes* a novel has been serialized, along with another novel, ran 24 pages in last issue. Short stories can be as long as they must be; the same with poetry. Some articles of special value to get the mag into literary places have been given special preferences; *Paranoia, Nixon, and Psychiatry* plus an excerpt from a novel *Iagotello* to exemplify paranoia, printed in Vol 2 Fall 1977; *The Vico Connection to James Joyce's Ulysses* pp 7-15 Voll 2 #3&4 Winter 77; *Queen Tiy,* the first liberated woman in histry (King Tut's mother) pp 7-23 Vol III, 1978. All the articles written by Vincent Campo and all scholarly work. No censorship of content." circ. 600. 2/yr. Pub'd 2 issues 1979; expects 2 issues 1980, 2 issues 1981. sub. price: $5.00; per copy: $2.00 + 75¢ mailing; sample: none. Back issues: We have every few back issues. We save a few for past purposes. Of which we've got none yet. Discounts: none. 125pp; 5½X8; of. Reporting time: immediate, one or two days. Payment: one magazine to non-members. Copyrighted. Ads: $100.00/$50.00. CCLM, COSMEP, NYSWP.

NEWSFRONT INTERNATIONAL, Collective, 4228 Telegraph Avenue, Oakland, CA 94609, (415) 654-6725. 1975. Articles, interviews, news items. "Translations and compilations from the progressive world press. We also published two pamphlets, *Portugal: Key Documents of Re Revolutionary Process* 1975. *Second Class, Working Class: an International Women's Reader* 1979" circ. 1,200. 11/yr. Pub'd 11 issues 1979; expects 11 issues 1980, 11 issues 1981. sub. price: $12.00; per copy: $1.00; sample: free. Back issues: 1st issue $1.00 each, additional $0.75. Discounts: bookstores, 60/40. 20pp; 8X11½; of.

NEWSLETTER, Long Island Poetry Collective, Inc., Board of Directors, PO Box 773, Huntington, NY 11743. 1974. Criticism, reviews, news items. "Features include: calendar of regional literary events (Long Island-NY City), 4-10 reviews per issue, an extensive small press markets column, and other informational materials of useto readers/writers of poetry." circ. 600. 8/yr. Pub'd 8 issues 1979; expects 8 issues 1980. sub. price: $3.50 mailed first class; per copy: $0.50; sample: $0.50. Back issues: vol 3 (1976-1977) $5.00/ 10 issues; vol 4 (1977-78) $5.00/7 issues. 24pp; 8½X7; of. Reporting time: 2-4 weeks. Payment: in copies. Not copyrighted. Pub's reviews: 60 in 1979. §poetry (or poetry in combination with short fiction, graphics, etc.). Ads: none. CCLM.

NEWSREAL, Joan Rosen, Box 40323, Tucson, AZ 85717, 887-3982. 1974. Poetry, articles, interviews, reviews, music, letters, news items. "Length of material no more than 2 typewritten pages double spaced. Biases no sexist material. Recent contributors: Skip Williamson (cartoonist), Paul Krassner (writer), David Armstrong (writer)." circ. 15,000. 12/yr. Pub'd 12 issues 1979; expects 12 issues 1980, 12 issues 1981. sub. price: $6.00; per copy: free; sample: free. Back issues: $1.00. Discounts: trade, sometimes; mostly paid advertisement. 24-32pp; 10¼X16; of. Payment: none. Pub's reviews: 2 in 1979. §Music, energy, environmental, non-fiction, women. Ads: $375.00/$207.00/$5.75 col in. APS.

Nexus Press, Michael Goodman, 608 Forrest Road, NE, Atlanta, GA 30312, (404) 577-3579.

NHM Publications, Nancy H. McKeithan, 1517 Seabrook Avenue, Cary, NC 27511, (919) 467-2596.

THE NIAGARA MAGAZINE, Neil Baldwin, 195 Hicks St., Apt. 3B, Brooklyn, NY 11201. 1974. Poetry. "We are looking for poetry which reflects a deep commitment to temporal and/or spiritual landscapes. We continue to seek a dynamic poetry which uses space, enjambments, tensions in unusual ways; I have a personal aversion to 'flat,' sentence like, genteel poems. We publish the very well-known and also the very new—as long as it's exciting, projective, positive poetry. Although we have shifted locales from Buffalo to NYC, I consider the force and vitality of 'NIAGARA' to be a state of mind. I suggest you send for a sample copy before submitting work." circ. 500 plus. 2/yr. Pub'd

2 issues 1979; expects 2 issues 1980. sub. price: $5.00; per copy: $2.00; sample: $2.00. Back issues: No. 3, (Irish issue,) $1.50. No. 7, (Winter 1977), $2.00; No. 9, (Fall 1978, Robert Creeley interview), $2.50; No. 10/11 (fall 1979), $2.00. Entire back run available to libraries for $30.00. Please write for details. Discounts: 40% trade discount. 52pp; 8½X6¾; of. Reporting time: 12 weeks at most. Payment: copies. Copyrighted, we will transfer copyright in writing, upon request. no ads. CCLM, NYSSPA.

NICOTINE SOUP, Sea Of Storms, Laura Brown, Eric Brown, Robert C. Davidson, P.O. Box 22613, San Francisco, CA 94122, (707) 795-2098. 1975. Poetry, fiction, art, photos, cartoons, long-poems, collages, concrete art. "Contributors: Laurel Spear, Randy Mott, Robert Scotelero, Neil Shepard, Nancy Weber. Biases: We publish writers and artists who are under-published or unpublished. No particular length requirements." circ. 500. 3/yr. Pub'd 4 issues 1979; expects 3 issues 1980, 3 issues 1981. sub. price: $4.00; per copy: $1.50; sample: $1.00. Discounts: Libraries, 20%; Bookstores, 40%; Jobbers, 40%; Distributors, 50%. 36pp; size Varies; of. Reporting time: 2 months. Payment: none. Copyrighted, reverts to author. Ads: No ads. COSMEP, CCLM, CODA.

Nighthawk Press, Cliff Martin, Frank Scott, PO Box 813, Forest Grove, OR 97116. 1979. Photos, criticism, music, news items. "Contemporary music criticism, history, discography and reference" avg. press run 1,000-2,000. avg. price, cloth: $14.95; paper: $9.95. Discounts: 5 books plus 40%; (retailers) 25 books plus 50% (wholesalers) 10% on standing orders (libraries). 200pp; 5½X8½; of. Reporting time: 2-4 weeks. Payment: varies with individual book, typically small advance and std royalty. Copyrights for author. COSMEP, PNWBPA.

Nikmal Publishing, Selma H. Lamkin, 698 River St., Mattapan, MA 02126, (617) 361-2101. 1978. avg. press run 25. Expects 3 titles 1980, 1 title 1981. 5 titles listed in the *Small Press Record of Books in Print* (9th Edition, 1980). avg. price, paper: 4 - 8 - 13 - set $22.50. 85pp; 5X7; †of. Copyrights for author.

NIMROD, Francine Ringold, Arts and Humanities Council of Tulsa, 2210 So. Main, Tulsa, OK 74114. 1956. Poetry, fiction, articles, art, photos, interviews, parts-of-novels, long-poems, plays. "Recent contributors: David Ray, Winston Weathers, Stephen Kennedy, Paulette Millchap, Carol Haralson, H.L. Van Brunt, E.M. Broner, Lance Henson, Paul Scott, Stanley Sulkin, Ellen Bass, Isaac Bashevis Singer, Victoria Ocampo, Judith Johnson Sherwin, Cynthia MacDonald, Peter Viereck, Jorge Luis Borges, Toni Morrison, Lucille Clifton, Kofi Awoonor, James Allen McPherson. Double issue for 1977, Vol. 21, No. 2 and Vol. 22, No. 1 — published *New Black Writing: Africa, West Indies, the Americas* . Bonus subscription including *New Black Writing* (a double issue) and *Nimrod*, '78 — $5.00. *Nimrod*, spring/summer 1978 Vol. 22, No. 2 contains the work of James Purdy, William Peden, William Stafford, Kate Green, and others and features translations from Armenian, Spanish, French, Paraquayan, Hungarian, and Latin poets. The forthcoming issue: Nimrod Prize Issue will feature the winners of the second annual Nimrod Literary Awards: $500.00 first prize and $250.00 second prize for fiction and poetry. Submissions for the second annual prize will be welcomed from September, 1980 through January 25, 1981. Copies of first annual prize issue may still be purchased at $2.25." circ. 1,000 (counting subscriptions & direct sales). 2/yr. Pub'd 2 issues 1979; expects 2 issues 1980. sub. price: $6.00; per copy: $3.25; sample: $2.25. Back issues: $1.50 each up through Vol. 19, No. 2. 125pp; 6X9; of. Reporting time: 12-16 weeks. Payment: up to $5 a page. Copyrighted, reverts to author. §Poetry. Ads: $85/$50. CCLM, COSMEP.

NIT&WIT: Literary Arts Magazine, Leonard J. Dominguez, Kathleen J. Cummings, Publisher, 1908 W. Oakdale Ave., Chicago, IL 60657, (312) 248-1183. 1977. Poetry, fiction, articles, art, photos, cartoons, interviews, satire, criticism, long-poems, letters, parts-of-novels, reviews, news items. "All poems & short stories typewritten, photograph (black and white glossies) and graphics (black and white) will be thoughtfully considered. Work will be returned if accompanied with a self-addressed, stamped envelope. *Nit&Wit* requests that manuscripts be limted to 2,000 words." circ. 5M. 4/yr. Pub'd 2 issues 1979; expects 4 issues 1980, 4 issues 1981. sub. price: $5.95/yr, $10.00/2 yrs; per copy: $1.00; sample: $1.00. Back issues: $1.50. Discounts: Negotiable. 48pp; 5½X8½; of. Reporting time: 6-8 weeks. Payment: copies. Copyrighted, reverts to author. Pub's reviews: 0 in 1979. Ads: $225.-00/$130.00/$35.00 smallest size. COSMEP MIDWEST.

"NITTY GRITTY", Goldermood Rainbow Press, Bill Wilkins, Editor, 331 W. Bonneville, Pasco, WA 99301, 509-547-5525. 1974. Poetry, fiction, articles, art, photos, cartoons, interviews, satire, criticism, reviews, letters, concrete art. "Articles, commentary, fiction: maximum 10,000. Poetry-mostly short. Reviews-short: maximum 500 words. Cartoons-humor-photos." circ. 4,000. 2/yr. Pub'd 3 issues 1979; expects 2 issues 1980. sub. price: $10.00; per copy: $6.00; sample: $6.00. Back issues: $6.00. Discounts: trade 40%. 250pp; 8½X11; †of. Reporting time: 120 - 180 days. Payment: fiction $15, poetry & photos $2, cartoons & art work $5, commentary-personal experiences-reviews-articles $10. Copyrighted, rights do not revert. Pub's reviews: 30 in 1979. §all small press. Ads: $50/$30/$20

1/4/none. COSMEP, CCLM.

No Dead Lines, John Daniel, Venetia T. Gleason, 241 Bonita, Portola Valley, CA 94025, 415-851-1847. 1975. Poetry, fiction, art. "We experiment with alternative forms of fine book publishing. Emphasis on poetry, prose, and graphics. Each of our books is unique. Write for free catalog." avg. press run 300. Pub'd 6 titles 1979; expects 2 titles 1980, 2 titles 1981. 11 titles listed in the *Small Press Record of Books in Print* (9th Edition, 1980). avg. price, paper: $6.00. Discounts: 40% to bookstores & contributors. 50pp; 5½X8½; of. Reporting time: 2 weeks. Payment: authors get 2 free copies of their work, 40% discount thereafter. Copyrights for author.

No Tickee/No Washee Enterprises Ltd (see BILE)

Noble House Publishing, Robert Miller, 256 South Robertson, Beverly Hills, CA 90211, (714) 675-1230. 1979. Photos, news items. "Published one book, *Gringo*, 241-page book about a young man's unjust arrest and imprisonment in Mexico - his mistreatment, frustrations, and eventual comic escape. Upon returning to the US, Robert Miller appeared on TV and radio talk shows and before the US Senate, talking about his ordeal. Reaction and comments by Dan Rather of *60-Minutes* and Jane Fonda are included on back cover, as are excerpts from articles written in the Los Angeles Times and People Magazine about Mr. Miller and his experiences. The book has a wide audience appeal, in that the young man was innocent, and suffered this abuse while visiting the nearby country of Mexico, a popular tourist attraction for Americans of all ages." avg. press run 2,000. Pub'd 1 title 1979. avg. price, cloth: $10.95. 241pp; 6X9; †lp. Copyrights for author.

Nobodaddy Press (see also POETRY IN MOTION), David Lehman, Stefanie Green, Joel Black, 100 College Hill Rd., Clinton, NY 13323, 315-853-6946. 1976. Poetry, long-poems. "*The Reading of an Ever-Changing Tale,* a chapbook of poems by John Yau. Special limited editions of avant-garde poetry, 'High Quality Publishing.' The first 50 copies of an edition are signed by author and by artist (cover design). *Day One,* a book of poems, by David Lehman" avg. press run 500 copies. Pub'd 2 titles 1979. 6 titles listed in the *Small Press Record of Books in Print* (9th Edition, 1980). avg. price, paper: $3.50. Discounts: The usual trade discount of 40 percent. 28-40pp; 5½X8½; †of/lp. Reporting time: It varies. Payment: Author receives 100 copies. Copyrights for author. CCLM.

NOE VALLEY POETS WORKSHOP, Cassandra Publications, 7397 Boris Court #9, Rohnert Park, CA 94928. 1974. Poetry. "We publish only books by workshops members. We publish only books and the prices vary." circ. 500. 1-2/yr. Pub'd 5 issues 1979. 1 title listed in the *Small Press Record of Books in Print* (9th Edition, 1980).

NOK Publishers International, Chivuzo Ude, Luther Henkel, 150 Fifth Ave, Suite 826, New York, NY 10011, (212) 675-5785. 1973. Poetry, fiction. "We are devoted to publishing the growing amount of research available on Africa and to providing a publishing forum for authors involved in this area. We publish academic, scholarly and cultural books." avg. press run 2,000-3,000. Pub'd 5 titles 1979; expects 12 titles 1980, 20 titles 1981. avg. price, cloth: $18.00; paper: $4.95. Discounts: 40% retail bookstores, 10% to Univ. libraries, 20% for foreign and book jobbers. 300pp; 6X9; of. Copyrights for author. COSMEP.

Nolo Press, PO Box 544, Occidental, CA 95465, (707) 874-3105. 1971. "Our books are written to help the average person take care of his or her own legal problems. We now have 20 books covering such 'how to do your own' divorce, estate planning, homestead, name change, corporation, immigration, etc." avg. press run 7,000. Pub'd 2 titles 1979; expects 2 titles 1980, 3 titles 1981. 15 titles listed in the *Small Press Record of Books in Print* (9th Edition, 1980). avg. price, paper: $8.95. Discounts: trade 1-4 books, none; 5-9 books, 25%; 10 or more, 40%. Reporting time: we don't use outside writers. COSMEP.

Nor Publications (see also NEW OREGON REVIEW), 537 N.E. Lincoln St, Hillsboro, OR 97123.

Nordic Books, Niels Malmquist, PO Box 1941, Philadelphia, PA 19105, (215) 574-4258. 1978. Photos. "Subsidized book on Scandinavia, literature, articles, translations, etc., also Vikings. Will also consider non-subsidized material. Currently one title: translation of Nordahl Grieg's poems of the sea *Around Cape The Good Hope* translated by Lars Egede-Nissen." avg. press run 1,500-2,000. Pub'd 1 title 1979; expects 1 title 1981. 1 title listed in the *Small Press Record of Books in Print* (9th Edition, 1980). avg. price, cloth: $6.95; paper: $3.25. Discounts: Trade. 48pp; 5½X8½; of. Reporting time: 2 weeks. Payment: On individual basis. Copyrights for author.

Norman Bethune Institute, Canadian Cultural Workers' Committee, PO Box 727, Adelaide Station, Toronto, Ontario M5C 2J8, Canada. 1970. Poetry, fiction, articles, art, photos, cartoons, interviews, criticism, music, plays, news items. "NBI is a research institute and publisher of progressive books. It has published books and pamphlets on a wide range of subjects, from the politics and economics of Canada to the National liberation struggles of the peoples of various countries of Asia, Africa and Latin America, to books of poetry and culture, the struggles of the immigrants in Canada against racial discrimination and violent repression, books about the People's Socialist Republic of Albania, posters of various kinds." avg. press run 2,000-5,000. Pub'd 36 titles 1979; expects 55 titles 1980. avg. price, cloth: $6.50. Discounts: 20% discount on orders of 10 copies or more. 16-600pp; 5½X8⅜; of.

Noro Press (see also BEYOND RICE, A Broadside Series; NORO REVIEW), Geraldine Kudaka, P.O.Box 1447, San Francisco, CA 94101. 1979. Poetry, fiction, articles, art, photos, interviews, satire, criticism, reviews, long-poems, plays. "Noro Press has in the workings a magazine (NORO REVIEW) and an anthology. The anthology, to be released Spring 1982, is of erotica. It covers a broad range including interpersonal relationships, gay love, true confessions, sado-masochism, etc. Seeking visual art, poetry, short fiction, articles and criticism. Payment will be made upon publication at $5.00 per printed page. Include SASE" avg. press run 1,200. Pub'd 1 title 1979. avg. price, paper: $4.00; other: $6.00 per single copy. Discounts: 40% for orders of more than 10 plus postage. 96pp; 5½X8½. Reporting time: 4-6 weeks. Payment: erotic anthology: $5.00 per printed page; all others in copies. Copyrights for author.

NORO REVIEW, Noro Press, Geraldine Kudaka, P.O.Box 1447, San Francisco, CA 94101. Poetry, fiction, plays. "NORO REVIEW is a literary magazine focussing on but not limited to Asian American/multi-cultural writers. Will consider poetry of any length, fiction up to 30 pages, and one act plays" circ. 1,200. Reporting time: 4-6 weeks. Payment: copies. Copyrighted.

NORTH AMERICAN MENTOR MAGAZINE, John Westburg, Publisher, John Westburg, Mildred Westburg, General Editors; Martial Westburg, Art Editor, 1745 Madison Street, Fennimore, WI 53809. 1964. Poetry, fiction, articles, art, photos, satire, criticism, reviews, parts-of-novels, long-poems, plays. "We offer an annual poetry contest, with cash awards and certificates of merit. Contestants must be paid subscribers. Write for contest rules." circ. 350-500. 4/yr. Pub'd 4 issues 1979; expects 4 issues 1980. sub. price: $11.00; per copy: $4.00; sample: $1.25. Back Issues: Volume 1-2, $150.00; Volume 3-4, $50; all others, $3.00 per number. Discounts: None. 60-90pp; 8½X11; †of. Reporting time: 2 to 3 months. Payment: 1 copy. Copyrighted, does not revert to author. Pub's reviews: 4 in 1979. §Art, anthropology, poetry, fiction, history, literary criticism, and political science. Ads: none. CCLM.

THE NORTH AMERICAN REVIEW, Robley Jr. Wilson, Univ. Of Northern Iowa, Cedar Falls, IA 50613, 319-266-8487/273-2681. 1815. Poetry, fiction, articles, reviews, long-poems. "Environmental focus." circ. 3,000. 4/yr. Pub'd 4 issues 1979; expects 4 issues 1980, 4 issues 1981. sub. price: $8.00; per copy: $2.00; sample: $1.50. Back issues: face price. Discounts: Agent 20 percent; bulk (10 or more) 30 percent. 80pp; 8½X11; of. Reporting time: 8 weeks. Payment: $10.00 per published page; 50 cents a line for poetry. Copyrighted, assigned on request of author. Pub's reviews: 33 in 1979. §poetry & short fiction. Ads: $300.00/$175.00. CCLM, COSMEP.

North American Students of Cooperation (see also CO-OP: The Harbinger of Economic Democracy), Margaret Lamb, Editor, Box 7293, Ann Arbor, MI 48107, (313) 663-0889. 1971. Articles, cartoons, interviews, satire, reviews, letters. "1,000-4,000 words. Articles should be related to cooperatives, esp. consumer co-ops, or similar efforts at social change. Double-spaced. Returned only if accompanied by stamped self-addressed envelope" avg. press run 3,500. Pub'd 4 titles 1979; expects 5 titles 1980, 6 titles 1981. 11 titles listed in the *Small Press Record of Books in Print* (9th Edition, 1980). avg. price, paper: $1.75. Discounts: 40%. 48pp; 6X9; of. Reporting time: 2 weeks. COSMEP.

North Atlantic Books (see also Io (named after moon of Jupiter)), Richard Grossinger, 635 Amador Street, Richmond, CA 94805, 415-236-1197. 1973. Poetry, fiction. "Authors: Richard Grossinger, Diane Di Prima, Edward Sanders, Lindy Hough, Irene McKinney, Bernadette Mayer, Don Byrd, Gerrit Lansing, Wayne Turiansky, Theodore Enslin, Paul Kahn, Josephine Clare, Bobby Byrd, Alex Gildzen, Janet Rodney, Robert Caswell, Roy Rappaport, Edward Whitmont, David Henderson." avg. press run 2,000. Pub'd 4 titles 1979; expects 5 titles 1980, 5 titles 1981. 9 titles listed in the *Small Press Record of Books in Print* (9th Edition, 1980). avg. price, cloth: $20.00; paper: $5.95. Discounts: refer to Io. 250pp; 6X9; of. no unsolicited manuscripts. Payment: 10%. Copyrights for author.

North Country Press, P.O. Box 12223, Seattle, WA 98112. 1975. "We are only a book publisher, not a magazine. Our only book is The World Of A Giant Corporation, an unauthorized report on General Electric, by John Woodmansee with Ralph Nader, Derek Sheaver, and others, paperback $2.95." 1 title listed in the *Small Press Record of Books in Print* (9th Edition, 1980). Discounts: 40 percent trade thru us or our distributor, carrier pigeon; please write for info on higher discounts to wholesalers, indicating quantity & payment schedule to be used. of. Although we correspond with anti-corporate groups, we are not seeking any new manuscripts.

North Star Press, John N. Dwyer, P.O. Box 451, St. Cloud, MN 56301, (612)253-1636. 1969. Poetry, fiction. "Books only. Main theme is middle western Americana. Prefer not over 50M word mss. Not presently soliciting mss. Have full list hu fall, 1981." avg. press run 2500-3000. Pub'd 4 titles 1979; expects 4 titles 1980, 4 titles 1981. 20 titles listed in the *Small Press Record of Books in Print* (9th Edition, 1980). avg. price, cloth: $8.00; paper: $6.50. Discounts: regular trade 40%; large order single title will give 2½ to 3% additional. 160pp; 6X9, 5½X8½; of. Reporting time: 2 weeks. Payment: 10%. Copyrights for author. Minn Book Publ Roundtable.

‡**NORTH STONE REVIEW, Tendon Press,** University Stn. 14098, Minneapolis, MN 55414. CCLM.

North West Arts (see THE ARTFUL REPORTER)

THE NORTH WIND, Beaver Lodge Press, Susan Walsh, Co-Editor; Pam Martin, Editor, Box 65583, Vancouver 12, B. C. V5N 5K5, Canada. 1974. Articles, art, reviews. "We would like articles on medieval and renaissance crafts, skills, manners etc. of about 500 to 1,000 words, from *any* culture. This is a newsletter/research organ of the Northern Society for Creative Anachronism. People associated with SCA (and there are about 4,000 of them) will know what we want. Rigour demanded, i.e. proper footnotes and references are required." circ. 200. 10/yr. Pub'd 12 issues 1979; expects 12 issues 1980, 10 issues 1981. sub. price: $7.00; per copy: $0.50. 24pp; 21X28 cm; †mi/of. Reporting time: 2 weeks. Payment: copies. Copyrighted. Pub's reviews: 10 in 1979. §If they relate to medieval skills or history. Ads: Inquire.

NORTHEAST/JUNIPER BOOKS, John Judson, 1310 Shorewood Dr., LaCrosse, WI 54601. 1962. Poetry, fiction, articles, art, interviews, criticism, reviews, parts-of-novels, long-poems. "We solicit any work of quality that has a human being behind it whose words help shape his and our awareness of being human. This has always come before fashion, reputation or ambition in our eyes. Juniper books are chapbooks. A subscription includes two NE's and 4 Juniper books per year, 2 haika books plus gifts." circ. 4-500. 2/yr. Pub'd 10 issues 1979; expects 10 issues 1980. sub. price: $15.00/$22.00 for complete sub including 2 fine printed poetry bks per-yr plus NE and all Juniper Books.; per copy: $2.50; sample: $2.00. Back issues: write for information/most are available but in very small quantities. 60-80pp; size varies; †of/lp. Reporting time: 6-8 wks. Payment: 2 copies. Copyrighted, reverts to author. Pub's reviews. §poetry, crit., experimental fiction. no ads. CCLM.

✓ **NORTHEAST JOURNAL,** Miles Parker, Editor-in-Chief; Tina Letcher, Indu Suryanarayan, Associate Editors, P.O. Box 235, Annex Sta, Providence, RI 02901. 1969. Poetry, fiction, articles, art, photos, interviews, satire, criticism, reviews, long-poems, plays. "*Northeast Journal* was previously published under the name of *Harbinger*. The staff is open to any work of quality. Unknown writers are welcome to submit. *Northeast Journal* is presently funded by a matching grant from the CCLM, National Endowment for the Arts & Rhode Island Council for the Arts." circ. 600. 2/yr. Pub'd 1 issue 1979; expects 1 issue 1980, 2 issues 1981. sub. price: $3.50; per copy: $2.00; sample: free with 9x6 SASE - 60¢ U.S. postage. Discounts: 33% to bookstores. 60pp; 5½X8½; of. Reporting time: 3-6 months. Payment: 1 yr subscription. Copyrighted, reverts to author. Pub's reviews: 5 in 1979. §poetry, fiction, biography, criticism. CCLM, COSMEP.

NORTHEAST RISING SUN, Cherry Valley Editions, Pamela Beach Plymell, Joshua Norton, Brown Miller, Hugh Fox, Carl Weissner, Jorg Fauser, Box 303, Cherry Valley, NY 13320, 607-264-3204. 1976. Articles, criticism, reviews, interviews, letters, news items. circ. 2,000. 8/yr. Pub'd 8 issues 1979; expects 8 issues 1980. sub. price: $10.00; per copy: $1.50; sample: $1.50. Discounts: 40 percent - 50 percent. 32pp; 5½X8½; of. Reporting time: a. s. a. p. Payment: pay at going rate for reviews. Copyrighted, reverts to author. Pub's reviews: 100 in 1979. §all literary. Ads: $50.00/$35.00. CCLM, NYSSPA, COSMEP/EAST.

Northeastern University Press, Robilee Smith, Editor, Northeastern Univ. Press, P.O. Box 116, Boston, MA 02117, 617 437-2783. 1977. "Scholarly books only." avg. press run 500. Pub'd 3 titles 1979; expects 5 titles 1980, 5 titles 1981. 1 title listed in the *Small Press Record of Books in Print* (9th Edition, 1980). avg. price, cloth: $16.95; paper: $8.95. Discounts: 10% to libraries and teachers; 20% to distributors. 250pp. Copyrights for author.

Northern House (see also STAND), 19 Haldane Terrace, Newcastle upon Tyne NE2 3AN, United Kingdom. 21 titles listed in the *Small Press Record of Books in Print* (9th Edition, 1980).

NORTHERN LIGHT, George Amabile, Co-Editor; Douglas Smith, Co-Editor, 605 Fletcher Argue Bldg., Univ. of Manitoba, Winnipeg, Manitoba R3T2N2, Canada, 204-474-8145. 1968. Poetry, reviews, letters. "Any length poem is possible, though we've found that few longpoems are really sustained. We want poetry which uses the subtle rhythms of speech, strong images, fresh metaphor, intense patterns of verbal music, which are original and subtle, and a central coherent theme or context. We don't like chatty poems, 'street' poetry which is often illiterate and boring, literary puzzles, word games, typographical doodling, abstract prose laid out in lines to look like poetry, or meaningless 'free association'. Manuscripts without SASE will be destroyed. Recent contributors include Pat Lane, Elizabeth Brewster, Alan Safarik, Kenneth McRobbie, Thomas McGrath, Susan Musgrave, Peter Wild, Robert Bagg, Richard Emil Braun, etc. We prefer to publish young Canadian Poets, and also do reviews of recent books of Canadian poetry." circ. 1,000. 2/yr. Expects 2 issues 1980, 2 issues 1981. sub. price: $3.65; per copy: $2.00; sample: $2.00. Back issues: Full set (including far point 1-8) $50.00. Discounts: 10% agencies 40% student rate (bulk) for classroom use. 64pp; 8⅝X5⅝; of. Reporting time: 1 mo. Payment: 5 copies. copyright: NL & U. of M. Press. Pub's reviews. §Recent books of Canadian poetry. Ads: $100.00/$65.00/$40.00. COSMEP, CPPA.

NORTHERN LINE, Poetry Leeds Publications, Dr. Mark Burke, 75 Outwood Lane, Leeds, W. Yorks LS18 4HU, United Kingdom, 0532-588995. 1978. Poetry, fiction, articles, art, photos, cartoons, reviews. "*Northern Line* is the only regular British magazine to concentrate wholly on work by children & teenagers - contributors must have been born 1960 or later. Only bias is in favour of printing the best work available from all over Great Britain - art-work, poetry *short* prose-fiction." circ. 2,000. 4/yr. Pub'd 4 issues 1979; expects 4 issues 1980. sub. price: $6.00; per copy: $1.50; sample: $1.50. Back issues: current issue: #10; back issues $1.00 each (all rates include postage, etc.). Discounts: negotiable: British rates £1.80 (our year sub), 45p single copy. 28-32pp; 6X9; of. Reporting time: 3 months. Payment: copies. Copyrighted, reverts to author. Pub's reviews: 30 in 1979. §Anything to do with young people's creativity & mags, anthologies of young people's work. Ads: $40.00/$25.00. PLP, ALP.

NORTHERN NEIGHBORS, Dyson Carter, PO Box 1210, Gravenhurst, Ont. P0C 1G0, Canada. 1949. "Staff produced-we do not accept submissions." circ. 12,000. 11/yr. Expects 11 issues 1980, 11 issues 1981. sub. price: $4.00; per copy: $.75; sample: $.25. Back issues: $1.00 per copy. 28pp; 9X11; of. Payment: none.

Northland Publications, Stanley J. Goodwin, Box 12157, Seattle, WA 98102. avg. price, paper: $2.40. Discounts: 40-60%. 84pp; 4½X7.

NORTHWEST CHESS, Robert A. Karch, PO Box 613, Kenmore, WA 98028, (206) 486-5430. 1947. Fiction, articles, art, photos, cartoons, interviews, reviews, letters, news items. "We are interested in chess-related material of all kinds. There's no need for a 'regional slant'; chess is much the same in the Northwest as it is elsewhere. Longer material would probably be broken into parts for consecutive issues" circ. 1100 mostly in the Northwest. 12/yr. Pub'd 12 issues 1979; expects 12 issues 1980, 12 issues 1981. sub. price: $6.00 USA, $10 foreign; per copy: $0.50; sample: $0.50. Back issues: from $0.25 to $1.00 each, depending on year. Discounts: Free exchange with other chess mags/30 percent disc. to agents/$3.00 per year to institutional residents in the USA. 32pp; 7X11; of. Reporting time: 2 weeks. Payment varies from contributors' copies to about $15.00 for articles. Not copyrighted. Pub's reviews: 20 in 1979. §chess and impact of computers on chess. Ads: $30.00/$15.00/$0.05. COSMEP, AUSCJ.

Northwest Matrix, Charlotte Mills, Nancy Clark, PO Box 984, Waldport, OR 97394, 503-563-4427. 1975. Fiction, articles, criticism. "NW Matrix is a feminist publishing house. We only publish woman authors. 1. We're interested in women's history, anthropology, politics and literature; 2. Essays or short papers on same topics for essay series 'Current feminist topics'. 3. Fiction, biography, history (non-sexist) for young adults." avg. press run 1,200. Pub'd 1 title 1979. avg. price, paper: $4.00. Discounts: 40 percent for all orders over 5 for each title. 150pp; 5¼X8¼; of. Reporting time: 1-3 mos. Payment varies. Copyrights for author. COSMEP, WIP.

NORTHWEST REVIEW, University of Oregon Press, Michael Strelow, Editor; Deb Casey, Fiction Editor; Jay Williams, Poetry Editor, 369 P.L.C., University of Oregon, Eugene, OR 97405, 503-686-3957. 1957. Poetry, fiction, art, photos, reviews, parts-of-novels, long-poems, plays. "Recent contributors: Wm. Stafford, John Woods, Greg Kuzma, Douglas Blazek, in poetry; Albert Drake, Jerry Bumpus, Joyce Carol Oates in fiction. Bias: Quality in whatever form. No other predisposition." circ. 2,000. 3/yr. Pub'd 3 issues 1979; expects 3 issues 1980. 2 titles listed in the *Small Press Record of Books in Print* (9th Edition, 1980). sub. price: $6.00; per copy: $2.50; sample: $2.00. Back issues: $2.50 all except double issues or specially priced issues. Discounts: bookstore/agencies:20% consignment & 40% wholesale. 132pp; 6X9; of. Reporting time: 6 weeks. Payment 3 copies. Copyrighted. Pub's reviews: 15 in 1979. §literature/poetry fiction:special Northwest interest materials. Ads: $100.-00/$60.00. CCLM, COSMEP.

NORTHWOODS JOURNAL, Northwoods Press, Inc., Robert W. Olmsted, Managing Editor; Paul Hodges, Editor, PO Box 249, Stafford, VA 22554, (703) 659-6771. 1972. Poetry, fiction, articles, art, cartoons, interviews, satire, criticism, reviews, letters, long-poems. "Bias against writing about writing. Fiction to about 3,000 words. Bias Pet Peave *We hate SASE of less than full #10 size!* $2 reading fee required for now. Subscribers - we send several back issues so writers will only submit totally inappropriate stuff *once.*" circ. 300. 4/yr. Pub'd 8 issues 1979; expects 4 issues 1980, 4 issues 1981. sub. price: $6.00; per copy: $2.00; sample: $2.00. Back issues: $2.00 if available, most are not. Discounts: None. 60pp; 5½X8½; †of. Reporting time: 2-10 weeks. Payment: $1.00 per page minimum. Copyrighted, does not revert to author. Pub's reviews: 24 in 1979. §all small press or self published works. Ads: No ads accepted.

Northwoods Press, Inc. (see also NORTHWOODS JOURNAL), Robert W. Olmsted, President, PO Box 249, Stafford, VA 22554, (703) 659-6771. 1972. Poetry, fiction, news items. "Request author's guide before submitting anything" avg. press run 1,000-2,000. Pub'd 13 titles 1979; expects 34 titles 1980, 15 titles 1981. 52 titles listed in the *Small Press Record of Books in Print* (9th Edition, 1980). avg. price, cloth: $12.95; paper: $3.95; other: $25.00 collector's. Discounts: 2% per book after 1st to 50% max. 120pp; 5½X8½; of. Reporting time: 1 day to 3 months. Payment: individual agreement, basically 10% first 2,500; 12½% next 2,500; 15% all over 5,000. Copyrights for author.

NOSTALGIAWORLD, Dennis F. Sullivan, PO box 231, North Haven, CT 06473, 203-239-4891. 1978. Articles, art, photos, cartoons, interviews, reviews, music. "Unsolicited nostalgia materials will not be acknowledged or returned without return postage and self-addressed envelope. The right is reserved to edit material submitted for publication. Now accepting articles and pictures on TV shows, movies, broadway musicals, records and recording artists. Emphasis on music personalities." circ. 10,000. 6/yr. Pub'd 6 issues 1979; expects 6 issues 1980, 12 issues 1981. sub. price: $15.00; per copy: $1.25; sample: $1.25. Back issues: $2.00. Discounts: Apply, apply, apply. State quantity. 28pp; 12X17; of. Reporting time: 60 days. Payment: apply. Copyrighted, does not revert to author. Pub's reviews. §TV, movie stars, movies, broadway musicals, records and recording artists. Ads: $95.-00/$50.00/$0.10.

NOSTOC, Arts End Books, Marshall Brooks, Editor; Bill Costley, Editor-At-Large, Box 162, Newton, MA 02168. 1973. Poetry, fiction, articles, criticism, reviews, parts-of-novels. "We have no biases; no special requirements. We publish both known and unknown writers. Interested in small press history." circ. 500. Minimum of 2 issues/yr. Pub'd 2 issues 1979; expects 2 issues 1980, 2 issues 1981. sub. price: $3.00; per copy: $.75; sample: $.75. Back issues: rates on request. Usual trade discount. 30pp; 5½X8½; †lp/of. Reporting time: immediately. Payment: copies. Copyrighted, reverts to author. Pub's reviews: 30 in 1979. §small press history. Ads: rates on request.

Not-For-Sale-Press, Lew Thomas, 243 Grand View Ave, San Francisco, CA 94114, 415-647-4290. 1975. Articles, art, photos, interviews. "*8 x 10,* 1975, compiled by Lew Thomas, 48 pgs. 21 photos. *PERFORMANCES AND INSTALLATIONS,* Kesa. 1976, 62 pages, 50 photos." Pub'd 1 title 1979; expects 3 titles 1980. 9 titles listed in the *Small Press Record of Books in Print* (9th Edition, 1980). avg. price, paper: $8.95. Discounts: 40% trade, 55% wholesale. 48-120pp; 8X10, 9X12; of.

NOT GUILTY!, The Not Guilty Press, Derek Pell, P.O.Box 2563, Grand Central Station, New York, NY 10017. 1975. "Absurdist texts & documents. Recent contributors: Paul Eluard, Peter Payack, Opal Louis Nations, Ed Woods, Paul Gogarty, Ed Sanders, Charles Haseloff, Richard Kostelanetz, Tuli Kupferberg, Marcel Marien. Please read before submitting manuscripts" circ. 250. irreg. Pub'd 2 issues 1979. sub. price: $8.00/yr; per copy: $1.75. Back issues: Vol.1, #2 ($2.50); Vol. 1, #3 (op); vol 1, #4 ($2.50); vol 1, #5/6 ($3.50). Discounts: 50% on cash orders. Standard 40% on all others. 80pp; 5½X8½; of. Reporting time: from here to eternity. Payment: 2 copies. Copyrighted, reverts to author. Pub's reviews: 23 in 1979. §Fiction, poetry, surrealist humor. NYSSPA, ASPCA.

The Not Guilty Press (see also NOT GUILTY!), Derek Pell, P.O.Box 2563, Grand Central Station, New York, NY 10017. 1968. Poetry, fiction, satire, long-poems, collages. "Sorry, no unsolicited manuscripts." avg. press run 250-500. Pub'd 2 titles 1979; expects 4 titles 1980, 4 titles 1981. Discounts: standard 40%. of. Copyrights for author. NYSSPA, ASPCA.

NOT MAN APART, Friends of the Earth, Tom Turner, Editor; Eleanor Smith, Managing Editor, 124 Spear Street, San Francisco, CA 94105. 1970. Poetry, articles, art, photos, cartoons, reviews, letters. "Suggest reading a sample issue before submitting. We concentrate on national and global environmental issues, with a political perspective. Also review books of environmental concern." circ. 25,000. 12/yr. Pub'd 12 issues 1979; expects 12 issues 1980, 12 issues 1981. sub. price: $15.00; per copy: $1.25; sample: free. Back issues: $.25 copy. 24pp; 11½X15 (tabloid); of. Reporting time: varies 2-8 wks. Payment: copies. Copyrighted, does not revert to author. Pub's reviews: 20-30 in 1979. §environment, food, eco-fiction (whatever you take that to mean). Ads: $420.00/$260.00/$0.50.

NOTES & QUERIES: for Readers & Writers, Collectors & Librarians, E.G. Stanley, J.D. Fleeman,

D. Hewitt, Pembroke College, Oxford OX1 1DW, United Kingdom. 1949. 12/yr. sub. price: £5($13.00); per copy: 50p ($1.30).

NOTES FROM THE UNDERGROUND, Franson Publications, Michael J. Dunn, 4291 Van Dyke Place, San Diego, CA 92116. 1975. Poetry, articles, interviews, reviews, letters. "Send submissions to editor: Michael J. Dunn, 28614 25th Place South, Federal Way, WA 98003." irreg. sub. price: no subscriptions. Back issues: Vol I (issues 1-10) softbound, $10.00; Vol II (issues 11-20) softbound, $16.00. Discounts: 40%/5 copies. 150pp; 11X8½; of. Reporting time: 2 weeks. Payment: royalties. Copyrighted, reverts to author. Pub's reviews.

NOTTINGHAM MEDIAEVAL STUDIES, Antonia Gransden, The University, Nottingham NG7 2RD, United Kingdom. 1957. Articles. "Articles on mediaeval language, literature, history, etc. concerning the whole of Europe making up to some 20 pp of print @550 words per page." circ. 500. 1/yr. sub. price: £3.50; per copy: £3.50. Back issues: £3.50. Discounts: £3 (trade price). 100pp; 7X9½. Reporting time: 2 mos.

NOUMENON, Brian Thurogood, Sagittarius Publications, 40 Korora Road, Oneroa, Waiheke Island, New Zealand, WH-8502. 1976. Articles, art, photos, cartoons, interviews, satire, criticism, reviews, music, letters, news items. "Science fiction magazine" circ. 600. 10/yr. Pub'd 10 issues 1979; expects 9 issues 1980, 10 issues 1981. sub. price: US $12.25/10 Airmail; $7.00/10 seamail; per copy: $0.75; sample: free. Back issues: detailed card available. Discounts: Trade 33⅓%. 29pp; 6¼X9; †of. Reporting time: 1 month. Payment: negotiable. Copyrighted, reverts to author. Pub's reviews: 150 in 1979. §Science fiction. Ads: $30.00/$15.00.

Noumenon Press (see also INTERSTATE), Loris Essary, Mark Loeffler, PO Box 7068, University Station, Austin, TX 78712. 1974. Poetry, fiction, art, photos, music, long-poems, collages, plays, concrete art. "Available titles are Carl D. Clark, *Desire, Chasing A Cow;* Susan Bright Buchanan, *Container;* [Tamara O'Brien, *Affairs;* (out-of-print; available by special arrangement only)] Jeff Woodruff, *Farm To Market;* Paul B. Miner, *Your Mother Wears Combat Boots;* Loris Essary, *Ending;* David Gene Fowler, *Hit Man Reduction,* Dirk H. Van Nouhuys *The Synthesis of Alcuen L. Adams, 205 W 11th,* Loris Essary *Stele.* Manuscripts are currently by invitation only and writers should submit their work to INTERSTATE magazine. A sample copy of a book is available for $2.50." Pub'd 2 titles 1979; expects 3 titles 1980. 12 titles listed in the *Small Press Record of Books in Print* (9th Edition, 1980). of. Reporting time: Immediately. Payment: copies. Copyrights for author.

John L Noyce, Publisher (see also LIBRARIANS FOR SOCIAL CHANGE; STUDIES IN LABOUR HISTORY), John L. Noyce, P.O. Box 450, Brighton, Sussex BN1 8GR, United Kingdom. 1970. Articles, cartoons, interviews, news items. "Bibliographies, directories, etc. of use to the Alternative Community, etc; and a series on Alternative Technology (10 titles in this series so far). Also Librarianship." avg. press run varies. 14 titles listed in the *Small Press Record of Books in Print* (9th Edition, 1980). Discounts: 25 percent. 10-200pp; size A4; †mi/of. Reporting time: we try. Payment: 10 percent royalty plus free copy. Copyrights for author.

NRG, Skydog Press, Dan Raphael, David Whited, 228 S.E. 26th, Portland, OR 97214, (503) 231-0890. 1975. Poetry, fiction, art, music, letters, parts-of-novels, long-poems, collages, concrete art, photos. "Solid bias—spatial (in Communicative Cybernetics)—to be reacted w/—the work as 4 dimensional resultant of words/meaning/energy rampant in the associational/re-membering matrix-organism of mind; gut-sense disorientation/travel. Kempton, Grabill, Beining, Helmes, Essary, Rhammings, Mr Nips, Dec." circ. 400. 3/yr. Pub'd 3 issues 1979; expects 4 issues 1980. sub. price: $2.25; per copy: $.75; sample: stamps. Back issues: $0.75 12,9-6, 3-2; $1.50 10 & 11. Discounts: negotiable. 12pp; 11X17; of. Reporting time: less than 1 month. Payment: copies. copyright reverts to author. Pub's reviews: 3 in 1979. §Visual, experimental. no ads. CCLM.

NUTRITION ACTION, Center for Science in the Public Interest, Tom Monte, 1755 'S' Street, N. W., Washington, DC 20009, (202) 332-9110. 1974. Articles, art, photos, cartoons, interviews, criticism, reviews, letters, news items. circ. 20,000. 12/yr. Pub'd 12 issues 1979; expects 12 issues 1980, 12 issues 1981. sub. price: $10.00/yr; per copy: $1.00; sample: free. Discounts: Full-time students and people 65 years of age $7.50; bulk orders of 10 or more subscriptions, $6.00 each. 16pp; 8½X11; of. Reporting time: 1 month (approx.). Payment: negotiable, but not much. Copyrighted, reverts to author only if requested. Pub's reviews: 6 or 7 in 1979. §food/health/nutrition/fitness/gardening/related areas.

NUTRITION HEALTH REVIEW, Vegetus Publications, Frank Ray Rifkin, Andrew Rifkin, 143 Madison, New York, NY 10016. 1976. Poetry, fiction, articles, art, photos, cartoons, interviews, satire, criticism, reviews. "Subjects relating to Nutrition, Vegetarianism, Animal Welfare" circ. 110,000. 4/yr. Pub'd 8 issues 1979; expects 8 issues 1980, 8 issues 1981. sub. price: $8.00-2 yr, 8 issues; per copy: $1.25; sample: $1.25. Back issues: $1.25. Discounts: 50% for retail stores. 32pp; size tabloid; of. Reporting time: 60 days. Payment: negotiable. Copyrighted. Pub's reviews: 30 in 1979. §Nutrition, health, psychology. Ads: $1200.00/$600.00/$250.00. COSMEP.

O

O Press, Michael Lally, 190 A Duane Street, New York, NY 10013. 1974. Poetry. "I do only books-no unsolicited ones-all 'poetry' or poets' writing-titles include: *Theory of Emotion* by Diane Ward and *Facade* by David Drum-Forth coming: Books by Tim Dlugos, Doug Lang, etc." avg. press run 300. Pub'd 1 title 1979; expects 1 title 1980, 1 title 1981. 4 titles listed in the *Small Press Record of Books in Print* (9th Edition, 1980). avg. price, paper: $2.00. 32pp; size varies; of.

The Oak Arts Workshop Limited, Rupert Mallin, General Editor, 10 Snow Hill, Clare, Sudbury, Suff, United Kingdom. 1975. Poetry, fiction, articles, art, photos, cartoons, interviews, satire, criticism, reviews, letters, parts-of-novels, long-poems, collages, plays, concrete art. avg. press run 300. Pub'd 2 titles 1979. avg. price, paper: £1.00. Discounts: 40%. 80pp; size A4; †mi/of/lp. Reporting time: 1 month. Payment: copies plus small cash payment, depending on funds. Does not copyright for author. ALP, ALM.

OASIS, Oasis Books, Ian Robinson, 12 Stevenage Road, London SW6 6ES, United Kingdom. 1969. Articles, poetry, fiction, art, photos, reviews, interviews, criticism, music, letters, long-poems, plays, collages, concrete art. "Single author issues only. Write before submitting. Any length & style, high quality essential. International in content; we publish a good proportion of material in translation. We do not favour 'big name' contributors, but beginners face stiff competition. Submissions must be accompanied by usual return postage—sorry, no time to comment on rejections. Recent contributors: D.E.Steward (USA), John Perlman (USA), I.P.Taylor (U.K.), Peter Dent (U.K.), Matthew Sweeney (Eire), Robert Vas Dias (USA), Elaine Randell (U.K.), Richard Caddel (U.K.), Robin Fulton (Scotland)" circ. 500+. 5/yr. Pub'd 5 issues 1979; expects 5 issues 1980, 5 issues 1981. sub. price: £5.00 for 10 issues or International Money Order; per copy: 70p ($1.50); sample: 70p ($1.50). Back issues: £1.00/£2.00. Discounts: books-trade 25 percent single copies, 5 or more 40 percent. 16pp; size A5; †of. Reporting time: as soon as possible — usually one month. Payment: copies. Copyrighted, reverts to author. Ads: £8/£4/£2 1/4 page. ALP (U.K.) & IPD.

Oasis Books (see also OASIS), Ian Robinson, 12 Stevenage Rd., London, England SW6 6ES, United Kingdom. 1969. Poetry, long-poems. "Oasis Books publish high-quality poetry and prose from the UK, North America and from other languages in translation, by both established and less well known poets in the form of booklets or full-length volumes. Mostly solicited mss only. Some recent titles: SIX MODERN GREEK POETS (tr. John Stathatos); SNATH, Martin Booth; *Half a Century of Kingston History* F. Sommer Merryweather; *HMS Little Fox* Lee Harwood; *Boston Brighton* Lee Harwood; *37 Poems* Werner Aspenstrom; *Casino* John Ash; *The Manual for the Perfect Organization of Tourneys* Paul Evans; *Athens Blues* Yannis Goumas; *Snapshots* Antony Lopez; *Tracts of the Country* John Wilkinson; *White Flock* Anna Akhmatova; *A Night with Hamlet* Vladimir Holan; *Selected Poems* Jean Claude Renard; *Deathfeast* Takis Sinopoulos; *Window* Leon Stroinski; *The Water Spider* Marcel Bealu; *Fading into Brilliance* David Chaloner; *Stones* Takis Sinopoulos; *How the Snake Emerged from the Bamboo Pole but Man Emerged from Both* Marvin Cohen" avg. press run 500. Pub'd 5 titles 1979; expects 5 titles 1980. 21 titles listed in the *Small Press Record of Books in Print* (9th Edition, 1980). avg. price, paper: $1.50 to $4.50. Discounts: 40% over 5 copies, 25% otherwise (trade only). 36-100pp; size A5; †of/lo/lp. Reporting time: 1 wk to 1 mo. Payment: by arrangement. Copyrights for author. ALP, IPD (Independent Press Distribution).

OBSIDIAN: BLACK LITERATURE IN REVIEW, Alvin Aubert, English Dept., Wayne State Univ., Detroit, MI 48202. 1975. Poetry, fiction, articles, interviews, criticism, reviews, parts-of-novels, long-poems, plays. 3/yr. Pub'd 3 issues 1979; expects 3 issues 1980, 3 issues 1981. sub. price: $5.50; per copy: $2.00. Back issues: $2.00. Discounts: 10 percent discount to subscription agencies. 100pp; 5½X8½; of. Reporting time: 2 - 4 weeks. Payment in copies. Copyrighted, reverts to author. Pub's reviews: 8 in 1979. §Black literature in English worldwide. Ads: $50.00/$30.00/$0.30. CCLM, COSMEP.

Occasional Productions, David D. Edwards, Editor & Publisher, 251 Parnassus Ave, San Francisco, CA 94117. 1978. avg. press run 1,500. Expects 1-3 titles 1980. 1 title listed in the *Small Press Record of Books in Print* (9th Edition, 1980). avg. price, paper: $4.95. Discounts: 40% to book dealers; 20%

classroom use. 128pp; 7X7; †of. Copyrights for author.

OCCASIONAL REVIEW, Realities, Soos, 1976 Waverly Ave., San Jose, CA 95122, (408) 251-9562. 1979. Articles, interviews, criticism, reviews. circ. 600. Pub'd 2 issues 1979; expects 5 issues 1980, 8 issues 1981. sub. price: 2 issues, $1.00; per copy: $0.71; sample: $0.71. Back issues: Issue #1. $1.50. 24-36pp; 5½X8; †mi. Reporting time: 2-3 weeks. Payment: copies. Copyrighted, reverts to author. Pub's reviews: 30 in 1979. §Poetry, literature, criticism, drama, education, Spanish language, magazines. Ads: $15.00/$10.00. COSMEP.

OCCIDENT, James A. Powell, John Talbot Hawkes, Paul Lake, Florence Verducci, 103 Sproul Hall, University of California, Berkeley, CA 94720. 1881. Poetry, fiction, interviews, criticism, reviews. "OCCIDENT seeks to publish the best in poetry, fiction, and criticism. Our particular interests are well-crafted poetry and criticism of poetry informed by a knowledge of poetics, both modernist and traditional. We are interested in critical essays on Ezrea Pound, the Objectivist school, and subsequent poetry that has carried forward or adapted their procedures, as well as essays on modern poetics. We have also published articles on Yvor Winters and on poetry and rhetoric. We are especially interested in work — criticism as well as poetry — that seeks to extend poetry's purview beyond its current narrowly prescribed bounds, poetry that strives to engage the full range of human experience — public, historical, political, and economic, as well as personal, private, and subjective. We are not interested in disembodied poetry: formal and rhythmic attention are imperative, whether their artifice derives from traditional or modernist sources. In fiction we are interested in both mainstream and experimental work, our only criterion being high quality. We also regularly include translations. Recent contributors include John Hawkes, Donald Davie, Raymond Carver, Thom Gunn, Phillip Levine, Seamus Heaney, John Peck, Leonard Michaels, Carl Rakosi, C.H.Sisson, Charles Tomlinson and Les Murray" circ. 1,000-1,500. 3/yr. Expects 1 issue 1980, 3 issues 1981. sub. price: $8.00/3 issues; institutions $15.00/3 issues; per copy: $3.00; sample: $3.00. 52-64pp; 8½X11; of. Reporting time: 4-6 weeks. Payment: 5 copies. Copyrighted, reverts to author. Pub's reviews: 12 in 1979. §poetry, short fiction, novels, poetics, criticism. Ads: $150.00/$80.00/$40.00(1/4 pg).

THE OCHLOCKONEE REVIEW, Steven W. Huss, 3190 Whirlaway Trail, Tallahassee, FL 32308, (904) 893-5325. 1979. Poetry. "Three issues expected in 1980." circ. 200. 3-4/yr. sub. price: $4.00; per copy: $1.50; sample: $1.50. 25pp; 4X5¾; of. Reporting time: 4-6 weeks. Payment: 2 copies. Copyrighted, reverts to author. Pub's reviews. §Poetry, chapbooks, small magazines.

Tom Ockerse Editions, Thomas Ockerse, 37 Woodbury Street, Providence, RI 02906, 401-331-0783. 1967. Poetry, fiction, articles, art, photos, collages, concrete art. "The intended purpose of T.O.E. is to publish monographs of works by artists whose work is structured by a primary commitment to concrete language, i.e., self-describing/self-referal." avg. press run 300-1,000. Pub'd 1 title 1979; expects 2 titles 1980. 12 titles listed in the *Small Press Record of Books in Print* (9th Edition, 1980). avg. price, cloth: $20.00; paper: $4.00; other: $100.00. pp varies/no limit; size varies; of/lp/silkscreen/x-erox. Payment varies. Copyrights for author.

Kathleen P. O'Donnell, Kathleen P. O'Donnell, 103 Bryn Mawr Avenue, Lansdowne, PA 19050, 259-9391.

Odin Press, Livia Raynes, PO Box 536, New York, NY 10021, (212) 744-2538. 1977. "Terms are net 30 days, FOB New York, NY 10021. Orders up to 100 lbs will be shipped via United Parcel Service or USPS special fourth class rate. Shipments over 100 lbs will be shipped Motor Freight. Refunds, less the cost of shipping, will be made for books returned in saleable condition within nine months of purchase date. For additional information contact Livia Raynes, Editor Odin Press, PO Box 536, New York, NY 10021." avg. press run 2,500. Pub'd 1 title 1979. avg. price, cloth: $10.95; paper: $2.95. Discounts: 1-9, 25%; 10-24, 40%; 25-99, 43%; 100-299, 46%; 300 or more, 50%. 208pp; 4¼X5½; of. Reporting time: 3 months. Payment: advance up to $2,000.00; royalty 10-15%, depending on volume. Copyrights for author. COSMEP, NESPA.

Odyssey Publishing Company, Route 3, Box 698, Yakima, WA 98901, (509) 452-5531. 1979. avg. press run 10,000. Pub'd 1 title 1979. 1 title listed in the *Small Press Record of Books in Print* (9th Edition, 1980). avg. price, paper: $4.00. 150pp; 5½X7; †of.

OFF OUR BACKS, Vickie Leonard, Carol Anne Douglas, Mary Klein, Alice Henry, Janis Kelly, Fran Moira, Tacie Dejanikus, Lin Jansen, Wendy Stevens, 1724 20th st. N.W., Washington, DC 20009, 202-234-8072. 1970. Art, articles, photos, cartoons, interviews, criticism, reviews, letters, news items. "Consider ourselves a radical feminist *news* journal, with prison, struggle, culture, & health & reviews section. Free to prisoners." circ. 15,000. 11/yr. Expects 11 issues 1980. sub. price: $7.00 Indiv.; $20.00 Institutions (Inc. libraries); $7 Canadian; $13 foreign; $12 contributing subsc.; per copy: $0.75; sample: $0.75. Back issues: $0.75. Discounts: for 5 or more copies monthly: 35¢ of 75¢ cover.

282

price; billed/paid quarterly. 36pp; 10½X14; of. Reporting time: 3 months. Payment: copies. Copyrighted, reverts to author. Pub's reviews: 35-40 in 1979. §women. Ads: $200.00/$100.00/10¢. COSMEPA, NESPA.

THE OFFSHORE CREWMAN'S NEWSLETTER (see Offshore Research Service)

Offshore Press, Anthony Petruzzi, 294 Mt Auburn Street, Watertown, MA 02172, (617) 924-1860. 1979. Poetry, photos, long-poems. avg. press run 500. Pub'd 1 title 1979. 1 title listed in the *Small Press Record of Books in Print* (9th Edition, 1980). avg. price, paper: $6.00. 32pp; 8½X10; of. Reporting time: 1 month. Copyrights for author. NESPA, NESPD.

Offshore Research Service (THE OFFSHORE CREWMAN'S NEWSLETTER), John R. Rochelle, Glenn Swetman, Charles Collins, PO Box 2606 NSU, Thibodaux, LA 70301, (504) 446-5676. 1976. "Offshore Research Service is a private orgainization currently researching and publishing modest priced literature about employment and training opportunities in the rapidly expanding offshore marine industry. The first publication to emerge from ORS was *Employment Opportunities in the Louisiana Offshore Marine Industry;* this work is primarily about jobs aboard crewboats and supply vessels servicing the offshore exploration, production and marine construction." avg. press run 500. Pub'd 1 title 1979; expects 2 titles 1981. 1 title listed in the *Small Press Record of Books in Print* (9th Edition, 1980). avg. price, paper: $5.00. Discounts: 1-4 books, 20%; 5-24, 40%; 25-49, 43%; 50-99, 46%; 100 or more, 50%. 30-50pp; 8½X11; of. Copyrights for author.

THE OHIO REVIEW, Wayne Dodd, Ellis Hall, Ohio University, Athens, OH 45701, 614-594-5889. 1959. Poetry, fiction, articles, interviews, reviews. circ. 1,400. 3/yr. Pub'd 3 issues 1979; expects 3 issues 1980. sub. price: $10.00; per copy: $3.50; sample: $2.00. Back issues: $2.50 per or $1.00 each with subscription. Discounts: Varies, sent on request. 130pp; 6X9; lp. Reporting time: 90 days. Payment: Rates vary: copies plus min. $5.00 per page prose; $10.00 per poem. Copyrighted. Pub's reviews: 30 in 1979. §Poetry, fiction, books, including all chapbooks. Ads: $120.00/$75.00. CCLM.

The Ohio State University Libraries Publications Committee (see UNDER THE SIGN OF PISCES: Anais Nin and Her Circle)

OHIOANA QUARTERLY, James P. Barry, Editor, 1105 Ohio Dept Bldg., 65 S. Front St, Columbus, OH 43215, 614-466-3831. 1929. Articles, reviews, art. "Pub'd by the Ohioana Library Assn. Reviews by staff and guest reviewers. Length of review varies from 40 to 400 words. Ohio authors or books on Ohio only. Articles on Ohio authors, music, other arts in Ohio, up to 2M words." circ. 1,200. 4/yr. Pub'd 4 issues 1979; expects 4 issues 1980, 4 issues 1981. sub. price: $8.50 (membership); per copy: $2.50; sample: gratis. Back issues: $2.50. Discounts: $6.00 to libraries. 48pp; 6X9; of. Reporting time: 2 weeks. Payment: Copies only. Copyrighted, rights do not revert, but we grant permission for full use by author. Pub's reviews: 260 in 1979. §Books about Ohio or Ohioans. Books by Ohioans or former Ohioans. New magazines pub'd in Ohio. Ads: none. CELJ.

OINK!, Paul Hoover, Maxine Chernoff, 7021 N. Sheridan Rd, Chicago, IL 60626. 1971. Poetry, fiction, art, long-poems, collages. "*Oink!* is now publishing special issues only. No unsolicited manuscripts will be considered. See #13, special Russell Edson issue; #14, Paul Hoover issue; #15, Peter Kostakis issue" circ. 750. Irreg. Pub'd 2 issues 1979. 3 titles listed in the *Small Press Record of Books in Print* (9th Edition, 1980). price per copy: $2.50. Back issues: #1-$20, #2-$20, #3-$15, #4-$5, #5-13-$2.00, #14 & #15-$2.50. Discounts: 60/40 to bookstores. pp varies; 5½X8½; of. Reporting time: no submissions requested. Payment: copies only. Copyrighted, reverts to author. §poetry, prose poems, especially, translations. CCLM.

Oklahoma State University Press (see CIMARRON REVIEW)

Old Adobe Press, B. Young, J. Hasley, P.O. Box 115, Penngrove, CA 94951, [Haslam]707-763-7362. 1971. "Temporarily inactive." avg. press run 500-1,000 1st printing; 2,500 2nd printing. Pub'd 1 title 1979; expects 1 title 1980. 1 title listed in the *Small Press Record of Books in Print* (9th Edition, 1980). avg. price, paper: $1.95-$4.95. Discounts: 1 copy 20%, 2-3 30% 4 or more 40%. 150pp; 5X8; of/lp. Payment: standard. all titles copyrighted in authors name. COSMEP, COSMEP-WEST.

OLD COURTHOUSE FILES, Paul E. Clark, Diana Huf, J.W. Moses, Dinah Wernick, Box 74, Albright College, Reading, PA 19603. 1979. Poetry, fiction, interviews, satire, criticism, parts-of-novels, long-poems, plays. "We are seeking well-crafted works—experimental or traditional—new or previously published. Our only bias is thematic: we prefer writings that affirm life, that confront the impersonal and the false in technocratic society." circ. 150. 4/yr. Pub'd 2 issues 1979; expects 4 issues 1980, 4 issues 1981. sub. price: $7.00; per copy: $2.00; sample: $1.50. Back issues: $2.50. Discounts: query. 50pp; 6X8½; of. Reporting time: 3-12 weeks. Payment: copies. Copyrighted, reverts to author.

Old Hickory Press (see also OLD HICKORY REVIEW), Charles T. Stanfill, Robert Michie, PO Box 1178, Jackson, TN 38301. 1974. Poetry. "Poetry chapbooks by Tennessee and Mid-South poets. We have published Kenneth Lawrence Beaudoin, Neil Graves, Isabel J. Glaser, and Robert Michie. One short story collection by Dorothy Stanfill." avg. press run 300. Pub'd 2 titles 1979; expects 2 titles 1980, 1-2 titles 1981. 4 titles listed in the *Small Press Record of Books in Print* (9th Edition, 1980). 40pp; of. Reporting time: 1 month. Payment: variable. Copyrights for author.

OLD HICKORY REVIEW, Old Hickory Press, Charles T. Stanfill, Editor; Robert Michie, Poetry Editor; Dorothy Stanfill, Fiction Editor, PO Box 1178, Jackson, TN 38301. 1969. Poetry, fiction, reviews, long-poems. "Crafted with care contemporary poetry. Fiction 2,500 maximum. We do our own reviews. Recent poetry by William Virgil Davis, William Dubie, Paula Rankin, Kenneth L. Beaudoin, Norman H. Russell, Errol Miller, Ed Orr, Glenn Ray Tutor, and fiction by Susan Sibley and Frances Goldwater. Interested in work by new as well as established writers." circ. 400-500. 2/yr. Pub'd 2 issues 1979; expects 2 issues 1980, 2 issues 1981. sub. price: $4.00; per copy: $2.00; sample: $2.00. Back issues: on request. 50-70pp; 6X9; of. Reporting time: 1-3 weeks. Payment: 2 comp. copies of issue in which work appears. Copyrighted, reverts to author. Pub's reviews: 3 in 1979. §Contemporary poetry.

Old Pages Books Co (see also FLY BY NIGHT), Gary Nargi, PO Box 921, Huntington, NY 11743. 1980. Poetry, fiction, criticism, parts-of-novels. avg. press run 500. Pub'd 2 titles 1979. avg. price, paper: $2.50; other: free pamphlets projected. mi, of. Reporting time: immediate, acknowledgement when we hold pieces. Payment: copies. Copyrights for author.

THE OLD RED KIMONO, Ken Anderson, Jo Anne Starnes, Humanities, Floyd Junior College, PO Box 1864, Rome, GA 30161, 404-295-6312. 1972. "Submissions of short poetry and short fiction are read September 1-March 1. Recent contributors include Corinne Bliss, Malcolm Glass, Lyn Lifshin, Rose Mary Prosen, and Reg Saner. SASE." circ. 1,000. Pub'd 1 issue 1979; expects 1 issue 1980. 64pp; 8X11; of. Reporting time: 3 months. Payment: 2 copies. Copyrighted.

Oleander Press, Will Marston, 17 Stansgate Ave., Cambridge CB2 2QZ, United Kingdom. 1960. Poetry, plays. "We aim to fill in gaps left by commercial and academic publishers e.g. 'Celtic: A Comparative Study' (1980) 'Basque Language and Literature' (1981) rejected by university presses as being 'too minority a subject' or reprints of Arabian travel classics considered 'too specialized a field' by commercial publishers, such as *The German Left*. Ideas for scholarly titles or reprints in this field welcome. 28 vols. already in 'Cambridge Town, Gown & County' series. Other series on Indonesia, Libya, Travel, and (in abeyance due to lack of support) drama and poetry" avg. press run 2,500. Pub'd 12 titles 1979; expects 12 titles 1980. 63 titles listed in the *Small Press Record of Books in Print* (9th Edition, 1980). avg. price, cloth: $12.00; paper: $5.00. Discounts: booksellers 33%. 48-200pp; lp/IBM. Always send letter first with SASE. Payment: by arrangement. Copyrights for author. ALP.

Oleander Press/U.S., 210 Fifth Ave., New York, NY 10010. 3 titles listed in the *Small Press Record of Books in Print* (9th Edition, 1980).

The Olive Press Publications, Addis Lynne Norris, PO Box 99, Los Olivos, CA 93441. 1978. avg. press run 7,500. 1 title listed in the *Small Press Record of Books in Print* (9th Edition, 1980). avg. price, cloth: $8.95; paper: $4.95. Discounts: 40% over 5 copies. 250pp; 6X9.

Omangoo Press, Rt 171, P064, Woodstock Valley, CT 06282, 203-974-2511. 1974. Articles, art, photos, interviews, letters, news items. "Books on Fruitarianism & Live Food related to Spirituality and Healing. We publish books on healing, vegetarianism, spiritual. Recently published books: V. Kulvinskas, M.S., N.D. *Survival Into 21st Century,* introduction by Dick Gregory, art: Peter Max. $8.95 —*Nutritional Evaluation Of Sprouts,* $2.45—Abramowski, M.D., *Fruitarian Diet For Regeneration* $1.00. *Love Your Body-Poorman's Vegetarianism* $2.50." avg. press run 10,000. avg. price, paper: $9.00; other: $2.50. Discounts: jobbers 60 percent, trade 40 percent, agent 10 percent, classroom 25 percent. 320 pp max, 100 pp min; 8X11; of. Reporting time: 3 months. Payment: yes. Copyrights for author.

Ommation Press (see also MATI; SALOME: A LITERARY DANCE MAGAZINE), Effie Mihopoulos, 5548 North Sawyer, Chicago, IL 60625. 1975. Poetry. "Ommation Press is no longer publishing *The Ditto Rations Chapbook Series* (the chapbooks already published are still available for purchase, send SASE for list of titles), which has completed its proposed 20 titles. However, a new series, *Offset Offshoots* has been started (Lyn Lifshin, Christine Zawadiwsky, Rochelle Ratner, Douglas MacDonald). Manuscripts are always welcome for consideration, particularly by women, but please include sufficient postage for return of manuscript." avg. press run 200. Pub'd 4 titles 1979; expects 4 titles 1980. 81 titles listed in the *Small Press Record of Books in Print* (9th Edition, 1980). avg. price, paper: $2.00 *Offset Offshoot,* $0.50 *Ditto Rations.* Discounts: 40% discount on purchase of ten or more copies.

25-50pp; 8½X11; 5X9; †of. Reporting time: 2 weeks. Payment: 50 copies of book. Copyrights for author. CCLM, COSMEP Midwest.

ON DIT, Andrew Fagan, Geoff Hammer, Union Buildings, Adelaide University, Adelaide 5001, South Australia, 223-2685. 1932. Poetry, fiction, articles, photos, cartoons, interviews, satire, criticism, reviews, letters, news items. "We print what students submit." circ. 4,500-5,000. 18/yr. Pub'd 22 issues 1979; expects 22 issues 1980, 22 issues 1981. sub. price: $6.00; per copy: $0.30; sample: $0.30. Back issues: $0.30 each if available. Discounts: 20% for regular advertisers. 16pp; 290X430; of. Reporting time: one week. Copyrighted, reverts to author. Pub's reviews: 40 in 1979. §Criticism, opinion. Ads: $220.00/$120.00.

ON STAGE, Irene Diana Bayshore, PO Box 4040, Fullerton, CA 92634. 1968. Articles, photos, interviews, criticism, reviews, letters, plays, news items. "American Community Theatre Association (ACTA), a division of ATA. Concentration on community and regional theatre, reader participation and manuscript submissions welcomed. Length of mss of no concern. Summer 1978 issue marks editorial reorganization. Focus on Los Angeles as regional theatre. Original play by John Cassavetes, interview with Gena Rowlands, book review by Meade Roberts. Request editorial guide and information for single copy prices. Individual membership, annual dues: $30.00, student membership: $15.-00. Also family and institional dues categories." circ. 758. 4/yr. Pub'd 4 issues 1979; expects 2 issues 1980, 4 issues 1981. 64pp; 8½X11; of. Reporting time: immediate. Payment: 2 copies. Copyrighted, reverts to author. Pub's reviews. §Books and periodicals pertaining to theatre; dramatic works.

ON THE BEACH, Judith Ann Young, Robert G. Young, PO Box 1245, Newport, OR 97365, (503) 265-2400. 1978. Poetry, articles, photos. "Articles of interest to Oregon tourists, 250 words" circ. 10,000. 8/yr. Pub'd 8 issues 1979; expects 8 issues 1980, 8 issues 1981. sub. price: $9.00; per copy: $0.75; sample: free. 24pp; 8⅜X10⅞; of. Reporting time: 30 days. Payment: 5¢ per word. Ads: $500.-00/$275.00.

Onaway Publications, Ona C. Evers, Manager, 28 Lucky Drive, San Rafael, CA 94904, (415) 924-0884. 1977. "How-To books" avg. press run 1,500. Pub'd 2 titles 1979; expects 1 title 1980, 1 title 1981. 1 title listed in the *Small Press Record of Books in Print* (9th Edition, 1980). avg. price, paper: $4.45. Discounts: 1-9, 20%; 10-99, 40%; 100 & over, 50%. 80pp; 5½X8½, 8½X11; of. no submissions at this time; staff written. COSMEP.

ONE, David Chaloner, 16 Rosemary Avenue, London N3 2QN, United Kingdom. 1971. Poetry, fiction, articles, criticism, reviews. "Andrew Crozier, Tony Towle, James Schuyler, Douglas Oliver, Michael Palmer, Peter Riley, Lee Harwood, John James, Anne Waldman, Gerard Malanga, Ian Patterson, John Welch, John Hall, Martin Wright, Anthony Barnett, Peter Schjeldahl, Tim Longville, Jim Burns, Peter Ackroyd, Andre Du Bouchet, Martin Thom, Peter Philpott, Paul Green." irreg. Pub'd 2 issues 1979. Discounts: 33⅓% trade. 50pp; size A4; mi. Reporting time: varies. rights remain with authors/credit appreciated. Pub's reviews.

ONEARTH IMAGE, Findhorn Publications, Dennis Evanson, John White, Findhorn Foundation, The Park, Forres, Morayshire 1V360TZ, Scotland, 030-93-2582. 1979. Poetry, fiction, articles, art, photos, cartoons, interviews, reviews. "The purpose of *Onearth Image* magazine is to provide readers with a planetary view of the unfolding spiritual attitude and way of life that is currently creating a new culture. Each issue has a different theme. Includes articles written by members of the Findhorn Community as well as contemporary spiritual leaders. Recent contributors: David, Spangler, Donald Keyes, Barbara Mary Hubbard." circ. 5,000. 6/yr. Pub'd 2 issues 1979; expects 6 issues 1980, 6 issues 1981. sub. price: £4.50, $13.70; per copy: £0.75, $2.25; sample: Including postage and packing, airmail to Americas. Discounts: UK: 1-2, 25%; 3 or more, 35%. Overseas: 1-2, 25%; 3-9, 33⅓%; 10 or more, 40%. 28pp; 12¼X8¾; †of. Reporting time: 1 month. Payment: By arrangement, usually by free copies. Copyrighted. Pub's reviews: 3 in 1979. §Metaphysics, the spiritual life, occult philosophy, communities. IPG.

Ontario Library Association (see also EXPRESSION; REVIEWING LIBRARIAN), Lawrence A. Moore, Fay Blostein, 73 Richmond Street, W., Suite 402, Toronto, Ontario M5H 1Z4, Canada, (416) 762-7232. 1900. avg. press run 2,500. Pub'd 2 titles 1979; expects 4 titles 1980. 5 titles listed in the *Small Press Record of Books in Print* (9th Edition, 1980). avg. price, paper: $9.00. Discounts: 20% (10 or more). 200pp; size varies; of. Payment: 10% (1-500), 20% (all additional) quarterly.

THE ONTARIO REVIEW, Raymond J. Smith, Editor; Joyce Carol Oates, Assoc Editor, 9 Honey Brook Drive, Princeton, NJ 08540. 1974. Poetry, fiction, articles, art, photos, interviews, criticism, reviews. circ. 1,000. 2/yr. Pub'd 2 issues 1979; expects 2 issues 1980. sub. price: $7.00; per copy: $3.50; sample: $3.50. Back issues: $3.50. 116pp; 6X9; of. Reporting time: 4 weeks. Payment: $5.00 per page. Copyrighted, reverts to author. Pub's reviews: 22 in 1979. §Poetry, fiction. Ads: $100.-

00/$60.00. COSMEP.

Oolichan Books, Ron Smith, John Marshall, P.O. Box 10, Lantzville, British Columbia V0R2H0, Canada, 604-390-4839. 1975. Poetry, fiction, plays. "*Oolichan Books* generally publishes *full-length* manuscripts of poetry, fiction and drama...although we do plan to publish two chapbooks in the coming year, but only because we believe each is of exceptional quality. We prefer letters of inquiry with sample writing. Apart from our main interest in poetry and fiction we are also interested in statements on poetics or collections of letters which reveal something of the stance of the writer & and his/her attitude to the language. We attempt to maintain a balance between established and newer authors. Generally we are not interested in the mass market book (unless it has something to say and, to be blunt and pragmatic, will provide us with the means to publish more serious fiction & poetry) but rather in books which indicate how the writer sees through language. Recent contributors include: Robert Kroetsch, John Newlove, Robin Skelton, Ken Cathers, Robert Stallman, George Woodcock, John Marshall, Yves Troendle, M. Carmichael. Daphne Marlatt. We are also interested in books on labor history or leftist politics." avg. press run 750-2,000 depending on author. Pub'd 5 titles 1979; expects 8 titles 1980, 8 titles 1981. avg. price, cloth: $12.95; paper: $5.95; other: Special editions, signed & numbered. $15.00. Discounts: 40% trade agent or jobber, 20% libraries. 76-160pp; 6X9; lp. Reporting time: 1-3 months. Payment: 10 percent. Copyrights for author. ACP, LPG, BCPA.

Open Books, Susan Moon, 1631 Grant, Berkeley, CA 94703, 415-548-2208.

OPEN CELL, Jennifer McDowell, Paula Friedman, Harlan Jones, Milton Loventhal, PO Box 5602, San Jose, CA 95150. 1969. Poetry, fiction, art, photos, reviews, music, parts-of-novels, plays. "Prose pieces should not exceed 10 pages. Two to 6 poems per submission is preferred. Enclose SASE. Recent contributors. Julia Vinograd, George Kauffman." circ. 1,000. 2/yr. Pub'd 1 issue 1979; expects 1 issue 1980, 1 issue 1981. sub. price: 5 issues $2.00/institutions: 5 issues $5.00; per copy: $.50; sample: $.25. Back issues: Issues 1-6: $3.00 each others, $1.00 each. Discounts: one-third off. 8pp; 19X11; of. Reporting time: 6 month. Payment: copies. Copyrighted. Pub's reviews. §women's auto-biographies. Ads: $50.00/$25.00/$10.00 for 2" x 2". CCLM.

OPEN PLACES, Eleanor M. Bender, Thomas Dillingham, Bk. Review Ed., Box 2085, Stephens College, Columbia, MO 65215, 314-442-2211. 1966. Poetry, reviews. "No new work will be considered until *after* Sept. 1, 1981." circ. 1000. 2/yr. Pub'd 2 issues 1979; expects 2 issues 1980. 5 titles listed in the *Small Press Record of Books in Print* (9th Edition, 1980). sub. price: $4.00; per copy: $2.00; sample: $2.00. Back issues: Nos. 1-27 $40.00 p.p. Discounts: 40% trade. 64pp; 8½X5½; lp. Reporting time: 2-6 wks. Payment: $8/page + copies. Copyrighted. Pub's reviews: 12 in 1979. §poetry, small press poetry books. no ads. CCLM, COSMEP.

OPEN ROAD, Vancouver News Group, Box 6135, Station G, Vancouver, B.C. V6R 4G5, Canada. 1976. Poetry, articles, art, photos, cartoons, interviews, satire, criticism, reviews, letters, parts-of-novels, news items. circ. 14,000. 4/yr. Pub'd 3 issues 1979; expects 3 issues 1980, 3 issues 1981. sub. price: Instit. $20.00; per copy: $1.00; sample: free. Back issues: #2,5,6 - $5 ea; #8,9,10,10½ - $2 ea. 20pp; 11½X16¾; of. Reporting time: 3 months. Payment: none. Pub's reviews: 10 in 1979. §Anarchism, anti-authoritarianism, feminism, prisons, community organizing, anything with an anti-authoritarian slant to it. All popular struggles.

Open Sesame Publishing Co., David Shiang, 1609½ San Pablo Avenue, Berkeley, CA 94702, (415) 526-6204. 1979. Criticism. "Open Sesame has published one book to date but hopes to publish many more in the future. Queries welcome." Expects 1-2 titles 1980, 1-2 titles 1981. 1 title listed in the *Small Press Record of Books in Print* (9th Edition, 1980). Discounts: 20-60%; depends upon the number of copies purchased. of. Reporting time: 4-6 weeks. Payment: Royalty rates are fairly standard. Copyrights for author. COSMEP, WIP.

Openings Press, Dom Silvester Houedard, John Furnival, Rooksmoor House, Woodchester, Glos, United Kingdom. 1964. Concrete art. "No unsolicited mss." avg. press run 250-500. Pub'd 10 titles 1979. 10 titles listed in the *Small Press Record of Books in Print* (9th Edition, 1980). avg. price, paper: £1.50; other: 25p. Discounts: 33⅓%. variedpp; size varied; of/silk-screen. Payment: copies. ALP.

OPINION, James E. Kurtz, Editor, P.O.Box 3563, Bloomington, IL 61701. 1951. Articles, satire, criticism, reviews. "We want strong articles on theology, philosophy and sociology-but not long articles. We don't care who you are as long as you know how to write and can back your stuff with accurate research, facts." circ. 3,000. 12/yr. Pub'd 12 issues 1979; expects 12 issues 1980. sub. price: $5.00; per copy: $.50; sample: $.30. Back issues: $.50 each. Discounts: none. 16pp; 8½X11; of. Reporting time: 3 weeks. Payment: copies only. Not copyrighted. Pub's reviews. §All areas. Ads: $25.00/$12.50/$.10.

286

THE ORCADIAN, G. GA. Meyer, c/o W. R. Mackintosh, THE ORCADIAN Office, Kirkwall, Orkney, United Kingdom. 1854. Articles, photos, reviews, letters, news items, interviews, criticism. circ. 10,000. 52/yr. sub. price: £11.96; per copy: 27p; sample: 27p. 8pp; 558X410mm; †lp. Pub's reviews. Ads: £400/£200/20p line. NS/SMPA.

ORE, Eric Ratcliffe, Manag. Editor; Brian Louis Pearce, Adv. Ed., The Towers, Stevenage, Herts, England SG1 1HE, United Kingdom. 1954. Articles, poetry, reviews, criticism, long-poems. "No sick material or unpatriotic material. No concrete work. Ideally based on the past of ancient Britain as a faith for the future. Occult-white-Arthurian legend/ancient British." circ. 650. 2-3/yr. 11 titles listed in the *Small Press Record of Books in Print* (9th Edition, 1980). sub. price: 35p; sample: 10p. Back issues: price by arrangement. Discounts: 33% trade, 12½% libraries. 40pp. Reporting time: 2 wks. Payment: by arrangement. Ads: 2p/word. ALP.

Oregon Historical Society (see also OREGON HISTORICAL QUARTERLY), Priscilla Knuth, Executive Editor; Thomas Vaughan, Executive Director; Bruce T. Hamilton, Book Editor, 1230 S.W. Park Avenue, Portland, OR 97205, 503-222-1741. 1873. Articles. "Thomas Vaughan, Terence O'-Donnell, Bruce T. Hamilton" avg. press run 2,500. Pub'd 5 titles 1979; expects 9 titles 1980, 10 titles 1981. avg. price, cloth: $18.57; paper: $6.86. Discounts: 40% trade, 20% library. 200pp (varies); size varies w/book; of. Reporting time: 1 year. Payment: 10 percent (varies). Copyrights for author.

OREGON HISTORICAL QUARTERLY, Oregon Historical Society, 1230 S.W. Park Ave., Portland, OR 97205. 1900. Articles, photos, reviews. circ. 7M. 4/yr. Pub'd 4 issues 1979. sub. price: $10.00; per copy: $2.00; sample: $2.00. 112pp; 6X9; of. Reporting time: 6 weeks. Payment: none. Copyrighted. Pub's reviews: 15 in 1979. §Regional history. Ads: No ads.

‡**OREGON TIMES MAGAZINE, New Oregon Publishers, Inc.,** Tom Bates, Editor; Dave Kelly, Man. Editor, 208 SW Stark, Suite 500, Portland, OR 97204. 1971. Poetry, fiction, articles, photos, interviews, criticism, reviews, plays. "We can use up-to-date news on Oregon and the Pacific Northwest as it applies to the environment and left-leaning politics." circ. 6,000. 12/yr. sub. price: $8.00; per copy: $.75; sample: free. Back issues: $.35 apiece. Discounts: Students, senior citizens $6.00 yr. 64pp; 8½X11; of. Reporting time: 2 weeks. Pub's reviews. §Oregon and Northwest. Ads: $234/$117/none.

Oriel, Peter Finch, Meic Stephens, 53 Charles St., Cardiff, Wales CF14ED, United Kingdom, 0222-395548. 1974. Poetry, art. "Publications are confined to Welsh and Anglo-Welsh authors together with material about Wales. Unsolicited mss. are not requested. In existence are a number of fine edition poster poems an illustrated book about Dylan Thomas. A new series of spoken work records. Catalogues available." avg. press run 2,000. Pub'd 20 titles 1979; expects 20 titles 1980. 13 titles listed in the *Small Press Record of Books in Print* (9th Edition, 1980). Discounts: 33⅓-50%. of/lp. Payment: By arrangement. Does not copyright for author.

THE ORIGINAL ART REPORT (TOAR), Frank Salantrie, P.O. Box 1641, Chicago, IL 60690. 1967. Articles, interviews, satire, criticism, reviews, letters, news items. "Exclusive interest in fine art (visual) in Midwest and elsewhere in the world as it affects people, society, and art. Material must take advocacy position, one side or another. No puffy previews, reviews, profiles. Prefer controversial treatment of subject matter." circ. 100-1,000. 12/yr maximum. sub. price: $12.00/12 issues; per copy: $1.25; sample: $1.25. Back issues: $2.25 each if available. Discounts: 25 to same address-$8.50 each/special artist discount-32½% off-pay $7.50 for individual subscription. 6-issue sub $6.95. 6pp; 8½X11; of. Reporting time: 1-2 weeks. Payment: 1 cent/word; max 1000 words. Pub's reviews. §fine art (visual)/related.

Original Press, Verdi Throckmorton, 561 Milltown Road, North Brunswick, NJ 08902, (201) 249-5543.

ORIGINS, Ms. L. Wilson, Mr. H. Barrett, Box 5072, Station E, Hamilton, Ontario L8S4K9, Canada, 416-528-0552. 1967. Poetry, art, fiction, articles, cartoons, reviews, news items. circ. 500. 4/yr. Pub'd 4 issues 1979; expects 4 issues 1980, 4 issues 1981. sub. price: $5.00 individuals, $6.00 insit; per copy: $1.50; sample: sample. Back issues: $0.50 when available. Discounts: Bulk, classroom. 40pp; 5½X8½; †of. Reporting time: 4 weeks. Payment: Prose, $5.00; Art, $5.00. Poetry complimentary copy, book reviews $3.00. Copyrighted, reverts to author. Pub's reviews: 12 in 1979. §Canadian poetry and stories. Ads: $40.00/$25.00.

Orion Press (see also EUREKA REVIEW), Roger Ladd Memmott, 90 Harrison Avenue, New Canaan, CT 06840. 1975. Poetry, fiction. avg. press run 500-1,000. Discounts: 25%-40%. 150pp; 5½X8½; of. Reporting time: 8 weeks. Payment: Copies or monies, if available. Copyrights for author. CCLM, COSMEP.

ORNAMENT, A Quarterly of Jewelry and Personal Adornment, Robert K. Liu, Carolyn L. E. Benesh, PO Box 35029, Los Angeles, CA 90035, 213-652-9914. 1974. Art, criticism, reviews, letters, news items. "Street Address: 1221 S. LaCienega, Los Angeles, Ca 90035. Formerly published under the name of *The Bead Journal* which terminated with Volume 3, No. 4. As of Volume 4, No. 1 published under the name of *Ornament.*" circ. 4,000. 4/yr. Pub'd 4 issues 1979. sub. price: $14.00; per copy: $3.50; sample: $4.00. Back issues: same as current except vol 2, which are $2.50 each. Discounts: 40% on wholesale orders, 15% to subscription agents. 72pp; 8X11; of. Reporting time: 4-6 weeks. Payment: copies of the magazine in which article appears. Number depends on lenth of article. Copyrighted, reverts to author. Pub's reviews: 110 in 1979. §Jewelry, ancient, ethnic, contemporary, forms of personal adornment. Ads: $340.00/$190.00/$20.00 for 4 lines-25 words. COSMEP/Int'l Guild of Craft Journalists, Authors & Photographers/American Crafts Council.

ORPHEUS, Illuminati, P. Schneidre, c/o Illuminati, 1147 So Robertson Blvd, Los Angeles, CA 90035, 213-273-8372. 1975. Poetry, long-poems. "Contributors have included Charles Wright, James Merrill, Charles Bukowski, James Tate,Paul Monette, Richard Howard." circ. 1,100. 3/yr. Expects 4 issues 1980, 4 issues 1981. sub. price: $5.00; per copy: $1.95; sample: $1.95. Back issues: Unavailable. Discounts: Bookstores, 50%; all others on request. 100pp; 5X8; †of. Reporting time: 2 weeks. Payment: by private arrangement. Copyrighted. Ads: $50.00/$25.00. CCLM, COSMEP.

OSIRIS, Andrea Moorhead, Box 297, Deerfield, MA 01342. 1972. Poetry, fiction, interviews, criticism, reviews, long-poems. "*OSIRIS* is apolitical. Prints texts in English, French, Spanish, Italian, without translation. Recent contributors: Michel Cosem (France), Robert Martean, Cecile Cloutier (Quebec), Martin Robbins, Raymond Federman, Ruth Federman (USA)." circ. 500. 2/yr. Pub'd 2 issues 1979; expects 2 issues 1980, 2 issues 1981. sub. price: $4.00; per copy: $2.00; sample: $2.00. Back issues: $3.00 #1-4. 40pp; 6X9; of. Reporting time: 4 weeks. Payment: 2 copies. Copyrighted, reprint with credit line to *OSIRIS*. Pub's reviews. §Spanish poetry. Ads: /$25/query. CCLM.

OTHER PRESS POETRY REVIEW, Paul Gotro, Terry Galvin, 2503 Douglas College, New Westminister, British Columbia, Canada, 522-6038. 1976. Poetry, fiction, articles, art, photos, parts-of-novels, long-poems, plays, concrete art. "J. Michael Yates, Eugene McNamara, Harold Enrico, Leona Gom, Eric Ivan Berg, Micheal Bullock, Derk Wynand." circ. 400. 4/yr. sub. price: $6.00; per copy: $1.50; sample: free. 32pp; of. Reporting time: 1 month. Payment: in copies. §poetry, short fiction.

Other Publications, Alan Davies, 826 Union Street, Brooklyn, NY 11215, (212) 789-8361. 1971. Poetry, long-poems. avg. press run 500. Pub'd 1 title 1979; expects 1 title 1980, 1 title 1981. 4 titles listed in the *Small Press Record of Books in Print* (9th Edition, 1980). avg. price, paper: $3.50; other: $10.00 signed. Discounts: 40% bookstores. 50pp; 6X9; of. Reporting time: 1 month. Copyrights for author.

Other Scenes, John Wilcock, Box 4137, Grand Central Station, New York, NY 10017, 212-582-3112. 1967. Articles, art, news items, interviews, letters, collages, concrete art, photos. "Literature, alternative, occult, sociology, travel. Secondary address: BCM-Oscenes, London WC IV, U.K." avg. price, paper: 50¢. of. Reporting time: 48 hours. Payment: low. Does not copyright for author.

Otto F. Reiss, Publ. (see ART AND ARCHAEOLOGY NEWSLETTER)

OUR GENERATION, 3981 boul St Laurent, Montreal, Quebec H2W 1Y5, Canada. 1961. Articles, photos, interviews, criticism, reviews. circ. 5,000. 4/yr. Pub'd 4 issues 1979; expects 3 issues 1980. sub. price: $7.50; per copy: $2.00; sample: free. Discounts: none. 48pp; 7X9¼; of. Reporting time: 3 mos. Payment: none. Copyrighted, does not revert to author. Pub's reviews: 15 in 1979. §public affairs-women-anarchist-social critique-Canada & Quebec. Ads: $100/$50. CPPA.

Out & Out Books, Joan Larkin, Ellen Shapiro, Jane Creighton, 476 Second St, Brooklyn, NY 11215, 212-499-9227. 1975. Poetry, articles. "Book-length manuscripts of special interest to women. 7 vols. of lesbian poetry and 2 prose non-fiction published. Currently not soliciting manuscripts except for lesbian pamphlet series (series documenting ideas important in the evolution of lesbian feminism)." avg. press run 2,000. Pub'd 3 titles 1979; expects 3 titles 1980. 21 titles listed in the *Small Press Record of Books in Print* (9th Edition, 1980). avg. price, paper: $3.50. Discounts: 40% trade discount. 72pp; 5½X8½; of. Reporting time: 3 months. Payment: 10% of retail. Copyrights for author. COSMEP, WDG.

Out of the Ashes Press, Walt Curtis, Norman Solomon, Anson Wright, P.O. Box 42384, Portland, OR 97242. 1971. Poetry, fiction, photos, parts-of-novels, long-poems, collages. "We are interested in experimental/high quality literature. We are interested in collections of poetry and fiction which are from an insurgent perspective— non-rhetorical, pro-feminist, anti-imperialist, innovative, non-commercialized, searching, sensitive, explosive, what we can make possible. We cannot consider submissions that are only a few pages long; we cannot really consider extremely long (over about 200 pages) manuscripts either. All stuff sent should have a S.A.S.E. enclosed. Recent books: *Going Critical: Anti-nuclear Pamphlet* by Norman Solomon; *Journey Across America* By Walt Curtis; *Openings, Selected Writings* by Anson Wright; *Mothers and Fathers: Being Parents, Remebering Parents* by Solla Carrock. *Mala Noche*, short story by Walt Curtis; *Now: a Narrative Document*, prose by Norman Solomon; *Jericho*, novel by Anson Wright." avg. press run 2,000. Pub'd 4 titles 1979. 7 titles listed in the *Small Press Record of Books in Print* (9th Edition, 1980). 64pp; 8X10; of. Reporting time: variable. Payment: contributors' copies (for anthologies) authors' copies.

OUT THERE MAGAZINE, Rose Lesniak, Editor, 156 W 27th, 5-W, New York, NY 10001, 212-675-0194. 1972. Poetry, articles, long-poems, interviews, letters, collages, concrete art, reviews. "Especially interested in quality. Experimental, non-sexist, non-elitist. No art for art sakes material. Seeking graphic-poetry collaborations for calendar." circ. 1,000-2,000. 1/yr. Pub'd 1 issue 1979; expects 1 issue 1980. price per copy: $2.50. Back issues: (1-8) $10.00 (No. 8-11 $2.00). Discounts: 40% to bookstores. 100pp; 8½X11; of. Reporting time: 1-2 months. Payment: 2 copies, some money-depending on grant $. Copyrighted, reverts to author. Pub's reviews: 3 in 1979. §All quality criticisms of firm statements. Ads: $200.00/$100.00. CCLM, COSMEP.

OUTCOME, The Outcome Collective, c/o 78A Penny Street, Lancaster, England, United Kingdom. 1976. Poetry, fiction, articles, art, photos, cartoons, interviews, reviews, collages, news items. circ. 1,600. 2-3/yr. Pub'd 3 issues 1979; expects 2 issues 1980, 2 issues 1981. sub. price: £1.50; per copy: 50p; sample: 50p. Back issues: issues 3-8 (inclusive) £2, single back issues 40p. Discounts: negotiable. 36-40pp; size A4; of. Copyrighted. Pub's reviews: 2 in 1979. §Lesbian, gay literatue, sexual politics publications. Ads: £50/£25.

OUTERBRIDGE, Charlotte Alexander, English A323, College of Staten Island, 715 Ocean Terrace, Staten Island, NY 10301, (212)390-7654. 1975. Poetry, fiction, interviews, satire, reviews, parts-of-novels, plays. "Slight bias toward form, craft & against clearly socio-political statements. Among contributors: Reg Saner, Colette Inez, Philip Dacey, Floyd Skloot, Paula Rankin, Bin Ramke, Barry Spacks, Alyce Ingram, R.J. Bixby, Marilyn Throne, Warren Miller." circ. 500-1000. 2/yr. Pub'd 6 issues 1979. sub. price: $4.00; per copy: $2.00 single, $4.00 double; sample: $2.00. Back issues: $1.50. Discounts: 20% for 10 or more. 65pp; 5½X8½; of. Reporting time: 6-8 weeks. Payment: 2 copies. Copyrighted, reverts to author. Pub's reviews. §poetry, fiction, novels. COSMEP/CCLM/SPR.

OUTPOSTS, Outposts Publications, Howard Sergeant, 72 Burwood Road, Walton-On-Thames, Surrey KT12 4AL, United Kingdom. 1944. Poetry, reviews, criticism, articles. "OUTPOSTS is the oldest independent poetry magazine in the UK. It was founded to provide a satisfactory medium for those poets, recognised or unrecognised, who are concerned wtih the potentialities of the human spirit, and who are able to visualize the dangers and opportunites which confront the individual and the whole of humanity. Although recent contributors have included famous poets like Ted Hughes, Peter Porter, George MacBeth, Vernon Scannell, Kingsley Amis, Thomas Blackburn & etc the magazine makes a special point of introducing the work of new and unestablished poets to the public." circ. 1,500. 4/yr. Pub'd 50 issues 1979; expects 4 issues 1980. sub. price: $10.00; per copy: $2.50; sample: $2.50. Back issues: Price varies. Discounts: 10% publishers 10% series. 40pp; size demi 800; lp. Reporting time: 2 weeks. Payment: Depends on length of poem. Copyrighted, reverts to author. Pub's reviews: 80 in 1979. §Poetry, criticism of poetry. Ads: $80.00/$50.00. ALP.

Outposts Publications (see also OUTPOSTS), Howard Sergeant, 32 Burwood Rd, Walton-on-Thames, Surrey KT12 4AL, United Kingdom, Walton-on-Thames 40712. 1944. Poetry. avg. press run 250-500. Expects 60 titles 1980, 60 titles 1981. 12-120pp; lp. Reporting time: one month. Payment: by separate arrangement with each author according to size of collection. Copyrights for author.

OUTRIGGER, Outrigger Publishers LTD, Tim Pickford, 4 Miami St, East Mangere, Auckland, New Zealand. 1974. Poetry. "1980 is last year of production." circ. 250. 6/yr. Pub'd 6 issues 1979; expects 6 issues 1980. sub. price: NZ $7.00 plus $2.00 postage; per copy: $2.00; sample: $2.00. Discounts: 33⅓% bulk orders. 40-50pp; size A5; †mi. Reporting time: 2 months. Payment: copies. Copyrighted. Pub's reviews: 7 in 1979. §Poetry only. Ads: No ads.

Outrigger Publishers LTD (see OUTRIGGER; PACIFIC QUARTERLY/MOANA; MIORITA)

Over the Rainbow Press, Box 7072, Berkeley, CA 94707. 1974. "Non-sexist children's books. Titles: *The Forest Princess* by Harriet Herman (74); *Return of the Forest Princess* by Harriet Herman (76)." avg. press run 2,500. 2 titles listed in the *Small Press Record of Books in Print* (9th Edition, 1980). avg. price, paper: $2.95. Discounts: 5-9, 35%; 10 or more, 10%. 38pp; 8X10. Copyrights for author.

The Overlook Press, Mark Gompertz, Ingrid Josephson, Route 212, PO Box 427, Woodstock, NY

12498, (914) 679-6838. 1971. "We are distributed by Viking Press, although special sales are based in Woodstock, NY and are handled by Alfred Mayer, President. Our editorial offices are located at 667 Madison Avenue, New York, NY 10021. Phone: (212) 688-0920. We specialize in art and design books, although we also publish general non-fiction, fiction, and poetry. We have published *Milton Glaser: Graphic Design, The Art of Natural History, Animal Illustrators and Their Work* by S. Peter Dance, and will soon publish *Images From the Bible: The Paintings of Shalom of Safed, The Words fo Elie Wiesel.* Our last project was *Industrial Design* by Raymond Loewy. For this title we published a deluxe edition with a signed lithograph, and we will do the same for *Images From the Bible.*" Pub'd 18 titles 1979; expects 14 titles 1980, 13 titles 1981. Reporting time: 4-6 weeks. AAP.

‡OVO MAGAZINE, Jorge Guerra, P.O. Box 1431, Station A, Montreal, Quebec H3C2Z9, Canada, 514-861-8094. 1970. "OVO MAGAZINE is a Quebec based photographic publication which is published quarterly. OVO is dedicated to the promotion of photography as a means of social improvement and communication. Publishes 2 separate versions, French and English. Issues are now thematic (prisons, immigration, etc)." circ. 6,000. 4/yr. Pub'd 4 issues 1979; expects 4 issues 1980. sub. price: $6.00 4 issues-U.S. $8.00-for. $10.00-yr; per copy: $2.00. Back issues: $1.00. Discounts: 30% discount on orders of more than 6 copies. 48pp; 8½X11¾; of. Reporting time: 1 to 2 weeks. Payment: varies. Copyrighted. Pub's reviews: 6 in 1979. §photography. Ads: $300.00/$150.00. CPPA.

Owl Creek Press (see also THE MONTANA REVIEW), Rich Ives, Laurie Blauner, 520 S Second, W, Missoula, MT 59801, (406) 728-0479. 1979. Poetry, fiction, articles, long-poems. "We are interested in quality translations in both poetry and fiction." avg. press run 1,000. avg. price, cloth: $10.00-$15.00; paper: $3.00-$5.00. Discounts: standard. 5½X8½; †lp. Reporting time: 2-4 weeks. Payment: 10%. NEA.

Owlseye Publications (see also POETALK QUARTERLY), Elizabeth Harrod, Tom Plante, Ann Emerson, 1403 Northside, Berkeley, CA 94541, (415) 526-4209. 1979. Poetry, interviews, criticism, reviews, letters. "For *Poetalk Quarterly* reviews of small press & university press poetry, limit one page. For annual poetry supplement Owlseye limit poems to one page. Deadline for supplement 20 September. US and Canada Subs. $3.00/year; single issue Spring, Summer, Fall $1.00. Foreign subscriptions: $5.00/year. Winter issue single copy $1.50. Magazine & supplement copyrighted. All rights reserved to individual authors." avg. press run 1,000. avg. price, other: single copy $1.00, back issues $1.50. Discounts: 1 copy, none; 5 copies, 30%; 10 copies, 40%. 20pp; 7X8½; †of. Reporting time: immediately to 2 months. Payment: copies. CCLM.

Ox Head Press, Don Olsen, 414 N 6th St, Marshall, MN 56258. 1966. Poetry, satire. "3 to 6 poems per pamphlet. Robert Bly, *The Loon.* $3.00. Philip Dacey *The Condom Poems,* $2.00. *Parodynthology* $2.00." avg. press run 300-500. Pub'd 2 titles 1979; expects 2 titles 1980, 2 titles 1981. 3 titles listed in the *Small Press Record of Books in Print* (9th Edition, 1980). avg. price, paper: $2.00. Discounts: Varies; no discount on single copies. pp varies; 4¼X6¼; †lp. Reporting time: week to a month. Payment: $25 & up plus 25 copies. Copyrights for author.

Oxford University Press (see BRITISH JOURNAL OF AESTHETICS; MUSIC AND LETTERS)

Oxus Press, John Stathatos, 16 Haslemere Rd., London N.8., United Kingdom. 1976. Poetry, long-poems. "The Oxus Press publishes contemporary poetry in English, European poetry, and modern Greek poetry in translation. Titles include *The Last Days of the Eagle* by David Grubb, *In Passage* by John Stathatos, *Biography & Other Poems* by Nassos Vayenas, and *Danger In The Streets* by Yannis Ritsos. British & o'seas distributors are Independent Press Dist., 12 Stevenage Rd, London SW6 6ES to whom all orders shoul be addressed." avg. press run 300-1,000 plus. 7 titles listed in the *Small Press Record of Books in Print* (9th Edition, 1980). Discounts: 33⅓ off. †of. Regret no unsolicited mss considered. Payment: 10 percent on full length books. ALP/IPD.

OXYMORON: Journal Of Convulsive Beauty, Alphaville Books, Jack Grady, 728 Hinman Avenue, Evanston, IL 60602. 1976. Poetry, fiction, parts-of-novels, collages. "Bulletin of the *Alphaville Sleep & Dream Lab.* International Surrealism. Price structure includes surface mail postage & Oxymoron supplements, issued irregularly, free of charge to subscribers. Delivery outside North America $2.00 additional per volume. Magazine exchanges and dream materials with SASE/IRC enclosed are invited. Annual. No mss. solicited yet for Vol 2 (1981)." circ. 999. 2/yr. Expects 2 issues 1980. sub. price: Volume one, (complete in one issue): $5.00 individuals; $10.00 institutions; per copy: $5.00 individuals; $10.00 institutions, postpaid; sample: $5.00 individuals; $10.00 institutions, postpaid. 64pp; 11X8½; †of/lp. reports: in spurts. Pays honoraria plus copies. Copyrighted, reverts to author. Pub's reviews. §International Surrealist Movement News. Ads: inquire. Global Psychoactivity.

Oyez, Robert Hawley, PO Box 5134, Berkeley, CA 94705. 1964. Poetry, criticism. "Books usually designed by Graham McIntosh. Usually report promptly by not reading at this time." avg. press run

500-1,000. Pub'd 4 titles 1979. avg. price, cloth: $8-$10; paper: $2.00-$6.00. 60-80pp; 5½X8½. Payment: 10% royalties and copies. Copyrights for author.

P

P.E.N. American Center, John Morrone, 47 5th Ave, New York, NY 10003. "We publish the *Grants and Awards available to American writers*. The booklet is a directory of financial assistance for the writer. The 1980/81 edition is considerably updated, and includes 37 new awards." avg. price, cloth: $3.00 + $0.50 (postage) for individuals, $6.00 + $0.50 (postage) for libraries and educators.

P.E.N. BROADSHEET, Peter Elstob, Fleur Adcock, Poetry Editor, 7 Dilke Street, Chelsea, London SW3 4JE, United Kingdom, 01-352-9549. 1975. Poetry, fiction, criticism. "Poetry is paid for at £5.00; short story (1,000 words), £20.00. A preliminary letter is advisable" circ. 1000. 2/yr. Pub'd 2 issues 1979; expects 2 issues 1980, 2 issues 1981. sub. price: £1.50 including postage; per copy: 60p; Writer's Day Issue 75p; sample: 50p. Back issues: 50p. 24pp; 21mm X 30mm. Payment: £5 poems; £20 short story (max. 1000 wds.). Copyrighted, reverts to author. Pub's reviews: 20 in 1979. §Literature, biography, Belles Lettres. Ads: £7.50/£4.

Pachart Publishing House (see also THE ASTRONOMY QUARTERLY; THE ETHNODISC JOURNAL OF RECORDED SOUND), Box 35549, Tucson, AZ 85740, (602) 297-4797. 1970. Art, music. "Astronomy & Astrophysics Series (11 vols); The Astronomy Quarterly Library (5 vols); Stochastic Press (1 vol); The Astronomy Quarterly (3 vols); The Ethnodisc Journal of Recorded Sound (11 vols)." COSMEP, RMBPA.

PACIFIC HORTICULTURE, W. George Waters, Box 485, Berkeley, CA 94701, (415) 524-1914. 1976. Articles. "We use authoritative articles on western gardening and related subjects (design, history, plant exploration, etc). These are illustrated with good botanical drawings, photographs (many in color) and well reproduced on good stock. We are establishing a reputation for gardening literature. Our book reviews are, therefore, candid-criticizing content and style." circ. 10,000. 4/yr. Pub'd 4 issues 1979; expects 4 issues 1980, 4 issues 1981. sub. price: $8.00, Foreign $10.00; per copy: $2.50; sample: $2.50 + $0.50 mailing. Back issues: most available at sample copy prices. Discounts: 40% for purchases in lots of 10 copies. 64pp; 10X7; of. Reporting time: 1 month usually, but variable. Copyrighted, reverts to author. Pub's reviews: 20-30 in 1979. §Books on plants, gardening and related subjects. Ads: $175.00/$75.00/$0.30 min $12.00. PHF.

Pacific Northwest Humanist Publications (see HUMANIST IN CANADA)

PACIFIC POETRY AND FICTION REVIEW, Campanile Press, Rex Stock, Editor; Dawn Kolokithar, Assoc. Editor; Dave Zielinski, Assoc. Editor, English Office, San Diego State University, San Diego, CA 92182, 714-266-0675. 1973. Poetry, fiction, articles, art, photos, interviews, satire, criticism, reviews, parts-of-novels, long-poems, plays. "We are seeking poetry, short fiction, graphic art, reviews, plays. Contributors: Glover Davis, Ritsos, Robert L. Jones, Borjes, Bruce H. Boston... Chandler Brossard, Jerry Bumpus, Gerald Butler." circ. 500. 2/yr. sub. price: $8.00 indiv.; $13.50 instit.; per copy: $4.00 - $7.00; sample: $3.00. Back issues: $1.00. Discounts: none. 115pp; 6X9; of. Reporting time: 6-8 weeks. Payment: 1 copy. Not copyrighted.

PACIFIC QUARTERLY/MOANA, Outrigger Publishers LTD, Norman Simms, P.O.Box 13-049, Hamilton, New Zealand. 1973. Poetry, fiction, articles, criticism, reviews, music, long-poems. "Oral and literary traditions, translations, essays, interviews, reviews" circ. 800. 4/yr. Pub'd 4 issues 1979; expects 4 issues 1980. sub. price: $12.00/yr indiv; $18.00/yr institution; per copy: $5.00; sample: $5.00. Back issues: $5.00 each. Discounts: trade retail 33⅓ percent; subscription services 10 percent. 120-180pp; size A5; of. Reporting time: 3 mos. Payment: copies. Copyrighted. Pub's reviews: 60 in 1979. §Literature, ethnic, tribal, oral traditions, criticism, translations, music, art, crafts. Ads: $100.-00/$60.00.

PACIFIC RESEARCH, Leonard M. Siegel, 867 W Dana #204, Mountain View, CA 94041, 415-969-1545. 1969. Articles, reviews. "Usually behind schedule" circ. 800. 4/yr. Expects 5 issues 1980. 1 title listed in the *Small Press Record of Books in Print* (9th Edition, 1980). sub. price: $10.00-U.S.; $12.00-Foreign/2 yr; per copy: $1.50; sample: free. Back issues: $1.00 for Vol 9 #2 and before (shorter format). 24-32pp; 8½X11; of. Reporting time: 1 month. Payment: $50.00-$100.00. Pub's reviews. §US economy & foreign policy; Asia; Latin America. Ads: Exchange ads for similar publications.

PADAN ARAM, David Joselit, Cynthia Zarin, Sarah Relyea, 52 Dunster Street, Harvard U, Cambridge, MA 02138, 495-2807. 1975. Poetry, fiction, art, photos, reviews, long-poems, concrete art. "We try for a sparse, clean layout, and prefer publishing several poems by the same author rather than single pieces. Award winning graphics. Recent contributors include Robert Bly, Peter Mattair, James Richardson, and Cedric Whitman." circ. 14,000. 4/yr. Pub'd 4 issues 1979; expects 4 issues 1980. sub. price: $4.00; per copy: $.50; sample: $0.50 postage. Back issues: Price on request for available issues. 16pp; 11X13; lp. Reporting time: 4-6 weeks. Payment: none. Copyrighted. §poetry and short fiction. Ads: $134.40/$71.40.

Padma Press, Carol Stetser, PO Box 56, Oatman, AZ 86433. 1976. Photos. "*Padma Press* publishes high-quality black and white photography books, postcards and posters. In print-*Black And White-1977, Chopping Wood, Carrying Water-1978, Continuum, An Autobiography at Thirty-1979*" avg. press run 2,000. Pub'd 1 title 1979; expects 1 title 1980. 3 titles listed in the *Small Press Record of Books in Print* (9th Edition, 1980). avg. price, paper: $6.95. Discounts: 40 percent trade. 56pp; 8½X11; of. not accepting unsolicited manuscripts at the present time. Payment: negotiable. Does not copyright for author.

Padre Productions (see also COLLECTOR'S ITEM; WESTERN PUBLISHING SCENE), Lachlan P. MacDonald, PO Box 1275, San Luis Obispo, CA 93406, 805-543-5404. 1973. Fiction, articles, art, photos, reviews, news items. "Padre Productions concentrates on Western travel, especially unconventional books illustrated with line drawings, and on antiques and collectibles (illustrated by photos and drawings); however, art, children's, self-help and general titles are of interest. One poetry anthology scheduled." avg. press run 3,500, usually 3,000 paperback and 500 hardcover. Pub'd 4 titles 1979; expects 2 titles 1980, 8 titles 1981. avg. price, cloth: $7.50; paper: $4.95. Discounts: 1-4 copies 20 percent; 5-100 40 percent. Payment with order. Fully returnable 90 days to 1 year if resalable condition. Trade. 160pp; 5½X8 & 6X9; of. Reporting time: 10 days-2 weeks. Payment varies according to involvement, usually 10 percent. Copyrights for author. COSMEP.

PAID MY DUES: JOURNAL OF WOMEN AND MUSIC, Calliope Publishing Inc., Karen Corti, Kathryn Gohl, P.O. Box 6517, Chicago, IL 60680. 1974. Articles, art, photos, cartoons, interviews, criticism, reviews, music, letters, news items. "Reviews 700-1,000 words; articles not more than 5,000. Interest in how-to articles. We have a definite feminist editorial stance" circ. 2,500-3,000. 4/yr. Pub'd 4 issues 1979; expects 3 issues 1980, 3 issues 1981. sub. price: $10.00/$15.00 instit.; per copy: $2.50; sample: $2.25 plus 53¢ postage. Back issues: Vol 1 no longer available; Vol 2, 3 each issue $2.25 plus 53¢ postage. Discounts: Bulk rate (5 or more) 30% or 35% prepaid, would give same discount for classroom use; will give 20% to jobbers on institutional sub rate of $15.00 per year. 44pp; 8½X11; of. Reporting time: 1-3 months. Payment: $10.00 per thousand words; $4.00 per photo or graphic; will pay at higher rate in exchange advertising. Copyrighted, reverts to author. Pub's reviews: 3 in 1979. §Folk, jazz, classical interests, women musicians, songwriters, composers, conductors. Ads: $225.00/$125.00/$1.00 per line of 33 char.

PAINTBRUSH: A Journal of Poetry, Translations & Letters, Ishtar Press, Inc., Ben Bennani, Dept. of English, Riyadh University, P.O.Box 2456, Riyadh, Saudi Arabia. 1974. Poetry, articles, interviews, criticism, reviews. "Richard Eberhart, Denise Levertov, David Ignatow, George Keithley, Joseph Bruchac, Douglas Blazek, Charles Levendosky, Sam Hamill, G. Wilson Knight, and others." circ. 500. 2/yr. Pub'd 2 issues 1979; expects 2 issues 1980. sub. price: $5.00 in U.S./$6.00 Foreign; per copy: $3.00; sample: $3.00. Back issues: 2,3,4, $2.00/5,6 $3.00. Discounts: 20-40%. 65pp; 5½X8½; of/lp. Reporting time: 1-2 weeks. Payment: copies also monies when available. Copyrighted, reverts to author. Pub's reviews: 15 in 1979. §poetry & translations. Ads: $75/$35. CCLM, COSMEP, Associated Writing Programs.

PAINTED BRIDE QUARTERLY, Painted Bride Press, Louise Simons, R. Daniel Evans, Kate Britt, 527 South St, Philadelphia, PA 19147, 215-925-9914. 1973. Poetry, art, photos, criticism, reviews, music, long-poems. "*PBQ* is a literary journal of the arts: poetry, reviews, essays, performance, art work and photography. Publish eclectic material. Many different first-rate poets. No fiction. Include SASE." circ. 1,000. 4/yr. Pub'd 4 issues 1979; expects 4 issues 1980, 4 issues 1981. sub. price: $6.00; per copy: $1.50 single issue or $3.00 double issue, plus 50¢ postage; sample: $2.00 single, $3.50 double. Back issues: Vary-several rare issues. single issue 72pp; 6X9; of. Reporting time: 3-6 months. Payment: 2 copies. Copyrighted. Pub's reviews: 8 in 1979. §literature, performance. Ads: $50/$30. CCLM, COSMEP.

Painted Bride Press (see PAINTED BRIDE QUARTERLY)

Pajarito Publications (see also DE COLORES: Journal of Emerging Raza Philosophy), Jose Armas, Managing Editor; Helena Quintana, Linda Morales Armas, P.O.Box 7264, Albuquerque, NM 87104,

292

505-242-2839. 1973. Poetry, fiction, articles, art, interviews, criticism, reviews, music, letters, long-poems, collages, plays, concrete art. avg. press run 2000. Pub'd 4 titles 1979; expects 4 titles 1980, 4 titles 1981. 12 titles listed in the *Small Press Record of Books in Print* (9th Edition, 1980). avg. price, cloth: $8.00; paper: $6.00; other: Journal: $3.00 indiv.: $5.00 instit. Discounts: Bookstores 40% on 5 books or more; libraries 10%. 88pp; 9X6; of. Reporting time: 4 months. Payment: in copies. Copyrights for author. CCLM, RAYAS.

Pakka Press (see also JOYCEAN LIVELY ARTS GUILD REVIEW), Jack Sughrue, Box 459, East Douglas, MA 01516, (617) 476-7630. 1979. Poetry, fiction, articles, art, interviews, reviews, long-poems. "Mostly poetry and graphics" avg. press run 500. Pub'd 2 titles 1979. avg. price, paper: $3.50. Discounts: 40%. 72pp; 5X7; of. Reporting time: not accepting submissions at present. Payment: 25% above costs. Copyrights for author. COSMEP, NESPA, SPRIL.

EL PALACIO, Museum of New Mexico Press, Richard Polese, Editor, P.O. Box 2087, Santa Fe, NM 87503, (505) 827-2352. 1913. Articles, art, photos, reviews. "Issues planned yr in advance; several articles per year by commission. Enquiries required in advance on freelance. College-level popular style; 2,500-5,000 words, art supplied by author. Museum related topics, Southwest or Western slant (usually). Recent contributors: Dorothy Dunn Kramer, Betty Toulouse, Nancy Warren, Joan M. Burroughs, James R. Morgan, Yedida K. Stillman" circ. 2,000 plus. 4/yr. Pub'd 4 issues 1979; expects 4 issues 1980, 4 issues 1981. sub. price: $10.00; per copy: $2.50; sample: $2.50. Back issues: $3.00 for copies from 1918-1969/face value thereafter. Discounts: 40% trade-15% inst. 48pp; 8½X11; of. Reporting time: 2 wks-2 mos. Payment: $50.00. Copyrighted, does not revert to author. Pub's reviews: 28 in 1979. §anthro, archeology, history, fine arts folk art-western or southwest topic, natural history, geography. no ads.

Paladin Enterprises, Inc., Peter C. Lund, President and Publisher; Devon Christensen, Senior Editor; Timothy J. Leifield, General Manager, PO Box 1307, Boulder, CO 80306, (303) 443-7250. 1970. "Non-fiction manuscripts on military related subjects are given first consideration. These include weaponry technology, self-defense, survival, terrorism, political kidnapping. When accompanied with photos, ms are reviewed and returned within three weeks. Lenghth of material 25,000 to 35,000. SASE required. Recent works: *Life after Doomsday* by Bruce D. Clayton; *Crimson Web of Terror* by Robert Chapman; *The Pictorial History of U.S. Sniping* by Peter R. Senich" avg. press run 3,500. Pub'd 20 titles 1979; expects 22 titles 1980, 25 titles 1981. 52 titles listed in the *Small Press Record of Books in Print* (9th Edition, 1980). avg. price, cloth: $10.95; paper: $6.00; other: $3.00 (reprints of technical manuals). Discounts: $50-$100 retail value — 40% all titles except supplementary list; over $100 — 50% except supplementaty list; over $1000 — 55% except supplementary list. 175pp; 6X9 and 8½X11; of. Reporting time: 4 weeks. Payment: Standard 10, 12 & 15%. Copyrights for author.

PALERMO ANTIGRUPPO, Sicilian Antigruppo, Nat Scammacca, Crescenzio Cane, Villa Scanimac via Argenteria Km 4, 91100, Sicily, 0923-38681. 1968. Poetry, articles, satire, criticism, reviews, letters, long-poems, collages, concrete art. "3-5 pages in English and Italian. A poetry review of the Sicilian Antigruppo, a populist movement of pluralistic commitment, leftist. Contributors: Crescenzio Cane, Nat Scammacca, Lollini, Jack Hirschman, Guiseppe Zagarrio, Mariella Bettarini, Pietro Ter-minelli, Ignazio Apolloni, Carmelo Pirrera, Santo Cali, V. Bonanno." circ. 1,000. 3/yr. 24 titles listed in the *Small Press Record of Books in Print* (9th Edition, 1980). 44pp; 6X8; of/lp. Reporting time: 1 month. Payment: none. Copyrighted, reverts to author. Pub's reviews. §Poetry, poetics, criticism.

Palimpsest Workshop, John Alspaugh, Sally Doud, Joseph Robertson, 1421 Grove Avenue No.2, Richmond, VA 23220. 1978. Poetry, art, photos. "Poems through 3 pages in length, art & photos 5 x 7" avg. press run 500. Pub'd 1 title 1979; expects 1 title 1980. 1 title listed in the *Small Press Record of Books in Print* (9th Edition, 1980). avg. price, paper: $2.50; other: leather, $8.00. 50pp; 6X9; of. Reporting time: 8 weeks. Copyrights for author. COSMEP.

PAN AMERICAN REVIEW, Funch Press, Seth Wade, 1101 Tori Lane, Edinburg, TX 78539, 512-383-7893. 1970. "Good translations of Latin-American work (include originals) plus original poems, concrete poems, visual poems, poemdrawings, photographs, prose poems, drawings, fiction, articles, especially any material relating to Latin America. Some contributors: Neruda, Parra, Paz, Duran, Isla, Latta, Marvin Cohen, Lifshin, Lawder, Oliphant, Quagliano, Harley Elliott, Fritz Hamil-ton, Clarence Alva Powell." circ. 1,000-2,000. 2/yr. sub. price: $4.00; per copy: $2.00. Discounts: 40%. 64pp; 6X9; of. Reporting time: 1-4 weeks. Payment: copies. Copyrighted. COSMEP.

PANACHE, Panache Books, David Lenson, Candice Ward, PO Box 77, Sunderland, MA 01375, 413-367-2762. 1965. Poetry, fiction, parts-of-novels, long-poems, concrete art. "Not reading through 1981" circ. 750. Irregular. Pub'd 1 issue 1979; expects 1 issue 1980. sub. price: $2.50; per copy: $1.50; sample: $1.50. Back issues: Inquire for price list. Discounts: 40%. 64pp; 5½X8½; of/lp. Reporting time: one month. Payment: $3.00 page. Copyrighted, reverts to author. Ads: $25.00/$15.00. CCLM, COSMEP, NESPA.

Panache Books (see also PANACHE), David Lenson, Candice Ward, P.O. Box 77, Sunderland, MA 01375. 1965. Poetry, fiction, long-poems. "Not reading through 1981" avg. press run 500. Pub'd 2 titles 1979; expects 2 titles 1980. 4 titles listed in the *Small Press Record of Books in Print* (9th Edition, 1980). avg. price, paper: $3.50. Discounts: 40%. 64pp; 6X9; lp. Reporting time: 1 month. Payment: 10% of first press run. When 2nd printing occurs, contract will be renegotiated. copyright optional. NESPA, CCLM, COSMEP.

Pancake Press, Patrick Smith, 163 Galewood Circle, San Francisco, CA 94131, 415-648-3573. 1973. Poetry, long-poems. "Our principle interest is in first poetry books by writers who have fairly long experience. We want to do small first editions of poetry books which are the product of several years writing, and which have value as an autobiographical account of a significant social role—workers in all fields, sufferers of various passions, role-changers, all the democratic atoms of our national life." avg. press run 150. Pub'd 6 titles 1979. 3 titles listed in the *Small Press Record of Books in Print* (9th Edition, 1980). avg. price, paper: $5.00. Discounts: 25% for less than 25; 40% for 26-99; 48% 100 and over. 35-50pp; 5½ & 7X8½; of. Reporting time: 1 month. Payment: arranged by mutual consent. Does not copyright for author. COSMEP, WCPC.

Panda Programs, Georg Finder, Editorial; Kitty Futo, Graphics & Arts, 1872 W Lotus Place, Brea, CA 92621, (714) 990-6800. 1978. "All of our materials are introductory explanations of things that often scare children. No matter how bad it is, we imagine what we don't know about as much much worse than it usually really is. We are interested in subjects, and authors, who can help us to this." avg. press run 500-10,000. Pub'd 4 titles 1979; expects 8 titles 1980. 8 titles listed in the *Small Press Record of Books in Print* (9th Edition, 1980). avg. price, paper: $2.50; other: professional series/avail only to professionals, not the public. Discounts: 40-50% to distributors, group qty special pricing. 36pp; 8½X11; of. Reporting time: 45 days or less. Payment: varies.

PANDORA, An Original Anthology of Role-expanding Science Fiction and Fantsy, Spring Inc., Lois Wickstrom, 1150 St. Paul Street, Denver, CO 80206. 1973. Poetry, fiction, articles, art, cartoons, interviews, satire, criticism, reviews, music, letters, parts-of-novels, plays, news items. "Stories should be under 5,000 words, articles under 1,000 words, reviews 200-600 words, poems 20 lines or less, must be related to science fiction or fantasy. All contents of *Pandora* must be non-sexist, non-racist, non-stereotyped. Reviews, interviews, and articles should take this editorial preference into account." circ. 1,000. 4/yr. Pub'd 1 issue 1979; expects 3 issues 1980, 3 issues 1981. sub. price: $6.00; per copy: $2.50; sample: $2.50. Back issues: Set of first 4= $4.50; No. 1=$1.60; No. 2=$1.60; No.3=$2.00; No.4=$2.50. Discounts: Trade, 40%; bulk, 50%; recipient pays shipping. 64pp; 5½X8½; of. Reporting time: I try to report the same day I receive the manuscript. Payment: $.01 a word for stories, articles; $2.00 for poems; $10.00 for art (all one time use). Copyrighted, reverts to author. Pub's reviews: 15 in 1979. §Science fiction, fantasy, science (biology, chemisty, physics, esp, etc.). Ads: $30.00/$15.00/$0.05; National $60.00/$30.00/$0.05. COSMEP, SCBW, Feminist Writers Guild, Small Press Writers and Artists Organization.

PANDORA'S BOX, Joyce Farmer, Chin Lyvely, Box 845, Laguna Beach, CA 92652, (714) 494-7930.

THE PANHANDLER, University of West Florida, Pensacola, FL 32504, 904-476-9500. 1976. Poetry, fiction, art, photos, reviews. "Poetry 1-3 pages; fiction up to 15 ms. pp. Our only bias is toward poetry and fiction which exhibit technical proficiency and engage the reader. On the lookout for good new writers. Recently: Stephen Dunning, Malcolm Glass, Jim Hall, John Ower, David Kirby, Susan Ludvigson." circ. 1,500. 2/yr. Pub'd 2 issues 1979; expects 2 issues 1980, 2 issues 1981. price per copy: free on request w/ return postage; sample: free on request w/ return postage. Back issues: free on request w/ return postage. 48-64pp; 6X9; of. Reporting time: 2 weeks to 3 months. Payment: copies. Copyrighted, reverts to author. no ads. COSMEP.

Panjandrum Books (see also PANJANDRUM POETRY JOURNAL), Dennis Koran, L.J. Harris, 11321 Irva Ave., Ste.1, Los Angeles, CA 90025, (213) 477-8771. 1971. "Panjandrum Books (with Aris Books) publishes quality paperbacks on selected non-fiction subjects. Recently centering in the fields of health, diet, cooking, music, and literature. Panjandrum Press Inc publishes poetry and occasionally fiction." avg. press run 3-5,000; poetry: 1000. Pub'd 5 titles 1979; expects 7 titles 1980, 8 titles 1981. 32 titles listed in the *Small Press Record of Books in Print* (9th Edition, 1980). avg. price, cloth: $10-12; paper: $3-6. Discounts: Standard to bookstores and other retailers. Wholesalers please request further information.u. non-fiction: 150pp; poetry: 64pp; size varies; of. Reporting time: 1 month. Payment: varies. Copyrights for author. CCLM, WIP.

PANJANDRUM POETRY JOURNAL, Panjandrum Books, Dennis Koran, Ed-in-Chief; David

Guss, Assoc. Ed., 11321 Irva Ave. Ste.1, Los Angeles, CA 90025, (213) 477-8771. 1971. Poetry, fiction, art, photos, cartoons, reviews, collages. "eclectic; Rothenberg, Einzig, de Angulo, Bly, Ferlinghetti, Norse, McClure, Doria, Beausoleil, Vose, Weiss, Fraser, Vinograd, etc." circ. 2,000. 1/yr. Pub'd 2 issues 1979; expects 1 issue 1980, 1 issue 1981. sub. price: $10.00 Indiv., 3 issues; $14.00 Instit., 3 issues; per copy: $3.95; sample: Varies with issue ordered as sample, plus shipping. Back issues: PAN 1: $5.00; 2-3, o.p.; 4, $3.00; 5: $3.00; 6/7: $3.95. Discounts: Trade: 1, 20 percent; 2-3, 30 percent; 4-25, 40 percent; 25-up, 50 percent. No library disc. Jobbers: 1-3, 20 percent; 4-25, 40 percent; 26-up, 45 percent. 100-140pp; size usually 5½X8½; of. Reporting time: 1 month. Payment: As grants are avail.; $10.00/submission plus 2 copies of issue. Copyrighted, reverts with written permission. §all areas. no ads. CCLM, WIP.

Pantagraph (see SOU'WESTER)

Pantheon Press (see COSMOPOLITAN CONTACT)

Papa Bach Paperbacks (see also BACHY), John Harris, Reviews; Leland Hickman, Poetry and Prose; Rod Bradley, Art & Photography, 11317 Santa Monica Blvd, Los Angeles, CA 90025, (213) GRUBERG. 1972. Poetry, fiction, articles, art, photos, cartoons, interviews, satire, criticism, reviews, music, letters, parts-of-novels, long-poems, collages, plays, concrete art. "BACHY publishes serious poetry & fiction of highest quality, experimental or traditional, any length. Also related essays & reviews, black & white photography and graphic art" avg. press run 1000. Pub'd 3 titles 1979; expects 3 titles 1980, 4 titles 1981. avg. price, paper: $3.50; other: $3.00. Discounts: 40%. 170pp; 8½X11; of. Reporting time: 8 weeks. Payment: Author's copies only. Copyrights for author. CCLM, COSMEP, WIP.

PAPER AIR, Singing Horse Press, Gil Ott, Editor, 825 Morris Road, Blue Bell, PA 19422. 1976. Poetry, fiction, articles, art, interviews, criticism, reviews, music, letters, long-poems. "Correspondence is the substance of PAPER AIR. Each issue is a culmination of a moment of continuing dialogue among participants. Special issues on individual poets seem well suited to this*published John Taggart number 1979, Jackson Mac Low special summer 1980. Other central figures in the project include: Ron Silliman, Toby Olson, Karl Young, Craig Watson, David Miller" circ. 500. 2/yr. Pub'd 2 issues 1979; expects 1 issue 1981. sub. price: $8.00 indiv; $10.00 instit; per copy: $3.00; sample: $3.00. Back issues: $2.00 each, 1st 3 issues (Vol.1); Taggart issue $3.00. Discounts: 40% on orders of 3 or more copies. 72pp; 8½X11; of. individual attention. Payment: Individual arrangement. Copyrighted, reverts to author. Pub's reviews: 6 in 1979. §Poetry, essays. Ads: $100.00/$50.00. CCLM.

PAPER NEWS, Vanity Press, Tuli Kupferberg, 160 6th Avenue, New York, NY 10013, 212-925-3823. 1980. Poetry, cartoons, satire, music, news items. "Want short satire and found materials on humor of all kinds." circ. 500. irregular. 2 titles listed in the *Small Press Record of Books in Print* (9th Edition, 1980). price per copy: $0.25; sample: free. Back issues: $5.00 which lasts for infinity or the life of the paper (whichever is longer). Discounts: 40%. 16pp; 4½X5½; of. Reporting time: short. Ads: no ads.

Paperweight Press, L. H. Selman, 761 Chestnut Street, Santa Cruz, CA 95060, (408) 427-1177. 1975. Art. avg. press run 3,000. Pub'd 1 title 1979; expects 1 title 1980, 3 titles 1981. avg. price, cloth: $30.00. Discounts: 6 or more copies, 40%; Jobber 200 or more, 60%. 200pp; 8½X11; of. Payment: 5% cover price. Copyrights for author.

Papillon Press (see also LES PAPILLONS, A Journal of Modern Philosophical Inquiry), Beth J. Linn, Elizabeth J. Jeska, 3715 Talmadge Road, Toledo, OH 43606, (419) 474-6773. 1979. Fiction, articles, art, photos, interviews, reviews, news items. "Non-fiction books and some fiction. Papillon press is accepting articles pertaining to modern philosophical inquiry for a quarterly periodical, and for an anthology of philosophical articles which is now being compiled. Articles in the anthology will be slightly longer than those in the magazine, but all articles will be read as possible candidates for either publication. 'Every living soul has a personal philosophy of life, whether they know it or not,' comments B.J. Jeska, president of Papillon Press. 'We are looking for those writers who have given in-depth thought to their personal philosophies in light of the modern world.' Papillon Press specializes in philosophical and religious writings including: mysticism, yoga, meditation, theosophy, philosophy, health, psychology and varied realms of the metaphysical sciences. Fiction is also encouraged, but query first. A special issue of the periodical devoted to book reviews of recent releases in the metaphysical and philosophical sciences will be published each year. Articles should be 1,000 to 3,000 words. Previously published works will be considered. Send query, manuscript or request for writer's guidelines with SASE to Papillon Press, 3715 Talmadge Road, Toledo, OH 43606. No phone queries, please." avg. press run 500-1,000. Pub'd 1-2 titles 1979; expects 4 titles 1980, 4 titles 1981. avg. price, cloth: $9.95; paper: $6.95. Discounts: Standard. 250-350pp; 6X9; of. Reporting time: 2 months.

Payment: Standard 10%, some mss with subsidy. Copyrights for author. COSMEP.

LES PAPILLONS, A Journal of Modern Philosophical Inquiry, Papillon Press, Beth J. Linn, Elizabeth J. Jeska, 3715 Talmadge Road, Toledo, OH 43606, (419) 474-6773. 1979. Fiction, articles, art, photos, interviews, reviews, letters, news items. "We will not accept articles that lean toward any religious or political movement or those that express biases toward any ethnic group. We are looking for inquiry, not platforms. 1,100 to 3,000 words or less. *Les Papillons* explores the modern age with emphasis upon thought and attitude. Our writers come from many walks of life with divergent attitudes and expressions of life. The meaning of existence is explored in light of 'new age' trends. The audience is general-both scholars and laypersons. Writing should be simple and concise-to appeal to both audiences. Accepting: articles and book reviews. Photos and artwork with articles will be considered. Author must provide permissions to reprint if needed. A brief biography of the author should accompany articles. Include titles of published works if any. Biographies will be printed unless instructions otherwise are received. Poetry should be fitting to the theme of the publication-inspirational or speculative. Some artwork will be considered. Not necessary to query first. Artwork can be of any nature. Book Reviews: Current releases (two year limit) of books in the philosophical, metaphysical or religious sciences. We are not interested in totally negative reviews. If the book to be reviewed only warrants a negative review, don't waste your time, our time or page space with it. Submission Requirements: All copy typed, double-spaced with wide margins, one side of sheet. All pages should contain title, author and page number. Staple in left corner only or no binding. No handwritten manuscripts will be read or accepted. Miscellaneous: Copyrights will revert to author after publication. If an article is selected for an anthology being compiled, arrangements will be made separately for payment, rights and permissions. Previously published works will be considered-rigths to reprint are authors responsibility." 4/yr. Pub'd 4 issues 1979; expects 4 issues 1980, 4 issues 1981. sub. price: $12.00; per copy: $3.00; sample: $3.00. Back issues: No back issues at this time. Discounts: Classroom, 40%; Trade, 40%. 48pp; 6X9; of. Reporting time: 30-45 days. Payment: copies with plans for cash in the future. Copyrighted, reverts to author. Pub's reviews: 4 in 1979. Ads: $150.00/$75.00. COSMEP.

Parable Press, Bethany Strong, 136 Gray Street, Amherst, MA 01002, 413-253-5634. 1976. "Drama, fiction and non-fiction, graphics" avg. press run 1,000. Pub'd 3 titles 1979; expects 2 titles 1981. 2 titles listed in the *Small Press Record of Books in Print* (9th Edition, 1980). avg. price, cloth: $10.95; paper: $5.95. Discounts: 40% trade discount over 100 copies by arrangement. 400pp; 6X8; of. Copyrights for author. COSMEP, NESPA.

PARABOLA MAGAZINE, The Society for the Study of Myth & Tradition, D.M. Dooling, Publisher; Susan Bergholz, Exec Editor, 150 Fifth Avenue, New York, NY 10011, (212) 924-0004. 1976. Poetry, fiction, articles, interviews, criticism, reviews. "*PARABOLA* publishes articles of 3,000-5,000 words, reviews of 750 words on scholarly subjects but with a literate and lively style. Recent contributions are Huston Smith, Gary Snyder, Fritjof Capra, Robert Bly, P.L. Travers, Joseph Campbell, Jacob Needleman. Issues are organized by theme, androgyny, sacred dance, music/sound and silence, sacred space, earth and spirit among them." circ. 12,000. 4/yr. Pub'd 4 issues 1979; expects 4 issues 1980, 4 issues 1981. sub. price: $14.00; per copy: $4.00; sample: $4.00. Back issues: $6.50 (includes $1.50 postage and handling). Discounts: Trade, 30%; Bulk, 30%; Agency, 15%. 128pp; 6¾X10; of. Reporting time: 14 days. Payment: yes. Copyrighted, reverts to author. Pub's reviews: 65 in 1979. §Mythology, comparative religion, anthropology, folklore, novels, children's books, science fiction. Ads: $395.00/$275.00.

Parachuting Publications, Dan Poynter, P.O. Box 4232-Q, Santa Barbara, CA 93103, 805-968-7277. 1969. Photos, cartoons, news items. "I write, produce and market my own books. The author/publisher of 14 books, Dan Poynter is a consultant to the mail order and publishing industries" avg. press run 10,000. Pub'd 6 titles 1979; expects 7 titles 1980, 6 titles 1981. 13 titles listed in the *Small Press Record of Books in Print* (9th Edition, 1980). avg. price, cloth: $11.95; paper: $6.95. Discounts: start at 40 percent. 180pp; 6X9; of. Copyrights for author. COSMEP.

Parachuting Resources, Michael Horan, P.O.Box 1333, Richmond, IN 47374, (513) 456-4686. 1976. "I've printed 2 books: *Index to Parachuting 1900-1975*, and *Parachuting Folklore, the Evolution of Freefall* ." Expects 1 title 1980, 1 title 1981. 1 title listed in the *Small Press Record of Books in Print* (9th Edition, 1980). avg. price, cloth: $13.95; paper: $7.95. Discounts: Dealer: 40-50%. 214pp; 6X9; of. COSMEP.

PARACHUTIST, Paul C. Proctor, Director of Publications, 806 15th St. NW. Suite 444, Washington, DC 20005. 1958. Articles, photos, cartoons, reviews, news items. "Photographs" circ. 19,000. 12/yr. Pub'd 12 issues 1979; expects 12 issues 1980, 12 issues 1981. sub. price: $14.50; per copy: $1.50; sample: $1.00. 44pp; 8½X11; of. Reporting time: two weeks. Payment: no. Copyrighted, does not revert to author. Pub's reviews: 6 in 1979. §aviation sports. Ads: $470/$281/60¢ ($6 min.).

Paradise Loft, Carol J. Ott, 241 W 23rd Street, New York, NY 10011, (212) 675-7226.

Paradise Press, Susan King, 815 Ocean Front Walk #1, Venice, CA 90291, (213) 392-4098 and 478-4477. 1976. Poetry, fiction, art, photos, letters, long-poems, collages. avg. press run 300. Pub'd 2 titles 1979; expects 2 titles 1980, 3 titles 1981. 6 titles listed in the *Small Press Record of Books in Print* (9th Edition, 1980). avg. price, cloth: $15.00; paper: $6.00. Discounts: 50% on 5 or more copies. 30pp; size varies; †of/lp. Payment: 15% royalty. Copyrights for author.

PARAGRAPH: A QUARTERLY OF GAY FICTION, The Antares Foundation, N. A. Diaman, Editor; D.G.H. Schramm, Associate Editor, Box 14051, San Francisco, CA 94114. 1978. Fiction, art, satire. "The emphasis will be on literary excellence; a balance between lesbian and gay male work will be maintained in each issue; innovative, experimental and erotic material will be considered; foreign works in English translation." 4/yr. Pub'd 1 issue 1979; expects 1 issue 1980, 4 issues 1981. sub. price: $10/individuals, $12/foreign, $15/institutions; per copy: $3/indiv., $4/for., $5/inst.; sample: $3/indiv., $4/for., $5/inst. Discounts: 40%/trade prepaid. 72pp; 6X9; of. Reporting time: up to 8 weeks. Payment: contributors copies. Copyrighted, reverts to author.

PARCHMENT (Broadside Series), Perry Peterson, 524 Larson Street, Waupaca, WI 54981, (715) 258-2657. 1979. Poetry, art, letters. "*Parchment* is open to any poetry or art of merit. If haiku, submit at least five. Prefer inks and high-contrast art. All submissions must have SASE." circ. 100, signed & numbered. 6/yr. Pub'd 10 issues 1979; expects 6 issues 1980, 6 issues 1981. sub. price: $2.00; per copy: $0.50; sample: $0.50. Back issues: $0.50. 1pp; 8½X11; of. Reporting time: 2 months. Payment: 20 copies. Copyrighted, reverts to author.

Parenting Press, Betsy Crary, 7750 31st Avenue, NE, Seattle, WA 98115, 206-525-4660. 1979. Articles. "Non-fiction. Parent education" avg. press run 5,000. Pub'd 1 title 1979; expects 1 title 1980, 2 titles 1981. 1 title listed in the *Small Press Record of Books in Print* (9th Edition, 1980). avg. price, paper: $6.95. 100pp; 8½X11; of. Reporting time: 2 months. Payment: case-by-case.

PARIS REVIEW, George A. Plimpton, Editor; Fayette Hickox, Managing Editor, 45-39 171 Place, Flushing, NY 11358, 539-7085. 1952. Poetry, fiction, articles, photos, interviews, parts-of-novels, long-poems, collages. "Prose, fiction, poetry, interviews with eminent authors. Writing published tends to the contemporary modes." circ. 10,000. 4/yr. Pub'd 4 issues 1979; expects 4 issues 1980, 4 issues 1981. sub. price: 4 issues for $11.00; per copy: $3.50; sample: $4.10. Back issues: list available upon request. Discounts: 40% returnable, 50% non-returnable. 200pp; 8½X5¼; of. Reporting time: 6 weeks. Payment: Poems: $15-$100 depending on length, prose: $100-$200 depending... Copyrighted, reverts to author. Ads: $250.00/$150.00. CCLM.

PARIS VOICES, Ken Timmerman, Dan Hallford, John Cate, Antanas Sileika, c/o Shakespeare & Co., 37 rue de la Bucherie, Paris 75005, France, 806.44.95. 1977. Poetry, fiction, art, photos, criticism, reviews, parts-of-novels, long-poems. "*Paris Voices* is at the service of the expatriate literary community living in Europe. Little or no material is accepted from Britain or the U.S., unless written by a foreign national. Bias is for the well crafted, whether innovative or more traditional. Recent contributors include Stewart Lindh, Judith Mandelbaum, Patrick Henry, Anne Morgan, Jean Fanchette, Cecil Helman, John Bovey, John Kendrick, Patrice de la Tour de Pin." circ. 1,000. 3/yr. Pub'd 3 issues 1979; expects 3 issues 1980, 3 issues 1981. sub. price: $9.00; per copy: $2.25; sample: $1.00. Back issues: $2.00 depending on stock. Discounts: 30% trade, 40% bulk (more than 10 copies, 50% jobber. 80pp; 5X8; of. Reporting time: 3-6 weeks. Payment: 3 copies on publication. Copyrighted, reverts to author. Pub's reviews: 1 in 1979. §We're beginning a European small press review: also, American mags and small press books welcome, and will be acknowledged. We're also interested in trading subscriptions. Ads: $85.00/$50.00.

Parnassos (see THE CHARIOTEER)

PARNASSUS: POETRY IN REVIEW, Herbert Leibowitz, 205 West 89th Street, New York, NY 10024, (212) 787-3569. 1972. "Length varies from four pages to forty. Editorial policy is intentionally eclectic. Recent and forthcoming contributors: Adrienne Rich, Jonathan Williams, Guy Davenport, Elizabeth Sewell, Ross Feld, Paul Metcalf, Rosellen Brown, R.W. Flint, Michael Harper, Octavio Paz, Hayden Carruth, Alice Walker" circ. 1,500. 2/yr. Pub'd 2 issues 1979; expects 2 issues 1980, 2 issues 1981. sub. price: $10.00, $13.00 Libraries & Institutions; per copy: $5.00; sample: $5.00. Back issues: $3.75 each,$3.75, $4.25, $5.25, $7.25 for special issues. Discounts: 10% to magazine subscription agencies, 30-40% to bookstores. 250pp; 6X9¼; of. Reporting time: 3 weeks to 2 months. Payment: $25.00 average, occasionally more. Copyrighted, reverts on request. Pub's reviews: 40-50 in 1979. §Poetry. Ads: $175.00/$100.00/none. CCLM, COSMEP.

Paul G. Partington, Paul G. Partington, 7320 South Gretna Avenue, Whittier, CA 90606, (213)

695-7960. 1977. avg. press run 1,250. Pub'd 1 title 1979. 1 title listed in the *Small Press Record of Books in Print* (9th Edition, 1980). avg. price, cloth: $15.00. Discounts: 40% to jobbers and bookstores. 200pp; 8½X11; of.

Partisan Press, Helene Ellenbogen, Wayne Parker, PO Box 2193, Seattle, WA 98111, (206) 622-3132. 1978. Poetry, fiction, articles, art, satire, criticism, reviews. "Partisan Press is a new publishing project specializing in anarchist and left libertarian books, posters, and broadsides. We are planning four titles for our first year of publishing, which include two volumes of political theory (contemporary), a political autobiography (contemporary), and a technicl manual on police investigation methods. We intend to focus primarily on original material, and are open to the possibility of publishing fiction as well as non-fiction in the future. Our current planned titles range from 120 to 400 pages in length." avg. press run 3,000. Pub'd 4 titles 1979. avg. price, paper: $4.95. Discounts: Essentially three rates are anticipated: retail (single copies) full price; bookstores 40%; distributors 50-60%. 200pp; 5X8; of. Reporting time: 6 weeks. Payment: variable, 10-12%, no advances.

PARTISAN REVIEW, William Phillips, 128 Bay State Road, Boston, MA 02215, (617) 353-4260. 1934. Poetry, fiction, articles, interviews, criticism, reviews, parts-of-novels, long-poems, letters, plays. circ. 8,200. 4/yr. Pub'd 4 issues 1979; expects 4 issues 1980, 4 issues 1981. sub. price: $10.00, $9.00 Student Rate; per copy: $2.75; sample: $2.75. Back issues: $3.00. 164pp; 4¼X7⅜; of. Reporting time: 3 to 4 months. Payment: 1½¢ word, prose; 40¢ line poetry. Copyrighted. Pub's reviews: 18 in 1979. §books literature, politics, art, general culture, have backlog now. Ads: $200.00/$120.00. CCLM.

Partners In Publishing (see also PIP COLLEGE 'HELPS' NEWSLETTER), P.M. Fielding, Box 50347, Tulsa, OK 74150, (918) 583-0956. 1976. Articles, interviews, reviews, letters, news items. "We are only interested in material directed to persons who work with learning disabled youth or adults *or* material directed to the learning disabled young person or adult. Emphasis on college, vocational training or career information. Authors should have academic credentials or practical experience." avg. press run 2,000. Pub'd 2 titles 1979; expects 2 titles 1980, 1 title 1981. 1 title listed in the *Small Press Record of Books in Print* (9th Edition, 1980). avg. price, paper: $10.00. 140pp; 8X10; of. Reporting time: 1 month. Payment: varies. Does not copyright for author.

PASS-AGE: A Futures Journal, Robert Kahn, Timothy Wessels, PO Box 160, Dublin, NH 03444, 215-222-2735. 1975. Poetry, articles, art, photos, cartoons, interviews, reviews. "Stewart Brand, Susan Harris" circ. 1,000. 1/yr. Pub'd 1 issue 1979; expects 1 issue 1980, 1 issue 1981. price per copy: $3.50; sample: $3.50. Back issues: all back issues out of print. Discounts: 40% resale discount to distributors. 100pp; 8¼X10¾; †mi. Reporting time: several weeks. Payment: no cash, exchange finished copies of journal for contributors. Copyrighted, reverts to author. Pub's reviews: 1 in 1979. §Future studies, appropriate technology, alternative futures, economics. no ads. COSMEP.

PASTICHE: Poems of Place, The Pin Prick Press, Roberta Mendel, 3877 Meadowbrook Blvd., University Heights, OH 44118, 216-932-2173. 1980. Poetry. "Each month, two pages of vivid prose/poesy dealing with such diverse 'places' as cemeteries, school halls, the mind. No biases. Short poems (under 30 lines) preferred, but will look at longer ones and may excerpt. Will accept reprints if submitted with a release and *all* previous publication data. Some recent contributors: Cassie Edwards, Vivien C. Scarpa, Robert D. Hoeft, Shirley Aycock, Geoffrey Cook, Daniel Conroy, Eleanor Davidson Calenda, Roberta Mendel. Submissions may be accepted for The Pin Prick Press's other serial publications at the editor's discretion. *Pastiche: Poems of Place* is amenable to an exchange arrangement with other serial publications. For a fee, it will distribute other small press promotional materials with its own. *No SASE, no reply!*" circ. 100. 12/yr. sub. price: $10.00, $15.00 foreign; per copy: $1.00, $1.25 foreign plus $0.30 postage and handling. Discounts: by special arrangement. 2pp; 8½X11; of. Reporting time: ASAP. Payment: 1 copy of the issue in which their work appears. Copyrighted, on written request. COSMEP.

Patricia J. Sherman Real Estate Books, Patricia J. Sherman, 4011 Garden Avenue, Los Angeles, CA 90039, (213) 661-1194. 1976. "We are a two-title publisher of self-help real estate books co-authored by my husband and myself" avg. press run 2,000. Pub'd 1 title 1979. avg. price, cloth: $7.95; paper: $4.95. Discounts: Library, 25%; trade, 40%; jobber, 50%. 5X8; of. Does not copyright for author. COSMEP, NESPA, SCBC, WNBA.

PAUNCH, Arthur Efron, 123 Woodward Ave, Buffalo, NY 14214, 716-836-7332. 1963. Poetry, articles, photos, criticism, reviews, letters, long-poems. "*Paunch* continues to explore the theme of the human body in literature.No. 50-51 reprint of rare book (1959) by David Boadella, applying Reich to D. H. Lawrence, *The Spiral Flame*. The late 1978 issue, #52 included review articles on the life of Thomas Hardy, on Woman's Body and Literature, and Patricia Ellis Taylor's *The Missionary Position*

Reconsidered. Also, Charles Baxter's review of poems by the late Wendy Parrish, *Conversations in the Gallery*. #53-54, delayed until March, 1980, is devoted to the work of the late philosopher and aesthetician, Stephen C. Pepper, who, among other things, was instrumental in bringing Abstract Expressionism onto the American art scene. (Issue edited jointly with John Herold). Recent contributors include Gene Frumkin, Lyle Glazier, Michael McCanles, Cary Nelson, Phyllis Hoge, Ulf Goebel, Ellie Ragland Sullivan, Charles Hartshorne, Barry K. Grant." circ. 400. 2/yr. Pub'd 2 issues 1979; expects 2 issues 1980. 5 titles listed in the *Small Press Record of Books in Print* (9th Edition, 1980). sub. price: $4.00 indiv., $7.00 libraries; per copy: $2.00 single, $4.00 double issue.; sample: No samples. Back issues: Yes. All through No. 21, Oct. 1964; which was the first to be distributed publicly. Discounts: agents, $0.75 a year: classrooms, 20 percent: trade, 40 percent. Double: 172pp Single: 96pp; 5½X8½; of. Reporting time: 30 days. Payment: copies. Copyrighted, rights are handed over upon request to authors. Pub's reviews: 7 in 1979. §Poetry, literary criticism. no ads. Niagara-Erie Writers, CCLM, COSMEP.

THE PAWN REVIEW, Calliope Press, Michael Anderson, Editor; Thomas Zigal, Fiction Editor, 1162 Lincoln Ave #227, Walnut Creek, CA 94596. 1975. Poetry, fiction, articles, art, photos, cartoons, interviews, satire, criticism, reviews, music, letters, parts-of-novels, long-poems, collages, plays, concrete art. "*The Pawn Review* welcomes quality manuscripts, particularly from Texas writers. We publish short stories and poems primarily, and we try to publish one long story (5,000 words) and long poems (100 lines) per issue. In addition, we will consider translations, drama, b&w photographs and other genres. Recent authors include Speer Morgan, Edwin Honig, Peter Cooley, Warren Miller, Hollis Summers, Brian Swann, Les Standiford, Betsy Adams, William Virgil Davis, Susan Fromberg Schaeffer. Indexed in *Access Index*. Published by the Pawn Review Incorporated, a non-profit tax-exempt corporation." circ. 500. 2/yr. Pub'd 1 issue 1979; expects 2 issues 1980, 2 issues 1981. 4 titles listed in the *Small Press Record of Books in Print* (9th Edition, 1980). sub. price: $5.00; per copy: $3.00; sample: $3.00. Back issues: Vol 2, No. 2 available only. Previous issues available on limited loan basis for duplication. Discounts: Trade bookstores, on consignment: 40% University bookstores. 5-19, 25%; 20-49, 30%; 50+, 40%; plus shipping via Insured Library Rate or better, no returns. 92pp; 5½X8½ trimmed; of. Reporting time: 1-4 months. Payment: 1 copy; additional 25% discount. Copyrighted, reverts to author. Pub's reviews: 5 in 1979. §poetry from or by Texas poets/presses; poetry. Ads: $40.00/$25.00. COSMEP, CCLM, Texas Circuit, COSMEP/South,.

Paycock Press (see also GARGOYLE), Richard Myers Peabody Jr., Editor, PO Box 57206, Washington, DC 20037, 202-333-1544. 1976. Poetry, fiction, art, photos, satire, reviews, long-poems. "1979 titles: Poetry *I'm In Love With The Morton Salt Girl* by Richard Peabody. Fiction *The Love Letter Hack* by Michael Brondoli. 1980 titles: *Blank Like Me* by Harrison Fisher, *Jukebox* by Tina Fulker. Anthology: *1st Volume of D.C. Lit Mag Anthology*. Looking for fiction in 1981." avg. press run 350-500. Pub'd 2 titles 1979; expects 3 titles 1980, 2 titles 1981. 3 titles listed in the *Small Press Record of Books in Print* (9th Edition, 1980). avg. price, paper: $3.00. 60pp; 5½X8½; of. Copyrights for author.

Peace & Pieces Foundation, Maurice M. Custodio, Pres.; Todd S.J. Lawson, Vice-Pres.; William Samolis, Sec.; Efren Ramirez, Carol Carter, Ernesto Ferrera, Contributing Editors, Box 99394, San Francisco, CA 94109, 415-771-3431. 1971. "Non-profit, multicultural organization. No unsolicited manuscripts please. Recent titles include poetry *Astrolabes* by Elizabeth Keeler and prison poetry *Sweet Tomorrow* by Ross Laursen. Fiction *Contemporary Fiction: Today's Outstanding Writers* edited by Maurice Custodio, and satire-fiction *The 69 Days of Easter* by Todd Lawson, poetry *Light and Other Poems* by Ruth Weiss. Photography book by Asian photographer *In Pursuit of Images* Efren Ramirez. New book *The San Franciscans* by Todd S. J. Lawson for 1981 includes excusive interviews with philosopher Eric Hoffer, Mayor Feinstein, writers Scott Beach and Lawrence Ferlinghetti, et. al. We've published over 350 poets, writers, photographers and artists, sponsor bookfairs and festivals and have a video cassette (1/2 inch VHS) library of writers and poets, mostly California and West Coast. Also sponsor Video Prose and Poetry for the Deaf Program with interpreters. Not currently seeking manuscripts." avg. press run 500-3000. Expects 4 titles 1980. 8 titles listed in the *Small Press Record of Books in Print* (9th Edition, 1980). avg. price, cloth: $7.50; paper: $3.50. Discounts: 6-10 copies, 20%; 11-49, 40%, 50+, 50%; Libraries: 20%, Bookstores 40%. 140pp; 6X9. Reporting time: 4-6 weeks. Payment: 10-20% plus cash honoraria. Copyrights for author.

PEACE NEWS "For Non-Violent Revolution", Editorial Collective, 8 Elm Avenue, Nottingham, United Kingdom, 0602 53587. 1936. Poetry, articles, cartoons, photos, news items, letters. "London office: 5 Caledonian Road, London N1,Great Britain,01-837 9795" circ. 3,000. 25/yr. Pub'd 25 issues 1979; expects 25 issues 1980, 25 issues 1981. 3 titles listed in the *Small Press Record of Books in Print* (9th Edition, 1980). price per copy: 20p; sample: 10p. Back issues: 30p inc p&p. Discounts: 10% agencies, airmail subs; 20% agencies, surface subs; 33⅓% bookshops, surface mail. 20pp; size A4; of. Payment: material costs to graphic artists. Not copyrighted. Pub's reviews: 30 in 1979. §Health, conservation, alternatives, feminism, third world. Ads: £40/£21/3p(min. 30p). UAPS(E).

Peace Press, Richard Profumo, Dorothy Schuler, 3828 Willat Ave., Culver City, CA 90230, 213-838-7387. 1969. Fiction, art, photos, parts-of-novels. "Peace Press is an alternative printing & publishing collective." avg. press run 5,000. Pub'd 8 titles 1979; expects 8 titles 1980. 29 titles listed in the *Small Press Record of Books in Print* (9th Edition, 1980). avg. price, cloth: $11.00; paper: $7.00. Discounts: Trade: 1-4, 20 percent; 4-50, 40 percent; 50 plus, 45 percent. Text: 20 percent. Wholesalers inquire. 200pp; size varies; †of. Reporting time: 3 months. Payment: Quarterly. Copyrights for author. COSMEP, LPSC, COSMEP, WEST.

‡**PEBBLE, Best Cellar Press,** 118 South Boswell, Crete, NB 68333, 402-826-4038. "Poems, essays on poetry, review. I am involved with special issues. *A Book of Rereadings,* see ad copy in the Directory, and for next year, a long poem issue. Also the 10th anniversary issue." circ. 1,200. 1 to 2 issues per year. sub. price: $10.00 for 4 issues; per copy: $3.50; sample: There are no sample copies. Back issues: issues 1-10, complete, price on request. 150pp; 5½X8½; of. Reporting time: 1 week to 6 months. Payment: 2 copies, sometimes cash payment. Copyrighted. Pub's reviews.

PEDESTRIAN RESEARCH, L. Wilensky, PO Box 624, Forest Hills, NY 11375. 1973. "Biased serving the *pedestrian* viewpoint." circ. 500-1,000. 4/yr. Pub'd 4 issues 1979; expects 4 issues 1980, 4 issues 1981. sub. price: $3.00; per copy: $1.50; sample: $.25. Back issues: $1.50 past year, $3.00 more than a year old. Discounts: 25% on more than 5 issues sent to one address. 4pp; 8½X11; of. Reporting time: 1 month. Payment: optional. Pub's reviews. §Environment, pedestrians, ecology, pedestrian welfare interest, pedestrianism & environment.

PEEPHOLE ON PEOPLE, Charles N. Aronson, Writer Publisher, Charles N. Aronson, RR 1, 11520 Bixby Hill Road, Arcade, NY 14009, (716) 496-6002. 1978. Poetry, fiction, articles, art, photos, cartoons, interviews, satire, criticism, reviews, music, parts-of-novels, news items. "*POP* is a newsletter written, edited, published by Charles N. Aronson. It's very first issue will be 1-1 Jan 79. This first issue has gone out as a sample and as promo venture. Maximum length of material will probably be 2,500 words. *POP* does not solicit work from others. The basic idea behind *POP* is to make available to readers a newsletter magazine that does not cowtow and doesn't try to hurt, either, but does tell the truth whether it hurts circulation or not." circ. 6,000. 12/yr. Expects 12 issues 1981. sub. price: $12.00; per copy: $1.00. Back issues: Too new to have any back issues yet. Discounts: Fraid not. 8pp; 8½X11; of. Ads: no ads.

Pella Publ. Co (see also JOURNAL OF THE HELLENIC DIASPORA), P Pappas, S.E. Bronner, P.R. Craig, D Georgakas, 461 Eighth Ave, New York, NY 10001, 212-279-9586. 1976. Poetry, fiction, art, photos, cartoons, satire, criticism, music, long-poems, plays. "We are interested in modern Greek studies and culture, but also have a general list composed of new fiction and poetry by young writers and books on contemporary society and politics. We also publish books on the work of young artists." avg. press run 3,000. Pub'd 3 titles 1979; expects 10 titles 1980, 10 titles 1981. 7 titles listed in the *Small Press Record of Books in Print* (9th Edition, 1980). avg. price, cloth: $8.00; paper: $4.00. Discounts: Libraries 30%, Bookstores 40%, Bulk (50 copies or more) 50%. 176pp; 5½X8½; †of/lp. Reporting time: 4 to 6 weeks. Payment: Standard royalty arrangements. Copyrights for author. COSMEP.

PEMBROKE MAGAZINE, Shelby Stephenson, Editor; Norman Macleod, Founding Editor, PO Box 60, PSU, Pembroke, NC 28372, (919) 521-4214 ext 246. 1969. Poetry, fiction, articles, art, photos, criticism, reviews. "Archibald MacLeish, N. Scott Momaday, Simon J. Oritz, John Pauker, Joseph Bruchac, Blyden Jackson, Hugh MacDiarmid, Charles Olson, W.S. Graham, Diana Chang, Kay Boyle, Harald Littlebird, Jonathan Daniels, Guy Owen, Paul Green Felix Pollak." circ. 1,500. 1/yr-occasional supplementary issue. Pub'd 2 issues 1979; expects 1 issue 1980. sub. price: $3.00/yr-another $3.00 for supplementary issue, if published.; per copy: $3.00 (overseas $3.50); sample: $3.00. Discounts: 40% bookstores. 200pp; 6X9; of. Reporting time: 1-4 months. Payment: whatever we can. copyright reverts to author except for right of editor to reprint the magazine and to issue a PM anthology. Pub's reviews: 6 in 1979. §Native American poetry and novels. Ads: $40/$25. CCLM, COSMEP.

Peninhand Press (see also THE VOLCANO REVIEW), Thomas Janisse, PO Box 142, Volcano, CA 95689. 1979. Poetry, fiction, letters. "We have a strong interest in local mountain writers and artists." avg. press run 500. Pub'd 1 title 1979; expects 1 title 1980. avg. price, cloth: $11.00; paper: $4.00. Discounts: 1-4, 25%; 5 and over, 40%. 30pp; 5½X8½; lp. Reporting time: no unsolicited manuscripts at this time. Payment: copies. COSMEP.

Penmaen Press Ltd, Michael McCurdy, Joan Norris, Michael Peich, Old Sudbury Road, Lincoln, MA 01773, 617-259-0842. 1968. Poetry, fiction. "First edition wk preferable. No unsolicited manuscripts" avg. press run 1,000. Pub'd 4 titles 1979; expects 3 titles 1980. 10 titles listed in the *Small Press Record of Books in Print* (9th Edition, 1980). avg. price, cloth: $12.00-$40.00; paper: $4.00. Discounts: 1-4 copies 20 percent; 5-24 copies 40 percent; 25-49 copies 42 percent; 50-99 copies 44 percent; 100 or more 46 percent. 66pp; 6¼X9¾; †lp/of. Payment: 10% hardcover/7½% soft. Copyrights for author. NESPA.

PENNINE PLATFORM, Brian Merrikin Hill, 4 Insmanthorpe Hall Farm, Wetherby, West Yorks LS22 5EZ, United Kingdom, 0927-64674. 1966. Articles, poetry, art, photos, reviews, criticism. "The magazine is supported by the Yorkshire Arts Association. Tries to keep a high standard, both in poetry & art. Copyrighted for contributors who retain copyright. Associated with: Ruined Cottage Publications (same address) which has published (1977) *Hill* Brian Merrikin, two poems of pilgrimage. 1979 Smith, K.E. *The Dialect Muse.*" circ. 450. 3/yr. Pub'd 3 issues 1979; expects 3 issues 1980. 2 titles listed in the *Small Press Record of Books in Print* (9th Edition, 1980). sub. price: £1.50; per copy: 50p; sample: 50p. Back issues: 40p a copy. Discounts: Trade for books in bulk less 30%. 26pp; 6X8¼; of. Reporting time: varies. Payment: none. Copyrighted. Pub's reviews: 10 in 1979. §Poetry. Ads: £7.50.

THE PENNSYLVANIA NATURALIST, Ron Shafer, Jerry Shue, PO Box 1128, State College, PA 16801, (814) 238-1132. 1978. Articles, art, photos, letters, news items. circ. 7,000. 6/yr. Pub'd 2 issues 1979; expects 6 issues 1980. sub. price: $7.00; per copy: $1.50; sample: $1.50. Back issues: $1.25 through Dec-Jan '80 edition. 52pp; 8½X11; of. Reporting time: 6 weeks. Payment: variable, starting at 25 dollars for articles, six dollars for photos. Copyrighted, reverts to author. Pub's reviews. §Natural history, outdoor recreation, ecology/conservation. Ads: $150/$90.

Pennsylvania State University Press (see also THE SHAW REVIEW), Stanley Weintraub, S-234 Burrowes Building, University Park, PA 16802, 814-865-4242. 1951. Articles, interviews, criticism, reviews, letters. avg. press run 700. Pub'd 3 titles 1979; expects 3 titles 1980, 3 titles 1981. 60pp; 6X9; of.

Penny Postcard Press, J. T. Ledbetter, 1335 Norman, Thousand Oaks, CA 91360. 4X8½.

Penstemon Press, Kathleen Gray Schallock, 309 Debs Road, Madison, WI 53704, (608) 241-1132. 1978. Poetry, art. "I will be dealing primarily with the art book category, combining letterpress with lithography for the end product of a piece of artwork as opposed to a printing of literature combining visual and literary to produce a marriage of the two forms." avg. press run 50. Pub'd 3 titles 1979. avg. price, cloth: $50.00-$100.00. 10-40pp; †lp.

Pentagram Press (see also HAWK-WIND), Michael Tarachow, Box 379, Markesan, WI 53946. 1974. Poetry, fiction, articles, reviews, long-poems, news items. "The new —1892—C&P letterpress is set up & running real sweet, so I'm now doing mainly handset, letterpressed 1st editions of contemporary poetry & prose. New titles lp'ed include *Auspices,* by Cid Corman; *Habitat,* by Bob Arnold; *Star Anise* and *The Fifth Direction,* by Theodore Enslin; *Maize,* poetry by Gil Ott with graphics facing each poem by Carol Emmons; new offset titles include *Interlude,* poetry by Michael Tarachow with cover graphics by Carol Emmons; *Opus 31, No. 3,* Theodore Enslin; *The Master,* by Tom Clark. Forthcoming: *Anacoluthon* and *The Anatomic Works,* novellas by Tom Bridwell; *Weeds Wood Stone & Mettle,* poetry by Marilyn Kitchell; *August for Elegy,* Theodore Enslin; also as-yet untitled collections by Robie Liscomb & Barbara Moraff; all lp'ed; *Her Name,* By James Baker Hall, & *Toward a Further Definition,* a collection of essays by 26 alternative press editors telling more of what we do, & why; more anecdotal than factual, fortunately. Pentagram's doing fine-art printing at *reader's* prices—generally $4-$6 for a handmade book. An inquiry will get you a catalog; a few bucks a year will get you all the lp'ed postcards & b-sides I do (Taggart, Cultrera, Montag, Rosenblum, &c)—standing orders invited; query. *No unsolicited mss wanted, this is absolute; query first with SASE or yr just wasting yr time.*" avg. press run 200-2,000. Pub'd 5 titles 1979; expects 9 titles 1980, 9 titles 1981. 33 titles listed in the *Small Press Record of Books in Print* (9th Edition, 1980). avg. price, cloth: $17.50; paper: $4.00-$6.00; other: Limited signed $17.50. Discounts: 1 Book 0%, 2-4 20%, 5 plus more 35% No Returns. 24-280pp; size varies; †of/lp. Please query with SASE, before sending mss. Payment: Varies.

Pentangle Press, Robert Springer, 132 Lasky Dr., Beverly Hills, CA 90212, 213-278-4996. 1974. "Holography" avg. press run 2,000. Pub'd 2 titles 1979; expects 2 titles 1980. 2 titles listed in the *Small Press Record of Books in Print* (9th Edition, 1980). avg. price, cloth: $11.00; paper: $9.00. Discounts: retailers: 2-4 20%, 5-29 40%. 100pp; 6X9; of. Reporting time: 30 days.

PENUMBRA, Alice K. Boatwright, Fiction Editor; Charles A. Noon, Poetry; Christine Davidson, Children's Editor, Box 794, Portsmouth, NH 03801. 1979. Poetry, fiction, art, photos, cartoons, music, parts-of-novels, long-poems, collages, plays. "*Penumbra* is a quarterly magazine for writers from New Hampshire, Vermont and Maine. We are a regional magazine only to the extent that we offer writers from our area the opportunity to appear in print together. We don't have any preconceived notions about life in New England, but we hope to reflect something of it through our work. No length limits. Please *no* scifi, fantasy, ye olde New England. Poets should submit at least 3 poems. Some recent contributors: Larkin Warren, Marie Harris, Jean Pedrick, Elizabeth Knies, Ira Sadoff, David Walker, Donald Murray, to name a few (there are many more). Lots of good people, a good number of whom have never published before." circ. 1,000. 4/yr. Pub'd 4 issues 1979. sub. price: $4.00; per copy: $1.00; sample: $1.00. Discounts: up to 40% to bookstores, others to be negotiated. 16pp; 17X22; of. Reporting time: 6-8 weeks. Payment: free copies. Copyrighted, reverts to author. Ads: $15.00/$30.00/$45.00/$60.00.

The Penumbra Press, Bonnie P. O'Connell, Box 12, Lisbon, IA 52253. 1971. Poetry, fiction, art, photos, collages. "Editions usually number 200-250 copies. All releases are hand printed from hand-set type. Most editions are casebound, some come out in paperback. Recent: *Counting the Days* Jon Anderson, *Stepping Outside* by Tess Gallagher, *Sleeping On Doors* by Steven Orlen, *The Prayers Of The North American Martyrs* by Norman Dubie, *Anxiety And Ashes* by Laura Jensen, *Dear Anyone* by William Keens. We also publish '*The Manila Series*', pamphlets in which each release is housed in a manila envelope. Latest titles: *Keeping The Night* by Peter Everwine, *Ten Poems* by Rita Dove, which is Number 4 in the Manila Series. *Good Evening and other poems* by Abigail Luttinger, and *Cartography* by Debora Greger. Forthcoming: *The Train to Paris* by Brenda Hillman." Pub'd 1 title 1979; expects 3 titles 1980, 3 titles 1981. 6 titles listed in the *Small Press Record of Books in Print* (9th Edition, 1980). avg. price, cloth: $15.00; paper: $7.50. Discounts: 25% to dealers who purchase 5 or more copies. 30% to dealers who place a standing order for 5 copies of each release. 35pp; size varies; †lp. Reporting time: 2 weeks to 2 months. Payment: 10% of the edition. Copyrights for author.

PEOPLE & ENERGY, David Holzman, 9208 Christopher St, Fairfax, VA 22031. 1975. Articles, art, photos, cartoons, reviews, news items. circ. 2,000. 12/yr. Pub'd 6 issues 1979; expects 12 issues 1980, 12 issues 1981. 13 titles listed in the *Small Press Record of Books in Print* (9th Edition, 1980). sub. price: $12.00; per copy: $1.00; sample: SASE. Back issues: $0.80 copy. Discounts: $6.00 for 5 - 25 subscriptions; $5.00 for 26 or more subscriptions. 20pp; 8½X11; of. Reporting time: 2 weeks. Payment: not usually. Not copyrighted. Pub's reviews: 60 in 1979. §Energy, alternative technologies in housing, agriculture, transportation. Ads: none. COSMEP.

PEOPLE'S CANADA DAILY NEWS, PO Box 727, Adelaide Station, Toronto, Ontario M5C 2J8, Canada. 1970. Articles, photos, interviews, criticism, reviews, news items. "Carries material of various lengths from small news items to long documents in serialization. Basic content is to present the Marxist-Leninist analysis of CPC(M-L) on all issues-politics, economics, culture, etc. PCDN carries news of the struggles of the working class and people of Canada, the U.S. and all countries. It carries news and releases etc. from the parties and organizations of the Marxist-Leninist Communist Movement on the world scale. It carries, particularly at this period, in-depth analysis of the current economic and political crisis of the capitalist-revisionist world. Carries some reprints from the Albanian Telegraphic Agency, and from the journals of other Marxist-Leninist parties from time to time. Publication frequency, daily, except Sunday. INternational rates are $90.00 per year." 312/yr. Expects 296 issues 1980. sub. price: $65.00(Canada, U.S.), $90 elsewhere; per copy: $.15 from vendor, 50¢ by mail; sample: free. Discounts: No special discounts on straight subscriptions; however, for bulk orders of any issues or series of issues, discount can be negotiated. 4pp; 17X22⅝. Pub's reviews.

People's Canada Publishing House (see NEW LITERATURE & IDEOLOGY)

People's Computer Co. (see also RECREATIONAL COMPUTING; DR. DOBB'S JOURNAL OF COMPUTER CALISTHENICS & ORTHODONTIA), 1263 El Camino Real, Menlo Park, CA 94025, 415-323-3111. 1971. Articles, photos, cartoons, interviews, criticism, reviews, letters. "A non profit, educational company dedicated to demystifying personal and home computers." avg. press run 5,000-10,000. 3 titles listed in the *Small Press Record of Books in Print* (9th Edition, 1980). avg. price, paper: $2.00-$5.00. Discounts: 40 percent off retail to resalers; other discounts occasionally upon arragement. 48-64pp; 8½X11; of. Payment: none-we are non-profit. Copyrights for author.

PEOPLE'S NEWS SERVICE, PNS, PNS Collective, Oxford House, Derbyshire Street, London E2 6HG, United Kingdom, 01-739-3630. 1973. Articles, photos, cartoons, news items, interviews, reviews. "We are a fortnightly bulletin of home & international news. We spread information ignored by the conventional press, acting thus as an alternative news service." circ. 600. 25/yr. Pub'd 24 issues 1979; expects 25 issues 1980, 25 issues 1981. sub. price: £10.80 in UK & Eire, $42 airmail; per copy: 35p; sample: 50p. Back issues: negotiable. Discounts: no. 16pp; size A4; of. Reporting time: Variable. Payment: none. Yes. Pub's reviews: 120 in 1979. §Politics, women, prisons, media, third world, industry. no ads, negotible rates for inserts. APS.

PEOPLE'S YELLOW PAGES of the SAN FRANCISCO BAY AREA, Diane Sampson, Jan Zobel, P.O. Box 31291, San Francisco, CA 94131. 1971. Art. "No free lance other than art. No payment for art. Write for information-only local ads accepted." circ. 20,000. published once every 1½ yrs. Expects

1 issue 1980, 1 issue 1981. 1 title listed in the *Small Press Record of Books in Print* (9th Edition, 1980). price per copy: $5.00; sample: $5.00. Back issues: $1 to $3.50 depending on which issue. Discounts: 40% for 10 or more copies. 200pp; 8½X11; of. Payment: none. Copyrighted. Pub's reviews. §alternatives/women/gay/other liberation. Ads: Inquire for details.

The Pepys Press, Donald Vining, 1270 Fifth Avenue, New York, NY 10029, (212) 348-6847. 1979. "I am seeking diaries from World War II and show business diaries. Want to see no more than 20 page excerpts in first submission. Only genuine diaries, not compilations of letters or memoirs arranged in diary form. Though first publication is *A Gay Diary 1933-1946* and there will be succeeding volumes of this, the anthologies of World War II and show business (vaudeville, stage, film, radio, opera, dance) diaries will not be gay-certainly not entirely. Each anthology will, I hope, give up to 50 pages to a diary. I don't want just snippets in the end tho initially I don't want to see more than 20 pages." avg. press run 1,000. Expects 1 title 1981. avg. price, cloth: $14.95; paper: $9.95. Discounts: 40% to bookstores. 500pp; 5½X8½; of. Reporting time: 1 month. Outright payment (not large). Copyrights for author. COSMEP.

PEQUOD, David Paradis, Fiction; Mark Rudman, Poetry, 3478 22nd Street, San Francisco, CA 94110. 1974. Poetry, fiction, articles, criticism, parts-of-novels, long-poems, plays. "A journal of contemporary literature and literary criticism. Contributors: Paul Blackburn, Richard Hugo, Jane De Lynn, Tom McHale, Stephen Dobyns. We are not interested in receiving unsolicited submissions from people who are not familiar with PEQUOD. Poetry and criticism should be submitted to Mark Rudman, 817 West End Ave, NYC 10025; fiction to *Pequod* address above." 2/yr. Pub'd 2 issues 1979; expects 2 issues 1980. sub. price: 1 yr $5.00; 2 yrs $9.00; per copy: $3.00; sample: $3.00. Discounts: 40% trade. 100pp; 5½X8½; of. Reporting time: 2-3 months. Payment: $3-pages/$5-min/$30-max/4 copies. Copyrighted, reverts to author. CCLM.

Pequod Press, Rlene H. Dahlberg, 344 Third Ave, Apt 3A, New York, NY 10010, (212) 686-4789. 1977. Poetry, fiction, criticism. "At this point, the pieces must be fauly short, 9-12 pp. I intend to do fine press work, limited editions with original illustrations (100 copies) & offset trade edition (250-300 copies)." avg. press run 350-400. Pub'd 2 titles 1979; expects 3 titles 1980, 3 titles 1981. avg. price, paper: $7.50; other: $15.00. Discounts: 40% to trade. 16pp; 5X8½; †of/lp. Reporting time: At this point, I have all submissions for next few years. Payment: 25 copies (later, hopefully, 10%). Copyrights for author.

Peradam Publishing House (see also The Guide to Small Press Publishing), Arnold Wolman, Ted Wolter, P.O. Box 85, Urbana, IL 61801, 815-367-7070. 1971. Poetry, fiction, articles, art, photos, long-poems. "Keith Hitchcock, Gary Legare, Ted Wolter, Arnold Wolman, K.T. Moore, Bruce Sanders, Elvan, James Kleinhans, James Magorian, Susan Metz, Doris Ball, Carole Bersin." avg. press run 100 - 10,000. Pub'd 3-5 titles 1979. 28 titles listed in the *Small Press Record of Books in Print* (9th Edition, 1980). avg. price, paper: $1.00 - $5.00; other: Handmade books $10.00 - $200.00. Discounts: 40-50%. pp varies.; size Varies.; of/handmade. Reporting time: varies from 1 week to 3 months. Payment: 5-15% of retail price. Does not copyright for author. COSMEP.

Peregrine Smith, Inc., Richard A. Firmage, PO Box 667, Layton, UT 84041, 801-376-9800. 1970. Poetry, fiction, art, criticism, plays. "Books on Architecture, Arts, Crafts, History, Native Americans. Reprints." avg. press run 3,000-5,000. Pub'd 6 titles 1979; expects 10 titles 1980, 10 titles 1981. avg. price, cloth: $10.95 - $24.95; paper: $5.95 - $9.95. Discounts: 40% - 45%. 200pp; 5½X8½, 8½X11; of. Reporting time: 3 weeks to 3 months. Payment: 10%. Copyrights for author. AAP, Book Publishers Assoc. of Southern California.

PERFORMING ARTS JOURNAL, Bonnie Marranca, Gautam Dasgupta, P.O. Box 858, Peter Stuyvesant Station, New York, NY 10009, 212-260-7586. 1976. Articles, art, photos, interviews, criticism, reviews, music, plays. "Maximum length of article: 15 double-spaced typed pages. Biases: criticalorientation towards twentieth-century performing arts. Joseph Chaikin, Richard Schechner, Michael McClure, Edward Bond." circ. 4,000. 3/yr. Pub'd 3 issues 1979. sub. price: $11.00 individuals; $18.00 libraries & institutions; per copy: $4.00; sample: $4.00. Back issues: $4.50 (varies). Discounts: trade discount 40 percent. 144pp; 6X9; of. Reporting time: 2 months. Payment: none. Copyrighted. Pub's reviews: 50+ in 1979. §theatre, dance, music, film, video, performance. Ads: $165.00/$100.00. CCLM, COSMEP.

Pericarp Books (see Stone Country Press)

PERIODICS, Paul de Barros, Daphne Marlatt, PO Box 69375, Station K, Vancouver, B.C. V5K 4W6, Canada. 1977. Fiction, criticism, reviews, letters, parts-of-novels. "Bias is for good prose writing with an exploratory or innovative edge. Recent contributors include: Michael Rumaker, Fielding Dawson, George Bowering, David Young, Larry Eigner, Duncan McNaughton, Artie Gold, Kathy Acker, Michael Ondaatje, Barry Gifford, Paul Metcalf, Douglas Woolf, Dale Herd, Robert Duncan, Robert Kroetsch." circ. 500. 2/yr. Pub'd 2 issues 1979; expects 2 issues 1980. sub. price: $10.00; per copy: $3.00; sample: $3.00. Discounts: 40%. 82pp; 7X8½; of. Reporting time: 1 month to 3 months. Payment: 2 copies of issue. Copyrighted, reverts to author. Pub's reviews: 9 in 1979. §Books of stories, prose poems, novels, collections of letters, journals, literary biographies, some criticism, sources. Ads: $25.00. COSMEP, CCLM.

Peripatos Press, Jinx Walker, PO Box 550, Wainscottu, NY 11975. 1980. Poetry, art. "Interested in poetry by/for children; and children's art. Also how-to material. No limit on length; no bias." avg. press run 1000. Expects 1-2 titles 1980. avg. price, paper: $5.95. Discounts: Bookstores, wholesalers: 1-4 20%, 5+ 40%. No discounts on orders paid in less than 30 days. 120pp; 5½X8½; of. Reporting time: 2 weeks. Payment: in copies. Copyrights for author. COSMEP.

The Perishable Press Limited, Walter Hamady, Mary Hamady, PO Box 7, Mt. Horeb, WI 53572. Poetry, fiction, articles, art, cartoons, interviews, letters, long-poems, concrete art. avg. press run 150-200. Pub'd 6 titles 1979; expects 4 titles 1980, 6 titles 1981. avg. price, cloth: $39.37. Discounts: 30% to standing orders, institution or dealer or individual; 20% to dealers on printed letterhead. 22pp; 2½X3¼ and 12X15; †lp. Reporting time: as fast as possible. Payment: at least 10% in kind. Copyrights for author.

Perivale Press, Lawrence P. Spingarn, 13830 Erwin Street, Van Nuys, CA 91401, 213-785-4671. 1968. Poetry, fiction, criticism. "We specialize in translations from foreign poetry by individuals or regional-national groups and in anthologies. Small editions (750-1,000 copies) from 40 pp to 230 pp. Recently published: *Poets West,* edited by L.P. Spingarn. *Yiddish Sayings Mama Never Taught You* by Weltman & Zuckerman. *The Epigrams Of Martial, Tr.* by Richard O'Connell. *Contemporary French Women Poets, Tr.* by C. Hermey. *The Blue Door* & *Other Stories* by L.P. Spingarn. *Not-So-Simple Neil Simon* by Edythe M. McGovern. *Birds of Prey* by Joyce Mansour. *Tr.* by Albert Herzing" avg. press run 1,000. Pub'd 3 titles 1979; expects 3 titles 1980. 13 titles listed in the *Small Press Record of Books in Print* (9th Edition, 1980). avg. price, paper: $3.95. Discounts: trade: 40%; institution: 10%; student: 10%. 100pp; 5½X8½; of. Reporting time: 3 months. Payment: 10%-15% royalty, sliding. Will copyright for author if author pays fee. COSMEP.

Periwinkle Press, Jan Venolia, PO Box 1305, Woodland Hills, CA 91365, (213) 346-3415. 1979. "Periwinkle Press is a one-title publisher, so far. Not seeking authors." avg. press run 10,000. Pub'd 1 title 1979; expects 1 title 1980, 1 title 1981. avg. price, cloth: $6.95; paper: $3.95; other: $4.95. Discounts: Libraries, 20%; Bookstores, 40%; Disbributors, 50-55%. 103pp; 5⅜X7; of. Copyrights for author. COSMEP.

PERMAFROST, Greg Divers, Co-Editor; Linda Schandelmeier, Co-Editor; Gail Pepe, Art Director; Harley Stein, Assistant Editor, University of Alaska, Fairbanks, AK 99701, (907) 479-7193. 1977. Poetry, fiction, articles, art, photos, criticism, satire, reviews, parts-of-novels, long-poems. "*Permafrost* is not a regional magazine. We welcome material from outside Alaska and the Pacific Northwest region although we do encourage submissions from this area. Contributors include John Haines, William Stafford, Robert Hedin, Gunter Grass, Kay Boyle, Joseph Bruchac, John Morgan, Tom Lowenstein. Please enclose SASE." circ. 1000. 2/yr. Pub'd 2 issues 1979; expects 2 issues 1980, 2 issues 1981. sub. price: $5.00; per copy: $2.00, special issues $3.00; sample: Free upon request with 48¢ postage fee. Back issues: Vol. 1 No. 1., $5.00; other back issues $2.00 each. 64pp; 5½X8; of. Reporting time: 1 week to 1 month. Payment: copies. Copyrighted, reverts to author. Pub's reviews: 7 in 1979. §Books by writers of the Pacific Northwest & Alaska. no ads. CCLM/COSMEP.

Permanent Press, Robert Vas Dias, 52 Cascade Avenue, London, N10 England, United Kingdom. 1972. Poetry, long-poems. "Length: from 24 to 72 pages per book. Recent authors: Jackson Mac Low, Edward Dorn, Jennifer Dunbar, Elaine Randell, Nathaniel Tarn, Armand Schwerner, Janet Rodney, Toby Olson, Jonathan Griffin, Paul Blackburn." avg. press run 500. Pub'd 2 titles 1979; expects 2 titles 1980. 7 titles listed in the *Small Press Record of Books in Print* (9th Edition, 1980). avg. price, cloth: $12.95; paper: $6.00. Discounts: 40% to trade, no returns. 44pp; 6X8; of. Reporting time: 1 month. Payment: modest, plus copies. Copyrights for author. ALP.

The Permanent Press, Martin Shepard, Judith Shepard, Sagaponack, NY 11962, 516-324-5993. 1979. Fiction, satire, news items. "We publish original material, including both political books and books of whimsy." avg. press run 4,000. avg. price, cloth: $12.50; paper: $5.95. Discounts: 40-50%. 250pp; 5½X8½; lp. Reporting time: 8 weeks. Payment: 10-15% net. Some recieve very small advances, not all. Copyrights for author. COSMEP.

Permanent Press (see also BLANK TAPE), Box 371, Brooklyn, NY 11230. "Permanent press is not currently accepting submissions." avg. press run 500. Pub'd 1 title 1979; expects 2 titles 1980, 3 titles

1981. 6 titles listed in the *Small Press Record of Books in Print* (9th Edition, 1980). Discounts: Standard 40% to trade. of.

W. Perry, W. Perry, 23 Knickerbocker Drive, Neward, DE 19713. 1979. Fiction. "Novelette" avg. press run 200. Pub'd 1 title 1979. 1 title listed in the *Small Press Record of Books in Print* (9th Edition, 1980). avg. price, paper: $5.00. Discounts: Trade. 60pp; 4¼X6⅜; of. Copyrights for author.

Persephone Press, Gloria Greenfield, Pat McGloin, Deborah Snow, P.O. Box 7222, Watertown, MA 02172, (617) 924-0336. 1976. Fiction, art, photos. "Also publish nonfiction, political analysis and theory, history and reprints." avg. press run 5,000. Pub'd 2 titles 1979; expects 4 titles 1980, 6 titles 1981. 4 titles listed in the *Small Press Record of Books in Print* (9th Edition, 1980). avg. price, paper: $6.00. Discounts: 40% on trade orders, no minimum. 200pp; 5¼X8½; of. Reporting time: 1 month. Payment: 50% to authors, 50% to publishers, after expenses. Copyrights for author. COSMEP, Canadian Bookseller's Assn, NESPA, Women's Institute for Freedom of the Press.

Persona Press, N.A. Diaman, PO Box 14022, San Francisco, CA 94114, 415-861-6679. 1978. "*Ed Dean Is Queer* by N.A. Diaman, 1978, 224 pages, 5½ x 8½, paperback, offset $5.95. *The Fourth Well* by N.A. Diaman." avg. press run 1,000. Expects 2 titles 1980, 1 title 1981. 2 titles listed in the *Small Press Record of Books in Print* (9th Edition, 1980). avg. price, paper: $5.95. Discounts: 40% trade. 200pp; 5½X8½; lp.

Personabooks, Bari Rolfe, 434 66th Street, Oakland, CA 94609, 415-658-2482. 1976. Plays. "I also use expository and descriptive material, appropriate for textbooks." avg. press run 1,000. Pub'd 2 titles 1979; expects 1 title 1980. avg. price, paper: $4.00. Discounts: 40% to retailers. 100pp; 7X10; of. Reporting time: 1 month.

Personal Publications, Sam Rothensdyn, Editor, PO Box 9005, Washington, DC 20003, (202) 488-0800. 1980. Poetry, art, photos, cartoons. "We publish fine arts books and postcards; and plan some limited editions. Mostly erotic content." avg. press run 5,000. 4 titles listed in the *Small Press Record of Books in Print* (9th Edition, 1980). avg. price, paper: $3.00-$5.00; other: $0.35-$1.00. Discounts: up to 50%. of. Reporting time: 1-3 months. Payment: negotiated.

Petronium Press, Frank Stewart, 1255 Nuuanu Ave, #1813, Honolulu, HI 96817. 1975. Poetry, fiction, long-poems. "Biased toward fine printing and/or fine writing (the two together whenever possible). Biased toward the poem rather than the poet. Submissions are not encouraged. Publications to date include signed, limited-edition broadsides and portfolios of Gardner, Stafford, Logan, Denney, Merwin; books by Schmitz, Hoge, Edel, Quagliano, Hawaii's Asian-American writers. Forthcoming: a tri-lingual book of Philippine folktales." avg. press run 750. Pub'd 2 titles 1979; expects 2 titles 1980, 6 titles 1981. 10 titles listed in the *Small Press Record of Books in Print* (9th Edition, 1980). avg. price, cloth: $14.00; paper: $4.00; other: $4.00. Discounts: 40% to the trade. pp varies; 5½X7½; of/lp. Reporting time: 1 to 6 weeks. Payment: copies.

PHANTASM, Heidelberg Graphics, Larry S. Jackson, Editor and Publisher; Phillip Hemenway, Poetry Editor, PO Box 3606D, Chico, CA 95927, 916-342-6582. 1976. Poetry, fiction, articles, art, photos, interviews, satire, criticism, reviews, concrete art, news items, non-fiction. "Volume 4, 1979, took our readers to events across the country as well as includinga handset letterpressed chapbook with the six issues. We covered the National Poets for Poetry Rallies, Grace Paley's and E.L. Doctorow's San Francisco debate on 'The Writer and 'Political Commitment,' the Second International Moscow Book Fair, Oregon's conference about the impact of Native American resurgence upon contemporary American literature, and New York's Seventh World Poetry Therapy Conference. Exclusive features included tracing George Keithley's epic poem *The Donner Party* from his hike through the Sierras to its adaptation as an opera, a look at the virtues of vanity publishers, nd 'The Selling of Oscar Wilde.' Interviews with artist Chaim Gross and playwright William Luce coincided with biographical profiles. Guest columnists Jane Fonda, who was denied a position on the California Arts Council; Oleg Shestinsky, Sec oif the Board of the USSR Writers Union; andKate Wolf, folksinger/songwriter; offered diverse perspectives. We published 30,000 words of fiction in vol 4 by authors like John Shaw and Richard Lyons, the best contemporary poetry and translations, plus comprehensive book reviews. For vol 5 we will continue to make *Phantasm* an eclectic multi-cultural literary review, breaking the staid formats of trditional journals with a dash of independent western flavor. *Phantasm* is preserved in libraries from Sacramento to New York and indexed by the *American Humanities Index* and *Index To Periodical Fiction*. We welcome manuscripts and free lance articles congruent with our format." circ. 1,000. 6/yr. Pub'd 6 issues 1979; expects 6 issues 1980, 6 issues 1981. sub. price: $8.00 Individuals; $10.00 Libraries; per copy: $2.00 in bookstores; sample: $2.50 includes postage. Back issues: Write for back issue prices and index. Discounts: Subscription is only discount. 50 pluspp; 8½X11; †of/lp. Reporting time: 4 to 8 weeks. Payment is by copies and two dollars for poetry.

Copyrighted, reverts to author. Pub's reviews: 7 in 1979. §Poetry, graphics, biographies, current literary events. no ads. COSMEP, CCLM, SCCIPHC, WIP, RGWA.

PHANTASMAGORIA, Journey into the Surreal, Roberta Mendel, Editor-Publisher, 3877 Meadowbrook Blvd, University Heights, OH 44118, (216) 932-2173. 1980. Poetry, reviews, letters, news items. "Concise imagistic story poems that *move*, strange juxtapositions welcome; so, too, short witty nuggets of wisdom; reprints acceptable if accompanied by a release; also seeks review copies of small press publications — books, journals, pamphlets, broadsides, what-have-you; payment is one contributor copy. Send all queries, submissions, and review copies to Roberta Mendel, editor, 3877 Meadowbrook Blvd., University Heights, OH 44118. *No SASE, No Reply.*" circ. 100-200. 2/yr. Expects 2 issues 1980, 2 issues 1981. sub. price: $3.00 ($4.00 foreign); per copy: $2.00 ($3.00 foreign) plus $.30 postage and handling. Discounts: 25% for 20 or more of same issue. 12-16pp; 5½X8½; of. Reporting time: ASAP. Payment: copies. Copyrighted. Pub's reviews. §Poetry, small press (general, how-to, self-publishing). Ads: $15.00/$7.50/$3.00 for 3-5 forty character lines. COSMEP.

Philatelic Directory Publishing Co (see also THE PHILATELIC JOURNALIST), Gustav Detjen Jr., Box 150, Clinton Corners, NY 12514. 1976. "The directory is published as a handbook for philatelic writers and advance stamp collectors and students of Philately. In trying to expand its contents will consider the addition of any subject which is helpful to the philatelic writer and journalist." avg. press run 1,200. avg. price, paper: $12.00. Discounts: 33⅓ percent to the trade, larger quantities subject to negotiation. 48pp; 6X9; lp. Reporting time: 60 days. Payment: to be negotiated. Does not copyright for author. Society of Philaticians.

THE PHILATELIC JOURNALIST, Philatelic Directory Publishing Co, Gustav Detjen Jr., Box 150, Clinton Corners, NY 12514, 914-266-3150. 1971. Articles, letters. "Articles which are concerned with the problems of philatelic writers, which offer helpful suggestions, and which promote Philately." circ. 1,000 plus. 6/yr. Pub'd 6 issues 1979; expects 6 issues 1980, 6 issues 1981. sub. price: $6.00, $10.00 2 yrs, Library rate: $10.00 3 years; per copy: $1.00; sample: $1.00. Back issues: $1.00. Discounts: agents, 33⅓ percent; libraries special rate of $10 for three years. 16pp; 5½X8½; lp. Reporting time: 30 days. Payment: subject to negotiation. We do receive many free contributions in return for additional copies & ads. Not copyrighted. Pub's reviews: 84 in 1979. §Philately, postal service. Ads: $40.00/$25.00/$1.00 per line. COSMEP.

Jim Phillips Publications, Jim Phillips, PO box 168, Williamstown, NJ 08094, (609) 567-0695. 1972. Photos, news items. "Information and items needed for forthcoming books on WW II U.S. Airborne uniforms and equipment book, and U.S. Special Forces book." avg. press run 500-5,000. Pub'd 1 title 1979; expects 3 titles 1980, 3 titles 1981. avg. price, cloth: $5.95; paper: $3.95. Discounts: 40%. 35-400pp; 6X9; †of. Reporting time: 1 month. Payment: 50% after publication & ad costs. Copyrights for author.

Philmer Enterprises, Phyliss Shanken, #4 Hunter's Run, Spring House, PA 19477, 215-643-2976. 1976. Poetry, fiction, articles, art, long-poems. "At the moment, we can publish very few publications. Interest in gift books that can be illustrated by top quality artists. Interest in universal appeal for wide market, rather than traditional, elusive poetry." avg. press run 3,000. 2 titles listed in the *Small Press Record of Books in Print* (9th Edition, 1980). avg. price, paper: $3.95. Discounts: trade. 56pp; 5½X8½. Reporting time: 2 months. Payment: by arrangement with author. Copyrights for author. COSMEP.

PHOEBE, Editorial Board, G.M.U. 4400 University Dr., Fairfax, VA 22030. 1971. Poetry, fiction, articles, art, photos, interviews, reviews, parts-of-novels, long-poems. circ. 3,000. 4/yr. sub. price: $7.00; per copy: $2.00; sample: $2.00. 80pp; 8X10; of. Reporting time: 90 days. Payment: copies only. Copyrighted, reverts to author. Pub's reviews: 20 in 1979. §Chapbooks, first novels. Ads: Query. COSMEP.

THE PHOENIX, Morning Star Press, James Cooney, American Editor, Morning Star Farm, RFD, Haydenville, MA 01039, 413-665-4754. 1938. Poetry, letters, parts-of-novels, long-poems, plays. "We don't publish 'fiction'. We publish evocations of the human struggle told in stories, poems, diaries, novels, letters, woodcuts, line drawings & photos. We have no restrictions relative to the length of mss. or to the far ranging aspects of the struggle, past and present. We are most receptive to writings which intrinsically encourage uncompromising non-violent resistance to all assaults against the indivisibility of humanity and against the inherent human rights of individual conscience, freedom of speech and dissent. We are equally receptive to writings which nurture international reconciliations and healings of human society and help us find our way past the malign schisms of tribes, nations, races, absolutist religious & ideological dogmas, and the rival anti-human governments of this world." circ. 2,500-2,800. Irregular quarterly. Pub'd 4 issues 1979; expects 4 issues 1980. sub. price: $10.00

(4 nos); per copy: $3.00; sample: $2.50. Back issues: Very scant supply of recent issues. All copies of Vol. 1 & Vol. 2 (Spring 1938 through Autumn 1940) are long out of print but available in hardcover 2-volume facsimile reprint edition. 264-360pp; 5⅜X7⅝; †lp. Reporting time: usually 2-3 wks. Payment: copies plus a years subscription. Pub's reviews. §radical humanist literature. Ads: No paid ads. exchange notices & free notices only.

Phoenix Books/Publishers, Boye De Mente, Fern Stewart, P.O.Box 32008, Phoenix, AZ 85064, (602) 952-0163. 1970. "Have so far published only 8 books by outside writers; will not be considering new material until 1981" avg. press run 3,000-15,000. Pub'd 5 titles 1979; expects 4 titles 1980, 5 titles 1981. 21 titles listed in the *Small Press Record of Books in Print* (9th Edition, 1980). avg. price, cloth: $9.50; paper: $3.00-$9.95. Discounts: 2-4, 20%; 5-24, 40%; 25-49, 42%; 50-99, 45%; 100 and over, 50%. 176pp; 5½X8½; of. Reporting time: 4 weeks. Payment: 10%, 12½%, 15% based on sales (no advances). Copyrights for author. RMBPA (Rocky Mountain Book Publishers Assoc), COSMEP.

PHOENIX BROADSHEETS, 78 Cambridge Street, Leicester LE3 0JP, United Kingdom. 1972. Poetry, art, long-poems. "Sheets are free, from The Phoenix Theatre S.A.E. New Broom Private Press has a series of poems-cards-finely illustrated. S.A.E. for samples. Nos. 1-185 issues, some hand-coloured. Poetry mainly, sometimes excerpts from plays. Poets include: Brian Patten, Spike Milligan, Jack Woolgar, Charles Causley, Marlene Staniforth. Artists: Rigby Graham, Hans Erni, Toni Savage." circ. 2-300. infrequent. sub. price: free. 1pp; 9X5; †lp.

PhoeniXongs, James Durst, P.O. Box 622 (orders), 1652 Longvalley Drive (correspondence), Northbrook, IL 60062, 312-498-3981. 1973. Poetry, art, photos, cartoons, music, interviews, letters, articles. "We are primarily publishers of the work of songsmith James Durst." avg. press run 2,500. Expects 2 titles 1980. 3 titles listed in the *Small Press Record of Books in Print* (9th Edition, 1980). avg. price, cloth: $4.95; paper: $1.95. Discounts: Standard 40 percent trade. size Varies; of. COSMEP.

PHONE-A-POEM, Peter Payack, Founding Editor; Roland Pease, Associate Editor, Box 193, Cambridge, MA 02141, 617-492-1144. 1976. Poetry, satire, reviews. "*PHONE-A-POEM* is the Cambridge/-Boston 24-hour, free, recorded poetry hotline where you hear 3 minutes of poetry & poetry news. Poems are recorded by the poets themselves. I try to 'play' a broad selection of what's happening in poetry today. If somebody is doing it, you'll eventually hear it on *PHONE-A-POEM!*, *Phone-A-Poem* will consider 'high quality' cassette tapes of interesting poems that last no longer than 2½ minutes. 'Please include a copy of the poem with the cassette, plus a brief bio and SASE" circ. 1,500-2,000. 52/yr. Pub's reviews. §poetry, short short fiction, satire.

Photo-Art Enterprizes, Inc., John Zielinski, c/o Old Brick, 26 E Market, Iowa City, IA 52240, 319-338-2714. 1968. Photos. "We are not currently seeking submissions. Books in the past have been on Iowa: *The Amish: A Pioneer Heritage, Portrait of Iowa, Unknown Iowa: Farm Security Adminstration* photos 1936-1941, *Mesquakie* (indian) and proud of it." avg. press run 1,000. Pub'd 2 titles 1979; expects 2 titles 1980, 2 titles 1981. avg. price, cloth: $8.95; paper: $4.95. 5X8, 8X11; †of. Reporting time: no submissions.

PHOTOFLASH: Models & Photographers Newsletter, Ron Marshall, PO Box 7946, Colorado Springs, CO 80933. 1980. Articles, art, photos, interviews, reviews, letters, news items. "Since the Premier Issue has just been published, a circulation base has not been established yet. Because of this, advertising rates will be negotiated with individual advertisers based on our circulation at the time the ad is placed. *Photoflash* features fact-packed, tightly written mini-features and special reports regarding the interrelated fields of modeling & photography. *Please study a sample issue before submitting anything.* Previously unpublished photos of models are welcomed; compensation is credit line & contributor copies. Model releases and captions required. Send 5 x 7 to 8 x 10 black and white glossy photos only. Include a self-addressed stamped envelope that's large enough and has sufficient postage for return of material submitted. 'I will pay $10.00 each for *previously published* B&W glossy photos of models with detailed captions covering the photo, the model & the market..to show our readers what's selling & who's buying'. Model releases and SASE required. Editorial Office: Saks Building, Suite 8, 29 East Bijou Street, Colorado Springs, Co 80903." 11/yr. sub. price: $30.00; sample: $2.00. Back issues: issues are currently available by subscription only, except for sample or contributor copies. Discounts: half-price charter subscription, $15.00; special group rates for camera clubs, etc. will be considered; inquiries are welcomed. 6pp; 8½X11; of. Reporting time: 2-3 months. Payment: credit line & complimentary copies. Copyrighted, reverts to author. Pub's reviews. §Modeling & photography.

PHOTOGRAPHIC CALENDAR, Secession Gallery of Photography, Open Space, Tom Gore, PO Box 5207, Station B, Victoria, BC V8R 6N4, Canada. 1977. "Fine photographs." circ. 500. 1/yr. Pub'd 1 issue 1979; expects 1 issue 1980, 1 issue 1981. sub. price: $10.00; per copy: $10.00; sample: $10.00.

Back issues: $10.00. Discounts: 40%. 115pp; 6X8; †of. Reporting time: 4 months. Payment: in kind. Copyrighted.

THE PHOTOLETTER, Photosearch International, Jerry Sullivan, Editor, Photosearch International, Department 56, Osceola, WI 54020, (715) 248-3800. 1976. Photos, reviews, news items. *"The Photoletter* is a photo marketing newsletter (twice monthly) which pairs picture buyers with photographers" circ. 1500. Twice-monthly. Pub'd 22 issues 1979; expects 22 issues 1980, 22 issues 1981. sub. price: $46.00; sample: $2.00. Back issues: $2.00 each; 6 for $10.00. Discounts: schools: $34.00/yr. 4pp; 8½X11; of. Reporting time: one week. Payment: 10¢ word. Copyrighted, reverts to author. Pub's reviews: 4 in 1979. §photography. Ads: no ads.

Photosearch International (see THE PHOTOLETTER)

PHOTRON, Allan Beatty, PO Box 1040, Ames, IA 50010. 1971. Articles, criticism, reviews, letters, news items. "Single copy price: $0.75, 40p, or 4 international reply coupons. Also available for trade with other fanzines." circ. 400. Pub'd 1 issue 1979; expects 2 issues 1980. Back issues: inquire. 40pp; 5½X8½; of. Payment: copies. Copyrighted, reverts to author. Pub's reviews: 2 in 1979. §Science fiction, fantasy. Ads: Inquire.

Pi-Right Press (see also SILVER VAIN), Hank Louis, Barbara Barry, P.O. Box 2366, Park City, UT 84060. 1976. Poetry, fiction, articles, art, photos, parts-of-novels, long-poems. avg. press run 500. Pub'd 2 titles 1979; expects 3 titles 1980, 3 titles 1981. avg. price, paper: $3.00. Discounts: 40% booksellers. 80pp; 5½X8½; of. Reporting time: 3-4 weeks. Payment: 3 copies. Yes/yes. None.

PIECES, Bits Press, Lee Abbott, Gary Stonum, Robert Wallace, Dept of English, Case Western Reserve University, Cleveland, OH 44106, (216) 368-2340. 1979. Fiction. *"Pieces* seeks short fiction, preferably under 10 pages - particularly stories too short for the regular outlets. *Pieces* 1 featured work by Barbara L. Greenberg, Norman Lavers, Dennis Trudell, Catherine Petroski, Robley Wilson, Jr. *Pieces* 2 featured a scene omitted from the published version of John Updike's *Rabbit Redux."* circ. 900. 2/yr. Pub'd 1 issue 1979; expects 2 issues 1980, 2 issues 1981. sub. price: $2.00; per copy: $1.00; sample: $1.00. 32pp; 5½X8½; of. Reporting time: normally, one month. Payment: copies. Copyrighted, reverts to author.

PIEDMONT LITERARY REVIEW, Don R. Conner, Editor; John P. Dameron, Associate Editor, P.O.Box 3656, Danville, VA 24541, (804) 799-9049. 1976. Poetry, fiction, articles, satire, criticism, reviews. "All poetry forms and some...short prose as space permits. Cater to good taste, no overt sex" circ. 200. Quarterly. Pub'd 4 issues 1979; expects 4 issues 1980, 4 issues 1981. sub. price: $6.00; per copy: $2.00; sample: $1.50. Back issues: $1.50 per(donation). 40pp; 5X8; of. Reporting time: 8 weeks. Payment: copies. Copyrighted, reverts to author. Pub's reviews: 6 in 1979. §poetry. Piedmont Literary Society.

Pierian Press (see REFERENCE SERVICES REVIEW)

PIG IRON, Pig Iron Press, Jim Villani, Editor; Rose Sayre, Associate Editor; Terry Murcko, Poetry Editor; Jack Remick, Contributing Editor; Joe Allgren, Manuscript Editor, P.O. Box 237, Youngstown, OH 44501, 216-744-2258. 1974. Poetry, fiction, photos, cartoons, letters, long-poems, concrete art, art, collages, plays, articles. "The content of *Pig Iron* will accomodate those individuals from the general audience that are attentive to creative mobility and cultural change. Length: open. Style/bias: high-energy. Publish chapbooks none in 1976, none in 1977, three in 79-80 (expected 1,000 copies). Copyright for author, 10 percent to author. Size varies, paper only. Recent contributors: David Anderson, Guy Beining, Betsy Adams, George Smyth, Ken Fifer. Attentive to creative mobility & cultural change." circ. 1,000. 2/yr. Pub'd 1 issue 1979; expects 2 issues 1980, 2 issues 1981. sub. price: $7.00 for 2 issues, $13.00 for 4 issues, $18.00 for 6 issues; per copy: $4.00; sample: $2.50. Back issues: $3.00. Discounts: booksellers/3 or more copies 40%. 96pp; 8½X11; of. Reporting time: 3 weeks to 12 weeks. Payment: 2 copies, $2.00 per page. Copyrighted, reverts to author. no ads. COSMEP.

Pig Iron Press (see also PIG IRON), Jim Villani, Editor; Rose Sayre, Associate Editor; Terry Murcko, Poetry; Jack Remick, Contributing Editor; Joe Allgren, Manuscript Editor, P.O. Box 237, Youngstown, OH 44501. 1974. "Literary, alternative lifestyles." avg. press run 1,000. Expects 3 titles 1981. 3 titles listed in the *Small Press Record of Books in Print* (9th Edition, 1980). avg. price, paper: $2.00. Discounts: 40%. pp open; 5½X8½; of. Reporting time: 3 weeks to 4 months. Payment: 10% no advance. Copyrights for author. COSMEP.

Pig's Whisker Music, PO Box 27522, Los Angeles, CA 90027. 1 title listed in the *Small Press Record of Books in Print* (9th Edition, 1980).

THE PIKESTAFF FORUM, The Pikestaff Press, James R. Scrimgeour, Editor; Robert D. Sutherland, Editor, P.O. Box 127, Normal, IL 61761, (309)452-4831. 1977. Poetry, fiction, articles, art, photos, satire, criticism, reviews, parts-of-novels, long-poems, plays. "Poetry, prose fiction, drama, children's writing, reviews, commentary on contemporary literature. A regular feature, the 'Forum', will provide space for anyone to sound off on issues of importance to contemporary literature and/or the small-press scene. We are interested in writing that is clear and concise, that contains vivid imagery and concrete detail, and has human experience at the core. Traditional and experimental writing, established and non-established writers are welcome. Manuscripts should be accompanied by SASE. We publish as we have sufficient quality material to warrant an issue" circ. 1,000. Pub'd 1 issue 1979; expects 1-2 issues 1980, 2-3 issues 1981. sub. price: $10.00 for 6 issues; per copy: $1.00; sample: free on request with 40¢ stamp to cover postage. Back issues: $1.00. Discounts: Contributors, 50%; Bookstores, 25%. 32pp; size tabloid; of. Reporting time: within three months. Payment: 3 copies. Copyrighted, reverts to author. Pub's reviews: 3 in 1979. §small press publications. COSMEP, COSMEP-MIDWEST.

The Pikestaff Press (see also THE PIKESTAFF FORUM; THE PIKESTAFF REVIEW), James R. Scrimgeour, Editor; Robert D. Sutherland, Editor, P.O. Box 127, Normal, IL 61761, (309) 452-4831. 1977. "Projects include chapbooks and single-volume collections of individual authors; and books containing single works of considerable length. Comprehansive subscription: $20.00 for six issues of *Forum* & three issues of *Review*" Expects 2 titles 1980. 1 title listed in the *Small Press Record of Books in Print* (9th Edition, 1980). of. Reporting time: Within three months. Payment: Percentage of press run (to be negotiated). Copyrights for author. COSMEP, COSMEP-MIDWEST.

THE PIKESTAFF REVIEW, The Pikestaff Press, James R. Scrimgeour, Editor; Robert D. Sutherland, Editor, P.O. Box 127, Normal, IL 61761, (309) 452-4831. 1977. Poetry, fiction, art, photos, parts-of-novels, long-poems, plays. "A continuing anthology of poetry, prose fiction, drama, and graphic art. We are interested in work not previously published, high quality writing that is clear, conise, vivid, and memorable for what it tries to do and how it does it. Manuscripts should be accompanied by SASE. We publish as we have sufficient quality material to warrant an issue" circ. 500. Expects 1 issue 1980, 1-2 issues 1981. sub. price: $10.00/3 issues; per copy: $2.00. Back issues: $2.00. Discounts: Contributors, 50%; Bookstores, 25%. 6X9; of/lo. Reporting time: within three months. Payment: 3 copies. Copyrighted, reverts to author. Ads: none. COSMEP, COSMEP-MIDWEST.

Pikeville College Press (see also CUMBERLANDS), Leonard Roberts, College Box 2, Pikeville, KY 41501, 432-9227. 1971. avg. press run 500, 1,000. Pub'd 2-4 titles 1979; expects 2-4 titles 1980. avg. price, cloth: $4.50-$10.00; paper: $3.00-$6.00; other: $3.00-$6.00. Discounts: 15 edu insti, 30-40 booksellers; above 200 order 50%. 100 to 600pp; 5X8; of/lp. Reporting time: 1 to 2 months. Payment: 10 to 12½ percent. Copyrights for author. CCLM, COSMEP.

Pilgrim Press, Marion M. Meyer, Senior Editor; Esther Cohen, General Interest Editor, 132 West 31st Street, New York, NY 10001, (212) 594-8555. Fiction. "We publish full length books on religious, socially relevant, philosophical, health and welfare, & church stewardship related subjects. Warehouse address: Seabury Service Center, Somers, CT 06071. Formerly known as United Church Press." avg. press run 5,000-7,000. Pub'd 7 titles 1979; expects 34 titles 1980, 35 titles 1981. avg. price, cloth: $9.95; paper: $6.95. Retail discounts only.Special discounts for groups and organizations. 250pp; 8½X5¾; of. Reporting time: 1-2 months. Payment: Generally 10% royalty to author. Copyrights for author. APA.

THE PILGRIM WAY, James E. Johnston, PO Box 277, Cass Lake, MN 56633, (218) 335-6190. 1957. Poetry, fiction, articles. "Usually write everything myself. *The Pilgrim Way* is published for Pilgrims who confess they are strangers and Pilgrims on the earth. Non-institutional. To have Pilgrim Communes, the members being the Church or Assembly, practicing self sufficiency. Advocating decentralization to save lives in a nuclear war. Also, productivity. Opposing Abortion, euthanasia, sadistic hate campaigns, religious, land, wealth monopolies." circ. 500. 2-3/yr. Pub'd 1 issue 1979; expects 2 issues 1980, 3-4 issues 1981. sub. price: $2.50; per copy: $0.25; sample: $0.25. Back issues: $0.15. Discounts: subscription agent could keep $1.00 on sub. 20pp; 4½X6. Ads: //5¢.

PILGRIMS, Pilgrims South Press, Stephen Higginson, John Gibb, Associate Editor, P O Box 5469, Dunedin, New Zealand. 1976. Poetry, fiction, articles, art, photos, interviews, reviews, letters, satire, criticism, music, parts-of-novels. "Published work will include short stories, reviews, interviews, correspondence, photographs, art work/articles, essays. Each issue will contain a guest (paid). All mss. for return, include S.A.E and postage. Circ 1200; special issues 4M (i.e. Israeli & New Zealand Arts and Letters, July 1978)." circ. 2,500. 3/yr. Pub'd 3 issues 1979; expects 3 issues 1980. 3 titles listed in the *Small Press Record of Books in Print* (9th Edition, 1980). sub. price: NZ$5-85, overseas NZ$7-20; per copy: NZ$1-95; sample: NZ$1-95. Back issues: NZ$4-95 or double issue (Israel and New Zealand

Arts and Letters). 96pp; 240mm x 145mm; of. Reporting time: 3 weeks. Payment: copy and @ NZ$7-50/pp. Copyrighted, reverts to author. Pub's reviews: 20 in 1979. §all. Ads: $50/$35.

Pilgrims South Press (see also PILGRIMS), Stephen Higginson, John Gibb, Associate Editor, PO Box 5469, Dunedin, New Zealand. 1976. avg. price, cloth: NZ$4-50; paper: NZ$3-50; other: signed copies 1-20 NZ$12-50. Discounts: 40%. 210X150; lp. Reporting time: 6 weeks. Payment: yes. Copyrights for author. NZ Book Publishers Assoc.

PILLAR, B. E. Beveridge, Box B, St Cloud, MN 56301, (612) 251-3510 ext 256. 1902. Poetry, fiction, articles, art, photos, cartoons, interviews, satire, criticism, reviews, music, letters, long-poems, news items. "*Pillar* is a monthly publication, made by and for the inmates of the Minnesota Correctional Facility—St Cloud (hereafter referred to as MCF-SCL; formerly State Reformatory for men), located in St Cloud, Minnesota. *Pillar* is published with the approval of the Department of Corrections and the Administration of MCF-SCL. Opinions expressed herein are entirely those of the individual author(s), unless clearly stated to the contrary, and do not necessarily reflect policy or opinions of the State of Minnesota, the Department of Corrections, or *Pillar*. The subscription rate is $3.25 for twelve issues, with postage paid at St Cloud, MN 56301. In order to be considered for publication, all materials must meet editorial guidelines as set forth below: 1. Materials which are obscene, an MCF-SCL security violation, or personally offensive or derogatory to an individual will not be published. 2. Author(s) must identify themselves; if anonymity is desired, authorship may be kept confidential with the Editor, however, the Editor then takes full responsibility for content and authenticity, so in cases of controversy personal contact with the Edito should be arranted. 3. Credit must be given where it is due; plagiarism is unacceptable. 4. Anyone may submit material for publication, however, inmates of MCF-SCL recieve preferential consideration. 5. Any material submitted to *Pillar* becomes *Pillar* property, and, as such, is subject to routine editing. 6. Typed double-spaced materials are preferred, however, neatly printed double spaced materials (or kites) will also be considered. Illegible materials will be neglected. 7. All submitted materials will be reviewed, and appropriate responses made to the author promptly. 8. News items which are of unique interest to the inmate population of MCF-SC are desired, and clippings, etc., are welcome contributions, but the title and date of the publication from which they are taken, as well as the author's name, must accompany all such submissions. Unless proper accreditation accompanies such stories, they are unacceptable. 9. *Pillar's* goal is to provide a means of exposure to veiws, opinions, news etc., of inmates at MCF-SC. The preceding is a general list of *Pillar* policy. It should not be considered definitively complete, merely represenitive. Further applications to specific situations may be made upon request by writing to *Pillar*. Permission to reproduce material(s) is granted under the following conditions: sources must be accredited, permision to reproduce *Pillar* materials(s) is given for one printing only. Publish reviews of movies." circ. 1,300. 12/yr. Pub'd 12 issues 1979; expects 12 issues 1980, 11 issues 1981. sub. price: $3.25; sample: free. Back issues: $0.10 per copy & postage. Discounts: free exchange, comp. subs. to approved persons. 24pp; 8½X11; of. Reporting time: 1 month, except ongoing stories. Payment: in subscriptions. Pub's reviews: 3 in 1979. §Alternatives to incarceration, crime deterrence, etc. COSMEP.

The Pin Prick Press (see also PASTICHE: Poems of Place; SNIPPETS: A Melange of Woman; PHANTASMAGORIA, Journey into the Surreal), Roberta Mendel, 3877 Meadowbrook Blvd, University Heights, OH 44118, (216) 932-2173. 6 titles listed in the *Small Press Record of Books in Print* (9th Edition, 1980).

Pinchgut Press, Marjorie Pizer, Anne Spencer Parry, 6 Oaks Avenue, Cremorne, Sydney, N.S.W. 2090, Australia, 90-5548. 1948. Poetry, fiction. "Australian poetry and fiction in particular fantasy, so far." avg. press run 1,200-3,000. Pub'd 2 titles 1979; expects 2 titles 1980. 6 titles listed in the *Small Press Record of Books in Print* (9th Edition, 1980). avg. price, paper: $3.00-$5.00. of. Reporting time: quite quickly. Payment: 10% retail price.

PINCHPENNY, Tom Miner, Betty Goossens, c/o 916 22nd Street, #14, Sacramento, CA 95816. 1980. Poetry, cartoons. "All contributions welcome, but especially interested in strong, contemporary work: progressive, experimental poetry that speaks to today. Prefer young unknowns who submit sizeable selections with SASE's & autobiographical cover letters." circ. 100. 6/yr. Pub'd 6 issues 1979. sub. price: $6.00; per copy: $0.99; sample: $0.99. 28pp; 5½X8½; of. Reporting time: 1 month. Copyrighted, reverts to author.

Pine Row Publications (see also POTPOURRI FROM HERBAL ACRES), Phyllis V. Shaudys, Box 428, Washington Crossing, PA 18977.

PINECONE, White Pine Press, Dennis Maloney, 109 Duerstein St., Buffalo, NY 14210, (716) 825-8671. 1978. "*Pinecone* is a unique periodical appearing in varied formats including: postcards, broadsides, small chapbooks, cassette recordings and other. *The Zodiac Poems* by Robin Willoughby, a postcard chapbook; *Some Animals* postcards by Neruda, Lewandowski & others; *At the Carrying Place* 23 postcards from Stern, Simpson, Hollo, Bell, Ignatow; *I Am The Sun* Maurice Kenny." circ. 300. Pub'd 2 issues 1979; expects 2 issues 1980. sub. price: $4.00; per copy: $1.00. Discounts: under 5 - 20%, 5 & over - 40%. lp/of. Reporting time: 2 weeks to one month. Payment: copies. Copyrighted, reverts to author. COSMEP, CCLM.

Piney Branch Press, Jacob Fisher, 5000 Piney Branch Road, Fairfax, VA 22030, (703) 830-3185. 1978. avg. press run 500. Pub'd 1 title 1979. avg. price, paper: $3.95. Discounts: 40%. 300pp; 5½X8½; of.

Pink Triangle Press (see also THE BODY POLITIC- Gay Liberation Journal), The Body Politic Editorial Collective & Pink Triangle Press Collective, Box 639, Station A, Toronto, Ontario M5W1G2, Canada, 416-977-6320. 1975. Poetry, fiction, articles, art, photos, cartoons, interviews, criticism, reviews, letters, news items, non-fiction. "Will be seeking manuscripts and art works informed by a gay consciousness, the publication of which will in some way advance the cause of gay liberation." avg. press run 6,000. Pub'd 3 titles 1979. 3 titles listed in the *Small Press Record of Books in Print* (9th Edition, 1980). avg. price, paper: $6.00. Discounts: Fewer than 5:35%; 5-14:40%; 15-25:42%; 25 or more:45%. various methods of production. Reporting time: 1 month for Body Politic. Payment: negotiable.

PIP COLLEGE 'HELPS' NEWSLETTER, Partners In Publishing, P. M. Fielding, Box 50347, Tulsa, OK 74150, (918) 583-0956. 1976. Articles, interviews, reviews, letters, news items. "Very short, less than 150 words unless special enough to take several pages of the newsletter." circ. 500. 12/yr. Pub'd 12 issues 1979; expects 12 issues 1980, 12 issues 1981. sub. price: $20.00; per copy: $1.00; sample: free. Back issues: $1.00 for each back isssue or $10.00 for bound copy for each year Vol 1 - 1976, Vol 2 - 1977, Vol 3 - 1978. 4-8pp; 10X12; of. Reporting time: 1 month. Payment: copies. Not copyrighted. Pub's reviews: 24 in 1979. §Learning disabilities, college made easy, careers for LD adults.

THE PIPE SMOKER'S EPHEMERIS, Tom Dunn, 20-37 120th Street, College Point, NY 11356. 1964. Poetry, fiction, articles, art, photos, cartoons, interviews, satire, criticism, reviews, letters, parts-of-novels, collages, news items. circ. 5,000. 2/yr. Pub'd 1 issue 1979; expects 2 issues 1980, 2 issues 1981. 40pp; 8½X11; of. Reporting time: immediately. Payment: none. Copyrighted. Pub's reviews. §Tobacco, pipe smoking, books about books.

Pirate Press, Bill Griffiths, 107 Valley Drive, Kingsbury, London NW9 9NT, United Kingdom. 1971. Poetry. "Publications include contemporary poetry, especially on prison topics. Also microfiche editions" 5 titles listed in the *Small Press Record of Books in Print* (9th Edition, 1980). †of/duplicating. ALP.

Pitjon Press/BackBack Media (see also FROZEN WAFFLES), David Wade, Bro Dimitrios, 3215 Sec Ave West, Bradenton, FL 33505. 1976. Poetry, fiction, art, photos, interviews, reviews, long-poems, collages, plays, concrete art. "Hellish, getting the anthology off the ground; but I'm sure we'll make it." avg. press run 150-200; may expand to 500 or more. Pub'd 1 title 1979; expects 1 title 1980, 2 titles 1981. avg. price, cloth: $6.00; paper: $4.50; other: $4.50 or higher. Discounts: to be arranged. 80pp; size varies; of. Reporting time: From five seconds to five days. ESP sometimes attempted but we haight to admit our flower power has flown (or wilted). Payment: 1 copy per head; money later (as we becomme funded). Copyrights for author.

Pittore Euforico, Charles J. Stanley, PO Box 1132, Stuyvesant Station, New York, NY 10009. 1978. Poetry, fiction, art, photos, satire, music, letters, parts-of-novels, collages, concrete art. "Contributors include: Bern Porter, Charlie Morrow, Richard Kostelanez, Bill Jacobson, Bob Holman, Jeff Wright, Rainer Wiens, Laura Dean, Katherine Bradford. Titles include: *Colleagues* edited by Charles Stanley; *Maine Moments in New York* edited by Charles Stanley; *Yurtyet* edited by Charles Stanley; *The Adventures of Carlo Pittore* by Charles Stanley" avg. press run 750. Pub'd 4 titles 1979; expects 5 titles 1980. 14 titles listed in the *Small Press Record of Books in Print* (9th Edition, 1980). avg. price, paper: $6.00. Discounts: Trade 40%. 100pp; 8½X11; of. Copyrights for author. Maine Publishers and Writers Alliance, New York State Small Press Association.

PIVOT, Mayer Press, Joseph L. Grucci, 221 S. Barnard, State College, PA 16801, 814-238-8887. 1951. Poetry. "Length of material usually not more than 40-50 lines. Recent contributors: Eugene J. McCarthy, Paul West, Donald Newlove, Dorothy Roberts, John Balaban (Lamont Poetry Prizewinner)." circ. 1,500 - 2,000. 1/yr. sub. price: $4.00/3 issues; per copy: $1.50; sample: $1.00 plus $.50 postage. Back issues: $2.00; $45.00 for complete file. Discounts: Bookstores 33⅓ percent; Agents 40 percent. 48pp; 6X9; lp. Reporting time: 1-3 months. Payment: 2 author's copies. Copyrighted, reverts to author. Ads: $100.00/$55.00/$30.00. CCLM.

Place of Herons (see also WOOD IBIS), James Cody, Editor; Alma Perez, Editorial Assistant, PO Box 1952, Austin, TX 78768, (512) 472-0737; 476-7023. 1974. "See description under *Wood Ibis* for details, we are but/not confined to this description, necessarily." avg. press run 500-1,000. Pub'd 3 titles 1979; expects 6 titles 1980, 3-4 titles 1981. 2 titles listed in the *Small Press Record of Books in Print* (9th Edition, 1980). avg. price, paper: $3.00. Discounts: 40 percent for bookstores; varies with others. 10% for purchase of complete list; 15 titles available as of 6/79; 22 as of 6/80. 30-60pp; 5½X8½; of. Reporting time: varies, usually 2 weeks to 6 months. Payment varies, usually copies. Copyrights for author.

Placebo Press, Cecil Curtis, 4311 Bayou Blvd #T-199, Pensacola, FL 32503, (904) 477-3995. 1976. Poetry, fiction, articles, art, cartoons, satire. "Will be unable to accept any more manuscripts through 1980" avg. press run 200. Pub'd 12 titles 1979; expects 8 titles 1980, 12 titles 1981. avg. price, paper: $1.50. 64pp; 5½X8½, 8½X11; †mi. Reporting time: within a week on queries. No payment; we usually split the edition with author. Does not copyright for author.

Plain View, Inc., John C. Andrews, Susan Bright, 1509 Dexter, Austin, TX 78704, (512) 441-2452. 1979. Poetry, art, photos, cartoons, music, long-poems, collages, plays, concrete art. "We experiment with form & format. Our projects include a color xerox special edition of poetry on water colors, 2 films, 4 video tapes, an anthology of women's prison writing, a collection of graphic new music & a sequence of broadside performance scores. Recent artists: Susan Bright, Charles Geuser, Jeff Woodruf, women in the travis county jail, John Andrews, Beth Epstein." avg. press run 500. Pub'd 1 title 1979. avg. price, paper: $3.00 (chapbooks); other: Video tapes $75.00; watercolor collection $25.00. of. Reporting time: request only. Payment: by arrangement. Copyrights for author. Texas Circuit.

Plain Wrapper Press s.n.c., Richard-Gabriel Rummonds, Alessandro Zanella, Via Carlo Cattaneo, 6, Verona 37121, Italy, (045) 38943. 1966. Poetry, fiction, art, long-poems. "Only previously unpublished material, often bilingual, much emphasis on Latin American and Italian writers, original graphics. Recent Contributors: Anthony Burgess, Jorge Luis Borges, Jack Spicer, Frederic Tuten, P. P. Pasolini, Vittorio Sereni, Luigi Santucci, Andrea Zanzotto, Brendan Gill, Manuel Mujica Lainez. Don't encourage submissions; query first" avg. press run 100. Pub'd 3 titles 1979; expects 5 titles 1980. avg. price, cloth: $50.00 - $2,400.00. Discounts: Standing orders 20%; Trade 30%. 48-64pp; 14X25 cm, 28X38 cm; †lp. Payment: fixed fees, ranging from $150.00 to $7,000.00. Copyrights for author.

PLAINSPEAK MAGAZINE, Mike Ellsworth, PO Box 9167, Denver, CO 80209, (303) 744-9247. 1978. Poetry, articles, art, photos, cartoons, interviews, criticism, reviews, letters, long-poems, collages, news items. "We like articles about contemporary poets, less than 2,000 words. We print poetry that is clear, concise, direct and understandable—no avante garde or sappy love stuff. Recent Contributors: Allen Ginsberg, James Ryan Morris, Jess Graf. We do not like book-length poetry submissions; limit = 100 lines. Each issue we run a poetry contest (entry fee = $3.00) with over $100.00 in prizes." circ. 750. 2/yr. Pub'd 1 issue 1979; expects 2 issues 1980, 2 issues 1981. sub. price: $4.50; per copy: $2.75; sample: $1.75. Back issues: $1.75. Discounts: over 10 copies, $1.75 each; wholesale $1.40 each; jobber $1.15 each; consignment $1.95; librarian and teacher samples, free. 56pp; 8½X11; of. Reporting time: 8-10 weeks. Payment: $1.00 and one copy per page. Copyrighted, reverts to author. Pub's reviews: 6 in 1979. §Poetry, language, arts, music. Ads: $100.00/$55.00/$12.50.

PLAINSWOMAN, Jean Butenhoff Vivian, Editor; Joan Eades, Literary Editor, P.O. Box 8027, Grand Forks, ND 58202, (701) 777-4234. 1977. Poetry, fiction, articles, art, cartoons, interviews, reviews, letters, collages, news items. circ. 1300. 6/yr. Pub'd 12 issues 1979; expects 6 issues 1980, 6 issues 1981. sub. price: $6.00; per copy: $1.00; sample: $1.00. Back issues: $1.00. Discounts: 30%/issue. 16pp; 8½X11; of. Reporting time: 1 month. Payment: none at this time. Copyrighted, 2 yrs after publ. rights revert to author. Pub's reviews: 12 in 1979. §women & the law, women in general, women's history, women & politics; financial planning & management; literature. Ads: none.

Planetary Research, Jerry Katz, PO Box 1741, Santa Monica, CA 90406. "Our creations include *Kundalini* and *The Mystic Road to Inner Success*. Submit manuscripts on offbeat new age/occult subjects. 10,000-20,000 words." avg. price, paper: $2.95. 60pp; 8½X11, 5X7; of. Reporting time: 3 months. Payment: negotiable. Copyrights for author. COSMEP.

PLANTAGENET PRODUCTIONS, Recorded Library of the Spoken Word, Plantagenet Productions, Dorothy Rose Gribble, Westridge, Highclere, Nr. Newbury, Royal Berkshire RG15 9PJ, United Kingdom. 1964. "Recordings of poetry, philosophy, narrative and light work on cassette, tape, LP. Special orders undertaken. New tape/cassette issues; 'Poetry of Douglas Fraser'; E.M. Valk reads Oscar Wilde's *The Happy Prince* and his own translation of Wilhelm Hauff's *The Story of Caliph Stork*;

Hiawatha's Wedding Feast spoken by Dorothy Rose Gribble" erratic. Pub'd 1 issue 1979; expects 3 issues 1980. price per copy: LP-£2.25, £2, £1 cassette tape £2.25, £1.75 postage extra.

Plantagenet Productions (see also PLANTAGENET PRODUCTIONS, Recorded Library of the Spoken Word), Westridge, Highclere, Nr. Newbury, Berkshire RG159PJ, United Kingdom. Pub'd 1 title 1979; expects 1 title 1981. 34 titles listed in the *Small Press Record of Books in Print* (9th Edition, 1980). avg. price, paper: £1 plus postage.

Platyne Press, 2202 N Madelyn Avenue, Tucson, AZ 85712. 1976. "No unsolicited manuscripts" avg. press run 200. Pub'd 1 title 1979; expects 1 title 1980, 1 title 1981. 1 title listed in the *Small Press Record of Books in Print* (9th Edition, 1980). avg. price, paper: $7.50. Discounts: 5 or more 40%. 50pp; 5X8; †lp. Does not copyright for author.

Playwrights Canada, Shirley Gibson, 8 York Street, Toronto, Ontario M5J1R2, Canada, 416-363-1581. 1972. Plays. "Are bound by our constitution to only publish the work of Canadian citizens or landed immigrants." avg. press run 300. Pub'd 36 titles 1979; expects 40 titles 1980, 50 titles 1981. 13 titles listed in the *Small Press Record of Books in Print* (9th Edition, 1980). avg. price, cloth: $7.50; paper: $3.50. Discounts: 20-45 percent. 50pp; 8½X11 playscript; 6X9 paperback; †xerox/of. Reporting time: 2 months. Payment: 10%. Copyrights for author. Association of Canadian Publishers & Literary Presses Group.

Pleasant Hill Press, Eugene H. Boudreau, 2600 Pleasant Hill Rd, Sebastopol, CA 95472, (707) 823-6583. "My books are about the Sierra Madre in Mexico. Don't take submissions" avg. press run 1200. 3 titles listed in the *Small Press Record of Books in Print* (9th Edition, 1980). avg. price, cloth: $6.00; paper: $3.00. Discounts: 40%/bookstores. 90pp; 5½X8½; of.

Pleasure Dome Press (Long Island Poetry Collective Inc.) (see also XANADU), Anne-Ruth Baehr, Coco Gordon, Mildred Jeffery, Beverly Lawn, Lois Walker, Box 773, Huntington, NY 11743, (516) 549-1150. 1976. Poetry. "We are primarily interested in Long Island poets who are willing to assist in design and production. Publications include poetry postcards, chapbooks, full-length poetry collection in hard and soft-bound editions. We are not open to unsolicited mss. at this time, but welcome queries from regional poets, and suggestions for collaborative efforts. Recent Title: *Saying My Name Outloud* by Arthur Dobrin, 32 pp, soft ed, 1978; *Throat of Feathers* by Beverly Lawn, 64 pp, hard/soft eds, 1979." avg. press run varies according to project. Pub'd 1 title 1979; expects 1 title 1980, 1 title 1981. 6 titles listed in the *Small Press Record of Books in Print* (9th Edition, 1980). avg. price, cloth: varies; paper: varies; other: varies. Discounts: 10 percent on orders of $20.00 or more (includes XANADU and Newsletter subs.). pp varies; size varies; †lp/of. not currently considering unsolicited material. Payment varies. we buy all rights. CCLM.

PLEXUS, Bay Area Women's Newspaper, Feminist Publishing Alliance, Inc., A. Mac Mahon, C. Orr, K. D. F. Reynolds, A. Weinstock, Theresa Haynie, 545 Athol Avenue, Oakland, CA 94606. 1974. Poetry, articles, art, photos, cartoons, interviews, satire, criticism, reviews, letters, collages, news items. "New articles and reviews should be no longer than 500 words. Features can run from 1200 to 1500 words. Material of the feminist persuasion is sought, however, anything relevant to the lives of women struggling against sexism will be considered. Recent contributors have included Alta, Margo St. James, Priscilla Alexander. Articles of specific interest to women are sought. Prisoners in US free 1-year subsc. Pub's 4-6 reviews per issue, 2-12 short 'flashes' as well per issue. Recent contributors include: Dorothy Bryant, Mary Watkins, Jennifer Stone." circ. 12M. 12/yr. Pub'd 12 issues 1979. sub. price: $6.00 indiv., $10.00 instit. or library; per copy: $0.60; sample: free. Back issues: $.50 (as available). Discounts: $6.00/year to women's organizations. 20pp; 16X10; of. Reporting time: varies. Payment: six-month subc to contributors; token payment now available $5.00-$15.00. Copyrighted. Pub's reviews. §books by, for, and about women, theater, film, esp independent. Ads: $300.00/$175.00/$.75 a line. COSMEP.

PLOUGHSHARES, DeWitt Henry, Peter O'Malley, Box 529, Cambridge, MA 02139. 1971. Poetry, fiction, interviews, criticism, reviews, parts-of-novels, long-poems. "Maximum length for prose 6,000 words. We're biased towards new writers, towards writers in the Boston and New England areas, towards 'rediscovery' of neglected writers of interest to same. Because of our revolving editorship, status of issues in progress & contrast of emphasis from issue to issue, we suggest inquiry prior to submission. Recent contributors: James Merrill, Mark Halliday, Alice Mattison, Robert Pinsky, Frank Bidart, Allen Grossman, Margo Lockwood, Gail Mazur, Lloyd Schwartz, Seamus Heaney, Richard Yates, Gina Berriault, Andre Dubus,Stratis Haviaris, Ronald Sukenick, Fanny Howe, Larry Levis, Thomas Lux, Philip Damon, Jayne Anne Phillips, Susan Engberg, R.V.Cassill, Tom Flanagan, Benedict Kiely, Ted Hughes, Derek Mahon, John Mcgahern, Paul Muldoon, Norman MacCaig, Michael Longley" circ. 3,000. 4/yr. Pub'd 4 issues 1979; expects 4 issues 1980, 4 issues 1981. sub. price:

$10.00/4 issues (domestic); $12.00/4 issues (foreign); per copy: $3.50; sample: $3.50. Back issues: full set vol 1 - $15.00 or 1/1 $3.50; 1/2 $3; 1/3 $3.50; 1/4 $3.50; full set Vol 2 $10.00 or $2.50 each, except 2/4-$2.95; full set Vol 3 $10.00 or 3/1-$2.95, 3/2-$2.50, 3/3 & 4-$3.95; full set vol 4, $10.00 or 4/1-$2.95, 4/2-$2.95, 4/3-$3.50, 4/4-$3.50; 5/1-$3.50, 5/2-$3.50, 5/3-$3.50; 5/4-$3.50; 6/1-$3.50, etc. Discounts: 40% trade (5 copies or more); 10% agent. 220pp; 8½X5½; of. Reporting time: 3 mos. Payment: $5/p prose ($50 max); $10/poem. Copyrighted. Pub's reviews: 17 in 1979. §quality poetry, fiction, criticism. Ads: $100.00 (non-profit); $175.00 (trade)/$60.00 (non-profit); $100.00 (trade). CCLM, NESPA, Magazine Coop.

PLUCKED CHICKEN, Plucked Chicken Press, Will Petersen, Editor, Box 5941, Chicago, IL 60680, (312) 454-1177. 1977. Poetry, art, interviews, letters, long-poems. "Editor, WP, was managing editor for Corman's *Origin,* second series. As editor for *Bussei,* 1955-7 (Berkeley) published earliest poems of Snyder, Whalen, first poems of Kerouac. PC is a journal of 'conversations, essays, letters, drawings & poems'. First issue contains reproduced linocut picture, story, essay on Noh, conversations with light sculptor John David Mooney, woodcut artist Sidney Chafetz. Second issue contains poems by Snyder, Levy, Fineberg, Furuta, Gogisgi, Maloney, and features artist Tom Nakashima; PC3: artist Ben Freedman; PC4 83 pp on Noh. PC5 American and English poetry; etchings by Berg. PC6 features drawings of Karl Jacobson, poems by Moraff, Fitzsimmons" circ. 800. Occasional. Pub'd 2-4 issues 1979. sub. price: $15.00 for 4 issues. Donors receive signed stoneprints; per copy: $5.00; sample: $5.00. Back issues: PC1 &PC2 op; 3-6 $5.00 each. Discounts: 50% no consignments. 88pp; 8½X11; of. Reporting time: immediate response. Copyrighted, reverts to author. §Whatever strike the editor, individually, as of worth. No ads.

Plucked Chicken Press (see also PLUCKED CHICKEN), Will Petersen, Box 5941, Chicago, IL 60680, (312) 454-1177. 1977. Poetry, art, interviews, criticism, letters, parts-of-novels, long-poems. "Plucked Chicken Press founded by artist Will Petersen: hand-pulled editions of lithographs by artists. Plucked Chicken magazine an offshoot. Editor, WP, was managing editor for Cid Corman's *ORIGIN,* second series. As editor for *BUSSEI,* 1956-7 (Berkeley) published first poems of Snyder, Whalen, first poems of Kerouac. PC is a journal of 'conversations, essays, letters, drawings & poems'. Books by individual poets planned; with handpulled original stoneprints tipped in." avg. press run 800. avg. price, paper: $5.00; other: $12.00 for 4 issues; individual copies $5.00. 88pp; 8½X11; of. Reporting time: Immediacy attempted. Copyrights for author.

PLUM, Harvey Lillywhite, Eileen Silver-Lillywhite, 549 W. 113th St., #1D, New York, NY 10025, (212) 662-5385. 1978. Poetry, fiction, articles, interviews, criticism, reviews, parts-of-novels, long-poems. "We reserve 50% of *Plum* for not-yet-known writers. Other better-known contributors include Robert Mezey, Linda Pastan, Michael Benedikt, Colette Inez, Sherod Santos, Joyce Kornblatt, Ron Padgett, Rhoda Schwartz, A.G. Sobin, Judith Hemschemeyer, Dennis Schmitz, Naomi Lazard, Hiro Sato" circ. 1,000. 2/yr. Pub'd 1 issue 1979; expects 2 issues 1980, 2 issues 1981. sub. price: $5.00/2 issues; per copy: $3.00; sample: $2.50. Discounts: 40%. 80pp; 6¼X9; of. Reporting time: 1 month. Payment: copies. Copyrighted, reverts to author. Pub's reviews. §poetry, fiction, criticism, biographies. Ads: $100/$50.

PLUMBERS INK, Plumbers Ink Press, Marlene Kamei, Editor & Publisher, PO Box 2565, Taos, NM 87571, 758-8035. 1976. Poetry. "Prefer short to medium length poems. Interested in non-academic, modernist poetry. Like to see experimental work. Mss. not accompanied by a SASE will not be returned. Some recent contributors: Antler, Bobby Meyers, Andy Clausen, Gene Frumkin, Frieda Werden, Leo Romero, Kaye McDonough, James MacKie." circ. 200. 4/yr. Pub'd 4 issues 1979; expects 4 issues 1980, 4 issues 1981. sub. price: $6.00; per copy: $2.00; sample: $2.00. Back issues: $1.50 per single issue. 50-60pp; 5½X8½; of. Reporting time: 6 weeks to 2 months. Payment: 1 contributors' copy. Copyrighted, reverts to author. Ads: no ads. CCLM, COSMEP.

Plumbers Ink Press (see also PLUMBERS INK), PO Box 2565, Taos, NM 87571. 3 titles listed in the *Small Press Record of Books in Print* (9th Edition, 1980).

PNS (see also PEOPLE'S NEWS SERVICE), PNS Collective, Oxford House, Derbyshire Street, London E2 6HG, United Kingdom, 01-739-3630. 1973. Articles, photos, cartoons, interviews, reviews, news items. avg. press run 600. Pub'd 1 title 1979. 16pp; size A4; of. Reporting time: variable. Payment: none. Copyrights for author. APS.

POEM, Huntsville Literary Association, Robert L. Welker, PO Box 1247, West Station, Huntsville, AL 35807. 1967. Poetry. "Any length, any style, no biases except against pornography for the sake of pornography, propaganda for right, left, or center and biased for quality poetry. Recent contributors: T. Alan Broughton, Hannah Kahn, Larry Rubin, Charles Edward Eaton." circ. 500. 3/yr. Pub'd 3 issues 1979; expects 3 issues 1980, 3 issues 1981. sub. price: $5.00; per copy: $3.00; sample:

$1.50. Back issues: $3.00. 70pp; 4½X7⅓; lp. Reporting time: 30 days. Payment: copies. Copyrighted, granted on request. no advertisement. CCLM.

POEMS IN PUBLIC PLACES, Chris Cooney, Room 8, National Mutual Building, Wollongong, N.S.W. 2500, Australia. 1977. Poetry, art, photos, cartoons. "We accept poetry from poets in the following categories with priority given to (a) poets residing in the Illawarray region of New South Wales, Australia; (b) Australian poets living in Australia; (c) Australian poets." circ. 250. 3/yr. Pub'd 1 issue 1979; expects 4 issues 1980, 3 issues 1981. sub. price: $4.00; per copy: $1.00. Back issues: $0.70. 36pp; 13cm x 21cm. Reporting time: 4 months. Copyrighted, reverts to author.

POESIE - U.S.A., Pierre Chanover, P O Box 811, Melville, NY 11747. 1976. Poetry, art, photos. "*Poesie* USA is a quarterly magazine that encourages unpublished as well as published poets who have written poems in the French language. *Poesie* USA is the only poetry magazine written entirely in French in the United States. It serves the francophone and francophile community of North America." circ. 500 (circa). 4/yr. Pub'd 4 issues 1979; expects 4 issues 1980, 4 issues 1981. sub. price: $8.00/yr; outside U.S.A. $10.00; per copy: $2.00; sample: $1.00. Back issues: $2.00 each plus handling charges: 75¢ per issue. 48pp; 5½X8½; of. Reporting time: four weeks. Payment: in copies. Copyrighted, does not revert to author. §French Poetry. Ads: $75.00/$40.00/none. CCLM, COSMEP.

POET, Poet Press India, Dr. Krishna Srinivas, Dr. Mabelle A. Lyon, Edward L. Meyerson, Edwin A. Falkowski, 208 W. Latimer Ave., Campbell, CA 95008, 408-379-8555. 1960. Poetry, reviews. "40 line limit (poems only); free form, free verse (couplets thru ballads) in good taste; sase for fact sheet *before* submitting. Translations into English from 30 countries. N. Russell, O. Lysohorsky, R. Menon, M. Dei-Anang, H. McKinley, L. Pasternak-Slater, J. Negalha, L. Pennington, B. Cameron, A. Kastan." circ. 500. 12/yr. Pub'd 12 issues 1979; expects 13 issues 1980. sub. price: $18.00; per copy: $1.75; sample: $1.75. Back issues: $1.75. Discounts: none. 80pp; 5½X8½; lp. Reporting time: 30 days. Payment: none. Copyrighted, reverts to author. Pub's reviews: 21 in 1979. Ads: none. World Congress of Poets.

POET & CRITIC, Iowa State University Press, David Cummings, English Dept., ISU, 203 Ross Hall, Ames, IA 50011. 1964. Poetry, articles, art, interviews, satire, criticism, reviews. "Selected contributors comment on each other's work." circ. 500-1M. 3/yr. Pub'd 3 issues 1979. sub. price: $4.00; per copy: $2.00; sample: $1.00. 48pp; 6X9; of. Reporting time: up to 8 wks. Payment: copies only. rights revert upon permission. Pub's reviews: 6 in 1979. §Any poetry-related areas. no ads. CCLM, COSMEP.

Poet Gallery Press, Mike Pavlos, 224 West 29th St, New York, NY 10001. 1970. "A small press, founded originally to publish works of American writers living outside continental USA. Number of books published varies according to year-ECO conditions, etc. Have published a minimum of 2 titles per year since 1970 while have published (novels) fiction, drama, and poetry we have also published some experimental work." Pub'd 2-6 titles 1979. avg. price, paper: $5.50. Discounts: $3.00 to wholesaler. 70-120pp; 8½X11½; †mi/of/lp. Reporting time: 2 months. Payment: depends. Does not copyright for author. COSMEP.

POET LORE, Kate Curry, Managing Editor, 4000 Albemarle Street, N.W., Suite 504, Washington, DC 20016, (202)362-6644. 1889. Poetry, reviews. circ. 500. 4/yr. Pub'd 4 issues 1979; expects 4 issues 1980, 4 issues 1981. sub. price: $10.00 Indiv.; $15.00 Instit.; per copy: $3.50; sample: $2.50. Back issues: $2.50. 48pp; 6X9; of. Reporting time: 2 months to 4 months. Payment: 2 copies of issue. Copyrighted, rights revert to author. Pub's reviews: 11 in 1979. §Small press poetry books. Ads: $100/$55.

Poet Papers (see also THE RECORD SUN), Laimons Juris G, P.O. Box 528, Topanga, CA 90290. 1970. Poetry, art, photos, long-poems, collages. "Please: If sending materials for consideration enclose stamped self-addressed envelope! *No SASE-NO reply. American Refugee Poet* $3.50; *Walking Sheet* $2.00; *i.e.* $12.00; *A Man Without A Gun* $7.00; *A Thinker's Notebook* $6.00" avg. press run 5,000. Pub'd 2 titles 1979; expects 3 titles 1980, 4 titles 1981. 5 titles listed in the *Small Press Record of Books in Print* (9th Edition, 1980). avg. price, other: $6.10. Discounts: library-trade 20%. 150pp; 7X10; of/lp/silkscreen. Reporting time: 6 mos-1 year. Payment: copies of book. PAF (People's Antarctica Foundation).

Poet Press India (see also POET), Dr. Krishna Srinivas, Dr. Edwin A. Falkowski, 208 W. Latimer Ave., Campbell, CA 95008, 408-379-8555. 1960. Poetry, reviews, long-poems. "Pancontinental Premier Poets (Biennial Anthology of Poetry); Sixth, scheduled for the Fall-1980, 200 pgs." avg. press run 500. Pub'd 8 titles 1979; expects 8 titles 1980, 8 titles 1981. 18 titles listed in the *Small Press Record of Books in Print* (9th Edition, 1980). avg. price, paper: $1.75, up to $6.00 (over 100 pp.). Discounts: under 100 pages-$1.25, 3-$3.25, 5-$5.00. over 100 pages-$6.00, 2-$10.00, 5-$20.00. 96pp; 5½X8½; lp.

Reporting time: 30 to 90 days. Payment: open. copyright open (first rights). World Congress of Poets.

The Poet Tree, Inc (see also POET TREE NEWS; QUERCUS), Theresa Vinciguerra.

POET TREE NEWS, The Poet Tree, Inc, Theresa Vinciguerra, Box 25-4502, Sacramento, CA 05825, 456-5344. 1979. Articles, interviews, criticism, reviews, news items. "Some recent contributors have been Harold Leland Johnson and Ann Menebroker. We publish reviews and articles primarily relating to local poets and writers." circ. 200. 12/yr. Pub'd 3 issues 1979; expects 12 issues 1980, 12 issues 1981. sub. price: $12.00; per copy: free; sample: free. Back issues: not available. 4pp; 8½X11; of. Reporting time: 1 month. Payment: copies. Pub's reviews. §Poetry & fiction by authors in Sacramento and outlying areas. Ads: $25.00/$15.00/$0.25 per line.

POETALK QUARTERLY, Owlseye Publications, Elizabeth Harrod, Tom Plante, Ann Emerson, 23650 Stratton Court, Hayward, CA 94541, (415) 537-6858. 1979. Poetry, interviews, criticism, reviews, letters. "Reviews 1-2 pp., 7 x 8½. Poems for supplement: please limit to 1 page 6 x 8½. Recent contributors to supplement: Ray Craig, Noni Howard, Tom Plante. Subscription price for US & Canada $3/yr. Foreign subscriptions $5.00/year. Winter issue: $1.50 single copy. Business address: 1403 Northside, Berkeley CA 94702 USA." circ. 1,000. 4/yr. Pub'd 4 issues 1979; expects 4 issues 1980. sub. price: $3.00; per copy: $1.00; sample: $1.00. Back issues: $1.50 Vol 1 #1 oop. Discounts: 1 copy, none; 5 copies, 30%; 10 copies, 40%. 20pp; 7X8½; †of. Reporting time: immediately to 2 months. Payment: copies. Copyrighted, reverts to author. Pub's reviews: 64 in 1979. §We are interested in small press poetry, university press poetry, some criticism. Ads: $25.00/$15.00. CCLM.

POETIC JUSTICE, Publishing Associates, Bruce Taylor, 432 Heathcliff Drive, Pacifica, CA 94044, (415) 355-3630. 1979. Poetry, art, cartoons. circ. 500. 4/yr. Pub'd 2 issues 1979. sub. price: $5.95; per copy: $1.25; sample: $1.00. Back issues: $1.00. Discounts: 33⅓%. 32pp; 5X8; of. Reporting time: 10 days. Payment: copies. Copyrighted, reverts to author. Ads: $25.00/$15.00/$1.00 plus $0.10.

POETRY, John Frederick Nims, Box 4348, Chicago, IL 60680, (312) 996-7803. 1912. Poetry, reviews, long-poems. "Street address: 601 South Morgan Street, Chicago, IL 60607" circ. 8,000. 12/yr. Pub'd 12 issues 1979; expects 12 issues 1980, 12 issues 1981. sub. price: $18.00; per copy: $1.75 plus 25¢ post; sample: $1.75 plus 25¢ post. Back issues: $2 plus 25¢ post. 64pp; 5X9; of. Reporting time: 6 weeks. Payment: $10-page prose/$1-line verse. Copyrighted, reverts on request from author. Pub's reviews: 70 in 1979. §poetry. Ads: $165/$100. CCLM.

POETRY &c, Poetry & Press, Joann Castagna, PO Box 842, Iowa City, IA 52240. 1976. Poetry, fiction, articles, art, photos, cartoons, interviews, satire, criticism, reviews, letters, news items. "Contributors include: Mary Lane, John Yau, Mercy Bona, Jessie Ellison, Dan Campion, Elizabeth Eddy, Ruth Moon Kempher, etc. Special thanks to DC & JBM. Artwork by Sara Counts and Tim Sarro. We also publish postcards. We will continue to be the least expensive magazine in Chicago.Page size and number of pages per issue will be changing. Last issue was Vol 2 #12. No longer publishing." circ. 300-500. 12/yr. Pub'd 12 issues 1979. sub. price: $5.00; per copy: $1.00; sample: $1.00. Back issues: $10.00 for Volume I; $10.00 for Volume II. Discounts: 60/40 bookstores. 8pp; 11½X17; of. Reporting time: 1 month. Payment: copies/some cash from grants. Copyrighted, does not revert to author. Pub's reviews: 40 in 1979. §Only from Illinois writers/presses. Ads: $15.00/$0.05. CCLM, COSMEP-Midwest.

POETRY AND AUDIENCE, Stuart P Dorrian, The School of English, University of Leeds, Leeds LS2 9JT, United Kingdom. 1954. Poetry, reviews. "A market for serious, well crafted poems of no more than 25 lines." circ. 150. 12/yr. 2 titles listed in the *Small Press Record of Books in Print* (9th Edition, 1980). sub. price: £1.00; per copy: 20p; sample: free. 18pp; size quarto; of/duplication. Reporting time: 1 month.

Poetry & Press (see also AZIMUTH; POETRY &), Joann E. Castagna, Box 842, Iowa City, IA 52240. 1976. Poetry. "Will publish Jerome Sala's new book in 1979. No unsolicited manuscripts." avg. press run 1,000. Expects 1-2 titles 1981. Discounts: 60/40 to bookstores. 60-80pp; 5 1/2X8 1/2; of. No unsolicited material. Payment: To be arranged. Copyrights for author. CCLM, COSMEP.

POETRY AUSTRALIA, South Head Press, Grace Perry, 350 Lyons Rd., Five Dock, N.S.W. 2046, Australia. 1964. Poetry. circ. 1,600. 4/yr. Pub'd 4 issues 1979. sub. price: $10.00 (Aust)-$12.00 O/S; per copy: $2.50; sample: $1.00. Back issues: $3.00. 80pp. Payment: $8-per page. Pub's reviews: 24 in 1979. §poetry & prose.

POETRY BOOK AWARD, Realities, Soos, 1976 Waverly Ave., San Jose, CA 95122, (408) 251-9562.

POETRY CANADA REVIEW, Clifton Whiten, Publisher and Editor, PO Box 1280, Station A, Toronto, Ontario M5W 1G7, Canada, 922-9058. 1979. Poetry, articles, art, photos, cartoons, interviews, satire, criticism, reviews, news items. "*Layout to this point* 1. cover, feture poet phot & what's inside, 2. editiorial page, editorials & letters, etc., 3. in review by Len Gasparini, poems, etc., 4. international page (tentative), 5. poems, Canadian content, 6. & 7. feature poet, interview, impression, bibliography, selected poems, caricature, 8. Canadian poems, 9. schools page (tentative), 10. at the readings by Pat Smith & poems, 11. new voices, 12. pcr profiles" circ. 500. 4/yr. Pub'd 2 issues 1979. sub. price: $5.00 Individuals Canada; $6.00 U.S.; $7.50 overseas. $7.00 Libraries and inst. Canada; $8.00 U.S.; $9.50 overseas; per copy: $1.50; sample: $1.75(includes 3rd class individual postage and handling). Discounts: 20% schools — class sets over 10. 12pp; 11X17½; of. Reporting time: 1-3 weeks. Payment: copies. Copyrighted. Pub's reviews: 15 in 1979. §Poetry. Ads: $390.00/$250.00/$0.40. CPPA.

POETRY COMICS, The Happy Press, Dave Morice, Box 585, Iowa City, IA 52244, (319) 338-0084. 1979. Poetry, letters. "Beginning with issue No. 8, I will include cartoon strip versions of poems submitted by contemporary poets. The poems should be no longer than 14 lines, and they should be previously unpublished." circ. 200. 12/yr. Pub'd 4 issues 1979. sub. price: $5.00, 4 issues; per copy: $1.50; sample: $1.50. Back issues: $1.50. Discounts: 20% on orders of 10 or more copies of any assortment of issues. 22pp; 8½X11; of. Reporting time: 1 month. Payment: 5 copies. Copyrighted, does not revert to author. Ads: No ads.

POETRY EAST, Richard Jones, Kate Daniels, 530 Riverside Drive 4-B, New York, NY 10027, (212) 749-0841. 1980. Poetry, articles, art, photos, interviews, criticism, reviews, letters, collages, concrete art, news items. "Contributors include Tomas Transtromer, Stanely Kunitz, Gloria Fuertes, Philip Levine, Greg Orr, Robert Bly, Louis Simpson, Richard Shelton, Miklos Radnoti, W. H. Auden." circ. 1,000. 3/yr. sub. price: $8.00; per copy: $3.00; sample: $3.00. 108pp; 6X8½; of. Reporting time: 1 month. Payment: copies. Copyrighted, reverts to author. Pub's reviews: 4-5 in 1979. §Poetry, criticism, biography, literature, film, art, photography, etc. Ads: $100.00/$50.00.

POETRY FLASH, Richard Hoover, Publisher; Steve Abbott, Editor; Joyce Jenkins, Editor; Don Babb, Calendar Editor, 345 Fifteenth Street, Oakland, CA 94612, 415-836-1246. 1972. Poetry, articles, art, photos, interviews, criticism, reviews. "POETRY FLASH is the monthly review of Bay Area poetry events. We use calendar items, information interesting or useful to poets (places to publish, prizes, workshops, etc.) and reviews of books and readings. Monthly feature articles" circ. 5,000. 12/yr. Pub'd 12 issues 1979; expects 12 issues 1980. sub. price: $7.00; sample: $1.00. Back issues: $1 plus postage. 8pp; 8½X11; †of. Reporting time: one month. Payment: none. Copyrighted, reverts to author. Pub's reviews: 18-20 in 1979. §poetry/exploratory fiction/incisive thought. Ads: $125.00/$75.00/$10.00 column inch. CCLM, COSMEP, BAPC.

Poetry for the People, PO Box 12406, San Francisco, CA 94112, (415) 526-3254. 1975. Poetry. "We are an open collective-cooperative of poets doing a series of small chapbooks of our own and other poets' works, anthologies, etc. Authors in '79 include Opal Palmer, Jack Hirschman, John Curl, Rudy Breland, Rosemarie Hill. Forthcoming: Royal Kent, Kathy Barisione, Leslie Simon, Pancho Aguila, Randy Johnson. Additional address: PO Box 2307, Berkeley, CA 94702." avg. press run 500. Pub'd 6 titles 1979; expects 5 titles 1980, 5 titles 1981. 7 titles listed in the *Small Press Record of Books in Print* (9th Edition, 1980). avg. price, paper: $0.75. Discounts: 60/40. 20pp; 7X8½; mi, of. Reporting time: 2 months. Payment: author participates in production & costs, gets copies. Copyrights for author.

The Poetry in English Society (see VOICES - ISRAEL)

POETRY IN MOTION, Nobodaddy Press, David Lehman, Stefanie Green, Joel Black, 100 College Hill Rd., Clinton, NY 13323, 315-853-6946. 1976. Poetry, long-poems. "We may decide to expand operations and consider works of criticism and fine arts. We are committed to the development of new and unusual forms of publication, i.e. Broadsheets, poem post-cards, poem greeting cards, etc." circ. 500. 2/yr. sub. price: $4.00; per copy: $2.00; sample: $2.00. Discounts: The usual 40 percent off for bookstores, etc. 30-45pp; 8½X11; †of/lp. Reporting time: It varies. Copyrighted, reverts to author. §Poetry and the arts. CCLM.

Poetry in Public Places, Verna Gillis, Editor, 799 Greenwich St., New York, NY 10014, 212-242-3374. 1975. Poetry. "We place one poem per month in 2,020 buses throughout the state of New York. Poems should be no longer than 12 lines, keeping in mind the public nature of the project. All submissions should include a stamped, self-addressed envelope. Recent contributors include William Bronk, Robery Bly, George Oppen, John Taggart, Judith Johnson Sherwin." avg. press run 2,500. Pub'd 12 titles 1979; expects 12 titles 1980, 12 titles 1981. 48 titles listed in the *Small Press Record of Books in Print* (9th Edition, 1980). avg. price, other: $5.00 per card. Discounts: A full set of 12 poem cards is available to indivuduals at $50.00 per set, or to institutions and non profit organizations at a 40% discount. 1pp; 28X11; of. Reporting time: 6 to 8 months. Payment: $100.00 for the use of the poem. Copyrights for author.

Poetry Leeds Publications (see also NORTHERN LINE), Dr. M. Burke, 75 Outwood Lane, Leeds, W. Yorks LS18 4HU, United Kingdom, 0532-588995. 1978. Poetry, fiction, articles, art, photos, cartoons, news items. "Poetry Leeds Publications handles booklets by individual adult poets, 3 in series so far. PLP also brings out information broadsheets - aimed towards young people, explaining how to submit work, publication outlets and giving news about festivals, readings, and competitions. Any info gratefully received." Pub'd 3 titles 1979; expects 3 titles 1980. avg. price, other: 50p/$2.00 post& handling. Discounts: negotiable. mi, of. Reporting time: 6 months. Payment: copies. Copyrights for author. ALP.

THE POETRY MISCELLANY, Richard Jackson, Michael Panori, English Dept. Univ of Tennessee, Chattanooga, TN 37402, 615-755-4213; 624-7279. 1971. Poetry, interviews, criticism, reviews, long-poems. "David Wagoner, Denise Levertov, Mark Strand, Richard Wilbur, Donald Justice, Dan Masterson, Dara Wier, Carol Muske, Maxine Kumin,Marge Piercy, Lyn Lifshin, A.R. Ammons, Stanley Kunitz, Charles Simic, John Hollander, Linda Pastan, William Stafford, John Haines, Carol Oles, Constance Urdang, Carol Frost, Samuel Hazo, William Meredith, Laurence Raab, Cynthia Mac-Donald, Robert Pack, John Peck, Anthony Hecht, Barbara Howes, Donald Finkel, Michael Harper, Philip Booth, David Ignatow, Donald Hall, Steve Orlen, Heather McHugh, Stuart Dybeck, Sharon Olds, James Applewhite, Stanley Plumly. Review essays 3,000 words. We use translations too. Send translations with originals to Miller Williams, English Department, 333 Communications Center, University of Arkansas, Fayetteville, AK 72701" circ. 650. 1/yr. Pub'd 1 issue 1979; expects 1 issue 1980. sub. price: $3.00; per copy: $3.00; sample: $3.00. Back issues: Same price as current issues. Discounts: 30% for orders of ten or more to groups and individuals. 170pp; 6X9; of. Reporting time: 6-8 weeks. Payment: copies. Copyrighted, copyright reverts to author upon request, as for re-publication. Pub's reviews: 3 in 1979. §poetry, poetics. Ads: $50half page. CCLM.

POETRY NATION REVIEW, Carcanet Press, Donald Davie, C.H. Sisson, Michael Schmidt, 330 Corn Exchange, Manchester M4 3BG, United Kingdom. 1973. Articles, poetry, fiction, art, reviews, interviews, criticism, letters, long-poems. circ. 2,500. 6/yr. Pub'd 6 issues 1979; expects 6 issues 1980. sub. price: £6.90 ($18.00); per copy: £2.00; sample: £2.00. Back issues: I-VI £20.00 (Casebound 750pp). 65pp; size A4; of. Copyrighted, reverts to author. Pub's reviews: 85 in 1979. §Poetry and related.

POETRY NEWSLETTER, Richard O'Connell, Dept. of English, Temple University, Philadelphia, PA 19122. 1971. Poetry, interviews, long-poems, plays. "Poetry newsletter is now a quarterly. Recent contributors: Charles Angoff, Geoffrey Cook, Josephine Jacobsen, Anthony L. Johnson, D. S. Long, William Oxley, Edward Pitcairn, Kenneth Rexroth. The poetry is the news." circ. 500-1M. 4/yr. sub. price: $3.00; per copy: $1.00; sample: $1.00. Back issues: #1-#36 back issues available at $.50 ea. 30-40pp; 8½X10; of. Reporting time: 3-4 months. Payment: copies. Pub's reviews. §Poetry. no ads. CCLM.

POETRY NIPPON, The Poetry Nippon Press, Atsuo Nakagawa, 11-2, 5-chome, Nagaike-cho, Showa-ku, Nagoya 466, Japan. 1967. Poetry, articles, interviews, criticism, reviews, letters, news items, photos. "Translations of Japanese poems, poems on topical themes or Japan, Tanka, Haiku, one-line poems are solicited from non-members. Guest poems are also printed." circ. 500. 4/yr. Expects 4 issues 1980. sub. price: 23 Int'l Reply Coupons; per copy: 9 IRC's; sample: 3 IRC's. Back issues: 9 IRC's. Discounts: 30% for bulk order. 40pp; size A5; of. Reporting time: 1 year. Payment: Depends on ms. Copyrighted, reverts to author. Pub's reviews: 7 in 1979. §poetry books and magazines. Ads: $50/$30.

The Poetry Nippon Press (see also POETRY NIPPON), Atsuo Nakagawa, 11-2, 5-Chome, Nagaike-cho, Showa-ku, Nagoya 466, Japan, 052-833-5724. 1967. Poetry, articles, art, photos, interviews, criticism, reviews, letters, collages, concrete art, news items. "Translations of Japanese poems, poems on topical themes or Japan, Tanka, Haiku, one-line poems are solicited" Pub'd 25 titles 1979; expects 25 titles 1980. 1 title listed in the *Small Press Record of Books in Print* (9th Edition, 1980). avg. price, paper: $3.00 (single number), $6.00 (double number). Discounts: 30% for bulk order. 1-3pp; size A5; of. Reporting time: 1 year. Payment: Depends on ms. Copyrights for author.

POETRY NORTHWEST, David Wagoner, 4045 Brooklyn NE, Ja-15, Univ. Of Washington, Seattle, WA 98105. 1961. Poetry. circ. 1,300. 4/yr. Pub'd 4 issues 1979. sub. price: $5.00; per copy: $1.50; sample: $1.50. 48pp; 8½X5½; of. Reporting time: 1 month or less. Payment: copies and a years subscription. Copyrighted, does not revert to author. CCLM.

POETRY NOTTINGHAM, Poetry Nottingham Society Publications, Derek Greenwood, Chapel

House, Belper Lane End, Belper, Derbyshire OE5 2DL, United Kingdom. 1941. Articles, poetry, reviews, criticism, letters, concrete art, news items, art. "Poems in any form. Contributions only accepted from subscribers to the magazine or members of Nottingham Poetry Society. Overseas subscribers welcome. Rates on application." circ. 150. 4/yr. Pub'd 4 issues 1979; expects 4 issues 1980, 4 issues 1981. sub. price: £3.00; Membership of Society (inc. mag) £4.00; Husband/Wife joint membership £5.00; Student £2.00; per copy: 60p ea + p&p; sample: free (back number). Back issues: half price. Discounts: 15% to bookshops. 24pp; 8¼X6; of. Reporting time: 2-4 weeks. No payment. remains with authors. Pub's reviews. §Mainly members & subscribers own work. Ads: £5 per quarters (ie per issue).

Poetry Nottingham Society Publications (see also POETRY NOTTINGHAM), Derek Greenwood, Senior Editor, Chapel House, Belperlane End, Derbyshire DE5 2DL, United Kingdom. 1977. Poetry. "Members' or suhscribers' own poetry including graphics." avg. press run 100. Pub'd 1 title 1979; expects 2 titles 1980, 2 titles 1981. avg. price, paper: 60p. 16pp; 8¼X6; of/lp. Reporting time: 2-3 months.

POETRY NOW, E.V. Griffith, 3118 K Street, Eureka, CA 95501. 1973. Poetry. "*Poetey Now* appears in tabloid newspaper format and seeks to publish the best work available to us in all moulds. One 'poet profile' per issue, based on interview with a major contemporary poet. Photos of poets included throughout issue. Book 'reviews' are via sample—a few poems from the book being 'reviewed:-quoted in full without critical comment, just publisher's name, address and price of book. Special features include a 3-page spread in each issue of reprints from other little magazines. Contributors include William Stafford, John Haines, David Ignatow, Michael McClure, Russell Edson, Peter Viereck, Edward Field, Richard Eberhart, Ann Stanford, Mona Van Duyn, Karl Shapiro, Vassar Miller, Maxine Kumin, Edwin Honig, Gary Soto. Commencing in 1978, *Poetry Now* publishes an annual 'Newcomer's' issue, devoted to poets who have not appeared widely in magazines and who have not yet issued a book with a major publisher. One issue each year is devoted to 20th Century poetry in translation." circ. 2,500 plus. 6/yr. Pub'd 6 issues 1979; expects 6 issues 1980, 6 issues 1981. sub. price: $7.50; per copy: $1.50; sample: $1.50. Back issues: Issues 1 through 14 and 21 onward available at $1.50 each while stock lasts; 200-page Bicentennial issue (Nos. 15-18), $5.00. Discounts: classroom adoption: 85 cents per copy, with minimum order of 10 copies sent to single address. 48pp; 11½X15; of. Reporting time: 2 days to 2 wks. Payment: copies only, with three annual cash awards ($250-$100-$50). copyrighted; rights revert upon formal assignment. Pub's reviews: 144 in 1979. §poetry only. Ads: $150/$85/none. CCLM, COSMEP.

THE POETRY PROJECT NEWSLETTER, Vicki Hudspith, St. Mark's Church, The Poetry Project, 2nd Ave & 10th Street, New York, NY 10003, 674-0910. 1967. Poetry, interviews, reviews, letters, news items. "Recent contributors: Allen Ginsberg, Anne Waldman, Tony Towle, Jane DeLynn, Phillip Lopate, Ted Greenwald, Anselm Hollo, John Yau, Ron Padgett, Maureen Owen, Charles Bernstein, Paul Violi, Alan Davies, Ted Berrigan, Eileen Myles, Rose Lesniak, Vicki Hudspith, Alex Katz, Robert Bly. Frequency, monthly for 10 issues Oct - July." circ. 1,500. 10/yr. Pub'd 10 issues 1979; expects 10 issues 1980, 10 issues 1981. sub. price: $2.00 indiv., $5.00 libraries; sample: free. Back issues: not available except special circumstances. 4pp; 8X10; †mi. Copyrighted. Pub's reviews: 35-40 in 1979. §Poetry. CCLM, NYSSCA, NEA.

POETRY QUARTERLY (previously CURLEW), The Curlew Press, P.J. Precious, Harecott, Kettlesing, Harrogate, Yorkshire, United Kingdom, Harrogate 770686. 1975. Poetry, fiction, articles, art, photos, cartoons, interviews, satire, criticism, reviews, letters, parts-of-novels, long-poems, collages, plays, concrete art, news items. "To avoid contravening UK law, monies payable are deemed to be voluntary contributions." circ. variable. 4/yr. Pub'd 4 issues 1979; expects 4 issues 1980. sub. price: $12.00/£5.00 sub includes additional publications; per copy: $1.50/50P when available; sample: Free when available. Back issues: Some available on request. pp varies. up to 100; 5X8 and 8X14; of. Reporting time: By return of post when possible. Payment: none. Copyrighted, reverts to author. Pub's reviews: 18 in 1979. §Poetry, literature. Ads: £10.00/£5.00/10 words £1.00; 20 words £2.00, etc.(please count 1 dollar 50 cents per pound to cover bank charges in UK).

POETRY REVIEW, Roger Garfitt, 21 Earls Court Square, London SW5, United Kingdom, 01-373-7861. 1912. Poetry, long-poems, reviews, concrete art. circ. 2,900. 4/yr. Pub'd 4 issues 1979; expects 4 issues 1980. 3 titles listed in the *Small Press Record of Books in Print* (9th Edition, 1980). sub. price: $12.00 w-membership; per copy: $3.00. Back issues: Same as cover price. Discounts: -1/3 to trade. 60pp; size A5; of. Reporting time: 2 mos. Payment: £15 per poet for first poem, £20 for 2 poems. Copyrighted, reverts to author. Pub's reviews: 20 in 1979. §Poetry, criticism, etc. Ads: £40/£20/£10.

The Poetry Society of Australia (see also NEW POETRY; Prism Books), Robert Adamson, Editor;

Debra Adamson, Associate Editor, Box N110, Grosvenor Street P.O., Sydney, N.S.W. 2000, Australia. 1971. Poetry. avg. press run 500-1,000. Pub'd 4 titles 1979. avg. price, paper: $5.00. Discounts: 40% trade. 80pp; size varies; of. Reporting time: 2 months maximum. Payment: Contract, 20% of net. Copyrights for author. AIIPA.

POETRY TORONTO NEWSLETTER, Darina Smerek McFadyen, Vaughn Thurman, Sean O'Huigin, PO Box 181, Station P, Toronto, Ontario M5S 2S7, Canada. 1975. Poetry, articles, reviews. "Interested in reviews and especially previews of any live poetry events." circ. 600. 12/yr. Pub'd 12 issues 1979; expects 12 issues 1980, 12 issues 1981. sub. price: $5.00; $6.00 Institutions & outside Canada; per copy: $.50; sample: free. 24pp; 8½X5½; of. Reporting time: 4 weeks. Payment: copies only. COSMEP.

POETRY VIEW, Post-Crescent, Dorothy Dalton, 1125 Valley Rd., Menasha, WI 54952. 1970. Poetry. "Serious poetry to 24 lines-light verse 4-8 lines. Free verse preferred, fresh use of language-no religious, no overly sentimental. Enclose SASE with submissions, and queries. A tearsheet is sent to out-of-town contributors. Seasonal poems should arrive 2-3 months in advance." circ. 60M. 52/yr. Pub'd 52 issues 1979; expects 52 issues 1980. size -1/2p tabloid. Reporting time: 2-3 mos. Payment: $5 poem, month following publication. Not copyrighted.

POETRY WALES, Christopher Davies Publishers Ltd., J.P. Ward, 52 Mansel Street, Swansea SA1 5EL, United Kingdom, (0792) 41933. 1965. Articles, poetry, reviews, criticism, letters, long-poems. "Articles of not less than 2,000 words. All types of poetry considered. Originally biased towards Welsh, Anglo-Welsh poetry, or poetry by persons living in Wales. Now wider approach encompasing all British and US poets, writers and translations of foreign poets and critiques of same." circ. 1,000. 4/yr. Pub'd 4 issues 1979; expects 4 issues 1980, 4 issues 1981. sub. price: £4.40; per copy: £1.00; sample: 75p. Back issues: 50p. Discounts: trade 33⅓. 130pp; 5½X8½; of. Reporting time: 3-4 wks. Payment: by arrangement. Copyrighted, reverts to author. Pub's reviews: 40 in 1979. §Poetry, criticism, iterary history. Ads: £25/£15/£8 1/4.

Poets & Writers, Inc. (see also CODA: Poets & Writers Newsletter), 201 West 54th Street, New York, NY 10019, 212-757-1766. 1972. Articles, photos, news items. "Poets & Writers publishes a directory of fiction writers and poets who publish in the US and pamphlets of practical information for writers on subjects such as literary agents, reading series sponsors, copyright, literary bookstores." avg. press run 5,000-15,000. Pub'd 1 title 1979; expects 3 titles 1980, 3 titles 1981. 7 titles listed in the *Small Press Record of Books in Print* (9th Edition, 1980). avg. price, cloth: $18.00; paper: $10.00; other: $2.50 - $5.00 (25% for listed writers). Discounts: For directories: 2-49, 40%; 50 or more, 46%; to listd writers, 25%. directories, 256pp; pamphlets, 36pp; 8½X11; of. COSMEP, CCLM, NYSSPA.

Poets & Writers of New Jersey, Box 852, Upper Montclair, NJ 07043. "P&WNJ is a service organization for writers interested in NJ, and for organizations interested in the services of writers. Established in 1974, P&WNJ publishes an occasional newsletter for members (sample free for s.a.se.). An anthology of members' writing, *Advance Token To Boardwalk* ($3.95 plus 30¢ mailing costs) was published in 1977. Writers with an interest in NJ, and persons interested in programs of/about NJ writing or workshops are invited to make inquiry at the address above.".

POETS' LEAGUE of GREATER CLEVELAND NEWSLETTER, League Books, Kate Kilbane, Editor, PO Box 6055, Cleveland, OH 44101. 1975. Poetry, articles, reviews. "The newsletter runs reviews of local readings and poetry books, articles on poetry in general, articles on the Cleveland poetry scene, a calendar of poetry events, a poem or two per issue, and whatever else seems germane. Query. League Books is a distributor currently of four poetry titles: *Emergency Exit,* Cyril A. Dostal; title, Christopher Franke; *Big Mama,* Linda Monacelli*Editor, Barbara Angell, Mary Ann Cronin, Meredith Holmes, Sally Pirtle, Marguerite Beck Rex; & *Alone, But Not Lonely,* Elaine Ede Hornsby. *Big Mama* and *Alone, But Not Lonely* are out-of-print." circ. 800+. 6/yr. Pub'd 6 issues 1979; expects 6 issues 1980, 6 issues 1981. sub. price: $5.00 per six issues; sample: $0.25. 8-10pp; 8½X11; xerox. Payment: copies. Copyrighted, reverts to author. Pub's reviews. COSMEP.

POETS ON:, Ruth Daigon, Box 255, Chaplin, CT 06235, 203-455-9671. 1976. Poetry. "*Poets On:* explores basic human concerns through crafted poetry our first issue dealt with *Turning Points.* Each subsequent issue will have a basic theme-*Roots, Loving* etc. some of our contributors are William Stafford, Marge Piercy, John Tagliabue, Richard Eberhart, Philip Booth etc." circ. 400. 2/yr. Pub'd 2 issues 1979; expects 2 issues 1980. sub. price: $5.00; per copy: $2.50. Back issues: $2.50. 48pp; 5½X8½; lp. Reporting time: up to a month. Payment: 2 copies. Copyrighted, reverts to author. COSMEP.

POINT OF CONTACT/PUNTO DE CONTACTO, Pedro Cuperman, 110 Bleecker St. 16B, New York City, NY 10012, 212-260-6346. 1975. Poetry, art, photos, interviews, criticism, reviews. "Recent contributors: S.W. Snodgrass, Jean Franco, Eldridge Cleaver, Pedro Cuperman, Michel Beaujour, David Wevill, Christopher Middleton, Carlos Blanco Aguinaga, Raymond Panikkar, Noe Jitrik, Saul Yurkievich." circ. 1,500. Quarterly. Pub'd 4 issues 1979. sub. price: Institutional $22.00; Individual $12.00; per copy: $3.50; sample: $3.50. Back issues: $3.50. 100pp; 8X10; of. Payment: None. Copyrighted, does not revert to author. Pub's reviews. §Literature, criticism, political theory. Ads: $200.-00/$110.00.

Point Riders Press, Arn Henderson, Frank Parman, PO Box 2731, Norman, OK 73070. 1974. Poetry. "Publisher of books of poetry. 8 books in print (publish approx. 3/yr.)" avg. press run 1,000. Pub'd 3 titles 1979. 9 titles listed in the *Small Press Record of Books in Print* (9th Edition, 1980). avg. price, paper: $3.95. Discounts: Single copy 15%, 2 to 4 copies 25%, 5 or more 40%. 86pp; 6X8; of. Reporting time: 3-6 months, unsolicited mss discouraged thru 1981. Payment: in copies. Copyrights for author.

Poltroon Press, Alastair Johnston, Frances Butler, PO Box 5476, Berkeley, CA 94705. 1975. Poetry, fiction, art, photos, interviews, satire, criticism, letters, parts-of-novels, long-poems, collages, concrete art. "Tom Clark, Thomas Love Peacock, Tom Raworth. No bias towards first names of Tom or Tomassina but trend is developing. Now publishing Darrell Grey, Philip Whalen, H.D.L. Vervliet" avg. press run 150. Pub'd 6 titles 1979; expects 6 titles 1980, 6 titles 1981. 16 titles listed in the *Small Press Record of Books in Print* (9th Edition, 1980). avg. price, cloth: $15.00; paper: $4.00. Discounts: 40 percent on 5 or more, etc. 32pp; 8X10; †of/lp. Immediately return all unsolicited mss. Payment varies (often 25 percent of net sales). Copyrights for author.

Poly Tone Press, Nicholas Fotine, 16027 Sunburst Street, Sepulveda, CA 91343, 213-892-0044.

Polygonal Publishing House, Michael Weinstein, 80 Passaic Ave, Passaic, NJ 07055. 1976. avg. press run 2,000. Expects 2 titles 1980, 3 titles 1981. 2 titles listed in the *Small Press Record of Books in Print* (9th Edition, 1980). Discounts: 20% trade & bulk. of. Payment: 20%. COSMEP.

The Pomegranate Press, Ifeanyi Menkiti, PO Box 181, N. Cambridge, MA 02140. 1972. Poetry, fiction. "Poetry and experimental fiction-Joyce Carol Oates, James Merrill, Charles Bukowski, Adrienne Rich; a new short story by Oates w/ 10 silkscreened illus." avg. press run 200-900. Pub'd 1 title 1979; expects 3 titles 1980, 3 titles 1981. avg. price, cloth: $30.00-$50.00; paper: $8.00-$15.00. Discounts: 40% on orders of 5. 40pp; 6½X9; 10X12; †lp. Reporting time: 2 months. Payment: preferably 10 copies of the work, books 10% after expenses. Copyrights for author. COSMEP.

PONTCHARTRAIN REVIEW, Long Measure Press, Ken Fontenot, Editor, PO Box 1065, Chalmette, LA 70044, 504-242-0947. 1977. Poetry, fiction, interviews, reviews. "We are primarily interested in poetry that shows talent, though we occasionally accept a prose piece of fiction if it is not much longer than parable-size. Recent contributors are local poets but in the future we hope to have poets with reputations such as: Richard Hugo, David Ray, Louise Gluck, and Philip Levine. We usually do our own interviews and reviews but manuscripts are welcome with SASE." circ. 300. 2/yr. Pub'd 2 issues 1979; expects 2 issues 1980, 2 issues 1981. price per copy: $2.00; sample: $2.00. Back issues: $2.00. Discounts: We are willing to trade with other journals. 40pp; 6X9; †of. Reporting time: 3 weeks to 2 months. Payment: copies only. Copyrighted, reverts to author. Pub's reviews: 4 in 1979. §We are interested in reviewing books of poetry. Ads: $50.00/$25.00.

Poor Richards Press, P O Box 189, Forest Lake, MN 55025. 1 title listed in the *Small Press Record of Books in Print* (9th Edition, 1980).

Poor Souls Press/Scaramouche Books, Paul F. Fericano, Roger W. Langton, 1050 Magnolia No. 2, Millbrae, CA 94030. 1974. Poetry, satire. "Poor Souls Press used to be known as Scarecrow Books. But Scarecrow *Press* in New J threatened litigation if we did not change our name. Consquently, Paul Fericano has changed his name to Hugh Beaumont." avg. press run 500. Expects 3 titles 1980. 26 titles listed in the *Small Press Record of Books in Print* (9th Edition, 1980). avg. price, paper: $2.00. Discounts: usual. 36pp; 5½X8½; †of. Reporting time: Not accepting any new manuscripts at this time, until Moscow withdraws from the Soviet Union. §Payment: Lots of political favors. Copyrights for author.

PORCH, Porch Publications, James V. Cervantes, Editor; Greg Simon, Assoc. Editor; Steve Jaech, Assoc. Editor, c/o James V Cervantes, Dept of English, Arizona State University, Tempe, AZ 85281, 206-325-5614. 1977. Poetry, art, interviews, reviews, letters, long-poems. "Send only your best work, and at least 5 poems per submission, length irrelevant; reviews submitted must be substantial, at least typed, double-spaced pages, do not underestimate your reader; chapbook manuscripts have best chance with those published in the mag. Some poets published, so far: Thomas Brush, Michael Burkard, Norman Dubie, Tess Gallagher, Laura Jensen, Janine Pommy-Vega, Roger Weingarten,

W.S. DiPiero, Barry Goldensohn, Lorrie Goldensohn, William Keens, Pamela Stewart, Tom Absher, Clayton Eshleman, Dave Smith, George Keithley, Katherine Kane, Frank Graziano, James Bertolino, Stuart Friebert." circ. 500. 3/yr. Pub'd 3 issues 1979. sub. price: $5.00; per copy: $2.00; sample: $1.50. Back issues: Please inquire; Vol. 1, No. 1, No. 2 & No. 3 are out of print. Discounts: Individual rate applies to libraries & organizations; 40% discount on 5 or more to others. 60-100pp; 5½X8½; of. Reporting time: 1-3 weeks on submissions to mag; booked until 1980 on chapbook mss. Payment: 2 copies at present; hope to pay cash (however little) in the future. Copyrighted, reverts on request. Pub's reviews: 4 in 1979. §Poetry, fiction. Ads: $50.00/$25.00/exchange. CCLM.

Porch Publications (see also PORCH), James V Cervantes, Editor; Greg Simon, NW Editor & Reviews; Stephen Jaech, Contributing Editor, c/o James V Cervantes, Dept of English, Arizona State University, Tempe, AZ 85281. 1977. Poetry, interviews, criticism, reviews, long-poems. "Booked with chapbook mss until 1980; material for the Inland Boat pamphlet series selected by annual guest-editor(s): 1st yr., Dubie & Stewart; 2nd yr., Zimmer & Lindberg." avg. press run 300. Pub'd 1 title 1979; expects 3 titles 1980, 4 titles 1981. 3 titles listed in the *Small Press Record of Books in Print* (9th Edition, 1980). avg. price, paper: $3.00 chapbooks; $1.00 pamphlets. Discounts: 40%, 5 or more copies; 50% to contributors; 50% on 100 or more. 30pp; 5½X8½, 6X9; of. Reporting time: 1 month. Payment: Percentage of run/arranged. Copyrights for author. CCLM.

The Porcupine's Quill, Inc., Tim Inkster, Elke Inkster, 68 Main Street, Erin, Ontario N0B 1T0, Canada, (519) 833-9158. 1975. Poetry, fiction, art, criticism. avg. press run 500. Pub'd 19 titles 1979; expects 5 titles 1980. avg. price, cloth: $10.95; paper: $5.95; other: limited editions $40.00. Discounts: 1-5, 30%; 5 & over, 40%. 80pp; 6X9; †of. Payment: per contract. LPG ACP LCP.

Porphyrion Press, Coral Crosman, 4053 Middle Grove Road, Middle Grove, NY 12850, 518-587-9809. 1974. Poetry, fiction, art, photos. avg. press run LTD. 100-300, so far. Pub'd 1 title 1979. 1 title listed in the *Small Press Record of Books in Print* (9th Edition, 1980). avg. price, paper: $3.50. Discounts: standard 40 percent etc. 58pp; 5½X8½; of. not currently considering material. Copyrights for author. COSMEP.

Port City Press (see REVIEW)

PORTAGE, Dave Engel, Route 1, Box 128, Rudolph, WI 54475. 1975. Poetry, fiction, articles, art, photos, reviews. "Anything connected in some way with central Wisconsin or by a central Wisconsin writer. Last issue included Bertolino, Oldknow, Ginsberg, McKeown, Dreyfus." circ. 350. 1/yr. Pub'd 1 issue 1979; expects 1 issue 1980, 1 issue 1981. sub. price: $2.50; per copy: $2.50; sample: $2.50. Back issues: $1.50. Discounts: 20%. 80pp; 5½X8½; of. Reporting time: 2 weeks. Payment: one copy. Copyrighted, reverts to author. Pub's reviews: §Will review books about rural or small town Wisconsin (not Milwaukee or Madison).

Porter Sargent Publishers, Inc., 11 Beacon St., Boston, MA 02108, (617) 523-1670. 1914. "Titles include: *The Handbook of Private Schools, The Directory for Exceptional Children, The Politics of Nonviolent Action* by Gene Sharp, *Ganhi as a Political Strategist* by Gene Sharp, *Guide to Summer Lamps and Summer Schools* by Gene Sharp." Pub'd 4 titles 1979; expects 4 titles 1980, 5 titles 1981. avg. price, cloth: $25.00; paper: $8.00. 1,400pp; of. Reporting time: 3 months. Copyrights for author.

Portola Institute (see BRIARPATCH REVIEW: A Journal of Right Livelihood and Simple Living)

Post-Crescent (see POETRY VIEW)

POSTCARD ART/POSTCARD FICTION, Rosler, Martha, Martha Rosler, 2920 23rd Street, San Francisco, CA 94110. 1974. Fiction, art, photos. "I do all the writing myself. I chose mail as a means of dissemination because of its directness and because i wanted to raise questions about 'personal' and 'first-personal' communications, fiction, and autobiography. All my work is meant to relate the private, often female, sphere to the public, often male, sphere. Focuses of work have included food production, consumption, art careerism, and violence." circ. 600. 1-2/yr. Pub'd 1 issue 1979. sub. price: $1.75; per copy: $1.75; sample: $1.75. 12pp; size postcard; †mi/of. §arts, film/video, photography.

Potomac Asia Communications (see THE ASIA MAIL)

POTPOURRI FROM HERBAL ACRES, Pine Row Publications, Phyllis V. Shaudys, Box 428, Washington Crossing, PA 18977, (215) 493-4259. 1979. Articles, art, photos, interviews, reviews, letters, news items. "New in September 1979, this 'first-of-its-kind' publication is 'of the reader, by the reader, and for the reader'! Editor and subscribers share herbal tips, recipes, remedies, and experiences....along with seasonal and regional herb culture and usages. Letters and free ads ('Herb

Blurbs') are encouraged from the subscribers, who are herbal hobbyists or present or potential herb-business owners. I plan to recommend herbal publications in future issues and therefore welcome samples or copies for possible review." circ. 300. 4/yr. Pub'd 4 issues 1979; expects 4 issues 1980, 4 issues 1981. sub. price: $6.00; sample: $1.50. Back issues: complete 79/80 series (4 issues) for $5.00. Discounts: 20% per 10 subscriptions. 10pp; 8½X11; of. Reporting time: 4-6 weeks. Payment: free advertisement now; possibly free subscriptions later. Copyrighted. Pub's reviews. §Herbs, gardening, home businesses, cook-books. COSMEP.

Potto Publications, Jenifer Palmer-Lacy, 5235 Lymbar, Houston, TX 77096, (713) 569-1153. 1979. Poetry, fiction, art, long-poems. "200 Beall #113, Nacogdoches, TX 75961." avg. press run 300. Pub'd 2 titles 1979; expects 1 title 1980, 1 title 1981. 2 titles listed in the *Small Press Record of Books in Print* (9th Edition, 1980). avg. price, paper: $2.50. 20pp; 5½X8; of. Reporting time: 3 months. Payment: negotiable. Copyrights for author.

POW (Poetry Organization for Women), Sharon Lee, PO Box 2414, Dublin, CA 94566. 1977. News items. "Basically, *POW* is a network for womenpoets. I established this in 1977 because of the tremendous response I had to Women Talking/Women Listening...It was a way for all of us to keep in touch, share news, problems, find out technical/legal, meet other womenpoets for carpools, social activities and provide marketing information and opportunities for women to grow in their writing.. Now we have 250 subscribers across the country... We publish 'Book Recommends' books read by members which they 'chat' an informal recommendation. No pretense at review - only positive & *no critial* remarks." circ. 250. 7-8/yr. Pub'd 8 issues 1979; expects 8 issues 1980, 8 issues 1981. sub. price: $6.00; sample: SASE with $0.28 postage. 6-8pp; 8½X14. Payment: the joy of being a womanpoet among friends.

Powerlifting USA (see also POWERLIFTING USA), Mike Lambert, Box 467, Camerillo, CA 93010, (805) 482-2378. 1977. "This press will publish books and booklets pertaining to the sport fo powerlifting.. and strength training.. as well as books/booklets pertaining to camera repair/camera collections..particularly regarding antique cameras." avg. press run 3,000. Pub'd 2 titles 1979. avg. price, cloth: $13.95; paper: $8.95. 200pp; 8½X11; of. Payment: negotiable. COSMEP.

POWERLIFTING USA, Powerlifting USA, Mike Lambert, Box 467, Camarillo, CA 93010, (805) 482-2378. 1977. Articles, photos, interviews, news items. "Articles of 1,000 words or less are appropriate, on the sport of *Powerlifting.*" circ. 2,900. 12/yr. Pub'd 7 issues 1979; expects 12 issues 1980, 12 issues 1981. sub. price: $15.00; per copy: $1.50; sample: free. Back issues: all back issues are $2.00 each. Discounts: wholesale dealer rate is $0.90 per copy. 44pp; 8½X11; of. Payment: normally, $25.00 for an accepted article. Pub's reviews: 2 in 1979. §Strictly those related to the sport of powerlifting or strength training. Ads: $100.00/$50.00. COSMEP.

PRACTICAL PARENTING, Vicki Lansky, Kathryn Ring, 16648 Meadowbrook Lane, Wayzata, MN 55391, 612-933-5008. 1979. "Newsletter by parents & for parents to share tips, philosophies & good ideas." circ. 3,000-5,000. 6/yr. Pub'd 6 issues 1979. sub. price: $5.00, $6.00 Canada; sample: $1.00. Back issues: $1.50. Discounts: 10%. 12pp; 8½X11; of. Reporting time: 4 weeks. Payment: not more than $20.00. Copyrighted. Pub's reviews. Ads: not at this time.

Practices of the Wind (see also PRACTICES OF THE WIND), Nicolaus Waskowsky, c/o David M. Marovich, Box 214, Kalamazoo, MI 49005, (616) 343-0237. 1979. Poetry, long-poems. avg. press run 500. Pub'd 1 title 1979. 1 title listed in the *Small Press Record of Books in Print* (9th Edition, 1980). avg. price, paper: $3.00. Discounts: 2-5 copies, 20%; 6-10 copies, 40%; library 25%. 40pp; 5½X8½; of. Reporting time: 1 month. Payment: negotiable. Copyrights for author.

PRACTICES OF THE WIND, Practices of the Wind, Nicolaus Waskowsky, David M. Marovich, PO Box 214, Kalamazoo, MI 49005, (616) 343-0237. 1980. Poetry, long-poems. "ISSN #0196-822X. Please send inquiry with SASE before submitting manuscript." circ. 600. 1/yr. price per copy: $4.00; sample: $4.00. Discounts: 25% library. 64pp; 5½X8½; of. Reporting time: 1 month. Payment: 2 copies/negotiable. Copyrighted, reverts to author.

Prairie Poet Press (see AMERICAN POET)

Prairie Publishing Company, Ralph E. Watkins, Box 24 Station C, Winnipeg R3M 3S7, Canada, (204) 885-6496. 1969. "We are in the market for book length material dealing with the growth, discovery, and development of Western Canada. Historical material dealing with Manitoba." avg. press run 2,000 copies. Pub'd 4 titles 1979. 6 titles listed in the *Small Press Record of Books in Print* (9th Edition, 1980). avg. price, paper: $5.00. Discounts: 40 percent bookstores, 20 percent libraries & schools. 165pp; 6X9; of. Reporting time: 6 to 8 weeks. Payment: 10 percent. Copyrights for author. AMBP.

THE PRAIRIE RAMBLER, PO Box 505, Claremont, CA 91711, 714-621-8109. 1978. Satire, criticism. "Principally reprinting of quotations, past and present, which seem appropriate to these times. Would like to publish original material but find little time to write it and have been somewhat unsuccussful in obtaining from other sources. Not that we haven't tried." circ. 200. 12/yr. Pub'd 11 issues 1979; expects 12 issues 1980, 12 issues 1981. sub. price: $5.16; per copy: $0.43; sample: free upon request. Back issues: As long as supply lasts will send back copies for a small donation to cover postage. 8pp; 8½X11. Reporting time: we will acknowledge almost immediately. Ads: inquire.

PRAIRIE SCHOONER, Hugh Luke, 201 Andrews Hall, Univ. of Nebr., Lincoln, NB 68588. 1927. Poetry, fiction, articles, criticism, art, photos, interviews, reviews, parts-of-novels. circ. 1,500. 4/yr. Pub'd 4 issues 1979; expects 4 issues 1980, 4 issues 1981. sub. price: $9.00; per copy: $2.50; sample: $.50. 96pp; 6½X10. Reporting time: 1-2 months. Payment: copies of magazine, tearsheets, and prizes; payments depend on grants rec'd. Copyrighted, Unless author requests copyright transfer. Pub's reviews: 60 in 1979. §literature/general culture. Ads: $50/$35. CCLM, COSMEP.

PRAIRIE SUN, Prairie Sun Publications, Bill Knight, Box 876, Peoria, IL 61652, (309) 673-6624. 1972. Photos, interviews, criticism, reviews, news items. "1109 W Main Street, Peoria, IL 61650" circ. 25,000. 52/yr. Pub'd 47 issues 1979; expects 47 issues 1980, 52 issues 1981. sub. price: $12.00; per copy: free; sample: $0.50. 16pp; 10X15; of. Reporting time: 2 weeks. Payment: varies, $5.00-$35.00. Copyrighted, reverts to author. Pub's reviews: 20-25 in 1979. §Music, alternative energy, general counter-culture, politics. Ads: $225.00/$150.00. APS.

Prairie Sun Publications (see PRAIRIE SUN)

PRAXIS: A Journal of Cultural Criticism, Ronald Reimers, Nico Mayo, Gregg Gorton, PO Box 1280, Santa Monica, CA 90406. 1975. Poetry, articles, art, photos, cartoons, interviews, criticism, reviews. "Publish essays on aesthetics, art and literary criticism, and wide-ranging articles on social radicalism in the arts. *Praxis* No. 4 includes articles on *The Wizard of Oz,* Bertolt Brecht, Mondrian, structuralism, Genet's *The Balcony,* Gramsci, cultural resistance in Chile, political posters, etc. and poetry by Denise Levertov, Walter Lowenfels, Peter Klappert, Don Gordon, Thomas McGrath, Tanure Ojaide, Margaret Randall, H. Mullen, Ernesto Cardenal, Yannis Ritsos, Ricardo Alonso, Mary Lou Reker, etc." circ. 2,500. 2/yr. Pub'd 2 issues 1979; expects 2 issues 1980. sub. price: $7.00; per copy: $3.50; sample: $3.50. Back issues: write. Discounts: 40%. 160pp; 9X5½; of. Reporting time: 6 weeks. Payment: copies. Pub's reviews. Ads: $75.00.

The Pray Curser Press, Erwin R. Bergdoll, c/oErwin R. Bergdoll, Elm Bank, Dutton, VA 23050, 804-693-2823. 1976. "An irregular private press involved in graphic arts and lucid letters to produce prints, illustrated broadsides, brochures, portfolios and booklets, mostly in limited, numbered, signed editions. Emphasis is cheerfully on quality (de spiritus et materia), in a world which is, to use J. R. Oppenheimer's quaintly ironic comment, obviously going to hell. Cognoscenti are invited to express interest, make exchanges, contribute ideas & materials. Material used: woodblock prints, poems, short pieces." avg. press run 107. Pub'd 1 title 1979. 2 titles listed in the *Small Press Record of Books in Print* (9th Edition, 1980). Discounts: Negotiable. 1-2pp; 14X19; †lp/handpress. Reporting time: 1 week or less. Payment: free copies. copyright for author requested. BPHS, APHA, EBUWCK.

Precedent Publishing Inc., Louis Knafla, PO Box 1005, South Holland, IL 60473, 312-828-0420. 1973. "Books usually cloth in history, politics, philosophy, social science, humanities. No fiction for next several years. Editorial: 520 N Michigan Avenue, Chicago, IL 60611." avg. press run 1,500. Pub'd 2 titles 1979; expects 1 title 1980, 1 title 1981. avg. price, cloth: $17.50. Discounts: single copy, 10%; multiple, 20%; bulk consult on specific titles. 300pp; 6X9; of. Reporting time: 1 month usual. Payment: yes. Copyrights for author. COSMEP.

PRECISELY, RK Editions, Richard Kostelanetz, Stephen Scobie, Sheldon Frank, Paul Zelevansky, Dick Higgins, Loris Essary, Karl Young, PO Box 73, Canal Street, New York, NY 10013. "% Scobie, Dept of English, Univ. of Alberta, Edmonton, Alberta, T6G 2E5. Critical essays on experimental literature, expecially of the past twenty years in North America. $2.00 for one number, $10.00 for five numbers, $18.00 for nine numbers, $24.00 for twelve numbers, in the currency of the subscriber, mailed to his countryman. PRECISELY: Three Four Five will be devoted to criticism of VisuaL literature; PRECISELY: ten, eleven, twelve to criticism or Aural Literature; PRECISELY: Seven, eight, nine, to an anthology of author-contributed criticism." 2/yr. Pub'd 1 issue 1979; expects 4 issues 1980, 5 issues 1981. price per copy: $2.00; sample: $2.00. 64pp; 5½X8½; of. Reporting time: 1 month. Payment: Depends upon growth. Copyrighted, reverts to author. Pub's reviews. §Experimental literature.

PRELUDE TO FANTASY, Hans-Peter Werner, Editor, Route 3, Box 193, Richland Center, WI 53581. 1978. Poetry, fiction, articles, art, reviews, letters. "Artists should submit xerox copy rather than original artwork. All submissions must be accompanied by a SASE sufficient for return of submissions." circ. 75. 1/yr. Pub'd 1 issue 1979. price per copy: $1.00. Discounts: Trade only by mutual consent. 28pp; 5½X8½; of. Reporting time: probably 2-4 weeks. Payment: One free copy for all contributions. Copyrighted, reverts to author. Pub's reviews. §Fantasy, science fiction. Ads: negotiable.

PREMONITION TIMES, Roger Rejda, Joe Jochmans, Box 82863, Lincoln, NB 68501, (402) 477-8003. 1979. Articles, art, photos, interviews, satire, criticism, reviews, letters, news items. "The purpose of the *Premonition Times* is to serve as a clearing house for premonitions (dreams, visions, etc.) dealing with future events. Submissions sent to the Premonitions Center (same address as above) are sought nationally and internationally. They are then scientifically and objectively analyzed and cross-referenced with those on file, and reported in the *Times.* Sufficient numbers dealing with the same event constitute a 'Premonitions Alert'. Also presented are studies on prophecies (fulfilled and unfulfilled) of famous seers of today and yesterday; the premonition experience; divination; directed premonitions; and others. The 'Premonitions Center Questionnaire' is included with every other issue. Services include; the 'Premonitions Hotline', lectures, FM radio broadcasts." circ. 1,000. 12/yr. Pub'd 6 issues 1979. sub. price: $18.00; per copy: $1.75; sample: free. Back issues: $2.50; issue #1-#3, $3.75. Discounts: 20% special listing (write for). 30pp; 7X11½; †of. Reporting time: Premonitions research up to date within 2 weeks; prophecy research 13 years' background. Copyrighted, reverts to author. Pub's reviews. §Occult, prophecy, psychic phenomena, dream interpretation, psi events.

Prescott Street Press, Vi Gale, Editor, Publisher, 407 Postal Building, Portland, OR 97204. 1974. "We published one book in 1977. Will do three in 1978. Books are already scheduled. We will publish four books in 1979. They are scheduled, two books in 1980, they are scheduled." avg. press run 500 paper, 100 hardcover. Pub'd 3 titles 1979; expects 2 titles 1980. 8 titles listed in the *Small Press Record of Books in Print* (9th Edition, 1980). avg. price, cloth: $20.00; paper: $5.00; other: Poetry postcards $2.50. Discounts: Salal Series Postcards: $2.50 per pakt. (8 cards) usual trade discounts. Usual trade on books, also. 50-60pp; 6½X8¼; of/lp. Reporting time: 2 weeks. Payment: by arrangement. Copyrights for author. COSMEP, PSA, PEN.

Presidio Press, Adele D. Horwitz, Joan S. Griffin, 31 Pamaron Way, Novato, CA 94947, 415-883-1373. 1974. Fiction, articles, photos, interviews. avg. press run 5,000. Pub'd 23 titles 1979; expects 42 titles 1980, 20 titles 1981. avg. price, cloth: $12.95; paper: $6.95. Discounts: 1-4, 20%; 5-49, 40%; 50-99, 42%; 100+, 43%; special arrangement for large orders. 250pp; 6X9; of. Reporting time: 14 days. Payment: unique to each author. Copyrights for author. AAP, CWRT, NPC, ADPA, CAMP, WBPA, ABA, ALA, CLA, SOHA, AHA, OAH.

Press Gang Publishers, Press Gang Collective, 603 Powell Street, Vancouver, B.C. V6A 1H2, Canada, 253-1224. 1972. Fiction, articles. "We will be publishing a short story anthology in 1980 by and about women. We are interested in publishing analytical and/or historical works by and about women. We are feminists and anti-capitalists." avg. press run 5,000. Pub'd 1 title 1979; expects 1 title 1980, 2 titles 1981. 6 titles listed in the *Small Press Record of Books in Print* (9th Edition, 1980). avg. price, cloth: $10.50; paper: $4.00. Discounts: 40% to bookstores (if over 5 copies), 20% to libraries and schools. 120pp; 5½X8½; †of. Reporting time: 4-8 weeks. Payment: Varies. Copyrights for author. ACP, ABCPC.

Press of Arden Park, Budd Westreich, 861 Los Molinos Way, Sacramento, CA 95825. "Print miniatue books, letterpress & directory of private presses (letterpress)." avg. press run 100. Expects 4 titles 1981. 2 titles listed in the *Small Press Record of Books in Print* (9th Edition, 1980). avg. price, cloth: $15.00. 2X3; †lp.

Press Pacifica, Jane Pultz, Editor; Richard Pultz, Managing Editor, PO Box 1227, Kailua, HI 96734, 808-261-6594. 1975. Poetry, fiction, non-fiction. "We are a trade publisher and also the leading trade book wholesaler and library jobber in Hawaii. We represent many Hawaiian and mainland publishers. This year we will bring out four titles, three Hawaii oriented. However, we are always looking for books of wider scope: feminist material, history, biography, how-to-do books, etc.. We are not interested in books requiring color.Most of our books are black and white with line drawings or half-tones. We will not return material which does not include enough postage. We are truly interested in helping authors publish who have never done so. Always query with sample chapter and outline.We also provide publishing consultation for self-publishers. We have restricted our publihing to authors living in Hawaii for the time being." avg. press run 2,500 to 5,000 (1978). Pub'd 5 titles 1979; expects 6 titles 1980, 7 titles 1981. 11 titles listed in the *Small Press Record of Books in Print* (9th Edition, 1980). avg. price, cloth: $6.95-$9.95; paper: $1.95-$7.95. Discounts: Trade 25-44 percent discount, libraries 15-25 percent, no consignments. pp varies from 144 to 250; 5½X8½; 6X9;

8X10; of. Reporting time: 2 to 3 months. Payment: 10 percent first book. Copyrights for author. COSMEP, WBPA.

Press Porcepic Limited, W.D. Godfrey, Ellen Godfrey, 217-620 View Street, Victoria, B.C. V8W 1J6, Canada. 1971. "Publish fiction, poetry, literary criticisms, other books of social and political relevance by Canadian authors. James Reaney, Dorothy Livesay, Eli Mandel, Joe Rosenblatt. Editorial Offices West 217-620 View Street Victoria, British Columbia V8W 1J6" avg. press run 1,000-5,000. Pub'd 8 titles 1979. 37 titles listed in the *Small Press Record of Books in Print* (9th Edition, 1980). avg. price, cloth: $15.00; paper: $5.95. Discounts: Standard on over 10 copies; none on single copies. 6X9. Reporting time: 6 weeks. Payment: varies. Copyrights for author. COSMEP, ACP.

Press 22, Route 2, Box 175, Portland, OR 97231. "Book listed in SR should be ordered directly from author at — 3918 SW Garden Home Road, Portland, OR 97219." 1 title listed in the *Small Press Record of Books in Print* (9th Edition, 1980).

The Press of Ward Schori, Ward Schori, 2716 Noyes Street, Evanston, IL 60201, (312) 475-3241; 864-9797. 1961. "Primarily into miniature books-less than 3 inches high. Also publish sponsored books of poetry, local history. Print shop and former address: 1580 Maple Avenue, Evanston, IL 60201." avg. press run 500. Pub'd 3 titles 1979; expects 4 titles 1980, 2 titles 1981. 4 titles listed in the *Small Press Record of Books in Print* (9th Edition, 1980). avg. price, cloth: $10.00-$15.00. Discounts: To dealers, 20% on 2, 33⅓% on 5, 40% on 10 or more. †of/lp. APA.

Pressed Curtains (see also CURTAINS), Paul Buck, 4 Bower Street, Maidstone, Kent ME16 8SD, United Kingdom, 0622-63681. 1971. Poetry, fiction, art, articles, photos. "Publish contributors central to magazine" avg. press run 400. Pub'd 4 titles 1979; expects 6 titles 1980. 3 titles listed in the *Small Press Record of Books in Print* (9th Edition, 1980). avg. price, paper: $5.00; other: $12.00. 60pp; size A4; of. Reporting time: days. Payment: copies. Copyrights for author. ALP.

Priapus, 37 Lombardy Dr, Berkhamsted, Herts, United Kingdom. 10 titles listed in the *Small Press Record of Books in Print* (9th Edition, 1980).

Pride of the Forest, Barbara Johannah, PO Box 7266, Menlo Park, CA 94025.

Primary Press, Ernest Robson, Marion Robson, Box 105A, Parker Ford, PA 19457, 215-495-7529. 1970. Poetry, fiction, articles, satire, criticism, concrete art. "Our contributions consist of: our own work and anthologies. Our own compositions consist of: books experimenting to increase the information of poetry and relate this art to this culture with more relevance. We also publish chap books that are technical presentations of research in the acoustic-phonetic and visual parameters of poetry. Several of our books are determined by social/historical/philosophical interests. Our publications of others are exclusively anthologies. Our cassettes are compositions of phonetic music and social comment in some cases with technical realizations in collaboration with Frog Hollow Studios, San Jose, California. These realizations are electronically determined. Poets and Mathematicians, famous and unknown have contributed to our 1979 anthology *Against Infinity*." avg. press run 1,500. Pub'd 2 titles 1979; expects 2 titles 1980, 2 titles 1981. 11 titles listed in the *Small Press Record of Books in Print* (9th Edition, 1980). avg. price, cloth: $13.00; paper: $8.45; other: $1.95 chapbooks, $9.00 cassette. Discounts: trade 40%. 125pp; 6X9; 9X10½; of. Reporting time: rejects immediately; acceptances 1 year. Payment: by contract. Copyrights for author. COSMEP.

PRIMAVERA, Editorial Board, 1212 E 59th Street, Univ. of Chicago, Chicago, IL 60637, 312-753-3577. 1974. Poetry, fiction, art, photos, satire. "We are committed to encouraging new writers & artists. All work received will be read & *commented on* in a personal letter to you. Only women may submit. Please don't forget to type all literature & include S.A.S.E." circ. 1,000. 1/yr. Pub'd 1 issue 1979; expects 1 issue 1980. 5 titles listed in the *Small Press Record of Books in Print* (9th Edition, 1980). sub. price: $3.90; per copy: $3.90; sample: $3.90. Back issues: 1st issue $3.90; 2nd issue $3.90; 3rd issue $3.90, 4th issue $3.90, 5th issue $3.90. Discounts: Vol 1, 2, 3 $11.00; Vol 1, 2, 3, 4 $14.00; Vol 1, 2, 3, 4, 5 $17.00. 90pp; 8½X11; of. Reporting time: up to six months. Payment: 2 copies. Copyrighted, reverts to author. Ads: $125/$65/$6 per 5 lines, 25¢/wd add'l. COSMEP, CCLM.

PRIMIPARA, Impress Inc., Diane Nichols, P.O. Box 371, Oconto, WI 54153. 1974. Poetry, reviews. "Contributors *restricted* to Wisconsin residents only (anti-feminist work not accepted)—we're trying to establish a viable informal outlet for our state's women rather than leaning on N.Y. or CALIF. area markets." circ. 400. 2/yr. Pub'd 2 issues 1979; expects 2 issues 1980, 2 issues 1981. sub. price: $3.00; per copy: $1.75; sample: $1.00. Back issues: $1.00 each. 48pp; 8½X5½; of. Reporting time: 3 months. Payment: 1 copy. Copyrighted, reverts to author. Pub's reviews: 4 in 1979. §preference given to Wisc authors or Wisc based publications and women oriented.

The Print Mint, Inc. (see ARCADE-THE COMICS REVUE)

The Printable Arts Society, Inc. (see also BOX 749; RE:PRINT (AN OCCASIONAL MAGAZINE)), David Ferguson, Editor-in-Chief, Box 749, Old Chelsea Station, New York, NY 10011, (212) 989-0519. 1974. Poetry, fiction, art, photos, cartoons, satire, music, parts-of-novels, long-poems, collages, plays. avg. press run 5,000. of.

Printed Editions, Dick Higgins, PO Box 26, West Glover, VT 05875. 1972. "Printed Editions was formerly Unpublished Editions. Our principal US distributor is Bookslinger, PO Box 1625, 2163 Ford Parkway, St Paul, MN 55116. Our European distributor is McBridge Bros. & Broadley, Ltd. We are a coop of twelve artists, each doing sher own books (his or hers)." avg. press run 1,000. Pub'd 11 titles 1979. 27 titles listed in the *Small Press Record of Books in Print* (9th Edition, 1980). avg. price, cloth: $18.00; paper: $5.00; other: $20.00. Discounts: 40% per our distributors. 100pp; 6X9; of, lp. No mss. accepted; we are a coop of eight artists. Payment: 100% net. copyright in artists' names. COSMEP, NESPA, ALO.

Printed Matter, Inc., 7 Lispenard, New York, NY 10013, (212) 925-0325. 1976. 25 titles listed in the *Small Press Record of Books in Print* (9th Edition, 1980).

Prism Books (see also NEW POETRY; The Poetry Society of Australia), Robert Adamson, Box N110 Grosvenor St. P.O., Sydney, N.S.W. 2000, Australia. 1971. Poetry, photos, criticism, long-poems. "Published by NEW POETRY for The Poetry Society of Australia. These are well-produced limited editions of poetry from Australia's important new poets. In 1975 we published nine volumes, five of which were first books. To date: Kantarizis, Williams, Murray, Macrae, Maiden, Hewett, Porter, Thorne and Duncan." avg. press run 500-1,000. Pub'd 4 titles 1979. 13 titles listed in the *Small Press Record of Books in Print* (9th Edition, 1980). Discounts: 40% trade. 96pp; of/lp. Reporting time: 4 weeks. Payment: 2% (royalties).

PRISM INTERNATIONAL, John Simmons, Editor-in-Chief; Francois Bonneville, Managing Editor, 2075 Wesbrook Mall, University of British Columbia, Vancouver, BC V6T1W5, Canada, 604-228-2712. 1959. Poetry, fiction, criticism, reviews, parts-of-novels, plays. "Use translation of poetry and fiction in languages other than English (e.g., Spanish, French, Japanese)." circ. 500. 2/yr. Pub'd 2 issues 1979; expects 2 issues 1980, 2 issues 1981. sub. price: $7.00 indiv.; $10.00 libraries; per copy: $4.00; sample: $4.00. Discounts: Differs with the issue. 150pp; 6X9; lp. Reporting time: 4-6 weeks. Payment: $5.00 per printed page. Ads: $75.00/$35.00. CPPA.

PRISON, Donald Danford, Box 32323, 2605 State Street, Salem, OR 97310. 1978. Poetry, articles, satire, news items, letters. "Prefer short items, 500- words. This is a prison publication written mainly by prisoners and ex-prisoners. (I will accept some work by others relating to prison.) I want to cover all aspects of prison: psychiatry, sub-culture, 'rehab myth', the in-prison church, and so on. This is not a radical publication, even though some might consider it as such having never been exposed to any truth about the prison scene." circ. 5,000. 12/yr. Pub'd 5 issues 1979; expects 12 issues 1980, 12 issues 1981. sub. price: $6.00; per copy: $.75; sample: $.75. 12pp; †mi. Reporting time: 2-3 months. Pub's reviews. §Will consider reviews of prison related books and magazines. Ads: $0.20 word.

ProActive Press, James Craig, Marguerite Craig, P.O. Box 296, Berkeley, CA 94701, 415-549-0839. 1973. Fiction, articles, art. "We established the ProActive Press to assist in the co-creation of a caring society through humanistic politics. We are eager to share what skills we have with anyone who has a good, readable manuscript that offers a promising pro-life, pro-active program for humanizing social change. (We're not interested in more re-actions to the horrors we see and sense all about us.) Our *Synergic Power: Beyond Domination and Permissiveness* shows one kind of manuscript we're looking for. Also Utopian fiction." avg. press run 2,500. Pub'd 3 titles 1979; expects 3 titles 1980. 5 titles listed in the *Small Press Record of Books in Print* (9th Edition, 1980). avg. price, cloth: $8.95; paper: $4.95. Discounts: 40% trade, 20% text—both for orders of 5 or more books. 144pp; 5½X8½, 8½X11; of. Reporting time: Varies-query. Payment: varies-query. copyright by author's choice. COSMEP.

Proem Pamphlets, Michael Dawson, The Festival Office, Ilkley, W. Yorkshire LS29 8HF, United Kingdom, Ilkley 608925. 1976. Poetry. "The imprint was founded in order to provide a new outlet for poets who have not had the opportunity to publish a collection before. Each issue is devoted to one writer whose selection is introduced by an established poet. Initial issues have featured Tony Flynn (introduced by Douglas Dunn), Andrew Harvey(intro by John Wain), Melissa Murray (intro by Jon Silkin) and Larry Lanier (intro by Edward Lucie-Smith) in preparation: William Cooke (intro. Ted Walker). No submissions; established writers are invited to nominate contributors." avg. press run 750-1000. Pub'd 2 titles 1979; expects 2 titles 1980, 2 titles 1981. 5 titles listed in the *Small Press Record of Books in Print* (9th Edition, 1980). avg. price, paper: 40p. Discounts: 50% cash with order, 33⅓% net monthly, 25% sale or return. 20pp; 5½X8¼; of. Payment: negotiated for intro; share of income for new poet. Copyrights for author.

Programmed Studies Inc, Dick Whitson, P.O. Box 113, Stow, MA 01775, 617-897-2130. 1975. Articles. "Recently published programmed instruction course in seduction and lovemaking techniques: how to meet and bed girls—would like similar material for women" avg. press run 250. Pub'd 3 titles 1979; expects 3 titles 1980. 7 titles listed in the *Small Press Record of Books in Print* (9th Edition, 1980). avg. price, cloth: $29.95; paper: $4.95; other: $29.95. Discounts: up to 66%. 200pp; 8½X11; of/lp. Reporting time: 4 weeks. Payment: $25 to $200. Copyrights for author. COSMEP.

Programs in Communications Press, Jack Majors, 934 Pearl Suite J - 1, Boulder, CO 80302, 443-5514. 1976. "Consider books in area of interpersonal communications and personal growth only. Currently have only one book published, but would consider expanding offering with right authors. Particularly interested in publishing for college professors who would have outlets for their works in college classes." avg. press run 3,000. Expects 1 title 1980. avg. price, paper: $4.95. Discounts: 20% University Bookstores; 40% to retail stores; 50% to distributors, mail order houses, & other wholesalers. 164pp; 5½X8½. Reporting time: 2 months. Payment: Negotiated. Prefer author to contribute to printing costs. Copyrights for author.

Programs and Publications, Wendy Leebov Gollub, Sunny Shulkin, 321 Queen Street, Philadelphia, PA 19147, (215) 467-5291. 1979. avg. press run 3,000. Pub'd 2 titles 1979. avg. price, paper: $5.00. Discounts: 25% off to libraries, 30-40% off to stores, 50-60% off to distributors. 80pp; 8½X11; of. Reporting time: 1 month. Payment: flat fee. Copyrights for author. COSMEP.

Progresiv Publishr (see also CASE ANALYSIS; SOCIOLOGICAL PRACTICE), Kenneth H. Ives, Donald E. Gelfand, 401 E. 32nd #1002, Chicago, IL 60616, (312) 225-9181. 1977. Articles, reviews. "Pamphlet series *Studies in Quakerism.* Spelling reform book *Written Dialects N Spelling Reforms: History N Alternatives* (list $5.00). Forthcoming titles include: *Teaching Science as a Second Culture, Hazards of Program Evaluation, Inductive Religion,* lengths so far, 32 to 112 pages." avg. press run 150-300. Pub'd 2 titles 1979; expects 3 titles 1980, 1 title 1981. 9 titles listed in the *Small Press Record of Books in Print* (9th Edition, 1980). avg. price, paper: $2.00. Discounts: 5 or more 20%; 10 or more 40%. 45pp; 5X7. Reporting time: about a month. Payment: 10 copies.

Proletarian Publishers, P.O. Box 3925, Chicago, IL 60654. avg. press run 5,000. avg. price, paper: $4.95. Discounts: Bookstores-single or mixed titles: 20% 1-4; 30% 5-9; 40% 10 or more; 40% libraries & dist.; 20% libraries (college, public, school); 20% textbook. 250pp; 8X5.

Prologue Publications, Carol Rudoff, P.O. Box 640, Menlo Park, CA 94025, 322-5034. 1976. Articles. avg. press run 500 on up to several thousand. Pub'd 5 titles 1979; expects 2 titles 1980. 6 titles listed in the *Small Press Record of Books in Print* (9th Edition, 1980). avg. price, paper: $3.95. Discounts: trade 40 percent, bulk 50 percent, agent 12 percent. 72pp; 5½X8½; of. Reporting time: 6 weeks. Payment: 10 percent on sale. Copyrights for author. COSMEP.

Prometheus Books, Paul Kurtz, Editor-in-Chief, 1203 Kensington Ave, Buffalo, NY 14215. 1970. avg. press run 2,000. Pub'd 10 titles 1979; expects 17 titles 1980, 20 titles 1981. 1 title listed in the *Small Press Record of Books in Print* (9th Edition, 1980). avg. price, cloth: $14.95; paper: $7.95. Discounts: normal. 200-300pp; 6X9, 8½X5½; of. Reporting time: 1-2 months. Payment: yes. Copyrights for author.

Promise Publishing Corp., Dale Sinclair, 725 Market Street, Wilmington, DE 19801, 401-274-8496. 1978. Fiction, articles, music. "Newly organized in Boston and Rhode Island area moving to Delaware at above address 6-80. Publish and do PP mostly into fiction, how to books and sheet music publication. Other mailing address: 61 Halsey Street, Providence, RI 02906; PO Box 1534, Pawtucket, RI 02869." Pub'd 1 title 1979; expects 1 title 1980. 3 titles listed in the *Small Press Record of Books in Print* (9th Edition, 1980). avg. price, paper: $7.95. Discounts: Trade 20%. 325pp; 8½X11. Reporting time: 3 months. Payment: 50%. Copyrights for author.

PROP, Workspace Loft, Inc., Jessica Lawrence, Bob Durlak, Greg Haymes, Theo Dorian, Joachim Frank, Jan Galligan, Ed Atkeson, 4 Elm Street, Albany, NY 12202, (518) 436-9498. 1978. Poetry, fiction, articles, art, photos, cartoons, interviews, satire, criticism, reviews, music, letters, parts-of-novels, long-poems, collages, plays, concrete art, news items. "Open to contributions. Any style. Normal art in a normal world. Some recent contributors: Jan Galligan, Greg Haymes, Joachim Frank, Aaron Flores, Adriane Verschoor, Barbara Aubin, Ishvahni Leclair, Bart Platenga, Philemon, Roxanne Stormes, Jo Denali, Bowtie Blotto, Ed Atkeson." circ. 1,000. 4/yr. Pub'd 3 issues 1979; expects 4 issues 1980, 4 issues 1981. sub. price: $4.00; per copy: $1.00; sample: $0.75. Back issues: $1.50. Discounts: Contact Publishers (Workspace Loft, Inc. c/o Joachim Frank, 845 Park Ave., Albany, NY 12208; (518) 489-5059) Directly. 28pp; size varies; of. Reporting time: 8 weeks. Payment: No. Pub's reviews. §Art, film, experimental poetry, speculative fiction, photography, video, social theory, cultural anthro. Ads: ad exchange with other magazines and groups on equal space basis.

Proscenium Press (see also JOURNAL OF IRISH LITERATURE), Robert Hogan, P.O.Box 361, Newark, NJ 19711, (215) 255-4083. 1965. Plays. avg. press run 500-1000. Pub'd 4 titles 1979; expects 8 titles 1980. 6 titles listed in the *Small Press Record of Books in Print* (9th Edition, 1980). avg. price, cloth: $10.00; paper: $2.50. Discounts: 20%. 5½X8½; lp. Reporting time: varies from instantly to 6 months. Payment: usually only in copies. Copyrights for author.

Provision House, Ryan Petty, PO Box 5487, Austin, TX 78763, 452-1417. 1979. "We publish books and pamphlets that are useful, helpful, practical, interesting and/or fun. We are specially interested in how-to books, the sharing of experience that may be of service to others: how to do it; how to make it; how to survive it; how to cure it; how to thrive on it; how to avoid it; how to write it; how to say it; how to overcome it; how to make money from it or save money while accomplishing it. We publish books that fill a need or serve a purpose or answer a call. In August 1980 we will publish Joe Bruchac's book, *How to Start and Sustain a Literary Magazine: Practical Strategies for Publications of Lasting Value*. Last year we published Ryan Petty's *The Great Garage Sale Success Book*. We have several books presently under contract, including: *The Low-Salt, Low-Cholesterol, Good-Food-Anyway Cookbook, The Glove Compartment Legal Guide to Auto Emergencies*, and an as-yet-untitled book on time management. We are wide-open for submissions. Authors should query firt with a letter describing their projects, focusing on who needs to read a particular book being proposed, and why. Enclose SASE; ask for our free ctalogue." Pub'd 1 title 1979; expects 3 titles 1980, 4 titles 1981. avg. price, paper: $10.00. Discounts: write for unusual schedule with unusually good terms. of. Reporting time: 60 days. Payment: negotiated with author.

Pruett Publishing Company, Gerald Keenan, Managing Ed.; F.A. Pruett, President, 3235 Prairie Avenue, Boulder, CO 80301, 303-449-4919. 1959. Articles, art, photos, criticism, music. "We publish books of interest to the trans-Mississippi west: histories, railroadiana. Also special education titles and textbooks for el-hi and college levels. Examples are an extensive pictorial history of the California Zephyr, an Alaskan railroad book, a history of the American Indian in Colorado and a new social study series for the mentally handicapped child. Also publish regional outdoor guides such as *The Backpacker's Recipe Book* and *Tourguide to the Rocky Mountain Wilderness*." avg. press run will vary according to each book. Pub'd 25-33 titles 1979. 3 titles listed in the *Small Press Record of Books in Print* (9th Edition, 1980). avg. price, cloth: varies. Discounts: write for a copy of our complete schedule. pp will vary; 8½X11; 6X9; of. Reporting time: Within a few days, if we reject ms. Within 30-60 days, if ms. is under consideration. Payment: generally a royalty basis for authors. Copyrights for author. ABA, AAP.

Psychic Books, L. K. Ulery, Box 2205, Oxnard, CA 93030, (805) 488-8670. 1978. "Only a self-publishing author in the areas of psychology, philosophy, metaphysics, etc. Psychic energy and the power of the mind. Presently not considering outside material but hope to be in the position to consider other authors' work in 1979. Would only be interested in material in some way related and in keeping with our name Psychic Books." avg. press run 500. Expects 3 titles 1980, 3 titles 1981. 3 titles listed in the *Small Press Record of Books in Print* (9th Edition, 1980). avg. price, cloth: $7.75. Discounts: Trade, 40%; Libraries, 25%. 160pp; 5½X8½; of.

Psychohistory Press (see also THE JOURNAL of PSYCHOHISTORY; THE JOURNAL OF PSYCHOLOGICAL ANTHROPOLOGY), Lloyd deMause, Editor; Arthur Hippler, Editoru, 2315 Broadway, New York City, NY 10024. 1973. avg. press run 3M. Pub'd 6 titles 1979. 9 titles listed in the *Small Press Record of Books in Print* (9th Edition, 1980). avg. price, cloth: $12.00; paper: $6.00. Discounts: usual. 150pp; 7X9; of. Reporting time: 4 weeks. Copyrights for author.

PSYCHOTHERAPY DIGEST, Victor Kops Ph D, Editor, P.O. Box 1167, Del Mar, CA 92014, 714-481-7023. 1976. Articles, reviews. "The Digest reviews and summarizes the developments in psychotherapy. Therapists are encouraged to submit 500 to 800 word summaries of published or unpublished articles of unique programs, case histories, personal experiences, book reviews, etc." circ. 1,000. 6/yr. Pub'd 10 issues 1979; expects 6 issues 1980, 6 issues 1981. sub. price: $15.00; per copy: $1.50; sample: $1.50. Back issues: $1.50/issue. Discounts: Wholesale distributors and agents are generally given a 20% discount. 16pp; 8X11; of. Reporting time: 2-4 weeks. Payment: $25.00 per article accepted. Copyrighted, reverts to author. Pub's reviews: 4 in 1979. §Psychotherapy. no ads. COSMEP.

PTERANODON, Lieb/Schott Publications, Patricia Lieb, Carol Schott, PO Box 229, Bourbonnais, IL 60914. 1978. Poetry, fiction, interviews, long-poems. "*Pteranodon*: A literary magazine for poets and writers, published by Lieb/Schott Publications. Contains poetry, short stories, interviews, photography, art, workshops, etc. Send 4 to 6 poems at a time. Send only one short story 1,200 words, at a time. We publish unknown as well as known authors. We have a poetry contest with cash prizes during the making of each issue of *Pteranodon*. All winning poems and runners up are published in the magazine. Send SASE for contest rules. We have a different *accomplished* poet to judge each contest.

A one line book ad, containing book title, type of book, author, publisher, price, and the address that the book may be ordered from: $10.00. *pteranodon Chapbooks*: Interested authors should query with sample of 4 poems before submitting complete chapbook manuscript. Have published chapbooks by Glenn Swetman and Meg Files." circ. 500. 4/yr. Pub'd 3 issues 1979; expects 3 issues 1980. sub. price: $9.50; per copy: $2.50; sample: $2.50. Back issues: $2.50. 40-44pp; 8½X10½; of. Reporting time: 2 weeks to 2 months. Pays in copies, sometimes cash prizes. Copyrighted, reverts to author. Ads: $100.00/$65.00/$50.00.

PTOLEMY/BROWNS MILLS REVIEW, David C. Vajda, Box 6915-A Press Avenue, Browns Mills, NJ 08015, (609) 893-7594. 1979. Poetry, fiction, articles, satire, criticism, parts-of-novels, long-poems. "*Ptolemy* forty-eight pages, eclectic, mostly poetry, one/two issues per year. *Browns Mills Review* mostly short-short stories, short fiction, very open, one/two issues per year. Work in general, post modern, post contemporary, backward leaning, forward hunching, original, imitative, iconoclastic, crafted, leftward, stop." circ. 100-200. 2-3/yr. Pub'd 1-3 issues 1979. sub. price: $8.00; per copy: $2.00; sample: $1.00-$2.00. Back issues: $1.00-$2.00. Discounts: 50% per order, up to fifty. 20pp; 5½X8½; of. Reporting time: 1 week to 1 month. Payment: copies. Copyrighted, reverts to author.

THE PUB, Ansuda Publications, Daniel R. Betz, Alexander Gold, Reviews Editor, Box 123, Harris, IA 51345. 1979. Poetry, fiction, articles, art, satire, criticism, reviews, long-poems, plays, news items, parts-of-novels. "6,000 word maximum on fiction. No set limit on articles (query *first* on articles *only*). No set length on poetry but will not consider haiku or poetry with senseless rhyming. Canadians are welcome to send SASE with loose Canadian postage. Regulars are Laurel Speer & Merritt Clifton. Semi-regulars & others include Ted Krieger, James Miller Robinson, Nola Chapman, Rita Rosenfeld, & many more." circ. 200. 3/yr. Pub'd 4 issues 1979; expects 3 issues 1980, 3 issues 1981. sub. price: 3/$2.75; sample: $1.00. Back issues: #1, $0.75; #2, $0.90; #3, $1.00; #4, $1.00; #5, $1.25. Discounts: Query. 60pp; 5½X8½; †mi. Reporting time: immediately to 2 weeks, 1 month maximum. Payment: copies. Copyrighted, reverts to author. Pub's reviews: 37 in 1979. §Almost anything. Ads: Cheap! query — will also trade.

PUBLISHED POET NEWSLETTER, Daniel L. Morris, PO Box 1663, Indianapolis, IN 46206. 1980. Poetry, art, news items. 12/yr. sub. price: $15.00; sample: SASE. Back issues: $1.50 when available. 8-12pp; 7X8½; of. Reporting time: 2-4 weeks. Payment: $0.25 per line, $3.00 minimum, $5.00 minimum for art. Copyrighted, reverts to author. Pub's reviews. §Poetry and/or art.

Publishing Associates (see also FANTASY EXPRESS; GOLDEN GATE REVIEW; LAUGHING UNICORN; POETIC JUSTICE; RAINBOW'S END), 432 Heathcliff Drive, Pacifica, CA 94044, (415) 355-3630. 1979. Poetry, long-poems. "*Laughing Unicorn*: Earl Blanchard; *Poetic Justice*: Bruce Taylor; *MS Verses*: Renee French; *Fantasy Express*: Mark French; *Rainbow's End*: Geraldo Earl; *Golden Gate Review* : Renee French." avg. press run 500. Pub'd 9 titles 1979. avg. price, paper: $1.50. Discounts: 33⅓%. 32pp; 5½X8½; †of. Reporting time: 10 days. Payment: as arranged. Copyrights for author.

Puckerbrush Press, Constance Hunting, 76 Main St., Orono, ME 04473, 207-866-4868. 1971. Poetry, fiction, criticism. "Recent: *A Day's Work,* poems by Michael McMahon; *A Paper Raincoat,* poems by Sonya Dorman; No strictly 'women's' stuff please." avg. press run 150-300. Pub'd 2 titles 1979. 8 titles listed in the *Small Press Record of Books in Print* (9th Edition, 1980). avg. price, paper: $3.50. Discounts: 40%. 50-100pp; 6X9; of. Reporting time: 2-4 wks. Payment: 10% of each retail copy. copyright to author. NESPA, MWPA.

PUCK'S CORNER, R & J Kudlay, Robert Kudley, Joanne Kudlay, 105 Clark Street, Easthampton, MA 01027, (617) 281-3665. 1978. Poetry, articles, art, cartoons, criticism, reviews, letters, news items. "We are most interested in articles dealing with the antiquarian book trade. We use about 20 short poems (under 30 lines) per year." circ. 300. 12/yr. Expects 8 issues 1980, 12 issues 1981. sub. price: $8.00; per copy: $1.25; sample: $1.25. Back issues: Special Edgar Rice Burroughs (Sept.) issue $1.25. Discounts: 25% for 5-9 copies; 50%, 10 or more. 24pp; 8½X11; of. Reporting time: 1 month. Payment: up to 6 contributor's copies. Copyrighted, reverts to author. Pub's reviews: 4 in 1979. §Poetry, philosophy, books-on-books (production, design, etc.), book collecting, reference. Ads: $15.00/$8.00/$.02.

Pueblo Poetry Project, Joel Scherzer, Room 31, Union Depot, Pueblo, CO 81003. 1979. Poetry, art, photos, long-poems. "The Poetry Project is a federally funded program of the University of Southern Colorado. In 1979-80 we published an anthology of Pueblo poets and more than a dozen chapbooks, including: *Mojo* by Tony Moffeit, *Why Did I Laugh Tonight?* by Beth Ann Bassein, *Tapping Some Roots* by Ron Whitsitt, *Experiment in A* by Helen Roberts, *Gibbous* by Kim Cass-Nolan, *Hoodoo Woman* by Robbie Rubinstein, *A New Book* by Henry Darner, *My Skin Has Turned to Gray* by Joel Scherzer, *Delirium Trains* by Diane Rabson, *Speak Sunlight to Me* by John Senatore, *It's For You* by Bob

Cordova and *Management Does Not Guarantee This Machine to Work* by Rick Terlep. Submissions limited to Pueblo area." avg. press run 100. Pub'd 7 titles 1979; expects 8 titles 1980. 18 titles listed in the *Small Press Record of Books in Print* (9th Edition, 1980). avg. price, paper: $1.00. Discounts: 40%. 24pp; 5½X8½; of. Reporting time: 2 months. Payment: one-third of press run. Copyrights for author.

Pueo Press, Kimo Campbell, Editor; Aleen Vorhies, Production & Design, 810 College Ave, Kentfield, CA 94904, 415-456-6480. 1975. Fiction, photos. "We publish material on Hawaii and the Pacific. The type of material is not as important as the content." avg. press run 1,000. Pub'd 1 title 1979; expects 2 titles 1980. 2 titles listed in the *Small Press Record of Books in Print* (9th Edition, 1980). avg. price, paper: $6.95. Discounts: 1-4 copies, 30%; 5 or more, 40%. 85pp; 8¼X9. Reporting time: 30 days. Payment: Negotiable. Usually advance, plus profit share. copyrights for author if necessary. COSMEP.

PUERTO DEL SOL, Puerto Del Sol Press, Joseph Tuso, Box 3E, Las Cruces, NM 88003, 505-646-3932. 1961. Poetry, fiction, art, photos, interviews, reviews, parts-of-novels, long-poems, plays. "Emphasis on Chicano, Nat. Am. & Anglo writers. Some Latin American with trans." circ. 1,000. sub. price: $2.95; per copy: $2.95; sample: $2.95. Back issues: complete set $40.00 (vol 1 no. 1-vol 14 no. 2). Discounts: 40 percent general/50 percent jobber. 125pp; 6X9; of. Reporting time: 6 weeks. Copyrighted. Pub's reviews: 2 in 1979. §Chicano, Nat. Am., poetry, fiction. CCLM.

Puerto Del Sol Press (see also PUERTO DEL SOL), David Apodaca, Box 3E, Las Cruces, NM 88003. 1975. Poetry, fiction. "Joy Harjo: *The Last Song* $1.50. Leroy Quintana: *Hijo Del Pueblo,* New Mexico poems $2.00. Part of *Del Conejo* series for New Mexico writers." avg. press run 500. avg. price, paper: $2.00. Discounts: 40 percent/50 percent jobber. 30pp; 6X9; of. Reporting time: 6 weeks (solicited only). Payment varies. Copyrights for author.

Pulmac Enterprises, Inc., Alice Cowan, Middlesex Star Route, Montpelier, VT 05602, (802) 223-6326. 1977. Poetry. "Large print books" Pub'd 2 titles 1979. 1 title listed in the *Small Press Record of Books in Print* (9th Edition, 1980). avg. price, paper: $5.95. Discounts: Libraries, 20%; Distributors, 50%; Bookstores or equivalent, 1-2 copies, full price; 3-5, 15%; 6-9, 25%; 10-49, 40%; 50 +, 50%. 160pp; 5½X8½; of. Reporting time: 8 weeks. Payment: to be negotiated. Copyrights for author. COSMEP.

PULP, Sage Press, Howard Sage, 720 Greenwich St., New York City, NY 10014. 1974. Poetry, fiction, articles, art, photos, cartoons, interviews, satire, parts-of-novels, long-poems, plays. "Michael Heller, Archibald Henderson, Marge Piercy, Diana Chang, Lyn Lifshin, Philip Appleman, Richard O'Connell, Donald A. Sears. Consider all styles, no biases. Phyllis Witte, Lillie Howard, Margaret Diorio, Laurie Stroblas, Soichi Furuta, Isabel Arnaiz. Welcome translations. Send original. Karla M. Hammond, Seymour Epstein, Janet McCann, Alicia Ostriker, Chet Gottfried. Make check payable to Howard Sage." circ. 2,000. 2/yr. Pub'd 2 issues 1979; expects 2 issues 1980. sub. price: $2.00/$5.00 outside U.S.; per copy: $0.50; sample: $1.00 to Howard Sage. Back issues: $1.00 plus postage. 16pp; size tabloid 9¾X15; of. Reporting time: 1 week-1 mo. Payment: 2 copies. Copyrighted, reverts to author upon publication. Pub's reviews: 2 in 1979. §poetry, fiction. Ads: $150/$75/$1-for 28 wds. CCLM.

‡**PULP CONTENT, Pulp Press,** P.O. Box 3868 M.P.O, Vancouver V6B 3Z3, Canada.

Pulp Press (see also THREE CENT PULP; PULP CONTENT), Ed. Board, P.O. Box 3868 M.P.O., Vancouver V6B 3Z3, Canada. 1971. Poetry, fiction, art, satire, parts-of-novels, long-poems, plays, non-fiction. avg. press run 1,200-2,000. Pub'd 10 titles 1979; expects 15 titles 1980. 22 titles listed in the *Small Press Record of Books in Print* (9th Edition, 1980). avg. price, cloth: $8.95; paper: $3.50; other: $1.00-$2.00. Discounts: trade 40 percent: libraries 10 percent: wholesale (bulk) 50 percent. 108pp; 5¼X8; †of. Reporting time: 1 month. Payment: royalties negotiated after 1,000 copies sold. Copyrights for author.

PULPSMITH, The Generalist Assn., Inc., Harry Smith, Sidney Bernard, Tom Tolnay, 5 Beekman St., New York, NY 10038. 1980. "*The Smith,* a literary magazine in book format, has been a function of the Generalist Association, Inc. for 17 years. Now the Association is publishing *Pulpsmith* in its place. Pulpdiegest style and size, it contains essays on the phenonmena of the times, short fiction—mainstream and experimental—sci-fi, detective, mystery, romance, fantasy and lyrics and ballads. Original illustrations.u" circ. 10,000. 4/yr. Expects 2 issues 1980, 4 issues 1981. 18 titles listed in the *Small Press Record of Books in Print* (9th Edition, 1980). sub. price: $5.00; per copy: $1.50; sample: $1.00. Back issues: $1.50. Discounts: varies. 200pp; 5⅛X7⅜; of. Reporting time: 4 to 6 weeks. Payment: $10.00 to $100.00. Copyrighted, reverts to author. Pub's reviews. §Poetry, fiction, journalism. no ads. CCLM, COSMEP.

Pulse-Finger Press, Orion Roche, Box 18105, Philadelphia, PA 19116. 1967. Poetry, fiction, plays.

"Considering our size, we try to offer as close to a 'standard contract' as possible; usually what this amounts to, in the case of poetry, is a percentage of some 2-5%, and, in the case of fiction, 10-12%, depending on size of press run, estimation of prospective sales, etc. Advances for poetry are nominal, usually something between $100-250; fiction is normally a little more. We prefer contemporary themes and idioms; no limitations as to length, although, obviously, the size and number of our publications is inhibited by the market, ie., money. Printers like to be paid; lots of things we'd like to publish we just can't afford to because we don't think the public shares our good taste. Most of our distribution is local and via mail order. Absolutely *no* unsoliciteed mss. Please *do not* send threatening letters inquiring about the status of an unsolicited ms. unless SASE is enclosed along with the Anglo-Saxon outrages. I don't have the time; and for laughs, I read the Bible and Oswald Spengler." avg. press run 200-2,000. Pub'd 8 titles 1979; expects 10 titles 1980, 11 titles 1981. avg. price, cloth: $9.00. Discounts: 40% bookstores; 20% jobbers for singles; on a graduated scale up to 45% for larger orders, postage added. 250pp; 5½X8½; of. Reporting time: 3-6 months. Copyrights for author.

Purple Mouth Press (see also SKIFFY THYME), Ned Brooks, 713 Paul St, Newport News, VA 23605. 1975. "Fantasy." avg. press run 300-500. Pub'd 1 title 1979. 3 titles listed in the *Small Press Record of Books in Print* (9th Edition, 1980). avg. price, paper: $5.00. Discounts: 10 at 40%, 100 at 50%. 40-50pp; 8½X11; of, mi. Reporting time: 1-2 weeks. Payment: yes. Copyrights for author.

PURPLE PATCH, Geoff Stevens, 106 Walsall Road, Stone Cross, West Bromwich, West Midlands, United Kingdom. 1976. Poetry, fiction, articles, interviews, reviews, news items. circ. 200. quarterly. Pub'd 5 issues 1979; expects 4 issues 1980, 5 issues 1981. sub. price: £1.00; per copy: 21p. 16pp; 8X9½; †mi. Reporting time: varies. Payment: none. Copyrighted, reverts to author. Pub's reviews. §poetry, short stories, literary biographies.

Pushcart Press, Bill Henderson, P.O. Box 845, Yonkers, NY 10701, 212-228-2269. 1973. "Pushcart publishes THE PUBLISH-IT-YOURSELF HANDBOOK: Literary Tradition and How-To, edited by Bill Henderson, a complete guide on publishing without assistance of vanity or commercial publishers, including essays by Anais Nin, Stewart Brand, Alan Swallow, Leonard Woolf, Richard Kostelanetz, Len Fulton, Gordon Lish (plus 20 others). Complete bibliography and how-to section. Each year we will publish THE PUSHCART PRIZE: Best of the Small Presses, with the help of our distinguished contributing editors.We also recently published *The Little Magazine in America: A Modern Documentary History* edited by Elliott Anderson and Mary Kinzie. New titles in 1980 include *Published in Paris* by Hugh Ford (a history of small presses in Paris 1920-1940); *The Art of Literary Publishing,* edited by Bill Henderson (a collection of editors' essays on literary publishing); and *The Writers Quotation Book,* edited by James Charlton (300 quotes on the writer's craft)." Pub'd 1 title 1979; expects 4 titles 1980, 3 titles 1981. 9 titles listed in the *Small Press Record of Books in Print* (9th Edition, 1980). avg. price, cloth: $15.00; paper: $5.00. Discounts: 40% 6 or more copies. 500pp; 5½X8½; of. Payment: 10%. Copyrights for author. COSMEP.

The Putah Creek Press, Library Associates, University of California, Davis, CA 95616, (916) 752-3222. 1968. Poetry, art, photos, criticism. Pub'd 3 titles 1979; expects 2 titles 1980, 3 titles 1981. avg. price, paper: $5.00. Discounts: 20% to dealers. 6X9; 8½X11; of. Copyrights for author.

Pygmalion Press, Doug Rauch, Adrian Torcotte, 609 El Centro, South Pasadena, CA 91030, (213) 682-1211. 1973. Poetry, fiction. avg. press run 1,200-1,500. Pub'd 3 titles 1979; expects 3 titles 1980, 4 titles 1981. avg. price, paper: $3.95. Discounts: 40% to the retailer or jobber. 50pp; †of. Payment: individual arrangements. Copyrights for author.

THE PYRAMID GUIDE: International Bi-Monthly Newsletter, Bill Cox, 741 Rosarita Lane, Santa Barbara, CA 93105, (805) 682-5151. 1972. Poetry, articles, art, photos, cartoons, interviews, reviews, letters, news items. "1,000 words or less is best" circ. 6,000. 6/yr. Pub'd 6 issues 1979; expects 6 issues 1980, 6 issues 1981. sub. price: $13.00 foreign, $9.00 domestic; per copy: $1.50; sample: $1.00. Back issues: $1.00 each for issues 1-37, $1.50 each for current issue. Discounts: dealers 40% off. 12pp; 8½X11; of. Reporting time: variable. Payment: negotiable. Copyrighted. Pub's reviews: 20 in 1979. §Metaphysical, dowsing, world pyramids, anicent mysteries. Ads: $10.00 col inch.

PYRAMIDOLOGY MAGAZINE, Institute of Pyramidology, James Rutherford, Editor, 31 Station Road, Harpenden, Herts AL5 4XB, United Kingdom, Harpenden 64510. 1941. Articles, photos. "1,000 to 6,000 words. Religious bias. Recent contributors: Dorothy Norwood, Lt. Col. A.K. MacPherson, Eileen Bennett, Dr. V. Maragiogllio, C. Rinaldi, John Strong, Dr. Adam Rutherford." circ. 1,500. 4/yr. sub. price: $5.00 for members, $7.00 for non-members; per copy: $1.75; sample: $1.75. Back issues: Bound issues at $7.00 per year. Discounts: 40% on ten copies or more. 24pp; 5½X8½; of/lp. Reporting time: 1 month. Payment: negotiable. Copyrighted, reverts to author. §Pyramids of Egypt, theology, bible chronology.

Pyxidium Press, Richard Baronio, 462 Old Chelsea Station, New York, NY 10011, (212) 242-5224.

Quality Publications, Inc. (see also GREEN FEATHER), Gary S. Skeens, Exe. Editor; Robin Sue Humenik, Assoc. Editor, PO Box 2633, Lakewood, OH 44107. 1978. Poetry, fiction, articles. " *American Short Story Series:* (10 to 20 volumes) Length: 16,000 to 48,000 words. Eight to twelve stories per volume. Stories should deal with people, places with an American setting or background, and though we will consider all subjects a special interest will be paid to those of a western nature (either historical or contemporary). *Fiction:* All types of subject matter. Length: 40,000 to 75,000 words. *Non-fiction:* Areas of interest are Americana, Animals (wildlife, outdoor settings, Western US), History. Length: 45,000 to 80,000 words, though we will consider longer. *Query first with proposed idea. Poetry* : Any subject. Length: 48 pages minimum to approximately 80 pages, though longer manuscripts will be consider on occasion. *Query first with five to ten sample poems from collection.* Some recent contributor's include; Dyke Walton, Hy Young, Dave Diamond, Terry Miller, Janet Weiner. Street Address: Quality Publications, Inc., 15613 Chatfield Avenue, Cleveland, Ohio 44111." avg. press run 500. Pub'd 1 title 1979; expects 6 titles 1980. avg. price, cloth: $5.95; paper: $3.50. Discounts: 35-60%. 125pp; 5½X8½; of. Reporting time: 2 months. Payment: standard royalty contract. Copyrights for author. COSMEP.

Martin Quam Press, Ralph Scott, 1515 Columbia Drive, Cedar Falls, IA 50613, (319) 266-6242. 1978. Fiction, cartoons, letters. "Educational-psychological materials of a conservative nature." avg. press run 2,500. Pub'd 1-2 titles 1979. 1 title listed in the *Small Press Record of Books in Print* (9th Edition, 1980). avg. price, paper: $4.00. Discounts: 40% classroom, jobber, trade. 200pp. Reporting time: 30 days. Payment: 7.5%; or split payment arrangements based on publishing costs. Copyrights for author.

Quantal Publishing B, Anne N. Lowenkope, PO Box 1598, Goleta, CA 93017, (805) 964-7293. 1979. "I am interested in receiving manuscripts on Gestalt theories." avg. press run 5,000. 1 title listed in the *Small Press Record of Books in Print* (9th Edition, 1980). avg. price, paper: $8.95. Discounts: usual. 200pp; 6X9; of. Reporting time: 1 month. Copyrights for author. COSMEP.

QUARRY WEST, College V, UCSC, Sue Dunn, Lou Mathews, David Swanger, Carter Young, Eric Bolt, Eileen Drew, Rosy Liggett, College v, University of Calif, Santa Cruz, CA 95064. 1971. Poetry, fiction, articles, art, parts-of-novels, long-poems. "Joyce Carol Oates, Raymond Carver, J. B. Hall, Gary Ligi, Steven Dixon, Gary Soto, Susan Fromberg Schaeffer, Ronald Wallace, Greg Kuzma, Vern Rutsala, George Hitchcock, Sharon Olds, Lennart Bruce, Robert Peterson, Morton Marcus, Thomas Lux, William Matthews, Kathleen Fraser, William Everson." circ. 1,000. 3/yr. Pub'd 2 issues 1979; expects 3 issues 1980, 3 issues 1981. sub. price: $7.50; per copy: $2.50; sample: $2.00. Discounts: 40% 5 or more copies. 96pp; 7X8; of. Reporting time: 8 weeks. Payment: 2 issues and poster. Copyrighted. CCLM.

Quarterly Committee of Queen's University (see QUEEN'S QUARTERLY: A Canadian Review)

QUARTERLY REVIEW OF LITERATURE, Theodore Weiss, Renee Weiss, 26 Haslet Ave, Princeton, NJ 08540, 921-6976. 1943. Poetry, long-poems. "A unique poetry series in subscription. Each volume will include 4 to 6 collections of poems, translations, poetic plays or long poems. $500 prize awarded to each accepted manuscript. Brian Swann's *Living Time,* M. Slotznick's *Industrial Stuff,* E.G. Burrows's *Properties: A Play For Voices,* Reginald Gibbons's *Roofs, Voices, Roads,* and David Galler's *Third Poems: 1965-78* are the five books included in the first issue. Statements by each poet about his work, as well as biographies and photographs, introduce the poets" circ. 3,000. irregular. Pub'd 1 issue 1979; expects 1 issue 1980. 6 titles listed in the *Small Press Record of Books in Print* (9th Edition, 1980). sub. price: 2 volumes paper: $15; single $10; $20.00 institutional & hardback per volume; per copy: $20.00 (hardback) $10.00 (paper). Back issues: Scarce; available through us on request. Not all available; cost-roughly $20.00 per volume. Discounts: Bookstores: 10 percent on 1 copy, 40 percent on 3 or more. Agency subscription discounts: 10 percent. 250-350pp; 5½X8½; of. Reporting time: 6 weeks-2 months. New material accepted at specified period. Write for information. Payment: $500 each manuscript. Copyrighted, does not revert to author. Ads: $200.00/$125.00/$0.00. CCLM,

COSMEP.

Queens College Press (see also A SHOUT IN THE STREET: a journal of literary and visual art), Joseph Cuomo, General Editor, Writers & Artists Series, English Dept, Queens College, Flushing, NY 11367, 212-520-7238. 1977. Poetry, fiction, art, photos, interviews, long-poems, plays, nonfiction. "Send submissions only to A SHOUT IN THE STREET. We do not have staff to read submissions to book series." avg. press run 1,000. avg. price, paper: mag-$2.50. Discounts: 40 percent to bookstores; 50 percent to distributors. mag-96pp; size mag 6X9¼; †mag-of. Reporting time: magazine only-8 weeks. Payment: mag-copies + subscription. Copyrights for author. COSMEP.

QUEEN'S QUARTERLY: A Canadian Review, Quarterly Committee of Queen's University, Kerry (Dr.) McSweeney, Michael (Dr.) Fox, Queen's University, Kingston, Ontario K7L3N6, Canada, 613-547-6968. 1893. Poetry, fiction, articles, interviews, satire, criticism, parts-of-novels, plays. "Articles: 20-25 double-spaced pp. Recent contributors: Gwendolyn MacEwen, Dorothy Livesay, D. O. Hebb, George Woodcock, Joyce Carol Oates, Edgar Z. Friedenberg, Al Purdy" circ. 1,900. 4/yr. Pub'd 4 issues 1979; expects 4 issues 1980, 4 issues 1981. sub. price: $10.00 Canada; $11.00 Foreign; per copy: $2.50; sample: $2.50. Back issues: Depends on age; min. $2.50; max. $5.00. 192pp; 6X9; of. Reporting time: max, 1 month. Payment: $3 per printed page (short stories), $10 per poem 50 free offprints (articles), copies. Copyrighted. Pub's reviews: 280 in 1979. §serious books only; history, science, politics, philosophy, social science, literary studies, music, art, etc. Ads: $150/$85. CPPA.

QUERCUS, Theresa Vinciguerra, 25-4502, Sacramento, CA 95825, (916) 456-5344. 1979. Poetry. "*Quercus* publishes only poets in the Sacramento and outlying areas, because artistically it is a cooperative effort among the contributors, who help in the editing and selection of graphics, paper, and make other decisions regarding the final production. Payment is in 10 copies per contributor, plus each poet is featured at a local reading. Featured poets are paid anywhere from $5.00 to $20.00 for a reading. The Poet Tree, Inc. also publishes a monthly newsletter, *Poet Tree News* which accepts reviews of books and readings, plus info on contests and other matters relating to literary concerns. The subscription rate of $12.00 includes the monthly newsletter." circ. 200. 4/yr. Pub'd 1 issue 1979; expects 4 issues 1980. sub. price: $12.00; per copy: $2.00; sample: $1.00. Back issues: $1.00. Discounts: 40% for 10 or more copies. 20pp; 5½X8½; of. Reporting time: 1 month. Payment: 10 copies, plus being featured at a local reading. Copyrighted, reverts to author. Pub's reviews. §Poetry. Ads: $25.00/$15.00/$0.25 per line.

QUEST, Arleen Rogan, Managing Editor; Sara Shepard, Design & Production Editor; Jackie MacMillan, Marilyn Lerch, Lynn Gorshov, Gerri Traina, Tracy Thiele, Sarah Begus, Lisa Hoogstra, Isabelle Thabault, PO Box 8843, Washington, DC 20003. 1974. Poetry, articles, art, photos, cartoons, interviews, satire, criticism, reviews. "Only original, unpublished material is acceptable. Major articles should be no longer than 20 double-spaced typewritten pages (8½ x 11). QUEST is a national journal committed to the exposure of feminist political analysis and ideological development. Each issue covers a specific theme in-depth. Authors should write and request list of ideas and questions for particular themes of issues. QUEST is neither a news magazine, literary, or academic journal. We seek to be a forum for political exchange in the feminist movement. Recent contributors: Charlotte Bunch, Jo Freeman, Elizabeth Reid, Michelle Russell, Jane Flax, Deb Friedman." circ. 5,000. 4/yr. Pub'd 4 issues 1979. sub. price: $9.00/individuals; $25.00/institutions; $11.00/overseas, surface mail; $14.50/overseas, air mail.; per copy: $3.00 plus 35¢ postage; sample: $3.00 plus $.35 postage. Back issues: We now sell binder sets for volumes 1 and 2 because several of the nos. from those volumes are limited in number. Vol 1, $25.00; Vol 2, $25.00. Vols 1 & 2, $45.00. Single copies $3.00 + 35¢ postage. Discounts: trade 40% through Carrier Pigeon, 10% bulk, orders under 25, 20% orders 25 or over, agents, 20%. 96pp; 6X8¼; of. Reporting time: 6 months. Payment: In kind. Copyrighted, reverts to author. Pub's reviews: 2 in 1979. §women; feminism; social, political and economic change. Ads: $120.00/$70.00/none. COSMEP.

QUEST, Human Kinetics Pub. Inc., E. Dean Ryan, Box 5076, Champaign, IL 61820, 217-351-5076. 1975. Articles, reviews. "Scholarly journals." circ. 2,300. 2/yr. Pub'd 2 issues 1979; expects 2 issues 1980, 2 issues 1981. sub. price: $12.00; per copy: $7.00; sample: free. Back issues: $7.00. Discounts: 5%. 144pp; 6X9; of. Reporting time: 2 months. Copyrighted. Pub's reviews. §Sport, sport science, physical education. Ads: $150.00/$90.00.

Quest Press, Albert Eglash, Box 998, San Luis Obispo, CA 93406, (805) 543-8500. 1979. "Publishes books in the field of psychology. Current publications are limited to the field of communication: in these texts, a humanistic alternative to assertion training is being offered." Pub'd 3 titles 1979; expects 5 titles 1980. 10 titles listed in the *Small Press Record of Books in Print* (9th Edition, 1980). avg. price, paper: $20.00. Discounts: open to negotiation. 150pp; 8½X11; of. Payment: open to negotiation. Copyrights for author. COSMEP.

334

Quick Books (see LOOK QUICK)

Quicksilver Productions, Jim Maynard, Theresa Jaye Dickson, P.O.Box 340, Ashland, OR 97520, (503) 482-5343. 1973. avg. press run 12,000. Pub'd 6 titles 1979; expects 8 titles 1980, 9 titles 1981. 5 titles listed in the *Small Press Record of Books in Print* (9th Edition, 1980). avg. price, paper: $4.95. Discounts: Trade and jobbers, (trade discounts from 40% at 3 copies to 50%) at 1,000 mixed titles. 150pp; of. Reporting time: 2 months or less. Payment: 7½ to 10% of retail, paid twice annually. Copyrights for author. WIP.

QUILT, Ishmael Reed, Al Young, 2140 Shattuck Ave., Room 311, Berkeley, CA 94704, (415) 527-1586. 1980. Poetry, fiction, articles, art, photos, interviews, satire, criticism, reviews, parts-of-novels. "Multi-cultural fiction, poetry and criticism. Recent contributors: Bob Callahan, Frank Chin, Mei-mei Berssenbrugge, Jessica Hagedorn, Joy Harjo, Gearld Hobson, Deborah Major, Alurista, Floyd Salas, Ralph Ellison (interview), John A. Williams, Chancellor Williams, Ivan Van Sertima, Al Young, Ishmael Reed. No unsolicited manuscripts" circ. 2,500. twice yearly. Expects 2 issues 1980, 2 issues 1981. price per copy: $4.95. Discounts: standard to trade. 150pp; 5½X9; of. Payment: for special issues. Copyrighted. Pub's reviews. CCLM.

QUINDARO, Fred Whitehead, PO Box 5224, Kansas City, KS 66119, (913) 342-6379. 1978. Poetry, fiction, articles, interviews, criticism, reviews, news items. "Instigates, fosters and otherwise prints or encourages native and midwestern radical, socialist, communist and insurrectionary literature, of the past, present and all future generations. A shoestring publication for those who can scarely afford shoes, and a refuge for mad sinners. Has included Vincent Ferrini, Pablo Neruda, David Cumberland, Truman Nelson, a memorial meeting for Edward Dahlberg, etc." circ. 300. Pub'd 4 issues 1979. sub. price: $5.00; per copy: $1.50; sample: $1.50. 35pp; 8½X111; mi. Reporting time: 2 weeks. Payment: One or two copies and the honor of our company of visionaries. Copyrighted, reverts to author. Pub's reviews. §Radicalism, Saints and Sinner Visionaries, Communists, Anarchists, Socialists.

Quintessence Publications, Marlan Beilke, Irene Beilke, 356 Bunker Hill Mine Road, Amador City, CA 95601, 209-267-5470. 1976. Poetry, articles, art, photos, criticism, plays. "Initial publication is the 356 page *Shining Clarity: God And Man In The Works Of Robinson Jeffers,* [14th March, 1978]. Nominated for 1978 National Book Awards Category: contemporary thought. This book (hard-cover) is an indepth consideration of Jeffers' views of the human and the divine; hence, it is literary commentary more so than literary criticism. 50 complete Jeffers poems (one hitherto unpublished) included therein. Contributors: poets: Gary Elder and Bill Hotchkiss. Photographers: Horace Lyon and Karl Bissinger. Artists: Lumir Sindelar and Kenneth Jack. Critic: Dr. James D. Hart, Director, The Bancroft Library. The book will be issued in two states: 900 copies of trade edition; 100 copies in a slip-cased, signed edition featuring; bronze medal [weighing 2¾ths lb.] of Robinson Jeffers, unpublished black and white photographs, ms facsimile, etc." avg. press run 1,000. Pub'd 2 titles 1979. 8 titles listed in the *Small Press Record of Books in Print* (9th Edition, 1980). avg. price, cloth: $25.00; other: $100.00 (separate edition). Discounts: Trade, 5 or more copies-40 percent: others, by arrangement. 350pp; 8X6¼; †of/lp. Reporting time: 2 weeks. Payment: by arrangement. Copyrights for author.

QUIXOTE, QUIXOTL, Quixote Press and Quixote Center Press, The anti-capitalist renegade marxist wordslingers collective., PO Box 70013, Houston, TX 77007, 608-251-6401. 1868. Cartoons, art, letters, music, photos. "Fighting the rotten regionalist tradition promoted by the National Endowment to buy off the arts. Raking the embers of the 60s for fire in the 80s. Recent contributors: Red River Press, d.a. levy,charles bukowski, Karl Marx, Tom Horn, Portugee Phillips, Verona Tallina, Ed Ochester, rjs, Marge Piercy, New York Times investigative reporters. Have buried the genteel tradition of Warren Woessner and hexed jetset dilletantism of Kostelanetz. Appreciate seeing personal letters, manifestos, pro-revolutionary work. Special attention as ever to manuscripts from Madison, Cleveland, Poland, Texas and dirt on COSMEP or other elements of the petty bourgeiosie." circ. 500. 3 Angstroms/month-12 issues/yr. Pub'd 12 issues 1979; expects 25 issues 1980, 15 issues 1981. 5 titles listed in the *Small Press Record of Books in Print* (9th Edition, 1980). sub. price: $12.00; per copy: $1.00; sample: 50 zlty. Back issues: no, we have some side issues. Discounts: .001 percent to Bowker agents. 80pp; size varies; †of. Reporting time: 4 months to 40 years. Payment: copies, kewpies, cowpies. Copyrighted, to authors to stop that damn Reilly from ripping off. Pub's reviews: 40 in 1979. §satire, humor, fiction, marxist leninist maoist thought, anarchism, workers stuff. Ads: $3000.-00/$150.00/$0.07. CCLM, APS, LPS, CIO-AFL, NFL, BBC, PTA, TACL.

Quixote Press and Quixote Center Press (see QUIXOTE, QUIXOTL)

qwertyuiop, Reductio Ad Asparagus Press, Jim Coe, Editor, P.O. Box 15193, Columbus, OH 43215. 1977. Poetry, art, photos, cartoons, collages, concrete art. "Truly experimental; I publish some 'misses' as well as hits." circ. 100-200. 3-4/yr. sub. price: $5.00; per copy: $1.00; sample: $1.00. Back issues: out of print (hordes of collectors). 20-30pp; 8½X11; mi/of. Reporting time: immediately. Payment: Can't do it, except in copies. Not copyrighted. §Collage-art-photo; experimental writing; concrete.

R

R & D Services, Ron Playle, PO Box 644, Des Moines, IA 50303, 515-262-5397. 1971. "Publishes 'How-To-Win' booklets in many fields; money making opportunities, contests, etc." avg. press run 15,000. Pub'd 12 titles 1979; expects 12 titles 1980. 10 titles listed in the *Small Press Record of Books in Print* (9th Edition, 1980). avg. price, paper: $3.95. Discounts: trade: 50 percent & up, libraries: 25 percent. 32pp; 8½X11; of. Reporting time: 1 month. Payment: outright purchase (no royalty). Copyrights for author.

R & J Kudlay (see also PUCK'S CORNER), Robert Kudlay, Joanne Kudlay, 105 Clark Street, Easthampton, MA 01027, (617) 281-3665. 1978. Poetry, articles. "Most of our publications are the result of articles and authors first appearing in *Puck's Corner.*" avg. press run 300. Expects 5 titles 1980, 6 titles 1981. 4 titles listed in the *Small Press Record of Books in Print* (9th Edition, 1980). avg. price, paper: $1.50. Discounts: 50% (5 or more copies). 16pp; 6X9; of. Reporting time: 1 month. Payment: 15% (total paid upon publication). Copyrights for author.

R & M Publishing Company, Inc, Mack B. Dr. Morant, Bobby III Roberts, Ms. Mosezelle Nichols, PO Box 210, Marion, SC 29571, (803) 423-6711, 423-5047. 1978. "We publish all kinds of materials that are quality. However, we are most interested in socio-psychological materials in the form of proses and historical documentations, and educational, (How to materials)." avg. press run 1,-000-2,000. Pub'd 2 titles 1979; expects 1 title 1980. avg. price, paper: $3.50. Discounts: 40-60%. 5¼X8¼; lp. Reporting time: 4 to 5 weeks or less. Payment: negotiable. Copyrights for author. COSMEP.

RCP Publications (see also REVOLUTION), Box 3486, Chicago, IL 60654, 312-663-5920. "Most written by Bob Avakian, Chairman of Central Committee, RCP, or written under his direction." Expects 3 titles 1980, 3 titles 1981. avg. price, cloth: $12; paper: $5. Discounts: standard trade 40%, 20% for schools. 350pp.

RK Editions (see also PRECISELY), P.O. Box 73 Canal Sta., New York, NY 10013. 1977. Poetry, fiction, articles, art, photos, interviews, satire, criticism, reviews, music, long-poems, concrete art. "RK Editions is devoted exclusively to the works, mostly recycled and thus unavailable elsewhere, of Richard Kostelanetz. No submissions; this is not that kind of alternative publisher. RK is involved with other presses." avg. press run 1500. Pub'd 2 titles 1979; expects 3 titles 1980, 1 title 1981. 29 titles listed in the *Small Press Record of Books in Print* (9th Edition, 1980). avg. price, cloth: $20.00; paper: $5.00. Discounts: 40% to legitimate dealers, paying in advance, and including postage. As only a few copies remain of most titles, these never go on consignment; more plentiful titles such as *Grants & The Future of Literature,* can be consigned. 200pp; 6X9; of. Copyrights for author.

R.S.H. Publications Worldwide (see also CS JOURNAL), R. Sublett Hawkins, Publisher & Promoter.

RACCOON, St. Luke's Press, David Spicer, Editor, 1407 Union, Suite 401, Mid-Memphis Tower, Memphis, TN 38104, (901) 357-5441. 1976. Poetry, criticism, reviews. "Dark image, surreal, affirmative, woodsy; 15-35 lines. Poetry that expresses a need to be written; no brilliantly clever tidbits. First issue: Bruchar, Hogen, Stependev, Stokes, Cooley, Wild, Page, others. In association with St. Luke's Press." circ. 500. 1/yr. Pub'd 2 issues 1979; expects 2 issues 1980, 1 issue 1981. sub. price: $6.25; per copy: $6.25; sample: $6.25. Back issues: $5.00, #1 & #3 & #6 temporarily out-of-print. Discounts: Distributed nationally by Bookslinger and Spring Church and, to the trade, by Ebsco, Inc., and Faxon, Inc. under their respective schedules. 64pp; 6X9; of. Reporting time: 3 to 6 months. Payment: copies. Copyrighted, reverts to author. Pub's reviews: 6 in 1979. §Poetry. Ads: no ads. COSMEP.

Racz Publishing Co., Jeanette G. Racz, Business Manager, PO Box 287, Oxnard, CA 93032, (805) 642-1186. 1973. avg. press run 3,000. Pub'd 2 titles 1979; expects 2 titles 1980, 5 titles 1981. 6 titles listed in the *Small Press Record of Books in Print* (9th Edition, 1980). avg. price, cloth: $10.00; paper: $7.00. 200pp; 6X9; of. Payment: annually. Copyrights for author.

RADICAL AMERICA, Collective, 38 Union Square, Somerville, MA 02143, (617) 623-5110. 1967. Articles. circ. 5,000. 6/yr. Pub'd 6 issues 1979; expects 6 issues 1980. sub. price: $10.00; per copy: $2.00; sample: $2.00. Back issues: apply. Discounts: 40%. 80pp; 7X8½; of. Reporting time: month. Payment: none. Copyrighted, reverts to author. Pub's reviews: 20 in 1979. §politics/history/film/sociology/feminism. Ads: $100/$50/none.

RADICAL BOOKSELLER, Editorial Collective, R. B. Birchcliffe, Hebder Bridge, Yorkshire, United Kingdom. 1980. Articles, photos, cartoons, interviews, letters, news items. "Trade magazine, for libraries, booksellers, academics, and radical/alternative/socialist book buying public. Pilot isssue available. Offices shortly to move to Manchester (adress not yet known)." circ. 2,000-5,000. sub. price: £10.00; sample: £20.00. 16-24pp; size A4; of. Payment: minimal.

RADICAL TEACHER, Reamy Jansen, Susan O'Malley, 320 Riverside Drive #13D, New York, NY 10025. 1975. Articles, photos, interviews, criticism, letters, news items. "*Radical Teacher* is concerned with the unity of radical post-secondary, interdivciplinary, educational theory and practice, with special emphasis on three areas: classroom practice, such as descriptions of successful courses; the political economy of higher education, such as part-time teaching, retrenchment, the Carnegie Commission; revising the literary canon to include working class, feminist, Black and Thirld World writing. Business address: PO Box 102, Kendall Square Post Office, Cambridge MA 02139" circ. 1500. 4/yr. Pub'd 4 issues 1979; expects 4 issues 1980, 4 issues 1981. sub. price: $8.00/yr ($4.00/yr low income or unemployed); per copy: $3.00; sample: $3.00. Back issues: $2.00. Discounts: usually 40%. Back issues, 6-25 copies: $1.80/issue; over 25 copies: $1.20/issue. 40pp; 8 1/2X11; of. Reporting time: 2 months. Payment: none. Copyrighted, reverts to author. Pub's reviews: 1 in 1979. Ads: $75.00/$40.-00/$25.00 1/4 page.

RAGGED READIN', G.F. Edwards, Box 1461, Lawton, OK 73502, (405) 248-6870. 1976. Fiction, articles, interviews, reviews, letters, cartoons. "200-1500 words. Bennie Bengtson, Gerald Cielec, Al Manachino." circ. 1000. quarterly. Pub'd 1 issue 1979; expects 3 issues 1980, 4 issues 1981. sub. price: $4.00/6 issues; per copy: 75¢; sample: 75¢. Back issues: $1.00. Discounts: none. 24pp; 8½X11; †of. Reporting time: 15-90 days. Payment: 30¢/col inch on publication. Not copyrighted. Pub's reviews: 14 in 1979. §Books, small press mags. Ads: $15.00/$8.00/2½¢.

RAIN: JOURNAL OF APPROPRIATE TECHNOLOGY, The Rain Umbrella, Carlotta Collette, Mark Roseland, Co-editors, 2270 NW Irving Street, Portland, OR 97210, 503-227-5110. 1974. Articles, art, photos, cartoons, interviews, reviews, letters, news items, non-fiction. "Entries, blurbs, catalog-style, how-to, living lightly, community communications, short, networks, new ideas, right idea at the right time & place, models, patterns, solar, wind, energy conservation, recycling, small-scale neighborhood businesses, land use, utility rate reform, urban gardening, agriculture, video, alternative lifestyles, appropriate technologies, institutional size, scale & style." circ. 5,000. 10/yr. Pub'd 10 issues 1979; expects 10 issues 1980. sub. price: $15.00 ($7.50 Living Lightly); per copy: $1.50; sample: $1.50. Back issues: $1.00 each if still available, prior to August 1978; $1.50 from that date on. Discounts: 10 or more, 40 percent (60 percent of retail); 100 or more, 60 percent (40 percent of retail). 24pp; 8½X11; of. Reporting time: 2 months. Payment: None. Copyrighted, reverts to author. Pub's reviews. §Appropriate technologies in all areas of U.S. life. Ads: None.

The Rain Umbrella (see also RAIN: JOURNAL OF APPROPRIATE TECHNOLOGY), 2270 NW Irving St, Portland, OR 97210. 12 titles listed in the *Small Press Record of Books in Print* (9th Edition, 1980).

RAINBOW'S END, Publishing Associates, Ink Blot Press, Geraldo Earl, 432 Heathcliff Drive, Pacifica, CA 94044, (415) 355-3630. 1979. Poetry, cartoons. "Children's poetry (by and for)" circ. 500. 5/yr. Pub'd 2 issues 1979. sub. price: $5.95; per copy: $1.25; sample: $1.00. Back issues: $1.00. Discounts: 33⅓%. 32pp; 5½X8; of. Reporting time: 10 days. Payment: copies. Copyrighted, reverts to author. Ads: $25.00/$15.00/$1.00 + $0.10 word.

RAINCOAST CHRONICLES, Harbour Publishing, Howard White, Box 119, Madeira Park, BC V0N2H0, Canada. 1972. Poetry, fiction, articles, art, reviews, parts-of-novels. "The magazines prime concern is the history and culture of the British Columbia coast. We publish mainly articles on coast history, with the occasional poem or short story. Literary merit is at least as important as historical accuracy. Recent contributors have been Peter Trower, Pat Lane, John Kelly, Scott Lawrence, and many writers never published before." circ. 5M. Irreg. Pub'd 2 issues 1979. sub. price: $8.00/4 issues; per copy: $2.95; sample: $2.95. Discounts: schools & libraries 20%, bookstores 40%, distributors 50%. 56pp; 7½X10½; of. Reporting time: 4 wks. Payment: Articles $.05 a word; poems $25.00. Pub's reviews. §British Columbia history and literature. Ads: No ads.

Raindust Press, David Briscoe, Frank Higgins, PO Box 1823, Independence, MO 64055. 1975. "Have published 10 books by Dave Etter, Sylvia Wheeler, Peter Sears, Tom McAfee. One dollar a piece.will move to full length books this year." avg. press run 500. Pub'd 1 title 1979; expects 1 title 1980. avg. price, paper: $3.00. Discounts: 50% for classroom adoptions. 50pp; 5½X8½; of. Reporting time: 5 weeks. Payment: standard royalties.

Rainfeather Press, Steven B. Rogers, PO Box 831, College Park, MD 20740. 1978. Poetry, long-poems. "We are just getting started. Interested in printing series of chapbooks containing works of one particular poet or the work of a single translator (mainly for bilingual editions). Possibilities also exist for anthologies." Pub'd 2 titles 1979; expects 2 titles 1980. avg. price, paper: $2.50-$3.50. 25-40pp; 4¼X5½; †xerox. Reporting time: up to 1 month. Payment: 1-3 copies. Copyrights for author.

Raintree, Fredric Brewer, 4043 Morningside Dr, Bloomington, IN 47401, 812-332-6561. 1975. Poetry, satire, criticism, long-poems. "Have no interest in obscure, muddled writing. Recent writers: Phyllis Janowitz, Judith Roman, F. Richard Thomas, Roger Mitchell, Richard Pflum, Willis Barnstone, William Seibel. All mss. are solicited by Raintree. We do not read unsolicited material." avg. press run 100. Pub'd 8 titles 1979; expects 4 titles 1980, 7 titles 1981. 16 titles listed in the *Small Press Record of Books in Print* (9th Edition, 1980). avg. price, cloth: $10.00 to $75.00; paper: varies; from $4 to $8. Discounts: trade 1-4 copies 25%, 5-49 33%, 50-99 39%, 100-more 40%. pp varies; size varies; †lp. Reporting time: 1 month. Payment: royalties and copies. Copyrighted in name of author. Rights are negotiated.

Rainy Day Books, Richard W Jennings, 2812 W 53rd Street, Fairway, KS 66205, 913-384-3126. 1975. Poetry, fiction, art, photos. "Specialize in elementary educational materials dealing with self-aware-ness, preparation for adult conflict and crises, most recent titles: *LISA IS A CLOUD, EDWARD IS A RAINBOW, HAPPY APPLE AND THE MYSTERIOUS MONSTER FROM OUTER SPACE, YIKES!, POPCORN, THE TRAGIC TALE OF THE DOG WHO KILLED HIMSELF.*" avg. press run 5,000. Pub'd 2 titles 1979. 4 titles listed in the *Small Press Record of Books in Print* (9th Edition, 1980). avg. price, paper: $1.95. Discounts: 40% off retail to trade and educators. 48pp; 6X9; of. Reporting time: 30 days. Payment: negotiated. Copyrights for author.

Rainy Day Press, Mike Helm, PO Box 3035, Eugene, OR 97403, (503) 484-4626. 1978. "Rainy Day Press began as a way for me to have my own writing published, a direct result of my having read the *Publish-It-Yourself Handbook* and of my frustration at playing transcontinental ping-pong with my manuscripts. So far I have published a guide book for Eugene, Oregon, and a book on doing one's own legal work for adoption. At this point I am more interested in being a writer than a publisher, though one begets the other. I am not seeking manuscript submissions because I am primarily interested in getting my own writing projects off the ground" avg. press run 1,000. Pub'd 3 titles 1979; expects 4 titles 1980, 4 titles 1981. avg. price, paper: $4.25. Discounts: 40% with 25 books purchased, 30% for purchase of 15-24 books, 20% for 5-14 books, 10% for purchase of less than 5 books. 100pp; 5½X8½; of.

RAM, THE LETTER BOX, Eleanor Ramirez, Editor B.S. & A.; Alphonse F. (B.A.) Ramirez, 430 4th st, Brooklyn, NY 11215, (212) SO8-5415. 1976. "Poetry all types, also religious poetry, 16 line limit. Short paragraphs also on interesting topics. Subscription entitles poet to publication of approved poems in every issue. See our Rule & Regulations and obey all paragraphs. No off-color or obscene poems; if we receive, no return." circ. 200 or more. 4/yr. Pub'd 4 issues 1979; expects 4 issues 1980, 4 issues 1981. sub. price: $10.00 (plus $.40 each postage and handling for foreign countries); per copy: $2.50; sample: $2.50. Back issues: $2.50 each. Discounts: none. 40-50 pp or more—140-160pp; 5½X11. Reporting time: one month. Payment: None. Copyrighted, reverts to author. Ads: No ads.

Ram Publications, Ronald Fouts, Morris Jackson, Art Director, 1710 Connecticut Ave. NW, Washing-ton, DC 20009, (202) 338-4666. 1978. Art, photos. "No limit to length of material. Interested in photographic statements, travel/foreign photo-interest material. Recent contributors include E. Yanowitz, Lynnette Rushak, John T. Bledsoe, Jim Wilson, Bethann Thornburgh." avg. press run 5,000. Expects 1 title 1980, 5 titles 1981. avg. price, paper: $8.95. Discounts: Negotiable, in the area of 40-65% retail price. 80-100pp; 9X11; of. Reporting time: 2-4 weeks depending on subject matter. Payment: 10-12% of retail sales when work is by principal author. Copyrights for author.

RaMar Press, Ralph W. Elspass, Seven Lakes Box 548, West End, NC 27376, (919) 673-0571. 1979. Art. "First publication due in the spring of 1980. *Tips and Notes for the Artist* by Margy Lee Elspass. Over 250 illustrations. About 25,000 words." avg. press run 500-1,000. avg. price, paper: $10.00. Discounts: 10% schools, colleges, universities/25% libraries. 100pp; 8½X11; of. Copyrights for author.

Ramparts Press, Russell Stetler, Bo 50128, Palo Alto, CA 94303, (415) 325-7861. 1969. "Ramparts publishes books mainly on current affairs, politics, philosophy, sociology, econimics, gay liberation, nuclear power, marxst literary criticism, etc." avg. press run 8,000. Pub'd 4 titles 1979; expects 4 titles 1980, 4 titles 1981. avg. price, cloth: $14.00; paper: $5.95. Discounts: 5-49, 40% Trade; text 20%. 350pp; 5½X8; of. Reporting time: varies, 1-2 months. Payment: usually 10% on hardcover, 7½% on paperback. Copyrights for author.

rara avis, Jacqueline De Angelis, Aleida Rodriguez, P.O. Box 3095, Terminal Annex, Los Angeles, CA 90051. 1978. Poetry, fiction, criticism, reviews, parts-of-novels, long-poems, plays, articles, interviews. "We would like to see fresh use of language; revamping of the old style, or the most successful example of it. Recent contributors: James Krusoe, Eloise Klein Healy, Holly Prado, Lynn Luria-Sukenick.We have no preference as to length of material. We are especially interested in work by lesbians, Spanish translations and translations of women writers regardless of original language, reviews. We would like to see fresh use of language. Recent contributors include: Alice Bloch, Eloise Klein Healy, Judith Hemschemeyer, Alicia Ostriker, Holly Prado, Jane Rule." circ. 500-1000. 3/yr. Expects 3 issues 1980, 3 issues 1981. sub. price: $8.00; per copy: $3.00; sample: $3.00. Discounts: 40% bookstores for orders of 5 or more. 70pp; size varies but usually 5½X8½; of. Reporting time: 4-6 weeks. Payment: 2 copies. Copyrighted, reverts to author. Pub's reviews. §poetry, women, gays, translations. Ads: $75.00/$50.00/$25.00 for 1/4 page. CCLM, COSMEP.

RAS Communications/Blind Eye Publishing House/Blind Eye Books/Jasmine (see also SUNRISE), Randy Stables, 3620 52nd Avenue, Apt. 204, Red Deer, Alberta T4N 4J5, Canada, 406-347-2583. 1978. Poetry, fiction, art, cartoons, long-poems, concrete art. "No Profanity, No Pornography. Science fiction manuscripts needed, fantasy, manuscripts wanted, haiku, tanka, poetry, manuscripts needed. Longpoems needed." avg. press run 200. Expects 4-5 titles 1981. avg. price, paper: $3.75. Discounts: $9.00 for 3 copies, $18.00 for 6 copies, $20.00 for 10 copies. 50-60pp; 5½X8; of. Reporting time: 1 month. Payment: negotiable. Copyrights for author.

RASPBERRY PRESS (magazine), Susan Hauser, Rte. 6 Box 459, Bemidji, MN 56601, 218-751-8497. 1974. Poetry, articles, art, satire, letters, criticism. "No unsolicited submissions-return of unsolicited mss. immediately. Focus of each issue determined by whim of editor. R.P. 3 is poetry by Rich Behm. Work by: Carol Heckman, Beth Copeland, Tina Matthews, Judith Dunaway. R.P. 4/5 - a double issue, anthology format. R.P. 6 not scheduled." circ. 300. Annual. Pub'd 1 issue 1979; expects 1 issue 1980. 3 titles listed in the *Small Press Record of Books in Print* (9th Edition, 1980). sub. price: $2.00; per copy: $2.00; sample: $2.00. Back issues: R.P. 2, $1.00; R.P. 3, $2.00. Discounts: None. 50pp; size varies; †mi. Reporting time: 1 week. Payment: copy. Copyrighted. no ads.

Rat & Mole Press (see also STONY HILLS: The New England Alternative Press Review), Ritchie Darling, P.O. Box 111, Amherst, MA 01002. 1971. Poetry, fiction, satire, criticism. avg. press run 1,000. Pub'd 3 titles 1979; expects 4 titles 1980. avg. price, paper: $2.00. Discounts: bookstores, 40%; bulk order, 10%. 50pp; 5½X8½; 6X9; 7X8½; of/lp. Reporting time: 6 months. Payment: $10 per poem; prose by arrangement. Copyrights for author. COSMEP, NESPA.

The Rateavers, Bargyla Rateaver, Gylver Rateaver, Pauma Valley, CA 92061, (714) 566-8994. 1973. "Organic gardening and farming, conservation methods, reprints or abstracts, mostly." avg. press run 2,500-3,000. Pub'd 1 title 1979. 8 titles listed in the *Small Press Record of Books in Print* (9th Edition, 1980). avg. price, paper: $10.00. Discounts: none. 300pp; 5½X8½; of. Payment: percentage to author. Copyrights for author.

The Rather Press, Clifton Rather, Lois Rather, 3200 Guido Street, Oakland, CA 94602, (415) 531-2938. 1968. "We are a strictly self-contained private press, print only mss. we write ourselves, in editions of 150 usually. We do hard-cover books and small paperback items as gifts for friends." avg. press run 150. Pub'd 3 titles 1979; expects 3 titles 1980, 3 titles 1981. 10 titles listed in the *Small Press Record of Books in Print* (9th Edition, 1980). avg. price, cloth: $25.00. Discounts: 25% for purchase of 2 or more copies. 100pp; 6½X10; †lp.

Rationalist Press Association (see NEW HUMANIST)

Raven Publications (see also URBANE GORILLA), Ed Tork, 29 Parkers Road, Sheffield S10 1BN, United Kingdom, Sheff. 664-862. 1970. Poetry, fiction, articles, art, criticism, reviews, parts-of-novels, long-poems, news items. "ISSN 0142 - 128X" avg. press run 1,000. Pub'd 2 titles 1979; expects 2 titles 1980, 2 titles 1981. avg. price, paper: 75p/$5.00 (inc. p&p). Discounts: Rate on enquiry. 80pp; size A5; of. Reporting time: 2-3 months. Payment: None. Copyrights for author. ALP.

Raw Dog Press, R. Gerry Fabian, 129 Worthington Ave, Doylestown, PA 18901, (215) 345-7692. 1977. Poetry, photos, long-poems, collages. "Looking for books by authors who understand the terrible economics of poetry, very limited budget at present time. Manuscript length should be between 20-40 pages. When you try us, expect nothing and anything else is a bonus. Be sure to enclose the correct S.A.S.E. Published *Zip Codes Required* by R. Gerry Fabian and *The Circle is Never Broken* by Martin Willitts Jr. in 1980." avg. press run 300-500. Pub'd 1 title 1979; expects 2 titles 1980, 2 titles 1981. avg. price, paper: $2.00+; other: $2.00 & up. Discounts: Will negotiate and haggle with anyone. pp varies; 5X7; †of. Reporting time: 1 month. Payment: This varies with the material but we will work something out (copies +). copyright is agreed upon.

RE:PRINT (AN OCCASIONAL MAGAZINE), The Printable Arts Society, Inc., David Ferguson, c/o BOX 749, Box 749 Old Chelsea Station, New York, NY 10011. 1973. Poetry, fiction, satire, long-poems. "*RE:PRINT,* an occasional magazine, has been established to print and sell separately works of general interest that have been published in BOX 749 (another publication of Seven Square Press) and other magazines. We run 5000 of each issue and sell the copies until the print run is sold out. So far two stories have been published in the *RE:PRINT* series; we welcome the calling of our attention to other exceptional already-published work. Submissions only on request." circ. 5,000. 1/yr. price per copy: $.75; sample: $.75. 8-16pp; 4¼X11; †of. Payment: copies. Copyrighted. COS-MEP, NESPA.

REACHING, Lillie D. Chaffin, 105 Ratliffs Creek, Pikeville, KY 41501, 432-0500. 1978. Poetry. circ. 200. 1/yr. Pub'd 1 issue 1979; expects 1 issue 1980. sub. price: $1.50; per copy: $1.50; sample: $1.50. Back issues: $1.50. Discounts: 40%. 48pp; 4X5½; of. Reporting time: 1 week. Payment: copies. Copyrighted, reverts to author. §Poetry. Ads: $10.00/$5.00.

Real Free Press Foundation (see also WIPE OUT), R. Olaf Stoop, Martin Beumer, Dirk van Hasseltssteeg 25, Amsterdam, The Netherlands. 1965. Articles, interviews. "6-8 publications per year. Unasked submissions are unwanted." avg. press run 2,000. 15 titles listed in the *Small Press Record of Books in Print* (9th Edition, 1980). avg. price, paper: $2.50. Discounts: 30%. 32pp; 6½X9; of. APS.

Realities (see also OCCASIONAL REVIEW; POETRY BOOK AWARD), Soos, 1976 Waverly Ave, San Jose, CA 95122, (408)251-9562. 1974. "Currently publishing 24 page chapbooks by single authors. Persons with new projects in mind should contact me. Realities Library is a non-profit corp. Current seller is Poetry Book Award winner, James Marvelle: *Standing On My Head,* $1.95 + $0.95 postage." avg. press run 350-500. Pub'd 6 titles 1979; expects 3 titles 1980, 6-10 titles 1981. 16 titles listed in the *Small Press Record of Books in Print* (9th Edition, 1980).

Rebis Press, Betsy Davids, Jim Petrillo, P.O. Box 2233, Berkeley, CA 94702, 415-527-3845. 1972. Poetry, fiction, art, parts-of-novels, long-poems, concrete art. "We're overloaded and are not encouraging unsolicited mss. at this time. Publish 1-2 books a year." avg. press run 150-300. Expects 2 titles 1980, 1 title 1981. 5 titles listed in the *Small Press Record of Books in Print* (9th Edition, 1980). avg. price, other: $30.00. Discounts: Trade 40 percent. 32pp; size varies; †of/lp. Reporting time: 6 mos. or longer. Payment: royalties. Copyright for author.

REBUTTAL! The Bicentennial Newsletter of Truth, The First Ozark Press, Mary Bell, P.O. Box 1126, Branson, MO 65616. 1976. Criticism, reviews. "Vivid comment on national and international people, places, and events...with some emphasis on finding the truth in matters of political, educational, and medical nature. A look behind the mass media into what is really happening from the people's viewpoint. Staff-written." 24/yr. sub. price: $24.00 indiv; $36.00 instit.; per copy: $2.00; sample: $2.00. 4-8pp; 8½X11; †of. staff-written. Copyrighted. Pub's reviews: 15 in 1979.

RECON, Recon Publications, Chris Robinson, Editor; Lewis Bellis, Business Manager, P.O. Box 14602, Philadelphia, PA 19134. 1973. Articles, cartoons, interviews, reviews. "a monthly publication dealing with revolutionary military affairs: expose Pentagon planning, revolutionary strategy & tactics, GI movement, Third World struggles, women in the military, last issue 12/76." circ. 2,000. 12/yr. sub. price: $10.00; sample: $.50. Back issues: $20/year. 12pp; 8½X11; of. Reporting time: within a week. Payment: copies only. Pub's reviews. §politics/the military/history/geography. Ads: $40/$20/$.05-word. COSMEP.

Recon Publications (see also RECON), Chris Robinson, Editor; Lewis Bellis, Business Manager, PO Box 14602, Philadelphia, PA 19134. 1973. avg. press run 2,000. 5 titles listed in the *Small Press Record of Books in Print* (9th Edition, 1980). of. COSMEP.

THE RECORD SUN, Poet Papers, Laimons Juris G, PO Box 528, Topanga, CA 90290. 1969. Poetry, articles, art, photos, cartoons, satire, criticism, reviews, music, letters, collages. "All work submitted MUST have Stamped Self-Addressed envelopes - or we do not reply. Most of our contributors are subscribers (whom *The Record Sun* is printed for!)" circ. we print 7,000. 4/yr. Pub'd 4 issues 1979; expects 4 issues 1980, 4 issues 1981. sub. price: $4.00; sample: $1.00. Back issues: First Issue Anniversary Issue $2.00. Discounts: Deal with retailers directly. 3-6pp; 8½X14; of/xerox. Reporting time: 2 years (Editorship rotates-and our Editors travel frequently). Payment: copies. Copyrighted, reverts to author. Pub's reviews: 3 in 1979. §Poetry, photography, graphics, cartoons, joy, fun, satire, statistics, information. Ads: $50.00/$1.00.

RECREATIONAL COMPUTING, People's Computer Co., Bob Albrecht, Louise Burton, Ramon Zamora, 1263 El Camino, P. O. Box E, Menlo Park, CA 94025, 415-323-3111. 1971. Articles, photos, cartoons, interviews, criticism, reviews, letters. "A periodical for novices & intermediate uses of personal and home computers. Published by a non-profit, educational company dedicated to demystifying personal and home computers. Publications: *What To Do After You Hit Return* and others." circ. 5,000-10,000. 6/yr. Pub'd 6 issues 1979; expects 6 issues 1980. sub. price: $10.00; per copy: $2.00. Back issues: $2.50-$3.00 (depending on issue). Discounts to resellers, bulk subscriptions, and subscription agencies. 48-64pp; of. Reporting time: 6 weeks maximum. Payment: none. Copyrighted. Pub's reviews: 16 in 1979. §computers & computers in education, futurism, science fiction, puzzles & games. Ads: $400.00/$240.00.

Red Alder Books, David Steinberg, Box 545, Ben Lomond, CA 95005. 1974. Poetry, criticism, music, letters. "We have published two books to date-YELLOW BRICK ROAD, a collection of writings by people who are developing alternative life styles, and *Welcome, Brothers*, collection of poems on changing men's consciousness other books of the growing men's movement will follow." avg. press run 1,000. Pub'd 1 title 1979; expects 2 titles 1980, 2 titles 1981. 3 titles listed in the *Small Press Record of Books in Print* (9th Edition, 1980). avg. price, paper: $2.00. Discounts: 40% (5 or more); 20% (2-4). 100pp; 6X9; of. Reporting time: 2 weeks. Payment varies. Copyrights for author. COSMEP.

Red Candle Press (see also CANDELABRUM POETRY MAGAZINE), M.L. McCarthy, Basil Wincote, 19 South Hill Park, London NW3 2ST, United Kingdom. 1970. Poetry, long-poems. "Poetry. The Red Candle Press provides a (free) service to poets and does not aim to make a profit. We usually approach authors for an anthology. The usual agreement is that the Red Candle Press shall first cover its expenses from sales, and thereafter any profit shall be divided 50-50 with the author, if the book has a single author. Our expenses are the printer's fee and postage. We give the author five free copies. Contibutors to anthologies receive one free copy." avg. press run 500. Expects 2 titles 1980. 6 titles listed in the *Small Press Record of Books in Print* (9th Edition, 1980). avg. price, paper: £1.50p for poetry. Discounts: 1/3rd to booksellers. 90pp/poetry; 5½X8; of/lp. Reporting time: 1 to 3 months. Copyrights for author.

RED CEDAR REVIEW, Lynn Domina, Stephen O'Keefe, 325 Morrill Hall, Dept. of English, Mich. State Univ., E. Lansing, MI 48824, 517-355-9656. 1965. Poetry, fiction, art, photos, interviews, criticism, reviews, parts-of-novels, long-poems. "We have no particular editorial bias-clarity is appreciated, sentimentality isn't. Some recent contributors: William Stafford, Diane Wakoski, Hugh Fox, Judith McCombs, Barbara Drake, Charles Edward Eaton, Dan Gerber, Herbert Scott. We're also open to new writers; we generally try to comment on promising work that we don't accept. In some cases, we ask for resubmissions-no guarantees, of course. In addition to poetry and fiction, we'd like to receive reviews, interviews, and graphic art for consideration. Our two annual issues come out around Dec./Jan. and May/June, but submissions are considered year-round." circ. 400. 2/yr. Pub'd 2 issues 1979; expects 2 issues 1980. 2 titles listed in the *Small Press Record of Books in Print* (9th Edition, 1980). sub. price: $4.00; per copy: $2.50; sample: $2.00 for current issue, $1.00 for previous issues. Back issues: $1.00. 64pp; 8½X5½; of. Reporting time: 2 wks to 1 mo. Payment: 3 copies. Copyrighted, reverts to author. Pub's reviews: 0 in 1979. §Poetry, fiction, translations, books, chapbooks, magazines, anthologies. no ads. CCLM.

Red Clay Books, Charleen Swansea, 6366 Sharon Hills Rd, Charlotte, NC 28210, 704-366-9624. 1964. Poetry, fiction, art. avg. press run 2,000. Pub'd 4 titles 1979. 8 titles listed in the *Small Press Record of Books in Print* (9th Edition, 1980). avg. price, paper: $3.00. Discounts: 40 percent-trade; 20 percent-universities. 72pp; 6X9; of/lp. Reporting time: 3 months. Payment: negotiable. Copyrights for author.

Red Dust, Joanna Gunderson, PO Box 630, Gracie Station, New York, NY 10028. 1963. Poetry, fiction. avg. press run 1,000-1,500. Pub'd 4 titles 1979; expects 3 titles 1980. 24 titles listed in the *Small Press Record of Books in Print* (9th Edition, 1980). avg. price, cloth: $10.00; paper: $4.50. Discounts: libraries 20 percent; wholesalers & booksellers 1 copy-30 percent, 2 or more-40 percent, paperback 1-4 copies-20 percent, 5 or more-40 percent. 140pp; size varies; of/lp. Reporting time: 2 mo. Payment: $300 advance against royalty. we copyright for author in most cases. COSMEP.

RED FOX REVIEW, James Coleman, Thomas Hendrick, Mohegan Community College, Norwich, CT 06360. 1974. Poetry, fiction, art, photos. "A Regional Publication-Connecticut Writers. We sponsor a poetry contest yearly, $100.00 prize. 157 entries/1975, 246 entries/1977. Fiction contest 1979." circ. 1,500. 1/yr. Pub'd 1 issue 1979. sub. price: $2.00; per copy: $2.00; sample: $1.00. Back issues: $1. Discounts: 40%. 90pp; 7X10; lp. Reporting time: 1 month. Payment: copies only. Copyrighted. COSMEP, NESPA.

Red Herring Press, Robert Bensen, Rich Michelson, Kay Murphy, c/o Channing-Murray Foundation, 1201 W Oregon, Urbana, IL 61801, (217) 367-8770. 1978. Poetry. "Titles available: *Family Photographs* by Leslie Bertagnolli; *The Head of the Family* by Richard Michelson. *The Champaign Letters and Other Poems* by Forrest Robinson; *Equinox* by Kathryn Kerr; and *The Last Resort* by Robert Bensen. We publish high quality chapbooks (preferably first books), generally by present or former members of the Red Herring Poetry Workshop, as well as an annual anthology *Matrix.*" avg. press run 500. Pub'd 2 titles 1979; expects 4 titles 1980, 4 titles 1981. avg. price, paper: $3.00. Discounts: Standard 40%. 30-50pp; 7X8 1/2; of. Not soliciting manuscripts at this time. Payment: 20% press run. Copyrights for author. COSMEP.

Red Hill Press, Los Angeles & Fairfax (see also INVISIBLE CITY), John McBride, Paul Vangelisti, 6 San Gabriel Dr, Fairfax, CA 94930. 1969. avg. press run 750. Pub'd 3 titles 1979. 52 titles listed in the *Small Press Record of Books in Print* (9th Edition, 1980). avg. price, cloth: $10.00; paper: $3.00. Discounts: consult Small Press Distribution (Berkeley). 48-80pp; size varies moving to 9X5½; of. Reporting time: Extended. Payment: Copies. author's/translator's retain c-right. COSMEP, CCLM.

Red Ochre Press, Ed Baker, 8215 Flower Ave, Takoma Park, MD 20012. 1970. Poetry. "What we like; any style; as we can. We like a run of poems up to 64 pgs. Sound. Movement. Light. Space. The page, the paper, the piece uncluttered." avg. press run 250. Expects 1 title 1980. 4 titles listed in the *Small Press Record of Books in Print* (9th Edition, 1980). avg. price, paper: $3.00. Discounts: 10 copies or more-40% 1-9 copies-30%. 70pp; 6X9; of. Reporting time: 1 month. Payment: 25% of combination of net sales & number of copies produced. Copyrights for author.

Red Press, Tom Thompson, Editor, PO Box 197, North Sydney, NSW 2060, Australia. 1978. Poetry, fiction, photos, parts-of-novels, collages, long-poems. "Deliberately stupid works encouraged." avg. press run 500. 3 titles listed in the *Small Press Record of Books in Print* (9th Edition, 1980). avg. price, paper: $3.00. Discounts: 40% - 45% bookshops; 50% - 55% distributors. 50pp; 1/2 foolscap; of. Reporting time: no submissions sought 1980. Payment: 15% royalties, 1/2 total in advance on publication of books.

‡**RED WEATHER, Red Weather Press,** Bruce Edward Taylor, Patricia V. Alea, PO Box 1104, Eau Claire, WI 54701, 715-834-9870. 1976. Poetry, fiction, articles, interviews, criticism, reviews, parts-of-novels, long-poems. "Marge Piercy, Albert Goldbarth, Charles Wright, Carol Muske, Walter Lowenfels, Maura Stanton, Maxine Kumin." circ. 1,000 per issue. 3/yr. Expects 3 issues 1980. sub. price: $3.75; per copy: $1.25; sample: $1.25. Back issues: $1.25. Discounts: 40 percent to bookstores, classrooms, agents, jobbers 6 or more copies. 24pp; 11X17; of. Reporting time: 60 days. Payment: none. Copyrighted, reverts to author. Pub's reviews. §poetry, short stories. Ads: $30.00/$15.00. COSMEP.

Red Weather Press (see also RED WEATHER), Bruce Edward Taylor, PO Box 1104, Eau Claire, WI 54701, 715-834-9870. 1976. Poetry. "First Chapbook in series, *Everywhere The Beauty Gives Itself Away* by Bruce Edward Taylor" avg. press run 400. avg. price, paper: $1.25. Discounts: 40 percent on 6 or more copies. 22pp; 5X4; of. Payment: none on first print, 50 percent on 2nd and subsequent printings. Copyrights for author. COSMEP.

Reductio Ad Asparagus Press (see also qwertyuiop), Jim Coe, Box 15193, Columbus, OH 43215. 1977. Poetry, art, photos, cartoons, collages, concrete art. "Truly experimental; we publish some 'misses' as well as hits. Recently published *MOBIUS NOVEL* by the late Grant Pass." avg. press run 100-200. 3 titles listed in the *Small Press Record of Books in Print* (9th Edition, 1980). avg. price, paper: $1.00. 20-30pp; 8½X11; mi/of. Reporting time: immediately. Payment: copies only. Copyrights for author.

Reed & Cannon Co, Ishmael Reed, Steve Cannon, Joe Johnson, 2140 Shattuck #311, Berkeley, CA 94704. Poetry, fiction. "no unsolicited manuscripts" avg. press run 2,000. Pub'd 5 titles 1979; expects 3 titles 1980, 2 titles 1981. 3 titles listed in the *Small Press Record of Books in Print* (9th Edition, 1980). avg. price, cloth: $10.00; paper: $2.95-$5.95. Discounts: standard to trade. pp varies widely; size varies; of.

Robert D. Reed Publisher, PO Box 8, Saratoga, CA 95070, (378-4843. "Publishing my own works right now, but looking for additional titles in the how to area - would like to continue to publish reviews on various subjects, with broad appeal. The most complete tool available on how and where to research your ethnic-American cultural heritage - these books will save you hundreds of hours of research time. They include how to find info - supplies you with pertinent addresses for - genealogy

- historical societies - cultural institutes - libraries - archives - publishers - gives search hints and key words - directories - bibliographies - info centers - encyclopedias - newspapers - radio - churches, with many references. If anyone asked you for aid in researching their ethnic-American cultural heritage, these guides would direct them to every major source available - includes bibliography of current in print books. German, Polish, Jewish, Italian, Scandinavian, Russian, Black, Irish, Chinese, Native, Japanese, Mexican" avg. press run 1,000. Pub'd 12 titles 1979. 1 title listed in the *Small Press Record of Books in Print* (9th Edition, 1980). avg. price, paper: $2.95. Discounts: 1-5, $2.95; 6-10, $2.75; 11-25, $2.50; 26-50, $2.25; 50 up, $1.75, california res. add 6½% sales tax. 32pp; 5½X8½; †of. Reporting time: 1 month. Payment: varies. Does not copyright for author.

REFERENCE BOOK REVIEW, Donna M. Northouse, Editor; Cameron Northouse, John Payne, Box 19954, Dallas, TX 75219. 1976. Reviews. "*RBR* publishes reviews of reference publications in all fields; average length for reviews: 300-500 words." circ. 1,000. 3/yr. Pub'd 4 issues 1979; expects 4 issues 1980, 4 issues 1981. sub. price: $11.00; per copy: $3.00; sample: $3.00. Back issues: $3.00 per issue/$11.00 per volume. Discounts: 10% (jobber). 40pp; 5½X8½; of. Reporting time: 1 week. Payment: copies. Copyrighted. Pub's reviews: 400 in 1979. §Reference publications in all fields.

REFERENCE SERVICES REVIEW, Pierian Press, Cecily Johns, Editor; Tom Schultheiss, Managing Editor, P.O. Box 1808, Ann Arbor, MI 48106, 313-434-5530. 1972. Reviews. "Library/reference." circ. 3,000. Quarterly. Pub'd 4 issues 1979; expects 4 issues 1980. sub. price: $25.00; per copy: $7.50; sample: Free. Back issues: Available. Discounts: None. 100pp; 8½X11; of. Reporting time: 1 week. Payment: None. Pierian Press holds copyright. Pub's reviews: 500 in 1979. §All subjects in reference format. Ads: $400.00/$270.00.

REFLECT, William S. Kennedy, 3306 Argonne Avenue, Norfolk, VA 23509, (804) 857-1097. 1979. Poetry, fiction, articles, art, cartoons, reviews, letters. "One way to describe the editorial policy of *Reflect* is to say it presents the question: Did you ever think of that? Following the truth wherever it may lead takes us into diverse fields, including science, philosophy, the occult. We use two or three short stories each issue, 2,500 word maximum. Articles usually average 1,000 words. Recent contributors: Mildred K. Henderson (Editor of *Hob Nob,* David Vadja, Robert Whisler, Jonathan Lowe, Madine M. Johnson (Bluebells and Silver Spurs), Clara Holton, Ronald W. Grossman, Cassie Edwards, Lucile Coleman, Mildred K. Henderson, Clara Holton." circ. 200. 4/yr. Pub'd 4 issues 1979; expects 4 issues 1980, 4 issues 1981. sub. price: $3.00; per copy: $0.75; sample: $0.75. Back issues: $0.50 (if available). 36pp; 5½X8½; †mi. Reporting time: 2 weeks. Payment: one contributor's copy. Not copyrighted. Pub's reviews: 4 in 1979. §Literary, poetry, general small press. Ads: $0.10 per word.

Regmar Publishing Co., Jane Horton, PO Box 11358, Memphis, TN 38111, (901) 324-0991. 1971. Fiction. avg. press run 5,000. Pub'd 1 title 1979. avg. price, cloth: $9.95. Discounts: Trade 40%; Librarians 20%. of. Reporting time: 2 months. Payment: usual 10-12-15%. Copyrights for author.

William A. Reilly, Publisher, William A. Reilly, PO Box 63, 6 Crest Drive, Dover, MA 02030. 1970. "Writings of Diane & William Swygard." avg. press run 10,000. Pub'd 2 titles 1979; expects 1 title 1980, 1 title 1981. 9 titles listed in the *Small Press Record of Books in Print* (9th Edition, 1980). avg. price, paper: $1.95-$7.95. Discounts: 50% net 30 days. 60-206pp; 5¼X8; 5X7¾; lp. Payment: yes. Copyrights for author. COSMEP.

Release Press (see also SOME), Larry Zirlin, Harry Greenberg, Alan Ziegler, 411 Clinton Street, Apt 8, Brooklyn, NY 11231. 1973. Poetry, fiction, art, photos, collages. "Books in print are *City Joys* by Jack Anderson, *Sleeping Obsessions* by Mercy Bona, *Rome In Rome* by Bill Knott, & *Lucky Darryl,* a collaborative novel by Bill Knott & James Tate. *The Touch Code* by John Love, *The Vanishings* by Philip Graham & *Pond* by Gay Phillipps. Not on the lookout for any more material as we have enough to keep us busy. Small Press Dist. Inc. is our distributor—please order from them. *On Sundays We Visit The In-Laws* by Steven Schrader, *In Search of Fred and Ethel Mertz* by Karen Hubert, *Intimate Apparel* by Terry Stokes, *The Sleepless Night of Eugene Delacroix* by John Yaw." avg. press run 1,000. Pub'd 2 titles 1979; expects 3 titles 1980. 11 titles listed in the *Small Press Record of Books in Print* (9th Edition, 1980). avg. price, paper: $3.00. Discounts: query Small Press Distribution, Inc. 72pp; 5½X8½; of. Reporting time: varies. Payment: 10% of the press run, 50/50 after we 'break even'. Copyrights for author. CCLM.

RELIX, Leslie D. Kippel, Publisher; Steve Kraye, East Coast Editor; Jeff Tamarkin, Senior Editor; Clark Peterson, West Coast Editor, PO Box 94, Brooklyn, NY 11229, 212-998-2039. 1972. Poetry, fiction, articles, art, photos, cartoons, interviews, satire, criticism, reviews, letters, music, news items. "Also known as *Dead Relix*. RELIX covers rock music from the late 1960's to present. With accent on San Francisco groups. New focus of magazine on top groups, i.e. Pink Floyd, Led Zeppelin, The Who, Rolling Stones, with accent on new wave i.e. Clash, AC/DC, Plasmatics, etc." circ. 20,000. 6/yr. Pub'd

6 issues 1979; expects 6 issues 1980. 1 title listed in the *Small Press Record of Books in Print* (9th Edition, 1980). sub. price: $9.00; per copy: $1.75; sample: $1.75. Back issues: $3.00 and up. Discounts: stores: $1.15 C.O.D. per copy, min. order $25.00 (full returns after 10); distributors: 50% + credit terms available. 52pp; 8½X11; of. Reporting time: 6 weeks before publication. Payment: photos average $15.00; articles, minimum of $1.00 per col. inch, more for cover stories or major articles. Copyrighted, does not revert to author. Pub's reviews: 50 in 1979. §rock music. Ads: $500/$275/write for info.

RENEWAL, Michael K. Barling, 3A High St., Esher, Surrey KT10 9RP, United Kingdom. Articles, photos, reviews, news items, interviews, criticism, letters. 6/yr. sub. price: £1.75 ($4.30); per copy: 20p. Back issues: 49-53 12p (5 for 50p) 39,44-48 free. 40pp. Ads: 4p/wd (min £1.40).

RESEARCH, William R. Kell, Editor; Bob Fauteux, Associate Editor, Graduate School Research Development Center, 417 Johnston Hall, University of Minnesota, Minneapolis, MN 55455, (612) 373-3001. 1980. Poetry, cartoons. "*Research* vernacularizes the University of Minnesota's research enterprise across the entire range of scholarly disciplines, from the humanities & fine arts to the social, biological, & physical sciences. The magazine seeks poems (under 50 lines) which epitomize the quest for new knowledge, the creative process, the generation of ideas, and intellectual endeavor; or which capture specific instances of scholarly research. The magazine also seeks cartoons which address these same themes with insightful good humor. Quality of the first order is our criterion for acceptance." circ. 20,000. 4/yr. sample price: $2.00. 48pp; 8½X11; of. Reporting time: within two months. Payment: for poems, minimum of $1.00 per line, plus copies, on publication. For cartoons, will negotiate. Copyrighted, does not revert to author.

Resource Publications (see also MODERN LITURGY), William Burns, Editor; Doug Hughes, Advertising Manager, 7291 Coronado Dr, Suite 3, San Jose, CA 95070. 1973. Poetry, fiction, articles, art, photos, cartoons, interviews, criticism, reviews, music, letters, plays, concrete art, news items. "Interested primarily in creative ideas or examples of use in planning or leading worship, or religious arts." avg. press run 2,000-5,000. Pub'd 2 titles 1979; expects 4 titles 1980, 4 titles 1981. 15 titles listed in the *Small Press Record of Books in Print* (9th Edition, 1980). avg. price, paper: $3.00-$21.95; other: $5.95. Discounts: standard trade. 120pp; 5½X8½ to 8½X11; of. Reporting time: 8 weeks. Payment: editorial fee or royalty on sales. Copyrights for author. COSMEP, CPA, WIP.

RESOURCES, Richard Gardner, Box 134, Harvard Square, Cambridge, MA 02138, 617 876-2789. 1973. Satire. "RESOURCES is useful information about new products, services, publications, interesting organizations, new ideas and events. What's happening on the cutting edge of our changing society. Also, some amusing items from the trailing edge and a few so-so's from the vast middle of America (and the rest of the World)." circ. 10,000. 1 title listed in the *Small Press Record of Books in Print* (9th Edition, 1980). sub. price: $5.00/12 issues & index; per copy: $.50; sample: $.50. 8pp; 8½X11; of. Payment: no. Not copyrighted. Pub's reviews. §how-to/consumer information/technology. COSMEP, APS.

RESOURCES FOR FEMINIST RESEARCH, M. Stephenson, J. Newton, C. Zavitz, M. O'Brien, Ontario Institute for Studies in Education, 252 Bloor Street W., Toronto, Ontario M5S 1V6, Canada. 1972. Articles, reviews. "Documentation Sur La Recherche feministe/Abstracts, review essays, bibliographies, announcements." 4/yr. Pub'd 5 issues 1979; expects 4 issues 1980, 4 issues 1981. sub. price: $12.00/Canadian; $15.00/Foreign/$25.00/Institution; per copy: $3.50; sample: free to institutions and libraries. Back issues: $8.00/volume; $15/institutions. Discounts: write for details. 110pp; 8½X11; †of. Payment: none. Pub's reviews: 35 in 1979. §93/women's studies. Ads: exchange only.

RESURGENCE, Satish Kumar, Ford House, Hartland, Bideford, Devon, Wales, United Kingdom, 820317-0239D1. 1966. Articles, poetry, cartoons, photos, reviews, interviews, letters. "E. F. Schumacher, John Seymour, Vinoba Bhave, Philip Toynbee, Colin Ward." circ. 3,500. 6/yr. Pub'd 6 issues 1979. sub. price: $15.00 ($20.00 for Airmail); per copy: 70p or $2.50; sample: 70p or $2.50. Back issues: 70p each or $2.50. Discounts: to charities 12%. 44pp; size A4; of. Reporting time: month. Payment: none. Pub's reviews: 30 in 1979. Ads: £75/£40/£25 1/4 page/classified 7p per word.

REVIEW, Port City Press, Ronald Christ, Luis Harss, 680 Park Avenue, New York, NY 10021. 1968. Articles, criticism, reviews. "Latin American literature and art." circ. 3,000. 3/yr. Pub'd 2 issues 1979; expects 3 issues 1980, 3 issues 1981. sub. price: $7.00; per copy: $3.00; sample: free. 12 back issues at $30.00. Discounts: 15%. 92pp; 7X10; lp. Reporting time: 4-6 weeks. Payment: $50.00 per essay-translation. Copyrighted, reverts to author. Pub's reviews: 15 in 1979. §Latin American literature in translation & interdisciplinary texts on Lat. Am. topics. Ads: $100.00/$50.00.

REVIEWING LIBRARIAN, Ontario Library Association, Fay Blostein, 73 Richmond Street W., Suite 402, Toronto, Ontario M5H 1Z4, Canada, (416) 762-7232. 1974. Articles, reviews. circ. 1,100.

4/yr. Pub'd 4 issues 1979; expects 4 issues 1980, 4 issues 1981. sub. price: $10.00; per copy: $3.00; sample: free. Back issues: free. Discounts: Agent, jobber 20%. 48pp; 8½X11. Copyrighted, does not revert to author. Pub's reviews: 850 in 1979. §Media for elem/sec school use (books, mags, govt. pubs., non-print, reference, professional).

REVISTA CHICANO-RIQUENA, Nicolas Kanellos, Luis Davila, University of Houston, Houston, TX 77004, 219-980-6692. 1972. Poetry, fiction, articles, art, photos, interviews, satire, criticism, reviews, long-poems, plays. "Revista Chicano-Riquena is a journal of Chicano and Puerto Rican literature and art that also publishes articles of literary criticism, folklore, and popular culture. We publish the most renown Chicano and Puerto Rican writers as well as beginning writers." circ. 1,000. 4/yr. Pub'd 4 issues 1979; expects 4 issues 1980, 4 issues 1981. sub. price: $7.00 individuals; $10.00 institutions.; per copy: $3.00; sample: $3.00. Back issues: $3.00-$5.00. 64-170pp; 6X9; of. Reporting time: immediate acknowledgement; delayed acceptance or rejection. Payment: only on basis of CCLM grant; no fixed rate. Copyrighted, reverts to author. Pub's reviews: 12 in 1979. §Chicano and Puerto Rican literature, art, culture, etc. Ads: $60.00/$30.00/0. CCLM.

REVOLUTION, RCP Publications, Box 3486, Chicago, IL 60654, 32-663-5920. Articles. 12/yr. 75pp; of.

Reyn Publishing Co., Wilbur W. Bigelow, 14240 E 14th Street, San Leandro, CA 94578, (415) 352-5914. 1979. Articles, photos, cartoons, interviews, news items. "*Z-Cycle, Winning by a Force of a Fourth Type,* publication of recent book on the use of failure in our lives. Uses case study method to illustrate how people to failure. Very few know how to use failure." avg. press run 9,000. Pub'd 1 title 1979. 1 title listed in the *Small Press Record of Books in Print* (9th Edition, 1980). avg. price, cloth: $14.00; paper: $9.00. Discounts: 50% to wholesalers; 40% to retail. 280pp; 6X9. Reporting time: 30 days. Payment: standard. Copyrights for author. COSMEP.

RFD, RFD Collective, Rt 1 box 92 E, Efland, NC 27243. 1974. Poetry, fiction, articles, art, photos, reviews, letters, cartoons, interviews. "RFD is a Country Journal by gay men, for gay men. Any material relevant to building our community is considered." circ. 2,000. 4/yr. Pub'd 4 issues 1979; expects 4 issues 1980, 4 issues 1981. sub. price: $6.00; per copy: $2.00; sample: $2.00. Back issues: Nos. 3-15, $2.00 each; 16-18 $2.00. Discounts: bookstore 40 percent, dist. 51½ percent. 56pp; 8½X11 to 7¼X10½; of. Reporting time: 2 months minimum. Payment: copies. Not copyrighted. Pub's reviews: 2 - 3 in 1979. §Country concerns, spiritual realities, , faggotry, poetry alternatives. Ads: $100.00/$50.00/$0.15. CCLM, COSMEP.

Rhiannon Press, Peg Carlson Lauber, 1105 Bradley, Eau Claire, WI 54701, (715) 835-0598. 1977. Poetry, long-poems. "Concentration on midwest women's poetry. Line up chapbook authors on my own." avg. press run 200-250. Pub'd 1 title 1979; expects 2 titles 1980, 2 titles 1981. 2 titles listed in the *Small Press Record of Books in Print* (9th Edition, 1980). avg. price, paper: $2.50. 25 - 35pp; 5½X8½; of. Payment: copies of work or percentage of copies. Copyrights for author. COSMEP.

RHINO, Liz Peterson, Suzanne Brabant, Helen Cohen, Lee Berkson, 77 Lakewood Place, Highland Park, IL 60035, 312-433-3536. 1976. Poetry. "We're looking for good-excellent work by little-known writers, both short prose and poetry—neither to exceed 3 pgs., dble-spaced. (We would, however, like to see five poems or two prose works per writer.) Reports: 1 mo.; please supply SASE; Pays: 1 contributor's copy. Expects: 1 issue per year, 60 or more pages, Fall $2.00/ea. We print on high-quality paper. Please submit material between March 1 and May 31." circ. 600. annual. Expects 1 issue 1980. sub. price: $2.00 (paperback); per copy: $2.00; sample: $2.00. 60pp; 5½X8½; of. Reporting time: 1 month to 6 weeks. Payment: 1 contributor's copy. Copyrighted, reverts to author.

Richboro Press, Charles Moore, Box 1, Richboro, PA 18954, 215-355-6084. 1975. Articles. avg. press run 500. Pub'd 17 titles 1979; expects 12 titles 1980, 20 titles 1981. 13 titles listed in the *Small Press Record of Books in Print* (9th Edition, 1980). avg. price, cloth: $12.00; paper: $7.00. Discounts: Universal. 200pp; 5X7 / 7X10; †of. Reporting time: 2 wks. Payment: depends. Copyrights for author. COSMEP, COSMEPA.

RIO GRANDE WRITERS NEWSLETTER, Carol Moscrip, PO Box 40126, Albuquerque, NM 87107, (505) 266-3110. 1976. Interviews, reviews, news items. "Among members of RGWA are: Frank Waters, John Nichols, Norm Zollinger, Rudolfo Anaya, Tony Hillerman, Gene Frumkin, Stanley Noyes, Joy Harjo." circ. 300. 4/yr. Pub'd 4 issues 1979; expects 4 issues 1980, 4 issues 1981. sub. price: $6.00; sample: free. 6-8pp; 8½X11; of. Pub's reviews: 25 in 1979. §Southwestern contemporary writing of all kinds.

Rip Off Press Inc., PO Box 14158, San Francisco, CA 94114, (415) 863-5359. 1969. Cartoons. "We publish *funny* comics by top professioanls like Shelton, Crumb, Gonick, Richards." avg. price, other:

$1.25. of.

RIPPLES, Shining Waters Press, Karen Schaefer, Editor; Jim Schaefer, Publisher, 718 Watersedge, Ann Arbor, MI 48105. 1973. Poetry, long-poems, fiction, reviews, news items. "Unique publishing venture for developing poet and short fiction writer, as the first 3 issues are printed as newsletters of material being worked on, then final issue printed in formal format. Interested in natural , organic images of daily life around the perceiver." circ. 1,000. 4/yr. Pub'd 4 issues 1979. sub. price: $3.00; per copy: $.50 newsletter/$1.50 magazine; sample: $0.50/newsletter - $1.50 magazine - plus S.A.S.E. Back issues: variable. 40pp; 14X7; of. Reporting time: 1 day. Payment: copy. Copyrighted, reverts to author. Pub's reviews. §poetry/short fiction. Ads: $40.00. CCLM, COSMEP.

River Basin Publishing Co., Reinder Van Til, Robert A. Buntz Jr., Box 30573, St Paul, MN 55175, (612) 291-7470. 1979. "River Basin Publishing is a new small press dedicated to bringing out books and other studies that explore new and alternative ideas on technologies, energy and food sources and the re-thinging of political and social organizations. ex. *The Sane Alternative* James Robertson" avg. press run 5,000. Pub'd 1 title 1979; expects 5 titles 1980, 6 titles 1981. avg. price, cloth: $8.95; paper: $5.95. Discounts: Trade 40%, Distributors 50%. 152pp; 5½X8½. Payment: variable. Copyrights for author.

RIVER STYX, Big River Association, Michael Castro, Jan Castro, 7420 Cornell Ave., St. Louis, MO 63130, 314-725-0602. 1975. Poetry, fiction, art, photos, cartoons. "'Following the river, from mouth to source.' We've published works by Helen Adam, Michael Corr, Allen Ginsberg, Jerome Rothenberg, David Meltzer, Clayton Eshleman, John Knoepfle, Susan Mernit, Joe Bruchac, Carter Revard, Alejandro El-Romero, Ishmael Reed, Ntozake Shange, William Stafford, Quincy Troupe, Gary Snyder and many young, lesser known writers. Themes for 1980: *The Six Elements: Earth to Quintessence* Works connecting *In Any Way* will be considered." Bi-annual. Pub'd 2 issues 1979. sub. price: $5.00; per copy: $3.00; sample: $3.00. Back issues: $2.00 (issues 2 & 3). Discounts: 40 percent discount to stores, 50 percent discount with orders of 10 or more. 130pp; 5½X8½; †of. Reporting time: 2 months. Payment: 2 issues. Copyrighted, reverts to author. §Myth & poetics. Ads: None. COSMEP, CCLM.

RIVERSEDGE, Riversedge Press, Dorey Schmidt, Gen. Ed.; Patricia de la Fuente, Assoc. Ed., PO Box 1547, Edinburg, TX 78539. 1977. Poetry, fiction, art, photos, interviews, reviews. "*riversedge* wants high quality prose, poetry and graphics. The overall design of each issue is carefully planned. We have no biases, but like material to reflect both the culture of the Southwest and Rio Grande and the universals of human experience. Send $2.00 for a sample copy. We somtimes specific editorial comment on material submitted." circ. 500. 3/yr. Pub'd 3 issues 1979. sub. price: $7.00; per copy: $2.50 + .50 postage; sample: $2.00. Back issues: all $2.50 + .50 postage. Discounts: 40 percent discount to bookstores, bulk discount available. 64pp; 6X9; †of. Reporting time: 6 weeks. Payment: 2 copies. Copyrighted, reverts automatically, should cite RIVERSEDGE. Pub's reviews: 0 in 1979. §open to chapbooks or other collections of poetry. Ads: No ads. COSMEP.

Riversedge Press (see also RIVERSEDGE), Dorey Schmidt, Gen. Ed.; Patricia de la Fuente, Assoc. Ed, PO Box 1547, Edinburg, TX 78539. 1977. Poetry, fiction, art, photos. "We publish the magazine riverSedge and plan a series of chapbooks of fiction, art and poetry. At this point, we aren't taking unsolicited material for the chapbooks or broadside series." avg. press run 500-1,000. Expects 2 titles 1980, 2 titles 1981. 3 titles listed in the *Small Press Record of Books in Print* (9th Edition, 1980). avg. price, paper: $3.50. Discounts: 40 percent discount to bookstores, bulk discount available. 50 - 80pp; 6X9; †of. Reporting time: 6 weeks. Payment: arranged. Copyrights for author. COSMEP.

RIVERSIDE QUARTERLY, Leland Sapiro, Redd Boggs, Fiction; Sheryl Smith, Poetry; Mary Emerson, Art, PO Box 367, University Station, Garden City, NY 11530. 1964. Poetry, fiction, articles, art, satire, criticism, reviews, letters. "RQ prints reviews, essays on all aspects of science-fiction and fantasy, but emphasis is on current scenes rather than, e.g., gothic horror or fantasy in the Gilded Age. Some recent titles: '*Science Fiction As Will And Idea: The World Of Alfred Bester,*' '*Ursula Leguin's Archetypal Winter Journey,*' '*Mythology In Samuel Delany's Einstein Intersection.*' No maximum word length for essays or reviews, but fiction is restricted to 3,500 words. Contributors are urged to read several copies of the RQ (available at any major public or university library) before submitting MSS—and are warned that our standards are tough: RQ's rejects appear in the pro magazines." circ. 1,200. irreg. Pub'd 1 issue 1979; expects 1 issue 1980, 2 issues 1981. sub. price: $4.00, 4 issues; per copy: $1.00; sample: $1.00. Back issues: $1.00. 68pp; 8½X5½; of. Reporting time: 10 days. Payment: copies. Copyrighted, reverts to author. Pub's reviews: 2 in 1979. §science-fiction and fantasy. Ads: $75.-00/$50.00. CCLM.

ROAD/HOUSE, Todd Moore, 900 West 9th St., Belvidere, IL 61008, 543-9581. 1975. Poetry. "Some recent contributors to Road/House have been Harley Elliott, Kirk Robertson, Nila NorthSun,

Tom Montag, Albert Goldbarth, Ron Koertge, Thomas McGrath, etc." circ. about 200 (this varies). 2/yr. Expects 2 issues 1980. sub. price: $2.50; per copy: $1.50; sample: to people mostly free. Back issues: free until gone (libraries pay). Discounts: Road/House has no discount rates because it is given away, except in cases where libraries wish to subscribe. Then it is sold at the listed rate. 36-44pp; 5½X8½; of. Reporting time: usually 2 weeks. Payment: 2 or 3 copies to contribs depends on quantity available. Copyrighted, reverts when I assign them. Pub's reviews: 1 in 1979. §poetry only.

Rochester Routes/Creative Arts Projects (see also EXIT), 50 Inglewood Drive, Rochester, NY 14619. Poetry, fiction, art, photos, interviews, concrete art. "See entry under EXIT" avg. press run 1,000. 1 title listed in the *Small Press Record of Books in Print* (9th Edition, 1980). avg. price, paper: $2.00. 5½X8½. Reporting time: 1 month. Payment: payment in copies. Copyrights for author.

Rock Culture Books, Box 96, Scarsdale, NY 10583, (914)793-2649. 1976. Art, photos, music. "Non-fiction articles or booklength works, photos and artwork dealing with popular music only." avg. press run 2500. Pub'd 1 title 1979; expects 1-3 titles 1980. 1 title listed in the *Small Press Record of Books in Print* (9th Edition, 1980). avg. price, paper: $6.95. Discounts: Wholesaler and library discounts available. 100pp; 8½X11; of. Reporting time: deal with each project separately. Payment: depends on project; paid quarterly. Copyrights for author.

ROCKBOTTOM, Mudborn Press, Erasmus (Sasha) Newborn, 209 W. De La Guerra, Santa Barbara, CA 93101, 805-962-9996. 1976. Fiction, articles, interviews, criticism, music, letters, parts-of-novels, plays. "Rockbottom is published in Sept., Jan., and May as a journal of prose writing and associated arts (music, drama) with an emphasis on personal narrative, whether fictionalized story, interview, song, journalism, script, diary, or translations of same. Submissions are judged on human relevance, originality of style, and depth of perception. Models: Bukowski, Fox, Dawson, Drake, Sena, Grayson." circ. 1,000. 3/yr. Pub'd 3 issues 1979; expects 3 issues 1980, 3 issues 1981. sub. price: $10.00/3 issues; per copy: $3.50; sample: $3.50. Back issues: Complete backfile $50.00 (with reconstructed xerox version of #1). 128pp; 7X10; of. Reporting time: 1 month. Payment: copies only. Copyrighted, reverts to author. Ads: $100.00/$60.00/no classified. WIP, COSMEP, CCLM.

Rockfall Press, Charles L. Cutler, Cider Mill Road, Rockfall, CT 06481, (203) 349-8982. 1978. Expects 1 title 1980. 1 title listed in the *Small Press Record of Books in Print* (9th Edition, 1980). avg. price, cloth: $9.95. Discounts: negotiable. 189pp; 5½X8½; of. No submissions accepted.

Rocking Horse Press, Michele Palmer, 32 Ellise Road, Storrs, CT 06268, (203) 429-1474. 1977. Fiction. "Our specialty is children's books, esp. folk tales, animal stories, or rhymes, with appeal to 'all ages'. Not actively seeking material at present. Current titles: *Zoup Soup* and *A Mother Goose Feast* ." avg. press run 1M-3M. Pub'd 1 title 1979; expects 1 title 1980, 2 titles 1981. 2 titles listed in the *Small Press Record of Books in Print* (9th Edition, 1980). avg. price, paper: $1.50-$1.95. Discounts: Trade 40%; bulk rates available. 24pp; 4¼X6⅝; 5½X6½; of. Reporting time: 3-4 weeks. Payment: Will buy outright or pay by royalty. Copyrights for author.

ROCKINGCHAIR, Cupola Productions, John Politis, P.O. Box 27, Philadelphia, PA 19105, (215) WA5-3673. 1977. Reviews. "*ROCKINGCHAIR* is a review newsletter for popular music fans and librarians who buy records. Its main purpose is to help professional librarians in providing a better collection of recordings to meet the needs of their patrons. Popular recordings are reviewed for their artistic quality and their circulation potential. Please check sample copy before submitting any mss." circ. 550. 12/yr. Pub'd 12 issues 1979; expects 12 issues 1980, 12 issues 1981. sub. price: $10.85 (librarians) $12.95 (non-librn); per copy: $1.00 (librarians) $1.10 (non-librn); sample: $1.10. Back issues: $1.10 for back issues. Discounts: none at this time. 16pp; 7X8½; of. Reporting time: 4-6 weeks or less. Payment: copies for mini-articles, album & copies for record review. Copyrighted, reverts to author. libraries that subscribe are permitted reproduction of reviews for in-house use. Pub's reviews: 12 in 1979. §popular music, artists, recordings, spoken word discs, and tapes. no advertising. COSMEP.

ROMANIAN REVIEW, George G. Potra, Piata Scinteii 1, Bucharest, Romania, 173836. 1946. Poetry, fiction, articles, art, photos, interviews, criticism, reviews, music, letters, parts-of-novels, long-poems, plays, news items. "The *Review* is published in French, English, German and Russian language editions." 12/yr. Pub'd 12 issues 1979; expects 12 issues 1980, 12 issues 1981. sub. price: $12.00; per copy: $1.00. 160pp; 17cm x 24cm; lp. Reporting time: one month. Payment: royalties according to Romanian law. Copyrighted, reverts to author. Pub's reviews: 70 in 1979. §Romanian literature, arts, culture.

THE ROMANTIST, John C. Moran, Don Herron, Steve Eng, Saracinesca House, 3610 Meadowbrook Avenue, Nashville, TN 37205. 1977. Poetry, articles, art, interviews, criticism, reviews, photos. "H. Warner Munn, Donald Sidney-Fryer, Clark Ashton Smith, George Sterling, and kindred authors.

Purview is Modern Romanticism, especially Imaginative Literature (emphasis upon Fantasy) ; contains a regular section on F. Marion Crawford (1854-1909). Publishes only traditional (rimed) poetry." circ. 300-350. 1/yr. Pub'd 1 issue 1979; expects 1 issue 1980, 1 issue 1981. 1 title listed in the *Small Press Record of Books in Print* (9th Edition, 1980). sub. price: $5.50 incl postage; two or more copies (any issue) $5.00 each; per copy: $5.50 incl postage. Back issues: $5.50 incl postage. Discounts: 20% to 40% depending upon quantity. 80-100pp; 8½X11; of/lp. Reporting time: within one month. Payment: two copies (presently). Copyrighted, does not revert to author. Pub's reviews: 6 in 1979. §Fantasy, horror, weird, supernatural fiction, Romanticism, etc. Ads: $25.00/$13.00/$7.50.

Rook Press, Inc. (see also THISTLE: A MAGAZINE OF CONTEMPORARY WRITING), Ernest Stefanik, Cis Stefanik, P.O. Box 144, Ruffsdale, PA 15679. 1975. Poetry, criticism, articles. "Recent chapbooks include *Ten Vallanelles* by Tony Connor, *Witness: 'How All Occasions . . . '* by Ann Hayes, *The Elm's Home* by William Heyen, *Truth Lies In Paradox: Sonnets and Villanelles* by Norman N. McWhinney, *New Lives* by Anthony Petroski, *Step on the Rain: Haiku* and *Wake to the Bell: A Garland of Christmas Poems* by Raymond Roseliep, *The Duckweed Way: Haiku of Issa* and *Haiku of the Japanese Masters* translated by Lucien Stryk and Takashi Ikemoto, and *In Memory of Smoke* by Michael Waters. Anthologies published during 1977 include *Into the Round Air* (ed. Raymond Roseliep) and *The Sound of a Few Leaves: A Book of Weeks* (ed. Ernest & Cis Stefanik). Works scheduled for publication in 1978 include collections of poems by William Heyen, John Knoepfle, Kathy Mangan, Ralph J. Mills, Jr., and James Minor; a collection of essays by Raymond Roseliep; a collection of half-aphorisms by Norman N. McWhinney." avg. press run 300-500. Pub'd 10 titles 1979; expects 10 titles 1980, 10 titles 1981. 36 titles listed in the *Small Press Record of Books in Print* (9th Edition, 1980). avg. price, paper: $3.00. Discounts to booksellers, librarians, and individuals ordering direct: no discount on orders of less than $10; 1 copy, 0%; 2-5 copies, 20%, 6-10 copies, 30%, 11 or more copies, 40%. Only libraries receive deferred billing. 40pp; 14X21.5cm; of/lp. Reporting time: 4-8 weeks. Does not copyright for author.

ROOM, Gail Newman, Kathy Barr, P.O. Box 40610, San Francisco, CA 94140. 1976. Poetry, fiction, articles, art, photos, cartoons, interviews, satire, reviews, parts-of-novels, long-poems, collages. "We would like material with a wide range of styles and subject matter. We are also interested in journals, dream writing, articles on women writers, presses, and so on." circ. 750. 2/yr. Expects 2 issues 1980. sub. price: single copies only; per copy: $3.00; sample: $2.00. Back issues: $1.75. 72pp; 5½X8½; of. Reporting time: 3 mo. Payment: copies of mag., sometimes $15.00. Copyrighted, reverts to author. Pub's reviews: 7 in 1979. §women's books and publications. COSMEP.

ROOM OF ONE'S OWN, Growing Room Collective, Gayla Reid, Gail VanVarseveld, Eleanor Wachtel, Jean Wilson, PO Box 46160, Station G, Vancouver, British Columbia V6R 4G5, Canada, 604-733-6276. 1974. Poetry, fiction, art, photos, cartoons, interviews, criticism, reviews, parts-of-novels, long-poems, plays. "Good quality literary material by & about women, written from a feminist perspective." circ. 1,500. 4/yr. Pub'd 4 issues 1979. sub. price: $8.50-USA; $7.50-CA; $10.00 instituitons; per copy: $2.50; sample: $2.50. Back issues: depends on availablility — query issues wanted. Discounts: trade 30 percent, bulk-negotiable, agent-15 percent off institutional orders only. 80pp; 5½X8½; of. Reporting time: 6 weeks to 3 months. Payment: $3.50 per printed page. Copyrighted, reverts to author. Pub's reviews: 20 in 1979. §literature, women. Ads: $90/$50. CPPA.

ROQ Press (see also AQUILA MAGAZINE), Bob Quateroni, Executive Editor; Jane C. Musala, Editor; William A. Blair, Associate Editor, 116 Old Mill Road #G, State College, PA 16801, (814)-237-7509. 1975. Poetry, fiction, articles, art, photos, interviews, satire, reviews, music, letters, parts-of-novels. "Interested in craft and nature pamphlets. Need more *short* fiction (1000 words) and poems that don't look like they're written for a college poetry course." avg. press run 250. Pub'd 1 title 1979; expects 2-3 titles 1980. 2 titles listed in the *Small Press Record of Books in Print* (9th Edition, 1980). avg. price, paper: $2.00; other: $1.00 for crafts pamphlets. Discounts: none. 28pp; 5¼X8½; varies. Reporting time: 1-4 months. Payment: copies, Best poem of the year wins $25. Does not copyright for author. COSMEP.

Rose Publishing Co., Walter Nunn, 301 Louisiana, Little Rock, AR 72201, (501) 372-1666. 1973. Art, photos, cartoons. "Primarily books of nonfiction about Arkansas. Typical titles are 150-250 pp, usually cloth or trade paperback." avg. press run 2,000. Pub'd 7 titles 1979; expects 3 titles 1980, 4 titles 1981. 4 titles listed in the *Small Press Record of Books in Print* (9th Edition, 1980). avg. price, cloth: $9.95; paper: $6.95. Discounts: Trade, 5-24 copies, 40%; Classroom, 20% for college; 25% for public schools. 200pp; 5½X8½; of. Reporting time: 6 weeks. Payment: 10% of gross. Copyrights for author.

Rosler, Martha (see also POSTCARD ART/POSTCARD FICTION), Martha Rosler, 2920 23rd Street, San Francisco, CA 94110. 1974. Fiction, art, photos. "So far all works have been serial postcard 'novels' and other fiction, written by myself." avg. press run 1000. Pub'd 1 title 1979; expects 1 title 1980. 5 titles listed in the *Small Press Record of Books in Print* (9th Edition, 1980). avg. price, paper: $1.75.

348

12pp; 4½X6; †of/mi.

Ross Books, Franz Ross, Box 4340, Berkeley, CA 94704, (415) 841-2474. 1978. "Mostly how to, health & awareness, books also cookbooks. We have published poetry & one first time novel but don't do this very much." avg. press run 3,000-5,000. Pub'd 4 titles 1979; expects 2 titles 1980, 4 titles 1981. 13 titles listed in the *Small Press Record of Books in Print* (9th Edition, 1980). avg. price, cloth: $10.95; paper: $4.95. Discounts: 40% stores. 192pp; 6X9; of. Reporting time: 2 months. Payment: 8-10% of retail price. Copyrights for author.

Ross-Erikson Publishers, Inc., Robert Walton Brown, 1825 Grand Ave, Santa Barbara, CA 93101, 966-2691. 1973. Fiction, criticism. "Book length. See enclosed statement of purpose. Contributors-Agehauda Bhaiati, Kenneth Rexroth, Robert Duncan, Jerry Kamstra" avg. press run 3,000. avg. price, cloth: $11.95; paper: $4.95. Discounts: jobber 50 percent, salesman 10 percent of net. 250pp; 5½X8½; of/lp. Reporting time: 1 month. Payment: standard. Copyrights for author. LPS.

Rossi, B. Simon, PO Box 2001, Beverly Hills, CA 90213, (213) 271-3730. 1979. "Interested in material on self-help, non-fiction, super creative ideas for books. Useful informative manuscripts on the human behaviors, personal experiences and life are welcome. Interesting guides on how-to and useful information are also of interest." 1 title listed in the *Small Press Record of Books in Print* (9th Edition, 1980). avg. price, paper: $5.00. Discounts: 2-9, 20%; 10-24, 25%; 25-49, 30%; 50-99, 35%; 100-199, 40%; 200 or more, 50%. All orders are FOB Beverly Hills, CA. 100pp; 8½X5½; of. Reporting time: 3-5 weeks (return postage paid envelope must be included for return of material & quick response). Payment: negotiable. Copyrights for author.

ROUGH JUSTICE for the Single Homeless, Adrian Jones, Dave Roberts, Rick Skelton, Peter Walker, 90 St Mary Street, Cardiff, Wales, United Kingdom, Cardiff 36054. 1978. Articles, photos, cartoons, interviews, criticism, letters, news items. "Articles 300-800 words. Investigative reports, exposes of projects for single homeless people." circ. 1,500. 4/yr. Pub'd 4 issues 1979; expects 4 issues 1980, 4 issues 1981. sub. price: £2.00, overseas £3.00; per copy: 50p, overseas 75p; sample: 50p, overseas 75p. Discounts: bookshops 33%, others 20% on orders of 20 plus. 16pp; 8¼X11¾; of. Payment: none. Copyrighted. Pub's reviews: 4 in 1979. §Single homeless people, housing, poetry. Ads: £75/£40.

Roush Books, Kathy MacLennan, Box 4203, Valley Village, North Hollywood, CA 91607, (213) 762-3740. 1979. "*Kansas Boy* by J Patrick Desmond. True story of a boy who grew up in what is now our State of Kansas among the Osage Indians, 1866-1878. Also *A Voice Called* by the same author, the story of a youngs black boy's struggles to rid Africa of slave camps after he fled from his tribe." avg. press run 1,000. Pub'd 2 titles 1979. 2 titles listed in the *Small Press Record of Books in Print* (9th Edition, 1980). avg. price, paper: $5.95. Discounts: 25% libraries, 40% bulk, 50% agents (bookstores 40% cash). 100pp; 5½X8½; of/lp. Reporting time: approx 30 days. Payment: to be arranged, usually 10%. Copyrights for author. COSMEP.

The Rubicon Press, Jack McGovern, Carolyn Giovannini, 5638 Riverdsle Road S, Salem, OR 97302. 1972. Poetry, art. "We're interested in carrying on the tradition of publishing poetry in fine letterpress books. In association with Dusty Garage Books, book binders, Page Holleren prop., we've managed a modicum of success (see *A Little Thumb* by Jack McGovern). We're interested in learning. We're interested in growing. However, because of certain insidious economies we must only pursue one special project at a time. We're opened, but we're closed. Good luck." avg. press run 500. Pub'd 1 title 1979; expects 1 title 1980. 4 titles listed in the *Small Press Record of Books in Print* (9th Edition, 1980). avg. price, cloth: open; paper: $3.25. Discounts: open. 80pp; size varies; †lp. Payment: open. Copyrights for author.

RUDE, Acme Print & Litho, Joe Thomas, Publisher, 390 Douro Street, Stratford, Ont, Canada. 1977. "From politics to pornography, like a slap in the face, we do not print smut nor poetry" circ. 1M. monthly. Expects 12 issues 1980, 12 issues 1981. sub. price: $40; per copy: $5.00; sample: $7.50. Back issues: $10.00. Discounts: none. 100pp; 10X14; †of/lp. Reporting time: a.s.a.p. Payment: none until 1979. Not copyrighted. Pub's reviews. §everything except poetry. Ads: $1000/$600/50¢.

Rumour Publications, Judith Doyle, Fred Gaysek, Norman Fox, Brian Kipping, Judith Doyle, Barry Prophet, Kathy Acker, Fred Gaysek, Victor Coleman, Minette Robinson, 31 Mercer Street, Toronto, Ontario M5V 1H2, Canada. 1978. Poetry, fiction, art, photos, interviews, satire, criticism, music, letters, long-poems, collages, plays, concrete art. "Victor Coleman: *Captions For The Deaf*; Kathy Acker: *Kathy Goes To Haiti*; interested in new concepts and internatinal distribution.book formats." avg. press run 100-1,000. Pub'd 10 titles 1979; expects 12 titles 1980, 15 titles 1981. 13 titles listed in the *Small Press Record of Books in Print* (9th Edition, 1980). avg. price, cloth: $10.00; paper: $3.95; other: $2.00. Discounts: Booksellers, 30% 1-4; 40% 5-24; 42% 25-49; 44% 50-99; 46% 100 or more; School, college and trade, 20% 1-9; 25% 10 or more; Libraries, 25%. 50pp; size varies; of/lp. Reporting time: 1 month. Payment: 10% of retail price, x copies sold. Copyrights for author.

Runa Press, A. Quinn, Monkstown, Co Dublin, Eire, United Kingdom. 1943. "po" Reporting time: 14-21 days.

RUNE, Coach House Press, E. J. Carson, Brian Henderson, 81 St. Marys St., Box 299, St. Michael's College, Toronto, Ontario M5S1J4, Canada. 1974. Poetry, fiction, articles, art, interviews, reviews, letters, parts-of-novels, long-poems, concrete art. "Recent contributors-A. R. Ammons, bill bissett, Eli Mandel, Barry Goldensohn, J. M. Cameron, Norman Dubie, bp Nichol, Marshal McLuhan, Guenter Eich (trans), Ernst Jandl (trans), Jon Silkin, Daryl Hine, Louis Dudek, Joe Rosenblatt, Andrew Sukraski, Raymond Souster, Frank Davey, Richard Truhlar, Paul Dutton." circ. 300. 1/yr. Expects 2 issues 1980. sub. price: $2.50; per copy: $2.50. Back issues: $4.00 for No. 3, No. 1 & No. 2 are $6.00. Discounts: 30-40 percent consignment only. 80pp; 5½X8½; lp. Reporting time: 6 months (we're in no big hurry). Payment: no. Not copyrighted. Pub's reviews. §poetry/prose. Ads: $25.00/$12.50. CPPA.

Running Press, Lawrence Teacher, 38 South 19th Street, Philadelphia, PA 19103, 215-567-5080. 1973. "We publish large format quality trade paperbacks. Many of our books show people how to make or do things (*Fast Furniture, The Dome Builder's Handbook, Herb Grower's Guide, Shop Tactics*). *Energybook* 1 was the beginning of an on-going project which was continued with *Energybook* 2, published in the fall of 1976. Running Press has an horticultural authority, Richard Nicholls, who has written *The Plant Doctor, The Plant Doctor In His Vegetable Garden, The Handmade Greenhouse,* and *The Plant Buyer's Handbook.* We have also begun a line of reference works including a set of 12 glossaries on specific languages (i.e. banking, real estate, baseball), the *Running Press Dictionary Of Law, The Complete Encyclopedia Of Needlework, The Barefoot Doctor's Manual,* and *The Illustrated Running Press Edition Of The American Classic Gray's Anatomy.* Running Press is always interested in considering energy-, paramedical-, or medical-related manuscripts, and our interest in how-to is still strong. These manuscripts will be returned if accompanied by a self-addressed, stamped envelope." avg. press run 25,000. Pub'd 22 titles 1979; expects 22 titles 1980. 63 titles listed in the *Small Press Record of Books in Print* (9th Edition, 1980). Discounts: 1-4 20%, 5-24 40%, 25-49 41%, 50-99 42%, 100-249 43%, 250-599 44%, 600-999 45%, 1000+ 46%; 50% wholesale. of. Reporting time: 1 month. Payment: negotiable. AAP.

RUSSIAN LITERATURE TRIQUARTERLY, Ardis, Carl R. Proffer, Ellendea Proffer, 2901 Heatherway, Ann Arbor, MI 48104, 313-971-2367. 1971. Poetry, fiction, articles, art, photos, interviews, satire, criticism, reviews, letters, parts-of-novels, long-poems, plays, news items. "Russian or Soviet literary subjects." circ. 1,250. 3/yr. Pub'd 3 issues 1979; expects 3 issues 1980. sub. price: institutions-$35.00 cloth $25.00 pa; individual, $16.95; students $13.95; per copy: $7.00 current year. Back issues: $15.00 cloth/$10.00 pa. Discounts: none. 500pp; 6X9; of. Reporting time: 2 months. Payment: copies of issue. Copyrighted, reverts to author. Pub's reviews: 100 in 1979. §Russian literature/history/politics. Ads: $60.00/$40.00. CCLM, COSMEP.

S

S, Studio S Press, Tony D'Arpino, Editor; Attanasio DiFelice, E. Lee Bradley, 1600 Preston Lane, Morro Bay, CA 93442, 805-772-2715. 1978. Poetry, fiction, articles, art, photos, cartoons, interviews, satire, reviews, music, letters, parts-of-novels, long-poems, collages, plays, concrete art, news items. "New wave, experimental, conceptual. Biased toward futurism, anarchy, language. Clean xerox welcome. SASE. We consider the essay an actual art form and have similar feelings about advertising. Never Enough poetry!" circ. 2,000. 4/yr. Pub'd 4 issues 1979; expects 6 issues 1980. sub. price: $6.00; per copy: $1.75; sample: $1.75. Back issues: Sex & Death #1 & #2: $0.50 each. Discounts: standard rates. 40-90pp; of. Reporting time: 2-6 weeks. Payment: copies. Copyrighted, reverts to author. Pub's reviews. §All 45's, EP's, received will be listed if not actually reviewed. Ads: send for media kit. CCLM, COSMEP.

S-B Gazette (see STAR WEST)

The S & S Co., Alfred D. Niess, 11047 Antiock Road, Central Point, OR 97502, (503) 826-7870. 1967. Satire. "At present doing only self publishing *Monkeyshines For a Laughing Lunacy* 80 pages or more 5 1/2 x 8 1/2 paperback perfect bind for $4.95 per copy. It has two sections the first is humor, burlesques, and satire: the second is humorous poems, epigrams, and jokes. The first edition will be

500 books. Scheduled publication date is 12-1-78. We are looking for a simultanious or co-publish arrangement in or from another market area. Please submit only books already in print during 1979. Funds are limited so please include return postage if you wish your book back. We look for humor in any of its forms 80 pages or more in book. Our purpose is to add a smile to our times. Address up to May 25, 1981, Box 1425, Pomona, CA 91769." avg. press run 500+. Expects 1 title 1980, 1 title 1981. 1 title listed in the *Small Press Record of Books in Print* (9th Edition, 1980). avg. price, paper: $4.95. Discounts: 10% to libraries and institutions. 80pp; 5½X8½; of. Reporting time: 60 days maximum. Payment: 10%, if book sells well 15%. Copyrights for author.

S & S Press (see also KTQ:KITTY TORTURE QUARTERLY), D. W. Skrabanek, Anne R. Souby, PO Box 5931, Austin, TX 78763. 1978. Poetry, fiction, articles, art, cartoons, interviews, satire, reviews, plays, news items. "We are dedicated to the pursuit of whatever strikes our fancy." avg. press run 250-500. Pub'd 1 title 1979; expects 2 titles 1980, 2-3 titles 1981. 1 title listed in the *Small Press Record of Books in Print* (9th Edition, 1980). avg. price, paper: $2 to $6. Discounts: Trade 40%; libraries 20%. 36-150pp; 5X8, 7X8; of. Reporting time: 4-6 weeks (SASE). Payment: varies, average 5-10%. Copyrights for author. Texas Circuit.

SACKBUT REVIEW, Angela Peckenpaugh, 2513 E Webster Place, Milwaukee, WI 53211. 1978. Poetry, fiction, articles, art, photos, interviews, reviews, letters. "Prefer art that is pro-nature, advocating positive relations among living things, aesthetically pleasing, though not necessarily naive in its view of life. The style should be stimulating, whether through innovation of the imagination or due to the passion of the author. I am not fond of long poetry and do not want to circulate anything that is suicidal, war-like, enervating or pornographic. Decorative or antique art are fine." circ. 300. 4/yr. Expects 1 issue 1980, 3 issues 1981. sub. price: $3.50; per copy: $1.00; sample: $1.00 + $.50 postage. 32-40pp; 8½X5½; of. Reporting time: less than a month. Payment: at least 1 copy. Copyrighted. §Poetry, or collections of short stories; work by women a high priority, but anything non sexist and high quality intrigues: publications with emphasis on translation. Ads: $10/$5.

Sackett Publications, Ernest L. Sackett, 100 Waverly Drive, Grants Pass, OR 97526, (503) 476-6404.

Sagarin Press, Roy H. Sagarin, Nanci DeLucrezia, Box 251, Sand Lake, NY 12153. 1975. "Basically oriented to new ideas, creative non-fiction/poetry Ron Morris-circus writer/Lyn Lifshin/Gary Livingston. *Please note: so far I have published only books first under the Omphalos Press imprint and now as Sagarin Press. Siv Cedering Fox, Frederick Morgan, Peter Kane Default, Rochelle Owens, Daniella Gioseffi." avg. press run 1,000. Pub'd 5 titles 1979; expects 6-8 titles 1980. 9 titles listed in the *Small Press Record of Books in Print* (9th Edition, 1980). avg. price, cloth: $8.95 / $9.95; paper: $3.00 / $4.95. Discounts: 1-4 copies-25 percent, 5-49 copies 40 percent, etc. 60pp; 6X9, 7½X11½; of. Reporting time: 6 months or more. Payment: copies/royalties/contracts. Copyrights for author. COSMEP, NESPA.

Sage Press (see also PULP), 720 Greenwich St 4H, New York City, NY 10014. 2 titles listed in the *Small Press Record of Books in Print* (9th Edition, 1980).

Sagittarius Rising, Tracy Marks, P.O. Box 252, Arlington, MA 02174, (617) 646-2692. 1977. "Astrological books and booklets. Titles so far: *TURNING SQUARES INTO TRINES*: Astrological Essays, Tracy Marks; *DIRECTORY OF NEW ENGLAND ASTROLOGERS*: How to choose an Astrologer 64 entries by New England astrologers edited by Tracy Marks. *The Twelfth House* by Tracy Marks, 1978; *Art of Chart Synthesis* by Track Marks, 1979; *How to Handle Your T-Square* by Tracy Marks, 1979. Submissions for booklet series (6,000-18,000 words) only." avg. press run 3,000. Pub'd 2 titles 1979; expects 3 titles 1980, 3 titles 1981. 5 titles listed in the *Small Press Record of Books in Print* (9th Edition, 1980). avg. price, paper: $7.00. Discounts: 40% 6-25, 45% 26-50, 50% 51-100, 55% 101+. 180pp; 5½X8½; of. Reporting time: 2 months. Payment: No royalty or payment. Minimum charge for inclusion in directory. Does not copyright for author. COSMEP.

Saint Andrews Press (see also SAINT ANDREWS REVIEW), Ron Bayes, William Loftus, Edna Ann Osmanski, St Andrews College, Laurinburg, NC 28352, (919) 276-3652. 1969-70. Poetry, fiction, long-poems, plays. "Unlike the *St Andrews Review*, which welcomes unsolicited mss, the press solicits its ms—often from previous contributors to the magazine. Books average about 60 pp. Recent books: *Names, Dates, & Places* (Joel Oppenheimer), *Leave Your Sugar For The Cold Morning* (Warren Carrier). Forthcoming: *Here I Am!* (Dick Bakken), *Terra Amata* (Kathryn B. Gurkin), *Middle Creek Poems* (Shelby Stephenson), *The Medicine Woman* (Julie Suk), *St Sebastian's Arrows* (by the late Edgar A. Austin), and *Shanghai Creek Fire* (by Rob Hollis Miller). Following the above releases we plan genre celebrations of our first decade with works by Yukio Mishima (drama), Susan Sibley (fiction), a volume of poetry edited by Thad Stem and Sallie Nixon, and a volume of Ezra Pound criticism." avg. press run 500. Pub'd 4-5 titles 1979. avg. price, paper: $5.00. Discounts: 40%. 60pp; 6X9; lp. Reporting time:

Currently not accepting, query after Jan. 1981. Payment: 100 copies in lieu of royalty. Does not copyright for author. CCLM, COSMEP.

SAINT ANDREWS REVIEW, Saint Andrews Press, William J. Loftus, St. Andrews College, Laurinburg, NC 28352, 919-276-3652. 1970. Poetry, fiction, articles, art, photos, interviews, criticism, reviews, parts-of-novels, long-poems, collages, plays, non-fiction. "Pound Studies, Black Mountain Studies, Japanese Studies (esp. Mishima) continue to be interests, but we are not exclusivist and eagerly seek new talent. Recent contributors have included Rex McGuinn, Sister Bernetta Quinn, Jon Johnson, Sizzo DeRachewiltz, Yukio Mishima translated by Hiroaki Sato, Joel Oppenheimer, E. Waverly Land, John Cage, Tom Patterson, Martin Robbins, and John Williamson. We try to run at least one outstanding long poem each issue (e.g.: Judith Johnson Sherwin's *How The Dead Count.*" circ. 300-500. 2/yr. Pub'd 2 issues 1979; expects 2 issues 1980, 2 issues 1981. sub. price: $6.00; per copy: $3.00; sample: $1.50. Back issues: On request. Discounts: 40%. 120pp; 7X10; of. Reporting time: av 1 month during ac yr. Payment: copies. Copyrighted, reverts to author. Pub's reviews: 4 in 1979. §Books of poetry, fiction, no mags. Ads: $50.00/$25.00. CCLM, COSMEP.

ST. CROIX REVIEW, Angus MacDonald, Ed & Publ., Box 244, Stillwater, MN 55082, (612) 439-7190. 1968. Articles, cartoons, criticism, reviews, letters. "19th century liberalism" circ. 2,000. 6/yr. Pub'd 6 issues 1979; expects 6 issues 1980, 6 issues 1981. sub. price: $10.00; per copy: $2.00; sample: $1.00 postage & handling. Back issues: $2.00. Discounts: 50% for bulk orders, of 10. 48pp; 6X9; †of. Reporting time: 14 days. Payment: none. Copyrighted, does not revert to author. Pub's reviews: 50 in 1979. §social criticism. Ads: $100/$50.

Saint Heironymous Press, Inc., David Lance Goines, PO Box 9431, Berkeley, CA 94709, 415-549-1405. 1971. Poetry, art, concrete art. avg. press run 5,000. Pub'd 1 title 1979; expects 2 titles 1980. 7 titles listed in the *Small Press Record of Books in Print* (9th Edition, 1980). avg. price, paper: $9.50. Discounts: trade 40 percent (over $500 - 50 percent), Educational Institutions 20 percent. 56pp; size large format; †of/lp. Copyrights for author.

SAINT LOUIS HOME/GARDEN, Jack Bick, PO Box 29348, St Louis, MO 63127, (314) 965-1234. 1978. Articles, photos. "Local home and garden magazine dealing exclusively with Saint Louis, MO." circ. 20,000. 12/yr. Pub'd 8 issues 1979. sub. price: $12.00; per copy: $1.50; sample: $2.00. Back issues: $2.00. Discounts: over 50 $9.00 subscription. 88pp; 8½X11; of. Reporting time: query only. Payment: $75.00-$150.00 depending on length & photography. Copyrighted, does not revert to author. Pub's reviews. Ads: $725/$400/50¢.

ST. LOUIS JOURNALISM REVIEW, Focus/Midwest Publishing Co., Inc., Charles L. Klotzer, Publisher; Board of Editors, 928A N. McKnight, St. Louis, MO 63132, 314-991-1699. 1970. Articles, photos, cartoons, interviews, satire, criticism, reviews, letters, news items. circ. 6,000. 6/yr. Pub'd 6 issues 1979; expects 6 issues 1980, 6 issues 1981. sub. price: $7.00; libraries $9.60; per copy: $.75; sample: $.75 plus postage. Back issues: $2.00 plus postage. Discounts: 20% to subagencies, 40% to stores & outlets. 12-16pp; 11X16½; of. Reporting time: 4 weeks. Payment: $25.00 and up to $100.00 (or more). Copyrighted, does not revert to author. Pub's reviews: 10 in 1979. §journalism, particularly St Louis area, media, communications, press and broadcasting. Ads: $378.00/$195.00/$2.00.

St. Luke's Press (see also RACCOON), Phyllis Tickle, Managing Editor; David Spicer, Raccoon Editor, Suite 401, 1407 Union Avenue, Memphis, TN 38104, 901-357-5441. 1974. Poetry, fiction, criticism, parts-of-novels, long-poems, plays. "St. Luke's Press—we are publishers of book-length works in general literature. While we are interested in quality work from other sections, our primary function is to provide mid-south writers with a national audience and national distribution." avg. press run 2,000. Pub'd 3 titles 1979; expects 5 titles 1980, 5 titles 1981. 11 titles listed in the *Small Press Record of Books in Print* (9th Edition, 1980). avg. price, cloth: $8.95; paper: $6.95. Discounts: 40 percent trade; bulk, negotiable; wholesalers, 50 percent. pp Varies; size varies; of. Reporting time: 1-2 months. Payment: variable. Copyrights for author. COSMEP, COSMEP-SOUTH.

ST. MAWR, St. Mawr Jazz Poetry Project, John H. Kennedy, Box 356, Randolph, VT 05060. 1973 (print) 1977 (tape). Poetry, articles, art, interviews, music, long-poems, plays, news items. "*VEINS* is now a cassette mag. publishing jazz poetry, poetic drama, music; poetry, and interviews. All submissions should be on tape cassettes unless previous arrangements for us to do the recording have been made. Interested in multi-media experiments with music & poetry. Primarily interested in jazz poetry any length. International university circulation. Also interviews." circ. varies. irregular. Expects 3 issues 1980. sub. price: $12.00 per 180 minutes of tape; per copy: $3.50 or $3.00 plus SASE (3 oz.); sample: $0.24 stamp (back printed issues). Back issues: free for $0.24 stamp. Discounts: 40% bulk, min. 20. 45 min. per tape; 45 min. tape cassette; Magnetic tape cassette recorder. Reporting time: 3 weeks. Payment: copies. copyrights: if you are concerned, secure your own; assign us one time

352

rights. Pub's reviews. §poetry & music (also poetics). Ads which have redeeming artistic value will be published free. CCLM, NESPA.

St. Mawr Jazz Poetry Project (see also ST. MAWR), Box 356, Randolph, VT 05060. 1970. Poetry, art, music. "Unsolicited manuscripts not accepted." avg. press run 500. Pub'd 1 title 1979; expects 1 title 1980, 1 title 1981. avg. price, paper: $3.00. Discounts: 40% wholesale (minimum: 10). 50pp; 6X9; of/lp. Copyrights for author. CCLM, NESPA.

Salem Press, Inc. (see THE CONTEMPORARY LITERARY SCENE)

SALOME: A LITERARY DANCE MAGAZINE, Ommation Press, Effie Mihopoulos, Editor, 5548 N. Sawyer, Chicago, IL 60625, (312) 539-5745. 1975. Poetry, fiction, articles, art, photos, cartoons, interviews, criticism, reviews, music, plays, concrete art, satire, letters, long-poems, collages. "SALOME is a dance magazine that contains poems, short stories, plays, etc. about the dance; in all its forms. Please, do not send any material unrelated to the dance. Dance-related poems as special poem postcard issues of SALOME($2.00 a set), for which manuscripts are always welcome. Recent contributors: Bobbie Louise Hawkins, Ted Berrigan, Alice Notley, John Tagliabue, Richard Kostelanetz, Lyn Lifshin." circ. 500. 4/yr. Pub'd 4 issues 1979; expects 4 issues 1980. sub. price: $7.50; per copy: $2.00 (poem postcard issues); $4.00 (double issues); sample: $2.00 (postcards); $4.00 (double issue). Back issues: $4.00 each (double issue). Discounts: 40% 10 copies or more. 40pp; 8½X11; of. Reporting time: Immediately - 2 weeks. Payment: contributor's copy. Copyrighted, reverts to author. Pub's reviews: 50 books in 1979. §everything concerning dance, performing arts, (books, magazines, performances, etc.). Ads: $8.00/$40.00/$20.00. CCLM, COSMEP, MIDWEST.

THE SALT CEDAR, Tamarix, Don Snow, Editor; Lyn Chaffee, Assistant Editor, Rt 2, Box 170 B, Stevensville, MT 59870, (406) 777-5169. 1976. Poetry, fiction, articles, art, reviews, parts-of-novels, long-poems. "Hope to print more non-fiction prose & short stories in upcoming issues. Mostly interested in writing about the West, its landform, biota, community. Contribs: Peter Wild, Reg Saner, Lynn Strongin, Pamela Stewart, Lyn Hejinian, Phil Foss...We typeset & layout our own, and guarantee the purdiest little magazine in print." 2/yr. Pub'd 2 issues 1979. sub. price: $3.50; per copy: $2.00; sample: $2.00. Back issues: $2.00. Discounts: 40 percent for all. 30-40pp; 8½X11; of. Reporting time: 4-6 weeks. Payment: copies. Copyrighted, reverts to author. Pub's reviews: 5 in 1979. §poetry, non-fiction prose, natural history, environmental writings. CCLM.

SALT LICK, Salt Lick Press, PO Box 1064, Quincy, IL 62301.

Salt Lick Press (see also LUCKY HEART BOOKS; SALT LICK), James Haining, PO Box 1064, Quincy, IL 62301. 1939. "Open. Published materials by Bly, Lally, Burns, Searcy, Catelaz,Trammell, Hubert, Franck, Ahern, Siegel, Shuttleworth, Brown, Slater, Andrews, Silliman, Dante, Di Palma, et al." avg. press run 15,000. Expects 1 title 1980, 1 title 1981. 5 titles listed in the *Small Press Record of Books in Print* (9th Edition, 1980). avg. price, paper: $3.00. 68pp; 8½X11; †of/hand work. Reporting time: 10 days. Payment: copies and $ if available. Copyrights for author. COSMEP.

Salt-Works Press (see also SOMA-HAOMA), Tom Bridwell, Box 2152, Vineyard Haven, MA 02568, 617-385-3948. 1973. Poetry, fiction, articles, art, photos, criticism, long-poems, non-fiction. "Fine hand-set letterpress publications, hand-sewn, graphics, often use hand made paper (our own) for covers." avg. press run 300-400. Pub'd 10 titles 1979; expects 10 titles 1980. 38 titles listed in the *Small Press Record of Books in Print* (9th Edition, 1980). avg. price, cloth: $15.00; paper: $3.00-$5.00. Discounts: Standard. pp varies; 6X9; †lp. Reporting time: 6 weeks. Payment: Copies, plus. Copyrights for author.

SALTHOUSE, Salthouse Mining Company, D. Clinton, SALTHOUSE, Dept. of English, B. G. S. U., Bowling Green, OH 43403. 1975. Poetry, criticism, reviews, parts-of-novels, long-poems. "*Salthouse* and the Salthouse Mining Company is an eclectic enterprise, with a whimsical publishing schedule. For a glimpse of our work, please purchase a set of issues. Nos. 1-6 ($5) should be as good as any statement on what our philosophy is, has been and probably will be. Our interest is in work which centers on a number of disciplines: cultural anthropology of the Americas, experimental history of the Americas, criticism pertinent to the above areas, poetry and fiction which is flavored by a sense of anthropology, geography and history, and criticism of that kind of fiction and poetry. Were we rich, we'd publish at a more regular pace, but we are not rich, and it may take us several years to put out just one slim volume/issue. All our contributors need to be patient. Issue 7: *The Convade Papers* by Bill Herron (A very short mysterious novel about an interesting birthing phenomena): $1.25. Issue 8/9: *Sly Ohio* by Dennis Shramek (A wooly novel fragment about sexy Puritans): $3.00. Available autumn, 1980. The entire set (Issues No. 1-8/9) is available then for $10 (includes postage)." circ. 600. erratic. Pub'd 1 issue 1979; expects 1-2 issues 1980, 1 issue 1981. 1 title listed in the *Small Press Record of Books in Print* (9th Edition, 1980). sub. price: $3.00 for 2 issues/ $6.00 for 4 issues; per copy:

varies; sample: $2.00. Back issues: Nos. 1-6 at $5.00, single issue - $2. Discounts: 50% on orders of 10 or more for issues printed in 1979. pp varies; maximum 60 pages; 8½X11; of. Reporting time: maximum 6 months. Payment: complimentary issues. Copyrighted, reverts to author. Pub's reviews: 4 in 1979. §works which center on land or history. Ads: $30.00/$15.00. CCLM.

Salthouse Mining Company (see SALTHOUSE)

SAMISDAT, Samisdat Associates, Merritt Clifton, Editor-in-Chief; Robin Michelle Clifton, Reviews Editor; Tom Suddick, Contributing Editor; Adrian Rocha, Artist; Stella Popowski, Artist, Box 231, Richford, VT 05476. 1973. Poetry, fiction, art, satire, criticism, parts-of-novels, long-poems, plays. "We engage life for the living, for those of us daring to seize command of our destinies, Big Brother and his threat of nuclear apocalypse be damned! Our purpose is a awaken the mind & senses, overcoming numbing pop-culture, pigeonholing psychobabble, & religious & educationally imposed inner limits. We want fiction, poetry, & art done with confidence in subject, subtle style, flair, & most of all, with both deep thought and feeling. We seek communication, not internal whisperings & laments significant only to the author; message, not the so-called crafted emphasis on medium alone. Eco-freaks, outlaws, rebels, anarchists, & libertarians may find themselves among friends here—*but read us first!* We cannot be categorized or defined from a distance, or in general terms. We handle all submissions as personal correspondence. If we can help, we do so; asswipe we so identify. All photocopied manuscripts become asswipe, as do all without SASE, unread. Recent *Samisdat* writers: Catherine McAllister, James Miller Robinson, Tim Coates, Tom Cody, W.D. Ehrhart. The publish-or-perish crowd need not apply. We publish for a living—& on 37¢ an hour, have to love it as well. Canadian contributors should address Box 10, Brigham, Quebec, JOE 1J0" circ. 300-500. 4/yr. Pub'd 4 issues 1979; expects 4 issues 1980. sub. price: $12.00 for 500 pages, minimum; $20 for 1,000, our 1980 production. $100 brings all future issues and books.; per copy: $2.00; sample: $2.00. Back issues: query. Discounts: dicker. 64-88pp; 8½X5½; †of. Reporting time: Two seconds to two weeks. Payment: copies. Copyrighted, reverts to author. Pub's reviews: 360 in 1979. §We review & rate everything that comes in, if semi-relevant to writing & literature; exchange with anyone once, at least. We only review quality at any length, however, and are death on crudzines, vanity, & sheer self-indulgence. Ads: $15.

Samisdat Associates (see also SAMISDAT), Box 231, Richford, VT 05476. 1973. Poetry, fiction, criticism. "*Samisdat* books & chapbooks are published under a cooperative arrangement whereby authors supply cost of materials while we supply all necessary labor. Press runs are proportionately divided, usually half-and-half. We sell our share with *Samisdat* subscriptions; authors generally hawk theirs at readings, sometimes by mail, profiting 57 times on our 67 books to date. We won't take on an author unwilling to help us hustle, or interested in appearance & the mere fact of publication over & above building readership. We prefer authors already familiar with *Samisdat*, but do consider others, editing as strictly yet heterogeneously as for regular magazine issues. Recent authors include Jo Schaper, Andy Gunderson, Haywood Jackson, Dough Odom, Margaret Kingery, Everett Whealdon, W.D. Ehrhart, James Magorian, Corla Eugster, Gary Metras, Rita Rosenfeld, Gloria North, Kurt Nimmo, Real Faucher, Margaret Key Biggs, Peter Payack, Merritt Clifton and Robin Michelle Clifton. While our main series is literary, we have recently revived a non-fiction line including *The Samisdat Method: A Do-It-Yourself Guide To Offset Printing, and Relative Baseball,* a detailed statistical analysis of baseball's greatest players ($2.00 apiece)" avg. press run 400. Pub'd 12-15 titles 1979; expects 12-15 titles 1980. 54 titles listed in the *Small Press Record of Books in Print* (9th Edition, 1980). avg. price, paper: $1.00. 12-40pp; 8½X5½; †of. Reporting time: 2 minutes to 2 weeks. Copyrights for author.

SAMPHIRE, Michael Butler, Kemble Williams, Heronshaw, Holbrook, Ipswich, United Kingdom. 1968. Poetry. "Reviews used. Mag should be studied first." circ. 700 plus. 3/yr. Pub'd 3 issues 1979; expects 3 issues 1980. sub. price: £6.00; per copy: £1.50 (inc. airmail $2.00); sample: $2.00. Back issues: by arrangement. Discounts: 33⅓ percent. 48pp; 8½X5¾; lo. Reporting time: 6-8 wks. Payment: £2.00 per poem/page. Copyrighted. Pub's reviews: 9 in 1979. §Poetry, criticism. Ads: By arrangement.

Samuel Powell Publishing Company, 2125 1/2 I Street, Sacramento, CA 95816, (916) 443-1161. 1978. Fiction. avg. press run 1,500. Pub'd 1 title 1979. 1 title listed in the *Small Press Record of Books in Print* (9th Edition, 1980). avg. price, paper: $4.50. Discounts: 50% Distributors; 40% Bookstores. 120pp; 5½X8½. Copyrights for author.

SAN FERNANDO POETRY JOURNAL, Kent Publications, Richard Cloke, Editor in Chief; Shirley J. Rodecker, Associate Editor; Lori C. Smith, Associate Editor; Terry Buss, Associate Editor, 18301 Halsted Street, Northridge, CA 91325. 1979. Poetry. "No racist, chauvinist or pro-war material. Though regional to San Fernando Valley & Los Angeles, it is a *loose* regionalism & need not concern the region, nor need the author reside in it necessarily. Preference shown to authors residing in the general area once stolen from Mexico. Usual submission with SASE. Seeking peripheral, experimental, new frontiers-of-consciousness poetry. Entries with metre & rhyme will be used if subject is non-traditional. (Prefer themes with social consciousness, outward looking themes *Weltanschauung* —though we're not stubborn & will welcome good material on any theme or in any genre. Our crystal ball, however, tells us of much trouble ahead.)" circ. 500. 4/yr. Pub'd 3 issues 1979; expects 4 issues 1980, 4 issues 1981. sub. price: $8.00; per copy: $2.50; sample: $2.50, will exchange with other poetry mags, no chg. Back issues: Vol.I #1:$4.00; #2: $3.25. Back issue originals: prices will tend to rise in time. Discounts: Wholesale, 30%; Bookstores, 20%; Libraries, 20%. 60pp; 5½X8½; of. Reporting time: 30-60 days. Payment: None for less than 500 first run. 1 Free copy of mag. to each author, addition 20% discount. Copyrighted, reverts to author. Ads: $50.00/$25.-00/$10.00. COSMEP.

San Francisco Center for Visual Studies, David Howard, 49 Rivoli, San Francisco, CA 94117, (415) 285-7114. 1975. Photos, interviews. "Book contributors: Ansel Adams, David Howard, Jerry Uelsman, Ralph Gibson, etc. Primarily photography books concerned with contemporary photography and the history of photography!" avg. press run 2,000. Pub'd 1 title 1979; expects 1 title 1980. avg. price, paper: $6.95. Discounts: 40%. 88pp; 8½X11. We take no submissions. Copyrights for author.

SAN FRANCISCO REVIEW OF BOOKS, Ron Nowicki, 1111 Kearny Street, San Francisco, CA 94133, 415-HA1-9574. 1975. Articles, photos, cartoons, interviews, criticism, reviews, letters, news items. "Book reviews of titles from both large and small presses; current titles, but not best sellers. Minimum no. words: 600; Max. 2,000, with editor's ok. Recent contributors: Andrei Codrescu, Leonard Michaels, William Kotzwinkle, Raymond Carver, Stanley Weintraub, Gloria Frym, Valerie Miner, Chandler Brossard, Herbert Gold, Ron Silliman, Kay Boyle." circ. 20,000. 12/yr. Pub'd 11 issues 1979; expects 12 issues 1980. sub. price: $10.00; per copy: $1.00; sample: $1.00. Back issues: 75¢. Discounts: Usually 40 percent on consignments, 40 percent on outright purchases of 5 or more. 40pp; 11X15; of. Reporting time: 3-4 wks. Payment: 1 yrs. subscription plus copies. copyrighted, author must request rights, no problem. Pub's reviews: 300 in 1979. §Fiction, poetry, nonfiction, small press & fine print books. Ads: $500.00/$275.00/$12.00 col inch; repeat discounts. CCLM, COSMEP, ABA.

SAN FRANCISCO STORIES, George Matchette, Robert Monson, Charles Rubin, 625 Post Street, Box 752, San Francisco, CA 94109, (415) 752-7506. 1979. Fiction, parts-of-novels. "Stories or novel excerpts of 8,000 words or less. We try to print a variety of styles and subjects representative of the diverse ethnic and cultural segments of the community." circ. 1,000. 2/yr. price per copy: $3.25; sample: $3.25. Discounts: negotiable. 100pp; 5½X8½; of. Reporting time: 6-8 weeks. Payment: 2 copies. Copyrighted, reverts to author.

SAN JOSE STUDIES, A.N. Okerlund, San Jose State Univ., San Jose, CA 95192, 408-277-3460. 1975. Poetry, fiction, articles, art, photos, cartoons, interviews, satire, criticism, reviews, letters, long-poems. "*San Jose Studies* is published in February, May, and November. Manuscripts, books for reviewing, photo essays, and editorial communications should be sent to the editor at the above address, subscriptions and business communications should be sent to the managing editor at the above address. *San Jose Studies* publishes articles, literature, photographs, and art appealing to the educated public. Critical, creative, and informative writing in the broad areas of the arts, humanities, sciences, and social sciences will be considered. $100.00 annual award for best contribution published. Please limit contributions to a maximum of 5,000 words and avoid footnotes when possible. All mss. must be typewritten and double-spaced on standard 8½ x 11 white bond. The editorial board will need an original and one copy of the ms. SASE for return. Only previously unpublished work will be considered." circ. 400. 3/yr. Pub'd 3 issues 1979; expects 3 issues 1980. sub. price: $8.00; per copy: $3.50; sample: $3.50. Back issues: $2.00. Discounts: none. 112pp; 6X9; of. Reporting time: 2-3 mos. Payment: 2 copies. Copyrighted. Pub's reviews: 3 in 1979. §literature, history. Ads: $100/$60/none. Council of Editors of Learned Journals.

SAN MARCOS REVIEW, Gene Frumkin, David Johnson, P.O. Box 4368, Albuquerque, NM 87196. 1976. Poetry, articles, interviews, reviews, long-poems. "We are looking for poetry which begins with the uprooting of words, words which become unique, as if just born, but which then return to community, transformed, to participate in its myths, dreams, and passions." circ. 500. 2/yr. sub. price: $7.00/4 issues in U.S.-$8.00/4 issues other countries; per copy: $2.00; sample: free to libraries & educ. institutions. Discounts: 40% trade/20% bulk, classroom, etc. 60-80pp; 6X9; †of. Reporting time: 6-10 wks. Payment: 2 copies, payment. Copyrighted, reverts to author. Pub's reviews: 4 in 1979. §poetry. Ads: $40.00/$20.00.

San Pedro Press (see also WHETSTONE), Michael Bowden, Rural Route 1, Box 221, St David, AZ 85630. 1978. Poetry, art, photos, criticism, reviews. avg. press run 300. Pub'd 3 titles 1979; expects 3 titles 1980. avg. price, paper: $2.00. Discounts: 40% off for orders of 5 or more copies to booksellers. 56pp; 8½X5½; of. Reporting time: 1-6 weeks. Payment: contributor copies. Copyrights for author. CCLM.

Sanatana Publishing Society (see also VISHVAMITRA), Narada Muni, 3100 White Sulphur Springs Road, St. Helena, CA 94574, 707-963-9487. 1975. Articles, photos. "The Sanatana Publishing Society has as its primary purpose making the Sanatana Dharma available to the Western World through the publication of works by Swami Kripalvananda, Yogeshwar Muni, and others of our yogic tradition. We also publish works of related religious and philosophical interest, and new translations of important yogic scripture. Published materials range from short manuals and pamphlets to long books." avg. press run 2,000. Pub'd 1 title 1979; expects 1 title 1980, 1 title 1981. 5 titles listed in the *Small Press Record of Books in Print* (9th Edition, 1980). avg. price, paper: $2.00. Discounts: 1 copy net, 2-4 copies 20%,5-49 copies 40%, 50-99 copies 45%, 100-199 copies 48%, 200 or more copies 50%. 70pp; 4X6; of. Payment: no royalties. Copyrights for author. COSMEP.

Sand Dollar, Jack Shoemaker, Vicki Shoemaker, 1222 Solano Avenue, Albany, CA 94706. 1970. Poetry, articles, photos. "We are presently unable to consider unsolicited manuscripts. Recent books by Michael Davidson, Bill Berkson, Leslie Scalapino, Theodore Enslin, Wendell Berry, Ronald Johnson." avg. press run 1,000. Pub'd 5 titles 1979. 18 titles listed in the *Small Press Record of Books in Print* (9th Edition, 1980). avg. price, cloth: $15.00; paper: $4.00. of/lp. Reporting time: 1 month. Payment: 10% royalty. Copyrights for author.

Sand Project Press/US (see also BLUE PIG), 23 Cedar Street, Northampton, MA 01060. 1 title listed in the *Small Press Record of Books in Print* (9th Edition, 1980).

SANDSCRIPT, Cape Cod Writers Inc, Barbara Renkens Dunning, Editor; Jean Lunn, Poetry Editor, Box 333, Cummaquid, MA 02637, 617-362-6078. 1977. Poetry, fiction, photos, interviews, reviews, parts-of-novels. "Most contributors either live on Cape Cod or visit the Cape in the summer; however a limited amount of material is published by new writers from other areas." circ. 500. 2/yr. sub. price: $3.50; per copy: $2.00; sample: $1.50. Back issues: $1.50. Discounts: 50% discount to bookstores and in quanities of more than five. 50pp; 6X9; of. Reporting time: up to two months. Payment: 1 free copy. Copyrighted, reverts to author. Pub's reviews. §Fiction, poetry, magazines, children's books for our *CHILDREN'S PAGE.* Ads: $25.00/$15.00. NESPA.

The Sandstone Press, 321 East 43rd Street, New York, NY 10017, (212) 682-5519. 1971. Art, photos. avg. press run 500. Pub'd 1 title 1979; expects 1 title 1980, 10 titles 1981. Discounts: 40% to trade; negotiable on order for more than 50 copies; jobber negotiable. 125pp; 6X9; lp. Reporting time: 4-6 weeks. Payment: negotiable. Copyrights for author.

Sans Serif Press (see ALTERNATIVE FUTURES: THE JOURNAL OF UTOPIAN STUDIES)

SANTA BARBARA HARBOR NEWS, Jo McNally, PO Box 30802, Santa Barbara, CA 93105, 682-5545. 1979. "Now on Vol. 1, #5 first issue was May 1979 ISSN 01935925" circ. 1,800. 12/yr. sub. price: free distribution. 12pp; 8X12; †of. Reporting time: 1 week. Payment: based on column inch. Copyrighted. Pub's reviews. §The sea, boating, navigation, island lore. Ads: $35.00/$20.00/$1.00 for 15 words.

SAP Society for the Advancement of Poetics, Jess Graf, 14 Washington, c/o Jess Graf, Denver, CO 80203, 733-8288. 1976. Poetry, art, reviews. "Denver poetry plus guests" avg. press run 500. Pub'd 1 title 1979; expects 1 title 1980, 1 title 1981. avg. price, paper: $3.00-$4.00. 50pp; 5½X8½; of. Reporting time: 1 month. Payment: 2 copies. Does not copyright for author.

SAPPHO, Sappho Publications Ltd, Jacqueline Forster, BCM/PETREL, London WC1V6XX, United Kingdom. 1972. Articles, poetry, fiction, art, cartoons, photos, satire, reviews, news items, interviews, criticism, letters. "Contents contributed by readers/subscribers about women's/gays rights. Contributors: Jill Tweedie, Anna Raeburn, & Maureen Duffy." circ. 3,000. 12/yr. Pub'd 12 issues 1979; expects 12 issues 1980, 12 issues 1981. sub. price: U.K. subs. £7.00 1 year; overseas subs £8.40 12 months surface; per copy: UK: 60p plus 10p postage; overseas £1.00 surface. Back issues: £1.00 for 3. Discounts: 10% minumum on ads. 20pp; size A4; of. Reporting time: 1 month. Payment: none. Copyrighted. Pub's reviews: 6 in 1979. §Feminism, lesbianism. Ads: £40.00/£24.00/£16.00/£$10.00.

Sappho Publications Ltd (see also SAPPHO), Jackie Forster, Joan Young, BCM/Petrel, London WC1V6XX, United Kingdom. 1972. Poetry, fiction, articles, photos, cartoons, interviews, satire, criticism, reviews, letters, news items. "Monthly publication. Lesbian/feminist" avg. press run 1,000. 2 titles listed in the *Small Press Record of Books in Print* (9th Edition, 1980). avg. price, other: 65p sterling surface mail, £1.05 sterling airmail only USA/Canada. 36pp; size A4; of. Reporting time: varies. Payment: None. Copyrights for author.

SARCOPHAGUS, Ashford Press, M. J. Westerfield, RR1, Box 128, Ashford, CT 06278. 1975. Poetry, fiction, art, satire, parts-of-novels. "Quality material in any genre is welcomed. Individual poems generally should not exceed 2 typewritten pages. Religious & political material not normally used." circ. 500. 2/yr. Pub'd 2 issues 1979; expects 2 issues 1980, 2 issues 1981. sub. price: $5.00; per copy: $2.50. 50pp; 6X9; †of/lp. Reporting time: 2 weeks. Payment: in contributor copies, occasional cash awards for exceptional material. Copyrighted, reverts to author.

Saru, Drew Stroud, c/o Bradley, 110 W Kinnear Place, Seattle, WA 98119. 1979. Poetry. "I am primarily interested in accurate, imaginative translations of Japanese and Hispanic-Luso-American poetry. I am unsubsidized and print entirely at my own expense at present, so anyone submitting should be prepared to pay part or all of the cost of production." avg. press run 500. Pub'd 1 title 1979; expects 2 titles 1980. avg. price, cloth: $10.00; paper: $6.00. Discounts: depends on size or order. On large orders, can supply at very close to cost. of. Reporting time: will read immediately upon receipt. Payment: depends how much of production cost is shared by author.

The Saturday Centre (see also SCOPP), Patricia Laird, Kenneth Laird, Box 140 P.O., Cammeray, NSW 2062, Australia. 1972. "Work in any language (with English translation). Poems & short stories by little-known writers. Recent books by: Eric Beach; Philip Hammial; L.E. Scott; Kenneth Prunty; John-Peter Horsam. NB Contributors *must* send adequate postage for return or reply." avg. press run 500-1,000. Pub'd 4 titles 1979; expects 3 titles 1980, 6 titles 1981. 11 titles listed in the *Small Press Record of Books in Print* (9th Edition, 1980). avg. price, paper: $4.00. Discounts: 25% to agents, 40% to bookshops (firm orders only). 60pp; 4½X8¼; †of. Reporting time: less than 3 months, no promises to overseas contributors. Payment: arranged privately with author. Copyrights for author.

Scarecrow Press, Wm. R. Eshelman, Pres & Editor; Gary Kuris, Editor; Barbara Lee, Assistant Editor, P O Box 656, Metuchen, NJ 08840, 201-548-8600. 1950. Criticism. "Very varied list. Emphasis on reference books, scholarly monographs, some professional textbooks. Dominant subject areas include: Cinema, women, minorities, music, literature, library science, social work, parapsychology." avg. press run 1,000. Pub'd 100 titles 1979; expects 110 titles 1980, 110 titles 1981. 2 titles listed in the *Small Press Record of Books in Print* (9th Edition, 1980). avg. price, cloth: $12.00. Discounts: Net to libraries, etc; 10% to trade (we pay post). 250pp; 5½X8½; of. Reporting time: 1 week. Payment: 10 percent first 1,000 copies; 15 percent thereafter. Copyrights for author. AAP, ALA.

Scarf Press, Mark L. Levine, 58 E 83rd Street, New York, NY 10028, (212) 744-3901. 1979. "Books available from Ingram, Baker & Taylor, Brodart and Bookazine. Publisher of M.C.Gaines *Picture Stories from the Bible*: The Old Testament in Full Color Comic Strip Form" avg. press run 50,000. Pub'd 1 title 1979; expects 1 title 1980, 1 title 1981. 2 titles listed in the *Small Press Record of Books in Print* (9th Edition, 1980). avg. price, cloth: $9.95. 224pp. Copyrights for author.

The Sceptre Press, Martin Booth, The Sceptre Press, Knotting, Bedford MK44 1AF, United Kingdom. 1968. Poetry, fiction, long-poems, plays. "Length immaterial: catholic range of style and biases but no 'pop' or concrete work; recent contributors include Robert Creeley, Harry Guest, George MacBeth, Gavin Ewart, Ken Smith, Susan Musgrave, Denis Goacher, Peter Redgrove, Penelope Shuttle Alan Sillitoe, Ted Hughes, Sylvia Plath. Unknown poets welcome to submit, but always sending sae. The aim is to publish good verse in booklet form. Do please see what we publish before submitting." avg. press run 150-250. Pub'd 18 titles 1979; expects 18 titles 1980. 32 titles listed in the *Small Press Record of Books in Print* (9th Edition, 1980). avg. price, paper: £2 (US $4). Discounts: trade only. 20 plus pp (prose max. 10,000 words); size A5; 1p. Reporting time: 6 wks. Payment varies. copyright retained by author: registered by us.

SCHOLIA SATYRICA, R.D. Wyly, English Department, University of South Florida, Tampa, FL 33620, 974-2421. 1974. Poetry, fiction, articles, satire, criticism. circ. 310. 2 enlarged issues/yr. Pub'd 3 issues 1979; expects 2 issues 1980. sub. price: $3.50; per copy: $1.75; sample: $1.00. Back issues: $1.25. Discounts: 20 percent to subscription agencies, Faxon, Ebsco etc. 64pp; 5⅜X8½; of. Reporting time: 1-2 months. Payment: copies. Copyrighted, copyright reverts to author after pub. Ads: $50/$30.

The School of Living (see also THE GREEN REVOLUTION), Mildred J Loomis, Editor-Emeritus, RD 7, York, PA 17402. 1940. avg. press run 3,000. Pub'd 10 titles 1979; expects 10 titles 1980, 10 titles 1981. 3 titles listed in the *Small Press Record of Books in Print* (9th Edition, 1980). avg. price, other: $1.00; $8.00 year or donation. 32pp; 8½X11; of. Reporting time: 30 days. Payment: 1 year sub; 10 copies of mags. Does not copyright for author. APS (Alternate Press Syndicate).

Schroder Music Company, Ruth Burnstein, 2027 Parker Street, Berkeley, CA 94704, (415) 843-2365.

SCIENCE FICTION CHRONICLE, Algol Press, Andrew Porter, PO Box 4175, New York, NY 10017, 212-643-9011. 1979. Articles, photos, reviews, letters, news items. "*SF Chronicle* is a monthly newsmagazine serving the SF field through current news, market reports, letters, comprehensive coverage of events, conventions and awards, all mailed first class to subscribers." circ. 2,000. 12/yr. Pub'd 3 issues 1979; expects 12 issues 1980. sub. price: $12.00 (US and Canada); $18.00 (outside North America); per copy: $1.25; sample: $1.25. Back issues: all issues $1.00. Discounts: 50% trade, write: F&SF Book Co., PO Box 415, Staten Island, NY 10302. 16pp; 8¼X11; of. Reporting time: 1 week. Payment: 3¢ word. Copyrighted, does not revert to author. Pub's reviews: 7 in 1979. §SF, children's fantasy. Ads: $150.00/$80.00/$0.20.

SCIENCE FICTION & FANTASY BOOK REVIEW, The Borgo Press, Neil Barron, Box 2845, San Bernardino, CA 92406, (714) 884-5813. 1979. Criticism, reviews. "This is a monthly review magazine of the science fiction and fantasy field which began publication in February, 1979. ISSN 0163-4348. Editorial address: 1149 Lime Place, Vista, California 92083. Editorial phone: 714-726-3238." circ. 500+. 12/yr. Expects 11 issues 1980, 12 issues 1981. sub. price: $12.00, Library rate $15.00; per copy: $1.50; sample: $1.50; Free to libraries. Back issues: $1.50. Discounts: 20% to jobbers & library agents off library subscription rate. 16pp; 8½X11; of. Reporting time: 2 weeks. No payment for reviews other than free subscription; payment of 1¢ per word for short survey articles on particular writers or countries. Copyrighted, rights revert on request, but publisher retains right to reprint in whole or part. Pub's reviews: 821 in 1979. §Science fiction, fantasy, weird fiction, supernatural fiction, non-fiction about science fiction, science fiction art, science fiction movie books, non-print media (calendars, teaching aides, etc.) relating to science fiction. Ads: $99.00/$60.00/$1.00 per line for 48 character line.

SCILLONIAN MAGAZINE, Clive Mumford, c/o T. Mumford, St. Mary's, Isles of Scilly, Cornwall, United Kingdom. 1925. Articles, poetry, fiction, reviews, news items, interviews, letters, photos. "A voluntary local magazine run entirely for the islands." circ. 2,300. 2/yr. Pub'd 2 issues 1979; expects 2 issues 1980, 2 issues 1981. sub. price: £2.30; per copy: £1.15. Back issues: double single copy price. 125pp; 8½X5½. Reporting time: 3-4 weeks. Payment: nil. Copyrighted, reverts to author. Ads: £14.00/£8.00.

The Scoal Press, Scott Marber, 53 Pondview Circle, Brockton, MA 02401, 617-587-4275. 1979. Fiction, satire, parts-of-novels. "We are looking for full length fiction, preferably children's fantasy in the mold of *Alice in Wonderland, The Little Prince, James and the Giant Peach, The Wizard of Oz,* etc. Our first title, *A Lot of Lumps* by Scott Marber, was a 188 page, hardcover, fantasy endorsed as 'the best recent children's literature I've seen,' by John Wing, the host and manager of 'Pooh Corner', a children's radio hour on WRJR Hanover, NH." avg. press run 1,000. Pub'd 1 title 1979. avg. price, cloth: $8.95; paper: $4.95. Discounts: 50% wholesale, 40% retail, 30% libraries, 20% classroom. 192pp; 6X9. Reporting time: 3-6 weeks. Payment: negotiable. Copyrights for author. COSMEP.

Scop Publications, Inc. (see also MOVEMENT), Stacy Tuthill, Walter H. Kerr, Katharine Zadravec, 5821 Swarthmore Drive, College Park, MD 20740, (301) 345-8747. 1977. Poetry, fiction. "Scop Publications, Inc. recently incorporated as a non-profit press. Past contributors to anthologies: Linda Pasten, Josephine Jacobsen, Ann Darr, Gloria Oden, Clarinda Harriss Lott, Barbara Lefcowitz, Myra Sklarew, Katharine Zadravec. Publications: *Rye Bread: Women Poets Rising,* (1977) Ed. by Stacy Tuthill and Walter H. Kerr, anthology (144 pages). *Countdown In Bedlam* (1978) poems by Walter H. Kerr (96 pages). *Rasas & Lament of the Sudra* (1979) poems by Desmond O'Brien (96 pages), and *Second Rising,* an anthology edited by Stacy Tuthill." avg. press run 1,000. Pub'd 1 title 1979; expects 1 title 1980, 2 titles 1981. 5 titles listed in the *Small Press Record of Books in Print* (9th Edition, 1980). avg. price, paper: $5.00. Discounts: 40% to dealers. 96pp; 6X7½; of. Reporting time: Usually six weeks. Payment: copies. Copyrights for author. NESPD.

SCOPCRAEFT MAGAZINE, The Scopcraeft Press, Antony Oldknow, Editor; Hadrian Manske, Associate Editor, 3200 Ellis Street #16, Stevens Point, WI 54481, (715) 345-0865. 1966. Poetry, fiction, articles, art, photos, interviews, criticism, reviews, letters, parts-of-novels, long-poems, plays, news items. "This will be a magazine devoted to publishing material submitted by persons encountered by the editor in his role as driver/co-ordinator of the Plains Distribution Bookbus on its tours of the Upper Midwest States" circ. 300. 2/yr. Expects 2 issues 1980. sub. price: $7.50; per copy: $4.00; sample: $4.00. 8X7; †mi/of. Reporting time: varies. Copyrighted, reverts to author. Pub's reviews. §open.

The Scopcraeft Press (see also THE MAINSTREETER; THE FIFTH HORSEMAN; SCOPCRAEFT MAGAZINE), Antony Oldknow, Hadrian Manske, Associate Editor, 3200 Ellis Street #16, St Point, WI 54481. 1966. avg. press run 300. Pub'd 2 titles 1979; expects 2 titles 1980. 11 titles listed in the *Small Press Record of Books in Print* (9th Edition, 1980). avg. price, cloth: $7.95; paper: $2.95. 48pp; 8½X5½; of. Books by invitation and/or contract. Payment: According to contract. Copyrights for author.

SCOPP, The Saturday Centre, Patricia Laird, Joanne Burns, Rae Desmond Jones, Philip Hammial, Box 140 P.O., Cammeray NSW 2062, Australia. 1977. Poetry, fiction, art, photos, cartoons, satire, letters, long-poems, collages, concrete art. "Prefer multi-lingual material (with English translation). Prefer short poems (up to 36 lines). Encourage Black writers & new writers. Recent contributors: Bobbi Sykes, Margaret Diesendorf, L.E. Scott, J.J. Encarnacao, Zoltan Hegyi, Dezsery Andras, Pino Bosi, Enoe Di Stefano, Ivan Kobel, M. Kumashov, I.L. Church, E. Incekara." circ. 500. 3/yr. Pub'd 3 issues 1979; expects 3 issues 1980, 3 issues 1981. sub. price: $10.00 (Aust); per copy: $3.50 (Aust); sample: $3.50 (Aust). Discounts: 25% agents, 40% to bookshops if firm orders. 80pp; 4½X8¼; †of. Reporting time: no promises to overseas contributors. Payment: $5.00 per our page. Copyrighted. Ads: No ads.

Scotty Macgreger Publications, Scotty Macgreger, 10 Pineacre Dr., Smithtown, NY 11787. 1970. "Publishing poetry-educational books and records for children. Sell to libraries, schools, stores and smart people who want to buy for resale in their area." 4 titles listed in the *Small Press Record of Books in Print* (9th Edition, 1980).

Scranton Theatre Libre (see Libre Press)

SCREE, Duck Down Press, Kirk Robertson, Nila Northsun, PO Box 1047, Fallon, NV 89406, (702) 423-2220. 1973. Poetry, fiction, articles, art, photos, cartoons, interviews, satire, reviews, letters, parts-of-novels, long-poems, collages, concrete art. "In submissions we look for strong poems and fiction of intensity and place more emphasis on content than form. Any form is OK, we're mainly interested in what can be done with that form. We've published work strongly rooted in a sense of place—whether that place is absurdia or Arizona. Lately, the direction of the magazine seems to be towards fewer contributors/issue with more work from each. Say 3-10/issue, down from as many as 40 or more/issue. But this is tentative and if we receive enuff hi-power submissions to warrant it, issues with a larger number of contributors will appear.Prospective contributors should send 5-7 poems, 1-2 stories, or a sampling of artwork/photos and *must* include a SASE if they want a reply. Areas that we either continue to be interested in, or are becoming interested in include: work by and/or dealing with American Indians; work related to the visual arts — photography, collage, etc.; material from oral traditions; work that speaks strongly of the author's place — internal or external. Special issues on photography/poetry and the American Cowboy are planned. Some contributors: Masarik, Art Beck, John Bennett, Bukowski, Todd Moore, Kent Taylor, Ted Kooser, Gerald Haslam, Charles Potts, Judson Crews, Art Cuelho, Charles Plymell, Bern Porter, Wayne Ude, etc." circ. 500. 4/yr. Pub'd 4 (2 doubles) issues 1979; expects 4 (2 doubles) issues 1980. sub. price: $6.50 Individuals - $10.00 Institutions/ 4 numbers; per copy: $3.00 + $.70 postage; sample: $3.00 or exchange. Back issues: 1-8 $2.00 each + $.70 postage; 9/10,11/12, 13/14, 15/16, $3.00 each + $.70 postage. Discounts: 5 or more copies, 40 percent. 72-100pp; 5½X8½; of. Reporting time: fast. Payment: copies 3-6. Copyrighted, reverts to author. Pub's reviews: 50-60 in 1979. §Poetry/contemporary fiction/collage/little mags/photography/American Indian. Ads: Inquire. CCLM, WIP.

SCREEN, Society for Education in Film and TV, Mark Nash, 29 Old Compton St., London W1V 5PL, United Kingdom. 1969. Articles, art, photos, interviews, criticism, reviews, letters, news items. "Back numbers available from 1975" circ. 3,000. 4/yr. 1 title listed in the *Small Press Record of Books in Print* (9th Edition, 1980). sub. price: £7 or $20; per copy: £1.95/$6.00. Back issues: £1.90/$6.00. 128pp; 240mm X 170mm; of. Reporting time: 8 weeks. Payment: by arrangement. Copyrighted, joint copyright. Pub's reviews: 3 in 1979. §film/ video/media/cultural politics/photography. Ads: 1/1p £50; 1/2p £30.

SCREEN DOOR REVIEW, Arbitrary Closet Press, Richard Neva, 517 Bently, Eaton Rapids, MI 48827. 1972. Poetry, art, photos. "Art is anything I can get away with. Highly arbitrary biases. Includes the erotic: males, females, others. Take a chance. Known, unknown, anonoymous welcome. Temporarily in a state of cryonic suspension. Welcome letters" circ. 200. Pub'd 1 issue 1979; expects 1 issue 1980, 1 issue 1981. sub. price: $1.00; per copy: $1.00; sample: $1.00. Back issues: yes. 5X8; †lp/of/mi. Reporting time: Immediate. Payment: copies only. §poetry (short to medium length).

The Scribe Press (see also TAX NEWS), Fielding Greaves, PO Box 368, San Rafael, CA 94901, (415) 456-4198. 1976. Articles. avg. press run 500. Pub'd 4 titles 1979; expects 5 titles 1980, 5 titles 1981. 4 titles listed in the *Small Press Record of Books in Print* (9th Edition, 1980). avg. price, paper: $1.00. 8pp; 8½X11; of. Payment: negotiated flat rate. Copyrights for author. Company of Military Historians; AWE (Artists, Writers, Editors).

Sea Challengers, 1851 Don Avenue, Los Osos, CA 93402. 1977. avg. press run 10,000. Pub'd 1 title 1979; expects 1 title 1980. avg. price, cloth: $12.50; paper: $9.50. Discounts: 1 copy, 20%; 2-9, 40%; 10-49, 42%; 50-99, 44%; 100 and over books, 46%; jobbers ranges from 50-64% depending on various factors. 112-160pp; 6X9; 7X9. Payment: 10% of retail on each book sold on one book, 5% of retail on each book sold on two. Copyrights for author. COSMEP.

Sea Of Storms (see also NICOTINE SOUP), Laura Brown, Eric Brown, Robert C. Davidson, PO Box 22613, San Francisco, CA 94122, (707) 795-2098. 1975. Poetry, fiction, art, photos, long-poems. "Only one book published to date: *Mistaken,* poetry by Randy Mott, illustrated by Robynn Smith, 1978, 90 pages perfect bound. 2nd book, an anthology of short-stories by Vietnam veterans, in progress." avg. press run 1,000. Expects 1 title 1980, 1 title 1981. avg. price, paper: $3.75. Discounts: Libraries, 20%; Bookstores, 40%; Jobbers, 40%; Distributors, 50%. 80-100pp; 4¼X5½; of. Reporting time: 2-3 months on manuscripts. Payment: Arrangements made individually with author. Copyrights for author. CCLM, CODA, COSMEP.

Seacoast Press (see NEW ENGLAND SAMPLER)

Seahawk Press, Jerry Greenberg, Idaz Greenberg, 6840 S.W. 92nd Street, Miami, FL 33156, (305) 667-4051. 1956. "We publish books, posters, maps, postcards concerning corals and fishes of Florida, the Caribbean & the Bahamas. We also publish *Waterproof Guide To Corals & Fishes.*" avg. press run 10,000. Pub'd 2 titles 1979; expects 1 title 1980. 5 titles listed in the *Small Press Record of Books in Print* (9th Edition, 1980). avg. price, paper: $4.50. Discounts: 20% To 50%. 64pp; 6X9; †of.

The Seal Press, Barbara Wilson, Rachel da Silva, Hylah Jacques, 533 11th EAST, Seattle, WA 98102, 322-2322. 1976. Poetry, fiction. "Feminist fiction and poetry; children's titles and reprints. Recent contributors* Jody Aliesan, Barbara Wilson, Lisa Thomas; *I Change Worlds,* the autobiography of Anna Louise Strong; *Backbone 2,* a collection of fiction by NW women; coming: *Backbone 3,* a collection of non-fiction by NW women" avg. press run 500-1000. Pub'd 3 titles 1979; expects 4 titles 1980, 4 titles 1981. 9 titles listed in the *Small Press Record of Books in Print* (9th Edition, 1980). avg. price, cloth: $15.00; paper: $5.00. Discounts: standard. 100pp; 5X9; †of/lp. Reporting time: 2 months. Payment: 10% of press run. Does not copyright for author. COSMEP.

The Sean Dorman Manuscript Society (see also WRITING), Sean Dorman, 4 Union Place, Fowey, Cornwall PL23 1BY, United Kingdom. 1957. Poetry, articles. "Articles: 300 to 350 words. Poems: 8 to 20 lines. Letters to the editor: letters not paid for" avg. press run 500. Pub'd 1 title 1979. avg. price, paper: 50p. 46pp; 8X6½; †mi. Reporting time: 2 weeks. Payment: £3.00 on publication. Copyrights for author.

THE SEATTLE REVIEW, Nelson Bentley, Charles Johnson, Richard Blessing, Kate McCune, Manager, Padelford Hall GN-30, Univ. of Wash, Seattle, WA 98195, (206) 543-9865. 1977. Poetry, fiction, art, photos, interviews. circ. 1,000. 2/yr. Pub'd 2 issues 1979; expects 2 issues 1980, 2 issues 1981. sub. price: $3.50; per copy: $2.00; sample: $2.00. 80pp; 6X9; of. Reporting time: 8 weeks. Payment: $15 per poem; $5 per page of prose. Copyrighted, reverts to author. COSMEP.

SECESSION GALLERY NEWSLETTER, Secession Gallery of Photography, Open Space, Tom Gore, P O Box 5207 Stn B, Victoria, BC V8R 6N4, Canada, 604-383-8833. 1975. Criticism, reviews, letters. "Bibliographies and excerpts from the literature of photography are the two emphasised areas at present. The latter are about 750-1,500 words, and are based on the important books in the history of photography." circ. 200. 8/yr. sub. price: $10.00. Back issues: Bibliography reprints $2.00. 8pp; 8½X11; †mi/of. Reporting time: 6 weeks. Payment: negotiated. Copyrighted, reverts to author. Pub's reviews: 6 in 1979. §Photographic aesthetics and history.

Secession Gallery of Photography, Open Space (see also SECESSION GALLERY NEWSLETTER; PHOTOGRAPHIC CALENDAR), Tom Gore, P O Box 5207 Stn B, Victoria, BC V8R 6N4, Canada, 604-383-8833. 1977. Photos, criticism. "A series of photographically oriented things such as monographs, resource books, and the West Coast Photographers' Calender." avg. press run 1,000. Pub'd 4 titles 1979; expects 4 titles 1980, 4 titles 1981. 1 title listed in the *Small Press Record of Books in Print* (9th Edition, 1980). avg. price, cloth: $6.00; paper: $6.00. Discounts: 40%. 80pp; 5X7 to 11X17; †of. Reporting time: 6 weeks or post deadline. Payment: negotiated. Copyrights for author.

Second Aeon Publications, Peter Finch, 19 Southminster Road, PENYLAN, Cardiff, Wales CF2 5AT, United Kingdom, 0222-493093. 1967. Poetry, art, long-poems, collages, concrete art. avg. press run 300-1,000. Pub'd 1 title 1979. avg. price, paper: 50p. Discounts: By arrangement. 20pp; size A5; mi/of. Reporting time: 2 weeks. Payment: by arrangement. Does not copyright for author. ALP.

Second Back Row Press, Tom Whitton, Wendy Whitton, P.O. Box 43, Leura NSW 2781, Australia. 1973. "We have published 7 books on bookshops and we would be interested in further practical, how-to material for publication and/or distribution. We distribute over 25 presses from US, UK and Canada in Aust. and are always interested in more in alternative lifestyles area." Pub'd 7 titles 1979; expects 6 titles 1980. 8 titles listed in the *Small Press Record of Books in Print* (9th Edition, 1980).

Discounts: 40%. Reporting time: 1 month. Payment: 10%. Copyrights for author.

The Second Chance Press, Martin Shepard, Judith Shepard, Sagaponack, NY 11962, 516-324-5993. 1979. Fiction, news items. "We are a publishing company devoted to republishing books that could be considered modern day classics and that for any number of reasons have not received the recognition that we feel they deserve. All our books have been submitted by the authors themselves and in a few cases, by agents. We re-pulish six titles a year." avg. press run 4,000. Pub'd 6 titles 1979. avg. price, cloth: $12.50; paper: $5.95. Discounts: 40-50%. 250pp; 5½X8½; of. Reporting time: 8 weeks. Payment: none of the authors receive an advance they do receive 10 to 15% of net. Copyrights for author. COSMEP.

Second Class, Working Class, an International Women's Reader, 4228 Telegraph, Oakland, CA 94609. Articles, interviews, news items. "Articles on working women around the world, compiled from the international feminist press." avg. press run 2,000. Pub'd 1 title 1979. avg. price, paper: $3.00. Discounts: bookstore 60/40, bulk orders over 10, 10%. 64pp; 8X11½; of.

SECOND COMING, Second Coming Press, A.D. Winans, P.O. Box 31249, San Francisco, CA 94131, (415) 647-3679. 1971. Poetry, fiction, art, photos, interviews, satire, criticism, reviews, letters, parts-of-novels, long-poems, plays. "Open to all schools of poetry. Past contributors have included the late Wm. Wantling, Gene Fowler, Doug Blazek, Gerald Locklin, Lyn Lifshin, Anne Menebroker, Lynn Savitt, Terry Stokes, Gene Ruggles, Pancho Aguila, Charles Bukowski, Jack Micheline, Terry Kennedy, Al Masarik, etc" circ. 1,000-1,500. 2/yr. Pub'd 2 issues 1979; expects 2 issues 1980, 2 issues 1981. sub. price: $5.00/yr individual-$7.50/yr library; per copy: $2.00-$4.95; sample: $2.00-including postage and handling. Back issues: $5.00 each except Vol 1, No. 1, $50.00 (only 10 left), complete back list available $100.00. Vol. 2, No. 3 (Special Charles Bukowski issue $50.00). Discounts: 30 percent, 1-4 copies; 40 percent, 5 or more bookstores; 50 percent, 40 or more copies (plus postage and handling charge). 80pp; 5½X8½; 6X9; of. Reporting time: 1 day-30 days. Occasional modest payment as money permits. Copyrighted, rights revert back to author upon written request. Pub's reviews: none in 1979. §Poetry/novels. Ads: $75/$40. CCLM, COSMEP.

Second Coming Press (see also SECOND COMING), A.D. Winans, PO Box 31249, San Francisco, CA 94131, 415-647-3679. 1972. Poetry, fiction. "1 title in 1972: *3 Drums For The Lady:* Ann Menebroker. 5 titles in 1975: *Felon's Journal* by Gene Fowler, *7 On Style* by the late Wm. Wantling; *Love Letters* by George Tsongas; *No Capital Crime* by the late Ed. Lipman and *Tales Of Crazy John* by A. D. Winans. 3 titles published 1976. *Last House In America* by Jack Micheline; *To Keep The Blood From Drowning* by Doug Flaherty; *California Poets Anthology* featuring the work of over 70 leading California poets, 224 pages, with photos. 6 titles published in 1977 and 5 titles and 1 anthology published in 1978. 3 titles scheduled for 1979 and Jack Micheline's collection of short stories *Skinny Dynamite* in 1980" avg. press run 1,000. Pub'd 2 titles 1979; expects 1 title 1980, 4 titles 1981. 36 titles listed in the *Small Press Record of Books in Print* (9th Edition, 1980). avg. price, cloth: $10.00; paper: $3.50. Discounts: Same as magazine: 20 percent library only if this listed source is quoted. 64-72pp; 5½X8½; of. Reporting time: 30 days. Payment: 10 percent of press run, 50 percent of any profit after expenses are met. only copyrights for author upon arrangement. COSMEP, CCLM.

SECOND GROWTH: Appalachian Nature and Culture, Frederick O. Waage, Ginger Renner, Asst Editor; Linda Scott, Editorial Advisor, Appalachian Affairs, Dept. of English, East Tennessee State Univ., Johnson City, TN 37601, (615) 929-7466. 1975. Poetry, fiction, articles, art, photos, interviews, criticism, reviews, letters. "*Second Growth* has changed name and focus; Appalachian mountain area (Maine to Georgia) experienced through all forms of writing which present humanistic approaches to its ecology/natural history, and relate Appalachian culture, life-styles, arts to its natural space. Particularly interested in poetry, fiction, interviews, biographical/autobiographical narratives, non-'technical' writing by scientists and social scientists. *Second Growth is sponsored by the Institute for Appalachian Affairs, East Tennessee State University, Dr. Linda Scott, Director.* All subs. checks should be made out to the Institute. Personal correspondence with all interested writers desired; free copy with inquiry and SASE. *Photography and graphics strongly welcomed.* Recent contributors: Craigie Hemenway, Lee Pennington, Jim Wayne Miller, Lillie Chaffin, Gene Wilhelm, Jr" 4/yr. Expects 2 issues 1980, 4 issues 1981. sub. price: $5.00; per copy: $1.50; sample: free. 16pp; size tabloid; of. Reporting time: 2 months. Payment: copies. Copyrighted, reverts to author. Pub's reviews. §American poetry, nature, ecology, Appalachian arts, history, culture. Ads: $50/$25. COSMEP.

THE SECOND WAVE, Linda Stein, Marty Kingsbury, Jennifer Hagar, Miriam Kenner, Deb Gallager, Box 344 Cambridge A, Cambridge, MA 02139, (617) 491-1071. 1971. Poetry, fiction, articles, art, photos, cartoons, interviews, satire, criticism, reviews, letters, long-poems, plays, news items. "(All material must be related to the theme of feminism. She, the writer, should write only on issues relating to the theme of Women's Liberation, or women's relationship to other women. We do not want works glorifying marriage, traditional women's roles, etc.)" circ. 5,000. 2/yr; irregular. Pub'd 1 issue 1979; expects 2 issues 1980, 2 issues 1981. sub. price: $8.00 indiv.; $16.00 insti.; $12.00 overseas; per copy: $2.00 + 60¢ postage; sample: $2.00(incl. postage). 52pp; 8½X11; of. Reporting time: 1-3 months. Payment: 2 Copies. Copyrighted, reverts to author. Pub's reviews: 3 in 1979. §Small left press; feminist publications. Ads: $300/$155/1/3 $85/1/4 $50/1/6 $35.

Seed Center, DeRay, Sura, PO Box 658, Garberville, CA 95440, 493-6121. 1972. Poetry, fiction, non-fiction. "Generally oriented but not limited to self-awareness, self-discovery & metaphysical topics." avg. press run 3,500. Expects 3 titles 1980, 3 titles 1981. 14 titles listed in the *Small Press Record of Books in Print* (9th Edition, 1980). avg. price, cloth: $7.00; paper: $3.00. Discounts: Trade, jobber, bulk individual. 100-150pp; 4¼X7⅛; 6X9; of. Reporting time: varies-1 to 4 months. Payment: 8 to 15 percent paid quarterly. Copyrights for author. WBPA, WIP, COSMEP.

SEED SAVERS EXCHANGE, Kent Whealy, Rural Route 2, Princeton, MO 64673, (816) 748-3091. 1975. circ. 5M. annual (Feb). Pub'd 1 issue 1979; expects 1 issue 1980, 1 issue 1981. sub. price: $3.00; per copy: $3.00; sample: $3.00. Back issues: not available. 56pp; 7½X10; of. Copyrighted. Ads: No ads accepted.

THE SEEKER NEWSLETTER, LP Publications, Arleen Lorrance, Diane K. Pike, PO Box 7601, San Diego, CA 92107, (714) 225-0133. 1972. Poetry, articles, photos, cartoons, letters. circ. 1,000. 4/yr. Pub'd 4 issues 1979; expects 4 issues 1980, 4 issues 1981. sub. price: $10.00 or more; sample: free. Discounts: none. 28pp; 8½X11; of. Reporting time: 1 month. Payment: none. Not copyrighted. Ads: No ads.

SEEMS, Karl Elder, Editor; A. Lee Worman, c/o Lakeland College, Box 359, Sheboygan, WI 53081. 1971. Poetry, fiction, articles, reviews, parts-of-novels, long-poems. "Subscribe and we'll immediately send you our three most reecent back issues free; if you're disappointed, we'll return your money." circ. 250. 4/yr. Pub'd 3 issues 1979; expects 3 issues 1980, 4 issues 1981. sub. price: $6.00/4 issues; per copy: $1.50; sample: $1.50. Discounts: 25%. 35pp; 8½X7; of. Reporting time: 1-4 wks. Payment: copies. Copyrighted, reverts to author. CCLM.

Selene Books, Rowan Shirkie, P.O. Box 810, Sta. B, Ottawa, Ontario K1P 5P9, Canada, (613) 232-0098. 1977. Poetry, fiction, collages, concrete art. "Interested primarily in visual narratives: ie a combination of graphics and language as structure. Not for sale. Distribution made to other small presses in exchange for similar works or other experimental narrative forms." avg. press run 200-500. Pub'd 1 title 1979; expects 2-3 titles 1980, 4-5 titles 1981. 1 title listed in the *Small Press Record of Books in Print* (9th Edition, 1980). of. Reporting time: 2-3 weeks. copyrighted in Canada.

SELF AND SOCIETY, Bourne Press, Vivian Milroy, 62 Southwark Bridge Rd, London SE1 0AU, United Kingdom. 1973. Articles, poetry, cartoons, photos, reviews, news items, interviews, criticism, letters. "Material within field of humanistic psychology; length from 500 to 5000 words: popular science approach, not too much jargon. Recent articles on R. D. Laing, Aaron Esterson, Wilhelm Reich, Carl Rogers, Abraham Maslow, Sidney Jourard." circ. 3,500. 12/yr. Pub'd 12 issues 1979; expects 12 issues 1980. sub. price: £5.00; per copy: 45p. Discounts: 20%. 32pp; size A5; of. Reporting time: 1 month. Payment: nil. Copyrighted, reverts to author. Pub's reviews: 42 in 1979. §psychology (humanistic, growth movement). Ads: £30 per page/£20/10p. AHP.

SELF DETERMINATION JOURNAL, Alison Wells, Self Determination: A personal/Political Network, 2431 Forest Avenue, San Jose, CA 95128, (408) 984-8134. 1976. Poetry, fiction, articles, art, photos, cartoons, interviews, satire, criticism, reviews, letters, long-poems. "Contact editor by phone or with brief proposal. Topic areas vary (Major focus planned for 1979, media, violence-nonviolence). Focus on alternatives, both political and personal development in any area. See *Journal* for style, bias, etc. Authors: Willis Harmon, Jay Ogilvy, Michael Rossman, Kathy Bristol; interview with Carolyn Craven. Self Determination also publishes a resource directory, *NE=XUS*, and some political action guides" circ. 10,000. Quarterly. Pub'd 3 issues 1979; expects 3 issues 1980, 3 issues 1981. sub. price: $25.00 membership; per copy: donation. Back issues: donation. Discounts: libraries, $15.00; trade negotiable. 48+pp; 8½X11; of. Reporting time: 2 weeks. Payment: membership in exchange for contribution. Copyrighted, reverts to author. Pub's reviews: 30 in 1979. §human potential, politics, social change, health, education.

Self Published, Phyllis L. Gernes, R 3, Box 38B, Garden Valley, CA 95633, (916) 622-7590. 1979. Poetry, photos, interviews, news items. "Research into old manuscripts." avg. press run 1,000. Pub'd 1 title 1979. 1 title listed in the *Small Press Record of Books in Print* (9th Edition, 1980). avg. price, cloth: $9.95; paper: $5.95. Discounts: trade 40%, agent 30%. 209pp; 6X9; of. Copyrights for author.

SELF-RELIANCE, Institute for Local Self-Reliance, David Macgregor, 1717 18th St. NW, Washington, DC 20009, (202) 232-4108. 1976. Articles, cartoons, reviews. "Most articles are on issues related to urban decentralism and community self-reliance. We do accept and encourage unsolicited submissions on relevant topics." circ. 2,500. Bi-monthly. Pub'd 6 issues 1979; expects 6 issues 1980. sub. price: $8.00 Indiv; $15.00 Instit.; per copy: $1.00; sample: $1.00. Back issues: yes, $1.00. Discounts: 40% for orders of ten or more. 16pp; 8½X11; of. Reporting time: 2 weeks. Payment: yes. Copyrighted, reverts to author. Pub's reviews: 30-50 in 1979. §urban decentralism, energy, alternative technologies, urban planning. no ads. COSMEP.

SENECA REVIEW, James Crenner, Robert Herz, Hobart & William Smith Colleges, Geneva, NY 14456. 1970. Poetry, articles, interviews, reviews, long-poems. circ. 1,000. 2/yr. Pub'd 2 issues 1979; expects 2 issues 1980. sub. price: $5.00; per copy: $3.00; sample: $3.00. Back issues: $3.00. Discounts: 40% trade for stores. 84pp; 8½X5½; lp. Reporting time: 4-6 wks. Payment: copies. Copyrighted, does not revert to author. Pub's reviews: 3 in 1979. §poetry. Ads: $250.00/special small press rates/exchange. CCLM, NYSSPA.

SEPARATE DOORS, J. Craven, 911 W T Station, Canyon, TX 79016. 1978. Poetry, articles. "*SD* gives preference to lyric poems that illustrate the poet has a working knowledge of poetic technique; the assamption is that *good* free verse poetry is not free from careful attention to the relationship between sound and meaning." circ. 500. 1/yr. Pub'd 1 issue 1979; expects 1 issue 1980. sub. price: $1.50; per copy: $1.50; sample: $1.50. of. Reporting time: 1-4 weeks. Payment: copies. Copyrighted, reverts to author. Pub's reviews. COSMEP SOUTH.

SEPIA, Kawabata Press, Colin David Webb, Editor, Knill Cross House, Higher Anderton Road, Millbrook, Nr Torpoint, Cornwall, United Kingdom. 1977. Poetry, fiction, articles, art, reviews. "Shorter prose (under about 2,500 words preferred), shorter poems (under 40 lines preferred), short reviews (under 2,500 words preferred). Recent contributors: Wes Mogse, Nigel Gray, Tina Morris, George A. Moore, Andy Darlington." circ. 100. 4/yr. Pub'd 2 issues 1979; expects 4 issues 1980, 4 issues 1981. sub. price: £1; per copy: 25p; sample: 25p. Back issues: All sold out at present. 32pp; 6X8½; †mi. Reporting time: 14 days. Copyrighted, reverts to author. Pub's reviews: 19 in 1979. §Poetry, fiction.

Service Press Inc., Leonard Baldori, 6369 Reynolds Road, Haslett, MI 48840. 1978. Fiction, articles, photos, cartoons, news items. avg. press run 5,000. Pub'd 2 titles 1979. avg. price, paper: $4.50. Discounts: 40% on 1 dozen or more. 200pp; 8X10; of. Reporting time: 1 month. Payment: standard paperback, negotiable. Copyrights for author. COSMEP.

Servicios Internacionales, Leo Shaw, Box 941, Texas City, TX 77590, (713) 935-3491. 1969. "Humor books; all on slanted subject: 1,000 laughs: 900 gags, & 100 cartoons. Samples: Confucius say, all hilarious ribald saying of confucius. Retirement revelry: clean humor about retirees and senior citizens. Battle of the bulge: trials and tribulations of diets and dieters. Now on the press: unsafe to read at any speed: 1,000 laughs about safety engineers. Upcoming: completed mss on 30 slanted subjects, such as, Kalifunkens, Prune Pickers, Forty-Niners, Golden-Gaters, Kalifornifkators, Angelinos, Swiming Pools, Brides, Real Estate agents, anatomy. Underway: 148 books: all on slanted subjects: each with 900 gags and 100 cartoons." avg. press run 5,000. Pub'd 1 title 1979; expects 1 title 1980, 1 title 1981. avg. price, paper: $5.00. Discounts: 40%. 80-90pp; 8½X11; †of. Reporting time: no work for the public, unless exceptionally good humor books. Payment: 10%. Copyrights for author.

Sesame Press, Eugene McNamara, Peter Stevens, c/o English Dept Univ of Windosr, Windsor, Ontario N9B3P4, Canada. 1974. Poetry. "We publish only poetry by Canadian poets. We started out trying to offer an alternative to the sluggish attitude of the big presses (also their smugness, timidity etc.) and the in-group snobbery and elitism of too many small presses. We wanted to be more open (hence: *sesame.* Also our logo is a winged seed—well, like a sesame seed, or any kind of germ which might be catching—) and definitely not incestuous. We have published nothing from the home front —first four books were from poets in B.C., Moose Jaw, London, Ont. and Switzerland (an emigre Canadian) then we did one from Calgary, one from Hamilton, then Toronto and now finally *Landing* by Claude Liman in Thunder Bay Ont and *The Only Country in the World Called Canada* by Doug Beardsley in Victoria, B.C. Because of the current awfully inept poetry scene in Canada we may end up pulishing ourselves. By the end of 1979 we will publish our 14th and 15th titles" avg. press run 500. Pub'd 4 titles 1979; expects 4 titles 1980, 4 titles 1981. 5 titles listed in the *Small Press Record of Books in Print* (9th Edition, 1980). avg. price, paper: $3.00. Discounts: 40 percent. 50pp; 6X9; lp. Reporting time: 6 weeks. Payment: 50 copies on publication as full payment. Copyrights for author. COSMEP.

Seven Buffaloes Press (see also BLACK JACK & VALLEY GRAPEVINE), Art Cuelho, Box 249,

Big Timber, MT 59011. 1973. Poetry, fiction, art, photos, interviews, reviews, parts-of-novels, long-poems, collages. "Book length manuscripts are not being accepted at this time. I do publish some books, even novels; but the authors are those that have had work in my magazines." avg. press run 300-500. Pub'd 4 titles 1979; expects 6 titles 1980, 7 titles 1981. avg. price, paper: $3.50. Discounts: 1-5, 10%; 6-10, 15%; 11-15, 20%; 16-20, 25%; over 20 copies, 30%. 100pp; 5½X8½; †of. Reporting time: within a week; sometimes same day. Payment: negotiable. Copyrights for author. CCLM.

Seven Deadly Sins Press, Elizabeth Creager, David Vancil, Editor, 1117 B Mariposa, Austin, TX 78703. 1977. Poetry, fiction, articles, satire, long-poems. "The press is devoted to distributing unusual or potentiallly neglected works in the humanities. We like fresh, inventive writing, but this doesn't mean it has to be weird or chaotic. Formless, undisciplined work doesn't interest us. We have published Tom Whalen and Larry Fontenot" avg. press run 100-125. Pub'd 1 title 1979; expects 1 title 1980. 2 titles listed in the *Small Press Record of Books in Print* (9th Edition, 1980). avg. price, paper: $1.00-$1.50. 20-24pp; 5¼X8¼; 7X8½; †mi/of. Reporting time: query; up to 60 days. Payment: informal. Copyrights for author.

Seven Oaks Press (see also FORMAT), C. L. Morrison, 405 S. 7th Street, St. Charles, IL 60174, (312) 584-0187. 1978. Fiction, plays. "*The Adventures of Jamie* by Tom Bowie (242 pp.); *Defilement* by C. L. Morrison (235 pp). 3 plays for reading by Tom Bowie, 260 pp." avg. press run 1,000. Expects 4 titles 1980, 6 titles 1981. 5 titles listed in the *Small Press Record of Books in Print* (9th Edition, 1980). avg. price, cloth: $9.95; paper: $3.95. Discounts: Paper, 25%; hard, 40%. 250pp; 5X7; †of.

Seven Woods Press, George Koppelman, P.O. Box 32, Village Station, New York, NY 10014. 1971. Poetry, long-poems. "We have published long poems by William Doreski, Albert Goldbarth, and Nathan Whiting and are always open to submissions of book-length narratives of comparable quality." avg. press run 1,000. Pub'd 2 titles 1979; expects 2 titles 1980. 5 titles listed in the *Small Press Record of Books in Print* (9th Edition, 1980). Discounts: 40% trade wholesale. 72pp; of. Reporting time: varies. Payment: royalty 10%. Copyrights for author.

SEWANEE REVIEW, George Core, Editor; Mary Lucia S. Cornelius, Managing Editor, Univ. of the South, Sewanee, TN 37375. 1892. Poetry, fiction, articles, criticism, reviews, letters, parts-of-novels. "Publish book reviews, but books and reviewers are selected by editor." circ. 3,500. 4/yr. Pub'd 4 issues 1979; expects 4 issues 1980, 4 issues 1981. sub. price: $15.00 insti.; $12.00 indiv.; per copy: $4.25; sample: $4.25. Back issues: $5.50 for 1964 onward; $6.50 before 1964. Discounts: 15% to subscription agents. 200pp; 6X9; lp. Reporting time: 2 to 4 weeks after receipt. Payment: $10.00 p/prose; $0.60 line/poetry. We retain partial rights. Pub's reviews: 55 reviews, 175 books in 1979. Ads: $175.00/$110.00. CCLM.

SEZ: A Multi-Racial Journal of Poetry & People's Culture, Shadow Press, Jim Dochniak, Editor, PO Box 8803, Minneapolis, MN 55408, (612) 870-0899. 1978. Poetry, fiction, articles, art, photos, interviews, reviews, letters, long-poems, plays. "The only multi-cultural literary journal in Minnesota. Special attention given to regional Third World writers as well as writers whose work reflects ethnic and/or class consciousness. No 'art for art sake' or escapist literature wanted. Each issue is divided up into thematic sections; please inquire or suggest 'themes'. We are interested in publishing writers who are dealing with social issues and working for a more human society. Unsolicited mss. welcome with a SASE and short personal bio. Length: 2,500 words prose, etc., 10 pps. poetry. Recent contributors: Thomas McGrath, Mary McAnally, John Minczeski, Meridel LeSueur...." circ. 1000-2000. irregular. Pub'd 1 issue 1979; expects 2 issues 1980, 4 issues 1981. sub. price: $6.00 Individuals; $7.50 Libraries, Institutions; per copy: $1.50; sample: $1.50. Back issues: $1.25. Discounts: 40% trade, 50% bulk, distrib. etc. 32pp; 8½X11; of. Reporting time: 1 week to 6 months. Payment: 4 copies. Copyrighted, reverts to author. Pub's reviews: 25 in 1979. §Midwest regional, 'minority', men's & women's issues, cultural and literary traditions, folklore, political. Ads: inquire. CCLM, COSMEP.

SF COMMENTARY, Bruce Gillespie, GPO Box 5195AA, Melbourne, Victoria 3001, Australia, (03) 419-4797. 1969. Articles, interviews, criticism, reviews, letters, news items. "*Style:* Serious, but not standard academic style. 'Straight talk about science fiction', with a bias towards literary rather than scientific side." circ. 1,200. 5/yr. Pub'd 5 issues 1979; expects 5 issues 1980. sub. price: $6.00; per copy: $1.50; sample: 1 copy free. Back issues: $1.50. 16pp; size US Quarto; of. Reporting time: 3 weeks. Payment: none + copies of books for review/copies of issue where material appears. Copyrighted, reverts to author. Pub's reviews: 30 in 1979. §science fiction/criticism of SF/FANTASY cinema/general literature. Ads: $100.00/$60.00.

Shadow Press (see also DARK FANTASY), Howard Gene Day, Box 207, Gananoque, Ontario K7G2T7, Canada, 613-382-2794. 1973. Poetry, fiction, art. "Recent contributors include-Tevis Clyde Smith, Charles Saunders, Lew Cabos, Thomas Egan, Glenn Rahmen, Robert E. Howard. 3,000 words preferred-but not necessary" avg. press run 500-600. Pub'd 5-6 titles 1979. avg. price, other: $1.00. Discounts: 40 percent flat discount. 40-52pp; 5½X8½; of. Reporting time: 4-6 weeks. Payment: no royalty-flat -1/2 cent per word. Does not copyright for author.

Shadow Press (see also SEZ: A Multi-Racial Journal of Poetry & People's Culture), Jim Dochniak, PO Box 8803, Minneapolis, MN 55408, (612) 870-0899. 1978. Poetry, fiction, art, interviews, letters, parts-of-novels, long-poems, plays. "Shadow Press aims to publish and present writing and art work which is reflective of the struggle for New Human Images. Special attention given to writing and art work which is honest in its intention to add to the struggle for human dignity. NO ART FOR ARTS' SAKE, ESCAPIST, or DECADENT work, please. Attention also given to 'minorities', worker-writers, the economically disadvantaged, and work which reflects a cultural heritage. No unsolicited mss, but inquiries welcomed w/a SASE. Length relative to project: broadsides/1-5 pps., chapbooks/20-40 pps., books/50-100 pps., etc. (Projects for 1980 currently under consideration, & pending.)" avg. press run 1000. Pub'd 1 title 1979; expects 1 title 1980, 1 title 1981. 1 title listed in the *Small Press Record of Books in Print* (9th Edition, 1980). avg. price, paper: $3.50; other: $1.50/pamphlets; $1.00/broadsides. Discounts: 40% trade, 50% distrib., bulk negot. 32pp; 6X9; of. Reporting time: 1 week to 6 months. Payment: Inquire. Copyrights for author. COSMEP.

Shadowgraph Press (see SHADOWGRAPHS)

SHADOWGRAPHS, Shadowgraph Press, Richard Summers, PO Box 177, Bedford, MA 01730, (617) 465-2806. 1979. Poetry, fiction, art, photos, satire. "I am looking toward expanding my format to enable the use of longer pieces, and the inclusion of even more of the categories mentioned in types of material used." circ. 750. 4/yr. Pub'd 3 issues 1979; expects 4 issues 1980. sub. price: $10.00; per copy: $2.25; sample: $2.25. Back issues: $2.25. 75pp; 6X9; †of. Reporting time: 8-10 weeks. Payment: copies. Copyrighted, reverts to author. COSMEP.

SHAKESPEARE NEWSLETTER, Louis Marder, Univ. of Illinois, Chicago Circle, Chicago, IL 60680, 312-996-3289. 1951. Poetry, articles, criticism, letters, reviews, news items. "Short pithy poems-dozen lines or so. For articles-send your conclusions & I will let you know if I want the article." circ. 1,600. 6/yr. Pub'd 6 issues 1979; expects 6 issues 1980. sub. price: $4.00; per copy: $1.00; sample: $1.00. Back issues: $1 each $5 per yr for 6. Discounts: 3 years, $10.00. 8-10pp; 9¼X12; of. Reporting time: less than a month. Payment: 3 copies. Not copyrighted. Pub's reviews: 30 in 1979. §scholarly Shakespeareana. Ads: $355.00/$188.00. SNL.

Shameless Hussy Press, Angel, Alta, Box 3092, Berkeley, CA 94703. 1969. Poetry, fiction, art, photos, cartoons, satire, criticism, parts-of-novels, long-poems. avg. press run 3,000. Discounts: 40% to bookstores & bulk orders. 50pp; 8½X5½; of.

SHANKPAINTER, The Work Center Press, 24 Pearl St, Provincetown, MA 02657, 617-487-9960. 1969. Poetry, fiction. "Submissions to *Shankpainter* are restricted to fellows, former fellows, staff, former staff, visitors to the Fine Arts Work Center, and former visitors." circ. 800. 3/yr. Pub'd 2 issues 1979; expects 3 issues 1980, 3 issues 1981. sample price: free. Back issues: *Shankpainter* is not sold. Donations are appreciated. No back issues are available except for 1978. Discounts: We give our magazine away. 80-100pp; 7X10; †of. Payment: copies. Copyrighted, reverts to author. Ads: no ads.

SHANTIH, John S. Friedman, Co-Editor; Irving Gottesman, Co-Editor, Box 125, Bay Ridge St., Brooklyn, NY 11220. 1971. Poetry, fiction, articles, art, photos, cartoons, interviews, criticism, reviews, parts-of-novels, long-poems, plays, concrete art. circ. 1,000. Irreg. Pub'd 1 issues 1979; expects 2 issues 1980. sub. price: $12.00; per copy: $3.00; sample: $3.00. Back issues: Varies. Discounts: 40% dealers. 64pp; 8½X11; of. Reporting time: 6 weeks. Payment: Rarely. Copyrighted. Pub's reviews: None in 1979. §Foreign literature in translation. Ads: $500.00/$250.00/$2.00 a word. CCLM.

SHAVIAN—JOURNAL OF BERNARD SHAW, High Orchard Press, Robert Clare, Eric Ford, 125 Markyate Rd, Dagenham, Essex RM8 2LB, United Kingdom. 1941. Poetry, articles, art, photos, cartoons, interviews, satire, criticism, reviews, music, letters, plays, news items. "Research & scholarship on & about Bernard Shaw." circ. 600. 1/yr. sub. price: $8.00; per copy: $5.00; sample: $5.00. Back issues: $5.00. Discounts: agents 20%. 10pp; size A5; lo. Reporting time: 6 months. Payment: copies. Copyrighted. Pub's reviews. §Edwardian period. Ads: £15/page & pro rata.

SHAW NEWSLETTER, Shaw Society, E. Ford, High Orchard, 125 Markyate Road, Dagenham, Essex RM 82 LB, England. 1976. Poetry, fiction, articles, art, photos, cartoons, interviews, satire, criticism, reviews, music, letters, parts-of-novels, long-poems, collages, plays, concrete art, news items, non-fiction. "Brief items on and about G. Bernard Shaw, British writer (1856-1950). His life works, times, contemporaries, influences, causes which he espoused, e.g. vegetarianism." circ. 600. 3-4/yr. sub. price: $5.00. Discounts: Agents 20 percent. 4 pp per issue; size A5 upright; †of. Reporting time: 6 months. Pays in copies. Copyrighted. Pub's reviews. §Books magazines for review welcomed. See comments for suitable fields. Ads: $30.00 pro rata.

THE SHAW REVIEW, Pennsylvania State University Press, Stanley Weintraub, S-234 Burrowes Building, University Park, PA 16802, 814-865-4242. 1951. Articles, interviews, criticism, reviews, letters. circ. 700. 3/yr. Pub'd 3 issues 1979; expects 3 issues 1980, 1 issue 1981. sub. price: US & Canada, instit $10.00: indiv $7.50; all other countries, instit $11.00: indiv $8.50; per copy: $2.50; sample: $2.50. Back issues: Vol 1 through 13, $1.75; special back issues price for Vol. l4 through 2l: $3.00. Discounts: $1.00 to agents. 50pp; 6X9; of. Reporting time: immed. Payment: none. Copyrighted, does not revert to author. Pub's reviews: 2 in 1979. §connected to Shaw, his contemporaries or environment. Ads: none. CELJ (Council of Editors of Learned Journals).

Shaw Society (see also SHAW NEWSLETTER), E. Ford, High Orchard, 125 Markyate Road, Dagenham, Essex RM82LB, England. 1941. Poetry, fiction, articles, art, photos, cartoons, interviews, satire, criticism, reviews, music, letters, parts-of-novels, long-poems, collages, plays, concrete art, news items, non-fiction. "Advance knowledge of G Bernard Shaw (British writer 1856-1950) his life works, times, contemporaries, etc. & causes he exposed e.g. vegetarianism." avg. press run 600. avg. price, paper: $5.00. Discounts: Agents 20 percent. 4 pp per issue; size A5 upright; †of. Reporting time: 6 months. Pays in copies. Copyrights for author.

SHEBA REVIEW, The Literary Magazine for the Arts, Sharon D. Hanson, PO Box 86, Loose Creek, MO 65054, (314) 897-3924. 1977. Poetry, fiction, articles, art, photos, cartoons, interviews, satire, reviews, long-poems, news items. "Sheba Review, Inc., is a not-for-profit organization with tax-exempt status. Its objective is to promote the unknown writer and artist along with the acclaimed who originate or work in the midwest — with specific emphasis on those living and working in Missouri and Illinois. *Sheba Review* accepts unsolicited manuscripts (poetry, prose, photos, journalistic articles, letters, philosophical/religious/political commentary as it relates to art). A stamped, self-addressed envelope should accompany all material if the sender wishes unaccepted material to be returned. The *Sheba* staff, in its selection of material, tries to present a broad spectrum of thought and talent. Coverage is given to well-known artists and writers as well as 'undiscovered talent'." circ. 600+. 2/yr. Expects 2 issues 1980, 2 issues 1981. sub. price: $4.00; per copy: $2.50; sample: $2.50. Back issues: $3.00. 16-20pp; of. Copyrighted, reverts to author. Pub's reviews: 6 in 1979. §Any publication concerning literature & the arts.

The Sheep Meadow Press, Stanley Moss, 145 Central Park West, New York, NY 10023, 212-247-1759. 1976. Poetry. "Persea Books, Inc. 225 Lafayette Street, New York, NY 10012. Reg. trade discount." avg. press run 2500. Pub'd 2 titles 1979; expects 6 titles 1980, 4 titles 1981. avg. price, cloth: $7.95; paper: $3.95. Discounts: 43%. 102pp; 8½X5½; of. Reporting time: 3 months. Payment: 10%. Copyrights for author.

Sheer Press, Elaine Starkman, PO Box 4071, Walnut Creek, CA 94598.

Sheffield Free Press, c/o Ujamaa, 259 Glossop Rd, Sheffield, United Kingdom. APS.

SHELTERFORCE, John Atlas, Pat Morrissy, Robert Widrow, 380 Main St., East Orange, NJ 07018, (201) 678-6778. 1975. "SHELTERFORCE is a national housing publication that analyzes housing and urban problems and serves as a forum to exchange ideas concerning short- and long-term tactics and strategies for the housing movement. It is published by a group of housing activists, lawyers and planners in New Jersey." circ. 3,000. 4/yr. Pub'd 4 issues 1979. sub. price: $5.00/individual; $7.00/law office agency, organization; $10.00/instit., library; per copy: $1.00; sample: $1.00. Back issues: Complete set (10 issues), $9.00; Single copies, $1.25. Discounts: Bulk orders: 25+, 50¢; 50+, 25¢. 16pp; 11X16; lp. Reporting time: 2 months. Payment: none. Copyrighted. Pub's reviews: 4 in 1979. §housing, urban problems, politics, cities, environment. APS.

SHENANDOAH, Journalism Laboratory Press, James Boatwright, Richard Howard, Poetry, P.O. Box 722, Lexington, VA 24450, (703) 463-9111 ext 283. 1950. "Literary review featuring fiction, poetry, essays and reviews." circ. 1,200. 4/yr. Pub'd 4 issues 1979; expects 4 issues 1980, 4 issues 1981. sub. price: $5.00; per copy: $1.50. Back issues: $2.50. Discounts: 20% discount through agencies/50% bulk rate to bookstores. 100pp; 6X9; †of. Payment: by arrangement. Pub's reviews: 5 in 1979. Ads: $60/$35. CCLM.

Sheriar Press, 801 13th Avenue S., Myrtle Beach, SC 29582, (803) 272-5311. 1971. "We publish books by and about Avatar Meher Baba, the spiritual Master who lived in India from 1894 to 1969 and who traveled widely throughout the world during part of that time. His followers call him 'The Awakener,' for he established no religion or cult, but awakens the heart of man to find God as the real Self." avg. press run 3,000. Pub'd 2 titles 1979; expects 1 title 1980, 1 title 1981. avg. price, cloth:

$7.95; paper: $4.95. 160pp; 5½X8¼; †of.

John B. Sherrill, John B. Sherrill, PO Box 8623, Austin, TX 78712, (512) 451-4459. 1979. Poetry. "I am not a press, but a self-published poet with one book." avg. press run 250. Pub'd 1 title 1979. 1 title listed in the *Small Press Record of Books in Print* (9th Edition, 1980). avg. price, paper: $3.50. Discounts: 20% to libraries, 40% to all others. 60pp; 5½X8½; lp. Copyrights for author.

Shining Waters Press (see also RIPPLES), Karen Schaefer, Editor, 718 Watersedge, Ann Arbor, MI 48105. 1973. Poetry, fiction, reviews, long-poems, news items. of. Reporting time: 2 weeks on manuscripts. Payment: negotiable.

Shinn Music Aids, Duane Shinn, PO Box 192, Medford, OR 97501, 664-2317. 1966. Music. "Most publications are house-produced. Very little free lance material accepted." avg. press run 5M min.-25M max. Pub'd 12 titles 1979. 21 titles listed in the *Small Press Record of Books in Print* (9th Edition, 1980). avg. price, paper: $6.95. Discounts: 50 percent basic; single copy 25 percent-over gross 67 percent. 40pp; 8½X11; of. Reporting time: 4 weeks. Payment: flat rate. Copyrights for author.

Shire Press, Helen Garvy, PO Box 1728, Santa Cruz, CA 95061, 408-425-0842. 1971. avg. press run varies. Pub'd 2 titles 1979; expects 2 titles 1980. 3 titles listed in the *Small Press Record of Books in Print* (9th Edition, 1980). avg. price, paper: $2.00. Discounts: 40%. 5½X8½.

THE SHIRT OFF YOUR BACK, Two Geese Press, Cornelius Robert Eady, Sarah Micklem, 62 Spelman Hall, Princeton, NJ 08544. 1977. Poetry. "*The Shirt Off Your Back* is a new magazine that will be silkscreening poetry broadsides onto T-shirts. We will run off 5 shirts per month, 3 of which will be given to the poet, 1 shall be kept for ourselves and one will be put on display. We are looking for strong short poems from 8-10 lines long. We are looking for *poems,* not 'thoughts for the day'. Accepted poets can order extra shirts for $3.00 per shirt" 12/yr. Pub'd 1 issue 1979; expects 3 issues 1980, 12 issues 1981. sub. price: $60.00; per copy: $5.00; sample: $5.00. 1pp. Reporting time: 1 week to 4 months. Payment: 3 shirts. Copyrighted, reverts to author. Pub's reviews. §Poetry.

SHOCKS, Momo's Press, Stephen Vincent, Box 14061, San Francisco, CA 94114. 1973. Poetry, criticism, letters. "We usually do one large issue a year (100-150 pages). The issue has a particular focus. Most recently (1976) we did *The Androgyny Issue,* subtitled 'Men looking at the women in themselves, women looking at the men in themselves'. Just coming up is THE POETRY READING (issue). An exploration of how language can occur in our culture(s), it will contain articles on poetry w/video, dance, tape, pure voice, and a special w/SF Bay Area poetry typographers. Writers have included: Susan Griffin, Jack Anderson, Andrei Codrescu, Jessica Hagedorn, Ntzake Shange, Keith Assott, Michael Lally, Beverly Dahlen" circ. 1,500. 1/yr. price per copy: $5.00. Back issues: Total Series (Shocks #1-#9) $35.00 Shocks #5, The Day Book $2.50 Other past issues not available as singles. 6X9. Reporting time: 2 months. Payment: copies. Copyrighted, reverts to author. CCLM, COSMEP.

Sibyl-Child Press (see also SIBYL-CHILD: A Women's Arts & Culture Journal), Candyce Homnick Stapen, Doris Mozer, Susan B. Shannon, Joan Wood, Mary Louise O'Connell, Box 1773, Hyattsville, MD 20783, (301) 362-1404; (703) 683-0988. 1976. Poetry, fiction, articles, art, photos, cartoons, interviews, satire, criticism, reviews, letters, parts-of-novels, long-poems, plays, concrete art. "Art submissions should include commentary" avg. press run 1,000. Pub'd 2 titles 1979; expects 3 titles 1980, 3 titles 1981. avg. price, paper: $3.50. Discounts: no policy established at present—to be worked out on individual basis. 64pp; 5½X8½; of. New project, now accepting submissions. CCLM, COSMEP.

SIBYL-CHILD: A Women's Arts & Culture Journal, Sibyl-Child Press, Candyce Homnick Stapen, Doris Mozer, Susan B. Shannon, Joan Wood, Mary Louise O'Connell, P.O. Box 1773, Hyattsville, MD 20783, (301) 362-1404; (703) 683-0988. 1974. Poetry, fiction, articles, art, photos, cartoons, interviews, satire, criticism, reviews, music, letters, parts-of-novels, long-poems, collages, plays, concrete art. "Women's art and culture—Grace Cavalieri, Margery Goldberg, Barbara Holland, Wendy Stevens, Lois Van Houten, Joyce Tenneson Cohen, Polly Joan, Clarinda Harriss Lott, Candyce Homnick Stapen, Peg Kaplin" circ. 500. 3/yr. Pub'd 2 issues 1979; expects 3 issues 1980, 3 issues 1981. sub. price: $9.00; per copy: $3.50; sample: [same to individuals; free to institutions]. Back issues: VI Issue 1,$1.25; Issue 2 and 3 (double issue) $4.00; Issue 4 $2.00. Discounts: 20% to distributors (trade, jobbers, etc.); 10% to individuals in quantities of 5 or more. 64pp; 5½X8½; of. Reporting time: within a month. Payment: complimentary copies (2) plus tear sheets. Copyrighted, reverts upon written request provided that Sibyl-Child is credited as 1st publisher. Pub's reviews: 9 in 1979. §Women's studies, art, culture. Ads: $100.00/$50.00/$25.00. CCLM, COSMEP.

Sicilian Antigruppo (see also IMPEGNO 70; PALERMO ANTIGRUPPO), Nat Scammacca, Rolando Certa, Costtino Petalia, Villa Scanimac, via Argenteria Km 4, Trapani, Sicily, 0923-38681. 1968.

Poetry, fiction, articles, art, photos, interviews, satire, criticism, letters, parts-of-novels, collages, concrete art. "For our newspaper, a weekly, articles are usually up to 3½ typewritten pages. For our reviews any length. For books, essays, criticism on any subject no limit. Books of poetry, 64 pages. Languages; Italian, English and Sicilian. We are doing a series of 20 books of poetry of American poets completely in Italian and English, the languages face to face. Some writers and poets are: Crescenzio Cane, Ignazio Apolloni, Pietro Terminelli, Gianni Diecidue, Rolando Certa, Nat Scammacca, Franco DiMarco, Santo Cali, Carmelo Pirrera, L. Ferlinghetti, R. Bly, Rafaeli Alberti, Guiseppe Zaggario, Beppi DiBella, Ignazio Navarra, Cesare Zavattini." avg. price, paper: $4.00 - $5.00. Discounts: 33 percent. 150pp; mi/of/lp. Reporting time: 1 month. Payment: Regular contract 10 percent etc. Copyrights for author.

Signpost Press (see also THE BELLINGHAM REVIEW), Knute Skinner, Editor; Peter Nicoletta, Editor; Richard Dills, Editor; Joseph Green, Assistant Editor, 412 N. State, Bellingham, WA 98225. 1977. Poetry, fiction, art, photos, reviews. avg. press run 500. Pub'd 2 titles 1979. avg. price, paper: $2.00. 24pp; of. Payment: $50.00 plus 50 copies. Copyrights for author.

SIGNPOST, Louise Marshall, Barbara Diltz-Siler, 16812 36th Avenue W, Lynwood, WA 98036, 206-743-3947. 1966. Poetry, fiction, articles, art, photos, cartoons. "Editorial comment is heavily weighted for Pacific Northwest backpackers, ski tourers, snow shoers, etc. We rarely purchase outside material, but can 'pay' with extra copies." circ. 4,000. 16/yr. Pub'd 16 issues 1979; expects 16 issues 1980. sub. price: $10.00; per copy: $1.00. Back issues: $1.00 magazine issues; 50 cents newsletter. Discounts: 40 percent discount to retailers. 16pp; 10×15; of. Reporting time: 3 weeks. Payment: very low. Copyrighted, reverts to author. Pub's reviews. §outdoor non-motorized activities. Ads: $350.00/$180.00/$0.10-wd.$2.00 min.

Signpost Books, Cliff Cameron, 8912 192nd Street, SW, Edmonds, WA 98020, 206-776-0370. 1978. Articles. "We publish books on outdoor subjects for non-motorized persons, with emphasis on backpacking, camping, ski touring, snow-shoeing, bicycling, canoeing, etc. If subject has only regional appeal, it must be for the Pacific Northwest." avg. press run 5,000. Pub'd 9 titles 1979; expects 12 titles 1980. 20 titles listed in the *Small Press Record of Books in Print* (9th Edition, 1980). avg. price, paper: $5.95. Discounts: 10-24 books, 40%; 25-99 books, 45%; 100 or more, 50%. 128-144pp; 5½×8½; of. Reporting time: 4 weeks. Payment: 8-10 percent of retail price. Copyrights for author. PNBPA (Pacific Northwest Book Publishers Assoc).

SIGNS: A JOURNAL OF WOMEN IN CULTURE AND SOCIETY, University of Chicago Press, Barbara Charlesworth Gelpi, Editor, Center for Research on Women, Serra House, Stanford University, Stanford, CA 94305. 1975. Articles, criticism, reviews, letters. circ. 7,000. 4/yr. Pub'd 4 issues 1979; expects 5 issues 1980, 4 issues 1981. sub. price: $16.00 indiv.; $24.00 insti.; $14.40 students; per copy: $5.00 indiv.; $6.00 insti.; sample: $5.00 indiv., $6.00 instit. Back issues: Contact business office, University of Chicago Press, 11030 Langley Avenue, Chicago IL 60628, for this information. Discounts: Standard agencies. 300pp; 6X9; of. Reporting time: Contact editorial office, Center for Research on Women, Serra House, Stanford University, Stanford CA 94305, for this information, 3-6 months. Copyrighted, reverts to author. Pub's reviews: 18 in 1979. §Women. Ads: $165.00/$115.00.

SILVER VAIN, Pi-Right Press, Hank Louis, P. O. Box 2366, Park City, UT 84060, 801-649-8866. 1976. Poetry, fiction, art, photos, parts-of-novels, long-poems. "We are interested mainly in Western writers and Western views, although we are happy to consider quality writing of any flavor. We are interested in previously unpublished writers, as well as 'knowns'. We will consider any length. Recent contrib. — Sam Hamill, W. M. Ransom, Blair Fuller, Sheila Nickerson." circ. 500. 3/yr. Pub'd 2 issues 1979; expects 3 issues 1980, 3 issues 1981. sub. price: $10.00; per copy: $3.00; sample: $2.50. Back issues: $4.50. Discounts: 40% discount to booksellers. 80pp; 5½×8½; of. Reporting time: 3 weeks. Payment: 3 copies - $25.00 fiction, $5.00 poem. Copyrighted, reverts to author. Pub's reviews: 1 in 1979. §37/73. Ads: trade-outs only with other little mags. COSMEP, CCLM.

SILVERFISH REVIEW, Rodger Moody, Randall Roorda, PO Box 3541, Eugene, OR 97403, (503) 344-3535. 1978. Poetry, fiction, articles, art, photos, interviews, satire, criticism, reviews, letters, parts-of-novels, long-poems, collages, plays. "The only criteria for selection of material is quality. Recent Contributors: Poetry - Duane Ackerson, Susan Cobin, Barbara Drake, Stuart Dybek, Albert Goldbarth, John Morgan, Carolyn Stoloff, William Stafford, and Ingrid Wendt. Fiction - Beth Tasbery Shannon and Michael Strelow. Translations by Stuart Friebert. *SR number three* is a chapbook of poems by Frank Rossini, *Sparking the Rain.* We plan to devote the third of three issues each year to the work of an individual author: please enquire, or better yet, submit work for our regular issues, before sending a manuscript. Subscriptions are pleasing to us and (check our rates) dirt cheap to you. Our policy: the best for the least!" circ. 500. 3/yr. Pub'd 3 issues 1979; expects 3 issues 1980, 3 issues

1981. sub. price: $2.50; per copy: $1.00; sample: $1.00. 20% consignment, 40% wholesale discount to bookstores. 50% discount to distributors, jobbers, classrooms, etc. 48pp; 4¼X5½; of. Reporting time: 2-3 weeks. Payment: 3 copies. Copyrighted, reverts to author. Pub's reviews: 1 in 1979. §Contemporary poetry, fiction, aesthetics, and new magazines. Ads: $50.00/$25.00. COSMEP, CCLM.

Simon & Pierre Publishing Co. Ltd., Marian M. Wilson, Paula S. Goepfert, Box 280, Adelaide St. P.O., Toronto, Ontario M5C2J4, Canada, 416-463-5944 order desk 416-463-5945. 1972. Fiction, art, photos, plays, non-fiction. "Publish two illustrated drama series including one act and full length plays, and children's plays in cloth and paper binding, plus new fiction, photographic books and non fiction. All Canadian authors." avg. press run 2,500. Pub'd 11 titles 1979; expects 12 titles 1980. 16 titles listed in the *Small Press Record of Books in Print* (9th Edition, 1980). avg. price, cloth: $12.95; paper: $4.95. Discounts: Trade: 1-4, 20 percent; wholesalers 40 percent, 5 or more 40 percent; classroom & bulk discounts. 180-350 pp casebound, 64-120 pp plays in paper, 180-280 pp fiction in paper; 6X9, 8½X11; of. Reporting time: 2 weeks if rejected; 3 months if being considered for publication. Payment: average 10 percent royalty. Copyrights for author. COSMEP, ACP, CLEA.

SING HEAVENLY MUSE! WOMEN'S POETRY AND PROSE, Sue Ann Martinson, Editor; Brigitte Frase, Roseann Lloyd, Assoc. Editors, P.O. Box 14027, Minneapolis, MN 55414, (612) 822-8713; (612) 823-8030. 1978. Poetry, fiction, art, photos. "We are interested in publishing a variety of fine writing by women. Work by men is accepted if appropriate to the magazine. Contributors include: Meridel LeSueur, Barbara Holland, Ann Kelleher, Cary Waterman, Patricia Hampl, and Jane Navarre. Please inquire about artwork." circ. 800. 2/yr. Pub'd 2 issues 1979; expects 2 issues 1980, 2 issues 1981. sub. price: $6.00; per copy: $3.00; $3.50 by mail; sample: $2.00. Back issues: Special back issue price: $2.00. Discounts: 40% trade. 100pp; 6X9; of. Reporting time: 1-3 months. Payment: 2 copies. Copyrighted, reverts to author. Ads: please inquire. COSMEP.

SING OUT! The Folk Song Magazine, Rhonda Matter, Peter Wortsman, Sarah Plant, Mimi Bluestone, 505 Eighth Avenue, New York, NY 10018. 1950. Poetry, articles, art, photos, interviews, reviews, music, letters, news items. "We print music and lyrics of folk songs" circ. 10,000. 6/yr. sub. price: $11.00 indiv., $15.00 instit.; per copy: $2.00; sample: $2.00. Back issues: $0.50 to $8.00 depending on the date of issue. Discounts: Write to Circulation Department for complete back issue list. 48pp; 5⅞X8⅞; of. Reporting time: variable. Payment: copies. Copyrighted, reverts to author. Pub's reviews: 100 in 1979. §music, folklore, politics, arts, third world, ethnic materials, etc, women history labor. Ads: $500.00/$300.00/$75.00. COSMEP.

Singing Horse Press (see also PAPER AIR), Gil Ott, Editor & Publisher, 825 Morris Road, Blue Bell, PA 19422. 1976. Poetry, long-poems. "First title published 1980: *Drawing a Blank* by Craig Watson, $2.50." avg. press run 300. Pub'd 1 title 1979. 1 title listed in the *Small Press Record of Books in Print* (9th Edition, 1980). avg. price, paper: $2.50. Discounts: 40% order 3 or more copies, no consignment. 32pp; of. Reporting time: solicited material only. Payment: 10% of press run. CCLM.

Singing Wind Press, Karlene Gentile, 4164 West Pine, Saint Louis, MO 63108, 314-535-2118. 1975. Poetry, fiction, articles, art, photos, interviews, parts-of-novels. "Singing Wind Press does fine letterpress editions in poetry and children's literature and publishes fiction as well. Recent contributors include Speer Morgan, William Peden and Thomas McAfee in fiction; Thomas McAfee, Ted Schaefer, Larry Levis, Marcia Southwick, Kelly Cherry, Howard Schwartz, Robert Dyer, Jerred Metz and Carlos Suarez in poetry; Bernard McDonald in children's literature" avg. press run 1,000. Pub'd 2 titles 1979; expects 10 titles 1980. avg. price, cloth: $11.70; paper: $5.00. Discounts: 40%. 64pp; 8½X11; 5½X8½; †of/lp. Reporting time: 2 months. Payment: direct ms. payment or 10 percent; depending upon material & project. Copyrights for author. COSMEP.

Singlejack Books, PO Box 1906, San Pedro, CA 90733. 9 titles listed in the *Small Press Record of Books in Print* (9th Edition, 1980).

SIPAPU, Konocti Books, Noel Peattie, Route 1, Box 216, Winters, CA 95694, 916-662-3364; 916-752-1032. 1970. Articles, interviews, reviews. "A newsletter for librarians interested in third world studies, the counter-culture & alternative and independent presses. Konocti Books publishing work on similar themes. Make all checks out to Noel Peattie, Editor and Publisher, *SIPAPU*. No stamps accepted." circ. 400. 2/yr. Pub'd 2 issues 1979; expects 2 issues 1980. sub. price: $4.00; per copy: $2.00; sample: $2.00. Back issues: No special prices, but many back issues out of print. Complete file now microfilmed at University of Southern California. Discounts: books 40%. 32pp; 8½X11; of. Reporting time: 3 weeks. Payment: $0.04 per word. Copyrighted, released to author on request. Pub's reviews. §3d world/regional/special items. COSMEP, APS.

Sisters' Choice Press, Nancy Schimmel, 2027 Parker Street, Berkeley, CA 94704, (415) 843-2365. 1976. avg. press run 2,000. Pub'd 1 title 1979. 1 title listed in the *Small Press Record of Books in*

Print (9th Edition, 1980). avg. price, paper: $4.00. Discounts: 1 copy, none; 2-4, 20%; 5 or more, 40%. 56pp; 8½X11; of. Copyrights for author. COSMEP.

Sitnalta Press, Deirdre J. G. Porter, 1881 Sutter Street, #103, San Francisco, CA 94115, (415) 922-8223. 1978. Fiction, articles. "Bias: Non-mystical, rational material." avg. press run 2,000. Pub'd 1 title 1979; expects 2 titles 1980, 3 titles 1981. 2 titles listed in the *Small Press Record of Books in Print* (9th Edition, 1980). avg. price, paper: $8.00. Discounts: Trade/standard and negotiated. 200pp; 8½X5½; of. Reporting time: 30 days maximum. Payment: Trade/standard or as negotiated. Copyrights for author.

SKIFFY THYME, Purple Mouth Press, Cuyler Warnell "Ned" Brooks Jr., 713 Paul Street, Newport News, VA 23605, 804-380-6595. 1972. Art, cartoons. circ. 200-400. 1-2/yr. Pub'd 1 issue 1979; expects 1 issue 1980, 1 issue 1981. Back issues: none available. 18pp; 8½X11; †mi. Reporting time: a week. Payment: free copy. common law. Pub's reviews: 24 in 1979. §science fiction/fantasy/fantasy art/science fiction reference.

SKULL POLISH, Francis Poole, JoAnn Balingit, 4, rue Mohamed Bergach, Tangier Medina, Morocco. 1977. Poetry, fiction, art, reviews, collages. "Fiction of 1,000 words maximum length. Submissions must include SASE and international reply coupons." circ. 250. irregular. Pub'd 1 issue 1979; expects 2 issues 1980. sub. price: $3.00 (2 issues); per copy: $2.00 postpaid; sample: $2.00 postpaid. Back issues: unavailable. 36pp; 5X7; †of. Reporting time: 6 weeks. Payment: copies (2) of issue in which printed. Copyrighted, reverts to author. Pub's reviews: 8 in 1979. §Poetry, biography of literary figures, criticism, small press publications.

SKYDIVING, Michael Truffer, Po Box 189, Deltona, FL 32725. 1979. News items. circ. 6,000. 12/yr. Pub'd 6 issues 1979; expects 12 issues 1980. sub. price: $12.00; per copy: $2.00; sample: $2.00. Back issues: $2.00. Discounts: 40% standard, negotiable. 24pp; 11X14½; of. Reporting time: 2 weeks. Payment: yes. Copyrighted. Pub's reviews: 4 in 1979. §Aeronautics. Ads: $250.00/$175.00/$0.40. COSMEP.

Skydog Press (see also NRG), Dan Raphael, Mike Fish, 228 SE 26th, Portland, OR 97214, (503) 231-0890. 1978. Poetry, art, long-poems, collages, concrete art. "For the time being, are soliciting all our material. First titles: *Hollow Fox* by David Whited; *Polymerge* by Dan Raphael; all work is solicited from NRG contributors." avg. press run 400. Pub'd 3 titles 1979; expects 3 titles 1980. 2 titles listed in the *Small Press Record of Books in Print* (9th Edition, 1980). avg. price, paper: $1.50. Discounts: 40%. 24pp; 6½X9½; of. No outside submissions considered. Payment: 20% of press run. Copyrights for author. CCLM.

SKYWRITING, Blue Mountain Press, Martin Grossman, 511 Campbell St, Kalamazoo, MI 49007, 616-349-3924. 1971. Poetry, fiction, interviews, reviews, criticism. "*SKYWRITING* attempts to remain as open as possible, so there are no real biases concerning style. We are interested in quality poetry, and fiction as it presents itself, and have in the past published work by Barry Lopez, W.S. Merwin, Charles Wright, Ira Sadoff, Howard Norman, William Matthews, Russell Edson, Richard Shelton, Herbert Scott and John Woods. From our fifth issue on, we will 'feature' a poet, and present critical articles, interviews, more personal views, as well as the poet's newest work." circ. 500. 1/yr. Expects 2 issues 1980. sub. price: $6.00-3 issues; per copy: $2.00/$4.00 double issue; sample: $2.00/$4.00 double issue. Back issues: No. 1-$5.00; No. 2-$10.00; No. 3-$50.00; No. 4/5-$100.00; No. 6-$50.00. Discounts: 40% 5 copies minimum. 50pp; 9X6; of. Reporting time: 2-3 months. Payment: 2 copies. Copyrighted, reverts to author. Pub's reviews: 1 in 1979. §all areas. Ads: $60/$35. CCLM.

THE SLACKWATER REVIEW, Confluence Press, Inc., M.K. Browning, Spalding Hall, Lewis-Clark Campus, Lewiston, ID 83501, 208-746-2341. 1976. Poetry, fiction, articles, art, photos, interviews, criticism, reviews. "Prose 5-6 pages—poetry 1/2 to full page—focus on Northwest and Intermountain regional productions—do take unusually good materials from other areas. Wm. Stafford, Wm. P. Root, Jim Heynen, Richard Hugo." circ. 500-1,000. 2/yr. Pub'd 2 issues 1979; expects 2 issues 1980, 2 issues 1981. sub. price: $6.00; per copy: $2.50. Back issues: $2.00. Discounts: standard 40 percent retail; 50 percent wholesale. 100pp; 5½X8½; †of. Reporting time: 2-3 months. Payment: poetry 35 cents a line; prose 2 cents word *when funds allow!!*. Copyrighted, does not revert to author. Pub's reviews: 5-6 in 1979. §Books & chapbooks of Northwest & Intermountain Region Writers. CCLM.

Sleepy Hollow Restorations, Saverio Procario, James R. Gullichson, 150 White Plains Road, Tarrytown, NY 10591, 914-631-8200. 1972. Non-fiction. "Historical Material. American history and literature, pre-1900." avg. press run 2,000. Pub'd 2 titles 1979; expects 6 titles 1980, 6 titles 1981. 25 titles listed in the *Small Press Record of Books in Print* (9th Edition, 1980). avg. price, cloth: $15.00; paper: $3.00. Discounts: 40 percent trade, jobber. 300pp; 6X9; of. Reporting time: 1 month. Payment: 5-10 percent.

SLICK PRESS, Linda Williams, 5336 So. Drexel, Chicago, IL 60615. 1976. Poetry, fiction, art. "Am trying to publish unknown writers mostly." circ. 50 per issue. 2-4/yr. Pub'd 3 issues 1979; expects 4 issues 1980. sub. price: $8.00; per copy: $2.00; sample: Free only to bookstores, distributors, etc. $2.00 otherwise. 30-40pp; 8X11; †lp. Reporting time: asap. Payment: none at present. Copyrighted, reverts after 6 mos. time in the future. COSMEP, CCLM.

Slough Press, Charles Taylor, Pat Taylor, Duane Carr, Pat Carr, Ellis Taylor, Box 370, Edgewood, TX 75117. 1974. Poetry, fiction. "Slough Press in the future will be only interested in 'New Age' literature and nonfiction." avg. press run 500. Pub'd 4 titles 1979. 2 titles listed in the *Small Press Record of Books in Print* (9th Edition, 1980). avg. price, paper: $2.50. Discounts: Varies. 64pp; 5X4; †of. Reporting time: 2-3 weeks. Payment: Negotiable. copyright negotiable.

Slow Loris Press (see also SLOW LORIS READER), Anthony Petrosky, Patricia Petrosky, 923 Highview Street, Pittsburgh, PA 15206. 1971. Poetry, interviews, fiction. "*Slow Loris* broadside series IV: 25 signed folios: $150.00 each. From the Slow Loris poetry series: *Songs of Autumn,* Sigitas Geda*Trans. by Jonas Zdanys; *Green in the Body,* Robert Winner; *Polar Sun,* Sandi Picccione; and *Oblique Light,* Lynn Emanuel; *Interstate,* Marie Harris; *Father is a Pillow Tied to a Broom,* Gary Soto; *heart, Grain,* Nils Nelson; and *The Ancient Wars,* Paul Zimmer." avg. press run 500-1,000. Pub'd 4 titles 1979; expects 4 titles 1980. 28 titles listed in the *Small Press Record of Books in Print* (9th Edition, 1980). avg. price, cloth: $10.00; paper: $4.95-$5.95. Discounts: 1 copy no disc; 2-4: 20%; 5+: 40%; signed 2 or more 10%. 24-64pp; 6X9; lp/of. Payment: Copies. Copyrights for author. CCLM.

SLOW LORIS READER, Slow Loris Press, Patricia Petrosky, 923 Highview St, Pittsburgh, PA 15206. 1971. Reviews, photos, poetry, art, interviews, long-poems, fiction, articles, parts-of-novels. "*Rapport* changed to *Slow Loris Reader* in 1978. Submissions considered from October through May only." circ. 750. 2/yr. Pub'd 1 issue 1979; expects 2 issues 1980, 2 issues 1981. sub. price: $5.50/2 issues; per copy: $3.00; sample: $3.00. Back issues: $2.00 except for *Rapport* 1; $5.00 unsigned, $15 signed. Discounts: 1 copy, full price; 2-4, 20%; 5+, 40%. 80pp; 6X9; of. Reporting time: 2-4 months. Payment: contributor copies of magazine. Copyrighted. Pub's reviews: 3 in 1979. §poetry/translations/fiction. CCLM.

THE SMALL FARM, Jeff Daniel Marion, Rt 5 Cline Road Box 345, Dandridge, TN 37725. 1975. Poetry, reviews, long-poems. "Any poet is welcome who has good poems to offer, poems that take our earth consciousness in new directions, that leave us marked,changed by the experience of the poem. We believe in the importance of the creative act as a means of self-renewal as a vital connection with the organic flow of all life processes. Too, we see poetry as a striving to clarify the life we're living right now. We prefer in poetry a language that is alive, springy, a surface that is deceptively simple, underneath which are all the profundities, mysteries. We want a poetry that speaks to us now in a language that renews earth realities and possibilities, a poetry coming from, and committed to specific places. Contributors have included Wendell Berry, Robert Morgan, Frank Steele, Thomas Johnson, William Stafford, Robert Bly, Joe Bruchac, Greg Kuzma, Ted Kooser, Jim W. Miller, David Curry, and others." circ. 300. 2/yr. Pub'd 1 issue 1979. sub. price: $5.00 indiv., $6.00 libraries; per copy: $3.00-$5.00 (price varies depending on issue, inquire); sample: $5.00 plus postage. Back issues: inquire. 60pp; 5½X8½; of. Reporting time: 3-4 weeks. Payment: 2 copies. Copyrighted. Pub's reviews. §poetry/poetics.

SMALL MOON, Ed Cates, 52½ Dimick Street, Somerville, MA 02143. 1974. Poetry, art, photos, interviews, criticism, reviews, concrete art. "*Small Moon* publishes first translations, New England and West Coast writers and those in between. *Small Moon* #1 introduced Henrik Bjelke, Pen writer from Denmark, to U.S. readers. *Small Moon* #2 contained critical essays and excerpts from his novel, *Ocean Kiss.* First translations of Georgios Themelis' *Naked Window* (poems) in *Small Moon* #2. *Small Moon* #4 featured Polish poets Julian Tuwim and Jerzy Grupinski, and the German poet, Robert Musil, following a coterie of French poetry in issue #3. *Small Moon* #5/6 featured an extensive Italian contemporary poetry selection: Bartolo Cattafi, Rocco Scotellaro, Franco Fortini, Edith Bruck, David Maria Turoldo, Alfredo de Palchi, Alfredo Bonazzi, Pietro Cimatti, Rodolfo di Biaso, Leonardo Sinisgalli, Sandro Penna, Dario Belleza, Adriano Spatola, Giovanni Guidici, Andrea Zanzotto translated by Ruth Feldman and Brian Swann, Sonia Raiziss Giop, Frank Judge, W.S. Di Piero, Lawrence Venuti and Lawrence Smith, plus a special Armenian poetry supplement translated by Diana der Hovanessian. Recent contributors: Richardo de Silveria lobo Sternberg, Celia Gilbert, Robin Becker, Elizabeth McKim, Ron Schreiber, Cora Brooks, Martin Broekhuysen, Ed Cates, Stuart Friebert, Kent Wittenberg, Joyce Peseroff, Miriam Sagan, Beatrice Hawley, Lloyd Schwartz, Tony Fiusco, Rudy Kikel, William DeVoti, Douglas Worth." circ. 3,000. 2/yr. Pub'd 2 issues 1979. sub. price: $4.00; per copy: $1.50 + $.50 mailing; sample: $1.00. Back issues: $1.50 issue 5/6 (double issue). 20pp; of. Reporting time: 2 weeks to 2 months. Payment in copies. Copyrighted, reverts to author. Pub's reviews: 2 in 1979. §First translations, small presses, etc. Ads: write for information. CCLM, NESPA.

THE SMALL POND MAGAZINE OF LITERATURE, Napoleon St. Cyr, PO Box 664, Stratford, CT 06497. 1964. Poetry, fiction, articles, art, satire, concrete art, reviews. "Max: Fiction 2500 words, poetry approx 100 lines, other prose 2500 words. Recent contributors, some nobodies-some somebodies." circ. 300 plus. 3/yr. Pub'd 3 issues 1979; expects 3 issues 1980. sub. price: $4.75; per copy: $2.00; sample: $2.00. Back issues: Inquire. Discounts: Inquire. 36-40pp; 5½X8; of. Reporting time: 1-15 days. Payment: 2 copies. Pub's reviews: 6-9 in 1979. §only poetry (books). Ads: $30/$18. CCLM, COSMEP, NESPA.

THE SMALL PRESS REVIEW, Dustbooks, Len Fulton, Editor-Publisher; Ellen Ferber, Executive Editor; Pat Urioste, Contributing Editor ('Feedback'); Merritt Clifton, Contributing Editor ('The Watch'), P.O. Box 100, Paradise, CA 95969, 916-877-6110. 1966. Articles, cartoons, interviews, reviews, letters, news items. "In 1978 the *Small Press Review* was redesigned to include the Small Press Book Club. The Book Club chooses some ten small press books/magazines per 'Selectionlist' and offers them to Club members. A new 'Selectionlist' appears as the centerfold SPR monthly, and subscription to SPR constitutes membership in the Book Club. Dustbooks editors sort through 300-400 titles per month to develop each list for quality, range, and representation of what the small, independent presses and magazines are doing. We're always glad to send you a free sample copy of the latest SPR with the current 'Selectionlist' in it. Additionally, the *Small Press Review* seeks to study and promulgate the small press and little magazine (i.e. the *independent* publisher) worldwide. It was started in 1966 as part of an effort by its publisher to get a grip on small press/mag information since no one at the time (or for some years thereafter) seemed interested in doing it. It was also designed to promulgate the small press in a variety of ways. It links with other Dustbooks small-press info titles, updating the annual *International Directory of Little Magazines and Small Presses* and the annual *Small Press Record of Books in Print.* SPR is always on the lookout for competently written reviews (yes, we have a 'style sheet'—write for it), as long as they hold to a page in length and review a title published by a small press. SPR has a regular 'News Notes' section which gives info about small press activities, manuscript needs (*and there are many!*) and so on. We print print full-info listings monthly on twenty or so new small presses and mags. In the case of these latter listings, we generally utilize data from Int'l Directory report forms which come in to us throughout the year (if your magazine or press is not listed in either the *Int'l Directory* or *Small Press Record of Books in Print* please write to us for a form. If you fill out a form for the *Directory* you will automatically receive a form for the *Record* later.) Neither the *Small Press Review* nor Dustbooks itself receives grants of any kind from anywhere. Support is entirely by readers, subscribers and advertisers. Nor is there connection with any organization, small press or otherwise. NOTE: Canadian and foreign please remit in US funds only when ordering." circ. 3,000. 12/yr. Pub'd 12 issues 1979; expects 12 issues 1980, 12 issues 1981. sub. price: 10.00 Indiv. - $15.00 Inst.; per copy: $1.00; sample: free. Back issues: inquire. Discounts: $12/yr via agents. 16pp; 8½X11; of. Reporting time: 3 weeks. Not copyrighted. Pub's reviews: 100 in 1979. §anything published by a small press. Ads: $90/$55/$7.50 col. inch for SPR Mart.

SMITH'S JOURNAL, B. Reed Smith, 2009 Pinehurst Road, Los Angeles, CA 90068, 851-0375. 1978. Articles, cartoons, interviews, satire, criticism, reviews, letters, news items. "Biased toward autobiography, libertarian and anarchist ideas, especially when they all come together. Any political or social ideas as expressed thru autobiography, personal experience." circ. 5,000. 6/yr. Pub'd 1 issue 1979; expects 6 issues 1980, 10 issues 1981. sub. price: $5.00; per copy: $1.00; sample: $1.00. Back issues: $1.00. 16-24pp; 11¾X15½; of. Reporting time: 2 weeks. Payment: $.01 a word and copies. Copyrighted, reverts to author. Pub's reviews: §Autobiography, libertarian, third world, tax resistance. Ads: $100.00/$50.00. WIP.

SMOKE, Windows Project, Dave Ward, 23a Brent Way, Halewood, Liverpool, England L26 9XH, United Kingdom. 1974. Poetry, fiction, art, long-poems, collages, concrete art, photos, cartoons. "Tom Pickard, Jim Burns, Dave Calder, Roger McGough, Frances Horovitz" circ. 1,500. 3/yr. Pub'd 3 issues 1979; expects 3 issues 1980. sub. price: £1/6 issues incl. post.; per copy: 10p plus post; sample: 10p plus post. 44pp; size A5; of. Reporting time: as quickly as possible. Payment: £3.00 per contributor. No. no ads.

SmokeRoot (see also CUTBANK), Tom Rea, Kathy Callaway, Dept of English/Univ of Mont, Missoula, MT 59812. 1976. Poetry. "Chapbooks: 28pp maximum. Recent contributors: John Haines, Mary Swander, Rex Burwell, Madeline DeFrees." avg. press run 300. Pub'd 2 titles 1979; expects 2 titles 1981. 1 title listed in the *Small Press Record of Books in Print* (9th Edition, 1980). avg. price, paper: $2.25. Discounts: standard bookstore discount. 28pp; 5½X8½; †of. Reporting time: 4 weeks. Payment: by arrangement. Copyrights for author. CCLM.

SMU Press (see SOUTHWEST REVIEW)

THE SMUDGE, Douglas Mumm, PO Box 19276, Detroit, MI 48219. 1977. sub. price: $8.00.

Smuggler's Cove Publishing, Ben Dennis, Betsy Case, 107 W John, Seattle, WA 98119, (206) 285-3171. 1976. Art, photos. "Smuggler's Cove Books explore the myths and historical background of present lifestyles in concise, aware writing and in good photography and illustration. Design, architecture and nostalgia are among our special interests. The books are illustrated and directed mainly to an urban audience, though their appeal is general." avg. press run 10,000. Pub'd 1 title 1979; expects 1 title 1980, 1 title 1981. avg. price, cloth: $14.95; paper: $3.95-$9.95. Discounts: Retail: 1, 25%; 2-4, 33⅓%; 5-24, 40%; 25-49, 41%. Distributor: 2-4, 33⅓%; 5-9, 40%; 10-99, 46%; 100 up, 50%. 128pp; 9X9; of. Reporting time: 6 weeks. Payment: Standard Royalty.

Smyrna Press, Dan Georgakas, Leonard Rubenstein, Elias Bokhara, Judy Janda, Box 1803 GPO, Brooklyn, NY 11202. 1964. Poetry, fiction, art, parts-of-novels, collages. "We try to publish one-three books a year which combine the latest technical breakthroughs with a concern for social change that is essentially Marxist but undogmatic. Our current projects will combine art and politics as well as themes of sexual liberation. We can use good line drawings or woodcuts. We published three art books in 1976-77 which was a new departure for our press. Sample copies of literary books—50¢ sample copies of art books—$1.50." avg. press run 1,000 copies. Pub'd 3 titles 1979; expects 3 titles 1980. 10 titles listed in the *Small Press Record of Books in Print* (9th Edition, 1980). avg. price, cloth: $12.00; paper: $4.00; other: $1.50. Discounts: 40%. 60-96pp; 5½X8½; of. Reporting time: 2-3 weeks. Payment: copies and share of profits. Copyrights for author. COSMEP.

SNAPDRAGON, Ron McFarland, Editor; Margaret Newsome, Art; Patricia Hart, Production; Tina Foriyes, Editor, English Department, University of Idaho, Moscow, ID 83843, (208) 885-6156. 1977. Poetry, fiction, articles, art, photos, satire, music. "We are committed to publishing about 50% 'local' writers (not necessarily college students or faculty) and nearly all of our artwork is done locally. Have published Robert Bly, Henry Alley, Jason Weiss, Mona Simpson, Donald Levering, Olga Broumas, Rita Dove, William Studebaker, John Ditsky. Would like to see good prose (1-16 pages). Appreciate well-wrought urns of all varieties." circ. 300. 2/yr. Pub'd 1 issue 1979; expects 2 issues 1980, 2 issues 1981. sub. price: $3.00; per copy: $1.50; sample: $1.50. Back issues: $1.50 each. Discounts: $1.25 each for 6 or more copies (no postage costs assessed). 65pp; 7X8½; of. Reporting time: 2 weeks. Payment: copy. Copyrighted, reverts to author. Ads: $30(2 issues)/$10(2 issues). CCLM.

SNARF, Kitchen Sink Enterprises, Denis Kitchen, P.O. Box 7, Princeton, WI 54968. 1972. Art, cartoons, satire, letters. "Underground comic format-size ranges from -1/4 page strips to several pages long. Recent contributors: Robert Crumb, Justin Green, Will Eisner, Harvey Kurtzman." circ. 10,000-20,000. 2/yr. Pub'd 1 issue 1979; expects 2 issues 1980. sub. price: $4.00/ four issues postpaid; per copy: $1.00; sample: $1.00. Back issues: $1.00 postpaid. Discounts: 40% to bookstores, 60% discount to distributors. 36pp; 6¾X9¾; of. Reporting time: 2 wks. Payment: 10% royalty, pro-rated, minimum guaranteed: $25.00 pg and $90.00 cover. varies. §comix-oriented. no ads.

SNIPPETS: A Melange of Woman, The Pin Prick Press, Roberta Mendel, 3877 Meadowbrook Blvd., University Heights, OH 44118, 216-932-2173. 1980. Poetry. "Each month, two pages that touch on varied aspects of the feminine condition — paper dolls, shrews, feminists — all, and more, are represented. No biases. Short poems (under 30 lines) preferred, but will look at longer ones and may excerpt. Some recent contributors: Shirley Aycock, Bobbie Goldman, Geoffrey Cook, Cassie Edwards, Kit Knight, Arthur Winfield Knight, Roberta Mendel. Submissions may be accepted for The Pin Prick Press's other serial publications at the editor's discretion. Will accept reprints if submitted with a release and *all* previous publication data. *Snippets: A Melange of Woman* is amenable to an exchange arrangement with other serial publications. For a fee, it will distribute other small press promotional materials with its own. *No SASE, no reply!*" circ. 100. 12/yr. sub. price: $10.00, $15.00 foreign; per copy: $1.00, $1.25 foreign plus $0.30 postage and handling. Discounts: by special arrangement. 2pp; 8½X11; of. Reporting time: ASAP. Payment: 1 copy of the issue in which their work appears. Copyrighted, on written request. COSMEP.

Snow Press, Jessie Kachmar, PO Box 427, Morton Grove, IL 60053, 312-299-7605. 1976. Poetry. " *At This Time,* this press is limited to the work (poetry) of Jessie Kachmar Alternate address: 9300 Home Court, DesPlaines, IL 60016" avg. press run 1,000. 1 title listed in the *Small Press Record of Books in Print* (9th Edition, 1980). avg. price, cloth: $7.50; paper: $3.95. Discounts: 40% to book stores; and jobbers in quantities (10 or more). 102pp; 5½X8½. Copyrights for author.

SNOWY EGRET, Humphrey A. Olsen, Editor & Bus. Mgr.; Wm. T. Hamilton, Literary Editor; Gary Elder, West Coast Contributor; June Kemp, Artist; Dan Short, Artist, 205 S. Ninth St., Williamsburg, KY 40769, 606-549-0850. 1922. Poetry, fiction, articles, satire, criticism, reviews, music, letters, parts-of-novels, long-poems. "Emphasis on natural history and man in relation to natural history from literary, artistic, philosophical, historical points of view. Prose generally not more than 3,000 words but will consider up to 10,000; poetry generally less than page although long poems will be considered. Expanded coverage includes politics, population, play, aggression, space, solitude, human nature, sense and sensibility, in relation to nature. Rev. copies of books desired. Originality of material or originality of treatment and literary quality and readability important. Payment on publication plus checking copy. Recent contributors Gary Elder, Ron McNicoll, Merritt Clifton, Charles Fishman, Wm. D. Elliott, John Eastman, Conrad Hyers, Ed Zahniser. Additonal address: Dr. William T. Hamilton, Literary Editor, Dept. of English, Otterbein College, Westerville, OH 4308l" circ. 400. 2/yr. Pub'd 2 issues 1979; expects 2 issues 1980. sub. price: $4.00; per copy: $2.50; sample: $2.00. Back issues: all back issues $2.50. Discounts: 40 on single $2.50, same on 1/yr sub at $4.00. 50pp; 8½X11; †mi. Reporting time: 2 months. Payment: Prose, $2.00 mag page, poetry, min $2.00 a poem, $4.00 mag page on pub. Copyrighted. Pub's reviews: 31 in 1979. §people in relation to natural surroundings, fresh nature poetry, fiction, essays, criticism, philosophy, biography. Ads: None. CCLM, COSMEP-SOUTH.

SO & SO, As Is/So & So Press, John Marron, 2864 Folsom, San Francisco, CA 94110, 415-282-9570. 1973. Poetry, fiction, articles, art, photos, cartoons, interviews, reviews, letters, parts-of-novels, long-poems, concrete art. "Visual/concrete, projective verse, meditative/sitting space, descriptive of physical movement, conceptual, found (1-4 pages/person) John Giorno, Meredith Monk, Alan Davies, Ron Silliman, Laurie Anderson, Karl Kempton." circ. 300. 2/yr. Pub'd 1 issue 1979; expects 2 issues 1980, 3 issues 1981. sub. price: $5.00; per copy: $3.50; sample: $3.50. Back issues: $3.00/#2&3, $5/#1. Discounts: Will trade; 40% discount, minimum 5 copies to bookstores; 4 issue 2 yr subsc $12 inst; $10 indiv. 90pp; 8½X11; †of/mi/lp. Reporting time: 1 week to 6 months. Payment: 0-$5. Copyrighted, reverts to author. Pub's reviews: 1 in 1979. §dance, ethnopoetics, future ecology, medicine, poetry. Ads: $10/$8.

SOCIAL ANARCHISM, Carol Ehrlich, Howard J. Ehrlich, 2743 Maryland Avenue, Baltimore, MD 21218, (301) 243-6987. 1980. Poetry, fiction, articles, art, cartoons, satire, criticism, reviews, letters, parts-of-novels, long-poems, concrete art. "Materials must be congruent with a social anarchist and radical feminist perspective." 2/yr. sub. price: $3.50; per copy: $1.75; sample: $1.75. Discounts: 50% (15 or more/or with pamphlet orer). 60pp; 5½X8; of. Reporting time: 45 days. Payment: 5 copies. Pub's reviews. §Anarchism, feminism, radical arts, art & politics.

SOCIAL POLICY, Audrey Gartner, Managing Editor; Frank Riessman, Co-Editor; Colin Greer, Co-Editor, Room 1212, 33 W 42nd St, New York, NY 10036, 212-840-1279. 1970. Articles, art, photos, interviews, criticism, reviews, letters. "Articles run 2,000-4,000 words, on contemporary, social thought (education, economics, community development). Recent special issues dealt with 'self-help', 'older persons', 'mental health', 'organizing neighborhoods', 'consumer education'. Contributors include Michael Harrington, Lowell Levin, Stanley Aronowitz, S.M. Miller, Alvin Toffler." circ. 12,000. 5/yr. Pub'd 5 issues 1979; expects 5 issues 1980. sub. price: $13.00 Individuals, $20.00 Institutions; per copy: $3.00. Back issues: $3. Discounts: 10% agent. 64pp; 8½X11; lp. Reporting time: 2-4 weeks. Payment: none. Copyrighted, does not revert to author. Pub's reviews: 8 in 1979. §Nonfiction, social policy materials, esp. in area of economics and human services. Ads: $300/$180. COSMEP.

SOCIAL TEXT, Coda Press, Inc, Stanley Arorowitz, John Brenkman, Fredric Jameson, 700 West Badger Road, Suite 101, Madison, WI 53713, (608) 251-9662. 1979. Articles, criticism. "Recent contributors: Edward W. Said, Fredric Jameson, Stanley Aronowitz. Editorial address: 944 Van Hise Hall, University of Wisconsin, Madison, WI 53706" circ. 2,000. 3/yr. Pub'd 3 issues 1979. sub. price: $8.00; per copy: $3.00. Back issues: $3.00. Discounts: Distributors 50%, otherwise 40% wholesale. 152pp; 6X9; of. Reporting time: 2 months min. Copyrighted, reverts to author. Ads: $150.00/$80.00.

‡**SOCIALIST FULCRUM, Socialist Party of Canada,** Committee (Editorial), Box 4280 Station A, Victoria, B.C. V8X3X8, Canada. 1968. circ. 700. 4/yr. sub. price: $2.00 libraries $4.00 (2 year); per copy: $.25; sample: Free. 12-16pp; 8½X14; †of. no ads.

Socialist Party of Canada (see also SOCIALIST FULCRUM), Editorial Committee, Box 4280, Station A, Victoria, B.C. V8X 3X8, Canada. 1968. "Relevant critical letters printed and responded to." avg. press run 750. Pub'd 2 titles 1979; expects 4 titles 1980, 4 titles 1981. avg. price, paper: $0.40. Discounts: on application. 12-16pp; 8½X11; †of.

Society for Education in Film and TV (see also SCREEN), 29 Old Compton Street, London W1V 5PL, United Kingdom.

Society For Education Through Art (see ATHENE)

The Society for the Study of Myth & Tradition (see PARABOLA MAGAZINE)

Society Of Authors (see THE AUTHOR)

SOCIOLOGICAL PRACTICE, Progresiv Publishr, Donald E. Gelfand, 401 E 32nd, #1002, Chicago, IL 60616, (312) 225-9181. 1976. Articles, reviews. "Retain non-exclusive reprint rights, sharing resulting royalties." circ. 150. 2/yr. Pub'd 1 issue 1979. sub. price: $8.00 indiv., $16.00 instit.; 2 years $15.00, $30.00; per copy: $5.00 indiv., $10.00 instit. 80-100pp; 5½X8½; of. Reporting time: 1-3 months. Payment: 1 copy of issue plus 10 reprints. Copyrighted. Pub's reviews: 3 in 1979. §Applied sociology.

SOFT NEED, Expanded Media Editions, Pociao, Herwarthstr. 27, Bonn 5300, W-Germany, 02221/655 887. 1969. Poetry, fiction, art, photos, interviews, letters, collages, concrete art. "2-3 pages per author. Contributors: Burroughs, Ginsberg, Gysin, Patti Smith, Breger, Ploog, Hartmann." circ. 1,000. 1/yr. Pub'd 1 issue 1979. sub. price: $15.00 DM; per copy: 14.80 DM plus postage. Back issues: Brion Gysin Special, Claude Pelieu-Washburn Special. Discounts: 1-10 copies, 25%; 10-20 copies, 30%; 21-40 copies, 40%; over 40 copies, 50%. 120pp; 29.7X21; lp. Payment: 2 copies. Ads: 250/25.

Soft Press, Robert Sward, 28 Woodgate Drive, Toronto, Ontario M6N 4W3, Canada. 1970. Poetry, photos, collages. "No unsolicited material." avg. press run 1,000. Pub'd 1 title 1979; expects 1 title 1980, 1 title 1981. 7 titles listed in the *Small Press Record of Books in Print* (9th Edition, 1980). avg. price, paper: $4.95. Discounts: 1-3 copies, 20%; 4 or more copies, 40%. Distributors, 50-65% depending on order. 64pp; 6X9; of/lp. Payment: copies. Copyrights for author. COSMEP, ACP, BCPA (Assoc Canadian Publishers) (British Columbia Publishers Assoc).

SOJOURNER, THE NEW ENGLAND WOMEN'S JOURNAL OF NEWS, OPINIONS AND THE ARTS, Martha J. Thurber, Managing Editor, 143 Albany Street, Cambridge, MA 02139, (617)-661-3567. 1975. Poetry, fiction, articles, photos, interviews, criticism, reviews, letters, news items. "*Sojourner* has an open editorial policy - we attempt to present a forum for women, and we will consider anything for publication which is not agist, sexist, or homophobic. Recent contributorsinclude poetry by Robin Morgan and an interview with Adrienne Rich." circ. 10,000. monthly. Pub'd 12 issues 1979; expects 12 issues 1980, 12 issues 1981. sub. price: $8.00; per copy: $0.75; sample: $1.00. Back issues: $1.00. Discounts: 60% agent, 40% bookstore. 32pp; 11X17; of. Payment: none yet. Copyrighted, reverts to author. Pub's reviews: 100 in 1979. §feminism; women's issues; any book, film, etc., by a woman or about women. Ads: $480.00/$280.00/$5.00 for 4 lines, 30 characters.

Sol Press, R. Bruce Allison, 2025 Dunn Place, Madison, WI 53713, 608-257-4126. 1971. "Not accepting manuscripts. Also publish under the imprint Wisconsin Books." 3 titles listed in the *Small Press Record of Books in Print* (9th Edition, 1980). †of.

SOLAR AGE, Bruce Anderson, Bill D'Allessandro, Church Hill, Harrisville, NH 03450, (603) 827-3347. 1976. Articles, photos, cartoons, interviews, reviews, letters. circ. 30,000. 12/yr. sub. price: $20.00; per copy: $1.95. Back issues: $2.50. Discounts: jobbers - 50 percent; retail - 25-30 percent. 70pp; 8¼X11⅛; of. Reporting time: 2 months. Payment: negotiable. Copyrighted, does not revert to author. Pub's reviews: 12 in 1979. §Solar energy. Ads: $1,090/$695/$0.70. COSMEP.

Solo Press (see also CAFE SOLO), 750 Nipomo, San Luis Obispo, CA 93401. 7 titles listed in the *Small Press Record of Books in Print* (9th Edition, 1980).

SOMA-HAOMA, Salt-Works Press, Tom Bridwell, Box 2152, Vineyard Haven, MA 02568. 1973. Poetry, fiction, art, photos, music, long-poems. "Fine hand-set letterpress printing-limited runs of block prints & other graphics, silk-screening (often includes actual items). Real photos. Conceptually packaged-cans or boxes or whatever.." circ. 200. 2/yr. Pub'd 2 issues 1979; expects 2 issues 1980. sub. price: $24.00-2 issues; per copy: $12.00. Back issues: Available. Discounts: None. 80-120pp; 8½X11; †lp. Reporting time: 6 weeks. Payment: copies. Copyrighted. §poetry/photo/modern fiction. Ads: None.

SOME, Release Press, Harry Greenberg, Alan Ziegler, Larry Zirlin, 309 W. 104 St. Apt. 9D, New York, NY 10025. 1972. Poetry, fiction, articles, art, photos, reviews, long-poems. "We select material we ourselves would like to come across as readers. Recent contributors: Tate, Bly, Boggis, Stokes, Anderson, Benedikt, Gutstein, Loney, Knott, Piercy, Yau, Edson, Moritz, Kellman, Love, Phillipps, Inez, Orr, Seidman, Zavatsky, Lazar, Haymes, Safane, Lux, *some* 7/8 is in a box, including broadsides, photos, a pencil, a play, death warrents, a catalogue, etc. *Some*/9 is *Poets on Stage: The Some Symposium on Poetry Readings,* with almost 30 contributors, including: Levertov, Ginsberg, Lopate, Love, Atwood, Stokes, etc." circ. 1,250. 2/yr. Pub'd 2 issues 1979. sub. price: $5.00 individuals/$9.00 institutions; per copy: $2.50; sample: $2.50. Back issues: Inquire. Discounts: 40 percent discount for orders above

5. 72pp; 5½X8½; †of. Reporting time: 2-6 weeks. Payment: copies. Copyrighted, reverts to author. Pub's reviews. §all. no ads. CCLM.

SOME OTHER MAGAZINE, Barry Schwabsky, Robert Richman, 47 Hazen Court, Wayne, NJ 07470, (201) 696-9230. 1978. Poetry, fiction, articles, art, criticism, reviews, letters, parts-of-novels, long-poems, collages, plays. "The items circled above are those would consider for publication, though we haven't used all those types of material so far. We are primarily interested in publishing solicited material. We are biased towards the excellent. Among the contributors to number one are Dennis Barone, Daniel Hoffman, Allan Horing, John Yau." circ. 200. 2/yr. Expects 2 issues 1981. sub. price: $6.00; per copy: $2.00; sample: $2.00. Discounts: 40%. 40pp; 7X8; of. Reporting time: Quick enough to keep an uncluttered desk. Payment: Copies & subscription. Copyrighted, reverts to author. Pub's reviews. §Poetry, literary and cultural theory and criticism, fiction. Ads: $25.00/$15.00.

Somesuch Press, Stanley Marcus, PO Box 188, Dallas, TX 75221, (214) 748-1842. 1974. Fiction, articles, art. avg. press run 300. Expects 4 titles 1980, 6 titles 1981. avg. price, cloth: $40.00. Discounts: 40%, 10 or more copies, 33⅓%, 1-10 copies. lp. Reporting time: 1 month. Payment: By negotiation. Copyrights for author.

Somrie Press, Robert A. Frauenglas, 1134 E 72nd Street, Brooklyn, NY 11234, (212) 763-0134. 1 title listed in the *Small Press Record of Books in Print* (9th Edition, 1980).

SONG, Richard Behm, 808 Illinois, Stevens Pt, WI 54481, 715-344-6836. 1975. Poetry, articles, criticism, reviews, letters, long-poems. "*Song* maintains an editorial slant toward formal poetry, poetry written using rhyme and meter, poems which show the poet's awareness sound and sense. Recent contributors include Dacey, Judson, Tick, Galler, Oldknow, Langton, Turco, Court and many others." 2/yr and occasional ancillary publications. Pub'd 2 issues 1979; expects 2 or 3 issues 1980. 1 title listed in the *Small Press Record of Books in Print* (9th Edition, 1980). sub. price: $2.50; per copy: $2.50; sample: $2.50. Back issues: $2.50 each. Discounts: 20% on orders of 10 or more copies by educational institutions or workshops. pp varies: 50-100; 8½X5½; of. Reporting time: 4-16 weeks. Payment: 1 contributors copy. Copyrighted, reverts to author. Pub's reviews. §poetry/criticism/essays on craft of poetry. Ads: $20/$15.

Sono Nis Press, Robin Skelton, 1745 Blanshard Street, Victoria, B.C. V8W 2J8, Canada, (604) 382-1024 or (604) 382-5722. 1968. Poetry, criticism. avg. press run 2,000. Pub'd 10 titles 1979; expects 10 titles 1980, 10 titles 1981. avg. price, cloth: $16.00; paper: $5.95. Discounts: Trade: 20%, 1-4 copies; 40%, 4 plus. Institutional: 20%, Wholesale: 25%, 1-4 copies, 42%, 4 plus. 70-268pp; 6X9; †of, lp. Reporting time: 1 month. Payment: 10% retail price. Paid twice yearly. CBIC, ACP, CBA, ABPBC.

Sothis & Co. Publishing, Sara Scott, Editor-in-Chief; David Scott, Editor, P.O. Box 1166, Del Mar, CA 92014, (714) 481-9355. 1978. Poetry, fiction, photos, letters, parts-of-novels, long-poems. "We at Sothis are interested in producing or reprinting works which we feel have the possibility of eliciting high emotional states. This does not preclude any medium, as poetry, prose, letters may have this ability. It does, however, preclude much 'literature' of today and previous eras. Our production is aesthetically matched to help evoke what an author wished in his readers." avg. press run 4,000. Pub'd 2 titles 1979; expects 4 titles 1980, 8 titles 1981. 4 titles listed in the *Small Press Record of Books in Print* (9th Edition, 1980). avg. price, cloth: $8.95; paper: $6.95. Discounts: 40% to trade, net 30 days to libraries and institutions. 100pp; 6X9; †lp/of. Reporting time: 6-10 weeks. Payment: Variable: 7-15%. Copyrights for author.

SOU'WESTER, Pantagraph, Lloyd Kropp, Southern Illinois University, Edwardsville, IL 62026. 1960. Poetry, fiction, satire, long-poems. "We have no particular editorial biases or taboos. We publish the best poetry and fiction we can find." circ. 400. 3/yr. Pub'd 3 issues 1979; expects 3 issues 1980, 3 issues 1981. sub. price: $4.00; per copy: $1.50; sample: $1.50. Back issues: $2.00. Discounts: 20% off for orders over 4 copies. 92pp; 6X9; of. Reporting time: 4-6 wks. Payment: copies (also cash prizes). Copyrighted, reverts to author. Ads: No ads.

SOUNDINGS/EAST, Bernadette Darnell, English Dept., Salem State College, Salem, MA 01970, 745-0556. 1973. Poetry, fiction, interviews, parts-of-novels, long-poems, plays. "Our primary interest is poetry and short fiction. We will *consider* the other types of material I've indicated, but it's best to send a letter of inquiry first. Recent contributors: Denise Levertov, Lawrence Ferlinghetti, T. Alan Broughton, Camille Norton, Michelle Gillet, knowns and unknowns." circ. 2,000. 2/yr. Pub'd 2 issues 1979; expects 2 issues 1980, 2 issues 1981. sub. price: $2.00; per copy: $1.00; sample: free. Back issues: usually $1.00 per copy. Discounts: we charge $5.00 for three years. (Cheap to begin with. 50¢ per issue deducted for subscription service, etc.). 64pp; 5½X8½; of. Reporting time: 1-6 months, we do *not* read during the summer. Payment: two free copies, more if wanted. Copyrighted, reverts to

author. COSMEP.

SOURCE, LAD, Conceire Taylor, Editor-in-Chief; Charles Molesworth, Editor; Dennis Straus, Editor, Queens Council on the Arts, 161-04 Jamaica Avenue, New York, NY 11432, 291-1100. 1976. Poetry, fiction, articles, interviews, criticism, reviews, letters, parts-of-novels, art, satire. "Poetry should be of one page length but we have accepted longer material. We are looking for critisicm as well as essays and reviews on all topics as long as they are well written and interesting. Though we publish Ferrlinghetti, David Ignatow and others, we highlight poets who live or are from the Queens area of New York. At least 65% of our work comes from poets living in Queens. We have also received and have published work from writers in Canada, England, and as far west as California." circ. 500-1,000. 2/yr. Pub'd 2 issues 1979; expects 2 issues 1980, 2 issues 1981. sub. price: $2.50; per copy: $1.00; sample: $1.50. Back issues: $1.50. 48pp; 5½X8½; of. Reporting time: 6 months. Payment: copies. Copyrighted, reverts to author. Pub's reviews: 1 in 1979. §Poetry, critical pieces, fiction. Ads: $50.00/$25.00. CCLM, COSMEP.

THE SOURCE: A Bimonthly Magazine of Alternatives for the Sensitized Reader (see Vanilla Press)

‡SOUTH & WEST, Sue Abbott Boyd, Pinkie Gordon Lane, Jay Vines, 2406 So S Street, Fort Smith, AR 72901. 1962. Poetry, art, interviews. "The purpose of the magazine is to encourage new poets as well as give voice to those already established. Emphasis is on modern poetry, expression of new and young thought. This does not, however, mean prejudice against traditional poetry. All types of poems receive equal consideration. We prefer work that is individualistic, that reflects the personality of the writer. No subject is taboo that is handled in good taste. We prefer freshness to merely skillful execution of form. Poetry preferably not exceeding 37 lines, but will not reject a good, long poem." circ. 300. 4/yr. sub. price: $10.00; per copy: $2.50. 48pp; 6X9½; of. Reporting time: 1 month. Pays in copies. Copyrighted, reverts to author. §Poetry by new and established — no sentimentality first-love, true-love, lost-love poems. CCLM.

SOUTH CAROLINA REVIEW, Frank Day, Managing Editor; Richard Calhoun, Managing Editor; Robert Hill, Managing Editor, English Dept, Clemson Univ., Clemson, SC 29631, (803) 656-3229. 1968. Poetry, fiction, articles, interviews, satire, criticism, reviews. "Joyce Carol Oates, Mark Steadman, Stephen Dixon." circ. 600. 2/yr. Pub'd 2 issues 1979. sub. price: $3.50; per copy: $2.00; sample: $1.00. Back issues: $1.50. 84pp; 9X6; lp. Reporting time: 2 weeks. Payment: copies. Copyrighted. Pub's reviews: 22 in 1979. §poetry/literary history/criticism. CCLM.

SOUTH DAKOTA REVIEW, John R. Milton, Box 111, University Exchange, Vermillion, SD 57069, 605-677-5229. 1963. Fiction, poetry, art, articles, interviews, criticism, parts-of-novels. "Issues vary in content; not every type of material will be in each issue." circ. 700. 4/yr. Pub'd 4 issues 1979; expects 4 issues 1980, 4 issues 1981. sub. price: $6.00; per copy: $1.50; sample: No sample copies excpt at regular single copy price. Back issues: Most are available, send for price list. Discounts: 40 percent to bookstores. 100pp; 6X9; lp/of. Reporting time: Varies-average, 2 weeks. Payment: Copies, 1-4. We reserve our own reprint rights. Ads: contact editor. CCLM.

South End Press, PO Box 68, Astor Station, Boston, MA 02123, (617) 266-0629. 1977. Poetry, fiction, articles, art, criticism. "South End Press is committed to publishing books which aid people's day-to-day struggle to control their own lives. Our primary emphasis is on the United States, its political and economics systems, its history and its culture, and on strategies for its transformation. We aim to reach a broad audience through a balanced offering of books of all kinds, fiction and non-fiction, theoretical and cultural, for all ages and in all styles and formats." avg. press run 5,000. Pub'd 9 titles 1979; expects 15 titles 1980, 20 titles 1981. avg. price, cloth: $15.00; paper: $6.00. Discounts: Libraries, 20%, (standing order 25%); university bookstores 20%; bookstores 0%-43% depending on # of books ordered. 350pp; 5½X8¼; 6X9. Reporting time: 6-8 weeks. Payment: 8% of cover, twice yearly. Copyrights for author. ABA.

South Head Press (see POETRY AUSTRALIA)

Southbound Press, Rt 5, Shenandoah Drive, Seymour, TN 37865. 3 titles listed in the *Small Press Record of Books in Print* (9th Edition, 1980).

SOUTHEAST ASIA CHRONICLE, Southeast Asia Resource Center, Staff of Southeast Asia Resource Center, P.O. Box 4000-D, Berkeley, CA 94704, 415-548-2546. 1971. Articles, art, photos, cartoons, interviews. "Each issue covers one topic with several articles. Interprets current situation in/related to Indochina and throughout Southeast Asia. Sympathetic to revolutionary regimes in Indochina/supports friendly relations between U.S. and Vietnam, Laos, Cambodia. Recent authors: Banning Garrett, Linda and Murray Hiebert, Lou and Eryl Kubicka, Gary Porter and George Hildebrand, David Marr, E. Thadeus Flood, Khieu Samphan, Noam Chomsky. Free catalogue available on request." circ. 1200. 6/yr. Pub'd 6 issues 1979; expects 6 issues 1980. sub. price: $8.00 Domestic; $10.00 Foreign; $15.00 Foreign Airmail, $12 libraries and inst., $6.00 low income subsc.; per copy: $1.50 includes postage; sample: $1.50 includes postage. Back issues: varies. Discounts: varies. 28pp; 8½X11; of. Reporting time: 2-3 weeks. Pub's reviews. §Indochina, Southeast Asia.

Southeast Asia Resource Center (see also SOUTHEAST ASIA CHRONICLE), P.O. Box 4000 D, Berkeley, CA 94704, 415-548-2546. 1971. Poetry, fiction, articles, art, photos, cartoons, interviews, reviews, parts-of-novels, news items. "TRADITION AND REVOLUTION IN VIETNAM. Nguyen Khac Vien. The first serious political analysis by a Vietnamese writer available to a general English-language audience. CHILDREN OF VIET-NAM Tran Khanh Tuyet, editor. Stories and poems, with line drawings. Ages 4-9. BANH CHUNG BANH DAY (The New Year's Rice Cakes). Vietnamese children's folktale, with line drawings. Ages 6-10. Free catalogue available on request." Discounts: 40 percent to booksellers. of. Reporting time: please send letter first. Copyrights for author.

Southern Agitator, David Kronenwetter, 2115 Esplanade Avenue, New Orleans, LA 70119, 504-943-7041. 1978. Poetry, fiction, articles, art, cartoons, interviews, criticism, news items. "Question authority. Joe Blisley, Jim Bodie, Carlitos Barrow, Vince Whirlwind." circ. 1,300. 10/yr. Pub'd 2 issues 1979; expects 10 issues 1980, 10 issues 1981. sub. price: $5.00/10 issues; per copy: free; sample: free, donations. Back issues: donations limited. 20-36pp; of. Pub's reviews: 5-20 in 1979. §inquire. APS, COSMEP.

SOUTHERN EXPOSURE, Institute for Southern Studies, Bob Hall, Managing Editor, PO Box 531, Durham, NC 27702, 919-688-8167. 1973. Poetry, fiction, articles, art, photos, interviews, reviews, parts-of-novels, long-poems, collages, plays. "All material must be related to the South. Since issues are generally focused on particular themes, a query letter can be helpful. We'll let you know what topics we're planning to cover. Anything goes. We have published two regular issues and two special topic issues each year." circ. 10,000. 4/yr. Pub'd 4 issues 1979; expects 4 issues 1980. sub. price: $10.00 ($12.00-libraries); per copy: $4.00; sample: $4.00. Back issues: $2.50-$4.50. Discounts: 40% 5 or more. 120pp; 8½X11; of. Reporting time: 8 weeks. Payment: $75.00-$200.00. Copyrighted. Pub's reviews: 32 in 1979. §Southern; related to the South. Ads: $200.00/$100.00. COSMEP.

SOUTHERN HUMANITIES REVIEW, David K. Jeffrey, Barbara Mowat, 9090 Haley Center, Auburn Univ., Auburn, AL 36830, 205-826-4606. 1966. Poetry, fiction, articles, interviews, satire, criticism, reviews, parts-of-novels. "W.H. Auden, Joyce Carol Oates, Tom Sinclair, Bo Ball." circ. 650. 4/yr. Pub'd 4 issues 1979; expects 4 issues 1980. sub. price: $8.00; per copy: $2.50; sample: $2.50. Discounts: none. 100pp; 6X9; lp. Reporting time: 1 month. Payment: none. Copyrighted, reverts to author upon request. Pub's reviews: 200 in 1979. §Criticism, fiction, poetry. Ads: none.

SOUTHERN LIBERTARIAN MESSENGER, John T. Harllee, P.O. Box 1245, Florence, SC 29503. 1972. Poetry, articles, cartoons, satire, reviews, letters, art, news items. circ. 750. 12/yr. Pub'd 12 issues 1979; expects 12 issues 1980. sub. price: $4.00; per copy: $.35; sample: $.35. Back issues: $0.35 if available. 8-10pp; 8½X11; †mi/of. Reporting time: variable. No payment, except complimentary subscriptions. Not copyrighted. Pub's reviews: 10 in 1979. §libertarian, politics, economics, science fiction. Ads: $40.00/$20.00/$0.25. COSMEP, APS.

SOUTHERN POETRY REVIEW, Robert W. Grey, Editor, Dept. of English, Univ of N.C., UNCC Station, Charlotte, NC 28223. 1958. Poetry. "SPR is not a regional mag-though we have a special interest in young Southern talent. We emphasize variety and intensity. No restrictions on style, content or length. (We do not consider poems during the summer months.)" Circ. 700-1M. 2/yr. Pub'd 2 issues 1979; expects 2 issues 1980, 2 issues 1981. 2 titles listed in the *Small Press Record of Books in Print* (9th Edition, 1980). sub. price: $4.00; per copy: $2.00; sample: $1.00. Back issues: $2.00. Discounts: 30%. 80pp; 6X9; lp. Reporting time: 1 month. Payment: $3/poem plus contrib. copy. Copyrighted, reverts to author. no ads. CCLM, COSMEP, COSMEPA.

SOUTHERN PROGRESSIVE PERIODICALS UPDATE DIRECTORY, Craig T. Canan, PO Box 120574, Nashville, TN 37212. 1979. Art, photos, cartoons, reviews, concrete art, news items. "Need primarily graphics relating to struggles for progressive social change in the 'New South'. Contributors include Fred Wright, Tim Yeager." circ. 1,000. Pub'd 1 issue 1979. sub. price: $3.00; per copy: $1.50; sample: $1.50. Back issues: $1.50, all single copies $3.00 to libraries. Discounts: 1-4, $1.50; 5-24, $1.00; 25+, $0.75. 28pp; 7X8½; †of. Reporting time: 4 weeks. Payment: $1.00-$15.00. Copyrighted, reverts to author. Pub's reviews. §Progressive periodicals in 13 Southern states west to Texas and north to Kentucky and Virginia. Ads: $50.00/$25.00. COSMEP.

SOUTHERN QUARTERLY: A Journal of the Arts in the South, Peggy W. Prenshaw, Editor; Jac L. Tharpe, Advisory Editor; Thomas J. Richardson, Advisory Editor, Box 5078, Southern Stn., USM,

Hattiesburg, MS 39401, (601) 266-4180. 1962. Articles, art, interviews, criticism, reviews, music, letters, photos. "The editor invites essays, articles and book reviews on both contemporary and earlier literature, music, art, architecture, popular and folk arts, theatre and dance in the South. Particularly sought are survey papers on the arts and arts criticism — achievements, trends, movements, colonies. Forthcoming are special issues on Walker Percy, George Washington Cable's *The Grandissimes*, and images of the South in film. Inquiries and manuscripts should be addressed to *The Southern Quarterly*, Box 5078, University of Southern Mississippi, Hattiesburg, MS 39401" circ. 700. 4/yr. Pub'd 4 issues 1979; expects 4 issues 1980, 4 issues 1981. sub. price: $5.00; per copy: $2.50 (special issue prices may vary); sample: $2.50. Back issues: $1.50. Discounts: Subscription agency: $4.25. 100pp; 6X9; of. Reporting time: 3 months. Payment: 2 copies of journal. Copyrighted, reverts to author. Pub's reviews: 28 in 1979. §Studies of the arts in the South: literature, music, art, architecture, popular and folk arts, theatre and dance.

SOUTHERN REVIEW, T L Burton, E D Le Mire, Manfred MacKenzie, (Sydney), Dept. of English, Univ. of Adelaide, Adelaide, S. 5001, Australia. 1963. Poetry, fiction, articles, interviews, criticism, reviews, parts-of-novels. "Literary and inter-disciplinary essays; poems; short stories. M.L.A. Style Sheet. Articles for critical exchange section welcomed." circ. 700. 3/yr. Pub'd 3 issues 1979; expects 3 issues 1980, 3 issues 1981. sub. price: A$12.00/A$10.00 individuals; per copy: a$4.50 ($5.00 posted); sample: free. Back issues: $2.00 per issue to 1975. Discounts: agents A$8.00/students A$7.50. 96pp; 16cm x 24cm; of. Reporting time: 3 months. Payment: poems A$8.00/stories A$30.00. copyright vested in author. Pub's reviews: 5 in 1979. §literary criticism/literature and it's relation to history, philosophy, anthropology, etc. Ads: A$100/A$50.

THE SOUTHERN REVIEW, Donald E. Stanford, Lewis P. Simpson, Drawer D, University Station, Baton Rouge, LA 70893, 504-388-5108. 1935. Poetry, fiction, articles, interviews, criticism, reviews, letters, parts-of-novels, long-poems. "We emphasize craftsmanship and intellectual contest. We favor articles on contemporary literature and on the history and culture of the South. Recent contributors —Malcolm Cowley, Frank Kermode, Hayden Carruth, Roy Fuller, David Wagoner, Matthew Josephson, Thomas Parkinson, Martin Turnell, Howard Baker." circ. 3,000. 4/yr. Pub'd 4 issues 1979; expects 4 issues 1980, 4 issues 1981. sub. price: $5.00; per copy: $1.50; sample: free. Discounts: 30%. 220pp; 6¾X10; of. Reporting time: one month. Payment: poetry $20-$50 a page/prose $12-$20 a page. Copyrighted, reverts to author. Pub's reviews. §Contemporary Literature, Fiction, Poetry, Culture of the South. CCLM.

Southport Press, Dr. Travis DuPriest, Dr. Mabel DuPriest, Dept. of English, Carthage College, Kenosha, WI 53141, (414) 551-8500 (252). 1977. Poetry, fiction, plays. "We do hand printing of old and contemporary fiction and poetry. First imprint: portfolio of Wilma Tague's poetry. Currently accepting no unsolicited mss. New titles: *Medieval & Renaissance Prayers*; broadsides by Krister Stendahl (theology) & Lillie Chaffin (poetry)" avg. press run 100. Expects 2-3 titles 1980, 3 titles 1981. 3 titles listed in the *Small Press Record of Books in Print* (9th Edition, 1980). avg. price, cloth: $7.50; other: $1.00 broadsides (unbound). 10-25pp; 7X10; †lp. Reporting time: 2 weeks. Copyrights for author.

Southwest Research and Information Center (see also THE WORKBOOK), PO Box 4524, Albuquerque, NM 87106, (505) 242-4766. 1974. Articles, criticism, reviews, letters. "Resource information for citizen action of all kinds" avg. press run 2,000. Pub'd 6 titles 1979; expects 6 titles 1980. 4 titles listed in the *Small Press Record of Books in Print* (9th Edition, 1980). avg. price, paper: $2.00; other: $7.00 student, senior citizens; $10.00 individuals; $20.00 institutions; subscription. Discounts: 40% to Distributors. 48pp; 8½X10½; of. Reporting time: 2 weeks to 2 months. Payment: negotiable. COSMEP, WIP.

SOUTHWEST REVIEW, SMU Press, Margaret L. Hartley, Editor; Charlotte T. Whaley, Managing Editor, Southern Methodist Univ., Dallas, TX 75275, 214-692-2263. 1915. Poetry, fiction, articles, interviews, criticism, reviews, parts-of-novels. "Contemporary literature and discussion combining quality fiction and verse with studies in current affairs, historical research, literary criticism, accounts of achievements in the lively arts, essays of personal opinion, and book reviews." circ. 1,000. 4/yr. Pub'd 4 issues 1979; expects 4 issues 1980, 4 issues 1981. sub. price: $6.00; per copy: $1.50; sample: $1.00. Back issues: available on request. Discounts: 25 percent to agencies. 112pp; 6X9; lp. Reporting time: 3 months. Payment: prose, half cent perword; poems, $5.00 per poem. Copyrighted. Pub's reviews: 37 in 1979. §regional material, literature, poetry, social problems. Ads: $70.00 (one time), $60.00 (four times)/$37.50 (one time), $32.50 (four times).

THE SOUTHWESTERN REVIEW, Steve Glassman, PO Box 44691, Lafayette, LA 70504, (318) 264-6908. 1976. Poetry, fiction. "Interested in short articles on current developments in small/community/playwright theaters. Not currently accepting fiction or poetry. Recent contributors: William Pitt Root, Eugene Platt, Robert Grey, Robert Creeley, Ed Dorn, Stephen Spender, Venkatesh Srinivas

Kulkarni. Interview with Ernest Gaines. CCLM grantee." circ. 500 mag., 4,000 broadside. 2/yr. Pub'd 2 issues 1979; expects 2 issues 1980, 2 issues 1981. 60pp; 6X9. Payment: contributors' copies. Copyrighted.

Southwood Press (see ASPECT, Art and Literature)

Sovereign Press, Marguerite Pedersen, Editor, 326 Harris Rd, Rochester, WA 98579. 1968. Fiction, articles, art, photos, plays. "We limit our publications to works oriented on individual sovereignty; within that field we are looking for fiction, non-fiction, and art works of lasting merit. Recent contributors: John Harland, Melvin Gorham, Sanguine." avg. press run 2,500. Pub'd 2 titles 1979; expects 3 titles 1980, 4 titles 1981. 11 titles listed in the *Small Press Record of Books in Print* (9th Edition, 1980). avg. price, cloth: $8.95; paper: $2.00. Discounts: Libraries and booksellers: single or assorted titles, 1 to 4, 30%; 5 to 9, 40%; 10 to 99, 50%; 100 and over 55%. 120pp; 4X6¾; 5X8; of/lp. Reporting time: 1 month. Payment: individually arranged. Copyrights for author.

SPACE AND TIME, Gordon Linzner, 138 West 70th Street (4-B), New York, NY 10023. 1966. Poetry, fiction, art, cartoons, satire, long-poems, plays. "All material must be science-fction/fantasy oriented. Artwork is by assignment only. No firm length restrictions, but prefer stories under 10,000 words. Recent contributors: Janet Fox, Richard Tierney, Neal F. Wilgus, Charles De Lint, Charles Saunders, Andrew J. Offutt, Wayne Hooks, Charles Vess, Stephen Schwartz, Ron Wilber, Rich Bruning." circ. 250. 4/yr. Pub'd 4 issues 1979; expects 4 issues 1980, 4 issues 1981. sub. price: $6.00; per copy: $2.00; sample: $2.00. Back issues: all available back issues at once $30.00; otherwise sold separately under original cover price. Discounts: 40% on *all* orders of five or more copies of an issue. 60pp; 5½X8½; of. Reporting time: 2-3 months. Payment: 1/4¢ per word on acceptance; $2.00 per assigned illustation, plus contributor copy. Copyrighted, reverts to author. Ads: $10.00/$5.00/$0.005 per word.

SPARROW POVERTY PAMPHLETS, Sparrow Press, Felix Stefanile, Selma Stefanile, 103 Waldron St, West Lafayette, IN 47906. 1954. Poetry. "Please inspect a copy of *Sparrow Poverty Pamphlets* before submitting material. Over twenty-five years of poetry publishing we have acquired unbudgeable biases and tastes, and to this day 75% of the work that passes our desk is quite simply work that we do not want. Our only imperative is our personal view of literary excellence. Unlike the Pope we are fallible; nevertheless, *Sparrow* poems now appear in just about all the major anthologies, from Little, Brown to Untermeyer, from Donald Allen to Hall, Pack and Simpson, so we must do something right. (This brings money to our poets.) We have always been an open, eclectic publisher. In the past we have published Corman's word-count poems, Vassar Miller's sonnets, Gil Orlovitz's zany surrealism. What all our poets share in common is a vivid concern for poetry as heightened speech that moves the reader and listener as its own experience, a *new* experience, not a trend, or a guideline, not a fashion. Poetry as news of a real world. Recent poets: John Fandel, John Stevens Wade, Roger Pfingston, Tom Montag. Strict format: 20 to 32 typed pages, one poem per page. No carbons, xeroxes or otherwise duplicated manuscripts will be read. Bear in mind, those of you who read on the run: our pamphlets are devoted to the work of a single poet, issue to issue. We are no longer a poetry miscellany. If you can't come up with a 20 to 32 page manuscript, don't bother sending, and please note — the majority of the poems should be *unpublished*! We abhor query letters, which come mostly — though not always — from frumps and vaniteers. If you've got to ask what publications like *Sparrow* 'do', the chances are you're not much of a reader, or poetry fan. If you absolutely must write, be sure you include a self-addressed stamped envelope for reply, or we'll ignore you anyway. Manuscripts received without proper return postage and envelope will be destroyed" circ. 800. 3/yr. Pub'd 3 issues 1979; expects 3 issues 1980. sub. price: $6.00 indiv/$6.50 libraries; per copy: $2.00; sample: $2.00. Back issues: issues before No. 35 are collector's items, from $4.00-$25.00 each. Discounts: 40% to our agents/20% to classes more than 7. 32pp; 5½X8½; of. Reporting time: 3 to 6 weeks. Payment: 6 free copies of the pamphlet, plus modest advance against royalties, plus 20 percent of income after cost. Copyrighted. no ads. CCLM.

Sparrow Press (Vagrom Chapbooks; SPARROW POVERTY PAMPHLETS), Felix Stefanile, Editor; Selma Stefanile, Editor, 103 Waldron St., West Lafayette, IN 47906. 1954. Poetry, criticism. " *VAGROM CHAP BOOKS* by invitation only. Some poets published: Corman, Mills, Roseliep, Sister Maura" avg. press run 250-1,000. Pub'd 1 title 1979; expects 2 titles 1980. avg. price, paper: $3.00. Discounts: 40 percent to agents. 8-108pp; 5½X8½; of/lp. No submissions to Vagrom Chap Books. We do the inviting. Payment: 6 free copies, modest advance against royalties; plus 20 percent of income after cost. Our books sell. Copyrights for author. CCLM.

Special Aviation Publications, Nick Pocock, Alvena Prause Pocock, Box 672, Hillsboro, TX 76645. 1974. "Publishers of books. First title: *Did W.D. Custead Fly First?* by Nick Pocock. Presentation and discussion of evidence that little known aeronautical pioneer W.D. Custead flew before Wright

Brothers. Illustrated with photographs, maps and drawings. Aviation related only." Pub'd 1 title 1979; expects 1 title 1980. 1 title listed in the *Small Press Record of Books in Print* (9th Edition, 1980). avg. price, paper: $2.95. Discounts: 40 percent dealers. 5½X8; of. Reporting time: 1 month. ASWA.

Spectacular Diseases (see also LOOT; SPECTACULAR DISEASES), Paul Green, 83(b) London Road, Peterborough, Cambs, United Kingdom. 1975. Poetry, art, long-poems. "Bias toward the long poem, or material taken from work in progress. Four issues of magazine produced so far. Two books produced so far. Prices given for magazine only. Books vary per title." avg. press run 350. Pub'd 2 titles 1979. 2 titles listed in the *Small Press Record of Books in Print* (9th Edition, 1980). avg. price, paper: 75p. Discounts: Trade 33⅓%. 40pp; 5¾X8; of. Reporting time: 3-4 weeks , material usually solicited. Payment: copies only. Copyrights for author. ALP.

SPECTACULAR DISEASES (see Spectacular Diseases)

Spectre Press (see also CTHULHU), Jon M. Harvey, Publisher, 61 Abbey Road, Heathfield, Fareham, Hampshire, United Kingdom. 1976. Poetry, fiction, articles, art, cartoons, satire, long-poems, plays. "For example: *Lovecraftian Characters And Other Things,* an art portfolio by Jim Pitts; *The Compassion Of Time,* a general greetings card, illustrated and containing a short story, a collection of modern indian fairy stories by Manoj Das *The Man Who Lifted the Mountain.* And three anthologies of prose fictions and poetry: *Dreams Of A Dark Hue* and *Dark Words-Gentle Sounds.* Will publish any fantasy item of interest, of maximum length 20,000 words: collections of articles and/or fiction on aspects of fantasy; also one-author collections of prose, poetry and/or art work." avg. press run 750 copies. Pub'd 5 titles 1979; expects 2 titles 1980, 5 titles 1981. 9 titles listed in the *Small Press Record of Books in Print* (9th Edition, 1980). avg. price, cloth: varies; paper: varies; other: varies. Discounts: 10-30, 25%; 31-50, 33⅓%; 51-100, 40%; over 100, 50%. pp varies; size varies; of. Reporting time: 1-2 months. Payment: copies only. buys first U.K. rights only.

Spectrum Productions, Adrienne Schizzano, 979 Casiano Rd., Los Angeles, CA 90049. Poetry, fiction, plays. "We are interested in receiving inquiries (not mss.) in the field of translations of European drama before the twentieth century." 4 titles listed in the *Small Press Record of Books in Print* (9th Edition, 1980). COSMEP.

Speed Limit Press (MADOC), Mark Williams, 33 Bryn Glas, Hollybush, Cwmbran, Gwent NP4 4LG, Wales, 953 64798. 1977. Poetry, art, long-poems, concrete art. "Bill Wyatt, Barry Edgar Pilcher, Tina Fulker, George Cairncross, Dave Ward, Tina Morris, Richard Jones, Steve Sneyd. Largest publication to date *Magic City,* a 'realisation' of Cardiff by Barry Edgar Pilcher and Mark Williams, 64 pages of poems, prose, factoids, dreams, dialogues, scenarios, and extraneous 'found' material, all epiphanic. No specifics regarding length of material or bias." avg. press run 150. Pub'd 20 titles 1979; expects 10 titles 1980, 3 titles 1981. avg. price, paper: 15p. 30pp; 8X10, 5X8; †mi. Reporting time: maximum, one week. WASP.

THE SPHINX, editorship rotates among board members, English Dept, Univ Of Regina, Regina, SN S4S0A2, Canada. 1974. Articles, criticism, reviews. "4000 ww; sociological & pyschological approaches to literature;" circ. 250. 2/yr. Pub'd 2 issues 1979; expects 2 issues 1980, 2 issues 1981. sub. price: $3.50 indiv., $7.50 instit.; per copy: $2.00; sample: $2.00, free to institutions. 74pp; 8½X11; of. Reporting time: 5-6 weeks. Payment: none. Copyrighted. Pub's reviews: 14 in 1979. §fiction; criticism of above kinds.

THE SPHINX (in French language), Mounier, 7 rue de l'eveche, Beaugency 45190, France. 1978. Poetry, fiction, articles, art, photos, cartoons, interviews, criticism, reviews, music, long-poems, collages, concrete art, news items. "The most important part of the material is consecrated to poetry and to the new wave of art: Mail art, visual poetry, surrealism, work's in progress, beat generation, fluxus, dada and so on..Also much esoterism: Zen, occult, alchemy, Tarot and so on...Some recent American contributors: Allen Gingsberg, Henri Miller, Opal L. Nations, Bruce Hutchinson, Dick Higgins." circ. 500. Pub'd 4 issues 1979; expects 4 issues 1980, 4 issues 1981. sub. price: 35FF; per copy: 15FF; sample: Cost of sending: 5FF. Back issues: #1: 10FF; #2: 10FF; #3/4: 20FF (it's a special on the dead!). Discounts: 30%, Payments are made before sending. 60-80pp; 21cm x 27cm; of. Copyrighted. Pub's reviews: 150-200 in 1979. §New wave in art & poetry.

Spindrift Press, Richard N. Hayton, Writer & Publisher, P.O. Box 3252, Catonsville, MD 21228, (301) 944-3317. 1974. Fiction, satire. "In 1975 published *The King and The Cat* by Thomas Starling, a novel of political satire. $6.95/cloth.*The Garlic Kid* a WWII novel by Thomas Starling ($1.95/paperback) published in 1978. Hope for 1 or 2 books a year written from a radical perspective. At present submissions not solicited." avg. press run 1,000. Pub'd 1 title 1979; expects 1 title 1980, 1 title 1981. 2 titles listed in the *Small Press Record of Books in Print* (9th Edition, 1980). avg. price, cloth: $6.95; paper: $1.95. Discounts: 40% to bookstores. 225pp; 4½X7, 5½X8¼; of/lp. COSMEP.

Spinsters, Ink, Maureen Brady, Judith McDaniel, RD 1, Argyle, NY 12809, (518) 854-3109. 1978. Fiction, articles, criticism. "We publish one book and one monograph per year. We are a feminist press and only publish material written by women and of interest to women." avg. press run 3,000. Pub'd 2 titles 1979; expects 2 titles 1980. avg. price, paper: $4.50; other: $1.50 monograph. Discounts: Trade 40%, Class 20%, Distributor 50%. 120pp; 5X8. Reporting time: we only read certain months of the year. Payment: varies. Copyrights for author. COSMEP.

SPIRALS, Vivienne Verdon-Roe, PO Box 29472, San Francisco, CA 94129. 1977. Articles, letters. "Articles vary in length from 200 - 1,800 words. The publication aims to bridge the gap between mysticism and science. We are interested in probing the so-called 'unknown' and unorthodox, with the intention of finding and sharing new ideas and learning of value to mankind and both his inner and outer worlds. Subjects include metaphysics, psychic experiences, spirituality, healing, ancient civilisations and knowledge, earth energies, etc. Recent contributors include Marcel Vogel, Sir George Trevelyan, Ron Anjard, Frank Dorland (The Crystal Skull), Athene Williams (British psychic and author), Bill Cox, editor, *The Pyramid Guide,* Brad Steiger, author, George Hunt Williamson (explorer, mystic, author), Helen Wamback (psychologist), etc." circ. 1,000. 6/yr. Pub'd 6 issues 1979; expects 6 issues 1980, 6 issues 1981. sub. price: $3.00; per copy: $0.75; sample: $0.75. Back issues: $.50 (to subscribers). 16-20pp; 5½X8½; of. Reporting time: 5 days to 1 week. Payment: None. Our writers 'donate' articles. Not copyrighted. §We sometimes list small publications in our field (New Age), and occasionally include a book-review (same field). Ads: no ads.

SPIRIT & NATURE, Ananda Publications, Rambhakta, 14618 Tyler Foote Road, Nevada City, CA 95959. 1975. circ. 2,000. 4/yr. sub. price: $8.00; per copy: $2.00. Back issues: $2.00. 20pp; 8½X11; of. Pub's reviews: 1 in 1979. Ads: $75.00/$60.00/$50.00/$40.00/$30.00/$25.00. COSMEP.

Spirit Mound Press, Box 111, University Exch., Vermillion, SD 57069. 1974. Poetry, fiction, photos. "Do not publish regularly. Not open to submissions in 1979-1980" avg. press run 700. Pub'd 1 title 1979. 4 titles listed in the *Small Press Record of Books in Print* (9th Edition, 1980). avg. price, cloth: $5.95; paper: $2.95. Discounts: 40% to bookstores, dealers, and distributors. 75pp; 5½X8½, 6X9; lp. Copyrights for author.

THE SPIRIT THAT MOVES US, The Spirit That Moves Us, Inc. (Formerly Emmess Press), Morty Sklar, P.O. Box 1585, Iowa City, IA 52244, 319-338-5569; 319-337-9700. 1975. Poetry, fiction, articles, art, photos, reviews, parts-of-novels, long-poems, collages, concrete art. "My only prejudices are those of personal taste. Will publish anything that grabs me; prefer work that comes from feeling. I like translations from all languages. Recent contributors: William Kloefkorn, Linda Hasselstrom, Atukwei Okai (Ghana), Constantin Toiu (Romania), Allan Kornblum, David Ray, Emilie Glen, Anselm Hollo." circ. 800. 2/yr. Pub'd 3 issues 1979; expects 2 issues 1980, 2 issues 1981. 2 titles listed in the *Small Press Record of Books in Print* (9th Edition, 1980). sub. price: $5.00 (includes postage); $6.50 to libraries; per copy: $2.00 (includes postage); sample: $2.00 (includes postage). Back issues: 5-year set, 1) without Vol 1, #3 & Vol 2, #1: $25.00; 2) with Vol 1, #3 & Vol 2, #1: $50.00; both choices include *The Actualist Anthology, Cross-Fertilization: The Human Spirit as Place,* and *The Farm in Calabria* by David Ray. Bonus for 5-year sets: a set of 'poetry-with-drawings in the buses' 11 x 16 placards. Discounts: 40% for 5 or more, 25% for less than 5, (may mix issues or combine with books). 45% for prepaid; 50% for distributors; bulk rates available, for classes, etc. 48-144pp; 5½X8½; of. Reporting time: 5 minutes to a month. Payment: copies, money when possible. copyright By The Spirit That Moves Us, for the authors. Pub's reviews: 1 in 1979. §Any, as long as the review relates to the larger picture — such as concerns about 'esthetics', 'commitment', 'morality', etc. Ads: $40/$25. CCLM, COSMEP, PD.

The Spirit That Moves Us, Inc. (Formerly Emmess Press) (see also THE SPIRIT THAT MOVES US), Morty Sklar, Ed-Publ., P.O. Box 1585, Iowa City, IA 52244, 319-338-5569. 1974. Poetry, fiction, articles, art, photos, interviews, parts-of-novels, long-poems, collages, concrete art. "*The Spirit That Moves Us, Inc.* also puts poetry with drawings in the buses and presents free poetry readings. Sets of the placards and postcards are for sale to the public as well. Books to date: *Riverside* poems by Morty Sklar (1974: Letterpress); *The Poem You Asked For* poems by Marianne Wolfe (1977; Offset); *The Actualist Anthology* poems by Anselm Hollo, David Hilton, Cinda Kornblum, John Batki, Morty Sklar, Darrel Gray, Sheila Heldenbrand and 7 others who lived & interacted in Iowa City in the early 70's, (1977: Perfectbound or hardcover; 144 pages; photos & drawings). August 15, 1980: *Editors' Choice: Literature & Graphics from the US Small Press, 1965-1977* 504 pp; (work nominated by editors of mags and presses). April, 1980: *The Farm in Calabria* by David Ray; August, 1980, *Cross-Fertilization: The Human Spirit as Place* (anthology)." avg. press run 1,400. Pub'd 1 title 1979; expects 2 titles 1980, 1 title 1981. 4 titles listed in the *Small Press Record of Books in Print* (9th Edition, 1980). avg. price, cloth: $11.25; paper: $3.25; other: Poetry-With-Drawings (set of 10) 11 x 16 on colored stock — $6.00 the set; a replica of the above in 3.7 x 5.9 postcards — $1.50 the set. Discounts: 25% for less than 5; 40% for 5 or more (may mix titles); 45% prepaid; 50% to distributors. 16-504pp; 5½X8½; lp/of. Reporting time: 5 minutes to a month. Payment: 10 percent of run. copyrights revert to authors. COSMEP, CCLM.

Spiritual Community Publications, Parmatma Singh Khalsa, Box 1080, San Rafael, CA 94902, 415-457-2990. 1970. Articles, art, photos, interviews, reviews. "We encourage corrections, additions and advice." avg. press run 15,000. Expects 1 title 1980, 1 title 1981. 5 titles listed in the *Small Press Record of Books in Print* (9th Edition, 1980). avg. price, paper: $5.95. Discounts: 40% stores/50% distributors. 200pp; 5½X8½; of. Reporting time: 1 month. Copyrights for author. COSMEP.

The Spoon River Poetry Press (see also THE SPOON RIVER QUARTERLY), David R. Pichaske, Editor, PO Box 1443, Peoria, IL 61655. 1976. Poetry. avg. press run 750. Pub'd 4 titles 1979; expects 4 titles 1980, 4 titles 1981. 10 titles listed in the *Small Press Record of Books in Print* (9th Edition, 1980). avg. price, paper: $3.00. Discounts: Bookstores, 40%. 64pp; 5½X8½; of. Reporting time: 1 month. Payment: 35 copies free to author; further copies 40%. Copyrights for author.

THE SPOON RIVER QUARTERLY, The Spoon River Poetry Press, David R. Pichaske, PO Box 1443, Peoria, IL 61655. 1976. Poetry. "We want accessible poems that contain a thing, a voice, and a statement. Preference for midwest subjects, places, poets, idioms, feel" circ. 350. 4/yr. Pub'd 4 issues 1979; expects 4 issues 1980. sub. price: $6.00; per copy: $2.00; sample: $2.00. Discounts: 20% bulk, classroom, agent. 64pp; 5½X8½; of. Reporting time: 1 month. Payment: cont. copies. Copyrighted, reverts to author.

SPOOR, Ten Crow Press, Edward Cain, Star Rt Box 663A, Aberdeen, WA 98520, 206-648-2493. 1979-80. Poetry, fiction, articles, art, photos, interviews, reviews, parts-of-novels, long-poems, collages. "*Spoor* will also have at least one, possibly two original works of art (i.e. prints, photos, etc) for issue." circ. 300-500. 2/yr. Pub'd 2 issues 1979. sub. price: $20.00; per copy: $10.00. Back issues: $10.00/$20.00. Discounts: 30% to dealer. 50pp; 10X13; †of/lp. Reporting time: 6 weeks. Payment: issues plus expenses for art. Copyrighted, reverts to author. Pub's reviews. §Poetry, prose, visual arts, especially those connective of natual world.

SPRING: An Annual of Archetypal Psychology and Jungian Thought, Spring Publications Inc, James Hillman, Box 1, University of Dallas, Irving, TX 75061, 438-1123. 1940. circ. 3000. annual. sub. price: $10/yr; per copy: $10. Discounts: 40% trade 30% classroom and jobbers. 240pp; 6X9; of. Reporting time: 3 months. Payment: none. Copyrighted, does not revert to author. Pub's reviews. §psychology, myth, religious studies, literary criticism. Ads: $180/page, $90/half.

Spring Church Book Company, Britt Horner, Ed Ochester, PO Box 127, Spring Church, PA 15686. 1973. "We are a mailorder retailer of contemporary poetry from all publishers, with a strong emphasis on small press books; books listing at over $3.95 are sold at a discount. We do not handle broadsides and magazines. Catalog and update lists are free on request; we carry some 800 titles/year. Though we have issued books in conjunction with Quixote Press, we are not reading manuscripts at present" 6pp; 8½X11; of.

Spring Publications Inc (see also SPRING: An Annual of Archetypal Psychology and Jungian Thought), James Hillman, Box 1, University of Dallas, Irving, TX 75061, (214) 438-1123. 1940. Articles, criticism. "App. 240 pages, 20 page articles in magazine; James Hillman, Patricia Berry, Charles Boer, Edward Casey" avg. press run 3,000. Pub'd 5 titles 1979; expects 7 titles 1980, 7 titles 1981. 8 titles listed in the *Small Press Record of Books in Print* (9th Edition, 1980). avg. price, paper: $7.50. Discounts: 40% trade, 30% classroom and jobbers. 200pp; 6X9; of. Reporting time: 3 months. Payment: varies.

Sproing Inc. (see also PANDORA, An Original Anthology of Role-expanding Science Fiction and Fantsy), Eric Wickstrom, Lois Wickstrom, 1150 St Paul St, Denver, CO 80206. 1973. Poetry, fiction, articles, art, photos, cartoons, interviews, satire, music, letters, parts-of-novels, news items. "Right now we have a backlog of stuff by ourselves and friends that is waiting for us to afford the printing costs. Our basic theme is living our own lives within the establishment by helping them to leave us alone." avg. press run 2,000. Pub'd 3 titles 1979; expects 3 titles 1980, 3 titles 1981. 3 titles listed in the *Small Press Record of Books in Print* (9th Edition, 1980). avg. price, paper: $2.50. Discounts: 5 copies or more 40%, 100 copies or more 50%. 32-64pp; 8½X5½; of. Reporting time: ASAP usually a month or less. Payment: If it makes money beyond printing cost we split 50-50 on profits. Copyrights for author. COSMEP, SCBW.

Sprout Publications Inc, Herman Levy, Phillip Partee, 5241 Ocean Blvd, Sarasota, FL 33581, (813) 955-7522. 1979. "1 book thusfar: *The Layman's Guide to Fasting and Losing Weight* by Phillip Partee. Introduction by Dick Gregory (comedian author)" avg. press run 6,000. Pub'd 1 title 1979. avg.

price, paper: $3.95; other: $3.95. Discounts: 50% to Distributors, 40% to Retailers. 132pp; 5¼X8¼; of. Payment: none. Copyrights for author.

SPUR, Alan Burkitt, WDM, Bedford Chambers, Covent Garden, London WC2E 8HA, United Kingdom. 1972. Cartoons, photos, news items, letters. "Geared to needs of political lobbying and public awareness activists in Britain." circ. 3,000. 12/yr. Pub'd 12 issues 1979. sub. price: £8 or US $20.00; per copy: £.10; sample: S.A.E. 4pp; size A3; of. Reporting time: 1-2 wks. Pub's reviews: 10 in 1979. §World development, Third World, development education. Ads: no ads.

THE SQUATCHBERRY JOURNAL, Edgar Lavoie, Box 205, Geraldton, Ontario P0T1M0, Canada, 807-854-1184. 1975. Poetry, fiction, articles, art, photos, cartoons, interviews, satire, reviews. "This is a regional magazine featuring the fact and fiction, photographs and drawings, arising from experience in Northern Ontario." circ. 400. 2/yr. Pub'd 2 issues 1979; expects 2 issues 1980, 2 issues 1981. sub. price: $3.50; per copy: $2.00; sample: $2.00 or free, depending on circumstances. Back issues: $1.00 or free, depending on circumstances. Discounts: 6 copies/$1.50 each. 72pp; 6X9; of. Reporting time: almost immediately. Payment: a copy of the edition. Copyrighted, reverts to author. Pub's reviews: 2 in 1979. §only material featuring experiences of Northern Ontario. Ads: none permitted.

Stagecoach Pub. Co. Ltd., T. W. Paterson, P.O. Box 3399, Langley, BC V3A4R7, Canada. 1975. "Material used historical non-fiction mostly." avg. press run 10,000. Pub'd 6 titles 1979; expects 4 titles 1980. 15 titles listed in the *Small Press Record of Books in Print* (9th Edition, 1980). avg. price, cloth: $11.95; paper: $5.95; other: $2.95. Discounts: over 5, 37% (retailers); 20% schools, libraries, etc. 200pp; 6X9, 8½X11; of. Reporting time: 6 weeks. Payment: standard terms. Copyrights for author. ACP, BCPA.

STAND, Northern House, Jon Silkin, Lorna Tracy, David Wise, David McDuff, 19 Haldane Tce, Newcastle-on-Tyne NE23AN, United Kingdom. 1952. Poetry, fiction, reviews, criticism, art, interviews, letters. "U.S. Edition: Jim Kates, c/o 16 Forest Street, Norwell, MA" circ. 5,000. 4/yr. Pub'd 4 issues 1979; expects 4 issues 1980. sub. price: $7.50; per copy: $2.50; sample: $2.50. Back issues: $2.00. 80pp; 6-1/10X8; of. Reporting time: 1-2 mos. Payment: $16.00/poem; $20.00/1,000 words. Copyrighted, reverts to author. Pub's reviews: 30 in 1979. §literature, politics. Ads: $170.00 & pro rata. CCLM.

Standard Editions, P.O. Box 1297, Stuyvesant Station, New York, NY 10009. 1976. Fiction. "Standard Editions publishes books only. Our first two releases, both full length novels: *Abyss* by Dorothia Tanning & *Modern Love* by Constance De Jong. Constance DeJong, *The Lucy Amarillo Stories*, 90 pages, perfect bound (paper), edition of 1,000, published Sept 1978, fiction, a collection of short stories" avg. press run 1,000. Pub'd 2 titles 1979; expects 2 titles 1980. 3 titles listed in the *Small Press Record of Books in Print* (9th Edition, 1980). avg. price, paper: $3.50. Discounts: 40% to retail outlets. 200pp; 4¾X5¼; of. author holds copyright.

STAR WEST, S-B Gazette, Leon Spiro, Box 731, Sausalito, CA 94965. 1963. Poetry, cartoons, satire, concrete art. "Short, dynamic, multi-lingual poetry. Satire, Chicano, Black, etc, wide open. Ronald Crowe, Anna Moresi, Maria Auguello, Albert Chantraine, Mark Axelrod, Teresinka Pereira, Sonia Kury, Erin St. Mawr, Nazim Hickmet, Dora La Flamme, Felix Leon, Laureate, French Academy's David Gitin, Angela S. de Hoyos, Jean Coutsocheras, Paul Fericano, Sidney Tyler. Back issues available through Xerox University Microfilms." circ. 800-2,000. 4/yr. sub. price: $7.50; per copy: $1.50; sample: $1.50. 8½X14; of. Reporting time: 2 weeks. Payment: 5 copies. Not copyrighted.

STARDANCER, & (Ampersand) Press, Michael S. Prochak, Co-Editor; Chael Graham, Co-Editor, 415 3rd Street #3, Brooklyn, NY 11215, (212) 768-7841. 1975. Poetry, fiction, articles, art, photos, interviews, satire, criticism, music, letters, parts-of-novels, long-poems, collages, plays. "STARDANCERis an International Journal of the New Arts. Our goal is to provide a means whereby individuals may cast off outmoded and restrictive standards of art, literature, philosophy, self, and artistic achievement in order to ferret out and express creatively the evolutionary/revolutionary relationships between self, environment, era, art and the eternal present. We seek work of universal and lasting beauty and value — not of fashion or formula. Issue #5/6 (June 1980) is a special double issue of Work in Translation — the first of sevceral p roposed translation issues furthering international artistic contact. Issue #7 is devoted to the work of Russell Edson and Evolutionary experience. Issue #8 is an Anthology of New British Writers, to be co-edited by Dick Davis and Michael Prochak, and Issue #9 is an Anthology of New American Writers, to be co-edited by Terry Stokes and Chael Graham. All works for these two volumes must be nominated by established writers — we invite nominations and queries from any writers and artists interested in inclusion. Past contributors include Brian Swann, George Hitchcock, Greg Kuzma, James Reiss, John Ditsky, Dick Davis, Robert Lima, Rika Lesser, Russell Edson, and Paul JJ Payack. Because of the special nature of our coming issues, no submissions will be read unless previously queried or solicited until June 1982. International office: 10 South Street, Colchester, Essex, England" circ. 500-1,000. 2/yr, 1/yr after May 1, 1981. Pub'd 3 issues 1979; expects 2 issues 1980, 2 issues 1981. sub. price: $7.50; per copy: $3.50 to $5.00; sample: $4.00. Back issues: $2.50 #1, 2, 3. Only discount is for trade—30-40 percent, and bulk-10 copies min-40 percent. 120pp; 6X9; of. Reporting time: 1-3 months. Payment: $5.00 or subscription plus contributor's copies. Copyrighted, reverts to author. Pub's reviews: 2 in 1979. §New arts, literature, and anything of an evolutionary nature. Ads: $100.00/$50.00/must be cleared with us. CCLM.

Starogubski Press, Bonnie Bluh, 345 Riverside Drive, Suite 5J, New York, NY 10025. 1974. "An unfolding herstory of the modern day woman's movement in 6 European countries through fact, dialogues and personal commentary." 1 title listed in the *Small Press Record of Books in Print* (9th Edition, 1980). avg. price, paper: $4.50. Discounts: 40% bookstores on 3 books or more, 20% libraries & schools, 3 or more. 317pp; 5½X8; lp.

STARSHIP: The Magazine About Science Fiction, Algol Press, Andrew Porter, P.O. Box 4175, New York, NY 10017, 212-643-9011. 1963. Articles, art, photos, interviews, criticism, reviews, letters, news items. "*Starship* is published for the SF reader interested in the behind-the-scenes aspects of SF. It regularly publishes articles, interviews, criticism by award winning authors. *Starship* has been awarded the Hugo Award by The World SF Convention. Regular columnists: Frederik Pohl (publishing), Susan Wood (books), Vincent DiFate (art), and Robert Stewart (films). Some recent contributors: Ursula K. Le Guin, Samuel R. Delany, Jack Williamson, Poul Anderson, Vonda McIntyre, Joe Haldeman. Length of material 3-15,000 words." circ. 7,000. 4/yr. Pub'd 4 issues 1979; expects 4 issues 1980. sub. price: $8.60 (academic & libraries); $8.00 (individuals); per copy: $2.50; sample: $2.50. Back issues: #25 - #37, $2.25 each; #38 - #40, $2.50. Discounts: 40 percent trade discount. Write: F&SF Book Co., Box 415, Staten Island NY 10302. 84pp; 8¼X11; of. Reporting time: 1-3 weeks. Payment: 1-1.5 ¢/word for nonfiction. Copyrighted, does not revert to author. Pub's reviews: 90 in 1979. §S.F., children's fantasy. Ads: $180.00/$95.00/$0.15.

START, Start Press, Patrick Regan, Joanna Yorke, Paul Gater, Burslem Leisure Centre, Market Place, Burslem, Stoke-on-Trent, England ST6 3DS, United Kingdom, 0782-813363. 1978. Poetry, fiction, articles, art, interviews, criticism, reviews, music, letters, news items. "Mainly local material (i.e. Stoke-on-Trent) used, but will consider anything. No limits on length. Pieces of excessive length are serialised. English prices. For foreign prices, write and enquire. USA subscription £2.40." circ. 300. 4/yr. Pub'd 2 issues 1979; expects 4 issues 1980. sub. price: £1.10; per copy: 20p; sample: 10p + postage. Back issues: 10p + postage. 44pp; 8¼X11½; †mi. Copyrighted. Pub's reviews: 8 in 1979. §Poetry, music, fiction, arts. Ads: no ads.

Start Press (see START)

Stash, Inc. (see also JOURNAL OF PSYCHEDELIC DRUGS), Marsha Bishop, E. Leif Zerkin, M.D. David E. Smith, 118 South Bedford Street, Madison, WI 53703, 608-251-4200. 1967. "Stash attempts to present objective, unbiased drug information in the form of books and pamphlets. Stash does not advocate the use or non-use of psychoactive drugs (including alcohol, tobacco & caffeine), but rather hopes to educate readers and keep them up-to-date on the latest scientific, psychological and legal information available. Pamphlets may run anywhere from 10 to 30 pages in typeset form. Books would be of somewhat longer lenghth (90+ pages)." avg. press run 5,000. 11 titles listed in the *Small Press Record of Books in Print* (9th Edition, 1980). avg. price, paper: $5.00; other: $0.60 pamphlets. Discounts: We provide quantity discounts for our books and pamphlets. Price list available. of. Reporting time: 30 days. Payment: 10% of sales. Does not copyright for author.

Static Creation Press, Steven Boldt, 405 S. Geneva Street, Ithaca, NY 14850, (607) 277-4160. 1978. "I established the press to publish my own writing. I have neither the interest or money to publish anything further at this time and am definitely not looking for material." avg. press run 275. Expects 2 titles 1980. 2 titles listed in the *Small Press Record of Books in Print* (9th Edition, 1980). avg. price, paper: $6.00. Discounts: 40% trade. 225pp; 8½X11; †mi.

Station Hill Press (LOST PAPER; TRUMPS (A Periodical of Postcards)), George Quasha, Publisher & Director; Bruce McClelland, Managing Editor; Robert Kelly, Participating Editor; Charles Stein, Participating Editor; Franz Kamin, Participating Editor; Patricia Nedds, Book Arts Director; Susan Quasha, Visual Arts Director, Barrytown, NY 12507, (914) 758-4340. 1978. Poetry, fiction, art, photos, criticism, long-poems, collages, plays, concrete art. "Full-length books of poetry by Robert Kelly, George Quasha, Charles Stein, Frank Samperi, Clayton Eshleman, Bruce McClelland, Larry Eigner, Anselm Hollo. Prose-fiction by Maurice Blanchot, Paul Metcalf, Franz Kamin." avg. press run 1,500. Pub'd 6 titles 1979; expects 20 titles 1980, 20 titles 1981. 9 titles listed in the *Small Press Record of Books in Print* (9th Edition, 1980). avg. price, cloth: $10.00; paper: $3.50; other: special editions

$12.00-$50.00. Discounts: 50% distributor, none on single orders, escalating with qty. 64-150pp; 5¾X8¾; †of. Reporting time: no guarantee except by written arrangement. Payment: usually 10% of edition in copies. Copyrights for author.

Stephen Wright Press, Stephen Wright, Box 1341, F.D.R. Postal Station, New York, NY 10022, (212) 927-2869. 1978. Poetry, fiction, articles. "I have just begun my press and the first publication shall be a book I have written, *Brief Encyclopedia of Homosexuality,*/(approximate date of publication: November 2, 1978). The book is an original paperback, which is priced at $5.95. Approximate number of pages: 160. I belong to the Authors Guild and the Mystery Writers of America. At the present time, I am not a member of any publishing organization. This is not a magazine but a book. Applicable are gay and, to a lesser extent, lesbianism. Am planning the Stephen Wright Review, a miscellany. It will appear several times a year. I do not want submissions at present but inquiries for the Review." avg. press run 500-1,000. Expects 1 title 1980. 1 title listed in the *Small Press Record of Books in Print* (9th Edition, 1980). avg. price, paper: $5.95. Discounts: The usual discounts to the trade, to libraries, and to distributor(s). 160pp; 6X9; 5½X8½; of/lp. Do not submit manuscripts to Stephen Wright Press. Queries of every kind, however, are invited; and will be answered at once. Payment: All editions are the property of the author and therefore there are no royalties as such. The author who uses our services pays to get his/her book in print. copyright for author if request to do so.

STEPPENWOLF, Philip Boatright, Jean Shannon, PO Box 31174, Omaha, NE 62131. Poetry, articles, criticism, reviews. "Especially interested in the longer poem, translations (must be accompanied by a copy of the work in its original language), articles and critical comment. Request no more unsolicited mss. until further notice." CCLM.

THE STEREOPHILE, J. Gordon Holt, PO Box 1948, Santa Fe, NM 87501. 1962. Articles, cartoons, interviews, music. "Music of interest to record collectors, high fidelity buffs." circ. 7,000. 4/yr. Pub'd 2 issues 1979; expects 3 issues 1980, 4 issues 1981. sub. price: $16.00; per copy: $4.00; sample: $4.00. Back issues: $3.00. Discounts: Bulk discounts available on request. 88-108pp; 5½X8½; of. Payment: Varies, typically $100.00-$200.00 depending on length. Copyrighted. §Music reproduction and recording techniques. Acoustics and psyco-acoustics. Available on request.

The Stevenson Press, Mary Virginia Callcott, Robin Cravey, Callcott - Collinson, Inc., P.O.Box 10021, Austin, TX 78766, 255-8623. 1977. Fiction, art, photos, interviews, letters. "Length of material varies. We particularly emphasize our National History Series: USA - at least for now. Also our multi-media. Our first series (Ada DeBlanc Simond's *Let's Pretend: Mae Dee and Her Family*) is made up of six books, each of which has a cassette (audio) of the author reading her own stories. Main emphasis so far is Texas, turn of 1900. We have primary source material (century old love letters - over 80 - that tell a story) and much more. We have also done one video memoir - a video cassette - sort of oral history. We are regional, but hope the appeal is universal, and are beginning to branch out a bit." avg. press run 3,000. Pub'd 2 titles 1979; expects 9 titles 1980, 10 titles 1981. avg. price, cloth: $9.95; paper: $3.95 (soft cover, not paper); other: audio cassette $5.95. Discounts: vary. 5½X8¼; of. Reporting time: varies; we try to hold to a month or two. Authors are urged to query if we go beyond that time. Payment: 10% for first 5,000; 12.5% to 10,000; 15% thereafter. Copyrights for author.

THE STONE, Rich Jorgensen, 3978 26th St, San Francisco, CA 94131, 415-648-5392. 1967. Poetry, fiction, art, photos, cartoons. "Mostly we publish poetry of the body's land, love. The Stone is elemental." circ. 500. 1/yr. Pub'd 1 issue 1979; expects 1 issue 1980. 8 titles listed in the *Small Press Record of Books in Print* (9th Edition, 1980). sub. price: $2.00; per copy: $2.50; sample: $2.00 negotiable. Back issues: $2 if avail. Discounts: 40% to the trade. 96pp; 5½X8½; of. Reporting time: 1 week to 1 month. Payment: 2 copies/contributor. Copyrighted. CCLM.

Stone Circle Press, Carol Hauswald, PO Box 551, Bensenville, IL 60106, (312) 766-0223; (312) 620-0732. 1978. Poetry, art, photos, letters. "Compilations, non-fiction, how to, recipes, up for suggestion, current topics" avg. press run 2,000-8,000. Pub'd 2 titles 1979. avg. price, cloth: $8.95; paper: $5.95-$6.95. Discounts: negotiate. 128pp; 6X8; of. Reporting time: 6 weeks. Payment: negotiate. Copyrights for author. ABA.

STONE COUNTRY, Stone Country Press, Judith Neeld, Editor and Publisher; Pat McCormick, Art; Robert Blake Truscott, Reviews, 20 Lorraine Road, Madison, NJ 07940, 201-377-3727. 1971. Poetry, art, articles, interviews, criticism, reviews. "Poetry must make us see new. We look for concrete language; strong, uncommon imagery; mystery; tension; discovery. This is not a magazine for beginners. Styles can range from the traditional to the experimental and anywhere in between, but the poems must be honest and the language contemporary. We rarely publish poems over 40 lines in length, though will occasionally take a longer work of irresistible quality. We like to publish translations, accompanied by the original poem wherever possible. Submissions receive personal replies.

386

Recent contributors: Joyce Odam, Joan Colby, Martin Robbins, Stelios Yeranis, Diane Wakoski, A. McA. Miller, Tom O'Grady, Maxine Kumin, Janice Thaddeus, Eugenio Montale, others known and to-be-known. The Phillips Poetry Award of $25.00 is given each issue for the poem deemed best by a panel of poets and critics" circ. 900. 3/yr. Pub'd 3 issues 1979; expects 3 issues 1980. sub. price: $4.25; per copy: $1.75 current issue; sample: $1.50. Back issues: $1.50. Discounts: usual. 40pp; 5½X8; of. Reporting time: 6 weeks. Payment: Copies plus prize for poetry (see above); modest cash payments for cover art and prose commentaries/reviews. Copyrighted, reverts to author. Pub's reviews: 3 in 1979. §poetry. Ads: $16.00/$10.00/no classified. CCLM, COSMEP.

Stone Country Press (see also STONE COUNTRY; Pericarp Books), Judith Neeld, Editor and Publisher; Pat McCormick, Art Editor, 20 Lorraine Road, Madison, NJ 07940, 201-377-3727. 1976. Poetry, art. "Stone Country Press provides services for self-publishing poets with proven publishing records who have tired of the search for a book publisher that isn't backlogged or closed to new voices. We offer design, graphics, composition, printing and binding of softcovers from 8 to 80 pages. Our goal is your book; we only look for our expenses. SASE must accompany inquiries and mss. for quotes. Newer poets ask about our Pericarp Books." avg. press run 350. Pub'd 2 titles 1979; expects 3 titles 1980, 3 titles 1981. 10 titles listed in the *Small Press Record of Books in Print* (9th Edition, 1980). avg. price, paper: $3.50; other: + $.75 postage & handling. Discounts: by arrangement. 50pp; 5½X8½; of. Reporting time: 4 weeks. Payment: all sales receipts to author. Copyrights for author. COSMEP, CCLM.

Stone Press (see also HAPPINESS HOLDING TANK), Albert Drake, 1790 Grand River, Okemos, MI 48864. 1968. Poetry. "Small books and pamphlets. Published Peter Nye, Judith Root, Barbara Drake, and Judith Goren: recent chapbooks are *Beer Garden,* Lee Upton, and *Returning To Blind Lake On Sunday,* Jim Kalmbach, book, Earle Birney's *The Mammoth Corridors.* Also publish posters: Richard Kostelanetz, Harley Elliott, William Stafford, Earle Birney, Anselm Hollo, etc. Six posters for $1.25. Poetry Pack ($4) includes 2 issues of the magazine, 2 chapbooks, pamphlet, 3 posters, postcards, etc." avg. press run 300-500. Pub'd 2 titles 1979; expects 1 title 1980. 22 titles listed in the *Small Press Record of Books in Print* (9th Edition, 1980). avg. price, paper: $1.00. Discounts: 25 percent. 16-20pp; 8½X5½, 8½X7; †of. Reporting time: 1-3 weeks. Copyrights for author. CCLM.

STONE SOUP, The Magazine By Children, Children's Art Foundation, Inc., Gerry Mandel, William Rubel, Bx 83, Santa Cruz, CA 95063, 408-426-5557. 1973. Poetry, fiction, art, reviews, parts-of-novels, plays, photos, letters, long-poems. "All material written & drawn by children 3-13." circ. 8,000. 5/yr. Pub'd 5 issues 1979; expects 5 issues 1980. sub. price: $12.00; per copy: $2.50; sample: $2.50. Back issues: Prices upon request. Discounts: Schedule available upon request. 48pp; 6X8¾; of. Reporting time: 3 wks. Payment: 2 copies. Copyrighted. Pub's reviews: 10 in 1979. §childrens books. Ads: none. CCLM.

Stone Wall Press, Inc, Henry C. Wheelwright, 1241 30th Street NW, Washington, DC 20007. 1972. "Non-fiction—outdoor material regional to northeastern USA or national with photos or illustrations. Optimally combining pragmatic material with adventures, humor, and overriding sense of ecology" avg. press run 4-5,000. Pub'd 2 titles 1979; expects 5 titles 1980, 5 titles 1981. 16 titles listed in the *Small Press Record of Books in Print* (9th Edition, 1980). avg. price, cloth: $10.00; paper: $4.95. 175pp; 6X9; of. Reporting time: a week. Copyrights for author.

Stonehenge Books, Inc., Robert Emmitt, Executive Editor, 2969 Baseline Rd, Boulder, CO 80303, (303)444-4100. 1977. Fiction. "Stonehenge is a subsidizing publisher like a university press and will publish quality fiction (novels) sold and distributed by The Swallow Press, Chicago, now part of Ohio University Press. First two titles are Alex Blackburn, *The Cold War of Kitty Pentecost,* May 1979, and Robert Emmitt, *Acteon Homeward,* June 1979. Editorial Advisory Board includes, among others, Ron Sukenick, Rudolfo Anaya, John Williams, John Nichols, and Richard Hugo." avg. press run 1,-000-1,200. Pub'd 2 titles 1979; expects 5 titles 1980, 9 titles 1981. avg. price, cloth: $8.95; paper: $4.95. 250pp; 6X9; of. Reporting time: 6-9 weeks. Payment: Swallow gets 25% hardcover, 30% paperback, author receives remainder first receipts. Copyrights for author.

Stonehouse Publications, Lewis Watson, Sharon Watson, Timber Butte Road, Box 390, Sweet, ID 83670. 1974. Photos. avg. press run 10,000. Expects 1 title 1981. 1 title listed in the *Small Press Record of Books in Print* (9th Edition, 1980). avg. price, paper: $5.95. Discounts: Trade 40% any quantity, fully refundable. Mail order 46%, jobber & bulk 50%. Library 2 copies or more 20%. 100pp; 8½X11; of.

STONY HILLS: The New England Alternative Press Review, Rat & Mole Press, Diane Kruchkow, Box 715, Newburyport, MA 01950. 1977. Articles, art, photos, cartoons, interviews, criticism, reviews, letters, news items. "Reviews & articles on the New England small press scene, and important national events. Recently featured: Cosmep photos by Richard Morris; Boston Book Affair photos by Doug Mumm; Keith Rahmmings, Len Fulton and Diane Kruchkow on CCLM; Hugh Fox's Brazil Watch; in-depth reviews by Curt Johnson, Joe Bruchac, Karla Hammond, Robert Peters, Don Wellman, Robert Abel, Rudy Kikel, Helena Minton, Rich Mangelsdorff, William Dubie, Roberta Kalechofsky and others; Interviews with Terry Kennedy, Elizabeth McKim and Larry Eigner; and News Notes, listings, bookfair reports, poetry, letters, & etc. #8 lists books and magazines received in '79, and New England material published in '80. Index Available." circ. 4,000. 3/yr. Pub'd 2 issues 1979; expects 3 issues 1980, 4 issues 1981. sub. price: $3.00 individual; $4.50 institutions + $1.50 for first class mailing; per copy: $1.00 + 50¢ postage & handling; sample: $1.00. Back issues: $0.75 + $0.25 postge and handling. Discounts: more than 5 copies-40 percent. 16pp; 11X15; of. Reporting time: 1 month max. Payment: 5 copies. Copyrighted. Pub's reviews: 25 in 1979. §New England small press material. Ads: $75.00/$50.00. COSMEP, NESPA, CCLM.

THE STONY THURSDAY BOOK, John Liddy, 128 Sycamore Ave, Rath Bhan, Limerick, Ireland. 1975. Poetry, fiction, articles, art, photos, interviews, satire, criticism, reviews, letters, parts-of-novels. "Will also accept work in translation." circ. 1,000. 1/yr. Pub'd 1 issue 1979; expects 1 issue 1980, 2 issues 1981. sub. price: $4.30, in the event of 2 issues - $8.00; per copy: $4.30. Back issues: $2.00 for nos. 5 & 6. Discounts: 33 1/3% reverting to seller. 54pp; 7½X9½; of. Reporting time: 2 months. Payment: Usually in copies but hopefully in money from 1979. Copyrighted, reverts to author. Pub's reviews: 6 in 1979. §Poetry, story, novel, art, other magazines.

Story Press, Richard Meade, Editor; Carol Evans, Editor, 4142 Rose Avenue, Western Springs, IL 60558. 1977. Fiction. "Our press is currently dedicated to publishing collections of short story writers. Most of our writers have published in leading literary magazines, but have never published in book form. We never run more than 150 pages per book. In style we prefer stories which are emotional rather than intellectual, traditional rather than experimental in form. But we have no unalterable bias. Recent books: *The Hour of the Sunshine Now* by Norbert Blei, *The Monkey Puzzle Tree* by Florence Cohen." avg. press run 500. Expects 2 titles 1980, 2 titles 1981. 2 titles listed in the *Small Press Record of Books in Print* (9th Edition, 1980). avg. price, cloth: $12.50; paper: $4.00. Discounts: 40% trade and classroom discount. 128pp; 5¼X7½; lp. Reporting time: 2 months. Payment: 20% of profits after investment. Copyrights for author. COSMEP.

STORY QUARTERLY, F.R. Katz, Co-Editor; Dolores Weinberg, Co-Editor; Janine Warsaw, Co-Editor, 820 Ridge Road, Highland Park, IL 60035, 312-831-4684. 1974. Fiction, art, interviews, letters, parts-of-novels, satire. "*STORY QUARTERLY* seeks to be an open forum of the short story; featuring: a generous number of stories in a wide range of styles and forms. Also: guest columns on the state of the story; interviews with story writers; parts-of-novels, found fiction; letters to the editor. Our bias is toward instantly recognizable talent as opposed to instantly recognizable names. Please do not study the publication with an eye toward imitation/slant but send us your own truest work and vision. We would like to see more non-imitative break-through experimentation consistent with at least its own sense of control. Recent contributors: Jerry Bumpus, Kelly Cherry, Daniel Curley, Stephen Dixon, Gail Godwin, Phillip Green, Richard Kostelanetz, Joyce Carol Oates, Henry H. Roth, James Park Sloan, Meredith Sue Willis, Ben Brooks, Ann Beattie, Rosellen Brown, Norbert Blei." circ. 3,000. 2-3/yr. Pub'd 2 issues 1979; expects 2 issues 1980, 2 issues 1981. sub. price: $8.00; $12.00 library/institution, $15.00 foreign, four-issue subscription price; per copy: $2.75; sample: $1.75 (only sq #2/3). Back issues: $1.75 (only sq #2/3). Discounts: 40% bookstores; 20% distributors. 130pp; 6¾X9¾; of. Reporting time: 4 months. Payment: 5 copies, small gratuity, if finances permit, plus 1 copy. Copyrighted. Pub's reviews: 1 in 1979. §Fiction only. Ads: $250/$100. CCLM, COSMEP, IAC (Ill. Arts Council).

STRAIGHT AHEAD INTERNATIONAL, Time Capsule, Inc., Martha Cochrane, Editor, GPO Box 1185, New York, NY 10001, (212) 595-8448. 1980. Poetry, fiction, articles, art, photos, cartoons, interviews, satire, criticism, reviews, letters, parts-of-novels, long-poems, collages, plays, news items. "Work from women worldwide showing women's perspectives, socially relevant, personal work written with clarity, honesty, intensity." circ. 5,000. 4/yr. sub. price: $10.00; per copy: $3.00; sample: $2.00. Discounts: 25 subscriptions $8.00 each, 100 copes $2.00 each. 20pp; of. Reporting time: 6 weeks. Payment: pending due to funding. Copyrighted, reverts to author. Pub's reviews. §Women's issues, international scope. Ads: $1,000/$500. CCLM, COSMEP.

STRANGE FAECES, Opal L. Nations, Ellen Nations, 174 Thorndike Street #4, Cambridge, MA 02141. 1969. Poetry, fiction, art, photos, cartoons, satire, letters, parts-of-novels, collages, concrete art. "1) 4-5 page length 2) speculative 3) bias *for*- bad taste, inventive & unusual, bias *against* 99% small magazine so called poetry & interlectual claptrap 4) Mike Bulteau & Bruce Hutchinson. Submissions by request only." circ. 500. 3-4/yr, depending on funding. sub. price: $9.00 + postage and packing;

per copy: $3.00; sample: $3.00. Back issues: All sold. Discounts: 40 percent bookstores only. 50-60pp; size Varies with each issue.; of. Reporting time: immediate. Payment: none. rights remain with authors & artists. CCLM, COSMEP.

Strawberry Press (see also CONTACT/11: A Bimonthly Poetry Review Magazine), Maurice Kenny, PO Box 451, Bowling Green Station, New York, NY 10004, 212-522-3227. 1976. Poetry, art. " *Strawberry Press* publishes the poetry of Native American Indian poets only as it is felt that the open forum for Native American poets is closing to not only the young poets of this country, but to established poets as well who seem, often, to be ignored in both the small press nd established press except in the 'special issue' sense. Poets recently published include: Norman Russell, Joseph Bruchac, Wendy Rose, Lance Henson, Maurice Kenny, Rokwaho, Karoniaktatie, Carol Lee Sanchez, Duane Niatum, Peter Blue Cloud, Adrian C. Louis, and artists: Kahones, Sharol Graves and Helen Rundell. New poets published on broadsides: Mary Tall Mountain, William Oandasan, Joy Harjoy, Geary Hobson, Paula Gunn Allen." avg. press run chapbooks 500 in a limited issue: broadsides 250 in a limited issue. Pub'd 12 titles 1979; expects 3 titles 1980. 12 titles listed in the *Small Press Record of Books in Print* (9th Edition, 1980). avg. price, paper: varies; other: broadsides...$0.50/signed $1.50. Discounts: trade/jobber/classroom...40 percent. pp varies; size varies; of. Reporting time: 3 weeks. Payment to poet and artist, and copies. Copyrights for author. NYSSPA.

Street Editions, Wendy Mulford, 31 Panton St., Cambridge, England, United Kingdom. 1973. Poetry, long-poems, collages, concrete art, photos. "John James, Andrew Crozier, J.H. Prynne, Douglas Oliver, Alice Notley, Modern English, American, European Poetry." 10 titles listed in the *Small Press Record of Books in Print* (9th Edition, 1980). lo/lp.

STREET MAGAZINE, Street Press, Dan Murray, Graham Everett, Box 555, Port Jefferson, NY 11777. 1973. Poetry, fiction, articles, art, photos, cartoons, interviews, satire, criticism, reviews, music, collages, concrete art, news items. "Looking for poems, regional & human perspective, prose, graphics, photos, reviews, statements of writing. Returns up to 3 mos. Vol 1 No. 4: Interview with Jack Kerouac, plus poems and reviews. Vol 2 No. 1: Conversation with Robert Bly, plus poems and reviews. Vol 2 No. 2: Black Mountain Issue, poems, articles and perspectives. (available). Vol 2 No. 3: H. R. Hayes and Spanish America: translations of Spanish American poets; articles on and by H. R. Hayes. Vol 2 No. 4: Beat/Energy Issue: poems and articles on Energy. Early Greenwich Village memories and articles on Kerouac." circ. 750. 2/yr. Pub'd 3 issues 1979. sub. price: $6.00/4 issues; per copy: $2.00. Back issues: cost + postage. Discounts: 40%. 80pp; 5½X8; †of. Reporting time: 8 weeks. Payment: 2 copies. copyrighted, revert to authors. Pub's reviews. §poetry. CCLM, COSMEP.

Street Press (see also STREET MAGAZINE), Graham Everett, Dan Murray, Box 555, Port Jefferson, NY 11777. 1974. Poetry. avg. press run 500. Pub'd 3 titles 1979; expects 4 titles 1980, 6 titles 1981. 29 titles listed in the *Small Press Record of Books in Print* (9th Edition, 1980). avg. price, paper: $2.00. Discounts: 60/40. 48pp; 5½X8½; †of. Reporting time: 3 months. Payment: 10% of run. Copyrights for author. CCLM, COSMEP.

STROKER, Irv Stettner, Editor; Perry Gewirtz, Assistant Editor, 129 2nd Ave. No. 3, New York, NY 10003. 1974. Poetry, fiction, articles, art, photos, interviews, collages. "Prose-poems-art. Unsolicited mss. welcome. An unliterary literary review. Non-State subsidized, editors are out to lose their shirt, but have fune and make friends. Recent contributors: Henry Miller, Tommy Trantino, Mohammed Mrabet, Seymour Krim, Ignatius Sarsaparilla and newcomers." circ. 500. 4/yr. Pub'd 4 issues 1979; expects 14 issues 1980, 3 issues 1981. 5 titles listed in the *Small Press Record of Books in Print* (9th Edition, 1980). sub. price: $7.00 for 3 issues/$13.00 for 6 issues; per copy: $2.50; sample: $2.00. Back issues: $1.50. 40-48pp; 5½X8½; of. Reporting time: 4-6 weeks. Payment: contributor copies. Ads: $100.00/$50.00/$15.00.

STUDIA CELTICA, University Of Wales Press, J.E. Caerwyn Williams, University of Wales Press, 6 Gwennyth St., Cathays, Cardiff CF2 4YD, United Kingdom, Cardiff 31919. Articles. "Devoted mainly to philosophical and linguistic studies of the Celtic languages with some contributions on Celtic archaeology and early Celtic history." circ. 500. 1 double volume every 2 years. sub. price: £8.00 per double volume from volume XII-XIII due in 78. Back issues: £8 per double issue. Discounts: 33½% booksellers. 500pp; 9½X6; lp. Payment: none. Pub's reviews. §Celtic. Ads: none.

Studia Hispanica Editors, Luis A. Ramos-Garcia, PO Box 7304, University Station, Austin, TX 78712, (512) 458-5413. 1978. Poetry, fiction, articles, art, criticism, long-poems. "Studia Hispanica Editors is a non-profit international cultural exchange organization based at the Univ. of Texas, Austin, and the Univ. of Missouri - St. Louis. The press publishes originals in English, Spanish & Portuguese along with their translations. For the first time in Texas it serves the purpose to establish a genuine link between the American literature and the Latin American literature. The most recent achievements came in the approval and economical help from the National Endowment (Texas Commission on the Arts) to publish *A Bilingual Texas Poetry Anthology*. Edited by L.A. Ramos-Garcia & Dave Oliphant (Prickly Pear Press). This book will be out by December 1980. Another worthy publication will come from Brasil (Osman Lins) & Uruguay (Filisberto Herrandez). Those two well-known writers have sent two unpublished works to be included in the collection *Poiesis*, a cretive section for studia hispanica." avg. press run 500. Pub'd 1 title 1979; expects 2 titles 1980, 2 titles 1981. avg. price, paper: $5.00. Discounts: 30%. 115pp; †of, lp. Reporting time: 3-5 months.

STUDIA MYSTICA, Mary E. Giles, Editor; Kathryn Hohlwein, Art & Poetry Editor, Calif. State Univ., 6000 J Street, Sacramento, CA 95819. 1978. Poetry, fiction, articles, art, photos, interviews, reviews, music, letters, parts-of-novels, long-poems, collages, plays, concrete art. "Primary focus is interrelationship of arts and mystical experience. Interdisciplinary and discriptive in approach. We do *not* welcome speculative theology." circ. 750. 4/yr. Expects 4 issues 1980, 4 issues 1981. sub. price: $12.50 Indiv., $15.00 Institution; per copy: $3.25; sample: free. Back issues: Vol. 1, #1 $3.75; #2 $3.25: #3 $3.25; #4 $4.00. Discounts: Can be arranged with agents. 80pp; 5½X8½; †of. Reporting time: 3 weeks. Payment: Irregularly, some payment available for fiction and graphics. Copyrighted. Pub's reviews: 7 in 1979. §Mysticism, arts and religion.

STUDIES IN DESIGN EDUCATION AND CRAFT, John Eggleston, Keele University, Keele, Staffordshire ST5 5BG, United Kingdom, 0782-621111. 1966. Articles, cartoons, photos, reviews, news items, interviews, criticism, letters, concrete art. "Prints articles on new developments and practice of design education in schools and colleges." circ. 3,000. 2/yr. Pub'd 2 issues 1979; expects 2 issues 1980. sub. price: £8.00; per copy: £4.00; sample: £1.25. Back issues: £4.00. Discounts: 10 percent series disc/w ads. 80pp; 30cm x 21cm; of. Reporting time: max 1 mo. usually two wks. Payment: none. Copyrighted, rights held by magazine. Pub's reviews: 35 in 1979. §Craft, art, design, education. Ads: £50.00/£25.00.

Studies in Education Ltd. (see BRITISH JOURNAL OF IN-SERVICE EDUCATION)

STUDIES IN LABOUR HISTORY, John L Noyce, Publisher, John L. Noyce, P.O. Box 450, Brighton BN18GR, United Kingdom. 1976. Articles, reviews. "Radical 'Peoples' history-bias toward modern British-history." circ. 300 plus. 1/yr. Pub'd 1 issue 1979; expects 1 issue 1980, 1 issue 1981. price per copy: $5.00. Discounts: 10 percent to trade. 60pp; size A4; †of/dupli. Reporting time: we try. Payment: free copy. Pub's reviews: 12 in 1979. §Social History. Ads: details on application. U/APS (Europe).

Studio S Press (see also S), Tony D'Arpino, Editor, 1600 Preston Lane, Morro Bay, CA 93442, 805-772-2715. 1978. Poetry, fiction, articles, art, photos, cartoons, interviews, satire, criticism, reviews, music, letters, parts-of-novels, long-poems, collages, plays, concrete art, news items. "Studio S will continue publishing its series of pamphlets: Sex & Death, Anti-Vivisectionist, Standard Photoes, Standard Ads, etc. Also expect two titles 1980: *A Daring Model* by E. Lee Bradley and *Templum* by Attanasio DiFelice. Second address: PO Box 6592, San Francisco, Ca 94101." avg. press run 500-1,000. Pub'd 2 titles 1979; expects 4 titles 1980. avg. price, cloth: $5.95; paper: $3.95; other: $0.50. Discounts: standard rates. 40-60pp; of. Reporting time: 6-8 weeks. Payment: standard. Copyrights for author. CCLM, COSMEP.

THE SUBURBAN SHOPPER, Franklin Publishing Company, Kevin K. Kopec, PO Box 208, East Millstone, NJ 08873, 201-873-2156.

SUBVERSIVE SCHOLASTIC, Ramone Smith, Managing Editor, PO Box 10076, Columbus, OH 43201, (614) 267-2821. 1978. Poetry, fiction, articles, art, photos, cartoons, interviews, satire, criticism, reviews, music, letters, collages, plays, concrete art, news items. "Material should be concise and opinionated, of interest to highschool students. We're *for* social, political, economic equality. We're *against* oppression, capitalism, chauvinism, etc." circ. 5,000. 6/yr. Pub'd 8 issues 1979; expects 6 issues 1980, 6 issues 1981. sub. price: $5.00; per copy: $0.50; sample: $0.50. Back issues: $0.25. Discounts: $0.10 per copy plus postage for 10 or more copies. 24pp; 6X9; of. Reporting time: 1 month. Pub's reviews. §Any that would be or interest to high school students. Ads: $100.00/$50.00/$0.50. APS, CHIPS.

Sufi Order Publications (see also THE MESSAGE), Sikander Kopelman, Route 15, Box 270, Tucson, AZ 85715, 602-299-4597. 1977. Poetry, articles, art, interviews, music. "Sufi Order Publications is set up to spread the teachings of Hazrat Inayat Khan, Pir Vilayat Khan and other spiritual teachers. The works chosen reflect the Sufi ideals of love, harmony, beauty." avg. press run 6M. Pub'd 2 titles 1979; expects 3 titles 1980, 4 titles 1981. 10 titles listed in the *Small Press Record of Books in Print* (9th Edition, 1980). avg. price, cloth: $5.50; paper: $3.50. Discounts: 40%/bookstores; 25%/libraries. 300pp; 5½X8½; of. Copyrights for author.

SULPHUR RIVER, LuAnn Keener, 411 W Cedar #10, El Dorado, AR 71730, (501) 862-6487. 1977. Poetry. "Without conscious persuasion toward any style or school, *SR* seeks the best material available from both amateurs and established poets. Past contributors include Leon Stokesbury, Susan Wood, Walter McDonald, Joe Colin Murphy, and Lyn Lifshin." circ. 500. 2/yr. Pub'd 2 issues 1979; expects 2 issues 1980, 2 issues 1981. sub. price: $3.00; per copy: $1.50; sample: $1.50 (free to editors). 30pp; 4½X8½; of. Reporting time: 3 weeks. COSMEP.

SUMMER BULLETIN, Yorkshire Dialect Society, Ben T. Dyson, 47 Timothy Lane, Batley, West Yorkshire, United Kingdom, Batley 474238. 1954. Poetry, fiction, articles, criticism, reviews, news items. circ. 850. 1/yr. 40pp; 8X6; of.

H. Summer Enterprises, Harry Summer, P.O. Box 411, New York, NY 10014. 1979. Non-fiction. "*The Philosophy of Losing Weight...and Keeping it Off* is our first publication. We are also a book dealer for self-help mail order books." avg. press run 1,000. Pub'd 1 title 1979. 1 title listed in the *Small Press Record of Books in Print* (9th Edition, 1980). avg. price, paper: $2.50. Discounts: 1-5, 20%; 6-11, 40%; 12 or more, 50%. 48pp; 5½X8½; of. COSMEP.

Summer Stream Press, Dorothy R. Frost, David Duane Frost, PO Box 6056, Santa Barbara, CA 93111, (805) 967-5992. 1978. Poetry. "So far, this is a self-publishing venture. This press is now producing and marketing a series of cassette tapes under the general title: Poetic Heritage. #102180 Elinor Wylie/Amy Lowell; #103010 Sara Teadsale/Margaret Widdemer; #103150 Edna St. Vincent Millay; #103290 Emily Dickinson/Lizette Woodworth Reese" avg. press run 1,000. Expects 1 title 1980. avg. price, paper: $3.50. Discounts: 40%. 50pp; 5½X8½; of. Copyrights for author. COSMEP, WIP.

Summerthought Ltd., Peter Steiner, PO Box 1420, Banff, Alberta T0L0C0, Canada, 762-3919. 1969. Poetry, photos. avg. press run 10,000. Expects 4 titles 1980, 6 titles 1981. 8 titles listed in the *Small Press Record of Books in Print* (9th Edition, 1980). avg. price, cloth: $10.50; paper: $5.95. Discounts: 40 percent trade/20 percent classroom. 160pp; 6X9; lp. Reporting time: 2 weeks. Payment: 10 percent 12½ reprint. Copyrights for author. CBA.

SUN, Sun, Bill Zavatsky, 456 Riverside Drive-5B, New York, NY 10027. 1966 (as SUNDIAL). Poetry, fiction, interviews, criticism, reviews, letters, parts-of-novels, long-poems, plays. "No unsolicited material. Recent contributors: John Ashbery, Harvey Shapiro, George Economou, Rochelle Owens, Hugh Seidman, Ron Padgett, Phillip Lopate, Maureen Owen, etc." circ. 1,000. 2/yr. Expects 2 issues 1980, 2 issues 1981. sub. price: $10.00/3 issues; per copy: varies; sample: $3.50. Back issues: Inquire. Discounts: Trade 5 copies, 40%. 150-200pp; 5½X8½; of. No unsolicited material. Payment: copies. Copyrighted, reverts to author. Pub's reviews. §Books of poetry; books on or about poetry; translations of poetry; biographies of poets; anthologies of poetry, etc.; novels; criticism. Ads: $100.-00/$50.00. CCLM, COSMEP, NYSSPA.

Sun (see also SUN), Bill Zavatsky, 456 Riverside Drive, Apt 5B, New York, NY 10027, (212) 662-6121. 1975. Poetry. "No unsolicited manuscripts. Books by: Harvey Shapiro, Bill Zavatsky, Phillip Lopate, Peter Schjeldahl, Ron Padgett, Raymond Roussel, Francis Ponge, Max Jacob, Malcolm de Chazal, Marjorie Welish, Jaimy Gordon, Michael Heller, George Economou, Alan Feldman, Bill Knott, Paul Violi, Carolanne Ely, Michael O'Brien, James Schuyler, Tony Towle." avg. press run 1,500. Pub'd 6 titles 1979; expects 4 titles 1980, 7 titles 1981. avg. price, cloth: $7.95; paper: $4.00; other: Signed, ltd (to 26) $15.00. Discounts: 1-4 copies, 20%; 5-49 copies, 40%; over 50 copies, 43%. Agents and jobbers 10%. 80pp; 5½X8; of. Reporting time: no unsolicited manuscripts. Payment: privately arranged. authors receive a minimum payment of 100 copies of the edition, paperback. Copyrights for author. COSMEP, NYSSPA.

THE SUN, A MAGAZINE OF IDEAS, Sy Safransky, 412 W. Rosemary Street, Chapel Hill, NC 27514, 942-5282. 1974. Poetry, fiction, articles, art, photos, cartoons, interviews, satire, criticism, reviews, letters, parts-of-novels, long-poems, collages, news items. "Interested in articles on any subject, of any length, that enrich our common space." circ. 10,000. 12/yr. Pub'd 7 issues 1979; expects 12 issues 1980, 12 issues 1981. sub. price: $12.00; per copy: $1.25; sample: free. Back issues: Half-price. Discounts: varies. 48pp; 8X10½; of. Reporting time: 1 month. Payment varies, query first. Copyrighted, reverts to author. Pub's reviews: 10 in 1979. §all areas. Ads: $150.00/$80.00/$2.50 first ten words, 10¢ each add. COSMEP.

SUN & MOON: A Journal of Literature and Art, Sun & Moon Press, Douglas Messerli, Howard N. Fox, 4330 Hartwick Rd, #418, College Park, MD 20740, 301-864-6921. 1976. Poetry, fiction, articles, art, interviews, criticism, letters, parts-of-novels, plays, concrete art. "Primarily we print contemporary art and literature, but occasionally we reprint older material which is relevant to the literature and art of today. Recent contributors include Bruce Andrews, Eleanor Antin, Ascher/-

Straus, Charles Bernstein, Michael Brownstein, Clark Coolidge, Larry Eigner, Kenward Elmslie, Charles Henri Ford, Steve Gianakos, Barbara Guest, Michael Lally, Lucy Lippard, Bernadette Mayer, John Perreault, Gilbert Sorrentino, Anne Truitt, Tom Veitch, Anne Waldman, Jeff Weinstein, and Douglas Woolf" 2-3/yr. Pub'd 3 issues 1979; expects 3 issues 1980, 3 issues 1981. sub. price: $10.00 (Individuals) $15.00 (Institutions); per copy: $4.50; sample: $3.00. Back issues: $3.00 (issues 1 & 2 unavailable). Discounts: 40% for agents and bookstores. 150-250pp; 5½X8; of. Reporting time: 1-3 weeks. Payment: small honorarium for some issues. Copyrights all material unless copyrighted by author previous to publication. Pub's reviews: 4 in 1979. §Contemporary poetry and fiction, art and art related works. Ads: $100/$75. CCLM, Washington Writers Center, COSMEP.

Sun & Moon Press (see also SUN & MOON: A Journal of Literature and Art), Douglas Messerli, Howard N. Fox, 4330 Hartwick Road, #418, College Park, MD 20740, 301-864-6921. 1976. Poetry, fiction, art. "Sun & Moon Press publishes short books of poetry, fiction, art and critical theory. We are especially interested in texts that experiment with or are grounded in language-theory and/or that stress style. Recent publications include *Shade* by Charles Bernstein, *Cuiva Sails* by Ray DiPalma, *whos listening out there* by David Antin and *Plantin* by P. Inman" avg. press run 500. Pub'd 8 titles 1979; expects 8 titles 1980, 8 titles 1981. 9 titles listed in the *Small Press Record of Books in Print* (9th Edition, 1980). avg. price, paper: $3.00. Discounts: 20 - 40 percent. 30-60pp; 8½X11; †of/mi. Reporting time: 1 month. Payment: Royalty: 10% or in copies. Copyrights for author. CCLM, WWC (Washington Writer's Center).

Sun, Man, Moon Inc., Janice Baylis, Editor, P.O. Box 5084, Huntington Beach, CA 92646, 714-962-8945. 1976. "So far I've only printed my own dream materials. Am interested in materials which relate Jungian psychology to other topics such as art, literature, life, etc. Interested in works about symbolism. Non-fiction only." avg. press run 3,000. Expects 1 title 1980. 3 titles listed in the *Small Press Record of Books in Print* (9th Edition, 1980). avg. price, paper: $5.00. Discounts: Trade 40%; Bulk 45%; Agent 10%; Jobber 10%. 200pp; 5½X8½; 8½X11; of. Reporting time: 2 months. Payment: 12%. Copyrights for author.

sun rise fall down artpress (see also THE ACTS THE SHELFLIFE; Forbidden Additions; TRADE MAGAZINE), Miekal And, 838A Wisconsin St., Oshkosh, WI 54901, (414) 426-1732. 1977. Poetry, fiction, articles, art, photos, interviews, music, letters, parts-of-novels, long-poems, collages, plays, concrete art. "we're a collective press with membership open to anyone for $5/year. this entitles you to everything we publish for that year as well as involving you in the actual production of broadsides, chapbooks, mags and whatever else is dreamed up. we invite submissions of any length (we are always pleased to receive your poetic statements also) as well as correspondence. recent contributors include Doug Flaherty, Guy Beining, Keith Rahmmings, Martin J. Rosenblum, edward falco.u" avg. press run 300. Pub'd 4 titles 1979; expects 4 titles 1980, 4 titles 1981. 11 titles listed in the *Small Press Record of Books in Print* (9th Edition, 1980). avg. price, paper: $1.00 or barter. 25pp; 5½X8½; †of. Reporting time: couple of days. Payment: 10% of run. Does not copyright for author. COSMEP Midwest.

Sun-Scape Publications, Jaan Koel, PO Box 42725, Tucson, AZ 85733, 602-297-3424. 1975. Poetry, art, photos, interviews, music. "Sun-Scape Publications publishes the works of Kenneth G. Mills, Canadian author, poet, musician and teacher. A concert pianist for 23 years, Mr. Mills now gives his Unfoldments (his exciting verbal discourses, spontaneously given in rhythmic prose and poetry) to his students in Canada and the United States. Note: More information is available in introduction to both books. Sun-Scape Publications, PO Box 793, Station F, Toronto, Ontario, Canada M4Y 2N7 (416) 221-2461" avg. press run 5000. Pub'd 1 title 1979; expects 2 titles 1980, 2 titles 1981. 4 titles listed in the *Small Press Record of Books in Print* (9th Edition, 1980). avg. price, paper: $6.00; other: $14.00 (published cassettes with transcription booklets) These are cassettes of K.G. Mills' philosophical lectures called *Unfoldments.* Discounts: individuals, full retail price; institutions and libraries, 15%; retailers etc, 40%. 150pp; 7X8½; of. Copyrights for author.

SUN TRACKS: An American Indian Literary Magazine, Larry Evers, Department of English, Univ of Arizona, Tucson, AZ 85721, 884-1836. 1971. Poetry, fiction, articles, art, photos, interviews, parts-of-novels, long-poems. "We publish literary material by and about American Indians." circ. 1,000. 1/yr. Pub'd 1 issue 1979; expects 1 issue 1980. sub. price: $5.00; per copy: $5.00; sample: $5.00. Back issues: $5.00. Discounts: 20 percent on 10 copies or more. 100pp; 8½X11; of. Reporting time: 3 months. Payment: 3 copies. Copyrighted, reverts to author. §American Indian literature. CCLM.

SUNBURY (a poetry magazine), Sunbury Press, Virginia Scott, Joan Murray, Box 274 Jerome Ave Station, Bronx, NY 10468. 1973. Poetry. "'Affirming women, working class, Third World. Fay Chiang, Elouise Loftin, Joan Murray, Marge Piercy, Ellen Bissert, Quincy Troupe, Lorraine Sutton, V. Scott, Richard Oyama, Sharon Barba.'" circ. 1500. 3/yr. sub. price: $5.00; per copy: $1.75 plus post.;

sample: $1.75 plus postage. Back issues: $2.00 + 15% postage and handling. Discounts: 40% for ten copies or more. 88pp; 5⅜X8¼; of. Reporting time: 1-6 mos. Payment: in copies. Copyrighted, reverts to author. Pub's reviews. Ads: $100/$50. CCLM, COSMEP, NESPA.

Sunbury Press (see also SUNBURY (a poetry magazine)), Virginia Scott, Editor, Box 274 Jerome Ave Station, Bronx, NY 10468. 1973. Poetry, fiction, articles, criticism, reviews. "Affirming women, Third World, working class." avg. press run 1,000. Pub'd 3 titles 1979; expects 1 title 1980, 2 titles 1981. 8 titles listed in the *Small Press Record of Books in Print* (9th Edition, 1980). avg. price, paper: $2.00. Discounts: 60-40 consignment. 150pp; 5⅜X8¼; of. Reporting time: 1-6 months. Payment: copies. CCLM, NESPA, COSMEP.

Sunflower University Press (see also JOURNAL OF THE WEST), Robin Higham, President; Patricia P. Clark, General Manager, Box 1009, Manhattan, KS 66502, (913) 532-6733. 1978. Satire, reviews. "Paper and hardback books on theme issues or on contract with subsidy." avg. press run 500. Pub'd 1 title 1979; expects 2 titles 1980, 4-8 titles 1981. 8 titles listed in the *Small Press Record of Books in Print* (9th Edition, 1980). avg. price, paper: $8.00. Discounts: 25% on a no-returns basis and we pay shipping. 120pp; 7⅜X9¾; †of. Reporting time: 3 months. Payment: Probably after 1,000 copies sold. Copyrights for author.

Sunken Forum Press (see also Montreal Poems), Keitha K. MacIntosh, Dewittville, Quebec J0S1C0, Canada, 514-264-2866. 1974. Poetry, fiction. "Solicited mss accepted. *Sunken Forum Press* published *Shattered Glass & Other Fragments,* poetry fiction by Keitha MacIntosh in 1976. (still available, retail $3.50). Other Montreal poets are being published this year. *Montreal Poems III* now available, $3.00 retail. Guest poet Al Purdy plus Louis Dudek, Artie Gold, Stephen Morrissey & sixteen other Montreal poets. *Montreal Poems IV:* Women's Issue, $3.00 retail." avg. press run 1,000. Pub'd 10 titles 1979. avg. price, paper: $3.00. Discounts: 20-30 percent. 50pp; 8X10; of. Reporting time: 1 month. No payment. Copyrights for author.

SUNRISE, RAS Communications/Blind Eye Publishing House/Blind Eye Books/Jasmine, Randy Stables, 3620 52nd Avenue, Apt. 204, Red Deer, Alberta T4N 4J5, Canada, 406-347-2383. 1978. Poetry, fiction, articles, art, cartoons, interviews, satire, reviews, letters, long-poems. "Science fiction, fantasy, fiction, limited to eight pages. I also want wood cut prints and I also want haiku, tanka, long haiku, haiku-in-sequence. No Profanity, No Porno stuff. All submissions must be typed double spaced on 8½ x 11 paper. All submissions must be accompanied by SASE, and include a brief biographical sketch." 6/yr. Expects 1 issue 1980, 4 issues 1981. sub. price: $6.00; per copy: $2.00; sample: $2.00. Back issues: $1.50 per copy, $2.00 for 2 copies. Discounts: $10.00 for 15 copies, $20.00 for 30 copies. 30-40pp; 8½X11; of. Reporting time: 1 month. Payment: 1 free copy of *Sunrise.* Pub's reviews. §Science fiction, fantasy, poetry, haiku; tanka.

Sunrise Press, John Leibolo, PO Box 742, Chandler, AZ 85224, 967-4251. 1976. Poetry, fiction, long-poems, plays. "Length of material is limited to less than 150 printed pages. All subjects considered." avg. press run 500-1,000 copies. avg. price, cloth: $8.95. Discounts: negotiable. 111pp; 8½X11; of. Reporting time: 2 weeks. Payment: negotiable. Copyrights for author.

The Sunstone Press, James Clois Smith Jr., Gerald Hausman, PO Box 2321, Santa Fe, NM 87501, (505) 988-4418. 1971. Fiction, art. avg. press run 5,000. Pub'd 6 titles 1979; expects 8 titles 1980, 8 titles 1981. 71 titles listed in the *Small Press Record of Books in Print* (9th Edition, 1980). avg. price, cloth: $10.00; paper: $3.95; other: $3.95. Discounts: Standard. 128pp; 6X9; 8½X11; of. Reporting time: 90 days. Payment: Royalty only. Copyrights for author. COSMEP, RMPG.

SUPRANORMAL, 1983, Robert G. Sheppard, Tony Parsons, 15, Oakapple Road, Southwick, Sussex BN4 4YL, United Kingdom. 1974. Poetry, interviews, music, collages, concrete art. "1983 is a magazine on CGO cassette. Side two is usually a feature of some kind, on issue two, Lee Harwood, half an hour of his poetry. Future issues will include work by Stefan Themerson (-1/2 hr), Bob Cobbing (-1/2 hr), Allen Fisher, Jeff Nuttall, Paul Evans, Robert G. Sheppard." price per copy: £1.30. Discounts: trade discounts 33⅓%.

Survival Cards, Lee Nading, Publisher, P.O. Box 1805, Bloomington, IN 47402. 1976. avg. press run 10,000. Pub'd 1 title 1979; expects 1 title 1980, 1 title 1981. 1 title listed in the *Small Press Record of Books in Print* (9th Edition, 1980). avg. price, other: $2.75 (vinyl laminate). Discounts: 15-99 (40%), 100-199 (45%), 200-299 (50%), request jobber discounts. 10pp; 3X5; of.

SURVIVOR, c/o Rochester Routes, 50 Inglewood Drive, Rochester, NY 14619. 1977. Poetry, fiction, articles, art, photos, interviews, criticism, reviews, music, letters, plays, news items. "We suspended publication in 1978 to review funding sources; we may be resuming publication in early 1979. See last year's Directory for policies." circ. 1,500. 6/yr. price per copy: $1.00. Back issues: $4.00. Discounts: Address financial inquiries to Kenneth Browne, Business Manager, 300 Alexander St, Rochester, NY 14607. 32pp; 8½X11; of. Reporting time: 2 months. Payment: 3 copies. Copyrighted, reverts to author. Pub's reviews. §Poetry, fiction, criticism, art, photography, humanities, the arts, etc. Ads: $100.00/$60.00.

Survivors' Manual, A. S. McIntosh, 2823 Rockaway Avenue, Oceanside, NY 11572, (516) 766-1891. 1968. Poetry, criticism, letters, long-poems, collages. "Book length ms. Performance poetry, criticism of contemporary poetry incorporating coherent, well-thought-out visions for the future." avg. press run 500. Pub'd 3 titles 1979; expects 2 titles 1980. 4 titles listed in the *Small Press Record of Books in Print* (9th Edition, 1980). avg. price, paper: $3.00. Discounts: 40% bookstore, 50% jobber, 30% classroom. 100pp; of. Reporting time: 1 month. Payment: individually worked out. Copyrights for author.

Sussex Whole Earth Group (see WHOLE EARTH)

The Swallow Press Inc., Donna Ippolito, 811 W. Junior Terrace, Chicago, IL 60613, 312-871-2760. 1946. Poetry, fiction, articles, art, photos, interviews, criticism, long-poems, plays, news items, non-fiction. "We distribute the books of: Artists & Alchemists" avg. press run 2,000-5,000. Pub'd 20 titles 1979; expects 20 titles 1980. 10 titles listed in the *Small Press Record of Books in Print* (9th Edition, 1980). avg. price, cloth: $14.95; paper: $4.95. Discounts: 1 copy 10 percent; 2-4, 30 percent; 5-49, 40 percent; 50-99, 41 percent; 100-199, 42 percent; 200-299, 43 percent; 300-399, 44 percent; 400-499, 45 percent; 500-up, 46 percent. Short discount 20 percent. SCOP 40 percent. 250pp; 6X9. Reporting time: 3-6 months. Payment: Standard royalty 10 percent cl, 7½ percent pa. copyright in author's name. ABA.

Swamp Press (see also TIGHTROPE), Jo Mish, Frank Pondolfino, Ed Rayher, Bob Rayher, 4 Bugbee Road, Oneonta, NY 13820. 1975. Poetry, art, satire, criticism, reviews, letters, long-poems. "Fine papers used in all magazines & chapbooks. Handset, letterpress." avg. press run 250. Pub'd 10 titles 1979; expects 8 titles 1980, ? titles 1981. 6 titles listed in the *Small Press Record of Books in Print* (9th Edition, 1980). avg. price, cloth: $12.50; paper: $2.50. Discounts: Dealers: 20%/hardcovers, 40%/softcovers. 20-40pp; size varies; †lp. Reporting time: 6 weeks. Copies/chapbook payment worked out with authors. Does not copyright for author. COSMEP, NYSSPA.

SWEDISH BOOKS, Jan Ring, Sven Arne Bergmann, Tom Geddes, Karin Petherick, Mary Sandbach, Mike Western, Box 2387, S-40316 Goteborg, Sweden, 031-119113. 1978. Poetry, fiction, articles, art, photos, cartoons, criticism, reviews, letters, parts-of-novels. "Bibliographical information on (a) translations from Swedish and (b) original works in English on Swedish literature, writing, and Sweden." circ. 1,000. 4/yr. Pub'd 3 issues 1979; expects 4 issues 1980. sub. price: $16.50; per copy: $5.00. Back issues: $7.50. Discounts: by agreement. 50pp; 7X9; of. Reporting time: 2-3 months. Payment: in principle. Copyrighted, reverts to author. Pub's reviews: 45 in 1979. §Sweden, Scandinavian countries and literature (viz Danish, Norwegian, Swedish, Iceland, Finland).

SWIFT RIVER, Tree Toad Press, Deborah Robson, Box 264, Leverett, MA 01054. 1973. Poetry, fiction, articles, art, cartoons, music, parts-of-novels, long-poems. "Mostly fiction. Willing to devote whole issues to something special. No xerox unless very clean and not submitted elsewhere (include a note). Tree Toad Press and *Swift River* are active; Woolman Press and *Port Townsend Journal* publications are available from us." circ. 350+. 1-3/yr. Pub'd 1 issue 1979; expects 2-3 issues 1980, 2-3 issues 1981. sub. price: $6.00/2 issues; per copy: $3.00; sample: $3.00 or $1.00 & 6 X 9 SASE. Discounts: usual bkstore rate on orders of 5+. 50-125pp; 5½/x 8; of/lp/silkscreen. Reporting time: 1 week - 6 mos. Payment: copies, money when available (minimal amount). Copyrighted. Ads: $40.00/$25.00. COSMEP, NESPA.

SWIM LITE NEWS (newsletter), Loggeerhead, Gretchen Schreiber, Box 7231, Shawnee Mission, KS 66207, 816-566-2174. 1979. Articles, interviews, reviews. "Rt 1, Box 178A, Bates City, MO 64011." circ. 500. 4/yr. Pub'd 1 issue 1979. sub. price: $4.00; per copy: $1.25; sample: $1.25. Back issues: $1.25. Discounts: 20-40%. 4pp; 8½X11; †of. Copyrighted. Pub's reviews. §Health, physical fitness.

Sybex Incorporated, Rodnay Zaks, 2344 Sixth St, Berkeley, CA 94710, 415-848-8233. 1976. "Sybex is a technical press specializing in books about microcomputing for the personal, business and technical fields." avg. press run 50,000. Pub'd 8 titles 1979; expects 20 titles 1980. avg. price, cloth: $20.00; paper: $10.95. Discounts: query. 300pp; 8½X11; of. Reporting time: 2-3 weeks.

Sydenham Press (see also MAMASHEE), Margaret Drage, RR 1, Inwood, Ontario N0N 1KO, Canada. 1977. Poetry, fiction, art, criticism, reviews, news items. avg. press run 225. avg. price, paper: $1.50; other: $1.50 plus mailing costs. 48pp; 8½X11. Reporting time: 3 months.

Sydon, Inc., Sy M. Kahn, Don Gray, c/o Drama Dept, University of the Pacific, Stockton, CA 95211. 1965. Poetry. "Has not published in recent years, tho probably will within next year. We are not currently seeking material." avg. press run 300. 4 titles listed in the *Small Press Record of Books in Print* (9th Edition, 1980). avg. price, paper: $2.50. 50pp; lp. Payment: 10% royalties. Copyrights for author. COSMEP.

SYNCLINE, Syncline Press, Lucy Lakides, Robert Ely, Ellen Lakides, 7825 S. Ridgeway, Chicago, IL 60652. 1977. Poetry, fiction. "Each year, Syncline Press publishes one magazine issue and a special double issue featuring the work of one author. This year we published *Antonio Salazar is Dead,* a collection of prose-poems by J.L. McManus, and it's available for $3.00. Past magazine issues include work by Daniel Campion, Jennifer Moyer, Dennis Mathis, Ralph J. Mills Jr., Peter Aristedes, W.D. Ehrhart, Barry Silesky, James Magorian, Maxine Chernoff. We want an author's best work. Don't send resumes: if we want one, we'll ask for it. We are interested in translations of contemporary Greek poetry if accompanied by original text. Manuscripts sent without SASE are thrown away. Most importantly, we are not a vanity press, which means we don't use Syncline as a vehicle to see ourselves in print." circ. 250-500. 3/yr. Pub'd 3 issues 1979; expects 3 issues 1980, 3 issues 1981. sub. price: $5.00/3 issues (1 yr); per copy: $3.00; sample: $2.00. Back issues: Issues #1, $2.00; #2, $2.00; #3, $2.00; #4/5, $3.00. Discounts: 25% in quantity (10 or more). 48-60pp; 5½X8½; of. Reporting time: 4-8 weeks. Payment: contributor's copy. Copyrighted, reverts to author. Ads: $25.00/$15.00.

Syncline Press (see SYNCLINE)

Synergistic Press (see also CHANGE), Bud Johns, 3965 Sacramento St., San Francisco, CA 94118, 415-EV7-8180. 1968. Poetry, articles, art, letters. "Our interests are wide ranging, which is best shown are our four titles in print: *The Ombibulous Mr. Mencken,* a humorous biography of H. L. Mencken; *Last Look At The Old Met,* a personal portrait in drawings and text of the old Metropolitan Opera House, *Not a Station But a Place,* an art and text portrait of the Gare de Lyon in Paris and *Bastard In The Ragged Suit,* the published work of a leading protetarian writer of the '20s and '30s, with selections from manuscript fragments and drawings during the last two decades of his life when he didn't submit his work for publication, plus a biographical introduction. To date all of our titles have been developed internally and that probably be true of a majority of our titles in the immediate future. Average $6.80 (high $12.50, low $2.95), all cloth to date." avg. press run 3,000-5,000. Pub'd 1 title 1979; expects 1 title 1980, 2 titles 1981. 4 titles listed in the *Small Press Record of Books in Print* (9th Edition, 1980). avg. price, cloth: $7.75; paper: $5.95. Discounts: trade: single copies, 30 percent; 2-5, 35 percent; 6-11, 37 percent; 12-49, 40 percent; 50 or more, 44 percent; wholesaler/jobber discounts upon request. pp varies, have published from 52-216; of. Reporting time: 1 month. To date payment has varied with title. Copyrights for author.

SYNERGY, Energy Earth Communications, Inc., Ahmos Zu-Bolton, Lorenzo Thomas, Harryette Mullen, Box 1141, Galveston, TX 77553. 1978. Poetry, fiction, articles, interviews, criticism, reviews. "Arts and culture of the South & Southwest." 2/yr. sub. price: $4.95; per copy: $2.50. 80-100pp; 8½X11; of. Reporting time: up to 6 months. Payment: copies. Copyrighted, to contributors. Pub's reviews. §Poetry, fiction, folklore. Ads: $100.00. CCLM.

Synerjy (see also SYNERJY: A Directory of Energy Alternatives), Jeff Twine, Box 4790, Grand Central Station, New York, NY 10017, (212) 865-9595. 1974. "Bibliography directory of solar, wind, wood, energy, etc. Publications, products, facilities." avg. press run 500. Pub'd 2 titles 1979; expects 2 titles 1980. 2 titles listed in the *Small Press Record of Books in Print* (9th Edition, 1980). avg. price, paper: $14.00. Discounts: $24.00 for 1 yr subscription. of.

SYNERJY: A Directory of Energy Alternatives, Synerjy, Jeff Twine, Box 4790, Grand Central Station, New York, NY 10017, (212) 865-9595. "Bibliographic directory of solar, wind, wood, water, energy; heat transfer & storage of energy. Publications, products, facilities. July issues are yearly cumulations." circ. 400. 2/yr. Pub'd 2 issues 1979; expects 2 issues 1980, 2 issues 1981. sub. price: $24.00; per copy: $14.00. Back issues: $50.00 for 6 cumulative back issues. Discounts: $20.00 yr for standing order. 100pp; 8½X11; of. Copyrighted, reverts to author.

Syntaxophone Publications (see also JOE SOAP'S CANOE), Rupert Mallin, Keith Dersley, Martin Stannard, 10 Snow Hill, Clare, Sudbury, Suffolk, England. 1975. Poetry, articles, reviews, letters, long-poems. "Poetry of any length considered. Non-academic bias. Looking for interesting work to publish in a series of booklets." avg. press run 200. Pub'd 3 titles 1979; expects 2 titles 1980, 3 titles 1981. avg. price, paper: 30p. Discounts: 40% for 5 copies. 24pp; size A5, A4; †mi. Reporting time: 3 weeks. Payment: copies at present. Copyrights for author. ALP, ALM.

SYSTEMS & METHODS, GBC Press, Howard Schwartz, Editor, 630 So. 11th St., Box 4115, Las Vegas, NV 89106, (702)382-7555. 1974. "This magazine reviews systems being sold and contains articles on gambling. Each issue is numbered as a volume. #1 thru #28, general gambling. Starting with #19, pari mutuel type only." circ. 2,000. 6/yr. Pub'd 6 issues 1979; expects 6 issues 1980, 6 issues 1981. sub. price: $15.00; per copy: $3.00. Back issues: Six consecutive issues on one order $10.00/single copies $2.00. Discounts: Trade 50%; Jobber 62%:. 64pp; 5½X8¼; †of. Reporting time: 30 days approx. Payment: Depends on type and length. Copyrighted, reverts to author. Pub's reviews: 6 in 1979. §On pari mutuel type events. no ads. BPASC/ABA Affiliate.

SZ/Press, Suzanne Zavrian, Daniel Kurland, P.O. Box 383, Cathedral Station, New York, NY 10025. 1977. Poetry, fiction, art, parts-of-novels, long-poems, concrete art. "1-2 books per year, approx. $3.00 each. Poetry, prose, experimental arts." avg. press run 600. Pub'd 1 title 1979; expects 1 title 1980, 3 titles 1981. 1 title listed in the *Small Press Record of Books in Print* (9th Edition, 1980). avg. price, paper: $3.00. 64pp; of. Reporting time: 6 weeks. Payment: copies for the moment. Copyrights for author.

T

T.A.A.S. Association, Inc., Robert Evans, PO Box 2150, Jacksonville, FL 32203. 1972. Reviews. "The Afro-American Social Research Association, Inc. 655 Jessie Street Jacksonville, Florida (U.S.A.)." avg. price, paper: $2.00. Discounts: 1-50, $1.00 each; 51-1,000, $0.75; 1,001 and up, $0.50. 3pp; 4½X5½; †of. Copyrights for author.

TRT Publications, Inc., J. G. Brotchie Jr, S. W. Brotchie, Candice Keays, PO Box 486, Beverly, MA 01915, (617) 927-1986. 1968. Fiction, articles, photos, concrete art. "Full length books, assigned subject matter." avg. press run 2,500-5,000. Pub'd 3 titles 1979; expects 2 titles 1980, 2 titles 1981. avg. price, paper: $4.95. Discounts: 40% off retail to stores, distributors by arrangement. 150pp; 5½X8½; of. Reporting time: 2 weeks. COSMEP, APGA.

Tadpole Press (see Cadenza Press)

TAI CHI, Marvin Smalheiser, Editor, 3605 Sunset Blvd, Los Angeles, CA 90026, 213-665-7773. 1977. Articles, interviews, reviews, letters, news items. "Articles about T'ai Chi Ch'uan, I Ching, Zen, meditation about 700 words each." 6/yr. Pub'd 6 issues 1979; expects 6 issues 1980, 6 issues 1981. sub. price: $2.50; per copy: $.50; sample: $.50. 6pp; 8½X11; of. Reporting time: 2 weeks. Copyrighted. Pub's reviews.

Talespinner Publications, Inc., Jay Johnson, Nina Johnson, Lee Gilchrist, Betty Gilchrist, P.O. Box 19087, Minneapolis, MN 55419, (612) 825-0087. 1978. Fiction, art. "We primarily are a publisher of stories designed to entertain children, primary age to 4th grade. Pre-school material is also welcome. Manuscripts with max. length of 2,500 words on fantasy, fantasy-adventure, realistic fiction about 'real' children, sex-fair stories, fairy tales, etc. are what we're interested in-by previously-unpublished authors *only* (small press authors-ok; commercially 'exposed' authors-no). Artists-submit a character sketch and a setting sketch appropriate for a children's story, to be kept for future reference. Recent contributors have ranged from a great-grandmother to a Japanese novelist to a carpenter to advertising execs to young mothers. We're fascinated by contributors who love to share their talents w/children." avg. press run 2,000. Pub'd 2 titles 1979; expects 1 title 1980, 3 titles 1981. 2 titles listed in the *Small Press Record of Books in Print* (9th Edition, 1980). avg. price, paper: $1.50. Discounts: 40% to bookstores; 50% to distributors; for orders of 5 or more paperbacks, 25% for 1-4 copies; 20% classroom; 10% library; mail order: include 50¢ per copy (for postage/handling) and 10¢ for each additional copy. Remit payment within 30 days of receipt of books. *Libraries:* please waive postage and handling charges if you give Talespinner Publications a 'standing order' for new titles. 36pp; 5½X8½ and 8X8; of. Reporting time: 5-6 weeks. Payment: Cash honorarium, 40% discount on purchase of printed work. COSMEP.

Talonbooks, David Robinson, Karl Siegler, Peter Hay, Drama, 201-1019 East Cordova, Vancouver, British Columbia V6A 1M8, Canada, 604-255-5915. 1967. Poetry, fiction, art, photos, long-poems, plays, criticism, letters. *"Talonbooks* is one of the leading Canadian literary publishers. The press publishes almost exclusively only poetry, drama and fiction-and is the major publisher of contemporary drama in Canada. Also, Talonbooks, P.O. Box 42720, Los Angeles, CA 90042." avg. press run poetry-1,000; drama-4,000; fiction-2,000-3,000 (first printings). Pub'd 5 titles 1979; expects 15 titles 1980, 15 titles 1981. 98 titles listed in the *Small Press Record of Books in Print* (9th Edition, 1980). avg. price, paper: $2.95-$7.95. Discounts: 1 copy, 20%; 5 copies, 40%; - 500 copies, 46%; libraries, 10%. 128pp; 5½X8½; of. Reporting time: 3-6 months. Payment: 10% royalty of retail sale price. Copyrights for author. ACP, COSMEP, CBA.

Tamal Vista Publications, P. W. DeFremery, 222 Madrone Ave, Larkspur, CA 94939, 924-7289. 1976. *"The Stripper's Guide to Canoe-building"* avg. press run 2. 3 titles listed in the *Small Press Record of Books in Print* (9th Edition, 1980). avg. price, paper: $8.95. Discounts: 0-4 equals 0; 5-99: 40%; 100-149: 42%; 150 and up: 44%; wholesellers 50 percent. 96pp; 9X12; of. Reporting time: 1 month. Copyrights for author. COSMEP.

Tamalpa Press, Gloria North, 15 Estelle Avenue, Larkspur, CA 94939, 461-2465. 1978. Poetry. avg. press run 500. Expects 2 titles 1980, 1 title 1981. 1 title listed in the *Small Press Record of Books in Print* (9th Edition, 1980). avg. price, paper: $2.95. Discounts: 40%. 104pp; 5½X8½. Not open for submission at present.

TAMARACK, Tamarack Editions, Allen Hoey, 909 Westcott Street, Syracuse, NY 13210, (315) 478-6495. 1977. Poetry, long-poems. "Tamarack functions as a kind of on-going anthology, preferring to use at least three shorter poems or one or two longpoems by each contributor. In this way, we hope to let our audience see more of the range of each poet's voice. If we cannot find at least one of your poems we like, you are likely not for us. We are not interested in artless polemic, though well-crafted poems empty of human feeling will not find a home here either. Our focus is rural, perhaps even agrarian. Recent contributors include Graham Everett, R.T. Smith, Patrick Bizzaro, Ray Freed, Steve Lewandowski, Joan Colby, Tom Montag, et al." circ. 300. 2/yr. Pub'd 2 issues 1979; expects 2 issues 1980, 2 issues 1981. 24 titles listed in the *Small Press Record of Books in Print* (9th Edition, 1980). sub. price: $4.00/individual; $5.00/institution; per copy: $2.50/individual; $3.00/institution. Discounts: 40% to all on purchases of 5 copies or more for retail sales. 64pp; 5½X8½; †of. Reporting time: 2 to 6 weeks. Payment: copies. Copyrighted, reverts to author. Pub's reviews: 4 in 1979. §Poetry.

Tamarack Editions (see also TAMARACK), Allen Hoey, Cynthia Hoey, 909 Westcott Street, Syracuse, NY 13210, (315) 478-6495. 1975. Poetry, art, long-poems. "Occasional books, pamphlets, chapbooks & broadsides, by invitation, frequently based upion material rec'd for magazine. Most of the books and pamphlets are two-color, limited editions. Recent publications by William Heyen, Anthony Piccione, Graham Everett, R.T. Smith. A chapbook by Dave Smith will be available in the near future" avg. press run 300 to 350 copies. Pub'd 5 titles 1979; expects 5 titles 1980, 5 titles 1981. avg. price, cloth: $10.00; paper: $3.00/$4.00. Discounts: 40% on purchases of at least 5 copies for retail sale. pamphlets, 12-24pp; chapbooks 28-36pp; full-length 48+pp; 5½X8½; †lp/of. no unsolicited submissions for press. Payment is in copies, 10% of run. Copyrights for author.

Tamarack Press (see also WISCONSIN TRAILS), Howard Mead, Jill Weber Dean, Sue McCoy, P.O.Box 5650, Madison, WI 53705, 608-831-3363. 1975. "We conduct no major business by phone.-Tamarack press is interested in books about nature/environment/heritage/folklore/nostalgia:'Celebrate the Earth' theme/travel/recreation: Wisconsiana theme" avg. press run 7,500. Pub'd 4 titles 1979; expects 4 titles 1980, 5 titles 1981. 13 titles listed in the *Small Press Record of Books in Print* (9th Edition, 1980). avg. price, cloth: $20.00; paper: $5.00-$10.00. Discounts: Universal discount schedule. 100-150pp; 9X12; of. Reporting time: Queries: 1 week; outline & sample chapters: 1 month. Payment: 15% of net cash receipts (the equivalent of 10% of list price) if author supplies all materials needed for book. Y. AAP, RPA, COSMEP.

Tamarisk, Dennis Barone, Deborah Ducoff-Barone, 188 Forest Ave, Ramsey, NJ 07446, 201-327-7469. 1975. Poetry, fiction, art, photos, collages. *"Tamarisk* grew out of *APOCALYPSE.* Tamarisk, that old testament tree, to be before Apocalypse. Quieter, smaller, smarter; of any length—printing what comes, in someway, by way of ear, not mail. Forthcoming 'single artist' issues to include works by William Wilson and Barry Schwabsky. Magazine issues have featured work by John Cavanagh, David Abel, Cid Corman, and John Cline. That is the plan and there is a plan — a single artist issue and a magazine issue each year. Our plan, most likely, does not include you. Having small, scalelike leaves and clusters of pink flowers—*Tamarisk.*" avg. press run 250. Pub'd 1 title 1979; expects 2 titles 1980, 2 titles 1981. 3 titles listed in the *Small Press Record of Books in Print* (9th Edition, 1980). avg. price, paper: $1.00. 40pp; 5½X8½; of. Reporting time: 2 yrs to not at all. Payment: copies. Copyrights for author. NESPA.

Tamarix (see also THE SALT CEDAR), Route 2, Box 121 A, Stevensville, MT 59870, (406) 777-3674. avg. press run 500. Pub'd 2 titles 1979. Reporting time: 4-6 weeks.

Tanam Press, Reese Williams, 40 White Street, New York, NY 10013. 1979. Fiction, art. "Some recent contributors completed or in progress for 1979-1980: Susan Sontag, R Buckminster Fuller, Theresa Cha, Mike Roddy, Werner Herzog." avg. press run 3,000. Pub'd 3 titles 1979; expects 4 titles 1980, 6 titles 1981. 6 titles listed in the *Small Press Record of Books in Print* (9th Edition, 1980). avg. price, cloth: $10.00; paper: $6.00; other: $7.98 (record albums). Discounts: 20% to schools & libraries; retail: 3-25, 40%; 25 or more, 45%; distributors, jobbers 50%. of. Reporting time: 1 month. Payment: varies. Copyrights for author.

TANGENT, Tangent Books, Vivienne Finch, William Pryor, 58 Blakes Lane, New Malden, Surrey, England KT3 6NX, United Kingdom. 1975. Articles, poetry, fiction, art, photos, reviews, criticism. "*Tangent* is a confluence of contemporary writings - contributors to current issue include Bill Penn, Frank Samperi, Ken Edwards, Robert Hampson, Cory Harding, Harry Guest, Peter Sinclare etc. Prefer large selection of work by one author - plus translations, articles/essays on poetics. Second address: Waye Cottage, Chagford, Devon, England" circ. 1,000. 2/yr. Expects 2 issues 1980. sub. price: £3.00-£7.50; per copy: £1.50-£4.00; sample: postage. Back issues: By arrangement-usually postage. Discounts: trade 33⅓%. 70pp; size A4; of. Reporting time: 1 month. Payment: copies. Copyrighted, reverts to author. Ads: £20 per page & pro rata. ALP.

Tangent Books (see also TANGENT), Vivienne Finch, William Pryor, 58 Blakes Lane, New Malden, Surrey, England KT3 6NX, United Kingdom, 01-942-0979. 1974. Poetry, fiction, articles, art, photos, interviews, criticism, music, parts-of-novels, long-poems, collages, concrete art. "Tangent Books produce five publications a year, at least two of which are translations. Poetry collections already available are: THE MOONLIGHT SONATA by Yannis Ritsos, IN THE SLEEP-TRAP by Paul Snoek, STRANGERS IN AMBER by Yann Lovelock, illustrated front covers, printed in litho and/or letter-press. Usual trade discounts of 33⅓%. All mss must be accompanied by a stamped addressed envelope. Books published: *Mountain Poems* by Kate Ruse-Glason, *Background Music* by David Miller." avg. press run 1,000. Expects 4 titles 1980. 6 titles listed in the *Small Press Record of Books in Print* (9th Edition, 1980). avg. price, cloth: £1.50. Discounts: 33⅓% Trade, Independent booksellers, specialist small press shops 40%. 50pp; size A4; of. Reporting time: 1 month. Payment: Copies. Copyrights for author. ALP.

TAR RIVER POETRY, Peter Makuck, Department of English, East Carolina University, Greenville, NC 27834. 1960. Poetry, reviews. "Among recent featured contributors have been William Stafford, Susan Fromberg Schaeffer, A. Poulin, Jr., Frederick Morgan, Samuel Hago, Philip Dacey, A.R. Ammons, David Ignatow, Gary Miranda, Ralph Mills, Jr., Laurence Lieberman, Robert Phillips." circ. 1,000. 2/yr. sub. price: $4.00; per copy: $2.00; sample: $2.00. Back issues: $2.00. 56pp; 6X8¾; of. Reporting time: 6 to 8 weeks. Payment: Contributors copies. Rights reassigned to author upon request. Pub's reviews: 10 in 1979. §poetry. Ads: no ads.

THE TARAKAN MUSIC LETTER, Sheldon L. Tarakan, 25 W Dunes Lane, Port Washington, NY 11050, (516) 883-0941. 1979. Articles, reviews. "Discographical articles of 1,000 to 1,500 words. Newsletter is geared toward helping librarians in the development of phonograph record and tape collections. Articles are often of a retrospective nature, although current materials in the areas of classical music, jazz, popular music, show and movie music, etc., are also used." circ. 1,500. 5/yr. Pub'd 2 issues 1979; expects 5 issues 1980. sub. price: $22.50; per copy: $5.00; sample: free to libraries only. Back issues: $5.00 per issue. Discounts: 10% to jobber, 10% for bulk orders of 10 or more to same address. 8pp; 8½X11; of. Reporting time: within two weeks. Payment: copies. Copyrighted. Pub's reviews: 0 in 1979. §Books relating to phono records and audio tapes. Ads: rates upon request. COSMEP.

Taurean Horn Press (see also MINI-TAUR SERIES), 601 Leavenworth #45, San Francisco, CA 94109. 1974. Poetry. "Publications in print: *Honeydew*, an anthology; *Blind Annie's Cellar* by Paul Vane. MINI-TAUR SERIES. *Black Birds & Other Birds* by Mary Francis Claggett; *The Neighborhood* by Bernard Gershenson" avg. press run 500. Pub'd 1 title 1979; expects 1 title 1980, 1 title 1981. 5 titles listed in the *Small Press Record of Books in Print* (9th Edition, 1980). avg. price, paper: $4.00-$5.00. Discounts: 40% to book trade. 90pp; of. Reporting time: 1 week to 1 month (Have yet to accept unsolicited ms.). Payment: copies and/or other arrangements agreed upon prior to publication. Copyrights for author. WIP.

Taurus Press of Willow Dene, Paul Peter Piech, 2 Willow Dene, Bushey, Heath, Herts WD2 1PS, United Kingdom. 1959. Articles, poetry, art, satire, long-poems. Pub'd 3 titles 1979; expects 5 titles

1980, 5 titles 1981. 80 titles listed in the *Small Press Record of Books in Print* (9th Edition, 1980). avg. price, cloth: £5 to £50; paper: £1 to £4. Discounts: 25%. 24 to 48pp; †lp. Payment: 25 copies to author. Copyrights for author. ALP, BPS, LCPPP.

TAX NEWS, The Scribe Press, Fielding Greaves, 819 A Street, Suite 21, San Rafael, CA 94901, (415) 456-7910. 1977. Articles, cartoons, letters, news items. "Newsletter for local taxpayer organization: Marin United Taxpayers Association." circ. 5,000 +. 5 or 6. Pub'd 5 issues 1979; expects 5 issues 1980, 6 issues 1981. sub. price: $6.00; per copy: gratis; sample: SASE. Back issues: gratis - while they last. 4pp; 11X17; of. Payment: none. Not copyrighted. Ads: no ads.

TAXING & SPENDING, Institute for Contemporary Studies, A. Lawrence Chickering, Jane S. Caspari, 260 California Street, Suite 811, San Francisco, CA 94111, (415) 398-3010. 1978. Articles, cartoons, news items. "Articles on tax & expenditure limitations, local & national coverage. First issue authors include A. K. Campbell, Gordon Tullock, Jacob Atrin, Milton Friedman." circ. 2,000. 5/yr. Pub'd 4 issues 1979; expects 4 issues 1980, 4 issues 1981. sub. price: $15.00; per copy: $4.00. 96pp; 7X10; of. Reporting time: 1-3 months. Payment: an honorarium, $300-$500. Copyrighted, does not revert to author. Ads: $250 ($150 publishers)/$135 ($80 publishers). COSMEP.

TBW Books, Thea Wheelwright, Box 58, Day's Ferry Road, Woolwich, ME 04579, (207) 442-7632. 1978. "Non-fiction: Books on calligraphy and related subjects and books of historical interest to Maine readers." avg. press run 2,500-3,000. Pub'd 3 titles 1979; expects 5 titles 1980, 4 titles 1981. Discounts: Library 20%, schools 20%. The Bond Wheelwright Co., Freeport Me 04032 handles bookstore distribution/on titles that retail for $10 or less. of. Reporting time: about a month. Payment: 10% up to 15%. Arranged per title. Copyrights for author.

Teachers & Writers Collaborative (see also TEACHERS & WRITERS MAGAZINE), Miguel A. Ortiz, 84 Fifth Avenue (at 14th St.), New York, NY 10011, 212-691-6590. 1968. Articles, interviews, reviews. avg. press run 3,000. Pub'd 3 titles 1979; expects 2 titles 1980. 11 titles listed in the *Small Press Record of Books in Print* (9th Edition, 1980). avg. price, paper: $4.00. Discounts: none. 160pp; 6X9; of. Reporting time: one month. Payment: advance on royalty. Copyrights for author.

TEACHERS & WRITERS MAGAZINE, Teachers & Writers Collaborative, Miguel A. Ortiz, 84 Fifth Ave (at 14th St.), New York, NY 10011, 212-691-6590. 1967. Articles, interviews, letters. circ. 2,500. 3/yr. Pub'd 3 issues 1979; expects 3 issues 1980. sub. price: $5.00; per copy: $2.00; sample: $2.00. Back issues: $2.00 an issue. Discounts: none. 50pp; 8½X11; of. Reporting time: one month. Payment: $25.00-$50.00. Copyrighted, does not revert to author. Pub's reviews: 2 in 1979. §Education.

TEACHER UPDATE, Teacher Update, Inc., Nicholas A. Roes, Donna M. Papalia, Box 205, Saddle River, NJ 07458, (201) 327-8486. 1977. Articles, criticism, reviews, news items. "*Teacher Update* is a monthly newsletter for teachers — prek-3, as well as administrators, educators, etc. No paid space ads accepted. Inserts considered. Contact reader service dept. *TU* consists mostly of classroom ideas." circ. 5,500. 10/yr. Pub'd 10 issues 1979; expects 10 issues 1980, 10 issues 1981. sub. price: $12.00; per copy: $1.20; sample: $1.00. Back issues: $1.00 per single copy (discount schedule on request). Please contact us for discount info. 4-8pp; 8½X11; †of. Reporting time: 3 months. Payment: If accepted and in teacher update format. Copyrighted. Pub's reviews: 10 in 1979. §Early childhood education. COSMEP.

Teacher Update, Inc. (see also TEACHER UPDATE), Nicholas A. Roes, Donna M. Papalia, Box 205, Saddle River, NJ 07458, (201) 327-8486. 1977. Articles, criticism, reviews, news items. "We publish educational, consumer, and general interest books. Titles have been plugged on Nat'l (Network) TV, wire services, radio, etc. Only 5 titles chosen yearly but given well co-ordinated PR campaign." avg. press run 5,000. Pub'd 2 titles 1979; expects 3 titles 1980, 5 titles 1981. 5 titles listed in the *Small Press Record of Books in Print* (9th Edition, 1980). avg. price, cloth: $8.95; paper: $3.50. Discounts: 25%, library, classroom; 40%, bookstore. Special requests considered. 125pp; 5X7; of. Reporting time: 3 months. Payment: by arrangement. Copyrights for author. COSMEP.

Technical Documantation Services, Ed Foote, Ross Howell, Bill Kramer, Hi Gibson, Gibson Cookie, 56 S. Patterson, No. 108, Santa Barbara, CA 93111, (805) 976-7342. 1976. "The TDS books are strictly slanted to square dancers and include all levels of square dancing and round dancing (a part of square dancing). We publish our own materials and have not, as yet, contracted to publish any other author" avg. press run 1,000. Pub'd 2 titles 1979; expects 4 titles 1980, 1 title 1981. 5 titles listed in the *Small Press Record of Books in Print* (9th Edition, 1980). avg. price, paper: $5.95. Discounts: wholesale $4.00 (20 each, minimum); bulk $5.00 (15 minimum). 104pp; 4½X8; 8½X11; †of. Payment: 25¢ per copy sold. Copyrights for author. COSMEP.

Tejas Art Press, Robert Willson, 1000 Jackson-Keller Ro`d, Apt 274K, San Antonio, TX 78213, (512) 340-0285. 1979. "All of our books will be illustrated fully, by author or our staff. At present all books stay with the 100 page size, none smaller. Thus a poet must have that much material to submit. Our special interests are poetry and drama, with almost exclusive attention to Texas and the Southwest Indian. Present books under preparation: 1. Poetry by Catherine E. Whitmav. Illustrated, ink. 2. Translations of Aztec poetry, by John Cornyn. Illustrated. We use some small flat runs of color over line drawings." avg. press run 200. Pub'd 2 titles 1979. avg. price, paper: $3.85. Discounts: ask. 100pp; 7X8½; of. Reporting time: prompt, but write first. Payment: write. Copyrights for author. TC.

TELEPHONE, Telephone Books, Maureen Owen, Box 672, Old Chelsea Sta., New York City, NY 10011. 1969. Poetry, fiction, cartoons, letters, collages. "Britt Wilkie, Michael Flory, Janine Pomy Vega, Bob Dumont, Charlie Vermont, Ruth Krauss, Tony Towle, Susan Howe, David Moe, Richard Snyder, Erik Satie, Red Grooms, Carol Pierman, Joe Johnson, Maria Gitin, Peggy Garrison, Bruce Andrews, Joe Brainard." circ. 700. 2/yr. Expects 2 issues 1980. sub. price: $5.00-2 copies (All checks made out to: Maureen Owen); per copy: $2.00 (All checks made out to: Maureen Owen); sample: $2.00. Back issues: $10 per copy (most out of print). Discounts: none. 100pp; 8½X14; of. Reporting time: 1 month. Payment: none/copies. Copyrighted. Ads: none. CCLM, COSMEP, NESPA, WDG, BC.

Telephone Books (see also TELEPHONE), Maureen Owen, Box 672, Old Chelsea Sta, New York, NY 10011. Poetry, fiction. "In 1976 we'll publish books by Fanny Howe, Janine Pomy Vega, Yuki Hartman, Rebecca Wright. In 1978 I'll publish: *Delayed: Not Postponed* by Fielding Dawson; *Amtrak Trek* by Sotere Torregian; *The Secret History of the Dividing Line* by Susan Howe." avg. press run 750-1,000. Pub'd 3 titles 1979. 15 titles listed in the *Small Press Record of Books in Print* (9th Edition, 1980). avg. price, paper: $2.00 All cks made out to: Maureen Owen. 40pp; 5½X8½; of. Payment: In copies. Copyrights for author. CCLM, NESPA, COSMEP, WDG, BC.

TELOS, Telos Press, Paul Piccone, Sociology Dept, Washington Univ, St Louis, MO 63130, 314-889-6638. 1968. Articles, criticism, reviews. circ. 2,500. 4/yr. Pub'd 4 issues 1979; expects 4 issues 1980, 4 issues 1981. sub. price: $25.00; per copy: $6.00; sample: $6.00. Back issues: $6.00. Discounts: 30% bulk orders; 10% agent. 240pp; 6X9; of. Reporting time: 6 mos. Payment: none. Copyrighted. Pub's reviews: 40 books, 40 journals in 1979. §left-wing philosophy, lit. criticism, politics. Ads: $200.00/$125.00.

Telos Press (see also TELOS), Paul Piccone, C/O Sociology Dept, Washington Univ, St Louis, MO 63130, 314-889-6638. 1970. Articles, criticism, reviews. avg. press run 4,000. Expects 2 titles 1980, 2 titles 1981. 9 titles listed in the *Small Press Record of Books in Print* (9th Edition, 1980). avg. price, cloth: $7.00; paper: $3.00. Discounts: usual is 30%. Other can be arranged. 200pp; size varies; of. Reporting time: 6 months. Payment: no set policy. Copyrights for author.

TEMPEST: Avant-Garde Poetry, Earthwise Publications, Barbara Holley, PO Box 680-536, Miami, FL 33168, (305) 688-8558. 1979. Poetry, fiction, articles, art, cartoons, interviews, satire, criticism, reviews, long-poems, collages, concrete art, news items. "We also publish *Earthwise*: A Journal of Poetry (quarterly) and *Earthwise Newsletter,* bi-monthly. Current issue includes Larry Rubin, Lyn Lifshin, interview of Laurel Speer, (M.K. Biggs) and Aaron Kramer, others. Editor's home address is: 1571 N.W. 133 Street, Miami, FL 33167. Tel. 305-688-8558." circ. 300. 2/yr. Expects 2 issues 1980. sub. price: $6.00; per copy: $3.00 + postage; sample: $2.00. Back issues: $2.00. Discounts: $1.50 per lots of over 20 or consignment (write first). 40-60pp; 5½X8½; of. Reporting time: 3 months. Payment: $2.00 for a poem, slightly more for articles, woodcuts, stories, or interviews. $2.00 for b&w sketches. Copyrighted, reverts to author. Pub's reviews. §Poetry, ecology, news items of peoples of the earth. Ads: $10.00/$5.00/$0.10. COSMEP, CODA.

Ten Crow Press (see also SPOOR), Edward Cain, Star Rt Box 663A, Aberdeen, WA 98520, 206 648-2493. 1979-80. Poetry, long-poems. avg. press run 300. Pub'd 4 titles 1979. avg. price, paper: $5.00. Discounts: 30%. 50pp; size varies; †of/lp. Reporting time: 2 months. Payment: varies. Copyrights for author.

Ten Mile River Press, Duane BigEagle, William Bradd, 32000 North Highway One, Fort Bragg, CA 95437, (707) 964-5579. 1979. Poetry, fiction. "Submission of material is by invitation only." avg. press run 500. Pub'd 3 titles 1979; expects 15-22 titles 1980. avg. price, paper: $3.50. Discounts: 40% Trade. 35pp; 5½X8½; †of. Reporting time: submission by invitation only. Payment: 10% of run. Copyrights for author.

Ten Penny Players, Inc., Barbara Fisher, 799 Greenwich Street, New York, NY 10014, 212-929-3169. 1975. Poetry, fiction, plays. "Age range 3-12 years. Varying lengths: 8 pp - 34 pp. At present doing a series of read aloud and playscripts, fully illustrated by B Fisher and chapbooks of child poets/artists. We stress an integration of language and picture so that the material can be used either as a book to read or a book to perform." avg. press run 200 copies. Pub'd 2 titles 1979; expects 5 titles 1980, 5 titles 1981. 8 titles listed in the *Small Press Record of Books in Print* (9th Edition, 1980). avg. price, paper: $2.50. Discounts: Standard 60/40. 34pp; 4½X6; †of/lp. No unsolicited manuscripts please. Payment: Negotiable. Copyrights for author. NYSSPA, COSMEP, COSMEP EAST, WP.

Ten Speed Press, Philip Wood, Jackie Wan, George Young, PO Box 7123, Berkeley, CA 94707. 1971. Art, photos, cartoons, satire, letters. "We publish trade books" avg. press run 25,000. Pub'd 8 titles 1979; expects 8 titles 1980, 8 titles 1981. avg. price, cloth: $9.95; paper: $4.95. Discounts: usual trade: 40% to 50%. 200pp; 6X9; of. Reporting time: 2 weeks. Payment: 10% of list price. Copyrights for author.

Tendon Press (see also NORTH STONE REVIEW), Univ Sta. Box 14098, Minneapolis, MN 55414. 1 title listed in the *Small Press Record of Books in Print* (9th Edition, 1980).

TENDRIL, Moira Linehan, George Murphy, Chuck Ozug, Box 512, Green Harbor, MA 02041, 617-834-4137. 1977. Poetry, art. "Occasional graphics. Biases, poetry that is 'concise, imagistic, and evocative'. Recent contributors: A.R. Ammons, Joan Colby, Stephen Dobyns, M.R. Doty, Alan Feldman, Don Johnson, Denise Levertov, William Matthews, Carole Oles, Marge Piercy, Marieve Rugo, Dave Smith, William Stafford, Dabney Stuart, Judith Steinbergh, John Unterecker, Cary Waterman." circ. 750. 3/yr. Pub'd 3 issues 1979; expects 3 issues 1980, 3 issues 1981. sub. price: $6.00 individual/$8.00 institutional; per copy: $3.00; sample: $3.00. Discounts: negotiable. 120pp; 5½X8½; of. Reporting time: 4-12 weeks. Payment: If budget allows, otherwise, copies. Copyrighted, reverts to author. Ads: $40.00/$25.00/$15.00/$10.00. CCLM, NESPA.

TENNYSON RESEARCH BULLETIN, Tennyson Society Publications Board, Tennyson Research Centre, Central Library, Free School Lane, Lincoln LN2 1EZ, United Kingdom. 1967. Articles, criticism, letters. "Subs ($9.50 personal; $26.00 institutional) includes all publications issued in the year. Includes all notes and queries relating to *TENNYSON* and select articles up to 5,000 words. A cumulative index covering 1967 to 71 (Vol. 1) and 1972-76 (Vol. 2) has now been issued and is available free." circ. 500. 1/yr. 16 titles listed in the *Small Press Record of Books in Print* (9th Edition, 1980). sub. price: with membership. Back issues: Back numbers only 1967-73 $2.40; 1974-5 $3.60. Discounts: 25% trade. 21.5X13.7cm; lp. Reporting time: 1 month. Payment: nil. Copyrighted. §life & work of Tennyson. no ads.

Tenth House Enterprises, Inc., Hannelore Hahn, Tatiana Stoumen, PO Box 810, Gracie Station, New York, NY 10028, (212) 737-7536.

The Tenth Muse, Julia Jaeger, Box 1417, Pacifica, CA 94044, 993-5290.

Terra, Robert E. M.D. Arnold, PO Box 99103, Jeffersontown, KY 40299, (502) 239-5362. 1978. "Non-fiction." Expects 1 title 1980. 1 title listed in the *Small Press Record of Books in Print* (9th Edition, 1980).

Territorial Press (see also DACOTAH TERRITORY), P O Box 775, Moorhead, MN 56560. 2 titles listed in the *Small Press Record of Books in Print* (9th Edition, 1980).

Testamento Di Intenzionalita Di Alberto Faietti, Alberto Faietti, via Alghero, 8, Roma 00182, Italy, 06 779088. Poetry, long-poems. "Lire 10,000 (diecimila) or $12.00" avg. press run 1,000. Pub'd 1 title 1979. 8 titles listed in the *Small Press Record of Books in Print* (9th Edition, 1980). Discounts: 50%. 300pp; 6X8; †of. Copyrights for author.

Texas Center for Writers Press, James P. White, PO Box 19876, Dallas, TX 75219, 213-393-2413. 1974. Poetry, fiction. avg. press run 500-1,000. Pub'd 2 titles 1979; expects 3 titles 1980, 5 titles 1981. avg. price, cloth: $10.00; paper: $5.00. Discounts: Wholesalers 20%; Retailers 40%. Copyrights for author.

Texas Christian University Press (see DESCANT)

‡**TEXAS QUARTERLY,** Thomas M. Cranfill, Editor; Miguel Gonzales-Gerth, Editor, Box 7517 University Stn., Austin, TX 78712. 1958. Poetry, fiction, art, articles. "Interested in essays in the arts, humanities and social sciences, graphic art reproductions, poetry and prose fiction" circ. 1500. 4/yr. Pub'd 4 issues 1979; expects 4 issues 1980, 4 issues 1981. sub. price: $10.00/individual; $15.00/institution; per copy: $4.00. 160pp; 9½X6¾; †lp/of. Reporting time: 3 weeks. Payment: 2 copies, 50 reprints of articles only. Copyrighted, does not revert to author. Pub's reviews: 4 in 1979. §arts, humanities, social sciences, poetry, prose fiction. Ads: $100/$60.

THE TEXAS REVIEW, Paul Ruffin, English Department, Sam Houston State University, Huntsville, TX 77340. 1976. Poetry, fiction, articles, photos, interviews, reviews. "Because of the size of our magazine, we do not encourage the submission of long poems or exceptionally long short stories. We'll probably expand soon to incorporate photography, critical essays on literature and culture, etc." circ. 500 to 750. 2/yr. Pub'd 2 issues 1979; expects 2 issues 1980. sub. price: $3.00; per copy: $1.50; sample: $1.00. Back issues: $1.50. 148pp; 6X9; of. Reporting time: 4 weeks. Payment: copies, subscription (1 year). Copyrighted, reassigned to author upon request. Pub's reviews: 16 in 1979. §Poetry, fiction,. no advertising. COSMEP, CCLM.

THALIA: Studies in Literary Humor, Jacqueline Tavernier-Courbin, Dept of English, Univ of Ottawa, Ottawa KN1 6N5, Canada, (613) 231-5955. 1978. Articles, criticism, reviews, cartoons, interviews. circ. 500. 2/yr. Pub'd 3 issues 1979; expects 2 issues 1980, 2 issues 1981. sub. price: $12.00; per copy: $6.00; sample: $4.00. Back issues: $12.00 for Volume I and $12.00 for Volume II. Discounts: by direct query only. 75pp; 8½X11; lp. Reporting time: varies with ms content. Payment: none. Copyrighted. Pub's reviews: 2 in 1979. §any area connected to humor. Ads: none.

That New Publishing Company, Welmon WalkerJr, Phillip E. Walker, Sr. Editor, 1525 Eielson St, Fairbanks, AK 99701, 907-452-3007. 1976. Photos. "At this time we will only consider nonfiction; it may be of any type. We are particularly interested in money saving information works of any length and books on Alaska." avg. press run 3,000. Pub'd 3 titles 1979; expects 4 titles 1980, 5 titles 1981. 2 titles listed in the *Small Press Record of Books in Print* (9th Edition, 1980). avg. price, cloth: varies; paper: varies; other: varies. Discounts: 40% retail, 50% wholesale. pp varies; 5½X8½ and 8½X11; of. Reporting time: 6 to 8 weeks. Payment: Standard royalties are paid to author twice a year. Copyrights for author. COSMEP.

THEATER, Joel Schechter, Editor, 222 York Street, New Haven, CT 06520, (203) 436-1417. 1968. Articles, interviews, criticism, reviews, letters, plays. "*Theater* is concerned with contemporary activity in the world of theater, publishing essays, articles, reviews of recent performances around the country, new plays, interviews with practicing professionals. Recent issues have been devoted to Literary Managers, Artaud, Contemporary American playwrights, Ingmar Bergman. Recent contributors have included Jacques Derrida, Andrei Serban, Robert Brustein, Martin Esslin, Robert Lowell, Sam Shepard, and more." circ. 2,300. 3/yr. Pub'd 3 issues 1979; expects 3 issues 1980, 3 issues 1981. sub. price: $9.00 Individuals, $10.00 Libraries; per copy: $3.50; sample: $3.50. Back issues: Bulk discounts Discounts: Agents: 25%; Bookstores: 3-40%; Bulk: 10-15% (back issues only). 112pp; 9½X9½; of. Reporting time: 8 weeks. Payment: $25.00-$40.00. Copyrighted, does not revert to author. Pub's reviews: 5 in 1979. §New books on theater, new plays. Ads: $200.00/$150.00. COSMEP.

THEATRE, Ira J. Bilowit, Debbi Wasserman, 55 West 42nd Street #1218, New York, NY 10036, (212) 221-6078. 1977. Articles, art, photos, interviews, criticism, reviews, plays. "Query first, with SASE. Send xerox of writing samples." circ. 10M. 8/yr. Pub'd 3 issues 1979; expects 10 issues 1980, 7 issues 1981. sub. price: $12.00; sample: $2.00. Discounts: on application. 52-64pp; 8X11; of. Reporting time: queries answered promptly. Payment: $10.00-$200.00. Copyrighted, does not revert to author. Pub's reviews: 12-15 in 1979. §Theatre and performing arts. Ads: $795.00/$500.00. COSMEP.

THEATRE DESIGN AND TECHNOLOGY, U.S. Institute for Theatre Technology, Inc., Arnold Aronson, Kate Davy, Kate Davy, Managing Editor & Advertising Director; Jarad Saltzman, Herb Greggs, Ann Wells, Fred M. Wolff, Associate Editors, 1024 Holmes Avenue, Charlottesville, VA 22901, 804-295-7990. 1965. Articles, photos, interviews, reviews, letters, news items. "*Scope* of the *Journal* includes the range of interests set forth in the Institute's statement of policy: 'The Institute's first concern is the physical aspects of the theatre, as its architecture, engineering, administration, and the basic conditions of presentation. All these phases stand obviously at the service of the final fruition in the theatre, the presentation itself, where the skills of actor and playwright and director are the most conspicuous, aided by all the intricate collaboration of the stage through services of the designer, costumer, lighting designer and the various technicians.' Articles will reflect the opinion of the stated author in every case: except for officially designated Institute notices, opinions stated do not necessarily constitute sentiment of the Institute or recommended practice. Opinionated statements which tend to stimulate serious thought and thus further the art of the theatre are always to be encouraged." circ. 3,100. 4/yr. Pub'd 4 issues 1979; expects 4 issues 1980, 4 issues 1981. sub. price: $12.00-libraries only; per copy: $3.50; sample: $3.50. Back issues: $3.50. Discounts: 10% for annual contract. 40pp; 8¼X11; of. Reporting time: 6 weeks. Payment: none. Copyrighted, held by magazine after publication unless author wishes separate copyright. Pub's reviews: 15 in 1979. §books only, scenography, theatre production, engineering, architecture. Ads: $250/$150. COSMEP.

THEATRE NOTEBOOK, W.A. Armstrong, Editor; Michael Boolt, Editor; George Speaight, Manager, 103 Ralph Court, Queensway, London W2 5HU, United Kingdom. 1945. Articles, photos, reviews. "Scholarly articles on British theatre history & technique. Articles up to 5000 words. Notes

& queries on subject. Free to members of Society for Theatre Research." circ. 1,250. 3/yr. Pub'd 3 issues 1979; expects 3 issues 1980, 3 issues 1981. sub. price: £5; per copy: £2. Back issues: £2.50. Discounts: 10% agent. 48pp; 8½X5½; of. Reporting time: 4-6 wks. Payment: none. Copyrighted. Pub's reviews: 20 in 1979. §Books on British Theatre History. Ads: £40/£24/£18 1/4.

THEOLOGIA 21, Dominion Press, A. Stuart Otto, Editor, PO Box 37, San Marcos, CA 92069, (714) 746-9430. 1970. Articles, reviews, letters. circ. 500. 4/yr. Pub'd 4 issues 1979. sub. price: $5.00; per copy: $1.50; sample: free. Back issues: 1976-79 complete, bound $21.00. Discounts: 30% to dealers, agencies. 4pp; 8½X11; of. No ms. accepted. Pub's reviews: 1 in 1979. §Theology (Christian).

THICKET, John Yearwood, PO Box 386, Woodville, TX 75979, 713-283-2516. 1976. Poetry, fiction, photos, interviews, reviews. "Non-profit corporation, behind on publication for lack of facilities. Operations now to be subsumed and fostered by Woodsman Publishing Co., Inc., of Wyoming. J. Yearwood is president and publisher. Bright re-vitalized future certain." circ. 1,000. 3/yr. Pub'd 1 issue 1979; expects 3 issues 1980, 3 issues 1981. sub. price: $7.50; per copy: $2.50; sample: $2.50. Back issues: $2.50. Discounts: 40%. 96pp; 6X9; †of. Reporting time: 2 week to 1 month. Copyrighted. Pub's reviews: 5 in 1979. §Poetry, lit crit (poetry), short fiction. Ads: $120.00/$60.00/$0.25.

Third Coast, Linda Fry Kenzle, D. C. Kenzle, c/o International, 146 Broad Street, Lake Geneva, WI 53147. 1976. Poetry, fiction, articles, art, photos, cartoons, interviews, satire, reviews, music, parts-of-novels, long-poems, collages, plays, concrete art. "We are interested in *experimental* work, like offbeat multi-medium work as appeared in *Gathering: A Free Will Anthology* and head-turning poetry as in *Confessions of a No-Good Bum* and *Prism*. Our underground comix work is limited to the new wave style." avg. press run 500. Pub'd 10 titles 1979; expects 3 titles 1980, 5 titles 1981. avg. price, paper: $2.50. Discounts: Bulk rates on request. 35pp; 5½X8½; †of. Reporting time: As soon as we can. Payment: contributor copies. Copyrights for author.

THIRD COAST ARCHIVES, Moonfire Press, Eddee Daniel, Lynn Kapitan, 3061 N Newhall Street, Milwaukee, WI 53211, 414 964-0173. 1976. Poetry, fiction, art, long-poems, concrete art, photos, cartoons. "Our goal is to present contemporary poetry, including haiku, in a creative format through the use of illustration and graphic design." circ. 200-500. Quarterly (with a year-end double issue). sub. price: $5.00; per copy: $1.00 plus 25¢ postage and handling per issue number; sample: $1.00 plus 25¢ postage and handling per issue number. Back issues: Numbers 1,2,3 are $5.00 each; all others are $1.00 per number. Discounts: 40 percent plus postage on 5 copies or more. 32-70pp; 8½X5½; of. Reporting time: usually 2 to 8 weeks. Payment: copy. Copyrighted, reverts to author.

THIRD EYE, P.T. Lally, William Cannon, 189 Kelvin Drive, Buffalo, NY 14223, 716 832-4097. 1976. Poetry, long-poems. "Well-written free verse that transcends personal experiences. Would like to see poets with a logical pattern with punctuation that does not defy all sense of reason. Please: no Jesus poems, or dots in the shape of birdies that are supposed to be concrete poems. Just stick to basics and try and there will be a place for you here." circ. 500. 2/yr. Pub'd 3 issues 1979; expects 2 issues 1980, 2 issues 1981. sub. price: $2.50; per copy: $1.25; sample: $1.00. Back issues: $1. Discounts: None. 48pp; 8½X6¾; of. Reporting time: 3 weeks. Payment: Three copies, small cash payment when possible. Copyrighted, reverts to author. no ads.

THE THIRD PRESS REVIEW, Joseph Okpaku, 1995 Broadway, New York, NY 10023, (212) 724-9505. 1975. Articles, interviews, reviews. "Leopold Sedar Senghor, Wole Soyinka, Sol Gordon, Ph. D., Richard Kostelanetz." 6/yr. Pub'd 6 issues 1979. sub. price: $9.00; per copy: $2.00. Back issues: $3.00. 70pp; 8½X11; of. Reporting time: two months. Payment: Nominal. Copyrighted, reverts to author. Pub's reviews. §African Studies/Black writings. Ads: Upon request.

THIRD WORLD, Third World Journalists/Periodistas del Tercer Mundo, Neiva Moreira, Editor-in-Chief; Fernando Molina, Editor; Cedric Belfrage, Consulting Editor, Apartado 20-572, Mexico City, D.F. 20, Mexico, 559-30-13. 1979. Articles, photos, cartoons, interviews, news items, letters. "'A magazine on the Third World made by Third World journalists.' The English edition of *Cuadernos del Tercer Mundo,* an international magazine published in three languages (Spanish, Portuguese and English) by an independent, nonprofit association of militant professional journalists from over 40 countries. It basically aims to provide alternative information on the Third World, promote awareness on the causes of underdevelopment and the means to overcome it, and support cooperation among progressive sectors throughout the world." circ. 6,000. 6/yr. Pub'd 3 issues 1979; expects 6 issues 1980, 12 issues 1981. sub. price: $20.00 for 12 issues, $12.00 for 6 issues (prices apply throughout the world including air mail); per copy: $2.00; sample: free upon request. Back issues: $3.00 (prices apply throughout the world, including air mail). Discounts: 40%. 80pp; 6½X9; of. Reporting time: 3-4 weeks. Payment: occasional. Copyrighted. Ads: $800.00/$400.00.

Third World Journalists/Periodistas del Tercer Mundo (see THIRD WORLD)

Third World Press, Haki R. Madhubuti, 7524 So. Cottage Grove Ave., Chicago, IL 60619, (312) 651-0700. 1967. "Non-fiction, history, culture, politics, children's books." avg. press run 5,000. Pub'd 10 titles 1979; expects 9 titles 1980, 9 titles 1981. avg. price, cloth: $10.00; paper: $4.00. Discounts: trade 40% - 50%. 210pp; of/lp. Reporting time: 3 months. Payment: Regular Book Contest. 10% paid every 6 months. Copyrights for author.

Third World Publications Ltd., 151 Stratford Road, Birmingham B111RD, United Kingdom, 021-773-6572. 1972. "UK agents for Tanzania Publishing House & distributors for the East African Publishing House, & progressive South African publishers, and most UK organisations campaigning on Third World issues." avg. price, cloth: £4.00; paper: 20p to £7.50. Discounts: Trade: 33⅓ percent. Bulk: 10 percent (over £20.00 value) larger discounts negotiable on big orders.

Thirteenth House, Bill Koehnlein, PO Box 362, Huntington Station, NY 11746. 1979. "Mostly reprints; no unsolicited mss" avg. press run 1,000. Pub'd 1 title 1979. avg. price, paper: $3.50. of.

13th MOON, Ellen Marie Bissert, Editor, 13th Moon, Inc., Drawer F, Inwood Station, New York, NY 10034, 212-569-7614. 1973. Poetry, fiction, articles, art, photos, interviews, criticism, reviews, letters, parts-of-novels, long-poems, collages, plays, concrete art, news items. "*13th Moon* is a literary magazine publishing quality work by women. Eclectic, but particularly interested in feminist and lesbian work. Issues include work by Adrienne Rich, Marge Piercy, Audre Lorde, Alix Kates Shulman and Olga Bromas as well as visual poetry by Amelia Etlinger and Mirella Bentivoglio. Current issues also contain a critical article on Monique Wittig's *Les Guerilleres* by Marcelle Thiebaux and a comprehensive overview of Colonial Women Poets by Pattie Cowell. Open." circ. 4,000. 2/yr. Pub'd 2 issues 1979; expects 2 issues 1980. 1 title listed in the *Small Press Record of Books in Print* (9th Edition, 1980). sub. price: $6.00/for 3 issues; per copy: current issue: $2.25; sample: $2.25 plus 50¢ postage. Write for back issue information. Discounts: the usual 40% discount on orders of 5 or more. 108pp; 6X9; of. Reporting time: 2 weeks to 4 months. Payment: copies. Copyrighted, reverts to author. Pub's reviews: 15 in 1979. §Small press books by women/literature by women/women's literary history by women. Ads: $50/$30. CCLM, NESPA.

Thirty Press, Ltd. (see also CRUSADE), John Caron, Editor-in-Chief, 19 Draycott Place, London SW3, UK. 1955. Articles, photos, interviews, reviews, letters, news items. Pub'd 2 titles 1979.

THIS, This Press, Barrett Watten, 1004 Hampshire Street, San Francisco, CA 94110. 1971. Poetry, fiction, interviews, long-poems. "Recent contributors: Clark Coolidge, Bob Perelman, Lyn Hejinian, Robert Grenier, Ron Silliman, Alan Davies, Bernadette Mayer, Bruce Andrews, Ted Greenwald, Kit Robinson." circ. 450. annual. Pub'd 1 issue 1979; expects 1 issue 1980, 1 issue 1981. price per copy: $2.50; sample: $2.50. Back issues: 2: $7.50, 3: $5.00, 4-6: $3.00, 7-8: $2.00, 1: negotiable. 80-96pp; 7X8½; of.

THIS AND THAT, Victoria Andreyeva, Box 86, 527 Riverside Drive, New York, NY 10027, (212) 866-2200. 1980. Poetry, fiction, art. "Additional address: *Gnosis,* Earl Hall Center, Columbia University, New York, NY 10027. Bilingual magazine in English and Russian for children from ages 6 to 12. One of its main purposes is to help the children of recent Russian emigrees adjust to the American Culture by teaching american poetry, history, art, etc while at the same time including Russian poems, stories so that not a complete loss of their culture occurs. Includes tongue-twisters, sections on learning the Russian and American alphabet, poetry submitted by children and facing tranlations of material wherever possible. This magazine is also addressed to American children who wish to learn about Russian childrens world of learning." circ. 1,000. quarterly. Pub'd 1 issue 1979. price per copy: $1.00 plus postage; sample: $1.00 plus postage. 30pp; 8½X11; of. Payment: $20.00 for submissions, $25.00 translation. Ads: on an exchange basis/half page.

THIS MAGAZINE, Lorraine Filyer, Managing Editor, 70 The Esplanade, Third Floor, Toronto, Ontario M5E 1R2, Canada, 364-2431. 1966. Poetry, fiction, articles, art, photos, cartoons, interviews, criticism, reviews, letters. "2,000-3,000 words. Socialist with a Canadian viewpoint." circ. 7,000. 6/yr. Pub'd 6 issues 1979; expects 6 issues 1980, 6 issues 1981. sub. price: $7.50 U.S.; $6.50 CDN; per copy: $1.25; sample: $1.00. Back issues: $2.00. Discounts: 10% to agencies. 48pp; 8¼X11⅜; of. Reporting time: 6 weeks. Payment: $25.00 to freelance writers. Copyrighted, reverts to author. Pub's reviews: 6 in 1979. §Labour, education, politics. Ads: $300.00/$185.00/$25.00. CPPA.

This Press (see also THIS), Barrett Watten, 1636 Ocean View Ave., Kensington, CA 94707. 1974. Poetry, fiction, long-poems. "Titles: *The Maintains* by Clark Coolidge, 104 pp, $3.00; *The Dolch Stanzas* by Kit Robinson, 32 pp, $1.00; *Decay* by Barrett Watten, 32 pp, $1.00. 1978: *You Bet!* by Ted Greenwald, 80 pp, $2.50; *Quartz Hearts* by Clark Coolidge, 64 pp, $2.00; *Series* by Robert Grenier, 144 pp, $4.00; *Ketjak* by Ron Silliman, 96 pp, $3.50. Distributed through SBD (Small Press Distribution) at above address. *Country; Harbor; Quiet; Act; Around;* by Larry Eigner. Selected prose. 160 pp., $4.00

paper, $10.00 cloth." avg. press run 300-1,000. Pub'd 2 titles 1979; expects 5-6 titles 1980. 7 titles listed in the *Small Press Record of Books in Print* (9th Edition, 1980). of.

THISTLE: A MAGAZINE OF CONTEMPORARY WRITING, Rook Press, Inc., Ernest Stefanik, Cis Stefanik, PO Box 144, Ruffsdale, PA 15679. 1976. Poetry, fiction, articles, interviews, criticism. *"Thistle* publishes poems, short fiction *by poets,* criticism on contemporary writers, essays, and interviews. Numbers scheduled for publication in 1978 include a special issue guest edited by William Heyen containing critical article on David Ignatow, William Stafford, and Lucien Stryk, and a special issue on Raymond Roseliep guest edited by Vincent Heinrichs." circ. 250. 3/yr. Pub'd 3 issues 1979; expects 3 issues 1980, 3 issues 1981. sub. price: $6.00; per copy: $2.00; sample: $2.00. Discounts: 10% to agencies; not sold in bookstores. 40pp; 14X21.5; of. Reporting time: 4-8 weeks. Payment: 2 copies. Copyrighted, reverts to author.

Thistledown Press, Glen Sorestad, Sonia Sorestad, Neil Wagner, Susan Wagner, 668 East Place, Saskatoon, Saskatchewan S7J2Z5, Canada, 374-1730. 1975. Poetry, art. avg. press run 1,000 copies. Pub'd 5 titles 1979; expects 5 titles 1980, 5 titles 1981. 9 titles listed in the *Small Press Record of Books in Print* (9th Edition, 1980). avg. price, cloth: $12.00; paper: $5.00. Discounts: bookstore/jobber: 5 or more 40 percent. 70pp; 7X8½; of. Reporting time: 1 month-6 weeks. Payment: 10 books plus 10 percent net profit. Copyrights for author. Assoc of Canadian Publishers, Literary Press Group.

THOMAS HARDY YEARBOOK, Toucan, G Stevens-Cox, Mt Durand, St Peter Port, Guernsey CI, United Kingdom. 1970. Articles, poetry, photos, news items, interviews, criticism, letters. "1,000-3,000 words" circ. 1,500-3,000. 1/yr. Pub'd 1 issue 1979; expects 1 issue 1980. sub. price: £3.00; per copy: £3.00; sample: £3.00. Back issues: £5.00. 100pp; size Qto; lp. Reporting time: 1 month. Payment: by arrangement. Pub's reviews. Ads: £30.

THOREAU JOURNAL QUARTERLY, Marie Olesen Urbanski, Editor; Nancy MacKnight, Poetry Editor; Wade Van Dore, Poetry Editor; Kathryn Allen, Assistant Editor; Margaret Whalen, Assistant Editoru, 304 English-Math Bldg, English Dept., Univ. of Maine, Orono, ME 04473, 207-581-7307. 1968. Poetry, articles, criticism, reviews, plays, news items. "Primarily a literary journal, concerned with Thoreau's writing, as well as his ideas. Material about other members of the transcendental circle also considered. Recent articles: Sam B. Girgus, *The Mechanical Mind: Thoreau and McLuhan;* Fred Durden, *Thoreau and Frost.* Elizabeth Hanson, *The Indian Metaphor in Thoreau's A Week."* circ. 500. 4/yr. Pub'd 4 issues 1979; expects 4 issues 1980. sub. price: $5.00 indiv, $6.00 libr, $7.00 overseas; per copy: $1.25; sample: $1.25. Back issues: $6.00 per year. 30pp; 6X9; of. varies. Payment: copies only. Copyrighted. Pub's reviews: 8-10 in 1979. §Thoreau.

THE THOREAU SOCIETY BULLETIN, Walter Harding, The Thoreau Society, Inc., SUNY, Geneseo, NY 14454, (716) 245-5513. 1941. Articles, reviews, letters, news items. "Ideally 500-1,000 words. Edwin Way Teals, B.F. Skinner, Loren Eiseley." circ. 1,200. 4/yr. Pub'd 4 issues 1979; expects 4 issues 1980, 4 issues 1981. 2 titles listed in the *Small Press Record of Books in Print* (9th Edition, 1980). sub. price: $3.00; per copy: $0.50; sample: free. Back issues: $0.50. 8pp; 8½X11; of. Reporting time: 1 month. Payment: none. Pub's reviews: 15-20 in 1979. §Anything by or about Henry David Thoreau. Ads: No ads.

Thorp Springs Press (see also HYPERION A Poetry Journal), Paul Foreman, Foster Robertson, 803 Red River, Austin, TX 78701. 1971. Poetry, fiction, plays. avg. press run 1,000. Pub'd 10-12 titles 1979. 41 titles listed in the *Small Press Record of Books in Print* (9th Edition, 1980). avg. price, cloth: $7.50 - $8.00; paper: $3.00; other: pamphlet $1.00. Discounts: Bkst/40 percent returns in saleable condition if in 6 months; jobbers/10 percent 1-10 copies / 20 percent 11-50 copies. 90pp; 8½X5½; of. Reporting time: Up to 1 year. Copyrights for author. COSMEP-SOUTH, COSMEP, Texas Circuit.

‡THREE CENT PULP, Pulp Press, Pulp Press Ed. Board, Box 3868 M.P.O., Vancouver V6B 3Z3, Canada. 1972. Poetry, fiction, articles, art, photos, cartoons, interviews, satire, criticism, reviews, letters, parts-of-novels, concrete art. "New poetry, fiction, drama, art, and occasional political and literary essays. Has published over 175 authors and artists from 4 continents. Entirely supported by subscribers." circ. 1,100. 24/yr. Pub'd 24 issues 1979; expects 24 issues 1980. sub. price: $10.00 (24 issues); per copy: $0.03; sample: free. Back issues: complete volumes only $25 ea (scarce). Discounts: 100 percent to bookstores. 4pp; 5½X8½; †of. Reporting time: 1 month. Payment: copies. Copyrighted, reverts to author. §literary/political. CPPA.

Three Continents Press, Donald Herdeck, Editor, 1346 Connecticut Ave. N.W., Suite 1131, Washington, DC 20036, 202-457-0287; 457-0288. 1973. Poetry, fiction, criticism. avg. press run 2,000. Expects 10 titles 1981. 18 titles listed in the *Small Press Record of Books in Print* (9th Edition, 1980). avg. price, cloth: $15.00; paper: $6.00. Discounts: 20% (30 days payable) to discount houses and bookstores on small orders (up to $50.00); 30% on pre-pd for discount houses & bookstores. Individual orders must be pre-paid. 250pp; 5½X8½, 6X9; lp/of. Reporting time: 120 days. Payment: 10%, figured semi-annually on actual sales; modest advances. copyrights for author at author's expense. COSMEP.

Three Mountains Press, Denis Carbonneau, P.O. Box 50, Cooper Station, New York, NY 10003, 212-989-2737. 1975. Articles, interviews, news items. "Also publish books about books, books on book collecting, bibliography" avg. press run 500. Pub'd 1 title 1979. 2 titles listed in the *Small Press Record of Books in Print* (9th Edition, 1980). Discounts: 1-10 20%, 11-20 33%, 21+ 40%. of. Reporting time: within 4 weeks. Payment: by arrangement. Copyrights for author.

THREE RIVERS POETRY JOURNAL, Three Rivers Press, Gerald Costanzo, P.O. Box 21, Carnegie-Mellon University, Pittsburgh, PA 15213. 1972. Poetry, articles, reviews. "Recent contributors include Dave Smith, Charles Wright, Vern Rutsala, Jay Meek, Gerald Stern, Linda Pastan, Stanley Plumly, Leonard Nathan, Paula Rankin, and Patricia Goedicke. We continue to publish work in each issue by new writers. We are able to read manuscripts only between September 1 and April 30. We do not wish to receive xerox copies of poems, nor are we able to accept submissions bearing postage due. Reviews are by invitation only, from previous contributors." circ. 1,000. 2/yr. Pub'd 2 issues 1979; expects 2 issues 1980. sub. price: $5.00/4 issues; per copy: $1.50; sample: $1.50. Back issues: available only through Xerox University Microfilms. Discounts: 40% on five or more copies. 60pp; 8½X5½; of. Reporting time: 2 weeks-2 mos. Payment: copies. Copyrighted, reverts to author. Pub's reviews: 20 in 1979. §Poetry/poetics. Ads: exchange ads only. CCLM.

Three Rivers Press (see also THREE RIVERS POETRY JOURNAL), PO Box 21, Carnegie-Mellon University, Pittsburgh, PA 15213. "We do not presently contemplate publishing books under his imprint in 1980-81." of.

THREE SISTERS, Kevin McNamara, Box 969, Georgetown University, Washington, DC 20067, (202) 625-4172. 1971. Poetry, fiction, articles, art, photos, criticism, reviews, parts-of-novels, long-poems, plays. "Concerning copyright: authors may receive written permission of the editor if they wish to reproduce their work elsewhere after it has been printed in *Three Sisters.*" circ. 2,500. 2/yr. Pub'd 3 issues 1979; expects 3 issues 1980, 2 issues 1981. sub. price: $3.50; per copy: $2.00; sample: $2.00. Back issues: $2/issue. Discounts: 30%. 58pp; 6X9; of. Reporting time: 4-6 weeks. Payment: copies. Copyrighted, does not revert to author. Pub's reviews: 10 in 1979. §Literature.

THE THREEPENNY REVIEW, Wendy Lesser, Editor; Thom Gunn, Consulting Editor; Al Young, Consulting Editor, PO Box 335, Berkeley, CA 94701, (415) 849-4545. 1979. Poetry, fiction, art, interviews, criticism, reviews. "Length of material: Reviews should be 1,000-3,000 words, covering several books or an author in depth, or dealing with a whole topic (e.g., the current theater season in one city, or the state of jazz clubs in another). Fiction should be under 8,000 words; poems should be under 40 lines. Special features: Though primarily a literary and performing arts review, *The Threepenny Review* will contain at least one essay on a topic of current social or political concern in each issue. Interested essayists should first submit a letter of inquiry. Recent Contributors: Millicent Dillon, Thom Gunn, Julius Novick. *SASE must accompany all manuscripts.*" circ. 10,000. 4/yr. Pub'd 4 issues 1979. sub. price: $4.00; per copy: $1.00. 32pp; 11X17; of. Reporting time: two weeks to three months. Payment: none, except free subscriptions. Copyrighted, reverts to author. Pub's reviews. §Fiction, poetry, essays, philosophy, urban planning, sociology, social theory. Ads: $500.00/$275.00. COSMEP, Media Alliance.

THROUGH THE LOOKING GLASS, P.O.Box 22061, Seattle, WA 98122. "Free to prisoners and poor people" 12/yr. sub. price: $5.00/yr. 16pp; 8½X14.

Thumbprint Press, Todd Walker, Editor; Becky Gaver, PO Box 3565, College Station, Tucson, AZ 85722, 602-327-1569. 1965. Poetry, art, photos. avg. press run 250. Pub'd 3 titles 1979; expects 3 titles 1980, 3 titles 1981. 9 titles listed in the *Small Press Record of Books in Print* (9th Edition, 1980). avg. price, paper: $8.00; other: $15.00 (portfolios). Discounts: 1/3 to retailer, 2/3 to us (varies with distributor). 60pp; 5½X7; †of. Copyrights for author.

Thunder City Press (see also THUNDER MOUNTAIN REVIEW), Steven Ford Brown, Editor, PO Box 11126, Birmingham, AL 35202. 1975. Poetry, fiction, art, photos, interviews, criticism, reviews. "We have published books by Pier Giorgio Di Cicco, Michael Swindle, Charles Entrekin, DC Berry, Alan D. Perlis, James Mersmann, Emily Borenstein, Ed Ochester, Andrew Glaze, Susan Fromberg Shaeffer, Georg Trakl, Aldo Pellegrini, B. Jay Schapiro, Philip Shirley, and M.R. Doty. Looking for work that ends the virtual necessity for the World. ***Also a broadside series with Richard Brautigan, Donald Hall, Gary Snyder, Ann Deagon, Robert Bly, Pier Giorgio Di Cicco, Leonard Michaels, Galway Kinnell, Denise Levertov, Philip Levine, John Beecher, James Seay, Howard Nemerov, Diane Wakoski,

Georg Trakl, Charles Entrekin." avg. press run 500. Pub'd 5 titles 1979; expects 5 titles 1980, 6 titles 1981. 26 titles listed in the *Small Press Record of Books in Print* (9th Edition, 1980). avg. price, paper: $3.00; other: $10.00 signed & numbered. Discounts: To book jobbers and book stores. 40pp; 5½X11; †of. Reporting time: 1 month. Payment: Copies, book promotion, reviews, etc. Copyrights for author.

Thunder Creek Publishing Co-operative, Geoffrey Ursell, Editor, PO Box 239, Sub #1, Moose Jaw, SK S6H 5V0, Canada. 1975. Poetry, fiction, art, criticism, plays. avg. press run 750. Pub'd 4 titles 1979; expects 5 titles 1980. 2 titles listed in the *Small Press Record of Books in Print* (9th Edition, 1980). avg. price, paper: $4.00. Discounts: 40% to retailers; 20% from orders of 10 or more. 58pp; 6X9; lp. Reporting time: 3-4 weeks. Payment: 10% of list price, 5 free copies, additional copies at 40% discount. Copyrights for author. ACP.

THUNDER EGG, Cris Burks, Aileen Marie Hays, 707 W Waveland, Apt 509, Chicago, IL 60613, (312) 935-3461. 1977. Poetry, art, photos. "Contributors should submit 3 to 5 poems, 2-3 photos, graphics or artwork. Open to new poets as well as established poets." biannual. Pub'd 1 issue 1979; expects 2 issues 1980, 2 issues 1981. sub. price: $5.00; per copy: $2.50; sample: $2.50. Back issues: Vol 1, No 1, $2.00. 48pp; 5X8½; of. Reporting time: 1 month to 3 months. Payment: 2 copies. Copyrighted, reverts to author. §poetry.

THUNDER MOUNTAIN REVIEW, Thunder City Press, Steven Ford Brown, Editor, PO Box 11126, Birmingham, AL 35202. 1978. Poetry, art, photos, interviews, criticism, reviews. "*Thunder Mountain Review* is a magazine of poetry, translations and reviews. Rather than a regional magazine our contributors come from Canada, South America, Europe, and from all over the U.S. I am receptive to prose poems, and good translations especially. Also reviews though I have two reviewers. Please query first. I am interested in interesting use of language, image and ideas. Open to the experimental, the dazzling surrealist. Recent contributors have included Siv Cedering Fox, Joseph Bruchac, Thomas McAfee, Terry Stokes, Karla Hammond, Colette Inez, Michael Swindle, Dave Smith, Ann Deagon, Victor Contoski, Carolyn Stoloff, Stephen Stepanchev, George Myers Jr., Michael McMahon, Christine Zawadiwsky, Michael Waters, Stephen Dunn, Patrick Bizzaro, Peter Wild, Linda Pastan, Brian Swann, Olga Cabral, and Sonya Dorman. Recent translations have included Enrique Anderson Imbert, Eugenio Montejo, Pablo Neruda, Ramon Palomares, Rilke, George Trakel, Vicente Aleixandre, Angel Levia, Leon Felipe, Willem van Toorn, Robert Desnos, Eugenio Montego, Chandrakant Deotale, Gunter Grass, Manuel del Cabral, Artur Lundkvist, Ofelia Castillo, Cesar Moro, etc." circ. 500. 2/yr. Pub'd 1 issue 1979; expects 2 issues 1980, 2 issues 1981. sub. price: $6.00; per copy: $3.00; sample: $3.00. Back issues: Negotiable. Discounts: Negotiable. 52pp; 5½X8½; †of. Reporting time: Usually 1 week but sometimes longer. Payment: 1 copy plus discount. Copyrighted, reverts to author. Pub's reviews: 2 in 1979. §Contemporary literature, special interest in poetry. Ads: $50.00/$25.00. CCLM, COSMEP-SOUTH.

Thunder's Mouth Press (see also ANOTHER CHICAGO MAGAZINE), Lee Webster, 1152 S East Ave, Oak Park, IL 60304. 1976. Poetry, fiction, art, photos, criticism, reviews, long-poems, articles, cartoons, interviews, satire. "Fiction manuscripts occasionally require a longer reporting time, according to the length of the manuscript. Book or chapbook size submissions be accompanied by at least 2 SASE and authors bus/home phone numbers." avg. press run 500. Expects 1 title 1980, 2 titles 1981. avg. price, paper: $2.50. Discounts: 60/40 on order of 10 or more. 32-64pp; 5½X8½; †of. Reporting time: 6-8 weeks. Payment: On individual basis. Copyrights for author. COSMEP, CCLM.

Tib Publications, D. W. Carrey, Thelma Meyers, 2922 N. State Road 7, Suite 107, Margate, FL 33063, (305) 973-2862. 1976. "We publish non-fiction only. Business or consumer oriented. Will consider publishing 'how-to' works at author's expense and we will do the marketing. Full details on request." avg. press run 1,000. Pub'd 3 titles 1979; expects 3 titles 1980, 5 titles 1981. 5 titles listed in the *Small Press Record of Books in Print* (9th Edition, 1980). avg. price, paper: $8.00. Discounts: 40% on 10 or more, distributors negotiable. 80pp; 5½X8½; of. Reporting time: 2 weeks. Payment: 10%. Copyrights for author. COSMEP.

Tiburon Press, Robert Miller, Pat Martin, Robert Banning, Jennifer Jones, Lockbox 17034 Ballard, Seattle, WA 98107, (206) 782-1437. 1977. Articles, art, cartoons, reviews. "Self-help and how-to articles 500-2,500 words. Shorter pieces suitable for inclusion in syndicated columns. Longer articles suitable for chapters in self-help and how-bo books." avg. press run 10,000. Pub'd 1 title 1979; expects 1 title 1980, 1 title 1981. avg. price, paper: $4.95. Discounts: 60% list. 64-96pp; 8½X11; of. Reporting time: 2 weeks. Payment: negotiable, generally flat fee. Copyrights for author. PNBPA.

Tide Book Publishing Company, Rose Safran, Mary Nykoruk, Box 268, Manchester, MA 01944, (617) 526-4887. 1979. Fiction, articles, art, interviews, news items. "Currently specializing in popular sociological issues. Most recent title is *Don't Go Dancing Mother* by Rose Safran; subject matter is social gerontology. All titles will be brief. Line drawings are used. Will produce only quality trade paperbacks." avg. press run 2,000-5,000. Pub'd 1 title 1979. 1 title listed in the *Small Press Record of Books in Print* (9th Edition, 1980). avg. price, paper: $3.95. Discounts: 40% single copy trade, jobber 50%, salesman 10% of the net sale, inquire about bulk. 100pp; 6X9; lp. Reporting time: ASAP. Payment: no fixed arrangements. Copyrights for author. NESPA.

Tide Publications (see also THE LESBIAN TIDE), Jeanne Cordova, Sharon McDonald, 8706 Cadillac Avenue, Los Angeles, CA 90034, 90034, (213) 839-7254. 1971. Poetry, fiction, articles, art, photos, cartoons, interviews, satire, criticism, reviews, music, letters, parts-of-novels, long-poems, plays. avg. press run 10,500. avg. price, paper: $1.00. 40pp; 8½X11; of. Reporting time: Bimonthly. Payment: By arrangement, $5.00-$25.00. Copyrights for author.

Tideline Press, Leonard Seastone, P.O. Box 786, Tannersville, NY 12485, (518) 589-6344. 1972. Poetry. "Like to keep the text under 30 pages. Style preference varies: must be something that takes me someplace, grabs me by the throat and makes the blood to rise. Recently: Ronald Baatz, Mariquita Platov, Lyn Lifshin, Leonard Seastone, Peter Wild, Sheila Heldenbrand, Stephen Sossaman, Thomas Johnson, Jean Follain, Rose Drachler, George Crane, Phillip Foss, Jr." avg. press run 100 numbered, signed. Pub'd 4 titles 1979; expects 6 titles 1980, 6 titles 1981. avg. price, cloth: varies; paper: $20.00 - $30.00. Discounts: 30%. pp varies; size varies; †lp. Reporting time: usually same day SASE. Payment: copies. Does not copyright for author.

TIGHTROPE, Swamp Press, Jo Mish, Ed Rayher, Robert Rayher, Frank Pondolfino, 4 Bugbee Road, Oneonta, NY 13820. 1975. Poetry, art, articles, long-poems, photos, satire, criticism, reviews, letters. "Handset, letterpress on fine papers. We do appreciate writers who remember the sounds of words. The three rules of the imagists would be good to look at before submitting. We make handwritten comments on all materials received" circ. 300. 2/yr. Pub'd 2 issues 1979; expects 2 issues 1980, 2 issues 1981. sub. price: $3.00; per copy: $2.50; sample: $2.00. Back issues: See samples. Discounts: dealers 40%. 28pp; 4½X6, 9X12; †lp. Reporting time: 6 weeks. Payment: copies, $5.00/piece accepted. Copyrighted, reverts to author. COSMEP, NYSSPA.

Timber Press, Richard Abel, Senior Editor, P.O. Box 92, Forest Grove, OR 97116, 503-357-7192. 1976. Art, articles, photos. "Main emphasis is Northwestern subject matter, horticulture, crafts, natural sciences, art, architecture and forestry." avg. press run 4,000. Pub'd 3 titles 1979; expects 5 titles 1980, 8 titles 1981. 16 titles listed in the *Small Press Record of Books in Print* (9th Edition, 1980). avg. price, cloth: $9.95; paper: $4.95; other: $25.00+ special editions, limited. Discounts: 1, 20%; 5, 40%; 50, 41%; 100, 42%; 250, 44%; 500, 46%. 200pp; 8X5; of. Reporting time: 7 days. Payment: By arrangement. Copyrights for author. ABA, PNWPA (Pacific Northwestern Publishers Assn.), COSMEP.

Timberline Press, Clarence Wolfshohl, Box 294, Mason, TX 76856, (915) 347-5573. 1975. Poetry. "Print chapbooks of 20-50 pages (prefer shorter 20-30 pp). We look at all poetry sent, but lean toward nature poetry with a sense of place or good lyrical, imagistic poetry. Actually, our taste is eclectic with quality being our primary criterion. In the past year we have published a collection of prose poems *Woman Chopping* by Emily Borenstein and a selection of poems *Dream in Pienza and Other Poems* by Toni Ortner-Zimmerman, both New York state poets." avg. press run 200. Pub'd 2 titles 1979; expects 1 title 1980, 2 titles 1981. 7 titles listed in the *Small Press Record of Books in Print* (9th Edition, 1980). avg. price, paper: $2.00-$3.00. Discounts: 40% copy price. 25-45pp; 5½X7; †lp. Reporting time: 30 days. Payment: 50-50 split after expenses. Copyrights for author.

TIME BARRIER EXPRESS, Ralph M. Newman, PO Box 206, Yonkers, NY 10710, 914-337-8050. 1974. Articles, photos, cartoons, interviews, criticism, reviews, letters, news items, non-fiction. "*TIME BARRIER EXPRESS* magazine covers the history of rock & roll music, particularly from the 1950's and 60's. Special emphasis on the artists of that era and on the collection of their recordings. Special features include complete discographies and labelographies, vintage photos and reports of current events in this field." circ. 20,000. 6/yr. Pub'd 6 issues 1979; expects 6 issues 1980. sub. price: $9.00; per copy: $2.00; sample: $2.00. Back issues: available back issues are $1.50. Discounts available on orders of 10 or more to the same address. 80pp; 8½X11; of. Reporting time: 2 months before publication. Payment: negotiable. Copyrighted, reverts if requested. Pub's reviews: 90 in 1979. §Magazines, fanzines, books and recordings which encompass the subjects described above. Ads: please inquire about ad rates.

TIME CAPSULE, INC., Time Capsule, Inc., Marc Crawford, General PO Box 1185, New York, NY 10001, (212)595-8448. Poetry, fiction, articles, art, photos, reviews, letters, parts-of-novels. circ. 2,000. 4/yr. Pub'd 2 issues 1979; expects 4 issues 1980, 4 issues 1981. sub. price: $5.00; per copy:

$1.50; sample: $1.00. Back issues: $1.00. Discounts: Unavailable until 1980. 20pp; 12X18; of. Reporting time: 6 weeks. Payment: $50.00. Copyrighted, reverts to author. Pub's reviews. §Fiction. Ads: $1,000.00/$700.00. CCLM, COSMEP.

Time Capsule, Inc. (see STRAIGHT AHEAD INTERNATIONAL; TIME CAPSULE, INC.)

Timeless Books, Teri Gray, Swami Padmananda, P.O. Box 60, Porthill, ID 83853, (604) 227-9220. 1977. "To date we have published 2 books, *Kundalini: Yoga for the West* and *Aphorisms of Swami Sirinanda Radha,* both by Swami Sirinanda Radha. Two articles have been published in booklet format: *Kundalini: An Overview* and *The Aspirant,* both dealing with the spiritual life. The focus of our approach is bringing the Eastern teachings to life in the Western context. Booklets average about 20 pages; *Kundalini: Yoga for the West* is 400 pages hard bound. At present we are not accepting manuscripts. Our address in Canada is Box 9, Kootenay Bay, B.C. VOB 1X0" avg. press run books: 5,000; booklets: 1,000. Pub'd 3 titles 1979; expects 3 titles 1980, 3 titles 1981. 3 titles listed in the *Small Press Record of Books in Print* (9th Edition, 1980). avg. price, cloth: $19.95; paper: $5.00; other: booklets: $1.-00-$2.50. Discounts: Books and booklets, 40% over five copies. 250pp; 6X9; †of. Copyrights for author. COSMEP.

Timely Books, Yvonne MacManus, Jo Anne Prather, PO Box 267, New Milford, CT 06776, (203) 354-0866. 1978. Fiction. "We publish both fiction and non-fiction, primarily (but not restricted to) cause oriented themes. Concentrating at present on reprints (in trade paperback format) of formerly publ. works which deserve another go round in the market place." avg. press run 2,000-4,000. Pub'd 2 titles 1979; expects 2 titles 1980. avg. price, paper: $5.95. Discounts: 3-5 copies, 20%; 6-10 copies, 30%; 11-25 copies, 35%; 26 and up, 40%. 176pp; 5½X8½; of. Reporting time: 6-8 weeks. Payment: varies - usual trade paperback. Copyrights for author.

Times Change Press, Moonlight, Tom Wodetzki, Box 187, Albion, CA 95410. 1970. Articles, criticism. avg. press run 5,000. Pub'd 4 titles 1979; expects 4 titles 1980. 25 titles listed in the *Small Press Record of Books in Print* (9th Edition, 1980). avg. price, cloth: $9.00; paper: $3.00. Discounts: 40% to retail. 150pp; 5¼X7; of. Reporting time: 1 month. Payment: some money, not alot. Copyrights for author. COSMEP, WIP.

TINDERBOX, Alice Cabaniss, Co-ordinating Editor, 334 Molasses Lane, Mt. Pleasant (Charleston), SC 29464, 884-0212. 1978. Poetry, art. "SASE essential for manuscript return: no xerox or simultaneous, typewritten only. Quality experiential contemporary poetry, eclectic range since ten editors represent two coasts & wide variance in taste. No inspirational verse or long sagas, please. #8 has work by Wm Stafford, Mike Rose, Norm Levine, A.J. Wright, Peter Brett, Pat Groth, others." circ. 300. 4/yr. Expects 3 issues 1980, 4 issues 1981. sub. price: $6.00; per copy: $2.00; sample: $2.00. Back issues: #1 not available, #2, $2.00, #3 and #4 not available. Discounts: 25% to bookstores. 48pp; 5½X8½; of. Reporting time: 6 weeks if good, 6 days if unsuitable. Payment: 2 copies & the pleasure of good company. Copyrighted, reverts to author. Ads: $50.00/$30.00.

TINTA, Tommie Davidson, Connie Marina, Sonia Zuniga-Lomeli, Alejandro Hogan, Gladys Blacut, Spanish Dept, University of California, Santa Barbara, CA 93017, 961-3161. 1979. Poetry, fiction, articles, art, interviews, criticism, reviews, letters, parts-of-novels, long-poems, collages, plays. "No length limits. All material must deal in some way with Latin America, Spain or Portugal — either written by authors from these areas or having themes or settings relating to these areas. We are very receptive to creative literary criticism of contemporary Latin American Spanish and Portuguese fiction, drama and poetry. We also welcome book reviews and interviewsof literary figures." circ. 1,000. 2/yr. sub. price: $3.00; per copy: $2.00; sample: $1.00. Back issues: $1.50. Discounts: 40% to all orders over 5. 60-80pp; 6X9; of. Reporting time: 1 month maximum. Payment: 2 copies, plus one year subscription. Copyrighted, reverts to author. Pub's reviews. §Latin American literature, Spanish and Portuguese literature, literary translations.

TIOTIS POETRY NEWS, M.O.P. Press, Shirley Aycock, Rt. #19, Box 53C, Fort Myers, FL 33908, (813) 482-0802. 1978. Poetry, cartoons, satire, reviews, letters, news items. "No definite length limit, however nothing book-length. Hope to avoid all bias, except bad taste. First issue to be printed Feb. '79. Must subscribe to be eligible to submit poetry and vote for best of issue. Prizes of $5.00 to be awarded top four." circ. 200. 4/yr. Pub'd 4 issues 1979; expects 4 issues 1980, 4 issues 1981. sub. price: $4.00; per copy: $1.25; sample: $1.25. Back issues: 65¢. Discounts: No submission/vote privilege, 30%. 32pp; 7X8½; †mi. Reporting time: 2 weeks. Payment: Prizes as described above. Copyrighted, reverts to author. Pub's reviews: 1 in 1979. Ads: $12.00/$7.00/$0.05. COSMEP, UAPAA, POW(Poetry of Women), FSPS, NFSPS.

Tired Teddybear Productions (see also INTRINSIC: An International Magazine of Poetry & Poetics), Michael Zizis, Mary Ellen Kappler, Box 485, Station P, Toronto, Ontario M5S 2T1, Canada,

(416) 534-0139. 1978. Poetry, fiction, interviews, long-poems. "Tired Teddybear Productions is a childrens press. We are always looking for stories for children that serve to fire the imagination of children." avg. press run 2,500. Discounts: 40%-60% per volume sales.

Tiresias Press (see also THE HELEN REVIEW), Carol Polcovar, Dorothy Friedman, 190 Pacific Street, Brooklyn, NY 11201, (212) 834-0345. 1978. Poetry, fiction, art, photos, interviews. "Tiresias Press published *The Helen Review,* poetry cards (hand silk screened). Our first books will be a collectors series - done by a poet & artist. Riddle - Carol Polcovar; Outside Thunder - Dorothy Friedman; Women of Fes - Translated by Rochelle Ratner. No unsolisited manuscripts. Queries accepted." Pub'd 3 titles 1979. avg. price, paper: $5.00-$7.50. Discounts: 40%. 50pp; 8X6; of. Payment: 10% copies. Copyrights for author.

Titanic Books, Terence Winch, Doug Lang, Diane Ward, Bernard Welt, 1920 S St. NW #506, Washington, DC 20009, (202) 483-5195. 1977. Poetry, long-poems. "So far we've published three books, *Native Land,* by Ted Greenwald, *The Alphabet Work,* by Kenward Elmslie, and *In the Mood,* by Michael Lally. Each has been essentially a single work, not a collection, and we intend to stick to that idea— and also to keep our books relatively short (not over thirty pp.) and inexpensive (not over three dollars). We will not be considering unsolicited manuscripts" avg. press run 200. Pub'd 2 titles 1979; expects 3 titles 1980, 3 titles 1981. 3 titles listed in the *Small Press Record of Books in Print* (9th Edition, 1980). avg. price, paper: $2.50. Discounts: 40% to bookstores. 20-30pp; 8½X11; of. Payment: 25% of press run. Yes.

TITMOUSE, Linda Hoffman, Avron Hoffman, 720 West 19th Ave., Vancouver, B.C., Canada. 1939. Poetry, fiction, cartoons, satire, collages. "Dedicated to the hidden treasures of contemporary life; the far-out & the easy-to-read, non sexist & non-racist element of a dwindling counter-culture. Recent contributors, *Nicanor* Parra, *Nicanor* Snyder, *Nicanor* Edson & *Nicanors* Jaffee, Becker, & Cohen. *Bureaucratic and financial inquiries should be directed to Intermedia Press, Box 3294, Vancouver, B.C., Canada.*" circ. 400. irreg. sub. price: $4.00; per copy: $4.00; sample: $4.00. 53pp; 8½X5½; of. Reporting time: varies. Payment: copies. COSMEP.

TLM Press (see also IMPACT, An International Publication of Contemporary Literature & the Arts; LITERARY MONITOR: The Voice of Contemporary Literature), Gary Lagier, Editor; Thomas Piekarski, Associate Editor, 1070 Noriega, Sunnyvale, CA 94086, (408) 733-9615. 1975. "In addition to the two referenced magazines, *TLM Press* also publishes chapbooks & books - mostly poetry, some fiction. We also do some (highly selected) publishing for hire. But this is scheduled around our own activities. We can not do nay hardbound books." avg. press run 500 plus. Pub'd 3 titles 1979; expects 4 titles 1980. avg. price, paper: $3.50. 48-60pp; 5½X8½; of. Reporting time: Less than 6 weeks. Payment: 10 percent of run. Copyrights for author. CCLM, COSMEP, WIP, AWP.

TOCHER, Alan Bruford, School of Scotish Studies, 27 George Square, Edinburgh EH8 9LD, United Kingdom. 1971. Poetry, interviews, music. "All contents taken from archives of the School of Scotish Studies, mostly from tape recordings but including some MS. donations covering Scots and Gaelic traditional tales, songs and other lore or memories. Regular features on notable folksingers or storytellers (e.g. Jeannie Robertson), and on subjects such as witchcraft, tall tales, or illicit distilling. English translation with all Gaelic material, staff music with all songs." circ. 1M. 3/yr. sub. price: £1.50; per copy: 50p. Back issues: 30p (1971-76), 40p (1977-78, 50p (1979). Discounts: 1/3 to trade & bulk orders. 64-72pp; size A8; lo. Copyrighted. Pub's reviews: 10 in 1979. §Scotland. Ads: inserts only £15.

Todd Tarbox Books, Todd Tarbox, Shirley Tarbox, 1637 East 36th Place, Tulsa, OK 74105. 1975. "Children (stressing creativity)" avg. press run varies. Pub'd 2 titles 1979; expects 5 titles 1980. 4 titles listed in the *Small Press Record of Books in Print* (9th Edition, 1980). avg. price, cloth: Varies.; paper: varies; other: Varies. Discounts: Write for details. pp varies.; size varies; of/lp. Reporting time: 4 weeks on solicited manuscripts. Variety of payment arrangements. copyright varies. Bookbuilders Of Boston.

Tofua Press, Elizabeth Rand, Editor & Publisher, 10457-F Roselle Street, San Diego, CA 92121, 714-453-4774. 1973. Photos, letters. "We publish books on the South Pacific, cookbooks, real estate law, and California history." avg. press run 3,000-10,000. Pub'd 4 titles 1979; expects 4 titles 1980, 3 titles 1981. 13 titles listed in the *Small Press Record of Books in Print* (9th Edition, 1980). avg. price, cloth: $19.95; paper: $4.95; other: $4.95 (@lastic comb-bound). Discounts: trade. 120-450pp; 5½X8½; of. Reporting time: 1 month. Payment: 7½% retail to 15,000 copies, 8% over 15,000. Copyrights for author. COSMEP.

Tomato Publications Ltd., Liza Cowan, Penny House, 70 Barrow Street, New York, NY 10014. 1975. Articles, art, cartoons, interviews, satire, criticism, reviews, music, letters, news items. "First book:

1,100. 1/yr. Pub'd 1 issue 1979. sub. price: $8.00; per copy: $4.00; sample: $4.00. Discounts: 1 copy 20%; 5 or more, 40%. 180pp; of. Reporting time: 2 wks - 1 mo. Payment: copies only. Authors retain rights. §materials relating to the Kabbalah and Jewish mysticism. CCLM, BCF (Before Columbus Foundation).

Tree Books (see also TREE), David Meltzer, P O Box 9005, Berkeley, CA 94709. 1970. Poetry, articles. "Specifically interested in translations of kabbalist texts." avg. press run 250-350. Pub'd 4-5 titles 1979. 4 titles listed in the *Small Press Record of Books in Print* (9th Edition, 1980). avg. price, paper: $2.50-$4.00. Discounts: 20-40%. Variespp; of. Reporting time: 4-8 weeks. Payment: 10% of edition. CCLM, BCF (Before Columbus Foundation).

Tree Frog Press Limited, Allan Shute, 10717 106th Avenue, Edmonton, Alberta T5H3Y9, Canada, 403-425-1505. 1971. Fiction. "Children's literature." avg. press run 3,000. Pub'd 3 titles 1979; expects 4 titles 1980. 9 titles listed in the *Small Press Record of Books in Print* (9th Edition, 1980). avg. price, cloth: $5.95; paper: $3.95. Discounts: 40 percent (bulk negotiable). 64pp; size varies; of. Reporting time: 6 weeks. Payment: on contract basis. Copyrights for author. APA, ACP.

Tree Line Books, Harold Schmidt, Box 1062, Radio City Station, New York, NY 10019. 1978. Poetry, fiction, plays. Pub'd 1 title 1979; expects 2 titles 1980, 2 titles 1981. 1 title listed in the *Small Press Record of Books in Print* (9th Edition, 1980). Copyrights for author.

Tree Shrew Press, Richard M. Swiderski, 32 Evergreen Road, Holliston, MA 01746, (617) 429-7618. 1979. Poetry, photos, collages, concrete art. "We are devoted to the publication of poetic constructions, that is objects assembled from printed sheets, and employ a wide range of processes and materials." avg. press run 100. Pub'd 3 titles 1979. †lp. Reporting time: 2 months. COSMEP.

Tree Toad Press (see also SWIFT RIVER), Deborah Robson, Box 264, Leverett, MA 01054. 1973. Poetry, fiction, art. "Especially interested in short fiction chapbooks" avg. press run 350. Expects 1 title 1980, 1 title 1981. Discounts: standard. 56pp; 5½X8; of/lp. Reporting time: 1 week to 3 months. Payment: varies. Copyrights for author. COSMEP, NESPA.

‡**TREES, Acorn,** Joan Dibble Shambaugh, 185 Merriam Street, Weston, MA 02193. 1975. Poetry, fiction, art. "Use material in the nature of the title, word also used in its symbolic form." circ. 250. 1/yr. price per copy: $1.50; sample: $1.50. 25pp; 6X8; of. Payment: copies. Copyrighted. COSMEP.

Trek-Cir Publications, R. L. Rickert, PO Box 898, Valley Forge, PA 19481, (215) 337-3110. 1978. Poetry, fiction, art, cartoons. "We are not yet using unsolicited materials from outside sources." avg. press run 500-1,000. Expects 1 title 1980, 2 titles 1981. 1 title listed in the *Small Press Record of Books in Print* (9th Edition, 1980). avg. price, cloth: $8.00; paper: $5.00. Discounts: Negotiable, 25% to 40%. 75-100pp; 8X10; of.

TRELLIS, Maggie Anderson, Editor, P.O. Box 656, Morgantown, WV 26505, 304-845-7118. 1973. Poetry, articles, criticism, interviews, letters, long-poems. "Work by invitation only as magazine reflects current interests of the editor. Unsolicited mss are not being considered. Recent contributors: Denise Levertov, Irene McKinney, Jayne Anne Phillips, Tillie Olsen, Adrienne Rich. 1979 issue: Women and children. Future issues will be organized around single themes." circ. 1,000. irregular. Pub'd 1 issue 1979. price per copy: $4.50; sample: $2.00. Back issues: 1st supplement $2.50. Discounts: 20% on ten or more copies; 40% on ten or more if prepaid. Inquire for classroomm rates. 100pp; 8½X11; of. Reporting time: 2 weeks to 1 month. Payment: 2 copies. Copyrighted, reverts to author. §Poetry. CCLM.

TRENDS (see Wilfion Books, Publishers)

Trent University (see also JOURNAL of CANADIAN STUDIES/Revue d'etudes canadiennes), Ralph Heintzman, Trent University, Peterborough, ON K9J 7B8, Canada. 1966. Articles, criticism, reviews. avg. press run 1,800. Pub'd 4 titles 1979. Discounts: 15%. 120pp; 7½X10; of. Reporting time: 3 months.

Triad Press, Jane Segerstrom, PO Box 42006 1-D, Houston, TX 77042, (713) 789-0424. 1980. Art, photos. "Triad Press seeks book length, non-fiction manuscripts which meet current needs, are well-written, have a practical, non-academic approach, and which inspire. Photocopy OK, SASE. An example is *Look Like Yourself & Love It!,* a highly illustrated $14.95 trade paperback, publication date 9/10/80, which guides the reader toward developing a positive visual impact that incorporates personal uniqueness—for men and women." avg. press run 5,000-10,000. Pub'd 2 titles 1979. 1 title listed in the *Small Press Record of Books in Print* (9th Edition, 1980). avg. price, paper: $5.00-$19.00. Discounts: 1:none; 2-4:20%; 5-9:30%; 10-24:40%; 25-49:42%; 50-99:45%; 100-199:48%; 200+:50%. 168pp; 8½X11; of. Reporting time: 4 weeks. Payment: standard royalties, advance-on-completion. Copyrights for author. COSMEP.

Triad Publishing Co. Inc., Lorna Rubin, Lenore Freeman, PO Box 13096, Gainesville, FL 32604, (904) 373-5308. 1978. Photos. "Any non-fiction, adult and juvenile." avg. press run 10,000. Pub'd 2 titles 1979; expects 3 titles 1980, 3 titles 1981. avg. price, cloth: $9.95; paper: $3.95. Discounts: trade, professional. 64-450pp; 6X9; of. Reporting time: 1-3 months. Payment: 10% cover price, once yearly. Copyrights for author.

TRIBUTARY, Lee Thorn, 3755 E 32nd Street, Tucson, AZ 85713, (602) 748-1551. 1979. Poetry, reviews. "*Tributary* is a review of self-published literature (primarily poetry). Will also publish poems and criticism of works that are widely but inadequately reviewed in the establishment press." 4/yr. Expects 1 issue 1981. sub. price: $10.00; per copy: $2.50; sample: $2.50. 5½X8½; of. Reporting time: days. Payment: two copies. Copyrighted. Pub's reviews. §Poetry, fiction, politics, sex, sociology. Ads: No ads.

Tricontinental Editora Ltda. (see CADERNOS DO TERCEIRO MUNDO)

Trike, David Christopher Arnold, Keith Shein, 277 23rd Avenue, San Francisco, CA 94121. 1976. Poetry, fiction, art, photos, long-poems, collages, concrete art. avg. press run 500. Pub'd 2 titles 1979; expects 3 titles 1980. avg. price, paper: $4.00. Discounts: 40% for bookstores. pp varies; size varies; of/lp. Payment: 10% of press run. Does not copyright for author. WIP, COSMEP, LPS.

Trinity Press, Charles J. Chickadel, Box 1320, San Francisco, CA 94101. 1972. 3 titles listed in the *Small Press Record of Books in Print* (9th Edition, 1980). avg. price, paper: $5.95. Discounts: To the trade. 208pp; 8½X5½; of. COSMEP, CCLM.

TRIQUARTERLY, Elliott Anderson, Editor; Jonathan Brent, Co-Editor; Michael McDonnell, Managing Editor, 1735 Benson Avenue, Northwestern Univ., Evanston, IL 60201, 312-492-3490. 1964. Fiction, art, photos, criticism, parts-of-novels. circ. 5,000. 3/yr. Pub'd 3 issues 1979; expects 3 issues 1980, 3 issues 1981. 4 titles listed in the *Small Press Record of Books in Print* (9th Edition, 1980). sub. price: $12.00; per copy: $5.95; sample: $2.00. Back issues: price list on request. Discounts: available on request. 256pp; 6X9; of. Reporting time: 4 to 6 weeks. Payment varies. Copyrighted, rights revert to author upon request. Ads: $225.00/$125.00. CCLM.

TRIVIUM, Gomer Press, Colin Eldridge Dr., Dept. Of History, St. David's University College, Lampeter, Dyfed SA48 7ED, United Kingdom, 0570-422351 ext 37. 1966. Articles, reviews, criticism. "Articles: av. length - 5,000 words. Book reviews: av. length - 500 words. Bias: towards the humanities." circ. 300. 1/yr. Pub'd 1 issue 1979; expects 1 issue 1980. sub. price: £5/individuals; £5.00/institutions. 180pp; size A5; lp. Reporting time: 3-4 weeks. Payment: None. copyright vested in editor of TRIVIUM. Pub's reviews: 20 in 1979. §humanities; books only. Ads: £25/£12.50.

Troisieme-Canadian Publishers, Douglas Ogden Holmes, P.O.Box 4281, Grand Central Station, New York, NY 10017, (212) 940-0954. 1974. Fiction. "New to publishing business; two books published so far" avg. press run 2,000-5,000. Expects 2 titles 1980, 2 titles 1981. avg. price, cloth: $9.95. Discounts: trade: 50%; libraries and schools: 20%. 275pp; 5X8½. Reporting time: 1 month. Payment: no advance; 50% royalties to author. Copyrights for author.

TROUSER PRESS, Trans-Oceanic Trouser Press, Inc., Ira A. Robbins, Editor-in-Chief; Scott Isler, Editor; Jim Green, Assoc. Ed., 212 5th Ave, #1310, New York, NY 10010, 212-889-7145. 1974. Articles, photos, interviews, criticism, reviews, music, letters. "General rock music, especially British rock music. Reviews 300-600. Interested in any quality rock music. Features 2,000-6,000 words" circ. 40,000. 12/yr. Pub'd 11 issues 1979; expects 12 issues 1980, 12 issues 1981. sub. price: $12.00; per copy: $1.50; sample: $1.25 + 50¢ postage. Back issues: available numbers 14-49 at $1.75 each. Discounts: contact David Fenichell. 68pp; 8⅜X10⅞; of. Reporting time: 1 month. Payment: $25-50 for features. copyrighted, rights do not revert. Pub's reviews: 2 in 1979. §rock music, pop culture. Ads: $725.00/$420.00/$0.30.

Trucha Publications, Inc., Angelita Cosmos, PO Boxx 3534, San Antonio, TX 78211. 1970. Poetry, fiction, satire, criticism, plays. "The conscious publication of bilingual bicultural expressions transcending any ethnic origin, but very identifiable as Chicano. It is also the celebration of a dual experience in an English and Spanish speaking world which has resulted in a rich and rhythmic language." avg. press run 2,000. Pub'd 4 titles 1979; expects 5 titles 1980. avg. price, paper: $3.50. Discounts: varies according to volume, average 30%. 150-200pp; 6X9; †of. Reporting time: 3 months. Payment: varies.

Truedog Press, Inc. (see also MAXY'S JOURNAL), Mac Bennett, Craig Chambers, 216 West Academy Street, Lonoke, AR 72086, (501) 676-2467. 1977. Poetry, fiction, photos, cartoons, satire, reviews, parts-of-novels, long-poems, plays. "Play, one-act only. Although mail is received in Ark, mag in published at Nashville, TN" avg. press run 500+. Pub'd 1 title 1979; expects 2 titles 1980, 3 titles 1981. avg. price, paper: $2.00. 50pp; 6X9; of. Reporting time: 2 months. Payment: Contingent. COSMEP.

TRULY FINE PRESS, A Review, Truly Fine Press, Jerry Madson, P.O. Box 891, Bemidji, MN 56601. 1976. Poetry, satire, reviews, fiction, interviews, collages, concrete art, news items. "Have published Jon Miller, Richard Kostelanetz, d.h.lloyd, Gerald Locklin, Keith Rahmmings, Roberta Metz, Lyn Lifshin, James Magorian to name a few. Plus review of Bukowski." circ. 500. 2/yr. Pub'd 2 issues 1979; expects 2 issues 1980, 2 issues 1981. 2 titles listed in the *Small Press Record of Books in Print* (9th Edition, 1980). sub. price: $1.00 or 2 (9 X 12 envelopes) plus 45¢postage on each; per copy: 50¢ or 9 X 12 envelope with 45¢postage; sample: Free. 12pp; 11X17; of. Reporting time: 2 weeks to 6 months. Payment: 3 copies. Not copyrighted. Pub's reviews. §small press works.

Truly Fine Press (see also TRULY FINE PRESS, A Review), Jerry Madson, P.O. Box 891, Bemidji, MN 56601. 1973. Poetry, fiction. "Truly Fine Press has in the past published a pamphlet series. And also published Minnesota's first tabloid novel. Must query first" avg. press run varies. Pub'd 1 title 1979. 5 titles listed in the *Small Press Record of Books in Print* (9th Edition, 1980). avg. price, cloth: varies; paper: varies; other: Varies. pp variespp; size varies; †mi/of/lp. Reporting time: 2-4 weeks. Copyrights for author.

TRUMPS (A Periodical of Postcards) (see Station Hill Press)

TSA'ASZI', Lonna Lawrence, CPO Box 12, Pine Hill, NM 87321, (505) 783-5503. 1971. Poetry, fiction, articles, art, photos, cartoons, interviews, long-poems. "This magazine is produced by Navajo high school students about Navajo culture. Materials must be relevant to Navajo culture and preferably student produced." circ. 1,200. 4/yr. Pub'd 4 issues 1979; expects 4 issues 1980, 4 issues 1981. sub. price: $8.00; per copy: $2.50; sample: $2.50. Back issues: $1.50. Discounts: 25% of single issues to dealers. 72pp; 8½X11; †of. Reporting time: 2 weeks. No payments. Copyrighted, reverts to author. §Navajo culture. No ads.

‡THE TULANE LITERARY MAGAZINE, Sally Savic, Jessica Bagg, Marion Enochs, Peter Cooley, University Center, New Orleans, LA 70118. 1970. Poetry, fiction. "*The Tulane Literary Magazine* publishes material by Tulane students and outside contributors. Recent outsiders have included James Wright, W.S. Merwin, Allen Ginsberg. Material is considered only between September and April of each year and in no case will be returned unless an SASE is enclosed." circ. 500. 2/yr. Pub'd 2 issues 1979; expects 2 issues 1980, 2 issues 1981. sample price: free. 12pp; 10X12. Reporting time: 1 month. Copyrighted, reverts to author.

Tundra Books Of Northern New York, M. Engelhart, 51 Clinton, P.O. Box 1030, Plattsburg, NY 12901. 1971. Fiction, art, cartoons, concrete art. "Children's books. Letter of inquiry imperative *before* submission of manuscript" avg. press run 7,500. Pub'd 25 titles 1979; expects 10 titles 1980, 10 titles 1981. 2 titles listed in the *Small Press Record of Books in Print* (9th Edition, 1980). avg. price, cloth: $9.00; paper: $5.00. Discounts: standard. pp varies; size varies. Payment: standard. Copyrights for author. AIGA.

Turkey Press, Harry E. Reese, 6746 Sueno Road, Goleta, CA 93017, 685-3603. 1974. Poetry, fiction, art, long-poems. "Hand-set books of poetry, using linoleum blocks and line drawings on occasion, in limited, numbered editions. Ordinarily a trade edition in paperback, and a signed de luxe hand-bound copy in boards. Has published the following poets: Ray Di Palma, Philip Suntree, Randy Blasing, Glen Martin, Harry Reese, Robert Gibb, James Hickson, Robert Pinsky, Michael Hogan, William Lewis, and others. James Reinbold in fiction." avg. press run 300-500. Pub'd 6 titles 1979; expects 6 titles 1980. 13 titles listed in the *Small Press Record of Books in Print* (9th Edition, 1980). avg. price, cloth: $25.00; paper: $3.50; other: special editions have special prices. Discounts: we have a subscription series — $100.00 per year. pp varies; size varies; †lp. Reporting time: 2 months. Payment: as negotiated. Copyrights for author.

Turner Publishing, Inc., Sandra Haas, PO Box 1967, Washington, DC 20013, (202) 546-8747. 1977. Articles, photos, criticism, reviews, letters, news items. "Primarily renovation/rehabilitation oriented; houses in cities." avg. press run 5,000. Pub'd 1 title 1979; expects 2 titles 1981. 1 title listed in the *Small Press Record of Books in Print* (9th Edition, 1980). avg. price, paper: $5.00. Discounts: Trade, 40%; Libraries, 20%. 200pp; 5X8. Payment: Negotiable. Copyrights for author.

TURTLE, Richard Hill, 25 Rainbow Mall, Niagara Falls, NY 14303. 1979. Articles, art, photos, news items. circ. 10,000. 4/yr. Pub'd 3 issues 1979. sub. price: $2.00; per copy: $0.50; sample: free. Discounts: 12 issues for $5.00. 12pp; 11X17; of. Reporting time: 30-45 days. no payments. §Indian art and culture. Ads: $300.00/$175.00.

‡**Turtle Island Foundation (see also NEW WORLD JOURNAL),** 2845 Buena Vista Way, Berkeley, CA 94708. 9 titles listed in the *Small Press Record of Books in Print* (9th Edition, 1980).

Turtle Lodge Press, Marie H. Walling, 12411 N 67th Street, Scottsdale, AZ 85254, (602) 948-3565. 1979. Fiction. "Address for publication purposes: PO Box 4956, Scottsdale, AZ 85254. At present interested only in self-published or co-authored material." avg. press run 5,000-25,000. Pub'd 2 titles 1979; expects 4 titles 1980. 1 title listed in the *Small Press Record of Books in Print* (9th Edition, 1980). Discounts: To craft wholesalers, 50 plus 10 plus 20. Direct to bookstores: 40%. To school and library wholesalers, varies. of. Reporting time: not accepting mss at this time. AAA (Ariz Author's Assn), COSMEP, RNA (Religion Newswriters Assn).

TUUMBA, Tuumba Press, Lyn Hejinian, 2639 Russell Street, Berkeley, CA 94705. 1976. Poetry, fiction, articles, letters, parts-of-novels, long-poems, plays. "Each issue will be devoted to the work of one writer or the written work of one artist; this may include fiction, poetry, essays, interviews, statements, and manifestoes. Contributors include: Barbara Baracks, Susan Howe, Lyn Hejinian, Kenneth Irby, Ron Silliman, Bruce Andrews, Barrett Watten." circ. 400. 6/yr. Pub'd 6 issues 1979; expects 6 issues 1980, 6 issues 1981. sub. price: $9.00; per copy: $2.00; sample: $2.00. Back issues: $2.00. Discounts: usual to stores & distributors. 24pp; 6X9, 5½X8½; †lp. Reporting time: immediate. Payment: 40 copies. copyrights for author. Ads: none. COSMEP.

Tuumba Press (see also TUUMBA), Lyn Hejinian, 2639 Russell St, Berkeley, CA 94705. 1976. Poetry, fiction, articles, letters, parts-of-novels, long-poems, plays. "avant-garde literature in fine letterpress chapbook series" avg. press run 450. Pub'd 6 titles 1979; expects 6 titles 1980, 6 titles 1981. 19 titles listed in the *Small Press Record of Books in Print* (9th Edition, 1980). avg. price, paper: $2.00. Discounts: usual to bookstores and distributors. 24pp; 5½X8½; †lp. Reporting time: immediate. Payment: 40 copies to author. Copyrights for author. COSMEP.

TUVOTI Books (see also THE UNSPEAKABLE VISIONS OF THE INDIVIDUAL), Arthur Winfield Knight, Kit Knight, P.O. Box 439, California, PA 15419. 1971. Poetry, fiction, articles, art, photos, interviews, satire, criticism, reviews, letters, parts-of-novels, long-poems, collages. "Beat literature: Jack Kerouac, Allen Ginsberg, William S. Burroughs, Michael McClure, Gregory Corso, Carolyn Cassady, etc." avg. press run 2,000. Pub'd 3 titles 1979; expects 1 title 1980, 1 title 1981. 15 titles listed in the *Small Press Record of Books in Print* (9th Edition, 1980). avg. price, paper: $10.00. Discounts: query. pp varies; size varies; of/lp. Reporting time: 2 months. Payment: anthologies: generally 2 contributor's copies, individual work, generally 10% of run. copyrights to either author or us/ but in latter case rights revert to author. CCLM, COSMEP.

TWELFTH KEY, Penny Kemp, 14 4th Street, Toronto Islands, Toronto, ON M5J 2B5, Canada. 1976. Poetry. "At least one issue per volume will be thematic; at least one per volume devoted to 1-4 poets. Please write for a flyer." circ. 500. 3/yr. Pub'd 3 issues 1979; expects 3 issues 1980. 2 titles listed in the *Small Press Record of Books in Print* (9th Edition, 1980). sub. price: $15.00; per copy: $6.50; sample: $3.50 + postage. Back issues: Volume 1, $3.50 each. 90pp; 7X8½; of. Reporting time: 14 days. Payment: one copy of the issue concerned. Copyrighted, reverts to author. Ads: none.

23 CLUB SERIES, Intrepid Press, Allen DeLoach, P.O. Box 1423, Buffalo, NY 14214. 1971. "Experimental prose." irreg. Back issues: Available. Discounts: none. 8½X11; of. mss by request. Payment: copies only. Copyrighted. no ads. COSMEP.

The Twickenham Press, Anthony J Beesley, Barbara Beesley, 31 Jane Street, New York, NY 10014, (212) 741-2417. 1980. Poetry, fiction, satire, long-poems, plays. "There will be a post office box. In Oct. we will be publishing an off-beat psycho-historical novel entitled *Klytaimnestra, Who Stayed at Home* ; the author, Nancy Bogen is a professor of English literatue and a feminist. In 1981, we hope to publish two plays *Nature's Gentleman* by George Hickenlooper and *The Art of Love* by Robert Kornfeld, in conjunction with showcases of these works." avg. press run 1,000. 1 title listed in the *Small Press Record of Books in Print* (9th Edition, 1980). avg. price, paper: $7.00. Discounts: 20% to libraries; 40% to dealers; no returns. 250pp; 5½X8¼; lp. Reporting time: long. Payment: standard. COSMEP.

Two-Eighteen Press, Tom Johnson, P. O. Box 218 Village Station, New York City, NY 10014, 212-255-1723. 1974. "So far just a one-man show." avg. press run 1,000. 2 titles listed in the *Small Press Record of Books in Print* (9th Edition, 1980). avg. price, paper: $4.00. Discounts: Dealers 40 percent, distributors 50 percent. 100pp; of. Reporting time: 1 week. Does not copyright for author.

Two Geese Press (see THE SHIRT OFF YOUR BACK)

TWO HANDS NEWS, B. Madden, 1125 Webster, Chicago, IL 60614. 1976. "News of poetry scene in Chicago, with Chicago/Midwest poetry Calendar. Reviews of readings and books, commentary and interviews with national and local poets. Special issues have been on Cavafy, Kerouac, Bly" circ. 1,000. 6/yr. Pub'd 6 issues 1979; expects 6 issues 1980, 4 issues 1981. 1 title listed in the *Small Press Record of Books in Print* (9th Edition, 1980). sub. price: free or $5.00 first-class mail subscr.; sample: free. Back issues: $1.00-$10.00. 8pp; 11X8; of. Pub's reviews: 38 in 1979. §poetry only.

TWO STEPS IN, Peter Herring, Susan Sutton, John R. Louchard, Marjorie B. Faris, Lara Gabriel, Paul Lake, 532 Emerson Street, Palo Alto, CA 94301, 321-7950. 1975. Poetry, fiction, articles, art, photos, criticism, music, parts-of-novels, long-poems, collages, plays. "We are very receptive to new or unpublished writers and artists. No dry poetry & prose. Especially receptive to innovative fiction, & to new forms, crossovers between mediums. Artists & photographers should consider submissions as small shows. Those wishing to submit music or music criticism should send a query first." circ. 1,000. 2/yr. Pub'd 2 issues 1979; expects 2 issues 1980, 2 issues 1981. sub. price: $4.00; per copy: $2.00; sample: $2.00. Discounts: Trade, 40%. 70-80pp; 7X8½; †of. Reporting time: 1 month. Payment: 2 copies. Copyrighted, reverts to author.

Twowindows Press, Don Gray, 2644 Fulton St., Berkeley, CA 94704, (415) 849-1897. 1967. Poetry, fiction, art, parts-of-novels, plays, photos. "We tend to do small but well made books. Ms should run 12-32 pp. in book form. Style and content open. Discount schedules: See Serendipity Books Distribution" avg. press run 250-500. Pub'd 4 titles 1979. avg. price, cloth: $12.00; paper: $4.00. 32pp; †lp. Reporting time: varies. Payment: 10% of edition. Copyrights for author.

Tyndall Creek Press, David Beecher, 10 Titicus Mountain Road, c/o J M Eichroot, New Fairfield, CT 06810. 1971. Poetry. "Publishers of contemporary American oetry. Exclusive dealer for our books: 'Books Unlimited' 155 Harvard Ave., Allston, Mass. 02134. Submission of ms. by inquiry but all ms. will be returned within 30 days if correct postage and envelopes are provided. $2.50, $3.00 & $5.00 per book. Buys book rights only" Discounts: 40% off to wholesalers 50% in volume or frequency. 68-86pp; 5½X8; of. Reporting time: 1 month. Payment: free copies. COSMEP.

TYPE & PRESS, Garamond Press, Fred Williams, 24667 Heather Court, Hayward, CA 94545. 1974. Photos, interviews, letters. "Articles on historical heritage of printing, letterpress printing techniques and private presses. Up to 1800 words." circ. 250. quarterly. Pub'd 4 issues 1979; expects 4 issues 1980, 4 issues 1981. sub. price: $1.50; per copy: 30¢; sample: 30¢. Back issues: 30¢. Discounts: none. 4-8pp; 7¼X10¼; †lp. Reporting time: 2 weeks. Payment: none. Not copyrighted. §letterpress printing, history, techniques, etc. Ads: none/$13.50/free to subscribers for lp equip. APA, NAPA, AAPA, APHA.

TZADDIKIM, Judaic Book Service, Steven L. Maimes, 3726 Virden Avenue, Oakland, CA 94619. 1972. Art, criticism, reviews, poetry, photos. "TZADDIKIM is a catalogue-bibliography of specialized Judaic books. TZADDIKIM REVIEW contains book reviews and book notes. We sell, distribute and publish Jewish Books. All books are available by mail order." circ. 4,000. irreg. Pub'd 1 issue 1979; expects 1 issue 1980. 2 titles listed in the *Small Press Record of Books in Print* (9th Edition, 1980). sub. price: $2.00; per copy: varies; sample: $1.00. Discounts: Free to libraries, trade $0.50 each. 24pp; 8½X5½; of. Reporting time: 2 weeks. Payment: copies/books. Copyrighted. Pub's reviews: 35 in 1979. §Jewish books/Jewish mysticism/poetry/folklore/scripture/Hasidism. Ads: Inquire for rates.

U

U.S. Institute for Theatre Technology, Inc. (see also THEATRE DESIGN AND TECHNOLOGY), Kate Davy, Arnold Aronson, 1024 Holmes Ave, Charlottesville, VA 22901.

US1 Poets' Cooperative (see also US1 WORKSHEETS), Rotating board, 21 Lake Drive, Roosevelt, NJ 08555, (609) 448-5096. 1973. Poetry. "We are again reading manuscripts for US1 WORKSHEETS. For cloth prices inquire Wm. Wise & Co., Mountain Ave., Union, NJ" avg. press run 1,500. Expects 1 title 1980. 1 title listed in the *Small Press Record of Books in Print* (9th Edition, 1980). avg. price, paper: $4.95. Discounts: Inquire. 195pp; 6X9; of. Reporting time: i week to 4 months. Payment: copies. Copyrights for author. CCLM.

US1 WORKSHEETS, US1 Poets' Cooperative, Rotating panel, 21 Lake Drive, Roosevelt, NJ 08555, 609-448-5096. 1973. Poetry, fiction, articles, art, photos, cartoons, interviews, satire, music, parts-of-novels, long-poems. "Fiction should not be over 15 double-spaced pages. Poetry must be shorter than book length. A wide range of tastes represented in the rotating panel of editors. No restriction on subject or point of view. We read unsolicited mss., but accept very few." circ. 1,000. 2-3/yr. Expects 2 issues 1980, 2 issues 1981. sub. price: $4.00 (7 issues); per copy: $0.75; sample: $0.75. Back issues: Inquire. No. 1 and No. 2 have become quite rare. Discounts: inquire. 12pp; 11½X17; of. Reporting time: 1 week to 4 months. Payment: 2 copies. Copyrighted, reverts to author. Pub's reviews: none in 1979. §contemporary poetry and fiction. CCLM.

Uldale House Publ, 1 Uldale Dr, Egglescliffe, Cleveland TS16 9DW, United Kingdom. 1 title listed in the *Small Press Record of Books in Print* (9th Edition, 1980).

ULULATUS, Jay Vines, P.O. Box 397, Fort Smith, AR 72902, (501) 783-4956. 1978. Poetry, articles, interviews, long-poems. "*Ululatus* wants poets who express themselves through their poems, of themselves, their meaning in their world and environment as we are today. Always it is the poet first, but he/she must reveal themselves within their own position of reality. We do not want poems that are lies. Not currently taking submissions due to lack of funds. Back issues are still available, but no new issue will appear until mid-1981; no one seems quite as interested anymore. Current subscriptions will, of course, be filled" circ. 500-1000. 3/yr. Pub'd 2 issues 1979; expects 4 issues 1980. sub. price: $5.00 for 5 consecutive issues; per copy: $1.00; sample: $1.00 postage for 2 issues. Back issues: $1.00 postage for 2 issues. 40pp; 5½X8½. Reporting time: 4 weeks to 3 months. Payment: copies only. Copyrighted, reverts to author. Pub's reviews. §Books of poetry.

UMBRAL, A Quarterly of Speculative Poetry, Steve Rasnic Tem, 2330 Irving Street, Denver, CO 80211. 1978. Poetry, articles, art, photos, satire, reviews, letters, long-poems. "*Umbral* prints 1) poems rendering current technology and scientific concepts lyrically or commenting on them directly; 2) poems using the language of science figuratively; 3) science fiction and fantasy poems; 4) satires, fables, and prose poems; and 5) generally 'speculative' poetry — highly imaginative poems of personal & social myth. Recent contributors: Russell Edson, Chris Howell, Adam Hammer, Duane Ackerson, Yusef Kommunyaka, Carol Berge, Sonya Dorman, Sandra McPherson, Dave Smith, Dick Allen, Jack Anderson, Lynn Strongnin, Albert Goldbarth, Adrianne Marcus, Bill Tremblay Diane Ackerman, Patricia Goedicke, Peter Viereck." circ. 300. irreg,2-3/yr. Pub'd 3 issues 1979; expects 3 issues 1980, 3 issues 1981. sub. price: $6.00/4 issues; per copy: $1.50; double issue (4/5) $3.00; sample: $1.50. Back issues: #2,3-$1.50; #4/5-$3.00. Discounts: Varies, 40% average. 48pp; 5½X8½; of. Reporting time: 1 month most of the time. Payment: None at present, hope to later. Copyrighted, reverts to author. Pub's reviews. §Poetry, fantasy, science fiction, science & poetry. Ads: $20.00/$12.00.

THE U*N*A*B*A*S*H*E*D LIBRARIAN, THE "HOW I RUN MY LIBRARY GOOD" LETTER, Marvin H. Scilken, Editor; Mary P. Scilken, Assoc. Editor, G.P.O. Box 2631, New York, NY 10001. 1971. Articles, cartoons, satire, criticism, reviews. "U*L seeks long (and especially short) articles on innovative procedures; forms used in libraries. Articles should be complete to enable the reader to 'do it' with little or no research. Single paragraph 'articles' are ok with U*L. We ask for non exclusive rights." 4/yr. Pub'd 4 issues 1979; expects 4 issues 1980. 1 title listed in the *Small Press Record of Books in Print* (9th Edition, 1980). sub. price: $15.00 Foreign & Canadian postage add 10%; per copy: $4.00 foreign postage add 10% including Canada. Back issues: (all are in print) are $4.00 each add 10 percent foreign including Canada postage. 32pp; 8½X11; of. No payment. Copyrighted. Pub's reviews. §library subjects only.

UNCLE NASTY SERIES, Rob Earl, 73 Ware Street, Bearsted, Mainstone, Kent, England ME14 4PG, United Kingdom, (0622) 36436.

UNDER THE SIGN OF PISCES: Anais Nin and Her Circle, The Ohio State University Libraries Publications Committee, Richard R. Centing, 1858 Neil Avenue Mall, Columbus, OH 43210. 1970. Articles, photos, interviews, criticism, reviews. "Want biographical and bibliographical articles about Anais Nin and her circle (Henry Miller, *et al*). Studies on the art of diary keeping. Length of material limit: ten pages double-spaced. Style: informal or MLA- take your pick. Note: make checks for subscriptions payable to: The Ohio State University Libraries Publications Committee." circ. 400. 4/yr. Pub'd 4 issues 1979; expects 4 issues 1980. sub. price: $7.50 a year, 1980.; per copy: $2.00; sample: $2.00. All back issues in print at $5.00 a volume (1970-1979). 20pp; 5½X8½; of. Reporting time: 2 weeks. Payment: one copy. Copyrighted, does not revert to author. Pub's reviews: 6 in 1979. §books about autobiography/modern women writers/anything on Henry Miller and Lawrence Durrell/Nin's circle or times. Ads: $20/$10.

UNDERCURRENTS, Godfrey Boyle, 27 Clerkenwell Close, London, England EC1R 0AT, United Kingdom. 1972. Articles, cartoons, photos, satire, reviews, news items, interviews, letters. "A mag essentially of radical science and alternative technology, with emphases also in freak science stuff." circ. 8,000. 6/yr. sub. price: £2.50; per copy: 45p; sample: 45p. Back issues: all 50p. Discounts: 30% min. 52pp; size A4; lo. Reporting time: weeks.

420

‡**UNEARTH: The Magazine of Science Fiction Discoveries,** Jonathan Ostrowsky, John M. Landsberg, PO Box 779, Cambridge, MA 02139, (617) 876-0064. 1976. Fiction, articles, art, reviews, letters, parts-of-novels. "We publish speculative fiction of all kinds — science fiction, fantasy, etc. We lean toward material with strong characters and conflicts. Stories run from 2,500 to 12,000 words. We demand that contributors be at least somewhat familiar with the genre." circ. 5,200. 4/yr. Pub'd 4 issues 1979; expects 4 issues 1980, 4 issues 1981. sub. price: $5.00; per copy: $1.25; sample: $1.75. Back issues: No. 1, $3.50; No. 2, 3, 4, $2.50 each; No. 5, $3.00; No. 6, $2.75; No. 7, $1.75. Discounts: Wholesale discount 50% (negotiable), retail, bulk, classroom, all other — 40%. 128pp; 4¼X6¼; of. Reporting time: 1 to 6 weeks. Payment: Fiction $.005 word, $20.00 minimum; articles $.01 word. Copyrighted, does not revert to author. Pub's reviews: 25 in 1979. §Science fiction and fact, fantasy, horror. Ads: $100.00/$55.00/$.20. COSMEP.

UNICORN: A Miscellaneous Journal, Karen Rockow, Editor; Stuart Silverman, Assoc. Editor, 345 Harvard St. 3B, Cambridge, MA 02138, 617-354-0124. 1967. Articles, cartoons, interviews, satire, criticism, reviews, letters, collages, concrete art. "We are looking for all types of non-fiction, particularly lively articles and reviews (serious and whimsical) on all topics. We favor well-written pieces on the more off-beat and fun aspects of popular culture, folklore and literature; we also have an offbeat foods column: 'The Galumphing Gourmet;' use MLA style for any footnotes. Please-no intellectualese, studied incomprehensibility or pomposity, we pay $10.00 for front covers; $5.00 for back covers. Summer: Box 118, Salisbury, VT. 05769, 802-352-4236." circ. 700. irregr. Expects 1-2 issues 1980. sub. price: 3 issues; $4.00 Indiv., $5.00 Libraries, $4.50 Overseas; per copy: $1.50 Indiv., $2.00 Libraries; sample: $1.50. Back issues: All in print at single issue prices. Discounts: 35% on 10 or more. 28-32pp; 8½X11; of. Reporting time: 2-4 wks (summers longer). Payment: $5 honararium for essays plus copies & off prints. Copyrighted. Pub's reviews: 0 in 1979. §popular culture, folklore, gardening, progressive education, childrens lit. Ads: Query. CCLM, COSMEP.

UNICORN, Debbi Gambrill, Editor-in-Chief; Catherine Connor, Associate Editor; Lisa Almeda, Associate Editor, 4501 North Charles Street, Baltimore, MD 21210, 301-323-1010(ext. 356). 1975. Poetry, fiction, art, photos. "Shorter prose preferred; please send no more than 5 items per submission. Recent contributors: Linda Pastan, Jesse Glass Jr., Dan Johnson, Paul Lake, Lyn Stefenhagens, Katharyn Machan Aal." circ. 1,200. 4/yr. Pub'd 4 issues 1979; expects 4 issues 1980. sub. price: $4.00; per copy: $1.00; sample: $1.00. Back issues available-what we have on hand, at $0.75 per copy. Discounts: none. 28pp; 5½X8½; of. Reporting time: 8-10 weeks, longer in summer months. Payment in copies (three). Copyrighted, reverts to author. §Poetry and fiction. COSMEP, COSMEP-South, CCLM, PEN, Prison Writer's Project.

Unicorn Press, Teo Savory, Editor, P.O. Box 3307, Greensboro, NC 27402. 1965. Poetry, fiction. "All Unicorn books are printed on acid-free paper, bound between real Davy board by hand and all editions are sewn, not glued. We are not able to report on unsolicited manuscripts" avg. press run 500(chapbooks); 2,000(full-length books). Pub'd 10 titles 1979; expects 12 titles 1980. 37 titles listed in the *Small Press Record of Books in Print* (9th Edition, 1980). avg. price, cloth: $10.00-$15.00; paper: $4.00-$5.00; other: Chapbooks: varies. Discounts: 40% to bookstores. 12 to over 250pp; 5½X8½; †lp. Payment: 10% of all sales. Copyrights for author. COSMEP.

Union Park Press, William A. Koelsch, PO Box 2737, Boston, MA 02208. 1978. Articles. "At present the press confines itself to material on gay life and liberation in Boston and New England. It has so far published one book, A. Nolder Gay's *The View From the Closet,* a collection of essays on gay life and liberation originally published in Boston gay newspapers." avg. press run 1,850. Pub'd 1 title 1979; expects 1 title 1981. 1 title listed in the *Small Press Record of Books in Print* (9th Edition, 1980). avg. price, paper: $3.00. Discounts: 1-4 copies, 20%; 5 or more, 40%. 108pp; 5¼X8¼; of. Reporting time: 1 month. Copyrights for author. COSMEP.

UNITED ARTISTS, United Artists, Bernadette Mayer, Lewis Warsh, Flanders Road, Henniker, NH 03242. 1977. Poetry, interviews, long-poems. circ. 500. 4/yr. Pub'd 4 issues 1979; expects 4 issues 1980, 4 issues 1981. 4 titles listed in the *Small Press Record of Books in Print* (9th Edition, 1980). sub. price: $8.00; per copy: $2.00; sample: $2.00. 80pp; 8 1/2X11; †mi.

United Artists (see also UNITED ARTISTS), Lewis Warsh, Bernadette Mayer, Flanders Road, Henniker, NH 03242. 1977. Poetry, interviews, long-poems. avg. press run 750. Pub'd 5 titles 1979; expects 5 titles 1980. 11 titles listed in the *Small Press Record of Books in Print* (9th Edition, 1980). avg. price, paper: $3.00. 80pp; 7X10; of.

Unity Press, Doug Davis, 235 Hoover Rd., Santa Cruz, CA 95065, 408-427-2020. 1971. "'Books for Whole Living'" avg. press run 10,000 copies. Pub'd 4 titles 1979; expects 8 titles 1980, 12 titles 1981. 19 titles listed in the *Small Press Record of Books in Print* (9th Edition, 1980). avg. price, cloth: $12.95;

paper: $5.95. Discounts: 2-100 copies, 43%; 101-200 copies, 44%; 201 and up, 45%. 196pp; 5½X8½; of. Reporting time: 2 weeks. Payment: standard trade royalties. Copyrights for author. COSMEP.

UNIVERSAL HUMAN RIGHTS, Earl M Coleman Enterprises, Inc, Richard P. Claude, Editor in Chief, PO Box 143, Pine Plains, NY 12567, (518) 398-7193. 1979. Articles, reviews. "A quarterly journal offering scholars in the fields of law, philosophy, and the social sciences a forum in which to present transnational and international research within the scope of the Universal Declaration of Human Rights." 4/yr. Pub'd 4 issues 1979. sub. price: Inst $39.50; Indiv $19.50; per copy: $12.50; sample: free. Back issues: $12.50. Discounts: 10% agents & jobbers, for other rates contact publisher. 104pp; 6X9; of. Reporting time: 1 month. Copyrighted. Pub's reviews: 6 in 1979. §Human rights, social science, philosophy or law perspective. Ads: $200.00. SPA.

UNIVERSITY JOURNAL, Murray F. Markland, Graduate School, CSU, Chico, Chico, CA 95926. 1974. Poetry, fiction, articles, art, interviews, satire, criticism, reviews, letters, parts-of-novels, plays. "5-700 words. We do not publish unsolicited material from off-campus" circ. 1,500. 2/yr. Pub'd 3 issues 1979; expects 2 issues 1980, 2 issues 1981. sub. price: $5.00; per copy: $2.50. 28pp; 8½X11; †of. Reporting time: 6 weeks. Pub's reviews.

University of California Press (see also FILM QUARTERLY), Ernest Callenbach, University of California Press, Berkeley, CA 94720, (415) 642-6333. 1945. Criticism, reviews, interviews. avg. press run 7,500. avg. price, other: $2.00. Discounts: 10% off subscription price for subscription agents. 62pp; 6¾X8⅜; of. Reporting time: 2-3 weeks. Payment: 3 cents per word. copyright for publisher.

University of Chicago Press (see also SIGNS:A JOURNAL OF WOMEN IN CULTURE AND SOCIETY), 11030 Langley Avenue, Chicago, IL 60628, 312-568-1550.

University of Oregon Press (see also NORTHWEST REVIEW), John Witte, Editor; Deb Casey, Fiction Editor; John Addiego, Poetry Editor, 369 PLC, University of Oregon, Eugene, OR 97403, (503) 686-3957. 1957. Poetry, fiction, articles, art, photos, interviews, criticism, reviews, letters, long-poems, plays, concrete art. "Recent contributors in poetry: Gerald Stern, Olga Broumas, Wm. Stafford, David Wagoner; in fiction: Richard Kostelanetz, Joyce Carol Oates" avg. press run 2,000. Pub'd 3 titles 1979; expects 3 titles 1980, 3 titles 1981. avg. price, cloth: $9.95; paper: $2.50 (special issues $5.00 and $6.95). Discounts: 20% consignment; 40% wholesale. 150pp; 6X9; of. Reporting time: 6-8 weeks. Payment: 3 copies. Copyrights for author. CCLM, COSMEP.

University of the Trees Press, Christopher Hills, Ann Ray, Debbie Rozman, Norah Hills, PO Box 644, Boulder Creek, CA 95006, 408-338-3855. 1975. avg. press run 10,000. Pub'd 10 titles 1979; expects 10 titles 1980, 10 titles 1981. 16 titles listed in the *Small Press Record of Books in Print* (9th Edition, 1980). avg. price, cloth: $18.95; paper: $9.95. Discounts: 40 percent retail, 50 percent distr. 300pp; size varies; of. Payment: 10 percent. Copyrights for author.

University Of Utah Press (see WESTERN HUMANITIES REVIEW)

University Of Wales Press (see EFRYDIAU ATHRONYDDOL; STUDIA CELTICA; Y GWYDDONYDD; BULLETIN OF THE BOARD OF CELTIC STUDIES; WELSH HISTORY REVIEW; LLEN CYMRU (Board of Celtic Studies))

UNIVERSITY OF WINDSOR REVIEW, Eugene McNamara, c/o University of Windsor, Windsor, Ontario N9B3P4, Canada. 1966. Poetry, fiction, articles, art, criticism, reviews. "We try to offer a balance of essays, fiction, poetry, and reviews—but we seem to have developed into a platform for some really excellent fiction and poetry especially: W.D. Valgardson, Joyce Carol Oates, Tom Wayman etc." circ. 750. 2/yr. sub. price: $3.50; per copy: $1.75; sample: $1.75. Back issues: please write. Discounts: 40 percent. 100pp; 5¾X9; lp. Reporting time: 6 weeks. Payment: $25.00 for story or essay, $10.00 for poem. Copyrighted, reverts to author. Pub's reviews: 15 in 1979. §current fiction and poetry. Ads: No ads. COSMEP.

University of Wisconsin Press (see CONTEMPORARY LITERATURE)

UNIVERSITY PUBLISHING, Leonard Michaels, William McClung, Christine Taylor, 2431B Durant, Berkeley, CA 94704, (415) 548-0585. 1976. Articles, interviews, criticism, reviews. "*University Publishing*, an international quarterly, reviews books from the nearly 100 university presses. We believe university imprints are different from commercial or private imprints, and that observing the sum of university publishing engages the mind in unexpectedly rich ways. Each issue includes articles and columns as well as reviews, and a complete list of the news books printed by university presses during the previous quarter. Each issue is organized around a theme, War, Film, Music, Poetry, that has been illuminated by scholars from several disciplines. *Univesity Publishing* is as beautiful and lucid as we can

422

make it." circ. 10,000. 4/yr. Pub'd 2 issues 1979; expects 3 issues 1980, 4 issues 1981. sub. price: $6.00; per copy: $2.00; sample: $2.00 plus postage. Back issues: $2.50 per issue. Discounts: Bulk rates: one year subscription for 25, $150.00. 32pp; 13X17; of. Reporting time: 1 quarter. Copyrighted. Pub's reviews: 35 in 1979. §University Press Books, any subject. Ads: $400.00/$250.00. COSMEP.

University Statistical Tracts, Sol Weintraub, 75-19 171st Street, Flushing, NY 11366, (212) 969-7553. 1977. "College mathematics texts." avg. press run 2,500. Pub'd 1 title 1979; expects 1 title 1980, 2 titles 1981. avg. price, paper: $9.95. Discounts: 20-40%. 450pp; 11X8½; †of. Reporting time: 3 months. Payment: Standard. Copyrights for author. COSMEP.

UNMENDABLY INTEGRAL: an audiocassette quarterly of the arts, Full Track Press, Joe Cuomo, Editorial Director, c/o Full Track Press, PO Box 55, Planetarium Station, New York, NY 10024. 1978. Poetry, fiction, interviews, long-poems. "*Unmendably Integral:* an audiocassette quarterly of the arts is published by Full Track Press on high quality cassette tape (also available on broadcast quality 7¼ips open reel). The purpose of *Unmendably Ingegral* is to present a wholistic, people's-culture approach to the arts, focusing on those writers and artists whose work is of particular relevance to the culture we live in. Usually, each issue is concerned with the work of one individual writer or artist (issue #1: Meridel Le Sueur; #2: Roman Vishniac; #3: James Purdy with readings by the writer & an interview providing a context for the work of that writer or artist." 4/yr. Pub'd 3 issues 1979; expects 5 issues 1980, 4 issues 1981. sub. price: $35.00; per copy: $10.00; sample: $10.00. Back issues: $10.00 per issue. Discounts: 15% to agents. 90 minute cassette. Reporting time: 2 months on 7½ips open reel or high quality cassette only. Copyrighted.

UNMUZZLED OX, Michael Andre, Erika Rothenberg, 105 Hudston Street #311, New York City, NY 10013. 1971. Poetry, fiction, articles, art, photos, interviews, criticism, reviews, music, letters, parts-of-novels. "I try to edit a magazine which would be my favorite magazine if I didn't even edit it. That leads me to publish favorite people, like Creeley, Corso, Berrigan, Lewitt, Rivers, Eleanor Antin, James Wright, Ray Johnson. It's fun, as well, to try to create a personality for the magazine which, through design and patter, would embody the collective spirit of our contributors; we haven't succeeded. Secondary address: Box 550 Kingston Canada. Publication frequency: 1 volume of up to 4 numbers per year" circ. 4,500. 4/yr. 5 titles listed in the *Small Press Record of Books in Print* (9th Edition, 1980). sub. price: $8.00; per copy: $3.50; sample: $5.00. Back issues: 1-6:$12 each 7-21 cover price. Discounts: 40%. 140pp; 8½X5½; of. Reporting time: 2 weeks. Payment: none. Copyrighted. §art, literature, music, politics. Ads: $65/$35. CCLM.

THE UNREALIST: A Left Literary Magazine, The Unrealist Press, Peter J. Laska, 1243 Pine View Drive, Morgantown, WV 26505. 1977. Poetry, fiction, articles, interviews, satire, criticism, reviews. circ. 500. 1/yr. Pub'd 1 issue 1979; expects 2 issues 1980. sub. price: $5.50, 2 issue sub; per copy: $3.00; sample: $3.00. Discounts: Inquire. 60-100pp; 8½X11. Reporting time: 1-2 months. Payment: author's copy. Copyrighted, reverts to author. Pub's reviews: 5 in 1979. §Poetry, fiction. Ads: Inquire, will exchange ads. COSMEP-SOUTH.

The Unrealist Press (see also THE UNREALIST: A Left Literary Magazine), P. J. Laska, Editor, 1243 Pine View Drive, Morgantown, WV 26505. 1977. Poetry. Discounts: Inquire.

THE UNSPEAKABLE VISIONS OF THE INDIVIDUAL, TUVOTI Books, Arthur Winfield Knight, Kit Knight, PO Box 439, California, PA 15419. 1971. Poetry, fiction, articles, art, photos, interviews, satire, criticism, reviews, letters, parts-of-novels, long-poems, collages, non-fiction. "Jack Kerouac, William Burroughs, Gary Snyder, Allen Ginsberg, Gregory Corso, Lawrence Ferlinghetti, Carolyn Cassady, Michael McClure, Carl Solomon, Herbert Huncke, Diane Di Prima, John Clellon Holmes, Philip Whalen, Neal Cassady, & Peter Orlovsky. Particularly interested in beat writing. Have used photographs by Elsa Dorfman, Fred W. McDarrah & Jill Krementz and Larry Keenan, Jr. Vol. 8, *The Beat Journey,* $7.50. Vol. 9, *Alchemical Poem* by Gregory Corso, broadside reproduced in holograph in an edition of 500 numbered copies, $5.00" circ. 2,000. 1/yr. Pub'd 3 issues 1979; expects 1 issue 1980, 1 issue 1981. sub. price: $8.00; per copy: varies; sample: $3.00. Back issues: Vol 1(No 1,2,3), $60; Vol. 2(No 1,2,3), $35; Vol. 3(No 1,2,3), $15; Vol. 4(The Beat Book), $10. Vol. 5 (The Beat Diary), $10.95. Vol. 6 (*Neal in Court* by Jack Kerouac),$5.00; Vol. 7 (*Bowling Green Poems* in a edition of 250 signed copies by John Clellon Holmes), $10.00. Prices subject to change on collector's editions. Discounts: query. 176pp; 8½X11, 5½X8½; of. Reporting time: 2 months. Payment: 2 contributor's copies. Copyrighted, reverts to author. Pub's reviews: 0 in 1979. §literary-esp. Beat literature. Ads: $500.00/$250.00. CCLM, COSMEP.

Upland Press, PO Box 7390, Chicago, IL 60680, (312) 266-2087.

URBAN & SOCIAL CHANGE REVIEW, Karen Wolk Feinstein, Boston College, McGuinn Hall, Chestnut Hill, MA 02167. 1967. Articles, photos, criticism, reviews. "Articles usually 12-20 typewritten pages. Theme: Urban & Social Change. bias: Article should have implications for application to solve social problems or ameliorate urban crisis." circ. 2,500. 2/yr. Pub'd 2 issues 1979; expects 2 issues 1980, 2 issues 1981. sub. price: $8.00; per copy: $4.00; sample: free. Back issues: $3.00. 32-40pp; 8½X11; lp. Reporting time: 2 months. Payment: none. Copyrighted, does not revert to author. Pub's reviews: 50-100 in 1979. §urban studies, social problems, social change. Ads: $200.-00/$100.00/$75.00.

URBANE GORILLA, Raven Publications, Ed Tork, 29 Parker Rd, Sheffield S10 1BN, United Kingdom. 1970. Poetry, fiction, articles, art, criticism, reviews, parts-of-novels, long-poems, news items. circ. 1,000. 2/yr (bi-annual). Pub'd 2 issues 1979; expects 2 issues 1980, 2 issues 1981. sub. price: £1.20 ($10.00); per copy: 75p or $5.00 inc. p&p; sample: 90p or $5.00 inc. p&p. Back issues: 90p or $5.00 inc. p&p. Discounts: Rate on enquiry. 80pp; size A5; of. Reporting time: 2-3 months. Payment: none. Copyrighted. Pub's reviews: 27 in 1979. §Poetry, mags, books. Ads: £20.00 equals $35.00/page pro rata. ALP.

Sherry Urie, Sherry Urie, RFD, West Glover, VT 05875, (802) 525-6966. 1978. Poetry, fiction. "Manuscripts welcome. Vermont and other New England material given priority. Non-fiction preferred." avg. press run 2,000. Expects 2 titles 1980, 2 titles 1981. 2 titles listed in the *Small Press Record of Books in Print* (9th Edition, 1980). avg. price, paper: $3.95. Discounts: 1-4 copies, 20%; 5-24 copies, 40%; 25-99 copies, 45%; 100 up, 50%. 200pp; 5½X8½; of. Reporting time: 4-6 weeks. Payment: Arranged on an individual basis. Copyrights for author.

Urion Press, A.H. Rosenus, Box 2244, Eugene, OR 97402. 1972. Fiction. "Fiction, history, reprints. Please send letter of inquiry first" avg. press run 2,500. Pub'd 1 title 1979. 5 titles listed in the *Small Press Record of Books in Print* (9th Edition, 1980). avg. price, cloth: $9.95; paper: $5.95. Discounts: bkstrs 40% on orders over 3/jobbers 50% on orders over 10/. 250pp; of. Reporting time: 1 month. Copyrights for author. COSMEP.

UROBOROS, Allegany Mountain Press, Ford F. Ruggieri, Helen Ruggieri, 111 N. 10th St., Olean, NY 14760, 716-372-0935. 1974. Poetry, fiction, articles, art, photos, cartoons, interviews, satire, criticism, reviews, music, letters, parts-of-novels, long-poems, collages, concrete art. "Length: fiction up to 6000 words; criticism/reviews up to 500 words; poetry-no restrictions; art work-no restrictions; photographs-8 x 10" glossies. Style: poetry, fiction, art-no restrictions; criticism, reviews on small press literature only. Biases: contemporary & ancient myth, folk tales, archetypal perceptions, experimental edges, visions, dreams, satire, sense of humor. Generally open to anything that moves, means and/or is." circ. 500. 2/yr. Pub'd 2 issues 1979; expects 2 issues 1980, 2 issues 1981. sub. price: 3 issues for 5 dollars; per copy: $2.00; sample: $2.00. Discounts: 2-5 copies: 25%; 6-10 copies: 30%; 11-24 copies: 440%; 25+ copies: 50%. 80pp; 5½X8½; †of. Reporting time: 6-8 weeks. Payment: copies. Copyrighted. Pub's reviews: 3 in 1979. §poetry, fiction, state of the arts. Ads: $50/$25. CCLM, COSMEP, NYSSPA.

URTHKIN, Larry Ziman, P O Box 67485, Los Angeles, CA 90067, 213-556-3033. 1977. Poetry, fiction, art, photos, parts-of-novels, long-poems. "Short pieces, up to 500 words." circ. 300. 1/yr. Pub'd 1 issue 1979; expects 1 issue 1980, 1 issue 1981. sub. price: $5.00; per copy: $5.00; sample: $5.00. Back issues: $5.00. No discounts. 120pp; 8½X11; 5½X8½; of. Reporting time: 1-3 weeks. Payment: 1 copy per contributor. Copyrighted, reverts to author. COSMEP, WIP.

UZZANO, Uzzano Press, Robert Schuler, Editor, 511 Sunset Drive, Menomonie, WI 54751, (715) 235-6525. 1975. Poetry, art, photos, parts-of-novels, long-poems. "All issues of the journal are single author chapbooks or books. We have issued chapbooks and books by Dave Etter, John Knoepfle, William Kloefkorn, Thomas McGrath, Ray Smith, Raymond Roseliep, and many others. Primarily interested in Midwestern poetry but will look at high quality fiction. Inquire before sending manuscripts" circ. 500-1,000. 4/yr. Pub'd 4 issues 1979; expects 4 issues 1980, 4 issues 1981. sub. price: $7.50; per copy: $2.50; sample: $2.50. Back issues: $2.50 for issues 1-16. Discounts: 1-4 copies, 20%; 5 or more copies, 40%. 64pp; 5½X8½; of. Reporting time: 4-6 weeks. Payment: 100 copies to each author of a book or chapbook; cash when available. Copyrighted. Ads: none. CCLM.

Uzzano Press (see also UZZANO), Robert Schuler, Editor, 511 Sunset Drive, Menomonie, WI 54751, (715) 235-6525. 1976. "Uzzano Press prints chapbooks and books of poems. To date we have published *Bixby Creek Poems* and *Four From Kentucky* by William Witherup, *Open Songs* by Thomas McGrath, and *The Yellow Lamp* by Ray Smith. Inquire before sending mss." avg. press run 500-1,000. Pub'd 2 titles 1979; expects 2 titles 1980, 2 titles 1981. 12 titles listed in the *Small Press Record of Books in Print* (9th Edition, 1980). avg. price, paper: $2.50. Discounts: 1-4 copies, 20%; 5 or more copies, 40%. 64pp; 5½X8½; of. Reporting time: 4-6 weeks. Payment: 100 copies to author. Copyrights for author.

V

V. A. C. (Vereinigung Aktiver Kultur) (see also WURZEL), Ders U. Flurey, U Box, 6671 Menzonio, Switzerland. 1972. "*Only* wurzel, info letters, posters, tarot (psychedelic tarot), tarot (cards)" avg. price, paper: contribution free (int. stamp); other: psych. tarot: 25.sfr/cards: 5. sfr. pp varies; of. Payment: 15% royalty. Copyrights for author.

Vagabond Press, 1610 N. Water, Ellensburg, WA 98926. 1966. Poetry, fiction, articles, art, photos, interviews, reviews, letters, parts-of-novels, plays. "Query before submitting" avg. press run 900. Pub'd 3 titles 1979; expects 2 titles 1980. 11 titles listed in the *Small Press Record of Books in Print* (9th Edition, 1980). avg. price, cloth: $8.00; paper: $3.00. Discounts: 40% trade; orders over $30.00, 50%; 20% book jobbers. 200pp; 6X9; †of. Reporting time: 3-4 weeks. Payment: by agreement. Copyrights for author.

Vagrom Chapbooks (see Sparrow Press)

VAJRA BODHI SEA, Buddhist Text Translation Society, Bhkshuni Heng Ch'ih, Editor-in-Chief; Bhikshuni Heng Ch'ing, Editor; Bhikshuni Heng Tao, Editor; Upasaka Liu Kuo Chi, Editor of Chinese Half, 1731 15th St, Gold Mountain Monastery, San Francisco, CA 94103, 861-9672. 1970. Poetry, fiction, articles, art, photos, interviews, reviews, letters. "*VAJRA BODHI SEA* is the monthly journal of the Sino-American Buddhist Association, printing translations of Buddhist texts, biographies of Buddhist Masters, feature articles, World Buddhist News, poetry, language lessons, and a calendar of Buddhist Holidays and events. For publishing operations: City of 10,000 Buddhas, Talmage, CA 95481. Beginning with the September 1978 issue, *Vajra Bodhi Sea* has been published bi-lingually (Chinese-English). Complimentary subscription available with 'Sustaining' membership in Sino-American Buddhist Assn. Sustaining memb. available with $500 donation (three year term)" circ. 4,000. 12/yr. Pub'd 12 issues 1979; expects 12 issues 1980. 1 title listed in the *Small Press Record of Books in Print* (9th Edition, 1980). sub. price: $22.00; per copy: $2.00; sample: $2.00, free copies to universities and public libraries (sample copy one time only). Back issues: Prices vary from $100.00 to $2.00 dependent on rarity of issues. Discounts: bulk, non-profit organization (the publication is a second class periodical). 48pp; 11X8½; of. Payment: $22.00 per year (same for all). Copyrighted, reverts to author. §buddhism. Ads: No advertising.

VALHALLA, Merging Media, Rochelle Dubois, 59 Sandra Circle A-3, Westfield, NJ 07090, 232-7224. 1970. Poetry, fiction, articles, art, photos, interviews, criticism, reviews, music, letters, parts-of-novels, collages, plays, concrete art, news items. "Received $600 CCLM grant for VALHALLA 7, Women's Fiction" circ. 500. 1/yr. Pub'd 1 issue 1979; expects 1 issue 1980, 1 issue 1981. sub. price: $3.00; per copy: $3.00; sample: $3.00. Discounts: 40%/bookstores etc. no consignment. 50-75pp; 6X9; of. Reporting time: 1 month. Payment: Copies except for *Valhalla 6,* over age 50 contributors to be paid if funded by CCLM. Copyrighted, reverts to author. Pub's reviews: 2 in 1979. §Send titles & flyers first. Ads: $25/$15/. CCLM/COSMEP.

Valkyrie Press, Inc., Marjorie Schuck, Publisher, President, Owner, 2135 1st Street South, St. Petersburg, FL 33712, 813-822-6069. 1972. Poetry, fiction. "We are book publishers with our own full-scale modern book production and printing equipment including typesetting, layout, design, camera, offset presses, bindery. In our just now beginning eight years of existence, our complete list totals over 175 books, both cloth and paper, on such subjects as art, biography, juvenile, classical studies, fiction, folklore, health, history, how-to, humor, occult, philosophy, photography, poetry, religion, self-awareness, spiritual, and translations. We have recently entered into a cooperative publishing arrangement with the Lorber Verlag (publishers) of Bietigheim, Germany. Our recent major royalty book *Angel City,* by Patrick D. Smith, author of *Forever Island* and other novels, is scheduled to be produced by CBS-TV into a two-hour feature movie. It will also be translateed into Japanese and Russian. Several other of our books have received major and notable reviews. See listing in the *Literary Market Place.* We operate on a flexible, generous Publisher-Author Contract: straight royalty, cooperative, and/or subsidy-with a widescale promotional and publicity program." avg. press run 1,000. Pub'd 15 titles 1979; expects 15 titles 1980. 50 titles listed in the *Small Press Record of Books in Print* (9th Edition, 1980). avg. price, cloth: $6.95; paper: $4.95. Discounts: 40% and up. 128pp; 5½X8½; †of. Reporting time: 2-6 mos. Payment: 3 contract bases - see comments above. Copyrights for author. CCLM, COSMEP.

Van Dyk Publications, Adrian C. Jr. Van Dyk, 10216 Takilma Road, Cave Junction, OR 97523, (503) 592-3430. 1975. Poetry, long-poems. "Van Dyk Publications is a self-publishing business. I write, edit, design, and publish my own books of poetry under my own name, Adrian C. Van Dyk Jr. I take care of all distribution, wholesaling, collection, and production. All publicity and advertising is done by myself. The only thing I hire out, is a printer, because I do not have my own press. I have successfully published four books of poetry since 1974, with the first one in a second printing and also the third. I was titled 'Poet Laureate' in 1974, and have been selected to appear in 'Who's Who in Poetry' by the National Society of Poets. My work has been endorsed by such eminent authors as Jessamyn West McPherson and Lawrence Ferlinghetti. My Master's degree in English is from Sonoma State University in Rohnert Park, California. I do not solicit manuscripts from other authors, however Van Dyk Publications does intend to publish another author, Dianna Janyce, in 1979- the title *Dreams & Rainbows*." avg. press run 800. Pub'd 1 title 1979; expects 1 title 1980, 1 title 1981. 4 titles listed in the *Small Press Record of Books in Print* (9th Edition, 1980). avg. price, paper: $3.50. Discounts: 40% on orders of 10 copies or more. 75pp; 6X10; of. Copyrights for author. NSP (National Society of Poets).

VANDERBILT POETRY REVIEW, c/o Rochester Routes, 50 Inglewood Drive, Rochester, NY 14619. 1972. "*The Vanderbilt Poetry Review* published poetry, poetry translations and interviews. Past issues included established poets like Auden, Bly, and Heyen as well as new and younger writers. We also published special issues devoted to contemporary Canadian poetry and to contemporary Italian poetry. Due to funding problems, we have suspended publication. Back issues Nos. 1-4 may be purchased at the above address for $5.00 each." Back issues: No. 1-4 $5.00 each. 64pp; 5½X8½; of.

VANESSA POETRY MAGAZINE (see also The Many Press), John Welch, 15 Norcott Road, London, England N16 7BJ, United Kingdom@. 1976. Poetry, criticism, reviews. avg. press run 250. Pub'd 1-2 titles 1979. avg. price, paper: $1.50. 36pp; size A5, A4; †of. Reporting time: 2 months. Payment: in copies. Copyrights for author. ALP, ALMS.

Vanguard Books, Arlee Frantz, Managing Editor, P.O. Box 3566, Chicago, IL 60654, (312) 942-0774. 1975. "Publishers and distributors of literature reflecting current social struggles. Reprints, and original material: full length books. Looking for manuscripts of a socially progressive nature: histories, biographies, autobiographies, analysis, or fiction." avg. press run 5,000. Pub'd 1 title 1979; expects 4 titles 1980, 4 titles 1981. 29 titles listed in the *Small Press Record of Books in Print* (9th Edition, 1980). avg. price, cloth: $8.50; paper: $4.95; other: $2.95. Discounts: bookstores 1 copy, 20%; 2-4 copies, 30%; 5 or more copies, 40%; jobbers and distributors: 40%; Textbook dis. with full return privileges 20%, libraries 20%. 250pp; 5½X8½, 4¼X7; of. Reporting time: 2-6 months. Payment: arranged on an individual basis. Copyrights for author. COSMEP, ABA.

Vanilla Press (THE SOURCE: A Bimonthly Magazine of Alternatives for the Sensitized Reader), Jean-Marie Fisher, Publisher; Nell Morningstar, Managing Editor, 2400 Colfax Ave., South, Minneapolis, MN 55405, 612-374-4726. 1975. Fiction, art, photos, cartoons, satire. "Now interested primarily in regional material, Midwest writers and artists. Controversial material, national writers; no poetry for a few years, no fluff." avg. press run 1,000-5,000. Pub'd 1 title 1979; expects 2 titles 1980, 4 titles 1981. 8 titles listed in the *Small Press Record of Books in Print* (9th Edition, 1980). avg. price, cloth: $9.95; paper: $3.00-$3.50. Discounts: Bookstores 40%, distributors 50%; no rates for less than 3 books. 72pp; 7X8½; 5½X8½; of. Reporting time: 3-6 months. Payment: After Vanilla Press breaks even on cost of books, author receives standard royalties. Copyrights for author.

Vanity Press (see also PAPER NEWS), Tuli Kupferberg, 160 6th Avenue, New York, NY 10013, 212-925-3823. 1980. Cartoons, satire, music. "Will accept little (if any) unsolicited work. Interested in aphoristic forms, cartoons, 'funny' advetisements, documents, ephemera (found materials)." avg. press run 1,000. Pub'd 2 titles 1979. avg. price, paper: $0.50. Discounts: 40%. 32pp; 4¼X5½; of.

Variety Press, Judith King, 5214 Starkridge, Houston, TX 77035, (713) 721-5919. 1979. avg. press run 2,500. Pub'd 1 title 1979. 1 title listed in the *Small Press Record of Books in Print* (9th Edition, 1980). avg. price, paper: $5.95. Discounts: 1-4, 20%; 5-24, 40%; 25-49, 43%; 50-99, 46%; 100 up, 50%. 176pp; 5½X8½; of.

VECTOR, British Science Fiction Assoc. Ltd., Mike Dickinson, 269 Wykeham Road, Reading RG6 1PL, United Kingdom, 0734-666142. 1958. Articles, art, cartoons, photos, reviews, interviews, criticism, letters, satire. "The official organ of the BSFA. Publishes serious critical material on science fiction. No limit on length of articles. Recent contributors include J.G. Ballard (interviewed), Brian Aldiss, John Brunner, Ian Watson, John Clute, Mark Adlard, Ursula Le Guin, Edmund Cooper, James Blish." circ. 900. 4/yr. Pub'd 6 issues 1979; expects 4 issues 1980, 4 issues 1981. sub. price: 4 issues - $6.00 (Air mail - $12.00) (Institutions - $8.00 + $2.00); per copy: $1.50; sample: $1.00. Back issues: Most available. Write for price list. Discounts: 33⅓ to dealer. 48pp; size A5; lo. Reporting time: 3

weeks. No payment. Copyrighted, reverts to author. Pub's reviews: 74 in 1979. §Science fiction, fantasy and related subjects. Ads: £30.00 or $50.00/other sizes pro rata.

VEGA, Vega, JoAnn Amadeo, 252 No. 16th Street, Bloomfield, NJ 07003. 1976. Poetry, fiction, art, cartoons, letters, long-poems. circ. 350. 6/yr. Pub'd 6 issues 1979; expects 6 issues 1980, 6 issues 1981. sub. price: $12.00; per copy: $2.00; sample: $2.00. Back issues: $2.00. Discounts: free copies to waiting rooms and nursing homes while the supply lasts. 64pp; 8X11; †of. Reporting time: within 1 month. Payment: $10.00 award best poem per issue/contest; 1 free copy to 3 runner up poems, 2 free copies to spotlight poet, 2 free copies for cover design. Copyrighted, reverts to author. Pub's reviews: 70 in 1979. §Poetry.

Vega (see VEGA)

VEGATABLE BOX, James Ulmer, 4142 11th NE #3, Seattle, WA 98105, (206) 632-2518. 1978. Poetry, art, photos, interviews, reviews, long-poems. "No biases. Recent contributors: James Bertolino, William Matthews, Anselm Hollo, Sam Hamill, Terry Stokes, Richard Blessing, Ted Kooser, Rosmary Waldrop." circ. 250. 2/yr. Pub'd 1 issue 1979; expects 2 issues 1980. sub. price: $3.00; per copy: $1.50; sample: $1.50. Back issues: none availabe at present. Discounts: negotiable. 40pp; 5½X8½; †of. Reporting time: 4-6 weeks. Payment: 2 copies of the magazine. Copyrighted, reverts to author. Pub's reviews: 1 in 1979. §Contemporary poetry. Ads: negotiable, exchange ads. OAC, CCLM.

Vehicle Editions, Annabel Levitt, 238 Mott Street, New York, NY 10012, 226-1769. 1974. Poetry, art, long-poems, collages, letters, fiction. "Vehicle Editions generally does not accept submissions. Editor seeks authors to represent a broad range. Some past and forthcoming authors include: Simon Schuchat, Annabel Levitt, Jayne Anne Phillips, Christopher Knowles, Michael Lally, Ted Berrigan, Bill Berkson, Barbara Guest, Alice Notley. In some cases authors assist in production." avg. press run 400-2,500. Pub'd 3 titles 1979; expects 4 titles 1980, 4 titles 1981. 4 titles listed in the *Small Press Record of Books in Print* (9th Edition, 1980). avg. price, cloth: $25.00; paper: $5.00. Discounts: 40/60 bookstores; 50/50 distributors. 20-100pp; 5X7; †of/lp. Payment: varies. Copyrights for author. NYSSPA.

Vehicule Press (see also DAVINCI MAGAZINE), Si Dardick, Guy Lavoie, D. Vessey, Madeleine Duefresne, Jill Smith, Johanne Pagean, PO Box 125, Station La Cite, Montreal, Quebec H2X 3M0, Canada, 514-861-8982. 1973. Poetry, fiction, art, concrete art. "Vehicule Press publishes and distributes. Write for our current catalogue. We distribute art books/editions, bookworks, poetry, art catalogues and small press publications. In 1977 we published books by George Bowering, John McAuley, Claudia Lapp and Andre Farkas and a comprehensive survey of writing in Montreal called *Montreal—English Poetry of the Seventies* edited by Farkas and Norris. For 1978: *Inter-Sleep,* by Opal L. Nations, *I Don't Know* by David McFadden, *No Parking* by Tom Konyves, *The Trees of Unknowing* by Stephen Morrissey. Vehicule Press also published 1980: *Violent Duality: A Study of Margaret Atwood* by S. Grace; 1980: *Continuation* by Louis Dudek, *Spreading Time* by Earle Birney." avg. press run 500-1,000. Pub'd 7 titles 1979; expects 8 titles 1980. 14 titles listed in the *Small Press Record of Books in Print* (9th Edition, 1980). avg. price, cloth: $14.00; paper: $4.00; other: $3.00 plus 50¢ charge on all orders for postage. Discounts: Trade 40 pc, distributors/50 pc, universities-20 pc. 80pp; 5¼X8¼; †of. Reporting time: 60 days. Payment: Copies plus royalties. Copyrights for author. CBIC.

Velvet Flute Books, Joyce Strauss, Publisher, 6050 Canterbury Drive, E119, Culver City, CA 90230, (213) 776-5429. 1979. Fiction, art. avg. press run 1,000. Pub'd 1 title 1979. avg. price, paper: $4.95. Discounts: 20% Libraries, 40% bookstores. 100pp; 8X9; of.

Venice West Publishers, Nettie Lipton, 3050 S. Ventura Road, Oxnard, CA 93030, (805) 483-7818.

Ventura Press, Raymond Barrio, P.O. Box 1076, Guerneville, CA 95446. 1965. Fiction. "My own private self-publishing press." avg. press run 500. Pub'd 1 title 1979; expects 1 title 1980. 3 titles listed in the *Small Press Record of Books in Print* (9th Edition, 1980). avg. price, cloth: $8.50; paper: $3.75. Discounts: 5 or more 40%. 200pp; 5½X8½; of. No submissions accepted. Copyrights for author. WIP.

Veritas Press, Sarah Splaver Ph. D., 3310 Rochambeau Ave., New York, NY 10467, (212) 652-1540. 1978. "We published our first book, *Your Mind And Breast Diseases* a psychologist-breast cancer patient who did not have a mastectomy describes her experiences and discusses the relationships between the mind and breast diseases. In September 1978. Other materials we plan to put out will be in the fields of health and/or psychology." Expects 1 title 1980. avg. price, other: $8.95. Discounts: 10-19 titles, 10%; 20 or more titles, 20%. 5½X8½; of. We are not seeking submissions.

Veritie Press, Inc., Elizabeth Boyer, PO Box 222, Novelty, OH 44072. 1975. Fiction "Have published only two books in our first two years. *Marguerite De La Rogue, A Story Of Survival* and *Freydis And*

Gudrid both by Elizabeth Boyer. Both are historical novels based on fact. We are not yet ready to accept submissions." 3 titles listed in the *Small Press Record of Books in Print* (9th Edition, 1980).

‡**Verlag Pohl'n'Mayer (DEUTSCHHEFT)**, K.L. Pohl, K.H. Mayer, P. Box, D-8950 Kaufbeuren, West Germany, 089-333-980. 1972. Poetry, fiction. "We are editing young German and Austrian poets (Derschau, Broedl, Wagner) and call ourselves the testpilots of new German literature. In our mag *Deutschheft* you can find first published poems and stories written by wellknown German/Austrian and American writers (e.g. Enzensberger, Wondratschek, Rosei and Bukowski, Plymell, Ginsberg, Norse, Micheline)." avg. press run 1,000-5,000. Pub'd 3 titles 1979; expects 6 titles 1980, 8 titles 1981. 3 titles listed in the *Small Press Record of Books in Print* (9th Edition, 1980). avg. price, paper: books: DM 10.00; mags: DM 2.80. Discounts: 35%-50%. books: 100pp; mags: 40pp; size books: 20.5X13.5, mags: 24X18; of. Reporting time: books: 4 months; mags: 3 months. Payment: 10-15 percent of retail price. Copyrights for author.

VERMONT CHILDREN'S MAGAZINE, Ed Osborn, President, PO Box 941, Burlington, VT 05401, 425-2359. 1975. Poetry, fiction, art, photos, music, letters. "Our magazine is a collection of work done by Vermont elementary school children. We try to let their inclinations dictate the subject areas." circ. 5,000. 4/yr. Pub'd 2 issues 1979; expects 3 issues 1980, 4 issues 1981. sub. price: $5.00 for 4 issues; sample: $2.00. Back issues: our circulation precludes a stockpiling of past issues. Discounts: VT. elementary schools receive the magazine at cost (or less) as we are trying to support it with grants. 24pp; 8½X11; of. Reporting time: 2 months max. Payment: none-all contributors are children. Copyrighted, does not revert except by request. §children's literature, education, publishing. Ads: No advertising. CCLM, COSMEP.

Vermont Crossroads Press, Constance Cappel, President & Publisher, Box 30, Waitsfield, VT 05673, (802) 496-2469. 1974. Poetry, fiction, photos. "Publishing hard cover & soft cover books for the school-library market & the trade mkt. currently 40% children's books 60% adult-price range from $1.95-$9.50." avg. press run 5,000. Pub'd 6 titles 1979; expects 10 titles 1980. 5 titles listed in the *Small Press Record of Books in Print* (9th Edition, 1980). avg. price, cloth: $5.95; paper: $4.95. 150pp; 6X9, 8½X12; of. Reporting time: 2 month. Payment: 10% of retail, twice yearly. Copyrights for author. COSMEP

Vesta Publications Limited, Stephen Gill, Editor-in-Chief, PO Box 1641, Cornwall, Ont. K6H 5V6, Canada, 613-932-2135. 1974. Poetry, fiction, criticism, plays. avg. press run 1,000. Pub'd 14 titles 1979; expects 12 titles 1980, 19 titles 1981. 32 titles listed in the *Small Press Record of Books in Print* (9th Edition, 1980). avg. price, cloth: $10.00; paper: $4.00. Discounts: wholesalers 50%, libraries 10%, no shipping charges to American customers or other customers outside Canada. 120pp; 5X8; †of. Payment: 10% paid annually. COSMEP, CPA.

Vietnam Veterans Chapel, Dr. Victor Westphall, Box 666, Springer, NM 87747, 483-2833. 1978. "Pub'd *Trial by Combat: 1993*" avg. press run 2,000. avg. price, paper: $5.00. Discounts: 30%. 140pp; 5½X8½; of. Copyrights for author.

VIEW, Robin White, 1555 San Pablo Avenue, Oakland, CA 94612, (415) 835-5104. 1978. Interviews. "Each issue is one interview with a contemporary artist. Each issue is 24 pp & includes photographs of work & a exhibition biography." circ. 500. 10/yr. Pub'd 10 issues 1979; expects 6 issues 1980. sub. price: $10.00; per copy: $1.50; sample: free. Back issues: $1.50. Discounts: 40% to any bookstore or gallery that resells issues. 24pp; 7X9; of. Copyrighted.

VIEWPOINT AQUARIUS, Jean Coulsting, Rex Dutta, c/oFish Tanks Ltd, 49 Blandford St., London W1 3AF, United Kingdom. 1971. Articles, interviews, criticism, reviews, letters, news items. "Very serious, informative, goes deeper than 'nuts and bolts' of the Orthodox, penetrating to the hidden laws within: for flying saucers, occult, yoga, meditation, Theosophy." 11/yr. Pub'd 11 issues 1979; expects 11 issues 1980, 11 issues 1981. sub. price: $12.00; per copy: $1.00; sample: free. Back issues: $1.00. 30pp; size foolscap; †mi. Pub's reviews: 20 in 1979. §UFO, occult, yoga, meditation.

VILE, Banana Productions, Anna Banana, Bill Gaglione, 1183 Church St, San Francisco, CA 94114. 1974. Fiction, articles, art, photos, cartoons, satire, reviews, letters, parts-of-novels, collages. "Average length, 500-1,000 words, occasionally use longer (good) work. Poetry, none-the-less new issue contains 21 poems, used mainly as space fillers-not a feature. Style-Dada-Iconoclastic. Current Fe Mail Art issue incl. works from: Jan Van Raay, Natalia L.L., Leavenworth Jackson, Joyce Cutler Shaw, Carol Law, Ruth Rehfeldt, Yoko Ono, Judith Barry, Barbara Aubin, Lucy Childs, Beth Anderson, Judith Hoffberg, Eleanor Dickenson, etc. Pub's reviews of art shows, events & performances. Not of books unless they are art-related." circ. 1,000. 1/yr. Pub'd 2 issues 1979. sub. price: $10.00; per copy: $5.00; sample: $5.00. Back issues: 1st issue out of print, 2nd issue $25.00, 3rd, 4th, 5th and 6th issues available at $5.00 each. Discounts: none. 100pp; 8½X11; of. Reporting time: 2-3 months. Payment:

copies only. Copyrighted. Ads: No ads accepted. CCLM.

VILLAGE CIRCLE, West Village Publishing Company, Kathleen Cha, PO Box 5361, Orange, CA 92667, (714) 633-1420. 1979. Articles, art, interviews, reviews, letters. "*Village Circle* is a 12 page publication featuring information pieces on what's happening for the family in Southern California, with emphasis on the 'art of parenting,' Parenting Book Reviews, Children's Book Reviews, Sports for the family, and family-oriented fillers. Some recent contributors are Dr. Charles Ara, Family Counsellor, Dr. Julie Chan, Reading Specialist, Andy McBride, Surf Soccer Player, and reader filler. Length of material has varied from 1,000 to 1,500 words, but we prefer as a rule 500 to 800 words for a short article. Short pieces (especially parenting tips, recipes, craft ideas) maximum length is 300 words." circ. 5,000. 11/yr. Pub'd 8 issues 1979; expects 11 issues 1980, 11 issues 1981. sub. price: $10.00; per copy: $1.00; sample: $0.50. Back issues: March-August, 1979 $0.65; October on, $0.75. Discounts: clubs, groups, classroom, etc 20% with minimum order of 10, graduating to 35% for 50, 40% for 75, jobber 60/40. 12pp; 8½X11; of. Reporting time: 10 days. Payment: complimentary issues. Copyrighted, reverts to author. Pub's reviews: 113 in 1979. §Children's fiction and non-fiction (ages pre-school to 6th grade level), parenting, family nutrition, children's cookbooks, arts & crafts books. Ads: $250/$150/$20 5-8 lines. COSMEP.

VINTAGE, Lucille Cyphers, 1111 Lincoln Place, Boulder, CO 80302, (303) 443-9748. 1977. Poetry, fiction, articles, cartoons, reviews, letters. "Writers must be at least 60 years old. Mss need not be typewritten. Priority given to unpublished authors, very brief items & the slightly unusual. Books reviewed need not be new ones (100-150 words). Poetry 4-12 lines. Fiction 1,500 maximum. General writings, such as essays & memories 200-600 words" circ. 400. 6/yr. Pub'd 4 issues 1979; expects 6 issues 1980, 6 issues 1981. sub. price: $4.50; sample: $0.75. 30pp; 8½X11; of. Reporting time: 1 month. Payment: Very limited. One $10.00 prize offered. Pub's reviews: 10 in 1979. CODA.

Violet Press, Fran Winant, PO Box 398, New York, NY 10009. 1971. Poetry, art, photos. "We are a lesbian feminist press. 1-2 books per year." avg. press run 1,500. avg. price, paper: $3.00. Discounts: 40% U.S.A. discount on orders of 3 or more copies of any title. 64pp; 5½X8½; of. Reporting time: 1-2 months. Payment: contributors' copies. Copyrights for author. COSMEP, NESPA.

VISHVAMITRA, Sanatana Publishing Society, Narada Muni, 3100 White Sulphur Springs Road, St. Helena, CA 94574, 707-963-9487. 1975. Articles, photos. "*Vishvamitra* is the newsletter of the Sanatana Dharma Foundation, featuring articles by Yogeshwar Muni, Swami Kripalvananda, and others of our tradition. Also included is information on the programs and activities of the Sanatana Dharma Founation, and news concerning the Sanatana Dharma in the West." circ. 10,000. 2/yr. Pub'd 2 issues 1979; expects 2 issues 1980, 2 issues 1981. sub. price: free; per copy: free; sample: free. Back issues: free. Discounts: free. 12pp; 11X17; of. Copyrighted, does not revert to author. COSMEP.

VISION MOUND: The Journal of the Religious and Spiritual Teaching of Bubba Free John, The Dawn Horse Press, Saniel Bonder, David Todd, PO Box 3680, Clearlake Highlands, CA 95422. 1976. circ. 3,000. 6/yr. Pub'd 11 issues 1979; expects 6 issues 1980. sub. price: $20.00; per copy: $3.50; sample: $3.50. Discounts: 40%. 50pp; 8½X11. Copyrighted. Pub's reviews. §Spirituality, health, sexuality. Ads: No ads.

VISIONS, Black Buzzard Press, Bradley R. Strahan, 2217 Shorefield Road, Apt 532, Wheaton, MD 20902, (301) 946-4927. 1979. Poetry, reviews, art, photos. "You may include matching pen and ink illustrations, send me only your best, most well crafted poetry. I don't care if you're a big name but we do expect poetry that is well worked (no poetasters please). Our aim is to showcase strong, open, imagistic poetry; vibrant work that draws the reader in, poems that can be appreciated by all people not just the literate. No obscure 'look ma I'm so great I can write about nothing and still fool the critics', stuff. Prefer poems under 40 lines (but will consider longer). Recent contributors: Barbara Lefkowitz, Andy Darlington, Karlis Frievalds, Merrill Leffler, Steinn Steinarr, Lyn Lifshin, Tina Fulker, Clarinda Harris Lott, Harold Black, Susan Sonde. Please don't submit more than 10 poems at a time (not more than twice a year unless requested). NO SASE, NO RETURN!" circ. 500. 3/yr. Pub'd 1 issue 1979; expects 3 issues 1980, 3 issues 1981. sub. price: $7.00; per copy: $2.50 add 50¢ per copy for overseas orders; sample: $2.50. Back issues: issue #1, $5.00 (while it lasts). Discounts: Schools & educational institutions & libraries (special 2 year subscription $13.50), bulk, 50 or more copies 30%. 55pp; 5½X8½; of. Reporting time: 2 days to 2 weeks. Payment: one contributors copy ($'s only when I get a grant). Copyrighted, reverts to author. Pub's reviews: 5 in 1979. §Poetry/ will exchange reviews (ie you review my mag, I'll review yours). Ads: $60.00/$40.00. CCLM, WAWC.

Vista Publications, Louise Bame, 3010 Santa Monica Blvd., Suite 221, Santa Monica, CA 90404, (213) 828-3258. 1978. "Primary interest home economics and related arts, quality books in paperback. Our first (and only) book so far *Pants Fit For Your Figure* point-by-point pattern adjustment, by

Louise Bame." avg. press run 2,000. Expects 1 title 1980, 1 title 1981. avg. price, paper: $7.95. Discounts: Bookstores: 1-4, 20%; 5 or more, 40%; Distributor 1-4, 25%; 5 or more, 50%;, (5 minimum); 10% to schools and libraries on orders of 10 or more. 87pp; 8½X11; of. Reporting time: We would reply to queries within 2 or 3 weeks, but at present are not inviting submissions. Copyrights for author.

Visual Studies Workshop Press, AFTERIMAGE, Nathan Lyons, 31 Prince Street, Rochester, NY 14607, 716-442-8676. 21 titles listed in the *Small Press Record of Books in Print* (9th Edition, 1980).

Vitality Associates, Donald Britton Miller, Alice M. Miller, P.O. Box 154, Saratoga, CA 95070, (408) 867-1241. 1977. Articles. "Career planning/management, improving individual and organizational vitality; organizational behavior/development; human resource management. Home address: 14600 Wild Oak Way,Saratoga, CA 95070." avg. press run 1M. Pub'd 1 title 1979; expects 2 titles 1980, 4 titles 1981. avg. price, paper: $7.50 + $1.00 postage & handling. 144pp; 5½X8½; 4¼X7; of. Reporting time: 1 month. Payment: negotiated. Does not copyright for author.

Voice of Liberty Publications, David W. Lundberg, 3 Borger Place, Pearl River, NY 10965, (914) 735-8140. 1979. "The focus of V of L Publications is the individual. Books published by V of L will evaluate ideals, institutions, and processes in terms of their effects on the individual. A tenet held by the publisher is that individuals grow to their full stature when they have elbow room to control their own lives. The publisher believes that many current trends in government, economics, and society are destroying individual freedom. Alienation, violence, and self-destructive acts are the results of this loss. The objective of V of L Publications is to harness the power of the mind and the power of the printed word to increase individual liberty and thus increase the stature of the individual." avg. press run 2,000. Pub'd 1 title 1979. 1 title listed in the *Small Press Record of Books in Print* (9th Edition, 1980). avg. price, cloth: $8.95; paper: $5.95. 224pp; 5½X8½; of. Reporting time: no unsolicited ms considered.

VOICES - ISRAEL, The Poetry in English Society, Haifa Publications, Reuben Rose, Ada Aharoni, Mark Levinson, 38 Nehemia Street, Nave Sha'anan, Haifa, Israel, 04-223332. 1972. Poetry. "We solicit intelligible and feeling poetry concerned with the potentialities of the human spirit, and the dangers confronting it. *Voices* is the only magazine entirely devoted to poetry written in English in Israel. Copyright to the poems printed is vested in the authors themselves; nevertheless we do request that our clearance should be obtained before any poem published by us is reproduced anywhere. International Reply Coupons should accompany the submissions. Some recent contributors: Barbara Noel Scott, Shin Shalom, Ruth Finer Mintz, Elias Pater, Roger White, Anna Sotto, Seymour Mayne, Ada Aharoni, Mark Levinson and Reuben Rose." circ. 500. 1/yr. Pub'd 1 issue 1979; expects 1 issue 1980, 1 issue 1981. sub. price: $2.50 surface mail, $5.00 airmail; per copy: $2.50 surface mail, $5.00 airmail; sample: $2.50 surface mail, $5.00 airmail. Back issues: soldout. Discounts: 25%. 100pp; 6X8 1/2; †of. Reporting time: 3 months. Payment: 1 complimentary copy. Copyrighted, reverts to author. Ads: $20.00/$10.00. PEN.

THE VOLCANO REVIEW, Peninhand Press, Thomas Janisse, PO Box 142, Volcano, CA 95689. 1979. Poetry, fiction, art, photos, interviews, letters, long-poems. "We have a strong interest in local mountain writers and artists." circ. 300. Pub'd 2 issues 1979; expects 3 issues 1980, 3 issues 1981. sub. price: $7.50; per copy: $3.00; sample: $2.00. Back issues: $3.00. Discounts: 1-4, 25%; 5 and over, 40%. 80pp; 5½X8½; of. Reporting time: no unsolicited manuscripts at this time. Payment: copies. Copyrighted, reverts to author. COSMEP.

Vortex Editions, B. Lateiner, 3891 La Donna, Palo Alto, CA 94306. 1979. avg. press run 1,000. Pub'd 2 titles 1979; expects 2 titles 1980, 3 titles 1981. 2 titles listed in the *Small Press Record of Books in Print* (9th Edition, 1980). avg. price, paper: $4.00; other: $2.00. Discounts: Trade available. 100pp; 6X9; 5X8; of. Copyrights for author.

Vulcan Books, Michael H. Caven, PO Box 25616, Seattle, WA 98125, (206) 362-2606. 1973. "Biases: accept nondemoninational spiritual books that reflect oneness of all and truth in all forms, totally non-bias. Two new imprints in 1979: Cavebridge Press: a college division for new age books, Blue Rose Press: a vanity publisher for new age thought." avg. press run 2,000-5,000. Pub'd 5 titles 1979; expects 7 titles 1980, 17 titles 1981. avg. price, cloth: $10.00; paper: $8.00. Discounts: Trade 40%; Distributor 50%; Classroom 20%. 300pp; 5½X8½; of. Reporting time: 8 weeks. Payment: Standard 10, 12½, 15 per cent list; semi-annual royalty. ABA, PNWBPA.

W. I. M. Publications, S. Diane Bogus, D. M. De Oca, PO Box 5037, Inglewood, CA 90310, (213) 774-5230. 1979. Poetry, long-poems. "This press has been established to publish the works of one author (the editor) primarily. It plans to expand to include royalty-subsidy publication of poetical and essay anthologies in 3 years. We are available for criticism of poetry and fiction. We make editorial suggestions. $2.00 per poem. $3.00 per page of fiction" avg. press run 1,000. Expects 2 titles 1981. 4 titles listed in the *Small Press Record of Books in Print* (9th Edition, 1980). avg. price, paper: $5.00. Discounts: 40% with agency letterhead. 65pp; 5X8; lp. Reporting time: 3-6 weeks. COSMEP, IPW.

A WAKE NEWSLITTER, Studies Of James Joyce's Finnegans Wake, Clive Hart, Fritz Senn, Department of Literature, University of Essex, Wivenhoe Park, Colchester, Essex CO4 3SQ, United Kingdom. 1962. Articles, criticism. "Articles on Joyces's Finnegans Wake, with occasional notes and articles on other books by Joyce. No other material normally included. Short articles preferred. The bias is exegetical rather than critical." circ. 700. 6/yr. Pub'd 6 issues 1979. 3 titles listed in the *Small Press Record of Books in Print* (9th Edition, 1980). sub. price: £8.00; per copy: £1.50; sample: free. Back issues: £6.00 p.a. £1.00 single copies. Discounts: none. 24pp; size A5; lo. Reporting time: 24 hrs. Payment: nil. Copyrighted. Pub's reviews: 3 in 1979. §Joyce criticism. no ads.

Walden Press, Frank Hamilton, 423 South Franklin Ave, Flint, MI 48503. 1965. Poetry, fiction. "Autobiographical material where author has found direction, need and energy to be creative and love others; also encourage seniors to retell the 1920's and 1930's" avg. press run 1,000. Expects 3 titles 1980, 4 titles 1981. 3 titles listed in the *Small Press Record of Books in Print* (9th Edition, 1980). avg. price, cloth: $9.95; paper: $3.95. Discounts: 50 percent. 140-185pp; lp. Reporting time: 1 week. Payment: 20 percent. Copyrights for author. Lib of Congress.

Horan Wall and Walker (see also HORAN WALL AND WALKER WEEKLY COMMUNITY INFORMATION), Stephen Wall, PO Box 8, Surry Hills, Sydney, NSW 2010, Australia. 1974. Reviews. "No unsolicited ms please." avg. press run 75. Pub'd 1 title 1979; expects 1 title 1980, 1 title 1981. 25pp.

HORAN WALL AND WALKER WEEKLY COMMUNITY INFORMATION, Horan Wall and Walker, Stephen Wall, PO Box 8, Surry Hills, Sydney, NSW 2010, Australia. 1974. Interviews, news items. "Alternative and main stream xeroxed publication on Sydney national and international leisure, arts, media, welfare, telecommunictions and community developement issues." circ. 75. 52/yr. Pub'd 50 issues 1979; expects 50 issues 1980, 50 issues 1981. sub. price: $250.00; per copy: $5.00; sample: $5.00 plus postage. 25pp; size A4. Copyrighted. Pub's reviews: 100 in 1979.

Walnut Press, Bruce Thompson, P O Box 17210, Fountain Hills, AZ 85268, 602-837-9118. 1976. "Length of material at discretion of author, no biases. Bruce S. Thompson, Janice Davis, Jill Morris, recent contributors. We need clever, unique childrens stories which are illustrated or adaptable for illustration for children 4 to 9 years old as exemplified by *Cook and Color With Recipe Rabbit* and the Scratch-Sniff-Color *The Merry Christmas Mice*" avg. press run 3,000-10,000. Pub'd 3 titles 1979; expects 6 titles 1980, 12 titles 1981. 6 titles listed in the *Small Press Record of Books in Print* (9th Edition, 1980). avg. price, cloth: $10.95 to $22.50; paper: $6.95-$8.95; other: $1.50-$4.95. Discounts: Query. 24-250pp; 6X9, 8½X11; of. Reporting time: 2 wks. Payment: standard contract. Copyrights for author. COSMEP, WBPA, AAA (Arizona Authors Association).

Wampeter Press, George E. Jr. Murphy, Director, Box 512, Green Harbor, MA 02041, (617) 834-4137. 1977. "Primarily interested in *first* books of poetry by poets who have otherwise published widely in periodicals and journals but who have yet to have their collected works printed. As such, we suggest as a guideline that at least 1/2 of any submitted manuscript consist of previously published material from as wide a number of publications as possible. (If you've pleased that many editors, we'll be impressed enough to give it a good reading.) Exceptions to this guideline will, of course be made should the quality of the ms. submitted warrant. We are also interested in collections by established writers. Recent books: *Burning Through* by Elizabeth McKim, *Lillian Bloom: A Separation* by Judith Steinbergh, *Serving Blood* by Gloria Still." avg. press run 750. Pub'd 1 title 1979; expects 3 titles 1980, 5 titles 1981. 10 titles listed in the *Small Press Record of Books in Print* (9th Edition, 1980). avg. price, paper: $3.95. Discounts: 1-10, 30%; 11-25, 40%; 25+, 50%. 80pp; 5½X8½; of. Reporting time: 1 month. Payment: 10% of press run. Copyrights for author.

THE WASHINGTON C.R.A.P. REPORT, William A. Leavell Jr., 3610 38th Avenue So. #88, St Petersburg, FL 33711, (813) 866-1598. 1979. News items. "This is a unique political newsletter for the national market about the federal goverment - Congress, the White House, etc. It is non-partisan, non-profit and goes to politically active individuals and groups in all 50 states. It does not sell advertising and exists on subscriptions ($12.00 per year). Capitalism Revised American Party" circ. 5,000. 12/yr. Pub'd 1 issue 1979. sub. price: $12.00; sample: free. 4pp; 8½X11; of. Reporting time: all inhouse or information passed on without cost.

WASHINGTON INTERNATIONAL ARTS LETTER, Daniel Millsaps, Box 9005, Washington, DC 20003, (202) 488-0800. 1962. "We publish financial information for the arts and artists. Federal actions and grants; private foundation and business corporation arts program information. And we have the following titles in books:*Grants and Aid to Individuals, National Directory of,* 221p, paper, 4th ed., $15.95; *National Directory of Arts Support by Private Foundations,* #3, 264p, paper, $65. *National Directory of Arts Support By Business Corporations,* 221 pages, paper, $65, 1st edition" circ. 15,030. 10/yr. Pub'd 10 issues 1979; expects 10 issues 1980. sub. price: Individuals(personal address & check) $24.50. Institutions: $48/year.; sample: $2.00. Back issues: Write for schedule. 8pp per issue; 8½X11 inches; of. Pub's reviews: 350 in 1979. §all arts. Ads: none.

WASHINGTON REVIEW, Jean Lewton, Managing Editor; Patricia Griffith, Fiction; Clarissa Wittenberg, Art; Anthony Harvey, Books; Jean Nordhaus, Poetry Reviews; Bernard Welt, Poetry; Mary Swift, P O Box 50132, Washington, DC 20004, 202-638-0515. 1975. Poetry, fiction, articles, art, photos, cartoons, interviews, satire, criticism, reviews, letters, parts-of-novels, collages, plays. "Articles: 2,000 words at most. Review: 500-1,000 words. Interested in in-depth articles on all arts, with particular emphasis on DC. Recent contributors: Myra Sklarew, Michael Lally, E. Ethelbert Miller, Dolores Kendrick, Tom Whalen." circ. 10,000. 6/yr. Pub'd 6 issues 1979; expects 6 issues 1980, 6 issues 1981. sub. price: $7.50; per copy: $1.25; sample: $2.00. Back issues: $3.00. Discounts: 15 percent bulk discount, 15 percent classroom, 10 percent agencies, 40 percent to bookstores for resale. 36 pp tabloid; 10¾X15; of. Reporting time: 2 months. Payment: In issues. Copyrighted, reverts to author. Pub's reviews: 80 in 1979. §Arts, history, philosophy, social commentary. Ads: $125.00/$75.00. COSMEP, CCLM.

Washington Writers Publishing House, Grace Cavalieri, Deirdra Baldwin, Robert Sargent, PO Box 50068, Washington, DC 20004, (703) 524-0999. 1975. Poetry. avg. press run 500. Pub'd 4 titles 1979; expects 3 titles 1980, 3 titles 1981. 13 titles listed in the *Small Press Record of Books in Print* (9th Edition, 1980). avg. price, paper: $2.50. Discounts: bulk orders-10 or more titles. 32pp; 6X9; of. Reporting time: About two months, submissions are made only once a year, usually in the late summers, with decisions made by the end of October. Payment: none. copyright held by authors.

Washout Publishing Co. (see also WASHOUT REVIEW), Susan Shafarzek, P.O. Box 9252, Scenectady, NY 12309. 1975. avg. press run 500. 1 title listed in the *Small Press Record of Books in Print* (9th Edition, 1980). avg. price, paper: $1.95; other: $1.50 back issues. 60pp; 5½X8½; of. Reporting time: 4-6 weeks. Payment: 2 copies. Copyrights for author. CCLM, COSMEP.

WASHOUT REVIEW, Washout Publishing Co., Nan C. Johnson, Sarah Provost, PO Box 2752, Schenectady, NY 12309. 1975. Poetry, art, photos. "Poems preferably under 40 lines; variety of styles. Recent contributors: Elaine Dallman, Mark Nepo, Janet Seery, Peggy Seely, Toni O. Zimmerman, Susan Baumann, Mary I. Cuffe, Lee Meitzen Grue, Joel Dailey, Madeleine Hennessy, Kathryn Poppino, Susan Shafarzek, Joan Colby, Dennis Holzman, Alice Fulton, Sydney Lea, Lyn Lifshin, Christine Zawadiwski." circ. 500. 4/yr. Pub'd 4 issues 1979; expects 4 issues 1980. sub. price: $5.00; per copy: $1.95; sample: $1.50. Back issues: $1.50. Discounts: 40%-10 or more copies, 33⅓%-1 to 9 copies. 64pp; 5½X8½; of. Reporting time: 2-5 weeks. Payment: in copies (2). Ads: none. COSMEP, CCLM.

Water Mark Press, Coco Gordon, Charles Fishman, 175 E Shore Road, Huntington Bay, NY 11743, (516) 549-1150. 1978. Poetry, art, collages. "I print a yearly *Poets of North America First Book Award* with guest editor and detailed schedule of submission of sample poems, then mss (guidelines available, send SASE). This edition of 500 is offset printed on archival papers, smythe sewn, and all covered with handmade paper wrappers. 50 are hardbound with cloth & handmade paper, contain at least one hard-done graphic on handmade paper, and are signed & numbered by artist and poet. 20 copies are specially handbound for Presentation purposes, are numbered 1-xx, & signed by poet, artist, & papermaker. $6.50 (soft) $25.00 (hard) $60.00 (Presentation) First Award winner: *Sympathetic Magic* by Michael Blumenthal, 96 pp., art of Theo Fried (original etching on linen paper in hardbound), editor, Charles Fishman. Ad in A.P.R., active promotion, & winner & first runner up invited to read on Water Mark Studio Reading Series (P & WR. assistance.) Entrance fee is $5.00 for 2nd award. I also print any serious, original & innovative works that I feel will & must make history, either straight poery (with original art) or poet/artist (responses) which are the outcome of collaborations between vital contemp. artists who respond to each others' language: poet/environmental artist, poet/musician, poet/sculptor, etc. Being an actively exhibiting visual artist since 1959, and an original editor for *Xanadu* & *Pleasure Dome Press,* I am continually aware of visual artists' & poets' works, & therefore do not encourage unsolicited submissions for these publications. I create handmade papers for tone & content of publications. I have my own Vandercook 320 letterpress, but due to acute toxic poisoning from solvents, have been forced to abandon using it, & therefore invite trade with letterpress printers of my handmade papers for printing services." avg. press run 300-500. Pub'd 1 title 1979; expects 2 titles 1980, 4 titles 1981. 3 titles listed in the *Small Press Record of Books in Print* (9th Edition, 1980). avg. price, cloth: $25.00; paper: $6.50 (handmade paper wrappers). Discounts: 10% on 10 books, 20% on 20 books or more. 5½X8½; of/lp. Reporting time: 1-2 months, sometimes within one week. Payment: cash advance, Contrib copies & royalties. Copyrights for author. ALO.

Waterfall Press, Susan Efros, Joan Levinson, 1357 Hopkins Street, Berkeley, CA 94702, (415) 527-7790. 1978. Poetry, fiction, art, photos, satire, parts-of-novels. "*Walking Vanilla* a feminist, satirical novel. Future feminist fiction and poetry. A collection of women's erotica to come! Submissions are welcome for future feminist editions." avg. press run 3,000. Pub'd 1 title 1979. 1 title listed in the *Small Press Record of Books in Print* (9th Edition, 1980). avg. price, paper: $5.00. Discounts: 40% for five or more orders. 150pp; of. Reporting time: 6 weeks. Payment: individualy determined. Copyrights for author. COSMEP.

WATERS JOURNAL OF THE ARTS, Rocky Karlage, 1413 W North Bend Road #7, Cincinnati, OH 45224. 1974. Poetry, fiction, art, criticism. "Work must be intelligent and 'hard-worked'. If we have a bias, it is quality. Wish to encourage short fiction, criticism. Recent contributors: Emil Efthimides, Albert Russo, Thomas Dawson, Chael Graham." circ. 200. irregular. 2 titles listed in the *Small Press Record of Books in Print* (9th Edition, 1980). price per copy: $0.50; sample: $0.50. 30-50pp; 5½X8½; †of. Reporting time: 2 weeks-1 month. Payment: 2 copies. copyright: common law/yes. Pub's reviews. §Contemporary poetry and criticism, fiction.

Watershed Intermedia (see also BLACK BOX MAGAZINE; BREATHINGSPACE), Alan D. Austin, Anne Becker, P.O. Box 50145, Washington, DC 20004, 202-347-4823. 1976. Poetry, interviews, music, plays. "*WATERSHED* issues single cassettes of authors reading/performing their poetry. There are three series: the '*Signature*' series, featuring the work of major, established poets not otherwise available on records or tapes; the '*Touchstone*' series featuring the work of newer poets who prefer audio to print; and the '*Archive*' series—recordings from the past generation which should have been available, but weren't." Pub'd 19 titles 1979; expects 24 titles 1980, 24 titles 1981. avg. price, other: $8.95 (cassette). Discounts: Trade: 40 percent min. 5. (45-60 min playing time); size Single audiocassettes.; Audiocassette duplication. Reporting time: Varies. Payment: Royalty. copyrights remain with authors; audio copyright (Form 'SR') held in trust for duration of contract. COSMEP, AII.

WAVES, Bernice Lever, Robert Casto, Ontario College of Art, 100 McCaul Street, Toronto, Ontario M5T 1W1, Canada, 416-977-5311. 1972. Poetry, fiction, articles, art, photos, interviews, satire, criticism, reviews, letters, parts-of-novels, long-poems, collages. "Fiction-1,000 to 10,000 wds. Reviews-500 to 2,500 wds. Our bias is towards reviews of Canadian writing but we print original poetry and fiction in English or French from any country. Recent contributors: Layton, Birney, Purdy, Bissett, Livesay, and interviews with Laurence and Atwood." circ. 1,000. 3/yr. Pub'd 3 issues 1979; expects 4 issues 1980. sub. price: $6.00 Indiv., $10.00 Libraries; per copy: $2.00; sample: $1.00. Back issues: $2.00 each. Discounts: 40% on orders of 5 or more. 88pp; 5X8; of. Reporting time: 2-4 wks. Payment: sample copies. Copyrighted, reverts to author. Pub's reviews: 15 in 1979. §contemporary fiction & poetry. Ads: exchange or $50.00 a page. CPPA.

WAYS & MEANS, Moore Publishing Company, Eugene V. Grace, Betty Mushak, Frank Reid, PO Box 3036, Durham, NC 27705, (919) 286-2250. 1979. circ. 100,000. 12/yr. Pub'd 1 issue 1979. sub. price: $25.00. 64pp; 8½X11; of. Copyrighted, does not revert to author. Pub's reviews: 4 in 1979. Ads: $3,000.00.

Webb-Newcomb Company, Inc., David Maryland Webb, Justine Webb Newcomb, 308 N.E. Vance Street, Wilson, NC 27893, (919) 291-7231; (919) 237-3161. 1975. Poetry, fiction, art, cartoons, photos. avg. press run 1,000. Pub'd 1 title 1979; expects 3 titles 1980. 2 titles listed in the *Small Press Record of Books in Print* (9th Edition, 1980). avg. price, cloth: $8.95 projected; paper: $4.95. Discounts: 40% to non-retailers. 55-100pp; 6X9; lp. Reporting time: 2 months. Payment: made semiannually, 20% of retail book copy, depends on cost of producing book. Copyrights for author.

WEBSTER REVIEW, Nancy Schapiro, Harry J. Cargas, Webster College, Webster Groves, MO 63119, 314-432-2657. 1974. "WEBSTER REVIEW publishes contemporary American and international literature. We are interested in fiction of any length, poetry, interviews, essays, and English translations of contemporary writing from all countries. Recent contributors have included: Yehuda

Amichai, Howard Schwartz, Jon Dressel, Edwin Honig, Tadeusz Rozewicz and Jean Follain." circ. 1,200. 4/yr. Pub'd 4 issues 1979. sub. price: $5.00; per copy: $1.25; sample: free. Back issues: $1.25. Discounts: 25%. 64pp; 7X5; of. Reporting time: 1 month. Payment: 2 free copies. Copyrighted. CCLM, COSMEP.

WEE GIANT, Margaret Saunders, 178 Bond Street, N., Hamilton, ON L8S 3W6, Canada, 525-2823. 1977. Poetry, fiction, art, photos, reviews. circ. 400. 3/yr. Pub'd 1 issue 1979; expects 3 issues 1980, 3 issues 1981. sub. price: $4.00; per copy: $1.35; sample: $1.00. Back issues: $2.00. 44pp; of. Reporting time: 3 weeks. Payment: 2 copies of the magazine. Copyrighted, reverts to author. Pub's reviews: 9 in 1979. §Poetry.

WEIRD TRIPS, Kitchen Sink Enterprises, Denis Kitchen, Box 7, Princeton, WI 54968, (414) 295-3972. 1973. Articles, art, cartoons, interviews, letters, news items. circ. 10,000. 1/yr. Pub'd 1 issue 1979; expects 1 issue 1980, 1 issue 1981. price per copy: $1.50 postpaid; sample: $1.50 postpaid. Back issues: $1.50 postpaid. Discounts: 40%, store; 60% to dist. 36pp; 7X10; of. Reporting time: 1-14 days. Payment: $20-$200 per article, $100 cover. Copyrighted, reverts to author. Ads: no ads.

WEIRDBOOK, Weirdbook Press, W. Paul Ganley, Box 35, Amherst Branch, Buffalo, NY 14226, (716) 839-2415. 1968. Poetry, fiction, articles, interviews, criticism, reviews. "*Weirdbook* is strictly fiction, some poetry and artwork (supernatural horror, fantasy, not science fiction) *Fantasy Mongers* is advertising oriented, with some articles (mystery, sf, fantasy, horror, collectors of pulps, books, fanzines, etc in these areas)" circ. 900-1,000. irregular. Pub'd 2 issues 1979; expects 1 issue 1980, 2 issues 1981. sub. price: $4.00-3 issues/$10.00; per copy: $3.00; sample: $3.00. Discounts: standard or better. 64pp; 8½X11; of. Reporting time: 6 weeks to 3 months usually. Payment: 1/2¢ a word (sometimes higher) for *Weirdbook*. Copyrighted, reverts to author. Ads: no ads. COSMEP.

Weirdbook Press (see also WEIRDBOOK), W. Paul Ganley, Box 35, Amherst Branch, Buffalo, NY 14226, (716) 839-2415. 1968. Fiction, art. "We publish 'special issues' of *Weirdbook* magazine, devoted to single authors and artists (or anything we choose). These are not automatically sent to *Weirdbook* subscribers. They are published in magazine format, but in a paper cover edition (perfect-bound) and a cloth bound edition (1,000 copies and 250 respectively)." avg. press run 1,250. Pub'd 1 title 1979; expects 1 title 1980, 1 title 1981. avg. price, cloth: $15.00; paper: $5.00. Discounts: Standard 40% off to dealers. 96pp; 8½X11; of. Reporting time: by invitation only. Payment: 10% of whatever we get for copies (to each author and each artist in a specific special issue). Copyrights for author. COSMEP.

WELLSIANA, The World Of H.G. Wells, High Orchard Press, Eric Ford, Exec; Royston King, Technical, High Orchard, 125 Markyate Rd, Dagenham, Essex RM8 2LB, United Kingdom. Poetry, fiction, articles, art, photos, cartoons, interviews, satire, criticism, reviews, music, letters, parts-of-novels, plays, news items. "Literary and sociological bias for worldwide dissemination of life, works, times, influences, contemporaries on and about, upon and from British Author H.G. Wells (1866-1946)." sub. price: £2; per copy: 50p; sample: £1. Back issues: in bulk 20% list. Discounts: agents 20%. size A5; lo. Reporting time: 6 months. Payment: copies. Copyrighted. Pub's reviews. Ads: £10 pro rata.

WELSH HISTORY REVIEW, University Of Wales Press, Kenneth O. Morgan, Ralph A. Griffiths, Queens College, Oxford, Oxford, United Kingdom. "Articles in English on various aspects of Welsh history" circ. 600. 4 parts per volume; 2 parts per year. Pub'd 2 issues 1979; expects 2 issues 1980, 2 issues 1981. sub. price: £1.50/part; per copy: £1.50 per double issue. Discounts: 33⅓%. 120pp.

WEST BRANCH, Karl Patten, Robert Taylor, Department of English, Bucknell University, Lewisburg, PA 17837, 717-524-4591. 1977. Poetry, fiction. "*West Branch* continues to seek the best work being written today, both poetry and fiction. We believe that the most effective poems and stories make their way on terms established in the work itself; therefore we strive to read without prejudice all the prose and poetry sent to *West Branch*, trying to keep our own ideologies separate from our judgments of what constitutes 'the best work being written today.' Contributors to past issues include David Ignatow, Colette Inez, John Wheatcroft, John Taylor, David Ray, Peter Balakian, Bruce Smith, Sonya Dorman, Marvin Cohen, Carolyn Stofoff, Martha Collins, David O'Dell, Victor Depta, Karla Hammond, H.E. Francis, Eve Shelnutt, Joseph Bruchac, Betsy Sholl, Stuart Friebert, Rolaine Hochstein, Joseph Nicholson, Errol Miller, Joan Colby, Deborah Burnham, Judith Vollmer, Constance Hunting, William Ford, Alyce Ingram, Pamela Hadas, Winston Wethers, and others." circ. 500. 2/yr. Pub'd 2 issues 1979; expects 2 issues 1980. sub. price: $5.00; per copy: $2.50; sample: $2.00. Back issues: #1 available in limited quantities for $3.50 each. Discounts: 20-40% to bookstores. 84-96pp; 5½X8½; of. Reporting time: 4 to 6 weeks. Payment: 2 copies. Copyrighted, reverts to author. §Small press fiction & poetry. Ads: $75.00/$40.00. CCLM.

434

WEST COAST PLAYS, Rick Foster, PO Box 7206, Berkeley, CA 94707. 1977. Articles, photos, interviews, reviews, plays. "Emphasis on publication of plays produced in West Coast theaters along with relevant articles, interviews, and reviews." circ. 1,000. Pub'd 1 issue 1979; expects 2 issues 1980, 2 issues 1981. sub. price: $10.00; per copy: $4.95; sample: $3.50. Discounts: Trade $3.00; Agency $4.50. 200pp; 5½X8¼; of. Copyrighted, reverts to author.

WEST COAST POETRY REVIEW, West Coast Poetry Review Press, William L. Fox, Bruce McAllister, 1335 Dartmouth Dr, Reno, NV 89509, 702-322-4467. 1970. Poetry, interviews, criticism, letters, long-poems, collages, concrete art. "See magazine. Looking for experimental/visual works of conventional material. Recent contributors: Emmett Williams and Dick Higgins, Ian Hamilton Finlay, Dennis Saleh, Hugh Fox with John Brockman, Carolyn Stoloff." circ. 500-2,000. 2/yr. Pub'd 1 issue 1979; expects 1 issue 1980. sub. price: $15.00 for 4 issues; per copy: $5.00; sample: $5.00. Back issues: Inquire. Discounts: 40% trade. 100pp; 6X9; of. Reporting time: 1 week. Payment: 2 copies. copyright permission (for reprints, etc.) must be obtained from publisher-all we ask is published notice of permission and a copy of book in which work appears. Pub's reviews. §poetry, fiction, experimental. Ads: exchange. CCLM.

West Coast Poetry Review Press (see also WEST COAST POETRY REVIEW), William L. Fox, Bruce McAllister, 1335 Dartmouth Dr, Reno, NV 89509, 702-322-4467. 1973. Poetry, fiction, art. " *The Road To Tamazunchale,* a novel by Ron Arias; *Going Places,* William Stafford; *Ground Zero,* Thomas Johnson; *Soft Where, Inc.;* Aaron Marcus (experimental typography and conceptual art); *Me Too,* Raymond Federman; *Selected Ponds,* Ian Hamilton Finlay (photos). Titles due from Mary Ellen Solt, George Hitchcock, Don Gordon, D. S. Long, Richard Kostelanetz and others. Query first." avg. press run 1,000. Pub'd 4 titles 1979; expects 4 titles 1980. 10 titles listed in the *Small Press Record of Books in Print* (9th Edition, 1980). avg. price, paper: $3.00. Discounts: 40 percent trade. 80pp; 6X9; of. Reporting time: 1 week. Payment: copies. Copyrights for author.

WEST END MAGAZINE, Gail Darrow Kaliss, c/o Kaliss, 31 Montague Place, Montclair, NJ 07042. 1971. Poetry, fiction, articles, art, photos, interviews, reviews, letters. "We try to publish work of high literary quality which also serves to promote postive social and personal change. Limited space for reviews, etc." circ. 1,000. 2/yr. Expects 2 issues 1980. sub. price: $5.00; per copy: $1.25; sample: $1.25. Back issues: 50¢ each issue in print, vol 3 no 1 thru vol 4 no 4. 48pp; 7X8½; of. Reporting time: 10 days to 3-4 months. Payment: In copies. copyrights return to authors. Pub's reviews. §Please query before sending reviews. CCLM.

West End Press, John Crawford, Editor and Publisher, Box 697, Cambridge, MA 02139. 1971. Poetry, fiction, art, photos. "Politically progressive material favored." avg. press run 1,000-2,000. Pub'd 10 titles 1979; expects 6 titles 1980, 6 titles 1981. 24 titles listed in the *Small Press Record of Books in Print* (9th Edition, 1980). avg. price, paper: varies. Discounts: 40% to stores; after 10 copies, 50%. 20% to faculty. pp varies; 5½X8½; of. Reporting time: up to 3 months. Payment: in copies — at least 10% of run. Copyrights for author.

WEST HILLS REVIEW: A WALT WHITMAN JOURNAL, Vince Clemente, Aaron Kramer, Helen Everett, Bets Vondrasek, Rufus Langhans, Helen Andrew, Walt Whitman Birthplace Assn., 246 Walt Whitman Road, Huntington Station, NY 11746, (516) 427-5240. 1978. Poetry, articles, criticism. " *West Hills Review: A Walt Whitman Journal* is conceived as a living memorial to America's great poet and devoted both to Whitman scholarship and to the contemporary poets, whom he has inspired and touched. *The Review* will emanate from his birthplace, West Hills Long Island and eill publish Whitman criticism, poems and prose pieces about Whitman, as well as what is best in contemporary American poetry. Some recent contributors: Gay Wilson Allen, Edwin H. Miller, Harold Blodgett, Roger Asselineau, William Stafford, David Ignatow, William Heyen, Robert Bly, Allen Ginsberg, Lawrence Ferlinghetti, Al Poulin Jr., Milton Kessler, John Logan, Richard Eberhart, Nobert Krapf, Raymond Roseliep, Norman Rosten." circ. 1,000. 1/yr. Pub'd 1 issue 1979; expects 1 issue 1980, 1 issue 1981. sub. price: $5.00; per copy: $2.50; sample: $2.50. Back issues: $2.50. 100pp; 6X9. Reporting time: 1 month. Payment: copies. Copyrighted, reverts to author. §Whitman scholarship, contemporary poetry. Ads: No ads.

WEST PLAINS GAZETTE, Russ Cochran, Publisher; Michael Cochran, Editor, PO Box 469, West Plains, MO 65775, 417-256-9677. 1978. Poetry, fiction, articles, art, photos, interviews, letters, news items. "We are a historic-based quarterly, with our content material focused on a relatively small part of the South Missouri/North Arkansas Ozarks..i.e., Howell County Missouri, and more specifically, West Plains, Missouri, the county seat of Howell County. Though we do include some articles covering current events, our main thrust comes in the from of historical articles about people and events connected with the earlier days of this region. In presenting this material, we rely heavily on old photographs and oral histories obtained from long-time residents of this area." circ. 6,500. 4/yr.

Pub'd 4 issues 1979; expects 4 issues 1980. sub. price: $12.00; per copy: $3.50 plus $1.00 p/h; sample: $3.50 plus $1.00 postage. Back issues: $3.50 per issue, including postage. Discounts: 30% in quantities of 100 or more (jobber price $2.45 per mag.) We service local retailers at $2.60 per/mag. 64-72pp; 10¾X14½; †of. Reporting time: 4-6 weeks. Payment: $25.00-$100.00, varies according to length, number of photographs. Copyrighted, reverts to author. Ads: $500.00/$250.00.

West Village Publishing Company (see also VILLAGE CIRCLE), Kathleen Cha, PO Box 5361, Orange, CA 92667, (714) 633-1420. 1978. Fiction. "West Village Publishing is a small press with emphasis on children's books and family-oriented material (eg. parenting books on teaching reading to children, family humor, etc.). We also publish a monthly newsletter for families in Southern California with some emphasis on Orange County. We do not solicit manuscripts over the transom. At this time we approach the authors and arrangements subsequestly made. Length varies according to the type of book, age level of children's book etc." avg. press run 5,000. Pub'd 1 title 1979; expects 4 titles 1980, 5 titles 1981. 1 title listed in the *Small Press Record of Books in Print* (9th Edition, 1980). avg. price, cloth: $6.95; paper: $4.50. Discounts: 60/40. 33pp; 7X10; of. Reporting time: 6 weeks. Payment: at this time the author and type of books has dictated the terms, arranged on individual basis. COSMEP.

WESTART, Martha Garcia, PO Box 1396, Auburn, CA 95603, 916-885-0969. 1962. Articles, art, photos, interviews, criticism, reviews, letters. circ. 7,500+. 24/yr. Pub'd 24 issues 1979; expects 24 issues 1980. sub. price: $8.00; per copy: $.50; sample: $0.50. Back issues: Available thru xerox University Microfilms. Discounts: on request. 20pp; 10X15; of. Reporting time: 2 weeks. Payment: $0.30 per column inch. Copyrighted, reverts to author. Pub's reviews: 12 in 1979. §Arts, art techniques, crafts, craft techniques. Ads: $180.00/$90.00/$0.10.

WESTBERE REVIEW, Morning Star Press, Charles Sackrey, 2504 E 4th Street, Tulsa, OK 74104. 1976. Poetry, fiction, articles. "10-15 pages maximum on prose" circ. 300. 2-3/yr. Pub'd 2 issues 1979; expects 2 issues 1980, 2-3 issues 1981. sub. price: $7.00 for 3 issues; per copy: $2.50; sample: free when available. Back issues: $2.50 per copy. 64-72pp; 5X9; lp. Reporting time: 2-3 weeks. Payment: 3 copies. Copyrighted. CCLM.

John Westburg, Publisher (see also NORTH AMERICAN MENTOR MAGAZINE), John E. Westburg, Gen'l. Ed.; Mildred Westburg, Gen'l. Ed; Martial R. Westburg, Art Ed., 1745 Madison Street, Fennimore, WI 53809, 608-822-6237. 1964. Poetry, fiction, articles, art, criticism, reviews. "Open for discussion on use of any kind of material in liberal arts or humanities." avg. press run varies, but short runs only, less than 3,000. Pub'd 2 titles 1979; expects 3 titles 1980. 26 titles listed in the *Small Press Record of Books in Print* (9th Edition, 1980). avg. price, cloth: between $5.00 and $10.00.; paper: between $5.00 and $10.00.; other: Between $5.00 and $10.00. Discounts: special rates to jobbers, wholesalers, retailers. 50-200pp; 8½X11 or 8½X5½; †of. Reporting time: 6 months or more. Payment varies, but negotiable, but generally no payment made except in copies. Copyrights for author. CCLM.

WESTERN AMERICAN LITERATURE, Thomas J. Lyon, UMC 32, Utah State Univ., Logan, UT 84322. 1966. Articles, reviews. circ. 900. 4/yr. sub. price: $8.00; per copy: $2.00. Back issues: cover price $1.00 to $2.00. 80pp; 6X9. Reporting time: 2 mos. Payment: 3 copies, tear sheets. Copyrighted. Pub's reviews: 100 in 1979. §Western American literature. Ads: $75/$40.

WESTERN CITY SUBTOPIAN TIMES, Hexagon Press, Ken Rolph, PO Box 269, Greenacre, NSW 2190, Australia, 02-724-4444. 1980. Poetry, fiction, articles, art, photos, cartoons, interviews, reviews, letters, parts-of-novels, plays. "This magazine absorbs the research output and extends its range of topics." 4/yr. Expects 3 issues 1980, 4 issues 1981. sub. price: (Overseas) A$4.00 surface mail, airmail add difference of surface and air for particular country. We can supply details; per copy: (Overseas) A$1.00 surface; sample: (Overseas) A$1.00 surface. Discounts: 40% to bookstalls, etc. available on sale or return within Sydney, Australia. 12pp; size A4 (210mm x 297mm); †of. Reporting time: 6 weeks. Payment: nominal. Copyrighted, reverts to author. Pub's reviews. §Contemporary religious expression and building community in newly established urban and suburban areas. Ads: write for details.

THE WESTERN CRITIC, Dwight Jensen, Box 591, Boise, ID 83701. 1969. Articles, art, photos, cartoons, interviews, satire, criticism, reviews, letters. "Will consider poetry, which we have printed, and fiction, which we never have." circ. 1,650. irregular. Expects 2 issues 1980, 4 issues 1981. sub. price: 12 issues, $7.50; per copy: $.75; sample: $.75. Back issues: $0.75 if available. 48pp; 8X11; of. Reporting time: 2-3 weeks. Payment: $5 to $100 per article, usually $15-$25. Copyrighted, reverts to author. Pub's reviews. §The west, the arts, ecology, food, or politics. Ads: $40/$25.

WESTERN HUMANITIES REVIEW, University Of Utah Press, Jack Garlington, Editor, University of Utah, Salt Lake City, UT 84112, 801-581-7438. 1947. Poetry, fiction, articles, art, interviews, satire, criticism, reviews, music, letters, parts-of-novels, long-poems, plays, concrete art. "We prefer 2-3,000 words; We print articles in the humanities, fiction, poetry, and film and book reviews. Recent contributors: Joyce Carol Oates, John Gardner, David Wagoner, Henry Nash Smith, Dave Smith, Fawn Brodie, Olivia Davis, William Stafford, Mary Oliver, Robert M. Adams." circ. 1,200. 4/yr. Pub'd 4 issues 1979; expects 4 issues 1980. sub. price: $15.00 (Institutions) $10.00 (Individuals); per copy: $2.50; sample: $2.50. Back issues: $3.00. Discounts: 25 percent to agents. 96pp; 6¾X10; lp. Reporting time: 1 month if rejected; longer if accepted. Payment: Up to $150.00 for stories and articles; up to $50.00 for poems; up to $50.00 for reviews. Copyrighted, reverts to author on request. Pub's reviews: 23 in 1979. §All but novels (we don't review them) Poetry, scholarly works in any area of the humanities. We don't use ads. CCLM, COSMEP.

WESTERN PUBLISHING SCENE, Padre Productions, Lachlan P. MacDonald, Editor, P.O.Box 1275, San Luis Obispo, CA 93406, (805) 543-5404. 1979. "Scheduled to begin Fall, 1979. *Western Publishing Scene* is regional, covering 13 Western states and all media, but especially books, presses large and small." 12/yr. Pub'd 2 issues 1979. sub. price: $18.00/yr; per copy: $2.00; sample: $2.00. 8pp; 8½X11; of. Reporting time: 10 days to 2 weeks. Copyrighted, reverts on request. Pub's reviews. §Self-publishing, fiction, non-fiction, poetry, publishing education. COSMEP.

WESTERN SPORTSMAN, J. B. (Red) Wilkinson, P.O. Box 737, Regina, Sask. S4P3A8, Canada, (306) 352-8384. 1968. "*The Western Sportsman* is a regional outdoor magazine covering two distinct areas-Alberta and Saskatchewan. We are basically interested in material relating to these two western Canadian provinces, however, we do purchase how-to and other informational articles if they are of sufficient interest to our western audience. Most of the editorial content is devoted to fishing and hunting articles, however we do publish many articles on camping, snowmobiling, canoeing, fly tying, dogs, and other outdoor-related subjects. We prefer to receive articles up to 2,500 words, accompanied by up to 10 black and white 8 x 10 glossy photos." circ. 19,000. 4/yr. Pub'd 4 issues 1979; expects 4 issues 1980. sub. price: $5.25 US, $8.25 other; per copy: $1.50; sample: $1.50. 96pp; 7X10; of. Reporting time: 3 to 4 weeks. Payment: $40 to $225. Copyrighted. Pub's reviews. Ads: $550.00/$325.00. OWC, OWAA, ABC.

Western Washington University (see also JEOPARDY), Humanities 350, WWU English Dept, Bellingham, WA 98225, 206-676-3118. Poetry, fiction, articles, art, photos, satire, criticism, long-poems. avg. press run 1,500-2,000. Pub'd 1 title 1979. avg. price, paper: $1.00. †of. Reporting time: varies.

WESTERN WORLD REVIEW, Robert E. Sagehorn, P.O. Box 366, Sun City, CA 92381. 1965. "Articles, reviews, criticism, essays. 'Good' non-fiction on politics, economics, media, philosophy or most anything." circ. under 500. 4/yr. Pub'd 4 issues 1979; expects 4 issues 1980, 4 issues 1981. 4 titles listed in the *Small Press Record of Books in Print* (9th Edition, 1980). sub. price: $4.00; per copy: $1.00; sample: $1.00. Discounts: inquire. 40pp; 8½X7; †of. Reporting time: 2 wks. Payment: copies only. Copyrighted. Pub's reviews: 8 in 1979. Ads: inquire. COSMEP.

Westport Press, Inc, Henry F. Foerster, PO Box 277, Los Altos, CA 94022, (415) 941-5474. 1978. avg. press run 1,500. Pub'd 2 titles 1979. avg. price, paper: $3.95. 120pp; 5½X8½; of. Reporting time: 6 weeks. Copyrights for author.

Westshore Inc, Sondra Taggart, 655 Redwood Highway, Mill Valley, CA 94941. 1975. "Audio cassettes".

Westwind Press, A.S. Parrish, Director, Route 1, Box 208, Farmington, WV 26571, 304-287-7160. 1974. Fiction, art. "*An Edge of the Forest* (reissue), *The Bluegreen Tree* (first edition), (Speaking as a Writer (first edition). All orders postpaid, unless/until book post rates go up, when minimal p & h charges will be added, retail orders to publisher excepted" Pub'd 1 title 1979; expects 1 title 1980. 3 titles listed in the *Small Press Record of Books in Print* (9th Edition, 1980). avg. price, cloth: $9.00. Discounts: Libraries: 2-5, 10%; 6 and up, 25%. Bookstores & Jobbers: 1-4, 25%; 5 & up, 40%. 76-202pp; 6X9; of. Very small staff, cannot consider unsolicited mss. Does not copyright for author. COSMEP, NFPW.

WEYFARERS, Guildford Poets Press, John Emuss, Margaret George, Margaret Pain, Susan James, 10 Ashcroft, Shalford, Guildford, Surrey, United Kingdom. 1972. Poetry. circ. 250. 3/yr. Pub'd 3 issues 1979; expects 3 issues 1980. sub. price: £1.40; per copy: 50p; sample: 50p. Back issues: 20p if available. 32pp; 8X6; lo. Reporting time: 2 mo. No payment. Copyrighted. Pub's reviews: 15 in 1979. §Poetry only. Ads: No ads.

WHAT'S NEW ABOUT LONDON, JACK?, London Northwest, David H. Schlottmann, 929 South

Bay Rd., Olympia, WA 98506, (206) 352-8622. 1971. Articles, interviews, criticism, reviews, letters, news items. "Jack London (author) news/fan magazine, a co-operative venture between subscriber & publisher. Subscribers (and others) send in any news they may find, along with all details available. Items vary from trivia to major. Of related interest, THE CHANEY CHRONICAL is a companion magazine devoted to London's father, and THE WOLF is an annual issued each January 12." circ. 235. irreg. Pub'd 4 issues 1979; expects 7 issues 1980, 10 issues 1981. sub. price: $5.00/10 issues; per copy: $.60; sample: postage/sample. 10-12pp; 8½X11; †mi. Reporting time: a.s.a.p. Payment: copy. Pub's reviews: 13 in 1979. §Jack London. Ads: 1¢/word classified.

Whatever Publishing/Rising Sun Records, Marcus Allen, Shakti Gawain, 158 E Blithedale, Suite 4, Mill Valley, CA 94941, 415-383-2434. 1978. Poetry, fiction, art, photos. "We have plenty of material for the next 2-3 years." avg. press run 3,000-5,000. Pub'd 4 titles 1979; expects 4 titles 1980. 8 titles listed in the *Small Press Record of Books in Print* (9th Edition, 1980). avg. price, cloth: $10.00; paper: $4.50; other: $7.98 albums, cassettes. Discounts: 40% to bookstores, 50-55% to distributors, 10% to individuals ordering 10 or more titles. 150pp; 5½X8½, 6X9; of. Reporting time: 4 weeks. Payment: Little or no advance, 10% royalty to authors, 2% royalty to artists (if book is illustrated); paid every quarter. Copyrights for author.

WHETSTONE, San Pedro Press, Michael Bowden, Rural Route 1, Box 221, St David, AZ 85630. 1978. Poetry, art, photos, criticism, reviews. "Looking for quality poetry, regardless of 'school': every 3rd issue is a 10-20 pp pamphlet by a Southwest poet; which is reflective of our regional orientation. Some of our recent contributors: Peter Brett, Joseph Bruchac, James Cervantes, Jefferson Carter, M.R. Doty, Norman Dubie, Harley Elliott, Robert Gibb, Frank Graziano, Jeff Daniel Marion, Kirk Robertson, Pamela Stewart, Mark Vinz, and Peter Wild." circ. 250-500. 3/yr. Pub'd 3 issues 1979; expects 3 issues 1980. sub. price: $6.00; per copy: $2.00 + 40¢ postage; sample: $2.00 + 40¢ postage. Back issues: $2.00 + 40¢ postage. Discounts: 40% for 5 or more copies. 56pp; 8½X5½; of. Reporting time: 1-6 weeks. Payment: 2 copies of issue one appears in: 15% of first press run for pamphlets. Copyrighted, reverts to author. Pub's reviews. §Poetry, poetics, southwest, native american. Ads: by arrangement. CCLM.

WHISPERING WIND MAGAZINE, Jack B. Heriard, 8009 Wales Street, New Orleans, LA 70126, 241-5866. 1967. Articles, art, photos, cartoons, interviews, reviews, letters, news items. "Magazine for those interested in the American Indian; his traditions and crafts, past and present." circ. 1,000. 6/yr. Pub'd 10 issues 1979; expects 6 issues 1980, 6 issues 1981. sub. price: $6.95; per copy: $1.50; sample: $1.50. Back issues: included in each issue. Discounts: 5-9, $0.84; 10 plus, $0.75. 24pp; 8½X11; †of. Reporting time: 4-8 weeks. Payment: copies. Copyrighted. Pub's reviews: 15 in 1979. §American Indian. Ads: $114.66/$66.74/$0.21.

WHISPERS, Whispers Press, Stuart David Schiff, Editor; David Drake, Asst. Editor, Box 1492-W Azalea Street, Browns Mills, NJ 08015, 893-7425. 1973. Fiction, art. "1,000-8,000 words. Uses fantasy, terror and horror fiction. No science fiction. Recent contributors include Robert Bloch, Richard Matheson, Fritz Leiber, Manly Wade Wellman, Ray Russell, Frank Belknap Long, and William Nolan. Reviews solicited only." circ. 3,000. 1-2/yr. Pub'd 2 issues 1979; expects 1 issue 1980, 1-2 issues 1981. sub. price: $7.00 (equivalent of two double issues); per copy: $2.00, $4.00 (double); sample: $1.50, $2.50 for our double issues. Discounts: Standard 40% for 10 or more copies (may be mixed). 68-136pp; 5½X8; of. Reporting time: 3 months. Payment: 1¢ per word for unsolicited manuscripts, more to established writers. Copyrighted, reverts to author. Pub's reviews: 12 in 1979. §Fantasy, terror, horror, or science fiction. Ads: write for information.

Whispers Press (see also WHISPERS), Stuart David Schiff, Box 1492-W Azalea Street, Browns Mills, NJ 08015. 1977. Fiction. "We do *all* of our books by special arrangement with the authors. We *do not* solicit *any* manuscripts for books." avg. press run 3,500. Pub'd 2 titles 1979; expects 2 titles 1980, 2 titles 1981. avg. price, cloth: $12.00. Discounts: Standard 40%. 226pp; 6X9; of. Reporting time: we do not solicit book manuscripts. Payment: advance against royalites. Copyrights for author.

WHISTLER ANSWER, High Country Communications Ltd., Charlie Doyle, General Delivery, Whistler, B.C. V0N 1B0, Canada, (604) 932-5332. 1977. Poetry, fiction, articles, photos, cartoons, interviews, satire, criticism, reviews, art, letters, collages, music. "Feature length articles with emphasis on outdoor activities including skiing mainly. Counterculture (underground) bent with leftist political orientation. Recent contributors: Mark Loblaw, David McGonigal, Bob Colebrook, Jim Monahan, Russell Baker." circ. 5,000. 12/yr. Pub'd 12 issues 1979; expects 12 issues 1980, 12 issues 1981. sub. price: $5.00; per copy: $0.50; sample: free. Back issues: $0.75 or 2 for $1.00. 24pp; 10X15; of. Reporting time: varies. Payment: varies. Copyrighted, reverts to author. Pub's reviews: 1 in 1979. §Music, outdoors, skiing, lifestyles, politics. Ads: $160.00/$90.00/$0.10.

438

White Crescent Press (see also BEDFORDSHIRE MAGAZINE), B. Chambers, Crescent Road, Luton Beds, United Kingdom. 1947. avg. press run 3,000. Pub'd 4 titles 1979; expects 4 titles 1980, 4 titles 1981. avg. price, paper: 25p. 64pp; 8½X5½; †of. Payment: varies.

White Dot Press, Christopher Wienert, Editor, 407 Charter Oak Avenue, Baltimore, MD 21212, 301-435-7915. 1975. Poetry, long-poems. "White Dot Press publishes poetry only, and on a rather irregular basis. It's first book, which appeared in December 1975, was a self-publishing venture by the editor, entitled *The Everywhere Province.* A second book, *Collected Poems of Max Douglas,* was completed in January 1979. A third, much smaller title is due in the spring of '79." avg. press run 150-1,000. Pub'd 1 title 1979; expects 1 title 1980, 1 title 1981. 4 titles listed in the *Small Press Record of Books in Print* (9th Edition, 1980). avg. price, cloth: $10.00; paper: $4.00. Discounts: Trade & bulk up to 40%. pp varies; 6X9; of. Reporting time: open. Payment: by agreement. Copyrights for author.

The White Ewe Press (see also THE MILL), Kevin Urick, Box 996, Adelphi, MD 20783, 301-439-1470. 1976. Fiction. "Mostly interested in fiction. Recent titles include works by Albert Drake and George Myers, Jr. In 1978 I started the WEP Poetry Series; poets include Werner Low, John Elsberg, and Diane De Vaul. It wasn't deliberate, but to date all of my authors have first appeared in the magazine. My current publishing commitments are fairly extensive; due to time, energy, and financial limitations, it is highly unlikely I could take on any unsolicited manuscripts at the present time. And how are you, Mr. Wilson?" avg. press run 500 copies. Pub'd 3 titles 1979; expects 3 titles 1980. 7 titles listed in the *Small Press Record of Books in Print* (9th Edition, 1980). avg. price, paper: $3.00. Discounts: Trade 1-3, 10%; 4-10, 20%; 11-20, 30%; 21+, 40%. 88pp; 5½X8½; of. Copyrights for author.

White Mountain Publishing Company, Guy Lockwood, 13801 N. Cave Creek Rd, Phoenix, AZ 85022, 971-2720. 1976. Non-fiction. "Books, booklets. *Animal Husbandry & Veterinary Care For Self-Sufficient Living* by Guy Lockwood, D.V.M. now in print and on sale. Future work in progress. The 2nd edition is being published by: Charles Scibne's Sons, 597 Fifth Ave., New York, NY 10017. Revised edition title *Raising & Caring for Animals.*" avg. press run 5,000. Pub'd 2 titles 1979. avg. price, cloth: $10.95; paper: $7.95. Discounts: 50% plus 2% terms 60 days. 330pp; 5½X8½; of. Reporting time: can't predict. Payment: 10 percent gross or 50-50 profit w/investment. Copyrights for author. COSMEP.

WHITE MULE, Thomas Abrams, 201 E Emma, Tampa, FL 33603. 1975. Poetry, fiction, long-poems, plays. "Southern Surrealism: Van Brock, Patty Perry Minchen, Willie Reader, John Calderazzo, Hans Juergensen, Robert Smith, Ian Krieger, Ann Deagon, A. McA. Miller, Camille Symons, Linda Lappin, Charles Itzin, John Hatcher, Ed Perez, Evelyn Thorne, Lyn Lifshin, Erik Scott, David Dial. Experimental fiction; good mixtures of pornography and story; corn; whatever bends the surface humorously; violence; fairy tales; bullshit; something blue. Poetry that is imagistic, surrealistic, out of focus, or southern." circ. 500. 1/yr. Pub'd 1 issue 1979. sub. price: $5.00; per copy: $5.00; sample: $5.00. Back issues: priceless. 40pp; 7X8¼; of. Reporting time: 1 month limit; yet the mule is occasionally stuborn, and slow to act. Payment: copies and a smile. Copyrighted.

White Murray Press (LITERATUREGATE), Eric Baizer, PO Box 14186, Washington, DC 20044. 1971. "Articles outlining corruption at the National Endowment for the Arts and CCLM." Pub'd 3 titles 1979. 3 titles listed in the *Small Press Record of Books in Print* (9th Edition, 1980).

White Oak Publishing House, Mary J. Tripp, PO Box 3089, Redwood City, CA 94064, (415) 364-3882. 1976. "*Senior Citizens-A Guide to Entitled Benefits,* Mary J. Tripp, ed., White Oak Publishing House, paperback, 8 1/2 x 11, 181 pp., $7.95. A guidebook for seniors. This book answers questions in regard to Social Security, Medical Insurance, Supplemental Social Security, Social Activities, and much more. Typed in large, easy-to-read print. It is a book that serves as a friend and advisor to the elderly. ISBN 0-932556-01-9" avg. press run 3,000. Pub'd 1 title 1979; expects 1 title 1981. 2 titles listed in the *Small Press Record of Books in Print* (9th Edition, 1980). avg. price, paper: $7.95. Discounts: 1-4, 30%; 5-49, 40%; 50-99, 45%; 100 or more, 50%. 200pp; 8½X11; of.

WHITE PINE JOURNAL, White Pine Press, Dennis Maloney, Steve Lewandowski, 109 Duerstein St., Buffalo, NY 14210, 716-825-8671. 1973. Poetry, long-poems. "*White Pine* has become *White Pine Journal* with issue 24/25. *White Pine Journal* publishes a mixture of poetry, translations, short fiction, essays and graphics. Each issue contains a special translation section. The Journal will continue to focus on bio-regional concerns, particularly of the Northeast, and welcome essays reflecting these concerns." circ. 500-1,000. 4/yr. Pub'd 4 issues 1979; expects 4 issues 1980. sub. price: $8.00; per copy: $3.00; sample: $2.00. Back issues: On Turtle's Back, NY anthology $4.50 paper. Discounts: 40% trade discount 5 & over, 2-4, 20%; 1, 0%. 40-200pp; 5½X8½; of. Reporting time: 2 weeks-1 month. Payment: copies. Copyrighted. Pub's reviews. §Poetry. CCLM, COSMEP, NESPA, COSMEP-SOUTH,

COSMEP-EAST.

White Pine Press (see also WHITE PINE JOURNAL), Dennis Maloney, Steve Lewandowski, 109 Duerstein St, Buffalo, NY 14210. 1973. Poetry, long-poems. "In 1980 White Pine will publish the following books: *Great Horned Owl* by Jeanne Foster Hill; *Yarrow* by Michael Corr and *The View From Cold Mountain: Poems of Han-Shan & Shin-Te* translated by Arthur Tobias." avg. press run 500-1,000. Pub'd 2 titles 1979; expects 3 titles 1980, 3 titles 1981. 25 titles listed in the *Small Press Record of Books in Print* (9th Edition, 1980). avg. price, cloth: $10.00; paper: $3.00. Discounts: 1, 0%; 2-4, 20%; 5 & over, 40%. 40-80pp; 5½X8½; of. Reporting time: 2 weeks to 1 month. Payment: Copies. Copyrights for author. CCLM, COSMEP.

White Tower Inc. Press, Timothy Hall, Director; Richard White, Chief Editor, PO Box 42216, Los Angeles, CA 90042, (213) 254-1326. 1978. Articles. "We are a branch of a Calif. *non-profit* corporation, incorporated since 1971. Our focus is educational — we research and educate in all aspects of survival: wilderness, city, economic, spiritual, physical, etc. Our primary focus is to relay this data to newspapers and magazines and direct to the public. We regularly send out columns & articles to various magazines and newspapers, so far under our separate authors' names." avg. press run 1,000. Pub'd 5 titles 1979; expects 14 titles 1980, 20 titles 1981. avg. price, paper: $6.00 books, $0.35-$3.75 tracts, pamphlets and booklets; $0.10-$0.80 catalogs & flyers. Discounts: 10% educational; 40% to stores and dealers(minimum 10 copies); 50% to distributors. pp varies; size varies; †mi. Reporting time: 4-6 weeks. Payment: We submit basic contract, negotiable with author. Copyrights for author.

White Urp Press (see also ABBEY), 5011-2 Green Mt Circle, Columbia, MD 21044. 2 titles listed in the *Small Press Record of Books in Print* (9th Edition, 1980).

WHITE WALLS, Buzz Spector, Reagan Upshaw, Roberta Upshaw, PO Box 8204, Chicago, IL 60680. 1977. Poetry, fiction, articles, art, interviews, criticism, parts-of-novels, long-poems, collages, concrete art. "We are interested in writings by artists, art-related poetry, and fiction. Contributors include Ron Padgett, Barbara Guest, Dick Higgins, Jim Melchert, Agnes Denes, Lucio Pozzi, and John Perreault." circ. 750. 2/yr. Pub'd 1 issue 1979; expects 2 issues 1980, 2 issues 1981. sub. price: $5.00; per copy: $3.00; sample: $3.00. Discounts: Trade 40%, Jobber 40%, Classroom and bulk 20%. 48pp; 5½X8½; of. Reporting time: 1 month. Payment: 3 copies per contributor. Copyrighted, reverts to author. §Writings by artists, art criticism, concrete writing. AAP (Associated Art Publishers).

Whitfield, Joanne Whitfield, Vallie Whitfield, 1841 Pleasant Hill Road, Pleasant Hill, CA 94523, (415) 934-8054. 1964. Poetry, articles, art, photos, letters, parts-of-novels. "PO Box 23524, Pleasant Hill, California 94523. (Solicit manuscripts only from in-house staff). Do not take in materials. ISBN 0-930920" avg. press run 200-1,000. Pub'd 4 titles 1979; expects 2 titles 1980, 2 titles 1981. 4 titles listed in the *Small Press Record of Books in Print* (9th Edition, 1980). avg. price, other: $5.00-$25.00. Discounts: 10%, 20%, 30%, 40%. 200pp; 8½X11, 5½X8½; mi/of. Payment: Staff members only. Copyrights for author.

WHOLE EARTH, Sussex Whole Earth Group, Editorial Collective, 11 George St, Brighton, Sussex BN21RH, United Kingdom. 1974. Articles, art, photos, cartoons, interviews, reviews, letters, news items. "Major articles 1,500 words-short news articles. Large emphasis on graphics." circ. 1,500. 2-3/yr b'd 2 issues 1979; expects 3 issues 1980, 3 issues 1981. 1 title listed in the *Small Press Record of Books in Print* (9th Edition, 1980). sub. price: £3 sterling (dollar cheques: not acceptable). 24pp; size A4; of. Payment: none. Not copyrighted. Pub's reviews: 17 in 1979. §agriculture, community, crafts, ecology, foods, energy, lifestyle. Ads: inquire. APS.

Whole Image Graphics, PO Box 774, San Francisco, CA 94101, (415) 282-5221. 1978. Art, cartoons. "We publish comics, and distribute educational comics from all sources. Annotated bibliography of educational comic books available on request. Will consider suggestions for publishing new educational comics." avg. press run 20,000. Expects 1 title 1980, 4 titles 1981. avg. price, paper: $1.00. Discounts: 20% on orders over $20.00. 32pp; 7X10; of. Reporting time: 3 months. Payment: Writers, $10.00-$20.00/comic page advance on royalties, Artists: $30.00-$50.00/page advance. Copyrights for author.

Wide World Publishing, Elvira Monroe, PO Box 476, San Carlos, CA 94070, (415) 593-2039. 1976. Photos, articles, fiction. avg. press run 5,000. Pub'd 2 titles 1979; expects 2 titles 1980, 2 titles 1981. 7 titles listed in the *Small Press Record of Books in Print* (9th Edition, 1980). avg. price, paper: $3.-95-$4.95. Discounts: 40% trade, 55% jobber. 132pp; lp. Payment: authors are partners & share directly. Copyrights for author. COSMEP.

Wigan Pier Press, Sherri Cavan, 1283 Page Street, San Francisco, CA 94117, (415) 863-6664. 1979. Non-fiction. avg. press run 2,000. Pub'd 1 title 1979. avg. price, cloth: $15.00; paper: $6.00. Discounts: Bookstores 40%, Wholesalers 50%. 350pp; 5X8. Payment: yes. Copyrights for author.

Wild & Woolley, Pat Woolley, P.O. Box 41, Glebe NSW 2037, Australia, 02-699-9819. 1974. Fiction, cartoons, criticism. "Address (west): PO Box 67427, Los Angeles, CA 90067. Tel. 213-473-7366. We publish literary non-fiction, cartoon books, and books about recreational drugs. Our program is full until 1981. 5 books a year. Published 2 in 1979, intend 6 in 1980. So far we've published 37 books. Our Calif. address is only distribution. Editorial all from Sydney. Michael Wilding is no longer with Wild & Woolley. He can be contacted through Post-Modern Writing, Room N409, Woolley Bldg, Sydney University, Sydney 2006." avg. press run 1,000. 31 titles listed in the *Small Press Record of Books in Print* (9th Edition, 1980). avg. price, cloth: $9.95; paper: $4.95. Discounts: 40% retail stores, through Bookpeople. 128pp; 5½X8½; of. Reporting time: 3 months. Payment: royalties. Copyrights for author. COSMEP, AIPA, Poets' Union, Australian Society of Authors.

WILD FENNEL, Pauline Palmer, Editor, 2510 48th Street, Bellingham, WA 98225. 1970. Poetry, fiction, articles, art, cartoons, interviews, satire, criticism, reviews, letters. "Especially interested in humorous, personal essays. Some short fiction of the fantasy and sf genre. A very limited amount of poetry, but especially like short poems that show the poet as human with a sense of humor." circ. 200-500. irregular. Pub'd 2 issues 1979; expects 2-3 issues 1980. sub. price: $2.00; per copy: $1.00; sample: $1.00. 24-32pp; 8X10; of. Reporting time: 3-4 wks. Payment: copies only. Pub's reviews. §Science fiction, fantasy.

Wild Horses Potted Plant, Pamela Portugal, Helen Stephens, Jody Main, Nancy Portugal, 226 Hamilton Avenue, Palo Alto, CA 94301, (415) 326-6432. 1972. "Also: The Potted Plant in The Artifactory, 226 Hamilton Ave., Palo Alto, CA 94301. Phone: 415-326-6513 Published 2 books: *Potted Plant Organic Care, A Place For Human Beings,* and two booklets *Sprouts Are Good Sprout Booklet,* and *Sprout Booklet With Screen*" avg. press run 4,000. Pub'd 1 title 1979; expects 1 title 1980. 4 titles listed in the *Small Press Record of Books in Print* (9th Edition, 1980). avg. price, paper: $5.75. Discounts: 40-55. 160pp; 6¾X8½; of. Reporting time: infinite. Copyrights for author. ARTIFACTORY.

Wilfion Books, Publishers (TRENDS), Konrad Hopkins, Ronald Van Roekel, Directors, 12 Townhead Terrace, Paisley, Renfrewshire, Scotland PA1 2AX, United Kingdom. 1975. Poetry, fiction. "We publish three Series: *Contemporary Poets, Scotland Alive,* and *Genius of the Low Countries,* and distribute *Renfrewshire Men of Letters Series.* We also publish works from minority literatures (e.g., Dutch, maltese, Faeroese, etc.) in English translation; books on psychic/spiritual phenomena; and a literary magazine, *Trends,* twice yearly." avg. press run 500. 9 titles listed in the *Small Press Record of Books in Print* (9th Edition, 1980). avg. price, paper: $3.50. Discounts: 33⅓% (U.K.), 40% (U.S.A.) to bookseller; 20% libraries. 50-150pp; 6X8½; of. Reporting time: 1 month. Payment: royalty of 10%-15%; subsidies possible. Copyrights for author. SGPA.

WILLAMETTE VALLEY OBSERVER, Kenneth J. Doctor, Editor, 99 W. 10th Ave., Suite 216, Eugene, OR 97401, 503-687-0376. 1975. Poetry, fiction, articles, photos, interviews, satire, letters. circ. 10,000-15,000. 51/yr. Pub'd 52 issues 1979. sub. price: $13.00; per copy: $0.50; sample: $0.50. Back issues: $0.75. 32pp; 10¼X15; of. Reporting time: 1 mo. Payment varies. Copyrighted, reverts to author. Pub's reviews: 50 in 1979. §environment, art, music, children, sports, science, science fiction, fiction. Ads: $437.40/$218.70/$0.10. ONPA, NAAN.

William L. Bauhan, Publisher, William L. Bauhan, Dublin, NH 03444, 603-563-8020. 1960. Poetry, art. "Specialize in New England regional books; authors, non-fiction. Recent titles: *North of Monadnock* by Newton F. Tolman, *Is There a Doctor in the Barn* by Elizabeth Yates, *The Constant God* poems by Henry Chapin, *The Half-Seen Face* poems by Dorothy Richardson, *Document of a Child* by Justine Chase, *More Than Land* by Heman Chase" avg. press run 1,500-2,500. Pub'd 8 titles 1979; expects 7 titles 1980. 55 titles listed in the *Small Press Record of Books in Print* (9th Edition, 1980). avg. price, cloth: $7.50; paper: $4.95. Discounts: 40% off on 5 or more copies. flat 20% off on textbooks. ltd. editions. 150pp; 5½X8½; of/lp. Reporting time: month or so. Payment: 10% of list price; less on poetry & small editions. Copyrights for author. NESPA.

Moss William Publishing Co., Theda Salkind, PO Box 1555, New Springville, Staten Island, NY 10314. 1978. "Our aim is to publish non-fiction, primarily in the social sciences. Our first book is called *Slim Yourself* by Morton L. Arkava, Ph. D. It is a book intended for people interested in self-regulation of weight who are disciplined enough to use behavior modification principles." Pub'd

441

1 title 1979. avg. price, paper: $6.95. Discounts: 10-40% depending on quantity, 40% bookstores. 200pp; of, lp. Payment: 10% first 10,000 cc; 12½% next (individual agreement). COSMEP.

WILLOW SPRINGS, Tom Smith, Pub, PO Box 1063, Eastern Washington Univ., Cheney, WA 99004, 359-7061. 1977. Poetry, fiction, art, interviews, reviews, parts-of-novels, long-poems, plays. "Recent contributors: John Keeble, Brian Harris, Robert Wrigley, Ransom Jeffery, George Garrett, Quinton Duval, Phyllis Janowitz, James J. McAuley, George Venn, James Masao Mitsui, Colleen McElroy. We prefer submissions by writers who have read the Classics and Modern literature, as well as a good deal of contemporary writing. We encourage the submission of translations from all languages and periods." circ. 800. 2/yr. Pub'd 1 issue 1979; expects 2 issues 1980, 2 issues 1981. sub. price: $5.00; per copy: $3.00; sample: $2.50. Back issues: $3.00 each. Discounts: 40&. 90pp; 6X9; of. Reporting time: 1 month. Payment: up to $10.00 per page. Copyrighted, reverts to author. Pub's reviews. §Books of poetry, fiction, or non-fiction (criticism, naturalisst, political). Will not review other mags. We do encourage exchange. CCLM, COSMEP.

Donald D. Wilson, 121 Central Ave., Stirling, NJ 07980. 5 titles listed in the *Small Press Record of Books in Print* (9th Edition, 1980).

Wilson Brothers Publications, Robert S. Wilson, PO Box 712, Yakima, WA 98907, (509) 457-8275. 1978. Poetry, fiction, articles, art, photos, cartoons, interviews, satire, criticism, reviews, music, letters, parts-of-novels, long-poems, collages, plays, concrete art, news items. "We have published a series of paperback books entitled *Trolley Trails Through the West* of which seven volumes are now published, with two more planned for 1980, also a travelog entitled *Rambling Through British Columbia.* We are prepared to produce similar paperback books for others, any subject, from minimum of eight 5½ x 8½ pages to maximum of 56 pages of 8½ x 11 size. Books are staple bound, printed on 20 lb. white sulphite paper with 65 lb. Navajo or equivalent light card covers. Terms to author are 50% with order, balance on completion; we offer correction of punctuation, spelling, grammar, etc. if desired, and counsel regarding advetising and promotion." avg. press run 900. Pub'd 2 titles 1979; expects 1 title 1980, 1 title 1981. 9 titles listed in the *Small Press Record of Books in Print* (9th Edition, 1980). avg. price, paper: $3.00-$4.00. Discounts: Bookstores, 2-4 books, 10%; 5-9 books, 40%; 10 or more books, 50%; f.o.b. Yakima, any assortment. 28pp; 8½X11; of. Reporting time: 3 weeks. Payment: Terms to author are 50% with order, balance on completion; we offer correction of punctuation, spelling, grammar, etc. if desired, and counsel regarding advertising and promotion. copyright for fee of $12.50.

Wimmer Brothers Books (see also ELVIS THE RECORD), Janine Buford, Anderson Lou Ann, PO Box 18408, Memphis, TN 38118, (901) 362-8900. 1975. Interviews, news items. "Wimmer Brothers Books publishes two basic types of books. The first is cookbooks. We print and publish high quality spiral bound cookbooks for collectors. We also publish Presley books, about the late Elvis Presley. This sideline began in 1978 with the publication of Vester Presley's *A Presley Speaks,* followed by *Elvis: Portrait of a Friend* in 1979. We also designed and coordinated the publication of *I Called Him Babe: Elvis Presley's Nurse Remembers* with Memphis State University Press in 1979." avg. press run 5,000. Pub'd 1 title 1979; expects 3 titles 1980, 4 titles 1981. avg. price, cloth: $15.00; other: Spiral bound $4.00-$7.50. Discounts: 40% to stores, 50% to distributors. 256pp; 6X9; †of. Reporting time: 3-6 months. Payment: no advances, 10-15%. Copyrights for author. ABA.

WIN MAGAZINE, Lynn Johnson, Murray Rosenblith, Mary Jane Sullivan, Dan Zedek, Mark Zuss, 326 Livingston Street, 3rd Floor, Brooklyn, NY 11217. 1966. Poetry, articles, art, photos, cartoons, interviews, satire, criticism, reviews, letters, news items. "WIN is a weekly publication of the Peace Movement. We publish articles of interest to radical pacifist people and organizers of direct action campaigns, political analysis for and from the radical left. Recent contributors include Murray Bookchin, Harvey Wasserman, Miriam Wolf, Grace Paley, Art Waskow, the Berrigans, Claudia Dreifus, Marty Jezer, Staughton Lynd, David Morris, Rebecca Cantwell, Janet Gallagher, David McReynolds, and many others. Word length: 650-2000 words or more. No guidelines available, but anyone may request a sample copy for an idea of our style and bias. WIN is available on Microfilm from Xerox University Microfilms." circ. 5,500. 22/yr. Pub'd 44 issues 1979; expects 22 issues 1980, 22 issues 1981. sub. price: $15.00/yr individuals $20.00/yr libraries free/prisoners; per copy: $1.00; sample: free upon request. Back Issues: $1; bulk 10 or more 50% additional discount. Discounts: 40% to bookstores, 15% agency discount on ads, sub agents should write for info. 36pp; 8½X11; of. Reporting time: 4-6 weeks. Payment: none. Pub's reviews: 100 in 1979. §political, social change, nonviolence, sociology, anarchism, social and economic thought, nonviolent direct action experiences. Ads: $200/$125/$3 10 words. APS, LNS News Service.

WIND LITERARY JOURNAL, Wind Press, Quentin R. Howard, RFD Rt. 1 Box 809K, Pikeville, KY 41501, 606-631-1129. 1971. Poetry, fiction, articles, reviews, plays. "No set length on anything. No biases" circ. 500. 4/yr. Pub'd 4 issues 1979; expects 4 issues 1980. sub. price: $5.00, $6.00 instit,

$7.00 foreign; per copy: $1.50; sample: $1.50. Back issues: $2.00. Discounts: none. 80pp; 5½X8½; of. Reporting time: 2-4 weeks. Payment: copies only. Copyrighted, reverts to author. Pub's reviews: 25 in 1979. §Small presses only. CCLM, COSMEP, SSSL, AWP, Academy of American Poets.

Wind Press (see also WIND LITERARY JOURNAL), Rt 1 Box 810, Pikeville, KY 41501. 2 titles listed in the *Small Press Record of Books in Print* (9th Edition, 1980).

Windflower Press (see also THE BLUE HOTEL), Ted Kooser, P.O. Box 82213, Lincoln, NB 68501. 1967. Poetry, fiction, art. "Windflower Press publishes a magazine and books of poetry" avg. press run 500. Pub'd 1 title 1979. 8 titles listed in the *Small Press Record of Books in Print* (9th Edition, 1980). avg. price, cloth: $6.95; paper: $2.95. Discounts: 40 percent to bookstores for orders of 5 copies or more; 20 percent otherwise. 64pp; 5½X8½; of. Reporting time: 3 weeks. Payment: by contract. copyright by contract. COSMEP.

Windham Bay Press, Ellen Searby, Box 1332, Juneau, AK 99802, (907) 789-2288.

THE WINDLESS ORCHARD, Dr. Robert Novak, Indiana Univ Eng Dept, Ft. Wayne, IN 46805. 1970. Poetry, criticism. circ. 400. 4/yr. Pub'd 3 issues 1979; expects 4 issues 1980, 4 issues 1981. sub. price: $7.00 4 issues; per copy: $2.00; sample: $2.00. of. Reporting time: 1-9 weeks. Payment: 2 copies. Copyrighted. Pub's reviews.

WINDOW, Window Press, Dan Johnson, Paul Deblinger, Trisha Tatam, Nan Barbour, 4510 35th St. North, Arlington, VA 22207, 301-270-5424. 1976. Poetry, fiction, art, photos, interviews, reviews, letters. "No particular bias. Would prefer to print several poems by a given poet. Recent poems by Henry Taylor, Linda Pastan, William Claire, and John Engels. Other poets recently: Rod Jellema, David McAleavey, Stuart Friebert." circ. 750. 3/yr. Pub'd 3 issues 1979; expects 3 issues 1980. sub. price: $6.00 - 4 issues; per copy: $1.75; sample: $1.00. Back issues: $1.75. Discounts: 40 percent. 72pp; 5½X8½; of. Reporting time: 6 weeks. Payment: 2 copies. Copyrighted, does not revert to author. Pub's reviews: 1 in 1979. §poetry/criticism/fiction. Ads: $60.00/$40.00. WWC, COSMEP.

Window Press (see also WINDOW), Dan Johnson, Nan Barbour, Paul Deblinger, Trisha Tatam, Jeff Bradford, 4510 35th St. North, Arlington, VA 22207, (301) 270-5424. 1976. Poetry, fiction, art, photos, interviews, reviews. "No particular bias. Henry Taylor, Linda Pastan, Richard Dillard, Myra Sklarew, Harrison Fisher, William Claire, Stuart Friebert" avg. press run 500. Pub'd 3 titles 1979; expects 3 titles 1980, 3 titles 1981. avg. price, paper: $1.75; other: Library rate: $10.00 four issue subscription. Discounts: 40%. 60pp; 5½X8½; of. Reporting time: 6 weeks. Payment: pays 2 copies. Copyrights for author. COSMEP.

Windows Project (see also SMOKE), Dave Ward, 23a Brent Way, Halewood, Liverpool, England L26 9XH, United Kingdom. 1974. Poetry, fiction, art, photos, cartoons, long-poems, collages, concrete art. avg. press run 500. Pub'd 1 title 1979; expects 1 title 1980. avg. price, paper: 50P booklet/10P SMOKE. Discounts: 33 percent. 24pp; size A4 (booklet)/A5 (SMOKE); of. Reporting time: As quickly as possible. Payment: yes/negotiable.

Windsong Books International, Larry Little, Box 867, Huntington Beach, CA 92648. Articles, cartoons. avg. press run 5,000. Pub'd 1 title 1979. 1 title listed in the *Small Press Record of Books in Print* (9th Edition, 1980). avg. price, cloth: $10.95; paper: $4.95. Discounts: standard. 224pp; 5½X8½; of. Reporting time: not seeking submissions at this time.

Windy Row Press, Dane P. Cummings, MacDowell Road, Peterborough, NH 03458, (603) 924-3340. 1969. Poetry. "Add'l address 43 Grove Street, Peterborough, NH 03458" avg. press run 800. Pub'd 3 titles 1979; expects 1 title 1980, 2 titles 1981. 2 titles listed in the *Small Press Record of Books in Print* (9th Edition, 1980). avg. price, cloth: $5.50. Discounts: Bookstores: 33⅓% 1-4 copies; 40% 5 and over; schools and colleges 20%; libraries 25%. 64pp; 5¼X7⅝. Reporting time: 3 weeks. Payment: 10%. Copyrights for author.

The Wine Press, James Ramholz, Brooke Bergan, Michael Rychlewski, 6238 N Magnolia, Chicago, IL 60660. 1972. Poetry, fiction, articles, art, photos, interviews, criticism, reviews, letters, parts-of-novels, long-poems, news items. circ. 175-1,200. Expects 4 issues 1980. 10 titles listed in the *Small Press Record of Books in Print* (9th Edition, 1980). price per copy: varies. Discounts: 40% to bookstores. 12pp; 8½X5½; of/lp. Reporting time: immediately/three weeks. Payment: copies (10%); royalties by special arrangement. Copyrighted. Pub's reviews: 1 in 1979. §Poetry, philosophy, other literary forms, small presses and university presses.

Wingbow Press, Terence Nemeth, 2940 Seventh Street, Berkeley, CA 94710, (415) 549-3030. 1971. Poetry, fiction. Pub'd 6 titles 1979; expects 5 titles 1980, 6 titles 1981. avg. price, cloth: $15.00; paper: $5.00. Discounts: 40% to bookstores, 10 or more assorted; 50% to wholesalers. 120-200pp; of.

Reporting time: 2 months. Payment: royalty rate set per title, paid twice yearly. Copyrights for author. COSMEP.

Wings Press, Arnold Perrin, R2, Box 325, Belfast, ME 04915, (207) 338-2005. 1976. Poetry. "In 1979 we will begin a series of poets (one book each month) 24-40 pages of inter related poems by one author. The best we receive each month will be selected. We will not publish tritely rhymed or unimaginative poetry (our first responsibility is to the subscribers of the Wings Press Poetry Series), but we do seek readable, understandable poetry. Send two stamps for free book and guidelines. Recent contributors to Wings anthologies include: Frank Alesi, Dan William Burns, Polly Chase Cleary, A. T. Kemper, Ken Warner Lake, Marie L. Murphy, Emily Rosen, Ily Jean Till, Robert F. Whisler, Willy Wood, Anne Wurtz, and many others." avg. press run 250. Pub'd 6 titles 1979; expects 12 titles 1980, 12 titles 1981. 9 titles listed in the *Small Press Record of Books in Print* (9th Edition, 1980). avg. price, paper: $2.00. Discounts: 40% on 5 or more copies of any one title. 24-40pp; 5½X8½; †mi. Reporting time: 1 month. Payment: 20% royalties paid quarterly. Copyrights for author. MWPA (Maine Writers and Publishers Alliance).

Winter Trees Press, Jean Boudreau, Editor, 249 Division St., Fall River, MA 02721, 617-674-1687. 1977. Poetry. "No rhyming poetry, length 24 lines, no biases enclose sase with all inquiries." avg. press run 60 copies. avg. price, paper: $2.00. 24pp; 5½X8½; of. Reporting time: 1 month. Payment: Contributors copies. Copyrights for author.

WINTERGREEN, Wintergreen Collective, PO Box 1294, Kitchener, ON N2G 4G8, Canada. 1979. Poetry, articles, photos, cartoons, interviews, satire, criticism, reviews. "*Wintergreen* is a world-wide catalog of progressive periodicals-alternative, radical, spiritual, etc., in any language, & also groups, resources, centres, anthing.. If you would like to be included in future editions, please send *some different copies* of your peiodicals & any & all other info you have. Articles, photos, comix, etc, are wanted. See also *Alternative Research Newsletter,* which serves to up-date, gathers info for the catalog & the like. Subjects: abstracts, magazines, reference, spiritual, political, occult, bibliography, alterna-tives." circ. 1,000-1,500. 1/yr. Expects 1 issue 1980, 1 issue 1981. sub. price: write; per copy: write for price; sample: write. Back issues: write. Discounts: write. 150pp; 8½X11; of. Reporting time: Immediately. Pub's reviews. §Alternative culture, radical, mystical, underground, fringe culture. Ads: $60/$30/$0.10. APS.

WIPE OUT, Real Free Press Foundation, R. O. Stoop, Dirk Van Hasseltssteeg 25, Amsterdam, The Netherlands. 1966. Fiction, cartoons, satire. "Recent contributors: Joost Swarte, Peter Pontiac, Larry Todd." circ. 2,000. irregular. Pub'd 4 issues 1979; expects 2 issues 1980, 4-8 issues 1981. price per copy: $2.50; sample: $2.50. Back issues: $2.50. Discounts: 30%. 32pp; of. Reporting time: 1 year. Payment: 10%. Copyrighted, reverts to author. APM.

Wire Press (see also THE COFFEEHOUSE), Dino Siotis, 3448 19th Street, San Francisco, CA 94110. 1974. Poetry. "*Chroniche Of Exile-poems* by Greece's greatest poet, Yannis Ritsos. *Flash Blom* by Nanos Valaoritis, poetry, surrealist, 140 pages, $5.00, ISBN 0-918034-04-3. *Twenty Contempo-rary Greek Poets* edited by Dino Siotis and John Chioles, 132 pages, $4.95, ISBN 0-918034-03-5 (double issue of the *Cofferhouse* 7-8)." avg. press run 3,000. Pub'd 2 titles 1979; expects 3 titles 1980. 4 titles listed in the *Small Press Record of Books in Print* (9th Edition, 1980). avg. price, paper: $4.00. Discounts: 40 percent bookstores. 96pp; 8½X5; †of. Copyrights for author. CCLM.

WISCONSIN REVIEW, Linda Grabner, Senior Editor, Box 92 Halsey, University of Wisconsin-Oshkosh, Oshkosh, WI 54901, 414-424-2267. 1966. Poetry, fiction, art, photos, cartoons, interviews, reviews, long-poems, concrete art. "All submissions, SASE. Materials published are poetry, reviews, prose, art and photography. Printed in 2,000 copies four times per year, $4.00, single copy $1.25. We accept materials for publication on a yearly basis." circ. 1,500. 4/yr. Pub'd 4 issues 1979; expects 4 issues 1980. 3 titles listed in the *Small Press Record of Books in Print* (9th Edition, 1980). sub. price: $4.00; per copy: $1.25; sample: $1.25. Back issues: $1.00/issue. 32pp; 8½X11; of. Reporting time: 0-5 months. Payment: copies. Copyrighted, reverts to author. Pub's reviews: 8 in 1979. §poetry and shortstories.

Wisconsin Review, Charles Dahlen, Judith Wittig, Karen Waugh, Box 145 Dempsey Hall, Oshkosh, WI 54901, 414-424-2267. 1976. Poetry, fiction. "We usually only publish small chapbooks consisting of 16-30 pages. These are usually presented as a chapbook supplement with the magazine. If the author wishes extra copies they can be obtained for the cost of printing." avg. press run 1,000. avg. price, cloth: $0.67 (paperback). Discounts: none. 16-30pp; size varies with book; of. Reporting time: 0-3 months. Payment in copies. Copyrights for author. NONE.

WISCONSIN TRAILS, Tamarack Press, Jill Dean, Managing Editor; Sue McCoy, Asst. Editor, PO Box 5650, Madison, WI 53705, 608-831-3363. 1960. Articles, photos. "Tamarack Press at present is interested in books about nature and the environment, heritage, and folklore, and guides to city and countryside as well as outdoor sports. Submissions should contain outline and sample chapters." circ. 25,000. 4/yr. Pub'd 4 issues 1979; expects 4 issues 1980, 4 issues 1981. sub. price: $10.00; per copy: $2.50. Back issues: reg. issues $2.00/rare issues $4.00. Discounts: sub agency discount, all other universal disc. sched. 44pp; 9X12; of. Reporting time: 2-3 weeks-magazine; 2 month-books. Payment: on publication. Copyrighted, reverts to author. Pub's reviews. §outdoor sports/activities/anything dealing w/Wisconsin. AAP, RPA, COSMEP.

Wisdom Garden Books, Ken Reed, Richard DeLapp, Box 29448, Los Angeles, CA 90029, (213) 380-1968. 1974. "Non-fiction. Heavy on illustrations. How to. 80% Eastern rel./philosophy/consciousness. Also we are a small press distributor. Street address: 555 Rose Ave, Bldg. C, Venice, CA 90291." avg. press run 5,000. Pub'd 1 title 1979; expects 2 titles 1980, 4 titles 1981. 7 titles listed in the *Small Press Record of Books in Print* (9th Edition, 1980). avg. price, paper: $5.95. Discounts: 40% trade, lib. 2-up, 20%; jobber 50%. 175pp; 8⅜X10¼; 6X9; of. Reporting time: 2 mos. Payment: 8%, 1st 5,000; 10%, 2nd 10,000. Copyrights for author. ABA, SCBP.

THE WISHING WELL, Laddie Hosler, Box 664, Novato, CA 94947. 1974. Poetry, art, photos, cartoons, reviews, letters, news items. "*The Wishing Well* is the largest national magazine featuring hundreds of current self-descriptions (by code number) of gay women wishing to safely write/meet one another. Offers many original features not found elsewhere, including; group travel tours for gay women. Is a highly supportive, award winning, publication serving women in 50 states and Canada." circ. 2,000. 4/yr. Pub'd 4 issues 1979; expects 4 issues 1980, 4 issues 1981. sub. price: $40.00; per copy: $3.00; sample: $3.00. Back issues: from $1.50 to $3.00 depending on date of issue. 70pp; 7X8½; of. We publish material from members only with a few exceptions. Payment: none. Copyrighted. Pub's reviews: 40 in 1979. §Gay women, cartoon-art, book reviews (relating to readership), human rights, relating to women, bi-sexual women, human relationshps, growth. Ads: query.

WITCHCRAFT DIGEST MAGAZINE (THE WICA NEWSLETTER), Leo Louis Martello, Suite 1B, 153 West 80th St., New York, NY 10024. 1970. "Prospective contributors should familiarize themselves with our theology-philosophy as outlined in Dr. Martello's book *WITCHCRAFT: The Old Religion;* or Patricia Crowther's *Witch Blood: Autobiography of a Witch High Priestess* or her *The Witches Speak.* We're Pre-Christian Pagans, naturalists, and the Old Religion has NOTHING to do with Christian-defined Satanism, devil-worship etc. Anyone sending in a self-addressed stamped envelope will receive our FREE lists of Old Religion books and publications." circ. 3,500. 1/yr. sub. price: $1.25. Discounts: 40%. 24pp; 8½X11; of. Reporting time: immediately. Payment: 1 cent per word. Pub's reviews. §witchcraft, occult, psychology, religion. Ads: $100/$50/$.20.

Witwatersrand University Press (see ENGLISH STUDIES IN AFRICA-A Journal of the Humanities)

WLW JOURNAL: News/Views/Reviews for Women and Libraries, Women Library Workers, Carole Leita, Co-Editor; Carol Starr, Co-Editor, P O Box 9052, Berkeley, CA 94709. 1980. Articles, art, photos, interviews, criticism, reviews, cartoons, letters, news items, satire. "WLW Journal contains news and information of interest to members of this feminist library workers organization and any interested in reviews of feminist materials." circ. 500. 6/yr. Pub'd 6 issues 1979; expects 6 issues 1980, 6 issues 1981. sub. price: $12.00 for non-members. Membership ($15.00) includes newsletter.; per copy: $2.00; sample: free. Back issues: $2.00 each, as available. Discounts: $11.00/yr to vendors; $22.00/2 yrs. 32pp; 8¼X10¾; of. Reporting time: 2 months. Payment: none available at present; copies of issue sent free. Copyrighted. Pub's reviews. §feminism, libraries & information services, worker. Ads: $100/$50/$25 1/4 page.

Wolf House Books (see also THE LONDON COLLECTOR), Richard Werderman, Publisher, Box 209-K, Cedar Springs, MI 49319. 1971. "Books by and about Jack London." avg. press run 1,000. Expects 3 titles 1980. 7 titles listed in the *Small Press Record of Books in Print* (9th Edition, 1980). avg. price, cloth: $12.00. Discounts: 1-3, 25%; 4 or more 40%. 300pp; 6X9; of. Reporting time: 1 month. Payment: 10% of list. Copyrights for author.

WOLFSONG, Wolfsong Publications, R. Chris Halla, Gary Busha, Janet Halla, 509 W Fulton, Waupaca, WI 54981. 1978. Poetry, fiction, art, criticism, reviews, parts-of-novels, long-poems. "We have as our goal, publication of the best poetry, fiction, criticism and comment being written today. Editorial policy is based solely on literary merit. Some contributors have been Peter Wild, William Kloefkorn, Gary Busha. 1977 was *RIVER BOTTOM'S* last year as a magazine and press. Our plans for the future are to publish a pamphlet/chapbook series under the Wolfsong imprint. The new series will include poetry, fiction, criticism and anything else that impresses us." circ. 300-1000. irreg. Pub'd 4 issues 1979. sub. price: $10.00; per copy: $2.25; sample: $2.25. Discounts: 1-5 20%; 6-10 40%;

11-50 41%; 50 & up 50%. 20-60pp; 8½X5½; of. Reporting time: 1 mo. Payment: contributor's copies. Copyrighted. §poetry, fiction, literary criticism. Ads: inquire. CCLM, COSMEP MIDWEST.

Wolfsong Publications (see also WOLFSONG), R.C. Halla, Gary Busha, Janet Halla, 509 W Fulton, Waupaca, WI 54981. 1978. "Titles for 1978 include *Gold Mines* by Peter Wild, and *Stocker* by William Kloefkorn, *Waiting* by Debra Frigen, *Moon Rides Witness* by Dorothy Dalton" avg. press run 300-1,000. Expects 4 titles 1980, 5 titles 1981. 12 titles listed in the *Small Press Record of Books in Print* (9th Edition, 1980). avg. price, paper: $2.25. Discounts: 1-5 20%, 6-10 40%, 11-50 41%, 50 and up 50%. 20-60pp; 5½X8½; of. Reporting time: 1-2 months. Copyrights for author. CCLM, COSMEP MIDWEST.

THE WOMAN ACTIVIST, Flora Crater, 2310 Barbour Road, Falls Church, VA 22043. 1971. Articles. "The woman activist could be classified as a newsletter. I call it a political action bulletin for women's rights." circ. 300. 12/yr. Pub'd 12 issues 1979; expects 12 issues 1980. 12 titles listed in the *Small Press Record of Books in Print* (9th Edition, 1980). sub. price: $10.00; per copy: $1.00; sample: $.25. Back issues: $1.00. 8pp; 8½X11; of. Reporting time: 3 weeks. Payment: none. Pub's reviews: 2 in 1979. §women/politics/feminism. Ads: $.20 wd.

Woman Matters Press (see also AFFORDABLE CHIC NEWS), Barbara Schnipper, PO Box 153, Cabin John, MD 20731, (301) 229-6765. 1978. "Woman-supportive information published on matters related to career planning, cheap fashion know-how, consumer information, credit, health, and other issues of concern to women's lives. Most material is researched and written by the publisher, but inquiries are invited. Must be a topic of wide-interest, well-researched and well-written and accompanied by a SASE. Mostly self-publish own material but will buy articles outright. Each deal negotiable but rates are not high. Sometimes payable in copies." avg. press run 1,500. Pub'd 2 titles 1979; expects 1-2 titles 1980. 2 titles listed in the *Small Press Record of Books in Print* (9th Edition, 1980). avg. price, paper: $3.00. Discounts: Negotiable. 32pp; 5½X8½; of. Reporting time: 30-45 days. Copyrights for author. Washington Book Publishers Assoc., COSMEP-South, The Writer's Center of Glen Echo, MD.

WOMAN POET, Women-in-Literature, Inc., Elaine Dallman, Editor-in-Chief; Carolyn Kizer, Poetry Editor, PO Box 12668, Reno, NV 89510, (702) 825-8104. 1978. Poetry, photos, criticism, concrete art. "Unpublished fine poems of any length will be considered for our series of regional book/journals —*The West* (1980), *The Northeast* (1980), *The Midwest* (1981), *The South* (1981). Interviews and critical reviews of featured poets. We have an international readership interested in fine women's poetry. Well-written articles will let readers have deeper insights into—How is good literature written? What kind of women write it? What is their education? What does it take to write and to write well? Other material of human interest about writers will be presented. Recent contributors: Josephine Miles, Ann Stanford, Madeline DeFrees, Marilyn Hacker, Adrienne Rich, Audre Lourde, Mary Barnard, Lisel Mueller, Rosalie Moore, Adrianne Marcus, Diane O Hehir. We urge writers to inspect a copy before submitting. We are a non-profit corporation (literary-educational)—we welcome tax-deductible donations." circ. 4,000. 2/yr. sub. price: Indiv. $10.00; Instit. $16.00; per copy: $6.00 indiv., $9.00 instit.; sample: $5.50. Discounts: 1, 10%; 2-4, 20% (prepaid only); 5-24, 40%; write for classroom rates; 10 day trial copy on request to libraries, professors (prepaid only). 100pp; 8X9½; of. Reporting time: 3 weeks to 3 months. Payment: copies. Copyrighted. Pub's reviews. §Of selected poets; other poets' book in future. Ads: $200.00/$125.00/$85.00/$0.01. COSMEP, COSMEP-WEST.

WOMAN SPIRIT, WomanSpirit, Collective, Box 263, Wolf Creek, OR 97497. 1974. Poetry, fiction, articles, art, photos, cartoons, interviews, criticism, reviews, music, letters, long-poems, collages, plays. "Our audience is women. Only women contribute. We use 'she' and 'her' as generic terms. Unpublished women are encouraged to submit personal experiences, about their inner growth, and original art work (in black and white only). Originality, authenticity and positive attitudes towards women, their lives, changes and potential. 500 to 5000 words, graphics up to 8 x 10. Seasonal material (related to equinoxes and solstices) is used as appropriate and themes are developed which relate to cycles of monthly (moon) changes, yearly (sun) changes and life time development (aging). We are feminist, in the Women's Movement, see our magazine as going to the roots (radical) of women's experiences to rebuild a humane culture. We do not publish personal love poetry, love stories etc." circ. 5M. 4/yr. Pub'd 4 issues 1979. sub. price: $7.00 individual anywhere in world; $12.00 institutional; per copy: $2.50; sample: $2.00. Back issues: full set of six volumes: $50.00. Discounts available to bookstores and distributors, write for information. 64pp; 8½X11; of. Reporting time: 3-9 months. Payment: 2 copies. Copyrighted, reverts to author. Pub's reviews: 12-15 in 1979. §Ecology, folklore, native American, philosophy, spiritual, women, feminism. no ads; we carry announcements. CCLM.

Woman Works Press, Cheryl Howard, Annette Van Dyke, Rt 6, Box 309, Bemidji, MN 56601, (218) 751-0511. 1978. Poetry, photos. "The press was founded primarily to publish Annette Van Dyke's poetry and is not currently accepting submissions. Other contributor: Cheryl Younger, photography."

avg. press run 500. Pub'd 1 title 1979. avg. price, paper: $3.00. Discounts: 30%. 50pp; 5⅞X7-6/8; of.

WOMANCHILD, Womanchild Press, Julie Scheinman, Collins Road, Hardwick, RFD, Ware, MA 01082, 617-756-4426. 1976. Poetry, long-poems. "Wants poems of clarity in any style or form. Now accepting book-length mss for chapbook series. Recent contributors include Lifshin, Malanga, Gayle Harvey, Roberta Gould, S.R. Lavin." circ. 300. 1/yr. Pub'd 1 issue 1979; expects 1 issue 1980, 1 issue 1981. sub. price: $3.50; per copy: $3.50; sample: $3.50. Back issues: $5.00 for #1; very limited supply. Discounts: 10 or more 50% off, cash basis. 40-60pp; 6X9; †lp. Reporting time: 2-4 weeks. Payment: 3 copies. Not copyrighted. COSMEP.

Womanchild Press (see also WOMANCHILD), Julie Scheinman, Collins Road, Hardwick, RFD, Ware, MA 01082. 1976. Poetry, long-poems. "Publishes chapbooks by poets who have previously had poem(s) in *Womanchild.*" avg. press run 300. Pub'd 1 title 1979; expects 2 titles 1980, 2 titles 1981. 2 titles listed in the *Small Press Record of Books in Print* (9th Edition, 1980). avg. price, other: $3.00 for hand bound, papercover, unsigned. Discounts: 25% off on orders of 2-9 copies; 40% off on orders of ten or more. 40pp; 6X9; †lp. Reporting time: 2-6 weeks. Payment: arranged individually. Does not copyright for author. COSMEP.

WOMAN'S CHOICE, Woman's Choice Network, Louise Lacey, PO Box 489, Berkeley, CA 94701, (415) 527-1900. 1978. Poetry, fiction, articles, art, cartoons, interviews, letters, photos, satire. " *Woman's Choice* is a network of women (and some men) who address ideas from a feminine, intuitive, perspective. Contemporary oral history about feelings, experiences and insights into important issues and choices of our times. Written conversationally. No dogmas or answers; just stimulating ideas in the context of intimate friendship. *Woman's Choice* is the forum for these pieces: Articles, interviews, stories range from 50 to 6,000 words. Contributors do not have to subscribe. Write for sample issue and upcoming topics." circ. 1,000. 12/yr. Pub'd 12 issues 1979; expects 12 issues 1980, 12 issues 1981. sub. price: $18.00; per copy: $2.00; sample: free. Back issues: $2.00 each or 3/$5.00. Discounts: Request info. 12pp; 8½X11; of. Reporting time: 1-6 weeks. Payment: In contributors' copies and/or subscription. Copyrighted, reverts to author. Ads: No ads.

Woman's Choice Network (see WOMAN'S CHOICE)

Womanshare Books, Carol Newhouse, Dian Wagner, Nelly Kaufer, Billie Mericle, Sue Deevy, PO Box 681, Grants Pass, OR 97526. 1976. "Title of our book: *Country Lesbians*" avg. press run 2,000. avg. price, paper: $5.50. Discounts: 40% to bookstores.

WomanSpirit (see WOMAN SPIRIT)

WOMEN: A Journal of Liberation, Collective, 3028 Greenmount Ave, Baltimore, MD 21218, 301-235-5245. 1969. Poetry, fiction, articles, art, photos, cartoons, interviews, satire, reviews, long-poems, parts-of-novels. "Fiction & articles: 3,000 words or less. Art work & photos: black & white only. SASE with all work. Production schedule is irregular. Three issues to a volume; subscription by volume" circ. 10,000. 2-3/yr. Expects 3 issues 1980. sub. price: 1 vol./3 issues $6.00 individual; per copy: $2.00; sample: $1.00. Back issues: damaged copies $.50. Discounts: $1.05 prepaid, bulk; no returns. 64pp; 8½X11; of. Reporting time: 5 months. Payment: One free copy of issue. Copyrighted. Pub's reviews: 2 in 1979. §All areas. no ads. COSMEP.

†WOMEN AND LITERATURE, Janet M. Todd, Editor, Dept. English, Douglas College, Rutgers University, New Brunswick, NJ 08903. 4/yr. Pub'd 2 issues 1979; expects 4 issues 1980. sub. price: $10.00; per copy: $2.50; sample: $2.50. 66pp; 6X9. Reporting time: 4 months. Payment: copies. Copyrighted. Pub's reviews. §Books about women authors (George Sand, for example) and treatment of women in literature.

WOMEN ARTISTS NEWS, Midmarch Associates, Cynthia Navaretta, Exec. Editor; Cindy Lyle, Editor, Box 3304, Grand Central, New York City, NY 10017, 212-666-6990. 1975. Articles, art, photos, interviews, criticism, reviews, letters, collages, concrete art, news items. "300-500 word articles; emphasis on visual arts; coverage of dance, film, music, arts events, etc. Listing solo and group shows across the USA; opportunities for artists; artists' panels, symposia + conference reports; political news of interest to artists; interviews. 12 to 20 pages with b&w photos. Present ideas, philosophies and recent art phenomena. Frequently only publication of record reporting on N.Y. art-talk scene; many male subscribers." circ. 5,000. 10/yr. Pub'd 10 issues 1979. 2 titles listed in the *Small Press Record of Books in Print* (9th Edition, 1980). sub. price: $7.00 indiv; $10.00 insit.; per copy: $1.00; sample: $1.00. Back issues: $1.00. Discounts: jobber & agent 40%; bookstores, galleries 40%; classroom 40%. 12-20pp; 8½X11; of. Reporting time: 2—3 weeks. Payment: only in years when funded for payment to writers; pay regular regional contributors. Copyrighted, reverts to author.

Pub's reviews: 20 in 1979. §art, (visual arts, film, dance) women, arts legislation. Ads: $240/$125. CCLM, COSMEP.

WOMEN IN THE ARTS BULLETIN/NEWSLETTER, Women In The Arts Foundation, Inc., Sylvia Helm, 325 Spring St, New York, NY 10013, 212-691-0988. 1971 (for organization) 1973 (for newsletter). Photos, news items, articles, interviews, letters. "Length-200 to 1,000 words-must be on women's art movement or topics relevant to women artists." circ. 1,000. 10/yr. Pub'd 10 issues 1979; expects 10 issues 1980, 10 issues 1981. sub. price: $5.00 ($6.00 institution); per copy: 50¢; sample: free. Back issues: free for single copy; 50 cents/pc. otherwise. Discounts: trade-free, subscription in exchange for free subscription; 20 percent discount to jobber or agent. 6pp; 8½X11; of. No payment. Copyrighted. Pub's reviews. §women's visual art & writing. Ads: $110/$60.

Women In The Arts Foundation, Inc. (see also WOMEN IN THE ARTS BULLETIN/NEWSLETTER), 325 Spring St, New York, NY 10013. 3 titles listed in the *Small Press Record of Books in Print* (9th Edition, 1980).

Women-in-Literature, Inc., Elaine Dallman, Editor-in-Chief; Carolyn Kizer, Poetry Editor, PO Box 12668, Reno, NV 89510, (702) 825-8104. 1978. Poetry, photos, interviews, criticism. "Unpublished fine poems of any length, by women, will be considered for our series of regional book/journals— the West (1981), the Midwest, the Northeast, the South (1981). Interviews and critical reviews of featured poets. We have an international readership interested in fine women's poetry. Well-written articles will let readers have deeper insights into—How is good literature written? What kind of women write it? What is their education? What does it take to write and to write well? Other material of human interest about writers will be presented. Recent contributors: Josephine Miles, Ann Stanford, Madeline DeFrees, Rosalie Moore, Tess Gallagher, Olga Broumas, Mary Barnard, Sandra Gilbert, Kathleen Fraser, Adrianne Marcus, Diane O'Hehir. We urge writers to inspect a copy before submitting. We are a non profit corporation (literary-educational) and any donations to us are tax-deductible." avg. press run 4,000. Pub'd 2 titles 1979; expects 2 titles 1980. 3 titles listed in the *Small Press Record of Books in Print* (9th Edition, 1980). avg. price, cloth: $12.95 + $1.00 handling; paper: $6.00 + $0.50 handling, $9.00 instit. Discounts: 1, 10%; 2-4, 20% (prepaid only); 5-24, 40%; write for classroom rates; 10 day trial copy on request to libraries, professors (prepaid only). 100pp; 8X9½; lp. Reporting time: 3 weeks to 3 months. Payment: copies. Copyrights for author. COSMEP, COSMEP-WEST.

Women Library Workers (see also WLW JOURNAL: News/Views/Reviews for Women and Libraries), Carole Leita, Carol Starr, P O Box 9052, Berkeley, CA 94709, 415-654-8822. 1975. "Editor(s) Carole Leita, 4th Edition, APRIL 1980, share: a directory of feminist library workers (first edition published as *Sisters Have Resources Everywhere,* a directory of feminist librarians) is a directory of feminist library workers. Names, addresses and brief self-descriptions of women in the U.S. and Canada who are interested in sharing information, skills, and friendship with other feminists. Entries are geographically arranged; subject and name indexes are included." avg. press run 1,000. Expects 1 title 1980. 2 titles listed in the *Small Press Record of Books in Print* (9th Edition, 1980). avg. price, paper: $4.00 prepaid; other: $5.00 if invoiced. 60pp; 5½X8½; of. Reporting time: varies. Payment: none. Copyrights for author.

WOMEN STUDIES ABSTRACTS, ABC Letter Service of Rochester, Sara Stauffer Whaley, PO Box 1, Rush, NY 14543, (716) 533-1376; 533-1251. 1972. "Contains abstracts of articles from selected periodicals on all aspects of women's lives. Any periodical wanting to be considered for possible inclusion should write and send a sample copy. Authors of periodical articles on women should send a copy of the article and an abstract to WSA if they would like their material included." circ. 1,500. 4/yr. Pub'd 4 issues 1979; expects 4 issues 1980. sub. price: $25.00/individual; $45.00/ institutional; per copy: $6.00 ($10.00 to library); sample: $3.00, to libraries free. Back issues: 1972 (Vol. 1, minus nos. 1,2,3), $6.00; 1973 (Vol. 2, minus no. 2), $12.00; 1974 (Vol. 3), $15.00; 1975 (Vol.4), $25.00; 1976 (Vol. 5, minus no. 1), $20.00; 1977 (Vol. 6) $25.00. Discounts: To bookstores-40% off institutional rate. 96pp; 5⅞X9; of. Reporting time: 1 month. Payment: $100-$200 for bibliographic essay. Copyrighted, reverts to author. Pub's reviews. §Women. Ads: $100.00/$60.00. COSMEP.

WOMEN TALKING, WOMEN LISTENING, WTWL Press, Sharon Lee, Editor and Publisher, P.O. Box 2414, Dublin, CA 94566, 415-828-0671. 1975. Poetry. "Emerging voice of California women poets-extablished to provide exposure-commentary on changing womens roles-subjective history." circ. 1200. 1/yr. Pub'd 1 issue 1979; expects 1 issue 1980, 1 issue 1981. 1 title listed in the *Small Press Record of Books in Print* (9th Edition, 1980). sub. price: Volume V (1979-80) $3.00 plus 40¢ postage. $2.50 plus .065 tax and .40 post/handling. (CA res add .065 sales tax); per copy: $2.25 Vol. II, $2.50 Vol III et al; sample: $2.25 Vol. II, $2.50 Vol. III et al. Back issues: $2.25 Vol. II, $2.50 Vol. III et al. Discounts: 40% trade, 10% over 6 copies-post paid, 20% over 12 copies. 42-60pp; 7X8¼. Submissions from California women only 6-15 to 8-15. report by 9-15. Payment: copy poets special discount 1st 30 days. Copyrighted, reverts to author. CCLM, COSMEP, WIP, POW.

Women Writing Press (NY), Box 1035 Cathedral Sta, New York City, NY 10025. Poetry. "Women Writing Press (NY) is essentially an imprint which exists to distribute a self-published book. Manuscripts are not being solicited." 1 title listed in the *Small Press Record of Books in Print* (9th Edition, 1980). of.

Women's Action Alliance (see also WOMEN'S AGENDA), Ellen Sweet, Editor; Naomi Barko, Managing Editor, 370 Lexington Ave., New York, NY 10017. 1971. Articles, art, photos, cartoons, reviews, letters, news items. avg. press run 2,000. avg. price, other: $1.25. 16pp; 8¼X11; lp.

WOMEN'S AGENDA, Women's Action Alliance, Ellen Sweet, Editor; Naomi Barko, Managing Editor, c/o Women's Action Alliance, 370 Lexington Ave., New York, NY 10017. 1971. Articles, art, photos, cartoons, reviews, letters, news items. circ. 2,000. 6/yr. sub. price: $10.00 Indiv., $20.00 Organizations, $18.00 Indiv 2 years; per copy: $1.25; sample: $1.25. Back issues: $1.25. 16pp; 8½X11; lp. Copyrighted. Pub's reviews: 10 in 1979. §All areas concerning women and equal rights.

Women's History Research Center, Inc., Vicki Lynn Hill, '74 Ed; Louisa Moe, '75 Ed, 2325 Oak St, Berkeley, CA 94708. 1968. "Ordering address for 1975 edition of *Female Artists Past and Present* only: David Crosson, Archive of Contemporary History, University of Wyoming, Laramie, WY 82071" avg. press run 1,000. 2 titles listed in the *Small Press Record of Books in Print* (9th Edition, 1980). avg. price, paper: $5.00. Discounts: 30-40 percent discount to book dealers buying at least 5 copies. 100pp; 7X8½, 8½X11; of. COSMEP.

Women's Institute for Freedom of the Press (see also MEDIA REPORT TO WOMEN), Donna Allen, Editor, 3306 Ross Place, N.W., Washington, DC 20008, 202-966-7783. 1972. Non-fiction. "Studies of communication system, particularly as it affects women, is our major interest, although we will consider related material, especially documentary or source material, about women in media. 1977 published *Women in Media: a documentary source book* by Maurine Beasley and Sheila Silver, $5.95, paper, 200pp. Also annual Index/Directory of women's media." Pub'd 1 title 1979; expects 1 title 1980. 2 titles listed in the *Small Press Record of Books in Print* (9th Edition, 1980). avg. price, paper: $5.95; other: $8.00 for Index/Directory, $20.00 for subscription to *Media Report to Women*. Discounts: bulk-40 percent on 3 or more. 6X9, 8½X11; of. Reporting time: 2 months. Payment: negotiable. joint copyright WIFP and author.

Women's Studies, Wendy Martin, Dept. of English, Queens College, CUNY, Flushing, NY 11367. 1971. Articles, reviews. circ. 2,000. 3/yr. sub. price: $17.50. Back issues: Contact publisher. Discounts: Contact publisher. 100pp; 11½X6. Reporting time: 3 months. Payment: none. Copyrighted. Pub's reviews.

WOMEN'S STUDIES NEWSLETTER, Carolyn Brown, 176 Hagley Road, Stourbridge, W. Midlands DY8 2JN, United Kingdom, 038 43 5131. 1977. Poetry, fiction, articles, photos, cartoons, interviews, criticism, reviews, letters, news items. "Newsletter for people involved in women's education and women's studies to communicate, exchange ideas and information and generally express feelings about the issues which affect women's lives today. Feature articles 1,000-2,000 words; herstory (biographies of women); book reviews 400-700" circ. 1,500. 4/yr. Pub'd 4 issues 1979; expects 4 issues 1980, 4 issues 1981. sub. price: individual: surface £2.50; airmail £4.00/library and institution: surface £6.50; airmail £7.50; per copy: 70p; sample: 50p. Back issues: inquire. Discounts: inquire. 26pp; 6X8¼; of. Reporting time: up to 2 months. Payment: none. Not copyrighted. Pub's reviews: 28-36 in 1979. §Women's issues, health, politics, sexual politics. Ads: £15/£8.50/5p. APS.

WOMEN'S STUDIES NEWSLETTER, The Feminist Press, Florence Howe, Box 334, Old Westbury, NY 11568, 516-997-7660. 1972. Articles, reviews, art, photos, cartoons, interviews, news items. "News, issues, events in women's studies; articles are from 1,200 to 2,000 words usually. Subscription included as part of NWSA membership dues." circ. 2,000-2,500. 4/yr. Pub'd 3 issues 1979; expects 4 issues 1980, 4 issues 1981. sub. price: $7.00 individuals/$12.00 institutions/foreign: $10.00 individual/$15.00 institution; per copy: $2.00; sample: $2.00. Back issues: $2.00 each. Discounts: none. 32pp; 8½X11; of. Reporting time: 2-3 months. Payment: we do not pay contributors. Copyrighted, does not revert to author. Pub's reviews. §Women's studies. Ads: $125.00/$75.00/$0.25.

WOOD IBIS, Place of Herons, James Cody, Editor, PO Box 1952, Austin, TX 78768, (512) 472-0737; 476-7023. 1974. Poetry, fiction, articles, art, criticism, parts-of-novels, photos, cartoons, interviews, reviews, letters, long-poems, plays. "A journal of contemporary shamanism (for explanation of what we mean by 'shamanism' send $1.00 for a copy of the explicative essay, *Wood Ibis and Shamanism* : back country, nature, shamanism, ethnopoetry, tribalism, regionlism, Texas, the Southwest, North

America and the hemisphere; mythology, poetry, prose, essays, reviews, art. Contributing editors: Ricardo Sanchez (153 E. Truman Ave., Salt Lake City, UT 84115) and Reyes Cardenas (1208 6th Street, Sequin, TX 78155). Emphasis on Chicanos, Native Americans and Black Americans as well as Euro-Americans. Ongoing emphases on Celtic culture, white consciousness and Korean shamanism. Incoming material shapes the issues, issues do not shape the material, so we are open to new and unanticipated contributions. Our mandala is left imperfect so that the soul can escape. Coming issue on Texas and Oklahoma, featuring writes such as Foreman, Cody, Ramon & Ricardo Sanchez, Reyes Cardenas, Hillman, Behlen, Bigley, Steve Harris, Colin Murphey and Henry Allen. Art by S.T. Vaughn. Coming issues will include work by Gifford, Blue Cloud, Leggett, D. Clinton, Bruchac, Gary Elder, Tim Sagel, Jim Clark, Sharon Doubiago and Mike Lowery; translations by David McCann. Other emphases in issues will be Russia (a feature on/by Konstantin Kuzminsky), Big Bend and Central Texas. One issue in 1979 will be an anthology of writing from *P-79, One World Poetry Fetival,* Amsterdam Holland. Writing in English and Spanish, or both, welcome. Submissions must be accompanied by SASE. As our issues are very tightly edited, we occasionally find it necessary to return material already accepted. We regret this policy, but must reserve its option. Acceptances are made on the basis of quality only, not on identity with any group of publishing history. First timers and one-timers welcome. Emphasis is also placed on the value to community, even when literary quality may not be as strong. The closing of Black Elk's Hoop. A prayer for the return of Eden. Advancing/discovering practical myths for an emerging world. The Flowering Tree." circ. 1,000. Irregular, at least one a year. Pub'd 2 issues 1979; expects 1-2 issues 1980. sub. price: $6.00 Indiv., $12.00 Instit. for 4 issues; per copy: $1.50; double issue $3.00 plus postage; sample: $1.50; $3.00 for #' 3 & 4 plus postage. Back issues: No. 1/$5.00 ea. No. 2 $1.25 ea. plus postage. Discounts: 40% bookstores; 10% for 30 copies or more. 60-100pp; 8½X5½; of. Reporting time: Varies. Payment: Copies, hope to pay in cash in 1979. Copyrighted. Pub's reviews: 23 in 1979. §Nature, shamanism, ethnopoetry, tribal, regionalism, Texas, Native Americans, mythology, general poetry. Ads: $50.-00/$25.00.

Dr. Stella Woodall Publisher (see also ADVENTURES IN POETRY MAGAZINE), Dr. Stella Woodall, PO Box 253, Junction, TX 76849, 915 446-2004. 1968. Poetry, photos, cartoons, long-poems. "To the most outstanding poet in each edition is sent a copy of my awardwinning book: *Anthology of Texas Poems;* to the best poem published in each edition is sent a copy of *Anthology of Texas Poems.* The best poems of the year are published in *Adventures in Poetry Anthology.* Each edition of this quarterly internatinal magazine features the most outstanding poet, the latest poet laureate of Stella Woodall Poetry Society International, using these poets' photographs, biographies, and poems. A copy of my hard-back gold-award-winning book, *Anthology of Texas Poems,* is awarded to the author of the best poem in each edition of the international magazine. Each edition also features poets of one of our United States, using the photograph, biography, and a statement on poetry by the Governor of that state and the photographs, biographies, and poems of the President of that State's Poetry Society, and of that State's Poet Laureate. Poems by members of Stella Woodall Poetry Society International are given preference over the hundreds of poems submitted each quarter for publication in Adventures of Poetry Magazine. Membership dues are $15 anually. To become a member a poet must be recommended by a member and must submit his photograph, biography, and his best poem. For further information on membership poets should write to Dr. Stella Woodall, P.O. Box 253, Junction, Texas 76849." avg. press run 600. Pub'd 4 titles 1979; expects 4 titles 1980, 4 titles 1981. 4 titles listed in the *Small Press Record of Books in Print* (9th Edition, 1980). avg. price, cloth: $4.00; paper: free to members of Stella Woodall Poetry Society International. Extra copies and sample copies: $4.00 each; other: $4.00. 76-80pp; 8½X5½; of. Reporting time: Usually within one week sometimes longer.

Wooden Needle Press (see also THE MODULARIST REVIEW), R. C. Morse, 53-18 68th Street, Maspeth, NY 11378, (212) 672-9449. 1972. "We'll be starting to consider mss of poetry for chapbooks this year." avg. press run 400. Pub'd 2 titles 1979; expects 2 titles 1980, 2 titles 1981. 2 titles listed in the *Small Press Record of Books in Print* (9th Edition, 1980). avg. price, paper: $2.00. Discounts: 40% trade. 24pp; 5X8; of. Reporting time: 1-3 months. Payment: by contract. Copyrights for author. CCLM, NESPA.

THE WOODSTOCK REVIEW, Aesopus Press, Patricia Jackson, Marilyn Mohr, Annie Jung-Blythe, 27 Oriole Drive, Woodstock, NY 12498, (914) 679-7795. 1977. Poetry, art, reviews, long-poems. " *The Woodstock Poetry Review* is the original name of the magazine. Recent contributors: Carol Berge, Ed Sanders, Janine Vega, Marilyn Mohr, Susan Axelrod, Pearl Bond." circ. 400. 3/yr. Pub'd 3 issues 1979; expects 3 issues 1980, 4 issues 1981. sub. price: $6.00/yr; per copy: $2.00; sample: $1.50. Back issues: $1.50. Discounts: 25% discount in quantity, bookstores 40%. 40-50pp; 5½X8½; †of. Reporting time: 3 weeks to one month. Payment: copies. Copyrighted, reverts to author. Pub's reviews. §short literary reviews. Ads: none. CCLM.

The Word Shop, Michael Gosney, 3737 Fifth Avenue, Suite 203, San Diego, CA 92103, (714) 291-9126. 1976. Poetry, articles, art, photos, cartoons, interviews, long-poems. "Involved in new age publishing; yearly *Journal of Holistic Health.* Also ecologial and neo-spiritual works; *The Life and Adventures of John Muir.* Subsidy contractual arrangement with 40/60% distribution (author/publisher) split. In-house photo-typesetting and design. Editing and writing services." avg. press run 5,000. Pub'd 1 title 1979; expects 3 titles 1980, 4 titles 1981. 2 titles listed in the *Small Press Record of Books in Print* (9th Edition, 1980). avg. price, cloth: $12.00; paper: $7.00. Discounts: Bookstores, 40%; Distributors, 50%. 200pp; 8X10½; of. Reporting time: 2 months. Payment: 40% author/60% publisher with author paying for production of work, or other. Copyrights for author. COSMEP.

The Word Works, Inc., Deirdra Baldwin, Jim Beall, Karren Alenier, Bob Sargent, P.O. Box 4054, Washington, DC 20015, (703) 524-0999. 1974. Poetry. "We welcome inquiries including SASE" avg. press run 500. Pub'd 5 titles 1979; expects 5 titles 1980, 2 titles 1981. 11 titles listed in the *Small Press Record of Books in Print* (9th Edition, 1980). avg. price, paper: $4.00. Discounts: 40 percent. 50pp; 5½X8½; of. Reporting time: 3 mos. Payment: 10 percent of run. Y/Y.

The WorDoctor Publications, Rolf Gompertz, PO Box 9761, North Hollywood, CA 91606, 213-980-3576. 1974. "Self-publisher only, at this time. '*My Jewish Brother Jesus*' (Biblical novel)." avg. press run 1,000 copies. Pub'd 1 title 1979. 2 titles listed in the *Small Press Record of Books in Print* (9th Edition, 1980). avg. price, cloth: $6.95; paper: $3.95. Discounts: Distributors, jobbers, bookstores - 1 copy, 10%; 2-4 copies, 25%; 5-10 copies, 40%; 11 or more, 50%. 208pp; 5½X8½; of. Copyrights for author. COSMEP.

Words, Paul Johnston, Richard Spiegel, Mary Clark, 128A W 10th Street, Apt 3, New York, NY 10014, 242-8447. 1977. Fiction, criticism, parts-of-novels. "Publishes the work the 'The Company', the editors listed above-a communal effort for one another. Paul Johnston is an 80 year old man, a former letterpress printer, author of articles on printing & typography (+book: *Bibliotypographica*) + one novel published by Maurice Girodias' Olympia Press. These booklets are excerpts from his writing over the last 40 years. Contributions accepted." avg. press run 100. Pub'd 1-2 titles 1979; expects 2 titles 1980, 3 titles 1981. avg. price, other: Contribution appreciated. 10-40pp; 4¼X5½; of. No solicited ms.

The Work Center Press, SHANKPAINTER, Changes, 24 Pearl St, Provincetown, MA 02657, 617-487-9960. circ. 800. 1-3/yr. Pub'd 3 issues 1979; expects 1 issue 1980, 2 issues 1981.

THE WORKBOOK, Southwest Research and Information Center, PO Box 4524, Albuquerque, NM 87106, 505-242-4766. 1974. Articles, criticism, reviews. "Style-articles showing people who are concerned with specific problems & how they can become involved. Action oriented. Bias-politics are leftist oriented. Contributors-Michael Jacobson, Egan O'Connor. Richard Morgan, James Sullivan, Sandra Simons, Dan Butler, Steve Goldin." circ. 2,000. 6/yr. Pub'd 6 issues 1979; expects 6 issues 1980. sub. price: $7.00/yr students, senior citizens; $10.00/yr individuals, $20.00/yr institutions; per copy: $2.00; sample: free. Back issues: $1.00. Discounts: Trade-40% agent 40%. 48pp; 8½X10½; of. Reporting time: 2 weeks to 2 months. Payment: none. copyrighted by Southwest Research & Information Center. Pub's reviews: 300 in 1979. §Action oriented, dealing with environmental, consumer & social problems. Ads: none. COSMEP.

Workers' Press (see also APPEAL TO REASON), Jonathan Aurthur, Richard Santillan, Contributing Editor; John Moore, Contributing Editor; Jeff Frieden, Contributing Editor; Rudy Torres, Contributing Editor, PO Box 3774, Chicago, IL 60654. 1971. Articles, art, photos, cartoons, interviews, reviews. avg. press run 3,000. Pub'd 4 titles 1979; expects 4 titles 1980, 4 titles 1981. 4 titles listed in the *Small Press Record of Books in Print* (9th Edition, 1980). avg. price, paper: $2.50. Discounts: 40% stores, 50% distributors. 96pp; 5½X8½; of. Reporting time: 6 weeks. Copyrights for author.

Working Press, Bill Owens, Box 687-D, Livermore, CA 94550, (415) 447-5943. 1979. "Photo books. We also distribute photo books." avg. press run 1,000. avg. price, cloth: $19.95; paper: $9.95. Discounts: 20% library, 40% bookstores, 50% jobbers. 50pp; 9X9; of. Reporting time: 3 months. Payment: co-op arrangements. Copyrights for author. SPE/NPPA/ASMP.

Workshop Press Ltd., Norman Hidden, 2 Culham Court, Granville Rd, London N44JB, United Kingdom, 01-348-4054. 1967. "No unsolicited material required" 13 titles listed in the *Small Press Record of Books in Print* (9th Edition, 1980). Discounts: 33⅓ percent on bulk orders. lp. Reporting time: up to 1 mo. Payment: 10 percent royalty. Copyrights for author.

Workspace Loft, Inc. (see PROP)

THE WORLD, revolving citizenship, St. Marks Poetry Project, 2nd Avenue and 10th Street, New York, NY 10003, (212) 674-0910. 1967. Poetry, articles. circ. 750. 2/yr. Pub'd 2 issues 1979; expects 2 issues 1980, 2 issues 1981. sub. price: $4.00; per copy: $2.00; sample: $2.00. Back issues: price varies. Discounts: 40% trade. 60pp; 8½X11; †mi. Reporting time: varies. Payment: copies. Copyrighted, reverts to author.

WORLD NEWS, Skip Whitson, PO Box 4372, Albuquerque, NM 87106, (505) 255-6550. 1977. circ. 17,500. weekly. Pub'd 50 issues 1979; expects 50 issues 1980, 50 issues 1981. sub. price: $12.00; sample: $1.00. 8pp; 14X21½; of. Not copyrighted. Pub's reviews: 20 in 1979. §science fiction, politics, history. Ads: $688.00/$344.00/$0.10.

WORLD OF POETRY, John T. Campbell, Eddie-Lou Cole, Julie Joy, 2431 Stockton Blvd., Sacramento, CA 95817. 1975. Articles, art, photos, cartoons, interviews, satire, criticism, reviews, letters. "Slant to the beginner usually, using 'How To' format. Keep manuscript down to 2 or 3 pages typed. Recent contributors: Irma g. Rhodes, Leonard Nimoy, Marvin Miller. We need articles on current poets making news, with photos, etc." circ. 65,000. 4/yr. sub. price: $10.00; per copy: $1.00; sample: $1.00. Back issues: $1.00 each. Discounts: bulk, classroom, institution, agent: 50%. 4pp; 8½X11; †of. Reporting time: 2 weeks. Payment: $.05-$.10 per word. Copyrighted. Pub's reviews: 12 in 1979. §poetry. Ads: no.

Worldwatch Institute (WORLDWATCH PAPERS), Linda Starke, 1776 Massachusetts Ave NW, Washington, DC 20036, 202-452-1999. 1974. "Worldwatch Institute is a non-profit research organization attempting to identify emerging global trends and bring them to the public's attention through its Worldwatch Paper Series and work with the media. Current projects are on the role of technology, local and individual responses to global problems, energy strategies for a post-petroleum world, and strategies for accommodating human needs and numbers to the earth's resources in the next few decades. All research is done in-house." avg. press run 15,000 to 20,000 (with some distribution to press). Pub'd 10 titles 1979; expects 10 titles 1980, 10 titles 1981. avg. price, paper: $2.00. Discounts: $2.00 single copy; $1.50 for 2-10 copies; $1.25 for 11-50 copies; $1.00 for 51 or more. 50pp; 5⅜X8⅜; of. no submissions — all written in house. Copyrights for author.

WORLDWATCH PAPERS (see Worldwatch Institute)

THE WORMWOOD REVIEW, The Wormwood Review Press, Marvin Malone, Ernest Stranger, Art Ed., PO Box 8840, Stockton, CA 95204, 209-466-8231. 1959. Poetry, reviews, long-poems, collages, concrete art. "Poetry and prose-poems to 300+ lines reflecting the temper and depth of present human scene. All types and schools from traditional-economic through concrete, dada and extreme avant-garde. Special fondness for prose poems/fables. Each issue has yellow-page section devoted to one poet or topic (e.g. Bukowski, Wantling, Jon Webb, Micheline, Crews, Locklin, Koertge, Dick Higgins, Ian Hamilton Finlay, Steve Richmond, John Currier, Wm. Burroughs, etc)." circ. 700. 4/yr. Pub'd 4 issues 1979; expects 4 issues 1980, 4 issues 1981. sub. price: $4.50/yr, $6.00/yr institutions; per copy: $2.00; sample: $2.00. Back issues: Nos. 16-23, 25-76 ($2.00 per) Nos. 1-15 & 24 (priced upon request, when available). Discounts: $2.00 retail copy costs agent $1.20. 40-44pp; 5½X8½; of. Reporting time: 2-8 wks. Payment: 3-5 copies or cash equivalent. Copyrighted, rights reassigned on request to author. Pub's reviews: 85 in 1979. §Poetry/experimental prose. no ads accepted. CCLM.

The Wormwood Review Press (see also THE WORMWOOD REVIEW), Marvin Malone, Editor; Ernest Stranger, Art Editor, P O Box 8840, Stockton, CA 95204, (209) 466-8231. 1959. Poetry, reviews, long-poems, collages, concrete art. "Chapbook authors: Lifshin, Koertge, Locklin. Bukowski, David Barker; Crews and Weidman scheduled." avg. press run 700. Pub'd 1 title 1979; expects 1 title 1980, 1 title 1981. 5 titles listed in the *Small Press Record of Books in Print* (9th Edition, 1980). avg. price, paper: $2.00. Discounts: $2.00 retail copies cost agent $1.20. 40-44pp; 5½X8½; of. Reporting time: 2-8 weeks. Payment: 20 copies plus $2.50/poem. Copyrights for author. CCLM.

WOT, Dennis Reid, Ann York, 657 Andmore Drive, RR 2 Sidney, B.C. V8L 3S1, Canada, 385-1393. 1979. Poetry, fiction, photos. "Interested in spare realistic writing, obscure verbiage and surrealism discouraged." circ. 200. 2/yr. Pub'd 2 issues 1979. sub. price: $2.50; per copy: $1.25; sample: $1.25 (double for institutions). Discounts: 40% to bookstore on any amount. 48pp; 5½X8; of. Reporting time: 5 weeks. Payment: copy of magazine. Copyrighted, reverts to author. Ads: $50.00/$25.00.

WREE-VIEW, Norma Spector, Editor, 130 E 16th Street, New York, NY 10003. 1975. Poetry, articles, art, photos, cartoons, interviews, news items. circ. 4,500. 6/yr. Pub'd 6 issues 1979; expects 6 issues 1980, 6 issues 1981. sub. price: $3.00/yr; per copy: $0.35; sample: $0.35. Discounts: 40% off bundles of 5 or more. 12pp; size tabloid. Reporting time: 1 month. Payment: none. Not copyrighted. Pub's reviews: 2-3 in 1979. §Books re women, children, affirmative action, etc.

WRIT, Anjou, Roger Greenwald, Two Sussex Ave, Toronto M5S 1J5, Canada, 416-978-4871. 1970. Poetry, fiction, reviews, parts-of-novels, long-poems. "Sewn binding. We have an open policy; we're looking for good writing regardless of format or length; we'll print work that's intellectual and difficult if we think it's good and work that's colloquial, breezy, 'experimental' or whatever if we think it's good. We've printed large amounts of fiction and hope to continue doing so (numbers 4 & 10 were special fiction issues). Interested in translations of poetry and fiction not yet well known in English (enclose originals). We print only work that has not yet appeared in print." circ. 600. 1-2/yr. Pub'd 1 issue 1979; expects 1 issue 1980. sub. price: $9.00 for 2 issues not per calendar year; per copy: $4.50; sample: $3.00. Back issues: $2.50 each for Nos. 2, 3, 5, 7; $5.00 each for Nos. 1, 4, 6, 8, 9, 10. Discounts: bookstores 40% of sale price, subscription agencies none, classroom & other bulk purchases-by arrangement. 100pp; 6X9; of. Reporting time: Generally 6 weeks; longer May-August. Payment: Copies only. Copyright by the authors. Pub's reviews. §Poetry, fiction. Ads: $100/$60/or by exchange.

THE WRIT, Elizabeth M. Williams, 640 14th Place, N.E., Washington, DC 20002, (202) 397-7766. 1980. Poetry, fiction, articles, cartoons, interviews, satire, criticism, reviews, letters. "250-1,500 words (usually); publication begins January 1980 with Volume 1, Number 1" circ. 250. 4/yr. Pub'd 4 issues 1979; expects 4 issues 1980. sub. price: $6.00; per copy: $2.25; sample: $2.25. Discounts: Agent 15%, bulk and classroom rates on request. 24pp; 8½X11; of. Reporting time: 6 weeks. Payment: 5 copies. Copyrighted. Pub's reviews. §Law and law related items including fiction, plays, etc. Ads: $75.-00/$45.00/$0.35.

Writer's Guide Publications, Jerold L. Kellman, 9329 Crawford Avenue, Evanston, IL 60203, (312) 674-6476. 1 title listed in the *Small Press Record of Books in Print* (9th Edition, 1980).

Writer Unlimited Agency, Inc (see WRITERS INK)

WRITER'S NEWSLETTER, Thayr Richey, Editor; Donna Paulson, Anneke Campbell, 110 Morgan Hall, IU, Bloomington, IN 47401, (812) 337-3439. 1977. Articles, cartoons, criticism, reviews, letters, news items. *"Writer's Newsletter* provides a forum for writers to discuss writing and publishing concerns." circ. 1,000. 6/yr. Pub'd 6 issues 1979; expects 6 issues 1980, 6 issues 1981. sub. price: $3.00; per copy: $0.75; sample: $0.75. Discounts: Trade: 60/40 split. 20pp; 8½X5½; mi. Not copyrighted. Pub's reviews. §Poetry, fiction, small press books. Ads: Query Editor.

THE WRITER'S PAGE, Larry Goodell, Literary Editor, Box 429, Albuquerque, NM 87103, (505) 843-6440. 1895. Poetry, fiction, articles, art, photos, cartoons, interviews, satire, reviews, music, letters, parts-of-novels, long-poems, collages, plays, concrete art, news items. "This weekly has started *The Writer's Page* under new leadership featuring poetry, brief stories, reviews, and literary news items. Maximum for prose 2,000 words, but for exceptional merit 4,000-5,000 words possible. Prefer shorter poems which are clear and to the point, expressing social and environmental themes or just plain song. SASE a must." circ. 5,000. 26/yr. Pub'd 52 issues 1979; expects 52 issues 1980, 52 issues 1981. sub. price: $10.00; per copy: $0.25; sample: free. 12pp; 11½X17½; of. Reporting time: 2 weeks. Payment: 1 year subscription (52 issues). Copyrighted, reverts to author. Pub's reviews: 6 in 1979. §Poetry, fiction. Ads: $300.00/$150.00/$0.10.

Writers' Center Press (see also INPRINT), Jim Powell, Editor; Richard Grabman, Publications Director, Free University Writers' Center, 6360 N. Guilford Avenue, Indianapolis, IN 46220, (317) 253-3733. 1977. Poetry, fiction, criticism, letters, long-poems. "See *Inprint* for our editorial biases. Our chapbook Series publishes 16-32 pp. Published Elizabeth Krajeck Cohen's poetry *Cave Drawings* in October. Continues old Free University Press literary works which published *When I Danced* by Thomas Hastings (1977) and M.J. Phillips *21 Erotic Haiku* (1979), Alice Friman's *Song to My Sister.* Expected poetry by M. Belcher, Roger Pfingston & Richard Grabman. Other books scheduled include Thomas Hastings, Richard Grabman, and two anthologies of Indiana poetry and fiction." avg. press run 300-500. Pub'd 2 titles 1979; expects 6 titles 1980, 6 titles 1981. 4 titles listed in the *Small Press Record of Books in Print* (9th Edition, 1980). avg. price, paper: $2.00. Discounts: trade or classroom 40%. 24pp; 5½X8; of. Reporting time: 3-6 months. Payment: 5-10% of press run, plus discounts to author on add'l copies and 20% net profits (if any). Does not copyright for author.

Writers For Animal Rights (see also THE BLACK CAT), Phyllis L Fischer, Richard G Morgan, P.O. Box 1912OA, East Tennessee State University, Johnson City, TN 37601. 1975. Poetry, criticism. "We are interested primarily in chapbook-size collections of poetry and short monographs in the area of animal rights and welfare." avg. press run varies. avg. price, cloth: varies. Discounts: 40 percent discount to booksellers. of. Reporting time: varies. Payment: copies. Copyrights for author.

WRITERS FORUM, Alex Blackburn, University of Colorado at Colorado Springs, Colorado Springs, CO 80907, (303) 593-3155. 1974. Poetry, fiction. "We publish a book representing some of the best new American literature by authors, both established and unrecognized, resident in or associated with states west of the Mississippi. We will publish up to 5 poems, including long ones, by one author and fiction, including excerpts from novels, up to 15,000 words. Each book is introduced by an outstanding author/critic/teacher." circ. 1,000. 1/yr. Pub'd 1 issue 1979; expects 1 issue 1980, 1 issue 1981. sub. price: $5.95. Back issues: Vols. 1-5 lowcost microfiche. Discounts: 20%. 240pp; 5½X8½; of. Reporting time: 3-5 weeks. Payment: Free copies only, thus far. Copyrighted, reverts to author. AWP, CCLM, CODA.

Writers Forum (see also AND; KROKLOK), Bob Cobbing, John Rowan, 262 Randolph Ave., London W9, United Kingdom. 1963. Poetry, art, criticism, music, long-poems, concrete art. "Mainly members work." avg. press run 200. Pub'd 30 titles 1979; expects 25 titles 1980. avg. price, paper: 50p. Discounts: 1/3 off. 20pp; size size varies; †mi/of. Reporting time: 3 weeks. Payment: copies. copyrights on request. ALP.

WRITERS IN RESIDENCE, Armchair Press, Mark Berman, 123 Dorchester Road, Scarsdale, NY 10583. 1973. Poetry, fiction, art, photos, interviews, reviews, long-poems. circ. 300. 2/yr. Expects 1 issue 1980, 2 issues 1981. sub. price: $3.00; per copy: $1.50; sample: $1.00. Back issues: $1.00. Discounts: write for specific information. pp varies; size varies; of. Reporting time: 3 months. Payment: copies. Copyrighted. Pub's reviews. §poetry/fiction. Ads: $50.00/$25.00/$0.05 per word. CCLM.

WRITERS INK, Writer Unlimited Agency, Inc, David B. Axelrod, Joan C. Hand, 194 Soundview Drive, Rocky Point L.I., NY 11778, 516-744-6160. 1975. Articles, art, photos, cartoons, interviews, satire, criticism, reviews, collages. "Maximum article or story length 500 w. Though longer material might be serialized. Filler, humor for writers used. Limited to L.I. authors or items/ads of interest to L.I. literary scene." circ. 2,000. 4-10/yr. Pub'd 4 issues 1979; expects 4 issues 1980, 6 issues 1981. sub. price: $6.00; per copy: $0.60; sample: free. Back issues: specific issues by request, free if available. Discounts: None-but free to worthy folks or groups—sold, $6.00 yearly rate direct by 1st class mail from WU. 4-12pp; 5X7; of. Reporting time: immediately (maximum 2 weeks). Payment: 50 cents col. inch or $2.00 per photo. Copyrighted, reverts to author. Pub's reviews: 4 in 1979. §all aids to writers, general interest and of course, L.I. works, mags., books. Ads: $15.00/$8.00/$0.25. COSMEP, NESPA, LIPS, Lit. Assoc., East Enarts Council, Long Island Publ. Service.

WRITERS NEWS MANITOBA, Andris Taskans, 304 Parkview Street, Winnipeg, MB R3J 1S3, Canada, (204) 885-2652. 1978. Poetry, fiction, articles, art, interviews, satire, criticism, reviews, letters, parts-of-novels, long-poems, news items. "Length: up to 2,500 words prose, up to 6-16 pp poetry. Biases: Manitoba or Canadian literature. Contributors: Patrick Lane, Lorna Uher, Maara Haas, George Amabile, Robert Enright, Anne Szumigalski, Alexandre Amprimoz, Gregory Grace, Carolyn Zonailo, Paul Savoie." circ. 800. 5/yr. Pub'd 7 issues 1979; expects 5 issues 1980, 5 issues 1981. sub. price: $6.00; per copy: $1.25; sample: $1.00. Back issues: $2.00 (issues 1, 2 and 3 sold out). Discounts: 20%. 40-48pp; 4¼X5½; of. Reporting time: 2 months. Payment: 2 copies. Copyrighted, reverts to author. Pub's reviews: 26 in 1979. §Poetry, fiction, criticism. Ads: $100.00/$50.00/5¢ maximum 50.

WRITER'S NEWSLETTER, Thayr Richey, Anneke Campbell, 110 Morgan Hall, Indiana University, Bloomington, IN 47405, (812) 337-3439. 1978. Articles, cartoons, criticism, reviews, letters, news items. "Short (250-500 words) articles on writing/publishing poetry & fiction. Short reviews of same. Recent contributors: Brian O'Neill, Ralph Barns, Carol Burke, and Winifred Harner." circ. 500. 24/yr. Pub'd 6 issues 1979; expects 5 issues 1980. sub. price: $3.00; per copy: $0.75; sample: $0.75. Discounts: 60/40. 20pp; 5¾X8½. Reporting time: 1-2 months. Payment: copies. Pub's reviews. §Poetry, fiction, lit. crit., publishing, printing, writing. Ads: $45.00/$25.00.

Writers Press, Don Glassman, Box 805, 2000 Connecticut Avenue, Washington, DC 20008, (202) 232-0440. 1978. avg. press run 15,000. Pub'd 1 title 1979. 1 title listed in the *Small Press Record of Books in Print* (9th Edition, 1980). avg. price, paper: $4.00. Discounts: varies with size of order. of. AGNYC.

Writers' Publishing Company, Harry Titus, Box 309, Goleta, CA 93017, (805) 682-1445. 1978. Fiction. avg. press run 800. Pub'd 1 title 1979; expects 2 titles 1980. avg. price, cloth: $6.95; paper: $1.95. 152pp; 5½X8½. Reporting time: 30 days. Payment: standard book contract. Copyrights for author. COSMEP.

WRITING, Associated Creative Writers, Charles Brashers, 9231 Molly Woods Ave., La Mesa, CA 92041, 460-4107. 1979. Poetry, fiction, articles, interviews, reviews, letters, parts-of-novels, long-poems, plays. "No length limitation, but shorter pieces have best chances: long works have to earn all of their keep. Biased in favor of the 'well-made' story and poem with theme and meaning, but will entertain experimentation that scores in some other way. See the first issue, available in about 1,500 college and university libraries, for examples and commentary. Don't bother to send materials during June, July, and August. We're not at home." 6/yr. Expects 6 issues 1981. sub. price: $10.00; per copy: $1.95; sample: $1.00. Discounts: 40% to distributors, 20% to libraries. 24-32pp; 8½X11. Reporting time: Varies: we plan to have editorial meetings every two weeks. Payment: Chintzy: $5.00 per printed page, sorry, can't pay for small items. Copyrighted, reverts to author. Pub's reviews. §Books on

454

creativity and how to enhance it; books on writing techniques; books on theories of literature. Write for current rates: They'll vary according to our print run.

WRITING, The Sean Dorman Manuscript Society, Sean Dorman, 4 Union Place, Fowey, Cornwall PL23 1BY, United Kingdom. 1959. Articles, poetry. "Articles: 300 to 350 words unaltered tear-outs particularly welcome. If a little over-length, we will do the cutting. Ditto for poems of quality which normally should be between 8 and 20 lines, and of any style other than that of sheer incomprehensibility. Letters to the editor greatly sought but not paid for. The spring and summer issues are linked, carrying the same articles, poems and advertisements. Other items including letters to the editor, alter. The autumn and winter issues are similarly linked." circ. 400. 4/yr. Pub'd 4 issues 1979. sub. price: £1.50/$3.00; per copy: 50p/$1.00; sample: 50p/$1.00. Back issues: none available. 46pp; 8X6½; †mi. Reporting time: 2 weeks. Payment: £3.00 per article or poem. Copyrighted, reverts to author. Ads: $15/page.

WRITING IN HOLLAND AND FLANDERS, Singel 450, Amsterdam 1017 AV, The Netherlands, (020) 231056. 1956. Poetry, fiction, photos, parts-of-novels. "All material in the magazine comes from Dutch and Flemish authors. Their poetry and prose is presented in English translation for promotional purposes. The magazine is distributed to publisher's, libraries and interested private individuals, free of charge." circ. 4,000. 4/yr. Pub'd 4 issues 1979; expects 4 issues 1980. 48pp; size A5; lp. Copyrighted, reverts to author. Pub's reviews.

WTWL Press (see WOMEN TALKING, WOMEN LISTENING)

WURZEL, V. A. C. (Vereinigung Aktiver Kultur), Ders U. Flurey, Box 479, Basel 4002, Switzerland. 1976. Articles, art, interviews, criticism, news items. "In June 1980 change to Box 2822 CH 4002 Basel. Two issues and other information material in activity of big pw-wow of firsst land-community in Europe. Earth Star Union & University, U Box CH 6671 Menzonio" circ. 1,000. Pub'd 4 issues 1979; expects 2 issues 1980, 2 issues 1981. sub. price: 20 SFR; per copy: 1-/4-. Back issues: No. 1-6 in book form + index *Faksimile* 50. SFR. size A4; †of. Copyrighted. Pub's reviews. §Communitis, ind, tribe politics, mother earth, environment. Ads: 50 SFR/30 SFR.

X

X Press Press (see Downtown Poets Co-op)

XANADU, Pleasure Dome Press (Long Island Poetry Collective Inc.), Anne-Ruth Baehr, Coco Gordon, Mildred Jeffrey, Beverly Lawn, Lois Walker, Box 773, Huntington, NY 11743, (516) 549-1150. 1975. Poetry, art, photos, long-poems, reviews, news items. "Poems to 60 lines are most welcome, though longer work will be considered. We like to see at least 5 poems by an individual at one time. Poems with strong visual impact, concrete language: poems rooted in the human. Contributors include: Blazek, Bruchac, Fishman, Inez, McElroy, Miller, Swann, Terris and many others, known & unknown. S.A.S.E. must be included." circ. 1,000. 2/yr. Pub'd 2 issues 1979; expects 2 issues 1980, 2 issues 1981. sub. price: $3.50; per copy: $2.00; sample: $2.00. Back issues: $2.00 each. Discounts: 10 percent on orders of $20.00 or more, in any combination of titles (PLEASURE DOME PRESS also included.). 64pp; 5½X8½; of. Reporting time: 2-6 wks. (normally take longer on material that comes close). we buy copyright for author, reassign-upon request for reprints in collections of poems, anthologies. CCLM.

XENHARMONIC BULLETIN, Electronic Music Enterprises, Ivor Darreg, 349 1/2 W. California Ave., Glendale, CA 91203, 213-243-3477. 1974. Articles, reviews, music, letters. "*Xenharmonic* means a kind of music which does not sound like the ordinary 12-tone temperament as on the piano or organ keyboard. Encouragement for builders of new instruments and composers in new scale-systems. Will be open to contributors after 1977, letters welcome." circ. 200. 3-4/yr. Pub'd 2 issues 1979; expects 3 or 4 issues 1980. price per copy: $2.00; sample: SASE. Back issues: Available on request. 20pp; 8½X11; of. Pub's reviews. §Music, tapes, books on music.

XTRAS, From Here Press, William J. Higginson, Penny Harter, Box 219, Fanwood, NJ 07023, (201) 322-5928. 1975. Poetry, fiction, parts-of-novels, long-poems, plays, criticism. "*Xtras,* a cooperative periodical/chapbook series features writing in both verse and prose, emphasizing the experimental and work by relatively unpublished writers. Issues of *Xtras* are devoted to the work of one or a related group of writers who cooperate in publishing their own chapbooks, and receive a substantial number of copies in payment. Issues through mid-1981 are fully committed; no submissions can be accepted until then. Individual issues of *Xtras* feature translations from Japanese by WJH, longpoems by Penny Bihler, haiku and sequences by Alan Pizzarelli and Elizabeth Searle Lamb, workshop writings by teens and elderly, haiku and short poems by Allen Ginsberg, diary in haiku-prose by Rod Tulloss, etc." circ. 500-1,000. 3-5/yr. Expects 3 issues 1980, 4 issues 1981. sub. price: $6/4 issues; institutions, $10/4 issues; per copy: $2.00. Discounts: 40% to trade (5 mixed titles). 25-40pp; 5½X8½; †of. Reporting time: immed. Payment: copies. Copyrighted, reverts to author. Pub's reviews: 0 in 1979. §haiku, concrete poems, scores for performance pieces. Ads: No ads. COSMEP.

Y

Y GWYDDONYDD, University Of Wales Press, Glyn O. Dr. Phillips, 6 Gwennyth St., Cathays, Cadiff, Wales, United Kingdom, 0222-31919. 1962. Articles. circ. 850. 4/yr. Pub'd 4 issues 1979; expects 4 issues 1980. sub. price: £4.00 per year for four parts; per copy: £1.00; sample: £1.00. Discounts: booksellers 33⅓%. 50pp; size A4; lp. Copyrighted. Pub's reviews: 4 in 1979. §Science. Ads: £50.00/£25.00.

Y'lolfa, Talybont, Dyfed, Wales SY24 5ER, United Kingdom. "Prop; Robat Gruffudd, Printers and publishers interested in anything that will help the Welsh Revolution (Free Wales-Welsh Wales!) We do posters, paperbacks, funny cards, music, poetry, plays, 'Cymraeg' stickers and of course that awful magazine LOL. Send for free 16pp catalogue!" 8 titles listed in the *Small Press Record of Books in Print* (9th Edition, 1980).

THE YALE REVIEW, Kai T. Erikson, Editor; Sheila Huddleston, Managing Editor, 1902A Yale Station, New Haven, CT 06520. 1911. Poetry, fiction, articles, criticism, reviews, non-fiction. "Advertising, subscription office: Yale University Press, 92A Yale Station, New Haven CT 06520." circ. 5,000. 4/yr. Pub'd 4 issues 1979; expects 4 issues 1980. sub. price: $12.00/yr institutions $10.00/yr individuals; per copy: $3.00; sample: $3.00. Back issues: on request. Discounts: distributor, 50%, agent 20% bookstores 10%. 160 pp plus 12 to 24 pp front matter; 6⅜X9⅛; of/lp. Reporting time: 1-3 months. Payment: on publication. copyright Yale University, remaining so on publication by agreement with author. Pub's reviews: 31 reviews including 78 books in 1979. §literature, history, fiction, poetry, economics, biography, arts & architecture, politics, foreign affairs. Ads: $250/$115. CCLM.

YANAGI, Louis Patler, Bill Barrett, Box 466, Bolinas, CA 94924, 415-868-0292. 1974. Poetry, parts-of-novels, long-poems, art, photos, letters, collages. "General policy is to publish a large selection of a relatively few poets, with each issue edited for readability, cover-to-cover. Contributors: Tom Clark, Bill Berkson, Ed Sanders, John Wieners, Charles Olson, Frank O'Hara, Lawrence Kearney. The fourth issue of *Yanagi* is a *special* series of eleven original broadside poems each of which is a collaboration between poet and an artist of their choice. Size ranges from 8½ x 11 — 19 x 25, 300 copies, 26 signed." circ. 400. 1/yr. Pub'd 1 issue 1979. 8 titles listed in the *Small Press Record of Books in Print* (9th Edition, 1980). sub. price: Yanagi IV Special Broadside Series, 1977-8, $15.00; per copy: $15.00 for eleven broadsides, in portfolio; sample: variable. Back issues: Contact Sand Dollar Books, Albany, CA. Discounts: *Yanagi* 1-3 was distributed free to poets, donations were asked from bookstores and institutions. *Yanage IV*, see above. 80pp; 8½X11; †mi/of. Reporting time: 6 weeks. Payment: 2 copies. Copyrighted, reverts to author. §Poetry and poetics. CCLM, COSMEP.

YARDBIRD READER, Yardbird Wing Editions/Yardbird Publishing Co. Inc., P.O. Box 216, Fairmount Sta., El Cerrito, CA 94530. 1972. Music, letters, collages, concrete art. circ. 3,000. 2/yr. Pub'd 2 issues 1979. sub. price: $9.00; per copy: $4.95; sample: $3.50. Back issues: prior to 3 most recent issues—$3.00. Discounts: 40% regular bookstore; 27% college textbooks; 30% orders 5 or less. 200-336pp; 5½X8½; lp. Payment: copies; an occasional $25.00-$50.00 honorarium. Copyrighted. §fiction/poetry/plays. Ads: $150.00/$100.00/0. CCLM, COSMEP, WIP.

Yardbird Wing Editions/Yardbird Publishing Co. Inc. (see also YARDBIRD READER), Box 216, Fairmount Sta., El Cerrito, CA 94530. 1975. "Book length variable. We've published *Changing All Those Changes* by James P. Girard, *Zepplin Coming Down* by William Lawson, *Youth Law Handbook* by Berkeley Youth Alternatives." avg. press run 2,000. Pub'd 2 titles 1979. 8 titles listed in the *Small Press Record of Books in Print* (9th Edition, 1980). avg. price, paper: $5.00. Discounts: 40% general trade; 27% classroom. 250pp; 5½X8½; lp. Payment: 10% on 1st 5,000; 15% above 5,000. Copyrights for author. COSMEP.

Yarrow Press (see also CHOOMIA (A literary review)), Ann Guido, Jay Barwell, CHOOMIA, PO

Box 40322, Tucson, AZ 85719. 1975. Poetry, fiction, art, interviews, criticism, reviews, parts-of-novels, long-poems. "We do not publish books" avg. press run 500. avg. price, paper: $2.50. Discounts: 40% bulk over 10 copies. of. Reporting time: 1-2 months. Payment: copies. CCLM.

Years Press (see also CENTERING: A Magazine of Poetry), F. Richard Thomas, Dept. of ATL, EBH, Michigan State Univ, E. Lansing, MI 48824, (517) 332-5983. 1973. Poetry. avg. press run 300-400. Pub'd 1 title 1979; expects 1 title 1980, 1 title 1981. avg. price, paper: $1.50. 48-64pp; 7X8½; of. Mss. usually solicited. Payment: 5 copies. COSMEP, CCLM.

YELLOW BRICK ROAD, Emerald City Press, Robert Matte Jr., 2627 N Orchard, Tucson, AZ 85712, (602) 623-2932. 1974. Poetry, fiction, art, photos. "In poetry we consider anything of quality but shudder at, sleeve poems (heartthrob), traditional religious, and stuff pitting the poet against the universe. Content can range from surreal-absurd-humorous to heavy duty. Fiction must be under six pages double spaced. Poetry biases apply to style. We seek interesting graphics (B&W) as well as photographs, especially ones with roads. Every issue on special theme, i.e. the legends, laundromats, Momism, One Step Beyond, Down the Road. *Query* first with SASE for theme of upcoming issue. We welcome submissions from old pros and newcomers. We're just folks. Contributors have included: Ron Koertge, Emilie Glen, Harley Elliott, Charles Bukowski, Lyn Lifshin, Gerry Locklin, John Bennett, Doug Blazek, Gerda Penfold, G. P. Skratz, GOD, A. D. Winans, Charles Webb, Opal Nations, Michael Hogan, Geraldine King. Also publish poetry books. No unsolicited book manuscripts. Catalog sent upon request with SASE." circ. 400. Irreg. Pub'd 1 issue 1979; expects 1 issue 1980, 2 issues 1981. sub. price: $4.00/yr individuals, $5.50/yr institutions; per copy: $1.50; sample: $1.00. Back issues: YBR No. 1 $25.00; Nos. 2-6 $10.00; others $1.50. Discounts: 40% discount on five or more copies. 40pp; 5½X8½; of. Reporting time: 2 wks-2 months. Payment: contrib copies. Copyrighted, reverts to author. Pub's reviews: 15 in 1979. §poetry, short fiction, graphics. Ads: $50/$30/none. CCLM, WIP.

Yellow Moon Press, Robert B. Smith, 20 Tufts Street, Cambridge, MA 02139, (617) 492-2580. 1978. Poetry. "Most recent book by Connie Martin. Books in production will include work by Elizabeth McKin, Coleman Barks & Robert Bly. I am looking for work that is connected with mother earth & the process of understanding how we can better understand our connection to her & her spirituality." Pub'd 1 title 1979; expects 1 title 1980, 2-3 titles 1981. avg. price, paper: $3.00. Discounts: 60% press, 40% store. 24-32pp; 5½X8½; of. Payment: 50% of income after costs. Copyrights for author.

The Yellow Press (see also MILK QUARTERLY), Richard Friedman, Peter Kostakis, Darlene Pearlstein, 2394 Blue Island Ave, Chicago, IL 60608. 1972. Poetry, fiction. "Titles list includes books by Ted Berrigan, Paul Carroll, Maxine Chernoff, Richard Friedman, Paul Hoover, Henry Kanabus, Alice Notley and Barry Schechter." avg. press run 1,500. Pub'd 2 titles 1979; expects 3 titles 1980, 3 titles 1981. 10 titles listed in the *Small Press Record of Books in Print* (9th Edition, 1980). avg. price, cloth: $7.95; paper: $3.00; other: signed: $6.00 (paper), $15.00 (cloth). Discounts: bulk only, available through SBD: Small Press Distribution, 1636 Ocean View Ave., Kensington, CA 94707. 80pp; 5½X8½; of. No unsolicited book mss. currently being accepted. Payment: varying. Copyrights for author. CCLM, SBD (Small Press Distribution).

Yoknapatawpha Press, Lawrence Wells, Dean Wells, Box 248, Oxford, MS 38655, (601) 234-0909. 1975. "We specialize in books by or about William Faulkner, and Mississippi or Southern-related subjects. To date, most of our publications have been limited editions. We hope to expand in the trade book market." avg. press run 5,000. Pub'd 1 title 1979; expects 1 title 1980, 5 titles 1981. avg. price, cloth: $25.00; other: ltd editions $50.00. Discounts: 2-4, 20%; 5 plus, 30%; 50 plus, 40%. 150pp; 8X10. Reporting time: 3-6 weeks. Payment: 10%, quarterly. Copyrights for author.

Yorkshire Dialect Society (see SUMMER BULLETIN)

Young Davis Press, F.N. Wright, Chuck Davis, Norton Young, 1290 Whitecliff Road, Thousand Oaks, CA 91360, (805) 497-2505. 1977. Fiction. "Due to shortage of funds, accepting no mss. until further notice. *Whorehouse* still in print and available." avg. press run 3M. Pub'd 1 title 1979; expects 2 titles 1980. 1 title listed in the *Small Press Record of Books in Print* (9th Edition, 1980). avg. price, paper: $5.95. Discounts: 40%, 48% and 50%. 235pp; 6X9; of. Payment: will negotiate. Copyrights for author.

Young Publications, Lincoln B. Young, 531 N. Gay St. (PO Box 3455), Knoxville, TN 37917. 1957. Poetry. "Any length, any style, any subject except pornography or racist material." avg. press run 2,000. Pub'd 2 titles 1979; expects 2 titles 1980. 5 titles listed in the *Small Press Record of Books in Print* (9th Edition, 1980). avg. price, cloth: $17.95; paper: $10.00. Discounts: We offer discounts to booksellers and to contributors only. 300pp; 8½X7; †of. Reporting time: up to 6 months. No payment. Copyrights for author.

YOUTH AND NATION, Yaakov Fusfeld, 150 Fifth Avenue, New York, NY 10011, (212) 929-4955. 1934. Articles, art, photos, cartoons, interviews, satire, criticism, reviews, letters, news items. "Most contributions are political analysis." circ. 1,300. quarterly. Pub'd 4 issues 1979; expects 4 issues 1980, 4 issues 1981. sub. price: $2.50; per copy: $0.65; sample: $0.65. Back issues: if available, $0.65. Discounts: two years - $5.00 / 2½ years (10 issues) - $6.00. 32pp; 9¾X6¾; of. Payment: none. Not copyrighted. Pub's reviews: 4 in 1979. §Judaism, Socialism, Zionism, middle east. Ads: none.

Z

Z, Z Press, Kenward Elmslie, 104 Greenwich Avenue, New York, NY 10011. 1973. Poetry, fiction, long-poems, plays. "The editor strongly discourages the submission of unsolicited material, as the magazine is a one-man operation, and a real time pressure is at work. Recent contributors: Ashbery, Lally, Dlugos, Schuyler, Gooch, Coolidge, Wieners, Brownstein, Winkfield, Abbott, Nolan, Towle, O'Hara, Koch, Elmslie, Winch, Hawkins." circ. 1,200. 2/yr. Pub'd 1 issue 1979; expects 1 issue 1980. price per copy: $2.50; sample: $2.50. Back issues: $2.50. Discounts: 40% to bookstores. 120pp; 6X9. Reporting time: variable. Payment: none (except for 2 issues funded by CCLM). Ads: none. CCLM, COSMEP.

Z Press (see also Z), 104 Greenwich Avenue, New York, NY 10011. 25 titles listed in the *Small Press Record of Books in Print* (9th Edition, 1980).

ZAHIR, Diane Kruchkow, Weeks Mills, New Sharon, ME 04955. 1970. Poetry, fiction, articles, art, cartoons, interviews, criticism, reviews, letters. "No. 8 features New England poets. No. 9- features Spanish Journals of Hugh Fox, Dick Higgins on Immanentism, Sklar on Actualism plus plenty of great poetry. No. 10 - Guy Beining. No. 11 - Connie Fox. No. 12/13 - anniversary issue." circ. 1,000. irregular. Pub'd 1 issue 1979; expects 3 issues 1980, 2 issues 1981. 2 titles listed in the *Small Press Record of Books in Print* (9th Edition, 1980). sub. price: $4, 2 issues, ind; $6, 2 issues, inst; per copy: $2.50; sample: $2.50. Back issues: $2.00. Discounts: worked individually. 64pp; 5½X8½; of. Reporting time: 8 weeks. Payment: 1 or 2 copies. copyrighted. Pub's reviews. §poetry, fiction. Ads: $40.00/$25.-00. CCLM, COSMEP, NESPA.

ZANTIA: Stories and Poems by the Over-Sixty, Norma Gibson Maness, Zantia, Inc, P.O.box 1947, Annapolis, MD 21404, (301) 261-2549. 1978. Poetry, fiction, satire, letters, long-poems, plays. "Send poetry, stories, short plays and material for two features:*Letters from the Attic* and the *Grandchild's Page* . Prefer typed, double spaced, but will consider handwritten manuscripts. For *Letters from the Attic* send copies, not originals, of a few letters. Attach brief biographical data about writer and dates covered by the collection. *Grandchild's Page* manuscripts must be by a grandchild (of any age) about grandparent(s). Include self-addressed, stamped envelop with submissions to insure return of manuscripts" circ. 1,000. Quarterly. Expects 4 issues 1980, 2 issues 1981. sub. price: $8.00; per copy: $2.50; sample: $2.50. Back issues: $2.00 each with subscription order. Single back issue $2.50. 40pp; 8X10; of. Reporting time: 6 to 8 weeks. Payment: complimentary copies. Copyrighted, does not revert to author.

Zartscorp, Inc. Books, Lynn Zelevansky, Paul Zelevansky, 267 West 89th Street, New York, NY 10024, 724-5071. 1975. "Material used: experimental work of all kinds." avg. press run 500-1,000. Pub'd 1 title 1979; expects 1 title 1980, 1 title 1981. 2 titles listed in the *Small Press Record of Books in Print* (9th Edition, 1980). avg. price, cloth: $15.00; paper: $6.00. Discounts: 10 percent libraries/other: 1-4 books 20 percent/5-10 books 40 percent. 80pp; 8½X11; of. Author has copyright of work. We have copyright of book. COSMEP.

Zed Press, Roger VanZwanenberg, Editor; Robert Molteno, Editor, 57 Caledonian Road, London N19DN, United Kingdom. 1976. "A socialist, mail order publisher of books on revolution and imperialism in Third World. Our aim is provoke thought and reflect current debates in 5 main areas: Africa, Middle East, Asia, Women in Third World and Imperialism. U.S.A. address: 520 Riverside Avenue, Westport, Conn. 06880, USA." avg. press run 3,000. Pub'd 12 titles 1979; expects 18 titles 1980, 18 titles 1981. 36 titles listed in the *Small Press Record of Books in Print* (9th Edition, 1980). avg. price, cloth: $15.00; paper: $6.00. Discounts: Trade 40% Other discounts by special arrangement. 250pp; 5½X8½; of. Reporting time: 1 month. Payment: 10% cl; 7½% pa. Copyrights for author. COSMEP.

ZERO REVIEW, The Zero Press, G. P. Solomos, PO Box 13230, Philadelphia, PA 19101, (215)

458

222-4141. 1949. Poetry, fiction, articles, art, photos, criticism, reviews, letters, collages, plays, news items. "We look at all material sent in for consideration; however, most material used is solicited express from selected writers. For instance last issue (*Zero*: Winter 1979-80) contained previous and recent work by authors & poets such as Irving Thalberg, Samuel Beckett, Andrew Lovatt, James Baldwin, Toby Olson, Henry H. Roth, etc." circ. 5,000. 4/yr. Pub'd 1 issue 1979; expects 4 issues 1980. sub. price: $5.00; per copy: $1.50; sample: $1.00. Back issues: none available. Discounts: normal. 50pp; 8X10; of. Reporting time: depends on type of submission. Payment: occasional in cash, usually copies of publication. Copyrighted, reverts to author. Pub's reviews. §Literature, art, philosophy, politics, science. Ads: inquire. CLE, AAP.

ZERO ONE, Arthur Moyse, Jan Witte, 39 Minford Gardens, West Kensington, London W14 0AP, United Kingdom. 1970. "An elitist magazine. Anarchist orientated. Ill mannered and unapologetic. Will use any material withour permission. Will willingly read and return material with a stamped returned envelope but all ZERO ONE published material is either commissioned (unpaid) or simply stolen." circ. 350. 3/yr. Pub'd 3 issues 1979; expects 3 issues 1980, 3 issues 1981. sub. price: £3; per copy: £1; sample: none. 300pp; 8X10; lo. commissioned work only. No payment. Not copyrighted. Pub's reviews: 6 in 1979. §art, politics.

The Zero Press (see also ZERO REVIEW), G. P. Solomos, PO Box 13230, Philadelphia, PA 19101, (215) 222-4141. 1949. Poetry, fiction, art, photos, criticism, reviews, letters, parts-of-novels, collages, plays, news items. "The Zero Press was established in Paris (France) in the winter of 1948-49. The original editors were Asa Benveniste (now publisher of the Trigram Press, London) and Themistocles Hoetis (aka G. P. Solomos). It first published a literar quarterly *Zero* from Paris, Tangier, Mexico City, and New York City; publishing know (W.C. Williams, Christopher Isherwood, Wallace Stevens, J.P. Sartre, etc.) and (then) unknown (James Baldwin, Paul Bowles, Otto Friederich, Mason Hoffenberg, etc.) authors. In 1956 it published several books, stories, novels, literary anthologies, including *Brothers & Sisters* by Ivy Compton-Burnett, *A Thirsty Evil* (Seven stories) by Gore Vidal, *Zero Anthology* (Edited by T. Hoetis) including Marianne Moore, Constantine Cavafis, Lionel Ziprin, Robert Kelly, Samuel Beckett, J.P. Sartre, etc. among other publications." avg. press run 3,000. Pub'd 5 titles 1979. avg. price, cloth: $12.50; paper: $5.50. Discounts: normal trade rates. 200pp; 5½X8½; lp. Reporting time: solicited mss. only. Payment: normal contracts. Copyrights for author. CLE (Irish Book Publishers' Association)/AAP (Association of American Publishers).

Ziesing Bros.' Publishing Company, 768 Main St., Willimantic, CT 06226, 203-423-5836/8162. 1976. Poetry, fiction, articles, criticism, long-poems. "Taylor, Alexander: *Zadar*. Butterick, George F.: *Reading Genesis By the Light of a Comet.* Above are books of poems. We're also interested in remainders. We are currently remaindering James Scully's *Avenue of the Americas*. Scully, James: (Scrap Book) Scrap Book is a book of poems." avg. press run 1,000 copies. Pub'd 2 titles 1979. 9 titles listed in the *Small Press Record of Books in Print* (9th Edition, 1980). avg. price, paper: $2.95. Discounts: to the trade: 40%/to jobber: 50-55%. 50pp; 5¾X8¾; of. Reporting time: 2-3 months. Payment: contract. Does not copyright for author.

ZONE, Zone, Peter Cherches, Dennis Deforge, P.O. Box 733, NYC, NY 10009, 212-674-0602. 1976. Poetry, fiction, articles, art, photos, music, long-poems, interviews, satire, criticism, collages, concrete art. "ZONE is particularly interested in experimental, intermedia, and visual art." circ. 700. 2/yr. Pub'd 2 issues 1979; expects 2 issues 1980, 2 issues 1981. price per copy: $3.00; sample: $2.00. Discounts: 40% to bookstores. 64pp; 8½X11; of. Reporting time: 6-8 weeks. Payment: 3 copies plus reduced rates for extra copies. Copyrighted, reverts to author.

Zone (see also ZONE), Peter Cherches, Dennis DeForge, P.O. Box 733, NYC, NY 10009, 212-674-0602. 1976. Poetry, fiction, art, photos, interviews, satire, criticism, music, parts-of-novels, long-poems, collages, plays, concrete art. "Query first for books." avg. press run 700. Pub'd 2 titles 1979; expects 2 titles 1980, 2 titles 1981. 1 title listed in the *Small Press Record of Books in Print* (9th Edition, 1980). avg. price, paper: $3.00. Discounts: 40% to bookstores. 96pp; size varies; of. Reporting time: 6-8 weeks. Payment: 15% of press run and/or cash. Copyrights for author.

Zoographico Press, Ltd., Charles B. Murphy, 29 W Hubbard, Chicago, IL 60610, (312) 467-1088. 1979. Art, cartoons. "To date Zoographico is solely publishing the artwork of its founder, CB Murphy, which is describable as science fictionally surrealistic cartoons. So far I have published *January is Alien Registration Month* and have two titles in the works *The Nuclear Pup* and *One Hundred Alien Madonnas*. In the *not* near future I may take on other artists, but do not currently take submissions." avg. press run 250-500. Pub'd 2 titles 1979. 1 title listed in the *Small Press Record of Books in Print* (9th Edition, 1980). avg. price, paper: $6.75. Discounts: 40%. 75pp; 11X9½; of. Reporting time: don't take submissions now.

ZVEZDA, Mark Osaki, P.O. Box 9024, Berkeley, CA 94709. 1976. Poetry, fiction, art, photos, reviews, parts-of-novels, long-poems, collages, concrete art. "Not reading unsolicited material at this time. Inquiries are welcome however. Please send to: P. O. Box 9024, Berkeley, CA 94709." circ. 500 plus. 2/yr. sub. price: $4.00; per copy: $2.00; sample: $2.00. Back issues: $4.00 if available. Discounts: trade. 40-80pp; 8½X11; of. Reporting time: 1-3 months. Payment: 2 copies; some payment. Copyrighted, reverts to author. Pub's reviews. §Poetry, fiction/visual arts, graphics.

Subject Index

461

Cat's Pajamas Press
Chandler & Sharp Publishers, Inc.
Circinatum Press
LA CONFLUENCIA
Copley Books
THE DALHOUSIE REVIEW
THE ETHNODISC JOURNAL OF RECORDED SOUND
Genotype
Gerber Publications
Glenbow-Alberta Institute
Great Eastern Book Company
The Guide to Small Press Publishing
Hancock House Publishers
Institute for Polynesian Studies
Institute for the Study of Human Issues (ISHI)
Io (named after moon of Jupiter)
JOURNAL OF CALIFORNIA AND GREAT BASIN AN-
   THROPOLOGY
THE JOURNAL OF PSYCHOLOGICAL ANTHROPOLOGY
Kitchen Sink Enterprises
THE LEY HUNTER: The Magazine Of Earth Mysteries
LIBRARY REVIEW
Lycabettus Press
Malki Museum Press
Merlin Engine Works
Moon Publications
Oleander Press
Oregon Historical Society
P.E.N. BROADSHEET
EL PALACIO
Psychohistory Press
Pueo Press
ROMANIAN REVIEW
Ross-Erikson Publishers, Inc.
The School of Living
SCIENCE FICTION CHRONICLE
Three Continents Press
Tofua Press
Trado-Medic Books
John Westburg, Publisher
WESTERN WORLD REVIEW

ANTIQUES

ANTIQUE PHONOGRAPH MONTHLY
APM Press
COLLECTOR'S ITEM
CROP DUST
DIALOGUE
GILTEDGE: New Series
GRASS ROOTS
GREEN FEATHER
HARD CRABS
M.O.P. Press
MEN'S
Mosaic Press
NEWSREAL
OCCIDENT
Padre Productions
Paperweight Press
Precedent Publishing Inc.
Quality Publications, Inc.
THE SECOND WAVE
Sleepy Hollow Restorations
SOUTHERN QUARTERLY: A Journal of the Arts in the South
Ten Speed Press
W. I. M. Publications
THE WISHING WELL

ARCHITECTURE

Archinform
ASSEMBLING
Assembling Press
Bell Springs Publishing Company
Brick House Publishing, Co.
Capra Press
THE CHARIOTEER
Cheshire Books
Chronicle Books/Prism Editions
Erewon Press

GRASS ROOTS
Great Eastern Book Company
Jaks Publishing Co.
LANDSCAPE
Levenson Press
Lycabettus Press
Mandorla Publications
MODERN LITURGY
THE MODULARIST REVIEW
Mole Publishing Co.
Mosaic Press
Northeastern University Press
Oregon Historical Society
EL PALACIO
PASS-AGE: A Futures Journal
Peregrine Smith, Inc.
Point Riders Press
Prologue Publications
RK Editions
RAIN: JOURNAL OF APPROPRIATE TECHNOLOGY
ROMANIAN REVIEW
Smuggler's Cove Publishing
SOUTHERN QUARTERLY: A Journal of the Arts in the South
THEATRE DESIGN AND TECHNOLOGY
Timber Press
THE TOWN FORUM JOURNAL & COMMUNITY REPORT
Tundra Books Of Northern New York
Turner Publishing, Inc.

ARMENIAN

ARARAT

ARTS

& (Ampersand) Press
Acrobat Books Publishers
AIS EIRI
ALDEBARAN
All About Us
ALPHA
AMERICAN ARTS PAMPHLET SERIES
American-Canadian Publishers, Inc.
American Revolutionary Political Pamphlets
AND/OR NOTES
Angels Gate Press
THE ANGLO-WELSH REVIEW
ANN ARBOR REVIEW
ANOTHER SMALL MAGAZINE
ART & LITERARY DIGEST
Art Official Inc.
Artists & Alchemists Publications
ARTZIEN
ASPECT, Art and Literature
ASSEMBLING
Assembling Press
Astro Artz
ATHENE
BACK BAY VIEW
BALSAM FLEX SHEET
Banana Productions
THE BARAT REVIEW: A Journal of Literature and the Arts
BB Books
Bellerophon Books
Bellevue Press
THE BENNINGTON REVIEW
Bern Porter Books
BIKINI GIRL
BILE
Biohydrant Publications
BIRD EFFORT
BLUE UNICORN
Boardwell - Kloner
BOOK ARTS
Borealis Press Limited
BOTTOMFISH MAGAZINE
BRANCHING OUT
"BRILLIANT CORNERS": A Magazine of The Arts
BUCKLE
BUCKNELL REVIEW
BULLETIN OF THE BOARD OF CELTIC STUDIES

California Contemporary Craftspeople Publications
CALYX: A Journal of Art and Literature by Women
THE CAPILANO REVIEW
Capra Press
Caratzas Brothers, Publishers
Carolyn Bean Publishing, Ltd.
Catex Press
THE CENTENNIAL REVIEW
Ceolfrith Press
THE CHARIOTEER
Cheshire Books
Chicago New Art Association
CHICAGO REVIEW
CHOUTEAU REVIEW
Chronicle Books/Prism Editions
Cider Barrel Press
CINEMA/QUEBEC
Clamshell Press
Clatworthy Colorvues
Cobbers
COBBLESTONE
Coda Press, Inc
THE COFFEEHOUSE
COMBINATIONS, A JOURNAL OF PHOTOGRAPHY
CONCEPTIONS SOUTHWEST
CONTEMPORARY ART/SOUTHEAST
CORNFIELD REVIEW
CRAWL OUT YOUR WINDOW
Crawl Out Your Window Press
CREACION
CRISS-CROSS ART COMMUNICATIONS
CROSSCURRENTS
Crow
CRYPTOC: The Crypt of Comics
DANCE BOOK FORUM
DANCE HERALD
DANCE IN CANADA
Dance Motion Press
DARK HORSE
DAVINCI MAGAZINE
DECEMBER MAGAZINE
December Press
THE DEKALB LITERARY ARTS JOURNAL
DEPARTURES: Contemporary Arts Review
DESCANT
Doggeral Press
DREAMS
Ecart Publications
EDWARDIAN STUDIES
EL FUEGO DE AZTLAN
The Fault Press
FIFTH SUN
FILE MAG
Florida Arts Gazette
FOLLIES
FORMAT
FORMS: A Magazine of Poetry and Fine Art
FOUR DOGS MOUNTAIN SONGS
Fragments/The Valentine Press
Full Court Press
Full Track Press
The Future Press
GARGOYLE
GAZUNDA
GEGENSCHEIN, NeoNeo DoDo
THE GENEVA POND BUBBLES
Gilgamesh Press Ltd.
Glenbow-Alberta Institute
Gleniffer Press
GNOME BAKER
THE GOODFELLOW REVIEW OF CRAFTS
GRAND RIVER REVIEW/CAPITOL CITY MOON
Great Eastern Book Company
The Green Hut Press
Greenwood Press, Inc.
Griffin Books, Inc.
The Guide to Small Press Publishing
HAND BOOK
Hard Press

Heavy Evidence Press
HEIRS
HERESIES: A FEMINIST PUBLICATION ON ART AND POL-
    ITICS
The Heron Press
HIGH PERFORMANCE
The Hosanna Press
HOT WATER REVIEW
THE HUDSON REVIEW
THE HUNGRY YEARS
Illuminati
IMPEGNO 70
IMPULSE
INTERMEDIA
INTRINSIC: An International Magazine of Poetry & Poetics
IRON
Iron Press
Janus Press
JOE SOAP'S CANOE
JOURNAL OF ALTERNATIVE HUMAN SERVICES
JOURNAL OF CALIFORNIA AND GREAT BASIN AN-
    THROPOLOGY
KALLIOPE, A Journal of Women's Art
Karl Bern Publishers
Kelsey St. Press
KONGLOMERATI
Konglomerati Press
Kontexts Publications
Lancaster - Miller Publishers
LAOMEDON REVIEW
Leathern Wing Scribble Press
LEFT CURVE
Left Curve Publications
LIGHT: A Poetry Review
LODGISTIKS
LONG POND REVIEW
LOST AND FOUND TIMES
Lowy Publishing
LUMEN/AVENUE A
Luna Bisonte Prods
MAG CITY
MAGIC CHANGES
MAGIC SAM
The Maguey Press
MAIZE
Maize Press
Malki Museum Press
MATI
THE MERVYN PEAKE REVIEW
Mervyn Peake Society Publications
Metis Press
MEUSE
MIAMI INTERNATIONAL
Midmarch Associates
R. & E. Miles
MISSISSIPPI MUD
Mockingbird Press
MODERN LITURGY
THE MODULARIST REVIEW
THE MONGREL FOX
Moon Publications
Moonlight Publications
THE MOOSEHEAD REVIEW
MUSEUM OF TEMPORARY ART (MOTA) MAGAZINE
NEW ART EXAMINER
NEW BOSTON REVIEW
New Glide Publ.
NEW LETTERS
NEW VIRGINIA REVIEW
NEW YORK ARTS JOURNAL
NEWORLD
NEWSREAL
Not-For-Sale-Press
NOUMENON
Noumenon Press
The Oak Arts Workshop Limited
OHIOANA QUARTERLY
ONEARTH IMAGE
THE ONTARIO REVIEW

THE ORIGINAL ART REPORT (TOAR)
ORNAMENT, A Quarterly of Jewelry and Personal Adornment
The Overlook Press
PACIFIC QUARTERLY/MOANA
Padma Press
EL PALACIO
Paperweight Press
PARCHMENT (Broadside Series)
Penstemon Press
Pentangle Press
Peradam Publishing House
Peregrine Smith, Inc.
PERFORMING ARTS JOURNAL
The Perishable Press Limited
PERMAFROST
Personal Publications
PHOEBE
THE PHOTOLETTER
Pig Iron Press
Pikeville College Press
Pittore Euforico
PLUCKED CHICKEN
Plucked Chicken Press
POEMS IN PUBLIC PLACES
Poltroon Press
The Porcupine's Quill, Inc.
POSTCARD ART/POSTCARD FICTION
PRAXIS: A Journal of Cultural Criticism
Prescott Street Press
Printed Editions
PROP
PUBLISHED POET NEWSLETTER
The Putah Creek Press
QUEEN'S QUARTERLY: A Canadian Review
Quintessence Publications
RK Editions
RaMar Press
Rebis Press
Resource Publications
REVIEW
ROMANIAN REVIEW
Rosler, Martha
S & S Press
Saint Heironymous Press, Inc.
St. Mawr Jazz Poetry Project
SALOME: A LITERARY DANCE MAGAZINE
San Francisco Center for Visual Studies
SAN JOSE STUDIES
Sappho Publications Ltd
Scarf Press
SCREE
SCREEN
The Seal Press
Seven Oaks Press
SHADOWGRAPHS
SHEBA REVIEW, The Literary Magazine for the Arts
Simon & Pierre Publishing Co. Ltd.
Smyrna Press
SO & SO
SOCIAL TEXT
SOUTHERN QUARTERLY: A Journal of the Arts in the South
Spirit Mound Press
SPOOR
THE SQUATCHBERRY JOURNAL
STARDANCER
START
The Stevenson Press
STRAIGHT AHEAD INTERNATIONAL
STUDIA MYSTICA
SUN & MOON: A Journal of Literature and Art
Sun & Moon Press
sun rise fall down artpress
Survivors' Manual
SZ/Press
Tanam Press
TBW Books
Teachers & Writers Collaborative
TEACHERS & WRITERS MAGAZINE
Ten Crow Press

Ten Penny Players, Inc.
Ten Speed Press
THEATRE
THEATRE DESIGN AND TECHNOLOGY
Thumbprint Press
Timber Press
Todd Tarbox Books
Tomato Publications Ltd.
TRADE MAGAZINE
TRANSFORMACTION
The Transientpress
Treacle Press
TRIVIUM
TRULY FINE PRESS, A Review
Tundra Books Of Northern New York
Turkey Press
TURTLE
Two-Eighteen Press
TWO STEPS IN
UNIVERSITY JOURNAL
UNMENDABLY INTEGRAL: an audiocassette quarterly of the arts
UNMUZZLED OX
VALHALLA
VEGA
Vehicle Editions
Vehicule Press
Ventura Press
VIEW
VILE
WASHINGTON REVIEW
Washout Publishing Co.
WASHOUT REVIEW
Water Mark Press
WAVES
West Coast Poetry Review Press
WESTART
John Westburg, Publisher
WHITE WALLS
William L. Bauhan, Publisher
Windflower Press
WOMEN ARTISTS NEWS
WOMEN IN THE ARTS BULLETIN/NEWSLETTER
Women's History Research Center, Inc.
WREE-VIEW
Yoknapatawpha Press
ZONE
ZVEZDA

ASIA, INDOCHINA, CHINA

THE ASIA MAIL
Between The Lines
CHINA QUARTERLY
East River Anthology
THE ETHNODISC JOURNAL OF RECORDED SOUND
Great Eastern Book Company
Hwong Publishing Company
JOURNAL OF SOUTH ASIAN LITERATURE
Kelsey St. Press
Lawrence Hill & Company, Publishers, Inc.
LIBERO INTERNATIONAL
Merlin Engine Works
Moon Publications
Moonsquilt Press
NAMAZU
Oleander Press
PACIFIC RESEARCH
Phoenix Books/Publishers
The Scribe Press
SOUTHEAST ASIA CHRONICLE
Southeast Asia Resource Center
Ten Speed Press
Third World Publications Ltd.
Unicorn Press
Vesta Publications Limited
WOOD IBIS

ASIAN-AMERICAN

ANAPRESS

464

THE ASIA MAIL
Backpack Media
BRIDGE MAGAZINE
FROZEN WAFFLES
INTERRACIAL BOOKS FOR CHILDREN BULLETIN
NORO REVIEW
Oregon Historical Society
PULP
Vesta Publications Limited
WOOD IBIS

ASTROLOGY

Alta Napa Press

AVIATION

Iroquois House, Publishers
THE METRO
OCCIDENT
Parachuting Publications
Parachuting Resources
PARACHUTIST
S & S Press
SKYDIVING
Special Aviation Publications
Sunflower University Press

BIBLIOGRAPHY

THE AFRICAN BOOK PUBLISHING RECORD
Algol Press
AMERICAN LITERATURE
Americana Books
Angst World Library
ASSEMBLING
Assembling Press
Bern Porter Books
THE BIBLIOTHECK
The Black Cat Press
THE BOOK-MART
THE CHANEY CHRONICAL
CHECKLIST OF HUMAN RIGHTS DOCUMENTS
Critiques Livres
Croissant & Company
ECW Press
ELAN POETIQUE LITTERAIRE ET PACIFISTE
ESSAYS ON CANADIAN WRITING
FANZINE DIRECTORY
A GAY BIBLIOGRAPHY
Gay Task Force, American Library Association
Gleniffer Press
Greenwood Press, Inc.
HER Publishing Co.
Heresy Press
International General
Ithaca Press
JOURNAL OF MODERN LITERATURE
Library Research Associates
The Lightning Tree
LITERATURE OF LIBERTY
Robert L. Merriam
Nevada Publications
New London Press
NEWS FROM NEASDEN
John L Noyce, Publisher
Ontario Library Association
Paul G. Partington
RK Editions
RADICAL BOOKSELLER
Robert D. Reed Publisher
THE ROMANTIST
S & S Press
Scarf Press
STONY HILLS: The New England Alternative Press Review
Three Continents Press
Three Mountains Press
TZADDIKIM
WHAT'S NEW ABOUT LONDON, JACK?

BIOGRAPHY

ADVENTURES IN POETRY MAGAZINE

Algol Press
ASSEMBLING
Assembling Press
Astro Artz
The Boxwood Press
Capra Press
Clean Energy Press
Earl M Coleman Enterprises, Inc
CONNECTICUT FIRESIDE
CONSTALLATIONS
Croissant & Company
Crosley Inc
Edition Stencil
ETC Publications
Fels and Firn Press
The Future Press
Gleniffer Press
Griffin Books, Inc.
Heresy Press
Ithaca Press
JOURNAL OF MODERN LITERATURE
The Latona Press
Lawrence Hill & Company, Publishers, Inc.
Samuel P. Levine
The Lightning Tree
Maryland Historical Press
THE NEW AUTHOR
The Olive Press Publications
Parable Press
Presidio Press
QUEEN'S QUARTERLY: A Canadian Review
RK Editions
ROCKBOTTOM
Roush Books
Sagarin Press
Simon & Pierre Publishing Co. Ltd.
SMITH'S JOURNAL
SOUTH DAKOTA REVIEW
Synergistic Press
TBW Books
Three Continents Press
Vanilla Press
John Westburg, Publisher
Wimmer Brothers Books
Dr. Stella Woodall Publisher

BIRTH, BIRTH CONTROL, POPULATION

Air-Plus Enterprises
Bay Area ASPO News
The Chas. Franklin Press

BLACK

AFRICA CURRENTS
AMERICAN ARTS PAMPHLET SERIES
ASSEMBLING
Assembling Press
BLACK AMERICAN LITERATURE FORUM
THE BLACK POSITION
THE BLACK REVIEW
THE BLACK SCHOLAR: Journal of Black Studies and Research
CALLALOO
The Carolina Wren Press
CODA: The Jazz Magazine
DANCE HERALD
Diana Press, Inc
Energy Earth Communications, Inc.
THE ETHNODISC JOURNAL OF RECORDED SOUND
FREEDOMWAYS
Garrett Park Press
Heritage Press
HOO-DOO BlackSeries
Impact Publishers, Inc.
INTERRACIAL BOOKS FOR CHILDREN BULLETIN
Lawrence Hill & Company, Publishers, Inc.
LIVING BLUES
Maryland Historical Press
NOK Publishers International
OBSIDIAN: BLACK LITERATURE IN REVIEW
Paul G. Partington

Place of Herons
PULP
Sappho Publications Ltd
The Stevenson Press
SYNERGY
Third World Press
Three Continents Press
Vanguard Books
WOOD IBIS

WILLIAM BLAKE

BLAKE, AN ILLUSTRATED QUARTERLY

BOOK ARTS, CALLIGRAPHY

Epic
MEN'S
Parenting Press
Programs and Publications

BOOK COLLECTING, BOOKSELLING

ALA/SRRT NEWSLETTER
Americana Books
The Basilisk Press
The Black Cat Press
BOOK ARTS
BOOK BUYER'S GUIDE/MARKETPLACE
THE BOOK-MART
BOOK TALK
CONNECTICUT FIRESIDE
DENTAL FLOSS MAGAZINE
FINE PRINT: A Review for the Arts of the Book
FLY BY NIGHT
Franklin Publishing Company
Gleniffer Press
Heavy Evidence Press
Kensington Press
Libre Press
LITERARY MONITOR: The Voice of Contemporary Literature
Robert L. Merriam
Mosaic Press
Narbulla Agency
NEWS FROM NEASDEN
Parachuting Publications
THE PIPE SMOKER'S EPHEMERIS
PUCK'S CORNER
RADICAL BOOKSELLER
RAGGED READIN'
Stonehouse Publications
Three Mountains Press
Tideline Press
WEIRDBOOK
WESTERN PUBLISHING SCENE
WHISPERS

BOOK REVIEWING

ABRAXAS
ABSINTHE
AEOLIAN-HARP
ALA/SRRT NEWSLETTER
ALTERNATIVE RESEARCH NEWSLETTER
THE ANTIGONISH REVIEW
ASPEN ANTHOLOGY
Backpack Media
LE BEACON REVIEW
BIBLIOTHEQUE D'HUMANISME ET RENAISSANCE
THE BLACK CAT
BOOK BUYER'S GUIDE/MARKETPLACE
BOOK EXCHANGE
BOOK TALK
BOOKS & BOOKMEN
BOOKS IN CANADA: A National Review Of Books
BRICK: A Journal Of Reviews
BRITISH BOOK NEWS
C.S.P. WORLD NEWS
CAFETERIA
CANADIAN AUTHOR & BOOKMAN
Chicago New Art Association
THE CHOWDER REVIEW
COME-ALL-YE

Commen Cents
COMMON WORD
CONCH REVIEW OF BOOKS
CONNECTICUT FIRESIDE
CONRADIANA
CROSSCOUNTRY
CUTBANK
THE DALHOUSIE REVIEW
DECEMBER MAGAZINE
December Press
THE DICKENSIAN
Earthwise Publications
EN PASSANT/POETRY
ENGLISH STUDIES IN AFRICA-A Journal of the Humanities
FICTION INTERNATIONAL
FORESIGHT MAGAZINE
Franklin Publishing Company
FROZEN WAFFLES
The Future Press
GLENIFFER NEWS
GRASS ROOTS
THE GREEN REVOLUTION
GRYPHON: A Culture's Critic
INTERFACE: THE COMPUTER EDUCATION QUARTERLY
IOWA CITY BEACON LITERARY REVIEW
LAUGHING BEAR
LITERARY SKETCHES
LONG POND REVIEW
MODERN HAIKU
THE MRB NETWORK
NEW ART EXAMINER
NEW PAGES
NEWS AND LETTERS
News and Letters Press
NORTHEAST RISING SUN
NORTHWEST REVIEW
NOSTOC
OCCASIONAL REVIEW
OFF OUR BACKS
OHIOANA QUARTERLY
Ontario Library Association
PAINTED BRIDE QUARTERLY
Parachuting Publications
PEOPLE'S NEWS SERVICE
Pitjon Press/BackBack Media
PLEXUS, Bay Area Women's Newspaper
POETRY FLASH
Poetry Leeds Publications
POETRY QUARTERLY (previously CURLEW)
PORCH
PRECISELY
QUEEN'S QUARTERLY: A Canadian Review
RK Editions
RAIN: JOURNAL OF APPROPRIATE TECHNOLOGY
REFERENCE BOOK REVIEW
REVIEWING LIBRARIAN
RIO GRANDE WRITERS NEWSLETTER
ROAD/HOUSE
ROMANIAN REVIEW
ST. CROIX REVIEW
SAN FRANCISCO REVIEW OF BOOKS
Sappho Publications Ltd
SLOW LORIS READER
THE SMALL POND MAGAZINE OF LITERATURE
THE SMALL PRESS REVIEW
SOUTHERN QUARTERLY: A Journal of the Arts in the South
Southwest Research and Information Center
STONE COUNTRY
STONY HILLS: The New England Alternative Press Review
THEATRE DESIGN AND TECHNOLOGY
THE THIRD PRESS REVIEW
TRIVIUM
TZADDIKIM
University of Oregon Press
UNIVERSITY PUBLISHING
URBANE GORILLA
VECTOR
THE WESTERN CRITIC
WESTERN WORLD REVIEW

WRITERS INK

BUSINESS & ECONOMICS

AFRICA NEWS
Almar Press
American Business Consultants, Inc.
Beekman Publishers, Inc.
Beninda Books
Between The Lines
Bicentennial Era Enterprises
The Boxwood Press
Brattle Publications
Century Three Press
Commen Cents
Communication Creativity
CO-OP: The Harbinger of Economic Democracy
CO-OP MAGAZINE
La Cumbre Publishing Co.
Danbury Press
Editorial Services Co.
ETC Publications
Future Publishing Co.
THE GREEN REVOLUTION
Greenwood Press, Inc.
IN BUSINESS
Institute for Contemporary Studies
INTERCOM
International Human Systems Institute
Kitchen Sink Enterprises
LATIN AMERICAN PERSPECTIVES
Lawson Books
Lightbooks
LITTLE FREE PRESS
Manor Press
Master Key Publications
Mercantine Press
National Financial Publications
New Visions Press
Nikmal Publishing
North American Students of Cooperation
North Country Press
Onaway Publications
PACIFIC RESEARCH
PASS-AGE: A Futures Journal
Patricia J. Sherman Real Estate Books
PEOPLE & ENERGY
Programmed Studies Inc
QUEEN'S QUARTERLY: A Canadian Review
RAIN: JOURNAL OF APPROPRIATE TECHNOLOGY
REBUTTAL! The Bicentennial Newsletter of Truth
Reyn Publishing Co.
SELF-RELIANCE
Simon & Pierre Publishing Co. Ltd.
THE SMALL POND MAGAZINE OF LITERATURE
Stonehouse Publications
Sybex Incorporated
TAXING & SPENDING
Ten Speed Press
That New Publishing Company
Tiburon Press
Woman Matters Press

CALIFORNIA

Androgyne Books
Applezaba Press
California Living Books (Examiner Special Projects)
Copley Books
Genny Smith Books
VILLAGE CIRCLE

CANADA

Angle Lightning Press
ART & LITERARY DIGEST
BRITISH COLUMBIA HISTORICAL NEWS
CANADIAN CHILDREN'S LITERATURE
CANADIAN DIMENSION
CANADIAN LITERATURE
CANADIAN PUBLIC POLICY- Analyse de Politiques
CANADIAN THEATRE REVIEW

Highway Book Shop
House of Anansi Press Limited/Publishing Co.
JOURNAL OF CANADIAN FICTION
JOURNAL of CANADIAN STUDIES/Revue d'etudes cana-
    diennes
Prairie Publishing Company
Press Porcepic Limited
RAINCOAST CHRONICLES
Stagecoach Pub. Co. Ltd.

CELTIC

CARN (a link between the Celtic nations)
LLEN CYMRU (Board of Celtic Studies)
STUDIA CELTICA

CHICANO/A

AMOXCALLI
AZTLAN: International Journal of Chicano Studies
Bilingue Publications
CARTA ABIERTA
Cibola Press
DE COLORES: Journal of Emerging Raza Philosophy
LA CONFLUENCIA
Editorial Justa Publications, Inc.
EL FUEGO DE AZTLAN
EL FUEGO DE AZTLAN
Ink Blot Press
INTERRACIAL BOOKS FOR CHILDREN BULLETIN
Lawrence Hill & Company, Publishers, Inc.
MAIZE
Maize Press
MANGO
METAMORFOSIS
NEWS AND LETTERS
News and Letters Press
Pajarito Publications
Place of Herons
Pleasant Hill Press
PULP
REVISTA CHICANO-RIQUENA
RIVERSEDGE
The School of Living
Trucha Publications, Inc.
Ventura Press
WOOD IBIS

CHILDREN, YOUTH

Absolute O Kelvin (AOK) Press
Academy Chicago Limited
Albacore Press
Aldebaran Review
Andrew Mountain Press
Aura Publishing Co.
Auromere, Inc.
Avant-Garde Creations
The B & R Samizdat Express
Backroads/Caroline House
The Barnwood Press
Bayshore Books
The Bookstore Press
THE BREATH OF THE PEOPLE
Cadenza Press
California Street
CANADIAN CHILDREN'S LITERATURE
Canadian Women's Educational Press
Carousel Press
Cedar House Enterprises
The Center For Study of Multiple Gestation
Children's Art Foundation, Inc.
Cobblesmith
COBBLESTONE: The History Magazine for Children
Creative With Words Publications (CWW)
The Crossing Press
Ed-U Press, Inc.
FANTASY EXPRESS
C J Frompovich Publications
The Future Press
Gazelle Publications
Gleniffer Press

THE GREEN REVOLUTION
GROWING WITHOUT SCHOOLING
H.E.L.P. Books Inc.
Harden Publications
Harvest Press
Heinemann Publisher's (NZ) Ltd
Hiddigeigei Books
Hobby Horse Publishing
Impact Publishers, Inc.
In Between Books
Indian Tree Press
J&J Publishing
Kelsey St. Press
Kids Can Press
Knollwood Publishing Company
The Language Press
Lollipop Power, Inc.
Magic Circle Press
Manzanita Press
MJG Company
Montessori Learning Center
New Seed Press
The New York Literary Press
NORTHERN LINE
Panda Programs
Parable Press
Partners In Publishing
Peradam Publishing House
Peripatos Press
Pinchgut Press
PRACTICAL PARENTING
Press Gang Publishers
Programs and Publications
RAINBOW'S END
Rainy Day Books
Rocking Horse Press
The Scoal Press
Scotty Macgreger Publications
Simon & Pierre Publishing Co. Ltd.
Sproing Inc.
STONE SOUP, The Magazine By Children
SUBVERSIVE SCHOLASTIC
Talespinner Publications, Inc.
THIS AND THAT
THROUGH THE LOOKING GLASS
Tired Teddybear Productions
Tree Frog Press Limited
Tree Toad Press
Trek-Cir Publications
Tundra Books Of Northern New York
Turtle Lodge Press
Velvet Flute Books
VERMONT CHILDREN'S MAGAZINE
Vermont Crossroads Press
VILLAGE CIRCLE
Walnut Press
Webb-Newcomb Company, Inc.
West Village Publishing Company

CITIES

THE CO-OP OBSERVER
GRAND RIVER REVIEW/CAPITOL CITY MOON
Kitchen Sink Enterprises
LANDSCAPE
Lidiraven Books: A Division of Biogeocosmological Press
RAIN: JOURNAL OF APPROPRIATE TECHNOLOGY
SELF-RELIANCE
SHELTERFORCE
Turner Publishing, Inc.
URBAN & SOCIAL CHANGE REVIEW
WAYS & MEANS
White Tower Inc. Press

CLASSICAL STUDIES

ART AND ARCHAEOLOGY NEWSLETTER
Caratzas Brothers, Publishers
THE DALHOUSIE REVIEW
The Elizabeth Press
Lycabettus Press

Moon Publications
THE NORTH WIND
Raintree
Thumbprint Press
John Westburg, Publisher

PAUL CLAUDEL

CLAUDEL STUDIES

COMICS

ALTERNATIVE MEDIA
ARCADE-THE COMICS REVUE
ASSEMBLING
Assembling Press
Belier Press
COLUMBUS FREE PRESS
Cosmic Brain Trust
COSMIC CIRCUS
Flying Buttress Publications
FUNNYWORLD - The Magazine of Animation and Comic Art
The Future Press
The Happy Press
Heavy Evidence Press
Mosaic Press
NEWSREAL
POETRY COMICS
RAS Communications/Blind Eye Publishing House/Blind Eye Books/Jasmine
Real Free Press Foundation
Rip Off Press Inc.
S & S Press
SNARF
Third Coast
WEIRD TRIPS
Whole Image Graphics
Wild & Woolley
WIPE OUT
Zoographico Press, Ltd.

COMMUNICATION, MEDIA, JOURNALISM

Around Publishing
THE ARTFUL REPORTER
AUSTRALIAN SCAN: Journal of Human Communication
Banana Productions
Beekman Publishers, Inc.
The Bookery
Boyd & Fraser Publishing Company
CANADIAN AUTHOR & BOOKMAN
CANADIAN JOURNAL OF COMMUNICATION
Communicate Press
Communication Creativity
COMMUNICATIONS AND THE LAW
COPY CORNUCOPIA
Creative Book Company
The Direct Marketing Creative Guild
Donnelly & Sons Publishing Co.
DOUBLE HARNESS
F. Fergeson Productions
FLORAL UNDERAWL GAZETTE
FOLIO
FREELANCE
The Future Press
Gilgamesh Press Ltd.
Hollywood Film Archive
Hurtig Publishers
IMPULSE
Independent Publishing Fund of the Americas
INDEX ON CENSORSHIP
International General
THE INTERNATIONAL UNIVERSITY POETRY QUARTERLY
IPFA NEWS
KELLNER'S MONEYGRAM
Kitchen Sink Enterprises
THE LITTLE AROUND JOURNAL
LOST GENERATION JOURNAL
The Lovejoy Press
May-Murdock Publications
MEDIA HISTORY DIGEST

MEDIA REPORT TO WOMEN
Mercer House Press
MINORITY RIGHTS GROUP REPORTS
NEW PAGES
NEWS RELEASE FROM THE CHESS PRESS SYNDICATE
Parachuting Publications
Peace & Pieces Foundation
Peace Press
PEOPLE'S NEWS SERVICE
PRAXIS: A Journal of Cultural Criticism
Printed Editions
Programs in Communications Press
Quest Press
RK Editions
RAIN: JOURNAL OF APPROPRIATE TECHNOLOGY
Raintree
ROMANIAN REVIEW
ST. LOUIS JOURNALISM REVIEW
SCREEN
SOUTHERN PROGRESSIVE PERIODICALS UPDATE DI-
RECTORY
TYPE & PRESS
Horan Wall and Walker
HORAN WALL AND WALKER WEEKLY COMMUNITY IN-
FORMATION
Women's Institute for Freedom of the Press
WORLD NEWS
Writers Press

COMMUNISM, MARXISM, LENINISM

APPEAL TO REASON
THE CALL/EL CLARIN
CANADIAN SLAVONIC PAPERS
Canadian Women's Educational Press
Greenleaf Press
GUARDIAN
Ink Links Ltd.
International General
Lawrence Hill & Company, Publishers, Inc.
LEFT CURVE
Left Curve Publications
Liberator Press
NEWS AND LETTERS
News and Letters Press
Norman Bethune Institute
PEOPLE'S CANADA DAILY NEWS
PRAXIS: A Journal of Cultural Criticism
Proletarian Publishers
QUIXOTE, QUIXOTL
RCP Publications
RADICAL AMERICA
REVOLUTION
ROMANIAN REVIEW
SCREEN
Workers' Press
Zed Press

COMMUNITY

Aberdeen Peoples Press
Adventure Trails Research and Development Laboratories
ARAB AMERICAN ALMANAC
BLT Press (Bates, Lear, and Tulp)
Book Publishing Co.
Brick House Publishing, Co.
Canadian Women's Educational Press
Citrus House Ltd
CITY MINER
CLAIMANTS NEWSPAPER (Claimants Unite)
COMMUNITY ACTION
Community Collaborators
COMMUNITY DEVELOPMENT JOURNAL
COMMUNITY SERVICE NEWSLETTER
CONNECTION NEWS RELEASE
CO-OP: The Harbinger of Economic Democracy
Creative Book Company
DAWN
DOUBLE HARNESS
DUMP HEAP (Diverse Unsung Miracle Plants for Healthy Evo-
lution Among People)

Findhorn Publications
Florida Arts Gazette
FOLLIES
FREE VENICE BEACHHEAD
GRAND RIVER REVIEW/CAPITOL CITY MOON
THE GRAPEVINE WEEKLY
Grass-Hooper Press
GRASS ROOTS
THE GREEN REVOLUTION
Institute for Local Self-Reliance
JOURNAL OF ALTERNATIVE HUMAN SERVICES
LYNN VOICES
New Glide Publ.
NEW HUMANIST
NEW TIMES
NEWS AND LETTERS
News and Letters Press
THE NEWS CIRCLE
NEWSREAL
North American Students of Cooperation
ONEARTH IMAGE
PASS-AGE: A Futures Journal
PEACE NEWS "For Non-Violent Revolution"
PEOPLE & ENERGY
PEOPLE'S NEWS SERVICE
ProActive Press
RAIN: JOURNAL OF APPROPRIATE TECHNOLOGY
Red Alder Books
SELF-RELIANCE
Slough Press
STREET MAGAZINE
TOTAL LIFESTYLE- The Magazine of Natural Living
Turner Publishing, Inc.
Horan Wall and Walker
HORAN WALL AND WALKER WEEKLY COMMUNITY IN-
FORMATION
WOOD IBIS

COMPUTERS

Archinform
Bayshore Books
Boyd & Fraser Publishing Company
Chthon Press/Nonesuch Publications
COMPUTER MUSIC JOURNAL
CREATIVE COMPUTING
Creative Computing Press
The Crow's Mark Press
La Cumbre Publishing Co.
DR. DOBB'S JOURNAL OF COMPUTER CALISTHENICS &
ORTHODONTIA
INTERFACE: THE COMPUTER EDUCATION QUARTERLY
Liberty Publishing Company, Inc.
Minicomputer Press
Ted Nelson, Publisher
People's Computer Co.
RAIN: JOURNAL OF APPROPRIATE TECHNOLOGY
RECREATIONAL COMPUTING
Sybex Incorporated
Ten Speed Press

JOSEPH CONRAD

CONRADIANA

CONSERVATION

ABBEY NEWSLETTER
ANAPRESS
Brick House Publishing, Co.
BRITISH NATURALISTS' ASSOCIATION (PUBLISHERS)
Century Three Press
Clean Energy Press
CLEARWATER NAVIGATOR
CRY CALIFORNIA
DOUBLE HARNESS
Energy Publishing Company
FOURTH DIMENSION
Genny Smith Books
THE GREEN REVOLUTION
GREENPEACE (London) Newsletter
THE HARDHITTING INTERMITTENT NORTH IDAHO

NEWS
HIGH COUNTRY NEWS
HUMANIST IN CANADA
Lawrence Hill & Company, Publishers, Inc.
The Lightning Tree
El Moro Publications
THE NEW ENGLAND CONSERVATIONIST
NEWSREAL
NOT MAN APART
PASS-AGE: A Futures Journal
THE PENNSYLVANIA NATURALIST
PEOPLE & ENERGY
The Perishable Press Limited
PORTAGE
Porter Sargent Publishers, Inc.
Pueo Press
RAIN: JOURNAL OF APPROPRIATE TECHNOLOGY
The Rateavers
REBUTTAL! The Bicentennial Newsletter of Truth
SAMISDAT
The School of Living
Second Back Row Press
SECOND GROWTH: Appalachian Nature and Culture
THE SMALL POND MAGAZINE OF LITERATURE
TOTAL LIFESTYLE- The Magazine of Natural Living
Vermont Crossroads Press
Walnut Press
White Tower Inc. Press

COUNTER-CULTURE, ALTERNATIVES, COMMUNES

ALTERNATIVE RESEARCH NEWSLETTER
CONTRACULTURA
CO-OP: The Harbinger of Economic Democracy
Full Track Press
IN BUSINESS
LITTLE FREE PRESS
PIG IRON
WINTERGREEN

CRAFTS, HOBBIES

ABBEY NEWSLETTER
Alpine Publications
Apple Tree Lane
ART & LITERARY DIGEST
THE ARTFUL REPORTER
California Contemporary Craftspeople Publications
California Living Books (Examiner Special Projects)
Capra Press
Carma Press
Christopher Davies Publishers Ltd.
Chronicle Books/Prism Editions
Cider Barrel Press
COLLECTOR'S ITEM
COSMOPOLITAN CONTACT
Creative Arts Book Company
Design Enterprises of San Francisco
ETC Publications
Falconiforme Press Ltd.
FINE PRINT: A Review for the Arts of the Book
Full Court Press
Gerber Publications
Gleniffer Press
THE GOODFELLOW REVIEW OF CRAFTS
GRASS ROOTS
HOB-NOB
Hunter Publishing, Co.
INTERCOM
International Marine Publishing Co.
KITE LINES
Manor Press
Mayapple Press
Merlin Engine Works
R. & E. Miles
Minicomputer Press
Moon Publications
Naturegraph Publishers, Inc.
Ted Nelson, Publisher
New-Age Foods Publications
Onaway Publications

ORNAMENT, A Quarterly of Jewelry and Personal Adornment
EL PALACIO
Peregrine Smith, Inc.
Pleasant Hill Press
POTPOURRI FROM HERBAL ACRES
R & D Services
Richboro Press
Smuggler's Cove Publishing
STUDIES IN DESIGN EDUCATION AND CRAFT
The Sunstone Press
Tamal Vista Publications
Timber Press
Turtle Lodge Press
Vista Publications
WESTART

CRITICISM

ABRAXAS
Algol Press
American-Canadian Publishers, Inc.
AMERICAN LITERATURE
THE ANTIGONISH REVIEW
Ardis
ARENA SCIENCE FICTION
ARIZONA QUARTERLY
THE ARK RIVER REVIEW
ARTZIEN
ATTENTION PLEASE
AZIMUTH
THE BARD
BEAU FLEUVE SERIES
BIBLIOTHEQUE D'HUMANISME ET RENAISSANCE
Bilingual Review/Press
BIRD EFFORT
The Blue Oak Press
THE BODY POLITIC- Gay Liberation Journal
The Borgo Press
BOUNDARY 2
"BRILLIANT CORNERS": A Magazine of The Arts
CANADIAN AUTHOR & BOOKMAN
CANADIAN CHILDREN'S LITERATURE
CANADIAN FICTION MAGAZINE
CANADIAN LITERATURE
CANTO Review of the Arts
Capra Press
Cat's Pajamas Press
Chandler & Sharp Publishers, Inc.
THE CHARIOTEER
Chicago New Art Association
THE CHOWDER REVIEW
CINEASTE MAGAZINE
Clamshell Press
CLAUDEL STUDIES
COMMUNICATOR
CONCERNING POETRY
CONRADIANA
CONTACT/11: A Bimonthly Poetry Review Magazine
CONTEMPORARY ART/SOUTHEAST
THE CONTEMPORARY LITERARY SCENE
CONTEMPORARY LITERATURE
CONTEMPORARY POETRY: A Journal of Criticism
THE CRITICAL REVIEW
CRITIQUE: Studies in Modern Fiction
CROSSCURRENTS
DENVER QUARTERLY
DICKINSON STUDIES
THE DURHAM UNIVERSITY JOURNAL
The Ecco Press
ECW Press
The Elizabeth Press
Enitharmon Press
ESSAYS ON CANADIAN WRITING
Fels and Firn Press
FORGE
FORMAT
From Here Press
The Future Press
The Garlic Press
Gay Sunshine Press, Inc.

GOTHIC
THE GRACKLE: Improvised Music In Transition
The Graywolf Press
GREAT CIRCUMPOLAR BEAR CULT
Green Knight Press
THE GREEN REVOLUTION
GRYPHON: A Culture's Critic
THE GYPSY SCHOLAR: A Graduate Forum for Literary Criticism
HAPPINESS HOLDING TANK
HARPOON
Harvest Publishers
HARVEST QUARTERLY
Hearthstone Press
HIGGINSON JOURNAL
Higginson Press
THE HOLLINS CRITIC
HOLLOW SPRING REVIEW OF POETRY
House of Anansi Press Limited/Publishing Co.
HUMANIST IN CANADA
HYPERION A Poetry Journal
THE INTERNATIONAL FICTION REVIEW
INTERNATIONAL P.E.N. BULLETIN of SELECTED BOOKS
THE INTERNATIONAL UNIVERSITY POETRY QUARTERLY
INVISIBLE CITY
IOWA REVIEW
ISLANDS, A New Zealand Quarterly of Arts & Letters
JOURNAL OF CANADIAN POETRY
JOURNAL of CANADIAN STUDIES/Revue d'etudes canadiennes
JOURNAL OF MODERN LITERATURE
JOURNAL OF NARRATIVE TECHNIQUE
JUMP CUT, A Review of Contemporary Cinema
KOSMOS
L=A=N=G=U=A=G=E
LAPIS
Lapis Educational Association, Inc.
The Lightning Tree
LITERARY MONITOR: The Voice of Contemporary Literature
LITERARY SKETCHES
LONG POND REVIEW
MANASSAS REVIEW: ESSAYS ON CONTEMPORARY AMERICAN POETRY
MEANJIN QUARTERLY
The Menard Press
MISSISSIPPI REVIEW
MODERN LANGUAGE QUARTERLY
MODERN POETRY STUDIES
Mosaic Press/Valley Editions
NEW ART EXAMINER
NORTHEAST/JUNIPER BOOKS
NORTHEAST RISING SUN
Northeastern University Press
OCCIDENT
THE OCHLOCKONEE REVIEW
OFF OUR BACKS
Oleander Press
ONE
Open Sesame Publishing Co.
OUTPOSTS
Oyez
P.E.N. BROADSHEET
PARTISAN REVIEW
PAUNCH
Peace & Pieces Foundation
Pentagram Press
PEQUOD
Pequod Press
PHOEBE
PLEXUS, Bay Area Women's Newspaper
PLOUGHSHARES
POET & CRITIC
POETRY FLASH
THE POETRY MISCELLANY
POETRY NOTTINGHAM
POETRY WALES
POINT OF CONTACT/PUNTO DE CONTACTO
PRAXIS: A Journal of Cultural Criticism

PRECISELY
Press Porcepic Limited
Proem Pamphlets
QUEEN'S QUARTERLY: A Canadian Review
RK Editions
Raindust Press
Rat & Mole Press
RIVERSIDE QUARTERLY
ROCKBOTTOM
ROMANIAN REVIEW
THE ROMANTIST
RUNE
RUSSIAN LITERATURE TRIQUARTERLY
ST. CROIX REVIEW
Samisdat Associates
SCHOLIA SATYRICA
SENECA REVIEW
Seven Oaks Press
SHAKESPEARE NEWSLETTER
SHOCKS
SKYWRITING
Sleepy Hollow Restorations
SONG
SOUTHERN HUMANITIES REVIEW
SOUTHERN QUARTERLY: A Journal of the Arts in the South
Sparrow Press
THE SPHINX
STARSHIP: The Magazine About Science Fiction
STEPPENWOLF
STONY HILLS: The New England Alternative Press Review
TANGENT
TELOS
THALIA: Studies in Literary Humor
13th MOON
THISTLE: A MAGAZINE OF CONTEMPORARY WRITING
Three Continents Press
URBANE GORILLA
VECTOR
Ventura Press
Vesta Publications Limited
WEST HILLS REVIEW: A WALT WHITMAN JOURNAL
John Westburg, Publisher
THE WESTERN CRITIC
Wild & Woolley
The Wine Press
THE WISHING WELL
Writers For Animal Rights
THE YALE REVIEW
Yoknapatawpha Press

CUBA

AREITO

CULTURE

ZERO REVIEW
The Zero Press

DADA, SURREALISM

A
ABYSS
Alphaville Books
American-Canadian Publishers, Inc.
ANDROGYNE
Backpack Media
Banana Productions
BILE
BIRD EFFORT
BLADES
BLUE HORSE
Blue Mornings Press
COPULA
Crow
THE FAULT
The Fault Press
FROZEN WAFFLES
The Future Press
GEGENSCHEIN, NeoNeo DoDo
Heavy Evidence Press
HOT LOGARITHON

Intermedia Press
LATITUDES
Luna Bisonte Prods
MUSEUM OF TEMPORARY ART (MOTA) MAGAZINE
The Not Guilty Press
NRG
Old Pages Books Co
OXYMORON: Journal Of Convulsive Beauty
PANJANDRUM POETRY JOURNAL
PASTICHE: Poems of Place
Peace & Pieces Foundation
The Perishable Press Limited
PHANTASMAGORIA, Journey into the Surreal
PIG IRON
Pig Iron Press
Pitjon Press/BackBack Media
qwertyuiop
Reductio Ad Asparagus Press
SKYWRITING
Thunder City Press
THUNDER MOUNTAIN REVIEW
TOTAL ABANDON: A Literary and Arts Magazine
TRANSFORMACTION
TREES
TRULY FINE PRESS, A Review
ULULATUS
VILE
WHITE MULE

DANCE

AC Publications
AMERICAN DANCE GUILD NEWSLETTER
THE ARTFUL REPORTER
BALLET NEWS
Catalyst
DANCE BOOK FORUM
DANCE HERALD
DANCE IN CANADA
Dance Motion Press
DANCE SCOPE
THE DRAMA REVIEW
Duende Press
ENGLISH DANCE AND SONG
Footnotes
Jalmar Press, Inc.
LITTLE CAESAR
Lycabettus Press
MIAMI INTERNATIONAL
MODERN LITURGY
Moon Publications
NEWSREAL
Resource Publications
ROMANIAN REVIEW
SALOME: A LITERARY DANCE MAGAZINE
Simon & Pierre Publishing Co. Ltd.
SO & SO
Technical Documantation Services
THEATRE DESIGN AND TECHNOLOGY
Vehicle Editions

AUGUST DERLETH

August Derleth Society Newsletter

DESIGN

Archinform

CHARLES DICKENS

THE DICKENSIAN

EMILY DICKINSON

HIGGINSON JOURNAL
Higginson Press

DRAMA

AIS EIRI
Bern Porter Books
BIALA, PRAHRAN COLLEGE OF ADVANCED EDUCATION
CANADIAN AUTHOR & BOOKMAN
CANADIAN THEATRE REVIEW

THE CAPILANO REVIEW
The Carolina Wren Press
THE CHARIOTEER
CHIMERA-A Complete Theater Piece
Co-op Books Ltd.
CTR Publications
Curvd H&Z
DIMENSION
Dragon's Teeth Press
THE DRAMA REVIEW
DRAMATIKA
Dramatika Press
EDWARDIAN STUDIES
EVENT
Firestein Books
Folder Editions
Four Corners Press
GEORGE SPELVIN'S THEATRE BOOK
Harian Creative Press
Heirs Press
The Heron Press
Illuminations Press
JH Press
Litmus, Inc.
Love Street Books
THE METRO
MODERN LITURGY
Natalie Slohm Associates, Inc.
NEW VOICES
NORO REVIEW
Northeastern University Press
Oleander Press
ON STAGE
Orion Press
Personabooks
PHOEBE
Playwrights Canada
PRAXIS: A Journal of Cultural Criticism
PRISM INTERNATIONAL
Proscenium Press
Quintessence Publications
Resource Publications
ROCKBOTTOM
The Scopcraeft Press
SHAKESPEARE NEWSLETTER
Simon & Pierre Publishing Co. Ltd.
SNAPDRAGON
Spectrum Productions
Talonbooks
Tejas Art Press
Ten Penny Players, Inc.
THEATER
THEATRE DESIGN AND TECHNOLOGY
Thunder Creek Publishing Co-operative
Tree Line Books
The Twickenham Press
Vesta Publications Limited
WEST COAST PLAYS
John Westburg, Publisher
ZONE

DRUGS

And/Or Press
JOURNAL OF PSYCHEDELIC DRUGS
Stash, Inc.

EARTH, NATURAL HISTORY, ANIMALS

AKWESASNE NOTES
Alchemist/Light Publishing
Alex Aiken
Alpine Publications
Baja Trail Publications, Inc.
Bear Claw Press
Bear Tribe
THE BLACK CAT
BLACKBERRY
The Boxwood Press
Boyd & Fraser Publishing Company
Bradt Enterprises

BRITISH NATURALISTS' ASSOCIATION (PUBLISHERS)
Capra Press
Cheshire Books
THE CIRCLE
COEVOLUTION QUARTERLY
Creative Editions & Capitol Enquiry
Crow
DOUBLE HARNESS
ETC Publications
Falconiforme Press Ltd.
FARMING UNCLE
Gem Guides Book Co.
Genny Smith Books
George Sroda, Publisher
THE GREEN REVOLUTION
Hancock House Publishers
THE HOT SPRINGS GAZETTE
HOWL
Hurtig Publishers
Indian Tree Press
Io (named after moon of Jupiter)
Island Press - A Division of Round Valley Agrarian Institute
JC/DC Cartoons Ink
Kitchen Sink Enterprises
KUKSU: Journal of Backcountry Writing
The Latona Press
THE LEY HUNTER: The Magazine Of Earth Mysteries
The Lightning Tree
Mad River Press, Inc.
MANITOBA NATURE (formerly ZOOLOG)
MANY SMOKES
MEXICO WEST
Miocene Press
El Moro Publications
Mountain Press Publishing Co.
M-R-K Publishing
Michael F. Murphy Ph. D.
NATIONAL FISHERMAN
Naturegraph Publishers, Inc.
THE NEW ENGLAND CONSERVATIONIST
NOT MAN APART
PACIFIC HORTICULTURE
EL PALACIO
THE PENNSYLVANIA NATURALIST
Peradam Publishing House
The Perishable Press Limited
Pleasant Hill Press
QUEEN'S QUARTERLY: A Canadian Review
THE SALT CEDAR
SAMISDAT
The School of Living
Seahawk Press
SECOND GROWTH: Appalachian Nature and Culture
SNOWY EGRET
The Stevenson Press
Stone Wall Press, Inc
Survival Cards
TRT Publications, Inc.
Tamarack Press
Timber Press
Walnut Press
WESTERN WORLD REVIEW
WOOD IBIS

ECOLOGY, FOODS

ALTERNATIVES- Perspectives on Society and Environment
Amigo Press
Androgyne Books
APPLEWOOD JOURNAL
Aris Books
Autumn Press, Inc.
Bear Tribe
Bookworm Publishing Company
The Boxwood Press
Brick House Publishing, Co.
BRITISH NATURALISTS' ASSOCIATION (PUBLISHERS)
Brux Am Books
Bull Publishing Co.
Capra Press

Carousel Press
Cedar Creek Publishers
Center for Science in the Public Interest
Cheshire Books
Christopher Davies Publishers Ltd.
City Lights Books
CLEARWATER NAVIGATOR
Cobbers
Cobblesmith
COEVOLUTION QUARTERLY
COMMUNITY DEVELOPMENT JOURNAL
CONNECTICUT FIRESIDE
CONNECTION NEWS RELEASE
Creative Book Company
The Crossing Press
DAWN
The Dawn Horse Press
Delicious Desserts For Diabetics & Their Sugar Free Friends
DOUBLE HARNESS
DUMP HEAP (Diverse Unsung Miracle Plants for Healthy Evolution Among People)
The East Woods Press
ECOSYSTEMS
ELAN POETIQUE LITTERAIRE ET PACIFISTE
ETC Publications
Findhorn Publications
FOURTH DIMENSION
Fresh Press
Friends of the Earth
C J Frompovich Publications
The Garlic Press
GARLIC TIMES
Genny Smith Books
Geraventure Corp.
Gotuit Enterprises
GRASS ROOTS
THE GREEN REVOLUTION
GREENPEACE (London) Newsletter
Hancock House Publishers
Hays, Rolfes & Associates
HEALTH SCIENCE
HEALTHY LIVING
HUMANIST IN CANADA
John Muir Publications, Inc.
Joyful Press (formerly: T. I Opportunities)
Kitchen Harvest
The Lightning Tree
LIVING OFF THE LAND, Subtropic Newsletter
Louisiana Entertains
MANY SMOKES
McBooks Press
Moonsquilt Press
Mosaic Press
Natural Dynamics, Inc.
Natural Hygiene Press
NATURAL LIFE
Naturegraph Publishers, Inc.
New-Age Foods Publications
THE NEW ECOLOGIST
NEW ROOTS
THE NORTH AMERICAN REVIEW
NOT MAN APART
John L Noyce, Publisher
NUTRITION ACTION
NUTRITION HEALTH REVIEW
Omangoo Press
Panjandrum Books
PEACE NEWS "For Non-Violent Revolution"
Peace Press
PEDESTRIAN RESEARCH
PEOPLE & ENERGY
The Perishable Press Limited
Place of Herons
Pleasant Hill Press
Quicksilver Productions
RAIN: JOURNAL OF APPROPRIATE TECHNOLOGY
The Rateavers
RESURGENCE
Rosler, Martha

SECOND GROWTH: Appalachian Nature and Culture
SHAW NEWSLETTER
Shaw Society
Southwest Research and Information Center
Sproing Inc.
Stone Wall Press, Inc
Tofua Press
TOTAL LIFESTYLE- The Magazine of Natural Living
THE TOWN FORUM JOURNAL & COMMUNITY REPORT
UNDERCURRENTS
Walnut Press
Westport Press, Inc
White Mountain Publishing Company
White Tower Inc. Press
WHOLE EARTH
Wild Horses Potted Plant
Wimmer Brothers Books
Worldwatch Institute

EDUCATION

Adventure Trails Research and Development Laboratories
All About Us
American Business Consultants, Inc.
Amigo Press
Andrew Mountain Press
Arbor Publications
Ash Lad Press
ASSERT NEWSLETTER
ATHENE
The Avondale Press
Between The Lines
BILINGUAL REVIEW/La revista bilingue
The Boxwood Press
BRIARPATCH REVIEW: A Journal of Right Livelihood and
   Simple Living
BRITISH JOURNAL OF IN-SERVICE EDUCATION
Canadian Women's Educational Press
Carma Press
CEDAR ROCK
Charisma Press
Children's Art Foundation, Inc.
Christopher Davies Publishers Ltd.
Coast to Coast Books
Community Collaborators
LA CONFLUENCIA
CONSTRUCTIVE ACTION FOR GOOD HEALTH
Contemporary Curriculums
Creative Book Company
CREATIVE COMPUTING
Creative Computing Press
D.& E. Career Publishing Co.
Do It Now Foundation
DRUG SURVIVAL NEWS
Ed-U Press, Inc.
Edgepress
Editorial Justa Publications, Inc.
Editorial Services Co.
EDUCATIONAL CONSIDERATIONS
EMERGENCY LIBRARIAN
Endurance
ETC Publications
FEDERAL NOTES
The Feminist Press
GROWING WITHOUT SCHOOLING
H.E.L.P. Books Inc.
Harian Creative Press
Heinemann Publisher's (NZ) Ltd
The Helen Vale Foundation
House of Anansi Press Limited/Publishing Co.
HUMANIST IN CANADA
Impact Publishers, Inc.
IN TOUCH
INTERFACE JOURNAL: Alternatives in Higher Education
The International University Press
JOURNAL OF THE HELEN VALE FOUNDATION
Karl Bern Publishers
LAMISHPAHA
LIB ED
Masters Publications

Matagiri
Mercer House Press
MODERN LITURGY
Montessori Learning Center
NEW HUMANIST
Nikmal Publishing
Occasional Productions
Odin Press
Parenting Press
Partners In Publishing
PASS-AGE: A Futures Journal
PEOPLE & ENERGY
PIP COLLEGE 'HELPS' NEWSLETTER
Prometheus Books
Pruett Publishing Company
Martin Quam Press
QUEEN'S QUARTERLY: A Canadian Review
RADICAL TEACHER
RaMar Press
RECREATIONAL COMPUTING
ST. CROIX REVIEW
Scotty Macgreger Publications
SCREEN
Sea Challengers
Simon & Pierre Publishing Co. Ltd.
STONE SOUP, The Magazine By Children
STUDIES IN DESIGN EDUCATION AND CRAFT
SUBVERSIVE SCHOLASTIC
Survivors' Manual
Teachers & Writers Collaborative
TEACHERS & WRITERS MAGAZINE
TEACHER UPDATE
Teacher Update, Inc.
Ten Speed Press
Turner Publishing, Inc.
UNIVERSITY JOURNAL
John Westburg, Publisher
Whole Image Graphics
WOMEN'S STUDIES NEWSLETTER
WOMEN'S STUDIES NEWSLETTER

ENERGY

AERO SUN-TIMES
AFRICA NEWS
ALTERNATIVE SOURCES of ENERGY MAGAZINE
Autumn Press, Inc.
The Boxwood Press
Boyd & Fraser Publishing Company
Brick House Publishing, Co.
Capra Press
Cheshire Books
COEVOLUTION QUARTERLY
DOUBLE HARNESS
ECOSYSTEMS
Energy Publishing Company
Friends of the Earth
GREENPEACE (London) Newsletter
Hancock House Publishers
HIGH COUNTRY NEWS
HUMANIST IN CANADA
Institute for Local Self-Reliance
John Muir Publications, Inc.
Lawrence Hill & Company, Publishers, Inc.
Liberty Publishing Company, Inc.
The Lightning Tree
Lorien House
THE METRO
MID-ATLANTIC NEWS
Natural Dynamics, Inc.
NATURAL LIFE
THE NEW ECOLOGIST
NEW ROOTS
NOT MAN APART
Odin Press
Ontario Library Association
PASS-AGE: A Futures Journal
PEOPLE & ENERGY
RAIN: JOURNAL OF APPROPRIATE TECHNOLOGY
REBUTTAL! The Bicentennial Newsletter of Truth

The School of Living
Second Back Row Press
SELF-RELIANCE
Skydog Press
THE SMALL POND MAGAZINE OF LITERATURE
SOLAR AGE
Southwest Research and Information Center
STREET MAGAZINE
Synerjy
SYNERJY: A Directory of Energy Alternatives
TOTAL LIFESTYLE- The Magazine of Natural Living
Vanilla Press
Worldwatch Institute

ENGLISH

Arbor Publications
BOUNDARY 2
Boyd & Fraser Publishing Company
BROWNING SOCIETY NOTES
CANADIAN AUTHOR & BOOKMAN
THE CENTENNIAL REVIEW
Chandler & Sharp Publishers, Inc.
COLLEGE ENGLISH
THE DALHOUSIE REVIEW
Dolly Varden Publications
The Future Press
THE GYPSY SCHOLAR: A Graduate Forum for Literary Criti-
cism
HYPERION A Poetry Journal
JOURNAL OF NARRATIVE TECHNIQUE
LAUGHING BEAR
Libre Press
THE MAINSTREETER
THE MODERN LANGUAGE JOURNAL
New Victoria Publishers
NOTES & QUERIES: for Readers & Writers, Collectors & Li-
brarians
OCCIDENT
Oleander Press
PAUNCH
Pennsylvania State University Press
Peregrine Smith, Inc.
The Perishable Press Limited
Periwinkle Press
Poet Papers
PRAXIS: A Journal of Cultural Criticism
RADICAL TEACHER
SCHOLIA SATYRICA
SCOPCRAFT MAGAZINE
THE SHAW REVIEW
Simon & Pierre Publishing Co. Ltd.
Sleepy Hollow Restorations
THE SPHINX
THOREAU JOURNAL QUARTERLY
Thorp Springs Press
Tyndall Creek Press
John Westburg, Publisher
THE YALE REVIEW

ENTERTAINMENT

Dream Place Publications
Main Track Publications

EUROPE

INTERNATIONAL PORTLAND REVIEW

FANTASY, HORROR

W.D. Firestone Press
MYTHLORE

FASHION

Fashion Imprints Associates

FICTION

MAGAZINE
A SHOUT IN THE STREET: a journal of literary and visual art
ABBEY
Acorn
Acrobat Books Publishers

THE ACTS THE SHELFLIFE
Aesopus Press
THE AGNI REVIEW
AIS EIRI
Alcazar Press
THE ALCHEMIST
Alchemist/Light Publishing
ALDEBARAN
Allegany Mountain Press
AMBIT
American Artists In Exhibition, Inc.
Ampersand Press
Androgyne Books
Angst World Library
ANNEX 21
ANOTHER CHICAGO MAGAZINE
THE ANTIGONISH REVIEW
THE ANTIOCH REVIEW
APALACHEE QUARTERLY
Apple-wood Press
Applezaba Press
ARCADE-THE COMICS REVUE
THE ARGONAUT
Ariadne Press
THE ARK RIVER REVIEW
Armchair Press
Around Publishing
THE ARTFUL DODGE
THE ARTFUL REPORTER
AS IS
As Is/So & So Press
ASPEN ANTHOLOGY
ASPHODEL
Ata Books
Autolycus Press
Avant-Garde Creations
The B & R Samizdat Express
The Babbington Press
BACHY
Backpack Media
BACULITE
Banana Productions
Bartholomew's Cobble
Le Beacon Presse
Beekman Publishers, Inc.
THE BELLINGHAM REVIEW
THE BERKELEY MONTHLY
BERKELEY POETS COOPERATIVE
Berkeley Poets Workshop and Press
BEYOND BAROQUE
BIG MOON
BIG SCREAM
BIRD EFFORT
BLACK JACK & VALLEY GRAPEVINE
Black Sparrow Press
THE BLACK WARRIOR REVIEW
BLANK TAPE
Blind Alley Press
BLUE HORSE
THE BLUE HOTEL
Blue Moon Press, Inc.
Blue Mountain Press
Blue Wind Press
BOGG
BOMBAY GIN
Borealis Press Limited
Boss Books
BOX 749
Brick/Nairn
Broken Whisker Studio
Burning Deck Press
Cadmus Editions
CALLIOPE
Cambric Press
CANADIAN AUTHOR & BOOKMAN
CANADIAN FICTION MAGAZINE
THE CAPILANO REVIEW
Capra Press
The Carolina Wren Press

JAM TO-DAY
Janus Press
Jelm Mountain Publications
JEOPARDY
JOURNAL OF CANADIAN FICTION
JUICE
Just Buffalo Press
JUST PULP: The Magazine of Popular Fiction
KANSAS QUARTERLY
KARAKI
KARAMU
Kawabata Press
KEEPSAKE POEMS
Kelsey St. Press
Kent Publications
Dr. Albert R. Klinski
KUDOS
LAKE STREET REVIEW
Lakes & Prairies Press
Lame Johnny Press
Lamplighters Roadway Press
LAUGHING BEAR
Laughing Bear Press
THE LAUREL REVIEW
Lawrence Hill & Company, Publishers, Inc.
LETTERS
Libra Press
The Lightning Tree
Lintel
Lion Enterprises
LITERARY MONITOR: The Voice of Contemporary Literature
LITTLE CAESAR
THE LITTLE MAGAZINE
Little Red Hen, Inc.
LONDON MYSTERY MAGAZINE
LONG POND REVIEW
Longship Press
LOOK QUICK
LOONFEATHER: Minnesota North Country Art
LOST GLOVE
Lost Roads Publishers
THE LOUISVILLE REVIEW
LOWLANDS REVIEW
LUCKY HEART BOOKS
LUDD'S MILL
LUNCH
Lynx House Press
M. N. Publishers
M.O. Publishing Company
THE MADISON REVIEW
Maelstrom Press
MAELSTROM REVIEW
Mafdet Press
Mainespring Press
MAMASHEE
Maro Verlag
MATI
Matrix Press
MATTOID
MAXY'S JOURNAL
MEANJIN QUARTERLY
MERLIN PAPERS
Micah Publications
THE MIDATLANTIC REVIEW
Miles & Weir, Ltd.
MILK QUARTERLY
THE MILL
MISSISSIPPI MUD
MISSISSIPPI REVIEW
MISSISSIPPI VALLEY REVIEW
Mixed Breed
THE MODULARIST REVIEW
MODUS OPERANDI
Molly Yes Press
THE MONTANA REVIEW
Montreal Poems
MONUMENT IN CANTOS AND ESSAYS
THE MOONSHINE REVIEW
Moore Publishing Company

Mosaic Press/Valley Editions
Motheroot Publications
Mountain Union Books
Mudborn Press
Nada
NEBULA
New Bedford Press
NIR/NEW INFINITY REVIEW
NEW LETTERS
NEW MEXICO HUMANITIES REVIEW
THE NEW RENAISSANCE, An International Magazine of Ideas
    & Opinions, Emphasizing Literature & The Arts
New Traditions
NEW VOICES
THE NEWSCRIBES
NIMROD
"NITTY GRITTY"
No Dead Lines
Noro Press
NORO REVIEW
THE NORTH AMERICAN REVIEW
NORTHEAST/JUNIPER BOOKS
NORTHEAST JOURNAL
NORTHWEST REVIEW
NORTHWOODS JOURNAL
Northwoods Press, Inc.
Oasis Books
OCCIDENT
Old Adobe Press
OLD COURTHOUSE FILES
OLD HICKORY REVIEW
Old Pages Books Co
ONE
Oolichan Books
OPEN CELL
ORIGINS
Orion Press
Out of the Ashes Press
OUTERBRIDGE
Owl Creek Press
P.E.N. BROADSHEET
PACIFIC POETRY AND FICTION REVIEW
Pakka Press
PANACHE
Panache Books
THE PANHANDLER
Papa Bach Paperbacks
Parable Press
PARAGRAPH: A QUARTERLY OF GAY FICTION
PARIS REVIEW
PARIS VOICES
THE PAWN REVIEW
Paycock Press
Peace & Pieces Foundation
PEMBROKE MAGAZINE
Peninhand Press
Penmaen Press Ltd
Pentagram Press
PENUMBRA
The Penumbra Press
PEQUOD
Peradam Publishing House
Peregrine Smith, Inc.
PERIODICS
Perivale Press
PERMAFROST
Persona Press
PHANTASM
Philmer Enterprises
PHOEBE
Phoenix Books/Publishers
Pi-Right Press
PIECES
PIEDMONT LITERARY REVIEW
PIG IRON
Pig Iron Press
The Pikestaff Press
Pikeville College Press
Pinchgut Press

Pitjon Press/BackBack Media
PLOUGHSHARES
PLUM
Poet Gallery Press
The Pomegranate Press
PRAIRIE SCHOONER
Presidio Press
Press Porcepic Limited
Pressed Curtains
Printed Editions
PRISM INTERNATIONAL
PTOLEMY/BROWNS MILLS REVIEW
Puckerbrush Press
PUERTO DEL SOL
Puerto Del Sol Press
PULP
Pulse-Finger Press
PURPLE PATCH
Quality Publications, Inc.
QUARRY WEST
Queens College Press
QUILT
QUIXOTE, QUIXOTL
Raven Publications
RE:PRINT (AN OCCASIONAL MAGAZINE)
Rebis Press
RED CEDAR REVIEW
Red Clay Books
Red Dust
RED FOX REVIEW
Red Press
Regmar Publishing Co.
Release Press
RIPPLES
RIVERSEDGE
Riversedge Press
Rochester Routes/Creative Arts Projects
ROCKBOTTOM
Ross-Erikson Publishers, Inc.
S & S Press
Sagarin Press
Saint Andrews Press
SAMISDAT
Samisdat Associates
Samuel Powell Publishing Company
SAN FRANCISCO STORIES
SANDSCRIPT
The Saturday Centre
The Sceptre Press
The Scopcraeft Press
SCOPP
The Seal Press
THE SEATTLE REVIEW
THE SECOND WAVE
SEEMS
Selene Books
SEPIA
Seven Buffaloes Press
SHANKPAINTER
SHENANDOAH
Sicilian Antigruppo
SILVER VAIN
Simon & Pierre Publishing Co. Ltd.
SING HEAVENLY MUSE! WOMEN'S POETRY AND PROSE
Singing Wind Press
Sitnalta Press
SKYWRITING
SLICK PRESS
Slough Press
Slow Loris Press
SLOW LORIS READER
THE SMALL POND MAGAZINE OF LITERATURE
SMOKE
Smyrna Press
SNAPDRAGON
SO & SO
SOFT NEED
SOME
SOU'WESTER

SOUNDINGS/EAST
SOUTH CAROLINA REVIEW
SOUTH DAKOTA REVIEW
SOUTHERN REVIEW
SOUTHWEST REVIEW
THE SOUTHWESTERN REVIEW
Sovereign Press
Spectre Press
Spindrift Press
Spirit Mound Press
The Spirit That Moves Us, Inc. (Formerly Emmess Press)
THE SQUATCHBERRY JOURNAL
Standard Editions
Station Hill Press
Stonehenge Books, Inc.
Story Press
STORY QUARTERLY
STRAIGHT AHEAD INTERNATIONAL
STRANGE FAECES
Studio S Press
SUN
Sun & Moon Press
Sunbury Press
Sunken Forum Press
Sunrise Press
The Swallow Press Inc.
SWIFT RIVER
SYNCLINE
SZ/Press
Talespinner Publications, Inc.
Tanam Press
TELEPHONE
Texas Center for Writers Press
THICKET
THIRD EYE
13th MOON
THREE SISTERS
Thunder Creek Publishing Co-operative
Thunder's Mouth Press
TIME CAPSULE, INC.
Timely Books
Tiresias Press
TITMOUSE
TLM Press
Tombouctou Books
TOUCHSTONE
Trask House Books, Inc.
Traumwald Press
Treacle Press
Tree Line Books
Tree Toad Press
TREES
TRIQUARTERLY
Troisieme-Canadian Publishers
Truedog Press, Inc.
TRULY FINE PRESS, A Review
Truly Fine Press
THE TULANE LITERARY MAGAZINE
The Twickenham Press
Twowindows Press
US1 Poets' Cooperative
US1 WORKSHEETS
UNICORN
Unicorn Press
University of Oregon Press
URBANE GORILLA
Urion Press
UROBOROS
URTHKIN
UZZANO
Valkyrie Press, Inc.
Vanguard Books
Ventura Press
Veritie Press, Inc.
Verlag Pohl'n'Mayer
Vermont Crossroads Press
Vesta Publications Limited
VILE
WASHINGTON REVIEW

WATERS JOURNAL OF THE ARTS
Webb-Newcomb Company, Inc.
WEIRDBOOK
Weirdbook Press
WEST BRANCH
West Coast Poetry Review Press
West Village Publishing Company
John Westburg, Publisher
Western Washington University
Westwind Press
Whispers Press
WHISTLER ANSWER
The White Ewe Press
WHITE MULE
Wild & Woolley
Wild Mustard Press
WILLOW SPRINGS
Windflower Press
WINDOW
Window Press
WISCONSIN REVIEW
Wisconsin Review
WOLFSONG
THE WOODSTOCK REVIEW
WOT
WRIT
WRITER'S NEWSLETTER
WRITERS FORUM
WRITERS IN RESIDENCE
Writers' Publishing Company
XTRAS
YELLOW BRICK ROAD
The Yellow Press
Young Davis Press
Z
ZAHIR
ZONE
Zone

FILM, VIDEO

AFTA—The Magazine of Temporary Culture
AFTERIMAGE
ALTERNATIVE MEDIA
AMERICAN ARTS PAMPHLET SERIES
CAMERA OBSCURA: A Journal of Feminism and Film Theory
CANADIAN AUTHOR & BOOKMAN
CINEASTE MAGAZINE
CINEMAGIC
CLASSIC FILM/VIDEO IMAGES
CLASSIC IMAGES REVIEW
COPY CORNUCOPIA
CRISS-CROSS ART COMMUNICATIONS
DECEMBER MAGAZINE
December Press
Ecart Publications
EXCHANGE: A Journal of Opinion for the Ferforming Arts
Festival Publications
FILM
FILM CULTURE
Film Culture Non-Profit, Inc.
FILM LIBRARY QUARTERLY
FILM QUARTERLY
FUNNYWORLD - The Magazine of Animation and Comic Art
The Future Press
Hollywood Film Archive
Image and Idea, Inc.
International General
JUMP CUT, A Review of Contemporary Cinema
Kontexts Publications
Levenson Press
LITTLE CAESAR
THE MODULARIST REVIEW
Ted Nelson, Publisher
NEW HUMANIST
NOSTALGIAWORLD
PAUNCH
PRAXIS: A Journal of Cultural Criticism
RAIN: JOURNAL OF APPROPRIATE TECHNOLOGY
SCREEN

SOUTHERN QUARTERLY: A Journal of the Arts in the South
THEATRE DESIGN AND TECHNOLOGY
University of California Press
Windsong Books International
Women's History Research Center, Inc.

FOLKLORE

AC Publications
BITTERSWEET
Breakwater Books Limited
Cat Anna Press
Center for Southern Folklore
CENTER FOR SOUTHERN FOLKLORE MAGAZINE
THE CHARIOTEER
Children's Book Press/Imprenta de Libros Infantiles
Christopher Davies Publishers Ltd.
Cologne Press
COME-ALL-YE
LA CONFLUENCIA
CONSTALLATIONS
Creative With Words Publications (CWW)
Duir Press
THE ETHNODISC JOURNAL OF RECORDED SOUND
HOO-DOO BlackSeries
Jump River Press, Inc.
JUMP RIVER REVIEW
Legacy Books (formerly Folklore Associates)
The Lightning Tree
LORE AND LANGUAGE
Lycabettus Press
MALEDICTA: The International Journal of Verbal Aggression
Maledicta Press
Manzano Press
Mathom Publishing Co
The Middle Atlantic Press
Moonsquilt Press
Mosaic Press
THE NORTH WIND
Onaway Publications
PARABOLA MAGAZINE
The Perishable Press Limited
Perivale Press
Pleasant Hill Press
Rainy Day Press
Roush Books
Sleepy Hollow Restorations
STREET MAGAZINE
TOCHER
Tofua Press
Tree Books
Tree Toad Press
TSA'ASZI'
UNICORN: A Miscellaneous Journal
WISCONSIN TRAILS
WOOD IBIS

FRANCE, FRENCH

POESIE - U.S.A.

FUTURISM

And/Or Press

GAELIC

GAIRM
TOCHER

GAMES

Abyss/Augtwofive
ADVISORY BOARD RECORD
Avant-Garde Creations
Bonanza, Inc.
CASINO & SPORTS
CHIMERA-A Complete Theater Piece
Cincinnati Chess Federation
GBC Press
J'ADOUBE!
Kanthaka Press
Klutz Enterprises
KXE6S VEREIN R NEWSLETTER

Ted Nelson, Publisher
NORTHWEST CHESS
Service Press Inc.
Spectre Press
SYSTEMS & METHODS
Ten Speed Press
University Statistical Tracts

GARDENING

Adam Seed Publications
The Bookstore Press
Bookworm Publishing Company
Cheshire Books
Cobblesmith
DUMP HEAP (Diverse Unsung Miracle Plants for Healthy Evolution Among People)
Findhorn Publications
Geraventure Corp.
GRASS ROOTS
Harvest Press
Libre Press
LIVING OFF THE LAND, Subtropic Newsletter
North Atlantic Books
PACIFIC HORTICULTURE
PEOPLE & ENERGY
POTPOURRI FROM HERBAL ACRES
RAIN: JOURNAL OF APPROPRIATE TECHNOLOGY
The Rateavers
Richboro Press
SAINT LOUIS HOME/GARDEN
SEED SAVERS EXCHANGE
Ten Speed Press
Timber Press
TOTAL LIFESTYLE- The Magazine of Natural Living
White Tower Inc. Press
Wild Horses Potted Plant

GAY

THE ADVOCATE
THE ALTERNATE
Alyson Publications, Inc.
Avant-Garde Creations
BIG MAMA RAG
THE BODY POLITIC- Gay Liberation Journal
Calamus Books
Catalyst
Diana Press, Inc
DIGNITY
FAG RAG
FEMINARY
A GAY BIBLIOGRAPHY
GAY COMMUNITY NEWS
GAY INSURGENT
THE GAY LUTHERAN
GAY SUNSHINE: A Journal of Gay Liberation
Gay Sunshine Press, Inc.
Gay Task Force, American Library Association
GPU NEWS
INSIGHT: A Quarterly of LESBIAN/GAY CHRISTIAN OPINION
Leland Mellott Books
THE LESBIAN TIDE
Motheroot Publications
MOUTH OF THE DRAGON
National Gay News, Inc.
New Glide Publ.
OFF OUR BACKS
Out & Out Books
OUTCOME
PARAGRAPH: A QUARTERLY OF GAY FICTION
Peace & Pieces Foundation
PEACE NEWS "For Non-Violent Revolution"
The Pepys Press
Persona Press
Personal Publications
Pink Triangle Press
POETIC JUSTICE
Printed Editions
RFD

SAPPHO
Static Creation Press
Stephen Wright Press
Swish
Tide Publications
Union Park Press
Violet Press
W. I. M. Publications
THE WISHING WELL

GENEALOGY

Heritage Books Inc.

GERMAN

DIMENSION
NEW GERMAN STUDIES

GRAPHICS

Acme Print & Litho
Acorn
THE ALTERNATIVE PRESS
AND
ANTENNA
ATHAENA
BACKCOUNTRY
Basement Editions
BERGEN POETS
Big River Association
BIKINI GIRL
BIRTHSTONE
BLADES
BLANK TAPE
BLUE HORSE
Blue Wind Press
The Cabbagehead Press
Cherry Valley Editions
Chronicle Books/Prism Editions
CLOWN WAR
The Curlew Press
Curvd H&Z
DAIMON
The Direct Marketing Creative Guild
DRAGONFLY:A Quarterly Of Haiku
Dragonsbreath Press
EN PASSANT/POETRY
EVENT
THE FAULT
The Fault Press
FIFTH SUN
FINE PRINT: A Review for the Arts of the Book
FLOATING ISLAND
FRIENDS OF POETRY
The Future Press
GILTEDGE: New Series
GLASSWORKS
GRUB STREET
Halls of Ivy Press
Heresy Press
HEY LADY
Holmgangers Press
The Hosanna Press
HOT LOGARITHON
Ilkon Press
JAM TO-DAY
William Kaufmann, Inc.
KONGLOMERATI
Kontexts Publications
KROKLOK
LOCAL DRIZZLE
LONG POND REVIEW
Lowy Publishing
MATI
MILKWEED CHRONICLE
MR. COGITO
Morgan Press
NAZUNAH
The New Poets Series
NICOTINE SOUP
No Dead Lines

Oasis Books
PADAN ARAM
The Perishable Press Limited
PIG IRON
Pleasure Dome Press (Long Island Poetry Collective Inc.)
The Pray Curser Press
PULP
RAIN: JOURNAL OF APPROPRIATE TECHNOLOGY
Raven Publications
THE RECORD SUN
RIVER STYX
RUDE
Saint Heironymous Press, Inc.
THE SECOND WAVE
SHADOWGRAPHS
SKULL POLISH
SLICK PRESS
SO & SO
THE STONE
STRANGE FAECES
Swamp Press
13th MOON
Thistledown Press
THUNDER EGG
Tideline Press
TIGHTROPE
The Transientpress
Tree Shrew Press
Tree Toad Press
TREES
Trike
TRULY FINE PRESS, A Review
TWELFTH KEY
TYPE & PRESS
URBANE GORILLA
Vehicle Editions
VILE
WEST BRANCH
WESTERN PUBLISHING SCENE
Writers Forum
XANADU

GREEK

JOURNAL OF THE HELLENIC DIASPORA
Pella Publ. Co

HAIKU

AMOSKEAG: A Magazine of Haiku
Backpack Media
BONSAI
Bonsai Press
CANVASS
CICADA
Distant Thunder Press
DRAGONFLY:A Quarterly Of Haiku
The First Haiku Press
FROZEN WAFFLES
GUSTO
Gusto
GUTS AND GRACE
HIGH/COO: A Quarterly of Short Poetry
High/Coo Press
Houston Writers Workshop
HSA FROGPOND
Little River Press
MATI
MIDWEST CHAPARRAL
MODERN HAIKU
Pitjon Press/BackBack Media
Raw Dog Press
Rook Press, Inc.
SUNRISE
Swamp Press
TIGHTROPE
TOUCHSTONE
URTHKIN
XTRAS

HAWAII

Pueo Press

HEALTH

Adventure Trails Research and Development Laboratories
Alta Napa Press
And/Or Press
ASI Publishers, Inc.
Aslan Enterprises
Bear Tribe
Book Publishing Co.
Booklegger Press
Brick House Publishing, Co.
Bull Publishing Co.
Cedar Creek Publishers
Celestial Arts
Center for Science in the Public Interest
Cin Publications
CONSTRUCTIVE ACTION FOR GOOD HEALTH
The Crossing Press
Delicious Desserts For Diabetics & Their Sugar Free Friends
Do It Now Foundation
DRUG SURVIVAL NEWS
Endurance
Falkynor Books
Food For Thought Publications
FORESIGHT MAGAZINE
Freestone Publishing Collective
GARLIC TIMES
Golden Quill Publishers Inc
Golden West Books
GRASS ROOTS
THE GROVE
H.E.L.P. Books Inc.
HEALTH SCIENCE
HEALTHY LIVING
The Helen Vale Foundation
Hidden Valley Press
Himalayan Institute Publishers and Distributors
Images Press
Impact Publishers, Inc.
IN STRIDE
International Childbirth Education Association, Inc.
J&J Publishing
JOURNAL OF THE HELEN VALE FOUNDATION
JOURNAL OF PSYCHEDELIC DRUGS
Liberty Publishing Company, Inc.
Loggeerhead
LONG ISLAND CHILDBIRTH ALTERNATIVES QUARTERLY
Medic Publishing Co.
MEDICAL HISTORY
MEDICAL SELF-CARE
Natural Hygiene Press
Naturegraph Publishers, Inc.
North Atlantic Books
Northland Publications
NUTRITION ACTION
OFF OUR BACKS
Omangoo Press
Peace Press
Pentangle Press
Prologue Publications
RAIN: JOURNAL OF APPROPRIATE TECHNOLOGY
Rockfall Press
Ross Books
Sprout Publications Inc
H. Summer Enterprises
SWIM LITE NEWS (newsletter)
Tib Publications
Tide Book Publishing Company
Trado-Medic Books
Triad Publishing Co. Inc.
Unity Press
Valkyrie Press, Inc.
Veritas Press
The Word Shop
Worldwatch Institute

HISTORY

AIS EIRI
Akiba Press
ALBERTA HISTORY
American Studies Press, Inc.
Baja Trail Publications, Inc.
The Battery Press, Inc.
Bellerophon Books
Between The Lines
BIBLIOTHEQUE D'HUMANISME ET RENAISSANCE
Bicentennial Era Enterprises
Biscuit City Press
The Borgo Press
Briarpatch Press
BRITISH COLUMBIA HISTORICAL NEWS
BULLETIN OF THE BOARD OF CELTIC STUDIES
CANADIAN SLAVONIC PAPERS
Canadian Women's Educational Press
Capra Press
Caratzas Brothers, Publishers
Center for Southern Folklore
Chandonnet, Ann
Charles H. Kerr Publishing Company
Cheshire Books
Christopher Davies Publishers Ltd.
Coach House Press
COBBLESTONE: The History Magazine for Children
Communication Creativity
CONFEDERATE CALENDAR WORKS
LA CONFLUENCIA
Copley Books
Current Issues Publications
THE DALHOUSIE REVIEW
DAWN
Dharma Publishing
EAST EUROPEAN QUARTERLY
Glenbow-Alberta Institute
Golden West Books
Golden West Historical Publications
GRAND RIVER REVIEW/CAPITOL CITY MOON
Gray Beard Publishing
Great Basin Press
Greenwood Press, Inc.
Harvest Publishers
HARVEST QUARTERLY
Haskell House Publishers, Ltd.
Helaine Victoria Press
HER Publishing Co.
Heritage Books Inc.
Heyday Books
Historical Society of Alberta
THE HISTORY BOOK DIGEST
Hunter Publishing, Co.
Indian Publications
THE INSIDE TRACK
Institute for Polynesian Studies
Jaffe Books
Jelm Mountain Publications
THE JOURNAL of PSYCHOHISTORY
JOURNAL OF THE WEST
Kent Publications
Kitchen Sink Enterprises
Lame Johnny Press
LANDSCAPE
Library Research Associates
The Lightning Tree
LITERATURE OF LIBERTY
Maryland Historical Press
MAW: A MAGAZINE OF APPALACHIAN WOMEN
May-Murdock Publications
McNally & Loftin, West
THE METRO
MILITARY IMAGES MAGAZINE
Miocene Press
MODERN LANGUAGE QUARTERLY
Molly Yes Press
Moon Publications
Mowbray Company Publishers
Nevada Publications
NEW WORLD JOURNAL

North Star Press
THE NORTH WIND
Northeastern University Press
Oregon Historical Society
EL PALACIO
Paladin Enterprises, Inc.
Peregrine Smith, Inc.
Jim Phillips Publications
Piney Branch Press
Pleasant Hill Press
Prairie Publishing Company
Precedent Publishing Inc.
Presidio Press
Proletarian Publishers
Pruett Publishing Company
Psychohistory Press
Pueo Press
QUEEN'S QUARTERLY: A Canadian Review
RADICAL AMERICA
RAINCOAST CHRONICLES
Raintree
The Rather Press
Rose Publishing Co.
Roush Books
SALTHOUSE
The Sandstone Press
The Seal Press
Self Published
Sleepy Hollow Restorations
THE SMALL POND MAGAZINE OF LITERATURE
Socialist Party of Canada
Sono Nis Press
Spirit Mound Press
Stagecoach Pub. Co. Ltd.
The Stevenson Press
STUDIES IN LABOUR HISTORY
Summerthought Ltd.
Sunflower University Press
The Sunstone Press
Transport History Press
Vanguard Books
Veritie Press, Inc.
THE VOLCANO REVIEW
Walnut Press
WEST PLAINS GAZETTE
John Westburg, Publisher
WESTERN WORLD REVIEW
Whitfield
William L. Bauhan, Publisher
Wilson Brothers Publications

HOLOGRAPHY

Pentangle Press
Poet Papers
THEATRE DESIGN AND TECHNOLOGY
V. A. C. (Vereinigung Aktiver Kultur)

HOW-TO

A Harmless Flirtation With Wealth
Acrobus, Inc.
Almar Press
American Business Consultants, Inc.
Amity Books
Ana-Doug Publishing
Angst World Library
Apple Tree Lane
APPLEWOOD JOURNAL
Aris Books
Arlotta Press
Charles N. Aronson, Writer Publisher
Ashford Press
Bell Springs Publishing Company
Beninda Books
BITTERSWEET
Bonanza, Inc.
The Bookery
BOOKLEGGER MAGAZINE AND BOOKS
The Bookstore Press
Bookworm Publishing Company

Bradley David Associates, Ltd.
BRIARPATCH REVIEW: A Journal of Right Livelihood and
   Simple Living
Brick House Publishing, Co.
Brown Rabbit Press
Capra Press
Carma Press
Carousel Press
The Center For Study of Multiple Gestation
CHIMERA-A Complete Theater Piece
Chronicle Books/Prism Editions
Cin Publications
Cobblesmith
Commen Cents
Communicate Press
Communication Creativity
The Communication Press
Connection Press
COPY CORNUCOPIA
Creative Arts Book Company
Danbury Press
Design Enterprises of San Francisco
The Direct Marketing Creative Guild
Do-It-Yourself Publications, Co.
Dovetail Press Ltd
Dustbooks
Electronic Music Enterprises
EMPIRE: For the SF Writer
ETC Publications
Exponent Ltd.
Far Out West Publications
Fashion Imprints Associates
Flower Press
Freelance Publications
Fresh Press
Gamma Books
Garden Way Publishing Company
Gazelle Publications
Gemini Press
Ginseng Press
Gluxlit Press
Golden Quill Publishers Inc
GRASS ROOTS
Greatland Publishing Co.
HAPPINESS HOLDING TANK
Harlo Press
Hunter Publishing, Co.
International Marine Publishing Co.
Jaks Publishing Co.
Jalmar Press, Inc.
Jama Books
John Muir Publications, Inc.
Joyful Press (formerly: T. I Opportunities)
Klutz Enterprises
Lame Johnny Press
Legal Publications, Inc.
Light Living Library
LITERARY MONITOR: The Voice of Contemporary Literature
Lonely Planet Publications
Loompanics Unlimited
Louisiana Entertains
Master Key Publications
MEDICAL SELF-CARE
Mercantine Press
Merganzer Press
Merlin Engine Works
Minnesota Scholarly Press, Inc.
MJG Company
Molly Yes Press
Moon Publications
NEW ROOTS
Nikmal Publishing
Nolo Press
Occasional Productions
Onaway Publications
Panda Programs
Panjandrum Books
Parachuting Publications
Periwinkle Press

Phoenix Books/Publishers
Programmed Studies Inc
Promise Publishing Corp.
Provision House
Pushcart Press
Pygmalion Press
R & D Services
Racz Publishing Co.
RAIN: JOURNAL OF APPROPRIATE TECHNOLOGY
Rainy Day Press
Robert D. Reed Publisher
William A. Reilly, Publisher
Reyn Publishing Co.
Ross Books
Rossi
Running Press
S & S Press
Second Back Row Press
Shire Press
Southwest Research and Information Center
Sprout Publications Inc
Stonehouse Publications
H. Summer Enterprises
TRT Publications, Inc.
Tamal Vista Publications
That New Publishing Company
Tib Publications
Tiburon Press
TLM Press
Trans-Traffic Corporation, Publishing Division
The Transientpress
Tree Toad Press
Triad Press
Turner Publishing, Inc.
Unity Press
Vermont Crossroads Press
Vista Publications
Walnut Press
Westshore Inc
Whatever Publishing/Rising Sun Records
White Oak Publishing House
Windsong Books International
Wingbow Press
THE WOMAN ACTIVIST
THE WORKBOOK
WRITER'S NEWSLETTER

HUMANISM

Adventure Trails Research and Development Laboratories
Avant-Garde Creations
The Black Hole School of Poethnics
CIMARRON REVIEW
Dharma Publishing
ECO CONTEMPORANEO
Eco Contemporaneo Press
ECOSYSTEMS
Gleniffer Press
GRAND RIVER REVIEW/CAPITOL CITY MOON
Grass-Hooper Press
The Green Hut Press
THE HUMANIST
HUMANIST IN CANADA
HYPERION A Poetry Journal
Live-Oak Press
LP Publications
THE NEW ECOLOGIST
NEW HUMANIST
NEWS AND LETTERS
News and Letters Press
PEDESTRIAN RESEARCH
THE PHOENIX
Pilgrim Press
POETS ON:
Prometheus Books
RAGGED READIN'
REBUTTAL! The Bicentennial Newsletter of Truth
THE SEEKER NEWSLETTER
SELF DETERMINATION JOURNAL
Seven Deadly Sins Press

THE SMALL POND MAGAZINE OF LITERATURE
SOUTH & WEST
Southern Agitator
Spindrift Press
STREET MAGAZINE
Vanilla Press
Vermont Crossroads Press
THE WISHING WELL

HUMOR

A Harmless Flirtation With Wealth
ADVENTURES IN POETRY MAGAZINE
Alcazar Press
AQUILA MAGAZINE
Ariadne Press
Avant-Garde Creations
BARE WIRES
BLIND ALLEY
Breakwater Books Limited
THE BREATH OF THE PEOPLE
Celestial Arts
Celestial Gifts
COFFEE BREAK
Coffee Break Press
Cologne Press
The Communication Press
Curvd H&Z
Daisy Press
FRONT STREET TROLLEY
Fulcourte Press
Great Lakes Publishing
THE HARDHITTING INTERMITTENT NORTH IDAHO
   NEWS
HARVEST
Heavy Evidence Press
Hiddigeigei Books
Hurtig Publishers
Image and Idea, Inc.
JC/DC Cartoons Ink
Kangam
Samuel P. Levine
M.O. Publishing Company
M.O.P. Press
MANNA
MATRIX
Mockingbird Press
Moonlight Publications
Mosaic Press
Nanny Goat Productions
The Not Guilty Press
PAPER NEWS
Peace & Pieces Foundation
Perivale Press
Poor Souls Press/Scaramouche Books
Resource Publications
RESOURCES
Rip Off Press Inc.
ROQ Press
The S & S Co.
S & S Press
Servicios Internacionales
SNARF
Spindrift Press
STRANGE FAECES
THALIA: Studies in Literary Humor
Triad Publishing Co. Inc.
Tundra Books Of Northern New York
Valkyrie Press, Inc.
Vanity Press
Ventura Press
WILD FENNEL
Windflower Press
THE WISHING WELL
Dr. Stella Woodall Publisher
The WorDoctor Publications

ILLINOIS

POETRY &

INDEXES & ABSTRACTS

ABC Letter Service of Rochester
THE BRITISH ALTERNATIVE PRESS INDEX
CONNEXIONS
THE DALHOUSIE REVIEW
Greenwood Press, Inc.
LITERARY RESEARCH NEWSLETTER
New Glide Publ.
RAIN: JOURNAL OF APPROPRIATE TECHNOLOGY
WOMEN STUDIES ABSTRACTS

IOWA

IOWA WOMAN

IRELAND

JOURNAL OF IRISH LITERATURE
THE MONGREL FOX

JAMES JOYCE

JAMES JOYCE QUARTERLY
A WAKE NEWSLITTER, Studies Of James Joyce's Finnegans
   Wake

JUDAISM

Aura Publishing Co.
Biblio Press
YOUTH AND NATION

JACK KEROUAC

Fels and Firn Press

LABOR

APPEAL TO REASON
Between The Lines
Charles H. Kerr Publishing Company
CRIME AND SOCIAL JUSTICE: ISSUES IN CRIMINOLOGY.
Crime and Social Justice Associates, Inc.
Greenleaf Press
INDUSTRIAL WORKER
The Jacek Publishing Company
Kent Popular Press
Labor Arts Books
LABOUR LEADER
THE MILITANT
NEW UNIONIST
NEWS AND LETTERS
News and Letters Press
OFF OUR BACKS
PACIFIC RESEARCH
PEOPLE & ENERGY
Prairie Publishing Company
Pueo Press
Socialist Party of Canada
STUDIES IN LABOUR HISTORY
Turner Publishing, Inc.

LANGUAGE

Alta Napa Press
BA SHIRU
Barnhart Books
BILINGUAL REVIEW/La revista bilingue
Bilingual Review/Press
The Boxwood Press
BULLETIN OF HISPANIC STUDIES
BULLETIN OF THE BOARD OF CELTIC STUDIES
CANADIAN AUTHOR & BOOKMAN
CANDELABRUM POETRY MAGAZINE
Clamshell Press
CURTAINS
Dolly Varden Publications
HYPERION A Poetry Journal
IDO-LETRO
IF LIFE, THEN ONE AMONG AT LEAST FOUR
JOURNAL OF CALIFORNIA AND GREAT BASIN AN-
   THROPOLOGY
Kontexts Publications
Litmus, Inc.
LORE AND LANGUAGE

MALEDICTA: The International Journal of Verbal Aggression
Maledicta Press
Malki Museum Press
THE MODERN LANGUAGE JOURNAL
Moon Publications
NOTES & QUERIES: for Readers & Writers, Collectors & Librarians
NRG
Tom Ockerse Editions
Oleander Press
OSIRIS
PAPER AIR
Pressed Curtains
Primary Press
S
The Saturday Centre
SCOPP
Skydog Press
STAR WEST
Thorp Springs Press
TOTTEL'S

LATIN AMERICA

Between The Lines
Canadian Women's Educational Press
CHASQUI
THE ETHNODISC JOURNAL OF RECORDED SOUND
Gay Sunshine Press, Inc.
Institute for the Study of Human Issues (ISHI)
INTERNATIONAL PORTLAND REVIEW
LATIN AMERICAN PERSPECTIVES
The Maguey Press
MAIZE
Maize Press
NEWS AND LETTERS
News and Letters Press
EL PALACIO
Place of Herons
Plain Wrapper Press s.n.c.
PULP
REVIEW
The School of Living
Studia Hispanica Editors
TINTA
WOOD IBIS
Workers' Press

LAW

BULLETIN OF THE BOARD OF CELTIC STUDIES
Coker Books
COMMUNICATIONS AND THE LAW
THE LIBERATOR
THE WRIT
Writers Press

LESBIANISM

ALBATROSS
Avant-Garde Creations
Back Row Press
Catalyst
Cleis Press
CONDITIONS
Diana Press, Inc
Eggplant Press
FEMINARY
FOCUS: A Journal For Lesbians
Frog in the Well
A GAY BIBLIOGRAPHY
GAY COMMUNITY NEWS
Gay Task Force, American Library Association
Glad Hag Books
GPU NEWS
THE LESBIAN TIDE
LESBIAN VOICES
MAJORITY REPORT
Metis Press
Motheroot Publications
The Naiad Press, Inc.
National Gay News, Inc.

OFF OUR BACKS
Out & Out Books
PARAGRAPH: A QUARTERLY OF GAY FICTION
PEACE NEWS "For Non-Violent Revolution"
Persephone Press
Persona Press
PLEXUS, Bay Area Women's Newspaper
rara avis
Sappho Publications Ltd
The Seal Press
THE SECOND WAVE
Slough Press
Stephen Wright Press
Sunbury Press
13th MOON
Tide Publications
Timely Books
Tomato Publications Ltd.
WOMEN: A Journal of Liberation

LIBERTARIAN

AGAINST THE WALL
'THE CASSETTE GAZETTE'
City Lights Books
Confluence Press, Inc.
THE DANDELION
FRONTLINES
Handshake Editions
HOWL
Libre Press
LIMIT! (The National Newsletter Of The Libertarian Republican Alliance)
LITERATURE OF LIBERTY
Mockingbird Press
NEWS AND LETTERS
News and Letters Press
Partisan Press
PEACE NEWS "For Non-Violent Revolution"
ROUGH JUSTICE for the Single Homeless
SAMISDAT
SMITH'S JOURNAL
SOUTHERN LIBERTARIAN MESSENGER
WESTERN WORLD REVIEW

LIBRARIES

ALA/SRRT NEWSLETTER
AMOXCALLI
BOOKLEGGER MAGAZINE AND BOOKS
Celebrating Women Productions
EMERGENCY LIBRARIAN
EXPRESSION
FILM LIBRARY QUARTERLY
Gleniffer Press
HENNEPIN COUNTY LIBRARY CATALOGING BULLETIN
Homosexual Information Center Inc
Information Alternative
LIBRARIANS FOR SOCIAL CHANGE
THE LIBRARY IMAGINATION PAPER!
LIBRARY REVIEW
McFarland & Company, Inc., Publishers
John L Noyce, Publisher
RADICAL BOOKSELLER
RAIN: JOURNAL OF APPROPRIATE TECHNOLOGY
ROCKINGCHAIR
Scarecrow Press
SIPAPU
THE TARAKAN MUSIC LETTER
THE U*N*A*B*A*S*H*E*D LIBRARIAN, THE "HOW I RUN MY LIBRARY GOOD" LETTER
WLW JOURNAL: News/Views/Reviews for Women and Libraries
Women Library Workers

LITERARY REVIEW

AGENDA
THE AGENT
AKROS
THE ALTADENA REVIEW
The Altadena Review, Inc.

AMERICAN ARTS PAMPHLET SERIES
THE AMERICAN BOOK REVIEW
ANGEL EXHAUST
THE ANGLO-WELSH REVIEW
ANN ARBOR REVIEW
ANTAEUS
THE ANTIGONISH REVIEW
ARIZONA QUARTERLY
THE ARTFUL REPORTER
ASPEN ANTHOLOGY
THE ATLANTIC REVIEW
THE AUTHOR
BALTIC AVENUE POETRY JOURNAL
BARTLEBY'S REVIEW
LE BEACON REVIEW
BEDFORDSHIRE MAGAZINE
BIRD EFFORT
BLACK AMERICAN LITERATURE FORUM
THE BLACK POSITION
THE BLACK REVIEW
THE BLUEGRASS LITERARY REVIEW
BOOKS IN CANADA: A National Review Of Books
BOSS
BRITISH JOURNAL OF AESTHETICS
THE BULWER LYTTON CHRONICLE
CAFE SOLO
CAFETERIA
CALIBAN: A Journal of New World Thought & Writing
THE CALIFORNIA QUARTERLY
Cambric Press
CANADIAN AUTHOR & BOOKMAN
CANADIAN FICTION MAGAZINE
THE CANADIAN FORUM
CANADIAN LITERATURE
CANTO Review of the Arts
Carcanet Press
CENTER
THE CHANEY CHRONICAL
THE CHARIOTEER
CHARITON REVIEW
CHASQUI
CHICAGO REVIEW
CHOOMIA (A literary review)
CHOUTEAU REVIEW
THE CHOWDER REVIEW
COLORADO-NORTH REVIEW
CONFRONTATION
CONNECTICUT QUARTERLY
THE CONTEMPORARY LITERARY SCENE
CRAZY HORSE
CREAM CITY REVIEW
CREDENCES: A Journal of Twentieth Century Poetry and Poet-
ics
CRITIQUE: Studies in Modern Fiction
CULTURAL WATCHDOG NEWSLETTER
CUTBANK
THE DALHOUSIE REVIEW
DARK HORSE
DELTA Literary Review
DENVER QUARTERLY
DESCANT
DOUBLE HARNESS
DUCK SOUP
EAR MAGAZINE
EAST RIVER REVIEW
EDWARDIAN STUDIES
ELAN POETIQUE LITTERAIRE ET PACIFISTE
THE FAULT
FICTION INTERNATIONAL
THE FIDDLEHEAD
FIRELANDS ARTS REVIEW
FLY BY NIGHT
FOCUS: A Journal For Lesbians
FOLIO
FOREIGN POETS AND AUTHORS REVIEW
The Future Press
GARCIA LORCA REVIEW
GAY SUNSHINE: A Journal of Gay Liberation
GEGENSCHEIN

THE GEORGIA REVIEW
GILTEDGE: New Series
GLOBAL TAPESTRY JOURNAL
THE GRAMERCY REVIEW
Great Raven Press
GREAT WORKS
GREENSBORO REVIEW
THE HAMPDEN-SYDNEY POETRY REVIEW
HAND BOOK
HAPPINESS HOLDING TANK
THE HARVARD ADVOCATE
Harvest Publishers
HARVEST QUARTERLY
Hearthstone Press
HEIRS
THE HELEN REVIEW
HELIX
HELLCOAL ANNUAL
Hellcoal Press
THE HOLLINS CRITIC
HOLLOW SPRING REVIEW OF POETRY
HOME PLANET NEWS
Home Planet Publications
THE HUDSON REVIEW
HYPERION A Poetry Journal
INDEX ON CENSORSHIP
INDIAN Literature
INTERNATIONAL PORTLAND REVIEW
INTERSTATE
IRONWOOD
Ironwood Press
ISLANDS, A New Zealand Quarterly of Arts & Letters
JAMES JOYCE QUARTERLY
Jawbone Press
JOURNAL OF CANADIAN FICTION
THE JOURNAL OF COMMONWEALTH LITERATURE
JOURNAL OF MODERN LITERATURE
JOURNAL OF SOUTH ASIAN LITERATURE
JOYCEAN LIVELY ARTS GUILD REVIEW
Jules Verne Circle
JULES VERNE VOYAGER
KANSAS QUARTERLY
KAYAK
THE KENYON REVIEW
THE KIPLING JOURNAL
Kontexts Publications
KOSMOS
Kosmos
LAOMEDON REVIEW
LAPIS
Lapis Educational Association, Inc.
LAUGHING BEAR
LETTERS
LETTERS MAGAZINE
THE LIMBERLOST REVIEW
LINQ
LITERARY MONITOR: The Voice of Contemporary Literature
THE LITERARY REVIEW
THE LITTLE WORD MACHINE
LONG POND REVIEW
MADRONA
THE MALAHAT REVIEW
THE MASSACHUSETTS REVIEW
MATRIX
THE METRO
MICHIGAN QUARTERLY REVIEW
THE MICKLE STREET REVIEW
THE MIDWEST QUARTERLY
THE MISSOURI REVIEW
MONTEMORA
Motheroot Journal
MOUNTAIN REVIEW
MOVING OUT: Feminist Literary & Arts Journal
NANTUCKET REVIEW
NEW BOSTON REVIEW
NEW DEPARTURES
NEW EDINBURGH REVIEW
NEW ENGLAND REVIEW
NEW HUMANIST

NEW LITERATURE & IDEOLOGY
NEW OREGON REVIEW
NEW ORLEANS REVIEW
NEW PAGES
NEW VOICES
NEW WOMEN'S TIMES & NEW WOMEN'S TIMES FEMI-
    NIST REVIEW
NEW YORK ARTS JOURNAL
NEWORLD
NORTH AMERICAN MENTOR MAGAZINE
NORTHEAST RISING SUN
NOT GUILTY!
OBSIDIAN: BLACK LITERATURE IN REVIEW
OCCASIONAL REVIEW
OCCIDENT
THE OHIO REVIEW
OHIOANA QUARTERLY
OSIRIS
OTHER PRESS POETRY REVIEW
OUTRIGGER
Owlseye Publications
P.E.N. BROADSHEET
PANJANDRUM POETRY JOURNAL
PARIS REVIEW
PARNASSUS: POETRY IN REVIEW
PARTISAN REVIEW
PEMBROKE MAGAZINE
PENNINE PLATFORM
Pennsylvania State University Press
PERMAFROST
THE PHOENIX
THE PIKESTAFF FORUM
THE PIKESTAFF REVIEW
PILGRIMS
PLOUGHSHARES
POET & CRITIC
POETALK QUARTERLY
POETRY CANADA REVIEW
POETRY NATION REVIEW
THE POETRY PROJECT NEWSLETTER
PRAIRIE SCHOONER
PULPSMITH
QUERCUS
RACCOON
Raven Publications
RED WEATHER
REVISTA CHICANO-RIQUENA
THE ROMANTIST
ROOM OF ONE'S OWN
RUSSIAN LITERATURE TRIQUARTERLY
SAINT ANDREWS REVIEW
SAMISDAT
SAMPHIRE
SAN FRANCISCO REVIEW OF BOOKS
SAN FRANCISCO STORIES
SAN JOSE STUDIES
SAN MARCOS REVIEW
SCIENCE FICTION & FANTASY BOOK REVIEW
The Sean Dorman Manuscript Society
SF COMMENTARY
SHAVIAN—JOURNAL OF BERNARD SHAW
SHAW NEWSLETTER
THE SHAW REVIEW
Shaw Society
SHENANDOAH
SILVERFISH REVIEW
THE SLACKWATER REVIEW
SLOW LORIS READER
SMALL MOON
SOURCE
SOUTHERN HUMANITIES REVIEW
SOUTHERN REVIEW
THE SOUTHERN REVIEW
SOUTHWEST REVIEW
STAND
STARDANCER
STONY HILLS: The New England Alternative Press Review
SURVIVOR
Swamp Press

THE TEXAS REVIEW
13th MOON
THOREAU JOURNAL QUARTERLY
THE THOREAU SOCIETY BULLETIN
THREE RIVERS POETRY JOURNAL
THE THREEPENNY REVIEW
Thunder's Mouth Press
TIGHTROPE
TLM Press
TOWARDS
TRIBUTARY
UNDER THE SIGN OF PISCES: Anais Nin and Her Circle
UNIVERSITY OF WINDSOR REVIEW
UNIVERSITY PUBLISHING
UNMUZZLED OX
THE UNREALIST: A Left Literary Magazine
VANDERBILT POETRY REVIEW
VEGATABLE BOX
VISIONS
WAVES
WEBSTER REVIEW
WELLSIANA, The World Of H.G. Wells
WEST COAST POETRY REVIEW
John Westburg, Publisher
WESTERN AMERICAN LITERATURE
WESTERN HUMANITIES REVIEW
WHAT'S NEW ABOUT LONDON, JACK?
The Wine Press
Women's Studies
THE WORMWOOD REVIEW
The Wormwood Review Press
WRITERS NEWS MANITOBA
WRITER'S NEWSLETTER
WRITING
THE YALE REVIEW
Yarrow Press
ZERO REVIEW
The Zero Press

LITERATURE (GENERAL)

& (Ampersand) Press
Absolute O Kelvin (AOK) Press
Acme Print & Litho
ALIVE
ALPHA
ALTERNATIVE FUTURES: THE JOURNAL OF UTOPIAN
    STUDIES
American Revolutionary Political Pamphlets
ANN ARBOR REVIEW
Ansuda Publications
Ardis
Charles N. Aronson, Writer Publisher
Ashford Press
ASPECT, Art and Literature
Associated Creative Writers
Auriga
Author! Author! Publishing Co.
Authors' Co-op Publishing Co.
Autolycus Press
Aya Press
BACK BAY VIEW
BANGE DAGEN
THE BARAT REVIEW: A Journal of Literature and the Arts
THE BENNINGTON REVIEW
THE BIBLIOTHECK
Bilingue Publications
BIRD EFFORT
BLACK MARIA
Black Swan Books Ltd.
BLOODROOT
Bloodroot, Inc.
BOTTOMFISH MAGAZINE
BOXCAR
The Boxwood Press
Breitenbush Publications, Inc.
BRIARPATCH
Briarpatch Press
"BRILLIANT CORNERS": A Magazine of The Arts
BROWNING SOCIETY NOTES

BUCKNELL REVIEW
CAHIER
Calamus Books
CALLALOO
Calliopea Press
CALYX: A Journal of Art and Literature by Women
CANADIAN AUTHOR & BOOKMAN
Capra Press
Carcanet Press
CAROLINA QUARTERLY
Cassandra Publications
CENTRAL PARK
THE CHARIOTEER
CHELSEA
Christopher Davies Publishers Ltd.
Christopher's Books
City Lights Books
CITY MINER
Coach House Press
COFFEE BREAK
Coffee Break Press
DE COLORES: Journal of Emerging Raza Philosophy
CONCEPTIONS SOUTHWEST
CONNECTICUT FIRESIDE
CONNECTICUT QUARTERLY
CONTRABAND MAGAZINE
Contraband Press
Co-op Books Ltd.
CORNFIELD REVIEW
CRAWL OUT YOUR WINDOW
Crawl Out Your Window Press
CREACION
Crosscut Saw Press
CROTON REVIEW
Crowfoot Press
The Crow's Mark Press
CRYPTOC: The Crypt of Comics
CULTURAL WATCHDOG NEWSLETTER
CUMBERLAND JOURNAL
Dakota Press
DECEMBER MAGAZINE
December Press
THE DEKALB LITERARY ARTS JOURNAL
DELIRIUM
DIALOGUE
DIMENSION
Doggeral Press
EARTH'S DAUGHTERS
Earthwise Publications
Editorial Creacion
Entwhistle Books
The Fault Press
The Feminist Press
FEMINIST STUDIES
FICTION INTERNATIONAL
Five Trees Press
FOCUS: A Journal For Lesbians
FOCUS/ MIDWEST
FOUR DOGS MOUNTAIN SONGS
FRONT STREET TROLLEY
EL FUEGO DE AZTLAN
Full Court Press, Inc.
Funch Press
Futile
The Future Press
Gibbous Press
Giddyup Press
Gleniffer Press
Gluxlit Press
GNOSIS
Great Basin Press
Great Works Editions
GREENHOUSE REVIEW
Griffon House Publications
Ground Under Press
Growing Room Collective
Guernica Editions
Jean Guenot
THE HAMPDEN-SYDNEY POETRY REVIEW

Harian Creative Press
THE HARVARD ADVOCATE
Haskell House Publishers, Ltd.
Heinemann Publisher's (NZ) Ltd
HELIX
Hexagon Press
HILLS
HOB-NOB
HODMANDOD
HOLLOW SPRING REVIEW OF POETRY
Holmgangers Press
Holy Cow! Press
HOT WATER REVIEW
House of White Shell Woman
HYPERION A Poetry Journal
ILLUMINATIONS
IMPEGNO 70
INDIANA WRITES
INPRINT
INS & OUTS
Ins & Outs Press
INSIDE/OUT
Intermedia Press
Io (named after moon of Jupiter)
ION
Jelm Mountain Publications
"JOINT" CONFERENCE
JOURNAL OF MODERN LITERATURE
Kenmore Press
Konglomerati Press
Kropotkin's Lighthouse Publications
L.W.M. Publications
LAKE STREET REVIEW
Lame Johnny Press
Lancaster - Miller Publishers
LAPIS
Lapis Educational Association, Inc.
LAUGHING BEAR
Laughing Bear Press
Lawton Press
Leete's Island Books
Leland Mellott Books
LETTERS
LITERATURE OF LIBERTY
Little Wing Publishing
LIVE WRITERS! LOCAL ON TAP
The Lomond Press
Longship Press
Lorien House
LOST GENERATION JOURNAL
Lothlorien
LUCKY HEART BOOKS
M.O.P. Press
MAIN TREND
Mainespring Press
MAIZE
Maize Press
MANGO
THE MANHATTAN REVIEW
Mayapple Press
McBooks Press
The Menard Press
Merging Media
METAMORFOSIS
Metatron Press
MICHIGAN QUARTERLY REVIEW
MIDWEST ALLIANCE
MODUS OPERANDI
Moon Books
Motheroot Publications
Mothra Press
THE MRB NETWORK
MYTHLORE
NETHULA JOURNAL OF CONTEMPORARY LITERATURE
NEW COLLAGE MAGAZINE
New England Press
NEW ENGLAND REVIEW
NIR/NEW INFINITY REVIEW
THE NEW LAUREL REVIEW

ALTERNATIVE RESEARCH NEWSLETTER
ARULO!
THE BERKELEY MONTHLY
BRANCHING OUT
THE BRITISH ALTERNATIVE PRESS INDEX
The Carolina Wren Press
CENTER FOR SOUTHERN FOLKLORE MAGAZINE
CENTERING: A Magazine of Poetry
Children's Art Foundation, Inc.
CONFRONTATION
CONNECTICUT FIRESIDE
CROP DUST
Energy Earth Communications, Inc.
GRAND RIVER REVIEW/CAPITOL CITY MOON
GRAVIDA
Great Lakes Publishing
HAPPINESS HOLDING TANK
Harvest Publishers
HARVEST QUARTERLY
Heidelberg Graphics
Inky Trails Publications
INTERMEDIA
THE INTERNATIONAL UNIVERSITY POETRY QUAR-
TERLY
IOWA CITY BEACON LITERARY REVIEW
IRONWOOD
Ironwood Press
Konglomerati Press
LAUGHING UNICORN
Lothlorien
Jim Mann & Associates
MEDIA MANAGEMENT MONOGRAPHS
THE METRO
MOVING OUT: Feminist Literary & Arts Journal
NEW AMERICA
NEW MAGAZINE REVIEW
NEW PAGES
NEW POETRY
NEWS RELEASE FROM THE CHESS PRESS SYNDICATE
OREGON TIMES MAGAZINE
Poet Papers
POETRY QUARTERLY (previously CURLEW)
POETRY TORONTO NEWSLETTER
PRAIRIE SUN
Publishing Associates
RELIX
SEWANEE REVIEW
THE SMALL PRESS REVIEW
SOJOURNER, THE NEW ENGLAND WOMEN'S JOURNAL
OF NEWS, OPINIONS AND THE ARTS
STONE SOUP, The Magazine By Children
13th MOON
URBANE GORILLA
Vagabond Press
VERMONT CHILDREN'S MAGAZINE
WILLAMETTE VALLEY OBSERVER
WOMEN STUDIES ABSTRACTS
Years Press

MATHEMATICS

Applied Probability Trust
Ilkon Press
Liberty Publishing Company, Inc.
MATHEMATICAL SPECTRUM
Polygonal Publishing House
University Statistical Tracts

MEDIEVAL

Askin Publishers, Ltd.
Cherry Valley Editions
Mandorla Publications
THE NORTH WIND
NOTES & QUERIES: for Readers & Writers, Collectors & Li-
brarians
NOTTINGHAM MEDIAEVAL STUDIES
Raintree
Resource Publications

MEN

AMERICAN MAN
JOURNAL OF CALIFORNIA AND GREAT BASIN AN-
THROPOLOGY
THE LIBERATOR
Malki Museum Press
MEN'S
Programmed Studies Inc
RECON
Red Alder Books
RFD
Triad Press

MIDDLE EAST

ARAB AMERICAN ALMANAC
Between The Lines
Dream Place Publications
Great Eastern Book Company
ISRAEL HORIZONS
Lycabettus Press
MERIP REPORTS
M'GODOLIM
Moonsquilt Press
NEWS AND LETTERS
News and Letters Press
THE NEWS CIRCLE
Oleander Press
Three Continents Press
VOICES - ISRAEL

MILITARY, VETERANS

Alex Aiken
The Battery Press, Inc.
CONSTALLATIONS
DAWN
East River Anthology
Lancer Militaria
Libre Press
MILITARY IMAGES MAGAZINE
PACIFIC RESEARCH
Paladin Enterprises, Inc.
Jim Phillips Publications
Presidio Press
The Scribe Press

MUSIC

ALBUM
AMERICAN FIDDLERS NEWS
ANTIQUE PHONOGRAPH MONTHLY
APM Press
The Avondale Press
Bell Springs Publishing Company
BLITZ
The Bold Strummer Ltd
"BRILLIANT CORNERS": A Magazine of The Arts
Calliope Publishing Inc.
Celestial Otter
CODA: The Jazz Magazine
COMPUTER MUSIC JOURNAL
CROSSCURRENTS
DANCE HERALD
Dragon's Teeth Press
DREAMS
EAR MAGAZINE
Electronic Music Enterprises
ENGLISH DANCE AND SONG
THE ETHNODISC JOURNAL OF RECORDED SOUND
F. Fergeson Productions
FLORAL UNDERAWL GAZETTE
Glouchester Press (Music Publ)
THE GRACKLE: Improvised Music In Transition
IMAGINE
IMPETUS MAGAZINE
INDIAN HOUSE
JOURNAL OF CALIFORNIA AND GREAT BASIN AN-
THROPOLOGY
Kelsey St. Press
Legacy Books (formerly Folklore Associates)
LITTLE CAESAR
LIVING BLUES

Main Track Publications
Malki Museum Press
Manzano Press
Merlin Press
MIAMI INTERNATIONAL
MODERN LITURGY
Moon Publications
MUSIC AND LETTERS
MUSICAL OPINION
New Woman Press
Nighthawk Press
Northeastern University Press
NOSTALGIAWORLD
Pachart Publishing House
PAID MY DUES: JOURNAL OF WOMEN AND MUSIC
PAPER AIR
PhoeniXongs
Plain View, Inc.
PRAIRIE SUN
Promise Publishing Corp.
RELIX
Resource Publications
Rock Culture Books
ST. MAWR
St. Mawr Jazz Poetry Project
Shinn Music Aids
SING OUT! The Folk Song Magazine
SNAPDRAGON
SOUTHERN QUARTERLY: A Journal of the Arts in the South
THE STEREOPHILE
Sun-Scape Publications
TIME BARRIER EXPRESS
TOCHER
Tree Toad Press
TROUSER PRESS
Two-Eighteen Press
XENHARMONIC BULLETIN

NATIVE AMERICAN

AKWESASNE NOTES
ALBERTA HISTORY
Backpack Media
Bear Claw Press
Bear Tribe
Between The Lines
Capra Press
Cat's Pajamas Press
THE CIRCLE
LA CONFLUENCIA
Copley Books
Dakota Press
ETC Publications
FROM THE CENTER: A FOLIO
FROZEN WAFFLES
Glenbow-Alberta Institute
Heidelberg Graphics
Heyday Books
Historical Society of Alberta
INDIAN ARIZONA NEWS
INDIAN HOUSE
INDIAN TRUTH
THE INDIAN VOICE
INTERRACIAL BOOKS FOR CHILDREN BULLETIN
JOURNAL OF CALIFORNIA AND GREAT BASIN AN-
   THROPOLOGY
Lawrence Hill & Company, Publishers, Inc.
The Lightning Tree
LUMBEE NATION TIMES
MAIZE
Maize Press
Malki Museum Press
MANY SMOKES
The Middle Atlantic Press
EL NAHUATZEN
Naturegraph Publishers, Inc.
NEWS AND LETTERS
News and Letters Press
Oregon Historical Society
EL PALACIO

Peregrine Smith, Inc.
Place of Herons
San Pedro Press
SCREE
Slough Press
SOUTH DAKOTA REVIEW
The Stevenson Press
Strawberry Press
SUN TRACKS: An American Indian Literary Magazine
Sunbury Press
TSA'ASZI'
TURTLE
Unicorn Press
WHETSTONE
WHISPERING WIND MAGAZINE
WOOD IBIS

NEW ENGLAND

GARGOYLE
The Globe Pequot Press
NEW ENGLAND SAMPLER
Union Park Press
Sherry Urie

NEW ZEALAND

ISLANDS, A New Zealand Quarterly of Arts & Letters

NEWSLETTER

ADVISORY BOARD RECORD
ALA/SRRT NEWSLETTER
ALTERNATIVE MEDIA
AMERICAN DANCE GUILD NEWSLETTER
August Derleth Society Newsletter
BALSAM FLEX SHEET
Cadenza Press
CAROUSEL
Center for Women's Studies & Services (CWSS)
CODA: Poets & Writers Newsletter
COMMON WORD
COMMUNITY SERVICE NEWSLETTER
CONRADIANA
THE CO-OP OBSERVER
COSMEP NEWSLETTER
EAR MAGAZINE
EARTHWISE NEWSLETTER
EDITORIAL EYE
FEDERAL NOTES
FEMINIST BULLETIN
FIT
FRONTLINES
FUTURE STUDIES CENTRE NEWSLETTER
Gleniffer Press
HARD CRABS
HAWAII LITERARY ARTS COUNCIL NEWSLETTER
HOUSESMITHS JOURNAL
HSA FROGPOND
INDIAN TRUTH
INPRINT
KXE6S VEREIN R NEWSLETTER
Kxe6s Verein R Press
LAUGHING BEAR
LIFELINE
LOCUS: The Newspaper of the Science Fiction Field
THE LONGEST REVOLUTION
MATRIX
Moody Street Irregulars
MOODY STREET IRREGULARS
NEWSFRONT INTERNATIONAL
NEWSLETTER
Oregon Historical Society
THE ORIGINAL ART REPORT (TOAR)
PEEPHOLE ON PEOPLE
PIP COLLEGE 'HELPS' NEWSLETTER
POET TREE NEWS
POETRY NEWSLETTER
Poets & Writers, Inc.
POETS' LEAGUE of GREATER CLEVELAND NEWSLETTER
POW (Poetry Organization for Women)
PSYCHOTHERAPY DIGEST

THE PYRAMID GUIDE: International Bi-Monthly Newsletter
Quality Publications, Inc.
RESOURCES FOR FEMINIST RESEARCH
RIO GRANDE WRITERS NEWSLETTER
SCIENCE FICTION CHRONICLE
SIPAPU
SOUTHERN LIBERTARIAN MESSENGER
THROUGH THE LOOKING GLASS
WASHINGTON INTERNATIONAL ARTS LETTER
THE WISHING WELL
WORLD OF POETRY
WRITER'S NEWSLETTER
WRITER'S NEWSLETTER

ANAIS NIN

UNDER THE SIGN OF PISCES: Anais Nin and Her Circle

OCCULT

Alta Gaia Society
Arcane Order
Artists & Alchemists Publications
Ash-Kar Press
ASI Publishers, Inc.
Askin Publishers, Ltd.
ASTROLOGY '80—The New Aquarian Agent
ASTROLOGY NOW
Auromere, Inc.
Autumn Press, Inc.
Bear Tribe
Borderland Sciences Research Foundation
BOTH SIDES NOW
Cat Anna Press
Celestial Gifts
CONNECTICUT FIRESIDE
CONSPIRACIES UNLIMITED
Cosmic Brain Trust
COSMIC CIRCUS
CRCS Publications
Dimensionist Press
The Donning Company / Publishers
Gemini Press
Gibson-Hiller
Hesperidian Press
Io (named after moon of Jupiter)
JOURNAL OF BORDERLAND RESEARCH
JOURNAL OF SUPERSTITION AND MAGICAL THINKING
Kitchen Sink Enterprises
Llewellyn Publications
M.O. Publishing Company
MAGICAL BLEND
Magical Blend
THE METRO
Onaway Publications
ORE
Planetary Research
PREMONITION TIMES
Quantal Publishing B
Quicksilver Productions
Sagittarius Rising
SPACE AND TIME
SPIRALS
Sun, Man, Moon Inc.
Thirteenth House
Tree Books
Valkyrie Press, Inc.
Vanilla Press
VIEWPOINT AQUARIUS
WEIRD TRIPS
White Tower Inc. Press
WITCHCRAFT DIGEST MAGAZINE (THE WICA NEWS-
    LETTER)
WOOD IBIS

OUTDOORS, SPORTS, BOATING

Albacore Press
Baja Trail Publications, Inc.
Celestial Arts
Christopher Davies Publishers Ltd.
Chronicle Books/Prism Editions

Cobblesmith
Creative Arts Book Company
ETC Publications
Far Out West Publications
FIGHTING WOMAN NEWS
The Great Outdoors Trading Company
THE GROVE
Hancock House Publishers
Harvestman and Associates
Heyday Books
THE HOT SPRINGS GAZETTE
Human Kinetics Pub. Inc.
IN STRIDE
International Marine Publishing Co.
Io (named after moon of Jupiter)
JOURNAL OF SPORT PSYCHOLOGY
KITE LINES
Liberty Publishing Company, Inc.
Light Living Library
Loggeerhead
Masters Publications
Merganzer Press
MESSAGE POST
MEXICO WEST
Mountain Press Publishing Co.
The Mountaineers Books
Paladin Enterprises, Inc.
Parachuting Publications
Parachuting Resources
PARACHUTIST
Peregrine Smith, Inc.
Powerlifting USA
POWERLIFTING USA
Pruett Publishing Company
QUEST
Regmar Publishing Co.
SANTA BARBARA HARBOR NEWS
Seahawk Press
Service Press Inc.
SIGNPOST
Signpost Books
SKYDIVING
Stone Wall Press, Inc
Survival Cards
SWIM LITE NEWS (newsletter)
WESTERN SPORTSMAN
WHISTLER ANSWER
WISCONSIN TRAILS

PACIFIC NORTHWEST

Albacore Press
Gray Beard Publishing

PHILATELY, NUMISMATICS

Philatelic Directory Publishing Co

PHILOSOPHY

Alleluia Press
Alta Napa Press
Apeiron Press
Art Official Inc.
Artists & Alchemists Publications
THE ASTRONOMY QUARTERLY
Auromere, Inc.
Autumn Press, Inc.
Avant-Garde Creations
Bear Tribe
BERTRAND RUSSELL TODAY
Blue Heron Press
The Book Department
BOTH SIDES NOW
Brason-Sargar Publications
BRITISH JOURNAL OF AESTHETICS
C.S.P. WORLD NEWS
'THE CASSETTE GAZETTE'
Center for the Art of Living
Center Press
Center Publications
CHAIRMAN'S CHAT

Charisma Press
CHARISMA PRESS REVIEW
COLLABORATION
COSMOPOLITAN CONTACT
DAEDALUS, Journal of the American Academy of Arts and
  Sciences
The Dawn Horse Press
Derwyddon Press
Desserco Publishing
Dharma Publishing
Dominion Press
Dragon's Teeth Press
Edgepress
EFRYDIAU ATHRONYDDOL
Falkynor Books
FIFTH SUN
FILE MAG
Findhorn Publications
W.D. Firestone Press
FOURTH DIMENSION
Franson Publications
Gearhead Press
GESAR- Buddhist Perspectives
Gibson-Hiller
Giddyup Press
Great Eastern Book Company
Greenwood Press, Inc.
Handshake Editions
Himalayan Institute Publishers and Distributors
THE HUMANIST
HUMANIST IN CANADA
IF LIFE, THEN ONE AMONG AT LEAST FOUR
THE INDEPENDENT JOURNAL OF PHILOSOPHY
The Independent Philosophy Press
Inquiry Press
Jewel Publications
JOURNAL OF BIOLOGICAL EXPERIENCE
Journey Publications
The Language Press
LAPIS
Lapis Educational Association, Inc.
Lion Enterprises
LITERATURE OF LIBERTY
LODGISTIKS
LOVE
Mafdet Press
Matagiri
THE MESSAGE
Moonsquilt Press
Mu Publications
Ted Nelson, Publisher
THE NEW ECOLOGIST
NEWS AND LETTERS
News and Letters Press
NOTES FROM THE UNDERGROUND
ONEARTH IMAGE
OPINION
Papillon Press
LES PAPILLONS, A Journal of Modern Philosophical Inquiry
PAUNCH
Peace Press
Peradam Publishing House
PHANTASMAGORIA, Journey into the Surreal
Precedent Publishing Inc.
Primary Press
Proletarian Publishers
Prometheus Books
QUEEN'S QUARTERLY: A Canadian Review
R & J Kudlay
Seed Center
Sheriar Press
Sitnalta Press
Slough Press
Socialist Party of Canada
Sovereign Press
Sufi Order Publications
Sun-Scape Publications
TAI CHI
Tanam Press

TELOS
Telos Press
TOWARDS
Tree Books
TRULY FINE PRESS, A Review
Unity Press
UNIVERSAL HUMAN RIGHTS
University of the Trees Press
Vanilla Press
WESTERN WORLD REVIEW
Wild Horses Potted Plant
The Wine Press
Wisdom Garden Books
WOOD IBIS
Words
Ziesing Bros.' Publishing Company

PHOTOGRAPHY

A SHOUT IN THE STREET: a journal of literary and visual art
AFTERIMAGE
Afterimage Book Publishers
Alchemist/Light Publishing
ALDEBARAN
Angle Lightning Press
ANOTHER CHICAGO MAGAZINE
Backpack Media
Backroads/Caroline House
Banana Productions
The Black Cat Press
THE BLACK WARRIOR REVIEW
California Street
Camera Work Gallery
THE CAPE ROCK
Capra Press
Carolyn Bean Publishing, Ltd.
Chronicle Books/Prism Editions
Cider Barrel Press
Clatworthy Colorvues
Coach House Press
Coast to Coast Books
COMBINATIONS, A JOURNAL OF PHOTOGRAPHY
CONFEDERATE CALENDAR WORKS
Creative Eye Press
Curvd H&Z
DARK HORSE
DESCANT
The Dog Ear Press
DOUBLE HARNESS
Druid Books
Duck Down Press
Embee Press
EVENT
FLOATING ISLAND
Foolproof Press
FROZEN WAFFLES
The Garlic Press
Glad Hag Books
GLASSWORKS
Lorna Greene
Hancock House Publishers
HOT WATER REVIEW
Hurtig Publishers
Images Press
IMPULSE
JAM TO-DAY
JOURNAL OF CALIFORNIA AND GREAT BASIN AN-
  THROPOLOGY
KELLNER'S MONEYGRAM
Lightbooks
LONG POND REVIEW
Malki Museum Press
MILITARY IMAGES MAGAZINE
NIT&WIT: Literary Arts Magazine
Not-For-Sale-Press
OVO MAGAZINE
Padma Press
EL PALACIO
PAUNCH
Peace & Pieces Foundation

493

PHOEBE
Photo-Art Enterprizes, Inc.
PHOTOFLASH: Models & Photographers Newsletter
PHOTOGRAPHIC CALENDAR
THE PHOTOLETTER
PIG IRON
Powerlifting USA
Pueo Press
Queens College Press
Ram Publications
Riversedge Press
Salt-Works Press
San Francisco Center for Visual Studies
SCREE
SCREEN
SECESSION GALLERY NEWSLETTER
Secession Gallery of Photography, Open Space
SHADOWGRAPHS
SMALL MOON
SOMA-HAOMA
Sothis & Co. Publishing
Spirit Mound Press
SURVIVOR
Thumbprint Press
Thunder's Mouth Press
Tideline Press
URTHKIN
Valkyrie Press, Inc.
WEST BRANCH
WEST PLAINS GAZETTE
THE WINDLESS ORCHARD
Working Press
ZONE
Zone

POETRY

MAGAZINE
A
A SHOUT IN THE STREET: a journal of literary and visual art
ABBEY
ABERDEEN UNIVERSITY REVIEW
ABSINTHE
ABYSS
Abyss/Augtwofive
Acorn
THE ACTS THE SHELFLIFE
ADVENTURES IN POETRY MAGAZINE
AEOLIAN-HARP
Aesopus Press
AEVUM
AGENDA
THE AGNI REVIEW
AHNOI
Ahsahta
AIS EIRI
AKROS
ALCATRAZ
Alcatraz Editions
THE ALCHEMIST
ALDEBARAN
Aldebaran Review
ALEMBIC
Alice James Books
All About Us
Allegany Mountain Press
Alleluia Press
ALLIN
The Ally Press
Alphabox Press
Alta Napa Press
THE ALTADENA REVIEW
The Altadena Review, Inc.
THE ALTERNATIVE PRESS
AMBIT
American Artists In Exhibition, Inc.
AMERICAN POETRY REVIEW
Ampersand Press
AND
ANDROGYNE

Anemone Press
ANGEL EXHAUST
Angels Gate Press
ANGELSTONE
Angelstone
Angle Lightning Press
Anian Press
Anjou
ANN ARBOR REVIEW
ANNEX 21
ANOTHER CHICAGO MAGAZINE
Ansuda Publications
ANTENNA
Anti-Ocean Press
THE ANTIOCH REVIEW
Anvil Press Poetry
APALACHEE QUARTERLY
Apeiron Press
Apple-wood Press
Applezaba Press
AQUARIUS
AQUILA MAGAZINE
Arbitrary Closet Press
Arc Publications
Arcane Order
THE ARK
THE ARK RIVER REVIEW
Armchair Press
Artemisia Press
THE ARTFUL DODGE
ARULO!
AS IS
As Is/So & So Press
ASFA POETRY QUARTERLY
ASPEN ANTHOLOGY
ASPHODEL
ATHAENA
THE ATLANTIC REVIEW
Atlantis Editions
ATTENTION PLEASE
Author! Author! Publishing Co.
Avalon Editions
Aya Press
BACHY
BACKCOUNTRY
Backpack Media
BACULITE
Balsam Flex
BALTIC AVENUE POETRY JOURNAL
Baltic Avenue Press
Bard Press
BARDIC ECHOES
The Barnwood Press
Bartholomew's Cobble
BARTLEBY'S REVIEW
Basement Editions
The Basilisk Press
BB Books
Le Beacon Presse
Bear Claw Press
BEAU FLEUVE SERIES
BEFORE THE RAPTURE
Bellevue Press
THE BELLINGHAM REVIEW
BELOIT POETRY JOURNAL
BERGEN POETS
BERKELEY POETRY REVIEW
BERKELEY POETS COOPERATIVE
Berkeley Poets Workshop and Press
Bern Porter Books
BEYOND BAROQUE
BEYOND RICE, A Broadside Series
BIG MOON
Big River Association
BIG SCREAM
Biohydrant Publications
BIRD EFFORT
BIRTHSTONE
Bits Press

BITTERROOT
BLACK BOOK
BLACK BOX MAGAZINE
Black Buzzard Press
THE BLACK CAT
BLACK JACK & VALLEY GRAPEVINE
Black Sparrow Press
Black Swan Books Ltd.
THE BLACK WARRIOR REVIEW
BLACKBERRY
The Blackhole School of Poethnics
BLANK TAPE
Blind Alley Press
BLT Press (Bates, Lear, and Tulp)
BLUE BUILDINGS
Blue Heron Press
BLUE HORSE
THE BLUE HOTEL
Blue Moon Press, Inc.
Blue Mornings Press
Blue Mountain Press
The Blue Oak Press
BLUE PIG
BLUE UNICORN
Blue Wind Press
THE BLUEGRASS LITERARY REVIEW
Blues Press
Boa Editions
Boardwell - Kloner
BOGG
BOMBAY GIN
BONSAI
Bonsai Press
The Bookstore Press
Borderline Press
BOSS
Boss Books
BOX 749
BRAINWAIFS
Brason-Sargar Publications
BRAVO
Breitenbush Publications, Inc.
Brick/Nairn
"BRILLIANT CORNERS": A Magazine of The Arts
Broken Whisker Studio
Brown Rabbit Press
BUCKLE
Burning Deck Press
Byron Press
The Cabbagehead Press
Cadmus Editions
CAFE SOLO
CAFETERIA
THE CALIFORNIA QUARTERLY
CALLIOPE
Calliope Press
Calliopea Press
CAMBRIC POETRY PROJECT
Cambric Press
Camera Work Gallery
CANADIAN AUTHOR & BOOKMAN
THE CANADIAN FORUM
CANADIAN LITERATURE
CANDELABRUM POETRY MAGAZINE
CANVASS
THE CAPE ROCK
THE CAPILANO REVIEW
Carcanet Press
Cardinal Press, Inc.
CAROLINA QUARTERLY
The Carolina Wren Press
Carpenter Press
Cassandra Publications
Catalyst
Cat's Pajamas Press
Cliff Catton Press
The Cauldron Press
Cedar Creek Press
CEDAR ROCK

Cedar Rock Press
CELEBRATION
Celestial Otter
THE CENTENNIAL REVIEW
Center For Contemporary Poetry
Centergram Press
CENTERING: A Magazine of Poetry
Ceolfrith Press
The Chair
THE CHAIR
Chalardpro Books
Chandonnet, Ann
CHANDRABHAGA
THE CHARIOTEER
CHARITON REVIEW
Chariton Review Press
Charles River Books, Inc.
The Charles Street Press
CHAWED RAWZIN
Chawed Rawzin Press
Cheat Mountain Press
CHELSEA
Cherry Valley Editions
CHOCK
Chock Publications
CHOOMIA (A literary review)
Chowder Chapbooks
THE CHOWDER REVIEW
Christopher Davies Publishers Ltd.
Christopher's Books
THE CHUNGA REVIEW
Cider Barrel Press
Cider Mill Press
CIMARRON REVIEW
CINCINNATI POETRY REVIEW
Circinatum Press
CIRCLE
Circle Forum
City Lights Books
Clamshell Press
Cleveland State Univ. Poetry Center
CLOWN WAR
Coach House Press
CODA: Poets & Writers Newsletter
THE COFFEEHOUSE
Cold Mountain Press
COLLABORATION
COLLEGE ENGLISH
College V, UCSC
COLONNADES
COLORADO STATE REVIEW
Colorado State Review Press
COLUMBIA: A MAGAZINE OF POETRY AND PROSE
The Common Table
COMPASS
CONCERNING POETRY
CONNECTICUT FIRESIDE
CONNECTIONS MAGAZINE
CONTACT/11: A Bimonthly Poetry Review Magazine
Contact II: Publications
CONTEMPORARY POETRY: A Journal of Criticism
CONTRABAND MAGAZINE
Contraband Press
CONTRAST
Copper Beech Press
Copper Canyon Press/Copperhead
COPULA
Cornerstone Press
CORNFIELD REVIEW
CRAZY HORSE
CREATIVE PITTSBURGH
Creative With Words Publications (CWW)
Creekwood Press
Croissant & Company
CROP DUST
Cross Country Press, Ltd.
CROSSCOUNTRY
Crosscut Saw Press
The Crossing Press

Green Horse Press
The Green Hut Press
Green Knight Press
GREEN'S MAGAZINE
Lorna Greene
THE GREENFIELD REVIEW
The Greenfield Review Press
GREENHOUSE REVIEW
Greenhouse Review Press
THE GREYLEDGE REVIEW
Grilled Flowers Press
Ground Under Press
GRUB STREET
GRYPHON
Guildford Poets Press
GUSTO
Gusto
GUTS AND GRACE
Halty Ferguson Publishing Co.
HANGING LOOSE
Hanging Loose Press
HAPPINESS HOLDING TANK
The Happy Press
Hard Press
HARD PRESSED
Harian Creative Press
Harper Square Press
HARPOON
Hartmus Press
HARVEST
HAWK PRESS Hawk Press
HAWK-WIND
Hearthstone Press
Heavy Evidence Press
Heirs Press
Helikon Press
Helix House
HELLCOAL ANNUAL
Hellcoal Press
The Heron Press
Hesperidian Press
HEY LADY
The Heyeck Press
Hibiscus Press
HIGGINSON JOURNAL
Higginson Press
HIGH/COO: A Quarterly of Short Poetry
High/Coo Press
HILLS
Hippopotamus Press
HIRAM POETRY REVIEW
Hoddypoll Press
HODMANDOD
HOLLOW SPRING REVIEW OF POETRY
Holy Cow! Press
HOME PLANET NEWS
Home Planet Publications
HOO-DOO BlackSeries
The Hosanna Press
HOT WATER REVIEW
House of Anansi Press Limited/Publishing Co.
House of Keys
Houston Writers Workshop
HUERFANO
The Huffman Press
THE HUNGRY YEARS
Huntsville Literary Association
The Hurricane Company
HYPERION A Poetry Journal
Icarus Press
Ilkon Press
Illuminati
ILLUMINATIONS
Illuminations Press
IMAGE MAGAZINE
IMAGES
IMPACT, An International Publication of Contemporary Literature & the Arts
IN A NUTSHELL

In Between Books
IN THE LIGHT
INC.
INDIAN Literature
Indian Publications
Ink Blot Press
INKY TRAILS and TIME TO PAUSE
Interim Books
Interim Press
Intermedia Press
INTERNATIONAL POETRY REVIEW
INTERNATIONAL PORTLAND REVIEW
THE INTERNATIONAL UNIVERSITY POETRY QUARTERLY
The International University Press
INTREPID
Intrepid Press
INTRINSIC: An International Magazine of Poetry & Poetics
INVISIBLE CITY
IOWA CITY BEACON LITERARY REVIEW
IOWA REVIEW
Iris Press
IRON
Iron Mountain Press
Iron Press
IRONWOOD
Ironwood Press
Ishtar Press, Inc.
Islands
ISLANDS, A New Zealand Quarterly of Arts & Letters
Ithaca House
J&C Transcripts
J and J Press
The Jackpine Press
JACKSONVILLE POETRY QUARTERLY
JAM TO-DAY
Janus Press
Jawbone Press
JAZZ
Jazz Press
Jelm Mountain Publications
JEOPARDY
JOE SOAP'S CANOE
Journal Books
JOURNAL OF CANADIAN POETRY
JOURNAL OF NEW JERSEY POETS
JOYCEAN LIVELY ARTS GUILD REVIEW
JUICE
Jump River Press, Inc.
JUMP RIVER REVIEW
Jungle Garden Press
Just Buffalo Press
JUST PULP: The Magazine of Popular Fiction
KALDRON
KANSAS QUARTERLY
KARAKI
KARAMU
Karmic Revenge Laundry Shop Press
Kawabata Press
KAYAK
KEEPSAKE POEMS
Kelsey St. Press
Kenmore Press
Kent Publications
THE KENYON REVIEW
King and Cowen (New York)
King Publications
KONGLOMERATI
Konglomerati Press
Konocti Books
Kontexts Publications
KOSMOS
Kosmos
KRAX
KROKLOK
Kropotkin's Lighthouse Publications
KUDOS
KUDZU
KUKSU: Journal of Backcountry Writing

Kulchur Foundation
LAKE STREET REVIEW
Lame Johnny Press
Lamplighters Roadway Press
LAPIS
Lapis Educational Association, Inc.
LATITUDES
LAUGHING BEAR
Laughing Bear Press
LAUGHING UNICORN
THE LAUREL REVIEW
Laurentian Valley Press
Lawton Press
Leathern Wing Scribble Press
LETTERS
Libra Press
LIGHT: A Poetry Review
The Lightning Tree
THE LIMBERLOST REVIEW
LINES REVIEW
LINQ
Lintel
Lionhead Publishing
LITERARY MONITOR: The Voice of Contemporary Literature
Litmus, Inc.
LITTLE CAESAR
Little Dinosaur Press
THE LITTLE MAGAZINE
THE LITTLE REVIEW
Little River Press
Little Wing Publishing
Live-Oak Press
LOCAL DRIZZLE
The Lomond Press
Long Haul Press
LONG POND REVIEW
LONGHOUSE
Longhouse
LOOK QUICK
LoonBooks
LOONFEATHER: Minnesota North Country Art
LOOT
LOST AND FOUND TIMES
LOST GLOVE
Lost Roads Publishers
THE LOUISVILLE REVIEW
Love Street Books
The Lovejoy Press
LOWLANDS REVIEW
LUCKY HEART BOOKS
LUDD'S MILL
LUMEN/AVENUE A
Luna Bisonte Prods
LUNCH
Lycabettus Press
LYNN VOICES
Lynx House Press
M.O.P. Press
THE MADISON REVIEW
MADRONA
Maelstrom Press
MAELSTROM REVIEW
Mafdet Press
MAG CITY
MAGIC CHANGES
MAGIC SAM
Mainspring Press
THE MAINSTREETER
Malpelo
MAMASHEE
MANASSAS REVIEW: ESSAYS ON CONTEMPORARY
    AMERICAN POETRY
The Mandeville Press
THE MANHATTAN REVIEW
MANROOT
Manroot Books
The Many Press
THE MARGARINE MAYPOLE ORANGOUTANG EXPRESS
Maro Verlag

Matagiri
MATI
Matrix Press
MATTOID
MAXY'S JOURNAL
May-Murdock Publications
Mayapple Press
Meanings Press
MEANJIN QUARTERLY
Membrane Press
The Menard Press
MERLIN PAPERS
Merlin Press
Metatron Press
Michael Joseph Phillips Editions
THE MICKLE STREET REVIEW
THE MIDATLANTIC REVIEW
Midmarch Associates
MIDWEST CHAPARRAL
MILK QUARTERLY
MILKWEED CHRONICLE
THE MILL
MINI-TAUR SERIES
Minnesota Writers' Publishing House
MISSISSIPPI REVIEW
MISSISSIPPI VALLEY REVIEW
MR. COGITO
Mixed Breed
MODERN IMAGES
MODERN POETRY STUDIES
THE MODULARIST REVIEW
MODUS OPERANDI
Mojave Books
Momentum Press
THE MONTANA REVIEW
MONTEMORA
Montreal Poems
MONUMENT IN CANTOS AND ESSAYS
Moody Street Irregulars
MOODY STREET IRREGULARS
Moonfire Press
THE MOONSHINE REVIEW
Moonsquilt Press
Moore Publishing Company
THE MOOSEHEAD REVIEW
Morgan Press
Mosaic Press/Valley Editions
Mosaic Press
Motheroot Publications
Mountain Union Books
MOUTH OF THE DRAGON
Mu Publications
MUNDUS ARTIUM: A Journal of International Literature & Art
Nada
EL NAHUATZEN
Natalie Slohm Associates, Inc.
NAZUNAH
NEBULA
THE NEW AUTHOR
NEW COLLAGE MAGAZINE
NIR/NEW INFINITY REVIEW
NEW JERSEY POETRY MONTHLY
THE NEW JOURNAL
THE NEW LAUREL REVIEW
NEW LETTERS
NEW LITERATURE & IDEOLOGY
NEW MEXICO HUMANITIES REVIEW
NEW ORLEANS REVIEW
NEW POETRY
The New Poets Series
New Rivers Press, Inc.
New Traditions
NEW VOICES
NEW VOICES
New Woman Press
NEW WORLD JOURNAL
New Worlds Unlimited
The New York Literary Press
NEW YORK QUARTERLY

THE NEWSCRIBES
THE NIAGARA MAGAZINE
NIMROD
"NITTY GRITTY"
No Dead Lines
Nobodaddy Press
NOE VALLEY POETS WORKSHOP
Noro Press
NORO REVIEW
NORTH AMERICAN MENTOR MAGAZINE
THE NORTH AMERICAN REVIEW
North Atlantic Books
North Star Press
NORTHEAST/JUNIPER BOOKS
NORTHEAST JOURNAL
NORTHERN LIGHT
NORTHERN LINE
NORTHWEST REVIEW
NORTHWOODS JOURNAL
Northwoods Press, Inc.
NOSTOC
Noumenon Press
O Press
Oasis Books
OCCIDENT
THE OCHLOCKONEE REVIEW
Tom Ockerse Editions
Offshore Press
THE OHIO REVIEW
OINK!
OLD COURTHOUSE FILES
Old Hickory Press
OLD HICKORY REVIEW
Oleander Press
ONE
Oolichan Books
OPEN CELL
OPEN PLACES
Openings Press
ORIGINS
Orion Press
ORPHEUS
Other Publications
Out & Out Books
Out of the Ashes Press
OUT THERE MAGAZINE
OUTERBRIDGE
OUTPOSTS
Outposts Publications
OUTRIGGER
Owl Creek Press
Owlseye Publications
Ox Head Press
Oxus Press
Oyez
P.E.N. BROADSHEET
PACIFIC POETRY AND FICTION REVIEW
PADAN ARAM
PAINTBRUSH: A Journal of Poetry, Translations & Letters
PAINTED BRIDE QUARTERLY
Pakka Press
PALERMO ANTIGRUPPO
Palimpsest Workshop
PAN AMERICAN REVIEW
PANACHE
Panache Books
Pancake Press
THE PANHANDLER
Panjandrum Books
PANJANDRUM POETRY JOURNAL
Papa Bach Paperbacks
PAPER AIR
Paradise Press
PARCHMENT (Broadside Series)
PARIS REVIEW
PARIS VOICES
PARNASSUS: POETRY IN REVIEW
PASTICHE: Poems of Place
PAUNCH

THE PAWN REVIEW
Paycock Press
Peace & Pieces Foundation
PEMBROKE MAGAZINE
Peninhand Press
Penmaen Press Ltd
PENNINE PLATFORM
Penstemon Press
Pentagram Press
Pentangle Press
PENUMBRA
The Penumbra Press
PEQUOD
Pequod Press
Peradam Publishing House
Peregrine Smith, Inc.
Peripatos Press
Perivale Press
PERMAFROST
Permanent Press
Petronium Press
PHANTASMAGORIA, Journey into the Surreal
PHOEBE
PHOENIX BROADSHEETS
PhoeniXongs
PHONE-A-POEM
Pi-Right Press
PIEDMONT LITERARY REVIEW
PIG IRON
Pig Iron Press
The Pikestaff Press
Pinchgut Press
PINCHPENNY
PINECONE
Pirate Press
Pittore Euforico
Place of Herons
Plain View, Inc.
PLAINSPEAK MAGAZINE
PLANTAGENET PRODUCTIONS, Recorded Library of the
   Spoken Word
Pleasure Dome Press (Long Island Poetry Collective Inc.)
PLEXUS, Bay Area Women's Newspaper
PLOUGHSHARES
PLUCKED CHICKEN
Plucked Chicken Press
PLUM
PLUMBERS INK
POEM
POEMS IN PUBLIC PLACES
POESIE - U.S.A.
POET
POET & CRITIC
Poet Gallery Press
POET LORE
Poet Papers
Poet Press India
POETALK QUARTERLY
POETIC JUSTICE
POETRY
POETRY AND AUDIENCE
Poetry & Press
POETRY AUSTRALIA
POETRY CANADA REVIEW
POETRY COMICS
POETRY EAST
POETRY FLASH
Poetry for the People
POETRY IN MOTION
Poetry in Public Places
Poetry Leeds Publications
THE POETRY MISCELLANY
POETRY NEWSLETTER
POETRY NIPPON
The Poetry Nippon Press
POETRY NORTHWEST
POETRY NOTTINGHAM
POETRY NOW
THE POETRY PROJECT NEWSLETTER

POETRY QUARTERLY (previously CURLEW)
POETRY REVIEW
The Poetry Society of Australia
POETRY TORONTO NEWSLETTER
POETRY VIEW
POETRY WALES
POETS' LEAGUE of GREATER CLEVELAND NEWSLETTER
POETS ON:
Point Riders Press
Poltroon Press
The Pomegranate Press
PONTCHARTRAIN REVIEW
Poor Souls Press/Scaramouche Books
PORCH
Porch Publications
The Porcupine's Quill, Inc.
Porphyrion Press
Potto Publications
Practices of the Wind
PRACTICES OF THE WIND
PRAIRIE SCHOONER
PRAXIS: A Journal of Cultural Criticism
PRELUDE TO FANTASY
Prescott Street Press
Press Porcepic Limited
Pressed Curtains
PRIMAVERA
PRIMIPARA
Printed Editions
Prism Books
PRISM INTERNATIONAL
Proem Pamphlets
PTERANODON
PTOLEMY/BROWNS MILLS REVIEW
THE PUB
PUBLISHED POET NEWSLETTER
Publishing Associates
Puckerbrush Press
PUCK'S CORNER
Pueblo Poetry Project
PUERTO DEL SOL
Puerto Del Sol Press
Pulmac Enterprises, Inc.
PULP
Pulse-Finger Press
PURPLE PATCH
The Putah Creek Press
Pygmalion Press
Quality Publications, Inc.
QUARRY WEST
QUARTERLY REVIEW OF LITERATURE
Queens College Press
QUERCUS
QUILT
Quintessence Publications
QUIXOTE, QUIXOTL
R & J Kudlay
RACCOON
RAINBOW'S END
Raindust Press
Rainfeather Press
Raintree
Rainy Day Books
RASPBERRY PRESS (magazine)
Rat & Mole Press
Raven Publications
Raw Dog Press
RE:PRINT (AN OCCASIONAL MAGAZINE)
REACHING
Realities
Rebis Press
Red Alder Books
Red Candle Press
RED CEDAR REVIEW
Red Clay Books
Red Dust
RED FOX REVIEW
Red Herring Press
Red Hill Press, Los Angeles & Fairfax

Red Ochre Press
Red Press
RED WEATHER
Red Weather Press
Reed & Cannon Co
REFLECT
Release Press
Rhiannon Press
RHINO
RIPPLES
RIVER STYX
RIVERSEDGE
Riversedge Press
ROAD/HOUSE
Rochester Routes/Creative Arts Projects
Rook Press, Inc.
ROQ Press
The Rubicon Press
Runa Press
RUNE
Sagarin Press
Saint Andrews Press
SAINT ANDREWS REVIEW
St. Luke's Press
ST. MAWR
St. Mawr Jazz Poetry Project
Salt-Works Press
SALTHOUSE
SAMISDAT
Samisdat Associates
SAN FERNANDO POETRY JOURNAL
SAN JOSE STUDIES
SAN MARCOS REVIEW
San Pedro Press
Sand Dollar
SANDSCRIPT
SAP Society for the Advancement of Poetics
SARCOPHAGUS
Saru
The Sceptre Press
Scop Publications, Inc.
SCOPCRAEFT MAGAZINE
The Scopcraeft Press
SCREE
SCREEN DOOR REVIEW
Sea Of Storms
The Seal Press
The Sean Dorman Manuscript Society
THE SEATTLE REVIEW
Second Aeon Publications
SECOND COMING
Second Coming Press
THE SECOND WAVE
SEEMS
SENECA REVIEW
SEPARATE DOORS
SEPIA
Sesame Press
Seven Buffaloes Press
Seven Woods Press
Shameless Hussy Press
SHANKPAINTER
The Sheep Meadow Press
SHENANDOAH
John B. Sherrill
Shining Waters Press
THE SHIRT OFF YOUR BACK
SHOCKS
Sicilian Antigruppo
Signpost Press
SILVER VAIN
SING HEAVENLY MUSE! WOMEN'S POETRY AND PROSE
Singing Wind Press
SKULL POLISH
SKYWRITING
SLICK PRESS
Slough Press
Slow Loris Press
SLOW LORIS READER

THE SMALL FARM
SMALL MOON
THE SMALL POND MAGAZINE OF LITERATURE
SMOKE
SmokeRoot
Smyrna Press
SNAPDRAGON
SNIPPETS: A Melange of Woman
Snow Press
SNOWY EGRET
SO & SO
SOFT NEED
Soft Press
SOMA-HAOMA
SOME
SOME OTHER MAGAZINE
SONG
Sono Nis Press
Sothis & Co. Publishing
SOU'WESTER
SOUNDINGS/EAST
SOURCE
SOUTH & WEST
SOUTH CAROLINA REVIEW
SOUTH DAKOTA REVIEW
SOUTHERN POETRY REVIEW
SOUTHERN REVIEW
THE SOUTHERN REVIEW
SOUTHWEST REVIEW
THE SOUTHWESTERN REVIEW
SPARROW POVERTY PAMPHLETS
Sparrow Press
Spectacular Diseases
Spectre Press
Spectrum Productions
Spirit Mound Press
THE SPIRIT THAT MOVES US
The Spirit That Moves Us, Inc. (Formerly Emmess Press)
The Spoon River Poetry Press
THE SPOON RIVER QUARTERLY
SPOOR
Spring Church Book Company
STAR WEST
STARDANCER
START
Station Hill Press
STEPPENWOLF
THE STONE
STONE COUNTRY
Stone Country Press
Stone Press
THE STONY THURSDAY BOOK
STRANGE FAECES
Strawberry Press
Street Editions
STREET MAGAZINE
Street Press
STROKER
Studio S Press
SULPHUR RIVER
Summer Stream Press
SUN
Sun
Sun & Moon Press
sun rise fall down artpress
Sun-Scape Publications
SUN TRACKS: An American Indian Literary Magazine
SUNBURY (a poetry magazine)
Sunken Forum Press
SUNRISE
Sunrise Press
The Sunstone Press
SUPRANORMAL, 1983
The Swallow Press Inc.
Swamp Press
Swish
Sydon, Inc.
SYNCLINE
Syntaxophone Publications

SZ/Press
Talonbooks
Tamalpa Press
TAMARACK
Tamarack Editions
TANGENT
Tangent Books
TAR RIVER POETRY
Taurean Horn Press
Taurus Press of Willow Dene
Tejas Art Press
TELEPHONE
Telephone Books
TEMPEST: Avant-Garde Poetry
Ten Crow Press
Ten Penny Players, Inc.
TENDRIL
Testamento Di Intenzionalita Di Alberto Faietti
Texas Center for Writers Press
THICKET
Third Coast
THIRD COAST ARCHIVES
THIRD EYE
13th MOON
THIS
This Press
THISTLE: A MAGAZINE OF CONTEMPORARY WRITING
Thistledown Press
Thorp Springs Press
Three Continents Press
THREE RIVERS POETRY JOURNAL
THREE SISTERS
Thunder City Press
Thunder Creek Publishing Co-operative
THUNDER EGG
THUNDER MOUNTAIN REVIEW
Thunder's Mouth Press
Tideline Press
TIGHTROPE
Timberline Press
TIME CAPSULE, INC.
TINDERBOX
TIOTIS POETRY NEWS
Tiresias Press
Titanic Books
TITMOUSE
TLM Press
Tombouctou Books
Toothpaste Press
TOTTEL'S
TOUCHSTONE
TOUCHSTONE
TRADE MAGAZINE
Trask House Books, Inc.
Traumwald Press
Treacle Press
TREE
Tree Books
Tree Line Books
Tree Shrew Press
TREES
Trek-Cir Publications
TRELLIS
TRIBUTARY
Trike
Truedog Press, Inc.
TRULY FINE PRESS, A Review
Truly Fine Press
THE TULANE LITERARY MAGAZINE
Turkey Press
TUUMBA
Tuumba Press
TWELFTH KEY
The Twickenham Press
TWO HANDS NEWS
Twowindows Press
Tyndall Creek Press
US1 Poets' Cooperative
US1 WORKSHEETS

ULULATUS
UMBRAL, A Quarterly of Speculative Poetry
UNICORN
Unicorn Press
UNITED ARTISTS
United Artists
University of Oregon Press
THE UNREALIST: A Left Literary Magazine
The Unrealist Press
URBANE GORILLA
UROBOROS
URTHKIN
UZZANO
Uzzano Press
Valkyrie Press, Inc.
Van Dyk Publications
VANDERBILT POETRY REVIEW
VANESSA POETRY MAGAZINE
Vanguard Books
VEGA
VEGATABLE BOX
Vehicle Editions
Verlag Pohl'n'Mayer
Vermont Crossroads Press
Vesta Publications Limited
VILE
VINTAGE
VISIONS
VOICES - ISRAEL
Vortex Editions
W. I. M. Publications
Wampeter Press
WASHINGTON REVIEW
Washout Publishing Co.
WASHOUT REVIEW
Water Mark Press
WATERS JOURNAL OF THE ARTS
Webb-Newcomb Company, Inc.
WEST BRANCH
WEST COAST POETRY REVIEW
West Coast Poetry Review Press
WEST END MAGAZINE
WEST HILLS REVIEW: A WALT WHITMAN JOURNAL
WESTBERE REVIEW
John Westburg, Publisher
Western Washington University
WEYFARERS
WHETSTONE
White Dot Press
WHITE MULE
WHITE PINE JOURNAL
White Pine Press
WHITE WALLS
Wild & Woolley
Wild Mustard Press
Wilfion Books, Publishers
WILLOW SPRINGS
WIND LITERARY JOURNAL
Windflower Press
THE WINDLESS ORCHARD
WINDOW
Window Press
Windows Project
Windy Row Press
The Wine Press
Wings Press
Winter Trees Press
Wire Press
WISCONSIN REVIEW
Wisconsin Review
THE WISHING WELL
WOLFSONG
WOMAN POET
Woman Works Press
WOMANCHILD
Womanchild Press
Women-in-Literature, Inc.
WOMEN TALKING, WOMEN LISTENING
Women Writing Press (NY)

WOOD IBIS
Dr. Stella Woodall Publisher
Wooden Needle Press
THE WOODSTOCK REVIEW
The Word Works, Inc.
THE WORLD
WORLD OF POETRY
THE WORMWOOD REVIEW
The Wormwood Review Press
WOT
WRIT
WRITER'S NEWSLETTER
THE WRITER'S PAGE
Writers For Animal Rights
WRITERS FORUM
Writers Forum
WRITERS IN RESIDENCE
WRITERS NEWS MANITOBA
WRITING
WRITING IN HOLLAND AND FLANDERS
XANADU
XTRAS
YANAGI
Yarrow Press
Years Press
YELLOW BRICK ROAD
Yellow Moon Press
The Yellow Press
Yoknapatawpha Press
Young Davis Press
Young Publications
Z
ZAHIR
Ziesing Bros.' Publishing Company
ZONE
Zone
ZVEZDA

POLITICAL SCIENCE

Adventure Trails Research and Development Laboratories
AFRICA TODAY
ANTI-APARTHEID NEWS
APPEAL TO REASON
AREITO
BERKELEY BARB
Between The Lines
CANADIAN DIMENSION
CANADIAN PUBLIC POLICY- Analyse de Politiques
CANADIAN SLAVONIC PAPERS
Chandler & Sharp Publishers, Inc.
CHECKLIST OF HUMAN RIGHTS DOCUMENTS
Christopher Davies Publishers Ltd.
Earl M Coleman Enterprises, Inc
Critiques Livres
CURRENT (a reprint magazine)
Current Issues Publications
Dundee Publishing
EAST EUROPEAN QUARTERLY
ECOSYSTEMS
Golden West Historical Publications
Greenwood Press, Inc.
Griffon House Publications
Harvest Publishers
HARVEST QUARTERLY
THE HISTORY BOOK DIGEST
THE INDEPENDENT JOURNAL OF PHILOSOPHY
The Independent Philosophy Press
Ink Links Ltd.
INTERCONTINENTAL PRESS/INPRECOR
Jaffe Books
JOURNAL OF SOCIAL RECONSTRUCTION
Lawrence Hill & Company, Publishers, Inc.
LITERATURE OF LIBERTY
MERIP REPORTS
Merlin Press
THE METRO
MINORITY RIGHTS GROUP REPORTS
Mojave Books
THE NEW ECOLOGIST

NEW HUMANIST
NEW LITERATURE & IDEOLOGY
NEWS AND LETTERS
News and Letters Press
NORTHERN NEIGHBORS
OUR GENERATION
PACIFIC RESEARCH
PASS-AGE: A Futures Journal
Peace Press
Porter Sargent Publishers, Inc.
Precedent Publishing Inc.
Proletarian Publishers
RADICAL AMERICA
REBUTTAL! The Bicentennial Newsletter of Truth
RECON
ST. CROIX REVIEW
Socialist Party of Canada
UNIVERSAL HUMAN RIGHTS
THE WASHINGTON C.R.A.P. REPORT
John Westburg, Publisher
WIN MAGAZINE
THE WOMAN ACTIVIST

POLITICS

Adventure Trails Research and Development Laboratories
THE AGENT
Alchemy Books
ALTERNATIVE RESEARCH NEWSLETTER
ANOTHER CHICAGO MAGAZINE
Beekman Publishers, Inc.
Between The Lines
BOTH SIDES NOW
CADERNOS DO TERCEIRO MUNDO
THE CANADIAN FORUM
Canadian Women's Educational Press
CENTRAL PARK
THE CHELSEA JOURNAL
Christopher Davies Publishers Ltd.
City Lights Books
COLUMBUS FREE PRESS
CONNEXIONS
Creative Editions & Capitol Enquiry
CROSSCURRENTS
CUADERNOS DEL TERCER MUNDO
DAWN
DECEMBER MAGAZINE
December Press
Editorial Research Service
FAG RAG
FOCUS/ MIDWEST
Fulcourte Press
GREENPEACE (London) Newsletter
GUARDIAN
Guernica Editions
HERESIES: A FEMINIST PUBLICATION ON ART AND POLITICS
Hurtig Publishers
INQUIRY MAGAZINE
Institute for Independent Social Journalism, Inc.
ISRAEL HORIZONS
The Jacek Publishing Company
Kent Popular Press
Kitchen Sink Enterprises
LATIN AMERICAN PERSPECTIVES
LEFT CURVE
Left Curve Publications
LEFTWORKS
LIBERAL NEWS
Liberator Press
LIMIT! (The National Newsletter Of The Libertarian Republican Alliance)
MAIN TREND
Fran Metcalf Books
MIDWEST ALLIANCE
MINORITY RIGHTS GROUP REPORTS
Moon Publications
THE NEW ECOLOGIST
NEW GUARD
NEWS AND LETTERS

News and Letters Press
NEWSFRONT INTERNATIONAL
Norman Bethune Institute
OFF OUR BACKS
Oolichan Books
Out & Out Books
PAPER AIR
PEOPLE'S CANADA DAILY NEWS
Pig Iron Press
PLEXUS, Bay Area Women's Newspaper
Poetry for the People
POSTCARD ART/POSTCARD FICTION
ProActive Press
QUEEN'S QUARTERLY: A Canadian Review
QUEST
RCP Publications
RESURGENCE
REVOLUTION
River Basin Publishing Co.
Rosler, Martha
ST. CROIX REVIEW
The Scribe Press
THE SECOND WAVE
SELF DETERMINATION JOURNAL
SING OUT! The Folk Song Magazine
THE SMALL POND MAGAZINE OF LITERATURE
SOCIAL TEXT
South End Press
Southeast Asia Resource Center
SOUTHERN EXPOSURE
THIRD WORLD
THIS MAGAZINE
Thunder's Mouth Press
THE WASHINGTON C.R.A.P. REPORT
WAYS & MEANS
WEST END MAGAZINE
West End Press
WESTBERE REVIEW
WOMEN'S AGENDA
WREE-VIEW

PRINTING, PUBLISHING

ALTERNATIVE MEDIA
AZIMUTH
Biscuit City Press
BRIARPATCH
CANADIAN AUTHOR & BOOKMAN
Come! Unity Press
Communication Creativity
COPY CORNUCOPIA
COSMEP NEWSLETTER
The Direct Marketing Creative Guild
Editorial Experts, Inc
EDITORIAL EYE
Elpenor Books
FINE PRINT: A Review for the Arts of the Book
Fred A. Fleet II
FOCUS
Gleniffer Press
The Graywolf Press
HAPPINESS HOLDING TANK
INKY TRAILS and TIME TO PAUSE
Inky Trails Publications
KEEPSAKE POEMS
Kxe6s Verein R Press
LIBRARY REVIEW
M.O. Publishing Company
M.O.P. Press
Jim Mann & Associates
MEDIA MANAGEMENT MONOGRAPHS
Mudborn Press
NEW PAGES
Nordic Books
Padre Productions
Parachuting Publications
PEEPHOLE ON PEOPLE
The Pray Curser Press
Pulmac Enterprises, Inc.
RADICAL BOOKSELLER

Raintree
ROCKBOTTOM
S & S Press
The Sandstone Press
SCIENCE FICTION CHRONICLE
SOUTHERN PROGRESSIVE PERIODICALS UPDATE DI-
RECTORY
Southport Press
Stephen Wright Press
Stonehouse Publications
TIOTIS POETRY NEWS
Trinity Press
TYPE & PRESS
WESTERN PUBLISHING SCENE

PRISON

Aldebaran Review
Cardinal Press, Inc.
Coker Books
COMMUNICATOR
CONSTALLATIONS
THE COSMEP PRISON PROJECT NEWSLETTER
Creative Eye Press
CRIME AND SOCIAL JUSTICE: ISSUES IN CRIMINOLOGY.
Crime and Social Justice Associates, Inc.
Crosley Inc
DAWN
FROM THE CENTER: A FOLIO
INSIDE/OUT
"JOINT" CONFERENCE
King Publications
Kitchen Sink Enterprises
New Glide Publ.
NEWS AND LETTERS
News and Letters Press
Noble House Publishing
OFF OUR BACKS
PILLAR
Pirate Press
PRISON
RFD
STROKER
THROUGH THE LOOKING GLASS

PSYCHOLOGY

ADOLESCENCE
Adventure Trails Research and Development Laboratories
ANIMA
ASCENT
Ash Lad Press
ASSERT NEWSLETTER
Avant-Garde Creations
Birth Day Publishing Company
Borderland Sciences Research Foundation
BRAIN/MIND BULLETIN
Brason-Sargar Publications
Celestial Arts
Center for the Art of Living
Center Press
Chandler & Sharp Publishers, Inc.
CHANGE
CITY MINER
CLARITY
Connection Press
CONSTRUCTIVE ACTION FOR GOOD HEALTH
CRCS Publications
Dada Center Publications
Do It Now Foundation
Down There Press + (My Mama's Press)
DRUG SURVIVAL NEWS
E & E Enterprises
EDUCATIONAL CONSIDERATIONS
Erin Hills Publishers
ETC Publications
FAMILY THERAPY
Food For Thought Publications
Gay Sunshine Press, Inc.
Genotype
Ginseng Press

H.E.L.P. Books Inc.
Himalayan Institute Publishers and Distributors
Human Kinetics Pub. Inc.
THE HUMANIST
HUMANIST IN CANADA
Images Press
Impact Publishers, Inc.
Interface Press
International Human Systems Institute
Jalmar Press, Inc.
JOURNAL OF BIOLOGICAL EXPERIENCE
JOURNAL OF PSYCHEDELIC DRUGS
THE JOURNAL of PSYCHOHISTORY
THE JOURNAL OF PSYCHOLOGICAL ANTHROPOLOGY
JOURNAL OF SPORT PSYCHOLOGY
JOURNAL OF SUPERSTITION AND MAGICAL THINKING
The Language Press
LAPIS
Lapis Educational Association, Inc.
Libra Publishers, Inc.
Lidiraven Books: A Division of Biogeocosmological Press
Litmus, Inc.
LP Publications
Mandarin Press
M-R-K Publishing
NEW HUMANIST
North Atlantic Books
Occasional Productions
Onaway Publications
Peace Press
Programs in Communications Press
Prometheus Books
Psychic Books
Psychohistory Press
PSYCHOTHERAPY DIGEST
Martin Quam Press
QUEEN'S QUARTERLY: A Canadian Review
QUEST
Quest Press
Red Alder Books
Sagittarius Rising
The Scoal Press
THE SEEKER NEWSLETTER
SELF AND SOCIETY
Shire Press
SPRING: An Annual of Archetypal Psychology and Jungian
Thought
Spring Publications Inc
Starogubski Press
Sun, Man, Moon Inc.
Tide Book Publishing Company
Unity Press
University of the Trees Press
V. A. C. (Vereinigung Aktiver Kultur)
Velvet Flute Books
Veritas Press
Vitality Associates
WEIRD TRIPS
Westshore Inc
WOMAN'S CHOICE

PUBLIC AFFAIRS

THE ADVOCATE
THE ANTIOCH REVIEW
APPEAL TO REASON
CANADIAN DIMENSION
CANADIAN PUBLIC POLICY- Analyse de Politiques
Capra Press
Chandler & Sharp Publishers, Inc.
CO-OP: The Harbinger of Economic Democracy
COSMOPOLITAN CONTACT
J. DuHadway Craig
CURRENT (a reprint magazine)
DAWN
DEMOCRATIC LEFT
THE DEVELOPING COUNTRY COURIER
Editorial Research Service
FOCUS/ MIDWEST
FREELANCE

Frelance Publishing Co.
GARCIA LORCA REVIEW
GUARDIAN
Hancock House Publishers
House of Anansi Press Limited/Publishing Co.
HUMANIST IN CANADA
Independent Publishing Fund of the Americas
THE INDIAN VOICE
INQUIRY MAGAZINE
Institute for Contemporary Studies
Institute for Independent Social Journalism, Inc.
THE INSURGENT SOCIOLOGIST
IPFA NEWS
The Lightning Tree
MEN'S
Fran Metcalf Books
THE METRO
MID-ATLANTIC NEWS
THE NEW ECOLOGIST
New Glide Publ.
NEW GUARD
North American Students of Cooperation
OREGON TIMES MAGAZINE
PARTISAN REVIEW
PEDESTRIAN RESEARCH
RAIN: JOURNAL OF APPROPRIATE TECHNOLOGY
RECON
ROUGH JUSTICE for the Single Homeless
THE SMALL POND MAGAZINE OF LITERATURE
SOCIAL POLICY
SOUTHEAST ASIA CHRONICLE
TAXING & SPENDING
Third World Publications Ltd.
Thorp Springs Press
Timely Books
URBAN & SOCIAL CHANGE REVIEW
THE WESTERN CRITIC
Workers' Press
THE WRIT

REFERENCE

AMERICAN FIDDLERS NEWS
The Avondale Press
Barnhart Books
Biblio Press
Brattle Publications
Brown Rabbit Press
Festival Publications
The Garlic Press
Garrett Park Press
Greenwood Press, Inc.
Hays, Rolfes & Associates
The Hosanna Press
INFORMATION MOSCOW
Kanthaka Press
LITERARY RESEARCH NEWSLETTER
Maledicta Press
McFarland & Company, Inc., Publishers
Minnesota Scholarly Press, Inc.
New Glide Publ.
Nighthawk Press
Oleander Press
Ontario Library Association
PEOPLE'S YELLOW PAGES of the SAN FRANCISCO BAY
    AREA
Poets & Writers, Inc.
Poets & Writers of New Jersey
Presidio Press
Racz Publishing Co.
REFERENCE BOOK REVIEW
REFERENCE SERVICES REVIEW
RESEARCH
RESOURCES
Running Press
Scarecrow Press
Stephen Wright Press
Turner Publishing, Inc.
Variety Press
WASHINGTON INTERNATIONAL ARTS LETTER

White Oak Publishing House
Whitfield
THE WORKBOOK

RELIGION

Alleluia Press
Ananda Publications
ANIMA
Anti-Ocean Press
Ardis
Autumn Press, Inc.
THE AWAKENER MAGAZINE
Back Row Press
BEFORE THE RAPTURE
BERTRAND RUSSELL TODAY
Between The Lines
BOTH SIDES NOW
Buddhist Text Translation Society
BUZZ
Charisma Press
CHARISMA PRESS REVIEW
CLARITY
CRUSADE
CS JOURNAL
The Dawn Horse Press
Dharma Publishing
DIGNITY
Dominion Press
THE GAY LUTHERAN
GESAR- Buddhist Perspectives
GNOSIS
Great Eastern Book Company
Hexagon Press
HOLY BEGGARS' GAZETTE
HUMANIST IN CANADA
THE INQUIRER
INSIGHT: A Quarterly of LESBIAN/GAY CHRISTIAN OPIN-
    ION
Institute of Pyramidology
Iroquois House, Publishers
Jakubowsky
Jewel Publications
JOURNAL OF CALIFORNIA AND GREAT BASIN AN-
    THROPOLOGY
Kitchen Sink Enterprises
LAPIS
Lapis Educational Association, Inc.
LILITH
Loving Publishers
Lycabettus Press
Malki Museum Press
MANNA
MANY SMOKES
MASTER THOUGHTS
M'GODOLIM
MODERN LITURGY
Moon Publications
Moonsquilt Press
MOVEMENT
Nevada Publications
NEW HUMANIST
OPINION
Parable Press
PARABOLA MAGAZINE
Peace Press
W. Perry
Pilgrim Press
THE PILGRIM WAY
Poet Papers
Prometheus Books
PYRAMIDOLOGY MAGAZINE
Quantal Publishing B
RENEWAL
Resource Publications
Ross-Erikson Publishers, Inc.
ST. CROIX REVIEW
Sanatana Publishing Society
Scarf Press
Sheriar Press

Soft Press
SPIRIT & NATURE
STUDIA MYSTICA
Sun-Scape Publications
T.A.A.S. Association, Inc.
THEOLOGIA 21
Timeless Books
Top Stone Books
TREE
Tree Books
TZADDIKIM
VAJRA BODHI SEA
Vesta Publications Limited
VISHVAMITRA
Webb-Newcomb Company, Inc.
WESTERN CITY SUBTOPIAN TIMES
Wisdom Garden Books
WITCHCRAFT DIGEST MAGAZINE (THE WICA NEWS-
 LETTER)
The WorDoctor Publications

REPRINTS

Academy Chicago Limited
Askin Publishers, Ltd.
BOTH SIDES NOW
Charles River Books, Inc.
Earl M Coleman Enterprises, Inc
The Crossing Press
CURRENT (a reprint magazine)
Edition Stencil
Northeastern University Press
Peradam Publishing House
Peregrine Smith, Inc.
Press Pacifica
Proletarian Publishers
RE:PRINT (AN OCCASIONAL MAGAZINE)
THE RECORD SUN
The Seal Press
Timely Books

ROMANIAN STUDIES

MIORITA

SAN FRANCISCO

PEOPLE'S YELLOW PAGES of the SAN FRANCISCO BAY
 AREA

SCANDINAVIA

Nordic Books
SWEDISH BOOKS

SCIENCE

Adventure Trails Research and Development Laboratories
ALTERNATIVE SOURCES of ENERGY MAGAZINE
Aslan Enterprises
THE ASTRONOMY QUARTERLY
The Boxwood Press
Boyd & Fraser Publishing Company
BRAIN/MIND BULLETIN
BUCKNELL REVIEW
THE CENTENNIAL REVIEW
CHAIRMAN'S CHAT
Cheshire Books
CREATIVE COMPUTING
Creative Computing Press
DAEDALUS, Journal of the American Academy of Arts and
 Sciences
Dervy, A. J.
Dominion Press
FOURTH DIMENSION
Halls of Ivy Press
Inquiry Press
Interface Press
Kitchen Sink Enterprises
Levenson Press
Lidiraven Books: A Division of Biogeocosmological Press
The Lightning Tree
Mad River Press, Inc.
Mandarin Press

Manzanita Press
MEDICAL HISTORY
THE NEW ECOLOGIST
Open Sesame Publishing Co.
Pachart Publishing House
PASS-AGE: A Futures Journal
Pentangle Press
QUEEN'S QUARTERLY: A Canadian Review
RAIN: JOURNAL OF APPROPRIATE TECHNOLOGY
Sea Challengers
STREET MAGAZINE
Timber Press
Tofua Press
Triad Publishing Co. Inc.
UNDERCURRENTS
University of the Trees Press

SCIENCE FICTION

Algol Press
Angst World Library
ARENA SCIENCE FICTION
THE ARGONAUT
Around Publishing
Auriga
Authors' Co-op Publishing Co.
Avant-Garde Creations
BLANK TAPE
The Borgo Press
British Science Fiction Assoc. Ltd.
CAHIER
Carpenter Press
CENTER
CINEMAGIC
COBBLESTONE
DARK FANTASY
de la Ree Publications
Dimensionist Press
The Donning Company / Publishers
EMPIRE: For the SF Writer
FANZINE DIRECTORY
W.D. Firestone Press
FOCUS
Fragments/The Valentine Press
Franson Publications
The Future Press
GALILEO
GEGENSCHEIN
Gemini Press
Gluxlit Press
The Guide to Small Press Publishing
Harden Publications
Heavy Evidence Press
Heresy Press
Hobby Horse Publishing
IN ORBIT: A Journal of Earth Literature
JANUS
Jelm Mountain Publications
Kangam
Kent Publications
LETTERS
LOCUS: The Newspaper of the Science Fiction Field
LONG POND REVIEW
M.O. Publishing Company
Mafdet Press
MATI
MATRIX
MODUS OPERANDI
NOUMENON
PANDORA, An Original Anthology of Role-expanding Science
 Fiction and Fantsy
Peace & Pieces Foundation
PHOEBE
PHOTRON
Pig Iron Press
PRELUDE TO FANTASY
Purple Mouth Press
RAS Communications/Blind Eye Publishing House/Blind Eye
 Books/Jasmine
RIVERSIDE QUARTERLY

The Sceptre Press
SCIENCE FICTION CHRONICLE
SCIENCE FICTION & FANTASY BOOK REVIEW
SF COMMENTARY
Shadow Press
SKIFFY THYME
SPACE AND TIME
STARSHIP: The Magazine About Science Fiction
STRANGE FAECES
UMBRAL, A Quarterly of Speculative Poetry
UNDERCURRENTS
UNEARTH: The Magazine of Science Fiction Discoveries
UNICORN: A Miscellaneous Journal
Unity Press
URTHKIN
VECTOR
WEIRDBOOK
WHISPERS
Whispers Press
WILD FENNEL
Wilfion Books, Publishers
Zoographico Press, Ltd.

SCOTLAND

BIG PRINT

SENIOR CITIZENS

Dawn Valley Press
EXPANDING HORIZONS
Rockfall Press
ZANTIA: Stories and Poems by the Over-Sixty

SHAKESPEARE

THE BARD

G. B. SHAW

THE SHAW REVIEW

SOCIALIST

Alyson Publications, Inc.
APPEAL TO REASON
BERKELEY JOURNAL OF SOCIOLOGY
Between The Lines
THE BODY POLITIC- Gay Liberation Journal
CADERNOS DO TERCEIRO MUNDO
Canadian Women's Educational Press
Cardinal Press, Inc.
Charles H. Kerr Publishing Company
CLAIMANTS NEWSPAPER (Claimants Unite)
CRIME AND SOCIAL JUSTICE: ISSUES IN CRIMINOLOGY.
Crime and Social Justice Associates, Inc.
CROSSCURRENTS
CUADERNOS DEL TERCER MUNDO
DAWN
THE GAR
Gar Publishing Co.
GAY INSURGENT
LEFT CURVE
Left Curve Publications
LEFTWORKS
MERIP REPORTS
THE METRO
THE MILITANT
MOVEMENT
NEW UNIONIST
NEWS AND LETTERS
News and Letters Press
OUTCOME
Pink Triangle Press
PRAXIS: A Journal of Cultural Criticism
QUINDARO
RADICAL AMERICA
Smyrna Press
South End Press
Spindrift Press
THIRD WORLD
YOUTH AND NATION

SOCIETY

ADOLESCENCE
Adventure Trails Research and Development Laboratories
Alchemy Books
ALTERNATIVE FUTURES: THE JOURNAL OF UTOPIAN
  STUDIES
ALTERNATIVES- Perspectives on Society and Environment
AMERICAN MAN
ANTI-APARTHEID NEWS
Avant-Garde Creations
AZTLAN: International Journal of Chicano Studies
BERKELEY BARB
Between The Lines
Boyd & Fraser Publishing Company
BRANCHING OUT
Brick House Publishing, Co.
Chandler & Sharp Publishers, Inc.
CHANGE
Charisma Press
THE CHELSEA JOURNAL
Coda Press, Inc
COMMUNITY SERVICE NEWSLETTER
LA CONFLUENCIA
COSMOPOLITAN CONTACT
CRIME AND SOCIAL JUSTICE: ISSUES IN CRIMINOLOGY.
Crime and Social Justice Associates, Inc.
CROSSCURRENTS
CUMBERLAND JOURNAL
E & E Enterprises
ETC Publications
FAMILY THERAPY
FOCUS/ MIDWEST
FOLIO
GAY COMMUNITY NEWS
General Hall, Inc.
THE HUMANIST
Hyde Park Socialist
I.D.H.H.B., Inc
IN BUSINESS
Institute for Polynesian Studies
THE INSURGENT SOCIOLOGIST
JOURNAL OF CALIFORNIA AND GREAT BASIN AN-
  THROPOLOGY
THE JOURNAL OF PSYCHOLOGICAL ANTHROPOLOGY
JOURNAL OF SOCIAL RECONSTRUCTION
Kitchen Sink Enterprises
LEFT CURVE
Left Curve Publications
Libra Publishers, Inc.
The Lightning Tree
THE MIDWEST QUARTERLY
MONCHANIN JOURNAL
New Glide Publ.
The New South Company
NEW TIMES
North Country Press
NORTHERN NEIGHBORS
PEACE NEWS "For Non-Violent Revolution"
PILLAR
Piney Branch Press
Prometheus Books
PULPSMITH
Raintree
Red Alder Books
River Basin Publishing Co.
SELF AND SOCIETY
SOCIAL POLICY
SOCIALIST FULCRUM
Southwest Research and Information Center
SPUR
The Stevenson Press
Times Change Press
University of the Trees Press
URBAN & SOCIAL CHANGE REVIEW
WEIRD TRIPS
WIN MAGAZINE
THE WORKBOOK

SOUTH

Offshore Research Service

Rose Publishing Co.
SOUTHERN EXPOSURE

SOUTHWEST

Artemisia Press
BACULITE
BOOKS OF THE SOUTHWEST
The Maguey Press
Platyne Press
San Pedro Press
WHETSTONE

SPIRITUAL

Adam Seed Publications
ALTERNATIVE RESEARCH NEWSLETTER
Ananda Publications
Artists & Alchemists Publications
ASCENT
Ash-Kar Press
Auromere, Inc.
Autumn Press, Inc.
Avant-Garde Creations
THE AWAKENER MAGAZINE
BEFORE THE RAPTURE
Birth Day Publishing Company
The Book Department
Book Publishing Co.
BOTH SIDES NOW
Cat Anna Press
Cliff Catton Press
Center Publications
COLLABORATION
CS JOURNAL
Dada Center Publications
The Dawn Horse Press
Dharma Publishing
Dimensionist Press
Findhorn Publications
FORESIGHT MAGAZINE
Hidden Valley Press
HOLY BEGGARS' GAZETTE
I.D.H.H.B., Inc
Images Press
Jakubowsky
JOURNAL OF CALIFORNIA AND GREAT BASIN AN-
    THROPOLOGY
Journey Publications
Kanthaka Press
LADY-UNIQUE-INCLINATION-OF-THE-NIGHT
LAPIS
Lapis Educational Association, Inc.
Llewellyn Publications
LOVE
LP Publications
MAGICAL BLEND
Magical Blend
Malki Museum Press
Matagiri
THE MESSAGE
MODERN LITURGY
Moon Publications
ONEARTH IMAGE
Papillon Press
LES PAPILLONS, A Journal of Modern Philosophical Inquiry
W. Perry
Planetary Research
Psychic Books
Resource Publications
Sagittarius Rising
Sanatana Publishing Society
Seed Center
THE SEEKER NEWSLETTER
SPIRALS
SPIRIT & NATURE
Spiritual Community Publications
Sufi Order Publications
Summer Stream Press
Sun-Scape Publications
TAI CHI

Timeless Books
TOTAL LIFESTYLE- The Magazine of Natural Living
TREE
TZADDIKIM
Unity Press
University of the Trees Press
Valkyrie Press, Inc.
VISHVAMITRA
Vulcan Books
Whatever Publishing/Rising Sun Records
Wild Horses Potted Plant
Wilfion Books, Publishers
The Word Shop

TAPES & RECORDS

AFTA—The Magazine of Temporary Culture
ALBUM
Balsam Flex
BLACK BOX MAGAZINE
BLITZ
Cardinal Press, Inc.
Cosmic Brain Trust
COSMIC CIRCUS
The Crow's Mark Press
DIAL-A-POEM POETS LP'S
DOUBLE HARNESS
THE ETHNODISC JOURNAL OF RECORDED SOUND
Exponent Ltd.
IMPETUS MAGAZINE
INDIAN HOUSE
THE METRO
NOSTALGIAWORLD
PLANTAGENET PRODUCTIONS, Recorded Library of the
    Spoken Word
Realities
Resource Publications
ROCKINGCHAIR
THE STEREOPHILE
Summer Stream Press
Sun-Scape Publications
SUPRANORMAL, 1983
Tanam Press
THE TARAKAN MUSIC LETTER
TIME BARRIER EXPRESS
XENHARMONIC BULLETIN

ALFRED, LORD TENNYSON

TENNYSON RESEARCH BULLETIN

TEXAS

The Stevenson Press

THEATRE

THE ARTFUL REPORTER
The Black Cat Press
BRITISH THEATRE INSTITUTE NEWSLETTER & REPORT
BTI
CANADIAN THEATRE REVIEW
CHIMERA-A Complete Theater Piece
CLAUDEL STUDIES
CTR Publications
THE DRAMA REVIEW
DRAMATIKA
Dramatika Press
EXCHANGE: A Journal of Opinion for the Ferforming Arts
Footnotes
Four Corners Press
Greenwood Press, Inc.
JH Press
Jelm Mountain Publications
THE METRO
MIME JOURNAL
Moon Publications
New England Press
NEW HUMANIST
Northeastern University Press
ON STAGE
The Pepys Press
Peregrine Smith, Inc.

508

PERFORMING ARTS JOURNAL
Personabooks
Playwrights Canada
PRAXIS: A Journal of Cultural Criticism
Quintessence Publications
Resource Publications
Simon & Pierre Publishing Co. Ltd.
SOUTHERN QUARTERLY: A Journal of the Arts in the South
That New Publishing Company
THEATER
THEATRE
THEATRE DESIGN AND TECHNOLOGY
THEATRE NOTEBOOK
THE THREEPENNY REVIEW
WEST COAST PLAYS
WHITE MULE

THIRD WORLD, MINORITIES

AFRICA NEWS
Backpack Media
Between The Lines
CADERNOS DO TERCEIRO MUNDO
CALIBAN: A Journal of New World Thought & Writing
Canadian Women's Educational Press
CARTA ABIERTA
Children's Book Press/Imprenta de Libros Infantiles
CONCH MAGAZINE
Conch Magazine Ltd. (Publishers)
CUADERNOS DEL TERCER MUNDO
THE DEVELOPING COUNTRY COURIER
Energy Earth Communications, Inc.
FIFTH SUN
FROZEN WAFFLES
THE GREENFIELD REVIEW
Heirs Press
INTERRACIAL BOOKS FOR CHILDREN BULLETIN
Lawrence Hill & Company, Publishers, Inc.
Libre Press
LSM Information Center
MANGO
MINORITY RIGHTS GROUP REPORTS
NETHULA JOURNAL OF CONTEMPORARY LITERATURE
New Glide Publ.
NEWS AND LETTERS
News and Letters Press
John L Noyce, Publisher
OFF OUR BACKS
Oleander Press
PACIFIC RESEARCH
PEACE NEWS "For Non-Violent Revolution"
PEOPLE'S NEWS SERVICE
Pitjon Press/BackBack Media
Porter Sargent Publishers, Inc.
RAIN: JOURNAL OF APPROPRIATE TECHNOLOGY
The School of Living
SEZ: A Multi-Racial Journal of Poetry & People's Culture
Shadow Press
SOUTHEAST ASIA CHRONICLE
Southeast Asia Resource Center
SPUR
SUNBURY (a poetry magazine)
Sunbury Press
SYNERGY
THIRD WORLD
Third World Publications Ltd.
Trado-Medic Books
Unicorn Press
Worldwatch Institute
WREE-VIEW
Zed Press

DYLAN THOMAS

Oriel

H. D. THOREAU

THOREAU JOURNAL QUARTERLY

J. R. R. TOLKIEN

MINAS TIRITH EVENING-STAR

TRANSLATION

ALCATRAZ
Alcatraz Editions
ALEMBIC
THE ARK
Avalon Editions
Backpack Media
BEYOND BAROQUE
BIRD EFFORT
BLUE BUILDINGS
Boa Editions
BUCKLE
CALIBAN: A Journal of New World Thought & Writing
THE CHARIOTEER
CHARITON REVIEW
CHELSEA
Cherry Valley Editions
Clamshell Press
THE COFFEEHOUSE
Copper Beech Press
The Crow's Mark Press
CURTAINS
DIMENSION
DURAK: An International Magazine of Poetry
Engendra Press Ltd.
EXIT
Firefly Press
FOOTPRINT MAGAZINE
FOREIGN POETS AND AUTHORS REVIEW
FROZEN WAFFLES
Gabbro Press
Gay Sunshine Press, Inc.
Green Horse Press
Grilled Flowers Press
The Guide to Small Press Publishing
HYPERION A Poetry Journal
INKLINGS
Interim Press
Intermedia Press
INTERNATIONAL POETRY REVIEW
INVISIBLE CITY
IRONWOOD
Ironwood Press
Ishtar Press, Inc.
JAZZ
Jazz Press
KOSMOS
Kosmos
Leete's Island Books
LIGHT: A Poetry Review
THE LITTLE REVIEW
LONGHOUSE
Longhouse
LoonBooks
MATI
The Menard Press
MR. COGITO
Moonsquilt Press
Mudborn Press
MUNDUS ARTIUM: A Journal of International Literature & Art
Nordic Books
O Press
OCCIDENT
OINK!
Oleander Press
PAINTBRUSH: A Journal of Poetry, Translations & Letters
PEQUOD
Perivale Press
PHANTASM
PHOEBE
PINECONE
THE POETRY MISCELLANY
POETRY WALES
PONTCHARTRAIN REVIEW
Prescott Street Press
Pressed Curtains
PRISM INTERNATIONAL
PULP

509

QUARTERLY REVIEW OF LITERATURE
Rainfeather Press
Raintree
rara avis
Raven Publications
Red Hill Press, Los Angeles & Fairfax
Rochester Routes/Creative Arts Projects
RUSSIAN LITERATURE TRIQUARTERLY
Slow Loris Press
SLOW LORIS READER
Spectacular Diseases
THE SPIRIT THAT MOVES US
STAR WEST
STEPPENWOLF
STRANGE FAECES
Studia Hispanica Editors
Sun
SURVIVOR
Tangent Books
TINTA
TRANSLATION REVIEW
TRANSLATION
Translation
Tree Books
Twowindows Press
Unicorn Press
URBANE GORILLA
Valkyrie Press, Inc.
VANDERBILT POETRY REVIEW
WEBSTER REVIEW
John Westburg, Publisher
WHITE PINE JOURNAL
White Pine Press
Wild & Woolley
Wilfion Books, Publishers
YARDBIRD READER
Yellow Moon Press
ZONE

TRANSPORTATION, TRAVEL

Acrobus, Inc.
Alchemist/Light Publishing
And/Or Press
Baja Trail Publications, Inc.
BOXCAR
Bradley David Associates, Ltd.
Bradt Enterprises
Carousel Press
Chronicle Books/Prism Editions
Citrus House Ltd
Donnelly & Sons Publishing Co.
The East Woods Press
Eurail Guide Annual
Freelance Publications
Genny Smith Books
Golden West Books
Gotuit Enterprises
Greatland Publishing Co.
INFORMATION MOSCOW
THE INSIDE TRACK
Jaks Publishing Co.
Jama Books
Kitchen Sink Enterprises
Dr. Albert R. Klinski
Kurios Press
Lonely Planet Publications
Lycabettus Press
MEXICO WEST
MIAMI INTERNATIONAL
Miocene Press
Moon Publications
Mothra Press
Nevada Publications
THE NEW ECOLOGIST
Odyssey Publishing Company
Offshore Research Service
Oleander Press
ON THE BEACH
Padre Productions

PEOPLE & ENERGY
Phoenix Books/Publishers
RAIN: JOURNAL OF APPROPRIATE TECHNOLOGY
Ram Publications
Sol Press
Spiritual Community Publications
Summerthought Ltd.
Trans-Traffic Corporation, Publishing Division
Transport History Press
WEIRD TRIPS
Wilson Brothers Publications
THE WISHING WELL

MARK TWAIN

MARK TWAIN JOURNAL

U.S.S.R.

CANADIAN SLAVONIC PAPERS
Merlin Press

VISUAL ARTS

BEYOND RICE, A Broadside Series
KALDRON
Noro Press

WALES

THE ANGLO-WELSH REVIEW
Oriel
Y GWYDDONYDD
Y'lolfa

WALT WHITMAN

WEST HILLS REVIEW: A WALT WHITMAN JOURNAL

WOMEN

ABC Letter Service of Rochester
Academy Chicago Limited
AFFORDABLE CHIC NEWS
Air-Plus Enterprises
ALBATROSS
Alice James Books
All of Us
Alta Gaia Society
ANARCHISM: The Feminist Connection
Anemone Press
Angle Lightning Press
ANIMA
Ariadne Press
Artists & Alchemists Publications
ATLANTIS
Avant-Garde Creations
BARE WIRES
Bear Tribe
Between The Lines
BIG MAMA RAG
BLACK MARIA
BLOODROOT
Bloodroot, Inc.
BOOKLEGGER MAGAZINE AND BOOKS
Booklegger Press
BRANCHING OUT
BROADSHEET
CAFE SOLO
Calliope Publishing Inc.
CAMERA OBSCURA: A Journal of Feminism and Film Theory
Canadian Women's Educational Press
Cardinal Press, Inc.
The Carolina Wren Press
Carousel Press
Celebrating Women Productions
The Center For Study of Multiple Gestation
Center for Women's Studies & Services (CWSS)
Charles H. Kerr Publishing Company
CHRYSALIS: A Magazine of Women's Culture
Cleis Press
CONDITIONS
CONNECTION NEWS RELEASE
CONNECTIONS MAGAZINE
THE CREATIVE WOMAN

Daisy Press
Daughters Publishing Co., Inc.
Dawn Valley Press
Diana Press, Inc
Down There Press + (My Mama's Press)
EARTH'S DAUGHTERS
Embers Publications
FEMINARY
FEMINIST
FEMINIST BULLETIN
The Feminist Press
FEMINIST STUDIES
FIFTH SUN
FIGHTING WOMAN NEWS
Five Trees Press
Flower Press
FOCUS: A Journal For Lesbians
Foolproof Press
Freestone Publishing Collective
Frog in the Well
FRONTIERS: A Journal of Women Studies
GILTEDGE: New Series
Glass Bell Press
Gordon Publishing Co., Inc.
THE GREATER GOLDEN HILL POETRY EXPRESS
Growing Room Collective
Hartmus Press
HECATE
Helaine Victoria Press
HERESIES: A FEMINIST PUBLICATION ON ART AND POL-
    ITICS
House of Anansi Press Limited/Publishing Co.
House of White Shell Woman
HUMANIST IN CANADA
Impact Publishers, Inc.
Incunabula Collection Press
Independence Unlimited
International Childbirth Education Association, Inc.
INTERRACIAL BOOKS FOR CHILDREN BULLETIN
IOWA WOMAN
JOURNAL OF CALIFORNIA AND GREAT BASIN AN-
    THROPOLOGY
KALLIOPE, A Journal of Women's Art
Kelsey St. Press
Kids Can Press
Know, Inc.
THE LADDER
LADY-UNIQUE-INCLINATION-OF-THE-NIGHT
Lawrence Hill & Company, Publishers, Inc.
THE LESBIAN TIDE
LESBIAN VOICES
LETTERS MAGAZINE
LILITH
Lollipop Power, Inc.
Long Haul Press
LONG ISLAND CHILDBIRTH ALTERNATIVES QUAR-
    TERLY
THE LONGEST REVOLUTION
Loving Publishers
Magic Circle Press
MAJORITY REPORT
Malki Museum Press
MATI
MAW: A MAGAZINE OF APPALACHIAN WOMEN
Mayapple Press
MEDIA REPORT TO WOMEN
MEN'S
Merging Media
Merlin Press
Metis Press
THE METRO
MICHIGAN OCCASIONAL PAPERS IN WOMEN'S STUDIES
Midmarch Associates
MINORITY RIGHTS GROUP REPORTS
Moon Books
Motheroot Journal
Motheroot Publications
MOVING OUT: Feminist Literary & Arts Journal
Mudborn Press

The Naiad Press, Inc.
NAMAZU
Nanny Goat Productions
NEW DIRECTIONS FOR WOMEN
New Glide Publ.
NEW HUMANIST
New Victoria Publishers
NEW WOMEN'S TIMES & NEW WOMEN'S TIMES FEMI-
    NIST REVIEW
NEWS AND LETTERS
News and Letters Press
Northwest Matrix
OFF OUR BACKS
The Olive Press Publications
Ommation Press
OUR GENERATION
Out & Out Books
Over the Rainbow Press
PAID MY DUES: JOURNAL OF WOMEN AND MUSIC
PANDORA, An Original Anthology of Role-expanding Science
    Fiction and Fantsy
Paradise Press
PEACE NEWS "For Non-Violent Revolution"
Persephone Press
Philmer Enterprises
PLAINSWOMAN
PLEXUS, Bay Area Women's Newspaper
POSTCARD ART/POSTCARD FICTION
POW (Poetry Organization for Women)
PRACTICAL PARENTING
Press Gang Publishers
Press Pacifica
PRIMAVERA
PRIMIPARA
Programmed Studies Inc
PULP
QUEST
RADICAL AMERICA
RAIN: JOURNAL OF APPROPRIATE TECHNOLOGY
rara avis
Red Clay Books
RESOURCES FOR FEMINIST RESEARCH
Rhiannon Press
ROOM
ROOM OF ONE'S OWN
Rosler, Martha
SAPPHO
Sappho Publications Ltd
The Seal Press
Second Back Row Press
Second Class, Working Class, an International Women's Reader
THE SECOND WAVE
Shameless Hussy Press
Sibyl-Child Press
SIBYL-CHILD: A Women's Arts & Culture Journal
SIGNS:A JOURNAL OF WOMEN IN CULTURE AND SOCI-
    ETY
Simon & Pierre Publishing Co. Ltd.
SING HEAVENLY MUSE! WOMEN'S POETRY AND PROSE
Smuggler's Cove Publishing
SNIPPETS: A Melange of Woman
SOCIAL ANARCHISM
SOJOURNER, THE NEW ENGLAND WOMEN'S JOURNAL
    OF NEWS, OPINIONS AND THE ARTS
Spinsters, Ink
Starogubski Press
SUNBURY (a poetry magazine)
Sunbury Press
13th MOON
THROUGH THE LOOKING GLASS
Tide Publications
Timely Books
Times Change Press
The Transientpress
Triad Press
UNDER THE SIGN OF PISCES: Anais Nin and Her Circle
VALHALLA
Vanguard Books
Vanilla Press

Variety Press
Violet Press
W. I. M. Publications
Waterfall Press
THE WISHING WELL
WLW JOURNAL: News/Views/Reviews for Women and Librar-
  ies
THE WOMAN ACTIVIST
Woman Matters Press
WOMAN POET
WOMAN SPIRIT
Woman Works Press
WOMANCHILD
Womanchild Press
WOMAN'S CHOICE
Womanshare Books
WOMEN: A Journal of Liberation
WOMEN AND LITERATURE
WOMEN ARTISTS NEWS
WOMEN IN THE ARTS BULLETIN/NEWSLETTER
Women-in-Literature, Inc.
Women Library Workers
WOMEN STUDIES ABSTRACTS
WOMEN TALKING, WOMEN LISTENING
Women Writing Press (NY)
Women's Action Alliance
WOMEN'S AGENDA
Women's History Research Center, Inc.
Women's Institute for Freedom of the Press
Women's Studies
WOMEN'S STUDIES NEWSLETTER
WOMEN'S STUDIES NEWSLETTER
Worldwatch Institute
WREE-VIEW

WORKER

ALIVE
BANGE DAGEN
Between The Lines
THE CALL/EL CLARIN
Canadian Women's Educational Press
DEMOCRATIC LEFT
INDUSTRIAL WORKER
Labor Arts Books
Miles & Weir, Ltd.
New Visions Press
NEWS AND LETTERS
News and Letters Press
OFF OUR BACKS
QUIXOTE, QUIXOTL
Second Class, Working Class, an International Women's Reader
SUNBURY (a poetry magazine)

Regional Index

ALABAMA

ANGELSTONE, 316 Woodland Drive, Birmingham, AL 35209, (205) 870-7281
Angelstone, 316 Woodland Drive, Birmingham, AL 35209, (205) 870-7281
ASFA POETRY QUARTERLY, 820 North 18th Street, Birmingham, AL 35203, (205) 252-9241
BALTIC AVENUE POETRY JOURNAL, 1045 Fulton Avenue SW, Birmingham, AL 35211, 788-3307
Baltic Avenue Press, 1045 Fulton Ave. SW, Birmingham, AL 35211, 788-3307
Creekwood Press, Box 11191, Birmingham, AL 35202, (205) 870-4261
Thunder City Press, PO Box 11126, Birmingham, AL 35202
THUNDER MOUNTAIN REVIEW, PO Box 11126, Birmingham, AL 35202
THE BLACK WARRIOR REVIEW, P.O. Box 2936, University, AL 35486, (205) 348-5526
Akens-Morgan Press, Inc., Huntsville, AL 35801
Huntsville Literary Association, PO Box 1247, Huntsville, AL 35807
POEM, PO Box 1247, West Station, Huntsville, AL 35807
Doctor Jazz, PO Box 1043, Auburn, AL 36830, (205) 887-5066
SOUTHERN HUMANITIES REVIEW, 9090 Haley Center, Auburn Univ., Auburn, AL 36830, 205-826-4606

ALASKA

HARPOON, PO Box 2581, Anchorage, AK 99510, 276-1279
Chandonnet, Ann, PO Box A, Chugiak, AK 99567
PERMAFROST, University of Alaska, Fairbanks, AK 99701, (907) 479-7193
That New Publishing Company, 1525 Eielson St, Fairbanks, AK 99701, 907-452-3007
Windham Bay Press, Box 1332, Juneau, AK 99802, (907) 789-2288

ARIZONA

BONSAI, 1350 E Bethany House, #1, Phoenix, AZ 85014
Bonsai Press, 1350 E Bethany House, #1, Phoenix, AZ 85014
Do It Now Foundation, P.O. Box 5115, Phoenix, AZ 85010, 602-257-0797
DRUG SURVIVAL NEWS, P.O. Box 5115, Phoenix, AZ 85010, 602-257-0797
Golden West Publishers, 4113 N. Longview, Phoenix, AZ 85014
Horizons, PO Box 35008, Phoenix, AZ 85069
Hunter Publishing, Co., P.O. Box 9533, Phoenix, AZ 85068, 602-944-1022
INDIAN ARIZONA NEWS, 1777 W. Camelback Road A-108, Phoenix, AZ 85015, (602) 248-0184
Phoenix Books/Publishers, P.O.Box 32008, Phoenix, AZ 85064, (602) 952-0163
White Mountain Publishing Company, 13801 N. Cave Creek Rd, Phoenix, AZ 85022, 971-2720
Sunrise Press, PO Box 742, Chandler, AZ 85224, 967-4251
Walnut Press, P O Box 17210, Fountain Hills, AZ 85268, 602-837-9118
Turtle Lodge Press, 12411 N 67th Street, Scottsdale, AZ 85254, (602) 948-3565
PORCH, c/o James V Cervantes, Dept of English, Arizona State University, Tempe, AZ 85281, 206-325-5614
Porch Publications, c/o James V Cervantes, Dept of English, Arizona State University, Tempe, AZ 85281
Karl Bern Publishers, 9939 Riviera Drive, Sun City, AZ 85351
San Pedro Press, Rural Route 1, Box 221, St David, AZ 85630
WHETSTONE, Rural Route 1, Box 221, St David, AZ 85630
ARIZONA QUARTERLY, Univ. Of Arizona, Tucson, AZ 85721, Main Library 541-B (602) 626-1029
THE ASTRONOMY QUARTERLY, Box 35549, Tucson, AZ 85740, (602) 297-4797
BLUE MOON NEWS, c/o English Dept., University of Arizona, Tucson, AZ 85721, 602-884-1387
Blue Moon Press, Inc., c/o English Dept., University of Arizona, Tucson, AZ 85721, 602-884-1387
BOOKS OF THE SOUTHWEST, Univ. of Az Library, A349 Main Library, U. of AZ, Tucson, AZ 85721
CHOOMIA (A literary review), P.O. Box 40322, Tucson, AZ 85719
Daran Inc., 5730 N Via Elena, Tucson, AZ 85718
THE ETHNODISC JOURNAL OF RECORDED SOUND, Box 35549, Tucson, AZ 85740, (602) 297-4797
H.E.L.P. Books Inc., 1201 E. Calle Elena, Tucson, AZ 85718
HUERFANO, 5730 N. Via Elena, Tucson, AZ 85718
IRONWOOD, P.O.Box 40907, Tucson, AZ 85717
Ironwood Press, PO Box 40907, Tucson, AZ 85717
The Maguey Press, Box 3395, Tucson, AZ 85722, 602-623-9711
THE MESSAGE, Route 15, Box 270, Tucson, AZ 85715, 602-299-4597
Michael F. Murphy Ph. D., Dept of Microbiology, Univ Az College of Medicine, Tucson, AZ 85724, (714) 222-7254
NEWSREAL, Box 40323, Tucson, AZ 85717, 887-3982
Pachart Publishing House, Box 35549, Tucson, AZ 85740, (602) 297-4797
Platyne Press, 2202 N Madelyn Avenue, Tucson, AZ 85712
Sufi Order Publications, Route 15, Box 270, Tucson, AZ 85715, 602-299-4597
Sun-Scape Publications, PO Box 42725, Tucson, AZ 85733, 602-297-3424
SUN TRACKS: An American Indian Literary Magazine, Department of English, Univ of Arizona, Tucson, AZ 85721, 884-1836
Thumbprint Press, PO Box 3565, College Station, Tucson, AZ 85722, 602-327-1569
TRIBUTARY, 3755 E 32nd Street, Tucson, AZ 85713, (602) 748-1551
Yarrow Press, CHOOMIA, PO Box 40322, Tucson, AZ 85719
YELLOW BRICK ROAD, 2627 N Orchard, Tucson, AZ 85712, (602) 623-2932
Padma Press, PO Box 56, Oatman, AZ 86433

ARKANSAS

SULPHUR RIVER, 411 W Cedar #10, El Dorado, AR 71730, (501) 862-6487
M. N. Publishers, Route 2, Box 55, Bonnerdale, AR 71933, (501) 991-3815
MAXY'S JOURNAL, 216 West Academy Street, Lonoke, AR 72086, (501) 676-2467
Truedog Press, Inc., 216 West Academy Street, Lonoke, AR 72086, (501) 676-2467
Rose Publishing Co., 301 Louisiana, Little Rock, AR 72201, (501) 372-1666

Crosley Inc, 1515 Kitchen, Jonesboro, AR 72401, (501) 935-3928
TOTAL LIFESTYLE- The Magazine of Natural Living, P.O. Box 1137, Harrison, AR 72601
SOUTH & WEST, 2406 So S Street, Fort Smith, AR 72901
ULULATUS, P.O. Box 397, Fort Smith, AR 72902, (501) 783-4956

CALIFORNIA

POET TREE NEWS, Box 25-4502, Sacramento, CA 05825, 456-5344
Hollywood Film Archive, 8344 Melrose Ave., Hollywood, CA 90069, (213) 933-3345
Homosexual Information Center Inc, 6715 Hollywood Blvd 210, Hollywood, CA 90028
Acrobat Books Publishers, 420 1/2 N Larchmont Blvd, Los Angeles, CA 90004, 213-467-4506
ARAB AMERICAN ALMANAC, PO Box 74637, Los Angeles, CA 90004, (213) 483-5111
Archinform, PO Box 27732, Los Angeles, CA 90027, (213) 662-0216
Astro Artz, 240 So Broadway, 5th Floor, Los Angeles, CA 90012, 213-687-7362
AZTLAN: International Journal of Chicano Studies, University of California-Los Angeles, 405 Hilgard Avenue, Los Angeles, CA 90025,
    213-825-2642
BACHY, 11317 Santa Monica Blvd., Los Angeles, CA 90025, (213) GRU-BERG
BRAIN/MIND BULLETIN, P O Box 42211, Los Angeles, CA 90042
Center Publications, 905 S Normandie Ave., Los Angeles, CA 90006, 213-387-2356
Chicano Studies Research Center Publications, University of California-Los Angeles, 405 Hilgard Avenue, Los Angeles, CA 90025,
    213-825-2642
CHRYSALIS: A Magazine of Women's Culture, 1052 W. 6th Street, #330, Los Angeles, CA 90017, (213) 482-5120
Citrus House Ltd, 1335 N Citrus Ave, Los Angeles, CA 90028, (213) 469-7234
D.& E. Career Publishing Co., 5146 W Imperial, Los Angeles, CA 90045, (213) 374-7486
FAIRFAX FOLIO, 3039 Shasta Circle South, Los Angeles, CA 90065
FOLLIES, PO Box 41110, Los Angeles, CA 90041, (213) 254-4455
The Garlic Press, PO Box 24799, Los Angeles, CA 90024
THE GAY LUTHERAN, Lutherans Concerned, Box 19114A, Los Angeles, CA 90019, (213) 663-7816
THE GRAMERCY REVIEW, P.O. Box 15362, Los Angeles, CA 90015
Lorna Greene, 1240 1/2 North Havenhurst Drive, Los Angeles, CA 90046, (213) 654-2482
HIGH PERFORMANCE, 240 S. Broadway, 5th Floor, Los Angeles, CA 90012, (213) 687-7362
Illuminati, 1147 So. Robertson Blvd., Los Angeles, CA 90035, (213) 273-8372
Interface Press, P.O. Box 42211, Los Angeles, CA 90042, 213 257-2500
JAZZ, 3650 W Pico, Los Angeles, CA 90019
Jazz Press, 3650 W Pico, Los Angeles, CA 90019, (213) 821-2889
THE LESBIAN TIDE, 8706 Cadillac Ave., Los Angeles, CA 90034
Levenson Press, P.O.B. 19606, Los Angeles, CA 90019
LITTLE CAESAR, 3373 Overland Ave., #2, Los Angeles, CA 90034, 213-837-8255
Little Caesar Press, 3373 Overland Ave #2, Los Angeles, CA 90034, (213) 837-8255
Loving Publishers, 4576 Alla Road, Los Angeles, CA 90066, (213) 822-7413
MADRONA, 505 S Wilton Pl #203, Los Angeles, CA 90020
New Bedford Press, 5800 W Century Blvd., Suite 91502, Los Angeles, CA 90009, 837-2961
The New South Company, 924 Westwood Blvd., Suite 935, Los Angeles, CA 90024, 213 477-2061
NEWORLD, 6331 Hollywood Blvd #624, Los Angeles, CA 90028, 465-1560
THE NEWS CIRCLE, PO Box 74637, Los Angeles, CA 90004, (213) 483-5111
ORNAMENT, A Quarterly of Jewelry and Personal Adornment, PO Box 35029, Los Angeles, CA 90035, 213-652-9914
ORPHEUS, c/o Illuminati, 1147 So Robertson Blvd, Los Angeles, CA 90035, 213-273-8372
Panjandrum Books, 11321 Irva Ave., Ste.1, Los Angeles, CA 90025, (213) 477-8771
PANJANDRUM POETRY JOURNAL, 11321 Irva Ave. Ste.1, Los Angeles, CA 90025, (213) 477-8771
Papa Bach Paperbacks, 11317 Santa Monica Blvd, Los Angeles, CA 90025, (213) GRUBERG
Patricia J. Sherman Real Estate Books, 4011 Garden Avenue, Los Angeles, CA 90039, (213) 661-1194
Pig's Whisker Music, PO Box 27522, Los Angeles, CA 90027
rara avis, P.O. Box 3095, Terminal Annex, Los Angeles, CA 90051
SMITH'S JOURNAL, 2009 Pinehurst Road, Los Angeles, CA 90068, 851-0375
Spectrum Productions, 979 Casiano Rd., Los Angeles, CA 90049
TAI CHI, 3605 Sunset Blvd, Los Angeles, CA 90026, 213-665-7773
URTHKIN, P O Box 67485, Los Angeles, CA 90067, 213-556-3033
White Tower Inc. Press, PO Box 42216, Los Angeles, CA 90042, (213) 254-1326
Wisdom Garden Books, Box 29448, Los Angeles, CA 90029, (213) 380-1968
Creative With Words Publications (CWW), 8259 Fountain Avenue #5, West Hollywood, CA 90046, (213) 656-5358
Noble House Publishing, 256 South Robertson, Beverly Hills, CA 90211, (714) 675-1230
Pentangle Press, 132 Lasky Dr., Beverly Hills, CA 90212, 213-278-4996
Rossi, PO Box 2001, Beverly Hills, CA 90213, (213) 271-3730
Desserco Publishing, P.O. Box 2433, Culver City, CA 90230
Peace Press, 3828 Willat Ave., Culver City, CA 90230, 213-838-7387
Velvet Flute Books, 6050 Canterbury Drive, E119, Culver City, CA 90230, (213) 776-5429
THE AWAKENER MAGAZINE, 938 18th Street, Hermosa Beach, CA 90254, (213) 379-2656
Eurail Guide Annual, 27540 Pacific Coast, Malibu, CA 90265, (213) 457-7286
EURAIL GUIDE ANNUAL, 27540 Pacific Coast Hwy, Malibu, CA 90265
THE DELPHYS FORUM, P.O. Box 677, Pacific Palisades, CA 90272, 213-395-7787
Artichoke Press, 3274 Parkhurst Drive, Rancho Palos Verdes, CA 90274, (213) 831-1818
Poet Papers, P.O. Box 528, Topanga, CA 90290
THE RECORD SUN, PO Box 528, Topanga, CA 90290
BEYOND BAROQUE, 681 Venice Blvd. P.O. Box 806, Venice, CA 90291, (213) 822-3006
BEYOND BAROQUE LIBRARY of SMALL PRESS PUBLICATIONS, Beyond Baroque Foundation, 681 Venice blvd. P.O. Box 806,
    Venice, CA 90291, (213) 822-3006
FREE VENICE BEACHHEAD, PO Box 504, Venice, CA 90291, 823-5092
Paradise Press, 815 Ocean Front Walk #1, Venice, CA 90291, (213) 392-4098 and 478-4477
W. I. M. Publications, PO Box 5037, Inglewood, CA 90310, (213) 774-5230
Dervy, A. J., PO Box 874, Santa Monica, CA 90406, 213 395-6020

514

FIFTH SUN, 1134-B Chelsea Ave, Santa Monica, CA 90403, (213) 828-2918
Momentum Press, 512 Hill Street #4, Santa Monica, CA 90405
Planetary Research, PO Box 1741, Santa Monica, CA 90406
PRAXIS: A Journal of Cultural Criticism, PO Box 1280, Santa Monica, CA 90406
Vista Publications, 3010 Santa Monica Blvd., Suite 221, Santa Monica, CA 90404, (213) 828-3258
Morning Glory Press, 6595 San Haroldo Way, Buena Park, CA 90620
ACADEMY AWARDS OSCAR ANNUAL, 509 N. Harbor Blvd., La Habra, CA 90631, (213) 691-0737
Gem Guides Book Co., 5409 Lenvale, Whittier, CA 90601, 213-692-5492
MYTHLORE, PO Box 4671, Whittier, CA 90607
Paul G. Partington, 7320 South Gretna Avenue, Whittier, CA 90606, (213) 695-7960
COBBLESTONE, P.O. Box 1128, Los Alamitos, CA 90720
Fragments/The Valentine Press, P.O. Box 1128, Los Alamitos, CA 90720
Hwong Publishing Company, 10353 Los Alamitos Blvd., Los Alamitos, CA 90720, (213) 598-2428
Angels Gate Press, PO Box 1881, San Pedro, CA 90733
Miles & Weir, Ltd., Box 1906, San Pedro, CA 90733, 213-831-2012
R. & E. Miles, PO Box 1906, San Pedro, CA 90733, (213) 833-8856
Singlejack Books, PO Box 1906, San Pedro, CA 90733
Gotuit Enterprises, PO Box 2568, 1300 Golden Rain #9-C, Seal Beach, CA 90740, (213) 430-5198
Applezaba Press, 333 Orizaba, Long Beach, CA 90814, (213) 434-7761
Maelstrom Press, P O Box 4261, Long Beach, CA 90804
MAELSTROM REVIEW, P.O. Box 4261, Long Beach, CA 90804
THE ALTADENA REVIEW, P.O. Box 212, Altadena, CA 91001
The Altadena Review, Inc., PO Box 212, Altadena, CA 91001
Far Out West Publications, PO Box 953, South Pasadena, CA 91030, (213) 799-3754
Pygmalion Press, 609 El Centro, South Pasadena, CA 91030, (213) 682-1211
Golden West Books, PO Box 8136, San Marino, CA 91108, 213-283-3446
Electronic Music Enterprises, 349 1/2 W. California Ave, Glendale, CA 91203, (213) 243-3477
Festival Publications, P.O. Box 10180, Glendale, CA 91209
XENHARMONIC BULLETIN, 349 1/2 W. California Ave., Glendale, CA 91203, 213-243-3477
Samuel P. Levine, PO Box 174, Canoga Park, CA 91305, (213) 343-0550
Kent Publications, 18301 Halsted St, Northridge, CA 91324, 213-349-5088; 349-2080
SAN FERNANDO POETRY JOURNAL, 18301 Halsted Street, Northridge, CA 91325
TOWARDS, 17417 Vintage Street, Northridge, CA 91325, (213) 349-2780
Brason-Sargar Publications, PO Box 842, Reseda, CA 91335, (213) 851-1229
J&J Publishing, PO Box 1105, Reseda, CA 91335, (213) 345-3797
Mojave Books, 7040 Darby Ave., Reseda, CA 91335, 213-342-3403
Poly Tone Press, 16027 Sunburst Street, Sepulveda, CA 91343, 213-892-0044
Forest Primeval Press, 1335 Norman, Thousand Oaks, CA 91360
Penny Postcard Press, 1335 Norman, Thousand Oaks, CA 91360
Young Davis Press, 1290 Whitecliff Road, Thousand Oaks, CA 91360, (805) 497-2505
The Green Hut Press, 24051 Rotunda Rd, Valencia Hills, CA 91355, 805-259-5290
Periwinkle Press, PO Box 1305, Woodland Hills, CA 91365, (213) 346-3415
Lidiraven Books: A Division of Biogeocosmological Press, Box 5567, Sherman Oaks, CA 91413, (213) 892-0059
Creative Book Company, 8210 Varna Ave., Van Nuys, CA 91402, 213-988-2334
Legal Publications, Inc., PO Box 3723, Van Nuys, CA 91407, (213) 782-6545; 873-4939
Perivale Press, 13830 Erwin Street, Van Nuys, CA 91401, 213-785-4671
Halls of Ivy Press, 13050 Raymer Street, North Hollywood, CA 91605, (213) 875-3050
Roush Books, Box 4203, Valley Village, North Hollywood, CA 91607, (213) 762-3740
The WorDoctor Publications, PO Box 9761, North Hollywood, CA 91606, 213-980-3576
Main Track Publications, 12435 Ventura Court, Studio City, CA 91604, (213) 506-0151
THE PRAIRIE RAMBLER, PO Box 505, Claremont, CA 91711, 714-621-8109
Exponent Ltd., 2243 First Street, La Verne, CA 91750, (714) 595-3418
Bookworm Publishing Company, P.O. Box 3037, Ontario, CA 91761, 714-983-8548
Auromere, Inc., 1291 Weber Street, Pomona, CA 91768, (714) 629-8255
Master Key Publications, PO Box 519, Bonita, CA 92002, (714) 475-6060
J and J Press, 2441 Montgomery Avenue, Cardiff-by-the-Sea, CA 92007, (714) 753-2053
American Revolutionary Political Pamphlets, 704 Nob Avenue, Del Mar, CA 92014, 755-1258
CRAWL OUT YOUR WINDOW, 704 Nob Ave, Del Mar, CA 92014, 714-755-1258
Crawl Out Your Window Press, 704 Nob Ave, Del Mar, CA 92014, 714-755-1258
PSYCHOTHERAPY DIGEST, P.O. Box 1167, Del Mar, CA 92014, 714-481-7023
Sothis & Co. Publishing, P.O. Box 1166, Del Mar, CA 92014, (714) 481-9355
Communication Creativity, 5644 La Jolla Blvd., La Jolla, CA 92037, (714) 459-4489
Copley Books, 7776 Ivanhoe Avenue, P O Box 957, La Jolla, CA 92038, 714-454-1842
Moonlight Publications, PO Drawer 2850, La Jolla, CA 92038
Associated Creative Writers, 9231 Molly Woods Ave, La Mesa, CA 92041, 460-4107
Daisy Press, PO Box 883, La Mesa, CA 92041
Helix House, PO Box 1595, La Mesa, CA 92041, 714-460-4107
WRITING, 9231 Molly Woods Ave., La Mesa, CA 92041, 460-4107
Dolly Varden Publications, Box 2017, Oceanside, CA 92054, (714) 729-1736
The Rateavers, Pauma Valley, CA 92061, (714) 566-8994
CHAIRMAN'S CHAT, P O Box 696, San Marcos, CA 92069, 714-746-9430
Dominion Press, P O Box 37, San Marcos, CA 92069, 714-746-9430
MASTER THOUGHTS, PO Box 37, San Marcos, CA 92069, (714) 746-9430
THEOLOGIA 21, PO Box 37, San Marcos, CA 92069, (714) 746-9430
Borderland Sciences Research Foundation, P.O. Box 549, Vista, CA 92083, 724-2043
JOURNAL OF BORDERLAND RESEARCH, P.O. Box 549, Vista, CA 92083, 724-2043
A Harmless Flirtation With Wealth, P.O. Box 9779, San Diego, CA 92109, 714-234-9632
ANTENNA, 5014 Narragansett #6, c/o Gage, San Diego, CA 92107
BARE WIRES, P.O.Box 9779, San Diego, CA 92109, (714) 234-9632

Birth Day Publishing Company, PO Box 7722, San Diego, CA 92107, (714) 296-3194
Center for Women's Studies & Services (CWSS), P.O. Box 350, San Diego, CA 92101, 714-233-8984
FEMINIST BULLETIN, P.O. Box 350, San Diego, CA 92101, 714-233-8984
The Feminist Poetry & Graphics Center, 3040 Clairemont Drive, San Diego, CA 92117, 714-239-3664
Franson Publications, 4291 Van Dyke Place, San Diego, CA 92116
Giddyup Press, 4812 1/2 Del Mar, San Diego, CA 92107
THE GREATER GOLDEN HILL POETRY EXPRESS, 2829 Broadway, San Diego, CA 92102, 714-239-3664
JOURNAL OF ALTERNATIVE HUMAN SERVICES, Community Congress of S.D., 1172 Morena Blvd, San Diego, CA 92110, (714) 275-1700
Kensington Press, Box 16412, San Diego, CA 92116, (714) 284-4424
THE LONGEST REVOLUTION, Center for Women's Studies and Services, P.O.Box 350, San Diego, CA 92101, (714) 233-8984
LP Publications, (The Love Project), PO Box 7601, San Diego, CA 92107, (714) 225-0133
MAIZE, Box 8251, San Diego, CA 92102, 714-235-6135/714-455-1128
Maize Press, P.O. Box 8251, San Diego, CA 92102, 714-235-6135
NOTES FROM THE UNDERGROUND, 4291 Van Dyke Place, San Diego, CA 92116
PACIFIC POETRY AND FICTION REVIEW, English Office, San Diego State University, San Diego, CA 92182, 714-266-0675
THE SEEKER NEWSLETTER, PO Box 7601, San Diego, CA 92107, (714) 225-0133
Tofua Press, 10457-F Roselle Street, San Diego, CA 92121, 714-453-4774
Wild Mustard Press, PO Box 3237, San Diego, CA 92103, (714) 295-6870
The Word Shop, 3737 Fifth Avenue, Suite 203, San Diego, CA 92103, (714) 291-9126
Malki Museum Press, 11-795 Fields Road, Morongo Indian Reservation, Banning, CA 92220, 714-849-7289
ETC Publications, P.O. Drawer 1627-A, Palm Springs, CA 92263, 714-325-5352
Golden Quill Publishers Inc, PO Box 1278, Colton, CA 92324, (714) 783-0119
COSMOPOLITAN CONTACT, P. O. Box 1566, Fontana, CA 92335
Dimensionist Press, 5931 Stanton Avenue, Highland, CA 92346, 862-4521
WESTERN WORLD REVIEW, P.O. Box 366, Sun City, CA 92381
The Borgo Press, Box 2845, San Bernardino, CA 92406, (714) 884-5813
SCIENCE FICTION & FANTASY BOOK REVIEW, Box 2845, San Bernardino, CA 92406, (714) 884-5813
JOURNAL OF CALIFORNIA AND GREAT BASIN ANTHROPOLOGY, Department of Anthropology, University of California, Riverside, CA 92521, 714-787-3885
LATIN AMERICAN PERSPECTIVES, PO Box 5703, Riverside, CA 92517, (714) 787-5508
House of White Shell Woman, Box 1344, Brea, CA 92621
Panda Programs, 1872 W Lotus Place, Brea, CA 92621, (714) 990-6800
Ana-Doug Publishing, 1236 Cranbrook Place, Fullerton, CA 92633, (714) 871-4060
ON STAGE, PO Box 4040, Fullerton, CA 92634
Baja Trail Publications, Inc., P O Box 6088, Huntington Beach, CA 92646, (714) 536-8081
MEXICO WEST, P.O. Box 6088, Huntington Beach, CA 92646, 714-536-8081
Sun, Man, Moon Inc., P.O. Box 5084, Huntington Beach, CA 92646, 714-962-8945
Windsong Books International, Box 867, Huntington Beach, CA 92648
Amigo Press, 620 Lombardy Lane, Laguna Beach, CA 92651, (714) 494-2302
Nanny Goat Productions, Box 845, Laguna Beach, CA 92652, (714) 494-7930
PANDORA'S BOX, Box 845, Laguna Beach, CA 92652, (714) 494-7930
ABORTION EVE, Box 845, Luguna Beach, CA 92652, (714) 494-7930
IN STRIDE, 28570 Marguerite Parkway, Suite 103, Mission Viejo, CA 92692, (714) 831-0464
THE HUNGRY YEARS, PO Box 7213, Newport Beach, CA 92660, 548-3324
Malpelo, 1916 Court Avenue, Newport Beach, CA 92663
VILLAGE CIRCLE, PO Box 5361, Orange, CA 92667, (714) 633-1420
West Village Publishing Company, PO Box 5361, Orange, CA 92667, (714) 633-1420
POWERLIFTING USA, Box 467, Camarillo, CA 93010, (805) 482-2378
Powerlifting USA, Box 467, Camarillo, CA 93010, (805) 482-2378
Quantal Publishing B, PO Box 1598, Goleta, CA 93017, (805) 964-7293
Turkey Press, 6746 Sueno Road, Goleta, CA 93017, 685-3603
Writers' Publishing Company, Box 309, Goleta, CA 93017, (805) 682-1445
Psychic Books, Box 2205, Oxnard, CA 93030, (805) 488-8670
Racz Publishing Co., PO Box 287, Oxnard, CA 93032, (805) 642-1186
Venice West Publishers, 3050 S. Ventura Road, Oxnard, CA 93030, (805) 483-7818
TINTA, Spanish Dept, University of California, Santa Barbara, CA 93017, 961-3161
Golden West Historical Publications, PO Box 1906, Ventura, CA 93002
Bellerophon Books, 36 Anacapa Street, Santa Barbara, CA 93101, (805) 965-7034
Black Sparrow Press, PO Box 3993, Santa Barbara, CA 93105
Cadmus Editions, PO Box 4725, Santa Barbara, CA 93103
Capra Press, P.O. Box 2068, Santa Barbara, CA 93120, 805-966-4590
La Cumbre Publishing Co., 1761 Calle Poniente, Santa Barbara, CA 93101, (805) 966-5534
Doggeral Press, 417 Sea View Road, Santa Barbara, CA 93108, (805) 966-9966, 969-2500
Endurance, Box 2382, Santa Barbara, CA 93120, (805) 962-2034
FOUR DOGS MOUNTAIN SONGS, 417 Sea View Road, Santa Barbara, CA 93108
FRONTLINES, Box 40105, Santa Barbara, CA 93101, 805-963-5993
Harvest Publishers, 907 Santa Barbara Street, Santa Barbara, CA 93101
HARVEST QUARTERLY, 907 Santa Barbara Street, Santa Barbara, CA 93101
INKLINGS, 209 West De la Guerra, Santa Barbara, CA 93101, (805) 962-9996
Jama Books, PO Box 30751, Santa Barbara, CA 93105, (805) 687-9325
McNally & Loftin, West, Box 1316, Santa Barbara, CA 93101, (805) 964-7079
Mudborn Press, 209 W. De la Guerra, Santa Barbara, CA 93101, 805-962-9996
Parachuting Publications, P.O. Box 4232-Q, Santa Barbara, CA 93103, 805-968-7277
THE PYRAMID GUIDE: International Bi-Monthly Newsletter, 741 Rosarita Lane, Santa Barbara, CA 93105, (805) 682-5151
ROCKBOTTOM, 209 W. De La Guerra, Santa Barbara, CA 93101, 805-962-9996
Ross-Erikson Publishers, Inc., 1825 Grand Ave, Santa Barbara, CA 93101, 966-2691
SANTA BARBARA HARBOR NEWS, PO Box 30802, Santa Barbara, CA 93105, 682-5545
Summer Stream Press, PO Box 6056, Santa Barbara, CA 93111, (805) 967-5992

Technical Documentation Services, 56 S. Patterson, No. 108, Santa Barbara, CA 93111, (805) 976-7342
LUMBEE NATION TIMES, PO Box 911, Exeter, CA 93221, (209) 592-3327
CAFE SOLO, 7975 San Marcos, Atascadero, CA 93422
KALDRON, 441 North 6th St., Grover City, CA 93433, 805-481-2360
The Olive Press Publications, PO Box 99, Los Olivos, CA 93441
Sea Challengers, 1851 Don Avenue, Los Osos, CA 93402
El Moro Publications, P.O. Box 965, Morro Bay, CA 93442, (805) 772-3514
S, 1600 Preston Lane, Morro Bay, CA 93442, 805-772-2715
Studio S Press, 1600 Preston Lane, Morro Bay, CA 93442, 805-772-2715
ASSERT NEWSLETTER, PO Box 1094, San Luis Obispo, CA 93406, 805-543-5911
COLLECTOR'S ITEM, PO Box 1275, San Luis Obispo, CA 93406, 805-543-5404
Erin Hills Publishers, 1390 Fairway Dr, San Luis Obispo, CA 93401, (805) 543-3050
Impact Publishers, Inc., PO Box 1094, San Luis Obispo, CA 93406, 805-543-5911
Padre Productions, PO Box 1275, San Luis Obispo, CA 93406, 805-543-5404
Quest Press, Box 998, San Luis Obispo, CA 93406, (805) 543-8500
Solo Press, 750 Nipomo, San Luis Obispo, CA 93401
WESTERN PUBLISHING SCENE, P.O.Box 1275, San Luis Obispo, CA 93406, (805) 543-5404
The Boxwood Press, 183 Ocean View Blvd, Pacific Grove, CA 93950, 408-375-9110
J. DuHadway Craig, PO Box 42, Pebble Beach, CA 93953, (408) 624-0354
Apple Tree Lane, 2 Fair Oaks Lane, Atherton, CA 94025, (415) 323-4534
Bay Area ASPO News, PO Box 603, Belmont, CA 94002, (408) 243-1136
Down There Press + (My Mama's Press), PO Box 2086, Burlingame, CA 94010, 415-342-9867
Ink Blot Press, 6340 Mission Street, Daly City, CA 94014, (415) 992-1750
Cedar House Enterprises, PO Box 70, El Granada, CA 94018, 415-726-4096
Westport Press, Inc, PO Box 277, Los Altos, CA 94022, (415) 941-5474
DR. DOBB'S JOURNAL OF COMPUTER CALISTHENICS & ORTHODONTIA, 1263 El Camino, P. O. Box E, Menlo Park, CA 94025, 415-323-3111
Harvestman and Associates, PO Box 271, Menlo Park, CA 94025, (415) 969-0125
LITERATURE OF LIBERTY, 1177 University Drive, Menlo Park, CA 94025, 415-323-6933
People's Computer Co., 1263 El Camino Real, Menlo Park, CA 94025, 415-323-3111
Pride of the Forest, PO Box 7266, Menlo Park, CA 94025
Prologue Publications, P.O. Box 640, Menlo Park, CA 94025, 322-5034
RECREATIONAL COMPUTING, 1263 El Camino, P. O. Box E, Menlo Park, CA 94025, 415-323-3111
Merlin Engine Works, Box 169, Milbrae, CA 94040
Celestial Arts, 231 Adrian Rd., Millbrae, CA 94030
Poor Souls Press/Scaramouche Books, 1050 Magnolia No. 2, Millbrae, CA 94030
Fels and Firn Press, 1843 Vassar Ave., Mountain View, CA 94043, 415-965-4291
PACIFIC RESEARCH, 867 W Dana #204, Mountain View, CA 94041, 415-969-1545
LAUGHING UNICORN, 432 Heathcliff Drive, Pacifica, CA 94044, (415) 355-3630
POETIC JUSTICE, 432 Heathcliff Drive, Pacifica, CA 94044, (415) 355-3630
Publishing Associates, 432 Heathcliff Drive, Pacifica, CA 94044, (415) 355-3630
RAINBOW'S END, 432 Heathcliff Drive, Pacifica, CA 94044, (415) 355-3630
The Tenth Muse, Box 1417, Pacifica, CA 94044, 993-5290
No Dead Lines, 241 Bonita, Portola Valley, CA 94025, 415-851-1847
White Oak Publishing House, PO Box 3089, Redwood City, CA 94064, (415) 364-3882
Wide World Publishing, PO Box 476, San Carlos, CA 94070, (415) 593-2039
BBB Associates, PO Box 551, San Mateo, CA 94010, (415) 344-8458
Manroot Books, Box 982, So San Francisco, CA 94080
MANROOT, Box 982, South San Francisco, CA 94080
American Business Consultants, Inc., 1540 Nuthatch Lane, Sunnyvale, CA 94087, (408) 732-8931
IMPACT, An International Publication of Contemporary Literature & the Arts, 1070 Noriega, Sunnyvale, CA 94086, (408) 733-9615
LITERARY MONITOR: The Voice of Contemporary Literature, 1070 Noriega, Sunnyvale, CA 94086
TLM Press, 1070 Noriega, Sunnyvale, CA 94086, (408) 733-9615
The Heyeck Press, 25 Patrol Ct., Woodside, CA 94062
Alchemist/Light Publishing, P O Box 5530, San Francisco, CA 94101, (415) 655-0728
Alchemy Books, 681 Market, Suite 755, San Francisco, CA 94105, (415) 362-2708
THE ALTERNATE, 15 Harriet Street, San Francisco, CA 94103, (415) 346-4747
ANDROGYNE, 930 Shields, San Francisco, CA 94132, 586-2697
Androgyne Books, 930 Shields, San Francisco, CA 94132, 586-2697
Apple-Gems, PO Box 16292, San Francisco, CA 94116, (415) 587-9752
APPLEWOOD JOURNAL, PO Box 1781, San Francisco, CA 94101, (415) 668-6691
ARCADE-THE COMICS REVUE, Po Box 40474, San Francisco, CA 94140
As Is/So & So Press, 2864 Folsom, San Francisco, CA 94110, 415-282-9570
Ash-Kar Press, PO Box 14547, San Francisco, CA 94114
Banana Productions, 1183 Church St., San Francisco, CA 94114, 415-648-5174
BARTLEBY'S REVIEW, 3152 Lyon St., San Francisco, CA 94123
BEYOND RICE, A Broadside Series, P.O.Box 1447, San Francisco, CA 94101, 982-4316
BIRTHSTONE, 1319 6th Avenue, San Francisco, CA 94122
Black Stone Press, 393 Hayes Street, San Francisco, CA 94102, 863-1933
BOOKLEGGER MAGAZINE AND BOOKS, 555 29th St., San Francisco, CA 94131
Booklegger Press, 555 29th St, San Francisco, CA 94131
BOXCAR, PO Box 14337, San Francisco, CA 94114
Boyd & Fraser Publishing Company, 3627 Sacramento St., San Francisco, CA 94118, 415-346-0686
BRIARPATCH REVIEW: A Journal of Right Livelihood and Simple Living, 330 Ellis Street, San Francisco, CA 94102
Buddhist Text Translation Society, 1731 15th Street, Gold Mountain Monastery, San Francisco, CA 94103, 415-861-9672
California Living Books (Examiner Special Projects), 223 Hearst Building, Third & Market Streets, San Francisco, CA 94103, (415) 543-5981
Carolyn Bean Publishing, Ltd., 120 2nd Street, San Francisco, CA 94105, 415-957-9574
Children's Book Press/Imprenta de Libros Infantiles, 1461 9th Ave., San Francisco, CA 94122, 415-664-8500

Chronicle Books/Prism Editions, 870 Market Street Suite 915, San Francisco, CA 94102, 415-777-7240
Cin Publications, PO Box 11277, San Francisco, CA 94101, 861-5018
City Lights Books, 261 Columbus Ave., San Francisco, CA 94133, (415) 362-8193
CITY LIGHTS JOURNAL, 261 Columbus Avenue, San Francisco, CA 94133, (415) 362-8193
THE COFFEEHOUSE, 3448 19th Street, San Francisco, CA 94110
The Communication Press, P O Box 22541, San Francisco, CA 94122, 415-566-3921
COSMEP NEWSLETTER, PO Box 703, San Francisco, CA 94101, (415) 922-9490
Crime and Social Justice Associates, Inc., 131 Townsend Street, San Francisco, CA 94107, (415) 543-2079
CRY CALIFORNIA, 681 Market Street, Room 1059, San Francisco, CA 94105, 415-391-7544
Design Enterprises of San Francisco, P.O. Box 27677, San Francisco, CA 94127
Dryad Press, PO Box 29161, Presidio, San Francisco, CA 94129
Duir Press, 919 Sutter #9, San Francisco, CA 94109, (415) 441-8354
FANTASY EXPRESS, 159 Ralston Street, San Francisco, CA 94132, (415) 586-2209
FINE PRINT: A Review for the Arts of the Book, P O Box 7741, San Francisco, CA 94120, 415-776-1530
Friends of the Earth, 124 Spear, San Francisco, CA 94105, 415-495-4770
GAY SUNSHINE: A Journal of Gay Liberation, P.O. Box 40397, San Francisco, CA 94140
Gay Sunshine Press, Inc., P.O. Box 40397, San Francisco, CA 94140
Gibbous Press, 150 10th Avenue, San Francisco, CA 94118, 415-752-5898
GOLDEN GATE REVIEW, 159 Ralston Street, San Francisco, CA 94132, (415) 586-2209
HEIRS, 657 Mission St., San Francisco, CA 94105, (415) 824-8604
Heirs Press, 657 Mission St, San Francisco, CA 94105
Hiddigeigei Books, P.O. Box 5031, San Francisco, CA 94103
HILLS, 36 Clyde, San Francisco, CA 94107
Hoddypoll Press, 3841-B 24th Street, San Francisco, CA 94114
HODMANDOD, 150 10th Avenue, San Francisco, CA 94118, 415-752-5898
INQUIRY MAGAZINE, 747 Front Street, San Francisco, CA 94111, (415) 433-4319
Institute for Contemporary Studies, 260 California Street, Suite 811, San Francisco, CA 94111, (415) 398-3010
INTERMEDIA, P O Box 31-464, San Francisco, CA 94131
Intersection Inc., 756 Union St., San Francisco, CA 94133
KOSMOS, 2580 Polk Street, San Francisco, CA 94109, 415-928-4332
Kosmos, 2580 Polk Street, San Francisco, CA 94109, (415) 928-4332
LEFT CURVE, 1230 Grant St. Box 302, San Francisco, CA 94133
Left Curve Publications, 1230 Grant St, Box 302, San Francisco, CA 94133
Leland Mellott Books, 1461 Page Street, San Francisco, CA 94117, 431-2407
Live-Oak Press, PO Box 99444, San Francisco, CA 94109, (415) 771-4992
LOCUS: The Newspaper of the Science Fiction Field, Box 3938, San Francisco, CA 94119, 415-339-9196
Lost Roads Publishers, PO Box 11143, San Francisco, CA 94101
MADNESS NETWORK NEWS, PO Box 684, San Francisco, CA 94101, (415) 548-2980
MAGICAL BLEND, PO Box 11303, San Francisco, CA 94101
Magical Blend, PO Box 11303, San Francisco, CA 94101
MINI-TAUR SERIES, 601 Leavenworth #45, San Francisco, CA 94109
Momo's Press, PO Box 14061, San Francisco, CA 94114
Mothra Press, 1001-B Guerrero, San Francisco, CA 94110
New Glide Publ., 330 Ellis Street, San Francisco, CA 94102
NICOTINE SOUP, P.O. Box 22613, San Francisco, CA 94122, (707) 795-2098
Noro Press, P.O.Box 1447, San Francisco, CA 94101
NORO REVIEW, P.O.Box 1447, San Francisco, CA 94101
Not-For-Sale-Press, 243 Grand View Ave, San Francisco, CA 94114, 415-647-4290
NOT MAN APART, 124 Spear Street, San Francisco, CA 94105
Occasional Productions, 251 Parnassus Ave, San Francisco, CA 94117
Pancake Press, 163 Galewood Circle, San Francisco, CA 94131, 415-648-3573
PARAGRAPH: A QUARTERLY OF GAY FICTION, Box 14051, San Francisco, CA 94114
Peace & Pieces Foundation, Box 99394, San Francisco, CA 94109, 415-771-3431
PEOPLE'S YELLOW PAGES of the SAN FRANCISCO BAY AREA, P.O. Box 31291, San Francisco, CA 94131
PEQUOD, 3478 22nd Street, San Francisco, CA 94110
Persona Press, PO Box 14022, San Francisco, CA 94114, 415-861-6679
Poetry for the People, PO Box 12406, San Francisco, CA 94112, (415) 526-3254
POSTCARD ART/POSTCARD FICTION, 2920 23rd Street, San Francisco, CA 94110
Rip Off Press Inc., PO Box 14158, San Francisco, CA 94114, (415) 863-5359
ROOM, P.O. Box 40610, San Francisco, CA 94140
Rosler, Martha, 2920 23rd Street, San Francisco, CA 94110
San Francisco Center for Visual Studies, 49 Rivoli, San Francisco, CA 94117, (415) 285-7114
SAN FRANCISCO REVIEW OF BOOKS, 1111 Kearny Street, San Francisco, CA 94133, 415-HA1-9574
SAN FRANCISCO STORIES, 625 Post Street, Box 752, San Francisco, CA 94109, (415) 752-7506
Sea Of Storms, PO Box 22613, San Francisco, CA 94122, (707) 795-2098
SECOND COMING, P.O. Box 31249, San Francisco, CA 94131, (415) 647-3679
Second Coming Press, PO Box 31249, San Francisco, CA 94131, 415-647-3679
SHOCKS, Box 14061, San Francisco, CA 94114
Sitnalta Press, 1881 Sutter Street, #103, San Francisco, CA 94115, (415) 922-8223
SO & SO, 2864 Folsom, San Francisco, CA 94110, 415-282-9570
SPIRALS, PO Box 29472, San Francisco, CA 94129
THE STONE, 3978 26th St, San Francisco, CA 94131, 415-648-5392
Synergistic Press, 3965 Sacramento St., San Francisco, CA 94118, 415-EV7-8180
Taurean Horn Press, 601 Leavenworth #45, San Francisco, CA 94109
TAXING & SPENDING, 260 California Street, Suite 811, San Francisco, CA 94111, (415) 398-3010
THIS, 1004 Hampshire Street, San Francisco, CA 94110
TOTTEL'S, 341 San Jose, San Francisco, CA 94110, 415-285-2784
Trike, 277 23rd Avenue, San Francisco, CA 94121
Trinity Press, Box 1320, San Francisco, CA 94101

VAJRA BODHI SEA, 1731 15th St, Gold Mountain Monastery, San Francisco, CA 94103, 861-9672
VILE, 1183 Church St, San Francisco, CA 94114
Whole Image Graphics, PO Box 774, San Francisco, CA 94101, (415) 282-5221
Wigan Pier Press, 1283 Page Street, San Francisco, CA 94117, (415) 863-6664
Wire Press, 3448 19th Street, San Francisco, CA 94110
Frog in the Well, 430 Oakdale Road, East Palo Alto, CA 94303, 415-323-1237
Bull Publishing Co., P O Box 208, Palo Alto, CA 94302, 415-322-2855
Cheshire Books, 514 Bryant Street, Palo Alto, CA 94301, 415-854-0393
Cibola Press, P.O. Box 1495, Palo Alto, CA 94302
Five Trees Press, PO Box 327, Palo Alto, CA 94302
Fresh Press, 774 Allen Court, Palo Alto, CA 94303, (415) 493-3596
Genny Smith Books, 1304 Pitman Avenue, Palo Alto, CA 94301, 415-321-7247
INFORMATION MOSCOW, 970 San Antonio Road, Palo Alto, CA 94303, (415) 493-1885
Matrix Press, PO Box 327, Palo Alto, CA 94302
National Financial Publications, PO Box 50173, Palo Alto, CA 94303
Ramparts Press, Bo 50128, Palo Alto, CA 94303, (415) 325-7861
TWO STEPS IN, 532 Emerson Street, Palo Alto, CA 94301, 321-7950
Vortex Editions, 3891 La Donna, Palo Alto, CA 94306
Wild Horses Potted Plant, 226 Hamilton Avenue, Palo Alto, CA 94301, (415) 326-6432
Dream Place Publications, PO Box 9416, Stanford, CA 94305, (415) 494-6083
Klutz Enterprises, PO Box 2992, Stanford, CA 94306, (415) 327-3808
New Seed Press, P.O. Box 3016, Stanford, CA 94305
SIGNS:A JOURNAL OF WOMEN IN CULTURE AND SOCIETY, Center for Research on Women, Serra House, Stanford University, Stanford, CA 94305
THE ADVOCATE, 1730 S. Amphlett, Suite 225, San Mateo, CA 94402, 415-573-7100
Diablo Western Press, PO Box 766, Alamo, CA 94507, (415) 820-6338
Holmgangers Press, 22 Ardith Lane, Alamo, CA 94507
Owlseye Publications, 1403 Northside, Berkeley, CA 94541, (415) 526-4209
Alta Napa Press, Box 407, Calistoga, CA 94515
THE FOC'SLE, PO Box 21355, Concord, CA 94521, (415) 687-5673
POW (Poetry Organization for Women), PO Box 2414, Dublin, CA 94566
WOMEN TALKING, WOMEN LISTENING, P.O. Box 2414, Dublin, CA 94566, 415-828-0671
YARDBIRD READER, P.O. Box 216, Fairmount Sta., El Cerrito, CA 94530
Yardbird Wing Editions/Yardbird Publishing Co. Inc., Box 216, Fairmount Sta., El Cerrito, CA 94530
POETALK QUARTERLY, 23650 Stratton Court, Hayward, CA 94541, (415) 537-6858
TYPE & PRESS, 24667 Heather Court, Hayward, CA 94545
New-Age Foods Publications, PO Box 234, Lafayette, CA 94549
Working Press, Box 687-D, Livermore, CA 94550, (415) 447-5943
Whitfield, 1841 Pleasant Hill Road, Pleasant Hill, CA 94523, (415) 934-8054
Manhole Publications, 5641 San Luis Ct, Pleasanton, CA 94566
Reyn Publishing Co., 14240 E 14th Street, San Leandro, CA 94578, (415) 352-5914
Sanatana Publishing Society, 3100 White Sulphur Springs Road, St. Helena, CA 94574, 707-963-9487
VISHVAMITRA, 3100 White Sulphur Springs Road, St. Helena, CA 94574, 707-963-9487
THE FAULT, 33513 6th St., Union City, CA 94587
The Fault Press, 33513 6th St, Union City, CA 94587, 415-489-8561
Calliope Press, 1162 Lincoln Ave #227, Walnut Creek, CA 94596
DUMP HEAP (Diverse Unsung Miracle Plants for Healthy Evolution Among People), 2950 Walnut Blvd., Walnut Creek, CA 94598
THE PAWN REVIEW, 1162 Lincoln Ave #227, Walnut Creek, CA 94596
Sheer Press, PO Box 4071, Walnut Creek, CA 94598
GESAR- Buddhist Perspectives, 5856 Doyle St., Emeryville, CA 94608, 415-655-1025
Akiba Press, PO Box 13086, Oakland, CA 94611, (415) 339-1283
Diana Press, Inc, 4400 Market St, Oakland, CA 94608, (415) 658-5558
HOLY BEGGARS' GAZETTE, 3726 Virden Ave., Oakland, CA 94619
Jakubowsky, Box 209, Oakland, CA 94604, (415) 763-4324
JUICE, 1015 Rose Avenue, Oakland, CA 94611, 415-532-5621
LSM Information Center, LSM Press, P.O. Box 2077, Oakland, CA 94604, 635-4863
NEWSFRONT INTERNATIONAL, 4228 Telegraph Avenue, Oakland, CA 94609, (415) 654-6725
Personabooks, 434 66th Street, Oakland, CA 94609, 415-658-2482
PLEXUS, Bay Area Women's Newspaper, 545 Athol Avenue, Oakland, CA 94606
POETRY FLASH, 345 Fifteenth Street, Oakland, CA 94612, 415-836-1246
The Rather Press, 3200 Guido Street, Oakland, CA 94612, 531-2938
Second Class, Working Class, an International Women's Reader, 4228 Telegraph, Oakland, CA 94609
TZADDIKIM, 3726 Virden Avenue, Oakland, CA 94619
VIEW, 1555 San Pablo Avenue, Oakland, CA 94612, (415) 835-5104
Carousel Press, P.O. Box 6061, Albany, CA 94706, 415-527-5849
Little Dinosaur Press, 1222 Solano Avenue, Albany, CA 94706
Sand Dollar, 1222 Solano Avenue, Albany, CA 94706
Aldebaran Review, 2209 California, Berkeley, CA 94703
And/Or Press, P O Box 2246, Berkeley, CA 94702, (415) 849-2665
Aris Books, 526 Santa Barbara Road, Berkeley, CA 94707, 527-1958
Ata Books, 1928 Stuart Street, Berkeley, CA 94703, (415) 841-9613
Banyan Tree Books, 1963 El Dorado Avenue, Berkeley, CA 94707, 415-527-2499
BERKELEY BARB, P.O. Box 1247, Berkeley, CA 94701
BERKELEY JOURNAL OF SOCIOLOGY, 410 Barrows Hall, University of California, Berkeley, CA 94720
THE BERKELEY MONTHLY, 910 Parker Street, Berkeley, CA 94710, (415) 848-7900
BERKELEY POETS COOPERATIVE, P.O. Box 459, Berkeley, CA 94701, (415) 848-9098
Berkeley Poets Workshop and Press, P.O. Box 459, Berkeley, CA 94701
Blue Wind Press, P.O. Box 7175, Berkeley, CA 94707, 415-526-1905
THE BREATH OF THE PEOPLE, 1631 Grant Street, Berkeley, CA 94703, 415-548-2208

California Contemporary Craftspeople Publications, 1560 Beverly Place, Berkeley, CA 94706, (415) 525-5254
California Street, 723 Dwight Way, Berkeley, CA 94710, (415) 548-8273
CAMERA OBSCURA: A Journal of Feminism and Film Theory, PO Box 4517, Berkeley, CA 94704
Catex Press, 1150 Spruce St, Berkeley, CA 94707
Center Press, 2045 Francisco Street, Berkeley, CA 94709, (415) 526-8373
Christopher's Books, 850 Talbot Avenue, Berkeley, CA 94706, (415) 482-2198
CITY MINER, P.O. Box 176, Berkeley, CA 94701, 415-524-1162
Creative Arts Book Company, 833 Bancroft Way, Berkeley, CA 94710, 415-848-4777
CRIME AND SOCIAL JUSTICE: ISSUES IN CRIMINOLOGY., P.O. Box 4373, Berkeley, CA 94704
Crosscut Saw Press, 2940 Seventh Street, Berkeley, CA 94710
Current Issues Publications, 2707 Walker Street, Berkeley, CA 94705, (415) 549-1451
Dharma Publishing, 2425 Hillside Avenue, Berkeley, CA 94704
Editorial Justa Publications, Inc., P. O. Box 2131-C, Berkeley, CA 94702, 415 848-3628
EL FUEGO DE AZTLAN, 3408 Dwinelle Hall, Univ of Calif, Berkeley, CA 94720
Erewon Press, P.O. Box 4253, Berkeley, CA 94704
The Figures, 2016 Cedar, Berkeley, CA 94709, 415-843-3120
FILM QUARTERLY, University of California Press, Berkeley, CA 94720
FOLIO, 2207 Shattuck Ave., Berkeley, CA 94704
Foolproof Press, PO Box 647, Berkeley, CA 94701
EL FUEGO DE AZTLAN, 3408 Dwinelle Hall, Univ of Calif, Berkeley, CA 94720
Full Court Press, Box 4520, Berkeley, CA 94704, 415-845-7645
GARLIC TIMES, 526 Santa Barbara Road, Berkeley, CA 94707, 527-1958
THE GOODFELLOW REVIEW OF CRAFTS, PO Box 4520, Berkeley, CA 94704, 415-845-7645
Ground Under Press, 2913 Shattuck Avenue, Berkeley, CA 94705
Heyday Books, Box 9145, Berkeley, CA 94709, (415) 849-1438
ILLUMINATIONS, 1321-L Dwight Way, Berkeley, CA 94702, 415-849-2102
Illuminations Press, 1321-L Dwight Way, Berkeley, CA 94702, 415-849-2102
Images Press, P.O. Box 9444, Berkeley, CA 94709, 415-843-8834
JOURNAL OF BIOLOGICAL EXPERIENCE, 2045 Francisco Street, Berkeley, CA 94709, (415) 526-8373
JUMP CUT, A Review of Contemporary Cinema, P.O. Box 865, Berkeley, CA 94701, 415-548-1507
Kelsey St. Press, 2824 Kelsey St., Berkeley, CA 94705, 841-2044
Lancaster - Miller Publishers, 3165 Adeline Street, Berkeley, CA 94703, (415) 845-3782
LANDSCAPE, PO Box 7107, Berkeley, CA 94707, (415) 549-3233
Moon Books, P. O. Box 9223, Berkeley, CA 94709, 415-444-0465
NEW WORLD JOURNAL, 2845 Buena Vista Way, Berkeley, CA 94708
OCCIDENT, 103 Sproul Hall, University of California, Berkeley, CA 94720
Open Books, 1631 Grant, Berkeley, CA 94703, 415-548-2208
Open Sesame Publishing Co., 1609½ San Pablo Avenue, Berkeley, CA 94702, (415) 526-6204
Over the Rainbow Press, Box 7072, Berkeley, CA 94707
Oyez, PO Box 5134, Berkeley, CA 94705
PACIFIC HORTICULTURE, Box 485, Berkeley, CA 94701, (415) 524-1914
Poltroon Press, PO Box 5476, Berkeley, CA 94705
ProActive Press, P.O. Box 296, Berkeley, CA 94701, 415-549-0839
QUILT, 2140 Shattuck Ave., Room 311, Berkeley, CA 94704, (415) 527-1586
Rebis Press, P.O. Box 2233, Berkeley, CA 94702, 415-527-3845
Reed & Cannon Co, 2140 Shattuck #311, Berkeley, CA 94704
Ross Books, Box 4340, Berkeley, CA 94704, (415) 841-2474
Saint Heironymous Press, Inc., PO Box 9431, Berkeley, CA 94709, 415-549-1405
Schroder Music Company, 2027 Parker Street, Berkeley, CA 94704, (415) 843-2365
Shameless Hussy Press, Box 3092, Berkeley, CA 94703
Sisters' Choice Press, 2027 Parker Street, Berkeley, CA 94704, (415) 843-2365
SOUTHEAST ASIA CHRONICLE, P.O. Box 4000-D, Berkeley, CA 94704, 415-548-2546
Southeast Asia Resource Center, P.O. Box 4000 D, Berkeley, CA 94704, 415-548-2546
Sybex Incorporated, 2344 Sixth St, Berkeley, CA 94710, 415-848-8233
Ten Speed Press, PO Box 7123, Berkeley, CA 94707
THE THREEPENNY REVIEW, PO Box 335, Berkeley, CA 94701, (415) 849-4545
TREE, P.O. Box 9005, Berkeley, CA 94709
Tree Books, P O Box 9005, Berkeley, CA 94709
Turtle Island Foundation, 2845 Buena Vista Way, Berkeley, CA 94708
TUUMBA, 2639 Russell Street, Berkeley, CA 94705
Tuumba Press, 2639 Russell St, Berkeley, CA 94705
Twowindows Press, 2644 Fulton St., Berkeley, CA 94704, (415) 849-1897
University of California Press, University of California Press, Berkeley, CA 94720, (415) 642-6333
UNIVERSITY PUBLISHING, 2431B Durant, Berkeley, CA 94704, (415) 548-0585
Waterfall Press, 1357 Hopkins Street, Berkeley, CA 94702, (415) 527-7790
WEST COAST PLAYS, PO Box 7206, Berkeley, CA 94707
Wingbow Press, 2940 Seventh Street, Berkeley, CA 94710, (415) 549-3030
WLW JOURNAL: News/Views/Reviews for Women and Libraries, P O Box 9052, Berkeley, CA 94709
WOMAN'S CHOICE, PO Box 489, Berkeley, CA 94701, (415) 527-1900
Women Library Workers, P O Box 9052, Berkeley, CA 94709, 415-654-8822
Women's History Research Center, Inc., 2325 Oak St, Berkeley, CA 94708
ZVEZDA, P.O. Box 9024, Berkeley, CA 94709
BLUE UNICORN, 22 Avon Road, Kensington, CA 94707, 415-526-8439
Manzano Press, 85 Ardmore Rd, Kensington, CA 94707, (415) 526-6980
This Press, 1636 Ocean View Ave., Kensington, CA 94707
BERKELEY POETRY REVIEW, c/o Office of Student Activities, 103 Sproul Hall, Univ of Calif, Berkeley, CA 94720
Cosmic Brain Trust, 414 So 41st Street, Richmond, CA 94804, (415) 658-0233
COSMIC CIRCUS, 414 So 41st Street, Richmond, CA 94804, 415-658-0233
Hobbit House Press, 5920 Dimm Way, Richmond, CA 94805, 415-232-3428

Io (named after moon of Jupiter), 635 Amador Street, Richmond, CA 94805, 415-236-1197
North Atlantic Books, 635 Amador Street, Richmond, CA 94805, 415-236-1197
Joy Woods Press, PO Box 25, Bodega, CA 94922, (707) 874-3064
Connections Press, PO Box 454, Bolinas, CA 94924, (415) 868-1753
Four Seasons Foundation, PO Box 159, Bolinas, CA 94924
Tombouctou Books, Box 265, Bolinas, CA 94924, 415-868-1082
YANAGI, Box 466, Bolinas, CA 94924, 415-868-0292
INVISIBLE CITY, 6 San Gabriel Drive, Fairfax, CA 94930
Jungle Garden Press, 47 Oak Rd, Fairfax, CA 94930
Red Hill Press, Los Angeles & Fairfax, 6 San Gabriel Dr, Fairfax, CA 94930
Intermundial Research, Box 518, Inverness, CA 94937
MEDICAL SELF-CARE, Boxx 718, Inverness, CA 94937, (415) 663-1403
Pueo Press, 810 College Ave, Kentfield, CA 94904, 415-456-6480
Tamal Vista Publications, 222 Madrone Ave, Larkspur, CA 94939, 924-7289
Tamalpa Press, 15 Estelle Avenue, Larkspur, CA 94939, 461-2465
The Great Outdoors Trading Company, 24759 Shoreline Highway, Marshall, CA 94940, (707) 878-2811
Connection Press, P.O. Box 689, Mill Valley, CA 94941, 415-383-9163
Druid Heights Books, 685 Camino Del Canyon, Muir Woods, Mill Valley, CA 94941
Hartmus Press, 23 Lomita Drive, Mill Valley, CA 94941
Westshore Inc, 655 Redwood Highway, Mill Valley, CA 94941
Whatever Publishing/Rising Sun Records, 158 E Blithedale, Suite 4, Mill Valley, CA 94941, 415-383-2434
Chandler & Sharp Publishers, Inc., 11A Commercial Blvd., Novato, CA 94947, 415-883-2353
Presidio Press, 31 Pamaron Way, Novato, CA 94947, 415-883-1373
THE WISHING WELL, Box 664, Novato, CA 94947
Old Adobe Press, P.O. Box 115, Penngrove, CA 94951, [Haslam]707-763-7362
M-R-K Publishing, Rural Route #6, Petaluma, CA 94952, (707) 763-0056
Edgepress, Box 64, Point Reyes, CA 94956, 415-663-1511
FLOATING ISLAND, Floating Island Publications, P.O. Box 516, Point Reyes Station, CA 94956
Floating Island Publications, PO Box 516, Pt Reyes Sta, CA 94956
Cassandra Publications, 7397 Boris Court #9, Rohnert Park, CA 94928, 239-1253
NOE VALLEY POETS WORKSHOP, 7397 Boris Court #9, Rohnert Park, CA 94928
May-Murdock Publications, PO Box 343, 90 Glenwood, Ross, CA 94957, (415) 454-1771
Leaves of Grass Press, PO Box 3914, San Rafael, CA 94902
Onaway Publications, 28 Lucky Drive, San Rafael, CA 94904, (415) 924-0884
The Scribe Press, PO Box 368, San Rafael, CA 94901, (415) 456-4198
Spiritual Community Publications, Box 1080, San Rafael, CA 94902, 415-457-2990
TAX NEWS, 819 A Street, Suite 21, San Rafael, CA 94901, (415) 456-7910
Manzanita Press, P.O.Box 4027, San Raphael, CA 94903, (415) 479-9636
Artists & Alchemists Publications, 215 Bridgeway, Sausalito, CA 94965, 914-332-0326
THE BLACK SCHOLAR: Journal of Black Studies and Research, P.O. Box 908, Sausalito, CA 94965, 415-332-3130
COEVOLUTION QUARTERLY, Box 428, Sausalito, CA 94965, 415-332-1716
In Between Books, Box T, Sausalito, CA 94965, 388-8048
STAR WEST, Box 731, Sausalito, CA 94965
Green Horse Press, 471 Carr Avenue, Aromas, CA 95004, (408) 724-6863
Red Alder Books, Box 545, Ben Lomond, CA 95005
University of the Trees Press, PO Box 644, Boulder Creek, CA 95006, 408-338-3855
ECHOS, 391 Union Ave #D, Campbell, CA 95008, (408) 377-2505
POET, 208 W. Latimer Ave., Campbell, CA 95008, 408-379-8555
Poet Press India, 208 W. Latimer Ave., Campbell, CA 95008, 408-379-8555
BOTTOMFISH MAGAZINE, 21250 Stevens Crk., Cupertino, CA 95014, 408-996-4550
Genotype, 15042 Montebello Road, Cupertino, CA 95014, (408) 867-6860
Freestone Publishing Collective, 10001 E Zayante Road, Felton, CA 95018, (408) 335-3714
Resource Publications, 7291 Coronado Dr, Suite 3, San Jose, CA 95070
ALCATRAZ, 354 Hoover Road, Santa Cruz, CA 95065
Alcatraz Editions, 354 Hoover Road, Santa Cruz, CA 95065
ANOTHER SMALL MAGAZINE, 1014 N Branciforte, Santa Cruz, CA 95062, 426-8698
Children's Art Foundation, Inc., Box 83, Santa Cruz, CA 95063, 426-5557
Clatworthy Colorvues, 111½ Riverview St, Santa Cruz, CA 95062, 408-426-6401
College V, UCSC, College Five, UCSC, Santa Cruz, CA 95064
Embers Publications, c/o Maude Meehan, 2150 Portola Drive, Santa Cruz, CA 95062, 408-476-6164
GREENHOUSE REVIEW, 126 Escalona Dr., Santa Cruz, CA 95060, 408-426-4355
Greenhouse Review Press, 126 Escalona Dr., Santa Cruz, CA 95060, 408-426-4355
Harvest Press, P.O. Box 1265, Santa Cruz, CA 95061, 415-335-5015
INTERFACE: THE COMPUTER EDUCATION QUARTERLY, 116 Royal Oak, Santa Cruz, CA 95066, (408) 438-5018
KAYAK, 325 Ocean View, Santa Cruz, CA 95062
Kayak Press, 325 Ocean View, Santa Cruz, CA 95062
Paperweight Press, 761 Chestnut Street, Santa Cruz, CA 95060, (408) 427-1177
QUARRY WEST, College v, University of Calif, Santa Cruz, CA 95064
Shire Press, PO Box 1728, Santa Cruz, CA 95061, 408-425-0842
STONE SOUP, The Magazine By Children, Bx 83, Santa Cruz, CA 95063, 408-426-5557
Unity Press, 235 Hoover Rd., Santa Cruz, CA 95065, 408-427-2020
FEDERAL NOTES, PO Box 986, Saratoga, CA 95070, 408-356-4667
MODERN LITURGY, Box 444, Saratoga, CA 95070
Robert D. Reed Publisher, PO Box 8, Saratoga, CA 95070, (378-4843
Vitality Associates, P.O. Box 154, Saratoga, CA 95070, (408) 867-1241
LESBIAN VOICES, 330 South Third Suite B, San Jose, CA 95112, 408-289-1088
MANGO, PO Box 28546, San Jose, CA 95159
MERLIN PAPERS, PO Box 5602, San Jose, CA 95150
Merlin Press, P. O. Box 5602, San Jose, CA 95150

OCCASIONAL REVIEW, 1976 Waverly Ave., San Jose, CA 95122, (408) 251-9562
OPEN CELL, PO Box 5602, San Jose, CA 95150
POETRY BOOK AWARD, 1976 Waverly Ave., San Jose, CA 95122, (408) 251-9562
Realities, 1976 Waverly Ave, San Jose, CA 95122, (408)251-9562
SAN JOSE STUDIES, San Jose State Univ., San Jose, CA 95192, 408-277-3460
SELF DETERMINATION JOURNAL, Self Determination: A personal/Political Network, 2431 Forest Avenue, San Jose, CA 95128, (408) 984-8134
Lamm-Morada Publishing Co., Box 7607, Stockton, CA 95207, (209) 931-1056
Sydon, Inc., c/o Drama Dept, University of the Pacific, Stockton, CA 95211
THE WORMWOOD REVIEW, PO Box 8840, Stockton, CA 95204, 209-466-8231
The Wormwood Review Press, P O Box 8840, Stockton, CA 95204, (209) 466-8231
CAFETERIA, PO Box 4104, Modesto, CA 95352
Times Change Press, Box 187, Albion, CA 95410
The Dawn Horse Press, PO Box 3680, Clearlake Highlands, CA 95422, 994-9497, 994-9498
VISION MOUND: The Journal of the Religious and Spiritual Teaching of Bubba Free John, PO Box 3680, Clearlake Highlands, CA 95422
Island Press - A Division of Round Valley Agrarian Institute, Star Route 1, Box 38, Covelo, CA 95428
Ten Mile River Press, 32000 North Highway One, Fort Bragg, CA 95437, (707) 964-5579
Seed Center, PO Box 658, Garberville, CA 95440, 493-6121
Entwhistle Books, Box 611, Glen Ellen, CA 95442
Ventura Press, P.O. Box 1076, Guerneville, CA 95446
Adam Seed Publications, 1561 S. Fitch Mt. Rd., Healdsburg, CA 95448
Dada Center Publications, 2319 West Dry Creek Road, Healdsburg, CA 95448, 707 433-2161
Bell Springs Publishing Company, PO Box 640, Laytonville, CA 95454, 707-984-6746
Nolo Press, PO Box 544, Occidental, CA 95465, (707) 874-3105
Garcia River Press, PO Box 527, Pt. Arena, CA 95468, (707) 882-9956
Clamshell Press, 160 California Avenue, Santa Rosa, CA 95405
CONSTELLATIONS, PO Box 4378, Santa Rosa, CA 95402, (707) 526-6020
Frontier Press, P O Box 5023, Santa Rosa, CA 95402, 707-544-5174
Journey Publications, PO Box 3567, Santa Rosa, CA 95402, 707-539-1659
Lamplighters Roadway Press, 1162 W Sexton Road, Sebastopol, CA 95472
Pleasant Hill Press, 2600 Pleasant Hill Rd, Sebastopol, CA 95472, (707) 823-6583
Creative Eye Press, P.O. Box 620, Sonoma, CA 95476, (707) 996-4377
Mad River Press, Inc., RT 2, Box 151B, Eureka, CA 95501, (707) 443-2947
POETRY NOW, 3118 K Street, Eureka, CA 95501
The Forest Library Edentata, PO Box 349, Redway, CA 95560
Quintessence Publications, 356 Bunker Hill Mine Road, Amador City, CA 95601, 209-267-5470
WESTART, PO Box 1396, Auburn, CA 95603, 916-885-0969
ATTENTION PLEASE, 708 Inglewood Drive, Broderick, CA 95605
Hearthstone Press, 708 Inglewood Drive, Broderick, CA 95605, 916-372-0250
THE CALIFORNIA QUARTERLY, 100 Sproul Hall, Univ of Calif, Davis, CA 95616
The Putah Creek Press, Library Associates, University of California, Davis, CA 95616, (916) 752-3222
Self Published, R 3, Box 38B, Garden Valley, CA 95633, (916) 622-7590
Dragon's Teeth Press, Adams Acres, El Dorado Nat. Forest, Georgetown, CA 95634
Peninhand Press, PO Box 142, Volcano, CA 95689
THE VOLCANO REVIEW, PO Box 142, Volcano, CA 95689
Konocti Books, Route 1, Box 216, Winters, CA 95694
SIPAPU, Route 1, Box 216, Winters, CA 95694, 916-662-3364; 916-752-1032
Blarney Books, 6129 Shenandoah Drive, Sacramento, CA 95841
Creative Editions & Capitol Enquiry, PO Box 22246, Sacramento, CA 95822
Crow, 5430 Del Rio Rd, Sacramento, CA 95822, (916) 441-5358
Ellen's Old Alchemical Press, P.O. Box 161915, Sacramento, CA 95816, 916-455-9984
HARD PRESSED, P.O. Box 161915, Sacramento, CA 95816, 916-455-9984
Hibiscus Press, P.O. Box 22248, Sacramento, CA 95822
IN A NUTSHELL, P.O. Box 22248, Sacramento, CA 95822
Jalmar Press, Inc., 6501 Elvas Ave, Sacramento, CA 95819, 916-451-2897
PINCHPENNY, c/o 916 22nd Street, #14, Sacramento, CA 95816
Press of Arden Park, 861 Los Molinos Way, Sacramento, CA 95825
QUERCUS, 25-4502, Sacramento, CA 95825, (916) 456-5344
Samuel Powell Publishing Company, 2125 1/2 I Street, Sacramento, CA 95816, (916) 443-1161
STUDIA MYSTICA, Calif. State Univ., 6000 J Street, Sacramento, CA 95819
WORLD OF POETRY, 2431 Stockton Blvd., Sacramento, CA 95817
Heidelberg Graphics, P.O. Box 3606D, Chico, CA 95927, 916-342-6582
PHANTASM, PO Box 3606D, Chico, CA 95927, 916-342-6582
UNIVERSITY JOURNAL, Graduate School, CSU, Chico, Chico, CA 95926
Ananda Publications, 14618 Tyler Foote Road, Nevada City, CA 95959, 916-265-5877
I.D.H.H.B., Inc, Box 370, Nevada City, CA 95959
KUKSU: Journal of Backcountry Writing, Box 980 Alleghany Star Rt., Nevada City, CA 95959
SPIRIT & NATURE, 14618 Tyler Foote Road, Nevada City, CA 95959
Dustbooks, Box 100, Paradise, CA 95969, 916-877-6110
THE SMALL PRESS REVIEW, P.O. Box 100, Paradise, CA 95969, 916-877-6110
Naturegraph Publishers, Inc., P. O. Box 1075, Happy Camp, CA 96039, 916-496-5353
The Bookery, 8193 Riata Drive, Redding, CA 96002, (916) 365-8068
The Blue Oak Press, P.O. Box 27, Sattley, CA 96124, 916-994-3397

COLORADO

AFRICA TODAY, c/o G.S.I.S, Univ of Denver, Denver, CO 80208
Ananda Marga Publications, 854 Pearl Street, Denver, CO 80203, (303) 832-6465
BIG MAMA RAG, 1724 Gaylord, Denver, CO 80206

DENVER QUARTERLY, University of Denver, Denver, CO 80208, 303-753-2869
Eggplant Press, P.O. Box 18641, Denver, CO 80218, 303 841-1442
Moonsquilt Press, 2312 10th Street, Denver, CO 80211, 458-1070
PANDORA, An Original Anthology of Role-expanding Science Fiction and Fantsy, 1150 St. Paul Street, Denver, CO 80206
PLAINSPEAK MAGAZINE, PO Box 9167, Denver, CO 80209, (303) 744-9247
SAP Society for the Advancement of Poetics, 14 Washington, c/o Jess Graf, Denver, CO 80203, 733-8288
Sproing Inc., 1150 St Paul St, Denver, CO 80206
UMBRAL, A Quarterly of Speculative Poetry, 2330 Irving Street, Denver, CO 80211
All of Us, P O Box 4552, Boulder, CO 80306
Aslan Enterprises, P.O. Box 1858, Boulder, CO 80306, 303-449-1515
Blue Wolf, 1240 Pine Street, Boulder, CO 80302, (303) 442-4214
BOMBAY GIN, c/o Naropa, 1111 Pearl Street, Boulder, CO 80302, 444-0202
CRISS-CROSS ART COMMUNICATIONS, PO Box 2022, Boulder, CO 80306, (303) 443-0244
Dovetail Press Ltd, Box 1496, Boulder, CO 80306
EAST EUROPEAN QUARTERLY, Box 29 Regent Hall, University of Colorado, Boulder, CO 80309, (303) 492-6157
FRONTIERS: A Journal of Women Studies, c/o Women Studies, University of Colorado, Boulder, CO 80309, 303-492-5065
Great Eastern Book Company, PO Box 271, Boulder, CO 80306, (303) 449-6113
HOUSESMITHS JOURNAL, Box 1496, Boulder, CO 80306, (303) 449-2681
Paladin Enterprises, Inc., PO Box 1307, Boulder, CO 80306, (303) 443-7250
Programs in Communications Press, 934 Pearl Suite J - 1, Boulder, CO 80302, 443-5514
Pruett Publishing Company, 3235 Prairie Avenue, Boulder, CO 80301, 303-449-4919
Stonehenge Books, Inc., 2969 Baseline Rd, Boulder, CO 80303, (303)444-4100
VINTAGE, 1111 Lincoln Place, Boulder, CO 80302, (303) 443-9748
Adventure Trails Research and Development Laboratories, Laughing Coyote Mt., Black Hawk, CO 80422
COLORADO STATE REVIEW, 322 Eddy, English Department, Colorado State University, Fort Collins, CO 80523, (303) 491-6428
Colorado State Review Press, 322 Eddy, English Department, Colorado State University, Fort Collins, CO 80523, (303) 491-6428
Alpine Publications, 1901 South Garfield, Loveland, CO 80537, (303) 667-2017
COLORADO-NORTH REVIEW, University Center, Greeley, CO 80639, 303-351-4347
Artemisia Press, PO Box 6423, Colorado Springs, CO 80934, (303) 685-5766
Donnelly & Sons Publishing Co., PO Box 7880, Colorado Springs, CO 80933, (303) 593-8025
PHOTOFLASH: Models & Photographers Newsletter, PO Box 7946, Colorado Springs, CO 80933
WRITERS FORUM, University of Colorado at Colorado Springs, Colorado Springs, CO 80907, (303) 593-3155
BACULITE, P.O.Box 11151, Pueblo, CO 81001
LOOK QUICK, P.O. Box 222, Pueblo, CO 81002
Pueblo Poetry Project, Room 31, Union Depot, Pueblo, CO 81003
Grilled Flowers Press, PO Box 3254, Durango, CO 81301
ASPEN ANTHOLOGY, Box 3185, Aspen, CO 81611, 303-925-8750

CONNECTICUT

CONNECTICUT QUARTERLY, Box 68, Enfield, CT 06082, (203) 745-1603
HARVEST, P.O. Box 78, Farmington, CT 06032
Andrew Mountain Press, PO Box 14353, Hartford, CT 06114
The Book Department, 236 Tower Avenue, Hartford, CT 06120, (203) 728-3470
Bartholomew's Cobble, 19 Howland Road, West Hartford, CT 06107, 203-521-6053
Ashford Press, RR 1, Box 128, Ashford, CT 06278
SARCOPHAGUS, RR1, Box 128, Ashford, CT 06278
POETS ON:, Box 255, Chaplin, CT 06235, 203-455-9671
Rocking Horse Press, 32 Ellise Road, Storrs, CT 06268, (203) 429-1474
Curbstone Press, 321 Jackson Street, Willimantic, CT 06226, 423-9190
Ziesing Bros.' Publishing Company, 768 Main St., Willimantic, CT 06226, 203-423-5836/8162
Omangoo Press, Rt 171, P064, Woodstock Valley, CT 06282, 203-974-2511
RED FOX REVIEW, Mohegan Community College, Norwich, CT 06360
August Derleth Society Newsletter, 61 Teecomwas Drive, Uncasville, CT 06382, (203) 848-0636
The Globe Pequot Press, Old Chester Road, Chester, CT 06412, (203) 526-9572
The Jacek Publishing Company, 38 Morris Lane, Milford, CT 06460, 203-874-4544
NOSTALGIAWORLD, PO box 231, North Haven, CT 06473, 203-239-4891
Rockfall Press, Cider Mill Road, Rockfall, CT 06481, (203) 349-8982
Cider Mill Press, P O Box 211, Stratford, CT 06497
THE SMALL POND MAGAZINE OF LITERATURE, PO Box 664, Stratford, CT 06497
CONNECTICUT FIRESIDE, P.O. Box 5293, Hamden, CT 06518, 203-248-1023
Fireside Press, P.O. Box 5293, Hamden, CT 06518
Aura Publishing Co., 975 Elm Street, New Haven, CT 06511, (203) 397-3865
The Common Table, 216 Crown Street, Room 506, New Haven, CT 06510
Corinth Books Inc., 228 Everit St., New Haven, CT 06511
EMPIRE: For the SF Writer, Box 967, New Haven, CT 06511, 777-6952
Leete's Island Books, Box 1131, New Haven, CT 06505, (203) 481-2536
THEATER, 222 York Street, New Haven, CT 06520, (203) 436-1417
THE YALE REVIEW, 1902A Yale Station, New Haven, CT 06520
Timely Books, PO Box 267, New Milford, CT 06776, (203) 354-0866
IMAGINE, Box 2715, Waterbury, CT 06720, (203) 753-2167
EUREKA REVIEW, 90 Harrison Avenue, New Canaan, CT 06840
Orion Press, 90 Harrison Avenue, New Canaan, CT 06840
Tyndall Creek Press, 10 Titicus Mountain Road, c/o J M Eichroot, New Fairfield, CT 06810
Black Swan Books Ltd., PO Box 327, Redding Ridge, CT 06876, (203) 938-2716
Magic Circle Press, 10 Hyde Ridge Rd, Weston, CT 06883
The Bold Strummer Ltd, 1 Webb Rd,, Westport, CT 06880, 203-226-8230
Greenwood Press, Inc., 51 Riverside Avenue, Westport, CT 06880, (203) 226-3571
Lawrence Hill & Company, Publishers, Inc., 520 Riverside Ave., Westport, CT 06880, 203-226-9392

DELAWARE

W. Perry, 23 Knickerbocker Drive, Neward, DE 19713
JOURNAL OF IRISH LITERATURE, P O Box 361, Newark, DE 19711, (215) 255-4083
DELAWARE TODAY, 2401 Pennslyvania Avenue, Wilmington, DE 19806, (302) 655-1571
EN PASSANT/POETRY, 1906 Brant Rd, Wilmington, DE 19810
Promise Publishing Corp., 725 Market Street, Wilmington, DE 19801, 401-274-8496

DISTRICT OF COLUMBIA

THE AMERICAN SCHOLAR, 1811 Q St.NW, Washington, DC 20009, 202-C05-3808
Anemone Press, PO Box 441, Howard University, Washington, DC 20059, (202) 232-3066
Ariadne Press, 4400 P St., N.W., Washington, DC 20007, (202) 337-2514
BLACK BOX MAGAZINE, PO Box 50145, Washington, DC 20004, 202-347-4823
Center for Science in the Public Interest, 1755 'S' Street, N.W., Washington, DC 20009, (202) 332-9110
DIGNITY, 1500 Massachusetts Ave., NW, Suite 11, Washington, DC 20005, 202-861-0017
GARGOYLE, PO Box 57206, Washington, DC 20037, 202 333-1544
Glad Hag Books, PO Box 2934, Washington, DC 20013, (202) 399-0117
Institute for Local Self-Reliance, 1717 18th St NW, Washington, DC 20009
"JOINT" CONFERENCE, P.O. Box 19332, Washington, DC 20036, 202-234-1681
King Publications, P O Box 19332, Washington, DC 20036, 202-234-1681
The Lovejoy Press, 2128 Wyoming Avenue, Washington, DC 20008
Meanings Press, 902 Maryland Ave NE, Washington, DC 20002
MEDIA REPORT TO WOMEN, 3306 Ross Pl. N.W., Washington, DC 20008, 202-363-0812
MERIP REPORTS, P.O. Box 3122, Columbia Heights Station, Washington, DC 20010, (202) 667-1188
MID-ATLANTIC NEWS, 1110 Sixth Streeet, N.W., Washington, DC 20001, 202-387-8998
MUSEUM OF TEMPORARY ART (MOTA) MAGAZINE, PO Box 28385, Washington, DC 20005, 202-638-3400
NETHULA JOURNAL OF CONTEMPORARY LITERATURE, PO Box 50368, Washington, DC 20004
NUTRITION ACTION, 1755 'S' Street, N. W., Washington, DC 20009, (202) 332-9110
OFF OUR BACKS, 1724 20th st. N.W., Washington, DC 20009, 202-234-8072
PARACHUTIST, 806 15th St. NW. Suite 444, Washington, DC 20005
Paycock Press, PO Box 57206, Washington, DC 20037, 202-333-1544
Personal Publications, PO Box 9005, Washington, DC 20003, (202) 488-0800
POET LORE, 4000 Albemarle Street, N.W., Suite 504, Washington, DC 20016, (202)362-6644
QUEST, PO Box 8843, Washington, DC 20003
Ram Publications, 1710 Connecticut Ave. NW, Washington, DC 20009, (202) 338-4666
SELF-RELIANCE, 1717 18th St. NW, Washington, DC 20009, (202) 232-4108
Stone Wall Press, Inc, 1241 30th Street NW, Washington, DC 20007
Three Continents Press, 1346 Connecticut Ave. N.W., Suite 1131, Washington, DC 20036, 202-457-0287; 457-0288
THREE SISTERS, Box 969, Georgetown University, Washington, DC 20067, (202) 625-4172
Titanic Books, 1920 S St. NW #506, Washington, DC 20009, (202) 483-5195
Turner Publishing, Inc., PO Box 1967, Washington, DC 20013, (202) 546-8747
WASHINGTON INTERNATIONAL ARTS LETTER, Box 9005, Washington, DC 20003, (202) 488-0800
WASHINGTON REVIEW, P O Box 50132, Washington, DC 20004, 202-638-0515
Washington Writers Publishing House, PO Box 50068, Washington, DC 20004, (703) 524-0999
Watershed Intermedia, P.O. Box 50145, Washington, DC 20004, 202-347-4823
White Murray Press, PO Box 14186, Washington, DC 20044
Women's Institute for Freedom of the Press, 3306 Ross Place, N.W., Washington, DC 20008, 202-966-7783
The Word Works, Inc., P.O. Box 4054, Washington, DC 20015, (703) 524-0999
Worldwatch Institute, 1776 Massachusetts Ave NW, Washington, DC 20036, 202-452-1999
THE WRIT, 640 14th Place, N.E., Washington, DC 20002, (202) 397-7766
Writers Press, Box 805, 2000 Connecticut Avenue, Washington, DC 20008, (202) 232-0440

FLORIDA

Gerber Publications, PO Box 1355, Ormond Beach, FL 32074, (905) 677-9283
BOTH SIDES NOW, 1232 Laura St., Jacksonville, FL 32206
KALLIOPE, A Journal of Women's Art, 101 W. State Street, Jacksonville, FL 32202, 904-633-8340
T.A.A.S. Association, Inc., PO Box 2150, Jacksonville, FL 32203
D.D.B. Press, P O Box 20106, Tallahasaee, FL 32304, 904-224-0478
APALACHEE QUARTERLY, Po Box 20106, Tallahassee, FL 32304, (904) 224-0478
THE OCHLOCKONEE REVIEW, 3190 Whirlaway Trail, Tallahassee, FL 32308, (904) 893-5325
Dark House Press, Box 184, Fountain, FL 32438, (904) 722-4840
THE PANHANDLER, University of West Florida, Pensacola, FL 32504, 904-476-9500
Placebo Press, 4311 Bayou Blvd #T-199, Pensacola, FL 32503, (904) 477-3995
Triad Publishing Co. Inc., PO Box 13096, Gainesville, FL 32604, (904) 373-5308
THE DEVIL'S MILLHOPPER, c/o Lola Haskins, Box 178, LaCrosse, FL 32658, (904) 462-3117
SKYDIVING, Po Box 189, Deltona, FL 32725
Geraventure Corp., PO Box 2131, Melbourne, FL 32901, (305) 723-5554
LIVING OFF THE LAND, Subtropic Newsletter, PO Box 2131, Melbourne, FL 32901, (305) 723-5554
Falkynor Books, P O Box 8060, Hollywood, FL 33024, 305-581-4950
Tib Publications, 2922 N. State Road 7, Suite 107, Margate, FL 33063, (305) 973-2862
EARTHWISE: A Journal of Poetry, PO Box 680-536, Miami, FL 33168
EARTHWISE NEWSLETTER, PO Box 680-536, Miami, FL 33168, 305-688-8558
Earthwise Publications, PO Box 680-536, Miami, FL 33168, (305) 688-8558
MIAMI INTERNATIONAL, 2951 S. Bayshore Drive, Miami, FL 33133, (305) 443-5251
Seahawk Press, 6840 S.W. 92nd Street, Miami, FL 33156, (305) 667-4051
TEMPEST: Avant-Garde Poetry, PO Box 680-536, Miami, FL 33168, (305) 688-8558
Florida Arts Gazette, P.O. Box 397, Ft. Lauderdale, FL 33302, (305) 463-6891
Mixed Breed, Box 42, Delray Beach, FL 33444, (305) 276-8611
Backpack Media, 3215 Sec Ave West, Bradenton, FL 33505

FROZEN WAFFLES, 3215 Sec Ave West, Bradenton, FL 33505
Pitjon Press/BackBack Media, 3215 Sec Ave West, Bradenton, FL 33505
Bayshore Books, Box 848, Nokomis, FL 33555, (813) 485-2564
Americana Books, PO Box 481, Pinellas Park, FL 33565
INTERCOM, Box 305, Ridge Manor, FL 33525, 904-583-2343
Manor Press, Box 305, Ridge Manor, FL 33525
NEW COLLAGE MAGAZINE, 5700 North Trail, Sarasota, FL 33580, 315-355-7671, Ex 203
Sprout Publications Inc, 5241 Ocean Blvd, Sarasota, FL 33581, (813) 955-7522
DRAMATIKA, 429 Hope Street, Tarpon Springs, FL 33589
Dramatika Press, 429 Hope Street, Tarpon Springs, FL 33589
American Studies Press, Inc., 13511 Palmwood Lane, Tampa, FL 33624, (813) 961-7200; (813) 974-2857
GRYPHON, College of Arts & Letters, Room 370, Department of Humanities, Univ of South Florida, Tampa, FL 33620
THE HISTORY BOOK DIGEST, PO Box 18383, Tampa, FL 33679, (813) 837-0250
SCHOLIA SATYRICA, English Department, University of South Florida, Tampa, FL 33620, 974-2421
WHITE MULE, 201 E Emma, Tampa, FL 33603
KONGLOMERATI, PO Box 5001, Gulfport, FL 33737, 813-323-0386
Konglomerati Press, PO Box 5001, Gulfport, FL 33737, 813-323-0386
THE WASHINGTON C.R.A.P. REPORT, 3610 38th Avenue So. #88, St Petersburg, FL 33711, (813) 866-1598
THE BOOK-MART, PO Box 568, 3, St. Petersburg, FL 33731
Valkyrie Press, Inc., 2135 1st Street South, St. Petersburg, FL 33712, 813-822-6069
Energy Publishing Company, 1412 Ave H S W, Winter Haven, FL 33880, 813-293-2576
Kenmore Press, 3317 Thornhill Road SW, Winter Haven, FL 33880
M.O.P. Press, Rt 24, Box 53C, Fort Myers, FL 33908, (813) 482-0802
TIOTIS POETRY NEWS, Rt. #19, Box 53C, Fort Myers, FL 33908, (813) 482-0802

GEORGIA

THE DEKALB LITERARY ARTS JOURNAL, 555 N. Indian Creek Dr, Clarkston, GA 30021
Fulcourte Press, PO Box 1961, Decatur, GA 30031, (404) 378-5750
THE OLD RED KIMONO, Humanities, Floyd Junior College, PO Box 1864, Rome, GA 30161, 404-295-6312
CONTEMPORARY ART/SOUTHEAST, 3317 Piedmont Road NE #15, Atlanta, GA 30305
CRITIQUE: Studies in Modern Fiction, Dept. of English, Georgia Tech, Atlanta, GA 30332
DAIMON, P O Box 7952, Atlanta, GA 30357, 404-873-3820
House of Keys, P O Box 7952, Atlanta, GA 30357, 404-873-3820
Nexus Press, 608 Forrest Road, NE, Atlanta, GA 30312, (404) 577-3579
THE MOONSHINE REVIEW, Moonshine Cooperative, Rt. 2 Box 488, Flowery Branch, GA 30542, (404) 967-3326
THE GEORGIA REVIEW, Univ. of Georgia, Athens, GA 30602, 404-542-3481
BLUE HORSE, P.O. Box 6061, Augusta, GA 30906

HAWAII

Press Pacifica, PO Box 1227, Kailua, HI 96734, 808-261-6594
Institute for Polynesian Studies, Brigham Young University, Laie, HI 96762
Clean Energy Press, 3593-a Alani Dr, Honolulu, HI 96822, 808-988-4155
HAWAII LITERARY ARTS COUNCIL NEWSLETTER, PO Box 11213, Moiliili Station, Honolulu, HI 96814
Petronium Press, 1255 Nuuanu Ave, #1813, Honolulu, HI 96817

IDAHO

THE LIMBERLOST REVIEW, 704 S. Arthur Street, Pocatello, ID 83201
Little Red Hen, Inc., PO Box 4260, Pocatello, ID 83201, (208) 233-3755
Confluence Press, Inc., Spalding Hall, Lewis-Clark State College, Lewiston, ID 83501
THE SLACKWATER REVIEW, Spalding Hall, Lewis-Clark Campus, Lewiston, ID 83501, 208-746-2341
INKY TRAILS and TIME TO PAUSE, Inky Trails Publications, P.O.Box 345, Middleton, ID 83644
Inky Trails Publications, PO Box 345, Middleton, ID 83644
Stonehouse Publications, Timber Butte Road, Box 390, Sweet, ID 83670
Ahsahta, Boise State University, Department of English, Boise, ID 83725, 208-385-1246
THE WESTERN CRITIC, Box 591, Boise, ID 83701
THE HARDHITTING INTERMITTENT NORTH IDAHO NEWS, Rt. 1, Box 618, Bonners Ferry, ID 83805
Mole Publishing Co., Rt 1, Box 618, Bonners Ferry, ID 83805
SNAPDRAGON, English Department, University of Idaho, Moscow, ID 83843, (208) 885-6156
Timeless Books, P.O. Box 60, Porthill, ID 83853, (604) 227-9220

ILLINOIS

Clarence H. Hall, 3409 Altvater Road, Avon Park, IL 33825
RHINO, 77 Lakewood Place, Highland Park, IL 60035, 312-433-3536
STORY QUARTERLY, 820 Ridge Road, Highland Park, IL 60035, 312-831-4684
F. Fergeson Productions, Box 433, Lake Bluff, IL 60044, 312-864-7696
THE BARAT REVIEW: A Journal of Literature and the Arts, Barat College, Lake Forest, IL 60045, (312) 234-3000
Merganzer Press, 659 Northmoor Road, Lake Forest, IL 60045, (312) 234-7208
Snow Press, PO Box 427, Morton Grove, IL 60053, 312-299-7605
PhoeniXongs, P.O. Box 622 (orders), 1652 Longvalley Drive (correspondence), Northbrook, IL 60062, 312-498-3981
The Hosanna Press, 1230 Parkside Ave, Park Ridge, IL 60068, (312) 823-0401
The Black Cat Press, 8248 Kenton, Skokie, IL 60076, 677-9686
Stone Circle Press, PO Box 551, Bensenville, IL 60106, (312) 766-0223; (312) 620-0732
Cedar Creek Press, PO Box 801, Dekalb, IL 60115
Celestial Otter, 1923 Finchley Ct, Schaumburg, IL 60194, (312) 884-6425
MAGIC CHANGES, 1923 Finchley Ct, Schaumburg, IL 60194, (312) 884-6425
FORMAT, 405 S. 7th Street, St. Charles, IL 60174, (312) 584-0187
Kitchen Harvest, 3N 681 Bittersweet Drive, St. Charles, IL 60174, 312-584-4084
Seven Oaks Press, 405 S. 7th Street, St. Charles, IL 60174, (312) 584-0187
Epic, 1024 Judson Avenue, Evanston, IL 60202, (312) 475-8517

Greenleaf Press, PO Box 471, Evanston, IL 60204, 465-6156
The Press of Ward Schori, 2716 Noyes Street, Evanston, IL 60201, (312) 475-3241; 864-9797
TRIQUARTERLY, 1735 Benson Avenue, Northwestern Univ., Evanston, IL 60201, 312-492-3490
Writer's Guide Publications, 9329 Crawford Avenue, Evanston, IL 60203, (312) 674-6476
ANOTHER CHICAGO MAGAZINE, 1152 S. East, Oak Park, IL 60304
Cat's Pajamas Press, 527 Lyman, Oak Park, IL 60304
Independent Publishing Fund of the Americas, 119 S Cuyler, Oak Park, IL 60302
IPFA NEWS, 119 S Cuyler, Oak Park, IL 60302, 35695
MOJO NAVIGATOR(E), 527 Lyman, Oak Park, IL 60304
Thunder's Mouth Press, 1152 S East Ave, Oak Park, IL 60304
Eads Street Press, 402 Stanton Lane, Crete, IL 60417
LAPIS, 18225 Gottschalk, Homewood, IL 60430, (312) 798-5648
Lapis Educational Association, Inc., 18225 Gottschalk, Homewood, IL 60430, (312) 798-5648
Contemporary Curriculums, PO Box 83, Oak Lawn, IL 60453
Transport History Press, PO Box 201, Park Forest, IL 60466, (312) 799-1785
THE CREATIVE WOMAN, Governors State University, Park Forest South, IL 60466, (312) 534-5000, Ext. 2524
Precedent Publishing Inc., PO Box 1005, South Holland, IL 60473, 312-828-0420
Story Press, 4142 Rose Avenue, Western Springs, IL 60558
Academy Chicago Limited, 360 N. Michigan, Chicago, IL 60601, 312-782-9826
Apeiron Press, P.O. Box 5930, Chicago, IL 60680
APPEAL TO REASON, PO Box 3774, Merchandise Mart, Chicago, IL 60654
BEFORE THE RAPTURE, PO Box A3604, Chicago, IL 60690
BILE, 5228 South Woodlawn, Loft 3E, Chicago, IL 60615, 324-7859
BLACK MARIA, PO Box 25187, Chicago, IL 60625
THE BLACK POSITION, 7428 S. Evans Ave., Chicago, IL 60619
Boardwell - Kloner, 323 S Franklin, Room 804, Chicago, IL 60606, (312) 973-2816
"BRILLIANT CORNERS": A Magazine of The Arts, 7600 N Sheridan #104, Chicago, IL 60626, 312-761-3702
Broken Whisker Studio, PO Box 1303, (5D), Chicago, IL 60690
THE CALL/EL CLARIN, Box 5597, Chicago, IL 60680
Call Publications, Box 5597, Chicago, IL 60680
Calliope Publishing Inc., P.O. Box 6517, Chicago, IL 60680, (312) 929-5592
CASE ANALYSIS, 401 E 32nd, #1002, Chicago, IL 60616, (312) 225-9181
Center for the Art of Living, 2203 N Sheffield, Chicago, IL 60614, (312) 871-5681
The Center For Study of Multiple Gestation, Suite 463-5, 333 East Superior St., Chicago, IL 60611, (312) 266-9093
Charles H. Kerr Publishing Company, 600 W Jackson Blvd, Suite 413, Chicago, IL 60606, (312) 454-0363
Chicago New Art Association, 230 E. Ohio, RM. 207, Chicago, IL 60611, 312-642-6236
CHICAGO REVIEW, University of Chicago, 5700 S. Ingleside Box C, Chicago, IL 60637, 212-753-3571
DECEMBER MAGAZINE, 6232 N Hoyne #1C, Chicago, IL 60659, (312) 973-7360
December Press, 6232 N Hoyne, 1C, Chicago, IL 60659, (312) 973-7360
Elpenor Books, P O Box 3152, Merchandise Mart Plaza, Chicago, IL 60654, (312) 935-1343
Fashion Imprints Associates, 3523 Merchandise Mart, Chicago, IL 60654, 821-5922
GALLERY SERIES/POETS, 401 W. Ontario St., c/o Artcrest Products, Chicago, IL 60610
Gilgamesh Press Ltd., 1059 W Ardmore Avenue (literary division), Chicago, IL 60660, (312) 334-0327
Harper Square Press, c/o Artcrest Products Co., Inc., 401 W Ontario Street, Chicago, IL 60610, (312) 751-1650
HEALTH SCIENCE, 1920 Irving Park Road, Chicago, IL 60613, (312) 929-7420
IN THE LIGHT, 1249 W Loyola #207, Chicago, IL 60626
INDUSTRIAL WORKER, 3435 N Sheffield Rm 202, Chicago, IL 60657, 312-549-5045
Dr. Albert R. Klinski, 3928 N. St. Louis, Chicago, IL 60618, KE9-6159
Liberator Press, P.O. Box 7128, Chicago, IL 60680, 312-663-4329
LIVING BLUES, 2615 N. Wilton, Chicago, IL 60614
MATI, 5548 N. Sawyer, Chicago, IL 60625
Metis Press, PO Box 25187, Chicago, IL 60657
MILK QUARTERLY, 2394 Blue Island Ave, Chicago, IL 60608
Natural Hygiene Press, 1920 Irving Park Road, Chicago, IL 60613, (312) 929-7420
NEW ART EXAMINER, 230 E. Ohio, Chicago, IL 60611, 312-642-6206
NIT&WIT: Literary Arts Magazine, 1908 W. Oakdale Ave., Chicago, IL 60657, (312) 248-1183
OINK!, 7021 N. Sheridan Rd, Chicago, IL 60626
Ommation Press, 5548 North Sawyer, Chicago, IL 60625
THE ORIGINAL ART REPORT (TOAR), P.O. Box 1641, Chicago, IL 60690
PAID MY DUES: JOURNAL OF WOMEN AND MUSIC, P.O. Box 6517, Chicago, IL 60680
PLUCKED CHICKEN, Box 5941, Chicago, IL 60680, 454-1177
Plucked Chicken Press, Box 5941, Chicago, IL 60680, (312) 454-1177
POETRY, Box 4348, Chicago, IL 60680, (312) 996-7803
PRIMAVERA, 1212 E 59th Street, Univ. of Chicago, Chicago, IL 60637, 312-753-3577
Progresiv Publishr, 401 E. 32nd #1002, Chicago, IL 60616, (312) 225-9181
Proletarian Publishers, P.O. Box 3925, Chicago, IL 60654
RCP Publications, Box 3486, Chicago, IL 60654, 312-663-5920
REVOLUTION, Box 3486, Chicago, IL 60654, 32-663-5920
SALOME: A LITERARY DANCE MAGAZINE, 5548 N. Sawyer, Chicago, IL 60625, (312) 539-5745
SHAKESPEARE NEWSLETTER, Univ. of Illinois, Chicago Circle, Chicago, IL 60680, 312-996-3289
SLICK PRESS, 5336 So. Drexel, Chicago, IL 60615
SOCIOLOGICAL PRACTICE, 401 E 32nd, #1002, Chicago, IL 60616, (312) 225-9181
The Swallow Press Inc., 811 W. Junior Terrace, Chicago, IL 60613, 312-871-2760
SYNCLINE, 7825 S. Ridgeway, Chicago, IL 60652
Third World Press, 7524 So. Cottage Grove Ave., Chicago, IL 60619, (312) 651-0700
THUNDER EGG, 707 W Waveland, Apt 509, Chicago, IL 60613, (312) 935-3461
Traumwald Press, Suite 10, 3550 Lake Shore Drive, Chicago, IL 60657, (312) 525-5303
TWO HANDS NEWS, 1125 Webster, Chicago, IL 60614
University of Chicago Press, 11030 Langley Avenue, Chicago, IL 60628, 312-568-1550

Upland Press, PO Box 7390, Chicago, IL 60680, (312) 266-2087
Vanguard Books, P.O. Box 3566, Chicago, IL 60654, (312) 942-0774
WHITE WALLS, PO Box 8204, Chicago, IL 60680
The Wine Press, 6238 N Magnolia, Chicago, IL 60660
Workers' Press, PO Box 3774, Chicago, IL 60654
The Yellow Press, 2394 Blue Island Ave, Chicago, IL 60608
Zoographico Press, Ltd., 29 W Hubbard, Chicago, IL 60610, (312) 467-1088
Alphaville Books, 728 Hinman Avenue, Evanston, IL 60602
OXYMORON: Journal Of Convulsive Beauty, 728 Hinman Avenue, Evanston, IL 60602
PTERANODON, PO Box 229, Bourbonnais, IL 60914
ROAD/HOUSE, 900 West 9th St., Belvidere, IL 61008, 543-9581
Delicious Desserts For Diabetics & Their Sugar Free Friends, 747 Towne Drive, Freeport, IL 61032, (815) 232-6695
NEW TIMES, 1000 21st Street, Rock Island, IL 61201, 309 786-6944
Caroline House Publishers, PO Box 738, Ottawa, IL 61350, (815) 434-7905
MISSISSIPPI VALLEY REVIEW, Dept. of English, Western Ill. University, Macomb, IL 61455, 309-298-1514
DELIRIUM, PO Box 341, Wataga, IL 61488
Libra Press, PO Box 341, Wataga, IL 61488
PRAIRIE SUN, Box 876, Peoria, IL 61652, (309) 673-6624
The Spoon River Poetry Press, PO Box 1443, Peoria, IL 61655
THE SPOON RIVER QUARTERLY, PO Box 1443, Peoria, IL 61655
OPINION, P.O.Box 3563, Bloomington, IL 61701
THE PIKESTAFF FORUM, P.O. Box 127, Normal, IL 61761, (309)452-4831
The Pikestaff Press, P.O. Box 127, Normal, IL 61761, (309) 452-4831
THE PIKESTAFF REVIEW, P.O. Box 127, Normal, IL 61761, (309) 452-4831
Human Kinetics Pub. Inc., Box 5076, Champaign, IL 61820, 217-351-5076
JOURNAL OF SPORT PSYCHOLOGY, Box 5076, Champaign, IL 61820, 217-351-5076
QUEST, Box 5076, Champaign, IL 61820, 217-351-5076
Literary Herald Press, 408 Oak Street, Danville, IL 61832, (213) 446-5740
Afterimage Book Publishers, 305 S Cottage Grove, Urbana, IL 61801, (217) 384-7319
The Guide to Small Press Publishing, PO Box 85, Urbana, IL 61801, (217) 352-5476
Peradam Publishing House, P.O. Box 85, Urbana, IL 61801, 815-367-7070
Red Herring Press, c/o Channing-Murray Foundation, 1201 W Oregon, Urbana, IL 61801, (217) 367-8770
AMERICAN POET, 902 10th St., Box 35, Charleston, IL 61920
KARAMU, English Dept, Eastern Illinois Univ., Charleston, IL 61920, 217-581-5013
MODERN IMAGES, Box 912, Mattoon, IL 61920
SOU'WESTER, Southern Illinois University, Edwardsville, IL 62026
LUCKY HEART BOOKS, Box 1064, Quincy, IL 62301
SALT LICK, PO Box 1064, Quincy, IL 62301
Salt Lick Press, PO Box 1064, Quincy, IL 62301

INDIANA

Helaine Victoria Press, 4080 Dynasty Lane, Martinsville, IN 46151, (317) 537-2868
INPRINT, 6360 N. Guilford Ave, Indianapolis, IN 46220, (317) 253-3733
PUBLISHED POET NEWSLETTER, PO Box 1663, Indianapolis, IN 46206
Writers' Center Press, Free University Writers' Center, 6360 N. Guilford Avenue, Indianapolis, IN 46220, (317) 253-3733
Around Publishing, 541 Mentone, Mentone, IN 46539
THE LITTLE AROUND JOURNAL, PO Box 541, Mentone, IN 46539
GRYPHON: A Culture's Critic, RR 3, Box 127, Walkerton, IN 46574, 219-369-9394
Lion Enterprises, RR 3, Box 127, Walkerton, IN 46574, 219-369-9394
and books, 702 S Michigan, Suite 836, South Bend, IN 46618
Ted Nelson, Publisher, c/o the distributors, 702 So. Michigan, South Bend, IN 46618
Cedar Creek Publishers, 2310 Sawmill Road, Fort Wayne, IN 46825, 637-3856
Jewel Publications, 2417 Hazelwood Ave., Fort Wayne, IN 46805, 219-483-6625
THE WINDLESS ORCHARD, Indiana Univ Eng Dept, Ft. Wayne, IN 46805
Love Street Books, 2176 Allison Lane #13, Jeffersonville, IN 47130
The Barnwood Press, RR 2, Box 11C, Daleville, IN 47334, (317) 378-0921
Parachuting Resources, P.O.Box 1333, Richmond, IN 47374, (513) 456-4686
THE ARTFUL DODGE, 110 South Roosevelt, Bloomington, IN 47401, 332-6296
COLLEGE ENGLISH, Dept of English, Indiana University, Bloomington, IN 47401, 812-337-8183
INDIANA WRITES, 110 Morgan Hall, IU, Bloomington, IN 47401, (812) 337-3439
Michael Joseph Phillips Editions, 430 E Wylie, Bloomington, IN 47401, 317-255-2555
THE MINNESOTA REVIEW, Box 211, Bloomington, IN 47401
NAZUNAH, PO Box 1662, Bloomington, IN 47402, (812) 336-0572
Raintree, 4043 Morningside Dr, Bloomington, IN 47401, 812-332-6561
Survival Cards, P.O. Box 1805, Bloomington, IN 47402
WRITER'S NEWSLETTER, 110 Morgan Hall, IU, Bloomington, IN 47401, (812) 337-3439
WRITER'S NEWSLETTER, 110 Morgan Hall, Indiana University, Bloomington, IN 47405, (812) 337-3439
BLACK AMERICAN LITERATURE FORUM, Indiana State University, Parsons Hall 237, Terre Haute, IN 47809, 812-232-6311, Ext. 2760
HIGH/COO: A Quarterly of Short Poetry, Route 1, Battleground, IN 47920
High/Coo Press, Route 1, Battleground, IN 47920
SPARROW POVERTY PAMPHLETS, 103 Waldron St, West Lafayette, IN 47906
Sparrow Press, 103 Waldron St., West Lafayette, IN 47906

IOWA

FANZINE DIRECTORY, PO Box 1040, Ames, IA 50010
PHOTRON, PO Box 1040, Ames, IA 50010
POET & CRITIC, English Dept., ISU, 203 Ross Hall, Ames, IA 50011
BLUE BUILDINGS, 2800 Rutland, Des Moines, IA 50311, (515) 277-2709

R & D Services, PO Box 644, Des Moines, IA 50303, 515-262-5397
THE NORTH AMERICAN REVIEW, Univ. Of Northern Iowa, Cedar Falls, IA 50613, 319-266-8487/273-2681
Martin Quam Press, 1515 Columbia Drive, Cedar Falls, IA 50613, (319) 266-6242
Ansuda Publications, Box 123, Harris, IA 51345
THE PUB, Box 123, Harris, IA 51345
AZIMUTH, Box 842, Iowa City, IA 52240
Le Beacon Presse, 621 Holt Avenue, Iowa City, IA 52244, (319) 354-5447
LE BEACON REVIEW, 621 Holt Avenue, Iowa City, IA 52240, 319-354-5447
FOREIGN POETS AND AUTHORS REVIEW, 621 Holt, Iowa City, IA 52240, 319-354-5447
The Happy Press, Box 585, Iowa City, IA 52244, (319) 338-0084
Image and Idea, Inc., Box 1991, Iowa City, IA 52240
IOWA CITY BEACON LITERARY REVIEW, 621 Holt Avenue, Iowa City, IA 52244, (319) 354-5447
IOWA REVIEW, 308 EPB, Univ. Of Iowa, Iowa City, IA 52242, (319) 353-6048
IOWA WOMAN, Route 3, Box 202C, Iowa City, IA 52240, (319) 683-2659
M'GODOLIM, 621 Holt Avenue, Iowa City, IA 52240, 319-354-5447
EL NAHUATZEN, PO Box 2134, Iowa City, IA 52244, (319) 353-7170
Photo-Art Enterprizes, Inc., c/o Old Brick, 26 E Market, Iowa City, IA 52240, 319-338-2714
POETRY &, PO Box 842, Iowa City, IA 52240
Poetry & Press, Box 842, Iowa City, IA 52240
POETRY COMICS, Box 585, Iowa City, IA 52244, (319) 338-0084
THE SPIRIT THAT MOVES US, P.O. Box 1585, Iowa City, IA 52244, 319-338-5569; 319-337-9700
The Spirit That Moves Us, Inc. (Formerly Emmess Press), P.O. Box 1585, Iowa City, IA 52244, 319-338-5569
The Penumbra Press, Box 12, Lisbon, IA 52253
The * CWS Group Press, PO Box 543, 807 West 15th Street, Vinton, IA 52349, 319-472-3552
DENTAL FLOSS MAGAZINE, P.O. Box 546, 626 E. Main, West Branch, IA 52358, 319-643-2604
Toothpaste Press, PO Box 546, 626 E. Main, West Branch, IA 52358, 319-643-2604
CLASSIC FILM/VIDEO IMAGES, PO Box 4079, Davenport, IA 52808
CLASSIC IMAGES REVIEW, PO Box 4079, Davenport, IA 52808, (319) 323-9738

KANSAS

Kangam, PO Box 3354, Kansas City, KS 66103, (816) 931-1344
MIDWEST CHAPARRAL, 5508 Osage, Kansas City, KS 66106
QUINDARO, PO Box 5224, Kansas City, KS 66119, (913) 342-6379
Rainy Day Books, 2812 W 53rd Street, Fairway, KS 66205, 913-384-3126
Ghost Dance: THE INTERNATIONAL QUARTERLY OF EXPERIMENTAL POETRY, 6009 W 101st Place, Shawnee Mission, KS 66207, 351-5977
Ghost Dance Press, 6009 W 101st Pl, Shawnee Mission, KS 66207
Loggeerhead, PO Box 7231, Shawnee Mission, KS 66207, 816-566-2174
SWIM LITE NEWS (newsletter), Box 7231, Shawnee Mission, KS 66207, 816-566-2174
EDUCATIONAL CONSIDERATIONS, College of Education, K.S.U., Manhattan, KS 66506, 913-532-6367
JOURNAL OF THE WEST, Box 1009, Manhattan, KS 66502, (913) 532-6733 or (913) 539-3668
KANSAS QUARTERLY, Denison Hall, Kansas St. Univ., Manhattan, KS 66506, 913-532-6716
Sunflower University Press, Box 1009, Manhattan, KS 66502, (913) 532-6733
THE MIDWEST QUARTERLY, Pittsburg State University, Pittsburg, KS 66762, 316-231-7000
THE ARK RIVER REVIEW, c/o A.G. Sobin Box 14 WSU, Wichita, KS 67208, 316-832-1075
Gordon Publishing Co., Inc., 1302 N 5th Street, Salina, KS 67401, (913) 827-0569

KENTUCKY

Terra, PO Box 99103, Jeffersontown, KY 40299, (502) 239-5362
THE LOUISVILLE REVIEW, University of Louisville, Louisville, KY 40208, (502) 588-5921
THE BLUEGRASS LITERARY REVIEW, Midway College, Midway, KY 40347
Larkspur Press, Rt. 3 Severn Creek, Monterey, Owenton, KY 40359
CALLALOO, Department of English, University of Kentucky, Lexington, KY 40506, (606) 257-2614
SNOWY EGRET, 205 S. Ninth St., Williamsburg, KY 40769, 606-549-0850
CUMBERLANDS, College Box 2, Pikeville, KY 41501, 432-9227
Pikeville College Press, College Box 2, Pikeville, KY 41501, 432-9227
REACHING, 105 Ratliffs Creek, Pikeville, KY 41501, 432-0500
WIND LITERARY JOURNAL, RFD Rt. 1 Box 809K, Pikeville, KY 41501, 606-631-1129
Wind Press, Rt 1 Box 810, Pikeville, KY 41501
MOUNTAIN REVIEW, Box 660, Whitesburg, KY 41858
CRAZY HORSE, Murray State University, College of Humanistic Studies, Dept of English, Murray, KY 42071, (502) 762-2401

LOUISANA

THE NEW LAUREL REVIEW, PO Box 1083, Chalmette, LA 70044, 504-271-4209
PONTCHARTRAIN REVIEW, PO Box 1065, Chalmette, LA 70044, 504-242-0947
HER Publishing Co., P.O. Box 1168, Oakwood Shopping Center, Gretna, LA 70053
Long Measure Press, P O BOX 1618, Meraux, LA 70075, 241-7454
FRIENDS & FELONS, 2115 Esplanade Avenue, New Orleans, LA 70119, 504-943-7041
LOWLANDS REVIEW, 6048 Perrier, New Orleans, LA 70118
NEW ORLEANS REVIEW, Loyola University, New Orleans, LA 70118, 504-865-2294
Southern Agitator, 2115 Esplanade Avenue, New Orleans, LA 70119, 504-943-7041
THE TULANE LITERARY MAGAZINE, University Center, New Orleans, LA 70118
WHISPERING WIND MAGAZINE, 8009 Wales Street, New Orleans, LA 70126, 241-5866
Offshore Research Service, PO Box 2606 NSU, Thibodaux, LA 70301, (504) 446-5676
Acadian Publishing, Inc., Church Point, LA 70525, (318) 684-5417
THE SOUTHWESTERN REVIEW, PO Box 44691, Lafayette, LA 70504, (318) 264-6908
GOTHIC, 4998 Perkins Road, Baton Rouge, LA 70808, (504) 766-2906
THE SOUTHERN REVIEW, Drawer D, University Station, Baton Rouge, LA 70893, 504-388-5108
Louisiana Entertains, Rapides Symphony Guild, Box 4172, Alexandria, LA 71301, (318) 443-7786

MAINE

BLACKBERRY, Box 186, Brunswick, ME 04011
The Bookstore Press, Box 191, RFD 1, Freeport, ME 04032, 207-865-6495
Cobblesmith, Box 191, RFD 1, Freeport, ME 04032, 207-865-6495
Mercer House Press, P.O. Box 681, Kennebunkport, ME 04046, 207-282-7116
CONTRABAND MAGAZINE, P.O. Box 4073, Sta. A, Portland, ME 04101
Contraband Press, P.O. Box 4073, Sta A, Portland, ME 04101
Puckerbrush Press, 76 Main St., Orono, ME 04473, 207-866-4868
THOREAU JOURNAL QUARTERLY, 304 English-Math Bldg., English Dept., Univ. of Maine, Orono, ME 04473, 207-581-7307
TBW Books, Box 58, Day's Ferry Road, Woolwich, ME 04579, (207) 442-7632
The Dog Ear Press, PO Box 155, Hulls Cove, ME 04644
The Latona Press, RFD 2, Box 154, Lamoine, ME 04605
LoonBooks, PO Box 901, Northeast Harbor, ME 04662, (207) 276-3693
LETTERS, Box 82, Stonington, ME 04681, 207-367-2484
Mainspring Press, Box 82, Stonington, ME 04681, 207-367-2484
Great Raven Press, P.O. Box 813, Ft Kent, ME 04743, 834-6447
International Marine Publishing Co., 21 Elm Street, Camden, ME 04843, 207-236-4342
NATIONAL FISHERMAN, 21 Elm St., Camden, ME 04843, 207-236-4342
Bern Porter Books, 22 Salmond Road, Belfast, ME 04915, 207-338-3763
Wings Press, R2, Box 325, Belfast, ME 04915, (207) 338-2005
NEW ENGLAND SAMPLER, RFD #1, Box M119, Brooks, ME 04921, (207) 525-3575
THE NEW ENGLAND CONSERVATIONIST, Box 112A, Canaan, ME 04924, (207) 474-9125
ZAHIR, Weeks Mills, New Sharon, ME 04955
TRANET, Box 567, Rangeley, ME 04970, (207) 864-2252

MARYLAND

Gazelle Publications, 106 Hodges Lane, Takoma Park, MD 20012, (301) 585-8393
Red Ochre Press, 8215 Flower Ave, Takoma Park, MD 20012
THE MILL, Box 996, Adelphi, MD 20783
The White Ewe Press, Box 996, Adelphi, MD 20783, 301-439-1470
Heritage Books Inc., 3602 Maureen, Bowie, MD 20715, 301-464-1159
DICKINSON STUDIES, 4508 38th St., Brentwood, MD 20722, 301-864-8527
HIGGINSON JOURNAL, 4508 38th St., Brentwood, MD 20722, 301-864-8527
Higginson Press, 4508 38th Street, Brentwood, MD 20722, (301) 864-8527
AFFORDABLE CHIC NEWS, PO Box 153, Cabin John, MD 20731, (301) 229-6765
Woman Matters Press, PO Box 153, Cabin John, MD 20731, (301) 229-6765
FEMINIST STUDIES, c/o Women's Studies Program, Univ of MD, College Park, MD 20742, 301-454-2363
Rainfeather Press, PO Box 831, College Park, MD 20740
Scop Publications, Inc., 5821 Swarthmore Drive, College Park, MD 20740, (301) 345-8747
SUN & MOON: A Journal of Literature and Art, 4330 Hartwick Rd, #418, College Park, MD 20740, 301-864-692,
Sun & Moon Press, 4330 Hartwick Road, #418, College Park, MD 20740, 301-864-6921
New Visions Press, PO Box 2025, Gaithersburg, MD 20760, (301) 869-1888
Garrett Park Press, Garrett Park, MD 20766
CAROUSEL, The Writer's Center, Glen Echo Park, Glen Echo, MD 20768
Sibyl-Child Press, Box 1773, Hyattsville, MD 20783, (301) 362-1404; (703) 683-0988
SIBYL-CHILD: A Women's Arts & Culture Journal, P.O. Box 1773, Hyattsville, MD 20783, (301) 362-1404; (703) 683-0988
ABBEY NEWSLETTER, 5410 85th Avenue, Apt 2, New Carrollton, MD 20784, (301) 459-1181
Maryland Historical Press, 9205 Tuckerman St, Lanham, MD 20801, (301)577-2436 and 557-5308
Celestial Gifts, Box 175, Rockville, MD 20850
AS IS, 118 Fleetwood Terr., Silver Spring, MD 20910, (301) 587-0377
CS JOURNAL, P.O. Box 512-B, Silver Spring, MD 20907, 301-588-7896
Black Buzzard Press, 2217 Shorefield Road, Apt 532, Wheaton, MD 20902
VISIONS, 2217 Shorefield Road, Apt 532, Wheaton, MD 20902, (301) 946-4927
Liberty Publishing Company, Inc., 50 Scott Adam Road, Cockeysville, MD 21030
ABBEY, 5011-2 Green Mountain Circle, Columbia, MD 21044
AMERICAN MAN, Box 693, Columbia, MD 21045, (301) 997-1373
White Urp Press, 5011-2 Green Mt Circle, Columbia, MD 21044
M.O. Publishing Company, 14332 Howard Road, Dayton, MD 21036, (301) 774-2900
MODUS OPERANDI, 14332 Howard Road, Dayton, MD 21036, 301-774-2900
Icarus Press, P.O. Box 8, Riderwood, MD 21139, 301-821-7807
CONTRAST, Western Maryland College, Westminster, MD 21157
THE BLACK REVIEW, Black Berry Press, P.O.Box 9405, Baltimore, MD 21228
CELEBRATION, 2707 Lawina Road, Baltimore, MD 21216
The Charles Street Press, P.O. Box 4692, Baltimore, MD 21212
COMMON WORD, P.O. Box 4692, Baltimore, MD 21212
HARD CRABS, Md. Writers Council, 1110 St. Paul Street, Baltimore, MD 21202, (301) 685-5239
Heritage Press, PO Box 18625, Baltimore, MD 21216, (301) 383-9330
KITE LINES, 7106 Campfield Road, Baltimore, MD 21207, (301) 484-6287
The New Poets Series, 541 Piccadilly Rd., Baltimore, MD 21204, 301-828-8783
SOCIAL ANARCHISM, 2743 Maryland Avenue, Baltimore, MD 21218, (301) 243-6987
UNICORN, 4501 North Charles Street, Baltimore, MD 21210, 301-323-1010(ext. 356)
White Dot Press, 407 Charter Oak Avenue, Baltimore, MD 21212, 301-435-7915
WOMEN: A Journal of Liberation, 3028 Greenmount Ave, Baltimore, MD 21218, 301-235-5245
Spindrift Press, P.O. Box 3252, Catonsville, MD 21228, (301) 944-3317
ZANTIA: Stories and Poems by the Over-Sixty, Zantia, Inc, P.O.box 1947, Annapolis, MD 21404, (301) 261-2549
Camera Work Gallery, PO Box 32, Frostburg, MD 21532, (301) 689-5666
Antietam Press, P.O. Box 62, Boonsboro, MD 21713, (301) 432-8079
Hidden Valley Press, 7051 Poole Jones Road, Frederick, MD 21701, (301) 662-6745

MASSACHUSETTS

CALIBAN: A Journal of New World Thought & Writing, Box 797, Amherst, MA 01002
Food For Thought Publications, PO Box 331, Amherst, MA 01004, 413-256-6158
Green Knight Press, 45 Hillcrest Place, Amherst, MA 01002
Lynx House Press, PO Box 800, Amherst, MA 01004, (413) 773-7988
THE MASSACHUSETTS REVIEW, Memorial Hall, Univ. of Mass, Amherst, MA 01003, 413-545-2689
Parable Press, 136 Gray Street, Amherst, MA 01002, 413-253-5634
Rat & Mole Press, P.O. Box 111, Amherst, MA 01002
HOLLOW SPRING REVIEW OF POETRY, RD 1, Bancroft Road, Chester, MA 01011
PUCK'S CORNER, 105 Clark Street, Easthampton, MA 01027, (617) 281-3665
R & J Kudlay, 105 Clark Street, Easthampton, MA 01027, (617) 281-3665
Morning Star Press, Poplar Hill Road, RFD, Haydenville, MA 01039, 413-665-4754
THE PHOENIX, Morning Star Farm, RFD, Haydenville, MA 01039, 413-665-4754
New Traditions, Allen Coit Road, Norwich Hill, Huntington, MA 01050
SWIFT RIVER, Box 264, Leverett, MA 01054
Tree Toad Press, Box 264, Leverett, MA 01054
BLUE PIG, 23 Cedar Street, Northampton, MA 01060
Sand Project Press/US, 23 Cedar Street, Northampton, MA 01060
THE FOUR ZOAS JOURNAL OF POETRY & LETTERS, Box 461, Ware, MA 01082
The Four Zoas Press, Box 461, Ware, MA 01082
WOMANCHILD, Collins Road, Hardwick, RFD, Ware, MA 01082, 617-756-4426
Womanchild Press, Collins Road, Hardwick, RFD, Ware, MA 01082
Little River Press, 10 Lowell Avenue, Westfield, MA 01085, (413) 568-5598
Robert L. Merriam, Newhall Road, Conway, MA 01341, 413-369-4052
OSIRIS, Box 297, Deerfield, MA 01342
NEW ROOTS, Box 548, Greenfield, MA 01301, (413) 774-2257/774-2258
PANACHE, PO Box 77, Sunderland, MA 01375, 413-367-2762
Panache Books, P.O. Box 77, Sunderland, MA 01375
JOYCEAN LIVELY ARTS GUILD REVIEW, Box 459, East Douglas, MA 01516, (617) 476-7630
Pakka Press, Box 459, East Douglas, MA 01516, (617) 476-7630
Commonsense Books, Box 287, Bedford, MA 01730
SHADOWGRAPHS, PO Box 177, Bedford, MA 01730, (617) 465-2806
Tree Shrew Press, 32 Evergreen Road, Holliston, MA 01746, (617) 429-7618
Penmaen Press Ltd, Old Sudbury Road, Lincoln, MA 01773, 617-259-0842
Anthony Publishing Company, 218 Gleasondale Road, Stow, MA 01775, (617) 897-7191
The Babbington Press, P.O. Box 98, Stow, MA 01775, (617) 897-8535
Programmed Studies Inc, P.O. Box 113, Stow, MA 01775, 617-897-2130
Brick House Publishing, Co., 3 Main Street, Andover, MA 01810, (617) 475-9568
CANTO Review of the Arts, Canto, Inc., 9 Bartlet Street, Andover, MA 01810, 617-475-3971
Charisma Press, PO Box 263, St. Francis Seminary, Andover, MA 01810, (617) 851-7910
CHARISMA PRESS REVIEW, PO Box 263, Andover, MA 01810, 617-851-7910
GRAHAM HOUSE REVIEW, Bishop North, Phillips Academy, Andover, MA 01810
Ithaca Press, P.O. Box 853, Lowell, MA 01853
NEW VOICES, 24 Edgewood Ter, Methuen, MA 01844, (617) 688-1669
Chthon Press/Nonesuch Publications, 77 Mark Vincent Drive, Westford, MA 01886
TRT Publications, Inc., PO Box 486, Beverly, MA 01915, (617) 927-1986
Tide Book Publishing Company, Box 268, Manchester, MA 01944, (617) 526-4887
Micah Publications, 255 Humphrey St, Marblehead, MA 01945
STONY HILLS: The New England Alternative Press Review, Box 715, Newburyport, MA 01950
BLT Press (Bates, Lear, and Tulp), 72 Lowell Street, Peabody, MA 01960, (617) 531-7348
LYNN VOICES, 72 Lowell Street, Peabody, MA 01960, (617) 531-7348
SOUNDINGS/EAST, English Dept., Salem State College, Salem, MA 01970, 745-0556
William A. Reilly, Publisher, PO Box 63, 6 Crest Drive, Dover, MA 02030
TENDRIL, Box 512, Green Harbor, MA 02041, 617-834-4137
Wampeter Press, Box 512, Green Harbor, MA 02041, (617) 834-4137
THE NEW RENAISSANCE, An International Magazine of Ideas & Opinions, Emphasizing Literature & The Arts, 9 Heath Road, Arlington, MA 02174
Sagittarius Rising, P.O. Box 252, Arlington, MA 02174, (617) 646-2692
Alyson Publications, Inc., 75 Kneeland Street, Rm 309, Boston, MA 02111, (617) 542-5679
Ave Victor Hugo Publishing, 339 Newbury St., Boston, MA 02115
Bradt Enterprises, 409 Beacon Street, Boston, MA 02115, (617) 536-5976
Charles River Books, Inc., 59 Commercial Wharf, Boston, MA 02110, 617-742-9493
CREAMANIA, PO Box 92, Boston, MA 02199
GALILEO, 339 Newbury Street, Boston, MA 02115
GAY COMMUNITY NEWS, 22 Bromfield St., Boston, MA 02108, 617-426-4469
GROWING WITHOUT SCHOOLING, 308 Boylston Street, Boston, MA 02116, 617-261-3920
The Heron Press, 36 Bromfield St., Boston, MA 02108
Ishtar Press, Inc., Dept of English, Northeastern University, 360 Huntington Avenue, Boston, MA 02115
National Gay News, Inc., 22 Bromfield St, Boston, MA 02108, 617-426-4469
Northeastern University Press, Northeastern Univ. Press, P.O. Box 116, Boston, MA 02117, 617 437-2783
Porter Sargent Publishers, Inc., 11 Beacon St., Boston, MA 02108, (617) 523-1670
South End Press, PO Box 68, Astor Station, Boston, MA 02123, (617) 266-0629
Autumn Press, Inc., 1318 Beacon Street, Brookline, MA 02146, 617-738-5680
Kanthaka Press, P.O. Box 696, Brookline Village, MA 02147, 617-734-8146
THE AGNI REVIEW, P.O. Box 349, Cambridge, MA 02138, (617) 491-1079
Alice James Books, 138 Mount Auburn St., Cambridge, MA 02138
Apple-wood Press, Box 2870, Cambridge, MA 02139, (617) 964-5150
Brattle Publications, 4 Brattle Street, Suite 306, Cambridge, MA 02138, (617) 661-7467

COMPUTER MUSIC JOURNAL, 28 Carleton Street, Cambridge, MA 02142, 617-253-5646
DAEDALUS, Journal of the American Academy of Arts and Sciences, 7 Linden Street, Cambridge, MA 02138, (617) 495-4431, 4482
Firefly Press, 26 Hingham Street, Cambridge, MA 02138, (617) 661-9784
FOCUS: A Journal For Lesbians, 1151 Mass. Avenue, Cambridge, MA 02138
Halty Ferguson Publishing Co., 376 Harvard Street, Cambridge, MA 02138, 617-868-6190
THE HARVARD ADVOCATE, 21 South St., Cambridge, MA 02138, 617-495-7820
The Imaginary Press, Box 193, Cambridge, MA 02141
PADAN ARAM, 52 Dunster Street, Harvard U, Cambridge, MA 02138, 495-2807
PHONE-A-POEM, Box 193, Cambridge, MA 02141, 617-492-1144
PLOUGHSHARES, Box 529, Cambridge, MA 02139
RESOURCES, Box 134, Harvard Square, Cambridge, MA 02138, 617 876-2789
THE SECOND WAVE, Box 344 Cambridge A, Cambridge, MA 02139, (617) 491-1071
SOJOURNER, THE NEW ENGLAND WOMEN'S JOURNAL OF NEWS, OPINIONS AND THE ARTS, 143 Albany Street, Cambridge, MA 02139, (617)661-3567
STRANGE FAECES, 174 Thorndike Street #4, Cambridge, MA 02141
UNEARTH: The Magazine of Science Fiction Discoveries, PO Box 779, Cambridge, MA 02139, (617) 876-0064
UNICORN: A Miscellaneous Journal, 345 Harvard St. 3B, Cambridge, MA 02138, 617-354-0124
West End Press, Box 697, Cambridge, MA 02139
Yellow Moon Press, 20 Tufts Street, Cambridge, MA 02139, (617) 492-2580
URBAN & SOCIAL CHANGE REVIEW, Boston College, McGuinn Hall, Chestnut Hill, MA 02167
THE CIRCLE, 105 S Huntington Avenue, Jamaica Plain, MA 02130, (617) 232-0343
GARGOYLE, 40 St John St 2F, Jamaica Plain, MA 02130
Nikmal Publishing, 698 River St., Mattapan, MA 02126, (617) 361-2101
The Pomegranate Press, PO Box 181, N. Cambridge, MA 02140
NOSTOC, Box 162, Newton, MA 02168
DARK HORSE, Box 36, Newton Lower Falls, MA 02166, (617) 964-0192
ABYSS, P.O. Box C, Somerville, MA 02143
Abyss/Augtwofive, PO Box C, Somerville, MA 02143, 617-666-1804
GRUB STREET, PO Box 1, Winterhill Branch, Somerville, MA 02145
NEW BOSTON REVIEW, 77 Sacramento St., Somerville, MA 02143
RADICAL AMERICA, 38 Union Square, Somerville, MA 02143, (617) 623-5110
SMALL MOON, 52½ Dimick Street, Somerville, MA 02143
Offshore Press, 294 Mt Auburn Street, Watertown, MA 02172, (617) 924-1860
Persephone Press, P.O. Box 7222, Watertown, MA 02172, (617) 924-0336
The B & R Samizdat Express, PO Box 161, West Roxbury, MA 02132, 617-469-2269
Lakes & Prairies Press, 28 Elmwood Street (Rear), West Somerville, MA 02144
Acorn, 185 Merriam Street, Weston, MA 02193
TREES, 185 Merriam Street, Weston, MA 02193
Chowder Chapbooks, PO Box 33, Wollaston, MA 02170
THE CHOWDER REVIEW, PO Box 33, Wollaston, MA 02170
FAG RAG, Box 331, Kenmore Station, Boston, MA 02215, 617-426-4469
PARTISAN REVIEW, 128 Bay State Road, Boston, MA 02215, (617) 353-4260
Union Park Press, PO Box 2737, Boston, MA 02208
BACK BAY VIEW, 33 Karen Drive, Randolph, MA 02368, (617) 986-5704
The Scoal Press, 53 Pondview Circle, Brockton, MA 02401, 617-587-4275
Longship Press, Crooked Lane, Nantucket, MA 02554, (207) 722-3344
NANTUCKET REVIEW, P.O. Box 1234, Nantucket, MA 02554
Salt-Works Press, Box 2152, Vineyard Haven, MA 02568, 617-385-3948
SOMA-HAOMA, Box 2152, Vineyard Haven, MA 02568
Cape Cod Writers Inc, Box 333, Cummaquid, MA 02637
SANDSCRIPT, Box 333, Cummaquid, MA 02637, 617-362-6078
SHANKPAINTER, 24 Pearl St, Provincetown, MA 02657, 617-487-9960
The Work Center Press, 24 Pearl St, Provincetown, MA 02657, 617-487-9960
Winter Trees Press, 249 Division St., Fall River, MA 02721, 617-674-1687

MICHIGAN

Cobbers, 22725 Orchard Lake Road, Farmington, MI 48024, (313) 478-3322
Cat Anna Press, c/o Prescott, 328-D E. Whitcomb, Madison Hgts., MI 48071, (313) 588-6486
KT Did Productions, c/o English Dept, Oakland University, Rochester, MI 48063
MINAS TIRITH EVENING-STAR, PO Box 277, Union Lake, MI 48085
ANN ARBOR REVIEW, Washtenaw Community College, Fred Wolven, editor, Ann Arbor, MI 48106, (313) 973-3408
Arbor Publications, PO Box 8185, Ann Arbor, MI 48107, 313-662-5786
Ardis, 2901 Heatherway, Ann Arbor, MI 48104
Bear Claw Press, 1039 Baldwin Street, Ann Arbor, MI 48104, (313) 668-6634
CO-OP: The Harbinger of Economic Democracy, Box 7293, Ann Arbor, MI 48107, 313-663-0889
CO-OP MAGAZINE, Box 7293, Ann Arbor, MI 48107, (313) 663-0889
Crowfoot Press, PO Box 7631, Liberty Station, Ann Arbor, MI 48107, (313) 482-5394
THE INSIDE TRACK, 306 Westwood, Ann Arbor, MI 48103, (313) 668-7703
Mayapple Press, PO Box 7508, Liberty Station, Ann Arbor, MI 48107, (313) 971-2223
MICHIGAN OCCASIONAL PAPERS IN WOMEN'S STUDIES, 1058 LSA Building, The University of Michigan, Ann Arbor, MI 48109, (313) 763-2047
MICHIGAN QUARTERLY REVIEW, 3032 Rackham Bldg., University of Michigan, Ann Arbor, MI 48109, (313)764-9265
North American Students of Cooperation, Box 7293, Ann Arbor, MI 48107, (313) 663-0889
REFERENCE SERVICES REVIEW, P.O. Box 1808, Ann Arbor, MI 48106, 313-434-5530
RIPPLES, 718 Watersedge, Ann Arbor, MI 48105
RUSSIAN LITERATURE TRIQUARTERLY, 2901 Heatherway, Ann Arbor, MI 48104, 313-971-2367
Shining Waters Press, 718 Watersedge, Ann Arbor, MI 48105
BLITZ, PO Box 279, Dearborn Heights, MI 48127
BILINGUAL REVIEW/La revista bilingue, 106 Ford Hall Dept Bilingual Studies, Eastern Michigan University, Ypsilanti, MI 48197,

212-969-4035
Bilingual Review/Press, 106 Ford Hall, Dept Foreign Languages, Eastern Michigan University, Ypsilanti, MI 48197, 313-487-0042
JOURNAL OF NARRATIVE TECHNIQUE, English Dept, Eastern Michigan University, Ypsilanti, MI 48197, (313) 487-0151
Clover Press, Box 313, Detroit, MI 48231
Glass Bell Press, 5053 Commonwealth, Detroit, MI 48208, 313-898-7972
GREEN'S MAGAZINE, Box 313, Detroit, MI 48231
Harlo Press, 50 Victor, Detroit, MI 48203
MOVING OUT: Feminist Literary & Arts Journal, 4866 Third & Warren, Wayne State University, Detroit, MI 48202, 313 898-7972/313
   833-9156
NEWS AND LETTERS, 2832 E Grand Blvd, Detroit, MI 48211, 313 873-8969
News and Letters Press, 2832 East Grand Blvd. Rm 316, Detroit, MI 48211
OBSIDIAN: BLACK LITERATURE IN REVIEW, English Dept., Wayne State Univ., Detroit, MI 48202
THE SMUDGE, PO Box 19276, Detroit, MI 48219
Anti-Ocean Press, 540 W Maplehurst, Ferndale, MI 48220, (313) 547-0790
Fallen Angel, 1981 West McNichols C-1, Highland Park, MI 48203, 313-864-0982
NEW PAGES, 4426 South Belsay Rd., Grand Blanc, MI 48439
THE ALTERNATIVE PRESS, 3090 Copeland Rd, Grindstone City, MI 48467
AEOLIAN-HARP, 1395 James St., Burton, MI 48529
Walden Press, 423 South Franklin Ave, Flint, MI 48503
Inquiry Press, 4925 Jefferson Ave, Midland, MI 48640, 517-631-3350
THE CENTENNIAL REVIEW, 110 Morrill Hall, Mich. State Univ., E. Lansing, MI 48824, 517-355-1905
CENTERING: A Magazine of Poetry, ATL EBH, Michigan State University, E. Lansing, MI 48824
JOURNAL OF SOUTH ASIAN LITERATURE, Mich State Univ, Asian Studies Ctr., E. Lansing, MI 48823, 517-353-1680
RED CEDAR REVIEW, 325 Morrill Hall, Dept. of English, Mich. State Univ., E. Lansing, MI 48824, 517-355-9656
Years Press, Dept. of ATL, EBH, Michigan State Univ, E. Lansing, MI 48824, (517) 332-5983
THE GYPSY SCHOLAR: A Graduate Forum for Literary Criticism, Dept. of English, Michigan State U., East Lansing, MI 48824,
   517-355-7578
Arbitrary Closet Press, 517 Bently, Eaton Rapids, MI 48827
SCREEN DOOR REVIEW, 517 Bently, Eaton Rapids, MI 48827
Service Press Inc., 6369 Reynolds Road, Haslett, MI 48840
Loompanics Unlimited, PO Box 264, Mason, MI 48854, (517) 694-2240
HAPPINESS HOLDING TANK, 1790 Grand River, Okemos, MI 48864
Stone Press, 1790 Grand River, Okemos, MI 48864
GRAND RIVER REVIEW/CAPITOL CITY MOON, PO Box 15052, Lansing, MI 48901
Blue Mountain Press, 511 Campbell St., Kalamazoo, MI 49007, 349-3924
Blues Press, PO Box 91, Kalamazoo, MI 49005
Expedition Press, 420 Davis, Kalamazoo, MI 49007
Flower Press, 121 E Van Hoesen, Kalamazoo, MI 49002, 616-343-3809
Humble Hills Press, PO Box 7, Kalamazoo, MI 49004
Practices of the Wind, c/o David M. Marovich, Box 214, Kalamazoo, MI 49005, (616) 343-0237
PRACTICES OF THE WIND, PO Box 214, Kalamazoo, MI 49005, (616) 343-0237
SKYWRITING, 511 Campbell St, Kalamazoo, MI 49007, 616-349-3924
THE LONDON COLLECTOR, P.O. Box 209, Cedar Springs, MI 49319
Wolf House Books, Box 209-K, Cedar Springs, MI 49319
MIME JOURNAL, Performing Arts Center, Grand Valley State Colleges, Allendale, MI 49401
BIG SCREAM, 2782 Dixie, SW, Grandville, MI 49418, 616-531-1442
Nada, 2782 Dixie, SW, Grandville, MI 49418, 616-531-1442
BARDIC ECHOES, 125 Somerset Drive, N.E., Grand Rapids, MI 49503, (616) 454-2807
Gearhead Press, 835 9th NW, Grand Rapids, MI 49504, 459-7861
THE CHUNGA REVIEW, Box 158, Felch, MI 49831, (906) 246-3562

MINNESOTA

THE LIBERATOR, P.O. Box 189, Forest Lake, MN 55025
MEN'S, P.O. Box 189, Forest Lake, MN 55025
Poor Richards Press, P O Box 189, Forest Lake, MN 55025
CARLETON MISCELLANY, Carleton College, Northfield, MN 55057
ST. CROIX REVIEW, Box 244, Stillwater, MN 55082, (612) 439-7190
Carma Press, Box 12633, St Paul, MN 55112, 612-631-3120
CONSPIRACIES UNLIMITED, P O Box 3085, St Paul, MN 55165
THE DANDELION, 1985 Selby Ave, St Paul, MN 55104, 612-646-8917
Llewellyn Publications, PO Box 43383, St. Paul, MN 55164, (612) 291-1970
River Basin Publishing Co., Box 30573, St Paul, MN 55175, (612) 291-7470
The Ally Press, PO Box 30340, St. Paul, MN 55175, (612) 227-1567
ASTROLOGY NOW, Llewellyn Publications, P.O.Box 43383, St. Paul, MN 55164, (612) 291-1970
Back Row Press, 1803 Venus Ave., St. Paul, MN 55112, 612-633-1685
New Rivers Press, Inc., 1602 Selby Avenue, St. Paul, MN 55104
PRACTICAL PARENTING, 16648 Meadowbrook Lane, Wayzata, MN 55391, 612-933-5008
Cadenza Press, 3922 Arthur Street, N.E., Columbia Heights, MN 55421, (612) 788-0455
HENNEPIN COUNTY LIBRARY CATALOGING BULLETIN, 7009 York Ave. S., Secretary, Technical Services Division,Hennepin
   Co. Library, Edina, MN 55435, 612-830-4980
MILKWEED CHRONICLE, Box 24303, Edina, MN 55424, (612) 941-5993
Cleis Press, 3141 Pleasant Avenue, South, Minneapolis, MN 55408, (612) 825-8872
GREAT RIVER REVIEW, PO Box 14805, Minneapolis, MN 55414, 612-378-9076
Holy Cow! Press, P O Box 618, Minneapolis, MN 55440
International Childbirth Education Association, Inc., PO Box 20048, Minneapolis, MN 55420
LAKE STREET REVIEW, c/o CD/DM Books, Box 7188, Powderhorn Station, Minneapolis, MN 55407
LITTLE FREE PRESS, 715 E. 14th St., Minneapolis, MN 55404
NEW UNIONIST, 621 West Lake Street, Rm 301, Minneapolis, MN 55408, (612) 823-2593
NORTH STONE REVIEW, University Stn. 14098, Minneapolis, MN 55414

RESEARCH, Graduate School Research Development Center, 417 Johnston Hall, University of Minnesota, Minneapolis, MN 55455, (612) 373-3001
SEZ: A Multi-Racial Journal of Poetry & People's Culture, PO Box 8803, Minneapolis, MN 55408, (612) 870-0899
Shadow Press, PO Box 8803, Minneapolis, MN 55408, (612) 870-0899
SING HEAVENLY MUSE! WOMEN'S POETRY AND PROSE, P.O. Box 14027, Minneapolis, MN 55414, (612) 822-8713; (612) 823-8030
Talespinner Publications, Inc., P.O. Box 19087, Minneapolis, MN 55419, (612) 825-0087
Tendon Press, Univ Sta. Box 14098, Minneapolis, MN 55414
Vanilla Press, 2400 Colfax Ave., South, Minneapolis, MN 55405, 612-374-4726
Bobbi Enterprises, Rt 1, Box 44, Mt Iron, MN 55768, 735-8364
Minnesota Writers' Publishing House, RR #1, Box 148, Kasota, MN 56050, (507) 931-4120
Minnesota Scholarly Press, Inc., PO Box 2294, Manbato, MN 56001, (507) 387-4964
Ox Head Press, 414 N 6th St, Marshall, MN 56258
Knollwood Publishing Company, Box 735, Willmar, MN 56201, 612-235-4950
ALTERNATIVE SOURCES of ENERGY MAGAZINE, 107 S. Central Avenue, Milaca, MN 56353, 612-983-6892
PILLAR, Box B, St Cloud, MN 56301, (612) 251-3510 ext 256
North Star Press, P.O. Box 451, St. Cloud, MN 56301, (612)253-1636
DACOTAH TERRITORY, P.O. Box 775, Moorhead, MN 56560
Territorial Press, P O Box 775, Moorhead, MN 56560
LOONFEATHER: Minnesota North Country Art, Box 48, Hagg-Sauer Hall, Bemidji, MN 56601, (218) 755-2813
RASPBERRY PRESS (magazine), Rte. 6 Box 459, Bemidji, MN 56601, 218-751-8497
TRULY FINE PRESS, A Review, P.O. Box 891, Bemidji, MN 56601
Truly Fine Press, P.O. Box 891, Bemidji, MN 56601
Woman Works Press, Rt 6, Box 309, Bemidji, MN 56601, (218) 751-0511
THE PILGRIM WAY, PO Box 277, Cass Lake, MN 56633, (218) 335-6190

MISSISSIPPI

Yoknapatawpha Press, Box 248, Oxford, MS 38655, (601) 234-0909
MISSISSIPPI REVIEW, Box 5144, Southern Station, Hattiesburg, MS 39401
SOUTHERN QUARTERLY: A Journal of the Arts in the South, Box 5078, Southern Stn., USM, Hattiesburg, MS 39401, (601) 266-4180

MISSOURI

Editorial Research Service, P.O.Box 1832, Kansas City, MO 54141, (913) 342-6768
MARK TWAIN JOURNAL, Mark Twain Journal, Kirkwood, MO 63122
Singing Wind Press, 4164 West Pine, Saint Louis, MO 63108, 314-535-2118
Grass-Hooper Press, 4030 Connecticut Street, St Louis, MO 63116, (314) 772-8164
SAINT LOUIS HOME/GARDEN, PO Box 29348, St Louis, MO 63127, (314) 965-1234
TELOS, Sociology Dept, Washington Univ, St Louis, MO 63130, 314-889-6638
Telos Press, C/O Sociology Dept, Washington Univ, St Louis, MO 63130, 314-889-6638
Big River Association, 7420 Cornell Ave, St. Louis, MO 63130
The Cauldron Press, Dept of English, Univ. of Missouri, 8001 Natural Bridge Road, St. Louis, MO 63121, (314) 453-5541
Cornerstone Press, P.O. Box 28048, St. Louis, MO 63119, 314-487-4303
FOCUS/ MIDWEST, 928a N. McKnight, St. Louis, MO 63132, 314-991-1698
IMAGE MAGAZINE, P.O. Box 28048, St. Louis, MO 63119, 314-487-4303
RIVER STYX, 7420 Cornell Ave., St. Louis, MO 63130, 314-725-0602
ST. LOUIS JOURNALISM REVIEW, 928A N. McKnight, St. Louis, MO 63132, 314-991-1699
Autolycus Press, Box 23928, Webster Groves, MO 63119, (314) 645-2114
WEBSTER REVIEW, Webster College, Webster Groves, MO 63119, 314-432-2657
CHARITON REVIEW, Northeast Missouri State University, Kirksville, MO 63501, 816-665-5121 ext 2156
Chariton Review Press, Northeast Missouri State University, Kirksville, MO 63501, 816-665-5121 ext 2156
THE CAPE ROCK, English Dept, Southeast Missouri State, Cape Girardeau, MO 63701, 314-651-2151
THE INTERNATIONAL UNIVERSITY POETRY QUARTERLY, 1301 S. Noland Rd., Independence, MO 64055
The International University Press, 1301 S. Noland Rd., Independence, MO 64055
Raindust Press, PO Box 1823, Independence, MO 64055
Amity Books, 1702 Magnolia, Liberty, MO 64068, (816) 781-6431
CHOUTEAU REVIEW, Box 10016, Kansas City, MO 64111, (816) 561-3086
JOURNAL OF SUPERSTITION AND MAGICAL THINKING, P.O.Box 1832, Kansas City, MO 64141, (913) 342-6768
MIDWEST ALLIANCE, PO Box 4642, Kansas City, MO 64109, (816) 753-4587
NEW LETTERS, University of Missouri, Kansas City, MO 64110, 816-276-1168
THE LADDER, 7800 Westside Drive, Weatherby Lake, MO 64152
The Ladder Press, 7800 Westside Drive, Weatherby Lake, MO 64152
The Naiad Press, Inc., 7800 Westside Drive, Weatherby Lake, MO 64152, 816-741-2283
SEED SAVERS EXCHANGE, Rural Route 2, Princeton, MO 64673, (816) 748-3091
SHEBA REVIEW, The Literary Magazine for the Arts, PO Box 86, Loose Creek, MO 65054, (314) 897-3924
EXCHANGE: A Journal of Opinion for the Ferforming Arts, 129 Fine Arts Center, Missouri University, Columbia, MO 65211, (314) 882-2021
THE MISSOURI REVIEW, Dept. of English, 231 Arts & Science, University of Missouri-Columbia, Columbia, MO 65211
MONUMENT IN CANTOS AND ESSAYS, 4508 Mexico Gravel Road, Columbia, MO 65201
OPEN PLACES, Box 2085, Stephens College, Columbia, MO 65215, 314-442-2211
BITTERSWEET, Lebanon High School, 777 Brice St., Lebanon, MO 65536, 417-532-9829
LOST GENERATION JOURNAL, Route 5, Box 134, Salem, MO 65560, (314) 729-5669: (501) 568-6241
REBUTTAL! The Bicentennial Newsletter of Truth, P.O. Box 1126, Branson, MO 65616
WEST PLAINS GAZETTE, PO Box 469, West Plains, MO 65775, 417-256-9677
W.D. Firestone Press, 1313 South Jefferson Avenue, Springfield, MO 65807, (417) 866-5141
Mafdet Press, 1313 South Jefferson Avenue, Springfield, MO 65807, (417) 866-5141

MONTANA

BLACK JACK & VALLEY GRAPEVINE, Box 249, Big Timber, MT 59011
Seven Buffaloes Press, Box 249, Big Timber, MT 59011

AERO SUN-TIMES, 424 Stapleton Bldg., Billings, MT 59101, (406) 259-1958
Jaks Publishing Co., PO Box 5625, 1106 N Washington Street, Helena, MT 59601, (406) 442-5486
Calliopea Press, 701 Longstaff, Missoula, MT 59801, 406-549-6945
CUTBANK, English Dept., U. of Montana, Missoula, MT 59812
GILTEDGE: New Series, PO Box 8081, Missoula, MT 59807
THE MONTANA REVIEW, 520 S Second W, Missoula, MT 59801, (406) 728-0479
Mountain Press Publishing Co., 283 W Front, PO Box 2399, Missoula, MT 59806, (406) 728-1900
Owl Creek Press, 520 S Second, W, Missoula, MT 59801, (406) 728-0479
SmokeRoot, Dept of English/Univ of Mont, Missoula, MT 59812
THE SALT CEDAR, Rt 2, Box 170 B, Stevensville, MT 59870, (406) 777-5169
Tamarix, Route 2, Box 121 A, Stevensville, MT 59870, (406) 777-3674

NEBRASKA

ANNEX 21, Annex 21, U.N.O. 60th & Dodge Streets, Omaha, NB 68182
Best Cellar Press, 118 So Boswell Ave, Crete, NB 68333
PEBBLE, 118 South Boswell, Crete, NB 68333, 402-826-4038
AMERICAN FIDDLERS NEWS, 6141 Morrill Avenue, Lincoln, NB 68507, 402-466-5519
American Old Time Fiddlers Assoc., 6141 Morrill Avenue, Lincoln, NB 68507, (402) 466-5519
THE BLUE HOTEL, PO Box 82213, Lincoln, NB 68501
Century Three Press, 411 So 13th Street, Suite 315, Lincoln, NB 68508, (402) 474-6345
Mercantine Press, 4351 Washington Street, Lincoln, NB 68506, (402) 489-2626
PRAIRIE SCHOONER, 201 Andrews Hall, Univ. of Nebr., Lincoln, NB 68588
PREMONITION TIMES, Box 82863, Lincoln, NB 68501, (402) 477-8003
Windflower Press, P.O. Box 82213, Lincoln, NB 68501

NEVADA

NEW MAGAZINE REVIEW, PO Box 3699, N Las Vegas, NV 89030, (702) 734-6730
CASINO & SPORTS, 630 S. 11th St., Box 4115, Las Vegas, NV 89106, (702)382-7555
GBC Press, Gambler's Book Club, 630 S. 11th St., Box 4115, Las Vegas, NV 89106, (702)382-7555
Nevada Publications, Box 15444, Las Vegas, NV 89114, 702-871-1800
SYSTEMS & METHODS, 630 So. 11th St., Box 4115, Las Vegas, NV 89106, (702)382-7555
Duck Down Press, PO Box 1047, Fallon, NV 89406, (702) 423-2220
SCREE, PO Box 1047, Fallon, NV 89406, (702) 423-2220
Bonanza, Inc., PO Box 971, Reno, NV 89504, (206) 322-4900
Great Basin Press, Box 11162, Reno, NV 89510, (702) 826-7729
WEST COAST POETRY REVIEW, 1335 Dartmouth Dr, Reno, NV 89509, 702-322-4467
West Coast Poetry Review Press, 1335 Dartmouth Dr, Reno, NV 89509, 702-322-4467
WOMAN POET, PO Box 12668, Reno, NV 89510, (702) 825-8104
Women-in-Literature, Inc., PO Box 12668, Reno, NV 89510, (702) 825-8104

NEW HAMPSHIRE

AMOSKEAG: A Magazine of Haiku, 113 Comeau Street, Manchester, NH 03102
Bon Mot Publications, Box 606, Manchester, NH 03105
The First Haiku Press, 113 Comeau Street, Manchester, NH 03102
UNITED ARTISTS, Flanders Road, Henniker, NH 03242
United Artists, Flanders Road, Henniker, NH 03242
DEPARTURES: Contemporary Arts Review, 140 N. Main Street, Concord, NH 03301
PASS-AGE: A Futures Journal, PO Box 160, Dublin, NH 03444, 215-222-2735
William L. Bauhan, Publisher, Dublin, NH 03444, 603-563-8020
SOLAR AGE, Church Hill, Harrisville, NH 03450, (603) 827-3347
COBBLESTONE: The History Magazine for Children, 28 Main Street, Peterborough, NH 03458, (603) 924-7209
Windy Row Press, MacDowell Road, Peterborough, NH 03458, (603) 924-3340
NEW ENGLAND REVIEW, Box 170, Hanover, NH 03755, (802) 649-1005
New Victoria Publishers, 7 Bank St., Lebanon, NH 03766, (603) 448-2264
Independence Unlimited, 27 Gardner Street, Portsmouth, NH 03801, (603) 431-6530
PENUMBRA, Box 794, Portsmouth, NH 03801

NEW JERSEY

ARULO!, 252 No. 16th Street, Bloomfield, NJ 07003
VEGA, 252 No. 16th Street, Bloomfield, NJ 07003
Brux Am Books, PO Box 4052, Clifton, NJ 07012, (201) 667-4895
ALBATROSS, P.O. Box 2046, Central Station, East Orange, NJ 07019
SHELTERFORCE, 380 Main St., East Orange, NJ 07018, (201) 678-6778
From Here Press, Box 219, Fanwood, NJ 07023
XTRAS, Box 219, Fanwood, NJ 07023, (201) 322-5928
Karmic Revenge Laundry Shop Press, Box 14, Guttenberg, NJ 07093, 201-868-8106
East River Anthology, 75 Gates Ave, Montclair, NJ 07042
WEST END MAGAZINE, c/o Kaliss, 31 Montague Place, Montclair, NJ 07042
AHNOI, 707 90th Street, North Bergen, NJ 07047
Polygonal Publishing House, 80 Passaic Ave, Passaic, NJ 07055
LUNCH, 220 Montross Ave, Rutherford, NJ 07070
Poets & Writers of New Jersey, Box 852, Upper Montclair, NJ 07043
AGAINST THE WALL, PO Box 444, Westfield, NJ 07091
Merging Media, 59 Sandra Circle A-3, Westfield, NJ 07090, 232-7224
VALHALLA, 59 Sandra Circle A-3, Westfield, NJ 07090, 232-7224
Incunabula Collection Press, 277 Hillside Ave, Nutley, NJ 07110
Alleluia Press, Box 103, Allendale, NJ 07401, 201-327-3513
BERGEN POETS, c/o Mrs. Ruth Falk, 197 Delmar Avenue, Glen Rock, NJ 07452, (201) 444-3829
ACCCA Press, 19 Foothills Drive, Pompton Plains, NJ 07444, (201) 835-2661

Jim Mann & Associates, 7 Biscayne Drive, Ramsey, NJ 07446, (201) 327-8492
MEDIA MANAGEMENT MONOGRAPHS, 7 Biscayne Drive, Ramsey, NJ 07446, (201) 327-8492
Tamarisk, 188 Forest Ave, Ramsey, NJ 07446, 201-327-7469
de la Ree Publications, 7 Cedarwood Lane, Saddle River, NJ 07458
TEACHER UPDATE, Box 205, Saddle River, NJ 07458, (201) 327-8486
Teacher Update, Inc., Box 205, Saddle River, NJ 07458, (201) 327-8486
SOME OTHER MAGAZINE, 47 Hazen Court, Wayne, NJ 07470, (201) 696-9230
IF LIFE, THEN ONE AMONG AT LEAST FOUR, P.O. Box 282, Palisades Park, NJ 07650
NEW JERSEY POETRY MONTHLY, P.O. Box 824, Saddle Brook, NJ 07662, 201-445-9436
New Worlds Unlimited, PO Box 556, Saddle Brook, NJ 07662
BRAVO, 1081 Trafalgar Street, Teaneck, NJ 07666, (201) 836-5922
King and Cowen (New York), 1081 Trafalgar Street (John Cowen), Teaneck, NJ 07666, 201-836-5922
NEW DIRECTIONS FOR WOMEN, 223 Old Hook Road, Westwood, NJ 07675, 201-666-4677
E & E Enterprises, P.O. Box 405, Howell, NJ 07731, 201-364-1398
AFTA—The Magazine of Temporary Culture, 47 Crater Avenue, Wharton, NJ 07885, (201) 366-1967
JOURNAL OF NEW JERSEY POETS, Fairleigh Dickinson Univ., English Dept., 285 Madison Avenue, Madison, NJ 07940, 01-377-4700
THE LITERARY REVIEW, Fairleigh Dickinson University, 285 Madison Avenue, Madison, NJ 07940, 201 377-4050
STONE COUNTRY, 20 Lorraine Road, Madison, NJ 07940, 201-377-3727
Stone Country Press, 20 Lorraine Road, Madison, NJ 07940, 201-377-3727
CREATIVE COMPUTING, P.O. Box 789-M, Morristown, NJ 07960, 201-540-0445
Creative Computing Press, PO Box 789-M, Morristown, NJ 07960, 201-540-0445
Donald D. Wilson, 121 Central Ave., Stirling, NJ 07980
PTOLEMY/BROWNS MILLS REVIEW, Box 6915-A Press Avenue, Browns Mills, NJ 08015, (609) 893-7594
WHISPERS, Box 1492-W Azalea Street, Browns Mills, NJ 08015, 893-7425
Whispers Press, Box 1492-W Azalea Street, Browns Mills, NJ 08015
Air-Plus Enterprises, PO Box 367, Glassboro, NJ 08028, (609) 881-0724
THE MICKLE STREET REVIEW, 46 Centre Street, Haddonfield, NJ 08033, (609) 795-7887
Lightbooks, Box 425, Marlton, NJ 08053, (609) 983-5978
ASPHODEL, 613 Howard Avenue, Pitman, NJ 08071
Jim Phillips Publications, PO box 168, Williamstown, NJ 08094, (609) 567-0695
Cologne Press, PO Box 682, Cologne, NJ 08213, (609) 965-5163
THE ONTARIO REVIEW, 9 Honey Brook Drive, Princeton, NJ 08540
QUARTERLY REVIEW OF LITERATURE, 26 Haslet Ave, Princeton, NJ 08540, 921-6976
THE SHIRT OFF YOUR BACK, 62 Spelman Hall, Princeton, NJ 08544
US1 Poets' Cooperative, 21 Lake Drive, Roosevelt, NJ 08555, (609) 448-5096
US1 WORKSHEETS, 21 Lake Drive, Roosevelt, NJ 08555, 609-448-5096
Africa Research & Publications Project, P.O.Box 1892, Trenton, NJ 08608
BOOK BUYER'S GUIDE/MARKETPLACE, PO Box 208, East Millstone, NJ 08873, 201-873-2156
Franklin Publishing Company, PO Box 208, East Millstone, NJ 08873, 201-873-2156
THE SUBURBAN SHOPPER, PO Box 208, East Millstone, NJ 08873, 201-873-2156
Scarecrow Press, P O Box 656, Metuchen, NJ 08840, 201-548-8600
Great Society Press, 451 Heckman St. Apt. 308, Phillipsburg, NJ 08865, 201-859-6134
FOOTPRINT MAGAZINE, 150 West Summit St, Somerville, NJ 08876
LADY-UNIQUE-INCLINATION-OF-THE-NIGHT, Box 803, New Brunswick, NJ 08903
WOMEN AND LITERATURE, Dept. English, Douglas College, Rutgers University, New Brunswick, NJ 08903
Original Press, 561 Milltown Road, North Brunswick, NJ 08902, (201) 249-5543
GEORGE SPELVIN'S THEATRE BOOK, PO Box 361, Newark, NJ 19711, (215) 255-4083
Proscenium Press, P.O.Box 361, Newark, NJ 19711, (215) 255-4083

NEW MEXICO

AFTERBIRTH, Box 571, Placitas, NM 87043
Duende Press, Box 571, Placitas, NM 87043
Anonymous Owl Press, 3209 Wellesley NE #1, Albuquerque, NM 87107
BLAKE, AN ILLUSTRATED QUARTERLY, Dept. of English, Univ. of New Mexico, Albuquerque, NM 87131, 505-277-3103
BOOK TALK, 8632 Horacio Pl NE, Albuquerque, NM 87111, 505-299-8940
CENTER, P.O. Box 7494, Old Albuquerque Station, Albuquerque, NM 87194, (505) 247-9337
DE COLORES: Journal of Emerging Raza Philosophy, P O Box 7264, Albuquerque, NM 87104, (505) 242-2839
CONCEPTIONS SOUTHWEST, Box 20, UNM Post Office, Albuquerque, NM 87131, (505) 277-5656
LA CONFLUENCIA, P.O. Box 409, Albuquerque, NM 87103
The Doodly-Squat Press, P.O. Box 40124, Albuquerque, NM 87106
THE HOT SPRINGS GAZETTE, P.O. Box 40124, Albuquerque, NM 87106, 505-243-4272
INTERFACE JOURNAL: Alternatives in Higher Education, 505 Fruit Ave NW, Albuquerque, NM 87102
THE MARGARINE MAYPOLE ORANGOUTANG EXPRESS, 3209 Wellesley, NE 1, Albuquerque, NM 87107
NEW AMERICA, Humanities Room 324, University of New Mexico, Albuquerque, NM 87131, (505) 277-3929
Pajarito Publications, P.O.Box 7264, Albuquerque, NM 87104, 505-242-2839
RIO GRANDE WRITERS NEWSLETTER, PO Box 40126, Albuquerque, NM 87107, (505) 266-3110
SAN MARCOS REVIEW, P.O. Box 4368, Albuquerque, NM 87196
Southwest Research and Information Center, PO Box 4524, Albuquerque, NM 87106, (505) 242-4766
The Transientpress, Box 4662, Albuquerque, NM 87196, (505) 242-6600
THE WORKBOOK, PO Box 4524, Albuquerque, NM 87106, 505-242-4766
WORLD NEWS, PO Box 4372, Albuquerque, NM 87106, (505) 255-6550
THE WRITER'S PAGE, Box 429, Albuquerque, NM 87103, (505) 843-6440
TSA'ASZI', CPO Box 12, Pine Hill, NM 87321, (505) 783-5503
John Muir Publications, Inc., P.O. Box 613, Santa Fe, NM 87501, 505-982-4078
The Lightning Tree, PO Box 1837, Santa Fe, NM 87501, (505) 983-7434
Museum of New Mexico Press, PO Box 2087, Santa Fe, NM 87503
EL PALACIO, P.O. Box 2087, Santa Fe, NM 87503, (505) 827-2352
THE STEREOPHILE, PO Box 1948, Santa Fe, NM 87501
The Sunstone Press, PO Box 2321, Santa Fe, NM 87501, (505) 988-4418

INDIAN HOUSE, Box 472, Taos, NM 87571, (505) 776-2953
PLUMBERS INK, PO Box 2565, Taos, NM 87571, 758-8035
Plumbers Ink Press, PO Box 2565, Taos, NM 87571
Tooth of Time Press, Box 356, Guadalupita, NM 87722
Vietnam Veterans Chapel, Box 666, Springer, NM 87747, 483-2833
NEW MEXICO HUMANITIES REVIEW, Box A, New Mexico Tech, Socorro, NM 87801, (505) 835-5445
Bilingue Publications, PO Drawer H, Las Cruces, NM 88001, (505) 526-1557
PUERTO DEL SOL, Box 3E, Las Cruces, NM 88003, 505-646-3932
Puerto Del Sol Press, Box 3E, Las Cruces, NM 88003
American-Canadian Publishers, Inc., Drawer 2078, Portales, NM 88130, 505-356-4082
Iroquois House, Publishers, Box 15, Sunspot, NM 88349, (505) 437-2807

NEW YORK

MAGAZINE, 86 E 3rd Street, Apt 3A, New York, NY 10003, (212) 228-2178; (212) 243-1393; (212) 673-1511
Acrobus, Inc., 1324 Lexington Avenue, New York, NY 10028, 212-534-3265
AIS EIRI, 553 W. 51st St., New York, NY 10019, 212-757-3318
Algol Press, P.O. Box 4175, New York, NY 10017, 212-643-9011
ALTERNATIVE MEDIA, Box 775 Madison Square Station, New York, NY 10010, (212) 481-0120
American Artists In Exhibition, Inc., 799 Greenwich St., New York, NY 10014, 212-989-1595
THE AMERICAN BOOK REVIEW, PO Box 188, Cooper Station, New York, NY 10003, (212) 749-5906
American Dance Guild Inc, 1133 Broadway #1427, New York, NY 10010
AMERICAN DANCE GUILD NEWSLETTER, 1133 Broadway #1427, New York, NY 10010, (212) 691-7773
ANARCHISM: The Feminist Connection, 13 East 17 St., New York, NY 10003
Angle Lightning Press, 17 E. 84th Street, New York, NY 10028, 861-5926, 877-6239
ANTAEUS, 1 West 30th St., New York, NY 10001, 212-736-2599
AREITO, PO Box 1913, New York, NY 10001
ART AND ARCHAEOLOGY NEWSLETTER, 243 East 39th Street, New York, NY 10016
ASI Publishers, Inc., 127 Madison Ave, New York, NY 10016, 212-679-5676
ASTROLOGY '80—The New Aquarian Agent, 127 Madison Ave, New York, NY 10016, 212-679-5676
Author! Author! Publishing Co., 210 E 58th Street, New York, NY 10022
BALLET NEWS, 1865 Broadway, New York, NY 10023, 582-7500
Bard Press, 799 Greenwich Street, New York, NY 10014, (212) 929-3169
Basement Editions, 22 Catherine Street Floor #3, New York, NY 10038, (212) 925-3258
Belier Press, PO Box 'C', Gracie Station, New York, NY 10028
BIKINI GIRL, PO Box 319, Stuyvesant Station, New York, NY 10009, (212) 533-3561
BOOK ARTS, 15 Bleecker St, New York, NY 10012
BOSS, Box 370, Madison Square Station, New York, NY 10010
Boss Books, Box 370, Madison Square Station, New York, NY 10010
BOX 749, Box 749, Old Chelsea Station, New York, NY 10011
BRIDGE MAGAZINE, P.O. Box 477, New York, NY 10013, (212) 233-2154
Calamus Books, Box 689, Cooper Station, New York, NY 10003
CENTRAL PARK, 410 West End Ave., Apt 1E, New York, NY 10024
THE CHARIOTEER, PO Box 2928, Grand Central Station, New York, NY 10017
CHELSEA, Box 5880, Grand Central Station, New York, NY 10017
CINEASTE MAGAZINE, 419 Park Avenue South, New York, NY 10016
CINEMAGIC, 475 Park Ave, South, New York, NY 10016, (212) 689-2830
CODA: Poets & Writers Newsletter, 201 West 54th St., New York, NY 10019, 212-757-1766
COLUMBIA: A MAGAZINE OF POETRY AND PROSE, 404 Dodge, Columbia University, New York, NY 10027, 280-4391
Come! Unity Press, 13 E 17th Street, New York, NY 10003
CONTACT/11: A Bimonthly Poetry Review Magazine, PO Box 451, Bowling Green Station, New York, NY 10004, 212-425-5979
Contact II: Publications, PO Box 451, Bowling Green Station, New York, NY 10004, 212-522-3227
THE CO-OP OBSERVER, 241 W 23rd Street, New York, NY 10011, (212) 675-7226
COPY CORNUCOPIA, 516 Fifth Avenue, New York, NY 10036
Cykx Books, PO Box 299, Lenox Hill Station, New York, NY 10021, (212) 876-6577
DANCE BOOK FORUM, 22 West 77th Street #62, New York, NY 10024, 212-362-9921
DANCE HERALD, 243 West 63st, New York, NY 10023
Dance Motion Press, 22 West 77th Street #62, New York, NY 10024, 212-362-9921
DANCE SCOPE, 1133 Broadway #1427, New York, NY 10010, (212) 691-4564
Daniel Stokes, Publisher, 128 E 4th Street, New York, NY 10003
DEMOCRATIC LEFT, 853 Broadway, Suite 801, New York, NY 10003, (212) 260-3270
DIAL-A-POEM POETS LP'S, 222 Bowery, New York, NY 10012, 212-925-6372
The Direct Marketing Creative Guild, 516 5th Avenue, New York, NY 10036
Do-It-Yourself Publications, Co., 150 Fifth Ave., New York, NY 10011, (212) 242-2840
THE DRAMA REVIEW, 51 West 4th St. Room 300, New York, NY 10012, 212-598-2597
DREAMS, 76 Beaver Street, Suite 400, New York, NY 10005, (212) 996-0812
EAR MAGAZINE, 365 West End Avenue, New York, NY 10024, 212-475-8223
EAST RIVER REVIEW, 128 E 4th St, New York, NY 10003
Editorial Services Co., 1140 Avenue of the Americas, New York, NY 10036, (212) 354-5025
Equal Time Press, 463 West St. Apt H 960, New York, NY 10014
EUTERPE, 419 W. 56th Street, New York, NY 10019
FICTION, c/o Dept. of English, City College, 138th Street & Convent Ave., New York, NY 10031
Fiction Collective, Inc., c/o George Braziller, Inc., One Park Avenue, New York, NY 10016
FIGHTING WOMAN NEWS, P.O. Box 1459, Grand Central Station, New York, NY 10017, 212-228-0900
FILM CULTURE, G. P. O. Box 1499, New York, NY 10001
Film Culture Non-Profit, Inc., G. P. O. Box 1499, New York, NY 10001
FILM LIBRARY QUARTERLY, Box 348, Radio City Station, New York, NY 10019
FORGE, 47 Murray Street, New York, NY 10007, (212) 349-8788
Four Corners Press, 463 West Street, New York, NY 10014, (212) 989-1284
FREEDOMWAYS, Freedomways Associates, Inc., 799 Broadway Suite 542, New York, NY 10003

FREELANCE, 204 W 20th St, New York, NY 10011
Frelance Publishing Co., 204 West 20th St., New York, NY 10011
FROM THE CENTER: A FOLIO, PO Box 451, Bowling Green Station, New York, NY 10004, (212) 522-3227
Full Court Press, Inc., 15 Laight Street, New York, NY 10017
Full Track Press, PO Box 55, Planetarium Station, New York, NY 10024
FUNNYWORLD - The Magazine of Animation and Comic Art, PO Box 1633, New York, NY 10001, (212) 544-0120
The Future Press, P.O. Box 73, Canal St., New York, NY 10013
GEGENSCHEIN, NeoNeo DoDo, 111 Third Ave. #12C, New York, NY 10003, (212) 473-1883
GNOSIS, Earl Hall Center, Columbia University, New York, NY 10027, (212) 280-5113
Green Eagle Press, 241 W 97th Street, New York, NY 10025, 212-663-2167
GUARDIAN, 33 W 17th St, New York, NY 10011, 212-691-0404
HAND BOOK, 50 Spring Street, Apt. #2, New York, NY 10012
Hard Press, 340 East Eleventh Street, New York, NY 10003, (212) 673-1152
HERESIES: A FEMINIST PUBLICATION ON ART AND POLITICS, Box 766, Canal St Sta, New York, NY 10013, 212-431-9060
Hesperidian Press, 105 Riverside Drive, c/o Halpern, New York, NY 10024, 362-2831
HOME PLANET NEWS, P.O. Box 415 Stuyvesant Station, New York, NY 10009, (212) 534-2372
Home Planet Publications, P.O. Box 415 Stuyvesant Station, New York, NY 10009, (212) 534-2372
Ilkon Press, 210 Riverside Drive No. 6G, New York, NY 10025, 212-663-2579
INSIDE/OUT, GPO Box 1185, New York, NY 10001, (212) 595-8448
INSIGHT: A Quarterly of LESBIAN/GAY CHRISTIAN OPINION, P.O. Box 5110,, Grand Central Station, New York, NY 10017
Institute for Independent Social Journalism, Inc., 33 W 17th St, New York, NY 10011, (212) 691-0404
INTERCONTINENTAL PRESS/INPRECOR, 410 West Street, New York, NY 10014
Interim Books, Box 35, Village Station, New York, NY 10014
International General, P.O. Box 350, New York, NY 10013
INTERRACIAL BOOKS FOR CHILDREN BULLETIN, 1841 Broadway, New York, NY 10023, 212-757-5339
Inwood Press, c/o Teachers & Writers, 84 Fifth Avenue, New York, NY 10011
ISRAEL HORIZONS, 150 Fifth Avenue, Room 1002, New York, NY 10011, (212) 255-8760
JH Press, PO Box 294, Village Station, New York, NY 10014, 255-4713
JOURNAL OF THE HELLENIC DIASPORA, 461 Eighth Ave, New York, NY 10001, 212-279-9586
THE JOURNAL OF PSYCHOLOGICAL ANTHROPOLOGY, 2315 Broadway, New York, NY 10024, 212-873-3760
Kulchur Foundation, 888 Park Ave., New York, NY 10021, 988-5193
LAMISHPAHA, 1841 Broadway, New York, NY 10023, (212) 581-5151
L=A=N=G=U=A=G=E, 464 Amsterdam Avenue, New York, NY 10024, 212-799-4475
LETTERS MAGAZINE, P.O. Box 786, New York, NY 10008
LILITH, 250 W 57th, Suite 1328, New York, NY 10019, (212) 757-0818
THE LITTLE MAGAZINE, Box 207 Cathedral Station, New York, NY 10025
LOST GLOVE, c/o Kahaner, 161 W 86th Street, Apt 6A, New York, NY 10024
LUMEN/AVENUE A, PO Box 412, Stuyvesant Station, New York, NY 10009
MAG CITY, 437 East 12 St. No. 26, New York, NY 10009
MAIN TREND, PO Box 344 Cooper Station, New York, NY 10003
MAJORITY REPORT, 74 Grove St, New York, NY 10014, 212-691-4950
Mandarin Press, 210 Fifth Avenue, New York, NY 10010
THE MANHATTAN REVIEW, c/o P. Fried, 304 Third Avenue, 4A, New York, NY 10010
MARXIST PERSPECTIVES, 420 West End Avenue, New York, NY 10024, (212) 242-7777
THE MILITANT, 14 Charles Lane, New York, NY 10014, 212-243-6392
Mockingbird Press, 160 6th Avenue, New York, NY 10013, (212) 925-3823
MONTEMORA, The Montemora Foundation Inc., Box 336, Cooper Station, New York, NY 10003, 212-255-2733
MOUTH OF THE DRAGON, Box 957, c/o Bifrost, New York, NY 10009
NEW YORK ARTS JOURNAL, 560 Riverside Drive, New York, NY 10027
The New York Literary Press, 419 West 56th St., New York, NY 10019
NEW YORK QUARTERLY, PO Box 2415 G Central Stn., New York, NY 10017, 212-242-9876
NOK Publishers International, 150 Fifth Ave, Suite 826, New York, NY 10011, (212) 675-5785
NOT GUILTY!, P.O.Box 2563, Grand Central Station, New York, NY 10017
The Not Guilty Press, P.O.Box 2563, Grand Central Station, New York, NY 10017
NUTRITION HEALTH REVIEW, 143 Madison, New York, NY 10016
O Press, 190 A Duane Street, New York, NY 10013
Odin Press, PO Box 536, New York, NY 10021, (212) 744-2538
Oleander Press/U.S., 210 Fifth Ave., New York, NY 10010
Other Scenes, Box 4137, Grand Central Station, New York, NY 10017, 212-582-3112
OUT THERE MAGAZINE, 156 W 27th, 5-W, New York, NY 10001, 212-675-0194
P.E.N. American Center, 47 5th Ave, New York, NY 10003
PAPER NEWS, 160 6th Avenue, New York, NY 10013, 212-925-3823
PARABOLA MAGAZINE, 150 Fifth Avenue, New York, NY 10011, (212) 924-0004
Paradise Loft, 241 W 23rd Street, New York, NY 10011, (212) 675-7226
PARNASSUS: POETRY IN REVIEW, 205 West 89th Street, New York, NY 10024, (212) 787-3569
Pella Publ. Co, 461 Eighth Ave, New York, NY 10001, 212-279-9586
The Pepys Press, 1270 Fifth Avenue, New York, NY 10029, (212) 348-6847
Pequod Press, 344 Third Ave, Apt 3A, New York, NY 10010, (212) 686-4789
PERFORMING ARTS JOURNAL, P.O. Box 858, Peter Stuyvesant Station, New York, NY 10009, 212-260-7586
Pilgrim Press, 132 West 31st Street, New York, NY 10001, (212) 594-8555
Pittore Euforico, PO Box 1132, Stuyvesant Station, New York, NY 10009
PLUM, 549 W. 113th St., #1D, New York, NY 10025, (212) 662-5385
Poet Gallery Press, 224 West 29th St, New York, NY 10001
POETRY EAST, 530 Riverside Drive 4-B, New York, NY 10027, (212) 749-0841
Poetry in Public Places, 799 Greenwich St., New York, NY 10014, 212-242-3374
THE POETRY PROJECT NEWSLETTER, St. Mark's Church, The Poetry Project, 2nd Ave & 10th Street, New York, NY 10003, 674-0910
Poets & Writers, Inc., 201 West 54th Street, New York, NY 10019, 212-757-1766
PRECISELY, PO Box 73, Canal Street, New York, NY 10013

The Printable Arts Society, Inc., Box 749, Old Chelsea Station, New York, NY 10011, (212) 989-0519
Printed Matter, Inc., 7 Lispenard, New York, NY 10013, (212) 925-0325
PULPSMITH, 5 Beekman St., New York, NY 10038
Pyxidium Press, 462 Old Chelsea Station, New York, NY 10011, (212) 242-5224
RK Editions, P.O. Box 73 Canal Sta., New York, NY 10013
RADICAL TEACHER, 320 Riverside Drive #13D, New York, NY 10025
RE:PRINT (AN OCCASIONAL MAGAZINE), c/o BOX 749, Box 749 Old Chelsea Station, New York, NY 10011
Red Dust, PO Box 630, Gracie Station, New York, NY 10028
REVIEW, 680 Park Avenue, New York, NY 10021
The Sandstone Press, 321 East 43rd Street, New York, NY 10017, (212) 682-5519
Scarf Press, 58 E 83rd Street, New York, NY 10028, (212) 744-3901
SCIENCE FICTION CHRONICLE, PO Box 4175, New York, NY 10017, 212-643-9011
Seven Woods Press, P.O. Box 32, Village Station, New York, NY 10014
The Sheep Meadow Press, 145 Central Park West, New York, NY 10023, 212-247-1759
SING OUT! The Folk Song Magazine, 505 Eighth Avenue, New York, NY 10018
SOCIAL POLICY, Room 1212, 33 W 42nd St, New York, NY 10036, 212-840-1279
SOME, 309 W. 104 St. Apt. 9D, New York, NY 10025
SPACE AND TIME, 138 West 70th Street (4-B), New York, NY 10023
Standard Editions, P.O. Box 1297, Stuyvesant Station, New York, NY 10009
Starogubski Press, 345 Riverside Drive, Suite 5J, New York, NY 10025
STARSHIP: The Magazine About Science Fiction, P.O. Box 4175, New York, NY 10017, 212-643-9011
Stephen Wright Press, Box 1341, F.D.R. Postal Station, New York, NY 10022, (212) 927-2869
STRAIGHT AHEAD INTERNATIONAL, GPO Box 1185, New York, NY 10001, (212) 595-8448
Strawberry Press, PO Box 451, Bowling Green Station, New York, NY 10004, 212-522-3227
STROKER, 129 2nd Ave. No. 3, New York, NY 10003
H. Summer Enterprises, P.O. Box 411, New York, NY 10014
SUN, 456 Riverside Drive-5B, New York, NY 10027
Sun, 456 Riverside Drive, Apt 5B, New York, NY 10027, (212) 662-6121
Synerjy, Box 4790, Grand Central Station, New York, NY 10017, (212) 865-9595
SYNERJY: A Directory of Energy Alternatives, Box 4790, Grand Central Station, New York, NY 10017, (212) 865-9595
SZ/Press, P.O. Box 383, Cathedral Station, New York, NY 10025
Tanam Press, 40 White Street, New York, NY 10013
Teachers & Writers Collaborative, 84 Fifth Avenue (at 14th St.), New York, NY 10011, 212-691-6590
TEACHERS & WRITERS MAGAZINE, 84 Fifth Ave (at 14th St.), New York, NY 10011, 212-691-6590
Telephone Books, Box 672, Old Chelsea Sta, New York, NY 10011
Ten Penny Players, Inc., 799 Greenwich Street, New York, NY 10014, 212-929-3169
Tenth House Enterprises, Inc., PO Box 810, Gracie Station, New York, NY 10028, (212) 737-7536
THEATRE, 55 West 42nd Street #1218, New York, NY 10036, (212) 221-6078
THE THIRD PRESS REVIEW, 1995 Broadway, New York, NY 10023, (212) 724-9505
13th MOON, 13th Moon, Inc., Drawer F, Inwood Station, New York, NY 10034, 212-569-7614
THIS AND THAT, Box 86, 527 Riverside Drive, New York, NY 10027, (212) 866-2200
Three Mountains Press, P.O. Box 50, Cooper Station, New York, NY 10003, 212-989-2737
TIME CAPSULE, INC., General PO Box 1185, New York, NY 10001, (212)595-8448
Tomato Publications Ltd., 70 Barrow Street, New York, NY 10014
TRANSLATION, 307A Mathematics, Columbia University, New York, NY 10027, 212-280-2305
Translation, 307A Mathematics, Columbia University, New York, NY 10027, 280-2305
Tree Line Books, Box 1062, Radio City Station, New York, NY 10019
Troisieme-Canadian Publishers, P.O.Box 4281, Grand Central Station, New York, NY 10017, (212) 940-0954
TROUSER PRESS, 212 5th Ave, #1310, New York, NY 10010, 212-889-7145
The Twickenham Press, 31 Jane Street, New York, NY 10014, (212) 741-2417
THE U*N*A*B*A*S*H*E*D LIBRARIAN, THE "HOW I RUN MY LIBRARY GOOD" LETTER, G.P.O. Box 2631, New York, NY 10001
UNMENDABLY INTEGRAL: an audiocassette quarterly of the arts, c/o Full Track Press, PO Box 55, Planetarium Station, New York, NY 10024
Vanity Press, 160 6th Avenue, New York, NY 10013, 212-925-3823
Vehicle Editions, 238 Mott Street, New York, NY 10012, 226-1769
Violet Press, PO Box 398, New York, NY 10009
WITCHCRAFT DIGEST MAGAZINE (THE WICA NEWSLETTER), Suite 1B, 153 West 80th St., New York, NY 10024
WOMEN IN THE ARTS BULLETIN/NEWSLETTER, 325 Spring St, New York, NY 10013, 212-691-0988
Women In The Arts Foundation, Inc., 325 Spring St, New York, NY 10013
Women's Action Alliance, 370 Lexington Ave, New York, NY 10017
WOMEN'S AGENDA, c/o Women's Action Alliance, 370 Lexington Ave., New York, NY 10017
Words, 128A W 10th Street, Apt 3, New York, NY 10014, 242-8447
THE WORLD, St. Marks Poetry Project, 2nd Avenue and 10th Street, New York, NY 10003, (212) 674-0910
WREE-VIEW, 130 E 16th Street, New York, NY 10003
YOUTH AND NATION, 150 Fifth Avenue, New York, NY 10011, (212) 929-4955
Z, 104 Greenwich Avenue, New York, NY 10011
Z Press, 104 Greenwich Avenue, New York, NY 10011
Zartscorp, Inc. Books, 267 West 89th Street, New York, NY 10024, 724-5071
ARARAT, 628 Second Ave, New York City, NY 10016
The Ecco Press, 1 West 30th St, New York City, NY 10001, (212) 736-2599
Giorno Poetry Systems Records, 222 Bowery, New York City, NY 10012
Helikon Press, 120 West 71st Street, New York City, NY 10023
THE HUDSON REVIEW, 65 East 55th St., New York City, NY 10022, 212-755-9040
LIGHT: A Poetry Review, P.O. Box 1298D Stuyvesant PO, New York City, NY 10009
Midmarch Associates, 3304 Grand Central Sta, New York City, NY 10017, 212-666-6990
POINT OF CONTACT/PUNTO DE CONTACTO, 110 Bleecker St. 16B, New York City, NY 10012, 212-260-6346
Psychohistory Press, 2315 Broadway, New York City, NY 10024
PULP, 720 Greenwich St., New York City, NY 10014

Sage Press, 720 Greenwich St 4H, New York City, NY 10014
TELEPHONE, Box 672, Old Chelsea Sta., New York City, NY 10011
Two-Eighteen Press, P. O. Box 218 Village Station, New York City, NY 10014, 212-255-1723
UNMUZZLED OX, 105 Hudston Street #311, New York City, NY 10013
WOMEN ARTISTS NEWS, Box 3304, Grand Central, New York City, NY 10017, 212-666-6990
Women Writing Press (NY), Box 1035 Cathedral Sta, New York City, NY 10025
THE JOURNAL of PSYCHOHISTORY, 2315 Broadway, NY, NY 10024, 212-873-3760
ZONE, P.O. Box 733, NYC, NY 10009, 212-674-0602
Zone, P.O. Box 733, NYC, NY 10009, 212-674-0602
THE ARK, Box 322 Times Square Station, New York, NY 10108, 612-339-5162
Bradley David Associates, Ltd., Box 5279, 909 Third Avenue, New York, NY 10150, (212) 246-1114
New England Press, 45 Tudor City #1903, New York, NY 10117
Moss William Publishing Co., PO Box 1555, New Springville, Staten Island, NY 10314
Lintel, Box 34, St. George, NY 10301
GLASSWORKS, PO Box 163, Rosebank sta, Staten Island, NY 10305
OUTERBRIDGE, English A323, College of Staten Island, 715 Ocean Terrace, Staten Island, NY 10301, (212)390-7654
BERTRAND RUSSELL TODAY, P.O. Box 431, Jerome Ave., Bronx, NY 10468
GUSTO, PO Box 1009, Bronx, NY 10465, (212) 931-8964
Gusto, PO Box 1009, Bronx, NY 10465, (212) 931-8964
LITERARY RESEARCH NEWSLETTER, Department of English and World Literature, Manhattan College, Bronx, NY 10471, (212) 548-1400 Ext. 118
SUNBURY (a poetry magazine), Box 274 Jerome Ave Station, Bronx, NY 10468
Sunbury Press, Box 274 Jerome Ave Station, Bronx, NY 10468
Indian Publications, 1869 2nd Avenue, New York, NY 10467
Veritas Press, 3310 Rochambeau Ave., New York, NY 10467, (212) 652-1540
THE MIDATLANTIC REVIEW, P O Box 398, Baldwin Place, NY 10505
CROTON REVIEW, P.O. Box 277, Croton on Hudson, NY 10520, (914) 271-3144
CONNECTIONS MAGAZINE, Bell Hollow Road, Putnam Valley, NY 10579
Armchair Press, 123 Dorchester Road, Scarsdale, NY 10583
Rock Culture Books, Box 96, Scarsdale, NY 10583, (914)793-2649
WRITERS IN RESIDENCE, 123 Dorchester Road, Scarsdale, NY 10583
Sleepy Hollow Restorations, 150 White Plains Road, Tarrytown, NY 10591, 914-631-8200
CULTURAL WATCHDOG NEWSLETTER, 6 Winslow Road, White Plains, NY 10606, (212) 986-7152
Barnhart Books, Box 250, Bronxville, NY 10708, 914-337-7100
ATHAENA, 2 Sadore Lane, Yonkers, NY 10710
Pushcart Press, P.O. Box 845, Yonkers, NY 10701, 212-228-2269
TIME BARRIER EXPRESS, PO Box 206, Yonkers, NY 10710, 914-337-8050
Caratzas Brothers, Publishers, PO Box 210, 481 Main Street, New Rochelle, NY 10802, (914) 632-8487
The Elizabeth Press, 103 Van Etten Blvd, New Rochelle, NY 10804
Lawton Press, 673 Pelham Road, Apt 16E, New Rochelle, NY 10805, 914-636-3852
CENTERGRAM, 109 E. Main Street, Middletown, NY 10940
Centergram Press, 109 E. Main Street, Middletown, NY 10940
Library Research Associates, RD #5, Box 41, Dunderberg Road, Monroe, NY 10950, 914-783-1144
Voice of Liberty Publications, 3 Borger Place, Pearl River, NY 10965, (914) 735-8140
Danbury Press, PO Box 613, Suffern, NY 10901, (914) 357-0420
LITERARY MARKET REVIEW, 73-47 255th Street, Glen Oaks, NY 11004, (212) 343-7285
THE TARAKAN MUSIC LETTER, 25 W Dunes Lane, Port Washington, NY 11050, (516) 883-0941
THE GRACKLE: Improvised Music In Transition, Box 244 Vanderveer Station, Brookly, NY 11210
& (Ampersand) Press, 415 3rd Street, Brooklyn, NY 11215
ALA Social Responsibilities Round Table, c/o Eubanks, Brooklyn College Library, Brooklyn, NY 11201
ALA/SRRT NEWSLETTER, c/o Eubanks, Brooklyn College Library, Brooklyn, NY 11210
ANTIQUE PHONOGRAPH MONTHLY, 650 Ocean Ave., Brooklyn, NY 11226, 212-941-6835
APM Press, 650 Ocean Avenue, Brooklyn, NY 11226, 212-941-6835
ASSEMBLING, Box 1967, Brooklyn, NY 11202
Assembling Press, PO Box 1967, Brooklyn, NY 11202
BITTERROOT, Blythbourne Station, P.O. Box 51, Brooklyn, NY 11219, (914) 647-8861
BLANK TAPE, Box 371, Brooklyn, NY 11230
CLOWN WAR, P.O. Box 1093, Brooklyn, NY 11202
CONDITIONS, PO Box 56, Van Brunt Sta., Brooklyn, NY 11215, 212-857-5351/768-2453
CONFRONTATION, English Dept., Long Island University, Brooklyn, NY 11201
Downtown Poets Co-op, G.P.O. Box 1720, Brooklyn, NY 11202
Gridgraffiti Press, 3814 Maple Avenue, Brooklyn, NY 11224
HANGING LOOSE, 231 Wyckoff St, Brooklyn, NY 11217
Hanging Loose Press, 231 Wyckoff St, Brooklyn, NY 11217
Haskell House Publishers, Ltd., Box FF, Brooklyn, NY 11219, 212-435-0500
THE HELEN REVIEW, 389 Union Street, Brooklyn, NY 11231, (212) 875-2168
LIMIT! (The National Newsletter Of The Libertarian Republican Alliance), 1149 E 32nd Street, Brooklyn, NY 11210
Long Haul Press, Box 592 Van Brunt Station, Brooklyn, NY 11215, (212) 857-5351
Abraham Marinoff Publications, 400 Argyle Road, Brooklyn, NY 11218
Masters Publications, Box 1332, Brooklyn, NY 11201, (212) 596-1598
THE NEWSCRIBES, 1223 Newkirk Avenue, Brooklyn, NY 11230, (212) 282-8461
THE NIAGARA MAGAZINE, 195 Hicks St., Apt. 3B, Brooklyn, NY 11201
Other Publications, 826 Union Street, Brooklyn, NY 11215, (212) 789-8361
Out & Out Books, 476 Second St, Brooklyn, NY 11215, 212-499-9227
Permanent Press, Box 371, Brooklyn, NY 11230
RAM, THE LETTER BOX, 430 4th st, Brooklyn, NY 11215, (212) SO8-5415
Release Press, 411 Clinton Street, Apt 8, Brooklyn, NY 11231
RELIX, PO Box 94, Brooklyn, NY 11229, 212-998-2039
SHANTIH, Box 125, Bay Ridge St., Brooklyn, NY 11220

Smyrna Press, Box 1803 GPO, Brooklyn, NY 11202
Somrie Press, 1134 E 72nd Street, Brooklyn, NY 11234, (212) 763-0134
STARDANCER, 415 3rd Street #3, Brooklyn, NY 11215, (212) 768-7841
Tiresias Press, 190 Pacific Street, Brooklyn, NY 11201, (212) 834-0345
WIN MAGAZINE, 326 Livingston Street, 3rd Floor, Brooklyn, NY 11217
Beekman Publishers, Inc., 38 Hicks Street, Brooklyn Heights, NY 11201, (212) 624-4514
General Hall, Inc., 23-45 Corporal Kennedy Street, Bayside, NY 11360, (212) 423-9397
THE PIPE SMOKER'S EPHEMERIS, 20-37 120th Street, College Point, NY 11356
A SHOUT IN THE STREET: a journal of literary and visual art, English Dept. Queens College, Flushing, NY 11367, 212-520-7238
PARIS REVIEW, 45-39 171 Place, Flushing, NY 11358, 539-7085
Queens College Press, Writers & Artists Series, English Dept, Queens College, Flushing, NY 11367, 212-520-7238
University Statistical Tracts, 75-19 171st Street, Flushing, NY 11366, (212) 969-7553
Women's Studies, Dept. of English, Queens College, CUNY, Flushing, NY 11367
EXPANDING HORIZONS, 93-05 68th Avenue, Forest Hills, NY 11375, (212) LI4-9807
Folder Editions, 10326 68th Road, #A63, Forest Hills, NY 11375, 212-275-3839
PEDESTRIAN RESEARCH, PO Box 624, Forest Hills, NY 11375
Biblio Press, PO Box 22, Fresh Meadows, NY 11365, (212) 454-1922
THE MODULARIST REVIEW, 53 18 68th Street, Maspeth, NY 11378, (212) 672-9449
Wooden Needle Press, 53-18 68th Street, Maspeth, NY 11378, (212) 672-9449
Blue Mornings Press, PO Box 411, New York, NY 11357
Griffon House Publications, PO Box 81, Whitestone, NY 11357
BLACK ART: AN INTERNATIONAL QUARTERLY, 137-55 Southgate Street, Jamaica, NY 11413
SOURCE, Queens Council on the Arts, 161-04 Jamaica Avenue, New York, NY 11432, 291-1100
Cross Country Press, Ltd., PO Box 21081, Woodhaven, NY 11421, 212-896-7648
CROSSCOUNTRY, PO Box 21081, Woodhaven, NY 11421, 212-896-7648
KELLNER'S MONEYGRAM, 1768 Rockville Drive, Baldwin, NY 11510, (516) 868-3177
RIVERSIDE QUARTERLY, PO Box 367, University Station, Garden City, NY 11530
Fintzenberg Publishers, Box 301, Long Beach, NY 11561
Survivors' Manual, 2823 Rockaway Avenue, Oceanside, NY 11572, (516) 766-1891
The Feminist Press, Box 334, Old Westbury, NY 11568
WOMEN'S STUDIES NEWSLETTER, Box 334, Old Westbury, NY 11568, 516-997-7660
ADOLESCENCE, PO Box 165, 391 Willets Road, Roslyn Heights, L.I., NY 11577, (516) 484-4950
FAMILY THERAPY, 391 Willets Road, Roslyn Heights, L.I., NY 11577, (516) 484-4950
Libra Publishers, Inc., 391 Willets Road, Roslyn Heights, L.I., NY 11577, (516) 484-4950
HOT LOGARITHON, 301 Maple Avenue, Sea Cliff, NY 11579
Alcazar Press, 570 Windsor Street, Westbury, NY 11590, (516) ED4-3538
Freelance Publications, Box 8, Bayport, NY 11705, (516) 472-1799
GRAVIDA, Box 118, Bayville, NY 11709, (516) 628-3356
LONG ISLAND CHILDBIRTH ALTERNATIVES QUARTERLY, 15 Brewster Lane, East Setauket, NY 11733, (516) 689-8229
GNOME BAKER, Bo 337, Great River, NY 11739, (516) 277-3777
FLY BY NIGHT, PO Box 921, Huntington, NY 11743
Long Island Poetry Collective, Inc., PO Box 773, Huntington, NY 11743
NEWSLETTER, PO Box 773, Huntington, NY 11743
Old Pages Books Co, PO Box 921, Huntington, NY 11743
Pleasure Dome Press (Long Island Poetry Collective Inc.), Box 773, Huntington, NY 11743, (516) 549-1150
XANADU, Box 773, Huntington, NY 11743, (516) 549-1150
Water Mark Press, 175 E Shore Road, Huntington Bay, NY 11743, (516) 549-1150
Thirteenth House, PO Box 362, Huntington Station, NY 11746
WEST HILLS REVIEW: A WALT WHITMAN JOURNAL, Walt Whitman Birthplace Assn., 246 Walt Whitman Road, Huntington Station, NY 11746, (516) 427-5240
POESIE - U.S.A., P O Box 811, Melville, NY 11747
The Black Hole School of Poethnics, Box 555, Port Jefferson, NY 11777
The Blackhole School of Poethnics, Box 555, Port Jefferson, NY 11777
STREET MAGAZINE, Box 555, Port Jefferson, NY 11777
Street Press, Box 555, Port Jefferson, NY 11777
WRITERS INK, 194 Soundview Drive, Rocky Point L.I., NY 11778, 516-744-6160
LONG POND REVIEW, English Dept, Suffolk Community College, Selden Long Island, NY 11784
Scotty Macgreger Publications, 10 Pineacre Dr., Smithtown, NY 11787
BIRD EFFORT, 25 Mudford Avenue, Easthampton, NY 11937
Bird Effort Press, 25 Mudford Ave, Easthampton, NY 11937
The Permanent Press, Sagaponack, NY 11962, 516-324-5993
The Second Chance Press, Sagaponack, NY 11962, 516-324-5993
Peripatos Press, PO Box 550, Wainscottu, NY 11975
Harian Creative Press, 47 Hyde Blvd, Ballston SPA, NY 12020, 518-885-7397
Auriga, Box F, 8 Candlelight Court, Clifton Park, NY 12065, (518) 371-2015
JOURNAL OF SOCIAL RECONSTRUCTION, PO Box 143, Pine Plains, NY 12067
Sagarin Press, Box 251, Sand Lake, NY 12153
ALTERNATIVE FUTURES: THE JOURNAL OF UTOPIAN STUDIES, Human Dimensions Center, Rensselaer Polytechnic Institute, Troy, NY 12181, (518)270-6574
PROP, 4 Elm Street, Albany, NY 12202, (518) 436-9498
Washout Publishing Co., P.O. Box 9252, Scenectady, NY 12309
WASHOUT REVIEW, PO Box 2752, Schenectady, NY 12309
Embee Press, 82 Pine Grove Avenue, Kingston, NY 12401, (914) 338-2226
COLLABORATION, Matagiri Sri Aurobindo Center, Inc., Mt. Tremper, NY 12457, (914) 679-8322
Matagiri, Matagiri Sri Aurobindo Center, Mt. Tremper, NY 12457, (914) 679-8322
Tideline Press, P.O. Box 786, Tannersville, NY 12485, (518) 589-6344
Aesopus Press, 27 Oriole Drive, Woodstock, NY 12498, 914-679-7795
Information Alternative, Box 657, Woodstock, NY 12498
The Overlook Press, Route 212, PO Box 427, Woodstock, NY 12498, (914) 679-6838

THE WOODSTOCK REVIEW, 27 Oriole Drive, Woodstock, NY 12498, (914) 679-7795
DIALOGUE, Bard College, PO Box 95, Annanandale-on-Hudson, NY 12504, (914) 758-8506
Station Hill Press, Barrytown, NY 12507, (914) 758-4340
Philatelic Directory Publishing Co, Box 150, Clinton Corners, NY 12514
THE PHILATELIC JOURNALIST, Box 150, Clinton Corners, NY 12514, 914-266-3150
NEW VOICES, P. O. Box 308, Clintondale, NY 12515
HSA FROGPOND, RD 7 Box 265, Hopewell Junction, NY 12533, (914) 226-7117
Alta Gaia Society, Dutchess Avenue, Millerton, NY 12546, (518) 789-3865
Treacle Press, P.O.Box 638, New Paltz, NY 12561, (914)255-8447
CHECKLIST OF HUMAN RIGHTS DOCUMENTS, PO Box 143, Pine Plains, NY 12567, (518) 398-7193
Earl M Coleman Enterprises, Inc, PO Box 143, Pine Plains, NY 12567, (518) 398-7193
COMMUNICATIONS AND THE LAW, PO Box 143, Pine Plains, NY 12567
UNIVERSAL HUMAN RIGHTS, PO Box 143, Pine Plains, NY 12567, (518) 398-7193
CLEARWATER NAVIGATOR, 112 Market Street, Poughkeepsie, NY 12601, (914) 454-7673
ABSINTHE, Barryville, NY 12719, 914-557-8141
Indian Tree Press, Barryville, NY 12719, 914-557-8141
FARMING UNCLE, Box 91, Liberty, NY 12754
Spinsters, Ink, RD 1, Argyle, NY 12809, (518) 854-3109
BLUELINE, Blue Mountain Lake, NY 12812, (518) 352-7365
Natalie Slohm Associates, Inc., 49 West Main Street, Cambridge, NY 12816, (518) 677-3040
Cliff Catton Press, 195 Ridge Street #7, Glensfalls, NY 12801
COMBINATIONS, A JOURNAL OF PHOTOGRAPHY, Middle Grove Road, Greenfield Center, NY 12833, 518-584-4612
THE COSMEP PRISON PROJECT NEWSLETTER, C/O The Greenfield Review, Greenfield Center, NY 12833
THE GREENFIELD REVIEW, P.O. Box 80, Greenfield Center, NY 12833, 518-584-1728
The Greenfield Review Press, P.O. Box 80, Greenfield Center, NY 12833
Porphyrion Press, 4053 Middle Grove Road, Middle Grove, NY 12850, 518-587-9809
Celebrating Women Productions, PO Box 251, Warrensburg, NY 12885
Tundra Books Of Northern New York, 51 Clinton, P.O. Box 1030, Plattsburg, NY 12901
LATITUDES, 405 N. Highland Ave, E Syracuse, NY 13057, (315) 437-5994
Ed-U Press, Inc., Box 583, Fayetteville, NY 13066
AC Publications, PO Box 238, Homer, NY 13077, (607) 749-4040
Mathom Publishing Co, 68 East Mohawk St, Oswego, NY 13126, 315-343-3035
Lawson Books, PO Box 487, Seneca Falls, NY 13148
CONSTRUCTIVE ACTION FOR GOOD HEALTH, B 1104 Ross Towers, 710 Lodi St., Syracuse, NY 13203, 315-471-4644
The Crow's Mark Press, 851 Maryland Avenue, Syracuse, NY 13210
TAMARACK, 909 Westcott Street, Syracuse, NY 13210, (315) 478-6495
Tamarack Editions, 909 Westcott Street, Syracuse, NY 13210, (315) 478-6495
Cherry Valley Editions, Box 303, Cherry Valley, NY 13320, 607-264-3204
NORTHEAST RISING SUN, Box 303, Cherry Valley, NY 13320, 607-264-3204
Nobodaddy Press, 100 College Hill Rd., Clinton, NY 13323, 315-853-6946
POETRY IN MOTION, 100 College Hill Rd., Clinton, NY 13323, 315-853-6946
Molly Yes Press, R.D. 3, Box 70-B, New Berlin, NY 13411, 607-847-8070
Ash Lad Press, P.O. Box 396, Canton, NY 13617, 315-386-8820
FICTION INTERNATIONAL, St. Lawrence Univ., Canton, NY 13617, (315) 379-5961
AKWESASNE NOTES, Mohawk Nation, Rooseveltown, NY 13683, 518-483-2540
Flying Buttress Publications, PO Box 254, Endicott, NY 13760, (607) 785-5423
Swamp Press, 4 Bugbee Road, Oneonta, NY 13820
TIGHTROPE, 4 Bugbee Road, Oneonta, NY 13820
Almar Press, 4105 Marietta Drive, Binghamton, NY 13903, (607) 722-6251
Bellevue Press, 60 Schubert St., Binghamton, NY 13905, 607-729-0819
BOUNDARY 2, State University of New York, Binghamton, NY 13901, (607) 798-2743
Iris Press, 27 Chestnut St., Binghamton, NY 13905, 607-722-6739
Charles N. Aronson, Writer Publisher, RR1, 11520 Bixby Hill Road, Arcade, NY 14009
PEEPHOLE ON PEOPLE, RR 1, 11520 Bixby Hill Road, Arcade, NY 14009, (716) 496-6002
Moody Street Irregulars, P.O. Box 157, Clarence Center, NY 14032, (716) 741-3393
MOODY STREET IRREGULARS, P.O. Box 157, Clarence Center, NY 14032, (716) 741-3393
AEVUM, 4 Forest Place, Fredonia, NY 14063
The Basilisk Press, P.O. Box 71, Fredonia, NY 14063
GARCIA LORCA REVIEW, State Univ. of N.Y., Brockport, NY 14220
BEAU FLEUVE SERIES, P.O. Box 1423, Buffalo, NY 14214
BUCKLE, State Univ College/1300 Elmwood Av, English Dept., Buffalo, NY 14222, 716-886-7033
CONCH MAGAZINE, 102 Normal Avenue, Buffalo, NY 14213, 716-885-3686
Conch Magazine Ltd. (Publishers), 102 Normal Avenue, (Symphony Circle), Buffalo, NY 14213, 716-885-3686
CONCH REVIEW OF BOOKS, 102 Normal Ave., Buffalo, NY 14213, 716-885-3686
CREDENCES: A Journal of Twentieth Century Poetry and Poetics, Capen Hall, New York State University, c/o Poetry Collection,
    Buffalo, NY 14260, (716) 673-2917
EARTH'S DAUGHTERS, P O Box 41, Station H, Buffalo, NY 14214
Imp Press, PO Box 93, Buffalo, NY 14213, (716) 881-5391
INC., 111 Elmwood Avenue, Buffalo, NY 14201, (716) 885-6400
INTREPID, P.O. Box 1423, Buffalo, NY 14214
Intrepid Press, P O Box 1423, Buffalo, NY 14214
Just Buffalo Press, 111 Elmwood Avenue, Buffalo, NY 14201, (716) 885-6400
Labor Arts Books, 1064 Amherst St., Buffalo, NY 14216, 716-873-4131
MODERN POETRY STUDIES, 207 Delaware Avenue, Buffalo, NY 14202, (716) 847-2555
PAUNCH, 123 Woodward Ave, Buffalo, NY 14214, 716-836-7332
PINECONE, 109 Duerstein St., Buffalo, NY 14210, (716) 825-8671
Prometheus Books, 1203 Kensington Ave, Buffalo, NY 14215
THIRD EYE, 189 Kelvin Drive, Buffalo, NY 14223, 716 832-4097
Trado-Medic Books, 102 Normal Ave.(Symphony Circle), Buffalo, NY 14213, 716-885-3686

23 CLUB SERIES, P.O. Box 1423, Buffalo, NY 14214
WEIRDBOOK, Box 35, Amherst Branch, Buffalo, NY 14226, (716) 839-2415
Weirdbook Press, Box 35, Amherst Branch, Buffalo, NY 14226, (716) 839-2415
WHITE PINE JOURNAL, 109 Duerstein St., Buffalo, NY 14210, 716-825-8671
White Pine Press, 109 Duerstein St, Buffalo, NY 14210
TURTLE, 25 Rainbow Mall, Niagara Falls, NY 14303
THE HUMANIST, 7 Harwood Drive, Amherst, NY 14426, 716-839-5080
Boa Editions, 92 Park Avenue, Brockport, NY 14420, 716-637-3844
THE THOREAU SOCIETY BULLETIN, The Thoreau Society, Inc., SUNY, Geneseo, NY 14454, (716) 245-5513
SENECA REVIEW, Hobart & William Smith Colleges, Geneva, NY 14456
ABC Letter Service of Rochester, P.O. Box 1, Rush, NY 14543, (716) 533-1376 & (716) 533-1251
WOMEN STUDIES ABSTRACTS, PO Box 1, Rush, NY 14543, (716) 533-1376; 533-1251
AFTERIMAGE, 31 Prince Street, Rochester, NY 14607, 716-442-8676
EXIT, 50 Inglewood Dr, Rochester, NY 14619
MIORITA, Dept of F.L.L.L., Univ of Rochester, PO Box 13-049, Rochester, NY 14627
NEW WOMEN'S TIMES & NEW WOMEN'S TIMES FEMINIST REVIEW, 804 Meigs Street, Rochester, NY 14620
Rochester Routes/Creative Arts Projects, 50 Inglewood Drive, Rochester, NY 14619
SURVIVOR, c/o Rochester Routes, 50 Inglewood Drive, Rochester, NY 14619
VANDERBILT POETRY REVIEW, c/o Rochester Routes, 50 Inglewood Drive, Rochester, NY 14619
Visual Studies Workshop Press, 31 Prince Street, Rochester, NY 14607, 716-442-8676
Allegany Mountain Press, 111 N. 10th St., Olean, NY 14760, 716-372-0935
UROBOROS, 111 N. 10th St., Olean, NY 14760, 716-372-0935
Dundee Publishing, Box 202, Dundee, NY 14837, (607) 243-5559
DURAK: An International Magazine of Poetry, RD 1, Box 352, Joe Green Road, Erin, NY 14838
ALEMBIC, 1744 Slaterville Road, Ithaca, NY 14850, (607) 277-0827
EPOCH, 245 Goldwin Smith Hall, Cornell Univ., Ithaca, NY 14853, (607) 256-3385
Gamma Books, 307 Willow Ave, Ithaca, NY 14850, 607 539-7698
The Grapevine Press, Inc., 114 West State Street, Ithaca, NY 14850, (607) 272-3470
THE GRAPEVINE WEEKLY, 114 West State Street, Ithaca, NY 14850, (607) 272-3470
Ithaca House, 108 N. Plain St, Ithaca, NY 14850, 607-272-1233
McBooks Press, 106 North Aurora Street, Ithaca, NY 14850, (607) 272-6602
Static Creation Press, 405 S. Geneva Street, Ithaca, NY 14850, (607) 277-4160
J&C Transcripts, Box 15, Kanona, NY 14856, 607-776-3709
The Crossing Press, 17 W Main Street, Trumansburg, NY 14886, 607-387-6217
Celo Press, Route #5, Burnsville, NY 28714, (702) 675-4925

NORTH CAROLINA

The Jackpine Press, 1878 Meadowbrook Drive, Winston-Salem, NC 27106
RFD, Rt 1 box 92 E, Efland, NC 27243
COLONNADES, Box 2245, Elon College, NC 27244
Bakke Press, Rt. 3, Box 119-A, Hillsborough, NC 27278
LOVE, Box 9, Prospect Hill, NC 27314, (919) 562-3380
MANNA, Route 8, Box 368, Sanford, NC 27330
RaMar Press, Seven Lakes Box 548, West End, NC 27376, (919) 673-0571
GREENSBORO REVIEW, Dept English, North Carolina University — Greensboro, Greensboro, NC 27412
INTERNATIONAL POETRY REVIEW, Box 2047, Greensboro, NC 27402
Unicorn Press, P.O. Box 3307, Greensboro, NC 27402
NHM Publications, 1517 Seabrook Avenue, Cary, NC 27511, (919) 467-2596
ADVISORY BOARD RECORD, PO Box 2066 or 2204, Chapel Hill, NC 27514
CAROLINA QUARTERLY, Greenlaw Hall 066-A, Univ of N. Carolina, Chapel Hill, NC 27514, (919) 933-0244
The Carolina Wren Press, 300 Barclay Road, Chapel Hill, NC 27514, 919-967-8666
CHANGE, 1825 North Lake Shore Dr, Chapel Hill, NC 27514, 919-942-2994
FEMINARY, P.O.Box 954, Chapel Hill, NC 27514
FLORAL UNDERAWL GAZETTE, PO Box 2066 or 2204, Chapel Hill, NC 27514
HYPERION A Poetry Journal, c/o Hogan/300 Barclay Road, Chapel Hill, NC 27514
Institute for Southern Studies, P.O. Box 230, Chapel Hill, NC 27514
KXE6S VEREIN R NEWSLETTER, PO Box 2066 or 2204, Chapel Hill, NC 27514
Kxe6s Verein R Press, PO Box 2066 or 2204, Chapel Hill, NC 27514
Lollipop Power, Inc., P O Box 1171, Chapel Hill, NC 27514, 919-929-4857
NEWS RELEASE FROM THE CHESS PRESS SYNDICATE, PO Box 2204, Chapel Hill, NC 27514
THE SUN, A MAGAZINE OF IDEAS, 412 W. Rosemary Street, Chapel Hill, NC 27514, 942-5282
AFRICA NEWS, P.O. Box 3851, Durham, NC 27702, (919) 286-0747
AMERICAN LITERATURE, 6667 College Station, Durham, NC 27708, (919) 684-3948
Duke University Press, Box 6697 College Station, Durham, NC 27708, (919) 684-2173
Moore Publishing Company, PO Box 3036, Durham, NC 27705, (919) 286-2250
SOUTHERN EXPOSURE, PO Box 531, Durham, NC 27702, 919-688-8167
WAYS & MEANS, PO Box 3036, Durham, NC 27705, (919) 286-2250
TAR RIVER POETRY, Department of English, East Carolina University, Greenville, NC 27834
Webb-Newcomb Company, Inc., 308 N.E. Vance Street, Wilson, NC 27893, (919) 291-7231; (919) 237-3161
BRIARPATCH, Box 2482, Davidson, NC 28036, (704) 892-7644
Briarpatch Press, Box 2482, Davidson, NC 28036, (704) 892-7644
The East Woods Press, 820 East Boulevard, Charlotte, NC 28203, (704) 334-0897
Red Clay Books, 6366 Sharon Hills Rd, Charlotte, NC 28210, 704-366-9624
SOUTHERN POETRY REVIEW, Dept. of English, Univ of N.C., UNCC Station, Charlotte, NC 28223
Saint Andrews Press, St Andrews College, Laurinburg, NC 28352, (919) 276-3652
SAINT ANDREWS REVIEW, St. Andrews College, Laurinburg, NC 28352, 919-276-3652
PEMBROKE MAGAZINE, PO Box 60, PSU, Pembroke, NC 28372, (919) 521-4214 ext 246
The Hurricane Company, PO Box 426, Jacksonville, NC 28540, 919-353-4201
McFarland & Company, Inc., Publishers, Box 611, Jefferson, NC 28640, (919) 246-4460

Lorien House, PO Box 1112, Black Mountain, NC 28711, 704 669-9992
Ginseng Press, Rt 2, Box 1105, Franklin, NC 28734, 704-369-9735
MAW: A MAGAZINE OF APPALACHIAN WOMEN, PO Box 490, Mars Hill, NC 28754

NORTH DAKOTA

BLOODROOT, P.O. Box 891, Grand Forks, ND 58201, 701-775-6079
Bloodroot, Inc., P.O. Box 891, Grand Forks, ND 58201, (701) 775-6079
PLAINSWOMAN, P.O. Box 8027, Grand Forks, ND 58202, (701) 777-4234
Flying Diamond Books, RR2, Box D301, Hettinger, ND 58639, (701) 567-2646

OHIO

THE KENYON REVIEW, Kenyon College, Gambier, OH 43022, (614) 427-3339
COLUMBUS FREE PRESS, Box 3162, Columbus, OH 43210, 294-2062
LOST AND FOUND TIMES, 137 Leland Ave, Columbus, OH 43214
Luna Bisonte Prods, 137 Leland Ave, Columbus, OH 43214, (614) 846-4126
THE MODERN LANGUAGE JOURNAL, 314 Cunz Hall, Ohio State University, Columbus, OH 43210, 614-422-6985
OHIOANA QUARTERLY, 1105 Ohio Dept Bldg., 65 S. Front St, Columbus, OH 43215, 614-466-3831
qwertyuiop, P.O. Box 15193, Columbus, OH 43215
Reductio Ad Asparagus Press, Box 15193, Columbus, OH 43215
SUBVERSIVE SCHOLASTIC, PO Box 10076, Columbus, OH 43201, (614) 267-2821
UNDER THE SIGN OF PISCES: Anais Nin and Her Circle, 1858 Neil Avenue Mall, Columbus, OH 43210
CORNFIELD REVIEW, The Ohio State University Marion Campus, 1465 Mt. Vernon Avenue, Marion, OH 43302, (614) 389-2361
BLACK BOOK, ,Dept. of English, Bowling Green State Univ., Bowling Green, OH 43403
SALTHOUSE, SALTHOUSE, Dept. of English, B. G. S. U., Bowling Green, OH 43403
Papillon Press, 3715 Talmadge Road, Toledo, OH 43606, (419) 474-6773
LES PAPILLONS, A Journal of Modern Philosophical Inquiry, 3715 Talmadge Road, Toledo, OH 43606, (419) 474-6773
Fran Metcalf Books, 734 Millard Ave, Conneaut, OH 44030, (216) 599-7972
Hobby Horse Publishing, 10091 Hobby Horse Lane, Box 54, Mentor, OH 44060, (216) 255-3434
Veritie Press, Inc., PO Box 222, Novelty, OH 44072
FIELD, Rice Hall, Oberlin College, Oberlin, OH 44074
Bits Press, Dept of English, Case Western Reserve Univ, Cleveland, OH 44106, 216-368-2359
Cleveland State Univ. Poetry Center, Dept English, Cleveland State Univ, Cleveland, OH 44115, 216-687-3986
Deciduous, 1456 West 54th Street, Cleveland, OH 44102, (216) 651-7725
Everyman, 1456 West 54th Street, Cleveland, OH 44102
PIECES, Dept of English, Case Western Reserve University, Cleveland, OH 44106, (216) 368-2340
POETS' LEAGUE of GREATER CLEVELAND NEWSLETTER, PO Box 6055, Cleveland, OH 44101
GREEN FEATHER, PO Box 2633, Lakewood, OH 44107
Quality Publications, Inc., PO Box 2633, Lakewood, OH 44107
PASTICHE: Poems of Place, 3877 Meadowbrook Blvd., University Heights, OH 44118, 216-932-2173
PHANTASMAGORIA, Journey into the Surreal, 3877 Meadowbrook Blvd, University Heights, OH 44118, (216) 932-2173
The Pin Prick Press, 3877 Meadowbrook Blvd, University Heights, OH 44118, (216) 932-2173
SNIPPETS: A Melange of Woman, 3877 Meadowbrook Blvd., University Heights, OH 44118, 216-932-2173
Great Lakes Publishing, 2674 7th Street, Cuyahoga Falls, OH 44221, (216) 655-2996
HIRAM POETRY REVIEW, Box 162, Hiram, OH 44234, 216-569-3211
Kent Popular Press, Box 715, Kent, OH 44240, (216) 678-9355
LEFTWORKS, Box 715, Kent, OH 44240, (216) 678-9355
PIG IRON, P.O. Box 237, Youngstown, OH 44501, 216-744-2258
Pig Iron Press, P.O. Box 237, Youngstown, OH 44501
GUTS AND GRACE, Box 529, Massillon, OH 44648
Beninda Books, P.O. Box 9251, Canton, OH 44711
CAMBRIC POETRY PROJECT, 912 Strowbridge Drive, Huron, OH 44839, 419-433-4221
Cambric Press, 912 Strowbridge Dr., Huron, OH 44839, 419-433-4221
FIRELANDS ARTS REVIEW, Firelands Campus, Huron, OH 44839, 419-433-4221
Cincinnati Chess Federation, PO Box 30072, Cincinnati, OH 45230, (513) 232-3204
CINCINNATI POETRY REVIEW, Dept of English, University of Cincinnati, Cincinnati, OH 45221, 513-475-4484
J'ADOUBE!, P O Box 30072, Cincinnati, OH 45230, 513-232-3204
La Reina Press, PO Box 8182, Cincinnati, OH 45208, (513) 579-8798
LIVE WRITERS! LOCAL ON TAP, PO Box 8182, Cincinnati, OH 45208, (513) 579-8798
Mosaic Press, 358 Oliver Road, Dept. 11, Cincinnati, OH 45215, (513) 761-5977
WATERS JOURNAL OF THE ARTS, 1413 W North Bend Road #7, Cincinnati, OH 45224
THE ANTIOCH REVIEW, PO Box 148, Yellow Springs, OH 45387, 513-767-7386
COMMUNITY SERVICE NEWSLETTER, Box 243, Yellow Springs, OH 45387, 513-767-2161
Arlotta Press, 6340 Millbank Dr., Dayton, OH 45459
Gibson-Hiller, P O Box 22, Dayton, OH 45406, 513-277-2427
IMAGES, English Dept, Wright State Univ., Dayton, OH 45435
NIR/NEW INFINITY REVIEW, PO Box 804, Ironton, OH 45638
Croissant & Company, P.O. Box 282, Athens, OH 45701, 614-593-8339
THE OHIO REVIEW, Ellis Hall, Ohio University, Athens, OH 45701, 614-594-5889
Carpenter Press, Route 4, Pomeroy, OH 45769, 614-992-7520

OKLAHOMA

Full Count Press, 223 N. Broadway, Edmond, OK 73034, 341-8497
Point Riders Press, PO Box 2731, Norman, OK 73070
Griffin Books, Inc., 50 Penn Place - Suite 380, Oklahoma City, OK 73118, (405) 842-0398
G F E BOOK SHEET, Box 1461, Lawton, OK 73502, (405) 248-6870
RAGGED READIN', Box 1461, Lawton, OK 73502, (405) 248-6870
Evans Publications, 133 S. Main, P.O.Box 520, Perkins, OK 74059, (405) 547-2882
CIMARRON REVIEW, Oklahoma State University, Stillwater, OK 74074, (405) 624-6573
Academic Publications, Univ of Tulsa, 600 S. College, Tulsa, OK 74104

Cardinal Press, Inc., 76 N Yorktown, Tulsa, OK 74110, (918) 583-3651
Harden Publications, 5332 E 26th Street, Tulsa, OK 74114, (918) 936-8846
JAMES JOYCE QUARTERLY, University of Tulsa, 600 S. College, Tulsa, OK 74104
NIMROD, Arts and Humanities Council of Tulsa, 2210 So. Main, Tulsa, OK 74114
Partners In Publishing, Box 50347, Tulsa, OK 74150, (918) 583-0956
PIP COLLEGE 'HELPS' NEWSLETTER, Box 50347, Tulsa, OK 74150, (918) 583-0956
Todd Tarbox Books, 1637 East 36th Place, Tulsa, OK 74105
WESTBERE REVIEW, 2504 E 4th Street, Tulsa, OK 74104
CRYPTOC: The Crypt of Comics, 1001 Harvey Road, Seminole, OK 74868, (405) 382-3354

OREGON

Bicentennial Era Enterprises, PO Box 1148, Scappoose, OR 97056
Champoeg Press, PO Box 92, Forest Grove, OR 97116
MR. COGITO, Box 627, Pacific Univ., Forest Grove, OR 97116
Nighthawk Press, PO Box 813, Forest Grove, OR 97116
Timber Press, P.O. Box 92, Forest Grove, OR 97116, 503-357-7192
NEW OREGON REVIEW, 537 N.E. Lincoln St., Hillsboro, OR 97123, (503)640-1375
Nor Publications, 537 N.E. Lincoln St, Hillsboro, OR 97123
Breitenbush Publications, Inc., P.O. Box 02137, Portland, OR 97202
CIRCLE, P.O. Box 176, Portland, OR 97207
Circle Forum, P.O. Box 176, Portland, OR 97207
Coast to Coast Books, 2934 NE 16th, Portland, OR 97212, (503) 282-5891
DRAGONFLY:A Quarterly Of Haiku, 4102 N.E. 130th Pl., Portland, OR 97230
INTERNATIONAL PORTLAND REVIEW, P.O. Box 751, Portland, OR 97207
MISSISSIPPI MUD, 3125 S.E. Van Water, Portland, OR 97222
New Oregon Publishers, Inc., 208 SW Stark, Suite 500, Portland, OR 97204
NRG, 228 S.E. 26th, Portland, OR 97214, (503) 231-0890
Oregon Historical Society, 1230 S.W. Park Avenue, Portland, OR 97205, 503-222-1741
OREGON HISTORICAL QUARTERLY, 1230 S.W. Park Ave., Portland, OR 97205
OREGON TIMES MAGAZINE, 208 SW Stark, Suite 500, Portland, OR 97204
Out of the Ashes Press, P.O. Box 42384, Portland, OR 97242
Prescott Street Press, 407 Postal Building, Portland, OR 97204
Press 22, Route 2, Box 175, Portland, OR 97231
RAIN: JOURNAL OF APPROPRIATE TECHNOLOGY, 2270 NW Irving Street, Portland, OR 97210, 503-227-5110
The Rain Umbrella, 2270 NW Irving St, Portland, OR 97210
Skydog Press, 228 SE 26th, Portland, OR 97214, (503) 231-0890
Trask House Books, Inc., 2754 S.E. 27th Ave., Portland, OR 97202, 235-1898
CALYX: A Journal of Art and Literature by Women, PO Box B, Corvallis, OR 97330, 503-753-9384
ON THE BEACH, PO Box 1245, Newport, OR 97365, (503) 265-2400
Light Living Library, PO Box 190, Philomath, OR 97370
MESSAGE POST, PO Box 190, Philomath, OR 97370
JC/DC Cartoons Ink, 5536 Fruitland Rd NE, Salem, OR 97301, 585-6161
PRISON, Box 32323, 2605 State Street, Salem, OR 97310
The Rubicon Press, 5638 Riverdsle Road S, Salem, OR 97302
Northwest Matrix, PO Box 984, Waldport, OR 97394, 503-563-4427
THE ARCHER, P.O.Box 41, Camas Valley, OR 97416, (503) 445-2327
THE TOWN FORUM JOURNAL & COMMUNITY REPORT, Cerro Gordo Ranch, Dorena Lake, Cottage Grove, OR 97424, 503-942-7720
Town Forum Inc, Cerro Gordo Ranch, Cottage Grove, OR 97424
Avant-Garde Creations, P.O. Box 30161, Eugene, OR 97403
THE INSURGENT SOCIOLOGIST, c/o Department of Sociology, Univ. of Oregon, Eugene, OR 97403
NORTHWEST REVIEW, 369 P.L.C., University of Oregon, Eugene, OR 97405, 503-686-3957
Rainy Day Press, PO Box 3035, Eugene, OR 97403, (503) 484-4626
SILVERFISH REVIEW, PO Box 3541, Eugene, OR 97403, (503) 344-3535
University of Oregon Press, 369 PLC, University of Oregon, Eugene, OR 97403, (503) 686-3957
Urion Press, Box 2244, Eugene, OR 97402
WILLAMETTE VALLEY OBSERVER, 99 W. 10th Ave., Suite 216, Eugene, OR 97401, 503-687-0376
New Woman Press, Box 56, Wolf Creek, OR 97497
WOMAN SPIRIT, Box 263, Wolf Creek, OR 97497
Quicksilver Productions, P.O.Box 340, Ashland, OR 97520, (503) 482-5343
TOTAL ABANDON: A Literary and Arts Magazine, PO Box 1207, Ashland, OR 97520, 535-2283
Van Dyk Publications, 10216 Takilma Road, Cave Junction, OR 97523, (503) 592-3430
The S & S Co., 11047 Antiock Road, Central Point, OR 97502, (503) 826-7870
Sackett Publications, 100 Waverly Drive, Grants Pass, OR 97526, (503) 476-6404
Womanshare Books, PO Box 681, Grants Pass, OR 97526
Shinn Music Aids, PO Box 192, Medford, OR 97501, 664-2317

PENNSYLVANIA

Chalardpro Books, 802 Sixth Avenue, Coraopolis, PA 15108, 264-2236
Gemini Press, 625 Pennsylvania Avenue, Oakmont, PA 15139, 412-828-3315
CREATIVE PITTSBURGH, PO Box 7346, Pittsburgh, PA 15137, (412) 624-5934
Know, Inc., P.O. Box 86031, Pittsburgh, PA 15221
Motheroot Journal, 214 Dewey Street, Pittsburgh, PA 15218, (412)731-4453
Motheroot Publications, 214 Dewey St., Pittsburgh, PA 15218
Slow Loris Press, 923 Highview Street, Pittsburgh, PA 15206
SLOW LORIS READER, 923 Highview St, Pittsburgh, PA 15206
THREE RIVERS POETRY JOURNAL, P.O. Box 21, Carnegie-Mellon University, Pittsburgh, PA 15213
Three Rivers Press, PO Box 21, Carnegie-Mellon University, Pittsburgh, PA 15213
Trans-Traffic Corporation, Publishing Division, 666 Washington Road, Pittsburgh, PA 15228, (412) 341-0444

Fred A. Fleet II, 151 N Lincoln St, Washington, PA 15301, (412) 228-5061
TUVOTI Books, P.O. Box 439, California, PA 15419
THE UNSPEAKABLE VISIONS OF THE INDIVIDUAL, PO Box 439, California, PA 15419
Rook Press, Inc., P.O. Box 144, Ruffsdale, PA 15679
THISTLE: A MAGAZINE OF CONTEMPORARY WRITING, PO Box 144, Ruffsdale, PA 15679
Spring Church Book Company, PO Box 127, Spring Church, PA 15686
Dawn Valley Press, Box 58, New Wilmington, PA 16142
Montessori Learning Center, PO Box 767, Altoona, PA 16602, (814) 946-5213
AQUILA MAGAZINE, 116 Old Mill Road #G, State College, PA 16801, (814) 237-7509
THE PENNSYLVANIA NATURALIST, PO Box 1128, State College, PA 16801, (814) 238-1132
PIVOT, 221 S. Barnard, State College, PA 16801, 814-238-8887
ROQ Press, 116 Old Mill Road #G, State College, PA 16801, (814)237-7509
Pennsylvania State University Press, S-234 Burrowes Building, University Park, PA 16802, 814-865-4242
THE SHAW REVIEW, S-234 Burrowes Building, University Park, PA 16802, 814-865-4242
CUMBERLAND JOURNAL, P.O. Box 2648, Harrisburg, PA 17105
ANIMA, 1053 Wilson Avenue, Chambersburg, PA 17201, (717) 263-8303
Conococheague Associates, Inc., 1053 Wilson Ave, Chambersburg, PA 17201
THE GREEN REVOLUTION, P O Box 3233, York, PA 17402
The School of Living, RD 7, York, PA 17402
HOB-NOB, 715 Dorsea Road, Lancaster, PA 17601
BUCKNELL REVIEW, Bucknell University, Lewisburg, PA 17837
WEST BRANCH, Department of English, Bucknell University, Lewisburg, PA 17837, 717-524-4591
MILITARY IMAGES MAGAZINE, PO Box 300, Alburtis, PA 18011
FORMS: A Magazine of Poetry and Fine Art, 1724 Maple Street, Bethlehem, PA 18017
C J Frompovich Publications, RD 1, Chestnut Road, Coopersburg, PA 18036, (215) 346-8461
IN BUSINESS, Box 323, Emmaus, PA 18049, (215) 967-4135
The JG Press, Inc., Box 351, Emmaus, PA 18049, (215) 967-4135
Himalayan Institute Publishers and Distributors, RD 1, Box 88, Honesdale, PA 18431, (717) 253-5551
Libre Press, 529-530 Connell Bldg, Scranton, PA 18503
THE METRO, The Metro, Suite 529-530 Connell Bldg., Scranton, PA 18503, (717) 348-1010
FIT, 263 S Franklin Street, Apt E, Wilkes-Barre, PA 18701, (717) 825-5142
Deinotation 7 Press, Box 194, Susquehanna, PA 18847, (717) 853-3050
Raw Dog Press, 129 Worthington Ave, Doylestown, PA 18901, (215) 345-7692
Minicomputer Press, Box 1, Richboro, PA 18954, 215-355-6084
Richboro Press, Box 1, Richboro, PA 18954, 215-355-6084
Pine Row Publications, Box 428, Washington Crossing, PA 18977
POTPOURRI FROM HERBAL ACRES, Box 428, Washington Crossing, PA 18977, (215) 493-4259
Lakstun Press, Po Box 429, Bensalem, PA 19020, (215) 639-7261
CONTEMPORARY POETRY: A Journal of Criticism, Contemporary Poetry, Bryn Mawr College, Bryn Mawr, PA 19010, (215) LA5-1000
Kurios Press, Box 946, Bryn Mawr, PA 19010, 215-527-4635
COME-ALL-YE, P.O. Box 494, Hatboro, PA 19040, (215) 675-6762
Legacy Books (formerly Folklore Associates), P.O. Box 494, Hatboro, PA 19040, (215) 675-6762
Barn Hill, 825 Hallowell Drive, Huntingdon Valley, PA 19006, (215) 947-1646
Kathleen P. O'Donnell, 103 Bryn Mawr Avenue, Lansdowne, PA 19050, 259-9391
CHASQUI, Dept of Modern Languages, Swarthmore College, Swarthmore, PA 19081, (215) 447-7145
The Middle Atlantic Press, Box 263, Wallingford, PA 19086, 215-565-2445
AMERICAN POETRY REVIEW, 1616 Walnut St., Room 405, Philadelphia, PA 19103, 215-732-6770
Atlantis Editions, P.O. Box 18326, Philadelphia, PA 19120
Blue Flower, 1825 Pine Street, Philadelphia, PA 19104, (215) 382-1410
CHIMERA-A Complete Theater Piece, 5538 Morris Street, Philadelphia, PA 19144
Footnotes, 1300 Arch Street, Philadelphia, PA 19107
FOUR QUARTERS, LaSalle College, Philadelphia, PA 19141
A GAY BIBLIOGRAPHY, P.O. Box 2383, Philadelphia, PA 19103, (215) 382-3222
GAY INSURGENT, PO Box 2337, Philadelphia, PA 19103
Gay Task Force, American Library Association, PO Box 2383, Philadelphia, PA 19103, (215) 382-3222
HOT WATER REVIEW, PO Box 8396, Philadelphia, PA 19101
Hotwater, PO Box 8396, Philadelphia, PA 19101
HS Press, 5538 Morris Street, Philadelphia, PA 19144
INDIAN TRUTH, 1505 Race St., Philadelphia, PA 19102, 215-563-8349
Institute for the Study of Human Issues (ISHI), 3401 Market Street, Suite 252, Philadelphia, PA 19104, (215) 387-9002
JOURNAL OF MODERN LITERATURE, Temple Univ., Philadelphia, PA 19122
MEDIA HISTORY DIGEST, PO Box 867, William Penn Station, Philadelphia, PA 19105, (215) 787-9121
Nordic Books, PO Box 1941, Philadelphia, PA 19105, (215) 574-4258
PAINTED BRIDE QUARTERLY, 527 South St, Philadelphia, PA 19147, 215-925-9914
POETRY NEWSLETTER, Dept. of English, Temple University, Philadelphia, PA 19122
Programs and Publications, 321 Queen Street, Philadelphia, PA 19147, (215) 467-5291
Pulse-Finger Press, Box 18105, Philadelphia, PA 19116
RECON, P.O. Box 14602, Philadelphia, PA 19134
Recon Publications, PO Box 14602, Philadelphia, PA 19134
ROCKINGCHAIR, P.O. Box 27, Philadelphia, PA 19105, (215) WA5-3673
Running Press, 38 South 19th Street, Philadelphia, PA 19103, 215-567-5080
ZERO REVIEW, PO Box 13230, Philadelphia, PA 19101, (215) 222-4141
The Zero Press, PO Box 13230, Philadelphia, PA 19101, (215) 222-4141
How to Tutor Your Child in Reading, How-to, box 504, Exton, PA 19341, (215) 692-5358
PAPER AIR, 825 Morris Road, Blue Bell, PA 19422
Singing Horse Press, 825 Morris Road, Blue Bell, PA 19422
Primary Press, Box 105A, Parker Ford, PA 19457, 215-495-7529
Philmer Enterprises, #4 Hunter's Run, Spring House, PA 19477, 215-643-2976

Trek-Cir Publications, PO Box 898, Valley Forge, PA 19481, (215) 337-3110
OLD COURTHOUSE FILES, Box 74, Albright College, Reading, PA 19603

PUERTO RICO

CREACION, Apartado 111, Estacion 6, Ponce, PR 00731
Editorial Creacion, Apartado 111, Estacion 6, Ponce, PR 00731

RHODE ISLAND

ALDEBARAN, Roger Williams College, Bristol, RI 02809
Ampersand Press, Creative Writing Program, Roger Williams College, Bristol, RI 02809
CALLIOPE, Creative Writing Program, Roger Williams College, Bristol, RI 02809
THE GREYLEDGE REVIEW, Box 481, Greenville, RI 02828, (401) 231-2076
Biscuit City Press, P.O. Box 334, Kingston, RI 02881, 401-783-8851
JUST PULP: The Magazine of Popular Fiction, PO Box 243, Narragansett, RI 02882
Burning Deck Press, 71 Elmgrove Ave., Providence, RI 02906
Copper Beech Press, Box 1852 Brown Univ., Providence, RI 02912, 401-863-2393
DIANA'S ALMANAC, 71 Elmgrove Ave., Providence, RI 02906
Diana's Bimonthly Press, 71 Elmgrove Avenue, Providence, RI 02906, (401) 274-5417
Gray Flannel Press, P.O. Box 9181, Providence, RI 02940
HELLCOAL ANNUAL, Box 4 SAO, Brown University, Providence, RI 02912
Hellcoal Press, Box SAO, Brown Univ., Providence, RI 02912
MAN AT ARMS, 222 West Exchange Street, Providence, RI 02903, (401) 861-1000
Mowbray Company Publishers, 222 W Exchange Street, Providence, RI 02903, (401) 861-1000
NORTHEAST JOURNAL, P.O. Box 235, Annex Sta, Providence, RI 02901
Tom Ockerse Editions, 37 Woodbury Street, Providence, RI 02906, 401-331-0783

SOUTH CAROLINA

KUDZU, 166 Cokesdale Road, Columbia, SC 29210
TINDERBOX, 334 Molasses Lane, Mt. Pleasant (Charleston), SC 29464, 884-0212
SOUTHERN LIBERTARIAN MESSENGER, P.O. Box 1245, Florence, SC 29503
R & M Publishing Company, Inc, PO Box 210, Marion, SC 29571, (803) 423-6711, 423-5047
Sheriar Press, 801 13th Avenue S., Myrtle Beach, SC 29582, (803) 272-5311
SOUTH CAROLINA REVIEW, English Dept, Clemson Univ., Clemson, SC 29631, (803) 656-3229

SOUTH DAKOTA

The Cabbagehead Press, 214 E Main Street, Vermillion, SD 57069, (605) 624-8828
Dakota Press, Swes, University of South Dakota, Vermillion, SD 57069, 605-677-5281
SOUTH DAKOTA REVIEW, Box 111, University Exchange, Vermillion, SD 57069, 605-677-5229
Spirit Mound Press, Box 111, University Exch., Vermillion, SD 57069
Lame Johnny Press, Box 66, Hermosa, SD 57744, 605-255-4228

TENNESSEE

Authors' Co-op Publishing Co., Rt. 4, Box 137, Franklin, TN 37064, (615) 646-3757
The Battery Press, Inc., P.O. Box 3107, Uptown Station, Nashville, TN 37219
FRONT STREET TROLLEY, 2125 Acklen Ave., Nashville, TN 37212, 615-297-2977
THE ROMANTIST, Saracinesca House, 3610 Meadowbrook Avenue, Nashville, TN 37205
SOUTHERN PROGRESSIVE PERIODICALS UPDATE DIRECTORY, PO Box 120574, Nashville, TN 37212
SEWANEE REVIEW, Univ. of the South, Sewanee, TN 37375
Future Publishing Co., Jump Off Road, St Andrews, TN 37372, (615) 598-5320
THE POETRY MISCELLANY, English Dept. Univ of Tennessee, Chattanooga, TN 37402, 615-755-4213; 624-7279
THE BLACK CAT, P.O. Box 1912OA, East Tennessee State University, Johnson City, TN 37601
SECOND GROWTH: Appalachian Nature and Culture, Dept. of English, East Tennessee State Univ., Johnson City, TN 37601, (615) 929-7466
Writers For Animal Rights, P.O. Box 1912OA, East Tennessee State University, Johnson City, TN 37601
THE SMALL FARM, Rt 5 Cline Road Box 345, Dandridge, TN 37725
Southbound Press, Rt 5, Shenandoah Drive, Seymour, TN 37865
TOUCHSTONE, 4619 Sunflower Road, Apt 5, Knoxville, TN 37919, 615-588-5295
Young Publications, 531 N. Gay St. (PO Box 3455), Knoxville, TN 37917
Center for Southern Folklore, PO Box 40105, 1216 Peabody Avenue, Memphis, TN 38104, (901) 726-4205
CENTER FOR SOUTHERN FOLKLORE MAGAZINE, PO Box 40105, 1216 Peabody Avenue, Memphis, TN 38104, (901) 726-4205
ELVIS THE RECORD, PO Box 18408, Memphis, TN 38118, (901) 362-8906
Hays, Rolfes & Associates, PO Box 11465, Memphis, TN 38111, (901) 682-8128
RACCOON, 1407 Union, Suite 401, Mid-Memphis Tower, Memphis, TN 38104, (901) 357-5441
Regmar Publishing Co., PO Box 11358, Memphis, TN 38111, (901) 324-0991
St. Luke's Press, Suite 401, 1407 Union Avenue, Memphis, TN 38104, 901-357-5441
Wimmer Brothers Books, PO Box 18408, Memphis, TN 38118, (901) 362-8900
Old Hickory Press, PO Box 1178, Jackson, TN 38301
OLD HICKORY REVIEW, PO Box 1178, Jackson, TN 38301
Book Publishing Co., 156 Drakes Lane, Summertown, TN 38483, 615-964-3571

TEXAS

CLAUDEL STUDIES, University of Dallas Station, Irving, TX 75061
DUCK SOUP, 2000 Walnut Hill Lane, Irving, TX 75062, (214) 659-5279
SPRING: An Annual of Archetypal Psychology and Jungian Thought, Box 1, University of Dallas, Irving, TX 75061, 438-1123
Spring Publications Inc, Box 1, University of Dallas, Irving, TX 75061, (214) 438-1123
MUNDUS ARTIUM: A Journal of International Literature & Art, Box 688, Richardson, TX 75080
TRANSLATION REVIEW, Univ. of Texas-Dallas, Box 688, Richardson, TX 75080, (214) 690-2092
Slough Press, Box 370, Edgewood, TX 75117
Gluxlit Press, P O Box 11165, Dallas, TX 75223

New London Press, Box 7458, Dallas, TX 75209, 214-742-9037
REFERENCE BOOK REVIEW, Box 19954, Dallas, TX 75219
Somesuch Press, PO Box 188, Dallas, TX 75221, (214) 748-1842
SOUTHWEST REVIEW, Southern Methodist Univ., Dallas, TX 75275, 214-692-2263
Texas Center for Writers Press, PO Box 19876, Dallas, TX 75219, 213-393-2413
THICKET, PO Box 386, Woodville, TX 75979, 713-283-2516
DESCANT, English Department, TCU, Fort Worth, TX 76129
Special Aviation Publications, Box 672, Hillsboro, TX 76645
ADVENTURES IN POETRY MAGAZINE, PO Box 253, Junction, TX 76849, (915) 446-2004
Dr. Stella Woodall Publisher, PO Box 253, Junction, TX 76849, 915 446-2004
Timberline Press, Box 294, Mason, TX 76856, (915) 347-5573
Brown Rabbit Press, Box 19111, Houston, TX 77024, (713) 622-1844; 465-1168
CANVASS, 1714 Tabor, Houston, TX 77009, (713) 861-2337
Coker Books, Box 395, 3530 Timmons, Houston, TX 77027
Daughters Publishing Co., Inc., M5590 PO Box 42999, Houston, TX 77042
Houston Writers Workshop, Drawer 42331, Houston, TX 77042, (713) 461-6201
Joyful Press (formerly: T. I Opportunities), 9013 Long Point Road, Houston, TX 77055, (713) 467-4711; 465-3131
Lancer Militaria, PO Box 35188, Houston, TX 77035, (713) 522-7036
Lowy Publishing, 5047 Wigton, Houston, TX 77096, (713) 723-3209
Potto Publications, 5235 Lymbar, Houston, TX 77096, (713) 569-1153
QUIXOTE, QUIXOTL, PO Box 70013, Houston, TX 77007, 608-251-6401
REVISTA CHICANO-RIQUENA, University of Houston, Houston, TX 77004, 219-980-6692
TOUCHSTONE, Drawer 42331, Houston, TX 77042, (713) 461-6201
Triad Press, PO Box 42006 1-D, Houston, TX 77042, (713) 789-0424
Variety Press, 5214 Starkridge, Houston, TX 77035, (713) 721-5919
THE TEXAS REVIEW, English Department, Sam Houston State University, Huntsville, TX 77340
Energy Earth Communications, Inc., PO Box 1141, Galveston, TX 77553
HOO-DOO BlackSeries, PO Box 1141, Galveston, TX 77553
IN ORBIT: A Journal of Earth Literature, PO Box 1141, Galveston, TX 77553
SYNERGY, Box 1141, Galveston, TX 77553
Servicios Internacionales, Box 941, Texas City, TX 77590, (713) 935-3491
CEDAR ROCK, 1121 Madeline, New Braunfels, TX 78130, 512-625-6002
Cedar Rock Press, 1121 Madeline, New Braunfels, TX 78130
Tejas Art Press, 1000 Jackson-Keller Road, Apt 274K, San Antonio, TX 78213, (512) 340-0285
Trucha Publications, Inc., PO Boxx 3534, San Antonio, TX 78211
THE NEW AUTHOR, Route 1-Box 745, Aransas Pass, TX 78336
Biography Press, 1240 W. Highland Ave., Rt. 1 Box 745, Aransas Pass., TX 78336, 512-758-3870
BLIND ALLEY, P.O. Box 1296, Edinburg, TX 78539
Blind Alley Press, P.O. Box 1296, Edinburg, TX 78539
Funch Press, 1101 Tori Lane, Edinburg, TX 78539, (512) 383-7893
PAN AMERICAN REVIEW, 1101 Tori Lane, Edinburg, TX 78539, 512-383-7893
RIVERSEDGE, PO Box 1547, Edinburg, TX 78539
Riversedge Press, PO Box 1547, Edinburg, TX 78539
ABBA, PO Box 8516, Austin, TX 78712
Abba Books & Broadsides, PO Box 8516, Austin, TX 78712
Amistad Press, PO Box 5026, Austin, TX 78763, (512) 472-8992
THE ARGONAUT, PO Box 7985, Austin, TX 78712, (512) 478-2396
CARTA ABIERTA, Center for Mexican American Studies, Student Services Building 307, Texas Univ, Austin, TX 78712, (512) 471-4557
Cold Mountain Press, c/o Provision House, PO Box 5487, Austin, TX 78763
CONFEDERATE CALENDAR WORKS, PO Box 5404, Austin, TX 78763
DIMENSION, Box 7032, Austin, TX 78712, 512-471-4314
THE GAR, Box 4793, Austin, TX 78765, (512) 453-2556
Gar Publishing Co., PO Box 4793, Austin, TX 78765, (512) 453-2556
INTERSTATE, P.O. Box 7068, U.T. Sta., Austin, TX 78712
Journal Books, 704 Baylor Street, Austin, TX 78703
KTQ:KITTY TORTURE QUARTERLY, PO Box 5931, Austin, TX 78763
THE NEW JOURNAL, 704 Baylor Street, Austin, TX 78703
Noumenon Press, PO Box 7068, University Station, Austin, TX 78712
Place of Herons, PO Box 1952, Austin, TX 78768, (512) 472-0737; 476-7023
Plain View, Inc., 1509 Dexter, Austin, TX 78704, (512) 441-2452
Provision House, PO Box 5487, Austin, TX 78763, 452-1417
S & S Press, PO Box 5931, Austin, TX 78763
Seven Deadly Sins Press, 1117 B Mariposa, Austin, TX 78703
John B. Sherrill, PO Box 8623, Austin, TX 78712, (512) 451-4459
The Stevenson Press, Callcott - Collinson, Inc., P.O.Box 10021, Austin, TX 78766, 255-8623
Studia Hispanica Editors, PO Box 7304, University Station, Austin, TX 78712, (512) 458-5413
TEXAS QUARTERLY, Box 7517 University Stn., Austin, TX 78712
Thorp Springs Press, 803 Red River, Austin, TX 78701
WOOD IBIS, PO Box 1952, Austin, TX 78768, (512) 472-0737; 476-7023
SEPARATE DOORS, 911 W T Station, Canyon, TX 79016
CHAWED RAWZIN, 225 W. Crosby, Slaton, TX 79364
Chawed Rawzin Press, 225 W. Crosby, Slaton, TX 79364
CONRADIANA, Dept. of English, Box 4530, Texas Tech University, Lubbock, TX 79409
MJG Company, P.O. Box 7743, Midland, TX 79703, 915-682-3184
AMOXCALLI, PO Box 2064, El Paso, TX 79951, (915) 594-2222

UTAH

Peregrine Smith, Inc., PO Box 667, Layton, UT 84041, 801-376-9800

Pi-Right Press, P.O. Box 2366, Park City, UT 84060
SILVER VAIN, P. O. Box 2366, Park City, UT 84060, 801-649-8866
WESTERN HUMANITIES REVIEW, University of Utah, Salt Lake City, UT 84112, 801-581-7438
WESTERN AMERICAN LITERATURE, UMC 32, Utah State Univ., Logan, UT 84322

VERMONT

ST. MAWR, Box 356, Randolph, VT 05060
St. Mawr Jazz Poetry Project, Box 356, Randolph, VT 05060
Cider Barrel Press, Snake Road, S Newbury, VT 05066, (802) 866-5516
THE BENNINGTON REVIEW, Bennington College, Bennington, VT 05201, (802) 442-5401
LONGHOUSE, Green River R.F.D., Brattleboro, VT 05301
Longhouse, Green River R.F.D., Brattleboro, VT 05301
THE EVENER, Putney, VT 05346, (802) 387-4243
VERMONT CHILDREN'S MAGAZINE, PO Box 941, Burlington, VT 05401, 425-2359
Garden Way Publishing Company, Charlotte, VT 05445, (802) 425-2171
SAMISDAT, Box 231, Richford, VT 05476
Samisdat Associates, Box 231, Richford, VT 05476
Biohydrant Publications, R.F.D. 3, St. Albans, VT 05478
CURRENT (a reprint magazine), Editorial Office, R.D. #1, Barre, VT 05641, 802-476-4000
Pulmac Enterprises, Inc., Middlesex Star Route, Montpelier, VT 05602, (802) 223-6326
JAM TO-DAY, P.O. Box 249, Northfield, VT 05663
Vermont Crossroads Press, Box 30, Waitsfield, VT 05673, (802) 496-2469
Janus Press, Rt #2, West Burke, VT 05871
Printed Editions, PO Box 26, West Glover, VT 05875
Sherry Urie, RFD, West Glover, VT 05875, (802) 525-6966

VIRGINIA

PEOPLE & ENERGY, 9208 Christopher St, Fairfax, VA 22031
PHOEBE, G.M.U. 4400 University Dr., Fairfax, VA 22030
Piney Branch Press, 5000 Piney Branch Road, Fairfax, VA 22030, (703) 830-3185
April Dawn Publishing Company, Po Box 4433, Falls Church, VA 22044
Arcane Order, 2904 Rosemary Lane, Falls Church, VA 22042
JACKSONVILLE POETRY QUARTERLY, 2904 Rosemary Lane, Falls Church, VA 22042
THE WOMAN ACTIVIST, 2310 Barbour Road, Falls Church, VA 22043
Firestein Books, 11959 Barrel Cooper Court, Reston, VA 22091, (703) 860-1637
MANASSAS REVIEW: ESSAYS ON CONTEMPORARY AMERICAN POETRY, Communications Division, Northern Virginia Community College, Manassas, VA 22110
THE DEVELOPING COUNTRY COURIER, P.O.Box 239, McLean, VA 22101, (703) 356-7561
NEW GUARD, Woodland Rd, Sterling, VA 22170, 703-450-5162
BOGG, 2010 N. 21st Street, Arlington, VA 22201
WINDOW, 4510 35th St. North, Arlington, VA 22207, 301-270-5424
Window Press, 4510 35th St. North, Arlington, VA 22207, (301) 270-5424
THE ASIA MAIL, P O Box 1044, Alexandria, VA 22313
Editorial Experts, Inc, 5905 Pratt Street, Alexandria, VA 22310, 971-7350
EDITORIAL EYE, 5905 Pratt Street, Alexandria, VA 22310
The Huffman Press, 311 Madison St, Alexandria, VA 22314, 703-836-7160
Mu Publications, Box 612, Dahlgren, VA 22448
Dan River Press, PO Box 249, Stafford, VA 22554
NORTHWOODS JOURNAL, PO Box 249, Stafford, VA 22554, (703) 659-6771
Northwoods Press, Inc., PO Box 249, Stafford, VA 22554, (703) 659-6771
Greatland Publishing Co., 7 South Street, Front Royal, VA 22630, (703) 635-7180
CROP DUST, Route 2, Box 392, Bealeton, VA 22712, (703) 439-2140
Crop Dust Press, Route 2, Box 392, Bealeton, VA 22712, 703-439-2140
Community Collaborators, PO Box 5429, Charlottesville, VA 22905, 804-977-1126
THEATRE DESIGN AND TECHNOLOGY, 1024 Holmes Avenue, Charlottesville, VA 22901, 804-295-7990
U.S. Institute for Theatre Technology, Inc., 1024 Holmes Ave, Charlottesville, VA 22901
The Pray Curser Press, c/oErwin R. Bergdoll, Elm Bank, Dutton, VA 23050, 804-693-2823
LITERARY SKETCHES, Box 711, Williamsburg, VA 23185, 804-229-2901
THE CONTEMPORARY LITERARY SCENE, Dept. of English, Va. Commonwealth Univ., Richmond, VA 23284
Palimpsest Workshop, 1421 Grove Avenue No.2, Richmond, VA 23220
The Donning Company / Publishers, 5041 Admiral Wright Road, Virginia Beach, VA 23462, (804) 499-0589
NEW VIRGINIA REVIEW, PO Box 415, Norfolk, VA 23501, (804) 622-1991
REFLECT, 3306 Argonne Avenue, Norfolk, VA 23509, (804) 857-1097
Heresy Press, 713 Paul Street, Newport News, VA 23605, (804) 827-2631
Purple Mouth Press, 713 Paul St, Newport News, VA 23605
SKIFFY THYME, 713 Paul Street, Newport News, VA 23605, 804-380-6595
THE HAMPDEN-SYDNEY POETRY REVIEW, P.O. Box 126, Hampden-Sydney, VA 23943, 804-223-4381
THE HOLLINS CRITIC, P.O. Box 9538, Hollins College, VA 24020
Iron Mountain Press, Box D, Emory, VA 24327, 703-944-5363
SHENANDOAH, P.O. Box 722, Lexington, VA 24450, (703) 463-9111 ext 283
PIEDMONT LITERARY REVIEW, P.O.Box 3656, Danville, VA 24541, (804) 799-9049

WASHINGTON

LOCAL DRIZZLE, PO Box 388, Carnation, WA 98014, (206) 333-4980
The Chas. Franklin Press, 18409 90th Avenue W, Edmonds, WA 98020, (206) 774-6979
Signpost Books, 8912 192nd Street, SW, Edmonds, WA 98020, 206-776-0370
Medic Publishing Co., PO Box O, Issaquah, WA 98027, 392-5665
NORTHWEST CHESS, PO Box 613, Kenmore, WA 98028, (206) 486-5430
SIGNPOST, 16812 36th Avenue W, Lynwood, WA 98036, 206-743-3947

548

METAMORFOSIS, Center for Chicano Studies, GN-09, Washington University, Seattle, WA 98018, (206) 543-9080
LAUGHING BEAR, Box 14, Woodinville, WA 98072, 206-524-2314
Laughing Bear Press, Box 14, Woodinville, WA 98072, 206-524-2314
AND/OR NOTES, 1525 10th Ave., Seattle, WA 98122, 324-5880
and/or Services, 1525 10th Ave, Seattle, WA 98122
Angst World Library, 2307 22nd Ave. E, Seattle, WA 98112
L'Epervier Press, 762 Hayes #15, Seattle, WA 98109
Gray Beard Publishing, 107 W. John Street, Seattle, WA 98119, (206) 285-3171
Jawbone Press, 17023 5th Avenue NE, Seattle, WA 98155
MODERN LANGUAGE QUARTERLY, 4045 Brooklyn Ave. N.E., Seattle, WA 98105
Montana Books, Publishers, Inc., 3426 Wallingford Ave. North, Box 30017, Seattle, WA 98103
The Mountaineers Books, 719-B Pike Street, Seattle, WA 98101, (206) 682-4636
North Country Press, P.O. Box 12223, Seattle, WA 98112
Northland Publications, Box 12157, Seattle, WA 98102
Parenting Press, 7750 31st Avenue, NE, Seattle, WA 98115, 206-525-4660
Partisan Press, PO Box 2193, Seattle, WA 98111, (206) 622-3132
POETRY NORTHWEST, 4045 Brooklyn NE, Ja-15, Univ. Of Washington, Seattle, WA 98105
Saru, c/o Bradley, 110 W Kinnear Place, Seattle, WA 98119
The Seal Press, 533 11th EAST, Seattle, WA 98102, 322-2320
THE SEATTLE REVIEW, Padelford Hall GN-30, Univ. of Wash, Seattle, WA 98195, (206) 543-9865
Smuggler's Cove Publishing, 107 W John, Seattle, WA 98119, (206) 285-3171
THROUGH THE LOOKING GLASS, P.O.Box 22061, Seattle, WA 98122
Tiburon Press, Lockbox 17034 Ballard, Seattle, WA 98107, (206) 782-1437
VEGATABLE BOX, 4142 11th NE #3, Seattle, WA 98105, (206) 632-2518
Vulcan Books, PO Box 25616, Seattle, WA 98125, (206) 362-2606
THE BELLINGHAM REVIEW, 412 N. State Street, Bellingham, WA 98225, 206-734-9781
BIG MOON, 207 Texas, Bellingham, WA 98225, 206-671-4029
CONCERNING POETRY, English Department, Western Wash. University, Bellingham, WA 98225
JEOPARDY, Western Washington University, Humanities 350, WWU, Bellingham, WA 98225
Signpost Press, 412 N. State, Bellingham, WA 98225
Western Washington University, Humanities 350, WWU English Dept, Bellingham, WA 98225, 206-676-3118
WILD FENNEL, 2510 48th Street, Bellingham, WA 98225
Albacore Press, PO Box 355, Eastsound, WA 98245
Gododdin Publishing, PO Box 5242, Everett, WA 98206, (206) 334-6120
Garage #3, PO Box 1118, Stanwood, WA 98292
COFFEE BREAK, P.O. Box 103, Burley, WA 98322, 857-4329
Coffee Break Press, PO Box 103, Burley, WA 98322, 857-4329
Copper Canyon Press/Copperhead, P.O. Box 271, Port Townsend, WA 98368
The Graywolf Press, P.O. Box 142, Port Townsend, WA 98368, 206-385-1160
Circinatum Press, PO Box 99309, Tacoma, WA 98499, (206) 627-4816
SPOOR, Star Rt Box 663A, Aberdeen, WA 98520, 206-648-2493
Ten Crow Press, Star Rt Box 663A, Aberdeen, WA 98520, 206 648-2493
THE CHANEY CHRONICAL, 929 South Bay Rd, Olympia, WA 98506, (206) 352-8622
London Northwest, 929 So Bay Rd, Olympia, WA 98506
WHAT'S NEW ABOUT LONDON, JACK?, 929 South Bay Rd., Olympia, WA 98506, (206) 352-8622
Sovereign Press, 326 Harris Rd, Rochester, WA 98579
CRCS Publications, PO Drawer 4307, Vancouver, WA 98662, (206) 256-8979
Vagabond Press, 1610 N. Water, Ellensburg, WA 98926
Odyssey Publishing Company, Route 3, Box 698, Yakima, WA 98901, (509) 452-5531
Wilson Brothers Publications, PO Box 712, Yakima, WA 98907, (509) 457-8275
WILLOW SPRINGS, Pub, PO Box 1063, Eastern Washington Univ., Cheney, WA 99004, 359-7061
Bear Tribe, P O Box 9167, Spokane, WA 99209, (509) 258-7755
COPULA, W1114 Indiana Street, Spokane, WA 99205, 325-2985
MANY SMOKES, P.O. Box 9167, Spokane, WA 99209
Goldermood Rainbow Press, 331 W. Bonneville, Pasco, WA 99301, 509-547-5525
"NITTY GRITTY", 331 W. Bonneville, Pasco, WA 99301, 509-547-5525
Litmus, Inc., 525 Bryant, Walla Walla, WA 99362

WEST VIRGINIA

THE LIBRARY IMAGINATION PAPER!, 1000 Byus Drive, Charleston, WV 25311, (304) 345-2378
Mountain Union Books, c/o Bob Snyder, 1511 Jackson Street, Apt AB, Charleston, WV 25311
THE LITTLE REVIEW, Marshall University, Box 205, Huntington, WV 25701
THE LAUREL REVIEW, West Virginia Wesleyan College, Buckhannon, WV 26201, 303-473-8006
BACKCOUNTRY, Box 390, Elkins, WV 26241, (304) 636-6236
Cheat Mountain Press, Box 390, Elkins, WV 26241, (304) 636-6236
Glouchester Press (Music Publ), PO Box 1044, Fairmont, WV 26554, 304-366-3758
Westwind Press, Route 1, Box 208, Farmington, WV 26571, 304-287-7160
TRELLIS, P.O. Box 656, Morgantown, WV 26505, 304-845-7118
THE UNREALIST: A Left Literary Magazine, 1243 Pine View Drive, Morgantown, WV 26505
The Unrealist Press, 1243 Pine View Drive, Morgantown, WV 26505

WISCONSIN

SEEMS, c/o Lakeland College, Box 359, Sheboygan, WI 53081
Southport Press, Dept. of English, Carthage College, Kenosha, WI 53141, (414) 551-8500 (252)
Third Coast, c/o International, 146 Broad Street, Lake Geneva, WI 53147
MALEDICTA: The International Journal of Verbal Aggression, 331 S. Greenfield Ave., Waukesha, WI 53186, 414-542-5853
Maledicta Press, 331 S. Greenfield Ave., Waukesha, WI 53186, 414-542-5853
FRIENDS OF POETRY, Dept of English, University of Wisconsin, Whitewater, WI 53190, (414) 472-1036
The Language Press, P.O.Box 342, Whitewater, WI 53190, (414) 473-2767

CREAM CITY REVIEW, P O Box 413, English Dept, Curtin Hall, Univ of Wisconsin, Milwaukee, WI 53201
Distant Thunder Press, 1224 E Clarke Street, Milwaukee, WI 53212
GPU NEWS, PO Box 92203, Milwaukee, WI 53202, 414-276-0612
Heavy Evidence Press, P.O. Box 92893, Milwaukee, WI 53202
HEY LADY, 1819 N. Oakland Avenue, Milwaukee, WI 53202, (414) 272-3256
Liberation Publications, Inc., Box 92203, Milwaukee, WI 53202, (414) 276-0612
Membrane Press, P.O. Box 11601-Shorewood, Milwaukee, WI 53211
Metatron Press, 2447 N. 59th Street, Milwaukee, WI 53210, (414) 444-6266
Moonfire Press, 3061 N Newhall Street, Milwaukee, WI 53211, 414-964-0173
Morgan Press, 1819 N. Oakland Avenue, Milwaukee, WI 53202, (414) 272-3256
SACKBUT REVIEW, 2513 E Webster Place, Milwaukee, WI 53211
THIRD COAST ARCHIVES, 3061 N Newhall Street, Milwaukee, WI 53211, 414 964-0173
Lionhead Publishing, 2521 East Stratford Court, Shorewood, WI 53211, 414-332-7474
BELOIT POETRY JOURNAL, P.O. Box 2, Beloit, WI 53511
The Perishable Press Limited, PO Box 7, Mt. Horeb, WI 53572
PRELUDE TO FANTASY, Route 3, Box 193, Richland Center, WI 53581
ABRAXAS, 2322 Rugby Row, Madison, WI 53705
BA SHIRU, University of Wisconsin, 866 Van Hise, Madison, WI 53706
The Bieler Press, 4603 Shore Acres Road, Madison, WI 53716, (608) 222-3711
Coda Press, Inc, 700 West Badger Road, Suite 101, Madison, WI 53713, (608) 251-9662
CONTEMPORARY LITERATURE, 7141 Helen C. White Hall, University of Wisconsin, Madison, WI 53706
First Impressions, PO Box 9073, Madison, WI 53715, (608) 238-6254
JANUS, PO Boxx 1624, Madison, WI 53701, 267-7483; 241-8445
JOURNAL OF PSYCHEDELIC DRUGS, 118 South Bedford Street, Madison, WI 53703, 608-251-4200
THE MADISON REVIEW, Dept. of English, University of Wisconsin, Madison, WI 53706, (608) 263-3705
MODERN HAIKU, PO Box 1752, Madison, WI 53701, (608) 255-2660
THE MRB NETWORK, 1121 University Avenue, Madison, WI 53715, (608) 256-1946
Penstemon Press, 309 Debs Road, Madison, WI 53704, (608) 241-1132
SOCIAL TEXT, 700 West Badger Road, Suite 101, Madison, WI 53713, (608) 251-9662
Sol Press, 2025 Dunn Place, Madison, WI 53713, 608-257-4126
Stash, Inc., 118 South Bedford Street, Madison, WI 53703, 608-251-4200
Tamarack Press, P.O.Box 5650, Madison, WI 53705, 608-831-3363
WISCONSIN TRAILS, PO Box 5650, Madison, WI 53705, 608-831-3363
NORTH AMERICAN MENTOR MAGAZINE, 1745 Madison Street, Fennimore, WI 53809
John Westburg, Publisher, 1745 Madison Street, Fennimore, WI 53809, 608-822-6237
HAWK-WIND, Box 379, Markesan, WI 53946
Pentagram Press, Box 379, Markesan, WI 53946
THE PHOTOLETTER, Photosearch International, Department 56, Osceola, WI 54020, (715) 248-3800
PRIMIPARA, P.O. Box 371, Oconto, WI 54153
Druid Books, Ephraim, WI 54211
Dragonsbreath Press, Rt. #1, Sister Bay, WI 54234, (414) 854-2742
George Sroda, Publisher, Amherst Jct., WI 54407
PORTAGE, Route 1, Box 128, Rudolph, WI 54475
THE MAINSTREETER, 3200 Ellis Street #16, St Point, WI 54481
The Scopcraeft Press, 3200 Ellis Street #16, St Point, WI 54481
THE FIFTH HORSEMAN, 3200 Ellis Street #16, Stevens Point, WI 54481, (715) 345-0865
Land Educational Associates Foundation, Inc., 3368 Oak Avenue, Stevens Point, WI 54481, (715) 344-6158
SCOPCRAEFT MAGAZINE, 3200 Ellis Street #16, Stevens Point, WI 54481, (715) 345-0865
Swish, PO Box 754, Stevens Point, WI 54481, 715-344-0721
SONG, 808 Illinois, Stevens Pt, WI 54481, 715-344-6836
Jump River Press, Inc., 819 Single Avenue, Wausau, WI 54401, (715) 842-8243
JUMP RIVER REVIEW, 819 Single Avenue, Wausau, WI 54401, (715)842-8243
Center For Contemporary Poetry, Murphy Library, Univ of Wisconsin, La Crosse, WI 54601, 608-785-8511
Juniper Press, 1310 Shorewood Dr, La Crosse, WI 54601
NORTHEAST/JUNIPER BOOKS, 1310 Shorewood Dr., LaCrosse, WI 54601
RED WEATHER, PO Box 1104, Eau Claire, WI 54701, 715-834-9870
Red Weather Press, PO Box 1104, Eau Claire, WI 54701, 715-834-9870
Rhiannon Press, 1105 Bradley, Eau Claire, WI 54701, (715) 835-0598
UZZANO, 511 Sunset Drive, Menomonie, WI 54751, (715) 235-6525
Uzzano Press, 511 Sunset Drive, Menomonie, WI 54751, (715) 235-6525
GREAT CIRCUMPOLAR BEAR CULT, Box 468, Ashland, WI 54806
ALBUM, 218 N Douglas Street, Appleton, WI 54911, (414) 733-0160
POETRY VIEW, 1125 Valley Rd., Menasha, WI 54952
THE ACTS THE SHELFLIFE, 838a Wisconsin St, Oshkosh, WI 54901
Forbidden Additions, 838a Wisconsin St, Oshkosh, WI 54901
sun rise fall down artpress, 838A Wisconsin St., Oshkosh, WI 54901, (414) 426-1732
TRADE MAGAZINE, 838A Wisconsin, Oshkosh, WI 54901, (414) 426-1732
WISCONSIN REVIEW, Box 92 Halsey, University of Wisconsin-Oshkosh, Oshkosh, WI 54901, 414-424-2267
Wisconsin Review, Box 145 Dempsey Hall, Oshkosh, WI 54901, 414-424-2267
Kitchen Sink Enterprises, Box 7, Princeton, WI 54968, 414-295-3972
SNARF, P.O. Box 7, Princeton, WI 54968
WEIRD TRIPS, Box 7, Princeton, WI 54968, (414) 295-3972
PARCHMENT (Broadside Series), 524 Larson Street, Waupaca, WI 54981, (715) 258-2657
WOLFSONG, 509 W Fulton, Waupaca, WI 54981
Wolfsong Publications, 509 W Fulton, Waupaca, WI 54981

WYOMING

Jelm Mountain Publications, 304 So. 3rd Street, Laramie, WY 82070, 307-742-8053
HIGH COUNTRY NEWS, Box K, 331 Main St., Lander, WY 82520, 332-4877 (307)

Backroads/Caroline House, Box 370, Wilson, WY 83014, (307) 733-7730

AFRICA

East African Publishing House, PO Box 30571, Nairobi, Kenya, Africa, 557417 & 555694

ARGENTINA

CONTRACULTURA, C C Central 1332, Buenos Aires 1000, Argentina
ECO CONTEMPORANEO, C C Central 1933, 1000 Buenos Aires, Argentina
Eco Contemporaneo Press, C C Central 1933, 1000 Buenos Aires, Argentina

AUSTRALIA

ANAPRESS, 114 Albert Road, South Melbourne, Melbourne, Victoria 3205, Australia, 697-0100
ASPECT, Art and Literature, Scotland Island 2105 NSW, Sydney, NSW, Australia, 9972481
AUSTRALIAN SCAN: Journal of Human Communication, c/o Dept of Communication, Queensland Institute of Technology, GPO
  Box 2434, Brisbane, Queensland 4001, Australia, (07) 221-2411 Ext. 463
BIALA, PRAHRAN COLLEGE OF ADVANCED EDUCATION, 142 High St, Prahran 3181, Victoria, Australia
Communicate Press, PO Box 132, Toowong, Queensland 4066, Australia, (07) 370 1298
COMPASS, 11 Baker Street, Enfield, NSW 2136, Australia, (02) 7471592
THE CRITICAL REVIEW, History of Ideas Unit, Australian National University, P.O. Box 4, Canberra, A.C.T. 2600, Australia
GEGENSCHEIN, 6 Hillcrest Ave., Falconbridge, New South Wales 2776, Australia
GRASS ROOTS, Box 900, Shepparton, Victoria 3630, Australia
HECATE, G.P.O. Box 99, St. Lucia, Queensland 4067, Australia
The Helen Vale Foundation, 12 Chapel Street, St Kilda, Victoria 3182, Australia
HELIX, 119 Maltravers Road, Ivanhoe, Victoria 3079, Australia, 03-497-1741
Hexagon Press, P.O. Box 269, Greenacre, N.S.W. 2190, Australia, (02) 724-4444
JOURNAL OF THE HELEN VALE FOUNDATION, 12 Chapel Street, St Kilda, Victoria 3182, Australia, (03) 51-9861
LINQ, English Dept., James Cook University of North Queensland, Townsville 4811, Australia
Lonely Planet Publications, P.O. Box 88, South Yarra, Victoria 3141, Australia, 03 429-5268
MAGIC SAM, Box 164 Wentworth Building, Darlington, N.S.W. 2008, Australia
Mandorla Publications, R.M.B. 917, Dooralong, N.S.W. 2259, Australia, (043) 551219
MATTOID, c/o School of Humanities, Deakin University, Victoria 3217, Australia
MEANJIN QUARTERLY, University of Melbourne, Parkville, Victoria 3052, Australia, 341-6950
MEUSE, Box 61, Wentworth Bldg., Sydney University, NSW 2006, Australia
NEW POETRY, Box N110 Grosvenor St Post Office, Sydney, N.S.W. 2000, Australia

ON DIT, Union Buildings, Adelaide University, Adelaide 5001, South Australia, 223-2685
Pinchgut Press, 6 Oaks Avenue, Cremorne, Sydney, N.S.W. 2090, Australia, 90-5548
POEMS IN PUBLIC PLACES, Room 8, National Mutual Building, Wollongong, N.S.W. 2500, Australia
POETRY AUSTRALIA, 350 Lyons Rd., Five Dock, N.S.W. 2046, Australia
The Poetry Society of Australia, Box N110, Grosvenor Street P.O., Sydney, N.S.W. 2000, Australia
Prism Books, Box N110 Grosvenor St. P.O., Sydney, N.S.W. 2000, Australia
Red Press, PO Box 197, North Sydney, NSW 2060, Australia
The Saturday Centre, Box 140 P.O., Cammeray, NSW 2062, Australia
SCOPP, Box 140 P.O., Cammeray NSW 2062, Australia
Second Back Row Press, P.O. Box 43, Leura NSW 2781, Australia
SF COMMENTARY, GPO Box 5195AA, Melbourne, Victoria 3001, Australia, (03) 419-4797
SOUTHERN REVIEW, Dept. of English, Univ. of Adelaide, Adelaide, S. 5001, Australia
Horan Wall and Walker, PO Box 8, Surry Hills, Sydney, NSW 2010, Australia
HORAN WALL AND WALKER WEEKLY COMMUNITY INFORMATION, PO Box 8, Surry Hills, Sydney, NSW 2010, Australia
WESTERN CITY SUBTOPIAN TIMES, PO Box 269, Greenacre, NSW 2190, Australia, 02-724-4444
Wild & Woolley, P.O. Box 41, Glebe NSW 2037, Australia, 02-699-9819

AUSTRIA

THE INDEPENDENT JOURNAL OF PHILOSOPHY, Cobenzlgasse 13/4, A-1190 Vienna, Austria
The Independent Philosophy Press, Cobenzlgasse 13/4, A-1190 Vienna, Austria

BELGIUM

CAHIER, Lobergenbos 27, B 3200 Leuven, Belgium

CANADA

Absolute O Kelvin (AOK) Press, Box 485, Station P, Toronto, Ontario M5S 2T1, Canada, (416) 534-0139
Acme Print & Litho, 390 Douro Street, Stratford on Avon, Ontario N5A 3S7, Canada
ALBERTA HISTORY, 95 Holmwood Ave NW, Calgary Alberta T2K 2G7, Canada, 403-289-8149
THE ALCHEMIST, Box 123, LaSalle, Quebec H8R 3T7, Canada
ALIVE, P.O. Box 1331, Guelph, Ont., Canada
All About Us, Box 1985, Ottawa, Ontario K1P 5R5, Canada, (613) 238-2919
ALPHA, Box 1269, Wolfville, Nova Scotia B0P1X0, Canada, 542-2201 Ext 421
ALTERNATIVE RESEARCH NEWSLETTER, PO Box 1294, Kitchener, ON N2G 4G8, Canada
ALTERNATIVES- Perspectives on Society and Environment, Trent University, c/o Traill College, Peterborough, On K9J7B8, Canada
Anian Press, PO Box 69804, Station K, Vancouver, B.C. V5K 4Y7, Canada
Anjou, 235 Queen St West, Toronto, Ontario M5V 1Z4, Canada, 416-979-2555
THE ANTIGONISH REVIEW, St Francis Zavier University, Antigonish, Nova Scotia B2G1CO, Canada
ART & LITERARY DIGEST, Tweed, Ont K0K3J0, Canada
Art Official Inc., 217 Richmond Street West, Toronto, Ontario M5V 1W2, Canada, (416) 362-1685
ASCENT, Yasodhara Ashram Society, Box 9, Kootenay Bay, B.C. V0B 1X0, Canada, (604) 227-9220
ATLANTIS, Box 294, Acadia University, Wolfville, Nova Scotia B0P 1X0, Canada
The Avondale Press, P.O. Box 451, Willowdale, Ontario M2N5T1, Canada, (416) 773-5115
Aya Press, PO Box 303, Station A, Toronto, Ontario M5W 1C2, Canada, (416) 782-9984

Bellrock Press, 2050 MacKay Street, Montreal, QE H3G 2J1, Canada
Between The Lines, 97 Victoria Street North, Kitchener, Ontario N2H 5C1, Canada
Black Rose Books, 3981 Blvd., St. Laurent 4th Floor, Montreal, Que H2W 1V2, Canada
Blue Heron Press, PO Box 1326, Alliston, Ontario L0M 1A0, Canada, (705) 435-9914
THE BODY POLITIC- Gay Liberation Journal, Box 7289, Station A, Toronto, Ontario M5W1X9, Canada, 416-977-6320
BOOKS IN CANADA: A National Review Of Books, 366 Adelaide St East, Toronto, Ontario, Canada, 416-363-5426
Borealis Press Limited, 9 Ashburn Drive, Ottawa K2E 6N4, Canada, (613) 224-6837
BRANCHING OUT, Box 4098, Edmonton, Alberta T6E 4S8, Canada
Breakwater Books Limited, 277 Duckworth Street, St. John's, Newfoundland A1C 1G9, Canada, (709) 722-6680
BRICK: A Journal Of Reviews, Box 219, Ilderton, Ontario N0M 2AO, Canada, (519) 666-0283
Brick/Nairn, Box 219, Ilderton, Ontario N0M 2AO, Canada, (519) 666-0283
BRITISH COLUMBIA HISTORICAL NEWS, G.P.O. Box 1738, Victoria, BC V8W 2Y3, Canada, (604) 387-6671
C.S.P. WORLD NEWS, P.O. Box 2608, Station D. Ottawa K1P5W7, Canada, (613) 741-8675
Canada Publishing Co., Tweed, Ont K0K 3J0, Canada
CANADIAN AUTHOR & BOOKMAN, 24 Ryerson Ave, Toronto, Ontario M5T 2P3, Canada, (416) 868-6916
CANADIAN CHILDREN'S LITERATURE, P.O. Box 335, Guelph, Ontario N1H 6K5, Canada
CANADIAN DIMENSION, 801-44 Princess, Winnipeg, Manitoba R3B 1K2, Canada, 957-1519
CANADIAN FICTION MAGAZINE, PO Box 946, Station F, Toronto, Ontario M4Y 2N9, Canada, (416) 534-1259
THE CANADIAN FORUM, 70 The Esplanade, Third Floor, Toronto, Ontario M5E 1R2, Canada, 416-364-2431
CANADIAN JOURNAL OF COMMUNICATION, Box 272, Station R, Toronto, Ontario M4G 3T0, Canada, 425-6756
CANADIAN LITERATURE, University of British Columbia, 2021 West Mall, Vancouver, B.C. V6T 1W5, Canada, (604) 228-2780
CANADIAN PUBLIC POLICY- Analyse de Politiques, Arts Building, University of Guelph, Guelph, Ontario N1G2W1, Canada
CANADIAN SLAVONIC PAPERS, Centre for Russian & East European Studies, University of Toronto, Toronto, Ontario M5S 1A1, Canada
CANADIAN THEATRE REVIEW, 4700 Keele Street, Downsview, Ontario M3J1P3, Canada, 416-667-3768
Canadian Women's Educational Press, 280 Bloor St. W. Suite 313, Toronto, Ontario, Canada, (416) 922-9447
THE CAPILANO REVIEW, 2055 Purcell Way, North Vancouver, B.C. V7J3H5, Canada, 604-986-1911
Catalyst, 315 Blantyre Ave., Scarborough, Ontario M1N2S6, Canada
Charnel House, c/o Crad Kilodney, 134 Haddington Avenue, Toronto, Ontario M5M 2P6, Canada, (416) 482-1341
THE CHELSEA JOURNAL, 1437 College Drive, Saskatoon, Saskatchewan S7N0W6, Canada, 306-343-4561
CICADA, 627 Broadview Ave., Toronto, Ontario M4K 2N9, Canada
CINEMA/QUEBEC, c.p. 309, Station Outremont, Montreal, Quebec H2V 4N1, Canada, 514-272-1058
Coach House Press, 401 Huron St. (Rear), Toronto, Ontario M5S 2G5, Canada, (416) 979-2217
CODA: The Jazz Magazine, Box 87 Stn. J., Toronto, Ont. M4J4X8, Canada
Commen Cents, P.O. Box 3282, Station D, Willowdale, Ontario M2R 3G6, Canada
COMMUNICATOR, P.O. Box 2140, Springhill, Nova Scotia B0M 1X0, Canada
CONNEXIONS, 121 Avenue Road, Toronto, Ontario M5R 2G3, Canada, 960-3903
CROSSCURRENTS, 516 Ave K South, Saskatoon, Saskatchewan, Canada
CTR Publications, York University, Downsview, Ontario M3J1P3, Canada
Curvd H&Z, c/o 60 Fenley Drive, Weston, Ontario, Canada
THE DALHOUSIE REVIEW, Killam Library, Dalhousie University Press Ltd, Attn: Helen L. Gorman, Bus. Mgr., 4413 Halifax, Nova Scotia B3H4H8, Canada
DANCE IN CANADA, 100 Richmond Street, E. Suite 325, Toronto, ON M5C 2P9, Canada
DARK FANTASY, Box 207, Gananoque, Ontario K7G2T7, Canada, 613-382-2794
DAVINCI MAGAZINE, P.O. Box 125, Station LA CITE, Montreal, P.Q. H2X 3M0, Canada
Derwyddon Press, Lodge North, Box 7694, Station A, Edmonton, Alta T5J 2X8, Canada
DESCANT, P.O. Box 314 Station P, Toronto, Ontario M5S 2S8, Canada
DICO, PO Box 6204, Postal Station C, Victoria, B.C. V8P 4G0, Canada, 477-9654
ECLIPSE, 456 Piccadilly Street, London, Ontario N5Y 3G3, Canada, (519) 438-1526
ECW Press, 357 Stong College, York University, Downsview, ON M3J 1P3, Canada, (416) 667-3055
Edition Stencil, PO Box 2608, Station D, Ottawa, Ontario K1P 5W7, Canada, 741-9220
EMERGENCY LIBRARIAN, PO Box 46258, Station G, Vancouver VGR 460, Canada, 487-8365
ENERGY EFFICIENT HOMES, Box 640, Jarvis, Ontario N0A 1J0, Canada
Engendra Press Ltd., Box 235, Westmount Station, Montreal, Quebec H3Z 2T2, Canada, 514 933-1282
ESSAYS ON CANADIAN WRITING, 357 Stong College, York University, Downsview, ON M3J1P3, Canada, (416) 667-3055
EVENT, Douglas College, P.O. Box 2503, New Westminster, B.C. V3L5B2, Canada
EXILE, Box 546, Downsview, Ontario, Canada, 416-9679391/6673892
Exile Editions Ltd, 20 Dale Ave, Toronto, Canada, 416-667-3892
EXPRESSION, 73 Richmond Street, W., Suite 402, Toronto, Ontario M5H 1Z4, Canada, 416-762-7232
Falconiforme Press Ltd., Box 4047, Saskatoon, Saskatchewan S7K3T1, Canada
THE FIDDLEHEAD, The Observatory, Univ. New Brunswick, Fredericton, NB E3B 5A3, Canada, 506-454-3591
FILE MAG, 217 Richmond Street West, Toronto, ON M5V 1W2, Canada, (416) 977-1685
FOURTH DIMENSION, Box 10, Brigham, Quebec J0E 1J0, Canada
THE FRONT, P.O. Box 1355, Kingston, Ontario K7L5C6, Canada
The Front Press, P.O. Box 1355, Kingston, ON K7L5C6, Canada
Gabbro Press, 73 Marion Street, Toronto, Ontario M6R 1E6, Canada, 536-7235
Glenbow-Alberta Institute, 9th Avenue & 1st Street, SE, Calgary, AB T2G 0P3, Canada
Granny Soot Publications, 1871 East Pender Street, Vancouver, BC V5L 1W6, Canada
Greenwich-Meridian, 516 Ave K So, Saskatoon, Sask, Canada
Growing Room Collective, Box 46160, Station G, Vancouver, BC V6R 4G5, Canada, (604) 733-3529
Guernica Editions, PO Box 633, Station N.D.G., Montreal, Quebec H4A 3R1, Canada, (514) 254-2917
THE GUERNICA REVIEW, P.O. Box 633, Sta N.D.G., Montreal, Quebec H4A 3R1, Canada
Hancock House Publishers, 10 Orwell Street, N Vancouver, B.C. V7J 3K1, Canada, 604-980-4113
Harbour Publishing, P.O. Box 119, Madeira Park, BC V0N 2H0, Canada, (604) 883-2730
Highway Book Shop, Cobalt, Ontario P0J1C0, Canada
Historical Society of Alberta, 95 Holmwood Ave. NW, Calgary, Alberta T2K 2G7, Canada
House of Anansi Press Limited/Publishing Co., 35 Britain St., Toronto M5A1R7, Canada, 416-363-5444
HUMANIST IN CANADA, P.O. Box 157, Victoria, B.C. V8W2M6, Canada, 604-388-5323
Hurtig Publishers, 10560-105st, Edmonton, Alberta T5H2W7, Canada, 403-426-2359

IMPULSE, Box 901, Station Q, Toronto, Ontario, Canada
THE INDIAN VOICE, 102-423 West Broadway, Vancouver, British Columbia V5Y1R4, Canada, 604-112-876-0944
Intermedia Press, Box 3294, Vancouver, BC V6B 3X9, Canada
THE INTERNATIONAL FICTION REVIEW, Dept. of German & Russian, UNB, Fredericton, nb, Canada
International Human Systems Institute, 3136 Dundas Street West, Toronto, Ontario M6P 2A1, Canada, (416) 762-1363
INTRINSIC: An International Magazine of Poetry & Poetics, Box 485, Station P, Toronto, Ontario M5S 2T1, Canada, (416) 534-0139
ION, Dept of English, University of Victoria, Victoria, B.C., Canada, (604) 477-6911
JOURNAL OF CANADIAN FICTION, 2050 Mackay Street, Montreal, Quebec H3G 2J1, Canada
JOURNAL OF CANADIAN POETRY, PO Box 5147, Station F, Ottawa K2C 3H4, Canada, (613) 224-6837
JOURNAL of CANADIAN STUDIES/Revue d'etudes canadiennes, Trent Univ., Peterborough, Ont., Canada
KARAKI, 831 Kelvin Street, Coquitlam, B.C., Canada, 604-931-5417
Kids Can Press, 585½ Bloor Street W, Toronto, Ontario M6G 1K5, Canada
LAOMEDON REVIEW, Erindale College, 3359 Mississauga Road, Mississauga, Ontario L5L1C6, Canada
Laurentian Valley Press, 406 Elizabeth Street, Sault Ste. Marie, Ontario P6B 3H4, Canada, (705) 254-1285
LIFELINE, Cobalt, Ontario P0J1C0, Canada
Little Wing Publishing, General Delivery, Lund, B.C. V0N 2G0, Canada
LODGISTIKS, Lodge North, Box 7694, Station A, Edmonton, Alta T5J 2X8, Canada
THE MALAHAT REVIEW, P.O. Box 1700, Victoria, British Columbia V8W 2Y2, Canada
MAMASHEE, R R 1, Inwood, Ontario NON1KO, Canada, (519)844-2805
MANITOBA NATURE (formerly ZOOLOG), Manitoba Museum of Man and Nature, 190 Rupert Ave., Winnipeg, Manitoba R3B0N2, Canada
MATRIX, Box 510, Lennoxville, Quebec J1M 1Z6, Canada, (819) 563-6881
MFRC Publishing, 287 MacPherson Avenue, Toronto, Ontario M4V 1A4, Canada, (416) 961-0381
Miocene Press, 634 Tunstall Cres., Kamloops, BC V2C 3J1, Canada, 604-374-5644
MONCHANIN JOURNAL, Centre Monchanin, 4917 St-Urbain, Montreal, Quebec H2T 2W1, Canada, (514) 288-7229
Montreal Poems, Dewittville JOS 1CO, Canada, 514-264-2866
THE MOOSEHEAD REVIEW, Box 169, Ayer's Cliff, Quebec, Canada, 819-838-5921, 819-838-4801
Mosaic Press/Valley Editions, PO Box 1032, Oakville, Ontario L6J 5E9, Canada
Natural Dynamics, Inc., Box 640, Jarvis, Ont. N0A 1J0, Canada
NATURAL LIFE, Box 640, Jarvis, Ont N0A 1J0, Canada
NEBULA, 970 Copeland, North Bay, Ontario P1B3E4, Canada
NEW LITERATURE & IDEOLOGY, PO Box 727, Adelaide Station, Toronto, Ontario, Canada
Norman Bethune Institute, PO Box 727, Adelaide Station, Toronto, Ontario M5C 2J8, Canada
THE NORTH WIND, Box 65583, Vancouver 12, B. C. V5N 5K5, Canada
NORTHERN LIGHT, 605 Fletcher Argue Bldg., Univ. of Manitoba, Winnipeg, Manitoba R3T2N2, Canada, 204-474-8145
NORTHERN NEIGHBORS, PO Box 1210, Gravenhurst, Ont. P0C 1G0, Canada
Ontario Library Association, 73 Richmond Street, W., Suite 402, Toronto, Ontario M5H 1Z4, Canada, (416) 762-7232
Oolichan Books, P.O. Box 10, Lantzville, British Columbia V0R2H0, Canada, 604-390-4839
OPEN ROAD, Box 6135, Station G, Vancouver, B.C. V6R 4G5, Canada
ORIGINS, Box 5072, Station E, Hamilton, Ontario L8S4K9, Canada, 416-528-0552
OTHER PRESS POETRY REVIEW, 2503 Douglas College, New Westminster, British Columbia, Canada, 522-6038
OUR GENERATION, 3981 boul St Laurent, Montreal, Quebec H2W 1Y5, Canada
OVO MAGAZINE, P.O. Box 1431, Station A, Montreal, Quebec H3C2Z9, Canada, 514-861-8094
PEOPLE'S CANADA DAILY NEWS, PO Box 727, Adelaide Station, Toronto, Ontario M5C 2J8, Canada
PERIODICS, PO Box 69375, Station K, Vancouver, B.C. V5K 4W6, Canada
PHOTOGRAPHIC CALENDAR, PO Box 5207, Station B, Victoria, BC V8R 6N4, Canada
Pink Triangle Press, Box 639, Station A, Toronto, Ontario M5W1G2, Canada, 416-977-6320
Playwrights Canada, 8 York Street, Toronto, Ontario M5J1R2, Canada, 416-363-1581
POETRY CANADA REVIEW, PO Box 1280, Station A, Toronto, Ontario M5W 1G7, Canada, 922-9058
POETRY TORONTO NEWSLETTER, PO Box 181, Station P, Toronto, Ontario M5S 2S7, Canada
The Porcupine's Quill, Inc., 68 Main Street, Erin, Ontario N0B 1T0, Canada, (519) 833-9158
Prairie Publishing Company, Box 24 Station C, Winnipeg R3M 3S7, Canada, (204) 885-6496
Press Gang Publishers, 603 Powell Street, Vancouver, B.C. V6A 1H2, Canada, 253-1224
Press Porcepic Limited, 217-620 View Street, Victoria, B.C. V8W 1J6, Canada
PRISM INTERNATIONAL, 2075 Wesbrook Mall, University of British Columbia, Vancouver, BC V6T1W5, Canada, 604-228-2712
PULP CONTENT, P.O. Box 3868 M.P.O, Vancouver V6B 3Z3, Canada
Pulp Press, P.O. Box 3868 M.P.O., Vancouver V6B 3Z3, Canada
QUEEN'S QUARTERLY: A Canadian Review, Queen's University, Kingston, Ontario K7L3N6, Canada, 613-547-6968
RAINCOAST CHRONICLES, Box 119, Madeira Park, BC V0N2H0, Canada
RAS Communications/Blind Eye Publishing House/Blind Eye Books/Jasmine, 3620 52nd Avenue, Apt. 204, Red Deer, Alberta T4N 4J5, Canada, 406-347-2583
RESOURCES FOR FEMINIST RESEARCH, Ontario Institute for Studies in Education, 252 Bloor Street W., Toronto, Ontario M5S 1V6, Canada
REVIEWING LIBRARIAN, 73 Richmond Street W., Suite 402, Toronto, Ontario M5H 1Z4, Canada, (416) 762-7232
ROOM OF ONE'S OWN, PO Box 46160, Station G, Vancouver, British Columbia V6R 4G5, Canada, 604-733-6276
RUDE, 390 Douro Street, Stratford, Ont, Canada
Rumour Publications, 31 Mercer Street, Toronto, Ontario M5V 1H2, Canada
RUNE, 81 St. Marys St., Box 299, St. Michael's College, Toronto, Ontario M5S1J4, Canada
SECESSION GALLERY NEWSLETTER, P O Box 5207 Stn B, Victoria, BC V8R 6N4, Canada, 604-383-8833
Secession Gallery of Photography, Open Space, PO Box 5207 Stn B, Victoria, BC V8R 6N4, Canada, 604-383-8833
Selene Books, P.O. Box 810, Sta. B, Ottawa, Ontario K1P 5P9, Canada, (613) 232-0098
Sesame Press, c/o English Dept Univ of Windosr, Windsor, Ontario N9B3P4, Canada
Shadow Press, Box 207, Gananoque, Ontario K7G2T7, Canada, 613-382-2794
Simon & Pierre Publishing Co. Ltd., Box 280, Adelaide St. P.O., Toronto, Ontario M5C2J4, Canada, 416-463-5944 order desk 416-463-5945
SOCIALIST FULCRUM, Box 4280 Station A, Victoria, B.C. V8X3X8, Canada
Socialist Party of Canada, Box 4280, Station A, Victoria, B.C. V8X 3X8, Canada
Soft Press, 28 Woodgate Drive, Toronto, Ontario M6N 4W3, Canada
Sono Nis Press, 1745 Blanshard Street, Victoria, B.C. V8W 2J8, Canada, (604) 382-1024 or (604) 382-5722

THE SPHINX, English Dept, Univ Of Regina, Regina, SN S4S0A2, Canada
THE SQUATCHBERRY JOURNAL, Box 205, Geraldton, Ontario P0T1M0, Canada, 807-854-1184
Stagecoach Pub. Co. Ltd., P.O. Box 3399, Langley, BC V3A4R7, Canada
Summerthought Ltd., PO Box 1420, Banff, Alberta T0L0C0, Canada, 762-3919
Sunken Forum Press, Dewittville, Quebec J0S1C0, Canada, 514-264-2866
SUNRISE, 3620 52nd Avenue, Apt. 204, Red Deer, Alberta T4N 4J5, Canada, 406-347-2383
Sydenham Press, RR 1, Inwood, Ontario N0N 1KO, Canada
Talonbooks, 201-1019 East Cordova, Vancouver, British Columbia V6A 1M8, Canada, 604-255-5915
THALIA: Studies in Literary Humor, Dept of English, Univ of Ottawa, Ottawa KN1 6N5, Canada, (613) 231-5955
THIS MAGAZINE, 70 The Esplanade, Third Floor, Toronto, Ontario M5E 1R2, Canada, 364-2431
Thistledown Press, 668 East Place, Saskatoon, Saskatchewan S7J2Z5, Canada, 374-1730
THREE CENT PULP, Box 3868 M.P.O., Vancouver V6B 3Z3, Canada
Thunder Creek Publishing Co-operative, PO Box 239, Sub #1, Moose Jaw, SK S6H 5V0, Canada
Tired Teddybear Productions, Box 485, Station P, Toronto, Ontario M5S 2T1, Canada, (416) 534-0139
TITMOUSE, 720 West 19th Ave., Vancouver, B.C., Canada
Tree Frog Press Limited, 10717 106th Avenue, Edmonton, Alberta T5H3Y9, Canada, 403-425-1505
Trent University, Trent University, Peterborough, ON K9J 7B8, Canada
TWELFTH KEY, 14 4th Street, Toronto Islands, Toronto, ON M5J 2B5, Canada
UNIVERSITY OF WINDSOR REVIEW, c/o University of Windsor, Windsor, Ontario N9B3P4, Canada
Vehicule Press, PO Box 125, Station La Cite, Montreal, Quebec H2X 3M0, Canada, 514-861-8982
Vesta Publications Limited, PO Box 1641, Cornwall, Ont. K6H 5V6, Canada, 613-932-2135
WAVES, Ontario College of Art, 100 McCaul Street, Toronto, Ontario M5T 1W1, Canada, 416-977-5311
WEE GIANT, 178 Bond Street, N., Hamilton, ON L8S 3W6, Canada, 525-2823
WESTERN SPORTSMAN, P.O. Box 737, Regina, Sask. S4P3A8, Canada, (306) 352-8384
WHISTLER ANSWER, General Delivery, Whistler, B.C. V0N 1B0, Canada, (604) 932-5332
WINTERGREEN, PO Box 1294, Kitchener, ON N2G 4G8, Canada
WOT, 657 Andmore Drive, RR 2 Sidney, B.C. V8L 3S1, Canada, 385-1393
WRIT, Two Sussex Ave, Toronto M5S 1J5, Canada, 416-978-4871
WRITERS NEWS MANITOBA, 304 Parkview Street, Winnipeg, MB R3J 1S3, Canada, (204) 885-2652

FRANCE

'THE CASSETTE GAZETTE', Atelier A2, 83 rue de la Tombe-Issoire, Paris 75014, France, 327-1767
Critiques Livres, 173 avenue de la Dhuys, Bagnolet 93170, France, 360 56 90
ELAN POETIQUE LITTERAIRE ET PACIFISTE, 31 Rue Foch, Linselles 59126, France, (20)78.30.68
ENCRES VIVES, Castillon 09800, France
Jean Guenot, 85, rue des Tennerolles, Saint-Cloud 92210, France, 771-79-63
Handshake Editions, Atelier A2, 83 rue de la Tombe-Issoire, Paris 75014, France, 327-1767
PARIS VOICES, c/o Shakespeare & Co., 37 rue de la Bucherie, Paris 75005, France, 806.44.95
THE SPHINX (in French language), 7 rue de l'eveche, Beaugency 45190, France

GREECE

Lycabettus Press, P.O. Box 3391, Kolonaki, Athens, Greece, 363-5567

HOLLAND

ARTZIEN, Eerste Van Der Helststraat 55, Amsterdam, Holland, 768556
BANGE DAGEN, PO Box 812, Rotterdam 3000AV, Holland
Futile, PO Box 812, Rotterdam 3000AV, Holland
Ins & Outs Press, PO Box 3759, Amsterdam, Holland
INS & OUTS, PO Box 3759, Amsterdam, Netherlands, 278483/276868

Kontexts Publications, Eerste Van Der Helststraat 55, Amsterdam, Nthlnd, (020) 768556

Real Free Press Foundation, Dirk van Hasseltssteeg 25, Amsterdam, The Netherlands
WIPE OUT, Dirk Van Hasseltssteeg 25, Amsterdam, The Netherlands
WRITING IN HOLLAND AND FLANDERS, Singel 450, Amsterdam 1017 AV, The Netherlands, (020) 231056

INDIA

CHANDRABHAGA, Tinkonia Bagicha, Cuttack 753 001, Orissa, India, 20-566
Indian Academy of Letters, 35 Feroze Shah Road, New Delhi 110001, India
INDIAN Literature, 35 Feroze Shah Road, New Delhi 110001, India
Jaffe Books, Aymanathuparampil House, Kurichy P.O., Kottayam, Kerala, India

IRELAND

Blackrock Printers, Celtic League, 9 Br Cnoc Sion, Ath Cliath 9, Ireland
Co-op Books Ltd., 50 Merrion Sq., Dublin 2, Ireland
THE MONGREL FOX, 50 Merrion Square, Dublin 2, Ireland
MOVEMENT, SCM Publications, 168 Rathgar Road, Dublin 6, Ireland, Dublin 970975
THE STONY THURSDAY BOOK, 128 Sycamore Ave, Rath Bhan, Limerick, Ireland

ISRAEL

Haifa Publications, 29 Bar Kokhba Street, Tel Aviv, Israel

VOICES - ISRAEL, 38 Nehemia Street, Nave Sha'anan, Haifa, Israel, 04-223332

ITALY

Plain Wrapper Press s.n.c., Via Carlo Cattaneo, 6, Verona 37121, Italy, (045) 38943
Testamento Di Intenzionalita Di Alberto Faietti, via Alghero, 8, Roma 00182, Italy, 06 779088

JAPAN

FEMINIST, 6-5-8 Todoroki, Setagaya-ku, Tokyo 158, Japan, (03) 402-4028, 702-0289
LIBERO INTERNATIONAL, c/o Tohyama, 3-13-5, Shojaku, Settsu, Osaka, 564 Japan
NAMAZU, 2-12-2 Asahimachi, Abeno, Osaka, Japan
POETRY NIPPON, 11-2, 5-chome, Nagaike-cho, Showa-ku, Nagoya 466, Japan
The Poetry Nippon Press, 11-2, 5-Chome, Nagaike-cho, Showa-ku, Nagoya 466, Japan, 052-833-5724

MEXICO

CUADERNOS DEL TERCER MUNDO, Apartado 20-572, Mexico 20 DF, Mexico, 559-30-13
THIRD WORLD, Apartado 20-572, Mexico City, D.F. 20, Mexico, 559-30-13

MOROCCO

BLADES, 4, rue Mohamed Bergach, Tangier-Medina, Morocco
SKULL POLISH, 4, rue Mohamed Bergach, Tangier Medina, Morocco

NEW ZEALAND

BROADSHEET, P.O. Box 5799, Wellesley St. P.O., Auckland, New Zealand
HAWK PRESS Hawk Press, 30 Miro Street, Eastbourne, New Zealand, Wellington 628-648
Heinemann Publisher's (NZ) Ltd, Box 36064, Auckland, New Zealand, 489154
Islands, 4 Sealy Road, Torbay, Auckland 10, New Zealand, 4039007
ISLANDS, A New Zealand Quarterly of Arts & Letters, 4 Sealy Road, Torbay, Auckland 10, New Zealand, 4039007
NEW ZEALAND MONTHLY REVIEW, Box 345, Christchurch, New Zealand
NOUMENON, Sagittarius Publications, 40 Korora Road, Oneroa, Waiheke Island, New Zealand, WH-8502
OUTRIGGER, 4 Miami St, East Mangere, Auckland, New Zealand
PACIFIC QUARTERLY/MOANA, P.O.Box 13-049, Hamilton, New Zealand
PILGRIMS, P O Box 5469, Dunedin, New Zealand
Pilgrims South Press, PO Box 5469, Dunedin, New Zealand

NORTHERN IRELAND

DAWN, 168 Rathgar Road, Belfast 7 6, Northern Ireland

PORTUGAL

CADERNOS DO TERCEIRO MUNDO, Calcada de Combro 10-1, Lisbon 1200, Portugal

REPUBLIC OF IRELAND

CARN (a link between the Celtic nations), Celtic League, 9 Br Cnoc Sion, Ath Cliath 9, Republic of Ireland, Dublin 373957

ROMANIA

ROMANIAN REVIEW, Piata Scinteii 1, Bucharest, Romania, 173836

SAUDI ARABIA

PAINTBRUSH: A Journal of Poetry, Translations & Letters, Dept. of English, Riyadh University, P.O.Box 2456, Riyadh, Saudi Arabia

SCOTLAND

Aberdeen Peoples Press, 163 King St, Aberdeen, Scotland, 0224 29669
Alex Aiken, 48 Merrycrest Avenue, Glasgow G46 6BJ, Scotland
BIG PRINT, 163 King Street, Aberdeen, Scotland
Borderline Press, 96 Halbeath Road, Dunfermline, Scotland
Clo Chailleann, 9 Taybridge Road, Aberfeldy PH15 2BH, Scotland
Findhorn Publications, Findhorn Foundation, The Park, Forres, Morayshire 1V360TZ, Scotland, 030-93-2582
The Lomond Press, 4 Whitecraigs, Kinnesswood, Kinross KY13 7JN, Scotland, 059 284 301
Lothlorien, S2 Bath Street, Edinburg EH 15 1 HF, Scotland, 031 669 9332
ONEARTH IMAGE, Findhorn Foundation, The Park, Forres, Morayshire 1V360TZ, Scotland, 030-93-2582

SICILY

IMPEGNO 70, Via Argentaria Km.4, 91100 Trapani, Sicily
PALERMO ANTIGRUPPO, Villa Scanimac via Argenteria Km 4, 91100, Sicily, 0923-38681
Sicilian Antigruppo, Villa Scanimac, via Argenteria Km 4, Trapani, Sicily, 0923-38681

SIERRA LEONE

AFRICAN LITERATURE TODAY, Fourah Bay College, Univ. of Sierra Leone, Freetown, Sierra Leone

SOUTH AFRICA

ENGLISH STUDIES IN AFRICA-A Journal of the Humanities, Witwatersrand University Press, 1 Jan Smuts Ave., Johannesburg 2001, South Africa, (011) 39-4011 Ext. 794

SWEDEN

SWEDISH BOOKS, Box 2387, S-40316 Goteborg, Sweden, 031-119113

SWITZERLAND

BIBLIOTHEQUE D'HUMANISME ET RENAISSANCE, Librairie Droz S.A., 11r.Massot, 1211 Geneve 12, Switzerland
Ecart Publications, 6, Rue Plantamour, PO Box 253, Geneva CH -1211-1, Switzerland, 022-32.67.94/022-45.73.95
THE GENEVA POND BUBBLES, 6 Rue Plantamour, PO Box 253, Geneve CH-1211-1, Switzerland, 022-32-6794 & 022-45.73.95
Leathern Wing Scribble Press, 6 Rue Plantamour p.o.b. 253, Geneve CH-1211-l, Switzerland, 022-32-6794, 022 45.73.95
THE MERVYN PEAKE REVIEW, Les 3 Chasseurs, 1411 Orzens, Vaud, Switzerland
Mervyn Peake Society Publications, Les 3 Chasseurs, 1411 Orzens, Vaud, Switzerland
V. A. C. (Vereinigung Aktiver Kultur), U Box, 6671 Menzonio, Switzerland
WURZEL, Box 479, Basel 4002, Switzerland

UNITED KINGDOM

A, 47 Wetherby Mansions, Earls Court Square, London SW5 9BH, United Kingdom
ABERDEEN UNIVERSITY REVIEW, Dept Of Mathematics, Edward Wright Building, Dunbar Street, Aberdeen AB9 2TY, United
    Kingdom
AFRICA CURRENTS, Montagu Pubications, Montagu House, High Street, Huntingdon, Cambs., England PE18 6EP, United Kingdom
THE AFRICAN BOOK PUBLISHING RECORD, P.O. Box 56, Oxford 0X13El, United Kingdom, 0865-512934
AGENDA, 5 Cranbourne Court, Albert Bridge Road, London, England SW11 4PE, United Kingdom, 01-228-0700
Agenda Editions, 5 Cranbourne Court, Albert Bridge Rd, London, England SW114PE, United Kingdom, 01-228-0700
THE AGENT, 46 Denbigh Street, London SW1, England, United Kingdom
AKROS, Albert House, 21 Cropwell Road, Radcliffe on Trent, Nottingham NG12 2FT, United Kingdom
ALLIN, 27 Harpes Road, Oxford, United Kingdom
Alphabox Press, 47 Wetherby Mansion, Earls Court Square, London SW5 9BH, United Kingdom
AMBIT, 17 Priory Gardens, London, England N6 5QY, United Kingdom
AMERICAN ARTS PAMPHLET SERIES, Queens Bldg., Univ. of Exeter, Exeter EX4 4QH, United Kingdom
ANARCHIST REVIEW, Over the Water, Sanday, Orkney KW17 2BL, United Kingdom
AND, 262 Randolph Ave, London W9, United Kingdom
ANGEL EXHAUST, 59 Ilford House, Dove Road, London N1 3NA, United Kingdom, 01-354-1669
THE ANGLO-WELSH REVIEW, 1 Cyncoed Ave., Cyncoed Cardiff, Wales, United Kingdom
ANTI-APARTHEID NEWS, 89 Charlotte St., London W1P 2DQ, United Kingdom
Anvil Press Poetry, 69 King George St., London SE10 8PX, United Kingdom
Applied Probability Trust, Department of Pure Mathematics, The University, Sheffield S3 7RH, England, United Kingdom
AQUARIUS, Flat 3, 116 Sutherland Avenue, London W9, United Kingdom
Arc Publications, 6, Plane Street, Lydgate, Todmorden, Lancs, United Kingdom
ARENA SCIENCE FICTION, 6 Rutland Gardens, Birchington, Kent, England CT7 9SN, United Kingdom
THE ARTFUL REPORTER, 12 Harter Street, 4th Floor, Manchester, England M1 6HY, United Kingdom
Askin Publishers, Ltd., 16 Ennismore Ave., London W4 1SF, United Kingdom, 01-994-1314
ATHENE, S.E.A. Bath Academy of Art, Corsham, Wilts, United Kingdom
THE ATLANTIC REVIEW, 115-117 Shepherdess Walk, London, England N1 7QA, United Kingdom, 01-250-4011
THE AUTHOR, 84 Drayton Gardens, London, England SW10 9SD, United Kingdom
Avalon Editions, 9 Bradmore Road, Oxford OX2 6QN, United Kingdom
THE BARD, 10 Uphill Grove, Mill Hill, London NW7 4NJ, United Kingdom
BEDFORDSHIRE MAGAZINE, Crescent Rd., Luton Beds., United Kingdom
THE BIBLIOTHECK, National Library of Scotland, George IV Bridge; Edinburgh EHl lEW, Scotland, UK FK9 4LA, United Kingdom,
    (031) 226-4531
BOOK EXCHANGE, 9 Elizabeth Gardens, Sunbury-on-Thames, Middx TW16 S 9, United Kingdom, Sunbury 84855
BOOKS & BOOKMEN, P.O. Box 294, 2 & 4 Old Pye Street, Victoria St., London SW1P2LR, United Kingdom, 01-222-3533
BRAINWAIFS, Arts Centre, Micrlegate, York, England, United Kingdom, 795219
THE BRITISH ALTERNATIVE PRESS INDEX, PO Box 450, Brighton, Sussex BN1 8GR, United Kingdom
BRITISH BOOK NEWS, 65 Davies St., London W1Y 2AA, United Kingdom, 01-499-8011
BRITISH JOURNAL OF AESTHETICS, The univ. of Sussex, Sch. of Cultural & Comm. Studies, Arts Building, Falmer, Brighton,
    Sussex BN1 9QN, United Kingdom
BRITISH JOURNAL OF IN-SERVICE EDUCATION, British Journal of In-Service Education, Doncaster Metropolitan Institue of
    Higher Education, High Melton, Doncaster DN5 7SZ, United Kingdom
BRITISH NATURALISTS' ASSOCIATION (PUBLISHERS), 6 Chancery Place, The Green, Writtle, Essex, England CM1 3D4, United
    Kingdom, Chelmsford 420756
British Science Fiction Assoc. Ltd., 269 Wykeham Road, Reading RG6 1PL, United Kingdom, 0734-666142
BRITISH THEATRE INSTITUTE NEWSLETTER & REPORT, c/o 125 Markyate Road, Dagenham, Essex RM8 2LB, United Kingdom
BROWNING SOCIETY NOTES, Fitzwilliam College, Cambridge, England, United Kingdom, 0223 458657, ext 63
BTI, c/o 125 Markyate Road, Dagenham, Essex, England RM8 2LB, United Kingdom
BULLETIN OF HISPANIC STUDIES, School Of Hispanic Studies, The University, PO Box 147, Liverpool L69 3BX, United Kingdom
BULLETIN OF THE BOARD OF CELTIC STUDIES, Univ. of Wales Press, 6 Gwennyth Street, Cathays, Cardiff CF2 4YD, United
    Kingdom
THE BULWER LYTTON CHRONICLE, High Orchard, 125 Markyate Rd, Dagenham, Essex RM8 2LB, United Kingdom
BUZZ, 51 Haydons Road, South Wimbledon, London SW19 1HG, United Kingdom, 01-542 7661
Byron Press, The English Dept., Univ. Park, Nottingham, United Kingdom
CANDELABRUM POETRY MAGAZINE, 19 South Hill Park, London NW3 2ST, United Kingdom
Carcanet Press, 330 Corn Exchange Buildings, Manchester, England M4 3BG, United Kingdom, (061) 834-8730

Ceolfrith Press, 27 Stockton Road, Sunderland, Tyne & Wear SR27DF, United Kingdom, 0783-41214
The Chair, 161 Stokesley Crescent, Billingham, Cleveland TS23 1NQ, United Kingdom
THE CHAIR, 161 Stokesly Crescent, Billingham, Cleveland TS23 1NQ, United Kingdom
CHINA QUARTERLY, School of Oriental & African Studies, Malet St., London WC1E 7HP, United Kingdom
CHOCK, Rutherford College, Kent University, Canterbury, Kent CT27NX, United Kingdom, CHISLET 388
Chock Publications, Rutherford College, Kent University, Canterbury, Kent CT27NX, United Kingdom, CHISLET 388
Christopher Davies Publishers Ltd., 52 Mansel Street, Swansea SA1 5EL, United Kingdom, 0792 41933
Cienfuegos Press, Over the Water, Sanday, Orkney KW17 2BL, United Kingdom
CLAIMANTS NEWSPAPER (Claimants Unite), NFCU Publications (International), 134 Villa Rd, Birmingham, England B191NN, United Kingdom
CLARITY, 3 Greenway, Berkhamsted, Herts HP4 3JD, United Kingdom
COMMUNITY ACTION, P.O. Box 665, London SW1X 8DZ, United Kingdom
COMMUNITY DEVELOPMENT JOURNAL, Community Development Journal, Social Administration, The New University of Ulester, Coleraine NI, United Kingdom
CONNECTION NEWS RELEASE, c/o Release Publications Ltd., 1, Elgin Avenue, London W9, United Kingdom
CONTRIBUTORS BULLETIN (also FREELANCE WRITING), 5/9 Bexley Square, Salford, Manchester, England M3 6DB, United Kingdom, 061-832 5079
CRUSADE, 19 Draycott Place, London SW3 2SJ, United Kingdom
CTHULHU, 61 Abbey Road, Heathfield, Fareham, Hampshire, United Kingdom
The Curlew Press, Hare Cott, Kettlesing, Harrogate, Yorkshire, United Kingdom, Harrogate 770686
CURTAINS, 4 Bower Street, Maidstone, Kent ME16 8SD, United Kingdom, 0622-63681
DELTA Literary Review, 2 Bridge House Cottages, Finches Lane, Twyford, Winchester S021 1QF, United Kingdom
The Dickens Fellowship, 48 Doughty Street, London WC1 2LF, United Kingdom
THE DICKENSIAN, 48 Doughty St., London WC1N 2LF, United Kingdom
Dollar of Soul Press, 15 Argyle Road, Swanage, Dorset, United Kingdom
DOUBLE HARNESS, 9 Bradmore Road, Oxford OX2 6QN, United Kingdom
THE DURHAM UNIVERSITY JOURNAL, 43 North Bailey, Durham DH1 3EX, United Kingdom
ECOSYSTEMS, 73 Molesworth St., Wadebridge, Cornwall PL27 7DS, United Kingdom, 2996-7
EDWARDIAN STUDIES, High Orchard, 125 Markyate Road, Dagenham, Essex RM8 2LB, United Kingdom
EFRYDIAU ATHRONYDDOL, 6 Gwennyth St., Cathays, Cardiff, Wales, United Kingdom, Cardiff 31919
Eight Miles High Press, 44 Spa Croft Road, Teall Street, Ossett, W. Yorks WF5 0HE, United Kingdom
ENGLISH DANCE AND SONG, Cecil Sharp House, 2 Regents Park Rd, London NW1 7AY, United Kingdom
Enitharmon Press, 22 Huntingdon Rd, East Finchley, London N2 9DU, United Kingdom, 01 883 8764
ENVOI, Lagan Nam Bann, Ballachulish, Argyll, Scotland, United Kingdom
EPoCH, 2a Lebanon Rd, Croydon, Surrey CR0 6UR, United Kingdom
National Federation Of Claimants Unions Publications, 134 Villa Rd, Birmingham B19 1NN, United Kingdom
FILM, 81 Dean St., London W1V6AA, United Kingdom, 01 437 4355
FOCUS, 269 Wykeham Road, Reading RG6 1PL, United Kingdom
FOLIO, 202 Great Suffolk Street, London SE1 1PR, United Kingdom
FORESIGHT MAGAZINE, 29 Beaufort Av., Hodge Hill, Birmingham, England B346AD, United Kingdom, 021-783-0587
FREEDOM, In Angel Alley, 84B Whitechapel High St, London E1, United Kingdom, 01 247 9249
Freedom Press, In Angel Alley, 84B Whitechapel High St, London E1, United Kingdom, 01-247-9249
FUTURE STUDIES CENTRE NEWSLETTER, 15 Kelso Road, Leeds, W Yorks LS2 9PR, United Kingdom, Leeds 459865
GAIRM, 29 Waterloo St., Glasgow, Scotland G2, United Kingdom
Gairm Publications, 29 Waterloo St, Glasgow, Scotland G2, United Kingdom
Galloping Dog Press, 32 The Promenade, Swansea, West Glamorgan SA1 6EN, United Kingdom
GLENIFFER NEWS, 11 Low Road, Castlehead, Paisley PA2 6AQ, United Kingdom
Gleniffer Press, 11 Low Road, Castlehead, Paisley PA2 6AQ, United Kingdom, 041-889-9579
GLOBAL TAPESTRY JOURNAL, 1 Spring Bank, Salesbury, Blackburn, Lancs, England BB1 9EU, United Kingdom, 0254 49128
GREAT WORKS, 25 Portland Road, Bishops Stortford, Hertfordshire, United Kingdom
Great Works Editions, 25 Portland Rd., Bishops Stortford, Herts, United Kingdom
GREENPEACE (London) Newsletter, c/o 6 Endsleigh St., London WC1, United Kingdom
THE GROVE, Naturist Headquarters, Sheepcote, Orpington, Kent BR5 4ET, United Kingdom, Orpington 71200
Guildford Poets Press, 10 Ashcroft, Shalford, Guildford, Surrey, United Kingdom
Hans Zell Publishers Ltd., P O Box 56, Oxford OX1 3EL, United Kingdom
HEALTHY LIVING, 16 Ennismore Ave, London W4 1SF, United Kingdom, 01-994-1314
High Orchard Press, 125 Markyate Road, Dagenham, Essex, England RM8 2LB, United Kingdom
Hippopotamus Press, 26 Cedar Road, Sutton, Surrey SM25DG, United Kingdom, 01-643-1970
HOUSMAN SOCIETY JOURNAL, Penybryn House, Boot Street, Whittington, Oswestry, Salop SY11 4DG, United Kingdom, 069162313
HOWL, PO Box 19, Tonbridge, Kent, England, United Kingdom
Hyde Park Socialist, 21 Brightling Road, London SE4 1SQ, United Kingdom
IDO-LETRO, International Language (IDO) Society of Gt. Britain, 14 Stray Towers, Victoria Road, Harrogate, N. Yorkshire HG2 0LJ, United Kingdom
IMPETUS MAGAZINE, 68 Hillfield Avenue, Hornsey, London N8 7DN, United Kingdom, 01-348-2927
IN TOUCH, The Grail, 125 Waxwell Lane, Pinner, Middx HA5 3ER, United Kingdom
Independent Press Distribution, Administrator: Heidi Armbruster, c/o 12 Stevenage Road, London SW6 6ES, United Kingdom
INDEX ON CENSORSHIP, 21 Russell St., Covent Garden, London WC2B 5HP, United Kingdom, 01-836-0024
Ink Links Ltd., 271 Kentish Town Road, London NW5 2JS, United Kingdom, 01-267-0661
THE INQUIRER, 1-6 Essex Street, London WC2R 3HY, United Kingdom
Institute of Pyramidology, 31 Station Road, Harpenden, Herts AL5 4XB, United Kingdom, Harpenden 64510
Interim Press, 3 Thornton Close, Budleigh Salterton, Devon EX9 6PJ, United Kingdom
International Language (IDO) Society of Great Britain, 18 Lane Head Rise, Staincross Common, Mapplewell, Barnsley S75 6NQ, United Kingdom
INTERNATIONAL P.E.N. BULLETIN of SELECTED BOOKS, International PEN, 7 Dilke Street, London SW3 4JE, United Kingdom
IRON, 5 Marden Terrace, Cullercoats, North Shields, Tyne & Wear NE30 4PD, United Kingdom, 0632-531901
Iron Press, 5 Marden Terrace, Cullercoats, Northumberland, United Kingdom
THE JOURNAL OF COMMONWEALTH LITERATURE, School of English, Univ. of Leeds, Leeds LS2 9JT, United Kingdom
Kawabata Press, Knill Cross House, Higher Anderton Road, Millbrook, Nr Torpoint, Cornwall, United Kingdom

KEEPSAKE POEMS, 26 Sydney Road, Richmond, Surrey TW9 UEB, United Kingdom, 01 940 9364
THE KIPLING JOURNAL, 18 Northumberland Ave., London WC2N 5BJ, United Kingdom
KRAX, 63 Dixon Lane, Leeds, Yorkshire LS12 4RR, United Kingdom
KROKLOK, 262 Randolph Ave, London W9, United Kingdom
Kropotkin's Lighthouse Publications, c/o Housmans Bookshop, 5 Caledonian Rd., London N19DX, United Kingdom
L.W.M. Publications, 5 Beech Terrace, Undercliffe, Bradford, West Yorkshire, England BD3 0PY, United Kingdom
LABOUR LEADER, 49 Top Moor Side, Leeds LS11 9LW, United Kingdom
THE LEY HUNTER: The Magazine Of Earth Mysteries, PO Box 152, London, England N10 2EF, United Kingdom, 01-883-3949
LIB ED, 6 Beaconsfield Road, Leicester, England, United Kingdom, 0533-21866
LIBERAL NEWS, 1 Whitehall Place, London SW1A2HE, United Kingdom, 01 839 3658
LIBRARIANS FOR SOCIAL CHANGE, PO Box 450, Brighton, Sussex BN1 8GR, United Kingdom
LIBRARY REVIEW, 30 Clydeholm Road, Glasgow G14 OBJ, United Kingdom
LINES REVIEW, Macdonald, Edgefield Rd, Loanhead, Midlothian EH20 9SY, United Kingdom
THE LITTLE WORD MACHINE, 5 Beech Terrace, Undercliffe, Bradford, West Yorkshire, England BD3 0PY, United Kingdom
Liverpool University Press, School of Hispanic Studies, The Univ., P.O. Box 147, Liverpool L69 3BX, United Kingdom
LLEN CYMRU (Board of Celtic Studies), 6 Gwennyth Sr., Cathays, Cardiff, Wales, United Kingdom
LOL, Lolfa, Y, Talybont, Dyfed, Wales SY24 5ER, United Kingdom
LONDON MYSTERY MAGAZINE, 268-270 Vauxhall Bridge Rd., London SW1 1BB, United Kingdom
LOOT, 83(b) London Road, Peterborough, Cambs, United Kingdom
LORE AND LANGUAGE, The Centre for English Cultural Tradition and Language, The University, Sheffield S10 2TN, United Kingdom, Sheffield 78555 ext 4211
LUDD'S MILL, 44 Spa Croft Road, Teall Street, Ossett, West Yorkshire WF50HE, United Kingdom, Ossett 275814
The Mandeville Press, The Mandeville Press, 2 Taylor's Hill, Hitchin, Hertfordshire SG49AD, United Kingdom
The Many Press, 15 Norcott Road, London N16 7BJ, United Kingdom
MATHEMATICAL SPECTRUM, Dept of Pure Mathematics, The University, Sheffield S3 7RH, United Kingdom
MATRIX, 269 Wykeham Road, Reading RG6 1PL, United Kingdom
MEDICAL HISTORY, Wellcome Institute for the History of Medicine, 183 Euston Rd., London NW1 2BP, United Kingdom
The Menard Press, 23 Fitzwarren Gardens, London N19, United Kingdom
MINORITY RIGHTS GROUP REPORTS, MRG, 36 Craven St., London WC2N5NG, United Kingdom, 01-586-0439
MUSIC AND LETTERS, 32 Holywell, Oxford, United Kingdom
MUSICAL OPINION, Spring Road, Barn & Mouth, United Kingdom
Narbulla Agency, 4 Stradella Rd., Herne Hill, London SE24 9HA, United Kingdom
NEW DEPARTURES, Piedmont, Bisley, Stroud, Glos., England GL6 7BU, United Kingdom
THE NEW ECOLOGIST, 73 Molesworth Street, Wadebridge, Cornwall PL27 7DS, United Kingdom, 2996-7
NEW EDINBURGH REVIEW, 1 Buccleuch Place, Edinburgh, Scotland EH8 9LW, United Kingdom
NEW GERMAN STUDIES, Dept Of German, Univ. Hull, Hull HU6 7RX, United Kingdom, 0482 46311 (extn 7652)
NEW HUMANIST, 88 Islington High St, London N1 8EW, United Kingdom
NEWS FROM NEASDEN, 12 Fleet Road, London NW3 2QS, United Kingdom
Northern House, 19 Haldane Terrace, Newcastle upon Tyne NE2 3AN, United Kingdom
NORTHERN LINE, 75 Outwood Lane, Leeds, W. Yorks LS18 4HU, United Kingdom, 0532-588995
NOTES & QUERIES: for Readers & Writers, Collectors & Librarians, Pembroke College, Oxford OX1 1DW, United Kingdom
NOTTINGHAM MEDIAEVAL STUDIES, The University, Nottingham NG7 2RD, United Kingdom
John L Noyce, Publisher, P.O. Box 450, Brighton, Sussex BN1 8GR, United Kingdom
The Oak Arts Workshop Limited, 10 Snow Hill, Clare, Sudbury, Suff, United Kingdom
OASIS, 12 Stevenage Road, London SW6 6ES, United Kingdom
Oasis Books, 12 Stevenage Rd., London, England SW6 6ES, United Kingdom
Oleander Press, 17 Stansgate Ave., Cambridge CB2 2QZ, United Kingdom
ONE, 16 Rosemary Avenue, London N3 2QN, United Kingdom
Openings Press, Rooksmoor House, Woodchester, Glos, United Kingdom
THE ORCADIAN, c/o W. R. Mackintosh, THE ORCADIAN Office, Kirkwall, Orkney, United Kingdom
ORE, The Towers, Stevenage, Herts, England SG1 1HE, United Kingdom
Oriel, 53 Charles St., Cardiff, Wales CF14ED, United Kingdom, 0222-395548
OUTCOME, c/o 78A Penny Street, Lancaster, England, United Kingdom
OUTPOSTS, 72 Burwood Road, Walton-On-Thames, Surrey KT12 4AL, United Kingdom
Outposts Publications, 32 Burwood Rd, Walton-on-Thames, Surrey KT12 4AL, United Kingdom, Walton-on-Thames 40712
Oxus Press, 16 Haslemere Rd., London N.8., United Kingdom
P.E.N. BROADSHEET, 7 Dilke Street, Chelsea, London SW3 4JE, United Kingdom, 01-352-9549
PEACE NEWS "For Non-Violent Revolution", 8 Elm Avenue, Nottingham, United Kingdom, 0602 53587
PENNINE PLATFORM, 4 Insmanthorpe Hall Farm, Wetherby, West Yorks LS22 5EZ, United Kingdom, 0927-64674
PEOPLE'S NEWS SERVICE, Oxford House, Derbyshire Street, London E2 6HG, United Kingdom, 01-739-3630
Permanent Press, 52 Cascade Avenue, London, N10 England, United Kingdom
PHOENIX BROADSHEETS, 78 Cambridge Street, Leicester LE3 0JP, United Kingdom
Pirate Press, 107 Valley Drive, Kingsbury, London NW9 9NT, United Kingdom
PLANTAGENET PRODUCTIONS, Recorded Library of the Spoken Word, Westridge, Highclere, Nr. Newbury, Royal Berkshire RG15 9PJ, United Kingdom
Plantagenet Productions, Westridge, Highclere, Nr. Newbury, Berkshire RG159PJ, United Kingdom
PNS, Oxford House, Derbyshire Street, London E2 6HG, United Kingdom, 01-739-3630
POETRY AND AUDIENCE, The School of English, University of Leeds, Leeds LS2 9JT, United Kingdom
Poetry Leeds Publications, 75 Outwood Lane, Leeds, W. Yorks LS18 4HU, United Kingdom, 0532-588995
POETRY NATION REVIEW, 330 Corn Exchange, Manchester M4 3BG, United Kingdom
POETRY NOTTINGHAM, Chapel House, Belper Lane End, Belper, Derbyshire OE5 2DL, United Kingdom
Poetry Nottingham Society Publications, Chapel House, Belperlane End, Derbyshire DE5 2DL, United Kingdom
POETRY QUARTERLY (previously CURLEW), Harecott, Kettlesing, Harrogate, Yorkshire, United Kingdom, Harrogate 770686
POETRY REVIEW, 21 Earls Court Square, London SW5, United Kingdom, 01-373-7861
POETRY WALES, 52 Mansei Street, Swansea SA1 5EL, United Kingdom, (0792) 41933
Pressed Curtains, 4 Bower Street, Maidstone, Kent ME16 8SD, United Kingdom, 0622-63681
Priapus, 37 Lombardy Dr, Berkhamsted, Herts, United Kingdom
Proem Pamphlets, The Festival Office, Ilkley, W. Yorkshire LS29 8HF, United Kingdom, Ilkley 608925
PURPLE PATCH, 106 Walsall Road, Stone Cross, West Bromwich, West Midlands, United Kingdom

PYRAMIDOLOGY MAGAZINE, 31 Station Road, Harpenden, Herts AL5 4XB, United Kingdom, Harpenden 64510
RADICAL BOOKSELLER, R. B. Birchcliffe, Hebder Bridge, Yorkshire, United Kingdom
Raven Publications, 29 Parkers Road, Sheffield S10 1BN, United Kingdom, Sheff. 664-862
Red Candle Press, 19 South Hill Park, London NW3 2ST, United Kingdom
RENEWAL, 3A High St., Esher, Surrey KT10 9RP, United Kingdom
RESURGENCE, Ford House, Hartland, Bideford, Devon, Wales, United Kingdom, 820317-0239D1
ROUGH JUSTICE for the Single Homeless, 90 St Mary Street, Cardiff, Wales, United Kingdom, Cardiff 36054
Runa Press, Monkstown, Co Dublin, Eire, United Kingdom
SAMPHIRE, Heronshaw, Holbrook, Ipswich, United Kingdom
SAPPHO, BCM/PETREL, London WC1V6XX, United Kingdom
Sappho Publications Ltd, BCM/Petrel, London WC1V6XX, United Kingdom
The Sceptre Press, The Sceptre Press, Knotting, Bedford MK44 1AF, United Kingdom
SCILLONIAN MAGAZINE, c/o T. Mumford, St. Mary's, Isles of Scilly, Cornwall, United Kingdom
SCREEN, 29 Old Compton St., London W1V 5PL, United Kingdom
The Sean Dorman Manuscript Society, 4 Union Place, Fowey, Cornwall PL23 1BY, United Kingdom
Second Aeon Publications, 19 Southminster Road, PENYLAN, Cardiff, Wales CF2 5AT, United Kingdom, 0222-493093
SELF AND SOCIETY, 62 Southwark Bridge Rd, London SE1 0AU, United Kingdom
SEPIA, Knill Cross House, Higher Anderton Road, Millbrook, Nr Torpoint, Cornwall, United Kingdom
SHAVIAN—JOURNAL OF BERNARD SHAW, 125 Markyate Rd, Dagenham, Essex RM8 2LB, United Kingdom
Sheffield Free Press, c/o Ujamaa, 259 Glossop Rd, Sheffield, United Kingdom
SMOKE, 23a Brent Way, Halewood, Liverpool, England L26 9XH, United Kingdom
Society for Education in Film and TV, 29 Old Compton Street, London W1V 5PL, United Kingdom
Spectacular Diseases, 83(b) London Road, Peterborough, Cambs, United Kingdom
Spectre Press, 61 Abbey Road, Heathfield, Fareham, Hampshire, United Kingdom
SPUR, WDM, Bedford Chambers, Covent Garden, London WC2E 8HA, United Kingdom
STAND, 19 Haldane Tce, Newcastle-on-Tyne NE23AN, United Kingdom
START, Burslem Leisure Centre, Market Place, Burslem, Stoke-on-Trent, England ST6 3DS, United Kingdom, 0782-813363
Street Editions, 31 Panton St., Cambridge, England, United Kingdom
STUDIA CELTICA, University of Wales Press, 6 Gwennyth St., Cathays, Cardiff CF2 4YD, United Kingdom, Cardiff 31919
STUDIES IN DESIGN EDUCATION AND CRAFT, Keele University, Keele, Staffordshire ST5 5BG, United Kingdom, 0782-621111
STUDIES IN LABOUR HISTORY, P.O. Box 450, Brighton BN18GR, United Kingdom
SUMMER BULLETIN, 47 Timothy Lane, Batley, West Yorkshire, United Kingdom, Batley 474238
SUPRANORMAL, 1983, 15, Oakapple Road, Southwick, Sussex BN4 4YL, United Kingdom
TANGENT, 58 Blakes Lane, New Malden, Surrey, England KT3 6NX, United Kingdom
Tangent Books, 58 Blakes Lane, New Malden, Surrey, England KT3 6NX, United Kingdom, 01-942-0979
Taurus Press of Willow Dene, 2 Willow Dene, Bushey, Heath, Herts WD2 1PS, United Kingdom
TENNYSON RESEARCH BULLETIN, Tennyson Society Publications Board, Tennyson Research Centre, Central Library, Free School
 Lane, Lincoln LN2 1EZ, United Kingdom
THEATRE NOTEBOOK, 103 Ralph Court, Queensway, London W2 5HU, United Kingdom
Third World Publications Ltd., 151 Stratford Road, Birmingham B111RD, United Kingdom, 021-773-6572
THOMAS HARDY YEARBOOK, Mt Durand, St Peter Port, Guernsey CI, United Kingdom
TOCHER, School of Scotish Studies, 27 George Square, Edinburgh EH8 9LD, United Kingdom
Top Stone Books, 29 Station Road, Harpenden, Hertfordshire AL5 4XB, United Kingdom, Harpenden 64510
Toucan, Mt. Durand, St Peter Port, Guernsey, United Kingdom
TRANSFORMACTION, Harpford, Sidmouth, Devon EX10 0NH, United Kingdom
TRIVIUM, Dept. Of History, St. David's University College, Lampeter, Dyfed SA48 7ED, United Kingdom, 0570-422351 ext 37
Uldale House Publ, 1 Uldale Dr, Egglescliffe, Cleveland TS16 9DW, United Kingdom
UNCLE NASTY SERIES, 73 Ware Street, Bearsted, Mainstone, Kent, England ME14 4PG, United Kingdom, (0622) 36436
UNDERCURRENTS, 27 Clerkenwell Close, London, England EC1R 0AT, United Kingdom
URBANE GORILLA, 29 Parker Rd, Sheffield S10 1BN, United Kingdom
VECTOR, 269 Wykeham Road, Reading RG6 1PL, United Kingdom, 0734-666142
VIEWPOINT AQUARIUS, c/oFish Tanks Ltd, 49 Blandford St., London W1 3AF, United Kingdom
A WAKE NEWSLITTER, Studies Of James Joyce's Finnegans Wake, Department of Literature, University of Essex, Wivenhoe Park,
 Colchester, Essex CO4 3SQ, United Kingdom
WELLSIANA, The World Of H.G. Wells, High Orchard, 125 Markyate Rd, Dagenham, Essex RM8 2LB, United Kingdom
WELSH HISTORY REVIEW, Queens College, Oxford, Oxford, United Kingdom
WEYFARERS, 10 Ashcroft, Shalford, Guildford, Surrey, United Kingdom
White Crescent Press, Crescent Road, Luton Beds, United Kingdom
WHOLE EARTH, 11 George St, Brighton, Sussex BN21RH, United Kingdom
Wilfion Books, Publishers, 12 Townhead Terrace, Paisley, Renfrewshire, Scotland PA1 2AX, United Kingdom
Windows Project, 23a Brent Way, Halewood, Liverpool, England L26 9XH, United Kingdom
WOMEN'S STUDIES NEWSLETTER, 176 Hagley Road, Stourbridge, W. Midlands DY8 2JN, United Kingdom, 038 43 5131
Workshop Press Ltd., 2 Culham Court, Granville Rd, London N44JB, United Kingdom, 01-348-4054
Writers Forum, 262 Randolph Ave., London W9, United Kingdom
WRITING, 4 Union Place, Fowey, Cornwall PL23 1BY, United Kingdom
Y GWYDDONYDD, 6 Gwennyth St., Cathays, Cadiff, Wales, United Kingdom, 0222-31919
Y'lolfa, Talybont, Dyfed, Wales SY24 5ER, United Kingdom
Zed Press, 57 Caledonian Road, London N19DN, United Kingdom
ZERO ONE, 39 Minford Gardens, West Kensington, London W14 0AP, United Kingdom

BB Books, 1 Spring Bank, Salesbury, Blackburn, Lancs BB1 9EU, England, UK, 0254 49128

Balsam Flex, c/o I8 Clairview Road, London, SW I6, England
BALSAM FLEX SHEET, c/o I8 Clairview Road, London, SW I6, England
GAZUNDA, 73 Ware Street, Bearsted, Maidstone, Kent ME14 4PG, England, (0622) 36436
JOE SOAP'S CANOE, 298 High Road, Trimley St. Martin, Ipswich, Suff, England
Jules Verne Circle, 125 Markyate Road, Dagenham, Essex RM82LB, England
JULES VERNE VOYAGER, 125 Markyate Road, Dagenham, Essex RM82LB, England
KUDOS, 78 Easterly Road, Leeds LS8 3AN, England
SHAW NEWSLETTER, High Orchard, 125 Markyate Road, Dagenham, Essex RM 82 LB, England
Shaw Society, High Orchard, 125 Markyate Road, Dagenham, Essex RM82LB, England

Syntaxophone Publications, 10 Snow Hill, Clare, Sudbury, Suffolk, England
VANESSA POETRY MAGAZINE, 15 Norcott Road, London, England N16 7BJ, United Kingdom
Speed Limit Press, 33 Bryn Glas, Hollybush, Cwmbran, Gwent NP4 4LG, Wales, 953 64798
Thirty Press, Ltd., 19 Draycott Place, London SW3, UK

WEST GERMANY

Expanded Media Editions, Herwarthstr. 27, Bonn 5300, W-Germany, 02221/655 887
SOFT NEED, Herwarthstr. 27, Bonn 5300, W-Germany, 02221/655 887

KOMPOST, 6941 Lohrbach, Western Germany
Maro Verlag, Bismarckstr, 7½, D-8900 Augsburg, West Germany, 0821-577131
Verlag Pohl'n'Mayer, P. Box, D-8950 Kaufbeuren, West Germany, 089-333-980

Distributors

The following is a list of some 170 book distributors, book jobbers and magazine agents. Most of them have an active account with Dustbooks. Generally, an **Agent** (A) sells magazine subscriptions to libraries and other institutions (in the case of Dustbooks it handles the **Small Press Review**): a jobber (J) sells single copies of books to these same institutions; and a **distributor** (D) is a wholesaler who sells in quantity to bookstores, though will often mailorder single titles as the listings indicate. We suggest enclosing a SASE when writing for information to any of these listings; and always query before sending copies of books or magazines for possible distribution.

Abrahams Magazine Service Inc. 56 E. 13th St., NYC 10003 (A)
Academic Library Service, 141 N.E. 38th Terrace, Oklahoma City, OK 73105 (J)
ACP Distributors, 105 Pine Rd., Sewickley, PA 15143 (D)
Alesco, Box 1488, Madison, WI 53701 (J)
Aloe Book Agency, P.O. Box 4349, Johannesburg, Zambia 2000 (J)
American Jewish Congress, 15 East 84th St., NYC 10028 (J)
Americana West, P.O. Box 4373, Fresno, CA 93744 (D)
Ancorp Subscription Service, 3527 Broadway, Suite 401, Kansas City, MO 64111 (A)
Aquila Retail Services, P.O. Box 1, Portree, Isle of Skye, Scotland, United Kingdom, 1V51 9BT (A)
Aquinas Subscription Agency, 253 East Fourth St., St. Paul, MN 55101 (A)
Arthur J. Viders Company, Inc., 5017A North Grady, Tampa, FL 33614 (J)
Atlantis Distributors, 1725 Carondelet, New Orleans, LA 70130 (D)
Authors & Publishers Marketing Assoc., P.O. Box 3723, Van Nuys, CA 91407 (D)
BCN Agencies PTY Ltd., 161 Sturt St., Melbourne, Victoria, 3205 Australia (J)
Bacon Pamphlet Service, East Chatham, NY 12060 (J)
Bailey Subscription Agents, Ltd., Warner House, Folkestone, Kent, England, UK, CT19 6PH (A)
Baker & Taylor Co., P.O. Box 931, Clarksville, TX 75426 (J)
Baker & Taylor Co., P.O. Box 458, Commerce, GA 30529 (J)
Baker & Taylor Co., Gladiola Ave., Momence, IL 60954 (J)
Baker & Taylor Co., 380 Edison Way, Reno, NV 89502 (J)
Baker & Taylor Co., P. O. Box 6500, 6 Kirby, Somerville, NJ 08876 (J)
Ballen Booksellers, 66 Austin Blvd., Commack, L.I., NY 11725 (J)
Ballenger's Book Service, P.O. Box 2552, Salt Lake City, UT 84110 (J)
R.E. Banta, Bookseller, Crawfordsville, IN 47933 (J)
Richard S. Barnes, Bookseller, 909 Foster, Evanston, IL 60201 (J)
Berkeley Educational Paperbacks, 2480 Bancroft Way, Berkeley, CA 94704 (J)
Beverly Books INC., 36 E. Price St., Linden, NJ 07036 (J)
Big Rapids Distribution Co., 230 Adair St., Detroit, MI 48207 (D)
Blackwell North America, 10300 SW Allen Blvd., Beaverton, OR 97005 (J)
Blackwell North America, 1001 Fries Mill Rd., Blackwood, NJ 08012 (J)
Blackwell's AOB Dept., Hythe Bridge St., Oxford, United Kingdom, OXI 2ET (J)
Will H. Blackwell, 1803 Howard St., Jackson, MS 39202 (J)
P & H Bliss, P.O. Box 1079, Middletown, CT 06457 (J)
Book & Periodical Acq., Ltd., 33 Coronet Rd., Toronto, Canada, ON M8Z2L9 (J)
Book Business Project, The Visual Studies Workshop, 4 Elton St., Rochester, NY 14607 (D)
Bookazine Co. Inc., 303 West 10th St., NYC, NY 10014 (J)
Bookimpen Booksellers, Molenstraat 20, Den Haag Hind, Netherlands (J)
Bookpeople, 2940 Seventh St., Berkeley, CA 94710 (D)
Bookslinger, Jim Sitter, 2163 Ford Parkway, St. Paul, MN 55116 (D)

Booksmith Distributing Co., 450 Summer St., Boston, MA 02210 (J)
Bookspace, 3262 N. Clark, Chicago, IL 60657 (D)
Broadcast Marketing Corp., 4 East 52nd St., NYC, NY 10022 (D)
Brodart Inc., 500 Arch St., Williamsport, PA 17701 (J)
Campbell and Hall, 450 Summer St., Boston, MA 02210 (J)
Canebsco Subscription Services, 6 Thorncliffe Park Dr., Toronto, Ontario, Can. M4H 1H3 (A)
Carlisle Taylor, 115 E. 23rd St., NYC, NY 10010 (J)
Clark Subscription Agency, 17-19 Washington Ave., Tenaply, NJ 07670 (A)
Charles W. Clark Co. Inc., 564 Smith St., Farmingdale, NY 11735 (J)
Claude Gill Subscriptions, Aldermaston Court, Aldermaston, Reading, U.K. RG7 4PF (A)
Cloudland Literary Press Group Dist., 791 St. Clair Ave., West, Toronto, Ontario, Can. M6C 1B8 (D)
Collier Macmillan Dist. Serv. Ltd., 76 Bolsover St., London, U.K. W1P 7HH (J)
Coutts Library Service, 736-738 Cayuga St., Lewiston, NY 14092 (J)
Customer Book Service, Bx. 281 - Montgomery Cn., Rocky Hill, NJ 08553 (J)
Davis Agency, P.O. Box 2382, London, Ontario, Canada N6A5A7 (A)
Wm. Dawson & Sons, Ltd., 10-14 Macklin St., London, England, U.K. WC2B 5NG (J)
Dawson Subscription Agency, 6 Thorncliffe Park, Toronto, Canada ON (A)
Dekker En Nordemanns, O.Z. Voorburgwal 239, Amsterdam-C, The Netherlands (J)
Dewolfe & Fiske Inc., 10 Pequot Park, Canton, MA 02021 (J)
Diliart, Vallarta No. 1696, Gaudalajara, Mexico JA (J)
Dimondstein Book Co. Inc., 38 Portman Rd., New Rochelle, NY 10801 (J)
Distributors, 702 S. Michigan, South Bend, IN 46618
Distributors International, 1150 18th Street, Santa Monica, CA 90404 (D)
Drown News Agency, 15172 Golden West Circle, Westminster, CA 92683 (D)
E.B.S. Book Service, 290 Broadway, Lynbrook, NY 11563 (J)
Eastern Book Co., 131 Middle St., Portland, ME 04112 (J)
Eastern News Distributors, 111 Eighth Avenue, NYC, NY 10011 (D)
EBSCO Industries, 1st Avenue at 13th Streets, Birmingham, AL 35203 (J)
EBSCO Industries, 2727 Bryant St., 100, Denver, CO 80211 (J)
EBSCO Subscription Service, 840 Malcolm Rd., Burlingame, CA 94010 (A)
Edco-Vis Associates, Box 158, Middleton, WI 53562 (J)
Eddison Press Library Services, 22-24 Buckingham Palace Rd., London S.W. 1, U.K. (J)
Educational Services Div., 580 Bloomfield Avenue, Bloomfield, NJ 07003 (J)
El Camino Real, P.O. Box 25426-A, Denver, CO 80225 (D)
Ellsworth Magazine Service, 332 S. Michigan Ave., Chicago, IL 60604 (A)
Emery Pratt Co., 1966 W. Main Street, Owosso, MI 48867 (J)
Exclusive Books Pty. Ltd., P.O. Box 17554, Hillbrow, Rep. So. Africa 2038 (J)
F.W. Faxon Co. Inc., Bridget McDonough, 15 Southwest Park, Westwood, MA 02090 (A)
Reginald F. Fennell, Subscription Service, Jackson, MI 49201 (A)
Louis Goldberg, Library Book Supplier, 2018 Haines Street, Philadelphia, PA 19138 (J)
Grahame Library & Sub Centre, Attn. L. Barrett, 35-51 Mitchell St., N. Sydney N.S.W. Australia (A)
Gryphon House Distributors, P.O. Box 274, 3706 Otis Street, Mt. Ranier, MD 20822 (A)
R. Hill & Son Ltd., Gillies Avenue & Eden Street, Newmarket, Auckland 1, New Zealand (A)
R. Hill & Son Ltd., 20 Burlington Street, Crows Nest, N.S.W. Australia 2065 (A)
Lori Harding, Box 781, Uncan, Canada BC (D)
Hawaiian Magazine Distributors, 222 Koula St., Honolulu, HI 96813 (A)
Hennessy Company, 130 N. Main Street, Butte, MT 59701 (J)
Herbert Lang & Cie Ag., Munzhraben 2, CH-3000, Bern 7, Switzerland (J)
Hunter Publishing Co., P.O. Box 9533, Phoenix, AZ 85068 (A)
Ingram Book Co., Baltimore-Washington Industrial Park, 8301 Sherwick Ct., Jessup, MD 20794 (D)
Instructor Sub Agency, Instructor Park, Dansville, NY 14437 (A)
International Service Co., 333 Fourth Ave., Indialantic, FL 32903 (J)
International Univ Booksellers, 101 5th Avenue, NYC, NY 10003 (J)
Japan Publications Trading Co., P.O. Box 5030, Tokyo International, Tokyo, Japan 100-31 (J)
Jende-Hagan Co., P.O. Box 177, Frederick, CO 80530 (J)
Walter J. Johnson, Inc., 355 Chestnut/Bk Dpt., Norwood, NJ 07648 (J)
Joseph Poole & Co. Ltd., 86 Charing Cross Road, London, U.K. Wc2H OJB (J)
Josten's Library Service Div., 1301 Cliff Rd., Burnsville, MN 55337 (J)
Key Book Service, 425 Asylum Street, Bridgeport, CT 06610 (J)
Kinoe Shobo, Ltd., 34-4 Sakuragaoka 5-Chome, Setagaya-Ku, Tokyo, Japan 156 (J)
Kleins of Westport, 4450 Main Street, Westport, CT 06880 (J)
Kunst Und Wissen, D-7000 Stuttgart 1, Wilhelmstrabe 4, Postfach 46, West Germany (J)
Liberation Book Distributors, 16 East 18th Street, NYC, NY 10003 (D)

Liberation Info Dist., Attn: Hodari Ali, 1622 New Jersey Avenue, N.W., Washington, DC 20001 (J)
Liverpool Distributors, 1779 W. Adams Blvd., Los Angeles, CA 90018 (D)
McAinsh & Co. Limited, 1835 Yonge Street, Toronto, Canada ON M4S 1L6 (J)
McGregor Magazine Agency, Mt. Morris, IL 61054 (A)
Marshall Field & Co., 111 N. State Street, Chicago, IL 60690 (J)
Martinus Nijhoff B V, P.O. Box 269, H R 4309 Den Haa, The Netherlands G (J)
Maryknoll Publications, Maryknoll, NY 10545 (J)
Sandra Mattielli, Recreation Services Agency, Arts & Crafts, APO San Francisco, CA 96301 (A)
Meier & Frank Co., 1438 NW Irving, Portland, OR 97209 (J)
Mexican Book Service, Loft Bookshop in Village, St. Peters, PA 19470 (J)
Midwest Library Service, 11400 Dorsett Road, Maryland Hts., MO 63043 (J)
Moore-Cottrell Sub Agency, North Cohocton, NY 14868 (A)
Nespa, 45 Hillcrest Place, Amherst, MA 01002 (D)
New England Mobile Bookfair, 82-84 Needham Street, Newton Highlands, MA 02161 (D)
Olsson Enterprises, Inc., #1, 1900 L St., NW, Washington, DC 20036 (J)
Omnibus Book Center, P.O. Box 342, Becket, MA 01223 (J)
Pacific Whole Dist., P.O. Box 1041, Pacific Palisades, CA 90272 (D)
N.M. Peryer, CPO Box 833, Christchurch, New Zealand N (J)
Albert J. Phiebig, Books, P.O. Box 352, White Plains, NY 10602 (J)
Plains Distrib. Service, P.O. Box 3112, Rm. 500, Block 6, 620 Main, Fargo, ND 58102 (D)
R & R Technical Bookfinders, P.O. Box 1038, Littleton, CO 80160 (J)
Leigh M. Railsback, 1276 North Lake Avenue, Pasadena, CA 91104 (J)
Rayner Agency, P.O. Box 437, Elgin, IL 60120 (A)
Read-More Publications Inc., 140 Cedar Street, NYC, NY 10006 (A)
William Reeves Publ. & Booksellers, 1A Norbury Crescent, London, U.K. (J)
Regent Book Co., Inc., 107 Prospect Place, Hillsdale, NJ 07642 (J)
Relco, Inc., Donald Porter, 182 Grand Street, NYC, NY 10013 (D)
Reprint Distribution Service, P.O. Box 245, Kent, CT 06757 (D)
Rigley Book Co., P.O. Box 26012, San Francisco, CA 94126 (D)
Scholtens & Zoon B V 21 5063, Grote Market 43 44, Groningen, The Netherlands (J)
Scientia International Sub Agency, Lovestraede 4 A DK-1152, Copenhagen K. Denmark (A)
Second Back Row Press, P.O. Box 197, N. Sydney, NSW, Australia 2060 (D)
Sector Group Ltd., 516-522 West 19 Street, NYC, NY 10011 (D)
Select Press Book Service, Maple Street, Contoocook, NH 03229 (J)
Charles Sessler, Inc., 1308 Walnut Street, Philadelphia, PA 19107 (J)
Shar-Frey, Inc., 580 Bloomfield Avenue, Bloomfield, NJ 07003 (J)
Siler's Library Distributors, 2737 Bienville Avenue, New Orleans, LA 70119 (A)
Skylo Distribution, 1502 East Olive Way, Seattle, WA 98122 (D)
Small Press Distribution, Jeanetta Jones Miller, 1636 Ocean View Avenue, Kensington, CA 94707 (D)
Small World Books, 1407 Ocean Front Walk, Venice, CA 90291 (J)
Social Innovation, 3834 Fulton Street NW, Washington, DC 20007 (A)
Southern Library Bindery Co., 2952 Sidco Drive, Nashville, TN 37204 (J)
Spring Church Book Co., P.O. Box 127, Spring Church, PA 15686 (D)
Kurt Staheli & Co., Buchhandlung, Bahnhofstrasse 70, Zurich, Switzerland CH8021 (J)
Standard Book Suppliers, Adelaide, Australia 5000 (J)
Standing Orders Inc., 156 Fifth Avenue, NYC, NY 10010 (J)
Stechert Macmillan, 54 Rue Boissonade, Paris, France 75014 (J)
Stechert Macmillan Inc., 7250 Westfield Avenue, Pennsauken, NJ 08110 (J)
Sundance Paperback Distr., Newtown Road, Littleton, MA 01460 (D)
Swets Subscription Service, 347B Heereweg, Lisse, The Netherlands (A)
Tokyo Tsuhan Service Ltd., Odakyu Kyodo Bldg. 12F, P.O. Box 33, Chitose, Tokyo, Japan 156 (J)
Turner Subscription Agency, 235 Park Avenue, South, NYC, NY 10003 (A)
Frederick Ungar Publishing Co., 250 Park Avenue South, NYC, NY 10003 (J)
United Methodist Publ. House, P.O. Box 298, Dallas, TX 75221 (J)
United Methodist Publ. House, Fifth and Grace Streets, Richmond, VA 23261 (J)
Universal Per Ser/Riemann, Ebsco/826 S. NW. Highway, Barrington, IL 60010 (A)
University Press Book Service, 302 Fifth Avenue, NYC, NY 10001 (J)
Visual Studies Workshop, 31 Prince Street, Rochester, NY 14607 (D)
Weegar-Pride Book Co., Waterford Road, No. Bridgton, ME 04057 (J)
Western Book Distributors, Attn: Bruce Feldman, 2970 San Pablo Avenue, Berkeley, CA 94710 (D)
Western Book Distributors, 2441 Shattuck Avenue, Berkeley, CA 94704 (D)
Writers Inc/Van Oosten, 1411 4th Avenue Bldg. No. 1310, Seattle, WA 98101 (D)

ORGANIZATIONS

AAA	AMERICAN ANTHROPOLOGICAL ASSOCIATION
AABC	AFFILIATED TO ANARCHIST BLACK CROSS
AAP	ASSOCIATION OF AMERICAN PUBLISHERS
AASLH	AMERICAN ASSOCIATION FOR STATE AND LOCAL HISTORY
ABA	AMERICAN BOOKSELLERS ASSOCIATION
ABPA	AUSTRALIAN BOOK PUBLISHERS ASSOCIATION
ACP	ASSOCIATION OF CANADIAN PUBLISHERS
AGNYC	AUTHORS GUILD NEW YORK CITY
AIGA	AMERICAN INSTITUTE OF GRAPHIC ART
AII	AUDIO INDEPENDENTS INC
AIP	ARTISTS IN PRINT
AIPA	AUSTRALIA INDEPENDENT PUBLISHERS ASSOCIATION
ALMS	ASSOCIATION OF LITTLE MAGAZINES (UK)
ALO	ALLIANCE OF LITERARY ORGANIZATION
ALP	ASSOCIATION OF LITTLE PRESSES (UK)
APA	ALBERTA PUBLISHERS ASSOCIATION
APM	ANARCHIST PRESS MOVEMENT
APS	ALTERNATIVE PRESS SERVICE
ASCAP	AMERICAN SOCIETY OF COMPOSERS, ARTISTS AND PRODUCERS
ASW	AMERICAN SOCIETY OF WRITERS
ASWA	AVIATION-SPACE WRITERS ASSOCIATION
B OF B	BOOKBUILDERS OF BOSTON
BPS	BRITISH PRINTING SOCIETY
BPSC	BOOK PUBLISHERS OF SOUTHERN CALIFORNIA
CAPF	CANADIAN ALTERNATIVE PRESS FEDERATION
CBA	CANADIAN BOOKS ASSOCIATION
CBIC	CANADIAN BOOKS INFO CENTRE
CBPA	CONNECTICUT BOOK PUBLISHERS ASSOCIATION
CCLM	COORDINATING COUNCIL OF LITERARY MAGAZINES
CELJ	COUNCIL OF EDITORS OF LEARNED JOURNALS
CHA	CANADIAN HISTORICAL ASSOCIATION
CLE	IRISH BOOK PUBLISHERS ASSOCIATION
CNS	CANADIAN NEWS SERVICE
COSMEP	COMMITTEE OF SMALL MAGAZINE EDITORS AND PUBLISHERS
COSMEPA	COMMITTEE OF SMALL MAGAZINE EDITORS AND PUBLISHERS AUSTRALIA
CPPA	CANADIAN PERIODICAL PUBLISHERS ASSOCIATION
CRISP	COMMITTEE OF RHODE ISLAND SMALL PRESSES
EAA	EASTERN ARTS ASSOCIATION
EPAA	EDUCATIONAL PRESS ASSOCIATION OF AMERICA
FLG	FEMINIST LITERARY GUILD
GAA	GUILD OF ALTERNATIVE ARTISTS
GPNY	GAY PRESSES OF NEW YORK
IFA	INTERNATIONAL FICTION ASSOCIATION
IPA	INDEPENDENT PUBLISHERS OF AUSTRALIA
IPA	IRISH PUBLISHERS ASSOCIATION
IPG	INDEPENDENT PUBLISHERS GROUP
LCPPP	LONDON CHAPEL OF PRIVATE PRESS PRINTERS
LPG	LITERARY PRESS GROUP (TORONTO)

LPS	LIBERTARIAN PRESS SERVICE
LPSC	LITERARY PUBLISHERS OF SOUTHERN CALIFORNIA
MPA	MAGAZINE PUBLISHERS ASSOCIATION
MPW	MAINE PUBLISHERS AND WRITERS
MUTA	MARIN UNITED TAXPAYERS ASSOCIATION
NAAN	NATIONAL ASSOCIATION OF ALTERNATIVE NEWSWEEKLIES
NABD	NEW AGE BOOK DISTRIBUTION
NCPA	NORTHERN CALIFORNIA PUBLICISTS ASSOCIATION
NESPA	NEW ENGLAND SMALL PRESS ASSOCIATION
NYSSPA	NEW YORK STATE SMALL PRESS ASSOCIATION
NYSWP	NEW YORK STATE WATERWAYS PROJECT
OAC	OHIO ARTS COUNCIL
ONPA	OREGON NEWSPAPER PUBLISHERS ASSOCIATION
PA	PUBLISHERS ASSOCIATION
PANP	PEOPLE AGAINST NUCLEAR POWER
PBC	PHILADELPHIA BOOK CLINIC
PCBA	PACIFIC CENTER FOR THE BOOK ARTS
PHF	PACIFIC HORTICULTURAL FOUNDATION
PHS	PRINTING HISTORICAL SOCIETY
PPA	PERIODICAL PUBLISHERS ASSOCIATION
PRC/M	POETRY RESOURCE CENTER OF MICHIGAN
RCFP	REPORTER'S COMMITTEE FOR THE FREEDOM OF THE PRESS
RGWA	RIO GRANDE WRITERS ASSOCIATION
SAAA	ST. ALBANS ARTS ASSOCIATION
SCCIPHC	SUPERIOR CALIFORNIA CLUB OF INTERNATIONAL PRINTING HOUSE CRAFTSMAN
SGPA	SCOTTISH GENERAL PUBLISHERS ASSOCIATION
STWP	SOCIETY OF TECHNICAL WRITERS AND PUBLISHERS
TC	TEXAS CIRCUIT
UAPS(E)	UNITED ALTERNATIVE PRESS SERVICE (EUROPE)
WAWC	WASHINGTON AVA WRITERS CENTER
WASP	WELSH ASSOCIATION OF SMALL PRESSES
WBPA	WESTERN BOOK PUBLISHERS ASSOCIATION
WDG	WOMEN'S DISTRIBUTION GROUP
WIFP	WOMEN'S INSTITUTE FOR FREEDOM OF THE PRESS
WIP	WOMEN IN PRINT
WNBA	WOMEN'S NATIONAL BOOK ASSOCIATION
WP	WATERWAYS PROJECT
WPA	WESTERN PUBLISHERS ASSOCIATION
WWAC	WASHINGTON WRITERS CENTER
WWHS	WESTERN WORLD HAIKU SOCIETY
YAF	YOUNG AMERICANS FOR FREEDOM

Valery Nash
THE NARROWS* 62 pp. Paper $3.50

Marilyn Krysl
MORE PALOMINO, PLEASE, MORE FUCHSIA* 68 pp. Paper $4.00

AND OTHER FINE POETRY FROM CLEVELAND STATE UNIVERSITY POETRY CENTER

Stuart Friebert
UP IN BED
83 pp. Paper $2.95

Thomas Lux
THE GLASSBLOWER'S BREATH
71 pp. Paper $2.95

Stratis Haviaras
CROSSING THE RIVER TWICE
69 pp. Paper $2.95

Mark Jarman
NORTH SEA
70 pp. Paper $3.50

Franz Wright
THE EARTH WITHOUT YOU*
36 pp. Paper $3.50

Jan Haagensen
LIKE A DIAMONDBACK IN THE TRUNK OF A WITNESS'S BUICK
Viii + 55 pp. Paper $3.50

David Young
WORK LIGHTS: THIRTY-TWO PROSE POEMS
Viii + 45 pp. Paper $2.95

Bruce Weigl
A SACK FULL OF OLD QUARRELS
36 pp. Paper $2.50

Patricia Ikeda
HOUSE OF WOOD, HOUSE OF SALT*
62 pp. Paper $2.50

*Published with the aid of a grant from the Ohio Arts Council.

Department of English, Cleveland State University, Cleveland, Ohio 44115

The American Dust Series

The American Dust Series was originally conceived as a way to do something in honor of the celebration of the American Bicentennial. The first books in the series were: an anthology of writings by prisoners, an anthology of women writers, a story of the American Road in the 1970's, and a novel about New England farm life.

As the idea of the series outgrew and outlived its "occasional" origin, its shape also began to grow and change.

Chronicling and tracking the small press and independent publishing movement for 13 years, we at Dustbooks should know better than most that the thread that runs through American writing and publishing is diversity, variety. Thus the American Dust series continues by adding books not like the others, but unlike them, chronicling the geographical, stylistic, ethnic, and genre diversity and richness of writing in the contemporary Americas.

Dustbooks

Publishers of Small Press Information and General Trade Books

QTY	ISBN 0-913218	TITLE AND AUTHOR/EDITOR		PRICE	TOTAL

Small Press Information

	93-6	INTERNATIONAL DIRECTORY OF LITTLE		13.95/paper	_____
_____	94-4	MAGAZINES and SMALL PRESSES,		17.95/cloth	_____
_____		15th Edition, 1979-80	4-yr. sub.	42.00/paper	
_____			4-yr. sub.	54.00/cloth	
_____	96-0	DIRECTORY OF SMALL MAGAZINE/PRESS		9.95/paper	_____
		EDITORS and PUBLISHERS, 10th			
		Edition, 1979-80	4-yr. sub.	30.00	___
_____	95-2	SMALL PRESS RECORD of BOOKS in		17.95/cloth	_____
		PRINT, 8th Edition, 1979	4-yr. sub.	54.00	—
_____		SMALL PRESS REVIEW/SMALL			

		PRESS BOOK CLUB/monthly		Indiv.	Instit.	
			yr:	10.00	15.00	_____
			2 yrs:	16.00	23.50	_____
			3 yrs:	21.00	30.00	_____

Publishing How-To

	-75-8	THE CO-OP PUBLISHING HANDBOOK/	3.95/paper	_____
_____	-76-6	Michael Scott Cain	8.95/cloth	_____
_____	-79-0	GUIDE TO WOMEN'S PUBLISHING/Polly	4.95/paper	_____
_____	-80-4	Joan & Andrea Chesman	9.95/cloth	_____
_____		THE PUBLISH-IT YOURSELF HANDBOOK/	5.00/paper	_____
_____		Ed. by Bill Henderson	10.00/cloth	_____
_____		HOW TO PUBLISH YOUR OWN BOOK/	4.95/paper	_____
_____		L.W. Mueller	6.95/cloth	_____
_____		THE WRITER PUBLISHER/Charles N.	4.95/paper	_____
_____		Aronson	7.95/cloth	_____
_____	-47-2	AMERICAN ODYSSEY: A BOOKSELLING	4.50/paper	_____
_____	-46-4	TRAVELOGUE/Fulton & Ferber	7.95/cloth	_____
_____		THE PASSIONATE PERILS of PUBLISHING/	5.00/paper	_____
_____		Celeste West and Valerie Wheat		
_____		PUBLISH IT YOURSELF/Charles J. Chickadel	4.95/paper	_____
_____		INTO PRINT/Mary Hill and Wendell Cochran	6.95/paper	_____
_____		THE SELF-PUBLISHING MANUAL/Dan Poynter	9.95/paper	_____
_____		PRINTING IT/Clifford Burke	3.50/paper	_____

The "American Dust" Series

	-36-7	#2: MOVING TO ANTARCTICA: WOMEN'S	3.95/paper	_____
_____	-35-9	ANTHOLOGY Ed. by Margaret Kaminski	7.95/cloth	_____
_____	-34-0	#3: CAPTIVE VOICES: FOLSOM PRISON	3.95/paper	_____
_____	-33-2	WRITING	7.95/cloth	_____
_____	-49-9	#4: DARK OTHER ADAM DREAMING/	2.95/paper	_____
_____	-48-0	novel by Len Fulton	8.95/cloth	_____
_____	-29-4	#5: THE ENGLEWOOD READINGS/	2.50/paper	_____
_____	-30-8	Terence Clarke/poems	6.95/cloth	_____

____	-31-6	#6: NIGHT CONVERSATIONS WITH NONE	2.95/paper	____
	-32-4	OTHER/Shreela Ray/poems	6.95/cloth	____
____	-54-5	#7: ANTI-MATTER/C.M. Stanbury/	2.95/paper	____
	-55-3	novel	7.95/cloth	____
____	-50-2	#8: SELECTED ESSAYS/Rich Mangelsdorff	2.95/paper	____
____	-84-7	#9: AGAINST NATURE: WILDERNESS POEMS/	2.95/paper	____
	-83-9	Judith McCombs	7.95/cloth	____
____	-85-5	#10: CLEARING OF THE MIST/	2.95/paper	____
	-86-3	Richard F. Fleck/Novel	7.95/cloth	____
____	-25-1	#11: ARNULFSAGA/a longpoem/	2.95/paper	____
	-26-X	Gary Elder	7.95/cloth	____
____	-44-8	#12: THE POETRY of CHARLES POTTS/	2.95/paper	____
—		critique/Hugh Fox		
____	-91-X	13 OWLS BAY IN BABYLON _____	3.95/paper	
____	-92-8	Charles Black	9.95/cloth	

Novels/Poetry/Essays

____		THE GRASSMAN/Len Fulton/novel	2.95/paper	____
			7.95/cloth	____
____	-24-3	THE HONEY DWARF/Gene Detro/	2.50/paper	____
	-23-5	novel	5.95/cloth	____
____		THE FAR SIDE OF THE STORM/Western	4.00/paper	____
____		Anthology Ed. by Gary Elder	9.00/cloth	____
____	-42-1	MR. & MRS. MEPHISTOPHELES & SON/	2.50/paper	____
		Michael Lopes/poems		
____	-18-9	CONJURING A COUNTER-CULTURE/	2.50/paper	____
____		Walt Shepperd/essays	5.95/cloth	____
____	-22-7	THE DAYS OF TAO/Charles Baden	1.50/paper	____
		Powell/poems		
____	-20-0	PEEPLE/Hugh Fox/vignettes	2.00/paper	____
____		MIND DANCES/Hilary Fowler/poems	1.50/paper	____

Dustbooks
Box 100, Paradise CA 95969

Total _____

California Residents add 6% Sales Tax _____

Add Postage and Handling _____ $.95

Total Enclosed _____

NAME _____

ADDRESS _____

_____

BOOKSELLERS: 25% discount/2-10 copies;
40% 11-25; 50% 26 plus